THE GENTLE REBEL

★ ★ ★ ★ THE HOUSE OF WINSLOW / BOOK 4 ★ ★ ★ ★

Sequel to THE INDENTURED HEART

THE GENTLE REBEL

★

GILBERT MORRIS

BETHANY HOUSE PUBLISHERS

MINNEAPOLIS, MINNESOTA 55438

A Division of Bethany Fellowship, Inc.

Published by Bethany House Publishers
A Division of Bethany Fellowship, Inc.
6820 Auto Club Road, Minneapolis, MN 55438

Library of Congress Cataloging-in-Publication Data

Morris, Gilbert
   The gentle rebel / Gilbert Morris.
      p. cm. — (The House of Winslow ; bk. 4)

    1. United States—History—Revolution, 1775–1783—Fiction.
I. Title. II. Series: Morris, Gilbert. House of Winslow ; bk. 4.
PS3563.08742G4 1988
813'.54—dc19   88–18712
ISBN 1–55661–006–8   CIP

This one is for my redheads—

Alan Blake Morris and Zachary Alan
Morris

POWER IN THE BLOOD

Alan, my son, quite without intent
Wheeled around as I came in and bent
His head to one side grinning crookedly—
And from his eyes, my father looked at me.

A thousand times I'd seen my father twist
His head just so (sort of a starboard list)
Squint-eyed, as though peering through a haze,
Just as he looked at me through my son's gaze.

I saw my father clear in my son's light,
O, there is power in the blood all right!
That father's blood that cools and slows its pace
Will glow again in a grandson's face.

One day, perhaps, when I am gone from here,
I'll come again to look at Alan plain and clear;
Then he will halt, will stand in shocked surprise
To see *me* smile at him—through Zachary's eyes!

THE HOUSE OF WINSLOW SERIES

GILBERT MORRIS spent ten years as a pastor before becoming Professor of English at Ouachita Baptist University in Arkansas and earning a Ph.D. at the University of Arkansas. During the summers of 1984 and 1985 he did postgraduate work at the University of London and is presently the Chairman of General Education at a Christian college in Louisiana. A prolific writer, he has had over 25 scholarly articles and 200 poems published in various periodicals, and over the past years has had 15 novels published. His family includes three grown children, and he and his wife live in Baton Rouge, Louisiana.

CONTENTS

PART THREE
GUNS OVER BOSTON

PART ONE

FIRST BLOOD—LEXINGTON

★ ★ ★ ★

THE
HOUSE OF WINSLOW

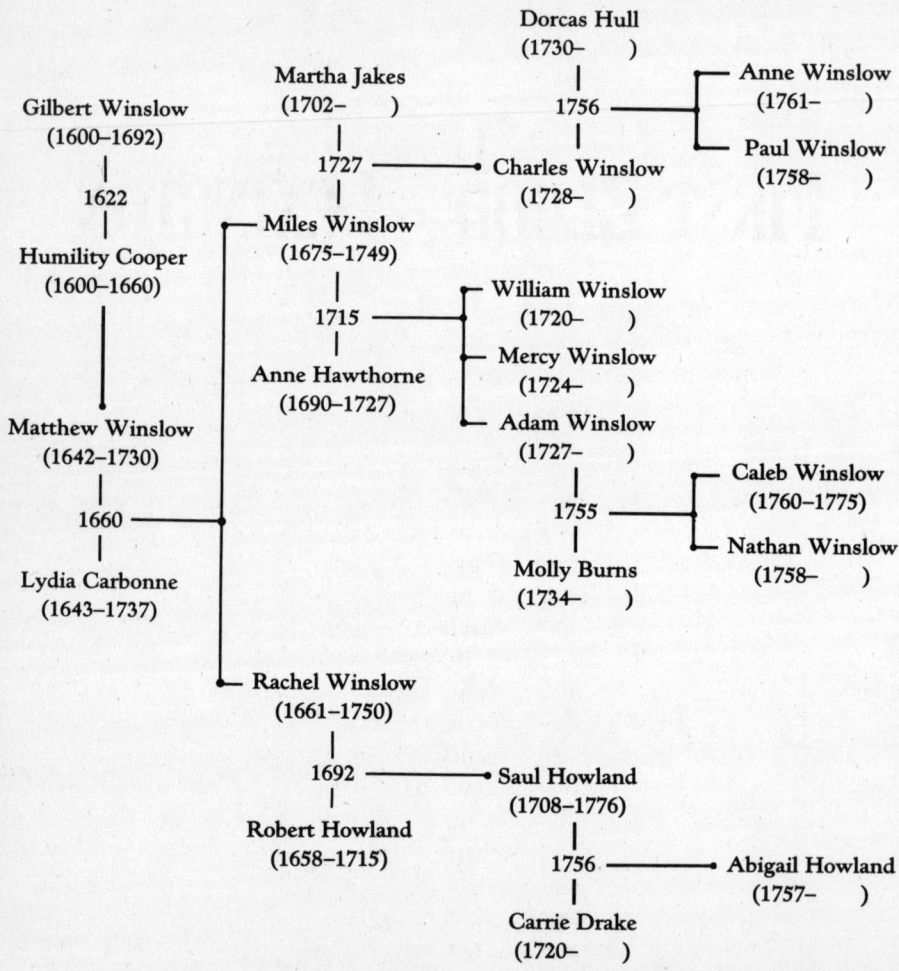

Dorcas Hull
(1730–   )

Martha Jakes
(1702–   )

Gilbert Winslow
(1600–1692)

1756 ————

Anne Winslow
(1761–   )

Paul Winslow
(1758–   )

1727 ————— Charles Winslow
(1728–   )

1622

Miles Winslow
(1675–1749)

Humility Cooper
(1600–1660)

1715 ————

William Winslow
(1720–   )

Mercy Winslow
(1724–   )

Anne Hawthorne
(1690–1727)

Adam Winslow
(1727–   )

Matthew Winslow
(1642–1730)

1755 ————

Caleb Winslow
(1760–1775)

Nathan Winslow
(1758–   )

1660 ————

Molly Burns
(1734–   )

Lydia Carbonne
(1643–1737)

Rachel Winslow
(1661–1750)

1692 ————— Saul Howland
(1708–1776)

Robert Howland
(1658–1715)

1756 ————— Abigail Howland
(1757–   )

Carrie Drake
(1720–   )

CHAPTER ONE

ALONE!

★ ★ ★ ★

If Julie Sampson had been born two years earlier or two years later, she would not have been in such a trap—or so she thought as she stood trembling in her small room, her back pressed against the wall.

If I were only twelve or thirteen, he'd leave me alone—or if I were seventeen, I'd be old enough to leave here!

She held her breath as heavy footfalls sounded on the stairs, came down the hall, then stopped abruptly outside her door. She suddenly pressed the back of her hand against her mouth to shut off the cry of terror that rose to her lips. The silence grew thick, so thick that between the solemn tickings of the clock she thought she could hear heavy breathing. Her eyes were riveted on the door as she waited for the pewter knob to turn. When the thought of escape through the small window beside her pierced her mind, she cast a quick glance at the snow that was drifting gently outside the glass.

She edged cautiously to her right. *I wonder if I would break my legs on the cobblestones?* she thought fleetingly, looking down at the walk that ran in front of the shop. She didn't really care—all she wanted to do was escape. She touched the catch on the window; then suddenly the footfalls retreated, going down the hall, and echoing down the stairs.

"Thank God!" she breathed, and then discovered that her legs were trembling so violently she could hardly stand, let alone make the jump to the walkway below. Dropping into the chair beside the small oak table, she hid her face in her hands and tried to think. She struggled to choke back the sobs that rose in her throat; finally, with great effort, she shook her shoulders, rose from the chair and walked to the washbasin at the foot of her bed. Dashing her face with cold water, she dried it with a thick, white cloth that hung at the end of the stand, then began to pace back and forth. Her mind whirled, filled with insistent but ineffective thoughts. She couldn't seem to sort them out, and any prayer she tried to utter seemed meaningless, an empty formula, a ritual learned from childhood.

She walked to the window, looking down over the wooden sign that said SILAS SAMPSON—CARTOGRAPHER in crimson letters, carefully scrolled. The sight of it evoked an image of her father, and as she thought of his slight figure bent over his desk, the tears flooded her eyes, and she dashed them away almost angrily.

I can't cry for him anymore! she thought. And then she looked across the street, resolutely past the sign swinging in the stiff January breeze, and saw a man wearing a heavy fur coat. Her lips grew firm, and snatching a heavy coat and a bonnet from the pegs on the wall, she stepped outside her room, walked down the hall and descended the stairs.

Her hope of passing through the shop without being noticed was dashed as a voice said, "Julie—where you going?"

Aaron Sampson suddenly appeared, interposing his bulk between her and the door, and as always she had to restrain herself to keep from flinching as he put his meaty hand on her shoulder. "I don't want you to go out in this weather," he said, and his grip changed to a caress that made her flesh crawl.

"Rev. Kelly asked me to come by today," she said quickly.

"The preacher? What's he want with you?"

"I—I think he wants some work done on his books."

"Oh, work is it?" Aaron Sampson cared nothing for preachers, but he dearly loved a dollar. Reluctantly, he let his thick hand slide off Julie's shoulder, stepped aside, and a sudden grin pulled the corners of his thick lips up as she slipped by him. "Might ought to tell that preacher that he'll be needed right soon, Julie!"

She closed the door quickly to shut off his words, but his coarse voice penetrated the three-inch oak with ease: "Might have a marrying job, ain't that right, girl?"

The hard lines of Philadelphia had been blurred by soft folds of new snow, and the rough street felt like thick carpet as Julie hurried to catch up with the tall minister. Her feet made no sound, and flakes as big as wafers stung her face. When she called out, "Rev. Kelly!" there was an echo in the icy air, as if her voice were frozen, too.

"Why, Julie!" Rev. Zachariah Kelly's skeletal thinness was disguised by the bulk of the fur coat, but the face that peered out from under a tri-cornered hat seemed even more pale and bony, framed as it was by the black hat and coat. "What are you doing out in this weather?"

"Oh, I—I just thought it would be good to get some fresh air." Julie's face flushed suddenly. She had lied to Aaron, and whatever the man's designs, her lack of truthfulness troubled her. Then she lifted her face and said quickly, "Rev. Kelly, you told my father once that you wanted him to make a map for you—of County Cork, I think it was?"

"Why, bless me, child!" He stared at her with kindly blue eyes, and then nodded. "I'd almost forgotten that—but so I did."

"Could—could I go home with you so we could talk about it? I can make the map—almost as good as Father could have done it if he . . . !"

Kelly's vision was weak, but he did not miss the sudden tears that rose to the girl's eyes at the mention of her father. He reached out, took her hand, and said gently, "It's very hard to lose a dear one, Julie—hard for anyone. But doubly so when we only have the *one* to lose." His mind went back two months when he had tossed the handful of dirt into the ground, hearing it strike the wooden coffin containing Julie's father with a dull *thud*, and he remembered that she had flinched at the sound as if the earth had struck her in the face—or as if a musket ball had smitten her in the heart. "You were very close to your father, Julie," he murmured. Then briskly, he took her arm and said, "Why, I think that's a splendid idea— that map of the old country! We'll just pop along to my study and I'll show you where I came from—and did you know, my dear, that all Irishmen are descended from kings?" He chattered away lightly, and was rewarded to see the lines fade from her smooth brow.

They passed under the shadow of Christ Church, an imposing virgin clothed in winter white, then walked around the path to the small cottage in the rear that almost touched the graveyard. Rev.

Kelly bustled Julie inside, and asked his wife to fix some tea and bring it to the study.

"There's no tea, you mind," Mrs. Kelly said with a mischievous smile. "Don't you remember, Zachariah?"

He stared at her blankly; then a grimace of annoyance swept his thin features. "Blast!" Then he laughed, and a twinkle lit his blue eyes. "When the Crown put that tax on tea, I got carried away with some of Sam Adams' talk—and when the Sons of Liberty dressed up like Indians and threw the King's tea into Boston Harbor, why, I joined the rest of the Bedlamites and threw all my tea in the fire!" He shrugged ruefully, then added as he guided Julie to his study, "That's the way it is with that sort of *repentance*—a man gets carried away with something, then has to live with it after the parade's over!"

Julie followed him into the large study lined with books. "Now, let's see," he muttered, staring at the two large tables against the wall almost buried with papers, drawings, books, and other scholarly material. "Ah! Here we have it!"

The minister extracted a large book from the midst of a stack of papers, opened it, and soon he and Julie were chattering away about longitudes, latitudes and other matters of the business. Rev. Kelly was not thinking of mapmaking, however, but of the young woman who stood beside him. Since the death of her father, Julie had been grappling with a problem that he could not quite identify. She had been a member of his church all her life, as had her father, and the two of them had been inseparable. Since his death, however, she had become more and more silent and her ruddy cheeks had grown pale.

He looked down on her, thinking not for the first time what an attractive girl she was. She was tall, and Kelly guessed that her five feet eight inches came from her mother's side, for her father had been slight—only a little over five six at best. She was no lightweight, and her transformation from childhood to womanhood was obvious—her blossoming figure was revealed by the simple gray gown she wore. Her shoulders were square, her arms rounded and strong. She had very black hair, thick and slightly curly. Her eyebrows, thick and dark, arched over eyes so dark that the pupils were difficult to see—eyes wide and almond shaped with long curling lashes. Her nose was straight and her rather square face and firm chin announced more than a hint of stubbornness.

She looks well enough, Kelly thought, but after they had talked of the map, settled the details of the price, he ventured to ask, "Now, Julie, tell me what's bothering you."

She looked startled; then a flush touched her cheeks. "Why— Rev. Kelly . . . !" Actually she had asked for this visit to try to tell him of her desperation, but now that he stood there, she could not force herself to say it.

"You know, Julie, I promised your father on his deathbed that I'd take care of you. As a matter of fact, if it weren't for your uncle, my wife and I would have had you come to live with us. We talked about it."

"Oh, could I do that, Reverend?" she asked quickly. Her eyes pleaded with him as she said nervously, "I'd do all the work! And I'm a very good cook, you know!"

Her quick response caught Kelly off guard, and looking into her face, he wished he had not mentioned the matter. "Why, my dear, we would love it—but Mr. Sampson is not at all sympathetic to the idea."

"You talked to him?"

"Why, yes, I did. It was only a few days after the funeral. I told him that it might be better for you to stay with us, but—"

"He said he wanted to keep me, didn't he?"

Aaron Sampson had said much more than that, Rev. Kelly remembered grimly. The burly man had cursed, his beefy face red, ending up by saying, "You preachers is all alike—out for all you can get! That milksop of a brother of mine, you pulled the wool over his eyes, but you don't get nothing off me, see? The girl stays here, and I've got the law on my side!"

Kelly's pale, thin face grew red at the memory of how the big man had practically thrown him out of the house, sending him out the door with a shove. "I'm afraid there's little hope that your uncle would permit you to come here, Julie," he said regretfully.

"I—I'm afraid of him, Rev. Kelly!"

"Afraid of him? Has he hurt you, Julie?"

"N-no."

"Mistreated you, has he?"

Her face burned, and she said in a whisper, "He—he won't leave me alone!"

Kelly felt a quick thrill shoot along his nerves—half anger and half fear. There was no mistaking the girl's meaning, but he stood there feeling impotent, having no clue as to how he could help her. *Her father was a fool!* he thought angrily.

Silas Sampson had been a good man, but weak in many ways, Kelly recalled. His wife had died when Julie was only six, and he had never remarried. Some had thought it wonderful the way he had let his daughter fill the place of a wife, but Kelly had thought it abominable, seeing that the child had been robbed of much that all children ought to know. But to be fair, he would have to admit that Silas had been a loving father; nothing had been too good for his Julie!

A year ago, he had fallen ill, very ill, and as his condition worsened, he became almost frantic. Kelly remembered well his visits, when the sick man had cried out, "I'm not afraid to die—but what will happen to my girl when I'm gone?"

The thought had tormented him, and nothing the minister or anyone else could say gave him any peace. Finally, he had surprised them all with a solution. He had sent for Rev. Kelly, and with fever glazing his eyes, he had said, "I—I have one relative, Reverend—a younger brother. We've not been close—in fact, Aaron and I haven't spoken in many years. But now I must call on him! He's all I have left!"

It had been, in Rev. Kelly's judgment, a bad decision. When Aaron Sampson had come to Philadelphia to live with his brother, he had been so unlike the frail cartographer that it was difficult for Kelly to believe they were related. Aaron was overbearing, arrogant, crude—in every respect the opposite of Silas. He had moved in, taken over the affairs of the business, and, with unbelievable callousness, waited for his only brother to die. Indeed, by the time Julie's father had slipped away, Aaron Sampson was spreading his elbows wide on the board.

Now looking down into Julie's pale face, Kelly was appalled. He knew only too well the power of men over women in the courts. No girl of Julie's age would have a chance against a full-grown man like Aaron Sampson. And the minister knew for a fact, having been told by that babbling fool of a lawyer, Will Spelling, that Julie's father had given Aaron Sampson everything! Nothing for the daughter. *The man was a fool!* Kelly thought again, but he only said gently, "Try not to worry, child. God is not unaware of our problems. I'll have another talk with your uncle."

"Please try to get him to let me come here!" Julie whispered, and the fear in her eyes was a living thing as he nodded.

After she left, Kelly walked into the kitchen and sat down at the table with his wife. She was a large woman, as thick as he was thin, a condition that gave rise to some ribald talk from the cruder elements of the town. But she was wise and had lived long enough with the tall preacher to know his thoughts. "You're worried about Julie, aren't you, Zachariah?"

He picked up the glass of cider she placed before him, tasted it, then set it down. "That man is after her, Bess!"

She stared at him, her lips growing white with pressure. "What will you do?"

He suddenly smote the table with his fist and shouted, "Nothing! Not a blasted thing!" Then he stared at her with a hopeless anger in his blue eyes, adding in a whisper, "There's not one blessed thing anyone can do, Bess!" He rose to his feet, and there was misery in every line of his tall body, for he was a true shepherd, and he loved this girl. The thought of Aaron Sampson's gross figure drew his lips together into a grimace, and he said bitterly, "The only hope—and it's a foul thought—is that he'll marry the poor child!" Then he left the kitchen, and went to the church, praying long—partly for the child and partly for himself, for forgiveness. For he was filled with a raging hatred for Sampson, and he well knew that until *that* changed, he could pray for nothing else.

Business was booming, and for the next month Julie was kept so busy (as was her uncle) that her fears subsided. Her father had trained her, and although it had been necessary to hire an assistant to fill the gap her father had left, the shop had prospered. Perhaps it was the constant talk of war with England that created a demand for maps, but whatever the cause, Julie had worked long days and many nights to keep up with the orders.

The new cartographer was a taciturn man named Isaiah Johnson. He was a good workman, but a heavy drinker, so he brought no levity into the shop. Aaron knew a little of the work, and was determined to learn more, and this was, perhaps, the reason why he had left Julie more or less alone. For all his crudeness, he was no fool; a shrewd man, he realized that the girl was profitable.

More to the point, he had gone into details with Will Spelling, and discovered that his grip on the property was not as firm as he had thought.

"Your name is on the paper," Spelling had pointed out, "but so is Julie's. In law, you and Julie are more or less partners—with you being the junior partner." The lawyer was a small man with close-set eyes, a catfish mouth, and no scruples. He smiled now, adding, "That's the way your brother wanted it, Aaron."

"Junior partner?" the huge man snorted, a wicked light in his small eyes. "Well, well—junior partner, is it? Well, there's a way around that!"

"I'm sure you've thought of it," Spelling said with a small smile. "And the girl's a likely looking filly!"

"Aye! And I think she'll make a better wife than a senior partner to me! Yes, indeed, Lawyer Spelling—I think we'll be needing to do a little more of your blasted paper work soon!"

It was nearly midnight when Julie made her way wearily up the steps, her fingers stained with ink and her eyes burning with fatigue. She undressed and washed, and had just donned her heavy nightgown when the door opened suddenly.

"Julie—we've got a little talking to do!"

Sampson stood there filling the doorway, and Julie's heart leaped with fear as she saw the cruel smile on his thick lips. Quickly she reached for the robe that lay on her bed, but as large as he was, Aaron moved quickly. He stepped forward, caught her by the arm, and the power of his hand was awesome.

"Please—" She swallowed and could only whisper, "Let me go, please—we'll talk in the morning."

He said nothing, but his grip on her arm tightened, and then his eyes glittered. His eyes ran over her, and she struggled vainly to pull away. "You ain't a baby, Julie," he said thickly. "You're a full-growed woman!"

Her ears were ringing, and the rank smell of the man sickened her. There was no one in the house; even if she screamed, no one could hear, and if anyone did, it was unlikely they would come. She stood there trembling and trying to break his grip, but it was hopeless.

He suddenly pulled her closer, putting his massive arms around her, and said, "You need a husband, Julie! And I'm him!"

"No!"

"I say you're going to marry me, girl, and don't make no mistake! The law says I'm your guardian—but we can't live here together alone—why, it wouldn't be decent!"

He leered down at her, grinning at the irony in his own words. "I'll leave!" she cried out. "I'll give up my share of the shop. I'll go live with the minister!"

"No, you'll marry me, Julie, and that's final!" Sampson drew her closer and attempted to speak more lightly. "Why, I know you're young, Julie, and I reckon you're afraid of men—seeing you ain't never had no fellows, that'd be natural. But I aim to treat you right—and Silas, he made me promise to do it."

"No!" Julie tried to pull away, but his arms held her in a powerful vise. "Father never said that!"

"Sure he did!" Aaron laughed, then pulled her face up and kissed her. "That's just a sample, Julie," he said. "I'll have a talk with that preacher tomorrow. Don't think we ought to put this thing off. You don't need no big wedding. Just have the parson come in tomorrow and do the job—or if he won't, I reckon I can find one who will!"

He laughed down at her horror-stricken face, kissed her again, then released her so abruptly that she nearly fell. "You get a good night's sleep now. I want you rested up, 'cause tomorrow you'll have a husband to keep happy!"

The door slammed, and in the silence Julie stood there, tears running down her face. She listened as his footsteps faded, then his door slammed. More than anything she wanted to fall across the bed and weep, but she knew that would be futile.

Finally, she went to the bed, knelt down, and for a long time she was still. The room was cold and quiet, and there was no sound at all except for a muffled word now and then as she prayed. Thirty minutes passed, then an hour. At last the clock in the hall struck one—a ghostly tone in the silence of the night, a round, mellow tone that seemed to touch her, for she suddenly raised her head, tears making crystal tracks down her cheeks.

But there was no fear in her dark eyes, and she slowly got to her feet and stood staring out the window into the darkness. The snow on the rooftops had turned to silver through the alchemy of moonlight, and there was not a soul stirring on the street.

Julie said, "Amen!" and then she knelt again, this time to pull a small traveling bag from underneath her bed. Opening it, she began to throw her clothes into it, her face set like flint. When the valise was packed, she paused, then picked up the Bible from the desk, placed it gently on the top of the clothes, shut the case and fastened it.

At last she walked to the door, pulled it open firmly, and without a backward glance, passed through the dark hall and out of the shop into the blackness of the night.

CHAPTER TWO

RUNAWAY

★ ★ ★ ★

Julie climbed down from the Conestoga wagon and, reaching up, took her small bag from the muscular hand of Matthew Perkins. The big man said as he passed it along, "You better think about going on with us, missy. Be right glad to have you."

"Do come!" his wife Ruth urged. She was a worn, middle-aged woman with still a few remnants of beauty, and she added a smile as she leaned over her husband to make a final plea to Julie. "You're all alone, and we'd be proud to share our home with you."

Julie looked up and for a moment was tempted, but quickly decided that their home was too close to Philadelphia. They had picked her up as she trudged along in the snow three days earlier, and they were such plain, simple people it had never occurred to them to doubt her story. She had told them that she was an orphan who was going to New York to work and live with an aunt. The lie had pained her, but she finally had said to herself, "It's *almost* the truth—I *am* going to live with an aunt."

She had left home with one thin fragment of a plan. Her mother's sister lived in Portsmouth, on the southern coast of England. The sisters had been close, and even though Julie's mother had been dead for years, Mrs. Collingwood had written at rare intervals, expressing some interest in her niece. Silas had spoken at times of a visit, but nothing had ever come of it. As Julie had prayed, the thought had come to her, and she conceived the idea of going to New York, there booking passage to flee the Colonies. She knew that Aaron would have the law looking for her, and the New World was a small place in which to hide—but England!

So she stood there in the snow with the Perkinses, looking very young. But there was a firmness in her voice as she shook her head and said, "I'm so grateful to you both, but—my aunt would be very disappointed if I didn't come! God bless you both!"

They said their farewells; then as the heavy horses pulled the big wagon down the rutted street, Julie turned and looked around at New York for the first time. The Perkinses had brought her to a section of town near the harbor, and she passed by a good many inns with names such as The King's Arms, The Merchant's Coffee House, The Blue Boar, and The Three Pigeons. It was late afternoon and she had eaten a good breakfast at dawn, but now the smell of cooking meat and fresh bread drifting out of the inns drew her, so she looked until she found a small one with the pretentious name of The Spread Eagle.

Going inside, she almost faltered. All the customers were men, except for an elderly couple who sat against the far wall. But hunger nudged her, and she took a small table next to the couple. The innkeeper was a rough-looking man with one eye covered by a black patch, but the meal he produced was good—beef and cheese with plenty of fresh hot bread and yellow butter. She ate hungrily, lingered over the steaming tea as long as possible, then got up and paid for the meal.

"Is it far to the harbor?" she asked.

"No more'n a quarter-mile down that way," he nodded with his head. Then he looked her over and added, "Be dark soon, miss. Best not be on the streets all alone."

"Oh, my brother will meet me, thank you." The words leaped easily to her lips, and she thought wryly, *It's getting easier to lie!* Then she hesitated and asked, "Do you have a room I could have for the night—in case I can't find my brother?"

"Right, miss. Cost yer a shilling with breakfast throwed in."

She gave him a coin. "I'll take it. Give me the key."

"Key was carried off long ago, miss—but I'll see you right. Don't allow no fancy tricks in my place! Not likely!"

It seemed the best thing, as it appeared unlikely that she would find a berth in a ship that evening. The man looked rough, but there was no guarantee that another place would be safer. She nodded and followed him up a small stairway that led to the upper floor. He opened a door, then stepped back, saying, "If you wants hot water later—or a late supper, just you call, miss."

"Thank you."

Julie waited until he left, then put her small bag on the bed. A pitcher of water and a basin on the table beside the bed beckoned, and she washed her face carefully, then put her coat on and started to leave. She reached the door, then paused suddenly, went to the bag and removed a purse containing most of the money she had. She counted out fifty pounds, dividing it into three parts. She put twenty pounds each in two leather bags and wrapped the other ten in a handkerchief and slipped it into a smaller bag with a long drawstring. This one she placed around her neck, allowing the bag to fall inside the front of her dress. She dared not leave any of the cash in an unlocked room, so she put one of the larger bags in her handbag and the other in her deep coat pocket. As she passed through the main dining room, the one-eyed innkeeper said, "Remember, miss, it won't do to be on the streets late."

She nodded, then walked rapidly down the narrow streets, filled with many more people than she was accustomed to. She saw more foreigners than was usual in Philadelphia—French, Spanish-looking men, swarthy fellows she took to be Portuguese, and many, many blacks, usually accompanying their owners on errands.

The harbor was a forest of masts, thicker than stalks in a field of corn—far more than most harbors. She wandered down the wharf, wondering how to find a ship bound for England, but there was no such thing as a passenger ship. She knew enough to realize that she would be fortunate to get a compartment on some sort of cargo ship headed back with a load of tobacco, furs, or lumber.

Twice she stopped men to ask about a ship, but neither of them knew of one. Then a tall man with a wolfish face came up to her, saying, "Hello, darling! Looking for someone?"

"No!" she said abruptly, then wheeled and walked back along the pier as rapidly as she could without breaking into a run. It was almost dark when she got back to the inn. She noted that a smallish woman with red hair was serving the customers their drinks. The smoke was thick and she felt uncomfortable there, so she ascended the stairs to her small room. There was no light, and when she had to go back downstairs to get a light for the candle on the small table, the red-haired woman looked at her in a sharp, peculiar way.

The room was cold, of course, with no heat at all except that which drifted up from the fireplace below, so she pulled the covers back and got under the heavy blankets fully dressed. For over an hour she read the Bible, and finally, putting it on the table, she blew the candle out. Sleep came almost at once, but she woke several times, awakened by the raucous laughter and shouts from the inn below, and more than once by bad dreams.

Finally the noise from downstairs subsided, and she slept an exhausted sleep.

The sound of the door opening brought her instantly awake— a very small sound, but in the silence of the room it seemed very loud. She sat bolt upright, clenching the covers to her breast as a thin line of light outlined the door as it opened, and in an unsteady voice she cried out, "You get out of here!"

Then the door swung open and a burly figure filled the opening as the one-eyed man bearing a brass lantern in his hand stepped inside and shut the door. He put his back to the door and said, "Well—looky whut we got here!"

"You—you better get out of here or I'll—!"

"You'll scream?" he asked with a rough laugh when she could not finish. "Go ahead, see what it gets you."

He pulled himself away from the door, and as he stepped beside her, she threw the covers back, and leaping from the bed started for the door. He caught her easily, and for one moment held her by the arm, looking down at her. There was a greedy look in his one black eye, and his breath came faster; then he said, "You're a pretty little thing, ain't you now?" He reached out with his free hand and with careless strength held her face. She knew it was in his mind to kiss her.

Then he gave her a shove and said, "Yer ain't got no need to fear—not from me. All I wants is the reward."

Julie stepped back suddenly as he released her, breathless with relief that he had no intention of molesting her. "Reward?"

"Aw, you know about that—don't be so innocent!" He reached into his inner pocket, pulled out a folded sheet and shoved it at her. "Soon as I seen you, I knowed you was familiar, but it didn't come to me till I was in bed. So I gets up, goes down to the harbor and finds out that I'm gonna make a pile of money off of you!"

Julie opened the paper and read in large print:

RUNAWAY GIRL—REWARD

The description that followed fit her; the handbill offered a reward of twenty pounds, and it was signed by Aaron Sampson of Philadelphia.

"Easiest twenty guineas I ever made!" the innkeeper laughed. Then he said, "You jes' come with me and we'll get going."

Julie's mind raced like a wild thing, and like a flash an idea leaped into her mind. She stood straight and looked right into the man's face, her voice steely as she said, "You'll get no twenty pounds—but you'll get a thrashing and a holiday in jail—that's what you'll get."

He stopped smiling, surprised at the sudden hardness that had crossed her face. "What's that?"

"You see that name—the man who's offering the reward?"

"Yeah, I see it—Aaron Sampson. What about it?"

"You may think you've seen some hard men here, but you've never run across one as mean as he is."

"Who is he?"

"My father," she lied easily. "I lied about meeting my brother. I'm going to meet my lover and we're going to England together and get married."

"That's a lie—but even if it ain't, your pa, he'll pay twenty pounds to get you back!"

Julie made herself shrug and look careless. "All right, have it your way."

Something about the easy way she gave in disturbed the man, and he hesitated. She caught it, and said, "What will happen is that I'll tell him you abused me, and he'll beat you half to death and then have you put in prison. He's a magistrate and knows the law—he's had people put in jail for less." A shadow of doubt had begun to cloud the single eye of the innkeeper, and Julie said, as though it had just occurred to her, "Of course, there's one way you can have the reward—and stay out of jail."

"How's that?" he asked quickly.

"Why, I'll give you the twenty pounds—if you promise to say nothing. We'll be gone tomorrow—then I don't care what you say to anyone."

"You ain't got no twenty pounds!"

Julie turned and picked up her small bag. Opening it, she plucked out the bag containing twenty pounds and tossed it at the man, who caught it. He pulled the strings opened, poured the coins out in his palm, and counted them. Then he looked up and said with admiration, "You're a shrewd one, you are! Gor!"

Julie feared any delay, for he could change his mind, so she fastened her small case, picked up her coat, which had fallen from the bed to the floor, and said, "Remember—I want nothing said about this—or I'll have a story to tell my father that'll get you drawn and quartered!"

"If you ain't something!" The innkeeper shook his head in admiration. "Blamed if you ain't a bold baggage!"

Julie left him, sweeping down the stairs and out into the street. The stars burned coldly in the dark sky, but rosy lights were breaking the darkness to the east as she hurried blindly down the street. There was no hope now of finding a ship in New York; the posters made capture almost a certainty. She moved quickly away from the waterfront area, and by the time the pale morning light washed across the streets, she was on the outskirts of town. Every time she passed anyone, she turned her face away like a guilty felon. She expected at any second to be stopped and hauled off to jail. Finally she halted, out of breath and shaky from fear. She found herself on a side street with only a few shops.

Some wagons were making their way out of town, and she knew her only hope was to get a ride in one of them, as she had with Matthew Perkins and his wife, but the thought nagged at her that the reward posters would be all along the coast, in every port, probably.

A bench made of a half-log with whittled posts for legs offered a moment's rest, so she sat down, and for half an hour tried to think of a plan. Nothing came to her, and finally she rose, intending to ask for a ride on one of the wagons, hoping for another miracle.

Just as she was about to move away, the door beside the bench swung open and a short man shaped like a barrel stepped outside with a shovel in his hand. He stopped upon seeing her, then smiled and said, "Well, you're here early, miss, but come on inside."

"Why, I was just—" she began; then she got a look at the merchandise inside the shop and stopped suddenly. She moved slowly, a thought coming to her, and she entered the shop followed by the owner.

"I could use a few things," she said, and for the next quarter of an hour she selected a small collection of items.

"This be all?"

"Yes. How much?"

"Well, let's see. . ." He added up the total, and she reached into her coat pocket to get the money.

"Something wrong, miss?"

Julie was searching her pockets frantically, but the leather pouch was gone. With a sickening feeling she remembered that the coat had fallen to the floor, and she knew that the heavy pouch must have slid out.

"I—no!" she said, then turning to one side, she pulled the purse-strings around her neck free, and opening the pouch, paid for the merchandise from its slender store. It took two pounds, and she resolutely put away the fear that touched her as the man wrapped the goods in a paper and handed them to her.

She left the shop so quickly that the shopkeeper came out to watch her disappear around a corner. "Funny sort of things for a young girl to want," he muttered, then started shoveling snow from the walk.

Julie walked down half a dozen streets, looking for some sort of privacy, and at last she found an old barn that was apparently deserted. She looked around furtively, then darted inside, her breath coming quickly. The place, she saw at once, was not being used, and she found a stall with a window that let a shaft of light into the darkness of what had been some sort of small harness room. She put her bag and the package on the floor, then slowly pulled the paper aside. Reaching down, she picked up a pair of scissors and held them up. She stared at them, then removed her bonnet and with a quick motion let her long hair down. It fell down her back, thick, black and lustrous, and she felt a momentary twinge of sadness, but then her lips tightened, and she reached back and awkwardly cut a long, thick tress. She held it up, looked at it for a long moment, then gave a half sob and dropped it to the floor and began snipping steadily.

Thirty minutes later, when the door of the abandoned barn swung open, the figure that stepped outside looked nothing like Julie Sampson!

The test came at once, for just as she slipped outside and was walking toward the main street, a man rounded the corner and walked right by her. Her heart almost stopped, but he only gave her a quick nod, said, "Morning," and without another word or look passed on down the street.

What he had seen was a young fellow, not over fifteen, with a soft cap pulled down over a head of roughly-cut black hair. To be sure, there was a little softness in the lad, something a little girlish in the curve of the cheeks—but no more so than in other city-raised lads.

Julie had deliberately scuffed the gray homespun shirt, the knee breeches and brown stockings in the dirt, as well as the heavy wool coat that hung down to her knees. The garments were too large and so poorly cut that they effectively concealed her developing figure.

She walked down the street carrying the case, which contained a few other masculine garments. All the clothing she had brought with her, along with personal feminine items, she had left in the loft, and the pile of hair she had buried.

It took great courage for Julie to join the growing stream of people on their way to work, but she knew no other way was possible.

I've got a chance! she thought. *If I'm careful and keep to myself, I can do it.*

So she made her way to the outskirts of town, was picked up by an old man with a wagon load of glass windows headed for New Haven. He was a foul-mouthed old man, and the things he said to the young "fellow" beside him made her cheeks burn, but she managed to cover her confusion, and as the wagon rumbled along, she tried to ignore the fact that she had only a few pounds. She had no idea how she would get across the sea to her aunt's, but one thing kept coming to her mind—a verse of scripture that Pastor Kelly seemed to love more than any other. He quoted it every time he preached, usually more than once. Now as the wagon bumped along over the rutted road and the old man told raw stories, Julie let that verse linger in her mind, saying it over and over again: "With God—nothing shall be impossible!"

During the weeks that followed, Julie felt as if she might wear that verse out, and more than once her faith almost failed. The pitifully small stack of coins dwindled rapidly, even though she spent money only for food—and not a great deal of that.

She traveled where the wagons went that picked her up, falling into a kind of aimlessness. Her idea of getting to England she clung to stubbornly, but there was no money for her passage, so she moved steadily up the coast, touching briefly at Newport, only to discover the reward posters there as well.

She had grown more assured with her disguise, discovering that people did not really care much, especially as the clothes she had bought grew dirty and worn. Sometimes she would stay in a barn and cut some wood for a meal with a farmer, but as she moved northward, the weather grew worse, and when she came to Boston on the third of February, a blizzard swept in from the west burying the city under ice and snow.

In desperation, Julie tried to find a ship that would take her in exchange for work, but nothing was available. Few ships made the trip in such weather, and those that did go were usually able to make up a crew of able-bodied seamen.

Her last coins went, and then she had nothing. She shoveled snow for some of the merchants, but most of the shops shut down, waiting for the warm breath of spring to thaw the city out.

On the third day after her money ran out, Julie touched bottom. She had gone up and down the streets asking for work with the few merchants who still opened their businesses, and found none. For two days she had eaten nothing, and her head was aching with fatigue.

Snow began to drift downward late in the afternoon, and with her stomach in a knot, she went to the harbor, stumbling through the falling snow, not really caring a great deal what happened.

The cold paralyzed her hands, and finally she sat down facing the forest of masts, all white and glittering with snow and ice. The sounds of the city were muffled by the thick, fleecy blanket of snow, and she realized that she would have to get up and find shelter in a barn or in an alley, but she had no will to do it.

Closing her eyes, she ignored the snow gathering on her head and whitening her clothing. She thought of her father and of those good times in the past. She remembered the church and Pastor Kelly with his thin face and hearty voice. She even remembered her mother, dead and buried—living only in her memories now.

Julie sat there, dozing and thinking of the sweet warm days of the past—and still the snow fell. Gently it fell, making a soft blanket that was no longer cold, but seemed warm—warm as her memories and her dreams.

Slowly she drifted into a gentle sleep like a little child.

CHAPTER THREE

A FAMILY DIVIDED

★ ★ ★ ★

Caleb Winslow was roused from a sound sleep by the sound of his brother's head hitting the oak headboard with a solid *THUNK!* He turned his head and grinned as a muffled oath broke the morning silence.

"Ministers aren't supposed to swear," Caleb said. By the thin gray light of the January sun he watched as his brother, holding the top of his head, swung his feet to the floor and sat up. "That must be a million times you've banged your head, Nathan. Appears to me you'd figure out a better way to wake up than beating your brains out every morning."

"Like what?" Nathan asked grumpily. "Cut my legs off and be a midget like you?" He stood up cautiously, avoiding the low, rough-hewn beam that dissected the small loft bedroom. He went to the oak washstand and, breaking the skim of ice from the water in the basin, began splashing his face, sputtering and wheezing. He worked up a thin lather and scraped at his cheeks with a razor.

Caleb watched with interest, and when Nathan was finished, he said, "Think I'll start shaving." He had said this since Nathan had started shaving two years earlier and had no real intention of acting on it.

"Shaving *what*?" Nathan grinned as he stripped off a flannel nightshirt and began pulling on his clothes. "Might as well look for whiskers on an egg as on your face. Got to be a man to grow something to shave, boy!"

Caleb's face flushed and he rolled out of bed and thrust his chin forward. "A little hair on your face don't make you a man!" His dark eyes flashed and he put his hands forward in a wrestling stance, adding, "You think you're more of a man than me, Nathan; why, you just come on, and we'll see!"

A sudden grin touched the lips of the older boy, and he regarded the stocky figure of his brother fondly. "You're getting too big to fool with." He rubbed the top of his head and added ruefully, "I keep growing *up* and you keep growing *around*, Caleb—looks like we could sort of *average out* somehow!"

The two did present a stark contrast. Caleb, at fifteen, was short but powerfully built. His chest was deep and pads of muscle swelled his upper body. His legs were thick and solid, and there was a ponderous quality to all his movements. He had a square chin, and even by the feeble morning light that streamed in, his dark coloring and dark eyes were visible.

He stood there, a solid figure, looking up at Nathan, and there was a trace of envy in his dark eyes as he took in his brother's tall form. Nathan was exactly six feet three inches tall, and though at seventeen he was two years older than Caleb, he had not filled out as he would later on. He had shot up like a weed for the past three years, his clothes becoming too short before they wore out. He had discovered his actual height by measuring the bed he shared with Caleb and found it to be exactly six feet and three inches long— which meant that if he got one inch too high in it, he would bash his head against the hard oak as he had done a few moments earlier. The only solution he could find was to sleep at an *angle*—a practice that did not make Caleb happy, since it meant sharing his half of the bed with his brother's long legs.

There was some awkwardness to Nathan's movements as he finished dressing and moved toward the door, for he had grown so fast that his coordination had not yet caught up with his stature. He had the cautious movements of a very tall man—always measuring low beams and door openings. In spite of this coltish awkwardness, there were traces of grace and strength as he moved through the door, and most people who saw him asked themselves, *What will he be like when he gets his full growth?*

But it was not only in height that the two differed; where Caleb had dark skin, blue-black eyes, and black hair, Nathan had auburn hair and the high complexion that frequently goes with that shade. His face was triangular, sloping down from a broad forehead to a pointed chin; his nose was rather short, but flared out at the base. Smallish ears almost hidden behind the hair, a wide mouth, straight eyebrows over a pair of startling light blue eyes—these were all part of the Winslow heritage that had come to him. He was almost delicate in feature, and some said he was pretty enough to be a girl. Yet there was a hint of stubborn strength in his features and a steadiness in his eyes that offset any touch of the feminine, and his long reach and developing strength had enabled him to hold his own in the youthful brawls that had come his way.

"Better get yourself dressed," Nathan called as he left the room. "I think Ma is frying donkers."

The fragrance of baking filled the house as they hurried down from the loft and into the broad hallway toward the kitchen. His mother turned as he entered, greeting him with a smile. "Good morning, Nathan."

"Morning, Mother." His appetite was ferocious, and the smell of cooking meat made his stomach rumble. His mother made donkers from the week's meat leftovers, chopped together with bread, apples, raisins and savory spices—fried and served with boiled pudding. He picked up a wooden spoon, filled it from the heavy black pot and jammed it into his mouth.

"Nathan, you'll burn your tongue off!" She took the spoon away from him, reached up and smoothed his hair down where it rose up in the back, and then pushed him toward the door. "You better get some firewood in before your father sees that empty wood box!"

"That's Caleb's job," he complained.

"Oh? You're too dignified to help around the house now that you're going to college?"

"I didn't say that!"

"You know Caleb does his work—and some of yours as well."

"All right, Mother, all right!"

He stalked outside to the woodpile, and a mixture of righteous indignation and guilt made him make four trips to the house, piling up the short chunks of red oak until the box overflowed. His mother said nothing, but watched him out of the corner of her eye, a furtive smile springing to her lips as he dumped the last load, then slumped into his chair, a picture of wounded innocence.

"You think *that's* enough to do for a spell?"

Molly Winslow's maiden name had been Burns, and she had the type of beauty often seen in women of Scottish blood. She looked ten years younger than her forty-one years, and her ash-blonde hair had no more gray in it than it had when Adam Winslow had first seen her as a child on the streets of London. She had the figure of a young girl, and only a few lines around her eyes revealed her age.

She nodded, but before she could answer, Caleb bustled into the kitchen. He came over to kiss his mother, as he always did, saying, "I'm starved, Ma!"

"After that supper you ate last night," Molly said tartly, "you're not likely to die of hunger." Her tone was sharp, but there was a fond light in her eyes as she looked at the boy. A stab of regret came to Nathan, mixed with envy, for he lacked the easy ways of his younger brother—especially where his parents were concerned. It was not that he loved them less than Caleb, but somewhere along the way an awkwardness had developed. Perhaps it was due to his tremendous height; it was, he recognized, much easier for both of them to see Caleb as a child—after all, who wants to reach up and caress a giant? But that resentful thought passed, and he knew that the wall between himself and his parents was the product of more than a few inches in his spine.

The outer door swung open, and Adam Winslow stepped inside, his dark eyes sweeping the room quickly. His tread was soundless as he came to stand beside his chair. "Morning. Food smells good." He greeted his sons, then sat down in an easy way, and while Molly was putting the food on the table, Adam sat there listening as Caleb chattered on about the trip to Boston. As he ran on, Nathan thought how odd it was that his brother talked so much, and he talked so little. *You'd think he was going to be the minister instead of me!* he thought suddenly.

As Nathan's mother put the hot bread on the table and sat down, suddenly he saw that room as he'd never seen it before—as if it were a painting with the title *Puritan Family at Breakfast*. It was a nice picture, too. They ate in the dining room on the Sabbath, and Mother set the table with china and silver, but on weekdays they ate in the kitchen. So in his mind he saw them sitting around the rough board table with the big fireplace, four of them but with an extra place set for five. His father claimed that the empty chair reminded them that they had an Unseen Guest with them at all times. It was a powerful image, and as a child Nathan had been a little afraid that God would come in and take His seat!

As his father asked the usual blessing, Nathan stole a glance at him, thinking that the Unseen Guest thing was one of the few outer traces of imagination Adam Winslow ever showed. Oh, he was creative enough at the forge, making beautiful rifles or even silver jewelry, but he had little of fancy in him in other ways.

Nathan thought that his father was the most *practical* looking man in the world. He was five feet ten and weighed one hundred eighty-five pounds, and if there was a stronger man in the county, he hadn't shown up to prove it. Adam had a square face with dark skin and darker eyes, and his hair showed only a few gray strands in the midst of the black. His hands were almost square, thick with pads of muscle and scarred from years of work with iron and wood. Nathan took a quick glance at Caleb and almost smiled, for there was something comical in the way his younger brother sat there, a mirror image of the father! They both had the same darkness, the same powerful frame, and despite the fact that Caleb was much more of a talker than his father, they thought in the same way.

"Did you pick up that last load from the warehouse, Nathan?"

"Yes, sir."

"You remember that bale of prime beaver that Louis left up in the loft—the one Dupree brought in last winter?"

"Yes, sir."

There was doubt in the way Nathan's father stared at him. He'd always made the annual trip to Boston to haul the furs, but this year he was so far behind in the forge that Nathan argued him into letting him do it—and somehow he had done even more—he had talked him into letting the two of them stay the rest of the summer with their Uncle Charles!

"I've been with you on the last five trips, Father," he'd pleaded, and then Mother had joined in so that finally a week earlier he'd agreed to let Nathan make the trip. Then Caleb had set up a howl to go, so the two of them were to leave the following day, on their own for the first time in their lives.

Now Nathan saw the questions in his father's eyes, and knew that if he decided his sons weren't to be trusted, he'd just take the furs himself. Right then Caleb jumped in, and for the first time in

Nathan's life he was glad his brother was such a talker!

Caleb knew his father, and he began talking cheerfully about how good it was for young fellows to learn responsibility and how glad he was to have an older brother. As always, he got his way. Nathan saw through it in a second, but he'd learned to accept the fact long ago that his father had a weakness for his younger son.

"It'll be good for them, Adam." Molly came over and put her arm around him, something which always gentled him down. "Charles wants them to come."

"I know. And I suppose the boys can learn something about business from him." His eyes fell on Nathan and there was a peculiar glint in his glance that the older son couldn't read. "But I can't see what good it will do a minister to know about business."

There it was. Nathan felt his face flush, for he resented the fact that his father had never put much stock in his call to the ministry. Ever since that day when Nathan had told his parents that he felt God wanted him to be a minister, the wall between him and his father had grown thicker. Now he said quickly, "Well, Father, I don't think it will do a minister any harm to know something of business."

"I suppose not."

Mother pulled at Father's arm, saying, "We'd better hurry if we don't want to be late for service, Adam." Then she smiled at Nathan and there was a gleam in her gray eyes as she said, "And it wouldn't look very good for you to be late, Nathan. Rev. Patterson might feel your dedication is lacking."

Adam snorted and there was a flash of anger in his dark eyes. "I wish he'd preach the gospel instead of singing the praises of King George!"

"He's not doing that, sir!" Nathan said, and was sorry at once.

Adam stared at the tall young man, his face settling down into an angry look that made Nathan wish he'd kept his mouth shut.

"Nathan, the man is no more than a mouthpiece for the Crown! He has a right to speak his mind, but he uses his pulpit for attacking loyal men in these Colonies—and he has no sense of justice!"

"Sir—I think that's not fair!"

"Not fair!" There was a thick silence in the room, and Nathan saw that they were into another of their arguments over politics. Adam Winslow had fought in the French and Indian War under Colonel Washington and sympathized with the group led by Sam

Adams who were out to challenge English authority. And it saddened Nathan, for his father was not an unreasonable man—quite the contrary. *But he's just as blind as the rest of that crew who want to push us into a war we can't win*! the boy thought.

"You think I'm *unfair*?" Adam demanded, stepping closer to Nathan. "Why, Patterson has branded my friends traitors from his pulpit! And you don't think it's *unfair* for a minister to use his office for a political platform?"

"You don't say that about those ministers who use their pulpits to demand freedom, Father," Nathan shot back, but over his father's head he saw his mother shaking her head violently, and it brought him up short. He realized that if his father got angry, he'd not let them go to Boston, so he said, "Oh, Father, I'm sorry we got into this. Let's drop it and go to service."

Adam was caught off guard with the sudden apology, and Nathan's mother came forward quickly, saying, "Yes, we have to go, Adam."

"All right, Molly."

Nathan and Caleb went quickly to hitch the team and saddle their own mounts. Nathan drove the wagon out of the stable to the front gate, and held the lines until his father helped his mother into the wagon. "Don't race those horses, boys," he said as he took the reins. "Not on the Sabbath."

Nathan said, "No, sir," then went to where Caleb sat on his horse. He mounted easily, and the two of them started down the road. As soon as they were out of hearing, Caleb said, "Why'd you have to start fighting with Father? If you'd kept on, he wouldn't have let us take the trip to Boston."

As they approached the white church just outside the village, Nathan thought of how his father had looked strangely at him when speaking of the founders of their family. Gilbert Winslow, the first of the family to come to America, had been a great and honored man, according to the family tales, as had his son Matthew. But once, in an unguarded moment, Adam had said to his son, "You're too much like Charles, Nathan."

As he pulled his horse down and allowed Caleb to catch up, Nathan thought about his uncle. Charles Winslow was the half brother of Adam, and there'd been some sort of scandal in his life, but Nathan could never find out exactly what it was all about. His uncle was a very successful businessman in Boston, and on the rare occasions when he'd come to Virginia, Nathan had been very impressed. He remembered him as a tall, handsome man with fair hair and bright blue eyes, and that he'd always given generous gifts to him and to Caleb. Slipping from his horse, he tied him to the post, thinking with excitement of the trip. Though he was older than Caleb and had gone to Harvard for one brief term of ten weeks, he was as excited as the younger boy about the trip, and some of it was the expectation of seeing his uncle again.

His parents pulled up fifteen minutes later, and his father said, "I told you not to race those horses, Nathan." There was displeasure in his dark eyes, and he led the way into the white frame building to their customary pew, speaking little to anyone.

Rev. Patterson was a short, broad man with a full, fair face and a strong Bristol accent. Nathan, although he agreed fully with the pastor's political sentiments, hoped fervently that his sermon would stay inside the covers of the Bible. His hopes were dashed, however, for the text was taken from that section of the Scriptures that teaches men to be obedient to those in authority. And those in authority, of course, were of the Royal House of Hanover—King George and his court of ministers.

Rev. Patterson was a man of strong opinions, and his displeasure with those who chose to challenge the authority of the Crown was intense. His eyes lingered longest on Adam Winslow, though there were many others in the congregation who were more adamant in their stand against royal policy than he.

Halfway through the sermon, Nathan heard Caleb snort and say under his breath, "Big jackass!" He dug his elbow into Caleb's ribs, hoping that nobody had heard, but there was a sullen "amen!" that came from his father, and Nathan slumped into his seat, wishing only that the service would end and they could get away.

After the sermon, Rev. Patterson posted himself at the door, and when the Winslows stepped up, he said with an angry light in his eyes, "Mr. Winslow, you should keep your sons in order!"

"Rev. Patterson, you should keep your sermons in order."

There was a sudden hush in the church, the humming of talk stopped abruptly. The position of a minister in the community was an elevated one, and few men would speak so harshly to one of them as Adam Winslow had just done.

"Sir, you are impertinent!" Patterson's face flushed richly, and he added angrily, "It's obvious, sir, that your rebellion against the

Crown has been expanded to include disloyalty against your church!"

Adam Winslow was an even-tempered man, but he had sat through a long line of political harangues masquerading as sermons, all directed at himself and some of his friends. Now the pastor chose to make the thing personal by singling him out, and it stirred him to anger. *There is something dangerous in him*, Nathan thought, and it startled him. He had seen his father aroused only once, years before. A large man had been mistreating a horse, and Nathan never forgot how his father had exploded into wrath, thrashing the bully so quickly and thoroughly that the story still lingered in the town.

"Rev. Patterson, when you preach the gospel, I am a faithful member of your flock. If you choose to depart from your calling and turn your pulpit into a political arena, I cannot respect you."

He might have said more, but Molly suddenly was there. She put her hand on his arm and said, "Adam—please!"

At once, he looked at her, and then said, "This is no place for argument. Excuse us, Pastor."

Nathan followed his parents, but the minister grasped his arms. "Nathan, you must try to talk to your father."

Nathan shook his head. "There is nothing I can say, Pastor. He just gets angry with me."

"I understand you're going to Boston."

"Yes, tomorrow."

"Be careful, Nathan!" Patterson's full face was still angry, and he added as the boy pulled away. "That's where all Sam Adams' gang is, and they'll pull us into a war if something isn't done!"

Nathan hurried away; this time he and Caleb followed the buggy down the road. As he expected, Caleb began to berate the minister. "Why, that preacher ought to be tarred and feathered!" he exclaimed. "I'll bet he gets his pay from ol' King George himself."

"Caleb, you're crazy!"

"No, I'm not!"

"You're just a kid—and not too smart at that!" The anger that had gnawed at Nathan spilled out, and he glared at Caleb, saying loudly, "What do you know? Oh, sure, there have been a few unfair taxes, but what do you think we can do about it?"

"We can fight!"

"Why, you *are* crazy, Caleb!" Nathan snapped. "England's the strongest nation in the world—and you think a few farmers like us can fight her?"

Caleb's dark face was stubborn. "England's thousands of miles away, Nathan, and this is a big country. All of us can shoot, can't we? How long can we stand for being treated like slaves?"

Nathan was shocked, for he had known men put into the stocks for saying less. "Caleb, that's *treason!*"

"It's the same as Father thinks!"

There was so much truth in Caleb's reply that Nathan was speechless. He shook his head in despair, and listened in silence all the way back to the house as Caleb talked endlessly about the matter.

Finally he said as they unsaddled the horses, "You'd better not say any of this to Father, Caleb. He'd never let you go to Boston with me."

"Yes, he would," Caleb argued, but caution kept him quiet, and the house, though filled with a certain restraint that evening, was unbroken by any political talk.

Molly lay quietly as the crowing of a cock broke through the silence of the morning. She felt the tension in Adam's body, and reaching out, touched his cheek. "You didn't sleep much."

"No."

"Neither did I."

He rolled over and peered at her in the dim light, then gave a quick laugh. "We know each other pretty well, don't we?"

"I guess when two people love each other like we do," she smiled, "their moods get all mixed up. When you're happy, so am I. And when you're troubled, I can't rest."

He shook his head, threw back the cover and got out of bed. Pulling on his clothes, he was silent, but when they were both dressed, he turned to her and said, "Should I let them go, Molly?"

"Yes."

He suddenly laughed. "You're always so certain of everything. I wish I were!"

She was almost as tall as he, so she only had to pull his head down a couple of inches to kiss him on the lips. "They'll be all right. They're good boys."

He stared at her, and there was an indecision in him that she had never seen. "Are they? I hope so."

"You're worried about Nathan, aren't you?"

"Yes, I am." He hesitated, then said, "He's too impulsive, Molly. Too much like Charles."

"No, he's not like Charles." Molly half turned to the window, then turned back, a thoughtful look on her face. "Oh, he *looks* like him, of course, and there's some of that wild Winslow blood, but deep down he's like you, Adam. I know you can't see it—but I can."

He struggled with the thought, then finally smiled and said, "You're right, I can't see it. So I'll just have to go on your judgment, Molly." He put his arms around her, and a fond light replaced the anxious look in his face. "It's been a long time since that first time I saw you. I think of that time often. How old were you?"

"Just eleven—and I thought you were the handsomest thing I'd ever seen."

"Will ye buy a handkerchief—only five bob!" He smiled at her, and added, "That's the first thing you ever said to me, wasn't it?"

"And you bought it, didn't you, dear?" Molly laughed and added, "If you'd known what you were getting into that morning, I think you'd have run away like a deer!"

"No. No, I wouldn't have. You've been my life, Molly."

She stood there, surrendering to his quick embrace, thinking of the strange manner of their courtship. She'd been an unfortunate child of eleven on the streets of London, mistreated by a drunken father. He'd been there on his first trip from home, and he'd been so moved by her plight that he'd paid her brute of a father all the money he had, getting her under his care as a bound girl—an indentured servant. She remembered how he'd been in love with Mary Edwards, and how, as the years had rolled by, Molly had been in love with him. And she remembered the shock in his eyes when he at last saw her as a woman—and fell in love. Since that time, they'd been truly man and wife, in spirit as in flesh.

Now she said, "Nathan will be all right. He's your son."

He stared at her, and his face relaxed. "We'll trust God to take care of them."

When they went downstairs, they found Caleb and Nathan had already fixed breakfast, a feat which amused them both. "Well, if I'd known a trip to Boston would produce this sort of thing," Adam smiled, "I'd have let you go long ago!"

Both boys were champing at the bit, anxious to go, so they ate a quick breakfast, and then it was time for them to leave. The wagons were loaded and the teams were in the village ready to go, so there was nothing to do but say goodbye.

But it was hard for Molly. Despite her brave words, it was the first time her boys were leaving to go farther than the small village, and there was a lump in her throat that would not go away.

She took Caleb's quick hug, and kissed him, then Nathan stood before her, a little embarrassed, as always, at showing affection. She pulled his head down, kissed him soundly, and said, "Take care of your brother, Nathan! Take very good care of him!"

"Ah, Mother," Caleb said with a wide grin. "It's me as will take care of him!"

Then the boys stood before Adam, and for once for some reason, Nathan did not feel intimidated. He looked into his father's eyes and saw there for the first time in years, an approval that he had always longed for.

Adam sought for words, but could only say what Molly had said. "Nathan, take care of your brother."

"Yes, sir." Nathan put his hand out awkwardly, but it was ignored and suddenly Adam put his arms around both boys, drawing them in with a powerful hug that took their breath, then released them.

"Get on your way now—and take care of each other."

They left, and all the way to town and for a long time after that, Nathan heard the words that his parents had spoken: "Take care of your brother." And he always remembered the strength of his father's arms in that last powerful embrace.

CHAPTER FOUR

COUNTRY COUSIN

★ ★ ★ ★

Ice glittered on the backs of the horses, and their frosty breath rose like miniature clouds of incense as Nathan pulled them to a halt in front of the two-story building that fronted the harbor with the sign THE WINSLOW COMPANY over the door.

"Wake up, Caleb." He nudged the small mountain of blankets huddled close beside him, and a smile touched his lips as a groan of protest emerged from the depths. "We're here—come out of there, boy."

"What is it?" The blankets parted, and Caleb reluctantly surfaced from the warm cocoon. He wore a black wool knitted cap pulled down to his eyebrows, a red and blue scarf swathed his face, so that all that could be seen of him was a sleepy pair of dark eyes.

"Go see where they want the load," Nathan said. "Looks like they might be closed." He watched with amusement as Caleb climbed down stiffly, then waddled across the snow to the big double doors. He looked like a walking barrel, for he hated cold and wore every garment he'd brought on the trip, in addition to a buffalo coat of Nathan's.

Been a hard trip, Nathan reflected as he watched Caleb disappear into the depths of the warehouse. *Bet not even Father could have done better!* Ice glittered in the short red stubbles of his beard, and he shook his head ruefully at his pride, knowing that his father would have made the trip faster.

But it *had* been a hard journey. Winter had closed like an iron fist, freezing the roads to slick ribbons, and near-blizzard cold had punished the horses terribly. Caleb had begun well, but for the last week he had done nothing but hug the fire at night and swath himself into every garment he could find during the day's trek. They had met with few travelers, and Nathan could not resist a heady gust of pride as he realized that he had brought the furs through when most men had sought the warmth of fire inside snug cabins.

As the big double doors swung open, he glanced down at his large hands, blue from the cold and calloused from handling the lines, and was pleased. There had been doubt in his father's eyes when they had parted, but the good feeling of accomplishing a hard task was a solid feeling in Nathan. "Hup, Babe—Dan!" He guided the team into the dark interior, climbed down and stamped his feet, which had no more feeling than the iron ring he tied up to.

"Mister Winslow didn't look for you." A thick-bodied man with a face blue from cold and red from drink stared at Nathan, and there was some resentment in his clipped New England speech as he added, "Don't have no help this time of day fer unloadin'."

"It'll wait for tomorrow."

"Them horses won't wait!"

If the man had been more civil, Nathan would have helped unhitch, but he was bone-tired and both he and Caleb were half-starved. "We're going to my uncle's house. How far is it?"

The big man's face flushed, but he said, "Three miles back down the old Turnpike—you must'a passed it comin' in—big white house with pillars." He gave them instructions in a grudging voice, then grinned sourly. "You'll have a nice little walk—may get there by dark."

Nathan stared at him, then said, "Caleb, we'll take Babe and Dan." The two brothers unhitched the horses, put a pair of hair hackamores on them, and led them outside. Nathan said tersely to the heavy man, "Get those other two animals unhitched and fed!" He mounted easily, but Caleb had to lead Dan to the watering trough and use it for a platform as he scrambled aboard, not without groaning.

The horses were just about played out, but three more miles would not kill them. As they plodded down the frozen road, the light beginning to fail, Caleb asked, "Uncle Charles won't be looking for us, will he?"

"I guess not, with all this weather. But he'll sure be glad to get the furs."

Caleb beat his hands together, then blew on them for warmth. "I can't remember much about him, Nathan. Is he like Father?"

There was a small interval of silence; then Nathan shook his head, a thoughtful stirring in his eyes. "No, Caleb, he's not like Father." He paused and the sound of the iron shoes on the frozen ground punctuated the cold silence, and a small smile touched his broad lips as he added, "But then, nobody else is like him, either!"

"Well, I sure hope they ain't finished supper yet," Caleb said. "My belly feels like my throat's been cut! I've sure heard a lot, though, about how fancy Aunt Dorcas is. She might bow up over having us at her best table, dirty as we are."

"Might be right," Nathan nodded, then added with a touch of warning in his voice, "Don't think they'll chuck us out for being trail worn—but you keep your revolutionary talk to yourself, Caleb. You mind what Father told us about Uncle Charles."

"Yaaaaa! Makes me sick!" Caleb scowled and gave Dan a hard kick. "Think of Winslows being a bunch of Tories!"

"That's what I mean!" Nathan said sharply, and he reached out and grabbed Caleb's arm strongly. "You keep that talk to yourself while we are here—and stay away from that rabble that calls itself Sons of Liberty, you hear me?"

Caleb turned suddenly, and his customary smile faded. His square face turned stubborn, and for one instant Nathan had the feeling that he was looking into his father's dark eyes. "I'll say what I think, Nathan—here or anywhere else!"

Hot words leaped to Nathan's lips, but he bit them off. He and Caleb had been through this many times, and it always ended with both of them white-lipped with anger. *No use to argue with him*, he thought wearily. *Mother and Father feel the same way, so it's no wonder he's getting to be a fire-eater.* But he only shook his head, saying in a reasonable tone, "Look, just keep your political opinions to yourself, Caleb—while we're here. Because if you don't, we'll get sent home quick, and Father won't ever let us do anything like this again."

The latter warning seemed to have some effect, for Caleb quickly shut off his protests and said only, "Well, guess you're right about that, Nathan—but it goes against the grain!"

Darkness fell quickly, and they managed to get lost inside the city, so that by the time they pulled up in front of a large white house on the outskirts of town, Nathan had to lean down and put his face to the sign. He made out the letters, straightened up, and said, "This is it. Come on."

A long ice-packed drive led to the house, and the rising wind made the frozen branches click overhead as they passed beneath. Tying their horses to an iron fence that set off a flowerbed, they mounted the high steps, and Nathan gave a couple of firm raps with the heavy brass knocker on the massive door.

Caleb shifted nervously as they waited, and finally he said, "Maybe we should have gone to the back door."

Nathan stared at him, then said, "What did that sign say over the door at the warehouse?"

Caleb thought, then answered, "The Winslow Company."

"That's right—and my name is Winslow. You go to the back door if you feel like it." He turned to hide a smile, for his taunt had done exactly what he'd expected—turned Caleb stubborn, which wasn't too hard to do in any case.

The door slowly opened, just a crack, and a black face appeared. "The family is at dinner. Is you expected?"

Nathan shot back, "Not *all* the family's at dinner. Go tell your master his nephews from Virginia are here!"

The steely quality in Nathan's voice must have startled the black man, for he quickly opened the door, and gave a nervous nod, saying, "Oh yas, indeed! You gentlemen come inside, please." He shut the door behind them and gave another nervous nod. "I'll tell Mistuh Winslow you is here!"

He turned to go, but at that moment, a voice called out from down the long hall, "Well—well! What's this? Is it you, Nathan?"

A tall man with bright blue eyes and reddish hair had emerged from a set of double doors and now came forward. He held out his hand, gave Nathan a firm grip, then slapped him on the shoulder, "My word! Are you *ever* going to stop growing, Nathan? And you, Caleb—" He turned to shake hands with the younger boy, and there was a light of amusement in his bright eyes. He laughed in delight, and reached out to give the boy a sudden hug. "Why, you're Adam Winslow!" He looked again and shook his head. "My word, you're the image of your father when he was your age, Caleb!"

"I take that as a compliment, Uncle Charles," Caleb said at once. He did not make quick judgments, and the instant warmth of Charles Winslow had caused him to throw up some sort of a wall. Nathan had seen it often, not only in Caleb, but in his father as well. Both of them were slow to judge, while he himself (often to his own chagrin!) gave his loyalty readily.

"We're a little late, Uncle Charles."

"Late!" Charles stared up at his tall nephew, then shook his head in wonder. "We didn't think you'd make it at all in this storm, Nathan!" Then he clapped their shoulders, saying, "You go get washed up—Benjamin, take my nephews to their room. Get them some hot water to wash with. We'll hold dinner until you can get there, boys."

"Yessuh, Mistuh Winslow!"

"Well, all our clothes are on the wagon, Uncle Charles," Nathan said, looking down at his mud-stained clothes. "We can't come to dinner like this!"

"You come as you are, Nathan," Charles said at once. "I don't think a little honest dirt from hard work will kill us!"

He gave them a smile, then turned and walked quickly back to the dining room off to the left of the wide hallway. It was an enormous room, for one of his demands for a house was that it be able to handle large dinner parties. Two massive fireplaces faced each other, and the heavy logs that popped and roared kept the room warm. The dining table was over twenty feet long, and it was covered with blinding white linen. Two giant chandeliers reflected their myriad candles on the silver that lay beside the five places set at the end next to the door.

"Mary, set two more places," Charles said to the black woman who stood by the wall.

"Two places? For whom?" Dorcas Winslow looked up sharply, her brown eyes reflecting her displeasure. She was an attractive woman, dressed in high fashion, even for a simple family dinner. Her dark brown hair shone in the candlelight, and the diamonds on her fingers winked as she raised a hand to pat it carefully. "I wasn't expecting anyone."

"It's Nathan and Caleb—just got in with the furs."

"Couldn't they wait until tomorrow?" Dorcas murmured. She loved ceremony, and any distractions that broke into the rituals of their affairs displeased her.

"Well, Mother, you couldn't ask them to sleep in the warehouse, could you now?"

The speaker was a young man who sat directly across from Charles, and there was a teasing note in his clear voice as he looked at Dorcas. "After all, they *are* family, aren't they?"

"I suppose, Paul," she said slowly, then added, "But they'll have to learn some manners if they stay here with us."

"I expect they'll have good enough manners," Charles said easily. "Virginians are just about the most hospitable people you'll find, Dorcas."

"Backwoods manners are not exactly what I like to see in my own home, Charles." She sighed and said, "I know you want them here, but it's going to be difficult."

"I do want them here," Charles said, and there was a sudden firmness in his voice. He was too heavy, and his face was marked with the signs of good food and too much liquor, but at times the vigor of his youth flared out, and at times like that the family had learned to avoid argument.

He picked up his wineglass, took a swallow, and looked around, saying, "We need some strong fresh blood in the business. I know you don't like Adam, Mama, but you'll have to admit he's a strong man—and I suspect these boys are just about the same."

"A stubborn man—I never trusted him!" Martha Winslow was seventy-two, but there was no weakness in her. She stared at her son with sharp black eyes, and added, "You were always a fool about Adam—but he never cared a pin for you—nor for any of us!"

Paul Winslow sat back, his quick mind analyzing the scene before him. He knew much of his family history, but he had never understood the hatred his grandmother had for her stepson, Adam Winslow. Once he had asked his father about it, but Charles had shook his head, saying, "She always hated him, Paul—even when he was a child. I think she was jealous of his mother—but she'd never admit it. Just don't think about it."

As the old woman stubbornly said, "You'll regret any dealings you have with that man!" Paul glanced at his mother and saw that she agreed with the sentiment—but for a different reason, he suspected. Suddenly he turned his head and caught the gaze of Anne Winslow, his fourteen-year-old sister. She had been listening quietly, but she missed little, Paul knew, and he winked at her, which made her drop her eyes.

"Adam's all right, Mother," Charles said adamantly, his face flushed as it often did when he was crossed. "He's kept his end of the business going well enough. And we need to keep the fur trade open. It's the most prosperous part of the company."

"Are they wearing Indian clothes, Father?" Anne piped up. She was a thin girl with her father's auburn hair and fair skin. Her bright blue eyes came from him as well.

Charles stared at her, then leaned back and laughed, "Indian clothes? Why, no, sweetheart, of course not!"

He was very partial to Anne, so he carefully explained how that some years ago, he and his brother Adam had divided the family business—with Adam moving to Virginia to handle the fur trade while he himself stayed in Boston to take care of the other aspects and the shipping. But Paul knew there was more to the separation than that; there had been almost no contact between the two families, and there had to be some reason.

He was still pondering on the matter when footsteps sounded and he looked up to see two young men enter. One was tall and fair, and looked so much like his own father it gave him a small shock. The other was short and dark.

"Well, here they are!" Charles stood up and waved a hand toward the two, saying gaily, "This is Nathan and this is his brother Caleb. Let me introduce you to your relatives, nephews. This is my wife, Dorcas; and my mother and your father's stepmother, of course, Mrs. Martha Winslow. This is my son, Paul, and my daughter, Anne."

Paul rose to his feet and walked around the table, saying with a smile, "Strange we haven't met—but better late than never, eh? Come now, you two sit down and eat."

Nathan and Caleb sat down, both feeling awkward, and as the black servant placed food before them, Nathan said, "I apologize for our clothing, but—"

"It's quite all right," Dorcas said in a tone that implied just the opposite.

"Did you see any Indians?"

Everyone laughed, but Anne's question eased the tension, and Nathan said, "No, Anne, it's too cold out for Indians, but I've seen lots of them back home, and I'll tell you some scary stories about them."

"You eat up now, and then you can tell us about Adam and Molly," Charles urged.

The food was good, and after Nathan and Caleb finished, Charles plied them with questions about Virginia—some about the family, but more about business. Nathan answered as well as he could, and his answers pleased their host.

All might have gone well, but suddenly Martha Winslow asked, "And has your father gotten rid of his erroneous ideas about the King?"

Before Nathan could answer, Caleb said loudly, "Why, ma'am, I expect my father's opinions on King George are about what any honest man's are—that he's a fool and not in the least interested in the freedom of his subjects in these Colonies!"

He's done it now! Nathan thought, but even as he tried to come up with some way to smooth the situation over, Paul Winslow took over. He said easily, "Now, Grandmother, we won't have any political arguments!" Getting up with a smile, he walked around and stood behind his mother and grandmother, and placing a hand on each of their shoulders, he said, "My cousins are probably worn out from a hard trip—and we have a lot of things to do in the next few weeks. There's a ball tomorrow night at Uncle Saul's and I want to show off my Virginia kinfolks. We'll have some of these pale Boston maidens falling at your feet, I can assure you!"

He went on easily, and Nathan drew a sigh of relief. *He knows how to handle them!* he thought with envy.

Later that night, when he and Caleb were finally in bed, he said, "You nearly ruined us with that rebel talk, Caleb. Keep quiet, you hear me?"

"You better worry about all those 'pale Boston maidens' Paul is going to throw at you," Caleb muttered faintly, then fell into a sleep so sound that he did not hear Nathan's drowsy reply. "You keep your mouth shut and I'll take care of the pale Boston maidens!"

"Oh, Abby, can't you hurry? The music's already started!"

Abigail Howland looked up from the French mahogany dressing table at Ellen Alden and gave a languid smile. "It will be the same crowd we've had for months, Ellen." She looked back into the mirror; then a thought struck her and she lifted a pair of hazel eyes to the tall girl who was pacing nervously back and forth across the room. "But I suppose you're thinking of Daniel being with Mercy Williams, aren't you? He's been giving her some pretty hot glances lately. If you don't make him propose to you pretty soon, she's going to get him."

Ellen was a slender girl with earnest brown eyes and auburn hair. "I—I wouldn't have a man I had to *force* into a proposal!" she said tightly.

"Mercy isn't as choosy as you, I think." Abby gave her shining brown hair a pat, then rose and led Ellen out of the room. As they went down the curving stairs, she said, "I can tell you how to get a proposal out of Daniel."

She spoke softly for a few moments; then suddenly Ellen's eyes opened wide and she cried, "No! I couldn't do *that*!—and neither could you, Abigail!"

"Men fight for land, for money, for power," Abby said. "But women fight for men!" She suddenly paused and nodded her head toward the milling crowd below. "There's Daniel—and I'll give you one guess as to who's dancing with him!"

"It's her!" Ellen moaned. "Oh, Abby, I love him so!"

"Well, let's see what can be done," Abby smiled. For the next half hour she busied herself with pushing Daniel Mains into the proposal that Ellen wanted to hear. Actually, it meant nothing to her, but Abigail Howland was bored with Boston, and it was a challenge to her. She herself had turned down more proposals than most girls ever had, but then she was beautiful, witty—and her father, Saul Howland, was one of the wealthiest men in Boston.

She enjoyed the only game possible for a woman—men; and it gave her some pleasure to maneuver the hapless Daniel Mains. In the space of thirty minutes she had devalued the character of Ellen's rival, elevated his opinion of Ellen herself, and when she left the two alone it was obvious that if she played her cards right, the tall girl had her fish hooked.

"At it again, Abby?" She turned with a smile to face Maury Simms, come to claim her for a dance. He was a tall, broad-shouldered man of twenty-six, who had been her suitor for a time, but had given up in despair. Now as they danced he said with a grin, "Giving Ellen a little help, are you?"

"I don't know what you mean, Maury," she said, but there was a smile on her red lips and she laughed aloud, saying, "Men are such fools!"

"Yes, we are, aren't we?" Maury had gotten over her, and it was one of her pleasures to be with a man who wasn't stalking her

or her father's money. "But not all of us. Paul Winslow's no fool—
not like me. I don't think you can maneuver him as you do the rest
of us."

"Oh, I don't want to maneuver anyone, Maury."

They finished the dance, then joined a group at the long table
crowded with wine and food. Emily Rauter was one of them, and
she smiled briefly, saying, "Your dress is beautiful, Abby."

"Thank you, Emily—you look wonderful."

Maury stood there with a broad smile on his face, thinking,
*They hate each other so well—both of them would like to tear the other's
face to rags with their fingernails.*

But that wasn't true—not so far as Abby was concerned. She
knew that Emily wanted Paul Winslow desperately, but it didn't
bother her. She had taken more than one man away from Emily.

"Who's that with Paul?"

They all looked across the room to see Paul Winslow coming
toward them, accompanied by a very tall young man with red hair.
"Oh, that must be Paul's country cousin," Maury said. Then a
thought struck him, and he said with a smile, "Better leave that
one alone, ladies—he's not available."

As he had suspected this statement made both women raise
their eyes for a closer look at the tall man. "What does that mean,
Maury?" Emily asked.

"Oh, well, in the first place, according to Paul, he's probably
a frightful patriot—which makes him ineligible right off—but even
worse, he's a minister. Parson of some sort."

"He may be a minister," Abby smiled, "but he's a man."

"Better leave him alone, Abigail," Emily said smoothly. "Paul
might not like your paying attention to his cousin."

"We'll have to see, won't we, dear?" Abby smiled, and moved
across the floor to meet the pair.

"Well, we don't need tigers in this country," Maury smiled at
Emily. "Not as long as you girls are around to eat each other alive."
Emily did not listen, for she was watching carefully as Paul intro-
duced his cousin to Abby.

"And this is the most beautiful woman in Boston, Nathan, Miss
Abigail Howland."

"Pay him no heed, Mr. Winslow," Abby smiled and held on to
Nathan's hand for a second longer than necessary. "You can't be-

lieve a word this man says—but a Virginian like yourself, why, a girl could trust you, I think."

Paul lifted his eyebrows; then a saturnine smile crossed his lips. "Well, I'll leave you two to get acquainted. And I forgot to tell you, Nathan, you two are kinfolks."

"What?" Nathan stared at Paul in confusion.

"Oh, I'll explain all that to you while we dance," Abby smiled up at him brilliantly and drew him into the dance. "My! It's so nice to dance with a really *tall* man!"

"What—what's this about our being kin to each other?" Nathan's thoughts were disjointed, for he had never seen a girl half so lovely. She wore some scent that seemed to paralyze him. As they moved through the dance, from time to time her body would brush against him, and he could not keep his thoughts straight.

"Oh, that's true enough," she said, and she spoke so softly that he had to bend down and put his face close to hers in order to hear. "Paul explained it to me once—he didn't want me to think that there'd be any—problem, with us being close kin." She laughed, and let her hand rest on his arm where it seemed to leave a mark. "Let's see, now—my grandmother was Rachel Winslow. She was your grandfather's sister. His name was Miles Winslow, I think. Oh, Nathan, that was ages ago."

As they floated across the floor, Nathan felt somewhat bewitched. He had spent little time with girls, and never with one this attractive, so he moved like a man in a dream for the next hour.

Paul was standing beside the wall, looking on when Emily came up and claimed him. "There are too few men here for you to be an observer. Dance with me!"

He agreed readily, and soon she had him laughing. She was a witty young woman, and it was not long before he found himself telling her of Nathan. Finally she said, "Well, he's a most attractive man, Paul. I'm surprised you let her dance for so long with him."

"Well, you know Abby, Emily. She'll do what she pleases."

"A woman should do what her *man* pleases, I think!"

He nodded. "I'll vote for that, but look, Nathan may not last long. Abby's taking him over to meet the officers. That's sort of like introducing the sheep to the wolves!"

Nathan did feel intimidated, for he was surrounded by a group of scarlet coated British officers. Miss Howland knew them all well, it seemed, and one by one he shook their hands; then they began shooting questions at him. A fine-looking man of forty, Major John Pitcairn, asked at once, "Well, Mr. Winslow, how blows the wind in the South? I know Mr. Washington. Is he going to get involved in this rebellion that seems to be brewing?"

Before Nathan could answer, a short, fat man with small, squinty eyes grunted, "Nonsense, Pitcairn! There'll be no rebellion! These Colonists are stupid, but not stupid enough to go up against the strongest power in the world—the British Empire!"

"Colonel Smith is correct!" A portly man with a bluff manner and bright brown eyes spoke up. This was General Thomas Gage, commander of the King's forces in Boston. "Washington is a gentleman, and I believe he's a loyal man. It's Sam Adams and Hancock who keep the pot boiling!"

"What do you think, sir?" Major Pitcairn asked Nathan. "Will there be a rebellion?"

Nathan felt every one of the King's officers watching him closely, and he cleared his throat before saying carefully, "As for me, I believe a revolution would be a disaster. I have to add that not all my family thinks in this way—"

"Good man!" Smith said at once, and the others nodded agreement.

"You must come with Paul to our mess, Mr. Winslow," Major Pitcairn said warmly. "He's there often, and we'd like you to join him."

"At your service, Major," Nathan said; then he felt a small hand close on his arm, and turned to find Abby.

"It's time for the refreshments you promised me, Mr. Winslow."

He followed her to the table, and she asked with an arch smile, "I understand you are a clergyman. Does that prevent you from taking a little wine?"

Actually it did, for Adam felt that wine was the first step to being a drunkard, but looking into her eyes, Nathan could not refuse, so he took a glass of wine and she toasted the King.

The one glass was a mistake, for it seemed to have so little effect that soon he was taking another. Dance followed dance, and each was punctuated by sparkling glasses of wine.

Nathan had never felt so wonderful in all his life! He was a fine fellow—a devil of a chap, really! And as the wine went down, his shyness fled, and soon he was laughing and talking with the most beautiful woman in Boston as if he'd done it all his life.

Hours later, he found himself with Abby in some sort of alcove, where she was showing him a picture of their mutual ancestor. He gazed into the strong face of Rachel Winslow, and then when he looked down to comment, Abigail's face was lifted. Her lips were red and she swayed against him. His head was swimming, but he could not stop himself. He took her in his arms, lowered his head, and then he kissed her. It was a powerful moment, for she did not draw back, but shared his kiss.

Then, she pulled away, and her voice seemed to come from afar as she said, "For a minister, you are quite a man, Nathan Winslow!"

Then she vanished into the crowd of dancers, and he suddenly discovered that for the first time in his life, he was drunk. He found that he had difficulty walking, for the floor seemed to shift and tilt under him, and he was acutely conscious of too much wine rolling around in his stomach.

Paul came to his rescue. Seeing his cousin's difficulty, he got him out of the house just in time for him to lose his supper, bundled him into a buggy, and finally helped him stagger upstairs. And it was Paul who said gently to the sleeping giant with the flushed face, "I think, Nathan, that Boston has been a little too much for you—or maybe I should say that Abigail Howland has been too much!"

CHAPTER FIVE

A Boy Named Laddie

★ ★ ★ ★

Despite the severe cold, Nathan had to push his way through heavy traffic that flooded the square. The bright scarlet coats of British soldiers added a dash of color to the somber old buildings, but he was jostled by chimney sweepers, sawyers, merchants, laddies, priests, carts, horses, oxen, and his ears buzzed with the talk that floated over the square.

He arrived at the British Coffeehouse, which occupied the first floor of a four-story, frame building painted a bilious yellow, and as soon as he pushed his way through the door, he heard his name called: "Winslow! Over here!"

Major John Pitcairn, seated at a small round table near the far wall, had to raise his voice to be heard, for the large room was packed with officers and their guests. Nathan threaded his way across the crowded room, nearly reeling from the scent of pipe smoke, stale whiskey, and unwashed male bodies.

Pitcairn pushed a bottle and a pewter cup toward him, saying, "Cold as the devil out there! Take some of that, my boy—it'll warm your insides!"

During the two weeks he'd spent at Boston, Nathan had learned how to handle the problem of drink. To say "No" created an instant problem, for almost everyone in the country drank some sort of liquor. Even ministers frequently received part of their pay in the form of kegs of beer, and *all* British officers drank a great deal. At first Nathan had refused, but that action had created such a discomfort on the part of the soldiers that he had learned to take a glass and simply give the appearance of drinking. He took the glass and sipped at it, but the sharp eyes of Pitcairn caught it, and he smiled. "Haven't done too much drinking since that night at Howlands', have you, Nathan?—or before either, I'd venture."

Nathan scowled and shifted uncomfortably in his chair, and finally he looked straight at the major and said, "I made a fool of myself that night, Major!" A flush touched his high cheekbones, and he shook his head, adding, "Shakespeare said 'God forbid I should put an enemy in my mouth to take away my brain'; I reckon that's what I did that night."

"It wasn't so bad as you remember it, Nathan," Pitcairn said with a sympathetic smile. "As I think on it, you may have been the most sober man in the house that night! At least three that I know of had to be *carried* out."

"That's them and not me!"

"Oh? Well, I wasn't watching you all the time. Maybe it was something you did with Abigail Howland that's got you as sensitive as a man without a skin?"

"I won't listen—!" Nathan half rose from his seat, his face twisted with anger, but looking at Pitcairn's honest face, he swallowed, sat down, and ducked his head. He drew a figure in the moist surface of the oak table, then looked up and there was a weak grin on his wide lips. "You're too sharp for me, Major."

Pitcairn sat there quietly, saying nothing until he refilled his clay pipe. Picking up the candle, he sucked the flame into the bowl until it glowed cherry red, then put it down carefully, a characteristic thing with him. He had learned to like this tall young man with the startling blue eyes, and for the past two weeks had spent several hours with him. He had not pried, but the young man had been open, and he had learned how his family was split by political opinion—Nathan's parents in Virginia strongly behind the patriot cause, while his Uncle Charles and his family were staunch loyalists. He had something to say to Nathan, and was hesitant.

"Well, you must have done *something* right with the young woman. You've been a pretty frequent guest at her house—and poor Paul must be cursing the day he ever took you there!"

"I—I'm sorry for that—about Paul, I mean."

"Oh, they weren't engaged." Pitcairn shook his head and

idded, "She's a real catch, my boy—looks *and* money. But I don't know if she'd suit your family."

Nathan shook his head sadly. "You're right about that. She's got little use for the rebel cause."

Pitcairn studied young Winslow, then made a quick decision. "Nathan, I sent for you because there's something you need to know."

Pitcairn's serious air was disturbing. "What is it, Major?"

"It's about your brother. He's getting involved with a radical group, and I think you ought to know it."

"Caleb? But he's just a boy!"

"That may be, but nonetheless he's taken up with a young man who works for your uncle—Moses Tyler, he's called."

"Why, I know Moses," Nathan said at once.

"We've had our eyes on him for some time. He's joined to the Sons of Liberty—perhaps you've heard of them?"

"Yes, but I thought they were harmless enough."

A rare anger touched Major Pitcairn's face, and he said, "Let's get out of here, Nathan. Too many ears to hear in this place."

He laid a coin on the table and Nathan followed him outside, both of them pulling their coats high to protect their faces from the bitter cold. "You ever hear of the Boston Massacre, Nathan?"

"Of course."

"Well, this is where it happened." Pitcairn waved his hand toward the square. "It was most unfortunate, Nathan. A band of unemployed laborers attacked a British sentry right over there, and a mob collected, throwing oyster shells and snowballs. In the confusion, somebody called out 'Fire!' and our men fired. Five men were killed and six were wounded."

"They shouldn't have fired on unarmed men, Major."

"No, certainly not, and a better officer would have prevented that. But it was a great opportunity for Sam Adams and James Otis! They got Paul Revere to do an engraving of the riot—you've probably seen it." A bitter smile touched Pitcairn's lips and he pointed at the Custom House, which was next to the British Coffeehouse. "Revere put a sign in the engraving on that building. Know what it was?"

"It was BUTCHER'S HALL." Nathan remembered the engraving well, for copies of it had been carried all over the Colonies. "But that's not treason, what Adams did."

"No, but it gave Sam Adams a beginning! And the next thing he did was organize the Boston Tea Party—*that* was a criminal act, Nathan."

"I suppose so," Nathan said slowly.

Pitcairn took the arm of the tall young man, his grip like steel, saying, "Nathan, Sam Adams was a business failure, one of those whining, nagging malcontents you want to poke in the nose—but just the sort you'd want on your side in an eye-gouging fight. He's a burr under the saddle, blast him! Such men breed revolutions, and they don't give a hang who has to die for it."

"And you say Caleb's been going to their meetings?"

They had just turned a corner and a blast of cold air struck them so hard that both men gasped. "See that old red brick building—the one with blue shutters?"

"What about it, Major?"

"That's Sam Adams' house—where they meet. The rest are no better, Nathan. Otis was a Massachusetts lawyer who couldn't handle his liquor. He was a Tory once, then switched over to a Whig position because he saw a dollar to be turned. And there's John Hancock—and he may be the worst of the lot—though he's smooth enough!"

"Rich, isn't he?"

"Oh yes, and how did he get that way? By smuggling tea! And that's why he got in on the tea party in the harbor—his profits were in danger. Nathan, the man's a criminal, and sooner or later the Sons of Liberty are all going to dangle from ropes." Major Pitcairn stopped fifty yards away from the red brick house. "I'd hate for your brother to be one to hang with them, Nathan, and that's why I've told you this."

Nathan thrust his hand out impulsively, and grasping the officer's hand, he burst out, "Thank you, Major!"

"Well, well, now you know—but what will you *do* about it, my boy?"

The question struck Nathan hard, for his mind was a total blank as to what could be done. He set his jaw, and there was a fire in his light blue eyes as he said, "I'll do *something*, Major—and you can bet on that!"

Major Pitcairn gave him a clap on the shoulder, but added a final word: "Our informer tells me they'll have a meeting tonight. I should try to keep the boy away if possible—but be a little careful,

Nathan. These men are revolutionaries—they'd think nothing of snuffing you out! Well, let me know if I can do anything."

Pitcairn wheeled and marched down the street, a trim, erect military figure, and Nathan moved to the shelter of a tiny inn across from the brick house. He took a seat and ordered a meal as an excuse for his presence. The food was slow in coming, and was badly cooked, but he never noticed. His brain was racing as he tried to think of some way to get Caleb free from trouble. He thought of sending him home, but knew at once that Caleb would never go. *Maybe if I write father—? But he'd probably be proud of Caleb, feeling as he does.*

He finished his meal, then realizing he couldn't stay in the inn until the group met, paid his bill and returned to the street. Snow lay in white stripes everywhere, and the flakes were getting larger. He looked up into the sky, then turned and walked slowly in the direction of the harbor. *I'll go to the warehouse and stay warm until later—then I'll do something.*

By the time he had covered the distance from the center of town to the waterfront, the snow was coming down as thickly as if some unseen giant were dumping it out of huge baskets. The flakes were huge, almost the size of a tuppence, and lay in drifts several inches deep along the shopfronts. The temperature had plummeted; by the time he turned off High Street and began walking along the docks, his cheeks were numb and his feet had no sensation as they struck the carpet of white that covered the wharfs.

Nathan moved closer to a long tobacco warehouse to avoid the icy blasts that stung his face. He glanced out at the harbor where the ships seemed to be frozen carcasses—their sharp outlines of masts and spars rounded into smooth curves by the blanket of snow.

But as he glanced out at the fleet, his half-frozen feet struck something. He tried to jerk his hands out of his pockets to catch himself, but he failed and his long body fell headlong into the snow!

"What the devil—!"

He yanked his hands out of his pockets and swept the snow from his face with a forearm. He rolled over and saw what appeared to be a bundle of rags under a white mound, and he lifted his heel to give it a savage kick, for the fall had knocked out his breath and one cheek was bleeding, scraped raw against the rough wood of the wharf.

"What—?" he gave a startled look, then lowered his boot, for he thought he saw a tiny movement beneath the mound. Scrambling to his knees he reached out and brushed the snow away and saw at once that the bundle was alive!

Fear struck him in the belly, and with hands that shook more from nervousness than cold, he tugged at the figure, which seemed to be swathed in some sort of ragged blanket. Pulling it to one side, he could barely make out in the gathering darkness a pale white face, eyes shut tight. "Hey! Wake up!" He shook the small figure, but there was no response.

"Got to find help!" he muttered. He got to his feet and looked wildly around, but he knew there was no doctor in the area. *Got to get him out of this cold!* He stooped and lifted the still figure, and was shocked at how light the lad was. Then it came to him what to do, and he plunged along through the snow. *The warehouse,* he thought—*it'll be warm there, and I can send somebody for the doctor!*

It was nearly a quarter of a mile to the company warehouse, and his lungs were on fire by the time he stopped, gasping in front of the door. There was no light inside, and he groaned as he saw the heavy padlock in place. Carefully he placed his burden down, extracted his key, then with numbed fingers managed to open the lock. Picking the boy up, he kicked the door open and stumbled inside. Even inside, the cold was bitter, but he made his way through the high-ceilinged area lit by a single lamp to the office at the rear. It was dark, and he felt his way to a small cot used by the foreman for quick naps. He groped along the desk, found the small candle, then ran back to the lantern in the warehouse area to light it. Cupping a hand around it, he hurried back to the office and stood there looking down at the small form he'd brought out of the storm.

Ought to be doing something! he thought, *but it's Saturday night.* For an instant he stood there in the cold silence, irresolute, still winded from his run through the storm.

Then he did something that was not customary, an involuntary reaction, something that just welled up in him. *"God, don't let this lad die!"* he prayed—then he blinked, surprised at what he'd done. Most of his praying was public, a form of rhetoric that he'd mastered by listening to others pray. Solitary prayer he'd given up on years before, for although he knew some—such as his mother— who spent much time praying, his own prayer life was a matter of form.

Then it came again, involuntarily: *"Oh, God! I didn't bring him here to die! Let him live! Please—let him live!"*

Again he was shocked at the emotion that drove his prayer, and at that instant he saw a flicker of an eyelid on the still pale face, and at the same time a moan passed through the lips turned blue by the cold.

"He's alive! Thank you, God!" Nathan rejoiced, and the pressure of fear lifted. He whirled and quickly built a small fire in the fireplace, set a kettle of water over it, then carefully added larger pieces to the fire until it crackled and began to drive the bitter cold out of his hands.

A small sound came from behind him; he turned from the fire to see the lad's arms moving, and he leaped to the cot. "All right, now, don't be afraid—you're all right!"

A pair of eyes, black as pools, suddenly peered up at him, and the blue lips moved painfully. "What—what—?"

"Don't try to talk, lad," Nathan said quickly. He stripped off the dirty blanket so thin it was no protection at all, and whipped off his own thick wool coat. Wrapping it around the boy, he noted the thin arms and hollow eyes. *Half starved*, he thought, then said, "I don't know much about taking care of frozen people, lad. Not much snow down in Virginia." He smiled as the huge almond-shaped eyes stared at him owlishly, then added, "I heard somewhere that you're supposed to rub snow on people who are just about frozen, so maybe—?"

He got up to go get some snow, but the dark eyes widened, and a thin hand clutched the coat closer. "No! I—I'll be all right."

The voice was weak, but color was coming into the thin cheeks, so Nathan said, "Well, guess we'll just let you thaw out, lad. Maybe pretty soon you can have a sip of tea—that sound all right?" He saw one quick nod, then the eyes closed, but he saw that the thin body was beginning to shake as feeling came back. "I'll see if I can find a doctor."

He got up, but to his surprise a hand flashed out and grabbed his sleeve, and there was fear in the dark eyes. "No—please—don't leave me!"

He hesitated, then said, "Well, I won't leave until we see how you do." The eyes closed, and the hand fell, as if that one effort had drained all strength from the cold flesh.

There was little he could do, then, but keep the fire going. He knew enough not to build up a roaring blaze, but slowly allowed the tiny fire to bring the temperature of the room above freezing. Thirty minutes passed, then an hour, and several times he got up and went to lean over the cot.

He saw a thin face with a set of thick, arching brows black as a crow's wing, the same color as the hair that looked as if it had been crookedly hacked with a blunt knife. He took in the straight nose, the square face and the firm chin, and thought, *A good-looking boy, but just about played out. If I hadn't stumbled over him, he'd have been gone by morning.*

The kettle began singing, and once again the eyes opened. "How about if you try to sit up and have a swallow of tea?" He put his arm around the boy, helped him to sit up, then said, "Might be good to get rid of this coat now—" He paused and asked, "What's your name, lad?"

There was a brief silence; then the boy slowly licked his cracked lips and said in a feeble voice, "Laddie. Laddie—Smith."

Nathan did not miss the hesitation over the last name, but he ignored it, saying, "Let's have the coat, and you try to get down a mite of this tea. I'm Nathan Winslow."

Laddie nodded, slipped out of the coat, and reached a thin hand for the huge cup that Nathan had found. The odor of the tea was rich in the cold room, and he had to use both hands to hold the cup, but when he began to drink, it was not in tiny sips, but in long swallows that made the thin throat contract.

"Hey, you'll founder yourself, Laddie!" Nathan reached out and pulled the cup back, then stared into the black eyes over it. "I found some biscuits and a bit of cheese. Why don't you come over to the desk and have just a little?"

The hunger in the dark eyes flared up, and at once he swung his legs from the cot and stood up—only to sway like a sapling in the wind.

"Easy, now!" Nathan put his arm around the thin shoulders and, guiding him to the chair, eased him down carefully, then put one biscuit and a thin slice of cheese on the top of the desk. "Eat that—real *slow*," he said, and sat down to watch. The boy wanted to thrust the whole morsel in his mouth, but with a struggle, took a tiny bite and sat there chewing it slowly, then washed it down with a swallow of scalding tea.

As Laddie ate, Nathan talked easily, telling how it was that he'd stumbled across what he thought was a sack of clothes. Then as the boy's eyes brightened with the food and tea, Nathan began trying to find out something about the waif. He saw at once, however, that it was not going to be easy, for his probing built an instant wall, and the dark eyes seemed to say "No Trespassing!"

Finally he got up to say, "Well, Laddie, I think I ought to roust a doctor out of his warm bed to have a look at you—and a good one, too!" He looked critically at the thin wrists and the hollow eyes and added, "We better have him strip you to the buff and be sure everything's—"

"No! I'm fine, Mr. Winslow!" Laddie lowered the cup so abruptly that some of the scalding liquid fell on his lap, but he did not seem to notice. "I don't want a doctor! Please, just let me stay until morning and I'll be able to take care of myself. I won't be a bother to you!"

There was fear in the dark eyes, but pride as well, and Nathan stood there perplexed. The lad was on the verge of starvation! Finally he said with a shrug, "Laddie, that storm out there is mighty likely to get worse, not better. You go back outside and you'll freeze." He hesitated, then asked, "You got any family? Anybody I can write to?"

"No. I got no folks."

The barren look in the dark eyes raked against Nathan's nerves, and he wondered if he'd have the nerve to make out as well as this youngster. His life had been easy; he'd never been hungry in his life, and suddenly he knew that he had to do something. The prayer he'd prayed came back to him, and he thought, *Well, if God's done His part, I've got to do mine!*

He looked down and asked quietly, "You need a place to stay, Laddie?"

The thin shoulders squared, and the full lower lip trembled ever so slightly, but the answer was clear: "I need a job, Mr. Winslow. I'll do any kind of work at all."

Nathan looked at the thin arms and said, "Well, guess you won't be loading bales of cotton right away, but I'm wondering if you can write and do sums?"

"Yes, sir!" Hope softened the youth's face, and he swallowed and added, "I'm very good with books."

"Why, that's good, because we need someone around here to help with that." *Which will come as a surprise to Uncle Charles!* he thought with a flash of humor. But he had worked with his uncle at the business for two weeks, and knew that there would be plenty for a clerk to do. Laurence Strake, the manager of the business, had even said something to that effect, hadn't he? *"Got to have a little help with the books, Mr. Winslow."*

"I—I'll work hard!"

"Sure, Laddie, but there's no hurry. We got to get some meat on your bones. Say, how old are you—twelve or thirteen?"

"At least." There was a glint in his eyes as he answered; then he smiled for the first time, and Nathan marveled at the even whiteness of perfect teeth. "Actually, I'm fifteen, Mr. Winslow."

"Pretty young to be alone, Laddie," Nathan said, and he laid his hand on the boy's thin shoulder. It surprised him when the boy drew back instantly, and he thought, *Someone's been mistreating him!* He stepped back and stroked his chin, saying, "Let's see, I'm staying with my Uncle Charles, and in that big old house of his there's got to be a place for one small clerk."

"Couldn't I just stay here? I could fix up something."

"No, no, that won't do," he shook his head. "Well, we'll stay here tonight; then I'll talk to Uncle Charles Monday. Maybe we could find a little room close by the business."

"I'll take anything, Mr. Winslow." Then Laddie stood up and went over to stand by the fire. As the frail figure looked down into the leaping flames, Nathan took in the ragged shirt, dirty, and so torn that he could see the heavy cotton undergarment beneath. He looked at the ancient trousers, so old and worn that they had no color left, and he smiled at how Laddie had to keep them up by a piece of string. The shoes, he saw, were far too large, and one of the soles flapped loosely as the boy moved.

"Tell you what, Laddie, I'll find some blankets somewhere, and we'll stay here until morning." His face lighted up and he added, "First thing, we get us a big hot breakfast; next we find you a room to rest up in for a day or so—then we hit my uncle up for a job. That sound good?"

The small figure did not move at first, then he turned and faced Nathan, dark eyes glittering with tears. It was a struggle to speak, but finally Nathan caught the words that came so softly he had to lean down to hear them.

"You—you saved my life, Mr. Winslow." The lower lip trembled, but the soft voice went on. "I heard a story once about people in some far-off place—I think it was maybe India. It said that when somebody saved a person's life—why, that person was supposed to serve the one that saved them as long as they live."

The fire crackled and spat in the silence that followed, and Nathan said, "Well, Laddie, this isn't India—so you don't have to serve *me* all your life."

He smiled at the earnest face, trying to make a joke out of it, but the boy said quietly and directly, looking right into Nathan's eyes, "I'll always want to serve and honor you, Mr. Winslow—as long as I live!"

It embarrassed Nathan, so he laughed; then a thought came to him, and he spoke before he thought: "I forgot all about Caleb and the Sons of Liberty!" Then he went to get the blankets, and Laddie stood there staring at the door he passed through. A thought came, bringing a strange smile—but whatever it was, there was no mention of it to Nathan when he returned with the blankets.

CHAPTER SIX

SONS OF LIBERTY

★ ★ ★ ★

As soon as a weak gray light came through the small window, Nathan painfully rolled out of his blankets and got to his feet. He had slept fitfully, not being able to get Caleb out of his mind, and the hard floor in the cold room had stiffened his muscles. He had banked the fire, so the water in the basin had a skim of ice on it.

"Laddie?" He walked over to the mound of blankets on the cot and gave one of the protrusions a slap. Instantly there was a muffled cry, and he laughed when the boy's head appeared from the opposite end, eyes startled with fear. "Couldn't tell that was your rump, but guess it's not the first swat you ever got on your backside, is it?"

Laddie stared at him, and finally gave a tiny nod, saying, "No, it's not."

"Well, pile out of there." He picked up Laddie's thin coat and considered it. "This won't do. You better wear mine."

Laddie got up and stood there unsteadily, then with a shake of his head reached for the ragged garment. "No, yours would be way too long. I'll make out."

"Well—we'll try it. There's an inn just down the street. Think you can walk, or you want me to carry you?"

"I can walk—but can we go by where you found me? I've got a sack with my things in it."

"It's on the way." He led the boy outside, locked the door, then put his hand on the thin arm, moving slowly down the empty street. They had not gone over a hundred yards before he felt the boy weaving. "Here, you can't make it like this, Laddie." He swept the small figure up into his arms and picked up his pace.

Once he glanced down and saw that the thin face was red with embarrassment, he gave a short laugh, saying, "Aw, Laddie, don't be so touchy. You're weak, that's all—you don't weigh no more than a bird! Why I've packed deer out of the woods for ten miles that weigh *twice* what you do!"

"I—don't want anyone to see me!"

"Well, they won't. In a couple of hours there'll be lots of folks going to church, but it's too early now—anyway, what if they do see?" Nathan had his left arm under the boy's legs, and with his right hand supported his side, and he gave him a quick grin. "I can feel every rib you got, Laddie—but we'll get you fat and pretty as a suckling pig before long!"

There was no answer, and he saw that the youth had buried his red face against his coat, and felt the thin form tremble both with cold and shame. He shrugged, then walked quickly to the spot where he'd found Laddie, knocked the snow from a mound, and swept up a small, lumpy cotton sack. "Got it! Now, let's get out of this weather."

The Blue Boar was one of the lesser inns of the harbor, a tiny place squeezed between a large tobacco warehouse and a ship repair yard. Laurence Strake, Charles's manager, had taken Nathan there for a meal or two. It was run by James Nelson, a former foretopman in the Royal Navy, before he had turned to innkeeping.

Nathan set Laddie up right, then banged on the door loudly, calling out, "Nelson! Nelson! Open up!"

A window overhead popped open, and a man's red face appeared, "Wot's this?"

"Can you fix us up with a room, Nelson—and some breakfast?"

The burly innkeeper scratched his bald spot, then nodded and said, "We got a place—be right down."

An hour later they were pushing away from the table, having filled up on a kidney pie, hot bread and butter with dollops of jam, and a rasher of bacon, all washed down by draughts of strong, hot India tea. Laddie had begun by eating ravenously, but soon had enough. "Stomach's shrunk, I expect," Nathan said. "Better eat lots of little meals, rather than stuffing yourself."

"I think so—but it was so *good!*" The food had brought color to Laddie's cheeks, and his eyes were much brighter.

Nathan got up and led the way up the crooked, narrow stairs to the room he'd arranged for. He pushed the door open, and Laddie followed him inside. "It's not much, but it won't be for long."

It was a small room, not over ten feet square, and most of that was filled by a massive bed with ropes supporting the shuck ticking. A small pine table with a cracked basin and a pewter pitcher completed the furnishings—but it was warm, for the heat from downstairs moved into it. "Have to keep your door open to keep warm," Nathan said.

"It's—nice." He looked at Laddie quickly and saw that the worn face was pale and beads of perspiration covered the smooth forehead.

"Maybe you ate a little too much," he frowned. "Look, you need to get cleaned up and into bed, Laddie. Why don't I get you out of those old clothes, give you a good wash? You must have something to sleep in, in here!"

He started to empty the bag on the bed, but was surprised when he heard, "Oh no, Mr. Winslow, you—you don't have to do that!"

"Why, it's no bother, lad! You'd do the same for me, I take it?"

Laddie looked at him strangely, then reached out and took the sack from him. "Please, I'm all right, really I am. I'll wash up and get into bed like you say."

He stared at the boy, then shrugged, "Well, be sure you do. I've got to get going. I'll tell Nelson's wife to feed you lots of broth and soup." He cocked his head, looked down with a frown. "I'll be gone all day and all night. But I'll be back first thing Monday morning, and you ought to feel a lot stronger by then."

"Yes, sir, and—thank you again!" Hesitantly, Laddie extended a hand. When Nathan's big paw closed around it, he was very careful not to press hard—it was such a fragile hand—and withdrew it quickly. "God bless you, Mr. Winslow."

Nathan was always embarrassed by gratitude of any form, and the look in the lad's dark eyes made him grunt, "Oh, nonsense!" Then he turned and left quickly. He paused only long enough to say, "Nelson, the boy's not well, so keep an eye out for him, will you?"

"Aye, sir, I'll do that—have me ol' woman make a spot o' fresh chicken broth fer the lad, I will." He rolled his eyes upward and shrugged a set of massive shoulders. "He ain't wot yer'd call a hearty lad, is he, now?"

"I'll make it worth your while, Nelson," Nathan said, then hurried out of the inn and looked around for a carriage. There were none stirring so early, but he managed to catch a ride with a farmer going his way. He washed, dressed in his best clothes and got downstairs just in time to have a quick breakfast with the family.

"You may be a little critical of Rev. Lockyear, Nathan," Charles said later as they got out of the carriage in front of a massive old church on the south side of town. "You're more in the line of Jonathan Edwards—the old school."

"I've heard that Rev. Lockyear is pretty high church," Nathan said.

"Oh, as to that, any Anglican minister would seem rather popish to you." He chuckled and lowered his voice so that the women who'd gone ahead couldn't hear, adding, "Your father went to school with Edwards and was converted under Whitefield, so you've pretty well grown up with a hell-fire and damnation sort of preaching. But it's different with the Church of England."

"They don't believe in hell?"

"Hell's not dignified enough for most of 'em." Charles laughed at the thought, then sobered. "You won't get much theology today, I'm afraid. Lockyear spends most of his pulpit time preaching the gospel of reconciliation—not man to God, but Whigs to Tories. If he *did* believe in a hell, he'd populate it with the likes of Sam Adams and his Sons of Liberty!"

They had reached the door, and once inside Nathan felt intimidated by the rich trappings: the massive altar in the fashion of Catholic churches, the silver and gold of the cups that reflected the glittering chandeliers overhead, and the rich walnut panels and pews carved by a master.

Not much like our plain little church back home. He followed the family down the aisle, noticing that the scarlet coats of British officers were liberally scattered throughout the congregation. He smiled at Major Pitcairn, sitting with General Gage and Colonel Smith, and then found what he was seeking: Abigail sitting with her parents in a pew close to the front. She turned and caught his eye, and the smile that came to her lips made him miss a step—

until he felt Paul beside him, and then was uncertain as to which of them she was smiling at. *Keeping us both running at her heels,* he thought, then sat down and took it all in.

The service was, indeed, strange to him. A trained choir hidden from view in a loft did most of the singing, and much of the service involved a ritual that called for the worshipers to respond, sometimes in Latin, and there was much standing and some kneeling on special pads. But the preaching was what he had come for, and he forgot the exotic surroundings when Rev. Lockyear mounted the pulpit, much in the manner of the captain of a ship of the line taking charge. He was a massive man, well over six feet, with a full face that reeked of authority. His voice was as big as the rest of him, and for the next hour the congregation was informed on the near-divinity of King George the Third, and how that the most powerful evidence of total depravity lay in the traitorous behavior of those who challenged any law of the British Parliament.

After thirty minutes of this, Nathan began to feel that he had been hit on the head once too often with a single idea, but looking around he saw that the congregation was drinking it all in. General Gage was leaning forward, his face intent, but Pitcairn was less intent. He caught Nathan's glance, gave a careful wink and a shrug, as if to say, *He does go on a bit, doesn't he now?*

Finally it was over, and Nathan outmaneuvered Paul neatly. He managed to place himself by Abigail, shook hands warmly with her parents, then drew her off to one side as soon as they were outside. "You've not forgotten about tomorrow night?" She had agreed to attend a lecture with him, a boring affair, but one which he felt safe inviting her to.

"I've thought of nothing else, Nathan." Her words were sweet to his ears, but he thought there was a mocking light in her eyes. She kept him off guard constantly, for she had more experience in courtship than he. She saw his face redden, and put her hand on his arm, saying softly, "I really have, Nathan. Oh, I don't care about the lecture, but it'll be good to have some time with you."

Warmth flooded him, and he opened his mouth to answer, but it was too late. The crowd came flooding out of the church, and Nathan was caught up with the small entourage that surrounded the general. Gage spotted him, nodded vigorously and said, "Well, now, Mr. Winslow, that was a most inspiring address by Rev. Lockyear, was it not?"

"Very powerful, General," Nathan answered dutifully.

Colonel Smith edged slightly between Nathan and Gage, as if the general were his personal property, not to be approached by a mere civilian. His small eyes narrowed, and there was a malevolent expression on his round face. "Not strong enough—not by half!"

"Why, Colonel, the Reverend practically delivered the rebels into hell—what more could you ask?" Pitcairn's handsome face was bland, but there was a glint of humor in his blue eyes. Nathan had noticed that he had no respect for Smith and lost no opportunity to poke fun at the man.

Smith's face grew crimson and his voice rose in real anger. "Ought to hang the lot of them!"

"Take a good deal of rope," Pitcairn answered mildly.

"Let me get them in front of a troop of British soldiers with loaded muskets, and I'd show you what I'd do!"

"Now, now, Colonel," Gage said with a shake of his head, "we must hope it doesn't come to that."

He went on speaking, but Pitcairn caught Nathan's eye, and giving a motion of his head, left the group. Nathan did not want to leave Abigail, but felt impressed to go. The officer made his way to a vacant spot, then said quietly, "There's a meeting of the Sons of Liberty tonight, at the place where I showed you."

"Thanks, Major," Nathan said. "Are you sure?"

"My informant has been accurate so far."

"I'll try to keep Caleb away." He paused, then asked, "You don't think Colonel Smith meant what he said, do you?"

"About shooting the rebels? I think it's possible. Most of us would have more sense, but there are enough like Smith to set the thing off, Nathan." He hesitated, then reached up and put a friendly hand on his shoulder, saying quietly, "You're putting yourself in a very bad place, I fear. You're being pulled in two directions, aren't you? Your family is one thing, and yet you've made some good friends—like me, I trust—on the other side. I hope it won't ever come to the point where you have to choose one way or the other."

Nathan looked down into the eyes of the officer and saw the honesty and simple honor written there. "I—I don't want to lose you as a friend, Major!"

"Nor I you—but I'm about in the same boat as you, Nathan. I've learned to respect Americans, most of them, and yet I'm a commissioned officer in the King's army, and I must obey orders."

"It'll work out, John." Nathan spoke with the optimism of a young man who had never seen his dreams turn to dust. He did not see the sudden compassion in his friend's eyes, for he had turned to go with Charles who was hailing him to the carriage.

Pitcairn turned to his friends, but there was a sadness on his face as he thought about the tall American who had come to mean so much to him.

Moses Tyler was fully satisfied with Caleb's reaction. He had taken his new friend to a simple Congregational church, then out to an inn for a good lunch, and now they were about to start a Sons of Liberty meeting.

Moses was a thin pock-marked boy of fifteen with faded blue eyes, but a strong chin and firm mouth. The eyes glinted out of an angular face, and his whitish hair was so long he brushed it away from his face with a habitual gesture.

He'd had a hard life, so there was an adult quality in him despite his slight form and youthful features. Born out of wedlock, he'd grown up as a bound boy—more a slave than a servant—and had never had a friend, at least not until Caleb Winslow had come to town. Moses was bound to Charles Winslow for another two years, and did the menial work at the company warehouse. He lived in a small room over a shop, and his only pleasures in life were found in his church activities and in the meetings with the Sons of Liberty. He'd been hired by one of the leaders to clean the place they used for a hall, and he'd stayed to listen at the meeting. Nobody paid him any heed, but he'd come back every time the society met, cleaning the place and being of general help, until finally Sam Adams had noticed him. "Boy—you are a patriot?" he asked directly.

"Yes, sir—that is, I wants to be."

"Then you shall be!" Adams had quickly found out that Moses had no family and plenty of free time, so he'd used the boy for chores and let him attend the less important meetings. Moses had never dared to say a word at any of these meetings; indeed, most of the time he had not the faintest notion what they were talking about, but once he said shyly to Adams after the fiery leader had addressed the group, "I liked what you said—about men being free, Mr. Adams."

"Did you now?" Adams was a stern man, slovenly in his personal habits and not given to light talk. He had a harsh way about him that kept most people at a distance, but there was a friendly light in his brown eyes as he looked at the boy. He put a hand on the thin shoulder, a most uncharacteristic gesture for him—and the first time any man had ever done such a thing to Moses. His shoulder seemed to burn under the weight of the hand; then Adams had nodded and said quietly, "When the trouble comes, Moses, it'll be boys like you, not old men like me, who'll have to make it work. Old men can make speeches, but it'll be you who'll have to look down a musket at a British soldier. And I think you'll be up to it!"

From that time on, Adams had always noticed the boy in small ways, and once had encouraged him to keep his eye out for any young fellow who might make a good Son of Liberty.

Looking around the crowded room, Moses leaned over and whispered "That's him, Caleb, that's Mr. Adams! And that's Mr. Revere with him."

"The silversmith? I've heard of him. Who's that coming in?"

"That's Dr. Warren. He's a real big shot in Boston."

Adams had turned from his talk with Revere, and seeing the two, came over and said, "Brought a guest, did you, Moses?"

Moses beamed, proud to be noticed. "Yes, sir! This is my friend Caleb Winslow."

Adams gave Caleb a straight look, then asked directly, "You're interested in our group, Mr. Winslow?"

"Well, I don't live in Boston, Mr. Adams, but I sure would be if I lived here."

"Where's your home?"

"I come from Virginia."

Revere had come up to listen. He was a full-faced man, with a heavy lower lip and sharp black eyes. "Virginia? Well, welcome to Boston!" He shook Caleb's hand and asked idly, "Don't suppose you know Colonel Washington?"

"Well, as a matter of fact, my father knows him pretty well." Caleb tried to keep his tone casual as he said, "My father was a scout with him and Braddock."

"Indeed!" Revere said, and he exchanged a quick glance with Adams, who looked more closely at Caleb. "Your name is Winslow? Any relation to Charles Winslow?"

"My uncle, sir." Caleb saw a dark look cross the faces of both men, and added hastily, "My father is his half brother—but they don't agree on politics."

"I see." Revere was rubbing his chin, a thought nibbling at him. Then he looked up with a smile and said, "Why, I've got it now! It was a few years ago, but I met your father—and your grandfather, as well."

"Really, sir?"

"Yes, I remember it now quite well. Your grandfather had come to Franklin to get a book printed, and I was in the shop. Matter of fact, I did the engraving for the frontispiece. It was quite a book—" He turned to Adams and said, "Here's a *real* American for us, Sam! This boy is a descendant of Gilbert Winslow from the *Mayflower.* You must have read that book of his; it was a bestseller for Franklin."

Adams stared at Caleb. "I am impressed, very much so."

"Wait now!" Revere said, and again struggled to remember; then it came. "Isn't your father a metal worker like myself?"

"He's a fine gunsmith, Mr. Revere."

"Ah, now, that's what I'd like to hear!" Adams' face was alive with interest, and he began to throw questions rapidly. In ten minutes Adams had his life history, the fact that he himself was a good gunsmith and that his family was strong for the cause. Finally he looked around and said, "Well, we must have more of your time, Mr. Winslow. I think you have a place in the Sons of Liberty."

"Why, that's kind of you, Mr. Adams," Caleb said. His heart was beating fast, and he was lightheaded. *Me—a friend of Sam Adams and Paul Revere! Just wait until I tell Father about this! He'll let me stay in Boston, I'll bet!*

The meeting began soon, but Caleb heard little of it. He was too engrossed with the personalities to listen to ideas. One thing he knew—for the first time in his life, he felt more like a man than a boy! "It's just great, Moses!" he said as the last speaker, Dr. Warren, ended and they all stood up. "I want to join with you."

"Let's go tell Mr. Adams."

They started toward the front, but at that instant there was a loud knock at the door. Revere was closest, and he moved to open it; there was caution in his face, and Adams said quietly, "Remember, we're just a group meeting to study history!" A small laugh sounded, but Adams frowned and they took their cue. "Open the door, Mr. Revere."

Caleb was never so surprised in his life, for there in the open door stood his brother Nathan!

"I'm looking for Caleb Winslow," Nathan said loudly, looking like a giant in the doorway, drawn up to his full height. There was a hard look on his face, and he suddenly met Caleb's eyes. "I see he's here."

"Why, yes, he is," Revere said. He smiled and put his hand out. "We're just finished, but won't you come in?"

"I have no business here—and neither does my brother." Nathan's voice was cold, and he ignored the hand, pushing past Revere to come and stand before the two boys. "Let's go, Caleb."

There was a sudden stillness in the place, an ominous and uncomfortable silence, and everyone looked right at Caleb.

He felt the pressure of their eyes, and though most of them were strangers to him, he felt Moses lean slightly against him, and it was enough to make him say, "I'll take care of myself, Nathan!"

"You're not taking care of yourself like this!"

"You have objections to our study group, Mr. Winslow?" Sam Adams did not move, but his deep-set eyes suddenly burned with the anger that always lurked just beneath the surface.

"Study group, you call it?" Nathan scoffed. "I think we all know exactly what it is you *study*! How to overthrow the King's true government!"

Revere said quietly, "I don't think Gilbert Winslow would have looked at it like that, my boy. He left England to make a world where men could be free. And I suspect your father feels that way, as well."

Nathan said angrily, "I will not argue politics with you, sir! Caleb, come with me!"

"No, I won't do it, Nathan."

Nathan stood there towering over the sturdy form of his brother, and he forced himself to say quietly, "Father said for me to take care of you, Caleb. I can't let you stay here with these men. You could end up in jail—or worse!"

"In that your brother may be accurate, young man." Dr. Warren suddenly moved out of the cluster in the rear and came to stand close to the brothers. He was a tall man with a fair complexion and a kind expression in his dark eyes. "It would not be fair to let you stay without knowing this well. All of us in this room are in danger—and it will probably get worse."

Nathan was taken off guard by the tall man's honesty. "Why, that's decent of you, sir."

The doctor glanced at Adams, and seemed to find what he sought. "Caleb, I suggest you go with your brother. Your father seems to have put you in his charge. Think about this, talk to your parents. Then make your decision."

Adams nodded. "Good idea, my boy. You do it."

"All right—but I know I'll be back."

Revere stepped back, but said to Nathan, "Give my regards to your parents for me, Mr. Winslow. I've often thought of them."

"I'll do that," Nathan said, then walked out of the room followed by Caleb, who was close to tears and bit his lips to hide it.

"Those lads are in for trouble," Dr. Warren murmured.

"That they are—and the tall one is in for the most grief," Adams nodded. "Well, there'll be many a family like that before this thing is over—split right down the middle."

"I wonder what Gilbert Winslow would have said about this?" Revere mused. Then he gave a rueful laugh. "He'd probably have whipped out a foil and run King George through! He was a real fighter, that one."

Adams looked toward the door, nodded slowly, then said, "We could do with some hot blood like that in this place. But it seems more likely that the real Winslow blood's in the young fellow—my hope's in him—not the older one."

"Maybe." Revere was rubbing his chin thoughtfully, but then he shook his head. "I remember that Gilbert Winslow, according to his book, got off the track himself when he was about this boy's age—but when he finally got his head pointed in the right direction, why, sir, he just about got the job done!—and this tall one has the same look about him!"

Nathan said nothing all the way back to the house, knowing that there was an iron stubbornness running through his brother. He had seen it many times as they had grown up together, and the one thing that he could not do with Caleb was force him to do something. When they were children, he had always been able to dominate Caleb physically, but no matter how much he was hurt, the boy *never gave up.* Knowing this, he determined to say nothing of the business. But Caleb felt differently.

As soon as they were in their room, he said, "Nathan, don't you ever do that again—not ever!"

Nathan made no attempt to avoid the charge, for his anger had gone, and it was replaced by a fear of what might happen. He shook his head sadly, then said, "Caleb, you don't know what you're getting into."

"I think I do!"

"I know you think so, but will you let me tell you how it looks to me?"

The request caught Caleb off guard. He'd expected hard talk, and now there was a plea on his brother's face that he'd rarely seen. "Well, I'll listen, Nathan."

"All right, here it is. You are forgetting one thing, and that is that we are *Englishmen*. Oh, I know King George is an idiot, probably insane! And I know that he's surrounded himself by men who are *not* fools, but are greedy and unscrupulous. And it doesn't take a smart man to see that we've been treated unfairly."

"Why, if you see that, Nathan," Caleb said in surprise, "why can't you see that we have to stand against them?"

"Say that we do," Nathan said slowly and with great intensity. "Say that we even do what Adams and Revere say we can do—defeat the Crown and set up our own government—which is impossible, but say that a revolution worked, where would we be then?"

"Why, we'd be free!"

"Not for long, Caleb. Have your forgotten Spain? She's already got a foothold in Florida and Louisiana. We'd be a little group of states with nothing in common—no army, no law, nothing to fight with. And if not Spain, it'd be one of the strong European nations like Prussia who'd get us."

"But we could be strong, Nathan, in time—"

"That's just it, Caleb," Nathan interrupted; "wouldn't *have* time! We'd be little and weak, and one of the wolves would pick us off sure as the world. Can't you see that?"

Caleb's face settled into the stubborn lines that Nathan had learned to dread, so he broke off at once. "Well, I'm sorry if I shamed you, Caleb, coming for you, but I—" The words stopped, and silently the tall young man who spoke so well on some things had no way to say what he felt. He wanted to say, *I came because I love you and you're my only brother and I don't want you to be hurt.* But his emotions were too subdued for that, so he merely put his hand on Caleb's shoulder and said, "I just want what's good for you, Caleb, that's all."

Caleb tried for a smile that didn't quite work. He said only, "I wish we thought the same about this thing, Nathan. I—I don't want to be against you." Then he whirled to hide his confusion and began to prepare for bed.

Nathan's heart was full, but there was no more to be said. He sat down at the desk and said, "I've got to write Father and Mother about this, Caleb. You know that?"

"Yes. You go ahead."

By the light of a candle, Nathan began to write. The scratch of his turkey-quill pen echoed in the quietness of the room. He could hear Caleb's steady breathing, but knew that he was not asleep. For over an hour he wrote, first about unimportant things, but finally he had to come to what he hated to put on paper:

> Finally, I have bad news for you about Caleb. He is physically well, but I must tell you he has joined himself to the Sons of Liberty—the radical "patriots" led by Sam Adams and others of that sort.
>
> It will be hard for you to read this, as it is hard for me to write it. Our opinions differ in this matter. But sitting here in the middle of the thing is different from being in the quiet backwaters of our little town. This place is like a powder keg, Father! You know how it is in a powder-making plant, with explosive powder everywhere, how they make people wear soft shoes with no nails that might give off a spark, and how nobody would *ever* think of striking a match? Well, if you can imagine a powder-making plant where wild, irresponsible men run down the aisles with torches and striking flint to steel right over the powder—that's what Boston is like!
>
> The Crown is sick of Boston's smuggling, and sick of the Sons of Liberty, so to protect Royal officials, 4,000 Redcoats have been stationed here under General Gage. That's one soldier for every four citizens, and the people refuse to house these men (which they are bound to do under the Quartering Act passed by Parliament). Many of these ill-fed, ill-paid men hire themselves out at menial jobs for low wages, incurring the bitter wrath of Boston's unemployed. Every day there is a street fight with mobs taunting the troops with cries of "bloody backs!" and all the while it is Sam Adams and his Sons of Liberty maneuvering in the background, fanning flames of revolt!
>
> I beg you, send for Caleb! He is hypnotized by the "romance" of being in a revolution that could well mean his life. As for me, I would like to stay, but will do as you instruct me.
>
> Your loving son,
> Nathan

CHAPTER SEVEN

A NEW CLERK

★ ★ ★ ★

When Laddie opened the door of his room to admit Nathan the next morning, the youth saw at once the marks of sleeplessness on his face. But Winslow smiled, saying, "Well, you look pretty good this morning."

"I'm fine. Mrs. Nelson fed me so much chicken soup, I'm about to sprout pinfeathers!"

"You feel like moving around a bit?" The boy nodded, plucked his ragged jacket from a wooden peg, and followed Winslow down the narrow stairs. "You had breakfast yet?"

"Oh, yes, I'm fine."

"Well, we'll go find you something to wear, then come back for a bite later."

Laddie felt very uncomfortable walking with Nathan down the street. Winslow was wearing buff trousers, a crisp white shirt with ruffles, a dark blue waistcoat and a wool cloak of a lighter hue. His auburn hair escaped here and there from beneath the blue and white tri-cornered hat, and he wore highly polished black boots to the knees. *I look like a beggar he's picked up from the gutter*, the lad thought, and when he led the boy into a shop filled with good clothing, it was worse.

"Yes, sir, may I be of help?" A short fussy-looking man with a prim moustache and a pair of silver-rimmed eyeglasses came up at once. He gave Nathan's figure an approving glance, but seemed not to notice Laddie at all.

"Yes, I want this young fellow suited out," Nathan said. He must have seen the supercilious look the clerk gave the ragged figure beside him, for he spoke with an edge to his voice. "I doubt you've got anything good enough to suit, but you can try."

That challenge seemed to change the man, for he straightened himself to his full five feet five and said indignantly, "You are mistaken, sir, grossly mistaken! We have just what the young gentleman needs!"

"We'll see. Now from the skin out, mind you—breeches, shirts, stockings, waistcoat, overcoat, a good hat, underclothes—anything else that's needed."

The light of pure greed brightened the clerk's narrowly spaced eyes, and he nodded so rapidly that his glasses almost fell off. "To be sure! Clothes make the man! And we'll have a new man here in no time, won't we, young fellow?"

A flash of humor appeared in the youth's dark eyes, but Laddie only nodded briefly, then turned to Nathan. "I can't let you spend all this on me, Mr. Winslow."

"You can pay it back out of your earnings," he shrugged. "You'll have to pass muster for my uncle—and his wife, which will be more difficult. I'll leave you here for an hour, all right?"

He gave an encouraging smile; then as he left the shop, the clerk at once began laying out the articles he had mentioned. It was a trying hour for Laddie, for men's clothing was something she knew little about. But she went at it carefully, choosing items that would be less revealing of the figure underneath. Some of the choices surprised the clerk, and he showed grave displeasure, but when Nathan returned at the appointed time, all the items were in a large bag ready to go.

"Get everything?" he asked, then at the lad's nod, asked the price and paid it without comment. "Let's go back to the Nelsons' place. I could use a bite now."

As they walked along the street, Nathan said, "We'll have to go out to my uncle's house, Laddie. I talked to Strake—he's the general manager—and he says he can use a clerk; you'll have to satisfy him before we get my uncle's approval."

They turned into The Blue Boar, and went upstairs, but Nathan called out as they went through the bar, "Nelson, let's have some battered eggs and some fresh fruit if you've got any—for the two of us."

When they were inside the door, Laddie opened the bag and began laying the items on the bed, saying, "Let me show you what I bought, Mr. Winslow—such nice things!"

He glanced down at the clothing, grinned and said, "Well, I don't want to see how they look with the *bed* wearing them, Laddie! Go on and put them on."

Laddie stared at him, and a red flush began creeping up the slender throat. Nathan looked at the boy in surprise and asked, "What's wrong?"

"N-nothing—but would you—would you mind waiting outside until I—get dressed?"

"Outside?" He could not have been more surprised if Laddie had asked him to jump out the window. Then he suddenly laughed and said, "Why, Laddie, I think you're ashamed because you're so skinny! Well, that's no matter to me—but I'll go on down and hurry Mrs. Nelson up with the breakfast. Quickly now, will you?"

He slammed the door as he left, thinking with a wry smile, *Pretty modest for a beggar!* But he was hungry and sat down, listening to Nelson tell one of his tall tales about how he'd saved his ship in the Indian Sea once.

Finally the breakfast was brought out by Mrs. Nelson, and he looked up at that same instant to see Laddie come down the stairs. He was so surprised at the change in the boy's appearance that for a moment he could only stare.

Nelson, however, was more vocal. He looked up from the mug of ale that he was sipping, and his eyes widened as he said, "Well, now! Lookee wot we got 'ere! A real gentleman is wot we got!"

Laddie crossed to the table, with no little grain of fear that they might see through the disguise. An examination of their faces drew a sigh of relief, however, for there was no indication of that.

Julie, in the guise of Laddie, had given much thought to the matter of concealing her sex, but the old plan of merely covering up with loose fitting, bulky clothes would not serve for this new life. Her quick mind had seen at once that she would have to dress like a clerk—but that meant wearing clothing much tighter and therefore more dangerous. All the time she had been choosing the clothing, this had been in her mind, and she had done well. She had, first of all, bound her upper figure tightly with a broad strip of cotton cloth ripped from her old clothes. Then she had donned the white stockings and a pair of buff knee breeches, the universal garment of young men everywhere. A light brown waistcoat, as loose-fitting as she dared, was buttoned up to where a white ruffle rose and covered her slender throat. Over all this she wore a dark brown broadcloth coat with wide double lapels and white ruffles from a shirt extending past the cuffs. A pair of high-topped brown boots covered her slender legs.

What Nathan saw was a thin young man with eyes perhaps too large and features more delicate than most his age, but looking very well in a suit of new clothes. He smiled and slapped his hand on the table. "Stab me!" he cried out with an approving smile, "I think that idiot of a clerk had *some* sense! Clothes *do* make the man, don't they, Nelson?"

"Why, I could get the lad a post as midshipman on the *Victory* right this day, sir! He's a proper gentleman, he is!"

"Well, and if he's good enough for the Royal Navy, why, he ought to be good enough for the Winslow Company," Nathan grinned. "Eat up, Laddie, then we'll get you gainfully employed!"

The interview with Laurence Strake took little time. Strake, a tall man with a lean face and sharp black eyes, shoved two papers toward Laddie. "Total up the figures on the one—and write a letter on the other," he demanded. He sat there and waited, surprise crossing his face when Laddie totaled the figures faster than he himself could have done and got it right. The letter pleased him even more. "Why, it's a fair hand you have, Smith! You've been well trained." He nodded to Nathan, adding, "I'm satisfied, but you'll have to gain Mr. Charles's approval."

"No problem there, but we'll have to go to the house. Come along, Laddie." They took the carriage and arrived just in time for an early lunch with the family.

"Now don't be nervous, Laddie. My uncle isn't a hard man." The servant admitted them, and he led the boy straight to the dining room. Charles looked up in surprise, as did the others. "Sorry to interrupt your meal," Nathan said hurriedly, "but when you finish, Uncle, could we have a word with you?"

"What is it, Nathan?" Charles asked, looking curiously at Laddie. "Who's this with you?"

"This is Laddie Smith, sir—it's a matter of business, but if you don't mind . . . ?"

Dorcas was staring at the pair, and she gave a quick frown toward her mother-in-law, then said sharply, "Get on with it, Nathan."

"Well, it's just that I remembered you and Mr. Strake spoke of needing a clerk last week, and I'd like to recommend this young man."

"A clerk?" Charles frowned, then nodded absently. "I believe we did have that in mind." He looked at Laddie more carefully, then said, "We'd thought of an older man—what's your age?"

"Oh, I took him by and Mr. Strake gave him a very strict examination," Nathan spoke up quickly. "He'll give you the result himself, but I can say he's ready to employ Smith at once."

"Well, it's Strake who'll have to work with him, so you may consider yourself hired, young fellow."

"Thank you, Mr. Winslow," Laddie said breathlessly. "I'll do my best for you."

"By the way, Uncle, Laddie here has been a little under the weather lately, so would it be all right if he started work in a few days—just until he can get his strength up?"

"He looks frail to me, Charles," Martha said.

"Clerks don't have to lift anything heavier than a pen, Mother," Charles said idly. "Yes, that'll be all right, Nathan. Anything else?"

"Well, as a matter of fact, we haven't spoken of wages, but if we could find a room here, we could count that as part of his wages."

Dorcas suddenly straightened up, her interest piqued. "You are competent with figures—and a fair penman?"

"I trust so, ma'am."

"Charles, Anne is doing very poorly with her studies. I suggest that it might be wise to let Smith have the room over the stable in exchange for lessons for her."

Always ready to do anything for his daughter, Charles gave Laddie a quick look, then asked, "Would this be acceptable with you, Smith?"

"Why, I'm no teacher, Mr. Winslow, but I'll give the young lady what pointers I can."

He put his hand out to Laddie, surprising the boy, and shook his hand warmly. "I'll have the room put in order at once—and this would be a good place for you to recuperate. Nathan, you've done well."

Anne jumped up and ran around the table, "Mama, can I show Mr. Smith his room, please?"

"All right, and tell Else to have it cleaned up." Dorcas was tight with money, and it pleased her to think that she had managed to wring a free service out of the young man. "You can begin your tutoring at once, young man. And I'll expect great improvement in my daughter's work."

"Yes, ma'am." Laddie turned to follow Anne out of the room, but paused to stop and say quietly to Nathan, "I must thank you again, Mr. Winslow."

After the two had gone, Charles said as he headed for the door, "Seems a fine chap—but a bit frail, as Dorcas says. Known him long?"

"Oh, not very—but I feel he'll make you a good clerk."

"You're very like your father, Nathan—the way you help people, I mean," Charles said. He paused and looked into his nephew's face. "I know Adam doesn't think too much of me, but I must tell you, I've long considered him the most honest man I've ever known." He paused; then a cloud crossed his face, and he said with a shrug as he wheeled to leave, "Indeed, perhaps the *only* honest man I've ever run across!"

A warm breeze drifted through the small window of Laddie's room, bringing in the odor of freshly turned earth and the sound of the martins building a nest outside the window. The iron hand of winter had relaxed a few days earlier, and warm spring winds had stirred the land to life.

Laddie looked down at the book before her, reading what she had written. Keeping a journal had never been a thing she cared to do, but in the isolation imposed by her secret, it had come to be a pleasure to be totally honest, even if only in a closely guarded journal. She looked back at the first entry, dated, Feb. 18, 1775, and smiled at the words:

"Here I am, like Jonah out of the whale's belly!"

She shook her head, thinking *I was pretty dramatic about everything then.* But as she slowly turned the pages, it struck her now that there was something dramatic in her life. It was a role she had to play, and unlike real actors who got off the stage and had a life of their own, she was *never* off stage—except for times like this alone in her room. She had a flair for capturing scenes on paper, and knew that she could write fiction if she turned her hand to it. As she read her own rather breathless accounts—how she had managed to keep up the charade of being a man, how in this case she was almost found out, how in that case she learned another useful trick for adding to the illusion of masculinity—she grew sober, and looked out the window, musing. *Sooner or later I'll be found out. A girl can't get by with pretending to be a man forever.*

Then she gave her head a rebellious shake, and read the entry she'd just made:

March 20, 1775

I had a strange thought tonight. Ever since I've been here with the Winslows, I've been so afraid of being found out! But that seems unlikely. I've become a student of masculine behavior—how to walk, for example, which is *nothing* like the same act performed by a woman! How to listen to male profanity without blinking an eye. I even take a night off at times and return boasting of my conquests over some beautiful woman—which Nathan scoffs at, saying I'm too young for such. I've learned to act the role well, but it's a hard thing!

But the thought I had tonight—it wasn't for me. For the first time I found myself worried about someone else. It comes to me now that I'm caught up in the Winslow family—only natural, since these people have become my whole world.

Charles Winslow is not a good man, perhaps, but he's treated me fairly enough. He is the half brother to Nathan's father, and from what I gather the two are not alike.

But Caleb is in trouble. I've seen how he's been cut out of the family here—and it's no wonder, since all these Winslows are Tories to the bone! He can't talk to Nathan, that's clear. So it came as little surprise when he began talking to *me*. I'm his age, and the only "man" he can speak to, so I've learned a lot from what he's said.

Nathan Winslow is the best young man in the world—but he's so in love with that painted flirt Abigail Howland that he can't see his own brother is being pushed outside!

She slammed the journal shut, slipped it into a cloth cover, put that into a box, and then carefully placed it in the false bottom of a small chest packed with her things.

She failed to understand the anger that raced through her when she thought of the problem, but it was, she knew, getting more severe. She closed the door, went across the fresh green grass from the carriage house and into the back door. The cook, a fat black woman named House Betty (to distinguish her from Field Betty), looked up, saying, "Dey's already havin' brekfust, Mistuh Smith."

It had been difficult at first, taking meals with the family, but during her first days, while giving Anne lessons, eating with the Winslows had evolved as the simplest way; now the first part of "Laddie's" work was tutoring the girl after breakfast, then she went into town to the business.

"Laddie, I showed Papa the letter I wrote," Anne said at once, her face beaming, "and he said it was the best he ever read!"

Charles smiled and nodded. "You've done wonders, Laddie—both here with Anne and at the office. I don't see what we ever did without you."

"It's easy to be a good teacher," Laddie said with a fond glance at Anne, "when you have a willing student."

Paul spoke up. "Let me say, Laddie, that the best day's work that Nathan here ever did in the business was to find you."

Nathan smiled, but there was a restraint in his manner. He was subdued, and Laddie wondered if there had been some sort of problem. She asked no questions, but later in the meal, Charles said with a peculiar look in his eye, "I think I mentioned a while back that someone from our office would have to go to New York very soon to learn that new bookkeeping system from Johnson? Well, it's got to be now. I want it set up here as soon as possible."

"Well, I can't go," said both Paul and Nathan at the same instant, then paused and looked at each other.

"Neither of you want to go?" Charles said in surprise, but there was a gleam in his blue eyes. "Well, that's too bad." Everyone at the table, except Anne, knew that the rivalry between the cousins for Abigail had grown so heated that they stayed awake nights scheming new ways to edge one another out.

The two of them began to bicker, each trying to shove the trip off on the other, and although they were polite enough, it was obvious that they were both determined to be the one left in Boston to court Abigail.

Finally Charles raised his hand for silence. "All right, I'll have Strake go." He watched as they settled down, then set off his little bombshell. "But it will be a shame—because he'll be wasted on Abigail."

"Abigail?" Paul demanded. "What's she got to do with a trip to New York?"

"Oh, didn't I mention that?" Charles tried to look surprised. "Why, she's gotten Saul and her mother to let her go for some shopping there, so we agreed that since she needed clothes and I needed someone there to learn some business, they might as well make the trip together. But it will be good for Abigail to spend some time in the company of a serious man like Strake, don't you think so, Nathan?"

Laddie gave a sudden grin at the blank expression on Nathan's face, but tried to look sorry when he glared balefully at her. "Why, Uncle Charles, I suppose I've been selfish about this whole thing." He put a look on his face that was revoltingly pious, and added smoothly, "I suppose I *could* make that trip."

Then Paul raised his eyebrows and said defiantly, "I'm going to New York, and that's that!"

The next fifteen minutes were tense, both young men ready to fight in order to go, but in the end Charles wearied of it. He raised his voice over the strident tones of his son, who was speaking much too loudly, and said, "All right! That's enough! I knew when this came up, there'd be no way for *one* of you to go—so *both* of you will go—and you'll have to go along as well, Laddie." He laughed at the surprise that crossed her face, and said, "You'll have to do the real work while these two pound each other over the fair lady."

"Charles, it's not dignified!" Dorcas said.

"Love hardly ever is," he said sourly.

"Please, Uncle Charles, I'd like to go along."

Caleb had said nothing for so long at the table that he was usually forgotten. Now he spoke up clearly, and added, "Will it be all right? Maybe I can learn something, too."

Charles stared at the young man, then slowly nodded, a strange expression on his face. *He looks so much like Adam!* "Well, it can't do any harm. You'll have to take the big carriage to hold all of you, but I have no objections."

"When do we leave, Father?" Paul asked.

"You'll pick Abigail up at ten in the morning." He gave them a sly smile and said, "I told her you'd *both* be going—and that seemed to please her a great deal."

It would! Laddie thought angrily. *She'll have them shooting each other in some fool duel before we get back!* Then she had to try to console

Anne, who felt left out. She took one quick look at Caleb, trying to fathom his motives, for it was one of the last things he'd have wanted to do—be away from the Sons of Liberty—but there was nothing on his face but a slight expression of satisfaction.

CHAPTER EIGHT

"A MAN IN LOVE IS BOUND TO BE A FOOL!"

★ ★ ★ ★

"I don't reckon Uncle Charles's big idea is going to work, is it, Laddie?"

The front wheel of the big wagon struck a pothole just as Laddie turned to look at Caleb, and the unexpected lurch threw her heavily against Caleb, who was driving. She pulled back quickly, took a tight grip on the seat, and asked, "What big idea?"

"Why, he got this whole thing up so's Abigail would have to choose between Nathan and Paul." He turned to face her, a sardonic smile on his lips. "But it sure has turned out different!"

Laddie's shoulders sagged, for the trip had been no pleasure for any of them. They had left Boston three days earlier, and the spring weather had been ideal for traveling. The roads were still heavily rutted from winter travel, but the inns had been fairly clean and the food mostly good. At their first night's stop, however, at a villainous place called The Blue Lion, Paul had spat out what was reported to be tea, and called to the innkeeper: "Sir, if this be tea, bring me coffee. If this be coffee, bring me tea."

And it was later at that same place that the sleeping accommodations almost caught up with Laddie. There were only two rooms; one, of course, was for Abigail, and the other for the rest of the party. All throughout the meal, Laddie's mind was racing, and when Nathan said, "Let's get some sleep—we've got a long trip tomorrow," panic had almost taken over, but the room, they found was so small that after one look, he had said, "This bed's too small for four. Caleb, you and Laddie will have to make out in the wagon tonight."

As she and Caleb had settled down that night, fortified with blankets, Caleb had said, "I like this better than that dirty old room, anyway. Don't you, Laddie? I'd just as soon camp out like this the whole trip." Laddie had quickly agreed, and then for a long time they had lain awake, listening to the spring peepers in a nearby creek and tracing out patterns in the icy points of light the stars made against the velvet sky.

Now as Caleb drove the wagon down the final stretch of road to where the silhouette of New York could be faintly seen, Laddie looked across at his stocky figure, thinking how strange it was that she should know more of him than Nathan. Caleb had spoken wistfully of how close they had been once, and his loneliness was a sharp pain that he exposed, she knew, only to her.

Now, she picked up on his comment, saying, "I guess men in love are generally fools."

"You got that right, Laddie!" Caleb nudged the off leader a touch with his buggy whip, and then gave a short laugh. "Don't know what my hurry is."

"Why'd you want to come along?" she asked.

He gave no direct answer, saying only, "Might as well be here as in Boston, I guess."

Paul took the reins when they got to the outskirts of New York and drove to the branch office, which was located in the center of the harbor. Hiram Johnson, the manager, was a short man with a full black beard and deep-set black eyes. "Won't take more'n two or three days to learn that system." He looked over the party and said innocently, "Reckon they's enough of you to handle the job?"

Paul looked a little foolish, and at that instant Laddie had an idea—an answer to the ever-present problem of where she would sleep. "If you've got a cot here, Mr. Johnson, I could stay here around the clock. That would be quicker, wouldn't it?"

"Sure, we can do that," the manager agreed, and Laddie saw that both Paul and Nathan were relieved.

"I'd like to stay, too."

Nathan stared at Caleb, and he opened his mouth to question

the boy, but at that instant, Abigail said, "I really need to get settled; if you'd be so kind as to take me to the hotel."

As Caleb and Laddie got their bags from the carriage, then watched the party drive off toward the inner city, Caleb said, "Looks like we ain't going to be bothered much with their company, are we, Laddie?"

There was something so childish about the way the two men followed around after Abigail, glaring at each other, that Laddie muttered angrily, "Like I said, men in love are bound to be fools!"

By the third day of the visit, Nathan would have agreed totally with Laddie's statement. He had begun well, showing up early at the office in the morning, but as the day wore on and Paul made no appearance, he grew moody. Finally at noon, he said, "Laddie, do you think you can handle this alone? I mean, I'm no clerk—so I might as well get out of your way." Then almost without waiting for an answer, he had walked quickly out of the office and had not returned.

But he did not better himself, for if he had felt useless at the office, he felt even more out of place following around after Abigail. When the trip had come up, he had thought, *Well, now I'll be able to get her alone—away from family and everyone.* But he never did that; in fact, he saw rather *less* of her than he had in Boston!

New York was a thriving beehive of a town, bursting at the seams, and filled with activities day and night. The streets teemed with people, including many sailors from the Royal Fleet that lay at anchor in the East River. Nathan was acutely aware that the threat of revolution lay always just beneath the surface, exactly as it had at Boston—which disturbed him. But he had little time to think about politics, for he found himself caught up in an almost frantic round of social activities led by Abigail and a group of young socialites.

They began in the mornings with tea in the lovely homes of the city, and Nathan was ill at ease. Paul and Abigail knew everyone, it seemed, and he stood on the outside looking in. He felt himself to be an outsider, a quaint colonial, a backwoodsman from Virginia, which was to some extent quite accurate. More than one pretty girl tried to draw his attention, but he was so single-minded in his pursuit of Abigail that he never noticed.

In the afternoons they prowled the streets of the Battery, took in the waxworks and the gardens, and later probed into the lower side of the city, attending a horse race and the many curiosities, peep shows, and wax museums that abounded on the lower side of Manhattan.

Then in the evenings, Abigail's friends scheduled dances in their large homes. These affairs were like small "balls" and lasted until the early hours of the morning, and Nathan felt out of place at them as well.

On the fourth night he stood with his back against the wall in a large Dutch-style mansion, watching the dancers weave across the polished floor. He had eaten little for the past two days, and his nerves were jangling from the constant frenzied activities and from lack of sleep. He had broken his own rule and had several glasses of wine, so his head was not clear.

He had danced several times, but only once with Abigail, and as he stood there, she danced by with Paul, looking up at him, laughing, and Paul suddenly threw his head back and laughed. Behind him someone said, "Make a lovely couple, don't they?" He glared at the overweight woman who had spoken to her equally overweight husband, then moved away.

For the next hour he grew more morose and he took several more glasses of wine from the refreshment table that groaned under the weight of food and drink. Finally, he thought, *A man's a fool to torment himself like this!* He caught a glimpse of Abigail dancing with a red-coated British officer, and impulsively plunged across the crowded dance floor, bumping into several couples, until he reached them.

"Abigail, I've got to talk to you!" he said urgently. Both Abigail and the officer, a compact young captain with a smooth face and a pair of cold blue eyes, turned to look at him in surprise.

"Why, Nathan!" she said. "What's the matter?"

"Come along; we can't talk here."

He took her arm and pulled at it, but found that the captain had anchored himself to her other arm. "You need better manners, fellow!" he said evenly. "Just you move along now."

Nathan stared at him, but did not release the arm he held. "Soldier, we'll get along very well without you."

The sharp rebuke fired the cold blue eyes of the officer, and he moved toward Nathan, but Abigail said, "Edgar! Please!" She placed her hand on his arm, smiled up and said, "Excuse us, will you, please?"

"Very well—but I'll have a word perhaps with you, sir, before you leave. We don't need your backwoods manners in this place!"

She patted his arm, then turned, pulling Nathan after her, through a door that led into the main hallway. He followed her until she led him through a set of French doors to a small porch that looked out onto a garden.

"Now, Nathan, what's the matter?"

"Well—" Suddenly he could say nothing, but felt foolish over his actions. He stood there in confusion, longing to say so much, yet somehow rendered speechless by her beauty.

She *was* beautiful—more than he had ever known! She stood there bathed in the pale moonlight that washed over her hair, and the night was so clear that he could see the curves of her cheeks, the arch of her lips. Yet coming out of the noisy ballroom into the almost holy quietness of the secluded garden had not cleared Nathan's mind, for now, looking down at her, he felt more confused than ever.

Finally she said, "What is it, Nathan? Tell me." And she leaned against him slightly, then raised her hand to place it on his cheek. "You've been so quiet lately. Are you angry with me?"

"No—but I feel like I'm out of your world, Abigail." He took her shoulders, and the fragrance of lilacs came to him, and he whispered, "You're so lovely, Abigail—and I feel so far away from you."

"Don't feel like that!" She smiled up at him, and then as he stood there, all the confusion of the trip seemed to fade. She was there, and she was lovely—so he simply leaned forward and kissed her. She did not hold back, but pressed herself against him, and the eagerness that he felt in her slim body struck him powerfully, so that he held her even tighter.

He drew back, and there was a softness in her eyes, a gentleness that she had kept hidden, and she said, "Nathan, you are . . ."

What she would have said, he never found out, for at that moment there was the sound of a door creaking, and Paul's voice said, "Quite a pretty scene—but a little public, don't you think?"

Nathan released Abigail and turned quickly to see him standing framed in the door. He waved a hand, and following his gesture, Nathan saw a man and a woman in a gallery across the garden watching them, and then looking to his right, several observers were standing at the large windows laughing and pointing at them.

"Nathan, you ought to have more sense!" Paul said more sharply. Then he took Abigail's arm, saying, "I think we'd better go."

"Take your hand off her!" Nathan said at once.

"Oh, don't be a fool!" Paul retorted.

Nathan's temper was even, as a rule, but once or twice in his life he had discovered that deep inside him there was the capacity for blinding rage—not just anger, much more intense than that. He had felt it once when a boy had smashed his favorite toy, and even at the age of ten he had so completely lost control of himself, bellowing and striking out, that his father had been shaken.

"Nathan, you must never let yourself go like that again!" he had said with a pale face. It had happened again, however, just two years earlier, when a man who'd been half drunk had pulled a pistol and shot Nathan's favorite dog. Nathan had no remembrance of his actions, but he'd finally come to himself with half a dozen men holding him with some difficulty, flat on his back. He had broken the man's jaw in two places, and left his face hopelessly shattered, and the shock of it had been so great that ever since he had been careful to avoid the black rage that he knew lurked deep within him.

Now, to his horror, he felt the thing, black and ugly, rising up again, and as before it seemed to deprive him of speech, to numb his brain and thought. He heard himself give a hoarse roar, felt his hands reach out and grasp Paul, and then he heard Abigail's frightened cry, which seemed to come from far away.

Sanity came sweeping back, and he found himself staring into the wide eyes of Paul, who seemed paralyzed by the awesome wrath that had leaped out of his tall kinsman without warning. Nathan wrenched himself away, whirled, ran headlong off the porch and across the yard, then disappeared down the street.

"I never saw him like that!" Abigail whispered. "He would have killed you!"

Paul's hand was not quite steady as he put it on her elbow and guided her inside. He said nothing, but there was a mixture of anger and wonder in his eyes as they left, and he cast one look down the dark street where Nathan had disappeared. *Yes—he would have killed me—and that's the dark side of the Winslow blood Father's tried to warn me of*, he thought grimly.

Laddie gave a start, coming out of a sound sleep on the couch.

A large hand was shaking her arm, and she opened her eyes to see Nathan, his face pale and angry, looking at her.

"Where's Caleb?"

"Caleb?" She sat up quickly, gave a look at the second cot that had not been used across the room. She threw the light blanket off and stood up. "I guess he hasn't come in yet." She gave him a careful look, then asked quietly, "What's the matter, Mr. Winslow?"

He stared at her, then shook his head. "Never mind, Laddie. I'm leaving here. Do you want to go with me or come with the others?"

"Why—" She stood there confused, knowing that something had happened, but not daring to pursue it. "I'll go with you—but what about Caleb?"

"I want him to go with me." He shook his shoulders, struck his hands together in a sudden burst of impatience, and asked tensely, "Has he been out late like this before?"

"Well—yes, he has. Guess he got bored watching me work on the books. But he's never been later than midnight."

Nathan stood there, a tall, silent shape, and then he said wearily, "Well, I'm not waiting until morning. Get your stuff ready. I'm going to hitch the horses."

He left her then, and she moved quickly to collect her few belongings. She put them into a small bag, then left the room, walking down a short hall to the door that led to the stable. Nathan was busy with the horses, and she said, "I'll help you."

They said nothing, but just as the last horse was harnessed into place the outer door opened, and Caleb walked in.

He was not alone; a tall man wearing high boots and a dark cloak was with him. Both of them paused abruptly, and Laddie saw the shock on Caleb's face as he spotted Nathan.

The tall man said something softly, and Caleb nodded. He walked toward the door to the hall and disappeared. Nathan dropped the lines over a steel ring fixed in the wall and went to stand before the man. "Who are you?" he asked abruptly.

A pair of steady gray eyes looked out at him from under a tricornered hat, then after a pause came the answer in a flat voice. "My name is Dawes."

"What's your business here?"

"Nothing with you, I think."

"I disagree. What are you doing with my brother?"

"Your brother? I see." Dawes nodded and said, "I have a little business affair with Caleb. Won't take but a minute."

A sound of footsteps drew Nathan's head around, and he saw Caleb come out the door with a flat leather pouch in his hand. He didn't look at Nathan, but simply walked forward and handed it to Dawes. "There you are."

"Thank you, Caleb." Dawes pushed the pouch into an inner pocket, reached out his hand and said, "You've been a great help to us. I'll be sure and tell—" Then he cut his words off, gave a quick look in Nathan's direction, and nodded as he wheeled and left the stable.

As the door closed softly, Caleb turned to face Nathan, his sturdy shoulders square in the dim light of the lantern. There was a stubborn look on his face, and he said, "I'll tell you before you ask, Nathan. I've brought those papers from Boston to give to Mr. Dawes as a favor to a friend of mine. That's all you need to know."

Nathan stood there, knowing at once that the "friend" was Sam Adams or Revere. He knew that every colony had formed a Committee of Safety—an armed force to be summoned when called—and it was kept alive by a link of messengers. He'd even heard of Dawes as one of the fire-eaters in the organization.

But there was nothing to say. Caleb stood there, daring him to speak, but he could not. He finally said, "I'm going back to Boston tonight. I want you to come with me."

Caleb shot a glance at Laddie, and she nodded, so he shrugged and said, "I'll get my things."

While he was gone, Laddie came up to stand before Nathan, and spoke quietly. "I can see you're in trouble, Mr. Winslow. I'm sorry for whatever it is." She put a light hand on his arm, and added very softly, "I'd help if I could."

He stood there trying to fight back the bitterness that welled up in him. His world seemed to have fallen apart, and he wanted to strike out. But he slowly made himself relax, and then he put his hand on her shoulder, feeling a quick rush of gratitude for the sympathy in Laddie's dark eyes.

"I know you would, Laddie, and that's a help." Then he shook his head. "Man sure does act like a fool sometimes, don't he now?" He gave her an embarrassed smile, then added, "And I guess I'm a bigger fool than most."

She wanted to put her arms around him and comfort him. He was so big—and yet there was something of the hurt child in him, crying out of his eyes.

But she carefully hugged herself and said, "No, you're not a fool, Nathan. You're just a little lost right now."

It was the first time he had ever heard Laddie use his given name, and it warmed him. He gave her a rough hug, then with a sharp laugh said, "Laddie, never get messed up with a woman!"

She looked up at him and smiled, her dark eyes gleaming. "I won't, Nathan," she promised.

CHAPTER NINE

DEATH AT LEXINGTON

★ ★ ★ ★

The earth grew warm in April, and the hot summer winds that thawed the cold ground not only stirred the buried seeds to life, but seemed to kindle the spirits of the men of Boston. The Sons of Liberty, ever-growing flickers of heat lightning that threatened to turn to actual bolts at any minute, were inundated with volunteers, and the Provincial Congress of Massachusetts met illegally but regularly in Cambridge, within sight of General Gage's sentries. Led by John Hancock, the Committee of Safety formed militia units, the Minute Men, subject to instant call.

Gage knew most of this, but hoped for something to bring a halt to the activities of the colonists. Instead, the first two weeks of April brought two developments that the general could not ignore. A group of patriots led by Major John Sullivan swept down on Fort William and Mary at Portsmouth, overpowered the guard, and made off with all the ammunition; the next day seventeen cannon were taken by another militant group in Boston itself.

A week later, on April 14, General Gage and Colonel Smith met to find some solution to the problem.

"General, we can't let this rabble build up their arms at the Crown's expense," Colonel Smith said heatedly to the commanding officer. "We've got to *strike*—we've got to hit hard enough to show them what comes of treason."

General Gage stared at Colonel Smith and bit his lower lip

nervously. He was now backed into a corner; London insisted he take action, not realizing how volatile the situation was. Now his options were gone, and he nodded wearily, "I suppose we must—but it's going to be a nasty affair, Colonel!"

"For *them*, General Gage," Smith grinned, "I'm sure it will. Now, where shall we direct the attack?"

Gage looked at the map on the wall, his mind trying and rejecting possibilities. "We must have an objective, of course," he said. "I have a bit of information that seems valid. The rebels have purchased a store of arms sufficient for fifteen thousand men, and one of our informers has given us the location." He stared at the man, grimaced, and said, "They've been pretty shrewd about it, I'm afraid."

"Shrewd, sir?"

"Yes. If they'd stored these arms in Boston, we'd nip them up in a lightning raid—they've put them far enough away so that a successful raid will be very difficult. You know how they watch our every move—we can't cross a street without every rebel in America knowing about it!"

"We can move at night, sir," Smith said eagerly. "And you haven't forgotten your promise that I am to lead the men in the first action?"

"No, I've not forgotten."

"Well, General Gage, where are these arms? I propose to strike them hard, sir!"

General Gage stared at the short, fat officer, and wished heartily that he had another man with more balance, but he did not. Slowly he raised his hand and placed a finger on the map.

"Concord. That's where we must strike!"

"We will scotch this snake, General!" Smith cried with excitement.

"Secrecy is my hope," Gage said slowly. "The raiding party will be composed of seven hundred men. Every eye in this city will be on them, so we must create a diversion—make them think we're going where we're not. Won't work too well, but I think these militia—what do they call them, Colonel?"

"Minute Men, sir."

"Well, it'll take more than a minute to collect an army! You will leave on the night of the eighteenth—but only you and I and Major Pitcairn will know the exact date."

"Major Pitcairn? But, sir, there are no Royal Marines here for him to command."

"I know, Colonel, but if you go down, there must be a commanding officer."

"Very well, sir, but don't trouble your head about me. *I* won't be the one who goes down if that rag-tag bunch of beggars dares to cross our path!"

Gage had been accurate in his prediction that it would be impossible to raise a sizable force without attracting attention. As the tempo of the British forces quickened, so did the eyes and mouths of a myriad of Colonials. Taverns such as The Green Dragon or The Bunch of Grapes hummed with rumors; Gage's orders detaching the grenadier and light infantry companies for extra maneuvers reached the Colonials almost as quickly as it did the British units. *Why? What were these picked troops, the elite, specially trained and equipped units of each regiment, going to do? You don't create a force of 700 picked men for nothing!*

Warren sent word by Revere to Lexington, where Sam Adams and John Hancock were lodging with the Rev. Jonas Clarke, close to the congress in Concord. Gage might have arrests in mind, and who were better subjects than Adams and Hancock? Lexington passed the word to Concord, and at once the village labored night and day, packing stores and shipping them west to Worcester.

Then came a new rumor of longboats and barges being made ready—perhaps to float Redcoats across the Charles for a quick landing on the Cambridge side where the roads led north to Lexington and Concord.

As the night of the eighteenth fell, few slept well on either side; a silence fell with the darkness, but it was the silence that one expects to be broken with the sharp sound of cannon fire or of marching feet.

Laddie was working late that night, as she had fallen into the habit of doing since the return from New York. Whatever peace she and Nathan had felt in the house of Charles Winslow had since then degenerated. Whenever Paul and Nathan spoke to each other at all, it was with a tight-lipped and sullen sort of formality, and their attitude cast a pall over the others. Laddie watched with disgust as the two of them pursued Abigail with a dogged persistence, and said once to Caleb, "They're all three acting like fools!"

Caleb had nodded, but the friction between him and Nathan had grown worse as the spring wore on. Laddie went for solitary walks, and often worked late—anything to keep out of the house. On this night, however, the constant shifting of men along the waterfront and down the dark streets rasped on her nerves. Several times she lifted her head suddenly, her heart beating faster, and went to peer out the window at the flickering lanterns that bobbed along the streets.

Finally the outer door slammed, and she jumped out of her chair, her fists clenched nervously as she waited for the inner door to open. Quick footfalls then, and when the door opened she saw Major John Pitcairn enter, his face drawn and a frown on his lips.

"Is Mr. Winslow here?" he said quickly. "Nathan, I mean."

"Why, no, sir, he's not. He went home about five o'clock."

The words ruffled Pitcairn's temper, and he struck his hands together sharply, saying, "Blast!" then turned to go, but he paused and turned to give Laddie a searching look. "You work for Mr. Winslow, don't you?"

"I'm Smith, Major. A clerk for Mr. Winslow."

He seemed to be weighing her in the balances of his mind; then finally he asked, "Are you a friend as well as an employee, Smith?"

"Why, yes, sir!"

Pitcairn bit his lips, and there was an agony of frustration in him, but finally he came close, saying in a low voice, "I want you to get word to Nathan. Tell him that Major Pitcairn said for him to get his brother out of Boston!"

"Sir—!"

"That's *all* I can say!" the words came out bitterly, and then he took Laddie's arm and his eyes burned into hers as he said with terrible intensity: "Tell him to get his brother out of Boston if he has to knock the young fool in the head and tie him hand and foot!"

Then he whirled and ran out of the room. As his footsteps echoed down the outer hall, Laddie stood there, her mind spinning. Then she dropped her ledger on the floor and ran toward the stable. She had obtained the use of a gentle mare to make the journey back and forth, and her first impulse was to get to Nathan, but then as she placed her foot in the stirrup, she suddenly halted. *I haven't seen Caleb all day,* she thought abruptly, and slowly she withdrew her foot, thinking hard in the dim lantern light.

He was around all morning—but after that I didn't see him all afternoon. Suddenly she knew he was somehow involved in the seething activities that ran along the nerves of the city. *But—where can he be now?*

Since their return from New York, Caleb had been morose—mostly with Nathan, but with her as well. He did his work, but the minimal camaraderie that she had shared with him had passed, and now he spent his free time with Moses Tyler. *Maybe he's with him now!* she thought, and ran outside and down the street. Moses lived in a single room over a gunsmith shop. *There's a light in his window!* she noted with a feeling of hope. She had to pass through the shop, asking the elderly man who sat at a workbench, "Is Moses here?"

The old man nodded, and she flew up the stairs. At the first knock, the door opened, and Moses stood there. She had shown some friendliness for the boy, but he was surprised at the visit. "Moses," Laddie said quickly, "I've got to find Caleb—it's very important!"

Instantly the boy's lips tightened, and suspicion flared in his eyes. "Don't know where he is," he said tightly.

She knew instantly that he was lying, and she realized that wild horses wouldn't drag information out of him—especially if he thought Nathan was involved. She knew from conversations with Caleb how much Moses distrusted the older brother.

"It's very serious, Moses," she forced herself to say calmly. "His mother is very ill—in fact, she's likely to die—and she's asking for Caleb."

The lie was hard for her, even though she was desperate, but she saw that it changed Moses.

"His ma is dying?" He shook his head and muttered, "Caleb, he sets a heap of store by his ma."

"Yes, and he's got to go to her—soon!"

Moses swayed back and forth, caught by indecision, and she forced herself to say nothing. Finally he said, "Well, he's gone—he ain't here."

"Where is he, Moses?"

He bit his lip, then said, "You can't tell anybody else."

"Where is he?!"

"Well—he's gone with his group—the Minute Men, you know?" Excitement lit his eyes, and he said, "The Redcoats is moving out tonight to raid Concord—and we're all going to see they don't do it! Caleb and me, we're in different groups, and he left nearly an hour ago . . . ! Hey, you keep shut, you hear me?"

But she was gone, down the stairs and out of the shop. Running at full speed, she entered the barn, then leaped into the saddle and drove the surprised animal out into the darkness.

It was a wild ride, for the streets were crowded, and she was by no means an expert rider. More than once the bulk of her mount sent a man spinning to the side, and curses followed her as she plunged on through the streets, but finally she passed out of the city and pounded wildly down the road toward the Winslow house.

She passed other riders on the road, and one of them shouted at her to hold up, but she did not pause, driving the mare until she pulled up in the front yard. Falling off the horse, she flipped the reins over a post and ran around the house, going in the back way. The family usually spent the evenings in the library or the small drawing room in the front of the house; through the back way, she might avoid being seen.

Running up the stairs, she went to the door of Nathan's room and knocked on it rapidly. His footsteps sounded, and when he opened the door and looked down at her, he said at once, "What's wrong, Laddie? Somebody sick?"

"Let me come in!" she whispered. She stepped inside and said at once, "I've got some bad news—Major Pitcairn just came by and he said to tell you to get Caleb out of Boston if you had to tie him up to do it."

"What? Why did he—"

"He couldn't say any more, Nathan, because he's a soldier, I think."

"A soldier? What's that got to do with Caleb?"

"Well, I guess he's not supposed to have anything to do with rebels. I—I started out here to tell you what he said; then I remembered that I hadn't seen Caleb all day. So I went to see Moses and asked him where Caleb was."

Nathan stared at her, beginning to understand. "What did Moses say?"

Laddie stood there, eyes troubled and finally the words came reluctantly, "Mr. Winslow, I know how you feel about the rebels—and I have to have your word that if I tell you what Moses said—you won't use it to hurt him."

"Why, you have my word, Laddie," Nathan said instantly. "I don't want any part of this revolution—I just want my brother safe."

"It's not that easy anymore. Moses said that Caleb is with a bunch of militia on the way to Concord to fight the Redcoats."

"What?" The news was so much worse than Nathan had expected that his mouth flew open, and he couldn't speak for a moment. Then he clenched his teeth and said, "All right, Laddie." He turned to pick up his coat, and headed for the door. She followed him down the stairs and out of the house, and he turned toward the barn. There were always good horses ready, and he started throwing a saddle on a tall bay.

"I'm going with you."

He paused, stared at her, and despite the shock that the news had etched on his lean face, he relaxed and even smiled. "Why, Laddie, I think you've done more than enough. And I thank you—but this is bad and likely to get worse."

"I'm going," she said stubbornly. "Saddle a horse for me while I go bring the mare in."

"But you could get shot!" he called as she left. She paid no attention, and Nathan stared at the door, then shook his head, muttering, "What a strange boy!"

In a few minutes they were on the road to Boston, and Laddie asked only one question as they turned toward Concord: "Aren't you going to take a gun, Mr. Winslow?"

"No, I'm not taking a gun." He made a big dark shape on the big bay, and she caught the gleam in his eyes as the moonlight shown in his face. "I'm not in this war, Laddie. I'll get Caleb out of it, and haul him back to Virginia, and that's all!" Then he drove his heels against the sides of his mount, and Laddie followed him as he raced along the strip of road turned silver by the pale moonlight.

They followed the Charleston road, making good time, but when they came to the spot where the road turned east, Nathan pulled up suddenly. Small groups of men were wandering around the crossroad, and there was an uncertainty about their actions that was disturbing. A tall man with a high-peaked hat was walking by, and Nathan said, "What's going on, Friend?"

"Why, it's the King's troops," the man said in a high nervous voice. He pointed down the Cambridge road, adding, "The hull army jest went down there—not mor'n an hour ago." He scratched his backside and looked around at the confusion, then shrugged and said, "I reckoned to get me a Redcoat—but they ain't no chance, now that they've got in front of us. Guess I'll get home to my woman."

Nathan started to move down the Cambridge road, but Laddie said, "Wait." He pulled back on his bridle, staring at her, but she was thinking of a map of the country. She had missed no chances to look at maps, and the Winslow Company had many. One of them was coming into focus in her mind.

"We can take the old road to Watertown. Then we can cut around in front of them where it joins the Cambridge road. That way we'll get to Concord before they do."

He stared at her in wonder. "How in the world do you know a thing like that?" he asked.

"Never mind—it's the only way."

And it worked exactly as she had said. The old road was overgrown in spots and rutted, but it lay only a quarter mile away from the new road, so they could actually hear the drums of the British as they passed by on their parallel course. Then they cut back two miles farther to the Cambridge road and passed on, coming into Lexington only an hour or so before dawn.

"These horses will never make it, Laddie," Nathan said. Both mounts were blowing and frothing. "Let's ask around. Maybe we can find someone to rent us some fresh mounts."

They tied the horses and walked across the open field where a fairly large number of men were standing around talking. All of them had muskets or rifles, but there didn't seem to be anyone in charge. Nathan moved around, but nobody was interested in renting horses; every eye was fixed on the road that led into Lexington from Boston.

"What are they doing, Nathan?" Laddie asked finally.

"Well, they're trying to get their nerve up to fight the Redcoats. But they'll never do it."

"Why, there's not more than fifty of them—and there must be six or seven hundred soldiers."

"They got more sense than to fight. Look, there's a farmhouse over there to the east. One of the men said we might get some horses there."

The two walked over to the house, but the woman who met

them said, "Have to ask my man 'bout horses. He's down there on the green somewhere. Ask fer Malcom Richards."

"This is no good!" Nathan grunted as they walked back. A pale gray light in the east revealed a line of trees, and he pointed at it. "Be dawn soon. We may have to *steal* some horses, Laddie!"

After searching for Richards unsuccessfully for forty-five minutes, the false dawn had given way to a red glow, and Nathan said, "We'll just have to ride our horses till they break down. Come on."

They had to pass through the field where the men seemed to have drawn together, and suddenly, one of them cried out, "There they are!"

And there was a sound like a bird singing afar off, but it wasn't a bird. It was a fife, and as they all stood there the sound of the drum's rattling came clearly on the dawn air.

"Form a line! Form a line!" One of the men on the green called out, and the men moved awkwardly to put themselves in some sort of order. They widened the line and stood there, muskets in their hands, staring at the red flash of uniforms now visible to the east.

Nathan and Laddie moved toward their mounts, but he said, "Let's rest them as long as we can—maybe we can let them go, then cut around them like we did before."

"I don't think there's a road for that." Laddie was suddenly cold and hot at the same time, for the column of red-clad troops was coming steadily on, and the rosy dawn touched their scarlet coats and their brass buttons with bright tips of light. Neither Nathan nor Laddie had ever seen trained troops, and they looked invincible as they marched inexorably toward the small bunch of farmers standing awkwardly on the green grass.

"They've seen us!" someone in the ranks said, and then two officers on horseback, flanked by two flag-bearers, rode forward. Rank after rank of Redcoats stretched back on the road; they did not quicken their pace but marched up to the edge of the common, stopping about one hundred and fifty paces away from the small group of farmers.

Suddenly Nathan gasped as if he'd been struck in the stomach, and he grabbed Laddie's arm with an iron grip. "Look! There's Caleb!"

He moved away toward the group, and Laddie followed. She saw him, then, at the end of a small group a little apart from the main body. He was staring at the British, his musket clasped in his hands, and he didn't see Nathan until suddenly he stood right in front of him.

"Caleb!" Nathan said with relief. "Thank God we found you!"

The shock of seeing his brother made Caleb's dark eyes widen, but then he said, "Nathan, get out of here!"

"Not without you." Nathan made his mistake then, for he put his hand on the other's arm and tried to pull him out of the line. "Look at that army, Caleb. Don't be a fool!"

Others in Caleb's group were watching with one eye, and Caleb yanked his arm away from Nathan's grip. "This is what I've got to do, Nathan. You don't belong here." Then he looked around Nathan and cried: "Here they come! Get out of here!"

"Fix bayonets!" came a shrill cry, and sunlight flashed on the metal. Then one of the officers spurred his horse, and Nathan turned with a shock to see Colonel Smith, sneering and calling out, "Column right!" The Redcoats wheeled to face the small group.

"Lay down your arms, you traitors!" Smith screamed. "Do you hear me? Get off the King's green!"

Then Nathan saw that the second officer was Major John Pitcairn. In the clear light of dawn their eyes met, and Nathan's lips moved in a prayer: *John! Don't let this happen! You're my friend!*

One of the farmers said, "Steady now. Just hold steady!"

Screaming wildly, Colonel Smith spurred his horse, but the words were not clear. He raised his saber, and Nathan at that instant saw a Redcoat raise his musket and fire. One of the farmers clutched his chest and fell to the ground, coughing. Then as Nathan whirled, the whole British front burst into a roar of sound and flame and smoke, and the ground shook with the fury of it.

Nathan turned in time to see a shot strike Caleb high on the chest. It drove him backward and instantly crimson blood gushed out as he went to the ground.

"Caleb!" Nathan cried out, and then Laddie screamed in his ear, "Look! The soldiers—they're charging!"

Nathan looked up to see the British advancing at a run through a ragged curtain of smoke. There was nothing to stop them, for the militia had turned and fled. Two Redcoats reached one man who was rolling on the ground and one of them drove his bayonet with all his force into the man's back.

Nathan reached down and picked Caleb up as if he were a

child, then raced across the green. Laddie followed, and both of them heard the yells of the Redcoats. Just as they reached the cover of the trees, musket balls sang close to their ears. They ran through a thicket, crashing through thorns and vines that tore their faces, and the only thing that saved them was the fact that the Redcoats were carrying packs that weighed over one hundred pounds.

Nathan ran until he was out of breath, then fell helpless to the ground, and as he looked down into the gray face of his brother, he heard far off, the tinny sound of drum and fife of the British Army.

CHAPTER TEN

THE VOW

★ ★ ★ ★

Time had passed, but Laddie had no idea how long she sat there watching helplessly as Nathan held the limp body of his brother. She had been vaguely aware of the sound of marching troops, but that had passed and now came the sound of voices floating to her, filtered by the woods.

Stiffly she got to her feet and Nathan raised his head to look at her as she came close. "He's dead, Laddie."

"I know."

"He was just a boy, and they killed him—the butchers!"

"Nathan, we have to leave here." Then she looked down and suddenly she cried out, "Nathan—look!" She dropped beside the two and put her hand on Caleb's throat, her eyes wide as she said urgently, "I can feel his pulse—and he's bleeding!"

Nathan stared at the face of his brother, not able to comprehend. It had never occurred to him that Caleb was alive, but now he saw the bright blood welling steadily from the wound, and he began to tremble. "Caleb!" he cried out, then said wildly, "We have to get a doctor!"

He started to rise, but Laddie said, "Nathan, we have to stop that bleeding or he'll die." Seeing that he was helpless with shock, she moved quickly. "Cut a bandage out of your shirt," she commanded, and she took the wounded boy's head, as Nathan ripped a strip from his white shirt. "Make a pad of it," she commanded, and she pulled Caleb's coat and shirt away, her heart nearly stopping at the sight of the bullet wound steadily throbbing, pulsing out the young man's lifeblood. Taking the cloth, she placed it on the wound, saying, "Hold it here—tight enough to stop the bleeding."

"I've got to go for a doctor!"

"No, you stay here. Some of the soldiers might still be there. I'll be back quick as I can."

His eyes pleaded with her, but she did not pause. As she left, she said, "Pray, Nathan!"

Then she was gone and he was alone. He sat there holding the pad, staring down at Caleb's pale face—and he tried to pray. His mind was cold with fear, and all he could say was, *"God!—God!"* over and over again. Time dragged on, and as he tried to pray, he seemed to hear his mother's voice repeating the last thing he'd heard her say: *Take good care of your brother, Nathan!*

The tears flowed and the fear grew worse as time went on, and he prayed aloud, "God—let him live—and I'll do anything you want!" His voice frightened a small gray squirrel that had moved to the ground from the top of a tall pine, and it dashed away, chattering angrily.

Finally, he heard the faint sound of voices coming from the direction of the village, and soon Laddie appeared with several men behind her. "There he is, Doctor!" she cried, and led the way to where Caleb lay.

A tall man gave Nathan a strange glance, then knelt and pulled the bandage back to look at the wound. He laid his head on Caleb's chest, listened, then stood up. "We'll move him to the Lewis place," he said. "Be careful as you can."

Nathan watched as four men gathered around and carefully picked the wounded boy up. As they moved slowly forward, Nathan asked, "How is he?"

"Very bad." The doctor shook his head and added, "I cannot offer you much hope, Mr. Winslow."

"He can't die!" Nathan whispered, but the doctor only shook his head and followed the others. Nathan stood there helplessly until Laddie came to touch his arm; then they followed. In less than half an hour, they had reached a small house located on a slight promontory overlooking Lexington. Silas Lewis, a thin, silver-haired man, and his wife Sarah lived alone there, and the doctor had Caleb placed in their bedroom.

Nathan and Laddie watched as he cleaned the wound, listened to the heart, then put a clean bandage on. He stood, and looked across the bed at Nathan. "I'm afraid the bullet has pierced the lungs."

"Can't you get it out, Doctor?" Laddie pleaded.

He looked at the pair, and there was compassion in his gray eyes. "It would be impossible." He moved toward the door, and paused long enough to say, "I would to God I could offer you hope, but the only hope now is in God."

"You're not leaving?" Nathan exclaimed with a start.

"I must," the doctor said, then asked with a curious look at Nathan, "You don't remember me, do you?"

"Why, no."

"I met you with your brother at a meeting. I'm Dr. Warren." He hesitated, then said, "He may wake up—or he may not. In any case, I cannot help him—and I am needed for other things. God help you, Mr. Winslow—God help us all!"

Then he was gone. Nathan swallowed hard, then slumped in the chair beside the bed. Laddie's throat ached, and she went to stand beside his chair. They could hear a clock ticking in the next room. Bright sunlight, like bars of solid gold, fell across the bright counterpane that covered Caleb, and the smell of freshly broken ground from the field drifted into the room. Slowly the hours passed, and Caleb lay there, his eyes closed, breathing so shallowly that at times there seemed to be no life at all. Once Mrs. Lewis came in and brought fresh water to bathe the dying boy's face, but Nathan did not seem to notice. He was crouched over the chair, his face pinched and thin, his eyes blank.

Laddie went out shortly after noon and stood on the front porch. The yard was filled with men, and their voices were tense and angry. One voice, louder than the rest, came from a powerfully built man with a Kentucky rifle in his hands. ". . . won't be no way for them lobster backs to git back to Boston 'cept on the Menotomy Road—and that's where we'll catch 'em."

"There ain't but a hundred of us—or less!" A thin, angry voice argued. "How we goin' to face all them Redcoats?"

"There's more of us than you think, Wilkins," the big man said slowly, and there was a grim smile on lips. "There's six assembly points spotted along the road, and the Committeemen west of Sudbury River and west of the Concord River will be at the North Bridge—and besides that, the Minute Men are come in from all over! I'd say we'll have maybe five hundred by the time them Redbacks come back down that road!"

A shout went up, and for the next fifteen minutes Laddie stood there trying to comprehend what was happening. She had just decided to go in when she heard someone call out "Laddie! Laddie Smith!" and turned to see Moses Tyler running up the hill.

He pulled up in front of her, his face red. "I—I seen Dr. Warren down on the road. He said that Caleb was shot—and he said . . ."

She saw him swallow hard; then when she said, "He's very bad, Moses," he began to cry. It was not a graceful crying. He dropped his musket and several of the men looked curiously as he slumped down with his back against the wall, sobbing and choking on the tears.

Finally when he grew quiet, he stood up and said, "I gotta see him, Laddie!"

"He won't know you, Moses."

"I gotta see him!"

Laddie looked into the boy's intense face, nodded, and led him inside. They passed into the room, where Nathan was slumped down, staring at Caleb's still face. "Nathan, Moses is here." Laddie was shocked to see hatred leap into Nathan's eyes. He leaped out of the chair and grabbed Moses by the arm, raising his fist to strike, but Laddie stepped between them, pleading, "Nathan—don't!"

He stopped, looked down at the small form of Tyler, and said bitterly, "Well, are you satisfied now? You've got him killed!" He whirled and plunged out of the room blindly, his feet echoing on the floor beyond.

"I better go with him, Moses," Laddie said quickly. "You can sit with Caleb."

She reached the porch in time to see Nathan walking rapidly across the yard, his head down. She moved quickly, catching up with him as he reached a copse of hickory trees. "Nathan—you can't leave!" she said.

He stopped abruptly, glared at her with anger lighting his eyes; then it faded and he seemed to sway from side to side, and he whispered, "I can't stay and watch him die, Laddie! I can't do that!"

"You're his brother, Nathan. What if he wakes up—and none of his people are there?"

He shut his eyes, stood there for a long time, it seemed; then he opened them and said, "All right—let's go back."

They made their way back to the porch, arriving at the same time as Dr. Warren. He looked at Nathan, then explained, "I thought I'd come back to see the boy."

Nathan said nothing, but Laddie replied, "Thank you, Dr. Warren."

They went inside, and Moses looked up with tears in his eyes. "Dr. Warren! He just woke up!"

"Caleb!" Nathan shouldered the doctor aside and knelt beside the bed. "Caleb!"

Laddie could see that Caleb's eyes were open, and he said weakly, "Nathan!"

The doctor had moved to the other side of the bed, his eyes searching the boy's face, and he put a hand on the pulse at Caleb's throat. "Dr.—Warren—" Caleb said, his eyes turning to him. "I knew you'd be in the fight." Then his eyes shifted back to Moses, and he asked in a reedy whisper, "Did we whip 'em, Moses?"

Moses started to speak, but couldn't for the tears that choked him. "What's wrong with Moses?" Caleb turned back to Dr. Warren. "Didn't we—turn the Redcoats back?"

Warren shook his head, his face a mask, then said, "You'd better talk to your brother, son." He gave Nathan a warning look and drew back.

Nathan knelt beside Caleb, and heard the labored breath and the rasp in the chest. But Caleb struggled to speak. "Nathan—I'm sorry—about the way it's been—with us."

"It's all right, Caleb," Nathan said, tears running down his cheeks.

"No—no, it's not all right—for brothers to have bad feelings." He lifted a hand and Nathan took it; then he said, "I know you don't believe in this war—" He paused and his eyes fluttered so that Dr. Warren leaned forward quickly, but then he seemed to grow stronger. "I guess I got shot, didn't I?"

"Yes, Caleb!"

"It hurts bad—Nathan." Then Caleb asked, "Am I going to die?"

Nathan sobbed, and Dr. Warren said quietly, "I'm afraid so, my boy."

The words did not seem to disturb Caleb. He lay there quietly, and the room was still. Finally he said, "Nathan, you tell Mother and Father about how I died—and say that I wasn't afraid!"

His eyes closed then, and Laddie's heart leaped, but he wasn't gone. He lay there, and for the next hour he seemed to float between two worlds. He would lie still for a time; then he would open his eyes and take up where he had left off. His mind was clear; he gave messages for some, and once he said, "Nathan?—it's a good thing I was converted at that meeting two years ago, wasn't it?" He smiled and said, "I'd hate to die if I hadn't found Jesus that time—I sure would be afraid to die . . ."

Finally he said, "What are the Minute Men doing, Moses?"

"Gettin' ready to fight the British, Caleb." Moses said. He had kept back to the wall, but now he came to reach a dirty hand out to his friend. "I—I wisht it was me 'stid of you that got shot!"

"No, you gotta go on and fight, Moses." He lifted his head and his voice grew stronger, his eyes fully open. "Oh, I can't help! I can't help you fight!"

"Caleb!" Nathan caught his brother, and the boy's eyes fixed on him.

"Nathan—they're going to fight the British! I got to help! I got to help!" He began to struggle and Nathan held him fast, and then suddenly he fell back. His chest pumped as he fought for breath; then he reached up and put his arm around Nathan's neck, whispering in a voice that rattled, "Nathan—I can't help!" Then suddenly he looked up at his brother. "You have to do it for me, Nathan!"

Nathan stared into Caleb's eyes and saw the life draining out, but again the arm around his neck tightened, and Caleb pleaded, "Nathan—you're my brother! Please—please, Nathan—go help them! Help them!" And then he opened his eyes and asked: "Will—you help—Nathan? For me . . . ?"

And Nathan cried with a loud voice that shook the room, "Yes! Yes, Caleb, I'll fight! Don't be afraid—I'll fight for you!"

He held the body close, and then he heard the words so faint that he barely caught them: "Nathan! Thank you, brother!"

Then Caleb went limp, and when Nathan laid him back, there was a smile on his lips. Dr. Warren reached out and closed his eyes, then said in a tight voice, "Brave boy! Brave boy!"

Nathan laid his hand on Caleb's hair, brushed it back, then rose and walked out of the room, his face a mask. He turned at the door, saying, "Laddie, stay with him till I get back." Then he was gone.

"They're a'comin'!" the rider shouted as he crested the hill. He was a small man, but he had a big voice, and he pulled his fine horse up with a flourish, filled with self-importance as the militia crowded around him. "I been to Concord, and I been watchin' the Redcoats comin' out of there—and they're shot all to pieces!"

"The Redcoats?" Dr. Warren demanded. He stood there, his gray eyes intense in the midday sun. "Who fought them?"

"Why, the Minute Men, 'course!" the rider said. He begged a drink and after a long pull from a bottle, he wiped his brow and said, "The British can't leave the road, and our men been shootin' them to rags from behind stone walls—must a'killed a hundred of the suckers at least!"

A shout went up, and Warren smiled. He had been hard put to it to hold the men together, for none of them were ready to face the British regulars in open battle on a field. But this was different! He got up on a stone, called for silence; then when it came, he said, "Well, here we are, and none of us thought we'd be fighting a war on a fine spring morning here in Lexington—but we are. It was not of our making. They shot our men down without mercy." A cry of anger followed this and he said, "We'll have the cost of that blood out of the Redcoats, won't we, men?"

"Tell us what to do, Warren!" a single voice yelled, and an echo of consent rose.

"All of you with muskets go over there—" He waited for the group to form, then said, "Mason Bates, you'll be captain of these. Those of you with rifles, I'll be your captain."

"Why don't we stay together?"

Warren smiled patiently at the tall man who asked the question. "Because a musket shoots one hundred paces and a rifle carries four hundred. Now, they're coming, so listen carefully. The Redcoats will have to stay on that road. They're hurt already, and we'll hurt them worse on the next ten miles. At least half that stretch is lined with stone walls. Get behind those walls, let them get twenty feet away, then rise up and cut them down!"

"But they'll fire a volley at us!"

"Fall down as soon as you shoot and let the volley go over your heads—then get up, run down the road and do it again!"

"There they come—just like I said!" the rider yelled. "I gotta ride some more!"

He tore down the road, yelling at the top of his lungs, but nobody watched. They were straining their eyes, trying to see the approaching Redcoats. Warren said, "You musketmen, get going! Riflemen, we'll wait here and give them a welcome."

The men with muskets scurried off, and Warren said, "We'll get behind that pile of logs next to the road." He led them to a pile of walnut logs that had been felled and trimmed, then said, "Keep down until they're in range—" He stopped suddenly and every man in the group turned to see what had stopped him. He was staring at a tall man who carried a fine Kentucky rifle in his hands— a rifle that the doctor had last seen on the wall of Silas Lewis's house. Dr. Warren studied him, then said quietly, "Mr. Winslow, I think you should think before you do this thing."

The men saw the tall man stare at the doctor, and his eyes were like blue ice. "I'll leave if you say so, Dr. Warren. But I'll be fighting whether you take me or not!"

Warren gazed steadily at Nathan, and finally he said, "As God wills then."

"No, as I will, Dr. Warren! I'll fight in this thing, but I won't blame it on God."

Warren's eyes flashed, but he only said, "Can you use a rifle?"

Nathan stared at him, and there was no trace of pride in his voice as he said, "I can shoot better than any man in your group." Then he waved the muzzle of the rifle toward the distant figure of a rider who had just appeared on the road. "I intend to prove that right now."

"It's too long a shot!" someone complained.

But Warren said, "If you want to be in this war, Winslow, you can begin right now."

Nathan nodded, and his face was pale. The officer was tearing down the road, and was yelling something. He stopped three hundred feet away, made his horse rear, then swung around and started back the other way. He had not gone twenty feet when Nathan's bullet struck him between the shoulder blades and he fell like a broken doll into the dust.

A yell went up, and one man struck Nathan on the shoulder, shouting, "You got him, Winslow!" But there was no joy on the young man's face, Warren saw, and he commanded, "Take cover!

They'll be here in ten minutes!" As the men scattered, he came to stand beside Nathan and said, "I'm sorry about your brother." He gave a curious stare at the silent young man, then shook his head and moved behind a tree.

Nathan Winslow reloaded and stood there in the fine summer air of April and waited for another target.

Major Pitcairn looked up wearily into the pale face of Charles Winslow. He had not slept all night, and the nightmare he had gone through had drawn deep lines into his face. "What is it, Mr. Winslow? I have to report to General Gage, so I can't—"

"Pitcairn, what *happened* out there?" Charles demanded. "We've heard rumors, but they can't be true!"

"Did you hear that we got shot to pieces?" Pitcairn rasped in anger. "Did you hear we lost over 250 men? Did you hear that some of the King's finest troops were routed by a bunch of farmers?"

Charles stared at him, dumbfounded, then said quickly, "I'm sorry to bother you, Major, but I've had word that my nephew might—"

"Nathan was there," Pitcairn said wearily. He passed a trembling hand over his face, then groaned, "Oh, my God, what have we done? What have we done?"

"You saw him?"

"He was right in front of our troops, Charles—and his brother was with him." He shook his head, whispering, "I pray God they survived!"

Then a voice called out that General Gage was waiting, and he left, saying only, "I can't tell you anything."

Charles wandered around a town gone mad, but could find no word of Nathan, so finally he went home. All that day he waited, but there was no word. The family had supper, and once Martha uttered something about "rebels." Charles snapped instantly, "Mother—shut your mouth or leave my table!" The old woman had stared at him, but he had stared back with an intensity that drove her to silence.

He was walking the floor after midnight when he heard a wagon come across the small bridge, and he threw down his cigar, picked up a lantern and ran outside. He ran to a small wagon that was pulling up in the yard and held the lantern up. He saw the haggard face of Nathan, and then his eyes went to the coffin in the rear, and the words stuck in his throat.

Nathan got down, and Charles saw that Laddie was there, too. There was nothing he could say, so he waited for Nathan to speak.

"I'm taking my brother home—to Virginia." His voice was dead, and so were his eyes, Charles saw. "I had Murchinson take care of him at the funeral parlor."

"Why, Nathan—" Charles began, but he was left alone with Laddie. He asked quickly, "What happened, Laddie?"

The dark eyes looked even darker in the yellow light of the lantern. "Caleb was killed at Lexington." And then she, too, walked away into the house.

Charles did not know what to do, so he stood there in the darkness. But fear touched him, and he retreated quickly inside. He paced the floor, and in a few minutes Nathan came down the stair with a bag. He stared at Charles, then said, "Goodbye."

Charles followed him out to the wagon, trying to reason with him, but it was useless. Nathan pulled himself up into the seat, and turned the team around, but a voice cried out, "Wait, Nathan!"

He pulled the team up, and Laddie, carrying an awkward bundle, pulled herself up into the wagon, sat down and looked full into Nathan's eyes. "I'm going with you to take him home. He was my friend."

Nathan looked at her, and for the first time since the shot had killed his brother, the emptiness that had filled him seemed somehow bearable. Laddie's eyes were huge in the darkness, but there was a stubborn set to the wide lips, so he nodded.

"All right, Laddie. Let's take Caleb home."

PART TWO

BAPTISM OF FIRE

★ ★ ★ ★

CHAPTER ELEVEN

"HE'S A MIGHTY FEARSOME MAN!"

★ ★ ★ ★

Spring washed over Virginia in a way that Laddie had never seen in New England, and after Caleb's funeral it became her habit to spend the cobwebby mornings roaming the open country that lay just over the ridge of Westfield. The columbines and wild violets perfumed the cool paths that wound in aisles beneath the gnarled oaks, and the cold spring-fed brooks, plump with sun perch, were shrill with the cries of peepers in the late afternoons.

Adam Winslow had brought Laddie to one of those swift streams that flung up fingers of white where the smooth green water struck an outcropping of rock. There was an abrupt elbow in the stream where the waters had gouged out a deep still pool under a huge white oak, and he had smiled at her, saying, "There's so many hungry fish in that pool, Laddie, you'll have to get behind that oak tree to bait your hook!"

Laddie thought of that moment as she sat with her back against the scaly trunk of the tree, and paused before putting a grasshopper on her hook, thinking as she often did of Nathan's father. *That was just three days after Caleb's funeral*, she thought, and the memory of that stark moment when the plain pine coffin bearing the body of Caleb had been lowered into the red Virginia clay came back vividly. *Adam Winslow was suffering himself—but he saw how out of place and miserable I felt.*

The grasshopper she held between thumb and forefinger

kicked his powerful hind legs, then registered its protest by spitting what looked like tobacco juice on her thumb. Ignoring this, she placed the point of the tiny hook just inside the hard collar forming the neck and threaded the struggling insect through the soft parts of the body. She took the limber cane pole, lifted it and dropped the bait into the green waters. One tiny round lead bullet was fixed a foot above the bait, which pulled him below the surface in a slow and natural way.

Mr. Winslow showed me that, too. As the thin line drifted down the stream close to a clump of willows, the scene from that time came to her.

"See—you just slip the hook in like this," Adam had said, and she had watched carefully as his thick fingers handled the delicate hook and the tiny grasshopper deftly. She had seen him pound a thick bar of white-hot steel at his forge with a fifteen-pound hammer, and his dexterity amazed her.

"Doesn't it hurt them, Mr. Winslow?" she had asked shyly. She had been uncomfortable in the presence of Nathan's parents since they had arrived. Nathan had been so stricken he had only mentioned that Laddie had been a friend of Caleb's; it had been Molly Winslow who had arranged a place for her to sleep and seen to her meals.

"Got no idea, son," Adam had answered, and he had suddenly paused to look at the struggling insect. He lifted his eyes and looked very much like his dead son at that moment, to Laddie at least, and then he had said very quietly, "Guess we don't ever know how much another creature is hurting, do we?"

"No, sir," she replied, then added, "But I've been wanting to tell you ever since I came how I grieve for you."

Adam Winslow was not a man that hung his emotions out for all to see, but Laddie saw his guard drop, and the pain in his dark eyes was so stark that she had dropped her gaze, unable to endure it.

She sat there watching the line arch into the swift water. As her grip tightened on the pole, she remembered how at that moment, he had gently let his thick hand rest on her shoulder, and he had said, "Molly and I—we appreciate your coming, Laddie. It means a lot to know that Caleb had a good friend who'd come all this way to see him home."

Suddenly the line snapped taut, and she cried out, "Gotcha!"

The lithe pole bent nearly double, and the line sliced wildly through the water as the fish tried to make it to the roots where it could shake off the hook. But she had too much skill. Slowly she played it, until finally she led it exhausted to the smooth bank. Carefully she reached into the water, slipped her hand inside its gaping gill, then lifted it out. "Oh, what a beauty!"

She admired the brilliant colors of the sun perch—deep blue, with green and red scales that glittered in the sunlight. "Must weigh a pound, at least," she said happily, then with a deft motion removed the hook before adding it to a string of at least fifteen others about the same size.

Plenty for all of us, she nodded; quickly she untied the stringer and tossed the few remaining grasshoppers into the stream. As they disappeared, snapped up by hungry fish, she picked up her Bible, stuffed it into a small canvas sack with the remains of a lunch, then quickly made her way up the creek. Twenty minutes later she was walking into the backyard of the Winslow house, and seeing Nathan's parents standing outside the forge, she held the stringer up with a whoop.

"Looks like Laddie fished the creek out again, Molly," Adam said, and a smile touched his broad lips. "Reminds me of how much Caleb liked to fish in that spot."

"Yes. He did."

Adam glanced quickly at Molly, and the look in her eyes made him move to her side and put his arm around her. "Sorry. I don't mean to keep mentioning him."

"No, that's as it should be," she said, and though her eyes half-filled with tears, she nodded and forced a smile. Patting his hand, she said, "He's still our son, even though he's with the Lord Jesus now. I won't let grief destroy my son for me—the way I've seen some do." She dashed the tears from her eyes, and two elements of her Scottish blood—the quiet beauty and the rock-ribbed faith—were very real to Adam as he stepped back, an approving light filling his eyes.

Passing through the gate, Laddie caught a glimpse of this fragment of drama, and felt as though she were intruding. She hesitated, but Adam moved toward her, saying, "That's a good mess of fish." He took them from her, admired them, then said, "Molly, Laddie and I will clean these if you'll cook them for us."

"Fish would be good," Molly smiled, then added, "Maybe Nathan will be back in time to eat supper with us." She turned and disappeared into the house.

"I'll clean the fish, Mr. Winslow," Laddie said quickly.

"All right." He walked alongside her toward the side of the forge, and as she stripped the fish from the stringer and put them on a rough slab nailed to a stump, he sat down, saying, "I always did like to watch another man work."

She looked nervously at him, for his dark eyes were so sharp that at times she was sure he would see through her masquerade, but there was no guile in his broad face. Unsheathing her knife, she began cleaning the fish—a job which she'd hated at first, but Adam had taught her how to do it easily. Holding the fish with one hand, she raked the scales off with a few quick strokes of the blunt side of the knife. Putting the knife down, she took the head, broke the backbone with a twist, then pulled head and entrails free with a quick jerk.

"You learn quick, Laddie," Adam remarked as she tossed the cleaned fish down and reached for another. "Can't believe a young fellow like you never cleaned a fish." He looked idly across the fields, then asked, "Where'd you say you were raised?"

"Philadelphia—" Laddie said, then realized with dismay that she'd given away too much. "Well—not really Philadelphia. We just lived there a little while, and then . . ." She invented a likely history for a young man, complete with parents dying conveniently early, and embroidered the tale with hard times and struggles to stay alive.

"Nathan tells me you're a good hand with books and figures."

"Oh—I learned a little here and there, Mr. Winslow—not so much as Nathan thinks."

He shifted, looked across the fields again, and as she cleaned the fish, she noticed that there was something restive in his manner. Finally he said quietly, "Nathan's unhappy."

"Well, yes, sir—but that's natural."

"No, it's not." Adam bit his lip, then shook his head, saying, "He's got something eating him up inside, Laddie—and it's not just his brother's death—though that's part of it." He sat there thinking; then suddenly he asked, "What is it, Laddie? What's wrong with him?"

"Why—" Laddie put the last fish on the stack, then picked up a rag and began to wipe her hands. "I've only known him for a few weeks," she said hesitantly.

"He won't talk to me—or to his mother," Adam said, and it was not a plea, just a statement of fact. "But it's plain that something happened in Boston."

"I—I can tell you a little, Mr. Winslow. Maybe I shouldn't, but I hate to see your family split." She bit her lip, then said, "Nathan's been seeing a young woman, Abigail Howland. I think he's in love with her."

"My brother Charles mentioned that in a letter."

"Did he tell you that Paul and Nathan have been fighting over her for weeks?"

"No."

"Well, they have. And the thing is—her people are Tory, and Nathan knows how you and Mrs. Winslow feel about such things."

"We don't agree, for a fact," Adam said painfully. He got up and said, "I guess Nathan's at Caleb's grave again. He goes there every day about this time. Somehow, it don't seem right, Laddie, for him to be grieving so hard over his brother."

"Don't you see, Mr. Winslow? He feels guilty. He thinks he should have gotten Caleb out of Boston before—"

She didn't finish, but he nodded. "He thinks I blame him, Laddie—but he's wrong on that. Caleb was only a boy, but he had a strong will. I doubt if I could have made him leave myself."

Laddie hesitated, then said, "Why don't you say that to him, sir? I think he needs to hear it."

"You think that?" Adam let the thought run through him, then said, "Thanks, Laddie." He turned and left the yard, walking in the direction of the village's small cemetery.

Laddie gathered up the fish and took them into the kitchen where Molly was rolling out a pie crust. Looking up, she asked, "Got them cleaned already, Laddie? Put them in that pot. Where's Adam?"

"He—went to get Nathan."

The hesitation in her voice caused Molly to look up quickly, and she studied Laddie's face carefully. "Oh?" she said finally. Then she looked down, saying quietly, "I hope Nathan will come to himself."

"So do I." Laddie knew that the death of Caleb had brought tremendous pain to this woman, and there was a desire to give some sort of comfort. There was a reticence in Molly Winslow that would never bring her to ask favors, but she needed someone to talk to. Laddie had learned during the weeks she had spent with the family that Molly Winslow was a woman of genuine Christian faith. It was not just that she was faithful in her duties to her church; there was an unmistakable spirit of love and joy in her that even the pangs of grief could not dim.

Laddie stood there, longing to say something. She looked at the pie crust taking shape. Suddenly she said, "Mrs. Winslow, if I wash my hands real good, maybe you'll let me help you fix supper?"

"Why—can you cook, Laddie?"

"I'm not really a cook," Laddie shrugged, "but anybody can fry fish, can't they? And somebody's got to peel those potatoes."

"I'd be pleased with your help." A smile touched Molly's lips. "Most men would die before they'd do a thing like peeling potatoes or cooking supper."

Laddie picked up a potato, drew her knife, and sitting down on a stool, she smiled and answered, "Except out camping—then all of us cook." She began paring thin strips from the potato, speaking of nothing important, but ten minutes later she had touched on the subject of Caleb. Then for the next half hour she told Molly Winslow of her son, how she had known him and admired him. She had not known him well, but thanked God for those times when Caleb had spoken with her for long hours, for now she had those times to share with the quiet-eyed woman who sat across from her, drinking in every word.

The pendulum clock ticked slowly, and as the meal took shape, the older woman began to speak. Grief had been so sharp within her heart that she had turned from every thought of Caleb, stifling memories as they rose within her, but now she began to speak of him—of simple things he had done as a child, of his quick mind and how it had often led him into mischief. And she laughed—for the first time since the funeral—as she told some of his pranks.

Finally the meal was ready, hidden beneath white napkins on the table, and suddenly Molly Winslow walked to stand beside Laddie, who was looking out the window. "You've been a blessing, Laddie," she said quietly; then she asked, "Are you a Christian?"

"Well, yes, Mrs. Winslow, though not a very good one . . ."

"I knew that you were. You have a gentle spirit, Laddie, and you've given my boy back to me somehow. I praise the Lord for sending you to me."

Laddie felt very awkward, but was spared having to respond, for there were footsteps on the porch, and looking up she said, "Here they are."

Molly turned quickly to see Nathan and Adam enter, and she said quickly, "Just in time, you two! Sit down before it gets cold!"

Laddie never knew exactly what Adam had said to his son at the cemetery, but Nathan, she saw at once, was not the same. He had been under a rigid constraint ever since he had come home, but now the bitter lines that had scored his lean face were softened. A new light shone in his eyes as he came across to give his mother a squeeze, saying, "Smells good, Mother. Hope you cooked enough."

Molly looked up with a startled expression, and gladness leaped into her gray eyes. She reached up and touched his cheek, saying, "There's plenty."

They all sat down and ate—especially Nathan. He had picked at his food for weeks, but now he attacked the fish and potatoes so avidly that Adam commented, "Laddie, you may have to go back to the creek and get another mess of fish for this boy."

Nathan said little, but finally after he put down the last of his pie, he leaned back and said, "Best meal I ever had."

"You need it, Nathan," Molly said. "You've lost weight."

He nodded and then said suddenly, "I've got something to say to you."

Adam looked up quickly, glanced at Molly, then said, "What is it, Nathan?"

A quiet settled over the small group, and suddenly, Laddie, feeling that this was family business, rose to leave. But Nathan said, "Sit down, Laddie. You've got a right to hear what I have to say." He clasped his fingers together, then began to review those last few weeks in Boston. He spoke evenly, without emotion, telling of his feeling for Abigail, his rivalry with Paul. He spoke of his friendship with Major Pitcairn and his admiration for some of the King's officers. Molly and Adam sat motionless as he spoke of how he had tried to get Caleb to stay out of politics.

"I should have tried harder with him—I see that now," he said quietly. The candle sputtered in the holder, and its flickering flames threw his wedge-shaped face into high relief, deepening the caverns of his eye sockets. "God knows I should have done *something*!" And here he paused and stared down at the table.

"Nathan," Molly returned, and she leaned over and put a hand on his. "You can't blame yourself for your brother's death. We always think of things we might have done—when we lose someone. But we know you tried."

"He was a strong-minded lad, you know that, son," Adam stated. "He would do what he thought was right. You can remember a time or two when there wasn't a thing *I* could do with him. He was a Winslow, right enough, and I never heard of any of that breed being very easily led. Don't blame yourself."

Nathan looked up with a smile trembling on his broad lips. "I—I know that, sir, but it's not going to be easy to live with."

"Life goes on, dear," Molly said. "You know we'll see Caleb again."

Nathan suddenly gave her a peculiar look. "This thing has changed me in more ways than one. For one thing—I'm not going to be a minister."

If he expected to shock his parents, Laddie observed, he was due for a disappointment, for neither of them were upset. Molly said only, "Nathan, I've always felt that you took up the calling too suddenly."

He stared at her, then laughed shortly, saying, "I've always known you felt that way, Mother—and it just made me more stubborn."

Adam was staring at his son, and a thought arose in him. "The Winslow men—most of 'em—have had this kind of a battle with God. You remember reading about Gilbert Winslow—how he wrestled with God from Europe to Plymouth Rock, vowing he'd never preach. But he did—and that's happened over several times."

"Well, that's out of my system."

"God will have His way with you, Nathan," Molly said firmly. "I promised you to God the night you were born—and God agreed to take you!"

Nathan gave an impatient shake of his head, but said only, "I don't have much faith—but all this is not what I wanted to tell you."

He got up and stood behind his chair. Silently he stared at them; then he told them about Caleb's death, and how he'd promised to fight for the cause. He went on quietly. "I don't feel as you do about all this—as a matter of fact, I think we'll all wind up either in jail or on a gallows." Then his lips grew firm, and he squared his shoulders in a way that Molly and Adam had seen a thousand times, and he said, "I don't believe very much in this fight that's coming—but Caleb did—and I'll do what I can for him, for my brother."

A silence fell on the room, which was broken when Adam said quietly, "That's not a real good reason for joining a revolution, Nathan—but I'll not try to change your mind. There'll be men fighting in this war for every cause under heaven—and not all of them will be good and pure." Pausing, he took a deep breath and went on slowly. "I guess going to war to keep your word to a brother is a reason that will do—until you get a better one!" Then he asked suddenly, "How you figure to get into this war, son?"

"Why—I have no idea, Father." Nathan suddenly was struck with a thought, musing quietly. "Can't just ride out and take potshots at the lobsterbacks from behind a tree, I suppose."

"No, I think there'll be a little better way than that," Adam said. He looked up and added, "I haven't told you, but Colonel Washington has sent for me."

"Colonel Washington? Do you know why?"

"Only one thing I can think of. Over the years he's asked me several times to join the Virginia militia—and I reckon he's going to ask a little harder."

"Will you do it?" Nathan asked.

"Well, I've told you some about the time I was a scout for him with Braddock." Adam shook his head, then said slowly, "He's a mighty fearsome man! If there's any man in this world I'd follow blind, I guess it'd have to be George Washington!"

"Colonel Washington—they's two gentlemen heah—name is Winslow."

The man at the writing desk looked up and studied the black man's intense face. "Send them in, Billy."

He stood up, a tall man with big bones, wide in the shoulder and wide at the hips. He brushed his hand across his pock-marked face in a gesture of weariness. His nose was large, his chin an ungainly wedge, and his reddish hair was thin in the back. He studied the door, then when it opened and the two men entered, he said, "Winslow, come in." Stepping forward, he extended his hand, and a smile softened the hard lines of his mouth. "Took a revolution to get you here, didn't it, Adam?"

"Yes, Colonel." Adam studied the tall man, noting that the years had aged him too much, but said only, "This is my son, Nathan. I thought you might like to hear firsthand about Lexington."

Washington's eyes did not leave Adam's face. "I heard about your boy. It was a hard thing."

"Yes, sir."

Washington stood there, something rock-like in his expression; then without warning his manner turned gentle. "I have no sons—but I can feel your grief, Winslow." The gentleness retreated again, and he said, "God only knows how many other young men will pay for this thing." Then he turned to Nathan and offered his hand. "You were there, Mr. Winslow?"

"Yes, sir."

"Tell me."

At first Nathan felt uncomfortable, for he was acutely aware that this was the richest man in Virginia, the top of the social heap. The most famous son of Virginia, his fame from his part in the French and Indian Wars had reached even Europe. But that passed, for Washington listened with such an intensity that Nathan lost himself in his tale.

Finally he finished, and the tall man sat there silently. *You can almost hear him thinking—putting it all together*, Nathan thought.

"It sounds like Braddock's last fight, Adam," he said finally. "You remember how they pinned us down and caught us in that murderous cross-fire?"

"If General Braddock had listened to you, sir, we'd have beaten them. He wanted to fight a European war—but the Indians wouldn't line up and let him shoot at them."

"That's what General Gage wants, I expect." Washington stood up and began pacing the floor. Finally he came and sat down again, and he asked at once, "Will you help with the militia?"

Adam shrugged. "I'll do whatever you want, Colonel. It's going to be a bad war, though."

"There is no good war," Washington murmured. "I've prayed that it would not come . . ." He fixed his eyes on Adam. "You'll be needed," he added quietly. He turned to Nathan. "You were in Boston on business?"

"Yes, Colonel. With my uncle."

"Do you intend to return, may I ask?"

Nathan swallowed, and shook his head. "I'd like to go into the militia with my father."

Washington stared at him, and Nathan grew uncomfortable under his eyes. "I would take it as a favor, Mr. Winslow, if you would go back to Boston—at least for a time."

"Sir?"

"The Congress will meet soon, and I have no doubt that it will declare hostilities. An army will have to be raised and arms collected. In the meantime, the British are in Boston. What will they do while our Colonies are trying to get ready to fight?"

"Why—I don't know, sir!"

"Neither do I, Nathan—but I would very much like to know." A gleam of humor touched Washington's cold gray eyes, and he said, "We are the fox—and the fox needs to know a great deal about the pack that's on his trail."

Nathan glanced at his father, then shook his head. "You want me to be a *spy*? I don't care for that at all. I want to be in the army."

"There *is* no army!" Nathan had heard of how Washington's temper could explode, and the evidence rose up before him. "As for being a spy, every man and woman in the Colonies will have to be a 'spy' if we are to win!"

"Sir," Nathan asked quickly, "just what *exactly* would you like me to do?"

The calm question seemed to please Washington. He lifted his hands and answered, "Rumors are worthless, Nathan. I will need to know *exactly* what the British are doing." His face grew suddenly glum, and he said, "It's asking a lot—but it's the job that needs doing right now. Later on, there'll be a place for you in the army."

Nathan looked at the tall man and replied quickly, "Yes, sir. I'll go back to Boston, if that's what you want." He had heard his father say many times that Washington could make men do what he wanted, and now he knew what that meant!

Washington smiled. "It will be most helpful."

An hour later, Adam and Nathan were on their horses headed home, each thinking of what was to come. Nathan finally broke the silence. "He didn't ask me if I believed in the cause, Father."

"No, he didn't." Adam thought back over the years, then shook his head. "Well, the colonel, he's got a way of taking men the way they are—and more times than not, he manages to use up whatever's in them to get what he wants done." Then he said, as he had before: "He's a mighty fearsome man, that big Virginian!"

CHAPTER TWELVE

A MAN'S LOYALTY

★ ★ ★ ★

"I hate to see him go back to Boston, Adam," Molly said. "He's all we have left now—and if half what we hear is true, fighting will break out there soon." It was two days after the meeting with Washington, and Nathan was leaving for Boston as soon as the team was hitched.

"That's right enough," Adam agreed. "The thing is spreading like wildfire. Don't guess there's a man who's not got wind of what happened in Lexington."

This was partly due, he realized, to a veteran postrider named Israel Bissel, who took a bulletin from Colonel Joseph Palmer of the news of Lexington. Bissel was not content with riding to Connecticut; he pushed on to the Sound, then west along its sandy borders, showing his news to all committeemen, shouting his news on greens and in taverns. April 23, Sabbath or no Sabbath, found him pelting into New York, where people clawed at his stirrups, demanding news and more news. Then he was off again, across the Hudson, across the Jersey flats. The last of his message was terse: "For the good of our country, and the welfare of our lives, and liberties, and fortunes, you will not lose a moment's time!"

Adam had been there when the Virginia militia companies came out, buzzing furiously over the seizure of Virginia powder and stores by Lord Dunmore, Royal Governor. By sundown of the twenty-eighth, all realized that the trouble was national, not local.

Colonel Washington dismissed the militia, but not without the passing of a resolution:

> We do now pledge ourselves to each other to be in readiness, at a moment's warning, to reassemble, and by force of arms, to defend the law, the liberty and rights of this *or any sister colony* from unjust and wicked invasion.

Adam turned his head to watch as Nathan drove the buggy out of the barn, Laddie beside him. "He has to go, Molly." There was nothing else to say, and Molly put a smile on as Nathan got down and came to stand before them. He stood tall in the bright morning sunshine, a steadiness in his smile, as he said cheerfully, "I don't know when I'll be back, but I'll think of you every day—both of you." He leaned down and kissed his mother, and she had to fight to keep from holding him and weeping. Then he shook hands with Adam, saying, "Father, you'll write from Philadelphia?"

"Yes." Adam stood there clasping his hand and could have cursed his close-mouthed ways. He had never been demonstrative—except with Molly, who had taught him better—and now he could do no more than hold on to Nathan's hand and finally clap him on the shoulder, saying, "I think you may want to go there—to give a word to—some of the leaders." He had not told Molly of the dangerous assignment; she thought he was going back to take up his duties with Charles.

Nathan turned and climbed back in, but Molly cried out, "Laddie, get yourself down and give an old woman a goodbye kiss!" Laddie hopped down sheepishly, and would have leaned over and given Nathan's mother a peck, but Molly grabbed her with a laugh, saying, "A good-looking boy like you has got to learn to take his kisses whenever he can—even from an old lady!" She was a strong woman, and she grabbed Laddie and gave her a hearty squeeze, then a resounding kiss on the cheek. "There!" she laughed as Laddie struggled and got free with a red face. "Now you know how it's done."

"Goodbye! God bless you," Laddie called after she regained her seat, and both of them looked back more than once and waved to the pair who stood at the gate until the buggy dropped over a hill and out of their line of view.

"They'll be lonesome with you gone," Laddie said.

"They'll miss you, too, Laddie. I never saw them take to anyone like they did to you." He gave the horses a touch with the whip and said, "I wish to God I didn't have to go back!"

They made the trip quickly, camping out beside small streams the first two nights, and Nathan's spirits seemed to lift. On the third night, one of the heaviest spring rains of the season caught them at dusk, and Nathan pulled up at a small inn, saying, "We can't camp out in this toad-strangler, Laddie. I'm ready for a home-cooked meal and a warm soft bed!"

The meal was good, but after they were finished, Nathan said, "You have a room for us?"

"That I have, sir!" The innkeeper was a barrel-shaped man with merry blue eyes, and he led them to an upstairs room with a large bed. He cracked the shutter, saying, "This will let some air in, sir, but you'd flood the place if you opened it full. Good night to you both."

Nathan stretched, yawned, and said, "I'm tired, Laddie. You must be, too. Let's go to bed."

Let's go to bed!

Laddie stood there, her heart pounding as Nathan stripped off his shirt; then as he started to remove his boots before taking off his trousers, she said with a gasp, "Nathan—I'm not really very sleepy right now."

He had yanked off one boot, and he sat there holding it as he stared at her. "Why not? You've not slept any more than I have."

"Oh, I don't sleep much," she said as he pulled off his other boot and stood to unbuckle his belt. She turned blindly and started for the door, but his voice caught her.

"Where you going?"

"I—I think I'll get my Bible and read." She caught a glimpse of him in his underwear slipping into bed, and she went on in a rush: "I—I don't want to keep you awake, Nathan. Maybe I'll just stay downstairs and read—until I get sleepy." She snatched up her Bible, which was in the top of her canvas bag, and started for the door.

"Oh, come on back, Laddie!" came the sleepy answer, and she heard the bed creak as he settled down. "The light won't bother me. Come on to bed when you feel like it—we need to get an early start tomorrow."

"All right, Nathan." With unsteady hands Laddie drew the single chair in the room next to a weathered oak table that held a single candle and sat down, her eyes fixed on the worn Bible feebly illuminated by the single candle.

Nathan sleepily looked across the room at the small figure. "You read that book a lot, Laddie," he observed. "Almost as much as my mother, I think." When there was only a nod for an answer, he asked, "What's your favorite book?"

"I think—Hebrews," Laddie answered.

"Hebrews?" Nathan yawned, then said sleepily, "Don't think I ever knew anyone who had that for a favorite. Why do you like it?"

"I don't know, Nathan—maybe because it's about Jesus being better than anything—better than Moses or angels or Aaron." She gave him a glance, then said quietly, "My favorite is this verse: 'For we have not a high priest who cannot be touched with the feeling of our infirmities, but was in all points tempted like as we are, yet without sin.' "

"Why do you like that?" Nathan was almost gone, his voice slurred with sleep.

"Because—I—I feel so *bad* sometimes, and I need someone who understands why I'm like I am. Have you ever felt like that, Nathan?"

But there was no answer, and she saw that he was sound asleep. Her own eyes were heavy, but she settled down in the chair and began to read. Hour after hour went by, and her eyes watered so that the letters swam together. She grew cold, and quietly pulled a coat out of her sack and covered up as best she could. She dozed as the clock downstairs sounded throughout the night, marking the leaden hours.

Finally, as a gray light touched the room, she painfully got to her feet and stretched her aching muscles. Glancing at the bed, she saw that Nathan was rolled over to one side, but his tossings had rumpled the covers and pillows on both sides.

A thought came to her, and she quietly put the coat back in her sack, removed her shoes and then rumpled her hair wildly. Holding her breath, she slipped into the bed, feeling the warmth of his body; then she gathered up her courage and gave his broad back a vigorous slap, at the same time saying, "Nathan! It's time to get up!"

She sat up and swung out of bed just as he rolled over and stared at her through half-open, sleep-drugged eyes. "Wha—wha's goin' on?" he muttered, still not awake.

Laddie was pulling on her boots as he sat up, and she gave him another slap on the bare shoulder. "I'll go down and get some hot water for you to shave with," she said. She stood up, stamped her feet, then made a show out of stretching, adding, "I never saw a man who kicks and talks in his sleep like you do! I'll never sleep in the same bed with you again!" *That'll take care of that little problem!* she thought with satisfaction.

"What? I don't talk in my sleep," he muttered, and then he called after her as she left, "See if you can round up some eggs— and some bacon, if they've got it, Laddie!"

While Nathan shaved, Laddie hitched up the team, and after a fine breakfast, they were on their way. The rains had stopped, and they camped out again for the rest of the trip, but they were both tired as they drew close to Boston.

"I don't understand all this," Nathan said suddenly. They were driving along at a rapid clip trying to make the city before dark, but in the dusk something was different as they topped the heights of Menotomy. "What in the world is *that*?"

Laddie looked down on the vast, darkening bowl and saw an immense, glowing horseshoe of scattered lights forming an arc about Charlestown and Boston. "It looks like a terrible lot of campfires," she answered.

He stared at the glowing dots that thickened in the central and western parts of the province, and nodded. "That's the army, Laddie, come from all over the Colonies." He touched the horse with his whip, and they moved along the road, passing several groups of armed men who seemed to be leaderless.

Laddie expected him to turn down the pike that led to the Winslow house, but he spun the rig around and made straight for the business district. "Aren't we going to the house?" she asked.

"No. I've got to talk to Sam Adams," he answered tersely, then added, "It won't be possible for me to see him during the day— and I've got a message from Colonel Washington for him."

The dark had closed across the sky as they pulled up a hundred feet from Adams' house. "We'll walk the rest of the way—and if you see anyone keeping an eye on the place, we'll walk right by the door."

"Why, Nathan?" she asked, keeping up with his long strides. He thought for a moment, then shrugged as he answered, "I guess you'll have to know a little about this business, Laddie. I'm doing a job for Colonel Washington."

When he explained briefly what he would be doing, Laddie said instantly, "Why, you'll be a spy, Nathan! They'll hang you for that if you get caught."

"Better not get caught, then," he grinned at her. "This is it." He knocked at the door, and it opened almost as if Adams had been waiting for a signal. "Mr. Adams, you may not remember me—"

"I remember you very well, Mr. Winslow," Adams said stonily. "What's your business here?"

The tone of Adams' reply revealed his dislike of the elder Winslow brother, and his face was forbidding in the lamplight. Realizing that words would not serve, Nathan plucked a pouch out of his pocket and handed it to him. "I think you'll recognize this gentleman's handwriting, sir."

"What's this?" Adams scowled, but he took the pouch and backed into the light, growling reluctantly, "Come in—come in!"

He broke the seal, pulled out a single sheet of paper, and as soon as his eyes fell on the paper, he gave an involuntary grunt, lifted his eyes to the pair with a new interest, then read the message.

"You know what's in this letter?" he asked.

"Not really, sir. I could guess that it describes the service I'm asked to carry out."

"Come into the study." Adams led them into the same room where Nathan had last seen him, at the meeting of the Sons of Liberty, and he winced as the image of Caleb's face came to him. "I know about your brother, Mr. Winslow," Adams said as he motioned to a couple of chairs. "I'm sorry. He was a fine boy." He sat down and asked, his intense eyes locking on Nathan's, "Is that why you've changed your politics—because of him?"

Nathan moved uneasily, for the question had no easy answer. He was silent so long that Adams grew impatient; then Nathan shrugged and replied, "I'll do what I can for the cause, Mr. Adams. To be perfectly frank with you, I'm not satisfied that this country can ever be independent." He lifted his chin and said steadily, "I made a vow to my brother as he was dying that I'd do the fighting he'd never be able to do—and that's what I will do, sir. If that's not enough for you, I'll trouble you no more!"

The anger that had leaped into Nathan's eyes seemed to please

Adams, and he said quickly, "It will be enough, Winslow. Others have less determination, I fear." Then his glance shifted to Laddie. "But who is this? Nothing in the message about two men."

"This is Laddie Smith, Mr. Adams. He was Caleb's friend, and he knows what the situation is. You can trust him—and since we can't be seen together, he'll be our point of contact."

"That sounds very well." Adams leaned back in his chair and grew silent. His face was lined with fatigue, and his voice was raspy as if he had been using it too much. Finally he said, "It's a good plan, Winslow. The Congress will authorize the army, and the commander in chief's first problem will be to make it work. Did you see the militia as you came through the heights?"

"Yes, sir. It looks like a heap of men," Nathan nodded.

"Lexington brought them here," Adams nodded. "It's the beginning. What matters is that a call went out, and men by the thousands from all walks of life answered it. Your brother's blood on the green of Lexington's grass isn't just marked by a day on a calendar, Nathan—it's a turning point for a whole continent!"

Adams spoke as if he were before a crowd of five thousand people, and both Laddie and Nathan saw clearly that this man had no reason for living but liberty for America. They sat there while he spoke of the terrible task that lay ahead, and finally he outlined the military situation.

"Artemas Ward, the senior general of Massachusetts, has been given command. He's an old man, heavy and with a bad case of kidney stones, but he's the best we've got until Congress appoints a man. And what a job he'll have!" Adams sighed, and added, "The men are there—thousands of them, but they're not an army— not yet."

"What's the problem, sir?"

"Why, most of them have strong local ties. A company from Sturbridge may march beside one from Barre, but they look with suspicion at each other. There are huge problems over rations, rank, pay, and most of these groups elect their own officers." Adams got up and said sourly, "Whoever the Congress appoints will have to turn all these fragments into an *American* army!"

"Who do you think will be commander?" Nathan asked.

"John Hancock wants it so bad he can taste it. He's got tons of money—but no military experience. How my cousin John Adams would love the office—but he can't wear a uniform!" He smiled dryly at this, then added, "I'll be at that meeting—and I've told a few others that choosing a commander in chief may be a harder fight that any battle in the field! But if we get the wrong man, we're doomed, Winslow." He shook his head; then for the next ten minutes they spoke of how information should be channeled.

"I welcome you, Winslow," Adams said as he led them to the door, "to the revolution." He shook hands with Nathan, then with Laddie. They made their way back to the carriage, and Nathan headed it toward the outskirts of town.

They spoke of the affair briefly; then Nathan gave a smile and put his arm across Laddie's shoulders, saying, "They'll hang you as well as me, Laddie, if they catch you. You sure you want to be in this thing?" The pressure of his arm gave Laddie a peculiar sensation, and she said quickly, "Yes! I don't know much about politics, Nathan, but I believe men ought to be free."

He seemed to forget that his arm was there, but let it rest on her shoulder for a few moments. Then he moved it, adding, "I guess freedom is a pretty scarce commodity in this world, Laddie— but if it's to be had, I guess it's worth fighting for."

"What's the matter with you, Major? You're sober as a Puritan preacher tonight!"

Major Pitcairn looked up to see Paul Winslow with Abigail Howland on his arm. He stood up at once, saying quickly, "I deny the charge, Winslow! But you've kept the most attractive woman at the ball captive all night long, so the fault is yours if I've been moping and feeling sorry for myself."

The truth was that the officer really was not enjoying the evening. The food and drinks had been excellent, the company drawn from the best in Boston, and there were, in fact, several attractive young women who had put themselves in his way. He was in a bad frame of mind and he knew it, but now he denied all, saying, "I say, Miss Howland, if you can tear yourself away from this fellow, put a poor soldier down for a dance, will you?"

"I've been waiting for you to ask me, Major," Abigail smiled. She had a way of making trivial remarks sound true.

The baggage can no more help flirting than she can help having hazel eyes! Pitcairn thought. It was common knowledge in Boston—at least in the upper levels of society—that Abigail was having quite a game with the Winslow cousins. *Looks like Paul has won by default,* he thought sardonically.

"I haven't congratulated you on your gallant conduct, Major," Abigail said. "Now, I demand that you tell me all the gory details."

The words raked across Pitcairn's memory, and he said a little sharply, "There was no gallantry that day—not on my part, at least."

"Why, you defeated the rebels, didn't you, John?" Paul asked in surprise.

"If General Percy hadn't gotten to us with a rescue party," he said with a tight-lipped grimness, "not a man of us would have lived to see Boston again!"

"But—I heard that the marksmanship of the rebels was terrible," Paul put in.

"It was good enough to beat the King's troops," Pitcairn said. "You have to remember, Winslow, these men were farmers and tradesmen, not professional soldiers or frontiersmen." He shuddered briefly, adding, "They cut us to pieces as it was—what will it be like if they get organized into a regular army?"

"Oh, they're a rabble in arms, Major!" Abigail insisted. "It's unthinkable that England could be defeated by a bunch of shopkeepers and farmers. Why, our armies have defeated Spain, France, and the best of Europe's trained might."

"That's true," Pitcairn nodded, "but it's just as true that these wars have so sapped our strength and scattered us all over the globe to keep the empire together that we have precious little in the way of troops to spare on this little theatre. And I don't think you realize how far this matter has gone."

"What do you mean, Major?" Paul asked.

"I mean that we are caught in this city, Paul. We are a good force here, but our scouts tell us that we are surrounded by thousands of men from all 13 Colonies. New Hampshire has sent a force under Colonel John Stark—and I can tell you now, he's a good soldier! Then there's Israel Putnam with 3,000 men from Connecticut, as well as Benedict Arnold and Nathan Greene, just to mention a few. South Carolina has voted to raise 2 infantry regiments of 750 men each and a squadron of 450 mounted rangers—and the list goes on and on!"

"Oh, Major, these troops aren't trained!"

"No, thank God—but all that it takes is *one* man who knows

how to whip an army together—and when *that* happens, we're in for a fight!"

"Come, Major!" Abigail said, and she smiled at him, adding, "What you need is more wine and some fun."

She pulled him away, leaving Paul alone. For the next half hour, Pitcairn did enjoy himself, for with such a beautiful woman, how could it be otherwise? Then she left him, and he moved back into the secluded area, taking a chair and watching the dancers sail by across the polished floor.

He was about to rouse himself and leave when a voice said, "Hello, John."

"Nathan!" Pitcairn rose at once as he looked up to see Nathan Winslow in front of him. "I didn't know you were in Boston."

"Just got back."

Pitcairn felt more uncomfortable than he ever had in his life. There was nothing of anger in Nathan's face, but neither was there the open friendliness that had been there before Lexington. There was a stubborn streak of honesty in the officer, and he went right to the issue. "Nathan, it does so little good—but I've grieved over the death of your brother. It was a foolish thing—so useless!"

Nathan gave Pitcairn a steady look, then shook his head, "I know it wasn't your fault, John. I bear you no ill will."

"That's like you, Nathan," Pitcairn said with some relief. Then he asked, "What will you do?"

"Go back to work, I suppose." The question, Nathan realized, meant more than that. *So it begins,* he thought suddenly. *A spy can never forget what he is—not for one second!* He added idly, "I suppose you've been busy?"

"Too true!" Pitcairn said ruefully. "I can't say that I understand General Gage!"

"How's that, John?"

"Why, a child can see what's happening! We're living in a state of siege, and it's just a matter of time until we have to do something about that army that's taking shape out there!" The major shook his head sadly, then added, "But the general just sits there, hoping it will all go away!"

Washington needs to know that! Nathan thought, then was saddened by the knowledge that John Pitcairn had spoken freely, as he would to a trusted friend. *Didn't take me long to learn how to use my friends—guess that's what a spy's life is like!*

"Nathan!" He turned quickly and found Abigail coming toward him, her hands outstretched. "You're back!"

"Just this minute, Abigail," he said, and taking her hands he kissed one of them, which brought a smile to her full lips. She appeared to have no memory of the scene at New York, or more likely she had chosen to forget it. "I've missed you."

"And I've been forlorn without you, Nathan," she pouted. "Now, come and dance with me! I've got so much to talk to you about!"

As they moved onto the floor, Paul Winslow came up to stand beside Pitcairn. He watched them silently, then said, "I'm surprised he came back."

"Are you? Why is that?"

"Because he's a Winslow!" The words were spoken with bitterness, and Paul smiled as Major Pitcairn stared at him in surprise. "Don't let him fool you, Major."

"Fool me? In what way, Paul?"

"He may smile and seem to be your friend—but he'll never forget that it was you who killed his brother."

"Why, I—!"

"Oh, I realize you didn't fire the shot," Paul shrugged. "But Nathan won't be able to make that distinction. It was a British bullet that killed Caleb, and he'll never forget it."

"But he's always been very unsympathetic to the rebel cause."

"That was because the conflict hadn't hurt *him*—but that's not true now."

"Oh, I think Nathan will show good judgment," Pitcairn protested uneasily.

"No, he won't!" The words leaped out, and Paul shook his head as he went on: "My father says that his brother Adam—that's Nathan's father—is the most stubborn man in the world, that he always was. And I think Nathan is his father all over again. You've hurt him—and I tell you flat out, John, you'd better not trust him!"

Pitcairn shook his head. "You're just saying all this because of Abigail, Paul. You're jealous and the girl has blinded you. Nathan Winslow is an honorable man."

"Oh, he is! And he thinks right now that his honor demands satisfaction for the blood of his brother. You can say what you please, Major, but I tell you that Nathan Winslow will never forget that day at Lexington!"

Pitcairn looked across the room, taking in the tall form of Nathan and the open face. Then he shook his head, saying, "He'll grieve for his brother—but in the end he'll do the wise thing."

"Winslows don't do the *wise* thing," Paul said as he turned to leave. "That's our record, I'm afraid."

It's all so different! Nathan thought. Abigail's face was framed in his vision, and the soft pressure of her body made his senses tingle, but he thought grimly: *She's so beautiful—but if she knew what was in my heart, she'd leave me right now!*

The music played on, and he held Abigail, danced, and smiled. But the thought came to him, clear as print on the page: *Sooner or later, this will end—all of it!*

CHAPTER THIRTEEN

A NEW COMMANDER

★ ★ ★ ★

The Boston Grenadier Corps, Laddie decided, was not particularly expert in drill; on the contrary, they handled their muskets rather clumsily, and the command "To the rear, march" on the part of the large drill master produced instant confusion. Several of the men wheeled at once—and ran head-on into those behind them, who plowed ahead heedless of the command.

"You clumsy dolts!" The drill master was over six feet tall, and he thrust his imposing bulk through the confusion, shoving men around as if they were made of straw. He lashed at them with a high tenor voice that carried like a trumpet, leaving no doubt as to his opinion of their parentage. At last he thrust his chin toward a man standing to one side. "Williams, keep them at it for an hour!"

Laddie followed him as he stomped away from the small field where the drill continued. "Mr. Knox?" He stopped abruptly and peered down impatiently. "Mr. Adams asked me to give you this."

"Adams?" Knox opened the envelope, and while he scanned the note, Laddie examined him curiously. He wore a splendid uniform, consisting of snowy white breeches, an emerald green coat with golden epaulets, and high-topped black boots that glistened in the sun. His face was full; a double chin lapped over the white scarf, and his bulk filled out the uniform like a sausage in its skin. He weighed almost three hundred pounds, but like many fat men, he was graceful and very quick in his movements. His heavy face was not dull, but dominated by a pair of sparkling blue-green eyes and a mobile mouth. He wore a white silk scarf around his left hand, which was apparently crippled in some way.

Laddie found herself the target of a penetrating gaze, and remembered what Sam Adams had said of the man: *He's a fat man and a bookworm—but don't let him fool you. Henry Knox has got a mind like a steel trap, and if any man in the Colonies knows more about cannon and ordnance, nobody's found out about it.*

"Come along, Smith. Got to wash the taste of that drill out of my mouth." He proceeded along the narrow streets so rapidly that Laddie had to practically run to keep up with him, and he kept up a lively conversation. "You ever see such clumsy cows? Can't walk across the street without falling down! They look good, though, don't they now? Every man of 'em's got to be five feet ten—that's the rule. Got a bunch of pretty uniforms, but my Lord, if they had to fight, they'd probably kill as many of each other as they would of the enemy!"

He led the way down twisting streets lined with tiny shops, and Laddie caught a glimpse of a sign that said METALWORK— PAUL REVERE over a large white building. "In here!" Knox said, and wheeled to pass under a sign that read NEW LONDON BOOK- STORE—HENRY KNOX, OWNER. He waded past a jumble of shelves and tables stuffed with flutes, wallpaper, telescopes, bread baskets, patent medicines—and books crammed into every inch of space.

"Go get your supper, Mullins," he said, sending an elderly clerk shuffling through the shop and out the door. "Now, young fellow," he said, shoving a chair toward Laddie, and settling down at a large desk, "you're going to Philadelphia, Adams says?"

"Yes, sir," Laddie answered. "Mr. Adams sent word for me to come and bring him some—information." She hesitated slightly, for she was still uncomfortable with the task that had been thrust upon her. Adams had gone to the Second Continental Congress in Philadelphia suddenly, but in a message to Nathan he had instructed: *Send Smith here with all information. Don't come yourself. See Henry Knox for what he may have.*

Nathan had stared at the brief note, then after reading it to Laddie, said, "He's a foxy one! Blasted note could fall into the hands of Gage himself and he'd be no wiser! So, I stay here, and you go with what we've got so far." To all protests, he had said, "I think they're watching me pretty close, Laddie, but no one would suspect you. And we won't put anything in writing; we'll put it in that sharp brain of yours!"

He had tousled her hair, flashed a quick smile, then begun drilling her on what information he had gleaned. Finally he had given her some money, saying, "Go see Knox—and be careful, Laddie! Wouldn't want anything to happen to you." She had thrust her hand out, and he had taken it, then instead of releasing it, had held it, opening it to look at her palm. "Mighty small hand you've got—like a scholar's hand should be." He had looked at her and she'd known instinctively he was thinking of Caleb, for he said, "I've lost too much, Laddie—you take care!"

Now she sat there as Knox stared at her, pondering her with a sharp glance. "Now, we're alone—what's this about?" He sat there and listened while Laddie haltingly explained what she was to do.

Finally when she had finished, he pulled the silk scarf from his left hand, and Laddie saw it was missing two fingers. "Shot them off while I was hunting," he said idly, then looked up and said, "Well, my boy, you're young for such a job, but if Adams vouches for you, I'll not say nay. I'll write out what I'd like to pass along, and—"

"Sir, it might be best if you just *tell* me instead of writing it down. That's the way Mr. Winslow's sending his information."

He stared at her, then commented skeptically, "Some of what Adams needs to know is technical. You might forget it."

"I don't think so, Mr. Knox."

He laughed, slapped his meaty thigh with his good hand, then got up and as he walked to a map on a large table, said, "By Harry, I like a man who knows what he can do! Come here." He waited until Laddie stood beside him, then pointed down at the map. "Here's Boston, and here's where the Redcoats are massed, and right *here* is where the Rhode Islanders are located, and here . . ."

He talked steadily for ten minutes, identifying the location of various units and then he turned and fixed his bright eyes on her. "Now, let's have that, Laddie Smith!"

Laddie easily rattled off the locations of units, and Knox's face glowed with pleasure. "Why, by Harry, that's one hundred percent!" He paused, and seeing something in Laddie's face, asked quickly, "What's the matter?"

"Well, sir, this map—it's not accurate."

"What?"

"It's out of proportion, Mr. Knox—and look, here, it doesn't show the road leading to Dorchester Heights—and this area is *not* flat, but is the highest point in the vicinity." Laddie had done a great deal of work on maps of that area before her father had died, and now she moved quickly, pointing out flaw after flaw in the map. She was so intent on what she was saying that she didn't see the glint of interest in Knox's moon face; finally she said, "Really, sir, you ought to get a better map."

She looked up into the blue-green eyes of the fat man, and flushed, but he said, "I take it you know quite a bit about maps, Laddie?"

"Oh—not really . . . !" Laddie grew flustered, but it was too late.

"Is it possible you've done some map-making yourself?"

"Just—just a bit, sir."

"I see." He sat there looking at her, then suddenly heaved his bulk up and said, "Sit down here, if you will, Laddie—I want you to write something for me."

She was surprised, but obeyed, and he dictated a few lines having to do with a book that he wished to order from London. He waited until she had finished, then reached out and took the paper. He glanced at it, then nodded and said, "Fine penmanship. My own writing is worse than you can imagine." He suddenly got up, and after rummaging through several shelves, came back and handed her three books. "Something for you to read in your spare time in Philadelphia."

Laddie sat there confused, looking at the books, all of which were dull-looking texts on military matters. Knox gave a hearty laugh. "All booksellers are a little odd, Laddie Smith. Pay me no mind. Well, let me give you a written note for Sam Adams. Lord, I'd like to be in Philadelphia! There's going to be fireworks there for sure! When you get back, will you drop by and give me a report, young fellow?"

"Yes, sir, I will." Laddie got up, and after Knox gave her a sealed packet, she left and hurried to catch the post carriage that made the trip to Philadelphia.

The Second Continental Congress had degenerated into something of a dogfight, and Laddie, who expected to see solemn and dignified proceedings from the cream of American life, sat through several days of the turmoil in shocked silence. She had made a quick trip, and had found Sam Adams with little trouble, but he had been up to his ears in the raging debate and had time only to get a brief report. He read the note from Knox, then hurriedly said, "Stick close, Smith. There'll be a time for what you've brought— and I don't want to have to waste time looking for you when that time comes. Knox says you write a good hand—I need a clerk, so stay handy." He had rushed off, but in the days that followed, often he had her write messages, sometimes delivering them to other committeemen.

She found a tiny room, and spent her nights reading the books Knox had given her. They were all on the use of cannon and artillery, and she waded through them dutifully, becoming mildly interested in the one that discussed the difficulties of moving guns from one place to another; she liked this one, for it had to do with maps and terrains, but she would much have preferred some lighter reading.

The days stretched out, became a week, and still the debate raged, it seemed nothing would ever be settled. One evening, just as dusk was falling, she walked to her old neighborhood and stood in the gathering darkness staring at the old shop. The sign that had read SILAS SAMPSON—CARTOGRAPHER was gone, and the new one said AARON SAMPSON—MAPS. Her heart leaped into her throat when, as she stood watching, a bulky form emerged and she recognized her uncle. The fear that swept over her grew as he crossed the street, and she almost ran in a blind panic when she realized that he would pass right by her!

It was dusk, but there was still light enough for him to see her face, and as he came close, he did give her a searching glance— and with a voice that shook a little, Laddie said, "Good evening to you."

Sampson didn't answer, but his small eyes met hers, and for one terrible second she thought that all was over, that he had seen through her disguise—but relief flooded her as he gave a grunt and passed on down the street.

Thank God! she breathed, and turned to enter the small inn down the street. She was apprehensive, for she had been slightly acquainted with the owners, and there was some risk. But as she took a seat, Mrs. Cowens merely glanced at her and said, "Yes, sir, what'll you be having?"

Laddie ordered a meal, then lingered over a pot of tea, and as she had hoped, Mrs. Cowens proved to be as loquacious as ever. She was a bright-eyed woman, big in bulk and a notorious gossip. It was not difficult for Laddie to get her started, and soon she led her into the area that most interested her. "I need a map of the area—don't suppose there's a cartographer close by?"

Mrs. Cowens soon gave a complete history of the Sampsons, including a detailed account of the disappearance of Miss Julie Sampson. "Ah—now there's something odd about that!

"I make no accusations, mind you—" She winked lewdly at Laddie, and went on to describe how the girl's father had died, and the brother had come to take over. "He's not as pleasant as the old man! But it was clear he'd got it in his head to marry the girl—'cause it was a good business, and she was a pretty little thing."

"You say she disappeared?" Laddie took a sip of tea and said in a disinterested fashion, "Maybe she just wanted to live somewhere else."

"Not likely, mister!" Mrs. Cowens sniffed. "She run off—that's wot she done! Why, didn't 'e offer a reward and didn't 'e have posters sent all over the country offerin' a reward for the gal?"

"Well, I guess he's given up by now."

"That 'e ain't, sir, for as Emily Shultz—she does Sampson's cleanin'—Emily says he's got to get hold of the girl 'cause he's in some kind of legal trouble over the business, and 'e needs her name on some sort of paper. Emily, she says Sampson raves like a crazy man and swears he'll get that gal if 'e has to turn every colony upside down!"

Laddie had heard enough, so she made her escape, and for long hours she walked the streets filled with a black despair. She finally went to her room, but slept fitfully, and the next day her eyes were gritty as she sat through the meeting.

Late that afternoon, however, the drama picked up. Washington had sat in the meeting day after day, dressed in a buff and blue uniform. Laddie had stared at him curiously, a tall, tall man, long-faced and wrapped in a deep mantle of silence. His silence was something almost physical and alive, while others raved and John Adams roared, "Oh, the imbeciles! The fools, with all their talk!"

One of the delegates sitting in front of Laddie asked another sitting beside him, "Who is he?"

"Well, nobody important. Name's Washington. He's a farmer from Virginia."

"Well, he *looks* important," the other said.

"He's rich—maybe as rich as Hancock."

"He never speaks?"

"No."

"Maybe he's got nothing to say?"

Later in the day, Sam Adams motioned to Laddie. He was talking to his cousin John, and he paused long enough to dictate a note; then as Laddie was writing it, Sam Adams asked, "How much is this Washington worth?"

"Got as much money as any man in America," John Adams said.

Sam gave him a sharp look, then said, "He's the one I want."

"Commander in chief? Hancock wants it like he wants heaven!"

Sam grinned at his cousin. "You want it, too, don't you, John?"

"Yes—but I can't wear a uniform."

"We've got to have somebody from the South, John—you know that!"

They both knew it, for the New England delegations were safe, but southerners would not follow a leader from that area. The two men talked about it at length; then Laddie heard John Adams say, "All right, Sam, I'll nominate him."

"Hancock will blow up!"

"He'll have to go along."

Late that afternoon, John Adams rose and talked about qualifications needed for a commander in chief. Most of the delegates thought he was speaking for Hancock, and Hancock himself was flushed and looked around the room with a smile.

Then Adams said, "Gentlemen, the qualifications are high, but we must not make a mistake in this matter. Do we have such a man? I say that we do, and I nominate George Washington of Virginia!"

Hancock's face turned pale, and Washington got up and left the room without a word.

And that had been it.

Washington was elected, and the country had a new leader.

Laddie was anxious to return to Boston, for there had been a flock of rumors about the wire-tight tensions of that city, but Adams had said, "I want Washington to hear your report." Two days later Laddie was startled as Sam Adams grabbed her arm and whispered, "Come along—Washington wants to hear what you've brought."

She followed him, her nervousness rising, and then she entered the large room where Washington sat at a desk flanked by two men. She recognized them as General Charles Lee and General Philip Schuyler.

"General, this is Laddie Smith," Adams said, then stepped back.

Washington looked up, and Laddie saw lines of fatigue on his craggy face, and his voice was raspy as he said, "What's the situation there, Mr. Smith?"

Laddie gave him the information from Nathan, and he looked interested at once. He said nothing, but when she had finished, he nodded and said, "Tell Mr. Winslow we appreciate his help."

The interview was over, but Laddie swallowed and said quickly, "General, Mr. Knox gave me some information on the location of troops around Boston."

"Henry Knox?" Washington's face broke into a smile, and he said, "I might have expected it." He looked at the thin, ugly man who was half-listening to the report, and said, "You must get to know Henry Knox, General Lee."

"Who is he?" Lee was an Englishman, had served in Europe and was reputed to be an excellent soldier.

"A bookseller from Boston," Washington smiled. "But he's studied gunnery out of his books—knows more about cannon than any man in America, I'd guess. I'm going to commission him and put him in charge of our artillery." Then he reached his hand out and said, "I'll take the report, Mr. Smith."

"Well, it's not in writing, General. Mr. Knox thought it might be safer that way. But I can give it to you orally."

"Sloppy work!" Lee sighed in disgust.

Washington said quickly, "Give me your report," and Laddie quickly outlined the position of the British, their numbers and their officers. Then she did the same with the American troops, and as she finished, Washington shot a knowing look at Schuyler, saying evenly, "We must hurry, General. I can't for the life of me imagine why General Gage hasn't hit our people!"

"He won't wait much longer—and our men there need you,"

Schuyler nodded. "We've got to make an army out of them quickly."

Washington turned to Laddie and said, "That's very complete, Mr. Smith. We are in your debt."

Adams motioned to Laddie, and when they were outside, he said, "Get back to Boston. Tell Knox what's happened, and tell Winslow to try to find out something about what Gage may do!" Then he put his hand out, a rare smile on his face. "You did well, my boy—very well!"

Laddie hurried away and was on the coach out of Philadelphia three hours later, pleased that it was over and she could go back to Boston. It shocked her to realize how the simple thought of seeing Nathan sent such a thrill of pleasure through her, and she shook her head angrily as the coach rolled along. *Don't think like that—you're nothing to him!*

Washington assembled a staff hurriedly, and on June 21 he set forth, accompanied by Lee and Schuyler and a brilliant escort. Crowds cheered them in every village as they passed through, but they had not ridden over twenty miles when they were met by a messenger on a lathered, wind-blown horse, who cried out his news: "General—there's been a battle!"

"Where?" Washington rose in his stirrups, and his face grew flushed.

"Place called Bunker Hill outside of Boston!"

Washington was a huge figure on his white horse, and he asked in an intense voice: "Did the militia fight?"

"Yes, General—like wildcats!"

Washington abruptly looked up to the blue sky, and half raised his hands. Suddenly he clapped them together in a vigorous gesture and cried out in a voice packed with emotion:

"Then the liberties of the country are safe!"

CHAPTER FOURTEEN

"THE WHITES OF THEIR EYES!"

★ ★ ★ ★

When Laddie returned to Boston, she found the reports of activity had not been exaggerated—for the city swarmed with British regulars. The newly landed generals—Sir William Howe, Henry Clinton, and handsome John Burgoyne—had come to settle the business of rebellion.

Nathan had picked her up in a bear hug when she had come into the warehouse to find him, saying, "Laddie! Bless God! you're back!" When he put her down, he laughed at her rosy face. "Sorry, Laddie. I guess no young fellow likes to be hugged by a big ugly chap like me, does he now?"

Laddie gave a shake of her head, pulled shut the coat that had popped open, and then smiled. "I guess once won't hurt, Nathan. I missed you, too."

He grabbed her arm, pulling her to The Blue Boar, and when Nelson saw Laddie, he called out, "Wife, 'ere's yer old tenant back again," and he gave Laddie a swipe on the shoulder.

"Bring us the best you've got, Nelson," Nathan smiled; then he turned to Laddie and his eyes, blue as cornflowers, shone as he said, "Lord, I've missed you, boy! Now, tell me everything."

Laddie told it all, and finally Nathan sat back and stared at her. "So Washington is our commander! By heaven, that's what we'll have to have if we're to get out of this thing with our necks whole."

"What's wrong? I thought our men had Boston surrounded? That's the word we got."

Nathan shook his head sadly, lines of worry creasing his smooth brow. "I've been spending a lot of time with the British officers. Guess it pays to court a Tory girl who moves in their circles," he added wryly, not heeding the sudden frown on Laddie's face. "And they know about what *we* know about those units around the city."

"They're good men, aren't they, Nathan?"

"Yes, but untrained and unequipped—and worst of all, they've got no leadership."

Nathan had been so glad to see Laddie that it warmed her to think of it, but in the next few days, he grew sober, and she knew he was fearful of a British attack.

When the attack came, it caught Nathan off guard. On the morning of the seventeenth, he was working at the warehouse, and Laddie looked up to see Henry Knox come in, his face tight with anxiety. She had introduced the two men, and there had been a mutual trust almost instantly.

"What's wrong, Henry?" Nathan asked, moving to meet him.

"There's the devil to pay, that's what!" Knox looked around to be sure they were alone, then said with great agitation, "General Ward's made a bad mistake—and the British are going to cash in on it. Haven't you noticed all the troops moving to the ships?"

"Why, I didn't think anything about it," Nathan said in surprise. "Howe's always got them doing some sort of training."

"Well, this is no drill! They're moving in force to attack!"

"Where?"

Knox shook his head and there was desperation on his round face. "I tried to get Ward to fortify Dorchester. It's high enough to command the neck of Boston peninsula—but he picked Charlestown across the James River."

"Why, that won't do!" Laddie said at once, a clear picture of the map of Boston springing to her mind.

"You see it, too?" Knox nodded with a grim smile. "Nathan is puzzled. Show him what the problem is."

Laddie took a sheet of paper, drew a rough map, saying, "See this thing that looks like a polliwog? Well, that's Charleston—there's Breed's Hill and Bunker Hill."

When Nathan still looked puzzled, she said, "Look, this thing sticks out into the water like a polliwog—it's attached by this little tail." She pointed to the thin narrow tail that tied the peninsula to the mainland. If our men are on these heights, all the British have to do is put men ashore at this neck—and our men'll be trapped like rats."

"Right!" Knox nodded savagely. "*You* see it—and *I* see it—why can't General Ward see it? By Harry, I wish General Washington were here!"

Nathan stared at him, then said, "What are you going to do, Henry?"

"Going to get myself killed, I suppose," Knox shrugged. "We've got no cannon, not much ammunition, not much of anything—but the fight's here! It's time to quit talking and fight, Nathan!"

He wheeled and Nathan caught up with him, his face tense. "I'm going with you."

Knox stopped, his eyes growing large. "Why, Nathan, you'll do more good where you are—getting information—"

"Perdition take it all! I'll not be a spy another day!" His eyes were electric, and stubbornness set his jaw. "I can find my way to Bunker Hill with or without you, Henry—but I'm *going*!"

Knox clapped him on the shoulder and said, "All right—but you need a musket."

"Right here!" Nathan ran to the small storeroom and came back with his Kentucky rifle, a small bore rifle, and a shotgun.

Knox stared at the weapons, then threw back his head and laughed. "By Harry, we'll get them far or near, eh, Winslow? Let's go."

"I'll take the shotgun." Laddie was holding out her hand, and Nathan was taken off guard.

"Why, Laddie," he said quickly, "you can't fight!"

"Why can't I?" There was a stubbornness on Laddie's full lips that matched Nathan's own, and there was determination in the dark eyes of the youth.

Knox stood to one side, his blue-green eyes quizzical. He had grown attached to these young people, and he had heard enough of Caleb's death from Laddie to know that Nathan Winslow was not ready to suffer another loss. *Nathan's taken Laddie for the brother he lost,* he thought. *Look at him! He can't bear to think of losing another one.* He said nothing, knowing that it was between the two of them, but he saw that Laddie was determined.

"I can find Bunker Hill, Nathan, just as well without you!"

Knox saw that Nathan was helpless, and he said, "Let the boy come, Nathan. Better with us where we can keep an eye on him, eh?"

Nathan nodded slowly, handing the shotgun to Laddie and the musket to Knox. "I'll get the powder and balls," he said quietly, and left Knox and Laddie alone.

"He's afraid for you, Laddie," Knox said gently.

"Well, so what?" The dark eyes flashed at him suddenly and Laddie added with just a trace of a quiver: "I'm afraid for *him*—but he can't see that."

Knox put his good hand on her shoulder and said quietly, "God will have to take care of you both, Laddie!"

"There's a lot of them, Nathan." Laddie looked down from the top of Breed's Hill, the barrel of the shotgun burning her hands. General Ward's orders had been to fortify Bunker Hill, the higher peak—but the order was misunderstood and Breed's Hill had been occupied instead. It was closer to the water, to the guns of the Royal Navy, and to the beaches where hostile troops would be landed.

The perfection of a June day wore on, and there was a moving blaze of color as the barges and longboats filled with scarlet-clad regulars unloaded one after another. Drums pounded, fifes cut shrill into the warm air, and a floating pageant lurched out across the Charles River to the silver splash of oars. Men in red and blue— the Royal Regiment of Artillery—trundled field-pieces into crafts, and H.M.S. *Lively* and *Falcon* increased their rate of fire.

"There's the Royal Marines," Nathan said. And although it was too far to recognize individuals, he knew that John Pitcairn would be leading his troops up the hill. *God! Don't let him get in front of my gun!* he breathed; then he saw Dr. Warren approaching to speak to Colonel Prescott, who was in charge. They were so close that Nathan heard Prescott say, "General Warren, you're senior in rank."

"No, I'm here as a volunteer, Colonel. I'll take my place with the others." He had a musket in his hand, and turning he saw Nathan and paused. A light touched his handsome face, and he smiled. "Might I join you, Mr. Winslow?"

"Certainly!" Nathan smiled grimly and said, "I'm in somewhat of a different frame of mind than when we first met at Sam Adams' home, Doctor."

"Sam's talked to me of you, Mr. Winslow. I'm proud to see you here." He nodded, then glanced down at the troops forming for a charge. "I think Gage must be senile, Nathan. He's going to make a frontal attack against men in fortified positions."

"I wonder why?"

"He has a contempt for us," Warren said, and then he added with a smile, "I think he'll not feel quite that way later on this afternoon!"

"There they come!" Prescott's voice cut across the air, and he cried out, "Don't shoot until you see the whites of their eyes, men!"

The forces on the beaches shifted, reshuffled, and the assault began—long scarlet-and-white lines, three deep, climbing like a slow surf toward the redoubt. On they came under the hot sun, each man carrying a load reckoned at 120 pounds.

Laddie heard a voice, and turned to see an elderly farmer, his musket steadily aimed at the Redcoats. "I thank thee, Lord, for sparing me to fight this day. Blessed be the name of the Lord." There was an incredible patience on his face, and Laddie said softly, "Amen!"

Sweat poured down Laddie's face as the lines came on. She counted ten companies across the broad British front, and ten more right behind—hundreds of red-coated men laboring in slow steps up the hill.

Slowly, inexorably, the grenadiers and Royal Marines came on. A voice said, "No firing—hold your fire!" Laddie's finger was on the trigger, and there was a taste of fear in her mouth—but it was fear of killing rather than of being killed. She could see their faces clearly now—some of them fat and some thin; some sunburned and some pale, and the whites of nervous eyes were in all the faces.

"Fire!" came a sudden command, and a ragged sheet of flame belched out from the hundreds of rifles and muskets in the hands of the Americans. As the smoke cleared, Laddie saw that entire ranks were down, men thrashing and screaming, while their comrades stepped over them. She heard balls whistling over her head, and ten feet to her right a man suddenly stood up, shot in the throat. He was trying to speak but only spewed out a ragged stream of bright scarlet blood, fell down, kicked the ground twice, then died.

"They're retreating!" Dr. Warren cried out, and it was so. The British were scrambling wildly down the hill, leaving their wounded behind.

"They won't try that again!" someone cried out.

But they were mistaken.

The second attack came with more power than the first, and the first man that Nathan identified was John Pitcairn. Nathan was firing and reloading like a machine, but as he straightened up to fire, he hesitated, for there, right in his sights was the major. He carried only a saber, and he held it high in the air, crying out encouragement to his men. His face was red with strain, but there was no fear on it, and Nathan found that he could not pull the trigger!

But even as he hesitated, a ball struck Pitcairn in the side, and he fell to the ground, clutching the sudden blossom of blood that appeared on his blue coat.

Men were dropping all along the line, but the toll on the charging Redcoats was terrible. The hill was covered with bodies—some still, and some feebly trying to crawl away, many writhing like cutworms. Time seemed to stand still, and Nathan could not remember a time other than this. He seemed to have been on the hill firing and taking fire forever, and it came as a shock when he heard Laddie crying out, "Nathan! They're leaving!"

He came out of the red haze of battle to see for the second time the British retreat. Then he heard Dr. Warren say, "I'm out of powder." Men up and down the line were saying the same, and Warren said, "If they try again, we're in trouble."

"They can't come up that hill again!" Nathan whispered. "It's like a slaughter pen!" Then he stood, grabbed a water bottle, and suddenly stepped out from the fortifications. Ignoring the startled cry of Warren and Laddie, he moved across the field of broken bodies until he came to where Pitcairn lay. He stopped and saw that the major's eyes were closed. "John—John!" he whispered, and as he knelt, the eyes suddenly opened, filled with pain.

"Nathan—is that you?" he whispered. He gave a slight cry as Nathan lifted his head and held the water bottle to his lips; then he drank deeply. There was a pale ivory cast to his fine face, and he tried to smile.

"John—I'm sorry!" The tears were running down Nathan's face, and he held the man as he would have held a child, closely as if to heal the terrible wound that was killing him.

Pitcairn looked up and his smile was gentle. "You must not grieve over this, Nathan. You must not."

"I can't help it!"

"You must not!" Then Pitcairn's body grew tense, and he said in a faint whisper, "The lights are going out—goodbye, my boy . . ." He coughed once, drew a strangled breath, and then relaxed.

Nathan sat there holding the shattered body of his friend, his mind blank and his heart crying out for grief. Finally, he felt a hand on his arm, and looked up to see Dr. Warren, his face stern. "Nathan—they're coming again!"

He followed Warren back and took his place beside Laddie, and slowly he began to see the field come into focus. He checked his powder, saw that he had only enough for one shot. Then he heard Prescott saying, "We'll fall back!"

And as the enemy charged, it became a nightmare! Men with no powder and no shot were defenseless against the bright bayonets of the grenadiers. They tried to use their muskets for clubs and took the bright blades in their stomachs; they tried to run, and the marines rammed the thin slivers of steel into their backs.

Nathan had pushed Laddie to the rear and had smashed the skull of one Redcoat when he saw Dr. Warren caught by two soldiers. The doctor raised his musket to use as a club, and both of them drove bayonets through his body. Warren fell to the ground and they plunged the bayonets into him again and again.

The sun was dropping, and the cool air washed over Laddie's face. "It's hard to believe we're alive, Nathan," she said, taking a deep breath.

"A lot of us aren't," he answered. They were sitting beside a small creek on a hill that overlooked Boston, and the paths were crowded with men who were going back to their homes.

They had rejoined Knox, and he looked at the dim forms of men filtering through the woods, many of them wounded. "There goes our army," he said slowly.

"You think it's over, Mr. Knox?" Laddie asked quietly. She had never seen the big man discouraged, and it troubled her.

He roused himself, and in the fading darkness, they saw him smile grimly. "They won't go far, Laddie."

"We lost, didn't we?" Nathan said.

Knox swore and said loudly, "No, we didn't lose! Howe bought that hill at the price of a thousand men, and we can't have lost more than two hundred. I'd like to sell him another worthless hill at the same price!"

"What's next?" Nathan asked, getting to his feet.

"We wait for Washington," Knox answered, heaving his bulk from the ground. Then he touched Nathan on the shoulder, saying, "You'd better be careful. The British aren't going to go easy on anybody who was on that hill today."

"I'm not going back," Nathan said. His face looked grim in the pale light, and he added, "I'll wait for General Washington."

Knox laughed and said, "Well, we'd all better stay together then. They'd have to find a pretty thick rope to hang Henry Knox, but they'd love to try it. I'm joining Washington as a staff officer. I'd like for you to come with me as part of my command—artillery."

"I know a little about rifles—but not much about cannon."

"We don't have any," Knox said dryly. "So you'll have time to learn until we get some." Then he said suddenly, "And I'll have you, too, Mr. Laddie Smith."

"Me, sir?"

"Yes, you." Knox moved to stand before Laddie, and his voice was gentle as he asked, "I don't think you'll stay in Boston either, will you? Not if Nathan goes."

"I—I don't want to be left behind." Laddie did not look at Nathan, but she felt his eyes on her.

"Knox, what will Laddie do in the army?" Nathan asked.

"I'd say make maps," Knox shot back. "We're going to need someone who can keep us from getting lost—and as far as I know there's not a qualified cartographer on hand." Then he shot a look at Nathan, saying mildly, "Laddie will be one of my aides, Nathan, not in the infantry. Safest place in a war is with the generals!"

Nathan saw that Knox was sincere, and he said to Laddie, "You won't stay out of this?"

"No—not if you don't, Nathan."

An owl sailed over, silhouetted against the darkening sky, and Nathan looked up as it dropped silently like a ghost into a small clump of bushes. There was the sound of a muffled struggle, then silence.

Nathan looked at the dark eyes of Laddie Smith and said with a smile, "I should have left you to freeze, boy! You're nothing but an aggravation to me." Then he laughed and ruffled Laddie's soft, dark hair, saying, "You're bound and determined to be a rebel, I see that plain."

Looking down at Laddie from his great height, Knox noted the soft eyes and the smooth-planed features. He smiled, saying as they turned to leave the grove:

"A rebel, yes—but, by Harry—*a gentle rebel!*"

CHAPTER FIFTEEN

LADDIE IN LOVE

★ ★ ★ ★

July 2, 1775, was a rainy Sunday in Cambridge. As the weather cleared, General George Washington rode into the rain-soaked college town and received from General Artemas Ward command of the entire military force of America. James Steven, a soldier on duty that day made a single bored notation: "Nothing hebbeng extroderly."

Nathan and Laddie had made one quick trip to the Winslow house to pick up their things. Charles had been the only one up as they entered, and there had been a heated argument, for he felt that Nathan was throwing his life away. "Why, you young fool, can't you see the end of this thing?" he'd cried out passionately, and in his agitation he'd seized Nathan by the arm and shaken him. "The King and Parliament *can't* let this rebellion succeed! It would give an invitation to every royal colony to rebel against England!"

"Uncle Charles, there's no point in discussing it." Nathan had pulled away from his uncle and said in a tone of utter finality, "I'm in this thing to the end, and Father is, too."

Charles had stood there, a sad look in his eyes. "It's the death of you, boy! Everything—everything will go. Abigail—have you thought about her?"

"Yes, I have."

"You know she's for the Crown, and she won't change?"

Laddie shot a glance at Nathan, noting the look of pain in his eyes, and then he had straightened up and said firmly, "I'm sorry, Uncle Charles, but it's what I have to do."

They had gathered their belongings and gone back to the rebel lines that night, and in the weeks that passed, both of them struggled to find their niche in the army that was being birthed in the hills around Boston.

Nathan wrote of this in a letter to his father:

August 2, 1775
Dear Father,

> I write this hastily, for the post is leaving in ten minutes. I am now a private in Henry Knox's command. General Knox is scraping up every firearm larger than a musket, and I have been given a tiny three-pounder, which barely qualifies!

> Laddie has been in the thick of things—for it turns out he has had some training in mapmaking and is a fine clerk. He is an aide of General Knox and has been made a sergeant! He is quite unbearable with his new rank! When he had the gall to try to give *me* an order this morning—grinning like a possum!—I threatened to turn him over my knee, and he faced up to me and said that would be mutiny and he'd have me flogged for it!

> Seriously, I am quite relieved to have him in that duty, for it will be much safer than being in the line. He's such a fragile youngster, and I would grieve to see him harmed.

> I understand that you will bring a troop of Virginia riflemen to the siege soon, so we will meet. Will Mother come with you? It would be impossible for her to stay with Uncle Charles, I think, but I hate for her to be alone. I will try to find a place in some small village where we can see her often.

> Your devoted son,
> Nathan Winslow

The troops around Boston lived in shelters made of whatever materials they could lay their hands on, and Laddie quickly realized that if she had not been made an aide to an officer, she would have been in bad shape. Some of the men knocked together rough shacks, a few had tents, but the majority simply lived on the ground between constantly soggy blankets.

All the staff officers had places in houses, and fear of discovery had clawed at Laddie until Knox had taken her to a small bungalow not far from the heights of Dorchester. "Lieutenant Mason and I will take the bedroom, Laddie, and you can bunk in the loft." Relief had flooded her; she would still be able to keep her sex a secret—at least for the time being.

Knox was a dynamo of activity, and he kept her close most of the time, roaring out memos, dictating reports, and spawning letters constantly. She learned to move through the confusion in his wake, and in a week had made herself indispensable to the huge man. To add to the confusion, it was often impossible to tell officers from enlisted men, for despite the efforts of General Washington to outfit the men in some semblance of a uniform, the Congress took no action. Washington finally authorized officers to adopt scarves, cockades, secondhand epaulets—whatever they could find to identify themselves.

As the weeks dragged on and the first American army took shape slowly under Washington's hand, Gage and his troops remained oddly passive in Boston. "I guess he thinks our army will give up and go home," Knox said once to Nathan; then he had added with a grimace, "And he could be partly right—with this eight-months Army of ours. By the end of the year, many of these units will be at the end of their agreed term of service, and will be free to go home."

But it never happened. When some of the men went home, short-term militia were called up to man the lines, while recruiting officers beat their drums in distant towns and hamlets. Many did stay past their time, and Nathan said once to Laddie, "It's Washington they stay for. He's not a man that troops will run after cheering and tossing their hats, but you just notice—when he passes by, men stand straighter and grip their muskets a little tighter—and they wind up writing letters back home trying to explain why it seems fitting for them to stay on after all."

September came, then October, and the hills put on their fall colors of yellow, red, and gold. Men who had been sleeping on the ground suddenly fell into a building frenzy, putting up shacks, and the sound of axes rang constantly as firewood parties fell on the hardwood groves.

On one of those days in late October, Laddie and Nathan went on a day's hunt at General Knox's suggestion. "By Harry, if I have to eat another plate of this stew, I'll give up food," he had groaned. "Winslow, you've mastered your drill with your gun, so take that rifle of yours and get us a buck—even if you have to mistake a nice cow for one! And Sergeant Smith, you go along to be sure he doesn't shoot himself." His smallish eyes had gleamed, for despite his ferocious words, he had noted that both Nathan and Laddie were worn thin with the efforts to put together some sort of artillery unit. "Both of you have done well," he said with a sudden warm smile. "Take a couple of days and forget about trying to kill the British."

Neither Nathan nor Laddie argued, and in less than two hours they were making their way out of the camp, headed toward the thick forests northeast of Boston, mounted on two large mules that would carry back the game. All day long they pushed deeper and deeper into the wilderness, and by dusk they were camped beside a large brook beneath a tremendous hemlock. Nathan had passed up several chances to knock down deer, choosing instead to knock down enough quail to feed them for the night. Laddie could scarcely believe how he could usually take their heads off with a single rifle shot, and as they were roasting them over a small fragrant fire that night, she finally said, "Nathan, if you can hit a tiny thing like that, a man wouldn't have a chance, would he?"

"Well, Laddie," he answered with a quick smile, "one big difference between shooting quail and men—the quail don't shoot back!" He was wearing a fringed hunting jacket, and his high-planed face was thrown into even sharper lines by the flickering of the fire. The trip had relaxed him, and the ease in tension made him look younger. He added thoughtfully, "Lots of men can hit a nailhead at a hundred yards, but nailheads aren't men, and it's a hard thing to take a human life." He looked at her across the fire and asked curiously, "Did you have any trouble pulling the trigger on Breed's Hill?"

"I—I don't think I could have done it," she said in her husky voice, "but the shotgun was loaded with bird shot. I guess that's all we had. It couldn't have killed anybody. I just aimed at the crowd and pulled the trigger, and I know it stung a few men." She thought about it, and when she looked at him, her strange almond-shaped eyes reflected golden glints from the sparks that rose from the fire. "I still don't know if I could shoot—if I *knew* I was going to kill a man."

He didn't answer at once, but her words troubled him, and he gave his attention to the bird he was roasting. "Hey, this is just about right." He pulled off a fragment of the toasted meat, juggled it in his hands to cool it, then tasted it, saying, "Laddie, this is *good!*" The two of them ate the quail, along with some biscuits and a couple of boiled potatoes they'd brought. They made tea in a small pot, and later Laddie brought out the plump wild blueberries she'd picked as they walked through the woods.

"I don't care if it takes a week to get some game," Laddie said finally. The sharp autumn air had brought a rich color to her face, and she pulled her short wool coat snugly around her, lay down on her blanket, and stared into the leaping flames of the fire. Sleepily, she murmured, "Nathan—how long will this war take?"

"How long?" Nathan laughed quietly and poked the fire with a stick, sending the tiny sparks upward to mingle in the tops of the trees with the real stars that glittered overhead. "Why, boy, it's not even *started* and you're already thinking about the end! But I guess you're thinking like lots of the fellows are—we'll spend the winter running the British out of our country; then we'll go home in time for spring planting and be done with King George."

She looked up, caught by the doubt that threaded his words, and asked, "You don't think it'll be like that?"

"No way it can happen. In the first place, we're probably going to *lose*, not win. Laddie, we got a bunch of farmers and shopkeepers with few guns—most of 'em never even *saw* a battle. We have no factories, no navy, no professional soldiers. And England has it all. Why, they got a hundred thousand men of their own troops, and if they're not enough they can hire that many more Germans or Hessians! You saw 'em march up that hill, like machines! What would have happened if we'd been in front of them without any protection—or if *we* had to charge up a hill like that against those trained troops?"

He took a sip of his tea, and there was a silence, broken only by the cry of some night bird—a lonesome sound that made her shiver and draw her blanket closer. She had been in the middle of such activity and such optimism for the past few weeks that defeat had not even been a thought in her mind. Now Nathan's face was so bleak in the firelight that she longed to put her hand on his, but said only, "Nathan, if you don't think we can win, why . . . ?"

"What am I doing here?" He finished the tea, put the cup away, then punched his blanket roll into shape and prepared to lie down. "I made a promise to Caleb, Laddie. I'll keep it. As long as there's a fight, I'll stay with it." A sudden cry in the woods startled them both, and he got to his feet, in one smooth movement seized his rifle and stood there, alert and waiting.

"Just a panther," he finally grunted. "Those critters sound like a woman screaming, don't they?" He laid the rifle down, threw a thick log on the fire, and seeing that she was still sitting, staring rigidly into the dark woods, he stepped closer. Reaching out, he grabbed her thick hair and pulled her startled face up; then giving her head a shake, he laughed and said, "Not scared of a little ol' panther, are you, Laddie?"

The gentle grasp he kept on her hair did not hurt, but his touch sent a shock along her nerves. Looking up into the wide blue eyes that laughed down at her, she could not control the sudden tremor that seemed to make her weak and vulnerable. For months she had kept a constant effort to erase all traces of her femininity from her speech, her movements—and now in one explosive instant the touch of Nathan's hand on her head sent everything crumbling!

I love you, Nathan Winslow! The words leaped to her lips, seemed to fill her breast, and she knew that if she lived to be an old woman, this scene would be fresh in her heart—his face framed by the naked branches of the hemlock, his smile gleaming brightly against his tanned face, the smell of leather and woodsmoke, along with the crackling fire and the gentle bubbling of the brook, and the touch of his hand on her hair—all would be there for her when she thought of this time. *I'll never have him—but I'll always remember this night—when I first knew I loved him!*

He had pulled her head up to smile at her, but he saw something leap into her eyes, and he thought it was fear. He crouched suddenly, and put his free hand on her shoulder, saying, "Laddie, don't be afraid! Panthers never attack men." The dark eyes he looked into blinked rapidly, and just a trace of a tremor touched the full lower lip. What he saw bothered him. Time ran on, and Laddie remained silent. Finally, Nathan said, "Laddie, ever since Caleb died, I've felt rotten—and it's mostly because I—I never really told him how much I cared for him. It's always been hard for me to tell people I care for them. Seems like some families are real good at that—kissing and hugging and always saying how they love each other. But I've not been that way."

The light touch of his hand was a torment to Laddie, but a delicious pain, and she was hypnotized by his closeness. She knew that she ought to move away, but she sat very still, unwilling to lose the slight pressure of his hands.

"What I mean," Nathan said gently, "is that I don't ever want to let that happen again—so that's why I want to tell you right now—I love you, Laddie—hard as it is for me to say such things—I do love you, boy!"

Laddie knew that he wanted her to speak, to say something of her feelings, but she was too full to trust herself. She waited until he released her, saying, "Well, I just wanted you to know."

He rolled up in his blankets, and she did the same, but she was biting her fist fiercely to keep back the choking sobs.

The fire burned on, sending ghostly shadows against the trees, and the wind sighed faintly through the bare treetops. Overhead the stars moved across the ebony sky, rank on rank, doing their great dance.

Finally, much later, the log that he had put on burned in two, snapped, and fell on the coals beneath, sending a shower of sparks upward. And in a voice that Nathan never heard, Julie Sampson—not Laddie Smith!—whispered faintly:

"And I love you—Nathan Winslow!"

The tall form under the blanket did not stir, but far off a lone wolf lifted his muzzle to the stars; his nocturnal cry echoed the sadness that filled the girl's heart.

Two days later they returned to camp, the mules loaded with the dressed carcasses of four deer and a canvas bag stuffed with wild turkey—enough to feed the whole unit! Neither of them had referred to that first night, and Laddie sensed that Nathan felt that her response had been too cold. She had tried to make it up, but the moment had passed, and by the time they returned to camp, Nathan was depressed. Although he had said only a little, Laddie had a suspicion that he was thinking of Abigail Howland. He had said once, "Guess Paul has been having it pretty well his own way with Abigail—with me stuck out here for months."

Knox greeted them with a shout of joy at the sight of the small mountain of game. "Roust that cook out!" he roared. Then he had thrown his arms around the two of them, practically picking Laddie off the ground in his massive arms. "Bless you both! I don't care right now if you never do another blessed thing right—I forgive you for the sake of that fresh meat!"

"Anything happen while we were gone?" Nathan asked.

"No, but something's *going* to happen!" Knox said. "There's a meeting of staff officers tonight, and I've got a plan to save our bacon—if I can get the His Excellency to buy it!"

"What kind of plan, sir?" Laddie asked.

"You'll find out, because I want you there with every map you can lay your hands on, Sergeant Smith!"

Nathan said suddenly, "You won't need me around for a little while, will you, sir?"

"Why, no, Nathan—" He paused, then said quickly, "I won't need you tonight—but if they like my plan, I want you handy."

"I'll be back day after tomorrow."

Knox stared at him, started to say something, but then shut it off. When he walked away, Laddie stared at him, then said quietly, "Don't do it, Nathan."

"Do what?"

"Oh, don't be so innocent!" She lifted her head and said scornfully, "You think I don't know what it is? You're going to sneak into Boston and see that woman!"

He stared at her; then a grin touched his lips. "Guess you know me too well, Laddie. But it's no risk. I'll go in after dark so the patrols won't get me."

She stared at him, then begged, "Nathan, please don't go! You know what they say—that they've already *shot* two men they caught spying!"

"I'm not spying."

"You think they'll believe that? Nathan, wait a while—please!"

He sobered, then said, "I'm sorry, Laddie. I know you're too young to understand this—but love makes you do crazy things."

He wheeled suddenly and walked away, and she stood there helplessly watching until he disappeared behind a line of tents.

She knew that he was gone at supper, for he did not appear to take part in the feast. Many hands were clapped on her shoulder, with a "Good job, Laddie!" and "Thanks for the meal, Sergeant!" but she could not swallow more than a few bites.

Later, she went with Schuyler and Knox to a large house where Washington was staying. His wife was there, a small woman with bright eyes and a quick word of welcome for all, but she soon disappeared, and the council began at once.

Washington spoke briefly, thanking each of his officers for their labors, then said in a tired voice, "Gentlemen, we have the British trapped, but we can't do anything with them."

"Your Excellency," Nathanael Greene, a tall, handsome officer, said, "I'm a Quaker, as you call us, and we are, in principle, opposed to fighting; but I can't see that waiting is getting us any closer to freedom. Can't we hit them head-on?"

Washington would have liked to do exactly that. Waiting was not his idea of war, but he shook his head, saying, "No, we're not yet ready for that sort of head-on fight. The answer, of course, would be to blast them out with heavy guns—but we have none. Until we can get some, we'll just have to pray that General Gage doesn't get inspired to move."

Knox stood up, the tallest man in the room except for Washington. "May I have your permission to offer a solution, sir?"

Washington had a deep affection for the officer, and he said with courtesy but little hope, "Certainly, Captain Knox."

Washington sat down, and Knox looked around the table at cynical Charles Lee, hot-tempered John Sullivan, the old Indian fighter Israel Putnam, John Grover of the 21st Massachusetts Regiment, Greene, and Schuyler. "Gentleman, guns are the answer, as the general points out. I propose to get some heavy guns, to place them on Dorchester Heights and blow the Redcoats out of their shirts!"

A look of disgust crossed the thin face of General Charles Lee. "Knox, it's impossible! We've tried to get guns from every possible source." Lee was always negative, and now he yawned and dismissed Knox's proposal with a wave of his manicured hand.

"Where do you propose to get the guns, Henry?" Washington asked, a trace of hope illuminating his face.

"Sergeant, hold up map Fourteen-C," Knox said, and Laddie quickly held it up with both hands. She felt Knox's heavy hand punching it, and he said one word:

"Ticonderoga!"

Washington stared blankly at Knox; then the idea brought a light to his gray eyes. "There *are* heavy cannon there—I'd forgotten!"

All of them were thinking of the wild raid under the command of Ethan Allen and his Green Mountain Boys and Benedict Arnold. The two of them had captured Fort Ticonderoga the previous May. The fort itself was falling in, and of no great use to anyone, but there were many cannon there.

"Henry!" Washington was visibly excited, a sight rarely seen. He stood to his feet and stared at the map. "Can it be done? Winter will catch you, and the roads are terrible."

Knox said at once, "General Washington, I will get those guns or die in the attempt!"

Washington slammed his fist down on the table. "We must have those weapons! Take any men you need—do what you have to!"

Lee said languidly, "Oh, it can't be done—not until spring, at least!"

But Knox was staring straight into his commander's eyes, and he said in a steady voice, "You shall have them, sir!"

The meeting went on for some time, but Laddie was dismissed, and went to bed. The next day, Knox moved through the camp like a whirlwind, picking men, choosing only the best and toughest. He stopped long enough to ask Laddie, "Where's Nathan?"

"I—I haven't seen him, sir—but you said he could have two days."

"All right, but as soon as you lay eyes on him, tell him I want him to go on this mission!"

All day Laddie looked for him, but Nathan didn't come. That night after supper, Knox came to her with an angry look on his round face. "I've got bad news, Smith." He stared at her, then said plainly, "Nathan's been captured."

"No!"

"Yes. One of our informers just brought word. There's no doubt of it."

"But, what will they do to him?"

He stared at the stricken countenance before him, then said, "They'll hang him, I'm afraid. He's been tried by a military court and sentenced to death."

"I've got to go to him!"

He shook his head. "It would not do, Laddie. You can't help him—and you might be taken as well."

She looked straight at him and said, "Sir, I've got to go. If you don't lock me up, I'll go."

He stared at her, then said, "By heaven, I'm sorry to hear it, Laddie! You know how fond I am of Winslow—" Then he groaned and said, "Go on then. I'll give you a pass—but it would be better if you didn't go."

Laddie said quietly, "He saved my life, Captain Knox. I've got to go—to do what I can!"

She turned and walked away, shoulders held square, and Knox suddenly swore, whirled and walked quickly away. *It would have been better if he'd been killed at Breed's Hill!* he thought grimly.

CHAPTER SIXTEEN

ESCAPE!

★　★　★　★

"Miss Abigail—dat man, he heah *agin!*"

The black girl entered the room reluctantly, keeping a respectful distance from the young woman who sat up in the bed and glared at her. "I *told* you to say I wouldn't see him! Why can't you ever do a single thing *right*, Susie?"

The slave blinked, then rolled her large eyes upward. "I done tole him 'zactly whut you said—but he jes' set there and say he ain't gonna move till you sees him." She shook her head with exasperation, adding, "It sho' is a shame yo poppa and momma both gone—I bet *dey* get shut of 'im!"

Abigail got up from the bed, smoothed her dressing gown, and walked across the room to stare out into the falling darkness. Her face was puffy with sleep, and she asked idly, "What sort of man did you say he was?"

"Oh, jes' a young man—sort of plain. He ain't no quality folks, Miss."

"I don't know anybody named Smith." Abigail went over to the mirror, sat down and began to brush her hair. Finally she said, "Oh, well, show him up, Susie. You can say I've been ill and can't come down."

"Yas, Miss Abigail." When the slave left, Abigail carefully brushed her hair, then moved to a plush couch, put her feet up and covered them with a brightly colored quilt. When the knock sounded on the door, she said, "Come in," and looked up to see Susie admit a young man.

"Yes, what is it?"

"You don't remember me, Miss Howland?"

Abigail stared in the failing light at the youth, but said, "I don't think we've met." Curiosity had caused her to let him in, but he was merely a plainly dressed youth in his late teens. The oval-shaped face and large eyes reminded her of someone, but she said, "I'm not well, Mr. Smith. I'll ask you to come back tomorrow and see my parents."

She blinked nervously as the man called Smith did not turn to leave, but stepped up so close that she could see determination in a pair of inky black eyes and a firm mouth. Fear rose in her, and she opened her mouth to call for the slave, but he said, "I'm here about Nathan Winslow."

"What! Who are you?" She threw back the quilt and stood to her feet, staring at her visitor. "I don't know you, and I'll ask you to leave!"

"You've seen me, Miss Howland," Laddie said. "I once worked for Mr. Charles Winslow. You saw me there when you came to visit his son—and I was at the warehouse when you came to go for rides with Nathan."

Abigail stared at her, then nodded slowly. "Yes—I think I do remember you—but what do you want?"

"I want to save Nathan's life," Laddie said evenly. "And you've got to help."

"It's impossible!" Abigail cried at once, and she walked to the small French desk and picked up a handkerchief. She dabbed at her eyes, and then twisted the kerchief into a knot. "Do you think we haven't tried? If you work for Charles Winslow, you must know he's talked to General Gage for *hours*—but the general says it's out of his hands."

Laddie did know that to be true, for she had gone straight to the Winslow house and asked Charles point blank what he was doing to get Nathan out of jail. He had stared at her, a haggard look in his eyes, and said wearily, "I've not slept a wink since he was taken—and I've used all the influence I have to get him out—but they're determined to make an example of him, Laddie. I've done all I can!"

She had left, and all day she had haunted the large building where the second story was used for a jail. In desperation she had gone inside and asked to see Nathan, claiming to be his brother, but the burly corporal had shaken his massive head, saying, "Not a bit of it! We got 'im clean, and we're gonna 'ang the blighter at dawn! And we don't mean 'e should cheat us by doin' away with 'imself, either! So it's no visitors 'cept them wot's got a pass signed by the general his own self!" A tall officer in shirt sleeves, his red coat hanging on a peg, looked up from across the room, where he sat idly reading a newspaper, then shrugged and looked back at the paper.

Laddie had left, noting carefully the details of the building. The room below was large, with several desks, but besides the corporal only two privates were on duty. *That's four in here—at least at night,* she thought, then glanced at the stairs at the back of the room. *No way to tell how many up there,* she thought as she left.

All night she walked the streets, and the next day she listened to the talk in the taverns, and found out that Nathan's hanging was to be a celebration of sorts. The Tories looked on it as an example for other traitors, and she heard bets made as to whether he would break his neck in the fall or die of strangulation, kicking wildly.

Her mind raced madly, and fear was a metallic taste in her mouth. *If only his father were here!* she thought. But there was no time. Finally in the early afternoon she passed by a church, and some impulse drove her to enter and take a seat in the dark recesses. A few candles burned on a table in the front, and a few people sat quietly with their heads bowed. She didn't even know what sort of church it was, but that didn't seem to matter.

The quiet soaked into her, and her fear lost some of its piercing sting as she began to pray. It was a strange time for her, for like most, she had always prayed calmly, rather routinely. But desperation numbed her now, and she began to weep, her chest heaving and great choking sobs racking her body. There was no eloquence, no fine phrase. *Help, O Lord! Oh, God, have mercy!* Over and over she cried out, as if she were dying herself. Never had she experienced such a paroxysm of grief and terror, and she remembered once what Rev. Zachariah Kelly had said in a sermon: "Men only seek God out of desperation." Now she knew it was so.

Finally her sobs ceased; suddenly a strange peace seemed to fill her mind, and the exhaustion and fear faded. She heard no voices and there was no mystic vision, but a passage of Scripture quietly drifted into her mind. At first she ignored it, thinking only of Nathan, but it came back, not once but several times:

> The Lord is my light and my salvation; whom shall I fear? The Lord is the strength of my life; of whom shall I be afraid? When the wicked, even my enemies and my foes, came upon me to eat up my flesh, they stumbled and fell. Though an host should encamp against me, my heart shall not fear; though war should rise against me, in this will I be confident.

The words were very familiar, for they had been the favorite verses of her pastor, Rev. Kelly. Many times he had quoted the entire twenty-seventh psalm from the pulpit, and she seemed to hear his voice as the words continued to flow through her spirit:

> Teach me thy way, O Lord, and lead me in a plain path because of mine enemies. Wait on the Lord; be of good courage, and he shall strengthen thine heart: wait, I say, on the Lord.

She got to her feet and left the church, and there was no trace of fear in her. As she made her way through the streets, she repeated the words: *"Teach me thy way, O Lord, and lead me in a plain path because of mine enemies."*

And there was still no fear in Laddie as she stood before Abigail and said, "There's not much time. They're going to hang him in the morning." She had come to the Howland residence because no other course had occurred to her. She had never been a believer in visions and dreams, but as she walked the streets after leaving the church, she somehow took the impulse to go to see Abigail as part of the "way" that she felt God was going to show her.

Abigail was trembling, and she collapsed on the sofa, moaning. "I've *tried* to help! Can't you understand that? I've had my father practically on his *knees* begging General Gage—and it's no use."

"Have you seen him?"

"I—wanted to. I even had Father get me a pass from General Gage!" She leaped up and ran to the desk. Picking up a sealed envelope, she held it up, then threw it back on the desk with a groan. "But Mother won't hear of it!"

"So it's no visitors 'cept them wot's got a pass signed by the general his own self!"

The words of the corporal echoed in her ears, and in that instant she knew what she had to do! There was no dreary planning, no wrestling with details; it sprang into her mind fully formed, and with a leap of her heart she remembered the words ". . . lead me in a *plain* path."

Carefully Laddie moved to stand in front of the desk, and asked quietly, "How did he get taken?"

"We don't know," Abigail whispered. She looked with a tremulous mouth at Laddie, adding, "He came to see me, of course." And despite the trembling lips, there was a flash of fire in her eyes, pride that a man would risk his life for her! "And I was so afraid! I tried to get him to leave—but he wouldn't listen!" She gave a small smile and shrugged, "Love makes people do strange things, don't you agree?"

Laddie thought of the plan she was determined on; there was a strange smile on her lips as she answered quietly, "Yes, a man will do strange things for love—and so will a woman." Then she demanded, "And why can't you use the pass—go see him, Miss Howland? If he's going to die for you, the least you could do is go say goodbye!"

Abigail dropped her head in confusion (exactly as Laddie had hoped!), and in one smooth motion, Laddie turned, picked up the pass and shoved it into her shirt. It took less than three seconds, and she said quickly, "I'm sorry to have bothered you, Miss Howland. I'll be going now."

Abigail looked up with a startled expression as Laddie reached the door, and she cried out loudly, "*I* can't go to him! Can't you see that?"

But the door closed, and in a matter of seconds Laddie was walking as fast as she could in the direction of the business district.

Two hours later she was opening the door of the Winslow warehouse. Quickly she moved to hitch the team of bays to the buggy—the same one, she noted with a slight shock, that they'd gone to New York in. She was thankful the guard had gone for the night, and even more grateful that she had kept her key!

Dark had fallen by the time the team stood stamping in the cold of the stable, and Laddie picked up the bulky package she'd brought with her. The office was still warm, and she pulled a small box out of the large sack, opened it, and withdrew two small flintlock pistols. Carefully she primed them with black powder and then, wrapping two balls in small fragments of cloth, shoved them home with the small ramrod. Carefully she put them aside, then turned to the large bag.

From it she pulled a fashionable dark blue dress, then one by one all the other garments that a young woman of fashion would be likely to wear. The clerk, she remembered suddenly, had been bewildered by a young man buying such garments, but he had not argued, for the price was high—taking Laddie's meager store of cash nearly to the last farthing.

She stared at the dress, stroking the fine material, and then she faltered—but in the silence as her fears rose, she seemed to hear Rev. Kelly's voice whispering: *Though an host should encamp against me, my heart shall not fear!* She tossed the dress down, stripped out of her male attire quickly, and in a few minutes she stood there, dressed in women's clothes for the first time in months. The freedom and looseness of the dress seemed strange to her, and she whirled and laughed as the skirt rose gracefully. There was no mirror except for the small one fixed over the washstand that some of the men used at times for shaving, but she donned the small bonnet with the flowing veil and stared into the mirror.

Several curls escaped the bonnet, ringing her face, and she had not trimmed her eyelashes in weeks, so they curled up over her large eyes. "I must say, Miss Sampson—you look quite ravishing!" Then she laughed shortly and threw her old clothes into the bag. The two pistols she carefully placed in the belt of the dress, far back at her sides so that they were covered by the short stylish red jacket which she put on.

She ran to the door, opened it, and after driving the team out, shut and locked it. Then she drove toward the jail, her jaw set and her heart steady with purpose.

The dropping temperature bit into her, even through the thick clothing, but she was glad, for the weather had driven most of the citizens indoors, and the streets were practically empty. She drove boldly up to the very door of the red brick building, got down quickly and tied the team to a hitching post. She retrieved the purse she had bought and, conscious of abandoning the masculine swagger she had picked up in past months, walked through the front door, her heart beating evenly.

"Why—wot's this?" The same burly corporal rose up from his chair as she entered, and he looked at her so hard that she was sure for one heartbeat that he remembered her. But he merely looked baffled and said, "You shouldn't be here, Miss!"

"Oh, that's quite all right, Corporal," she said sweetly, in the most feminine voice she could muster, "I have a pass to see Nathan Winslow." She smiled at him through the veil and took the sealed envelope out of the handbag.

He stared at her, then shook his beefy face from side to side. "I can't do that!" He looked nervously to his right and called out, "Lieutenant Fitzwilliam!"

The officer had been lying down on a cot, and he came to his feet slowly; then as he saw Laddie, straightened up and retrieved his coat from the peg on the wall. "What's this, Corporal?"

"Lady says she's got a pass to see Winslow."

Fitzwilliam had been buttoning his tunic—but he paused and stared at her, then shook his head. "That's quite impossible!"

Laddie held it out and said, "You refuse to honor an order from General Gage?"

The name seemed to shock the officer, for he suddenly arched his back and his pale face flushed red in lamplight. "Why—uh—I mean, certainly *not!*" He gingerly took the envelope, broke the seal, then extracted the paper inside. His mobile features revealed the shock that the note gave him, and he said at once in a conciliatory voice, "My apologies, Miss Howland. Of course, you may see the prisoner. I'll take you up myself."

"Thank you, Lieutenant," Laddie said, and took his arm. He said, "Corporal, I'll remain upstairs until this lady is ready to leave."

"Yes, sir!"

As she followed the officer up the stairs, she noted that the two privates, who had been playing cards, were watching with covert eyes, and she knew as soon as the officer was out of sight, the three of them would buzz with talk, but she put the thought of them from her mind.

"We have to keep a close watch, Miss Howland," Lieutenant Fitzwilliam said. He was burning with curiosity, and said carefully, "The prisoner—he's . . . ?"

"We—were to be married!" Laddie brought a sob into her voice and covered her face with her handkerchief.

"Oh—I—I'm sorry . . . !" Fitzwilliams muttered, then took a key as he paused before a heavy oak door fastened with a huge padlock and chain. As he inserted the key, he said apologetically, "You may see the prisoner alone—I'll be right here, so call when you're ready to leave. I'm afraid I must examine your handbag."

He looked through the bag, then pulled the lock free, swung the door open, saying, "Winslow! Miss Howland is here to see you!"

Laddie was behind the officer, who was a very tall man, and her first glimpse of Nathan came when he shifted and moved around her to the door. Nathan's face when she saw it was filled with joy, and then he looked full at her, and instantly there was a change. Laddie knew that the officer was watching, and she said, "Nathan!" and threw herself into his arms, so that he had to catch her. She clung fiercely to him until she heard Fitzwilliam sigh, and then the ponderous door swung to with a bang and the padlock rattled noisily.

Instantly Laddie pulled back and looked up into Nathan's bewildered eyes. He said harshly, "What sort of game is this? Who are you?"

Laddie reached up, yanked her hat off and grinned up at him. "Laddie Smith at your service!" She saw his mouth spring open and his eyes opened wide.

"Laddie!" he gasped. "I can't believe—!"

She shook her head and whispered fiercely, "That Redcoat is out there with his ear glued to the door, so don't talk so loud." He was still staring at her in unbelief, so she said with a smile, "I make a pretty good-looking girl in all this, don't I, Nathan? I think that fool lieutenant wanted to *kiss* me!" She pulled at the dress, adding, "This rig and all this padding is killing me! I don't see how women can stand to wear such clothes!"

"Laddie—you shouldn't be here!" Nathan came out of the shock that held him, and shook his head sternly. "I know you want to help, but there's no way. They'll hang you right beside me if—!"

"Nathan, I didn't come to get hanged!" Laddie snapped. "Now, listen to me—there's an officer out there, and downstairs there's a corporal and two privates. I've got the buggy right outside, and when we get out of here, we jump in and I'd like to see them catch us till we get through the lines!"

He stared at the fire in the dark eyes and said, "But they're all armed, Laddie."

"So are we!" Laddie reached inside the coat and pulled the two pistols out with a flourish. "Primed and ready to shoot!"

For the first time a light of hope leaped to his eyes, and he reached out and took one. Examining the load, he said with excitement, "By the good Lord—we just might make it!"

She nodded and said quietly, "That's right, Nathan—by the good Lord."

He shot a quick look at her, then suddenly dropped his head. He stood there struggling for a long moment, then lifted his face and sorrow was in his eyes. "I—I'd given up on God, Laddie."

"But He hasn't given up on you!" Laddie smiled. "Now, we've got to wait a few minutes; then we'll call the lieutenant in. Let me tell you what we're going to do . . ."

She spoke rapidly, and when she finished he said quickly, "I think we can do it!"

"All right, but we'd better wait a few minutes."

In the pause that followed, he looked at her and said, "Laddie, I—I've thought a lot about you these last few hours."

"You mean about Abigail!" she shot back instantly, then was sorry for it.

"Of her, too, of course, but that's different. I mean, I've thought of you, and of all I hated to leave, why, I guess my family was first—and by the Lord, I hated to leave you!"

"Did you, Nathan?"

"Yes." He reached out and grabbed her by the hair as he had at the creek in the woods, and he grinned suddenly, saying, "You're too pretty to be a boy, Laddie!" He laughed and gave her hair a harder tug as a thought struck him. "Why couldn't you have been a girl? Then we could have fallen in love and I wouldn't have gotten in all this mess!"

She gasped and pulled away, her face flaming. "Will you keep your hands off me!" She turned her back, and her breathing was shallow as she said, "Tell me how you got caught."

He told her how he had gone to Charles first, and had stayed there all day to keep out of sight of the patrols. Then, after dark, he'd gone to Abigail's; he ended by saying "So when I came out of the Howlands' a patrol was there and they picked me up."

"They were waiting for you?"

She turned to see a pain cross his face. "Yes," he said, and then said, "I think a servant at the Howlands' must have seen me."

She studied him, but said only, "Best to think that." Then she picked up her bonnet, tied it on, and arranged the veil. "I think you can call Lieutenant Fitzwilliam in now."

"All right." He walked to the door, and banging on it called out, "Lieutenant! Miss Howland is ready to go!"

He positioned himself to the side of the door, while holding one of the pistols in his left hand. When the door swung open, he did not wait, but reached out with a long arm, grabbed the officer by the jacket and pulled him inside in one smooth motion. Fitzwilliam found himself looking directly into the muzzle of a pistol, and the blue eyes that peered over it seemed no less threatening than the firearm held in the man's hand!

"Redcoat, you've got a very, very small chance to live," Nathan said quietly. "I'm a dead man, so I've got nothing to lose. Now, do you want to live—or not?"

Fitzwilliam's throat gave a convulsive swallow, and sweat popped out on his brow. He stared into Nathan's eyes and saw death, so he nodded quickly. "I'll do—anything! Just don't kill me!" he pleaded.

"All right, I promise you, if you do exactly what I tell you, you'll not be harmed. Now, you and I are going to the top of the stairs, and you're going to call the corporal. Tell him the lady is ill, and you want him to come upstairs."

"All right!"

The officer moved nervously as Nathan prodded him with the pistol, and when they got to the top of the stairs, Nathan opened the door, then placed the muzzle right under Fitzwilliam's ear, At once he called out loudly, "Corporal Dietz! The lady is ill! Come up and help me with her!"

"Now, back to the cell," Nathan said, and they moved back inside. Nathan said, "Put that pistol to his ear, Laddie, and shoot him if he blinks!"

They waited as Corporal Dietz dashed into the room—straight into the muzzle of Nathan's weapon. His mouth dropped open, but Nathan gave him no chance to think. He said, "Soldier, you want to live?"

Dietz hesitated, and there was a loud *CLICK* as Nathan pulled the hammer back, and the muzzle suddenly seemed very large to the corporal. He gasped, "Don't shoot!"

Nathan stared at him, then said harshly, "I'll tell you what I've told the lieutenant—if you do as you're told, you'll live. They can only hang me once, so I'll put a bullet in your brain if you even *blink!*"

The corporal nodded quickly, and Nathan moved back. "Lieutenant, take off your clothes."

"What?"

CLICK. The pistol that Laddie held to the officer's head cocked, and he at once cried out, "No!" and then began stripping off his uniform.

"Against the wall, both of you—Laddie, shoot them down if they move!" Nathan quickly undressed and put on the uniform of Fitzwilliam. When he buttoned up the tunic, he said, "All right, on your belly, Lieutenant!" Ignoring the officer's protests, he took the cords that Laddie had brought in the purse, then gagged him with a piece of cloth.

When Dietz stared stupidly at the officer, Laddie moved in front of him. "Pick me up, you stupid ox!" He blinked, but obeyed. As soon as she was in his arms, she pressed the muzzle of her flintlock directly over his heart and covered it with her coat. "Be pretty messy if this goes off, won't it?"

"And I'll be right behind you, Corporal," Nathan said. He picked up the purse Laddie had brought and shoved his weapon inside, then pointed the invisible flintlock at Dietz. "We're going down, and you're going to say to the guards, 'Both of you, go up quickly and guard the prisoner! The Lieutenant and I have to get the lady to a doctor!' You got that?"

"And tell them to keep that door locked tight until the two of you get back," Laddie added. She pressed the pistol hard against the thick chest and said, "I think the corporal is going to say his piece real well."

"Let's go," Nathan stated hurriedly, and he followed Dietz out of the door, then locked it carefully, putting the key in his pocket. "All right, we'll go down. Do it quick, and you've got a fair chance of staying out of hell for a little longer!"

They went down the stair in a rush, and Nathan kept his face turned away from the end of the room where he caught a glimpse of the two privates. Dietz performed as if his life depended upon it! He gave a stentorian yell that rattled the windows: "Get up to the prisoner, you two! Me and the lieutenant gotta get the lady to a doctor!" He dove for the door, screaming, "And don't open that cell for nobody till we get back!"

Nathan followed on his heels, and slammed the door, but not before he heard the soldiers running across the room and up the stairs. "Get in the back—on your face!" he commanded Dietz as Laddie unhitched the team and sprang to the seat.

"You gonna kill me!" Dietz protested, but Nathan forced him into the coach, face down in the back.

"We'll let you go if you keep your mouth shut! Drive on, Laddie!"

The horses leaped at the touch of Laddie's whip, and those few people who had braved the cold were surprised to see a carriage driving so fast along the icy streets.

Three hours later, Corporal Dietz found himself afoot and unharmed, but he could curse only in a whisper, for he was so close to the enemy lines he knew he'd be picked up. He slogged wearily back toward town, trying to make up a story that would satisfy the officers, but halfway there, decided that there *was* no such story. He thought better of returning, decided to become an ex-member of the King's forces, and went to the harbor where a certain ship was leaving at dawn for Calcutta.

As soon as they dumped Dietz and he disappeared down the road, Laddie said, "Nathan, I've got to get out of these clothes!"

"Well, you won't be near so pretty—but I guess you got a right to do just about anything you please." She grabbed the sack and sprinted into the woods behind a large oak tree, out of Nathan's line of vision. Her teeth were chattering as she changed back to her customary garb. Then she stuffed the feminine clothing in the sack and climbed back into the seat.

"That's better."

He didn't move, but sat there in the moonlight, staring out at the hills. The silence ran on, making her nervous, and finally he turned to her and said in an odd voice, "Sun's coming up pretty soon." He cleared his throat, then looked at her. "Thought it'd be my last one. Would have been, Laddie, except for you."

She shifted slightly, then met his eyes. "Well, that makes us even, doesn't it?"

"No, it doesn't." When she stared at him, he smiled and said, "I didn't risk anything when I got you out of the snow—but you stuck your neck in a noose for me tonight."

Laddie looked at him, then said quietly, "We better go, Nathan."

He stared at her. "You don't want thanks, do you, Laddie? But

I'll never forget it. Remember what you said once, the old Indian custom—If somebody saves your life, you belong to that person always?" His eyes held hers, and he said huskily, "So, I guess we kind of belong to each other somehow, don't we, Laddie?"

She couldn't speak for the lump in her throat until they had moved along for a few hundred yards, then she whispered, "I guess if you say so, Nathan, we must!"

He put his hand out, and her small hand was swallowed in his. "That's the way it is, then," he said as he released her. "Now, where you think we better go?"

"Why, I forgot to tell you, Nathan, we're on our way to catch up with General Knox. He's on his way to Fort Ticonderoga to get enough cannon to run the Redcoats out of Boston!"

He grinned at her, and said, "Guess I better change clothes, too, Laddie, or he'll shoot me for a lobsterback!" Then he laughed and said, "Ticonderoga, here we come!"

CHAPTER SEVENTEEN

CRISIS AT HALF MOON

★ ★ ★ ★

Laddie and Nathan caught up with General Knox three days later, and after he had listened to their story, he had stared at Laddie, finally saying, "I'm glad you're going to be along on this trip, Sergeant Smith. Getting this character out of jail took courage and initiative—but I've got the feeling this job we've got now is going to be *worse!*"

They pushed on as fast as the men could go, and at first the journey had been a joy to Laddie. She had reveled in the unexpected vistas of mountainous country, the vast, silent forests of New York State blanketed with fluffy, fast-melting snow. Nathan was never far from her side, and the two of them shared the campfire at night. He said little about Abigail; his close brush with death seemed to have freed him from the heaviness that he had carried, and at the same time made him more thoughtful. Often they would read Laddie's Bible long into the night, and Knox sometimes would stalk by, stare down at them, a puzzled light in his sharp eyes. He cared for nothing but guns and his idol, General Washington, so he was fascinated at the pleasure they seemed to get out of the old book.

The trip was uneventful until just outside of Albany. As they crossed a stream, a section of thin ice gave way, and Laddie plunged into the freezing waters up to her waist. Nathan had helped her out, saying, "We better build a fire and get you into some dry clothes."

"Oh, we'll camp in an hour," she had said. "I can wait until then."

It had been a poor decision, and all night she shivered, unable to shake off the biting cold that gripped her bones. The next day she had a slight fever and by night had begun to cough. Nathan watched her silently, unable to help, and on the second day, her temperature jumped and she couldn't eat. By late that afternoon, when they arrived in a small village called Half Moon, where the Mohawk and the Hudson met, she was so weak that Nathan practically carried her the last two miles. He wrapped her in blankets beside a fire that some of the men made, and sought out Knox.

"Sir, Laddie's got to have a doctor."

Knox shook his head, and gave a dubious look at the small settlement consisting of no more then twenty houses. "Not likely there'll be one here—but go see what you can find."

Nathan went into the village and asked a tall man who was chopping wood, "Is there a doctor in this town?"

"Doctor? No—nearest one is up river at Saratoga." He looked carefully at Nathan and asked, "You an army man?"

"Yes. This is Captain Knox's company." He studied the man carefully, for they had encountered quite a few ardent loyalists who hated them on sight. "We're going to Ticonderoga to get guns for General Washington."

The level gaze of the tall man did not waver; then he smiled and said, "Is that a fact? Wal, I hope you git enough to blow them lobsterbacks clean back to England! I'm Ezra Parker."

Nathan shook the hard hand that was offered. "Nathan Winslow. Most of the village feel like you do?"

"For a fact. We had a few Tories, but they felt so out of place they moved out. Whut's this about a doctor? You sick?"

"No, but we got a sick sergeant. Needs help bad."

Parker said slowly, "Wal, now, most of us use Sister Greene when we get hurt or sick."

"Sister Greene?"

"She's the preacher's ma." Parker laughed at Nathan's doubtful look, then said, "Don't blame you much for lookin' like that, Winslow, but I tell you true I'd trust Sister Greene's doctorin' a heap more'n I would most o' these sawbones! I got a wagon here, if you want a hand."

Nathan warmed to the man and said, "That'd be a kindness, Ezra."

Parker hitched his team and called to his wife, "Martha—I'm goin' to take a sick soldier to Sister Greene's house!" On the way to the camp, he listened avidly to the news about the war. "Some of our young fellows went when we got word about Lexington. I thought to go myself, but then Martha said to let them as had no children take care of the fighting."

They pulled up beside the fire, and Nathan said, "Stay where you are, Ezra. I'll get the boy." Then he reached down and picked Laddie up in his arms and carried her to the wagon. "Got to get you out of this weather, Laddie," he said, then added cheerfully, "This is Ezra Parker—he says they got a lady in this town that's good as a doctor."

Laddie smiled weakly, but her face was flushed and there was a hoarse rasping in her voice when she said faintly, "Glad to meet you."

Parker glanced at her, then whipped the horses up. "Young feller does look right peaked—but I got a heap of faith in Sister Greene." A thought struck him, and he exclaimed, "It just come to me, Nathan, Miz Greene, she's got a brother who's a general in the army."

"Nathanael Greene from Rhode Island?"

"That's the one. He's one of them Quakers, you know? And so is Sister Greene, and so is her boy, Dan."

"They don't believe in war, I hear?" Nathan said, and cast a doubtful look at Ezra. "They might not favor doing anything for a soldier."

"Ha! You don't know much 'bout them folks! They won't pull no trigger, but I guess Sister Greene would doctor ol' Slewfoot if he turned up at her door sick!"

"You a Quaker, Ezra?"

"Me? No, I'm a varmint!" Parker grinned. "They ain't many Quakers here—maybe thirty. But lots of the rest of us sort of look at Friend Daniel as our preacher. He don't stand fer being called *Reverend* nor no fancy name, so we just call him Friend Dan, even us sinners—of which we got a overabundance in Half Moon."

He drove into the village, down the main street, then turned off into a lane, pointing at a half-timbered house sitting back under a small grove of tall firs. He jumped down, nodded to Nathan as he tied up the team. "Bring 'im on in."

Nathan picked up Laddie, and as he walked up the path, the door opened and a woman came out. "Got a sick man fer you, Sister," Parker said. "This here is Nathan Winslow, and his sergeant has got the ague."

"Bring him in, Friend Nathan," the woman said. She was a tall woman in her fifties, straight and well-formed. Her hair was auburn with just a trace of silver, and there was a calmness in her brown eyes that Nathan liked at once. "We'll put him in the spare room." Nathan walked behind her down a short hall, turned into a small room, and then set Laddie down.

"Get into that bed, young man," Sister Greene said. "I'll come back in a spell with something that'll do thee good." She stared at Laddie and asked in that same even tone, "Thou art a man of God?"

Laddie looked quickly at her, nodded and said, "I'm a Christian."

"Good. Then we both know where thy healing's got to come from." Sister Green turned and opened a drawer, pulled a night shirt out, and handed it to Laddie. "Get into that."

As the woman left, Nathan said, "I'll be back tonight, Laddie, after roll call. You mind Sister Greene, now!"

He turned and left. As he passed Sister Greene, he said, "I don't like the way he looks, Sister."

"I should think not—he's got pneumonia."

Nathan swallowed and stared hard at the woman. "You—you real sure about that?"

"Yes. How long is thy unit staying here?"

"We'll pull out at dawn, but—!"

"Well, thee can leave the young man here."

"I can't do that!"

"He'll die if he's moved." Then in the same calm, even voice, she asked him exactly the same question she had asked Laddie: "Art thou a man of God?"

Nathan turned red and threw an awkward glance at Ezra, who seemed to be enjoying the scene. Finally he shook his head. "I thought I was once, Sister—but now, I guess I'm just kind of a seeker."

The door opened and Nathan was relieved at the interruption.

The man who walked in had the same chiseled features as Sister Greene—the same warm brown eyes and generous lips.

"Friend Dan," Ezra said, "this here is Nathan Winslow. He's done come to dump a sick soldier on you while he goes to play army."

Dan Greene glanced at Parker, and humor lit his eyes and drew a smile to his wide mouth. "Friend Ezra, when thee gets right with God, thee will have a little more tact." He had a deep baritone voice, and there was a solidness in his shoulders, a thickness in his chest that most ministers lacked. He shook hands with Nathan, his grip like a vise, and said, "I trust the sickness is not too bad."

"Pneumonia, Daniel," his mother said. "We'll keep him until Friend Nathan can come back for him."

"It's a lot to ask . . ." Nathan said uneasily. "I know you folks don't hold with armies and fighting—"

"We hold with helping those who need it, Friend Nathan," the man interrupted. "Thee can be assured your friend will get good care." His eyes studied Nathan, and he asked, "Is he your kin?"

Nathan quickly explained how he'd found Laddie, trying to soften the part he'd played, then said, "I lost a brother at Lexington—and Laddie Smith is . . . !"

He paused, and seeing how disturbed he was, Dan said, "Easy to see thee does care for the young man. But even if I say so, he's in the best hands for a man who's bad sick."

Nathan nodded, unable to speak, so he whirled and said, "I'll come back tonight."

Ezra followed him to the wagon, and said little on the way back to camp, for he saw that his new friend was tormented with doubts. When he stopped to let Nathan get out, he said with a plaintive note in his voice, "Guess it's times like this that sinners like you and me wisht we wuz Christians, Nathan. But reckon you got the boy in to folks who know how to get hold of God."

Nathan was worried and depressed all day, and finally when he came back after visiting the Greenes' house that night, he went straight to Knox. "Captain, Laddie's got pneumonia."

"Is it bad, Nathan?"

"I just came from there." His lips were tight and his eyes were miserable in the lamplight. "He was delirious, General—didn't even know me!"

Knox stared at him silently. "I'd like to let you stay with him,

Nathan—but I need every good man I've got."

"I know—I'll be leaving with you in the morning. But it'll be so hard—not knowing if he's dead or alive."

He had left then, and the next morning as the brigade filed through the town in the gray dawn, Nathan cast one last desperate look down the lane to the small house just barely visible in first light, and prayed fervently, *God—help Sister Greene!*

Even as he prayed that prayer, Daniel Greene was looking down the street at the troop. He turned and said to his mother, who was sitting at the table with a Bible open before her, "They're leaving. Don't think they'll be back for weeks, if what I heard is true. With this weather and these roads, those men are in trouble."

Sister Greene looked up at him and said, "I think we're in trouble, too, Daniel."

He gave her a quick look, for he could not remember many times when his mother had admitted having a problem. Her faith was unchanging, like a rock, and he went over to sit down across from her. "What is it, Mother?"

"That young man in there, Daniel."

"Thee thinks he'll die?"

"No. The sickness won't be unto death—but Sergeant Smith has a worse problem than ague or pneumonia." She paused and he waited. Waiting came easy for him, for the Quakers did much of it. Sometimes they would sit for two hours on hard, backless benches waiting until one of the Friends had the Inner Light touch his soul and a message was delivered.

Finally she lifted her eyes and said, "Sergeant Laddie Smith is living a lie, Dan."

"A lie? What sort of lie?"

"About an hour ago I went in, and the fever was so bad I knew I had to use cold packs to bring it down. That's when I found out—when I took his nightshirt off. Sergeant Smith is not a man, Dan. We've got a sick young woman to care for."

He stared at her, unable to believe what he heard. Finally he said, "That's bad! A woman with all those men!"

He got up and walked to look out the window as the last of the troops passed over the hill and disappeared; then he turned and said quietly, "I was mistaken about Winslow. He didn't seem like the sort to do this sort of thing—keep a loose woman."

"Loose or not—we've got to seek God, Daniel, or she'll be a

dead woman. I'll get the body healed—but thee must see to her soul."

Friend Daniel Greene said nothing, but doubt filled his brown eyes. Finally he said heavily, "God help her—poor child!" Then he got up and left the warmth of the fire, walking for the rest of the morning in the freezing cold.

GUNS OVER BOSTON

★ ★ ★ ★

CHAPTER EIGHTEEN

FRIEND DANIEL AND LADDIE

★ ★ ★ ★

Sometimes the cold gripped so fiercely that she shook in every joint, trying to burrow deeper into the warmth of blankets; then the heat would rise like a tide of fire and she would struggle feebly to throw off the covers. She was down in a cold, dark hole sometimes, being pulled deeper and deeper into an even blacker depth, and she wanted to sink into it—to escape the alternating agony of fire and ice that racked her body.

But every time she began to sink into a welcome oblivion, an insistent voice would come to her, just when she seemed about to slip into the utter depths; it would grow loud and the sound of it would draw her back to the light.

Time was not for her a stream that moved from one point to the other, but a vast ocean with no beginning and no end. Seconds, days, years had no meaning; the only things that marked time were the hands that touched her, bathing her with cool water and holding her head to put a cup of water to her parched lips. And even the voice and the hands were confusing, for in her delirium she somehow came to distinguish between one voice that was soft and quiet and another that was deep and powerful—and sometimes the touch of hands had that same difference.

At last she came out of the darkness, and the bright sunlight streaming in from a window across the room hurt her eyes. She closed them quickly, having glimpsed only a white ceiling and a wall covered with paper ornamented by yellow flowers. Lying there with her eyes shut, her other senses were flooded with signals— cool sheets against her body, the pressure of cool dampness on her forehead, a sour taste in her mouth, the smell of fresh bread baking, the acrid scent of camphor—and the sound of a man's voice.

The voice was very close but so quiet that she thought at first he was speaking with someone else in the room, but suddenly she realized with a faint shock that he was praying. Accustomed as she was to elevated language from ministers in pulpits (which she unconsciously imitated in her own prayers, to some degree), she was caught by the fact that whoever it was spoke with God on most familiar terms!

" . . . and so, Lord, it's been a hard fight, hasn't it?" The deep voice suddenly chuckled, and added, "I came pretty close to doubting Thee a time or two—but Thee never fails. Well, now, it's clear that Thee has pulled this young woman out of the pit as a brand plucked from the burning, and I thank Thee for keeping her alive— but Lord, we've got to do something about her soul! Lord, I'm not much of a preacher, but nothing is too difficult for Thee—so now that Thou has taken away the disease, I'm going to believe that the soul of this sinner will be made whole. And, Lord, when there's— well, friend, so thee is awake?"

He broke off suddenly as he found himself looking directly into a pair of black eyes that had opened and were regarding him intently. He had been holding a damp cloth on her head, and the position had brought his face within inches of hers, so always after that when she thought of him, she saw him this way, framed in her vision, his square face brown and tan. He had thick brown hair and heavy eyebrows the same color over deep-set brown eyes, and she could see clearly the dent in his straight nose and wonder what had broken it. He was a handsome man with very regular features, and a serene expression characterized both his face and his manner.

"I'd guess thee's a little dry," he said when she tried to speak and found her mouth parched. He removed the cloth from her head, picked up a cup, then put his arm under her shoulders and pulled her into a sitting position. "Drink as much of this as thee can."

She was so thirsty that she put both her hands on his, and in her eagerness spilled water down the white gown she was wearing. When it was gone, he gave her more; then she said in a voice rusty with disuse, "Thank you."

"Well, how does thee feel?"

She considered the question, then nodded. "I—feel weak." She looked around the room, then turned her eyes back on him. "How long have I been here?"

"How long? Well, they brought thee here five days ago. Does thee remember that?"

She suddenly remembered the room and nodded. "It's not clear—wasn't there a woman here?"

"My mother. She'll be back soon. Are thee hungry?"

The question hit her like a blow, activating her appetite, and she said urgently, "Yes!"

He laughed and got up. "I'll fix some eggs. It'll be nice not to have to pour broth down thee with a spoon for a change." He got up, adding as he left, "Don't try to get up yet. Thee would probably fall and break thy neck!"

He was gone for some time, and Laddie tried once to get out of bed. The room seemed to tilt, and she fell back and lay with her eyes closed, appalled at her weakness. He came back with a wooden tray containing a plate of scrambled eggs and a large glass of milk. "Can thee sit up and eat, or shall I feed thee?" he asked.

"Oh, I can eat!" she said quickly, and tore into the delicious eggs. She ate it all, and almost licked the plate, but felt his eyes on her. "I'm so hungry," she said as he took the tray away and set it down on the nightstand.

"Thee can have something more solid in a few hours." He sat down and gazed at her with a quizzical look in his eyes. "It's God's own mercy thee didn't die, young woman."

Young woman!

Laddie gave a gasp, and involuntarily she cried out, "You know . . . !" He took her meaning at once, and his mouth tightened as he nodded slowly. Something in his direct stare disturbed her, and she felt a flush creeping up her throat. *He thinks I'm a loose woman, living with the soldiers!* she thought instantly. There were in the young army, camp followers—low women who moved from man to man with no shame.

Her hand rose to her cheek, and Daniel Greene looked at her. *She looks so innocent!* he thought. The sickness had thinned her face, making her large eyes seem enormous. He found himself admiring the girl's beauty—which startled him considerably! He was the most eligible bachelor in the county, and had long ago grown indifferent to the charms of young women; so many had smiled at him.

I think I've gotten attached to her—like I did to the sick kitten I nursed back to health, he thought. *But she is a fetching girl—and she looks so young and innocent!* His experience with loose women was practically nonexistent, there being none in Half Moon—at least of the professional type—but he had always thought of them as being painted and lewd in manner. The girl he stared at had a dewy expression in her eyes, and a rosy flush that colored her slender neck and rose to give color to her smooth cheeks. He had seen a painting of the Madonna once in a museum in Philadelphia, and she looked more like that portrait of the Virgin Mary than a Jezebel!

She was twisting the sheet nervously, and suddenly she looked at him and whispered, "Does—everyone know—about me, I mean?"

"No. Just my mother and myself." He saw the relief in her eyes and was puzzled. *Why should a woman who lives with soldiers even care what people think? Maybe the officers wouldn't let her go with the troops if they knew her sex.*

"I'm sorry to be so much trouble," she said quietly. "Maybe I'll be well enough to leave soon."

"The soldiers won't be back for at least three weeks, maybe more," Greene said. He saw the distress that crossed her face and took it to mean she was longing for the private that had brought her. He searched for his name, found it, and said, "I promised Winslow we'd care for thee until the army comes back through with the guns."

Greene paused, and there was a change in his face. "Of course, we didn't know then—" He broke off, not knowing how to end his statement, and to his annoyance found that his own face was beginning to glow. He got up hastily, took the tray, and said, "I'll bring thee some hot water and towels. I'm sure thee must want to clean up."

Two hours later, his mother came in. "Well, she woke up," he said tersely.

There was a shortness in his words that drew her attention. "What's wrong, Daniel? Something bothers thee about the girl?"

Running his fingers through his crisp brown hair, he shook his head, then gave her an odd look. "There's something strange about her, Mother," he said. "She looks so—*innocent!* But she can't be—not living as she does."

Carrie Greene was Quaker to the bone, and if she had ever felt that God was moving in her spirit, she felt it now as she stood there staring at her son. He was the joy of her life—strong, as his father had been; from his boyhood, she had seen the fierce desire to serve God grow stronger until now he was, if anything, *too* single-minded. She had wondered once if he was so otherworldly that he gave too little thought to simple earthly things. She longed for grandchildren, but he had never shown an interest in any of the young women who practically announced their willingness to share his life. He was a fine farmer, but he performed those duties routinely, and he cared nothing for the prosperity that had come as a result of his skills.

I've not seen him so troubled, she thought suddenly, watching him pace the floor, and his agitation disturbed her. "I'll see if she needs anything." Anything that touched this son of hers touched her, and she could see that the young woman who lay in their house had managed to break through the tough shell of independence that her son had built around himself.

Slipping into the room, she found the girl asleep, but bathed and with her hair brushed. *She looks so young—and so beautiful,* the woman thought, and then: *No wonder Daniel was shaken by her.* She had lived long enough to know that there was something about a bad woman that drew men, and when one of them was as lovely as this one . . . !

Then the eyes opened, and the girl sat up, pulling the covers up to her chin. "Oh—I must have fallen asleep!"

"Well, thee'll sleep a lot for a few days." Sister Greene walked over and put her hand on the smooth forehead, then nodded. "Fever's gone. Thee'll get stronger now." She stared at the square face and into the almond-shaped eyes, trying to see into the spirit of the girl. "I'm Sister Greene. Thee has met my son, Daniel. What's thy name?"

"They—call me Laddie Smith—" She hesitated; then almost involuntarily she said, "But my real name is Julie Sampson." She gasped, shocked to find herself telling this, but there was something in the countenance of the woman who looked down at her that demanded honesty. She said hurriedly, "Please—don't tell anyone my real name. I—I'd be in trouble."

"I believe thee is already in trouble, child," Sister Greene said quietly. "But it will be as thee wishes. My son and I will keep thy secret."

"Thank you, Sister Greene!" Laddie bit her lip, then said, "I'll try not to be a bother until Nathan gets back."

"It'll be no bother." Sister Greene said, and her eyes suddenly seemed distant to Laddie, and for a long moment she appeared to be listening to some unheard voice. Then she looked into Laddie's eyes and said evenly, "I believe God sent thee to us. For what purpose, I have no word yet—but I will pray that the Light will be given." She suddenly stooped and kissed Laddie on the cheek, and a smile parted her lips. "Rest, now, and we'll talk later."

She left the room, and while Laddie wiped away the tears that had leaped to her eyes over the unexpected caress—the first she'd had from a woman since her mother had died—Sister Greene went back to find her son staring moodily out the window.

"I can see why the child disturbed thee, Daniel," she said at once, and there was a furrow on her smooth forehead. "There's something bound up in her heart."

"She's no child!"

"Well, not physically, I know, but there's a childlike quality in her—and I've had just a tiny word about her in my spirit. We must be very careful with this little one, son."

The two looked at each other, and finally Dan said, "I agree. We spend too much time on the ninety and nine—but this lost sheep has been put in our house for a purpose." He glanced toward the room where she lay, and added, "She's in love with Nathan Winslow—that's plain enough." The thought disturbed him somehow, and he got up and walked out of the room without bidding her farewell.

He's never done that before! she thought, and she too looked toward the room, wondering what changes could be thrust into her small world by the visitor who lay there.

In the days that followed, Laddie was glad that Nathan had left her pack, for it contained her journal—and she found it a relief to pour her heart out on the pages, saying those things that she dared not say aloud. One morning she sat at the table in her room, writing as the first rays of the sun peeped over the eastern hill and cast rosy gleams across her face:

December 27, 1775
It seems impossible that I've been here more than three

weeks! I remember how weak I was when I first came out of the fever, how Friend Daniel had to *carry* me to the table to eat; then later he would let me lean on his arm, practically carrying me on short walks across the floor. But yesterday, I outran him as we walked through the woods! He had a worried look on his face, and he called out, "Thee must be careful!" But I just laughed and called him a slowpoke!

They are so different! All the time I've been here, and they've never asked why I came here dressed like a man. Sometimes Friend Daniel will *almost* ask—but then he draws back—almost like he's *afraid* to know why I do it.

And it hurts me a lot not to tell them. Maybe I will soon. I guess I've been waiting for them to ask, and they've been waiting until *I* was ready—but it's been a strain despite their kindness.

They love God—both of them. Everything in their lives is based on that. They read the Bible all the time, it seems, and they pray more than I thought anybody *could* pray! They make me feel so worthless!

And they think I'm bad. That hurts so much! Before I leave here, I must tell them the whole story—I love them so much—and I can't bear to think they believe such things of me—though I can't blame them, for I know how it looks.

I went to church with them—only they call it "meeting." Everyone thinks I'm a man, so I had to sit with Dan and the men, while Sister Greene sat with the women. They both said later that it bothered them, so I don't think I'll go back.

We sat there for an hour and nobody said a word! Then a woman got up and said that God had spoken to her, and she gave a talk. Then there was another long silence; then Dan got up and preached. He is a real preacher! He's so quiet, usually, but he gets louder when he's preaching, and I felt the presence of the Lord like I never have in church!

I have to write this down. Several times I almost put it in this journal, but it sounded—funny. But now I'm sure.

Friend Daniel is in love with me.

That looks so—so *crazy* as I read the words, but it's so!

He doesn't know it himself—but I think his mother does. She's worried, and no wonder—her minister son falling in love with a wild girl who runs around with soldiers!

I don't know when I first noticed this—but I think it started because he took care of me when I was weak. He'd get attached to anything that was helpless! And as little as I know about men, he knows even *less* about women!

I remember the first time I saw how he was seeing me as a woman. I was staggering along beside him, weak as a cat, and he was guiding me. His mother was gone, and we were both laughing as my rubber legs kept bending and then I nearly fell, and he picked me up like I was a little girl, saying, "Enough of that!" and he carried me to a chair, but just before he put me down, he suddenly stopped and looked down at me, and I saw it come to him—I mean, that I *wasn't* a little girl! I was a woman wearing only a very thin robe, and I had my arms around his neck, and both of us stopped laughing. It was so quiet that I could hear my own heart pounding, and my silly face started burning like it always does when I get flustered! And his did, too! He put me down quick—like I was made of white-hot steel—and almost ran out of the room!

Since then, he's been—different. He talks to me a lot—mostly about the Bible, but he acts so awkward! Seems terrified to touch me!

And I have to put this down, too—I feel strange about him! I've loved Nathan so long, and then this Quaker minister holds me one time—and I have to put it down, that I'm just as nervous about *him* as he is about *me*!

I wish Nathan would come back! I'm so confused about *everything*.

Suddenly Laddie dropped her journal, ran to the bed and threw herself across it, her body shaken with sobs. She lay there weeping for a long time, not knowing why, unable to account for the sudden grief and fear that racked her. Finally, she got up, washed her face, and put the journal safely away.

"Laddie? Time to eat breakfast!"

The sound of Dan's voice came through the door, and her hands trembled as she reached out to open it. *Don't be a fool, Julie Sampson!* she thought fiercely. Then, lifting her head, she put a smile on her lips and left the room.

CHAPTER NINETEEN

NEW YEAR

★ ★ ★ ★

The last day of the year brought no relief from the numbing cold that had frozen the rivers and weighed the trees down with loads of glittering ice, but that did not deter those who had decided to see the new year in with a New Year's party.

"Thee missed Christmas," Dan said at breakfast, "which is what happens when thee takes up with Quakers—but I think we can safely go to the party tonight."

"Why, Daniel, thee has never gone to one of those parties before!" Sister Greene stopped pouring maple syrup over a pancake to stare at him in astonishment. "Some of the men will be drinking."

"Be a good chance to bear witness against it. I don't care for such things, but Julie would like it."

"Please—don't call me that!" Laddie said instantly, and then she was sorry for her sharpness and added, "It's just that if you use it to address me, Friend Daniel, you might let it slip in front of someone."

"Sorry." He shrugged and said, "Would thee like to go? I understand there's music and games."

"Wouldn't it be boring for you?"

"Oh, it won't hurt me—Laddie." He smiled and glanced at his mother. "Maybe thee should go as well, Sister Greene. Taste the fleshpots—see what they're like. No telling what thee has been missing all these years!"

"I believe I'll let thee do the tasting, son," his mother smiled. "One of us needs to keep in good standing with the Lord!"

Laddie had been bored, and as they walked over the snowy crust to the party, they laughed at a deer who scared itself by coming out of the woods face-to-face with them. It had jumped straight into the air, whirled and gone bounding away in that amazing graceful motion that is half run and half flight.

"Oh, beautiful!" Laddie cried out.

"It is. I can't shoot one to save my life." Dan gave her a smile and said, "Funny, I can kill a steer that I've raised quick enough—but I just can't shoot a deer."

"You would if you got hungry enough, I guess."

He nodded, then said, "This war—it's a bad thing for Friends."

"Bad for everyone."

"Yes—but some men—" he glanced at her and mentioned the name idly—"men like Nathan, why, they don't worry about killing in war."

She shook her head, and there was sadness in her voice. "Yes, he worries about it."

He considered that, then shrugged. "I suppose thee knows him—but with us, it's different. We don't believe in killing."

"Even to stay free, Friend Daniel?" She stopped and looked strangely at him. "You and your mother are the finest Christians I've ever known—but a lot of men are going to die for this new country. And—please don't be angry with me, Daniel—" She put her hand lightly on his arm, and despite her male garb and short hair, he thought he had never seen anything more lovely than her face framed against the snow. "You will enjoy the liberty that other men died to win for you."

"I'm not asking them to do it!" He was angry and turned away, but she caught up with him, again pulling at his arm.

"I don't fault you, Friend Daniel," she said, and then she smiled in the growing darkness, and added gently, "You and your mother are closer to God than anyone I've ever met. No matter what, I'll never forget you after we leave here."

He walked along beside her, shocked at the way her words had rocked him. *After we leave here.* She spoke no more of the war, and he only half heard what she said. He was thinking how empty the house would be without her. *Only a month—and she's the first thing I look for when I go into the house after being away!*

The party was in progress when they got to the schoolhouse. The desks were moved, and a line of tables along one wall was loaded with food and drinks. Over forty people were there, almost all of them young people, and over to one side several musicians were tuning up fiddles and dulcimers.

"Why, Friend Daniel!" A small well-formed girl in a pale blue dress left a group by the refreshment tables and came over to greet them. She had sparkling blue eyes and the most beautiful complexion Laddie had ever seen. "I can't *believe* you've actually come to a party—but it's about time." She turned to Laddie, her bright eyes taking in the neat uniform and the clearcut features. "And this is the soldier you've been keeping from all of us?"

"If thee would come to meeting, thee would have met our visitor. Laddie Smith, this is Faith Thomas. Faith, Sergeant Laddie Smith."

"You come with me, Sergeant," the girl said with a bewitching grin. She took Laddie's arm, saying with a toss of her head, "Friend Daniel, you go sit with the elders—Sergeant Smith is mine for the night."

Laddie had no choice, then, but to follow, and casting one helpless look at the minister, she soon found herself being introduced to a wide-eyed group of young people. The names came too fast for her, but she noted with a streak of humor, that the girls were impressed with the uniform; any presentable-looking young "male" creates a stir among the girls of a small community.

The young men were interested in the war, and they pressed close, asking about the army and the battles, but that stopped when the musicians struck up a tune, and Faith Thomas said, "You'll have to excuse us. Sergeant Smith has the first dance with me."

Laddie was stunned, but there was no time to protest, for the girl had stepped close, held out her hands, and suddenly they were dancing. Laddie had danced little, but she had observed much, and a strong natural sense of rhythm came to her aid, so that soon the two of them were moving easily across the floor.

What a flirt! Laddie thought as the young woman smiled and moved closer, whispering softly. Laddie was tall for a girl, and Faith had to look up, which gave her a chance to display her smile and her beautiful eyes to good effect. She said, "You're so young to be a soldier! And—I must say it, even if you think I'm too bold—you look so handsome in your uniform!"

Laddie said what the girl wanted to hear, and as they danced another dance, then a third, she began to be amused. They went to the table several times, and one tall young man attempted to claim Faith, but she said, "Oh, later, Hawk."

"Who is he?" Laddie asked. She looked over the girl's shoulder and got an angry stare from the young man that sobered her. "Is that your young man, Miss Thomas?"

"Oh, he thinks he is," she said with a smile; then she shrugged and said, "He's jealous—but he doesn't own me."

Dan had moved to one of the chairs by the wall, taking a seat by Ezra Parker, who had stared at him in amazement. "Preacher! I never thought I'd see the day."

Dan had grinned at him. "Thee won't come to meeting, Friend Ezra, so I've come to convert thee at a party."

"Well, fly right at it!" Ezra had a fondness for the young minister, and a deep respect that he gave to few men. He made no claims to be religious, but he had said often, *If I ever go get religion— it'll be the brand that young feller's got!* He sat there, and the two of them talked as the party went on. Several times Ezra excused himself, left the room and came back smelling strongly of alcohol, and most of the young men in the room did the same. As it grew late, Ezra brought Dan some apple cider, saying, "Don't reckon that'll hurt yore conscience, will it?"

"No. It's fine."

He spoke quietly, and Ezra followed his gaze to the couples on the floor. Then he said gently, "That young soldier—he was right sick, I hear?"

"Very ill, Friend Ezra."

The light blue eyes of Parker gleamed, and he said gently, "Well, he's apt to be a heap sicker 'fore long, Friend Daniel."

"What's that?" The Quaker stared at the tall, lanky man. "What does thee mean, Friend Ezra?"

"Wal, you know lots of Bible, Reverend, but you ain't too swift on young folks and partyin'—'course, you ain't had no practice. You ain't seen what's been shapin' up, have you?"

"I don't understand."

"Why, look at that!" Ezra pointed across the room and there was a wicked grin on his lips. "See my boy Hawk? You know he's been keeping company with Faith Thomas. He's already busted up two or three pretty strong young bucks when they come a'sniffin' around her! And looks like that leetle soldier is 'bout to have a dose of the same!"

Dan looked up with a startled expression, and one glimpse of what was happening across the room brought him to his feet, but quickly as he moved, he saw with dismay that it was too late.

Laddie had been amused by the situation, but after an hour of it, suddenly it had seemed silly. As the music ended, she moved with Faith to the table, and started to excuse herself so that she could go sit with Dan, but a rough hand suddenly seized her shoulder, whirling her about, and she found herself staring into the icy eyes of Hawk Parker. He had been drinking, and there was a raw rage in his sharp features.

Laddie struggled to free herself, but there was steel in the grip. "I guess you think that uniform makes you something special?" he said loudly.

"You're drunk, Hawk!" Faith said angrily.

"No, I ain't drunk—just want to let this here pretty boy of a soldier know he can't come around here and steal my girl!"

"Let go of me," Laddie said, struggling to free herself, and she caught a glimpse of Daniel hurrying across the room with alarm on his face. "I don't want . . . !"

"I don't gave a hoot *what* you want!" Hawk yelled, and with the speed of a striking snake he whipped his fist around and struck Laddie in the temple!

Laddie never saw the blow; bright lights flashed suddenly; then she sank into blackness, never feeling the hard floor that she fell back on.

Hawk stared at her with confusion in his eyes. He was very strong and accustomed to fighting strong men, so when his fist sent Laddie sailing back unconscious, he stood there confused by the cries of the women.

Daniel got there too late to stop the blow, but the sight of Laddie lying loosely on the floor with her face reddened by the blow triggered a black rage that he had not thought possible. His hand shot out, and he caught young Parker by the arm, whirling him around.

The liquor had befuddled the young man, and he was glad to see a strong man in front of him. He struck out at the minister wickedly, catching Daniel in the mouth with a tremendous blow, yelling loudly, "You keep out of this, preacher!"

He expected Greene to go down, for he had hit him as hard as he had ever hit any man, but the blow seemed to have no effect! The Quaker simply ignored it, and then he sent a terrible blow that smashed young Parker between the eyes. It drove the light out of his eyes, sent him hurtling back, and when he struck the wall, he was already unconscious.

The sound of Parker crashing into the wall brought sanity back to Greene, and he stood there horrified at the way the young man fell to the floor as if he were boneless.

There was a sudden silence, and then Ezra was beside him, looking down at the still form of his son. There was something like awe in his light blue eyes as he stared at the minister, and then he whistled softly and said, "Well—reckon you done the necessary, Friend Daniel—but I shore never thought any one feller could put the lights out on Hawk with one lick!"

"Is he—all right?" Daniel asked faintly. He felt sick and wanted to leave, for the shame of his violence seared his spirit.

"Oh, he'll have a sore head—but I would have whopped him with an axe handle anyway—for hittin' the soldier when he wasn't ready. He wasn't raised like that!"

Dan whirled and moved to where Laddie lay. He picked her up and carried her out of the room. Not one word was said until he passed through the door; then he heard the room humming wildly.

He was so shaken by the incident that he walked blindly down the lane. He had never struck another man in anger, and his mind swirled with the scene: he saw Parker's face as he reeled backward and hit the wall.

"Let me down!"

"What?" He realized that Laddie was struggling, trying to free herself. He set her down at once, and she swayed and held on to him for support. "I'd better carry thee."

"No! I—I'm just a little dizzy." She stood there, holding lightly to his arm, and they could hear a faint sound of music as the fiddles struck up again. She gave a rueful smile and touched her temple. "Never brought the New Year in like this," she said.

He looked soberly at her and shook his head. "Neither did I."

"What happened—after he hit me?"

He stood there silently, and the silver light of the moon high-lighted his features, painting his cheeks and throwing the hollows of his eyes into shadows. "I hit him," he said slowly, and he added after a moment, "I didn't know I had such capacity for hate in me."

She didn't move, but stood there looking up into his face, and what she saw was sorrow. She had heard enough of the Quaker faith to know how important it was for a man never to strike out, and she saw the raw pain in his eyes. "Dan—" she said softly, using his first name unconsciously, "don't feel bad. It was all my fault! I made a fool of myself!"

He didn't answer, and the silence grew heavy, broken only by the sound of a dog barking sharply at some unknown foe. Finally he shook his head and his shoulders drooped. "It's not your fault. I've been tried out before, Julie. All the time I was growing up there were boys who heard that Quakers would never fight—and more than once I've taken a blow in the face—and never hit back. Not until tonight."

She was shocked to see his firm lips tremble, and she whispered, "Dan—Dan, you were just trying to help me!" The pain he felt was so palpable it seemed to be ripping him apart, and she knew that the ugly incident had shaken his faith. She hated herself for provoking this doubt, and she reached up, not conscious of what she was doing, and put her hands on his cheeks. It was the gesture she would have used to comfort a child that had been terribly hurt, and she whispered, "Please don't grieve, Dan! I can't stand to see you hurt like this!"

Her eyes, he saw, were filled with tears, and her closeness suddenly shook him. He had long since mastered his emotions, never allowing them to rule any part of his life—but his guard was down. The raw rage that had exploded had left him empty, and now he was aware only that she was lovely in the moonlight, and that she cared for him.

There was no thought in what he did then. Her hands were warm on his cheeks, her lips half open, and she looked up with pleading in her luminous eyes. He put his arms around her, and she gave him one startled look, but she did not draw back. And when he slowly lowered his head and kissed her, there was a trembling innocence in her lips that shook him. Her hands on his cheeks were suddenly still, but as he held her closer, filled suddenly by a hunger, she put her hands behind his head pulling him close.

When he lifted his lips, she whispered, "Dan . . . !" and then she gave a sob and moved away from him.

The kiss had shaken him worse than the fight, and he stood there struggling with his thoughts. Finally he said, "We'd better get on."

"Yes!" She gave a half gasp, and they walked without speaking. The only sound was the crunch of snow under their feet.

Finally they got to the house, and he stopped her before they went inside. "I'm sorry—that I kissed thee."

She shook her head, and when she lifted her face, he saw the tears had made silver tracks down her cheeks. "I'm ashamed . . ." she whispered, and then she felt the deep sobs rising in her, and she whirled and dashed into the house.

He stood there, staring into the house, and finally he went to bed. But not to sleep. All night he lay there with his eyes open wide, staring blindly at the ceiling. He lived out the scene over and over, and the thought rose to torment him: *But she's another man's woman!* He tried to pray, but the heavens were brass. He cried out in agony to God, but his heart felt dead in his breast.

Laddie wept until there were no tears left, and then she sat staring vacantly out the window at the moonlit landscape. The very peaceful look of the fields and trees were a contrast to the storm that went on inside her.

When morning came, it was a relief to leave the bed, but breakfast was a quiet, strained affair. They looked at one another over the table, and though they smiled and spoke, Sister Greene went still, for she sensed that something had changed, and it brought fear into her heart for the first time she could remember.

They were almost finished with breakfast when there was the sound of a wagon stopping outside. Boots sounded on the steps; then a knock came. "I'll get it, Mother," Daniel said quickly. "I asked Edward Rollins to come by this morning." He moved to the door and opened it, but the greeting that was on his lips failed as he stared at the man who filled the doorway.

"Where's Laddie?"

Nathan's voice was sharp, and then he saw Laddie over Greene's shoulder, and shoved past the minister, his face breaking out into a wild grin. "Laddie! You're all right!" He reached out and grabbed her with a wild hug, not noticing her pale face. "I've been about crazy, Laddie, thinking you might be dead, and here you are, healthy as a bear!"

Laddie swayed as he shook her, and with a smile said, "Nathan—I'm so glad you're back!" Then she turned and looked straight into the eyes of Friend Daniel Greene, and said quietly, "Now I won't have to be a burden to these good people any more!"

CHAPTER TWENTY

THE GUNS OF TICONDEROGA

★　★　★　★

Henry Knox had not lost a pound, insofar as Laddie could tell. She had gone out with Nathan to the camp, and to her surprise, Daniel had accepted Nathan's invitation to go along. As they approached the site, Nathan pointed to where a group of soldiers were working on an enormous gun on a sled. "Look at the general, Laddie," Nathan grinned. "This trip has worn all the rest of us down to skin and bone—but Henry Knox stays fat as a seal!"

"Well, I see you didn't die, Sergeant!" Knox spotted them, and came to smile down at her. His cheeks were red and he was bristling with enormous energy. "By Harry, if I'd known you were going to live, I'd have had you at work rounding up oxen for me!" He gave a look at the worn animals that stood with lowered heads, eating listlessly.

"They're not going to make it, General," Nathan commented. "We've got to have some fresh animals. Maybe General Schuyler can help some more."

General Philip Schuyler, a wealthy New York State patrician, had secured eighty specially built sledges and eighty yoke of oxen. But thawed, mushy ground had hindered the caravan, and finally the snow came. The drivers had had to lash their beasts forward, the sledges slipping and sliding on runners. The capricious weather had tormented them, and now many of the oxen were useless.

"You've been here a month, Sergeant," Knox said. "We need

some patriots to help us get these guns to General Washington. Who would that be?"

Laddie said impulsively, "Captain Knox, I guess you're looking at him. This is Daniel Greene. I think he could get you some help—and he's a nephew of General Nathanael Greene."

"Well! Let me shake your hand, sir!" Knox beamed broadly and pumped Greene's hand vigorously. "Your relative is, in my opinion, the best of our young generals—I know that His Excellency shares that belief. Now, Mr. Greene, we must have oxen!" He gave the minister no chance to speak, but pulled him along the line of sleds, pointing out their virtues as if they were his beloved children. "We have fifty-eight pieces—four-pounders to twenty-four pounders. Beautiful, aren't they? And here is my favorite—" He rested his hand tenderly on one giant and said lovingly, "The men call this one The Old Sow—not a pretty name, but she'll do to shell the Redcoats out of Boston!"

"Sir—" Dan tried to speak, but Knox was a hard man to stop.

"We've brought this ordnance two hundred miles through the worst weather and over the worst roads in America! Everyone said it couldn't be done! And we have twenty-three crates of shot and one barrel of fine-quality British flints—all of which had to be freighted down Lake George in a collection of pirogues and batteaux."

"General Knox," Dan interrupted, "I—I must tell you—that I cannot help in this work." He gave Laddie a reproachful glance, then added, "I am one of the Friends—a Quaker, as you say. And it is against our doctrine to engage in war."

Knox stared at him steadily, then said, "General Greene is a Quaker, but he has thrown himself into the cause."

"I cannot answer for him—only for myself."

Knox's good-natured faced reddened. "I'm not asking you to *fight*—just to help with freighting equipment." He had spoken harshly, but he caught himself, and said reasonably, "Two groups have suffered much at the hands of the English—the Baptists and the Quakers. The Baptists have thrown themselves into this struggle, for they well know that if we do not free this land from English tyranny, they'll be crushed. Your own sect has been persecuted in England and in this country as well. If you will not fight, I call upon you to at least help in this way."

"I cannot do it." Daniel turned and walked away, his back stiff and unyielding.

Knox stared at him, then turned to Laddie. "I don't know what to make of such men!" Then he shrugged and said, "You two do the best you can. I've already sent to the villages close by, but we've *got* to have those oxen! If the British decide to attack, it may all be over!"

He stalked away, shouting furiously at a private who had let one of the cannon shift, then called back, "We'll take two days—have all the oxen you can ready by then. Promise them anything—but get them here!"

"I'll get my things," Laddie said, turning to go, but Nathan stopped her. There was a gleam in his light blue eyes and a quirk of humor turned the corners of his generous mouth upward.

"No, you stay there, Laddie. I'll scout around by myself—but you can do more good where you are. I want you to make that Quaker fight! Somehow there's got to be a way to make a patriot out of Friend Daniel Greene, and I want you to find it!"

> January 2, 1776
> I've tried to talk to Dan about helping us get the guns to Boston, but he won't do it. Nathan says that the people here won't volunteer, but he said if Dan would help, others would follow. Dan's such a good man—but stubborn!

Laddie stared at the words she'd just written despondently; then she gritted her teeth and began to write again, and there was a grim determination in her face.

> I think I know why Dan won't help, and it has nothing to do with his religion. Ever since Nathan came back, Dan's hated me! He thinks that Nathan and I are lovers, and he's jealous! I've suspected for weeks that he has feelings for me, and when he kissed me after the fight, he almost came out and said he loved me. But he thinks I'm bad!
> I'm going to tell him the truth! And I have to be honest about this, hard as it is—I think it might make Dan change his mind about helping with the guns if he knew the truth—but it's more than that. When he kissed me, I felt—oh, I don't know *how* I felt! But I do know that if I wasn't in love with Nathan, I'd never find a man that I'd be more likely to love than Dan!

She laid down the pen, carefully closed the journal, and put it away. It was early, but she knew that Dan and his mother took that time of the day to read the Bible and pray. She found them both in the small kitchen and said abruptly, "I have something to tell you both." They looked up, startled, and Laddie felt her face flush, but plunged ahead, "Last year my father died and left me in the charge of my uncle, Aaron Sampson . . ."

They sat there staring at her as she narrated her history, including the parts about Caleb's death, as well as revealing Nathan's love for Abigail Howland. Finally she said, "It's been hard, and I should have told you this a long time ago. You've been so good to me—even though you both thought I was a lewd woman living with soldiers."

It was Dan's turn to grow red, and he glanced at his mother. "I—I can't deny it," he said quietly. Then he looked up with a sudden smile that lighted his face, and the load that had burdened him seemed to roll away. "Thank thee for telling us, Laddie," he said.

"I knew in my spirit thee were not evil," Sister Greene said, and she rose to come over and embrace Laddie. She held her for a long moment, and when she drew back there were tears in her eyes. "I don't fault thee for anything, daughter. God has preserved thee in this strange way."

She turned and left the room abruptly, and Dan said in surprise, "Mother doesn't show her feelings much. She's been more concerned about thee than I thought. Even more than—"

"More than thee?" Laddie smiled quietly.

"That's what I was going to say." He had risen and came to stand beside her. Looking into her clear eyes, he seemed to have no words, and she saw the struggle that was going on inside him.

I must not hurt this man, she thought instantly, and as if he had discerned that thought, he said, "I've always been a pretty easy-going chap, Laddie—never had much to do with women. Matter of fact, I've had an idea that God wanted me to give my life completely to Him—and that was fine with me. But thee has changed all that," he finished with a light of wonder coming to his warm brown eyes, and he reached out and took her hand, looking at it as if he had found some strange and wonderful thing.

"Dan . . . !"

She spoke with a breathless quality in her voice, but he paid no heed. He looked directly at her and said evenly, as if he were commenting on the weather: "I love thee, Julie Sampson."

"You—you mustn't say that!" she whispered. His words set up an agitation in her heart, and she tried to turn away to hide her face, but he held her fast.

"I know thee love Nathan Winslow," he said quietly. "But he doesn't love thee, does he?"

"No! But he doesn't know I'm a woman!"

"And we both know why thee won't tell him, don't we?"

"I—don't know what you mean!"

"Thee won't tell him because thee knows thee'll lose him, Julie," he said remorselessly. "Thee know he'll hate thee for what thee've done to him. No man likes to be deceived, and even though thee *had* to do it, it'll make him feel like a fool!"

She pulled away from him, and the truth of his words stabbed her. She had said the same thing to herself a hundred times, had felt blind rage when she thought of Abigail in Nathan's arms—but as long as the words were unspoken, somehow she could still dream that he was hers.

Now she nodded slowly, and she looked at him steadily, saying, "I—I know all that—but I'll never let him know."

"Thee should," he insisted. Then he shrugged; suddenly a surprising grin touched his lips. "Well, one good thing will come out of all this."

"What's that?" she asked in surprise.

"I'll help with the guns." He smiled more broadly at her expression and said, "Thee is not the only one who is self-deceived, Julie. I've been saying that I wouldn't help because it went against my doctrine, but I knew all the time, it was really because I was jealous of Winslow."

"Oh, Dan, we're a couple of fools!" She looked at him and the grief in her face was replaced by an anxiety, and she put her hand lightly on his arm. "I—don't want to hurt you. I'm in love with Nathan."

He shook his head, a stubbornness in his face as he answered, "Thee thinks so, Julie—and no wonder. A young girl is rescued by a tall handsome young man in a romantic fairy-tale sort of affair—why, it would be more surprising if thee *didn't* have an infatuation for him!" Then he reached out and before she could stop him, he kissed her lightly, and smiled as her eyes widened. "But when thee kissed me that night, Julie, thee was not thinking of Nathan Winslow—but of Daniel Greene!"

"Why . . . !"

"Just give a little time, Julie," he said, and though there was a smile on his lips, she saw that he was deadly serious. "I'm coming with thee to Boston, and I'm staying so close that one of these days thee will fall in love with me."

She shook her head, but there was only wonder in her voice as she said quietly, "I don't think it will work—but Knox will be happy about the oxen."

She was right about that, for when the morning dawned for the caravan to leave, Knox was beaming with admiration at the fine array of animals that had been secured.

"By Harry, Friend Greene . . . !" he exclaimed as he looked at the train, all ready to pull out, manned by fresh, strong animals, "You may be a Quaker, but you've done more for this war by helping get these guns to Boston than you'll ever know!"

"I've had to bend my doctrine, Captain Knox," Greene admitted with a shrug.

"What will your fellow Quakers say about this?" Knox asked.

"They've already said it, I'm afraid." He reached into his pocket and pulled a paper out. Unfolding it, he said, "This is an affirmation of the traditional Quaker stand on war. It's just been sent out to all Friends." He read from the paper, his voice steady:

> It is our judgment that such who make religious profession with us, and do either openly or by connivance, pay any fine, penalty, or tax, in lieu of their personal services for carrying on war; or who do consent to, and allow their children, apprentices, or servants to act therein, do thereby violate our Christian testimony, and by so doing manifest that they are not in religious fellowship with us.

Knox stared at him. "Does that mean they're kicking you out?"

"That's about it, to put the matter bluntly."

Nathan had been listening to all this, and he suddenly grinned, saying, "Well, Friend Greene, you can always find a bunk with us! We can use a good man, eh, Laddie?"

Laddie smiled and nodded, but then Nathan added, "Laddie claims I snore too loud, so I reckon you two will have to share the blankets on the way to Boston. That all right with you?"

"I think it would be fine, Friend Nathan," Dan said with a smooth expression. What does *thee* think, Friend Laddie?"

But Sergeant Smith had turned and walked away abruptly with a scowl.

Nathan apologized for Laddie's behavior. "He's a strange

youngster, Dan," he said regretfully. "I've tried to toughen him up, but he's so blasted *sensitive!*" He clapped the other on the shoulder and grinned. "Well, we'll make a man out of Laddie Smith, won't we, Friend?"

The broad-shouldered Quaker looked at Nathan with a gleam in his eyes.

"Such a task may be harder than thee thinks, Friend Winslow!"

CHAPTER TWENTY-ONE

MESSAGE FROM BOSTON

★ ★ ★ ★

General Gage, out of favor in England because of the massacre at Bunker Hill, had been replaced by Sir William Howe, a man who fought and wenched doggedly. In November he had received orders from London to give up Boston and move south to New York, but he could not obtain the shipping to evacuate his men, so he settled back to stay until spring, occupying his time with a certain Mrs. Loring, the wife of his Commissary of Prisoners.

Washington created a small navy of privateers who darted in and out of the rocky harbors they knew so well. They nipped at the slow British merchantmen who came with supplies, and much of the food that did arrive was rotten. Captain John Manley of the schooner *Lee* scored a major coup when he took the British brigantine *Nancy* with her cargo of 2,000 muskets, 7,000 cannon balls, 10,500 flints, and a huge 13-inch mortar, which Israel Putnam christened "The Congress" by smashing a bottle of rum over its gaping muzzle.

Cut off by land and throttled by sea, the British made do with what they had. The Old North Church came down for firewood, as did the Liberty Tree, an arching elm under which Sam Adams and his rowdies had often met. Governor Winthrop's 100-year-old home in the middle of town went to the flames.

To fight boredom, if not the revolution, the British held elegant balls, and Abigail missed none of them. She was usually accompanied by Nathan's old rival, Paul Winslow, and the two of them arrived at Faneuel Hall one evening to attend a farce written by General John Burgoyne. Known to most as Gentleman Johnnie, Burgoyne had arrived in March with Howe and General Henry Clinton and declared, "What! Ten thousand peasants keeping five thousand of the King's men captive? Well, let *us* in and we'll soon make elbow room!" He was later to be called "General Elbow Room" by the troops for this remark.

But now Howe was gambling and gamboling with Mrs. Loring, so Burgoyne, a man of great concern for his men, had concocted the play for their entertainment. Paul led Abigail through the shouting ribald crowd, composed mostly of soldiers accompanied by many painted women, to a seat down close to the front.

"Noisy, aren't they?" He had to speak loudly to make himself heard, and added, "If they can fight like they can play, the rebels are doomed."

Abigail looked around and then smiled at Paul. "So far they haven't done much but get butchered at Bunker Hill and tear our town up. If Father hadn't been a faithful subject, they would have burned our house down."

"Ours too, I suppose," Paul shrugged. The British troops, frustrated with the remaining Bostonians who were thought to be signaling the rebels with burning gunpowder, had burned and pillaged the property of any American who could not prove his loyalty to the Crown.

Paul thought about it, then said, "It would be bad for us if the rebels came back. Some of the patriots who'd had their houses burned would be sure to come calling on every one of us who've stayed loyal to the King."

She stared at him with troubled eyes. "But—there's no chance of that, surely? They're just a rabble!"

"I hope you're right, sweetheart," Paul said. He had a dark streak of fatalism running through him, and he added as the curtain went up, "I'd hate to be at the mercy of our rebel 'neighbors.' I really think they'd be more dangerous to us than the soldiers in the army."

She turned to watch the play, but he saw that she had been shaken by the idea that she and her family might be on the losing side. The farce was taken from a play called *Maid of Oaks*, written by Burgoyne and produced in London by David Garrick. This humbler Boston production starred a caricature of Washington in a huge wig and rusty sword. The soldiers and their women roared with laughter at the farce, calling out lewd suggestions loudly, but as the play was nearly over, a sentry burst into the room crying out: "Turn out! Turn out! They are hard at it, hammer and tongs!"

The audience, thinking this was part of the play, clapped prodigiously, but the sentry yelled, "What the devil are ye about? The rebels are raiding Charles Town Neck, I tell you!"

There was a wild scramble then, as the officers and men saw that the threat was genuine, and Paul led Abigail through an almost empty hall to the carriage. On the way home, she said in a frightened voice, "Paul, can we lose?"

"No, not the war," he said moodily. "But we can lose here. If the rebels ever find out how weak we are—or if they ever get any cannon on those hills up there, it's all over."

"But—what will we *do*?"

"Get away, if we can, to England. But we'll lose everything. I talked with Father about it last week. He says there's no hope except maybe in Adam."

"Adam?"

"Nathan's father," he said with a strange smile at her. "Didn't Nathan ever tell you our family history?"

"No."

"He's more noble than I would have been. I didn't think your father would say anything, but I thought Nathan might."

"What's my father got to do with it?"

He chuckled and said, "Why your father and mine made a valiant stab at diddling Nathan's father out of his share of the family business years ago. Adam found out about it and just about shook my father's teeth out until Dad repented."

"My father never said a word!"

"Not too proud of that part of his life, I should think." Suddenly he laughed and clapped his thigh. "By George, it's funny now that I think of it! Here we've thrown our lots in with the British—sure that these rebels were going to lose. If the British win, Nathan and his father would be paupers and we'd be rich. Now, if Washington comes back with his army, Nathan and his family will be on top, and if we're not hanged for being traitors, we'll be poor as church mice." He laughed again, then gave her a sudden hard glance. "I think about this time you're having second thoughts about choosing me instead of Nathan, aren't you, sweetheart?"

"Don't be silly," she said quickly. But she was quiet on the ride home, and when he kissed her good night, she was preoccupied.

"May I come up?"

"Not tonight, Paul. I'm tired."

He looked at her cynically, then left immediately, but she tossed and turned long that night, unable to sleep. Finally she thought, *Nathan wouldn't let me suffer. He may be hurt, but he still loves me!* Then she smiled, stretched luxuriously, and felt much better.

Adam and Molly made their way through Cambridge, noting that most of the soldiers who filled the town had little in the way of uniforms. There were some exceptions, of course. The Rhode Islanders were there with their neat tents, each equipped with its own awning. The Twenty-first Massachusetts, men from Marblehead, had given up their occupations as shipwrights and fishermen, but not their seafaring heritage. Molly said quietly as they passed by, "How neat they look!"

Adam glanced at the troops, dressed in trim blue seacloth jackets and loose white sailor's trousers. "Look funny off a ship, don't they now? Make our boys look pretty sloppy."

He was now Captain Winslow of the Virginia Rangers—a rank which he had not wanted, but which General Washington had insisted on, and Molly was proud of him. She said as they approached the house that Washington used for a headquarters, "Our men are so different from the others!"

That was true. The Virginia riflemen had little in common with the other troops. They were tall, violent men with skins the color of tanned leather, and under Adam's command, they had marched seven hundred miles in three weeks, arriving in Boston with no one ill and no deserters.

The Virginians wore voluminous white hunting shirts and round, broad-brimmed caps with dangling fur tails. Their garb alone would have made them a target for attention, but their behavior provoked the other troops even more. They automatically pushed aside anyone who got in their way, and their height and obvious toughness awed most of the troops. They carried guns much longer and narrower than the familiar smoothbore muskets— and they won most of the loose money in camp by challenging all comers to shooting contests and winning every time—shattering bottles at three hundred yards. The Brown Bess would not even *carry* half that distance!

They fought anyone—kicking, biting, gouging out eyes—and if no stranger offered himself, they fought each other. Washington had said when giving Adam his commission, "It'll have to be you, Winslow. The officer of these men will have to be as tough as they are!"

They reached the house, and while the guard went inside to give his name, Adam said, "I'm glad you're here, Molly. This would be a lonesome place for me without you."

She smiled at him, a coquettish look in her eyes as she pinched his arm. "You think I'd let a good-looking thing like you loose in a place like this?"

"Not much danger," he grinned. "I wonder what General Washington wants?"

They did not have to wait long, for the door opened and Washington himself stepped outside, wearing a spotless uniform. Adam noted instantly that the air of expectancy he had come to know in this leader was obviously missing. The pressure had been enormous, and only a few days earlier he had written to his aide Joseph Reed:

> I have often thought how much happier I should have been
> if, instead of accepting a command under such circumstances, I
> had taken my musket on my shoulder and entered the ranks; or
> if I could have justified the measure to posterity and my own
> conscience, had retired to the back country and lived in a wig-
> wam.

But now the tall Virginian had a buoyancy in his walk, and his eyes shone as he said, "Captain Winslow—Mrs. Winslow, you are prompt."

"Yes, sir," Adam nodded. "I thought the matter might be urgent from the sound of your message."

"So it is," Washington smiled. "Mrs. Winslow, would you be pleased to ride in my carriage while I ride with your husband? It's only a short journey, but this weather is still sharp."

Adam put Molly into the carriage, then mounted a horse provided by an aide. As Washington wheeled his own horse, a magnificent white stallion, Adam thought, *How this man can ride a horse!* As they made their way out of Cambridge, heading for Boston, Washington chatted about small things, which left Adam mystified.

He didn't need me to go for a ride with him!

Then when they reached the turnpike, Washington pulled up and waved toward a small camp set off the road. "I think you'll be interested in this, Captain."

Adam knew at once what it was and exclaimed, "Knox made it with the guns!"

"Thank God, he did!" Washington said, and then he spurred his horse forward. They reached the camp, and as Adam swung down and helped Molly out of the carriage, Knox came out of a tent and almost ran to meet his commander.

Knox had a dramatic streak in him, and he drew himself up to his full height, saluted and said in a full voice, "Your Excellency— the mission is accomplished! Now the cause of liberty is safe!"

Washington laughed delightedly and said, "Henry, you are a little premature, but you have my thanks—indeed, the whole country owes you much, *Colonel* Knox!"

Knox's eyes flew open at his sudden promotion, and for once the huge bookseller was speechless. Then Washington said, "Now, you and I will have a talk on how to best use these little beauties of yours—and Captain and Mrs. Winslow here would like to see their son."

"Of course, General!" Knox said, and looking around he saw Nathan waiting at a respectful distance. "Come here at once—*Sergeant* Winslow!" He turned to Adam and Molly and said with a broad smile, "I'd make him a lieutenant if I could, sir! He and that young friend of his saved our necks on this trip!"

He turned to lead Washington into the tent, and Nathan came up to be embraced by his mother. "You're so *thin!*" she exclaimed.

"Been eating the bark off the trees," he said, looking down at her; then with a smile, he said, "Do I salute you, Captain Winslow?"

Adam looked up at his tall son and thought of the dark moods he'd had in the months since the war had started. There had been a wall between the two of them, and he hated it worse than he'd hated anything in his life. So in full view of the camp, he stepped forward and opened his arms. "Later, you can salute—but I'm so glad to see you—my son!"

Nathan found himself being held tightly by his father's iron-hard blacksmith arms, and as he returned the embrace, his eyes burned and he said, "I—I'm glad . . . !" and then he could say no more.

When Adam stepped back, there was a suspicious moisture in his own eyes and he said briskly, "Well, Sergeant, I believe I have it in my authority to take you into town and buy you a meal."

"And I want Laddie, too," Molly said. "I've thought about him so often."

Nathan's face changed, and Molly thought, *They've had a fight,* but he said, "He'll be glad to see you both. Talks about you a lot—but you'll probably have to take his buddy along. We picked him up on the trail and he and Laddie have been thick as thieves."

"Bring him along, son," Adam said quickly, and when Nathan went along the line of wagons to find Laddie, he said, "You notice something there?"

"Yes. Nathan could never hide his feelings—like you can."

"Me? You read me like a big-print Bible," Adam grinned. "But this new friend of Laddie's—I don't think Nathan cares much for him."

"Well, it may be some rough soldier leading the boy astray," Molly said. "But Nathan was always pretty possessive—like me." She gave him a swift look and said quietly, "I'm glad you did that—hugged him. He needs you, Adam."

"I guess I'm not very loving, Molly."

"Oh—you have your moments, Captain Winslow!" She laughed in delight as his face suddenly grew red, and said gently, "Let's not mention this girl he was seeing, Adam. Let him bring it up if he wants to."

Nathan returned with Laddie, and she was delighted to see them both. "And this is Friend Daniel Greene," she said, and Molly did not miss the admiration in Laddie's clear eyes as she introduced the handsome man in plain black clothes.

The five of them rode back to Cambridge crowded into the carriage, and the full story of the heroic trip after the guns poured out. The Quaker said almost nothing, but Laddie finally added, "If Friend Daniel hadn't rounded up all those oxen, I guess we'd still be perched on the bank of the Hudson River!"

"I didn't do all that much." He had a deep musical voice, Molly noted, and later when they got to the hotel where she and Adam had a room, they left the three long enough to go and clean up before meeting them for a meal.

"Well, what did you think of Friend Greene?" Adam asked at once.

"It's a good thing I'm an old married woman," she answered as she brushed her glossy hair back. "That Quaker is too handsome! What a shame it's all wasted on a preacher who doesn't need all those good looks."

"He *is* fine looking," Adam admitted. "And a husky fellow as well." He stared at her, admiring her long hair, then said, "I thought Quakers were against war and all that. Surprises me that he helped Knox out. But—he's not what we thought, is he? I mean, he's not a drinking or wenching man—likely to corrupt Laddie?"

"No, he'll not do that, I think." She said in a slow voice, then rose and said, "Let's go eat. I want to hear more about the trip."

For the next three days, Washington and Knox had their heads together, and the men were given permission to go into town often. There was little for Adam to do, and he said, "I know Washington—he's up to something. When it breaks, I don't reckon any of us will have any time for fun—so we better enjoy it."

It was a good time for Molly; she had seen little of Adam when he'd been so busy getting the Rangers organized, and the two of them spent a great deal of time with Nathan. They ate together every night, and Laddie was always included, as was the young Quaker.

They laughed a great deal, but Molly saw that beneath the surface, all three of the young people were somehow ill at ease. She said nothing to Adam, but finally on the third night, something happened that interrupted their holiday.

They were eating at an inn, and Adam was debating some theological point with Greene. The two had become good friends, differing on small matters of doctrine, but each sensing the goodness of the other. A young man in civilian clothes came in and asked, "Mr. Nathan Winslow?"

Nathan nodded, took the note he presented, and read it. The messenger, a tall young man still in his teens, waited, and finally Nathan looked up and asked, "Can you take an answer?"

"Yes, sir."

Nathan got up and went to the proprietor, and borrowing a quill, scratched a note on the back of the one he'd just received. He returned to the table, gave it to the messenger, who said, "I'll see she gets it, sir," and left.

The rest of them had tried not to appear curious, but Laddie blurted out, "It's Abigail, isn't it?"

Nathan flushed and said, "I'll have to be gone for a little while. Father, could you get me a pass for two days?"

Laddie stared at him, her face pale, and she turned to Adam. "Don't do it! He nearly got hanged last time he went to see that woman!"

"Nathan, it's too dangerous to go into Boston," Adam said quietly. "If you'll just wait a few days, I suspect you can walk in with the rest of us."

"I can't wait, sir," Nathan replied, his lips pale. "I have to go."

Adam stared at him, then nodded heavily. "I'll get you a pass. Come along."

"You are a bloody fool, Nathan Winslow!" Laddie cried out, and there was such anger in her that the words were blurred.

Molly watched as Nathan stared at Laddie. "I have to do it, Laddie." Then he turned and followed his father out of the room.

Molly got up and said abruptly, "Laddie, would you come with me? Excuse us please, Mr. Greene."

"Of course." Greene rose and watched Laddie follow Mrs. Winslow out of the inn, then sat there for a long time, staring at the table. He was thinking, *Winslow's a fool!—but then, so am I!*

Laddie followed Nathan's mother blindly out of the inn and down the street. She wanted to scream, but bit her lips, and by the time she and Molly entered the hotel room, Laddie was in control.

Molly took off her coat and went to look out the window. She stood there so long that Laddie grew nervous, saying finally, "What was it you wanted to talk to me about, Mrs. Winslow?"

Molly Winslow turned from the window and came to stand directly before her. Looking into her eyes, she said, "I wanted to ask you about Nathan . . ."

She paused and Laddie asked quickly, "Yes? What about him?"

"I wanted to ask you, Laddie—are you in love with him—as Daniel Greene is in love with you?"

The room grew still, the silence broken only by the sound of a soldier singing outside, and then Laddie fell into Molly's arms, crying as if her heart would break: "I don't know! I don't know! Oh, I'm so mixed up! Help me!"

Molly stood there holding the shaking body of the girl in her arms, praying, *God help us all!*

CHAPTER TWENTY-TWO

AT THE RED LION

★　★　★　★

"When did you find out about me?"

Molly had waited, holding the weeping girl until finally the sobs had ceased. She gave Laddie a handkerchief and watched silently as the girl wiped her face, then said with a small smile, "When you left Virginia, Laddie."

"What?"

"I suspected it for a time—but when I made you hug me just before you left—that made me sure." She sighed and reached out to touch a tear-stained cheek. "Men are so blind!" she snorted with a crisp shake of her head. "See just what they expect to see! Oh, I know you put on around men, stomp and swing your arms and such. But I think when you were with me, you forgot your act. You remember when you helped me cook supper? Child, there's not a man in the world who could peel a potato or move around as daintily as you did! The thought came to me, and so I watched you. Then when you were leaving, I hugged you real tight." Her lips turned up, and there was a gleam in her eyes as she said, "I've not had much experience hugging men, but I *knew* it was no man I was hugging!"

"Oh, Mrs. Winslow, I'm so miserable!"

"Well, that Quaker, *he* knows you're not a man," Molly said. "He hasn't taken his eyes off you. And you've kept Nathan fooled—and now you're in love with him—and Friend Daniel

Greene is in love with you! Sounds like a real bad play or book, doesn't it? What's your name?"

"Julie Sampson." She looked up and said, "Can I tell you all of it?"

"Of course, Julie." Molly sat there, listening to the girl, and when all was told, she smiled and said, "I guess you've got two mothers running scared—Sister Greene and me."

"Oh, you don't have to worry! Nathan's nutty over that Howland woman! He's put his head in a noose *twice* for her—and she doesn't give a tuppence for him!"

"You don't know that."

"I *do*!" Laddie shook her head violently, and paced the floor like a caged animal. "Why, if she cared *anything* about him, she'd not ask him to stick his head into the lion's jaws, would she?"

"Women have a lot of power over men, child," Molly said thoughtfully. "If he loves this woman, he'll go to her, no matter what it costs."

"I wish she were *dead*!"

"You haven't answered my question," Molly said. "Are you in love with Nathan?"

"Why, how could I be? He doesn't even know I'm a girl!"

"I didn't ask you how *he* felt, Julie—I asked if you loved *him*."

"I—I don't know. I thought I did—but then I met Daniel—and he treats me like a woman—and he does care for me."

"I see." Molly looked long into the eyes of the girl, then said, "Nathan will have to know."

"No!"

"Yes, for your own sake, and for his."

"He'll hate me!"

"That may be—but he'll never love you, will he?—not until he knows you're there to be loved—that you're not a boy but a lovely woman."

Laddie began to tremble, and as she looked up, her enormous eyes and soft lips trembling, Molly thought, *Nathan is my son, but he must be the blindest man on earth! This lovely child—and he never saw!* But she said, "You did what you had to do, child, to escape your uncle. But you're not alone now. No matter what Nathan feels, Adam and I will help you—and besides, I think from what I saw of Friend Daniel Greene, it would take a pretty powerful man to shake him loose from you!"

Laddie shook her head, then moaned, "Oh, if Nathan only hadn't gone to Boston! When he got taken before, I nearly died!"

"We'll have to pray, Julie," Molly said. "Do you think God answers prayer?"

"Oh, I know He does!"

"Then we'll pray that he'll be safe—and that God will open his eyes. He's lost his way, Julie," she stated quietly. "God may have to put him flat on his back with no way to turn before he finds his way."

Nathan,
    I must see you. Please meet me at the old Red Lion Inn on the turnpike. I will be there tonight at seven. Don't come to the house. It's too dangerous.

Sitting outside the ancient inn that shed yellow bars of light from its windows, Nathan thought of the note. As he waited in the darkness, he pictured the words that were burned across his brain. There was no signature, but he knew the writing. He had brought along a brace of pistols and kept to the back roads to avoid patrols. After darkness fell, he rode to the inn, let a hostler take his horse, then kept to the shadows of the stable, watching the road.

It was not more than thirty minutes after seven when a closed carriage drew up, and Nathan's eyes picked out the driver—the same young man who had brought the message. He pulled the team to a stop, leaned down and said something, then nodded and got down. He hitched the team and walked at a leisurely pace into The Red Lion Inn.

For five minutes, Nathan stood there in the darkness, wary, suspecting a trap, but nothing changed and he moved to the window and saw the driver at a table, settled down with a stein of beer.

Cautiously he moved to the coach and peered inside. He could see nothing, so he put his hand on the pistol in his belt and whispered softly, "Abigail?"

"Nathan!" The door opened, and he quickly stepped up and practically fell into Abigail's arms! She clutched him, pulling his head down, and her soft lips met his in a long kiss.

"Abigail, what's the matter?" he asked urgently when she drew back. "I've had a bad time—thinking all kinds of things."

She took his hand and held it to her cheek, then kissed the back of it, saying, "That's sweet, Nathan! But does there have to be something *wrong*? Can't it be that I just long to be with you?"

He thought of the note, and realized that it actually said nothing about her being in trouble. "I guess I just assumed you needed me."

Her perfume was heady, and she turned toward him and put her arms around his neck. The rounded softness of her body disturbed him, and her breath was sweet as she whispered, "Nathan, when I heard you were off on a dangerous mission and might not come back, I almost lost my mind!" He wondered how she knew about the mission, but he was so overcome by her embrace that he could not follow the thought.

The dim light from a crescent moon turned the snow silver and the yellow light from the lanterns on the front of The Red Lion were reflected in her eyes, which he could now see faintly.

He looked at her face, and the touch of her hands on his face distracted him. He sat there holding her, and her perfume seemed to drug his senses. He whispered hoarsely, "Abigail—I've thought about you every day."

"And I've thought of you every day, too, sweet—and every night!" She pulled him closer, and her lips brushed his cheek as she whispered, "I know you must think I'm shameless, but I've been so afraid!"

"But—I thought you and Paul . . . ?"

"Oh, Nathan, you know women are vulnerable! Paul is an attractive man, and I enjoy his company—but I didn't dream you'd let that frighten you off."

He felt suddenly weak and drew back, and then he said dryly, "Well, I wasn't exactly *frightened* off, Abigail. I was dragged off by a troop of dragoons—almost to the gallows!"

"I know, sweet, I know! It must have been awful!"

He laughed and said, "Well, I've enjoyed a few things more than waiting to be hanged."

"I had a pass from General Gage to see you—but I think that friend of yours took it!"

"He certainly did!" Nathan remembered again how he had felt when Laddie had come to him in prison, and he said slowly, "He saved my life, Abigail."

"Oh, you wouldn't have been executed," she said quickly. "Father had it all arranged with the general to get you pardoned—but you escaped before we could get there."

"Sorry to spoil your plan," Nathan said with a smile. "But at the time it seemed a little frivolous to hang around until the execution."

"It's so terrible! Let's don't even *think* about it, dear!" She leaned against him, her soft body sending involuntary signals along his nerves. "You're not angry with me, are you?"

"No, of course not."

"I knew you wouldn't be—but I was afraid that you'd never come back. That's why I sent for you."

"Does anyone know you're here?"

"Just Justin, the driver—and he wouldn't tell anyone."

He sat there thinking; then he said, "It's a bad time for us, isn't it?"

"Oh, I get so tired of it all—but it can't last forever, can it, Nathan?"

"It can last longer than I'd like—and it can be unpleasant for you."

"Father says we ought to leave—to go to New York—but Paul's father says it would be just as bad for loyalists there."

"The only safe place would be England, Abigail—or maybe Canada. Father is worried about Uncle Charles. He told him to leave at once for Canada, but he said he was too old to leave his home."

"Oh, Nathan, Father isn't well, and I'm so afraid! I don't know anything about politics—and everyone is saying that if Washington comes in with his army, we'll all be slaughtered!"

He laughed and put his arm around her. She was trembling and her weakness, as much as her beauty, stirred him deep inside, and he said, "You won't be slaughtered, Abigail."

"Nathan, you'll take care of me?"

She lifted her face, and her eyes had a golden gleam, the reflection of the lantern light, and he could no more help kissing her than he could help living. Her lips were soft, but they moved under his hungrily, and her arms drew him frantically closer, until finally he drew back, saying roughly, "Abigail—don't push me too far."

"I love you, Nathan," she whispered. "I know I've been too bold—but I—I was afraid I'd lost you!"

He sat there and for an hour they talked, and finally she said, "I've got to get home before I'm missed." They had embraced several times, and she pushed at her hair, laughing, "Nathan, when will I see you again?"

"It will be hard to arrange," he said, then added, "I'll be here again in three nights—that's as soon as I can get away."

"Oh, darling!" she breathed, and lifted her face for a final kiss. "That's so far away!"

Nathan thought of the guns they'd brought and said quickly, "If there's an attack on the town, you must get away at once, you and your family."

"But—what if we can't get out of town?"

"I don't think there'll be any trouble. General Washington has built discipline into the troops."

"But—everyone says that we'll be attacked by the patriots!" she said.

"If the city falls, I'll be there as soon as the lines are open. Stay in the house, and I'll get an order from headquarters giving you some protection."

"Oh, Nathan, I knew you'd take care of me!" She gave herself to him in one final embrace, then said, "Go tell Justin I'm ready, will you, sweet?"

He stepped out, went to the inn, and caught the eye of the driver. As he stood up, Nathan walked quickly to the barn, and he heard the team gallop out of town as he took his horse from the hostler.

The roads as he came nearer Cambridge were closely watched, and he had to show his pass to three patrols. He thought of what he'd said to Abigail about leaving town, and thought, *Too late— they'll never get through!*

When he got back to town, he went to bed, but as the dawn came, he got up without having slept. He ate breakfast, then was greeted by his father, who found him drinking a last cup of coffee.

"Glad you're back," Adam said. He sat down and poured himself a cup of the strong brew. "None of my business, son, but did you get your business done?"

"Yes, sir. But if I hadn't had that pass you got for me, it would have been impossible. The roads are crawling with our guards." He looked around and saw through the window of the mess shack that men were everywhere, running and calling urgently to each other. "What's going on?"

Adam smiled at him, sipped his coffee, then said, "Washington and Knox—they've decided to use those guns you brought back."

"When?"

The question came so sharply that Adam blinked. Then he said, "Well, it'll take a little doing, Nathan. If the British *see* us fortifying those heights, they'll come out and fight. We'll have to do it without their knowing it."

"Don't see how."

"It's strange, son, but I think God has moved into this thing." A light touched his father's eyes, and he leaned forward and said in a lively tone, "A young engineer named Rufus Putnam was just passing by General Heath's quarters, and he had to wait for the general. There were some old books there, and he spied a book on field engineering. He noticed in the book a diagram and a description of something called a 'chandelier'—which is a piece of French equipment new to him. It's a sectional wooden framework, they tell me, designed to hold in place 'fascines,' which is French for large, tightly-bound bundles of sticks. And, son, when you join these chandeliers together, you get a barrier as effective as a trench. Young Putnam told Heath, who told Washington, and the order's out to make hundreds of these things."

"You think they'll work?"

Adam shrugged and leaned back, his eyes dim with memory. "In the French and Indian War, I saw British troops stopped by heavy brush and timber—the general was there and saw it, too. These things are a heap tougher than any brush you ever saw— and if the Redcoats charge them—they'll be knocked down by our rifles!"

"It'll take a while, won't it, to build those things?"

"Not long as you might think. We've got a lot of men with nothing to do, and most of them are experts with an axe. Guess we'll be waiting for the right weather more than anything. Got to have a nice ground mist covering the base of Dorchester Heights, but with a full moon to light the top, so we can see what we're doing."

Nathan nodded, calculating days in his mind, then got up, saying, "How's Mother?"

"Worried about you." Adam grinned crookedly at him and said, "She and Laddie had quite a talk—mostly about you, I reckon. That boy gave you the hard side of his talk, didn't he?"

"Oh, he was just worried about me."

"I'd say so. But I guess Molly calmed him down—or maybe it was that Quaker preacher."

"He still here?"

"Oh, sure." Adam got up and took one final swig of his coffee. "Far as I can tell, he's settled in."

"For a man who doesn't believe in war, he's sure put himself in the middle of it."

"Isn't that a fact?" Adam looked out the window, straightened up and said, "The general said you and Laddie were to be in my company. But you know these boys—fact that you're a sergeant doesn't mean anything to them. You may have to pound a couple of them in the ground, just to show you've got a right to give orders."

"They're pretty tough, Captain," Nathan said with a grin. "Might be they'll pound me in the ground."

"Well, guess if one of them does that—*he'll* be the sergeant."

"Not likely. I'll use an axe handle on him!"

He worked all day with the company cutting saplings for the fascines, and after they had quit, he encountered Laddie. She was sitting outside Knox's tent working on a map that was pinned to a large table, and he was not surprised to see Daniel Greene bending over the same table, looking at something Laddie was pointing out.

"Hello, Laddie," he said. "You going into map-making, Friend Daniel?"

Greene flushed slightly, then shook his head. "Just trying to figure this thing out." He looked at the map, shook his head, and said, "Can't make much out of it."

Nathan went to stand between them, looking down from his great height at the map. "You draw this, Laddie?"

"Yes." Her tone was short, and he looked at her, noting that she was not smiling as usual.

"Something wrong?" he asked.

"No. Nothing's wrong."

He hesitated, then said, "Well, guess I'll get something to eat." He stood there staring at her, then said, "Now, you see I didn't get killed or anything."

"I'm glad of that," Laddie said steadily, then looked down at the map and cut him off, saying, "You see, Dan, if we can get these guns in place . . ."

Nathan walked away, and Daniel said quietly, "He's confused. Thee is not being fair to him."

She threw the stick she'd been using to the ground and said,

"Dan, I don't *care* what Nathan Winslow does! Let him kill himself over that woman if he wants to!"

"Thee is in love with him."

"That was before he started running around after her!"

Dan stared at her, and there was compassion in his brown eyes. "Julie, it's bad to deceive anybody—but the worst thing is to deceive thyself." He shook his head sadly and said, "I thought at first that Winslow was going to hurt thee—but I see now that he won't be the one—" He touched her arm gently and said quietly, "It'll be thee who will bring the grief!"

CHAPTER TWENTY-THREE

"I'LL DO WHAT I HAVE TO DO!"

★ ★ ★ ★

"This isn't an army—it's a theological seminary!" Henry Knox snapped impatiently.

The lights of Boston winked up like fireflies at the small group sitting around a cheerfully blazing campfire. For three weeks the plan to fortify Dorchester Heights had been delayed by weather, for though warmer breezes had come to melt the snow, Knox was forced to wait for a night when Boston itself would be beneath an umbrella of mist, while the heights would be clear enough to get the guns in place.

Adam had come most nights to sit with Nathan and Laddie as they waited, and Greene was usually there. Greene and Adam enjoyed talking about the Bible, and some of their finer points about the prophetic books grew heated. "Father," Nathan had grinned once when both men had lost their calm, "you and Dan get more worked up over the gray beard of that billy-goat in the book of Daniel than you do over shooting Redcoats!"

Colonel Knox had suddenly appeared, listened to the heated discussion, and made his disgusted remark. But he had sniffed the air like a hound on the scent. "This could be it," he remarked eagerly.

"Not enough mist to cover us," Adam commented. But he stood up and looked down the hill, adding, "Fog *is* rolling in, though . . ." He slapped his hands together impatiently, looked at

Knox, and asked, "What does the general say?"

Knox shrugged his heavy shoulders and grinned suddenly. "He's champing at the bit as usual." He laughed quietly and gave a sly look at Adam. "He ordered the chaplain to pray for mist on Boston. You think the Lord will hear the good chaplain, Captain Winslow?"

"I refuse to limit God," Adam answered with a smile. "If God can flood the earth, I suppose He can whip up a little mist."

Knox asked innocently, "But how does God settle on which prayer to answer? I mean—the British chaplain is praying for victory in this war, and our chaplain is asking God for the same thing. Now, He *can't* please both of them, can He?"

Adam knew full well that Knox loved to poke fun at such things, so he said, "You know that's a question no man can answer, Colonel. But I'll tell you one thing—General Washington is a praying man."

Knox suddenly flushed and said quickly, "You're right, Winslow—and I was wrong to speak in such a way. I know full well that if all the praying men in our army left, we would be lost. Matter of fact, I think this army comes about as close as any to the Model Army of Oliver Cromwell. The pastors all over are making it a holy war."

"Did you hear about Muhlenberg?" Nathan asked from where he sat propped up against a tree. "He was a Lutheran pastor from our state, over in the Shenandoah Valley. Right after Lexington he preached a red-hot sermon on the text, 'For everything there is a season, and a time for every matter under heaven.' Then at the end of his sermon, he threw off his pulpit robe and he was wearing the uniform of a colonel in the Continental Army."

"I've met him," Knox answered. "And there's that preacher from Chelsea, Philip Payson—captured two British supply wagons single-handed—and there's Major Craighead—he raised his own company and they say he alternates between fighting and preaching." He shot a sudden look at Dan, who was listening intently, and asked, "Friend Daniel, I talked to your uncle, General Greene, last week. He's anxious to see you. Said the two of you ought to get together, since you're both likely to be ex-Quakers for ignoring the rules."

Greene nodded his head, saying only, "I'd like to see him."

Then Nathan asked directly, "Are you going to get into this

war, Dan—I mean, sooner or later the fighting's going to start! We can't sit up on top of this blasted hill forever! What will you do then?"

"Haven't decided."

"Well, you'll have your chance soon." Knox stared down and said, "I'm thinking that fog is rolling in pretty thick—and if it stays still like this—and if it doesn't rain, but just stays damp—and if about twenty other things happen, we could move tomorrow or the day after. I'm going to bed. Sergeant Smith, you wake me up if that chaplain's prayers get answered."

"Yes, sir." Laddie watched Knox stalk away into the darkness, and Nathan got up and left the fire. Adam watched him go, and said quietly, "I hope he doesn't try to leave camp again." Twice in the last two weeks Nathan had managed to get free of duty and had disappeared, showing up the next morning looking hollow-eyed from lack of sleep. Laddie knew he was going to see Abigail, and was certain that Adam and Molly knew as much.

Adam got up, stretched, and said good night, then left the fire. It was late, but Laddie loved the sharp air, so she pulled her coat closer around her and sat there poking a stick at the fire. Finally she looked up and asked, "Have you heard from your mother?"

"Just today. Been waiting for a chance to give thee this." He reached into his pocket, extracted an envelope and passed it to her.

Laddie read her name on the front, broke the seal and held it up to the fire. As she read it her cheeks grew red, and finally she folded it up and put it in her pocket. She picked up the stick, poked the fire and watched the sparks swirl upward. Then she looked suddenly at him, and asked, "Do you know what she said, Dan?"

"No."

He had the Quaker habit of silence, which she had grown accustomed to. Most men would have asked at once what the letter said, but he sat there, a mild look on his square face, gazing at her across the fire. He was not like other men, she had discovered, and knew that his mother and his religion had melded him into a strange combination of strength and gentleness—a combination that she found most attractive.

"You haven't said a word about—about us," she said. "I guess you've changed your mind."

"No, I haven't." Again he sat there quietly, but he added after a time, "I don't change easily—but until *thee* has a change, I'll not be saying much about us."

"That's—that's sweet of you, Dan." She knew he was thinking of her feelings for Nathan, and she struggled to find something to say, but there was nothing. Finally she said, "Dan, do you think God is in this war—I mean, I hear all this talk about freedom and how it's God's will for us to fight for it. You never say anything."

"Haven't decided yet. But I'm pondering it." He shook his head and looked down at the dim lights of the city, saying quietly, "I think maybe that fog is getting thicker."

They sat there for an hour, talking quietly—and Laddie did not realize how much she had come to rely on being able to speak openly with someone. Finally, she said, "It's getting late. I'll see you in the morning, Dan. Tell your mother, when you write her, that I'll pray about—what she says."

She got up and left him, and for a long time Dan sat there watching the lights. Then he said aloud, "Well, Lord, I'll add my voice to that of the chaplain. Let it fog up so that the army can get this job done. I don't know what Thee has in mind for this country—but let me in on it, as soon as Thee finds it convenient."

The next morning Knox was up before dawn, pacing back and forth, and at noon he turned to Laddie and said, "Write this down, Laddie: 'General, we will fortify the hill as soon as possible. If you will give us the cover of a bombardment, it will be most helpful.' What's the date—March 2?" He signed the order and handed it to an orderly, saying, "Get this to His Excellency at once!"

All day long the camp hummed with activity, and all that night and the next what guns were available poured a steady stream of shot and shell down on Boston. Washington stayed up to count the shots and make sure that his limit of twenty-five shots was observed.

The next night was remarkably mild, and Boston was covered with a haze that made the top of Dorchester invisible. "All right," Knox snapped as dark fell, "Howe won't have his mind on us tonight, so get going!"

Nathan worked with the Virginians, and Adam was right beside him. He stopped to say, "We could have waited a year and not had a night this good! I reckon that chaplain's prayers are right forceful!"

Eight hundred men worked madly to place the pre-assembled chandeliers in position and load them with fascines—all of which were brought up the hill by three hundred amazingly quiet teams and drivers. Silently these men worked hour after hour in the moon-lit darkness. As dawn broke across the east, the last gun was rolled into place, and Knox said quietly, "Well, I've seen at least *one* miracle. To do a thing like this—*and nothing go wrong* . . . !" He took off his hat and added, "God has been with us."

General Howe was awakened abruptly by his aide, who was shaking him by the arm—an unprecedented action!—and saying in an agonized voice: "General—General! Wake up!"

Howe had spent part of the night gambling and part with Mrs. Loring, and his head ached from the prodigious amount of wine he had consumed. He struck out blindly at the aide, muttering angrily, "Get your bloody hands off me!"

But the aide pleaded, "Pardon me, sir, but you *must* come at once!"

"What the devil is it?" Howe demanded. He dragged himself out of bed and glared at the frightened aide; then he pulled himself together, knowing that it had to be serious for the lieutenant to behave so. "Is it an attack?"

"No, sir—"

"Well, let me get my pants on!" Howe dressed rapidly, then walked out of the bedroom where three of his staff officers were standing with ashen faces. "What's the matter?"

"Sir, look at that hill!"

Howe walked to the door and stared up at the heights; then he gasped, "Impossible!"

He looked up to see a fort on the hill where nothing had been the afternoon before. General Robertson came to stand beside him, and he said in an agitated voice, "General Howe, to do that in one night, the rebels must have had fifteen to twenty thousand men!"

Howe could not speak for a moment; then he said, "We must prepare for action, Gentlemen; the honor of the British Army demands an immediate attack on this rebel position." All morning he issued orders, and a plan emerged for two forces of two thousand men each to embark on the next tide. That afternoon files of infantry marched down to the longboats.

But at midnight a violent gale swept in from the south, making landings impossible. Windows were blown in, sheds overturned, and rail fences were actually blown away!

Howe had no choice but to cancel the mission, telling his generals the danger of the attack had been in his mind, but that he had thought the honor of his troops was of more concern. He ordered the evacuation of the city, and the boats were made ready.

The Boston Tories descended on Howe's headquarters. The most illustrious names of Massachusetts—Olivers, Saltonstalls, Mathers, Hutchinsons, Faneuels—gathered what few valuables they could carry to leave their homes—many never to see them again. Henry Knox's in-laws, the Fluckers, were among them.

Charles Winslow had stayed in town as this drama unfolded. He called Paul to his side and said with a pale face, "I won't leave this place."

"Well, if Uncle Adam will stand beside you, it may be all right. After all, he's part owner of the business." Paul grinned, and there was something cruel in his eyes as he added, "Maybe Adam's got enough honor for all of us, Father."

Charles turned pale, but did not respond. He asked instead, "What will Howland do? He's too sick to leave."

"I'll go see. He doesn't have a relative who's a patriot to stand between him and Sam Adams' Sons of Liberty." Then he paused and added, "Well, maybe he does at that." With this enigmatic word, he turned and left at once.

Charles left the city and went home, where his wife and his mother met him with fear in their eyes. Dorcas was weeping and clinging to him. "What will we do? What will happen to us, Charles?"

Charles Winslow did not answer her, but looked into the eyes of his mother. He said bitterly, "Well, Mother, you've hated my brother Adam all his life. You made life miserable for him when he was a child and despised him when he grew up."

"Charles—don't . . . !"

"But now this man—the best of the Winslows—is the only hope we have. If he doesn't help us—we're lost!"

Martha Winslow seemed to shrivel before his words, and she turned slowly and moved her arthritic joints painfully, leaving the room. Charles watched her, and his heart smote him. He shook his head and moved to go after her. "She's done no more than I have to Adam."

Anne clung to her mother, her freckles standing out against the pallor of her face. "Mother—will they kill us—the rebels?"

Dorcas held her tightly and whispered, "No! Your Uncle Adam

won't let them harm us!" And bitter tears flowed down her cheeks as she thought of the meanness she'd always shown toward Adam and his family.

When Paul entered the Howland mansion, he found Abigail alone in the parlor. Her face was serious, but she showed no fear. "Mother's with Father, Paul." She bit her lip, and added in a whisper, "I think he's dying."

Paul stared at her, then said, "I think you'd all better come with us. Adam won't let the rebels do anything to us."

"Father can't be moved," she said. "And if we do leave, they'll take everything."

He stared at her and she raised her head to meet his gaze. "We'll be all right, Paul. Don't worry about us."

"I see." He didn't move, but examined her carefully. Finally he said, "We're a great deal alike, you and I."

"Paul, we've been very close—"

"Well, *that's* a strange way of putting it!" he said angrily. "*We've been very close.* Can't you be more honest than that, Abigail?"

She flushed, but held her head imperiously higher, and there was a steely note in her voice as she said, "Paul, you just said that we're alike—and I agree. The world is coming to an end—our world. Yours is safe because Adam Winslow is going to look after you. My father's dying and my mother can't even look after herself—so I'll look out for us."

Paul stared at her, then shook his head. "I knew you weren't all sugar and spice—that image never fooled me for one instant, Abby—but I didn't look close enough. You're hard as flint."

"I'll do what I have to do," Abigail said quietly. Then she asked in a gentler tone, "So will you, Paul, won't you?"

He stared at her, then slowly nodded. "I suppose so—you know me as well as I know you." He moved his shoulders in some sort of weary gesture, then asked, "If it doesn't work out, come to me."

"It'll work out, Paul." Abigail smiled at him, and there was an adamantine light in her hazel eyes. She suddenly kissed him and clung to him fiercely, then pulled back and said, "Goodbye, Paul— at least for now!"

CHAPTER TWENTY-FOUR

OUT OF THE PAST

★ ★ ★ ★

Howe's army had not been defeated; it had been out-maneuvered by a larger force. This infuriated the British troops, and in their final days in Boston they took their frustration out on the old town. They broke into many houses, and military supplies that could not be taken aboard the fleet were smashed and thrown into the harbor.

Adam and Nathan spoke of the occupation of the city as the final evacuation of the British took place. Adam had been watching through a spy glass from a high point, and he suddenly snapped it shut and said, "Putnam will go in first. I'm going in with him."

"The folks who've been faithful to the cause have taken an awful whipping," Nathan commented. "If Charles didn't get his family away, they'll probably be ridden out on a rail along with the other Tories."

"He's not leaving with Howe," Adam stated. "I got a message from him two days ago. I'm going in with Putnam to be sure nothing happens to them."

Nathan broke in quickly, "Father, I hate to ask favors—but I need to go to the Howlands. They're worse off than the Winslows. Saul Howland died day before yesterday. That leaves Abigail and her mother alone."

Adam stared long at his tall son before saying, "I guess you have to do this, Nathan. Your mother and I don't know this woman, but you're a loyal boy, so we thought it'd be this way." He sorted out several ideas, then said, "One thing I can do, and that's get an official order placing the Howland estate under the protection of the army. The general says he wants law and order, and it'll just be a piece of paper—but maybe you can make it stick."

"Thank you, sir," Nathan said warmly. "It's what I wanted—but didn't dare ask."

Adam stared at him, doubt in his eyes. "Are you going to marry this woman, son?"

"Well, things have been so mixed up that we haven't talked about it . . ."

Adam wanted to warn him that it would be impossible to be loyal to the Continental Army with a wife who was a Tory, but he thought, *Nathan knows all that,* so he merely said, "I'll get the order and we can go in together with Putnam."

When the last Redcoat walked up the gangplank and Howe's fleet moved out of the harbor, Adam and Nathan were in the first unit that marched into the city. Doors and windows were packed with cheering crowds as they entered to the tune of *Yankee Doodle Dandy.* Back in Cambridge, Rev. Leonard gave a final church service for the siege of Boston, quoting from Ex. 14:25: ". . . And took off their chariot wheels, that they drave them heavily: so that the Egyptians said, Let us flee from the face of Israel; for the Lord fighteth for them against the Egyptians."

Adam said as Nathan left for the Howlands', "Be careful, Nathan. These folks have been hardly used, and they're liable to shoot first and argue later. You've got a piece of paper, but some of them have lost everything, and they see the Winslows and the Howlands as the enemy." He smiled and reached up to put his hand on Nathan's shoulder. "We've not been close until recently—and I'd hate for you to get killed over a house."

"I'll be careful." Nathan smiled and clapped his father on the shoulder. "You better take your own advice, Father!" He rode away, wondering at the way the war and the loss of Caleb had brought the two of them together.

Abigail and her mother were waiting for him. Mrs. Howland had aged ten years since the first time Nathan had met her. She was a tiny woman with smallish eyes that had been filled with pride—but now were so full of fear that it was hard for Nathan to look at her. Abigail said quickly, "You see, Mother? I told you that

Nathan would come. Now, you go upstairs and try to rest." A black woman stepped forward quickly, and Mrs. Howland went without protest, pausing only to whisper, "Thank you, Nathan!"

After her mother had gone, Abigail smiled and took Nathan's arm. Looking up into his face, she studied him, and finally said, "You'll never believe I care for you, will you, Nathan?"

"Why, of course . . . !"

She suddenly bit her lip and turned from him, her back straight. "No, you won't—because without you we would be lost. So you'll always ask yourself, *Does she really love me—or does she just need me?*"

He went to her, turned her around and looked into her eyes. "Abigail, you shouldn't talk like that. You need help right now, and I thank God that I can give it to you." She was trembling beneath his hands, and he took a deep breath and said, "I think we should get married as soon as possible. I know it's a bad time—with your father's death and all the trouble—but I want to take care of you!"

Abigail looked up at him, and there was an enigmatic light in her eyes. For a long moment she stood there, and he fully expected her to say no. Finally, however, she nodded slowly, whispering, "If that's what you want, Nathan." Then she raised her lips to him and he held her tightly.

Laddie came to Boston as part of Knox's staff on the eighteenth, along with Washington. The commander in chief made no dramatic speeches or gestures in taking over the city. When he attended services, the first to be held under the new flag of the Colonies— thirteen red and white stripes with the Union Jack in the corner— he asked Dr. Eliot, dean of the Boston clergy, to preach a sermon of devout thanksgiving, not of war. Dr. Eliot found his text in Isaiah, and George Washington of Virginia bowed his head to the words, "Look upon Zion, the city of our solemnities: Thine eyes shall see Jerusalem a quiet habitation, a tabernacle that shall not be taken down."

The next day, Knox called his staff together and put them to work. He was beaming with anticipation and said, "The Redcoats have made us a present of 250 cannon, Gentlemen! Thoughtful of them, by Harry! But we've got to train gunners for them—and fast!"

"You think we'll be going into action soon, Colonel Knox?" asked Lieutenant Harvester, a solid-bodied New Yorker.

"No doubt about it, Tom! Only question is—*where?* I'm no prophet, but I say it'll be New York. But what matters now is to get men trained." He gave orders rapidly, and sent the officers away, then turned to Laddie, saying, "I have a special job for you, Sergeant. We're going to be fighting this war for some time, I think, and all over this country. I want you to make my bookshop your headquarters, and before we leave this place, I want you to secure maps of every kind you can lay your hands on!"

"Yes, sir!"

"Go to every cartographer in Boston—go any place else you need to go. I'll see that you have leave and money—but I want a map for every place where we might engage the enemy, you understand? Here's the key to my shop. Mullins has kept it open, but here's a key for you. I'll be in and out, but you can fix up some kind of quarters for yourself."

"I'll do my best, Colonel," Laddie said, taking the key. "How long do you think we'll have?"

Knox shrugged his shoulders and said as he turned to leave, "That'll depend on how fast Howe and his brother, Richard Lord Howe, can get an army together and get back here! Maybe a month, more or less, is all we can count on, Smith—so get those maps quick!"

Laddie threw herself into the job, and as the days sped by she amassed a small mountain of maps and charts. She went to New York and brought back many more—so many that Mullins complained about the space she had usurped in Knox's store, but the owner had been highly pleased with what had been accomplished. When Laddie told him that the collection was fairly complete, he said, "Fine! Now you work on them—especially the New York area, because I'll eat my head if the Howe brothers don't show up there pretty soon! Washington thinks so, too. He's sending troops there every day. Better give me what you've got on that area right now."

During those first hectic days, Laddie had spent a great deal of her time alone. She had expected Daniel Greene to return to his home, but he made no move to do so. He had, she discovered, grown quite close to his uncle, General Greene, who evidently found his nephew to his liking. Daniel had brought the general by to meet Laddie, and she had found him to be a charming man. "Friend Daniel and I are in the same boat, Sergeant Smith," he said with a fond look at his nephew. "We Friends are a hard-headed lot—and the Lord practically sent the angel Gabriel to get me to join the army."

Laddie knew what hardships the general had undergone from his fellow Quakers, and she asked, "Are you making any progress toward converting Friend Daniel to your views, General Greene?"

"I think the Lord is doing a little along that line. My sister will disown me for making a soldier out of her boy, I suppose." Then he grew serious and said soberly, "It's never easy to find God, Sergeant, and when a thing like this revolution comes along—a man can get pulled to pieces trying to render unto Caesar what's his and unto God what's His!"

Laddie spent much time with Molly. The Winslows had rooms with a family living in town, but Adam was busy training his men, and Molly had little to do. She had dropped by Knox's bookstore, and the two of them had spent a pleasant hour. The visit was repeated, and often Laddie would spend the evening with the older woman.

But as Laddie came to love Molly more and more, a strange sort of constraint grew up between the two women concerning Nathan. His announcement that he was engaged to marry Abigail had shaken Laddie, though it had not been unexpected. As she spent more and more time with Molly, she saw that the engagement was a grief to Nathan's mother, and she wrote in her journal:

> April 3, 1776
>
> I feel so sorry for Molly and Adam! It breaks my heart to see the way they smile and never complain—when all the time they know that their only son is making a frightful mistake.
>
> Why is he so blind? I have to bite my tongue to keep from screaming at him that Abigail Howland is *using* him—but he wouldn't believe me, of course.
>
> But why do I get so furious? When I started keeping this journal, I vowed one thing—to *always tell the truth*. I've been saying that I hate Nathan because he's hurting his parents, and that's so—but it's not all of it. The truth is—I'm jealous of Abigail! Yes! Now I've put it down—and it seems ugly, but how many times have I thought of them together and hated them both?
>
> God forgive me for such thoughts!

It cost Laddie dearly to write the words, but it brought some sort of relief, although not for long. Two days after she made the entry, Molly stopped by the bookstore late one afternoon to say, "Come along, Laddie. You're having supper with us." It was not the first time she had done so, and Laddie always enjoyed being with her and Adam—but this time when she walked into the private dining room at the inn and saw Abigail sitting there with Nathan, she wished fervently she had not come.

"Why, it's Sergeant Smith!" Abigail said gaily, and she told the story of Laddie's theft of the pass as they ate. Her narration was witty, and it made the whole thing into some sort of romantic comedy. She ended by saying with a condescending smile, "Of course, Father had already seen to it that Nathan was in no danger."

Laddie had stared suddenly at Nathan, who seemed embarrassed, but said only, "Laddie had no way of knowing that, Abigail."

"Oh, I'm sure of that—I like to see young men have a little romantic flair—even if it gets out of hand at times."

Adam and Molly said little, and it was a relief for Laddie to make her excuses and get away as soon as she could. But all night long she tossed and turned, anger rising in her like a red tide. She tried to pray but finally gave up the attempt, and when she got up at dawn, her eyes were red and her heart filled with bitterness.

She dressed and tried to work, but was too angry to think. Finally she decided to return a map for further revision to Jacob Goldman, a map-maker who had been of great assistance to her. She picked up the document and was fifty yards down the street when she heard someone call, "Laddie!" and turned to find Nathan hurrying to catch up with her.

He looked haggard, and as soon as he stood beside her, he said, "I've wanted to talk to you."

"I've got to take this map to Goldman." The sight of him stirred an anger in her breast, and she turned coldly and continued on her way.

He fell into step with her, saying, "Laddie, you weren't very kind to Abigail last night. After all, she's lost her father—and she's all alone except for her mother—and you hardly said ten words to her."

Laddie struggled to hold back the hot words that leaped to her lips, but did not succeed. "Oh, she's got more than her mother, I think. She's got *you*, Nathan Winslow!"

He stopped suddenly and forced her to halt by taking her arm. He said angrily, "What's the *matter* with you?"

"Oh, nothing's wrong with me! I just somehow get upset when good people like Adam and Molly Winslow have to stand by and watch their only son make an idiot out of himself!" The anger that she had struggled with made her face pale, and she whirled and half ran down the street. When she saw that he was beside her, his face stubborn, she said, "Leave me alone!"

"No, I won't. I'm going with you; then we'll go someplace and talk."

"I don't want to talk to you, Nathan!"

"That's too bad, because you're going to whether you like it or not!"

She was so angry that tears gathered in her eyes, and to keep him from seeing them, she walked down the street, ignoring him. He said nothing else, but when she got to Goldman's he went inside with her.

Goldman was in the back of the shop talking to a tall bearded man, but he looked up and said, "Ah, Sergeant Smith!" and hurried over, a small, bald-headed man with a nervous smile. "You need more maps, is it?"

"No, I want to talk to you about this one. It won't take but a minute."

Nathan lounged back against the wall, and Laddie spread the map out on a table. For several minutes she carried on a conversation with Goldman, the two of them disagreeing over several points. Finally, Goldman said, "All right, I agree that the elevations are probably incorrect. Leave it with me and I'll make the changes from the 1743 chart."

Laddie said, "I think that will be much better. I'll drop by tomorrow, Mr. Goldman."

She turned to go, but there was someone standing right behind her. It was the customer Goldman had been talking with, and saying, "Pardon me," she moved to go around him.

When she stepped to one side, his hand shot out and caught her by the arm. "What are you doing?" she cried; then she looked up at the man—and found herself looking into the face of Aaron Sampson!

He looked very different, for he had grown a full beard—but the eyes were the same, and there was a smile of triumph on his full lips. "Well, now, I knew I'd find you someday, Julie, but I didn't think it'd be like this! Now I know why you've been able to keep yourself hidden from me!"

"You—let me go!" she cried out, and tried to break away, but his fingers bit into her arms like steel.

"Not likely!" he laughed loudly, and began to pull her toward the door.

"What the devil are you doing? Let go of him!" Nathan had stepped forward and his blue eyes glared angrily at the big man.

"Get out of the way. This is none of your affair," Sampson growled.

Nathan reached out and grabbed a handful of Sampson's coat. "Take your hands off him or I'll break your neck!"

Sampson looked up at Nathan, and the impulse to fight was in him, but he shook his head, saying, "Sergeant, I won't fight you—I won't have to, because the law will see to it that you mind your own business."

Nathan said hotly, "I don't know what the devil you're talking about—and I don't give a hang! This is Sergeant Laddie Smith of Colonel Henry Knox's staff, and I'll tell you just one more time— if you don't take your hands off him, I'll break your neck!"

Sampson shook his head and said, "You're wrong. This is my ward, Miss Julie Sampson of Philadelphia."

Nathan stared at him. "You're insane! Come along, Laddie!"

Sampson said at once, "I see that you have been deceived by this girl, Sergeant. But I can prove what I say with no trouble."

Laddie was standing there, fear washing over her, so weak that she could barely stand. She had had nightmares much like this, but she knew that there would be no awakening from this scene. She looked at Nathan, who was red with anger, and then she heard Sampson say, "Julie ran away last winter, and I've spent a lot of money trying to find her." He pulled a paper out of his pocket, handed it to Nathan, saying, "I've put these in every major city in the country—but I see now why they brought no results. I never thought she might become a man!"

Nathan read the description, and when he raised his eyes and looked at Laddie, he said, "You've made a mistake, Sampson."

"That'll be simple to prove, as I said." He looked at Laddie and said with a sly look in his eyes, "All you have to do is take your coat and your shirt off. A young fellow wouldn't mind doing that, now would he? Of course—a young lady *would* object."

Nathan glared at him, then said, "He doesn't have to do *anything*! We're leaving here."

"You're in Knox's force?" Sampson said. "I'm sure the colonel would ask the sergeant to do this very simple thing—because if he doesn't, I'll be right there with civil law to get it done! But there's a simpler way."

"And what's that?"

"Why, just look at her, Sergeant!" Sampson said with a smile. "It's written all over her face!"

"Laddie . . . ?" Nathan started to speak, but then he looked full in the white face of Laddie, and stopped abruptly. He had not for one second considered that Sampson might be telling the truth, but as the silence ran on, he seemed suddenly to be outside of himself, looking down from somewhere on the scene—seeing the three of them in a frame—and the look of guilt on the face of the person he'd been calling Laddie Smith was unmistakable!

He swallowed and could only whisper, "Laddie . . . ?" And then he saw the dark eyes fill with tears.

"It's true, Nathan, but . . . !"

He did not grasp the rest of her words, but wheeled and plunged out of the shop. As he fled blindly down the street, he thought he heard a voice crying his name.

CHAPTER TWENTY-FIVE

JULIE GOES TO A BALL

★　★　★　★

The story of a young woman masquerading as a soldier in the Continental Army spread like wildfire through Boston, and the soldiers themselves spawned ribald jokes. If Aaron Sampson had taken his ward away, it would have been easier for Nathan, but that didn't happen. As soon as Molly Winslow heard that Laddie had been discovered, she told Adam the whole story. The two of them had gone to Knox. He was thunderstruck by the affair, but after Molly gave him the extenuating circumstances, he had agreed to help. He had called Sampson to his office and told him that he would have to present legal proof of his relationship with the girl.

"But—I'll have to go to Philadelphia! The wench will run away again!" Sampson was livid with anger. He had been on the verge of leaving with Julie as a prisoner, and he glared at Knox.

"I'll have her detained. She's officially a member of my staff and under my authority. She'll be here when you get the evidence. That'll be all!" Knox snapped. He did not care for Sampson's looks, and after the man left, he stared at the small figure before him and shook his heavy head. "Well, by Harry! I never thought I'd be taken in by a snip of a girl!"

Julie looked up at him and saw that he was grieved, but not angry. "I'm so sorry, Colonel Knox," she whispered, and tears glittered in her eyes as she said, "Will you let him take me when he comes back?"

Knox was a gentle man, giant though he was, and he hated to hurt the girl anymore—but he had to tell her the truth. "I think the law will be on his side, Laddie—Miss Sampson, I mean." He came over and put his hand on her shoulder, adding, "Before he gets here your friends will think of some way to help you, I'm sure." Then he said briskly, "Now, I've talked this over with Mrs. Winslow, and since you have to stay somewhere, you can stay with her and Captain Winslow."

He had sent her to the Winslows, accompanied by Lieutenant Wilkins, who had given her a curious glance, but said only, "I hope things work out for you, miss." Molly had met her and when the door closed, she opened her arms and instantly Julie fell into them, the tears she had held back flowing freely. The older woman held the weeping girl, and finally said, "Well, that's done! Now we'll have some tea and talk."

Her matter-of-fact manner did as much as anything to calm Julie, and by the time Adam came in, she was able to greet him without a sign of distress. He took her hands, and there was a fondness in his dark eyes as he said gently, "This has been pretty bad, hasn't it?" Then his eyes twinkled and a smile touched his lips. "Going to be a little hard to get used to having a young woman around—Julie, is it? You must think all the Winslows are blind as bats, eh? Can't tell a young woman from a man!"

She knew he was trying to find some way to make her feel better, but the mention of Nathan disturbed her. "I don't think Nathan will ever forgive me, Captain Winslow."

"Nonsense! Of course he will," Adam said quickly. "He just needs a little time, child."

But three days went by, and while Julie grew to love the Winslows more than ever, Nathan did not come once to the house. Daniel, who was there every day, commented on it only once. "He's taking it pretty hard, Julie. Thinks the whole world sees him as a fool. But he'll come around—worse luck for me!"

But two more days went by, and Julie said sadly to Molly, "Nathan's never going to forgive me, and I—I love him so, Molly!"

"I know, Julie." Molly wanted to give some comfort, but doubt had filled her own heart, and there was nothing she could say.

But that evening before supper, Adam had come in and Molly saw at once that he was disturbed. "What's the matter?"

"Nathan—he's coming here tonight."

"How do you know, Adam?"

"Because I *ordered* him to come!"

"Oh, Adam, you shouldn't have done that!"

"I know it, Molly, but he's going to get himself in bad trouble if he doesn't pull out of this. I've tried to talk to him several times, but he just freezes up and says nothing. This morning one of the sergeants from the Maryland brigade made a remark about this thing—a dirty remark, and Nathan just about killed him! The man doesn't have a tooth left in the front of his head!—and it would have been all the same to Nathan if it had been an officer!" He shook his head and added, "He's acting like a child about this, Molly! He's got to act like a man—and like a Christian."

"And you think ordering him here will do that?"

"It can't be any worse than it is," he said grimly. "You see how hurt Julie is by the way he's acting."

Molly was disturbed by what Adam had done, but she said nothing to Julie, and when Nathan walked in that evening, she saw the girl's face turn pale as paper. But she had risen at once, and going to stand in front of him, she had said quietly, "Nathan, I've been wanting to tell you how sorry I am—for what I did to you."

Nathan stared down at her, searching her eyes to find something, and there was a combination of hurt and bitterness in his face. He said briefly, "I suppose it was something you had to do."

The coldness of his reply and the harsh light in his face struck her like a blow, and she bit her lip and said, "I'll never forget what you did for me, Nathan. I—I hope you'll be able to think of me a little more gently—after a while."

She had left the room, and Molly saw that Adam was as angry as she had ever seen him. Before he could speak, she said quickly, "Nathan, try to see it from her side—she was so alone, and you helped her as nobody else could. I've never seen a human being as grateful as she is to you."

"You knew about her, didn't you?"

"Well, yes—"

"And I found out that Daniel Greene and his mother knew. Why was *I* left out?"

"Oh, for heaven's sake, Nathan!" Adam exclaimed. "You sound like a spoiled brat, crying because you got left out! I've been so confounded proud of you—but now, I'm ashamed to see you filled with hate for a girl who's been through a terrible time!"

His words struck Nathan hard, for he treasured the approval of his father as much as anything in the world. But stubbornness pressed his lips together, and he said tightly, "I don't hate—her." Both of them saw how difficult it was for him to even mention the thing, and Molly knew the sensitive spirit that was in him. He was, to Adam, a man come to full strength, but she was aware that beneath the militant air, Nathan had a childlike quality.

The atmosphere was tense, and Nathan soon left, his head high and with a pallor under his tan. "Well, that wasn't exactly the best idea I ever had, was it, Molly?" Adam sighed, staring after him.

"I think you did the right thing," she said promptly, and came to put her arm around him. "He's so confused, Adam. But he's good at heart, so we'll just have to be patient until God gets him through this thing."

"There's not much time, though. Sampson could be back with those blasted legal papers any time." He sighed and turned to go look out into the darkness through the window. "I wish the Lord would do something quick."

"You know, I have an idea," Molly said slowly. "Maybe there's a way we can hurry things up." There was, he saw, a far-off light in her gray eyes; he had learned long ago that when his wife got such a look, things usually happened.

"Oh, Molly, I can't do it!" Julie wailed. She was standing in the middle of the floor staring at herself in the mirror. "Everybody will stare at me!"

"That's the idea, Julie—or part of it." Molly was on her knees working on the hem of the beautiful white dress that she and Julie had bought that afternoon. She stood up, stepped back, and gave the girl a critical look, then nodded. "You'll be the best-looking girl at the ball. But when—" A knock at the door interrupted her, and she said, "There's Friend Daniel. Now you mind what I told you."

"It'll never work!" Julie moaned, and she thought back to the day when Molly had come to her with the idea. *Nathan can't think of you as anything but a man, Julie—so we'll have to let him see you as a woman! There's a ball in three days, and Nathan will be there. We'll buy you the prettiest dress in Boston, pretty you up, and when Nathan sees you as a young woman, he'll just have to think differently!*

Julie, reluctant, had finally agreed, but now that the time had come, she stood there filled with apprehension as Molly admitted Daniel. "Why, Julie . . . !" Daniel came into the room, and stopped dead still as he caught sight of her, his eyes widening.

"Isn't she beautiful?" Molly beamed.

"Very." Daniel came closer, and Julie's color rose as he stared at her as if he'd never seen her before. Then he shook his head and smiled. "Well, I told thee, Mrs. Winslow, I feel pretty strange, a Friend going to a worldly ball." His eyes crinkled with humor and his smile broadened as he added, "But I reckon this young lady is going to need some protection—looking like that!"

"I don't want to go!"

"You have to," Molly said firmly, and began herding them toward the door. "I'd love to see Nathan when he gets his first glimpse of you in that dress! You'll have to tell me all about it when you get home."

Daniel had a carriage, and he helped her into it, then climbed in and took the lines. "We're going to be late."

"Dan, let's don't go to the ball!" she pleaded. "We can just drive around and talk."

He didn't answer for a time, waiting until they had passed along the wide streets lined with elms. Finally he glanced at her, huddled up and looking completely miserable. "To tell the truth, Julie, that's what I was going to try to talk thee into doing. Thee knows how I feel about thee, and it's a mark of grace that I'm willing to let Nathan see thee."

"He won't care, Daniel."

"Well, if he doesn't, you'll have faithful Friend Daniel Greene waiting for thee, Julie."

She didn't answer, and all too soon they pulled up in front of a huge mansion brightening the sky with a myriad of lights. Dan handed the lines to a servant, then helped her down. They passed up a walk as wide as a city street, then through a set of massive doors into a spacious foyer. Through a set of double doors on their right, they could see a large crowd, with music echoing around the two as they entered the room.

"Well, this is a little different from our Sabbath meeting, isn't it, Julie?" Dan said quietly, looking over the room with interest.

The brilliantly colored dresses of the women—red, green, blue—were highlighted by thousands of small candles set in the massive chandeliers overhead. Everyone seemed to be moving, some of them dancing and others going around the edges of the room, visiting the refreshment tables or engaging in conversation, and the hum of talk and laughter almost drowned out the small orchestra that played at the far end of the room. Many of the revelers were officers, and their buff-and-blue uniforms set them off from the civilians, who wore darker colors.

"Let's go over to the tables," Dan said. "Friends aren't much on dancing."

As Julie followed him through the crowd, she became aware that she was the target for many eyes. A woman dressed in a scarlet dress stared at her, then asked, loudly enough for her to hear, "Who is that?" Her escort, a tall major in the uniform of the 19th Maryland, leaned down and whispered in her ear, and the woman's eyes gleamed. "So—*that's* the one!" Then she had said something to a woman on her left, and the two of them had laughed.

By the time they reached the table, Dan had noted the sensation they were creating, and said, "Don't let it bother you. Some people aren't kind."

Julie stood there enduring the stares and the comments that were aimed at her, longing more than anything to run out of the room. Then suddenly someone stood before her, and she looked up to see Colonel Knox. He smiled down at her, then said, "My wife is a very jealous woman, Miss Sampson, so I'll probably pay for this—but I must have a dance with the loveliest woman in the room!"

Julie found herself dancing around the room before she had time to think. Knox, though large, was very light on his feet, and by the time the dance was over, Julie realized that he had asked her to dance in order to put his stamp of approval on her. "You've been so kind to me, Colonel," she whispered as he took her back to Daniel.

He gave her arm a squeeze and whispered, "You and that bunch of Christians will pray this thing out!" Then he was gone, but three officers jostled each other for her next dance, the winner being a smiling Virginian from Adam's company. He was followed by a tall captain from Glover's Marblehead fishermen, and then by a series of others.

Nathan and Abigail arrived late, but Daniel had been watching for them. He went across the room before they had a chance to speak to anyone else, saying, "Nathan, I haven't had the honor of meeting thy fiancee." He bowed as Nathan made the introductions, saying, "My congratulations to both of thee."

"Are you alone, Mr. Greene?" Abigail asked.

"No—but my partner has proved to be so popular that I'm quite left out." At that moment, Julie passed by not twenty feet away, floating on the arm of a youthful brigadier. "I believe thee knows her?"

Abigail straightened suddenly, her eyes narrowing, but it was Nathan that Dan was watching. His lips parted and his bright blue eyes recorded his incredulity. "That's *Laddie?*" he whispered, not conscious that he had used the familiar name.

"Not Laddie," Daniel corrected. "Miss Julie Sampson. Lovely, isn't she?"

The dress that Julie wore was pure white, with a voluminous skirt and a tight bodice that revealed her slim figure. Her hair was short but Molly had arranged it into a halo that framed her face with glossy black ringlets. She wore only one piece of jewelry, a gold locket with a green stone that glittered on her neck. Her skin was flawless, and Nathan, in shock, stared at the fully curved lips, the almond-shaped eyes, and the beautifully arched brows.

"I'm claiming your first dance, Miss Howland," Daniel said, and with a gleam in his brown eyes added innocently, "Nathan, I'm sure thee can get a dance with Miss Sampson if thee hurry." He moved so quickly that neither of them had time to react. "Now, Miss Howland . . ." he was saying as he took her hand and led her to the floor, "I'm just a poor parson, so you'll have to excuse my dancing . . . !"

Nathan stood there, tempted to follow Daniel and reclaim Abigail. The anger and bitterness he'd nourished for days over Julie's deception, however, had faded to some extent, and a sudden wave of curiosity ran through him. He quickly walked across the floor, stepped in front of a dandified young man who was pushing forward to claim the next dance, and said, "Will you dance with me, Miss Sampson?"

The sight of him towering above her touched Julie's nerves so sharply she could only nod and murmur, "Of course." The touch of his hand seemed to tingle, and as he guided her across the floor, there was a dreamlike quality about it.

He looked down at her, and thought suddenly, *Why, she's so small!* She was tall, but slim and fine-boned. Her head was down, and he stared at the classic lines of her face, the delicate features, marveling at her grace and beauty. Finally, she lifted her head and smiled at him with tremulous lips, whispering, "Do you hate me so much, Nathan?"

Her gentleness went straight through him like a knife, and he felt a rush of affection as the early times he'd had with her came flooding back. He started to speak, then noticed that they were the center of attention for many. "I have to talk to you," he said abruptly, and as they passed close to a pair of French doors, he led her off the floor. The doors opened to a low balcony that overlooked a large garden. The moon was bright overhead, and the muted sound of the music was almost ghostly on the air.

He paused, and looking down on her said, "I—I can't believe how terribly I've treated you—Julie." It was the first time he'd used her first name and it warmed her, as did his whole attitude.

"It wasn't your fault, Nathan. I know the things they've been saying—all the horrible jokes . . . !"

He shook his head and began to pace back and forth, his face twisted with shame. For several minutes he poured out on himself a litany of guilt, and she made no move to stop him. Finally he paused and she said, "Nathan—will you do me a favor?"

"Of course!"

She came to stand before him, putting out her hands. "Let's remember the good times, not these last few days!"

He took her hands, marveling that he'd never noticed how slender her fingers were. Her face was turned up to him, and he said, "That's good of you, Julie. I'd like that a lot. There were some good times, weren't there?"

Her lips parted and she said, "Oh, yes! You're the kindest man I've ever known! And—and I'll always love you!"

It was Nathan's turn to be shocked, and he thought he had misunderstood her. Bending down to put his face close to hers, he said, "I didn't hear you."

Julie knew that she was terribly wrong, but his gentleness had weakened her, and she slowly raised her hands and put them behind his neck, and pulling his head down, she whispered, "I said *I love you!*" And then she closed her eyes and kissed him full on the lips.

Nathan had never felt such a shock, and the touch of her soft lips was sweeter than anything he had dreamed existed. He held her, his arms going around her without thought, and the music that floated on the air seemed to brush against his mind.

"Well, Nathan? I see you and *Laddie* are getting along well!"

Nathan straightened up, whirled, and was appalled to see Abigail with Friend Daniel Greene standing at her side. She was furious, and he could not have uttered one word to save his soul.

Daniel had seen the kiss, and he knew something in his own soul of the bitter jealousy flashing out of Abigail's eyes. But years of developing Quaker-style patience came to his rescue, and as he looked at the three of them—he made himself smile. Putting a hand on Abigail's arm, he said, "Well, thee mustn't be too upset, Miss Howland. Nathan's mother tells me he was always an affectionate young fellow."

But Abigail did not smile. She grabbed Nathan's arm, snatched him away from Julie and practically dragged him off the balcony.

"Looks like Friend Nathan's in for a trip to the woodshed," Dan observed wryly. Then he said, "I've had about all the fun I can stand for one night. Is thee about ready to leave?"

"Yes!"

She followed him as he left the balcony, and when they pulled out of the driveway in the carriage, Daniel looked back at the house and shook his head, remarking, "Guess worldly pleasure's not all it's rumored to be. Always wondered about that."

CHAPTER TWENTY-SIX

A MATTER OF HONOR

★   ★   ★   ★

Day after day, units moved out of Cambridge and Boston, headed for New York, for Washington and his staff were convinced that Howe would strike there. Knox worked frantically training gunners to man the guns the British had left behind, and Adam kept the Virginia riflemen drilling constantly. "I expect we'll be leaving in a week, Molly," he said one night after supper.

"What will happen to Julie when we leave—if that scoundrel Sampson hasn't come by then?"

Adam shrugged and gave a disgusted grunt. "Don't know. I thought she might run away again. But don't guess she's got anywhere to run to." He stretched, then gave Molly a look of speculation. "I've had the idea that Quaker might marry her. That'd solve the problem."

"Yes—but I don't think she'd marry him."

"Good man." Then he gave her a closer look and demanded, "What's in your head? I know that look!"

"Oh—just thinking." She evaded his question, saying, "Charles wants us to come out tomorrow and have supper with them."

"Oh, Molly, I don't want to do that!"

"I know, Adam, but I think we should." She came over and sat down beside him. Taking his thick hand, she stroked it gently, tracing a long white scar in the shape of a fishhook that curled around his thumb. "I feel uncomfortable there, too, but we ought to go this time—for Charles's sake."

"I don't understand?"

"Why, he wants to thank you for saving his home—try to patch things up between you. He stopped by today while you were gone and asked. I tried to tell him we couldn't come, but he almost begged. I think maybe we ought to go this one time."

"Oh, blast!" he groaned. "I don't want any thanks . . . !" Then he threw up his hands and surrendered, as he usually did when she asked for something. "Well, we'll go—but get us away as soon as you can. Martha will be taking potshots at me as usual. Will Nathan come?"

"Yes, and Abigail—if she'll go. She and Nathan are having some sort of a fight. He won't say what—but Abigail is giving him a hard time. That's why he's been mooning around so much. She's dangling him, punishing him for something."

"He ought to whip her," Adam grinned. "Good beating every once in a while—that's what all wives need! But I guess he's too much in love to act sensibly."

Molly punched her husband playfully on the arm. "Better not let Nathan hear you say such things. He just might take you seriously!"

Julie, who was upstairs writing in her journal, felt the same way, but she dared not say it to Nathan. She wrote with a frown on her face, jabbing so viciously at the paper that she snapped the tip off her quill several times:

> I could pinch her silly head off! Or *his*! It's been nearly two weeks, and she's been absolutely *inhuman* to Nathan ever since she caught us kissing on the balcony.
>
> If he had any sense, he'd give her something to be jealous *about*! But he won't—he's so afraid he'll lose her.
>
> Well, the one good thing out of all of it is that I've gotten to see him almost every day. He goes to see Abigail. She either torments him for a little while and then sends him home, or else she won't see him at all.
>
> If I had a mind to do it, I could fix her! He's so sad, and I guess that one kiss really convinced him I was a girl! He's so gentle with me, and when he comes from her, humiliated, he's so vulnerable. He was telling me yesterday how bad he felt, and we were sitting close together on the couch. I really think if I'd given him *one* sign, he'd have kissed me again!

But I didn't. Even if that woman has driven him right into my arms (so to speak!), he'll never be any good to another woman—not the way she's got him bewitched!

And again, I looked all day for Aaron to come back. Ever since he left, every time a door opens, I tremble! It makes me almost ill to think of him—what he'll do when he has me back in Philadelphia!

God, help me! You're the Father of the fatherless!

She shut the journal, knelt and prayed for a long time, then left her room. Molly and Adam had already gone to bed, so she fixed a cup of tea and was sipping it when the door opened and Nathan came in. He had a heavy look on his face and there was gloom in his voice as he asked, "My folks already gone to bed?"

"Yes, they went early. Did you need to see them?"

He shrugged and turned to go. "It can wait until tomorrow."

"I just made some tea."

He came back and sat down, and the hot tea seemed to cheer him, but he seemed restless. "I'm not sleepy tonight. Hate to go to bed."

"Let's walk around the pond." The house that the Winslows had rented was on the outskirts of town, and the small pond that lay under the canopy of some huge chestnut trees had been a godsend to her. She had fished for the small perch that abounded in it, and in the late evenings had enjoyed it as she walked.

Nathan responded quickly. "If you're not sleepy, I'd like it."

The soft spring breeze had warmed the earth, bringing the peepers out, and they piped loudly, like ghostly sleigh bells until Nathan and Julie stepped onto the small beaten path that ringed the pond. The sudden silence made Julie laugh. "I think those frogs resent us. They think this pond is theirs, and we're trespassers."

"I guess so." Nathan looked up and saw the full moon and commented, "Look, Julie, there's some kind of a hazy ring around the moon—I wonder what it is?"

"I don't know much about the stars," she said. They moved on, and the pond was so still the reflection of the moon seemed solid as the reality. He reached down, picked up a stone and tossed it into the pond; it struck with a loud *plop*, and rapidly spreading circles broke up the image of the moon. As the tiny waves reached the shore, he murmured, "One little stone—and it changed the whole picture. Doesn't take much to mess things up, does it, Julie?"

She looked up at him quickly, knowing that he was thinking

of Abigail, and she hated what was happening to him. "Time changes things, Nathan." She motioned toward the pond. "See? The ripples are almost gone already, and it'll be like it was—smooth and clear."

"Life's not like that."

"No—because we're more than a pond," she agreed. There was a longing in her to say something that would take away the gloom that had come to mar his manner. Always he had been cheerful, even when things were bad, but he had lost that lightness of spirit. Finally she said, "Abigail will forgive you."

He stared at her, and shook his head. "She—she thinks that I've known all along that you were a girl. Says as close as the two of us were, I just *had* to know." His teeth gleamed in a quick smile, and he said ruefully, "I can see her point. Looking at you now, it seems downright impossible I didn't catch on!"

"Oh, I was clever," she said. "She'll get over it, Nathan."

"I guess so—" He stopped and turned to face her on the narrow path. He was so tall that she had to tilt her head to look up at him, and he put his hands on her shoulders and said, "Julie, I ought not to be bothering you with my troubles. You've got more than I have—and I'm worried about it. Maybe we ought to get a lawyer—you can't go back to Philadelphia with Sampson!"

She was totally conscious of his hands on her shoulders, but she let nothing show in her face. "It will be all right, Nathan."

"Well—" He dropped his hands suddenly as if they had been burned, and said awkwardly, "I—I guess we better get back."

"All right." They walked back, saying little, but when they got to the door, Julie spoke up. "Your uncle Charles came by today. He wants all of you to come to his house for dinner tomorrow—said for you to bring Abigail."

"Doubt if she'll come."

A streak of anger raced through Julie. "Tell her I'll be there—that'll make her come."

He shifted his shoulders uneasily, then said, "Might not be much fun for you. She's—upset with you."

Julie smiled as she turned to go in, amused by some thought. "She won't hurt me, Nathan. Good night."

Whether Abigail chose to attend the dinner at the Winslows because Julie would be there, Nathan was not certain. He looked across the table at Abigail, and thought he'd never seen anything more beautiful. She was wearing a blue silk dress that left her arms bare, and her rich brown hair was woven into a crown that sparkled with jewels. The dimples in her cheeks were often in evidence, for all evening she had been as charming as he had ever seen her.

She had kissed him when he came for her, the first time since the night of the ball, and on their way she had been animated as if nothing had happened between them. The change in her manner startled Nathan, making him somehow feel awkward. Her moods, he had discovered, were often like that, and he could not seem to adjust.

But the party is a success, he thought, looking around. Even Martha Winslow, his father's stepmother, seemed to be determined to keep things agreeable. Charles sat at one end of the table, with his wife on his right and Anne and Julie on his left. Nathan sat with his parents, and across from them Abigail sat between Paul and Martha.

They had eaten a sumptuous dinner, and the only thing that had marred the evening had been the fact that Paul was obviously drinking too much. He had been a little drunk even before the meal, and Nathan had noticed that he had eaten little but had emptied glass after glass of wine. His face was flushed, and there was an uncertainty in his speech and movement. Once his mother had said sharply, "Paul, you've had enough wine!" but he had paid no attention.

Charles Winslow had been less talkative than usual, but finally he cleared his throat and said in a voice that claimed attention, "I've been sitting here thinking how sad it is that our family has drifted so far apart. It's taken a war to get us all together at this table." He looked at Adam and spoke with a rueful shake of his head, "I'm no good at speeches, but this is one that I must make—"

He paused and looked awkward, then made a futile gesture with his hands. "Adam, I don't know how to put this, but you've saved the family—my family, anyway. God knows you had no reason to! We've not given you cause to love us." At this point his mother seemed to shrink, and Dorcas flushed and looked steadily down at the table. Charles seemed to struggle for words, found none, so he said in a whisper, "Thank you, Adam—for what you've done."

Adam was shifting uneasily in his chair, and he blurted out,

"Why, Charles, there's no need for all this! What sort of brother would I be if I didn't do what little I could for you? Let's say no more about it, if you please."

Charles smiled faintly and shook his head. "I know you didn't do it for thanks, Adam." His eyes lifted to the portrait of Miles Winslow, their father, on the wall, and he said, "I *look* like Father—but you've always *been* like him!"

The compliment took Adam aback, and he looked up at the painting. "He was a man, Charles, wasn't he? I wish we had more like him these days."

"Why, Captain Winslow, you shouldn't say that!" All eyes turned toward Abigail as she'd known they would. She gave Adam a smile and said, "I'm sure your father was a wonderful man—but you have a son who's going to do great things! The House of Winslow will be one of the great families in this new country!"

Nathan twisted uncomfortably in his chair as Abigail went on, and he said finally, "Oh, Abigail, I've done nothing. Everything I've done's been wrong!"

"That's not so!" Julie blurted out her thought, then tried to shrink into the chair. She had said not a word to anyone except Anne, feeling totally out of place.

Abigail stared at her, and she lost her smile for an instant, but quickly said, "I'm sure you must have high regard for Nathan, Miss Sampson." She paused and then added with a clipped edge to her words, "After all, it would be better I suppose for a woman who did what you did to have one man for a *friend*—than a whole squad!"

A shocked silence followed this taunt. They all realized that Abigail was accusing Julie of being a common woman—and Nathan of being a party to her behavior.

Abigail knew at once that she had gone too far, and tried quickly to modify the harsh charge. "I—I don't mean to imply . . ."

"We all know exactly what you mean, Abigail!" Paul stood up suddenly and there was a fine perspiration on his lip. His eyes were fixed on Abigail and his voice was harsh. He was usually so easygoing that the transformation was shocking.

"Paul, I'm sure Abigail meant nothing by the remark," Charles said quickly.

Paul stared at his father, then said in a quieter voice, "Father, you've told me many times lately that it was a sadness to you that after all Adam's done for you, there's nothing you can do for him, haven't you?"

"Why, yes, I have."

"Well, there's one thing we can do for him, and I propose to do it!"

"Paul! You're drunk!" Abigail said quickly.

"Yes, Abigail, I am drunk. And it's a shame that a man has to get drunk to do the right thing! But drunk or sober, my dear, we're going to have some truth tonight!"

"Paul, please don't do anything you'll regret." Abigail had been glaring at him angrily, but she suddenly grew gentle, and there was a softness in her tone.

"Regret?" he echoed, staring at her. He laughed harshly and said bitterly, "I've regretted just about everything I've ever done— but tonight I'm going to do the right thing." He settled back on his heels and stared at the Winslows. "Uncle Adam, as my father has said, you've saved our family—but he's wrong when he says there's nothing we can do for you—I'm going to save *your* family."

Adam and Molly had been mortified by the scene, and now Adam stared at his nephew. "Paul, I don't know what you're talking about."

"I'm talking, Uncle Adam, about Nathan."

"Nathan?"

"Oh, yes! And I'm talking about his intended bride, Miss Abigail Howland."

Nathan stood up suddenly, his eyes bright with anger. "Paul, shut your mouth!"

"No, I won't do that, Nathan," Paul said evenly, and then he got a strange look in his eye. "Honor—that's always been important to the Winslow men, hasn't it, Uncle Adam?"

"I hope so, Paul."

"Honor." Paul seemed to taste the word, then smiled sadly. "It's been just a word to me, I'm afraid. I've laughed at those who thought it was worth living for—or dying for. But lately, I've had to wonder if *I* wasn't the one who was wrong."

"Nathan, I want to go home!" Abigail uttered, her voice distraught, her face very pale.

"All right, Abigail. I'll take you," Nathan said.

He moved from his place, but Paul cried loudly, "Nathan, you've wondered who betrayed you when you went to Abigail?"

The question stopped Nathan in his tracks. Paul said evenly, "I turned you in."

"You!"

"Yes. I was in love with Abigail and you seemed to be winning her."

"Paul!" Charles's face seemed to be bloodless, and he cried out, "You betrayed your own flesh and blood?"

"Yes. But how did I know he was there?"

"I never told you that!" Abigail said loudly.

Paul reached into his pocket and pulled out several pieces of paper. "Nathan, you know Abigail's handwriting—here's the note she sent telling me you were coming to her house—and here's the one I got later that says our affair will have to stop—for a while—because she needs you to keep her from falling into the hands of the patriots."

Nathan took the notes, read one, then the other. He lifted his eyes, so filled with pain that Julie wanted to cry.

"I couldn't help it!" Abigail cried out, and then her face twisted and she ran out of the room sobbing.

Paul moved back and said with a hollow smile, "I'm sorry for you, Nathan, but not as sorry as I am for her—nor for me, because I love her. I know what she is—and I love her anyway. She would have ruined you, Nathan!" Then he turned and walked out of the room, and they heard the door slam as he left the house.

Nathan reached out and touched the notes to the tip of flame that rose from a candle, then put them into a silver dish. He watched the paper turn into blackened ash; then he looked at the silent group and said, "Uncle Charles, I hope you won't think too badly of Paul. When a man loves a woman—he's likely to do strange things, I guess." After a pause he asked quietly, "Are we ready to go home now?"

Adam and Molly came quickly to stand with him, and then he said, "Julie? Will you come with us?"

"Yes, Nathan, I'm ready," she whispered, and together they left the house.

CHAPTER TWENTY-SEVEN

THE FIERY TRIAL

★ ★ ★ ★

The morning after the disaster at Charles's house, Adam sent Nathan on a mission to collect some cannon and powder from a post in Rhode Island. When Molly pressed him, he said, "I could have sent someone else—but Nathan needs to get away." He grimaced and clapped his hands together in an abrupt gesture, exclaiming, "Molly, when he realized last night what that girl had done, it was like he'd taken a bullet in the brain!"

"I know, Adam." Molly's eyes were tired, and she tried to smile. "I think it's just as well for him to go away for a while."

"He was so depressed I was afraid he'd desert. His enlistment is up in two weeks—by that time we'll be moving on to New York for sure."

When Molly told Julie later that day what Adam had done, she had said quietly, "It's best that way. He was hurting so!" The older woman gave her a compassionate look and thought in her heart, *And so are you, child!*

As the days passed, Julie said little, but the thought of Aaron's return was never completely out of her mind. She ate little and her cheerful smile was rarely seen. There was little work for her to do, so after cleaning the house she spent long hours beside the small pond, sitting under the canopy of tender gold-green leaves. For hours she would read the Bible, especially the Psalms; then she would walk around the pond, praying silently. Praying and thinking. Fear would strike her like a knife, but each time it did, she would seek God, and a peace would settle over her.

Except for Molly, she saw almost no one, which was a blessing, for the inward journey she was struggling with required all her attention. She wondered at times about Daniel Greene, for the gentle Quaker had disappeared. Once she had asked Adam, but he had said, "Well, he was getting pretty close to his uncle, General Greene. Nathanael's a wandering man—maybe he took the young fellow off on one of his scouting trips."

Privately Julie thought he'd gone back home, and was disappointed, but as she became more and more engaged in her search for God's will, she thought of him fondly, but not often. Molly was a blessing, for the dark-eyed woman had the blood of the Covenanters in her veins, and knew what waiting on God was. Sometimes Julie would sit for hours listening as Molly read in a soft, firm voice out of the Bible, and although she said little of meaning or interpretation, there would be those times when she would read a verse, then pause for a long moment with her eyes closed—and then she would smile at Julie and comment on the meaning so that the verse would suddenly come alive to the girl.

It came as a surprise to her when Paul Winslow came down the path as she was walking late one afternoon. He stopped in front of her, saying, "Sorry to intrude on you, Miss Sampson." Fatigue had dulled his neat features, making him look older, and his manner was subdued. "Perhaps you'd rather not talk to me—I should not blame you."

"Would you like to walk with me, Mr. Winslow?" she asked, and her gentle answer brightened his eyes.

"Thank you." He stepped beside her, and for several minutes he said nothing. She could see he was changed; he was struggling with his thoughts, attempting to say something that came hard for him.

"You feel badly about Nathan, don't you, Mr. Winslow?" she said quietly, sensing that it was this that had brought him.

He stared at her, then smiled and nodded. "You're a very discerning young woman!" He bit his lip nervously, and threw his hands out in a helpless gesture. "What can I say? Father won't speak to me—and he's absolutely right . . . !"

His conscience, Julie saw, had been cutting him to pieces, and the light spirit that had bubbled out of him was gone. She said little as they walked and he spoke of his life, for she saw that he was looking for someone to hear his confession.

Finally he paused and said in a hopeless voice, "I—I don't know why I came to you with all this. Actually, I'm not much of a man to speak of myself about such things. I—I guess I wanted to tell Nathan how sorry I am, and you caught it instead." He had been staring down at the ground. Now he lifted his head, looked into her eyes and said , "Well, I'll leave you to—"

"Don't go, Paul." She called him by his first name unconsciously, for there was something young and vulnerable in him as he stood there. "Let's talk some more." He brightened, and for over an hour they walked, and this time she shared with him her struggle to find peace. As he listened, the simple faith in her voice held him. She made little of the precarious state of her life, but he knew of it, and admired her quiet courage.

Finally he left, saying, "You've been a help, Julie." Then a trace of his old humor touched his eyes and turned his lips up in the first smile she'd seen since he'd arrived. "You know what I'm going to do for you?" He paused solemnly and said firmly, "I'm going— to let you pray for me!"

She smiled at him. "I haven't waited for your permission, Paul."

He blinked, nodded, then turned abruptly and left. Later that night she told Molly of the visit.

"He's lost his way," Molly said. "But Winslow men have a habit of getting pulled out of the miry pit." Then she shook her head, saying, "That girl! She could have had one good man—but it wasn't enough for her!"

"Molly," Julie asked suddenly, "Doesn't the Scripture say we are to pray for those who despitefully use us? Are you praying for Abigail?"

Molly said, "Yes—but it's not hard, Julie. She hasn't used me ill."

"But the way she treated Nathan—?"

"She would have harmed us all much more if she'd married him, Julie!" Then she smiled and said, "And you mustn't forget— she's a Winslow, too! Oh, the blood's thinned some—but her grandmother was Rachel Winslow—and *her* great-grandfather was Gilbert Winslow." She paused and said thoughtfully, "I think about those people a great deal—and it's hard to keep in mind that they weren't gods—just people like us. But Gilbert threw his life on the altar for God, and Rachel went to the brink of death at Salem out of a love for God—so I'm not giving up on Abigail!"

Julie leaned against the wall, hands behind her. The quiet days had thinned her face, hollowed her cheeks somewhat, and her eyes were clear and speculative. "I feel so strange, Molly. The world is falling apart—trouble everywhere. And all I've done for days is walk around a pond."

"There never has been a time, Julie," Molly answered with a nod, "that the world *wasn't* falling apart. Gilbert Winslow saw his world fall apart when half of the Firstcomers died that first winter at Plymouth. His son, Matthew, was in prison with John Bunyan in the shadow of the gallows. That's the kind of world we live in—and it won't ever change." Her lips were relaxed as she spoke, and she added thoughtfully, "As for walking around a pond—you've been doing more than that, child. You've been trying to find out who you are to God—and who He is to you. And that's the most important job in this little life we have!"

"That's right, isn't it?" A look of wonder came into Julie's eyes and she whispered, "That's what God's been saying to me all this time—'Trust me!' " She laughed shortly, adding, "I was expecting some sort of lightning bolt to strike me—maybe fall out—like Adam said He did when he got converted."

"He did!" Molly laughed. "It was at one of George Whitefield's meetings, and Adam had tried just about everything—was about ready to give up—and all of a sudden, he just folded up. He got up looking stunned—and he's been walking with God ever since. So for some it's falling down at a meeting—for others, God speaks in a still, small voice—perhaps when walking around a pond!"

Two days after this conversation, Julie answered a knock at the door, opening it to see Dan standing there dressed in the uniform of General Greene's company. She stared at him in astonishment, and he laughed before she could move, giving her a kiss on the cheek. "Well, here I am, Julie," he smiled ruefully. "See what thee has done to a poor humble Friend?"

"Daniel! I can't *believe* it!"

"Neither could Mother! But she's not going to disown me. I just came from home, and thee know what, Julie? She wasn't surprised—said the Lord had already told her about it." He laughed in embarrassment, adding, "I wish He'd told *me*!"

"How in the world—?"

"Oh, my uncle had gone through the same struggle, thee knows. And officially I'm a chaplain—but that doesn't seem to mean much! I think when the fighting starts, there'll be at least two fighting Quakers in General Greene's company!"

She pulled him inside, glad to see him, pushing him into a chair, and demanding the details. They drank a pot of tea as he spoke of the great change that had come to his thinking. The china cup looked small in his large hands, and he sometimes spoke quietly of the inner struggle that had shaken him—then his eyes flashed as he spoke of the new vision that had caught his spirit. He didn't call it a *vision*, yet it was so strong that it made his eyes glow as he spoke of the emerging nation.

"It's not just a little movement, Julie," he said finally. "God is up to something with this country! The old world is tired—and the church of the living God is bound in chains. But in this land, why, it can be a place where we can all seek God in any way we choose!"

Finally, he caught himself, laughed and said, "I sound like a recruiting sergeant, don't I? But that's not why I came, Julie, although since thee is a part of what's happened to me, I wanted to share it with thee."

"I'm glad you came. I've missed you, Dan."

He stared at her, then said simply, "Did thee, Julie? Well, that may mean something, but I guess thee knows how I feel. I know thee thinks thee are in love with Nathan—but I finally decided that I could either keep my mouth shut—or I could say what I've been thinking."

"Dan—!"

"Don't stop me now, Julie! I'm a plain man—always will be. Not at all romantic or exciting." He considered this, and it was characteristic of him that he was anxious to be fair, even at such a moment. "So—I want thee to marry me."

Julie stood very still, and he added, "Maybe I'll never have what thee had to give the other fellow. I'll never ask for that. I can't give thee what he could—but I can give thee my name—and my love."

The clock ticked loudly on the shelf, and tiny motes floated in the brilliant sunshine that fell through the windows in bars that seemed almost solid. Tears rose to Julie's eyes and she said, "I can't let you do that, Daniel. It wouldn't be fair."

He nodded and there was a faint regret in his eyes—but a stubborn set to his jaw. "I may not be romantic, Julie," he said, "but I'm hard to discourage. I'll not bother thee, but thee are pretty likely to find me underfoot for a spell."

"You'll be off at the war."

"Woman, thee are talking to the only living *nephew* of General Nathanael Greene!" His eyes twinkled and he said proudly, "Why, dear Uncle Nathanael practically *insisted* that I take a good leave! So here I am, Julie—and like I say, I'm a hard man to discourage."

Julie shook her head, but though she often asked him to leave during the next three days, he settled down in a room close by, ignoring her urgings. He said nothing more about marriage or about Nathan, and his presence, for all her protests, was a comfort to her.

On a Friday afternoon, Adam came in with bitter news. The moment he entered the room and said "Julie!" she knew what it was.

"My uncle is back, isn't he?"

"I'm afraid so."

Molly asked quickly, "Adam, isn't there anything we can do?"

"He's got the papers—and Judge Evans says that Julie will have to go with him." He came up and tried to smile, saying, "Child, this isn't the end. We'll get a lawyer—a good one!"

Julie looked at him and asked quietly, "When—will I have to go?"

"On Monday, I'm afraid. General Knox held him off until after the Sabbath."

"I'll be ready—and I'd like to write your mother a letter, Daniel."

She left the room, and Daniel suddenly slammed his hand down on the table. "Well, devil fly off! I'd like to sink that man in the depths of the sea with a blasted millstone tied around his neck!"

He stood there, shocked at the force of his anger, then wheeled and left the room. "I'm going to see if my uncle knows a good lawyer in Philadelphia."

Molly waited until the door slammed, then came to stand beside Adam. "I'm afraid for her," she whispered. "She's so young and helpless!"

"Well, God's not!" Adam said, and the muscles in his thick arms tensed. She knew that he, like Daniel, longed for some way to throw himself physically into the matter, but he finally said, "This is going to be hard on Nathan. I thought he'd be back before now—but I got word from a courier—they're just twenty miles out of Boston with the guns. Be in some time late tomorrow, or Sunday at the latest." Then he shrugged and said in a gloomy tone, "I don't look for him to be too happy, Molly. He was in bad shape when he left—and this news isn't going to help, is it?"

Molly's lips tightened. "Saints are made by being put through the fire. I've heard you say the same many times. This is our son's time to go through his fiery trial, Adam—and all we can do is pray!"

CHAPTER TWENTY-EIGHT

"AS LONG AS WE LIVE!"

★ ★ ★ ★

Sunday Julie went to services with the Winslows and Daniel Greene. Adam shifted all through the sermon, and as soon as they were outside, Molly asked, "What is the *matter* with you, Adam?"

"This business has got to me, Molly. Can't stand the thought of that poor girl going off in that man's hands!"

They went home after church, and although Molly had fixed a large meal, none of them felt like eating much. The afternoon dragged on, and when night fell, Adam said, "Something must have happened to Nathan. He should have been here long before this."

At ten o'clock, Julie said, "I want to thank you both for all you've done for me." There was a wistful light in her eyes, and she added, "No parents could have been better to me than you've been."

"Why, we've done nothing!" Molly said.

"Yes, you have—and I wanted to tell you tonight how much I've learned to love all of you." She hesitated, and they saw that she was close to tears. "I'm going to bed now—good night—and God bless you!"

She left quickly and Adam and Molly went to bed soon after, but there was little rest for them. All night long, Adam tossed and turned, and finally just as dawn was breaking, there was the sound of a horse galloping down the street. The rider pulled up, and when they heard the knocking at the door, Adam said, "That's Nathan!"

He got up, pulled his clothes on, and hurried downstairs to unlock the door. Nathan stepped in, his face tense. "Hello, Father. She's still here, isn't she?"

"Well, yes," Adam said. "But Sampson's taking her back to Philadelphia today. Why are you so late?"

"Spring rains washed a bridge out—we had to go a long way around to another bridge—and then the courier you sent couldn't find us."

Molly came down the stairs belting a robe on, and Nathan put his arms around her and kissed her. "I've missed you!"

She stood in his arms, looked up into his face. He was so tall that he made her feel like a child, but there was something different about him, and she asked quickly, "Nathan—what's happened to you?"

He grinned down at her, then shot a look at Adam. "I could never fool her, could I, Father?"

"Neither could I, son." He too was staring at Nathan, and saw that there was no sign of the tension and gloom that he'd worn two weeks earlier. "Well, even I can see something's different. You left here looking like death—but you're not that way now."

"It's not a very long story," Nathan said, but there was a glow in his blue eyes, and excitement ran through his voice. "You were right, Father, about how I left here. I was mad and feeling sorry for myself—and I came pretty close to just leaving for good."

"I figured that," Adam nodded.

"It was in my mind most of the time. I'd made such a mess of things! If my enlistment had been up, guess I'd have done it—but I didn't want to be a deserter on top of everything else—so I decided to wait till I was out of the army, then pull out." His face grew sober, and he walked over to the window. The gray dawn was breaking up, and tiny shards of rose began to show in the east. He seemed to have forgotten them, and neither Adam nor Molly moved.

Finally he turned, and they were shocked to see tears in his eyes. "It was last Sunday—April 19." He struggled to get control of himself, then finally said huskily, "One year after—after Caleb died."

Molly put her hand to her mouth and turned away, and Adam set his jaw—but neither of them spoke. They had never seen Nathan so moved. He had rarely let his emotions show, but now they looked into his eyes and saw that somehow during the brief time he'd been gone, something had stripped him of the wall he'd kept between his inner self and the world. *His eyes,* Molly thought suddenly, *are like windows.* Looking into them she saw her son as she had never seen him—and she knew that Adam was seeing the same thing.

"I didn't even know what the date was. We'd camped beside a river, and late that afternoon one of the men mentioned that it was a year since Lexington—and it hit me hard! I walked off and left them—walking along the bank of the river. It all came back— about Caleb, and all night I just walked and walked—and cried. I never cried much, you remember? Well, I made up for it, I guess."

"We've all done our crying, son," Adam said gently.

Nathan shook his head and then went on. "I finally just wore out and sat down under a tree. The mosquitoes were bad, but I felt so terrible I didn't even care! I sat there, so mad that I couldn't even think! And I was ashamed of making such a fool out of myself— over Abigail! That, on top of grieving over Caleb, just about made me want to drown myself."

He stopped suddenly and looked at them so strangely that Molly asked, "What is it, Nathan?"

He shook his head, and the words seemed hard for him. "Well, I've been trying to think of a way to tell you about what happened to me under that tree—but there's no way except to just come out with it." He sobered and there was such a look of wonder in his eyes that Molly wanted to reach out and hold him. "I've been looking for God so long—even tried to be a minister to please Him. Read a thousand books of theology—and then He had to get me out under a tree with the bugs about to eat me alive before He'd speak to me!"

"You found the Lord!" Molly exclaimed, her eyes bright.

"Not quite as dramatic as your conversion, Father," Nathan said. "I didn't fall down, or anything like that—but for about two hours God brought up just about everything I'd ever done—and by dawn I was just too tired to fight, so I just called on God and told Him that I wasn't worth anything, but that if there was anything in me that He wanted—why He was welcome to it!" Then Nathan laughed and said with a joy they'd never heard: "And that's when Jesus Christ came in and took over!"

"Nathan! That's wonderful!" They all turned to find Julie standing in the hall. She'd already been up and dressed when he'd come, and she'd stood there listening to him. Now she came forward and there was a light in her face as she said, "I'm so *glad!*"

He stood there looking at her with a peculiar expression on his face, but he said only, "I'm glad I got here in time, Julie."

"I'm going to fix some breakfast," Molly declared. "Julie, you start the coffee while I get dressed."

As Julie cooked, Nathan related the fine details of his experience, and soon his parents were back, drinking it all in. They ate a good breakfast, and were just finishing when there was a loud knock on the door.

Adam got up, hesitated, then went and opened it.

Julie's courage almost failed her when she saw the bulk of Aaron Sampson fill the opening, and his coarse voice broke out loudly, "All right, where's the gal?"

Julie went at once to her room, picked up a bag containing what few things she was taking back, and returned swiftly. She saw that Adam's face was red, and he was saying, "The coach for Philadelphia doesn't leave until ten—!"

Julie didn't want to cause trouble for these people she loved, so she quickly stepped around Adam. "I'm ready."

Sampson was angry, and he glared at Adam. "I've got the papers all proper. That general has given me the runaround—but I'll have no more of it!" He grabbed Julie by the arm and jerked her out of the door. The pain of his grip made her cry out, but he said, "None of that! You've cost me a mint, you baggage! But, I'll have it back on you."

He was dragging her along toward the carriage he'd arrived in when suddenly his wrist was seized and Julie was plucked away from him. Sampson went reeling forward, falling heavily on the ground from a shove in the middle of his back.

"Get out of here, Sampson!"

The burly man looked up to see Nathan staring at him. He scrambled to his feet and cursed, but there was something deadly in the gaze that met his, so he shouted, "I'll have the law on you!"

Nathan asked, "Do you need help to get in that carriage?"

Sampson was a strong man, but he had felt the power of the soldier's grip, so he backed away, screaming, "You'll be jailed for this—I swear it!"

He drove off, whipping the horses and cursing all the way, and when he was down the road, the silence that fell was broken by Julie. "Nathan, you shouldn't have done that. You'll get into trouble."

"You can't go with that man, Julie!"

"I have to."

They went back into the house, and there was much talk about what to do, but an hour before the coach was to leave, Adam said, "We'll have to go. Nathan—they'll send as many men as they need to take her."

The four of them climbed into the carriage, and all too soon they were downtown. "There's Daniel," Molly said as they pulled up to the inn. The coach for Philadelphia was waiting, and Aaron Sampson was standing there with a tall man, obviously some sort of official.

"There she is!" he shouted. "Now, you do your duty!"

The officer came over as Adam pulled up and got out. "I'm Sheriff Marks, and I've got to ask you to surrender that young woman without making any trouble," he said quietly. "I know how you must feel, but he's within his legal rights."

While Adam was talking with the sheriff, Nathan jumped from the carriage to help his mother and Julie down. Dan hurried up to say, "Why, Nathan, you're back!" But he did not wait for a reply. Turning to Julie, he said, "I've been talking to my uncle, and he's given me a letter to Mr. Franklin—a personal friend of his. He's asking Franklin to get a good lawyer and to take a personal interest!"

"Why, that's so good of the general, Dan," Julie said, but there was little hope in her voice. She well knew that once her uncle got her in his grip, he cared nothing for the threats of the law.

Molly started to speak, but Nathan said loudly, "Wait a minute!" They all turned, surprised. Adam and the sheriff abruptly stopped their conversation, while Aaron Sampson threw an angry, malevolent look at him. An elderly couple about to mount the carriage paused to stare at Nathan. The driver, coming out of the inn with a large mail pouch, gave him a surprised look, thinking he was being stopped.

Nathan had their attention, and for one brief instant they stood there, as if time had stopped. The only sound breaking the silence was the impatient stamping of the horses' hooves. Julie had been standing between Dan and Nathan, and when he spoke she looked up at him, and her heart, struggling with fear ever since her first glimpse of Aaron Sampson in the doorway, somehow lightened.

Nathan had said practically nothing on the way to town. He had let others do the talking, but there had been a grim perplexity on his wedge-shaped face. Now he seemed to have reached a decision. He set his feet firmly, and reached down and took a grip on Julie's arm, his chin thrusting forward as he said, "You're not taking her back with you, Sampson!"

The beefy face of Sampson grew red, and he yelled, "You just try and hold her, Winslow! I got the law on my side. Sheriff, you hear what he says? Do your duty, man!"

Sheriff Marks moved a few steps toward Nathan, took in the aggressive set of his face, but said in an authoritative voice, "Now, Mr. Winslow, you must be reasonable about this thing. I don't like it myself, but it's the law."

"The law gives him the right to take her back to his home because he's her guardian."

"That's right."

Nathan took a firmer grip on Julie's arm and said, "Well, I have no objection to that—but he's not going to be her guardian after this morning."

"What kind of nonsense is that?" Sampson snorted. He moved closer to Julie, then took one look at Nathan's face and said quickly, "You get that girl in that carriage, Sheriff!"

"No you don't!" Nathan said. "She won't be in his charge if she's a married woman." He felt Julie's body tense, but he didn't look at her. "That's law, isn't it? When a woman marries, her husband is responsible for her?"

Sheriff Marks looked confused. He raised a hand and scratched his neck, staring first at Nathan then at Julie. "Well, I'm no lawyer, Winslow—I just—"

Suddenly Nathan felt Julie pull away and, looking down, saw that her face was red with anger. Her eyes were snapping, and there was a tremor of indignation in her voice as she spoke to him. "And what makes you think I'd marry *you*, Nathan Winslow?"

He stared down at her stupidly, for in his own mind the idea of marrying her had seemed simple, but she drew her arms together to her sides, and her enormous eyes flashed fire as she looked up at him and said through set teeth, "You needn't stand there looking like a martyr! Oh, wouldn't that be a great marriage—for the next forty years every time I did something you didn't like, you'd get that look on your face: *I married her to save her—now see how she pays me back!*"

"Why, it won't be like that—!" Nathan protested.

"Besides," Julie ran on swiftly, "you needn't think you're so righteous—Daniel's already asked me to marry *him!*"

Nathan's face went blank, and then he pivoted his head around to stare at Daniel. "Why, you can't marry him!"

"Oh, why can't I?" Julie challenged, looking up at Nathan. "You think nobody would marry me except to get me out of trouble? No man would love me for myself?"

Daniel said quickly, "My offer still stands, Julie. I don't mind saying before everyone that I love thee. Marry me."

"She's not marrying you, Greene—she's marrying *me!*"

Greene's face flushed, and he moved around to face Nathan, his broad shoulders suddenly tense. Anger laced his mild voice as he said, "Thee don't love her, Winslow! I'll admit she's in love with thee"—Nathan's head went back and he shot a wild glance at Julie, but the Quaker went on relentlessly—"but she'll get over that in time."

Sampson raised his voice, protesting, "Sheriff, do your duty!" But the officer was caught up in the drama. Julie was suddenly aware that she was the focal point of attention. Even people passing by had stopped to stare.

The sudden flash of anger that had swept through her faded. She lowered her head, her eyes swimming with tears, and she wished that it would all be over. Then she felt a hand under her chin, and looked up to see Nathan's face. There was a strange look in his eyes. He stared at her, and she saw him only in a blur, for the tears spilled over and rolled down her cheeks. He asked, "Is that right, Julie—what Greene said? Do you love me?"

She blinked and saw the gentleness in him that she'd learned to love. His hands were on her cheeks, and as he held her face, memories swept through her. Finally she whispered, "Yes! I guess I always will, Nathan."

He was silent, and then he said, "I've been so mixed up, Julie. I told you about finding God on the riverbank—but I didn't tell you what else I found."

"What, Nathan?" she asked.

"After I got straight with the Lord, I found out I could think straight about other things—and all I could think about was you. I've been God's worst fool about women—but somehow I know there'll never be anyone for me—except you, Julie!"

She knew that the spectators were leaning forward avidly, but she didn't care. Everything around them vanished, and she saw only his face, heard only his voice. Then she whispered, "It's just pity, Nathan—you don't love me."

"I had to find out that not all people find God the same way," he said quietly. "And I'm finding out now that not all men find love the same way—but believe me or not, Julie, I know in my heart I'll always love you. I wish we had *time!*—but we don't, because I'll be leaving to go with Washington. But I'll come back, Julie—and I want to come back to you—if you'll have me!"

Julie suddenly smiled, her face illuminated with joy, and she held her arms up, saying quietly, "I'll have you—and you'll have me!"

He kissed her, ignoring Sampson's cries of rage, and when he stepped back, they heard him say, "It ain't legal, I tell you—I'm her guardian! There ain't no wedding—and I'm taking her with me."

Sheriff Marks said regretfully, "I think he's within his rights. Now if you were actually *married*, why that'd be different—but you'll not find a minister to marry you right now, and even if there was one willing, it'd take a few days to get the papers done." He shook his head, adding, "Have to ask you to go with this man, Miss Sampson."

Julie moved away from Nathan, but suddenly she heard Dan say, "I don't think it'll be any problem—getting thee married—if that's what thee wants, Julie."

"Why, Friend Daniel," Adam spoke up, "you heard what the sheriff said! It'd take a miracle to get them married."

Greene pulled a paper out of his inner pocket and held it up. "Here's a license from General Greene authorizing a civil marriage. Boston is technically under martial law, so all licenses must be issued or approved by military authorities."

"Whose name is on that paper?" Sampson demanded.

"Well, it's not filled in yet." He came to stand before Julie and Nathan, and there was sadness in his fine eyes but a faint smile on his face. "I thought thee might change your mind and have me at the last minute, Julie, so I had my uncle give this to me—meant to write *my* name on it, but—if thee are sure of this thing, all I have to do is fill in Nathan's."

"Oh, Dan—" Julie almost sobbed, "I—don't want to hurt you—but I love him so much!"

"And thee, Nathan?"

"Friend Daniel," Nathan said quietly, "I love her now—but it's just the beginning."

"Well—that's it!" Greene said.

"No, it ain't!" Sampson said, his face contorted with rage. "You got a paper—but you ain't got no preacher. Come on, get in that coach!" His thought, as Julie knew, was to get her away at once, and once they were in Philadelphia, he would force her to marry him.

"Oh, we've got a minister here." Greene smiled as they stared at him, then waved his hand. "Chaplain Daniel Greene, at thy service—fully authorized by the commander in chief of the Continental Army to perform all prescribed duties—sermons, buryings—and marryings!"

"Daniel! Can you marry us?" Julie gasped.

"Well, it's not what I had in my mind—or in my heart—but I see that it's the way God is moving."

Aaron Sampson's face was pale as paste, and he whispered, "Sheriff—can he do that?"

Sheriff Marks had a broad smile on his face. "I can't go against George Washington and the Continental Army, can I?"

Sampson glared at them and said, "I don't believe it! You'll wait till I'm gone and then back out somehow!"

Daniel saw that the man meant it, so he said briskly, "Captain Winslow, would thee and thy wife come and stand here by the bride and groom? The rest of thee can be witnesses."

There was a dreamlike quality about it all, and the crowd grew larger as the party arranged itself in the street beside the coach. Julie could not believe what was happening, but there was reality in the hard squeeze that Nathan gave her hand, and she took her place with him in front of Dan, with Molly standing beside her, Adam by Nathan.

The traffic on the street had stopped, and eager spectators crowded close to see what was happening, whispered excitedly, then pushed closer, forming a circle around the small group.

Greene looked around at the curious faces, then raised his

voice, saying, "I don't know all the right words, but I think I know what a marriage is. The Scripture says that one of the wonders of all this world is 'the way of a man with a maid.' Out of the millions of men and women on this globe, one man and one woman come together, and each of them finds something in the other that's stronger than death! So they become *one* and are no longer two separate beings."

He looked steadily into Nathan's eyes and asked, "Nathan, does thee love this woman?"

"Yes!"

"Will thee forsake all others and love only her as long as thee both shall live?"

"I—I will!"

Greene's voice trembled only slightly as he said, "Julie, does thee love this man?"

"Yes!"

"Will thee love only him as long as thee both shall live?"

Julie looked up into Nathan's eyes, saw the love that was in him, and she nodded and said, "As long as we live!"

Then Greene said the words that tied them: "I pronounce thee husband and wife!"

And as Nathan bent down and kissed her, she clung to him fiercely for one brief moment; then she pulled away and smiled. Sampson climbed into the coach, screaming curses, and the growing crowd swarmed around to stare. But Adam put his arms around Molly and, smiling at her with shining eyes, said, "They've got a war to go through, Molly, but they've got each other, and they've got God!"

Molly kissed him, and he tasted the salt of tears on her lips, but there was victory in her clear eyes. She looked at Nathan and Julie, and said quietly, "They'll make it, Adam."

And then they moved forward to welcome the newest member of the House of Winslow.

THE
SAINTLY
BUCCANEER

THE
SAINTLY
BUCCANEER

★

GILBERT MORRIS

BETHANY HOUSE PUBLISHERS
MINNEAPOLIS, MINNESOTA 55438
A Division of Bethany Fellowship, Inc.

Manuscript edited by Penelope J. Stokes.

Cover illustration by Dan Thornberg,
Bethany House Publishers staff artist.

Published by Bethany House Publishers
A Division of Bethany Fellowship, Inc.
6820 Auto Club Road, Minneapolis, Minnesota 55438

Printed in the United States of America

Library of Congress Cataloging-in-Publication Data

Morris, Gilbert.
　　The saintly buccaneer / Gilbert Morris.
　　　　p. cm. — (The House of Winslow ; bk. 5)

　　1. United States—History—Revolution, 1775–1783—Fiction.
I. Title.　II. Series: Morris, Gilbert. House of Winslow ; bk. 5.
PS3563.08742S25　　1989
813'.54—dc19　　　　　　　　　　　　　　　　88–33337
ISBN 1-55661-048-3　　　　　　　　　　　　　　　CIP

To my special granddaughter — Laura Michelle Smith

All children are "special," of course, and all grandchildren are *extra* special—because all of them come from God; they are the fruit of the womb—the reward of the Lord. No two have the same laugh, the same fingerprints, and each of them forges a special golden chain to bind himself to the heart of a parent or a grandparent.

You are "special," Laura, because you have "special" parents. If it were not for their faith, you would not be alive on this earth! Stacy—my "special" daughter, the handmaiden of the Lord—and the light of her father's eyes! Ronnie, my "special" son-in-law who walked by faith!

You are "special," my Laura, because God has used you to increase the faith of others.

You are "special" because although God has not yet made you complete, He has given His promise that what He has begun he will complete.

And you are "special" because you exactly fill that space in my heart that no other child or grandchild could fill. Without you, I would be incomplete.

THE HOUSE OF WINSLOW SERIES

GILBERT MORRIS spent ten years as a pastor before becoming Professor of English at Ouachita Baptist University in Arkansas and earning a Ph.D. at the University of Arkansas. During the summers of 1984 and 1985 he did postgraduate work at the University of London and is presently the Chairman of General Education at a Christian college in Louisiana. A prolific writer, he has had over 25 scholarly articles and 200 poems published in various periodicals, and over the past years has had more than 20 novels published. His family includes three grown children, and he and his wife live in Baton Rouge, Louisiana.

CONTENTS

THE
HOUSE OF WINSLOW

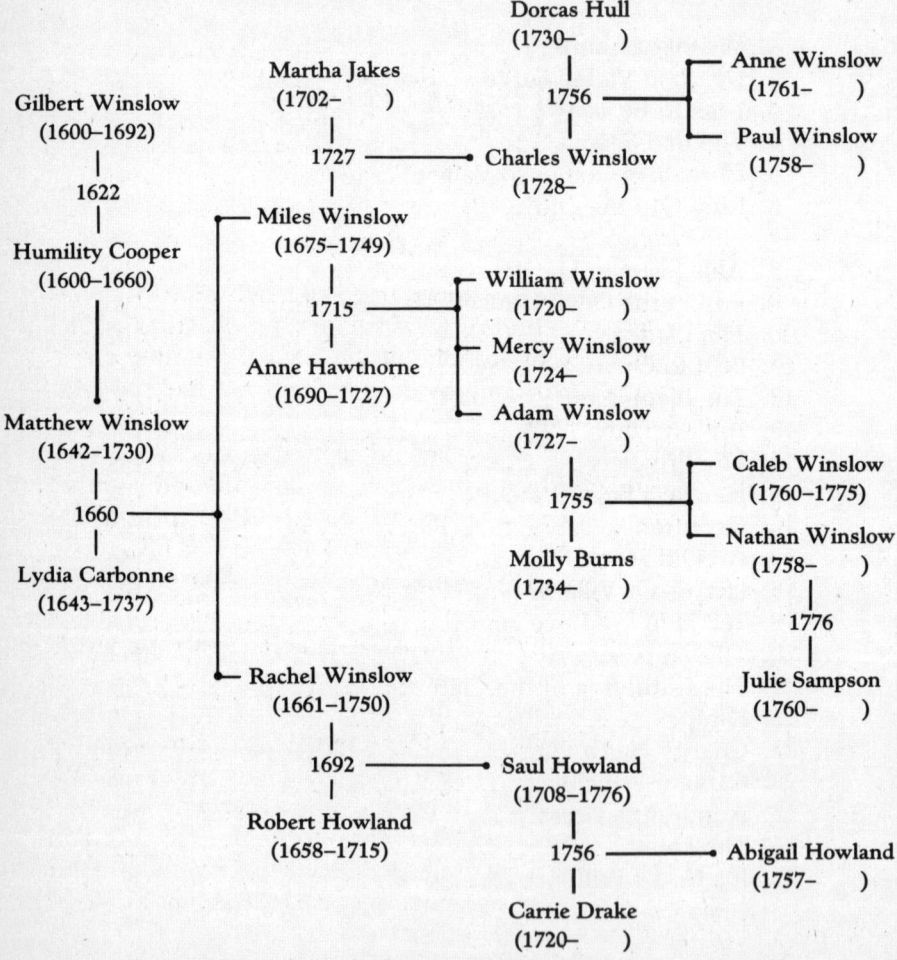

Gilbert Winslow
(1600–1692)
|
1622
|
Humility Cooper
(1600–1660)

Matthew Winslow
(1642–1730)
|
1660
|
Lydia Carbonne
(1643–1737)

Martha Jakes
(1702–   )
|
1727

Miles Winslow
(1675–1749)
|
1715
|
Anne Hawthorne
(1690–1727)

Rachel Winslow
(1661–1750)
|
1692
|
Robert Howland
(1658–1715)

Dorcas Hull
(1730–   )
|
1756

Charles Winslow
(1728–   )

William Winslow
(1720–   )

Mercy Winslow
(1724–   )

Adam Winslow
(1727–   )
|
1755
|
Molly Burns
(1734–   )

Saul Howland
(1708–1776)
|
1756
|
Carrie Drake
(1720–   )

Anne Winslow
(1761–   )

Paul Winslow
(1758–   )

Caleb Winslow
(1760–1775)

Nathan Winslow
(1758–   )
|
1776
|
Julie Sampson
(1760–   )

Abigail Howland
(1757–   )

CHAPTER ONE

VISITOR AT CAMP

★ ★ ★ ★

The bitter cold probed with icy fingers beneath Charity's thick fur coat, and it took an effort of will for her to ignore its grip. Her face had been stiffened by the bite of the frigid December wind, and despite the thick woolen gloves, she could not feel the reins that guided her rangy bay.

"Come on, Pompey!" she called out as the horse stopped suddenly. She was surprised at how weak her voice sounded, and her lips were stiff as wood as she spoke. Pulling the whip from the socket, she gave the tired animal a cut; and as he broke into a trot, she muttered, "Better find that camp pretty soon—else I'll be froze solid!"

The small black buggy careened along the frozen ruts, but in less than twenty minutes it crested a long hill, and there between a sweep of frozen meadowland on one side and a thick forest on the other, Charity saw with relief the campfires blossoming in the quick-falling darkness. An elderly woman with a wrinkled face but the body of a young girl had told her four hours earlier: "Ye'll find them soldiers at Valley Forge." Pointing toward the hills she had added, "Over there's the Schuylkill—ain't but a leetle ways to whur they is—was a forge thar once—but ain't nothin' there now—'cept Washington and them soldier fellers."

The horse sensed the end of the long journey and picked up his pace, so that she had to hold him back as she drew even with the first fires. Her first clear look at the men who stood around the feeble blaze brought a shock. She had pictured in her mind rows of sturdy tents with men dressed in neat uniforms; what she saw was a group of scarecrows! Their faces were blue with the cold, and their eyes looked enormous as they stared at her. And the clothing! Not a good coat or a pair of boots among the lot. Parts of the body showed through huge rents—one man even exposed a portion of bare, blue buttocks where the pants had worn away! Most of them looked deformed, elephantine, with their feet wrapped in blankets.

She saw them stare at her. Then several of them started toward her, their voices thin on the cold air. "Hup! Pompey!" she commanded quickly, and as she sped down between the ragged tents and flimsy huts, she heard their raucous, obscene cries fade behind her. She was not a girl given to idle fears, but there was a wolfish hunger in their faces.

Now the dusk was closing in and she grew a little desperate, searching for an officer. The huts grew closer together, and somewhere somebody was singing:

"Yankee Doodle went to London,

Riding on a pony—"

The space narrowed, forcing her to guide the horse between two rows of shacks that seemed to rise out of the ground, specter-like. Suddenly there was a shrill cry, and she caught a startled glimpse of a figure that darted from the shadows, rising up to grab Pompey's harness and pull him to an abrupt halt.

"Get out of my way!" she cried out, but even as she snatched the whip from its socket to slash at the man, she felt a pair of hands grab her and drag her off the buggy seat.

"Well, now! Whut we got here?"

Charity found herself in the grip of a huge man with yellowish teeth. He was grinning down at her, and his rank odor almost paralyzed her. He kept an iron grip on one arm and ran his free hand over her body, laughing in a shrill manner. "Looky here whut we done got us for a Chrismus gif', Sam!"

"Ain't that a fact, now?" Another man thrust his face close to hers, a thick-bodied man with a huge bulbous nose and small gleaming eyes.

"Let me go!" Charity tried to pull herself free, but the first man merely laughed at her struggles.

"You can take the wench first, Charlie," the one called Sam grinned. He nodded at Pompey, saying, "I'll cut us some steaks out of that there horse. Blast my eyes, but we'll have us steaks and a woman tonight—but keep her still so's them other fellers won't know 'bout it!"

Terror ran like fire through Charity, and she opened her mouth to scream, but the tall man named Charlie promptly clapped his dirty paw over her face and said, while dragging her to the shack to his left, "You take that beast and dress him out, Sam. Time you get back, you'll 'preciate a pretty leetle thing like this!"

Charity kicked and tried to claw at his face, but he laughed in evil delight. "Thet's right, honey, you keep it up! I likes a gal with some fight in 'er!"

Desperately she fought, and just as he was dragging her through the low door, she wrenched her head and his little finger slipped into her mouth. Instantly she bit down with all her might and tasted blood!

"Owww . . . !" The soldier instinctively shoved her away, yanking his hand free and sending her sprawling on the ground. But she was up like a flash and let out a piercing cry, "Help! Help me, somebody!"

She darted toward the buggy, but Sam grabbed her, and with a curse Charlie came racing after Charity, shaking the blood from his wounded finger. There was an ugly expression on his dirty face, and he snarled, "Bite me, will you? Well, maybe you need a lesson 'fore—!"

"Get away from that woman, both of you!"

Charity looked wildly toward her left, her eyes lighting on a very tall man dressed in a loose-fitting, shapeless gray smock. He had reddish hair curling out from beneath his fur cap, and the bluest eyes Charity had ever seen. A long rifle rested loosely in one hand. "I said let that woman alone," he commanded as the men around Charity began moving in.

Sam Macklin gave a quick look around and was reassured as he saw the ranks closing in, much like wolves circling a wounded deer. "Why, you fool!" he snarled and took one step forward, pulling a knife from his belt. "You git back there with the rest of your kind!" He gestured with the knife, the cold steel glittering in the fading light. "I'll cut your gizzard out, Winslow!"

"Do it, Sam!" Charlie urged wickedly. "Like to see one of them Virginia men cut right down the middle like a hawg!"

A chorus went up from the men and they closed around Charity, but the man named Winslow said evenly, as though he were making a remark about the weather, "I'd rather shoot a lobsterback than one of you; but I'm telling you now, one of you is going to die if you don't let that woman go."

"Aw, he's only got one shot!" Macklin shouted. "Git him!"

"Only one—want it, Sam?" Quick as a flash, Winslow brought the rifle up, and Macklin found himself staring down the cold steel muzzle. The blue eyes above it did not waver, but the voice matched the steel in his hands. "You think this is a good day to die? No? I didn't think you would. Miss, you come over here."

Charity jerked free of the hands holding her and ran to the tall man who seemed to hold the others with his eyes.

"You ain't gonna do it, Winslow!" Macklin breathed heavily, his face pale. He moved forward and said, "If he gets me, you boys cut him to pieces!"

With terror Charity saw he was not going to stop, that he was willing to take the bullet, and she knew the tall Virginian would not be able to resist the rest—but suddenly, there was the sound of a horse approaching, and a sharp voice cut through the air: "What the devil? What's that woman doing here?"

A man in a blue uniform pulled up, looking down at Charity. He had cold blue eyes, and she sensed the hurried withdrawal of the ragged men.

"I—I've come to see my brother," she answered quickly. "My name is Charity Alden."

He stared at her, a frown on his face. Then Winslow spoke. "I know him, General Wayne. He's in the hospital."

"All right. Take her there, Winslow." The steely eyes moved to Sam Macklin, and he said evenly, "I'll cut the heart out of any man who touches a decent woman. You understand that?" Without waiting for an answer, he turned to Winslow. "See to Miss Alden." He wheeled his mount and rode off swiftly into the maze of huts.

"I'll kill you for this, Winslow!" Macklin threatened.

"Sam, you can't even kill the lice that're crawlin' all over you," the tall Virginian grinned. Then ignoring the angry stares, he said, "I'll take you to your brother, Miss."

A lump seemed to have lodged in Charity's throat, and her legs wanted to give way. She had never known such terror, and without Winslow's help, she would have been lost. "I—I can't thank you enough, Mr. Winslow! But, won't those men try to get at you?"

He looked down at her from his great height and smiled. "Oh, they'll cuss and rare, but they're too beat to fool with revenge." He took Pompey's bit and laughed, "I think you'd better watch this horse day and night, though. We've eaten most of ours—and this one would be prime cut!"

"You know my brother—Curtis?" she asked, trying to keep up with his long paces.

"Sure. He's right down the line from one of my friends." He glanced at her curiously. "How'd you hear about him being hurt?"

"He sent word by a friend of his—Malcolm Ruggle." She bit her lip and asked the question that had been gnawing at her ever since the raw-boned Scot had come to Boston with his message. "Is he hurt bad?"

Winslow nodded slowly. "Bad enough." He hesitated, then added, "You see, it has to be *very* bad before we go to the hospital. Most things we take care of ourselves."

"He's . . . he's not going to die?"

Winslow put a hand on her shoulder, his eyes filled with compassion. "He's bad, miss—but God is able!"

God had played little part in Charity's life, and what she heard the Virginian saying was, *Only God can save your brother.* Fear shot through her at the thought. Winslow soon turned down an alley of sorts, a winding path between two rows of huts, and stopped before one of them. "I'll tell my wife about you—and we can leave the horse with a friend of mine."

He tied the horse to a slender stump, led her to the door, and called out, "Julie—we've got company!"

The room Charity entered was very dark, for there were no windows and only one small candle flickered, casting deep shadows over the interior. She had time to see a crude table, a small bed, and various objects hanging from pegs along the rough boards that made up the walls. There was an odor of bodies, cooking, and raw earth; it was much like a cave, she thought.

"This is Charity Alden, Julie—you've met her brother at the hospital. And this is my wife—and my son."

Charity's eyes rested on a young woman with black hair and eyes dark as pools. She was moving carefully, for she was very close to the time of giving birth. When she spoke her voice was very husky, and there was a gentle smile on her broad lips. "Welcome to Valley Forge, Miss Alden," she said. "Your brother is such a fine young man. I only wish we could have done more for him—but it's so crowded—and there's so little to do *with*."

"I'm going to take her there now," Winslow told her. "Tell Jed to watch the horse, will you?"

"Yes, Nathan." There was a calmness in the young woman that Charity envied, a stillness and a patience some women seemed to have. "Do you have any place to stay? No? Then you'd better come back here."

"Oh, I don't want to be a bother!"

Julie did not do more than smile, but turned and got a covered pot and handed it to her. "See if you can get your brother to eat something. I'll be praying for you."

The kindness of Julie Winslow caught at Charity, and she could only nod. Following Nathan outside, she commented as they walked along, "Your wife—she's so kind!"

"She's that."

Curiosity nibbled at Charity, and she asked tentatively, "Isn't she . . . nervous? About having a baby under such . . . conditions?"

"I tried to get her to go home, but she wants me to be with her when the boy comes."

"You seem sure about it—that it'll be a boy."

"Well, Julie says that's what God's told her—and I don't recall that she's ever missed when she says something like that."

Charity was flustered, for when people said "God told me to do this," it always made her slightly angry somehow. She didn't understand such things and felt they were attempting to be *spiritual* in some unfair way. But she could not feel resentment toward the kind young woman who had taken care of her brother.

"There's the hospital."

A long, low building was perched on top of a knoll, the wind tearing the spark-studded smoke that rose from the chimney, dissipating it into the darkness. She followed Winslow to the door, and a sentry in rags blocked their way. "No more room," he mumbled through blue lips.

"Want to visit, Soldier," Winslow answered shortly, his breath labored from the steep climb.

The sentry shrugged and stepped aside just as the door opened. A short man with a long gray apron splattered with blood came to stand inside the frame. He peered at the two of them through small spectacles. He had a long face, a thin nose and very red lips. "What's this?"

"This is Miss Alden, Doctor," Winslow said quickly. "She's come to see her brother."

The doctor peered at her and asked incredulously, "How in

the holy hades did you *get* here?" Then he caught himself, saying abruptly, "Oh, never mind."

"How is he, Doctor?"

"Your brother?" The question seemed to disturb him, and finally after a short pause, he shrugged. "Not well." Then an angry light leaped into his eyes, and he snapped bitterly, "How could he be doing *well* in a hellish place like this? No medicine—no bandages—nothing!"

"Maybe it'll help to have his sister here," Nathan offered hopefully.

The doctor stared at him, and finally said, "I trust it will help." The futility in his tone sent fear through Charity, and she stared at him as he stalked away to a path that led down the hill.

"Come along, Miss Alden."

Nathan stepped aside to let her enter. It was a simple log cabin thirty feet long at most, but there must have been more than a hundred men inside. They lay close together on beds built the length of the hut. Some of them were asleep, but most of them moved restlessly in the bitter cold. There was a continual groaning, and the stench was overwhelming.

She followed the tall Virginian to a tiny corner partitioned off in the back, and gave a gasp when she looked down at her brother's pale face, the hollows of his cheeks made deeper by the yellow glare of the lantern hanging from the ceiling.

"Curtis!" she cried, tears filling her eyes as she fell beside him. His thin hand was like ice, and for one brief instant terror filled her as she thought, *He's dead!* But then he stirred, and as she dashed the tears out of her eyes she saw that he had moved his head to face her. He was her baby brother, only sixteen, but he had been wild to become a soldier. Nothing she nor their father could say would keep him back—and now he lay dying in a miserable hut!

"Charity?" he asked in a thin, reedy voice—and when she leaned over and kissed him, he stared at her, his eyes enormous in his thin face. "How—did you get here?"

"Oh, Curtis!" She forced herself to smile. "Why, I heard you'd been wounded, so I just up and came to nurse you. I'll have you out of this place in no time!"

His eyes seemed to be all there was to him—all eyes and skin and bones. But then he smiled, and it broke her heart to see, for it made him look younger, childlike—and she could not speak for the tightness that gripped her throat.

"Sister—I'm—glad you came." His voice fell, and his eyelids dropped. "I—didn't want to—go out—by myself . . ."

He closed his eyes and his head lolled. Charity shot a look of fear at Nathan, but he shook his head. "Just fell asleep. He does that a lot. Maybe he'll eat a few bites when he wakes up again." He added, "I'll go give some of this to my friend over there while you sit with him."

Charity sat in the dim hut beside her brother for a long time. Nathan came back after a time, looked down, then left, leaving the soup with her. "Stay as long as you like; I'll take you home whenever you want."

As she continued the vigil, holding the thin hand, memories swept through her—mostly about the days when Curtis was a small boy. They had been very close, and now she was afraid. If she had been a woman of prayer, she would have prayed, but that part of her life had been perfunctory—a few memorized forms that meant nothing in this place of pain and darkness and death. Fear was not something lurking outside—it was a sharp blade slicing away at her deep down inside.

Her thoughts flew back and forth as she tried to think—but the fear that had paralyzed her since she had walked into the hospital seemed to have destroyed her power to think. She longed for her father or for her grandmother to be there. Always she had depended on them, and now they were far away. She was the only one who could help Curtis.

Finally she felt a hand on her shoulder and looked up with a start to see Winslow standing over her. He spoke quietly. "Charity—would you like to get Curtis out of this place?"

A sudden hope seized her, and she exclaimed with a wild urgency, "Oh, yes!"

"I've been praying on it," he replied slowly, his face still in the flickering lamplight. "And I think the Lord has told me that we better take Curtis home. I'll go get your buggy and tell Julie to fix up a place for him."

"Thank you!" was all she could say, and when he left, she let her hot tears fall on Curtis's thin hand. She moved her lips in a whisper. "Oh, God! Don't let him die!"

CHAPTER TWO

DEATH AT VALLEY FORGE

★ ★ ★ ★

Snowflakes large as shillings fell out of the sky—not drifting down gently but plummeting to the frozen earth. Charity had to stop frequently and clear her lashes, because the heavy flakes froze instantly as they touched her face. For the last week, since she had arrived at Valley Forge, she had made a daily journey from the Winslow hut to the hospital, taking food to several of Nathan's friends. He had been sent on some sort of military mission, and when Julie had started to put on her thin coat to make the trip, Charity had quickly insisted on taking her place.

"I hate to have you out in this weather, Charity," Julie had protested.

"Me? Why, I'm used to it, Julie," Charity had laughed as she slipped into her fur coat. "The last trip we made on *The Gallant Lady*, a snowstorm caught us. Father stayed at the wheel so long he froze his feet, and I almost did the same. I'm an old salt—and tough as boot leather!"

"But it's—"

"Julie, I want you to lie down and rest until I get back. Come on, now—let me cover you up." She practically forced her onto the low bed strung with rawhide, pulled a heap of ragged quilts over her, then impulsively leaned over and kissed her. "You've done so much for Curtis—and for me. Don't refuse me this one little thing!" Then she had darted over to pull the covers up on Curtis before leaving the hut.

The visits to the hospital had been difficult, for she hated the stench and squalor of the place. She had to carry the food past those who were starving, and the hollow eyes that followed her made her ache. They were dying, most of them, she realized, and they cried out silently for her to stop and talk. Some were young, not over fourteen, and they cried out for their mothers in their delirium. Charity forced herself to smile, spending most of the time that Curtis lay unconscious trying to bring some hope to the sick and wounded.

She made her way through the curtain of falling snow, muttering through stiff lips, "Worse than a fog off the Banks!" Finally she stumbled up to the hospital and entered. Dr. Williams looked up from where he was bending over one of the men, and rose instantly to come to her. "Glad you came, Charity," he nodded, his face grim. "Billy's bad—maybe you can stay with him a little."

"Is he . . . going to die, Dr. Williams?"

She had not liked the physician at first, thinking him surly and uncaring, but she had soon discovered that his gruff manner was a facade, that he hurt for the men under his care. She had discovered this on her third visit when he had drawn her to one side, saying harshly, "Wish you'd say a word to Sills—boy needs a little comfort."

"Which one is he?"

"Over there by the window. He's only fifteen—" She saw the look of pain surface in his face involuntarily. "Just the age of my own boy." Then the curtain dropped, and he went on, his lips tight. "Lost a leg last month, and it's gone to gangrene. Won't last long— but I expect he'd like a little word from a woman."

Billy Sills was a towheaded boy from Virginia, emaciated and bright-eyed with fever. He had been pathetically grateful when Charity had stopped and offered him a little of the thin stew, but it had been her presence rather than the food that had cheered him. She led him to talk, and soon she knew his family by name. His favorite sister was Melissa, "Missy"—and he used that name for Charity, saying, "You look a heap like her, you do."

Dr. Williams went on quietly. "We made a little place for him over by the corner," motioning to where a tattered blanket was tacked up. He hesitated, shook his head, then added, "Don't expect he'll know you. Been in a coma since this morning."

"I—I'll sit with him for a while." Charity worked her way around the room, making the food go as far as possible, speaking with a tight smile to the patients, then went to Billy with a mug of tepid water. Lifting the blanket, she sat down on the floor using her coat for a pad, and leaned closer to see the boy's face. The feeble yellow rays of a lantern barely enabled her to make out his features. His lips were drawn back and his eyes were fluttering, revealing a glimpse of the whites as they rolled up in his skull. His chest was rising and falling erratically, and the rasping sound of his breathing struck against her nerves. Desperately she wanted to run away, but she forced herself to mop his clammy brow with a bit of cloth from her pocket.

Her touch seemed to arouse him, for he rolled his head weakly from side to side. Then his eyes slowly opened and focused on her as she bent over him. He licked his dry lips, and his voice was a croak as he whispered, "Missy—that you?"

"Yes, Billy. It's Missy."

"Aw—I'm glad—you got here . . ."

She reached down, lifted his head, and put the water to his lips. He took a few quick swallows, then pulled his head back and looked up into Charity's eyes. "Missy—I ain't—gonna—make it."

"Billy . . . !"

"Good you came—though. Hate to die—Missy!"

Tears scalded her eyes and she set the cup down and reached out to embrace his emaciated form, holding him to her breast. "Billy—Billy!" she moaned, but could say no more, for her body was shaken by uncontrollable sobs. She held him like a baby, rocking back and forth and calling his name for a long time; then he pulled back and a spasm racked his body—a violent shudder that shook him until his teeth rattled.

"Missy!" he cried out, pulling at her weakly. "Don't let me die, sister! I—I'm afraid!" He gave a great wrenching cough, and when it passed, he asked, "Missy—you reckon—you could say—a prayer?" His eyes were enormous in the golden light of the lantern, and his lips trembled as he whispered, "I—I never got—religion, did I? Mother—she tried to—to talk about God—but I never did—"

Then his whole body arched and he began to kick the floor, his bare heel drumming in a horrible pattern. The blanket flew back, and Dr. Williams entered hastily, but even as he reached out, Billy took a deep breath, held it for a brief moment, and then his body went limp, the rattling cough raking against Charity's nerves.

"He's gone," the doctor said. He took the thin hands, folded them over the boy's chest, and dropped the blanket over the worn face. He pulled Charity to her feet and led her out of the space. She almost stumbled over a sleeping man, but Dr. Williams caught her with a surprising strength and helped her to the only open space in the room—a small cubicle where he kept his meager supplies and slept when he could on a cot made of saplings and rawhide. She was so blinded by tears she could see nothing, but suddenly felt Dr. Williams jerk to an abrupt halt. "Why, General Washington—I didn't know you were here."

Charity brushed the tears from her eyes and looked up to see two men standing in the open space. One was a thin man wearing a blue uniform greatcoat with black facing and silk scarf; the other, a very large man, over six feet. Charity looked at him with startled interest.

The general had a large nose, gray eyes, and deep pockmarks on his long face. He had very large hands, she saw, giving an impression of tremendous strength, though his eyes and voice betrayed a great weariness.

"How many, Doctor?"

"Well, not as bad as it might be—but we just this moment lost Billy."

"Billy Sills?" The gray eyes fell, and the big man stood there silently. Finally he raised his head, and Charity saw the pain etched across his face. "He was from my state. I know his parents, Colonel Hamilton. They are fine people."

This, she gathered, was Alexander Hamilton, the general's most trusted aide. "It's hard, Your Excellency." His voice was sharp and clipped, but he seemed almost boyish with violet eyes and lashes long and thick like a girl's. "It never gets easy, does it?"

Dr. Williams interjected, "This is Miss Charity Alden, Your Excellency. She came to see her brother—but she's been a great source of encouragement to all the men."

"We are in your debt, Miss Alden," the general returned, his gray eyes weighing her. As he took her hand in his, hers seemed lost in the massive grip. For a moment she felt the power of the man; then he released her hand, saying, "I hope your brother is doing well?"

"Not very well, sir." She bit her lip and added, "One of your Virginia men has taken us in—Nathan Winslow."

"That's Adam's son, isn't it?" Hamilton asked.

"Yes. I had to send Adam on a mission." Turning to Charity, Washington nodded, "Miss Alden, I pray that our merciful God will spare your brother. And we are grateful for your kindness to our poor men. Let me help you."

She put her arms into the coat he held for her, then said as she turned to go, "I'm—sorry about Billy."

"I'm sorry, too—for all of them."

She left the hospital quickly, and as she made her way back to the cabin, she wondered why the boy's death had affected her so deeply. The presence of Washington had taken the pain away momentarily, but now it swept back as the whining wind that purled around the evergreens and sent scuds of new snow everywhere reminded her of his cries.

What if Curtis should die like Billy?

The question came again and again, and by the time she got to the hut, she was so filled with fear for him that she did not even feel the cold.

Julie was sitting beside Curtis as she entered, and looking up she said, "He's been asking for you, Charity. See if you can get him to take a little broth."

"Why, sure I can, can't I, Curtis?" she asked with a forced heartiness. Taking the cup from Julie, she sat down and began to cajole him into swallowing a little of the broth. "I could always make you eat, couldn't I? Remember when you had measles, and I took care of you?"

A faint smile touched his pale lips. "I remember. Gave you the measles, didn't I?" he answered weakly.

"You sure did! Take another swallow—that's good! Now another. . . ."

He ate a little of the broth, then lay back wearily while she fussed over him. He had developed an alarming cough which would, on occasion, seize him in a frightful manner. It was as if a giant hand suddenly closed on him, shaking him from side to side and racking him until his breath was spent. It was getting worse, more frequent, and after a bout that made Charity want to cry out at his agony, he fell into a drugged and unhealthy sleep.

The two women did what they could, then sat down and talked as the stub of a candle sputtered in its own tallow. Charity was too exhausted by the death of Billy Sills and the tension over Curtis to say much, but Julie's voice had a soothing effect. Charity put her head back, closed her eyes, and listened as the young woman spoke of things other than disease and death.

Often the two had sat into the night, and Charity had listened as Julie told her of her meeting and marriage with Nathan. The story was so incredible that at first she had suspected the young woman was one of the most creative liars she'd ever met, but others in the camp had confirmed the story.

Julie had fled her home after her father's death to escape the rapacious attentions of her uncle. In desperation, she had disguised herself as a man, and Nathan had saved her from freezing to death on a wharf in Boston. Through a strange set of circumstances, she had joined the Continental Army as an aide to Colonel Henry Knox. Nathan, his attention occupied by a young woman he was courting, had never suspected her secret. He and his cousin, Paul Winslow, were engaged in such fierce competition for Abigail Howland that Nathan was blind to all else. Soon after Julie's secret finally got out, Nathan was made painfully aware of Abigail's deceit.

"I caught him as he was dropped, Charity," Julie had laughed as she recounted the story. "He was easy pickings."

But this, Charity discovered, was not true. The love of Nathan for Julie—and hers for him—was of a storybook quality, and the warmth in Julie's eyes when she spoke of her young husband spoke volumes.

Now as they sat there in the cold room, the hoarse breathing of Curtis was very loud in the quietness. Julie finally stopped speaking, and for a long time there was no other sound. In the dim light Charity saw that Julie's lips were moving, and she knew the girl was praying; it was something Charity had noted and been troubled about. Now the death of the boy was a fresh wound in her spirit, and she finally began to speak, telling her friend how it had been. She ended by saying, "It was so—*hard*! So awful, Julie!" Then she plunged in and added, "Julie—he said he didn't know God. Do you think he's in . . . ?"

Julie sat there for what seemed a long time; then she began to speak. At first it seemed to Charity the young woman had not heard what Charity had asked, for she said nothing about Billy or his death. She talked about God, about His love for man—and most of all she spoke of Jesus Christ and how He died on a cross to save all men. Her voice went on and Charity sat there listening. Finally Julie picked up her worn black Bible from the table by her side and, leaning over close to catch the feeble rays of the candle, read slowly: "This is a faithful saying, and worthy of all acceptation, that Christ Jesus died to save sinners, of whom I am chief."

Then she looked up, the tears shining in her eyes in the yellow light. "Charity, never question the love of God! No matter what you see in this world, remember that God sent His only Son, and Jesus died a terrible death on a cross. He died because He loves us all—you—and me—and Billy—and Curtis."

Charity swallowed, fighting back the sobs that rose to her throat. "But what about Billy?"

"I don't know, Charity," she answered quietly. "I *do* know that he will meet a loving God—and I never lose hope."

"I wanted to help Billy—but I couldn't!"

"I know, Charity." Julie put her hand on Charity's. "I think if you want to be able to help others—like Curtis and Billy—you've got to find your own peace with the Lord. Would you like that?"

Somehow the thought frightened Charity, and she said quickly, "Oh, I couldn't!" And she begged in a faltering voice, "Won't *you* help him, Julie? Please!"

The silence ran on and Charity saw that the other girl was praying. Finally Julie looked up and smiled. "Of course I will, Charity."

★　★　★　★

Three days later Curtis died. During those three days Charity was helpless. She took care of her brother's physical needs, but the presence of death was over the hut. Nathan came back, and he would sit for long hours beside Curtis, often with Julie by his side.

Julie would read the Bible aloud as she sat beside the dying boy, and once she said, "Maybe he doesn't understand it, Charity, but the scripture says, 'The entrance of thy word giveth light.' "

From time to time Curtis would rouse, always a little weaker, but he seemed to live on the prayers of the couple who was always there. He would hold on to Charity's hand, speaking of their early days, but he grew restless, his eyes searching for something, and only when Julie or Nathan would come and sit beside him would he relax.

On the day before he died, Julie was reading from the Gospel of John, late in the afternoon. Charity sat on the floor, her head leaning against the cot, and she heard the words:

> And as Moses lifted up the serpent in the wilderness, even so must the Son of man be lifted up: that whosoever believeth in him should not perish, but have eternal life. For God so loved the world, that he gave his only begotten son, that whosoever believeth in him should not perish, but have everlasting life. For God sent not his Son into the world to condemn the world, but

that the world through him might be saved.

"Does that mean me?" Curtis's voice interrupted the reading, and when Charity lifted her head, she saw that he had pulled himself up and was staring at Julie with a strange hope in his eyes. "Can I be saved, Julie?"

Julie said quietly, "Why, Curtis, Jesus *died* to save you. There's nothing God longs for more than to see us trust Him for salvation."

He lay back down and the silence ran on. There was an ache in Charity's throat, and she clenched her fists together until they hurt. Then she heard him say, "Would you help me, Julie?"

Julie sat there reading scripture after scripture, pausing to answer his questions, and finally she said, "I think you're ready to put your faith in Jesus, Curtis." She put the Bible down and got awkwardly to her knees, saying, "I'm in poor shape for this, but God is waiting. Let's pray—and you simply tell the Lord you have sinned, and that you want Jesus in your heart—"

She began to pray, and Charity went to kneel beside her, both of them bending over the thin form of Curtis. Charity never knew what happened. She found herself weeping uncontrollably, and with that, a sudden desire to pray. She tried, but there was something within her resisting.

Finally she looked up to see Julie struggling to get up. "Give me a hand, Charity," she gasped. As she was pulled to her feet, she laughed freely, tears running down her cheeks—but there was a light of joy in her eyes. "Your brother is in the family of God, Charity! Look at him!"

Curtis had tears in his eyes, but there was a smile on his lips as he exclaimed "Bless the Lord! Bless the Lord!" over and over again.

Julie put her arms around Charity. "It'll be your time one day. God has promised me that!"

Charity could not speak, but the peace that had come to the thin face of Curtis brought joy to her own heart.

Curtis died in his sleep the next day. He had awakened at dawn, and his eyes were clear as he held up his arms to kiss his sister for the last time. He gave a few messages for family and friends, said his farewell to Nathan and Julie, then looked at Charity, a quiet smile on his lips. "I'll be waiting for you." As he closed his eyes, Charity knew with a startling clarity and an aching heart that her brother would never open them again—not on this earth.

CHAPTER THREE

BACK TO BOSTON

★ ★ ★ ★

"Charity, I wish you'd change your mind." Nathan had come inside, slamming the door against the blast of freezing air that rattled the entire shack. His eyebrows were crusted white with ice, and there was a worried look in his eyes as he moved to where Charity sat beside Julie. "If this snow keeps up, you'll never make it through."

"I'll be all right, Nathan."

"Just wait until tomorrow, please, Charity," Julie whispered. Her voice was weak, and pain was dulling her eyes. Ever since Curtis's death, she had seemed to weaken, taking to her bed with a fever. Charity had grown to love the Winslows, but a plan had formed in her mind, and she smiled and leaned over to kiss Julie, saying, "Don't fret yourself about me, Julie Winslow." She felt the girl's arms close round her neck, and allowed herself to be held, then drew back and forced a smile, saying with artificial conviviality, "Now, you just take care of yourself and that big boy—if you're good, maybe I'll have a surprise for you!"

She pulled away, snatched up the small bundle containing her clothes, and dashed outside. The freezing cold bit at her lungs, causing her to catch her breath as the wind whipped tiny crystals of snow into her eyes.

"Everything's ready, Charity," Nathan informed her, motioning to the waiting buggy. "We had to do a little carpentry work to make the coffin fit, but it's all secure."

"Thank you, Nathan." Charity forced herself to walk toward the buggy, which had been stripped to accommodate the pine coffin that bore Curtis's body. When she had announced her intention of taking her brother back to be buried in the family plot, there had been incredulous looks on every face. But no persuasion could change her mind, so Nathan had made provisions for her trip. The back seat of the buggy had been ripped out, and an extension built on the floor, so that the coffin protruded past the rear wheels, and was tied down with ropes. The canvas top had been roughly sewn together to make a shelter over the front seat, providing at least some protection from the stormy weather. Most important, the wheels had been removed and a pair of runners thrust under a crudely built undercarriage, transforming the buggy into a sleigh. "If the snow gets deep," Nathan had told her, "you'll have a better chance with a sled than a buggy."

"Looks shipshape, Nathan," Charity stated, tilting her head back to smile up into his face. "Now, you listen to me! I'm going to make a record trip to Boston, and I'll be back here with a good doctor and supplies quicker than you can think!"

His mouth dropped open and he exclaimed, "Why, you can't do that, Charity!"

She slapped him on the chest and laughed shortly. "I never let any man tell me what I can or can't do! Now, you take care of your wife until I get back!"

Nathan stared at her; then a smile broke across his broad mouth. "Well, devil fly off! I reckon you'll do just that, Charity Alden! However," he added, his eyes twinkling, "you can argue all you like—but I'm sending a man with you."

"I don't need—!"

"This is Daniel Greene," he went on, ignoring her protests. "He's a preacher, but don't put too much stock in that. He appreciates a pretty woman well enough."

"Pay no attention to him, Miss Alden," the man who had stepped up interjected quickly. He was, Charity saw, a well-built individual, just under six feet. He had wide shoulders and warm brown eyes, and his voice was deep as the bass on an organ. "I need to get to Boston, and if thee would permit me to join thee, it would be most helpful."

"See? He can charm the birds out of the trees," Nathan grinned. Sobering, he added, "But most important, he's a chaplain in the Continental Army and a nephew of General Greene's. You get that pass from the general, Dan?"

"Yes, right here, Nathan."

"All right." Nathan hesitated, then reached out and hugged Charity. "Bless you, girl! God keep you."

Charity returned his hug and climbed into the buggy, noting that the chaplain did not attempt to help her but settled himself beside her as she took the reins. "Watch for me, Nathan," she called out. Turning her head back, she raised her voice, "Hup! Pompey!" and the sleigh lurched ahead so fast that Greene, giving her a startled look, had to grab at a brace.

Except for sentries and one squad bringing in firewood, there was no one stirring; all were buried inside the huts seeking relief from the biting cold. The sky was a clear gray, scored on the horizon by the naked black branches of trees, and the tiny crystals of snow bit like fire on Charity's face as the two made their way out of the camp. The smooth ride and the hissing sound of the runners over the frozen snow was so different from the lurching of a buggy over rutted roads that she delighted in the experience.

Looking at her from under the rim of a black-brimmed hat, Dan Greene noted her confident handling of the horse and the eager thrust of her firm chin. *Likes to have her own way*, he thought. There was an independence about her that was in abrupt contrast to the feminine grace of her face and figure. *Might give a husband a hard time!* was his first judgment, but as the miles spun on and the bleak sun rose feebly and she said nothing, he began to be interested, for not many women could hold their tongues like this one.

They were stopped twice by armed patrols—ragged Continentals who gave them a queer look, but let them through at once when they saw the pass signed by General Greene. "Better watch yourself, Chaplain," one of them warned. "Looks like a blizzard brewin' for sure."

As they drove on, Charity turned to look at him, and there was a directness in her glance that searched him thoroughly. "You're a Quaker, I take it?"

"That's right."

"I thought Quakers didn't believe in fighting."

"Well, that's what *I* thought, Miss Alden," Dan said wryly. "But my uncle somehow found his way into this war—and now I'm in it, too—though I can't say just how I reconcile my views as a man of peace with being in a shooting war."

She smiled at him quizzically, and then laughed out loud.

"Maybe you'll have to find some way to kill the Redcoats in a good Christian way!"

He shook his head sorrowfully as he murmured quietly, "Don't know about that."

She gave him a quick glance, feeling embarrassed at her satiric remark. "I didn't mean to make light of your beliefs, sir."

"No offense." He pointed at a deadfall down the road and asked, "How does some hot soup and tea sound?"

"Wonderful!"

She pulled the sleigh up to a line of trees and got down, stamping her feet to restore circulation.

"I'll build a fire if thee will get the food out of that box," Dan offered, and began at once breaking off small branches. He made the fire swiftly and efficiently, using a wad of punk lit by a spark from some flint and steel he carried in a small leather pouch, and soon the crackling fire had put some color and warmth into the bleak day. The singing of the small kettle sounded like a tiny trumpet on the cold air, and they sat down on a log to sip the scalding soup and coffee.

The intimacy of the meal and the warmth of the steaming food made them both more talkative, and as they ate, Charity learned more about the Winslows. The muscular chaplain, she discovered, knew their history well, and as he ate he spoke warmly of the couple. The solidness in his speech matched that of his body, but despite the slight strangeness of his Quaker speech, he had a way with words—managing somehow to convey a great deal with simple, direct language.

Finally they finished the meal, and she accepted his offer to drive. As they made their way down the desolate road, she asked abruptly, "What about Charles Winslow? Didn't I hear Julie say that he lives in Boston? I've heard of him, I think. A rich man?"

She did not miss the hesitation in Greene's manner nor the dubious quality in his deep voice as he replied slowly, "Well, yes— that's Nathan's uncle, his father's brother—or half brother."

"They don't get along?"

"Oh, yes, I suppose they do, but . . ." Dan searched for a phrase, then shrugged. "I really don't know much about it, Miss Alden. They had trouble at one time—but I heard that it's gotten better now. Why does thee ask?"

"I'm wondering why these Boston Winslows don't send some help to Nathan and Julie."

"Oh, Nathan would never ask! In the first place, I reckon Charles is a Loyalist." He guided Pompey skillfully around a fallen tree before continuing. "Well, there was some trouble between Paul and Nathan."

"Paul?"

"Paul Winslow—that's Charles's son."

"What kind of trouble?"

"Woman trouble!" The brown eyes of Dan Greene met the green eyes of Charity, and he grinned sourly, adding, "Both of them were in love with the same woman."

"This was before Nathan married Julie?"

"Yes." He sat silently. The restraint in his manner made her wonder. Finally he spoke. "Guess thee heard about the way Julie dressed up like a man and joined the Army?"

"I heard. Hard to think a woman could get by with that in the Army."

"Well, she did—mostly because she was General Knox's aide and didn't have to be around the troops. But the thing was, Nathan was in love with this rich girl named Abigail Howland—and so was Paul."

"Did she marry Paul?"

"No. She turned out to be a wench—and Paul Winslow was no better. The way it was, Nathan and Paul were both after her; but when it turned out she was a deceitful baggage, why, neither of them would have her."

"What about Julie? How did Nathan come to marry her?"

"She loved him." As the bleak words rolled from his lips, Charity shot a glance at Greene and read something in his square face that gave him away. *Why—he had been in love with Julie!* she thought.

She said only, "But, that's no reason for the Winslows to refuse to help their kin."

"Can't say. Nathan told me once that his uncle was pretty sick, so he may not even know about it. But they won't talk much about the rest of the family."

He changed the subject briefly, and then they settled down in silence for the long drive. As darkness fell, they found shelter at the home of a farmer. Charity fell asleep as soon as she hit the bed in the small room at the back of the house, but Greene sat up late talking about the war. They left at dawn after a good breakfast.

"I'm right sorry about your brother, Miss Alden," the farmer's wife said gently as she bade Charity goodbye.

"Thank you," she nodded.

The next two days were like the first, but the snow held off and they managed to find a place to sleep both nights. Late Wednesday afternoon, each lost in his own thoughts, Greene broke the long silence by saying, "I will leave thee here, Miss Alden."

Charity looked around in surprise, seeing only a small cluster of houses off the road ahead. "Aren't you going into Boston?"

"No. I have to find a man—and I can get a coach out of here."

She stopped the horse, and he reached back and pulled his small valise from where it was lodged. He got out and stood there looking up at her. "The rest of the journey will be safe now. I hope to see thee again."

She smiled warmly and thrust her hand out like a man, and he took it. "You've been a comfort, Chaplain Greene. Will I see you back at Valley Forge?"

He stared at her. "Thee is really going back with that doctor?"

"Didn't you hear me say it to Nathan?"

"Yes." Then he squeezed her hand, saying loudly, "Thee is a fine girl, Charity Alden! God bless thee!"

He stepped back, and she left him standing beside the road staring at her. As she closed the distance to Boston, she thought long about what he had said—and about what he had not said. "He was in love with Julie," she murmured as Pompey pulled the sleigh into the outskirts of the city. "But he loves Nathan—and Paul Winslow, why, he hates Nathan." She shook her head, remarking aloud, "Love sure is a messy thing!"

People turned to stare at the sleigh with the coffin protruding out of the rear, but she paid no heed. Charity dreaded her arrival, and as she drove along the waterfront, she sought for a way to make the news easier for her father. The harbor was a forest of icy masts, the pale sun reflecting in glittering flecks, dying them a deep reddish hue. She rode past the shops lining the shore, expertly guiding Pompey through the traffic. A mile farther she glanced out and saw *The Gallant Lady*. Seeing the ship should have lifted her spirits, for she had spent most of her life on board the three-masted schooner, the happiest part of her existence. But it brought no joy to her now as she caught sight of the weathered salt-box house perching on a high dune-like hill back off the rocky shore.

Her heart almost failed her then, but the lights gleamed in the low windows, and she straightened her back and set her jaw as she approached the house. The night was quiet except for the clopping of Pompey's hooves and the hissing of the runners along the icy road. She pulled the horse up at the picket fence, tied the reins, and stepped stiffly down. As she turned she saw the door open and her father framed in the lamplight. She could not see his face, and she could not move. There was no way to help, no way to shield him from the truth, so she stood there watching helplessly as he came slowly down the steps and walked down the path to the gate in his peculiar rolling gait, as if he were walking across the deck of a ship.

William Alden opened the gate and came to stand beside her. He was short and stocky, but not fat. His weathered red face, she saw, was pale in the fading light, and she leaned against him, suddenly weak, and whispered, "Father—I've—I've brought Curtis home!"

He did not answer, and she could feel his powerful heart beating. He stood there looking over her shoulder at the coffin, and when she pulled back, she saw that his eyes were filled with tears— the first she'd ever seen there in all her life.

In his erect frame, the heritage of the sea was noticeably strong in him. He came from a race that was all too familiar with the loss of sons, for the sea takes its toll of those who live on it. He had lost two brothers, and his own father had gone down in the South Seas when William was but a boy.

Now he slowly nodded and stated stoically, "We'll lay him beside the others tomorrow."

"Yes, Father."

As his eyes returned to her, he asked, "Did he die well, Charity?"

She nodded, her eyes filling with tears; but not wishing to seem weak, she dashed them away and spoke in a strong voice. "Yes. Yes, he died well." Taking his arm she said, "I'll tell you all about it." Then she hesitated, holding his arm firmly. "And I'll tell you why I have to go back to Valley Forge."

He stared at her in surprise and nodded, with just the touch of a smile on his lips. "All right—you'll do as you please, Charity. It's a way you have." Then they put the horse and the sleigh in the barn and went into the house.

CHAPTER FOUR

THE BAD SEED

★ ★ ★ ★

Charity pulled Pompey to a stop in front of the large white house with the eight pillars. She had passed by it often, for it was only two miles out of Boston, perched on a ridge of high ground, but as she got down from the buggy she considered it thoughtfully. *Not a poor man's house*, she thought as she wrapped the reins around an iron ring set in a huge oak. The freezing rain had put a bluish glaze of ice on the house, and she almost slipped once on the glassy surface of the tiled walk leading up to the front porch. A heavy brass knocker, sheathed in ice, was set in the center of the massive oak door. Breaking the ice, Charity lifted the knocker and gave a series of heavy blows on the door.

As she stood there waiting, she glanced back toward town, as if she could see the small cemetery where they had buried Curtis earlier in the day. It had been necessary to break up the frozen ground with steel crowbars to get below the frost line, and the memory of it now sent a quiver across her face as she seemed to see again the small group of mourners as they circled the stark hole in the frozen ground. The words of the minister had sounded thin on the cold air, and only the thought of how Curtis had called on God in the Winslows' rough cabin at Valley Forge kept her from giving way to the grief that had shaken her terribly.

The preacher had read from the Bible the words, *I am the resurrection and the life*, and then had made a few simple remarks about loss being made right when all God's people would be raised from the dust. *But that doesn't mean me!* The thought had raked across Charity's mind. Though not unfamiliar with death, this encounter with its presence had shaken her as never before.

The door swung open and a thin black woman peered at her. "Yas'um? Somethin' fo' you?"

"I'd like to see Mr. Winslow."

The slave looked at her, shook her head doubtfully, but opened the door wider, saying, "Mistuh Charles Winslow—he sick—but Miz Winslow will mebby see you."

The interior of the foyer was dark, but Charity's eyes adjusted as she followed the woman down a broad hallway. "Miz Winslow? Kin I come in?" the servant asked. A voice answered faintly, and she opened the door. Stepping back to let Charity in, she said, "Lady wants to see Mistuh Charles."

Charity entered, and as the door closed behind her, she walked toward the far side of the room where two women were sitting in chairs beside a large bay window. The younger of them was fashionably dressed, and she rose slowly, saying, "Yes? What is it?"

"My name is Charity Alden. I came to see Mr. Winslow, but I understand he's ill."

"What is your business with my husband?" There was a hardness in the woman's voice, as there was in her face. She spoke sharply as she would have to a servant. "I'm Mrs. Winslow."

Charity hesitated, not certain how best to speak of her errand. There was nothing in the face of the woman who stood opposite her that gave encouragement, but she was a direct girl accustomed to dealing with business.

"I've just come back from Valley Forge, Mrs. Winslow." She saw a flicker of interest in Mrs. Winslow's dark eyes and added quickly, "I was there to visit my brother, and I met Nathan Winslow and his wife."

"I suppose they sent you to beg for help?" The other woman was almost hidden by the large overstuffed chair she sat in, but the flickering light of the fire suddenly threw its beams across her face. She was, Charity saw, shrunken with age, and had the same hardness in her old eyes as in the countenance of the younger woman. "We've nothing for them," she rasped. "Let them get help from their precious 'Patriots'!"

"Don't upset yourself, Martha," Mrs. Winslow said; the words were a command, void of compassion. She gave Charity a direct look, saying, "This is Mrs. Martha Winslow—my husband's mother." Then she asked, "Do you have a message from my husband's people?"

"No—but I think you ought to know that Julie is quite ill, Mrs. Winslow," Charity told her. "The Army is starving—and if she doesn't get some decent food soon, I don't think she'll live. At best, she could lose the baby."

A strange angular light seemed to flicker in Dorcas Winslow's eyes, and as soon as she began to speak, Charity realized there was no hope of help from this person. She was an attractive woman, but it was not a gentle beauty; there was an adamant quality to her features, and even her figure was somehow rigid as she spoke in clipped tones: "I'm sorry you've made the trip for nothing, Miss Alden, but my husband is quite unable to have visitors. Even if he were, there's nothing he can do. We have nothing to do with this insane rebellion—and on the day when the King's power is once again in place, what you're asking us to do could be called treason!"

When Charity saw that neither of these two women would give any help, she prepared to leave. As she turned, a thought struck her and she faced them again. "If I can't speak with your husband, could I speak with your son?"

"Paul?" The request caught Mrs. Winslow off guard, and she lifted her head with a haughty anger. "I don't think you know very much about my son, Miss Alden. He has no reason to love Nathan Winslow!"

"I see." Charity considered the faces of the two women, then said, "Thank you for your time; I'll not intrude on you any longer."

She turned and left the room, almost running over the slave who had apparently been listening outside the door. She hurried down the hall, the black woman racing to open the door. There was a peculiar look on the servant's face as she said softly, "You kin fin' Mistuh Paul at the Black Horse Tavern."

Taken by surprise, Charity paused, searched the black face of the woman, and asked, "Why do you tell me that?"

A secretive air shrouded the woman's face, but there was a bright look of intelligence in her eyes. "Mistuh Adam—thet's Mistuh Nathan's pa—he wuz good to my pa. They is bof' good men, missy. I don' know if he'll help you. Mistuh Paul—he ain't good like Mistuh Charles and Mistuh Adam—but if he takes a notion to help you, he do it!"

Charity tried to remember what the burly chaplain, Dan Greene, had told her about Paul Winslow. "I heard he had trouble with Nathan. It doesn't seem likely he'll want to help him."

"Mistuh Paul—he do whut he want, missy! Him and Mistuh Nathan, they fight over that Abigail wench—but if Mistuh Paul ain't drunk, he mebby will remember dat it wuz Mistuh Adam who kept Mistuh Charles and all de rest of dis fambly from bein' put in jail when dem Redcoats got run outta Boston!"

"The Black Horse Tavern? That's down near the wharf." She smiled warmly and reached into her pocket to get a coin.

"No, missy!" the woman objected, drawing herself up. "I don' wants nuthin' fo' helpin' none of Mistuh Adam's folks! He was real good to me and my pa!" Her eyes opened in surprise as the young girl held out her hand, but she took it timidly. Then as she heard a call from inside, she lowered her voice. "You go see Mistuh Paul!"

★　★　★　★

The Black Horse Tavern was nearly full, even though it was only late afternoon. Jacob Spelling, the owner, looked with satisfaction across the low-ceilinged room that took up the entire first floor of the half-timbered building. Ordinarily he could have counted the customers on the fingers of one hand at such a time, but the cold weather had stopped all outdoor work, and most of the shops were closed for lack of business. The warmth of the tavern drew men, and Spelling smiled, calculating his profits; liquor and talk flowed freely as the men downed the potent ale and brandy.

Spelling moved with alacrity toward a table set in front of the wide window that provided a view of the harbor crowded with ships. He deftly removed an empty brown bottle, wiped the table, then poured a fresh drink into the pewter mug of the young man who sprawled carelessly in his chair. "Another bit, is it, Mr. Winslow? Just to keep this cold off your bones."

"Leave the bottle, Spelling." The speech of Paul Winslow was only slightly slurred, although he had been drinking for several hours. He picked up the tankard, motioned to the three men seated at the table, and offered languidly, "Drink up."

"What'll we drink to, Paul?" The speaker was a heavy young man with piercing eyes and a mouth like a catfish—wide and ugly.

"Didn't know you had to have something to drink to, Ralph."

"That's right, I don't!" Ralph Courtney grinned and downed his drink, then filled it again.

The other two men were obviously brothers, for they bore a strong family resemblance. They were both tall and rawboned, and both had the same shock of sandy hair and hooked nose. Mason Bright was twenty-eight; his brother Moses, two years younger. Like the other two men, they were well dressed and had a general air of prosperity that set them off from the rest of the men in the room.

"Let's drink to a timely demise of General George Washington," Paul suggested with a wicked grin, and leaned back waiting for the warnings he knew would follow his words. There was a raking look in his face, a dissatisfaction on his lips and in his eyes that dared trouble to come.

"Not so loud, you fool!" Mason Bright hissed, giving a nervous look around the room. "You want to get us all thrown in the hulks?"

"That's right," Moses spoke up. "I'd hate to spend Christmas in one of those things." He spoke of the rotting ships used as prisons for captives taken in battle.

Paul looked around the room and spat out contemptuously, "I don't see anybody here who could put any good Englishman in jail, do you, Ralph?"

Ralph Courtney had a boldness of his own, but it was mixed with a wily sense of self-preservation. He did not miss the sullen looks on the faces of the men sitting close enough to hear Winslow, and he put a restraining hand on Paul's arm. His wide mouth scarcely moved as he spoke quietly. "I reckon Mason's right this time. Our turn will come soon enough, Paul!"

There was a reckless light in Winslow's eyes, but he shrugged and growled, "Bunch of old women!" then took a long pull at his ale. He slumped back in his chair and stared out the window at the forest of masts that scored the harbor. "I'd like to get on board one of those and take a voyage to the South Seas."

"You better watch out, Paul," Ralph grinned, "or the press gang will get you!"

"They're not taking anybody now," Moses said. He shook his head and added in a low tone, "The rebels don't have enough ships to need more men."

"Different with the English," Mason went on. He glanced out at the ships and shook his head. "Got a letter last week from my cousin who's a second lieutenant on a King's ship. He said they're so short of men they're having to take the dregs out of the prisons to keep full crews."

"Well, I don't think we have to worry about getting pressed into His Majesty's Royal Navy here in Boston," Paul shrugged.

"No, but when you get to New York, you'd better watch your-self," Ralph insisted. "You done a lot of sailing, Paul, but from what I hear the lot of a sailor in the Royal Navy is pretty grim!"

"So I hear, but—" Paul Winslow stopped abruptly as a young woman in a heavy fur coat walked in through the front door and after taking a quick look around the room, went up to speak with Spelling.

"Well, what have we here, gentlemen?" he grinned. "Haven't seen a morsel that juicy in some time."

"She don't look like a tavern wench, for sure," Ralph leered. "Look at that!"

The girl had spoken with the burly Spelling who had motioned toward the table where the four young men were sitting. She had followed his gesture, then made her way toward them.

"Mr. Winslow?"

The four men all rose, and Paul stated, "I'm Paul Winslow."

There was a direct look in the young woman's eyes, but she hesitated slightly. "Could I—speak with you a moment, sir?"

"Of course," Paul agreed quickly, and giving a wink that she could not see, he said, "Would you gentlemen mind giving this lady a little privacy?"

She waited until the others left. "My name is Charity Alden, Mr. Winslow. I've just come from your home."

"Oh?" Winslow was not drunk, but his wits were moving rather slower than usual. He could not imagine why this beautiful creature had been to see his family, but he was bored, and any attractive woman he looked upon was a challenge to his skill. "Will you sit down, Miss Alden?"

"Thank you." She sat down and gave her attention to him, trying to think of the best way to gain his help. He was one of those men who have a neatness about them both in feature and in figure. He was of average height but there was a natural grace in his body, and as he took his seat, she knew he would do most things well. He was not massively built, but there was a depth to his chest that hinted of strength. He had a handsome face, his dark hair smoothly in place like a cap. His eyes were large and dark brown, the planes of his face smoothly joined to form a pleasing picture.

He came very close to having a feminine beauty—but there was nothing feminine about Paul Winslow, Charity saw at once. On the contrary! There was something of the predator in his smile, and she stirred uncomfortably as she forced herself to explain her mission. Quickly she told him of her trip to Valley Forge, and when she mentioned Nathan and Julie, his head shot up and he stared at her, an unreadable thought in his eyes. When she finished by telling of her visit with his mother and grandmother, he leaned back in his chair, a sardonic smile on his face.

"I don't imagine you got much encouragement from either of them, Miss Alden?"

"Well . . ."

He laughed and leaned across the table to put his hand on her arm, saying, "We have our family problems—Father would help you like a shot. But neither my mother nor my grandmother have any time for Nathan or his father."

The pressure of his hand made Charity uncomfortable. Not only was his touch too intimate, but she was aware that they were the target of all eyes in the crowded room. She pulled her arm free, her eyes flashing. "I'm going back with a doctor to help Julie, Mr. Winslow—with or without help!"

He looked at her with interest, then suddenly laughed. It was an easy laughter, the laughter of a man who finds amusement in many things. "Well, that's speaking right out," he remarked. "What do you want me to do?"

"I—I thought you might help get some supplies for me to take back."

"What kind of supplies?"

"Food, blankets, shoes—anything! They have nothing!"

Paul Winslow was a creature of impulse, and he blurted out without thinking, "I'll do that."

Her face lit up, showing an openness in her expression—a sudden trust. Winslow added, "When will you need the food?"

"I'm leaving tomorrow morning. I have to find a doctor who'll go with me, though."

"I'll get on it, Miss Alden," Winslow promised at once. "Maybe you could stop by here in a couple of hours to check over the supplies?"

"Oh, yes, I can do that," Charity said. She rose quickly and after an instant's hesitation put her hand out and gave him a firm grip. "I—I know you and Nathan have had . . . problems in the past. It's good of you, sir, to put it aside."

"Nothing at all, Miss Alden," he protested.

She gave him another smile. "I'll be back by six, Mr. Winslow."

As soon as she left the room, Winslow's friends came rushing back to pump him for details. When he told them what she wanted, Ralph's catfish mouth drew tight, and he gave a sharp look at this friend. "You're going to help him, Paul?"

"Why not?"

"He gave you a hard time with that Howland girl, didn't he?"

"Well—that's over."

Courtney said no more, but his question had changed Winslow's mood. He had offered his help on impulse, but the mention of Abigail Howland brought a scowl to his face. He threw himself into his chair, picked up his mug and drained it. "Spelling!" He raised his voice over the rabble of voices. "Blast you! Why can't you keep this cup filled?"

Ralph Courtney knew Paul Winslow well, and he saw immediately that the volatile element in the man had surfaced. *Winslow's a good chap,* he had confided to Mason earlier, *but he's as changeable as the wind!*

Courtney sat down and said nothing more about the girl. He was aware of Paul's sensitive nature, as sensitive as a man without a skin; and the loss of Abigail Howland to Nathan was something he had not forgotten. The afternoon wore on and they all drank steadily, especially Paul. There was a scowl on his face as he put down tankard after tankard of liquor, and Courtney knew that the man was building up to one of the fits of anger that came on him like a sudden squall.

The Bright brothers left, and the two men were left alone. Paul finally broke the silence, his voice husky with drink. "He cut me out, Ralph, didn't he? Took Abigail away from me!"

"Ancient history, Paul. Forget it."

"Never going to—forget it!"

"You're drunk, Paul."

"That is correct, my friend—but I'm sober enough to handle Miss Charity Alden."

Ralph peered at him sharply, then shook his head. "Better be careful, Paul. Girls like her have fathers and brothers who have the bad habit of calling fellows like us to account."

"Like to see 'em try it!" Winslow lifted his head and there was a gleam in his eyes. He got up and went over to the bar, and Ralph watched as some sort of argument went on. The husky tavern keeper shook his head, but finally seemed to agree to something reluctantly, and Paul came back to the table with a smile of satisfaction on his face.

"I don't like it, Paul."

"You don't have to like it. Go on home to your mother."

It was part of Winslow's manner to become insulting when he drank too much, and Ralph got up angrily. "All right, I will!"

He left, his back stiff with outrage, but Paul only laughed at him. He leaned back and there was a look of pleased anticipation on his face. The time ran by, and he drank little more.

Finally he looked up to see Charity enter, and he got up and went straight to her. "Well, you're back," he said warmly. "Did you get a doctor?"

"Yes!" There was an excitement in her green eyes, and he admired her flawless complexion as she continued. "He's really too old to make the trip, but he's a real Patriot! I was ready to pay him anything he asked, but when he found out it was for the son of one of General Washington's officers, why, he jumped at the chance!"

"Splendid!" Paul said. "Now, I've been working on the supplies, but there are still a few problems."

"Problems?"

"Oh, you know how difficult it is to get some things with the war and all." He snapped his fingers and said ruefully, "I say, Miss Alden, I'm just about starved, and I'll wager you haven't taken time to eat a bite, have you now?"

"Well, there's hasn't been much time—"

"Of course not," Paul agreed, adding quickly, "I've arranged to have the innkeeper bring a supper to one of the rooms upstairs. Why don't you join me?"

Charity looked startled, and he hurried on. "There are really a couple of items about the supplies that we ought to discuss."

"Well—I suppose it will be all right."

"Fine! Fine! Let me show you the way." He led her across the room, saying to Spelling as they passed by, "Oh, Innkeeper, you can bring that food along—and Miss Alden will be having a bite with me!"

As Charity walked up the stairs she felt the eyes of the men in the room follow her—and she had an impulse to turn and leave. The tavern was respectable enough, but it was the first time she had ever been in one alone. And while the supper upstairs had sounded harmless enough, as she entered the room and he closed the door, a shock of fear ran along her nerves. It was a bedroom, and though there was a table and two straight-backed chairs, there was something about the whole thing that seemed improper.

He talked easily about food supplies and drew her out on the hard conditions of the Army in camp, and soon a knock at the door came, and Spelling brought in a large tray and left it on the table.

"Well, this looks good—try some of this ale, won't you?" he offered with a smile and picked up one of the tankards while handing her the other one.

"Oh no, really, Mr. Winslow. I don't care for anything to drink."

He sipped his own drink, and then said, "Well, perhaps later."

She sat down at his urging and ate a little, but the uneasiness she felt increased. He began to drink steadily, talking all the while and refilling his tankard from a large jug.

At first the talk was about supplies, but soon the tenor of the conversation changed, and he began paying her personal compliments. He was, she realized, not entirely sober, and she got up at once, saying, "I must go."

He looked at her, then put his tankard down and got to his feet. "But, Charity, we've not had time to get to know one another." There was a light in his eyes that shot fear into her heart, and she turned to leave, only to find herself whirled around to face him.

"Let me go!" she cried out, struggling wildly, but his strength was tremendous. He held her as easily as if she were a child.

"Now, sweet, be still!" he admonished, and suddenly he pulled her close and kissed her full on the lips.

Charity's heart raced wildly, and she struggled in vain to free herself. He was, she saw, enjoying her struggles, and she stopped at once.

"Now, *that's* more like it!" he grinned, and his grip relaxed a fraction. It was not much, but it was, Charity thought swiftly, the best opportunity she was likely to have. If she tried to scream, he would clamp his hand over her mouth, and there was no way she could overcome his superior strength. She made herself smile and said, "Well, sir, you *are* a forceful man!"

"Ah," he smiled, "but I am hoping force will not be necessary, Charity."

"You startled me, Mr. Winslow!"

"Call me Paul," he said. His eyes fell to the food and he asked, "Shall we continue our meal, Charity?"

"Well, I could eat a little, Paul."

They sat down, and she began to eat—not much but enough

to keep him from questioning her. He ate nothing, but drank steadily, going to the door once and calling down to Spelling for more ale. He began to tell her about Nathan and soon his face grew angry. The more he drank the more she encouraged him, and soon he was so intoxicated that his speech was slurred and his movements clumsy.

All at once he looked across the table at her accusingly. "You're trying to get me drunk, aren't you?"

"No, Paul," she returned quickly. All the while she had been talking she had thought wildly, trying to find some way to escape, but there was no way. Then her eyes fell on a long whip-like rod nearly two feet long with a cup on one end—a candle snuffer. It was leaning against the wall next to the door, and she measured the distance to it carefully.

He rose unexpectedly and started around the table, saying, "Come here, Charity!"

She had only a brief second, but she leaned over and in one motion grabbed the rod and with all the strength in her arm slashed him across the face.

The force of the blow sent him reeling to the side, and the sharp, thin rod split his cheek from his ear to his lower jaw. The pain of it sliced through him, and he threw up his hands as she slashed at him again, taking the blow on his forearm. He stumbled backward, falling to the floor over a stool, and as he fell, she cried out, "You dog! I ought to cut you to ribbons!"

But he was struggling to his feet, and though the blood was running through the fingers he had clapped to his cheek, he was strong and dangerous. She struck at him once more. Then as he reeled backward, she threw the snuffer at him and with one sure motion, opened the door and fled so quickly down the stairs and across the broad taproom that Spelling's jaw dropped with amazement as she disappeared through the door.

He mounted the stairs swiftly and found Winslow cursing and raving. When Spelling looked at the cut, he said quietly, "You'll have to have a doctor stitch that up, Winslow—and even then, you're going to have a nasty scar." He stared at the young man, distaste in his eyes, and added, "I hope it heals badly! Maybe you'll learn to leave decent girls alone!"

CHAPTER FIVE

CHRISTMAS COMES TO VALLEY FORGE

★　★　★　★

Giant flakes of snow swirled earthward as the heavily loaded sled drawn by a matched set of roan geldings pulled over the rise. Dr. Aaron Bergen's head jolted as Charity yanked the team to an abrupt halt, and his nearsighted eyes peered around the frozen wasteland in confusion. "What's this?"

"Valley Forge," Charity said stiffly through frozen lips. "We made it." The strain of the hard journey was revealed by the lines around her eyes and mouth, and she had to force herself to keep her shoulders square. They had pulled out of Boston with the threat of a howling blizzard lurking in the lowering clouds, but by hard driving they had made the journey in record time.

As they continued down the slope, Dr. Bergen peered through the whirling flakes at the scarecrow-like men who were making some effort at marching their posts, staggering stiffly through the deep drifts. He shook his head, saying sadly, "Guess I've had the wrong idea about the Army, Charity."

"I know." She did not try to tell him that her own impressions had been the same, for the bitter cold made it necessary to limit words. Nothing had changed, she saw, as they passed along the rows of tents and shacks—except that the steadily falling snow had sculptured the rough, ill-built shacks into beautifully shaped, smooth structures. The leaning fieldstone chimneys breathed reluctant blue-white vapors that tried to rise but were immediately swept away by the moaning wind.

"This is it." Charity pulled the tired team to a stop in front of the Winslow hut, climbed down and stamped her feet to restore circulation. Dr. Bergen groaned slightly and staggered stiffly toward the cabin.

The door had opened as soon as the horses stopped and two men rushed out. "What'd I tell you, Father?" Nathan's face was split in a wide grin as he came forward to steady Charity, who was stumbling in the drifts lying in high ridges around the cabin. "This is Charity Alden—and I'd lay a wager this is some doctor she forced to come at gunpoint!"

The older Winslow stepped forward, and although he was shorter and darker, Charity saw at once that this man had the same strong face and calm assurance as his son. Charity was struck by the long scar that ran along one side of his face—it reminded her, with an agonizing stab, of her experience with Paul Winslow.

But Adam Winslow's manner soon put Charity at ease and helped her forget that frightening encounter. "My son puts a high value on you, Miss Alden," he said with a smile. "I tried to tell him it wouldn't be possible to get back in this weather, but he never doubted."

"Good heavens, Charity!" Nathan had lifted the tarpaulin, and his face was filled with astonishment as he stared at her. "Looks like you brought the whole store!"

"All we could pile on," Charity grinned. "Most of it is food, with as much warm clothing as we could carry—and Dr. Bergen brought all the medicine he could lay his hands on." She smiled and stepped toward the doctor to lay her hand on his shoulder. "I didn't have to threaten him at all, Nathan. He's a true Patriot—and when he found out that one of General Washington's officers had a need—why, he tore around like a crazy man getting supplies!"

"Never mind all that!" The doctor snorted and waved aside the thanks that the men tried to voice. "Where's my patient? I didn't freeze my tail off to stand here gossiping!"

"This way, Doctor," Nathan directed, a relieved look on his face and a grateful expression in his blue eyes that made all the effort worthwhile to Charity. "Father, you look after Charity, will you?"

"Of course." As the two disappeared through the low doorway, Major Winslow took the harness in his hand, then turned to

Charity. "Would you like to ride over to the quartermaster's shed? We have to get these supplies under armed guard at once, you know."

"No, thank you—I need some exercise, Major." She fell into step with him as they moved down the winding trail and asked, "How is Julie? I've been uneasy."

"Not good—but I feel much better now that you and the doctor are here. Our own doctor is pretty rough, and he's got enough patients to keep ten doctors busy." He paused and after a few steps he dropped his right hand on her shoulder and said, "We're in your debt—all of us."

"Oh, no!" Charity shook her head quickly, her cheeks rosy. "Your daughter-in-law was so good to my brother Curtis. If she hadn't talked to him about God, Major, I . . . don't think I could've had a peaceful day the rest of my life."

"I heard about it. We're all sorry about Curtis—but if he had to go, I'm glad he was under the blood."

Under the blood. The phrase would have sounded pious, almost sanctimonious, in the mouths of most men—but there was the same easy acceptance of God in Major Winslow that Charity had marveled at in his son and in Julie. It made her nervous—but at the same time she was drawn to that quality in the Winslows which made God as acceptable a topic of conversation as water or earth.

She listened as Major Winslow spoke of Julie's certain conviction that she would have a boy, and smiled with him as he shrugged and added quietly, "I'll not argue with her, Charity. When that girl says God has spoken, you can be absolutely sure she is right!"

"I think that's true, Major. She is as fixed as the pole star!" She halted abruptly and gave him a guarded look, saying, "I'd better tell you, sir, I went to see your family in Boston."

"My brother?"

"Well, no—that is, I went to see him, but he was ill. I spoke to his wife, but—"

She could not finish, and he smiled gently at her discomfort. "I would imagine you didn't get much encouragement from Dorcas—but I thank you for trying."

Charity bit her lip, and he saw that she was bothered, but he let the silence run on. Finally she continued. "There was a slave there at the house, named Cory. She told me to go see your nephew."

He saw instantly that she was uneasy, and shrugged. "She's a good girl, that Cory. Did you see Paul?"

By the time they pulled up to the quartermaster's building, he had the whole sordid story out of her, including how she had wounded Paul, and how shocked she was to see a similar scar on Adam Winslow's face. But there was a kindness in his dark eyes as he looked at her. "Don't blame yourself, Charity. It wasn't your fault." He sighed and shook his head sadly. "Paul's got the makings of a good man—but he's been spoiled beyond belief. He's spent his inheritance—and more beside. His father could never say no to him, and Dorcas is even worse. Why, he's spent enough on *boats* to start a business!"

"Boats?" Charity questioned. "What kind of boats?"

"Ah, yes," Adam smiled. "Nathan said you were a seafaring lass. Well, Paul started out with a small boat, got a bigger one, then bigger—and he's made quite a sailor of himself. I've often thought that it would have been a good thing if he'd gone to sea—but he doesn't have the discipline for that, I'm afraid."

Charity wanted to know more, but the sentries approached, and Major Winslow gave orders for unloading the sleigh. "There's plenty of room, I'm afraid," he remarked ruefully as the supplies were placed almost reverently in the large building by a brace of privates. "But it's a gift from God, all this; and in the name of His Excellency, I thank you, Charity."

"It's so *little*," she lamented sadly. She had noted that the hands of the soldiers unloading the food had trembled as they touched it, and that they had to put it down with force of will. The hunger of Valley Forge marked their eyes, and she whispered, "How can it happen, Major Winslow? How can our people let our men *starve*?"

"Some don't know," he answered. "But," he continued, anger raking his dark face and his mouth drawn to a thin line, "some don't care. Lots of people think we're fools out here, led by a madman who wants to make himself a king."

Charity looked at the pitiful heap of supplies, then at the wolf-lean faces of the soldiers, and she murmured, "It seems . . . impossible!"

"With God all things are possible, Charity!" There was such strength in Major Winslow's voice and such determination in his lean face that he frightened her. She had never seen such dedication as she found in these people, and knew instinctively that for this man the war was to the death. When he smiled, she was amazed at how these Winslow men, with all their strength, could have such gentleness! Then she thought of the drunken lust etched on the face of Paul Winslow, and she mused: *They're not all like Nathan and his father.*

★ ★ ★ ★

For the next four days Charity and Dr. Bergen worked from dawn until dusk, and even later. There were four long huts packed wall-to-wall with the sick and dying, and the pair of them were found long after sundown moving down the narrow aisles between bodies illuminated by the feeble yellow lantern light.

Dr. Bergen and Dr. Williams appreciated each other, but would not admit it. They had stared at each other suspiciously at first; then slowly, as each man discovered the quality of the other, they began to spend their spare time together arguing endlessly—and loudly!—over treatment of the sick men. Once Nathan and Charity had listened to them reach the yelling stage over a fine point of medicine, and Charity had whispered in wonder, "The way they scream at each other, you'd think they were the worst of enemies, wouldn't you?"

"Good men—both of them," Nathan had said, and it was true that Williams' load was lightened by the arrival of his colleague. As for Bergen, any sacrifice he might have made in coming became as nothing, for General Washington himself had made a visit, and his warm thanks to the little doctor had brought tears to Bergen's eyes. "Such a man!" Bergen had murmured huskily as he told Charity about it. "Such a man our general is! And did I tell you, Charity, he talked with me for half an hour—to me, Aaron Bergen!"

"What did he say, Dr. Bergen?"

"Oh, all about the men, of course." He shook his head and there was wonder in his bearded face as he said in such a low tone she had to lean forward to hear it: "He loves them—these men of his! How he loves them!"

When not at the hospital, Charity was with Julie, and it was a joy to her to see the improvement from the food and medicine. A rich glow had come to the pregnant woman's face, and the feebleness that had struck her down was replaced by a vigor that delighted not only Nathan but all of them.

Dr. Bergen argued loudly with Dr. Williams that it was the presence of a *real* doctor which made the difference, but privately he admitted to Charity that it was as much Julie's faith as his doctoring that had brought improvement, and Charity agreed.

Christmas Eve, Charity and Dr. Bergen made their rounds, taking such small fragments of food and drink as could be spared to the men. Julie was awake when they returned, and seeing the look on her face made Bergen question, "Is it something, Mrs. Winslow?"

"Maybe." There was no fear in Julie's face, but she moved carefully as she walked across the room to sit in the one chair. "I think it will be tomorrow."

"A Christmas child!" Bergen chuckled. "Well, send for me when it's time!" Then he wheeled and left the hut.

Charity went to sit on the floor beside Julie. The two of them had spent many hours in that position, with Julie listening as Charity spoke of her life. At other times Julie had read from her Bible, always amazing Charity at how the words of the old book—words she'd heard a hundred times—came to life as the young woman read them and commented on their meaning. Charity had never thought of the Bible as a book for life, but more as an ancient tome of philosophy that one could study or read for an hour. As for making it a principle or guide to *practical* matters—why, that had never entered her head, nor had she ever known another human being who thought of it like that.

The night wore on, and finally Julie went to bed, saying to her husband with a calm smile on her lips, "He'll be here tomorrow, Nathan. Our son."

Charity looked at the faces of the couple and wondered, *How many people are in warm, safe places, but don't have the peace and joy of these two in these miserable conditions!*

She slept fitfully in a corner of the hut, wrapped in a blanket and expecting at any moment to hear Julie call for help. But dawn came, and with it a knock on the door. She got to her feet to open it and was surprised to find the Quaker chaplain outside. "Why, it's you, Friend Daniel!" she said with a smile.

He beamed at her use of the title so beloved by the Quakers. "I'm glad to see thee, Miss Alden," he nodded, then added, "I thought thee might like to go to service with me."

"Service?"

"Christmas service," he said simply.

Hearing his voice Julie called, "Friend Dan, come in."

The burly Quaker entered, and as he bent over Julie, there was a light in his eyes that Charity did not miss. She had known from the way he had spoken of this woman that there was a special feeling for her—and now she saw the mixture of pain and admiration in his eyes.

"Is it well with thee, Julie?"

"Yes, very well. Now, you take this young woman along. I'll be all right," she added quickly, seeing Charity hesitate. "Nathan will be here in a few minutes."

"He's on his way," Greene informed her. "I thought Miss Alden might like to go to our service. His Excellency will be there—in fact, the whole Army will be attending."

"Preach the word, Friend Dan," Julie smiled. "Go along, both of you."

They moved outside and headed for the drill ground just as Nathan came hurrying along with Dr. Bergen. The snow had stopped and now reflected a ruby glow as the sun cast its first rays over the mountains. The shadows lay like long fingers over the camp, dark and sinister at first, but as they moved out of the heavy timber onto the flat plain used as a drill field by the troops, the light swelled into a brilliant display of color—blue-white ice, dark green firs, the crimson reflections of the sun on the snow, and overhead a sky that was for the first time in days a delicate pale blue instead of iron gray.

The Army had already arrived, closely packed in a fan-shaped formation. "There it is," Greene commented quietly. "The Continental Army of the United States."

"It's not very big, is it, Friend Dan?"

"No. Not big." He led her to where the officers were mounted in a cluster, then added clearly, "Not many, Miss Alden. But it's all pure grain—the chaff has been blown away. These are the men—these pitiful few—who will make this nation free, or it will become a slavish colony forever."

He said no more but led her to a small platform in the center of the semicircle made by the troops. She could see Washington clearly, and once again she was struck by the massive presence of the man. His eyes, she saw, were fixed on the ranks, and she knew, as did the men, that he was weighing the possibilities. Would they be enough? Would they stand fast? Would they stay when the skies were falling?

The other officers, including von Steuben, Mad Anthony Wayne, and Hamilton, never took their eyes off their commander. They waited, and finally Washington began to speak. His voice, rising and falling in even cadences, carried clearly across the open space to the rear ranks. When he spoke of "our country," there was something in the way he said it that made every man on that frozen field believe it was true.

They were starving, freezing, dead with fatigue. They had been deserted by their supporters, cornered and beaten by the British, scorned by the powerful nations of the world—but when Washington said *our country*, they believed it. There was a meaning to their suffering, and as Washington spoke simply of their sacrifice and of the suffering yet to come, they accepted it because he said so.

It was simple, Charity saw at once. Washington was the keystone to the arch; he held the Army together, and without him the whole experiment in democracy would fall to ruins.

Then he said, "And now, our chaplain will speak to us, to all of us. May Almighty God, who rules over this new nation as He rules over the stars in their courses, bless his words to our hearing."

Dan Greene stepped forward, opened his Bible, and read the words:

> Behold, a king shall reign in righteousness, and princes shall rule in judgment. And a man shall be as an hiding place from the wind, and a covert from the tempest; as rivers of water in a dry place, as the shadow of a great rock in a weary land.

Raising his head, he lifted up his voice and began to preach. "This scripture refers to the Lord Jesus Christ. One day He will come. Kingdoms may rise and fall, but He will come. That is the one certain thing in this earth—that one day the earth will be under the authority of Him who can do no wrong." Then he stopped, and when he paused, the silence was almost palpable in its intensity.

"But *until* He comes, the Lord of Glory," he cried out suddenly in a tone that rang like a great bell over the frozen ground, "we are men who must occupy this earth—and we believe that He, this almighty God who will come, wants us to live as free men and not as serfs!"

Charity stood there transfixed. This was no sermon delivered as a religious duty by a hired parson! It was a prophetic cry from the heart of one man, but it caught the hungers of all who listened; and as Dan Greene spoke of God's love and purpose, he forged it to the cause for liberty for which these men were asked to lay down their lives.

She couldn't remember much of the sermon, but she would

never forgot that scene—never! Washington, his face set like a flint, staring out at the troops. The ragged, bearded men with hollow eyes grown suddenly bright with hope. The hush that was broken by Greene's voice—and the ragged but powerful *Amen* that went up as he closed with prayer. She was certain that when she became an old woman, she would see this scene as sharply and clearly in her mind's eye as she had seen it with her physical eyes just now.

Commands were given, the troops were dismissed, and Dan came to stand beside her. "I expect thee is cold."

"No, I don't think so." She hesitated, then said, "I—I thought your sermon was moving."

He didn't answer, but took her arm and they made their way back to the hut. He seemed to be constrained, so she remained silent, but as they came in sight of the hut, he lifted his head quickly. "Look! There's Nathan—something's happened!"

He broke into a run, and Nathan shouted as he saw them, "He's here! By the good Lord—he's here!"

He was laughing, tears running down his face as Greene caught him in a bear hug, and the two of them danced around in the snow.

Dr. Bergen came outside, considered the two big men waltzing in the snow, and remarked with a grin, "Pair of blasted fools!" But there was light in his small eyes, and he nodded to Charity, "Go on in and greet the newest member of the House of Winslow."

Julie was sitting up, holding a white bundle. "Come and see him, Charity," she called, her eyes bright with joy.

Hesitantly, Charity approached the bed. As she knelt and Julie pulled the blanket back, she exclaimed, "Oh, he's got red hair!"

"Yes," Nathan voiced from behind her. "And he's got a name, too."

"A name?" Charity asked. "What is it?"

Julie had a playful look in her eyes, and she reached out to take Nathan's hand as she announced, "His name is Christmas. Christmas Winslow."

"Christmas?" Charity smiled. "What a wonderful name! I never heard of a man named Christmas."

"He came on Christmas—and the Lord has promised me that he'll be a blessing to his people—just as the Lord Jesus came to be."

Charity's eyes filled with tears and she put out a timid hand and stroked the fine red hair. "Christmas Winslow—may you be as good a man as your father and your grandfather!"

"Amen!" Dan Greene affirmed fervently, which was echoed by the rest as they sat gazing at the newest arrival at Valley Forge—and wondering what his life would be like.

CHAPTER SIX

RING OUT THE OLD

★ ★ ★ ★

"He'll make a fine American—and from the sound of that crying, he's got the lungs to be a preacher as well!"

Charity pressed herself against the rough log wall and stared at General Washington. If the room had seemed small before, now the general's bulk seemed to take all the available space. He was standing in the center of the floor, his head almost brushing the shakes of the ceiling, smiling down at Julie, who was holding the baby up for him to admire.

Christmas Winslow was the only person in the room not impressed with the imposing stature of General George Washington. He had just had his meal cut short, and his face was red with rage as he protested vigorously. Washington put out a finger gingerly, and the flailing hand of the baby encountered it, grasped it, and to everyone's surprise, Christmas stopped crying.

"You have a way with babies, Your Excellency," the tall, bald man standing to one side commented. This was Daniel's uncle, General Nathaniel Greene, one of Washington's most trusted officers.

Washington raised his head at Greene's statement, then looked back at the baby, saying with a wistful look in his gray eyes, "I love children." He said no more, but Charity knew, as did the others, that the great sorrow of his life was his lack of sons.

It had been a shock to Charity when she had opened the door to find the general standing there that morning. He had greeted her warmly by name and thanked her again for the supplies. She was not accustomed to the attention of famous men, and none was more famous than Washington. He was, she was amazed to find, a simple man. Though the richest man in America, yet he had laid his position and his fortune on the line for the cause of liberty. As he spoke with Nathan and Julie, Charity watched him intently and was taken off guard when he turned and faced her, saying, "I understand you're a ship owner, Miss Alden."

"Why—yes, sir. My people have always been sailors."

He began asking her about the ship, about cargoes and speed, and she answered his steady flow of questions a little bewildered. Once she glanced at Daniel and saw a faint smile on his face, but she had no time to think of that.

Finally Washington paused and looked at her silently, with some of the same calculation in his eyes that she'd noted when he'd looked at the troops during the Christmas service. The room was silent save for the small whistle of a teakettle on the small hearth. Finally he spoke. "I am become a beggar, Miss Alden."

"A beggar, Your Excellency?"

"Yes, a beggar." A bitterness ran along the edge of the general's thin lips, and he added curtly, "I must go with my hat in my hand to our Congress for the bare necessities of life for my poor men—"

"And often as not, they keep you waiting like some peasant!" Greene exploded. "It's an outrage, sir, an outrage!"

"I am the servant of the Congress, General Greene," Washington rebuked the older man gently, then fixed his eyes on Charity. "A ship is on its way from France with a hold full of supplies— cannon, powder, muskets, food—everything an army needs!"

"That's Franklin's work, I'd warrant!" Daniel exclaimed.

"Yes. He worked like a slave to get these supplies—and now it may all be wasted." He stopped and looked straight into Charity's eyes, adding slowly, "Unless we can find a Patriot who will help us. A Patriot with a fast ship."

It was all clear to Charity then, for she knew that the British fleet had sewn a tight web around the coast of America with the intent of strangling the flickering revolution by a blockade. It had been, she knew as well, a successful move, for the British Navy was paramount among the navies of the world. There had been no losses on the British side in single ship actions, so it was taken for granted that England's fleet was invincible.

There was only one thing the general could mean, and Charity voiced it. "You want me to bring the supplies to our shores at Boston?"

"Yes. The French ship cannot be caught even *close* to our shores," Washington nodded, pleased with her alertness. "The best we could do is arrange to send a ship to Port-au-Prince and transfer the supplies."

"Why, we make that run several times a year, Your Excellency," Charity replied, quickly analyzing the best routes and anticipating the dangers. "It would be no trick at all for *The Gallant Lady*."

"If the British stop you," Washington insisted with a warning shake of his heavy head, "your ship will be seized. You'll lose her."

Charity laughed at the idea. "Those wallowing hulks catch *my* ship? Not in a million years."

Washington was still apprehensive. "The Army must have food, clothing, and weapons. I've made General Greene quartermaster. If you feel you can do this, work it out with him. We have little to offer you in the way of reward, but if the gratitude of one old soldier is of any value to you, Miss Alden, you will have my heartfelt thanks—and that of my men."

For some reason, the simple words brought tears to Charity's eyes, for she knew this man would die before asking anything for himself. She blinked the tears back and stated, "Sir, if my father will agree, we will get your supplies." Then she added as an afterthought, "And Father usually lets me have my own way."

A laugh went up and Charity blushed, but the general nodded with a soft smile, saying just as he turned to go, "I believe, Miss Alden, that most of us men would let you have your own way. God bless you."

Washington turned and left, followed closely by the two Greenes, and as soon as the door slammed shut, the baby set up a howl that stopped the moment Julie began to feed him. Nathan smiled at the pair. Turning to Charity, he asked, "Do you really think you might be able to get those supplies?"

"Don't see why not. Like I told the general, no Britisher can catch the *Lady*. Besides, they'll never suspect our cargo, because they're used to seeing us make voyages in that area."

Nathan grinned at her. "You sure are a better looking sailor than any I've ever laid eyes on, Charity."

★   ★   ★   ★

For three days Charity did little but ponder Washington's

words. She helped Julie with the baby, but that young woman made such an astonishing recovery that by the last day of the year, she was able to carry on without help.

All morning on the thirty-first, Charity walked around the camp, being greeted constantly by the soldiers who had come to recognize her. The sight of a woman was a rare thing, and more than once she had seen the ugly face of lust, but every soldier in the Continental Army knew with an iron certainty that the man who touched Charity Alden would hang in the cold wind the next day.

She stood and watched as Baron von Steuben, that strange import from Europe, drilled a picked squad on a hard-packed field of snow. He howled and wept and cursed in German, and the men laughed at him, and then he would laugh at himself. But Charity had heard Major Winslow say, "That fat Prussian has made soldiers out of them! They'll never break and run again!"

During the afternoon, Charity walked along the perimeters of the camp, staring at the miserable huts and tattered tents, gazing from time to time into the hungry eyes of a sentry or some of the men on wood detail, wondering why they stayed.

The sun paled and seemed to cast no heat on the frozen ground as she finally returned late in the afternoon, weary from the overwhelming situation. A resolve had come to her, and the import of her decision brought no comfort, for she had seen neighbors and relatives who had paid a heavy price for throwing their strength into the battle for freedom.

Deep in thought as she walked, she was unaware of anyone until a shadow came across her path. Looking up, she saw that Dan Greene was standing patiently with his hands in his pockets. Something about his attitude told her he had been waiting for her.

"Getting dark, Miss Alden."

She fell in beside him, and he spoke of casual things, but finally he stopped and she halted as well, looking up at him.

"Has thee made up thy mind?"

"Yes—but how'd you know?" she asked.

"Ah, now, that's not been too hard." He kicked the snow off one of his boots, lifted his eyes, and gave her that gentle smile so often seen in his strong features. "Thee has been walking around for three days now practically talking to thyself. But I know what thee is going to do, Charity."

His use of her given name surprised and pleased her somehow, and she smiled up at him. "Oh, do you now, Dan? And what *am* I going to do?"

"Why, thee is going to get the supplies for the general," he answered and laughed at her expression, adding, "And I am going with thee!"

"What!"

"Surely thee didn't think the general would let thee go alone?"

"I don't need any help!"

He stared at her, shaking his head. "Oh, there's no doubt thee would do it, but my uncle is the quartermaster of the Continental Army, and he's assigned me to be liaison officer in this matter."

It irked Charity to see the assurance in Greene's face. She had made up her mind to go, but there had been nothing said about taking anyone along. She had spent years proving that she was as good a sailor as any man, and now it seemed that she had to prove it to the Continental Army. "Take you along? Are you a sailor? Can you skip up a foremast and set a top gallant? Can you navigate?"

He shrugged, ignoring her flash of anger, and admitted, "I'm no sailor, Charity. Matter of fact, the only time I ever got in a boat bigger than our little fishing skiff, I got so sick I couldn't hold my head up. So thee will have to help me along—if I'm allowed to go, that is. And the general would really prefer to have a member of his staff along to negotiate with the captain of the French ship."

His words soothed her ruffled emotions, and she laughed lightly and put her hand on his arm, hard as iron beneath her touch. "Well, maybe we'll make a sailor out of you, Dan. Don't know of any Quaker sailors, though."

He put his hard, square hand over hers and there was a queer feeling in her as he murmured softly, "It's a good thing thee is doing, Charity Alden—and God will bless thee for it."

Her face flushed as he pressed her hand. He was a powerful man, his thick chest and broad shoulders making her feel almost unsubstantial. He had, she realized, a physical strength that was prodigious—but it was the spirit which flared out of his warm brown eyes that she had learned to admire.

Finally he released her hand and looked off into the distance. "Listen!" Far off some bells were ringing. Church bells, probably, but far away, heard only as a silver tinkling that floated across the white frozen world.

"Ringing out the old year," he told her. Then he smiled. "And for thee, Charity Alden, the bells are ringing out a great deal. Thee is leaving the old world—coming into something new."

There was something almost prophetic in his deep voice, and a quick stab of fear ran through her. Her life had been fixed, and now she was moving out of it, into an unknown and uncertain time. She took a deep breath, and looking across Valley Forge, she whispered, "I think you're right, Dan—but it'll be all right."

"So help us God!" he murmured as if in a benediction.

★ ★ ★ ★

"What's the date?"

Dan looked up at Charity, who had come below to the small cabin used by the first mate, and answered, "The fifteenth, isn't it?" He rose and the top of his head almost brushed the low ceiling. He had almost beaten his brains out at first aboard the *Lady*, for the doors were just low enough to catch him right in the center of the forehead. "Look, I can't make head nor tails of this awful stuff! Now what in the world does *this* mean?"

Charity looked down at the problem in navigation that he was wrestling with, and then shook her head. Taking the book from him, she tossed it on the small desk, saying, "You've not got the head to make a navigator—but you make a fine foretopman, Dan!"

"Never mind that!" He grimaced, then forced a grin, thinking of the only time he'd climbed to the top pinnacle of the mainmast. A wind had been rocking the ship at anchor, and he'd made it to the top, but when he looked down, he immediately got sick and froze to the spar. His grip was so powerful that none of the sailors had been able to break his grasp, so Charity had gone aloft and, after a time of soft talking, had persuaded him to turn loose. He'd followed her down and fallen to the deck instantly.

The crew had laughed, of course, but when the mild-mannered Quaker had refused to be offended, they had been forced to like the man. He had, after all, proven himself to be the strongest man on board. Years of work on the farm had given his fingers a steel-trap grip; after he had put Stevens, the biggest man among the crew, on his back as if he had been a child, he had gotten along famously.

Greene had been accepted by William Alden almost at once. Charity's father was not an educated man, but he had a wisdom that lies deep in seafaring men, and he saw the quality of the husky Quaker almost at once. This had surprised Charity considerably, for she knew her father made up his mind slowly. She was, however, not at all unaware of Daniel Greene's ability to move among men—an ability she had observed as he gained the respect from the soldiers at Valley Forge.

Persuading her father to make the voyage had been simple. He had a slow-moving mind, but like a glacier, once in motion, he was difficult to stop. He blamed the British for his son's death, and had cast about in his mind for some way to repay them. So when he heard it was Washington's personal request, and was made to understand that the cargo would give the Continental Army what it needed to stand up to the hated English, he agreed at once.

The Gallant Lady carried a crew of fourteen as a rule, but none of them were told of the mission—with the exception of Alden's nephew, Thaddeus. Thad Alden was a young man of seventeen, the best sailor for his age out of Boston, many believed, and he was also part owner of the ship. His father had been Alden's only brother, and it had been a blow when he had been lost off the coast of Africa on another ship.

Thaddeus had been stand-offish with Greene, which puzzled the officer, for the boy was characteristically friendly with all others. Greene had finally asked Charity, "Why doesn't Thad like me?"

"Oh . . ." Charity had become flustered, and her face turned pink. "He's—he's jealous of you, Dan."

"Of me?"

"Well, not just *you*. He thinks—"

She could not finish and Greene smiled. "I see. The lad's in love with thee. Well, it'd be surprising if he weren't, Charity."

The compliment disturbed her, and she'd flounced off, muttering about how silly men were, but Greene had looked at her with a new light of interest in his eyes.

Since that time there had been an air of constraint between them, but now as she peered out the only small window in the cabin, she seemed herself again. "Father wants us to go pick up the papers from the harbor master before setting sail, and there are a few more things to bring from the chandler's shop. Want to come along?"

"Maybe we can get some more of that chowder at the inn," he said hopefully. "Still planning on leaving day after tomorrow?"

"We'll go out after dark. I don't think the British would stop us, but no sense taking chances."

One of the sailors, a squatty man with a bristling beard, followed them to the chandler's shop, shouldered the supplies, and headed back to the ship. They made their way to the harbor master's office, got the papers Captain Alden needed, then came outside onto the street. "Now, how about that chowder?" Greene suggested.

"All right," Charity smiled up at him. "But you better enjoy it, because I have the feeling that day after tomorrow you're going to hate the sight of food!"

"Give no thought for the morrow—or the day after, either, as the scripture says!" He walked with her along the cobblestone street, enjoying the warm air that had driven the chilling winds away from the city. She knew the city well, and pointed out several interesting spots to him. Finally they turned into The Eagle's Nest, a small tavern where she often came with her father. The food was good and reasonably priced, and the tavern was frequented by a more respectable spectrum of seafaring men than many of the others.

They sat down at a table against the back wall, and the innkeeper, a small man with a patch over one eye and several fingers missing, took their order. "One wouldn't think being an innkeeper would maim a fellow like that," Dan remarked.

"He was with Nelson at Trafalgar," Charity answered.

Greene shifted and lowered his voice. "Isn't it a little dangerous for us to be in here?"

Charity laughed at him, saying, "If you try to stay away from every man in Boston who fought on a King's ship, you'll be pretty lonely." She traced with her finger a design cut deep into the blackened oak table, and her face grew serious. "Don't worry about Tompkins. Most of the men who served in the British navy got their belly full. You don't know much about life on board a ship of the line—a fighting ship, do you, Dan?"

"Nothing at all."

"It's about as close to hell on earth as you want to come," she replied. There was a frankness in this girl that intrigued Dan. She was blunt, plain-spoken to the point of abruptness. It was her life on board ship since she was a child that had molded her, and her manner of thinking was almost masculine, in a way that contrasted sharply with the trim feminine lines of her figure and the grace of her features.

She spoke of the floggings that cut the flesh to the bone, the biscuits filled with weevils, the rotten salt pork that made up the boring and unhealthy diet. She was eloquent in her own way as she painted a stark and ugly picture of the brutal life that the common sailor endured for a pittance, which was often withheld from him for little or no cause—or which he lost in the brothels and gambling houses that lined the harbors of every deep-water port in the world.

The food came—steaming clam chowder with fragrant fresh-baked bread and a jug of clear cider to wash it down. They ate with enjoyment, and Charity more than once realized that this man—so foreign in so many ways, with his strange religion and ignorance of the sea—had some quality that was potent enough to bring a fellowship to her that she had known only with one other man.

They talked long, and were so engrossed in conversation that it came as a rude shock when a shadow fell across Charity's face and a venomous voice declared, "Here's the filthy vixen, Courtney!"

Both Charity and Greene were startled, and when she looked up, she saw Paul Winslow standing over them, a ragged bandage covering his left cheek. The man he'd called Courtney stood behind him, and he reached out and pulled at Winslow, saying in an urgent whisper, "Now, Paul, you don't want to get yourself involved with this woman!"

"Who says I don't? Blast you, Courtney. If you can't be a man, go home to Mama as you always do!" He grinned wickedly as the heavyset Courtney shrugged and stepped back. Then he turned and put his left hand on the bandage and stared angrily down at Charity. He was weaving slightly, his eyes glazed as he stood there. Then he reached out and grabbed Charity by the hair and gave a yank.

Greene was up in a flash, and his fist moved so fast that it was only a blur. Charity heard a solid *thunk*! and then her hair was free. She saw Winslow driven backward into Courtney by the powerful blow, and both of them careened into a table, falling to the floor with a crash of dishes.

"I think we can leave now," Greene said quietly. He took Charity's arm and they walked past the two men—Courtney struggling to his feet and Winslow lying as still as a corpse, with his mouth open and a livid bruise on his forehead where Greene's blow had landed.

They walked out of the tavern, which had fallen silent, and as soon as they were outside the impact of what had happened hit Charity. She began to tremble, and Greene held her arm firmly as they made their way back to the ship. "Let's not go on board, Dan," she said quietly. "Can't we just sit here a while?"

"Surely." He sat beside her, and soon she began to tell him the story. He listened silently, and finally, moved by the ugly account, he put his arm around her and she leaned against him. She was a proud girl, but the scene had frightened her, and she let him hold her until the trembling passed.

After a while she took a deep breath, pulled away from him, and looked up with some embarrassment in her face. "Sorry, Dan. Guess I'm not as tough as I thought. But it's all over now."

"Not quite over, I think." He stood up and she saw the man called Courtney coming down the street, his eyes fixed on them. "Maybe you better go aboard."

"No, I'll stay with you."

Courtney came straight up to them, and there was a reluctance in him. "A word, sir?"

"I'm standing here, friend," Dan said quietly. The odd greeting took the man off-guard, and Dan added, "How's Winslow?"

Courtney shifted, his catfish mouth drawn tight. He scuffed his feet, then said, "This is none of my doing, sir, but my friend demands satisfaction."

"A duel?"

"Certainly!"

"I let my dog take care of fighting of that sort."

Courtney shrugged. "I must tell you, sir, that if you refuse, my friend will take a horsewhip to you on the public street."

"Don't do it, Dan!" Charity whispered.

"I would pay attention to the lady, sir," Courtney suggested. "You would have no chance at all in such an affair with Paul Winslow. Much better that you leave town and never return."

Although Dan Greene's training in nonviolence was strong, it had been considerably weakened since he had left his home to join his uncle and Washington's troops. He was a chaplain, and a noncombatant, but because he had lived in the atmosphere of war too long, he responded instantly. "Name the time and the place, sir!"

"Tomorrow morning at dawn—there's a beach down there a quarter of a mile." He pointed with his left hand and added, "It'll be most private. We'll see to a physician, and you have your second there with you. The choice of weapons belongs to my friend, of course?"

"Anything!"

"The rapier, then—foils will be provided if you have none."

"At seven."

Courtney nodded and moved away. After walking a few paces, he quickly turned and came back, a queer light in his piercing black eyes. "I've done as Winslow asked—now I want to say one word on my own." He hesitated, then blurted out, "Man, don't do it! He's a devil! There's no man in this country—perhaps nowhere—that can touch him!"

"At seven," Greene repeated stubbornly.

Courtney stared at him, shaking his head. "Very well—at seven. But make your peace with God!"

No sooner had Courtney moved away than Charity was at Greene like a terrier. "You can't do it! He'll kill you!"

She argued and reasoned until he finally stated, "A man can't get off the earth because another man says so. That's one thing this war is about!"

"It's not the same thing! And besides, he's Nathan's cousin—doesn't that mean something to you?"

"I can't help that."

Charity argued until she was hoarse, but finally gave in. Looking up at Dan's stubborn face, she murmured resignedly, "All right, Dan—let's go on board."

He was surprised at her subdued manner, but agreed. They went down to the cabin, both lost in their own thoughts. After she left, he sat on the bunk staring at the wall for what seemed like hours.

She came in later with some soup. "I'm not hungry," he told her.

"Eat it and don't argue!" she snapped.

After they had eaten, he said simply, "Charity, I'd like to be alone if thee doesn't mind."

"All right, Dan."

She left without another word, and he lay down on his bunk, his mind in an agony of indecision. He hated the idea of violence, but he had already settled in his mind that he would fight for the honor of his country. Could he do less for his own honor—or for Charity's? *Is it pride?* he asked himself. *Will I be a coward? Can I face up to cold steel?*

Time passed, and his mind grew fuzzy. Once he started to get up to open the window, but to his astonishment he was drowsy. *How can I be sleepy facing death in a few hours?* he thought. As his eyelids grew heavy again, the outlines of the cabin lost their sharpness, and the sounds of the ship grew faint.

He awoke with a start, sitting up so abruptly that his head swam. There was an awful, bitter taste in his mouth, and as he stood up he was so weak he had to grab at the bulkhead to keep from pitching onto the floor. Then, suddenly, the floor tilted and he fell headlong to the deck. As the floor began to move in the other direction, he became sick—sicker than he had ever been in his life—a sickness that made him fearful—not that he would die but that he would live!

He crawled out of the cabin, up steep steps to the deck, where he pulled himself up to the rail and vomited violently.

"Are you all right, Dan?"

He turned and with an effort focused his eyes on Charity, who had come up behind him and was watching with compassion.

"We're—at sea!" he muttered. "How'd I sleep so long?"

"I dosed your soup with laudanum," she answered. "You were bound and determined to be a fool—and there's only one way to treat a fool!"

He grew indignant and started to argue, but the ship nosed down into the green waters, and he groaned and grew sick again.

She watched him carefully, then nodded. "We'll have lots of time to talk about it on the way to Port-au-Prince and before we get back to Boston, Dan."

★ ★ ★ ★

Six weeks later, in the mild March winds, Charity and Dan pulled up in front of Charles Winslow's house. "Are you sure you want to do this, Dan?" Charity asked.

"It's a thing that can't be avoided, Charity," he answered, his voice subdued. As he got out of the buggy and came to help her down, the memories of the voyage they'd just completed flashed across her mind. It had been entirely successful from a military point of view. They had met the French ship, transferred the cargo, and not a single English ship had challenged them on the return voyage. They'd dropped anchor at the rendezvous point—a natural harbor ten miles north of Boston—and wagons had been waiting. Henry Knox had gotten his cannon, and Washington's hungry men would eat well for the first time in many months.

Taking Dan's arm, Charity thought of the long days under the southern sun and the long warm nights on deck. The two of them had spoken little at first, but gradually the barriers had come down, and finally they had fallen under the spell of sail and surf and warm sunny skies.

One night off the coast of Port-au-Prince when the cargo was safely aboard, she had stood looking up into a sky alive with stars, and he had come to stand by her. Both of them were elated that their mission was accomplished—part of it, at least. They had talked excitedly long after the crew was asleep.

And then, they had grown quiet. The sea was laid out like green glass with flashes like gold flakes breaking up the reflection of the yellow moon. The waves were slapping the sides of the ship, and she became acutely aware of him as a man. He turned to her, his face still, but his eyes searching hers.

He had never touched her, and even now he seemed to be unaware that he had put his hands on her shoulders. She looked up, unable to move, and as he slowly let his arms go around her, she had unconsciously lifted her arms and put them around his neck. He pulled her close and kissed her slowly, and she returned his kiss.

Which of them pulled back first neither knew, but he held her just one moment, saying, "Charity Alden—thee is a woman to unsettle a man's mind!"

As they moved up the steps now and he knocked on the Winslows' front door, she still remembered the touch of his lips—and she wondered then, as she had since that night, what he thought of her. Neither of them had spoken of the kiss, but he had not forgotten, she knew.

"Yas'um?"

"We'd like to see Mr. Charles Winslow," Greene said to the slave, whom Charity recognized as Cory.

"Come in, please." The black woman did not speak further, but there was a bitterness in her eyes as she cast a look at Charity. "I'll see if Mistuh Winslow kin see you."

They waited in the spacious foyer, and the black woman came back, saying, "Come wif' me, please."

Charity was reluctant, but there was no way out, so she accompanied Dan to the same room where she had visited with Mrs. Winslow.

Charles Winslow was standing beside one of the tall windows, and he turned slightly to face the pair as they entered. "I'm Charles

Winslow," he said in a voice that barely carried across the room. His illness had marked him radically, making his cheeks hollow and giving his blue eyes an unhealthy bleak look—nonetheless, both Charity and Greene saw the resemblance to Nathan.

"I'm sorry to trouble thee, sir," Dan apologized, at the same time casting a look at the woman who sat glaring at them from a chair by the wall. He went on hurriedly, making no attempt to defend himself, but giving a straightforward version of the quarrel.

"Why have you come here, Mr. Greene?" Winslow inquired.

"I would like to settle the matter in a civilized way, sir." Greene stood straight, his face revealing no weakness as he put the matter into words. "I do not believe in duels, and if an apology will satisfy thy son, I will make it."

"Charles!" Dorcas Winslow started to her feet, her face distorted with rage, and rushed to stand before Dan and Charity, lifting her hand in a gesture of accusation. "How can you let that person into our home?"

She would have said more, her voice on the verge of a scream, but Winslow commanded sharply, "Dorcas, please leave the room!"

With a baleful glance at her husband, she ran out of the room weeping.

"I apologize for my wife, but there is some cause."

"Certainly, Mr. Winslow. These things are always unpleasant," Dan replied quickly. "I might add that thy nephew, Nathan, is my good friend, and thy brother, Major Winslow, is a man of whom I cannot speak too highly. That is why I am willing to apologize—even though there was provocation."

Winslow stared at the honest face of Dan Greene and then he walked to the window and stared out at the trees without a word. Dan and Charity exchanged glances, mystified. After a lengthy silence, Winslow spoke without turning. "I appreciate your generosity, sir—but it is no longer a matter of importance."

"But—Mr. Winslow, we must settle this matter!"

"There is nothing to settle, Mr. Greene." Winslow turned, and grief lined his face. "My son is dead."

The stark words hit like a blow, and when neither visitor spoke, Winslow added, "Three days after your quarrel, Paul went to New York. He disappeared, and no trace of him can be found."

"Mr. Winslow," Charity offered hopefully, "could he have been taken in the press—for the British Navy? I've heard they're impressing whomever they can get."

"That was my first thought," Winslow nodded. "But it was not the press. I have strong connections in England—particularly with the Navy. A post rank investigation was made, and my son was not taken in the press. The only other explanation is that he was murdered for his money and his jewelry."

"I hope not, Mr. Winslow," Greene expressed compassionately.

"There is no other answer." Charles Winslow stared woodenly at the floor and said quietly, "My son was last seen in a notorious brothel on the waterfront—in the worst district. He was drunk—as usual—and the authorities tell me that more than one man has been murdered, stripped, and thrown into the sea there."

"Sir, may I—?"

"I bid you good day." Winslow's face broke and he left the room abruptly, leaving them standing alone.

"We'd better go," Dan suggested. They made their way to the front door and left without another word. Standing beside the buggy, Charity exclaimed, "Such a waste! Such a waste!"

Dan nodded slowly, and said painfully, "He was a Winslow, Charity. I wonder how men of the same blood can be so different?"

There was no answer, and after helping her into the buggy and taking the reins, he drove slowly away from the magnificent home of the Winslows of Boston.

THE *NEPTUNE*

★ ★ ★ ★

His Majesty's ship *Neptune*, with thirty-two guns, slipped bow-first into the green trough between two steep waves, seeming to burrow into the cold brine like a huge mole tunneling into loam. Clarence Langley, first lieutenant, had not regained his sea legs. He was thrown forward and would have sprawled on the deck if Angus Burns, the second lieutenant, had not grabbed his arm and hauled him upright.

Langley cursed under his breath, and was rebuked instantly by the other. "Better give thanks to God ye didn't fall, Langley. If He hadna put me here, ye'd have made a pretty sight fallin' like a landlubber in full view o' the crew." Burns was a small man, slight in build and not over five six. He spoke with the thick burr of Scotland, and he would have been attractive except that a bout of scurvy off the African coast had cost him many of his teeth. He was religious to the bone, holding to the iron-forged, hyper-Calvinistic creed of his fathers, convinced that God's hand was in everything, that all of them were playing out roles that Jehovah had long ago written out in fine detail.

Langley opened his mouth to argue angrily, but casting a quick look at Burns's dour face, laughed and gave it up. "I'd as soon argue with the sun, as you, Angus." He clapped a hand on the smaller man's shoulder, and there was affection in his eyes as he added, "Well, I'm glad that God put you here to keep me from making a clumsy oaf of myself before the crew. This is the only decent uniform I've got—nothing fit to wear to the captain's table. I look like a scarecrow!"

Burns grunted, taking in the tall form of the first lieutenant, noting the neat brown hair and regular features. The Scotsman placed no value on outer appearance, and it was Langley's seamanship and honesty that drew him rather than his dashing appearance. He shrugged, glanced down at his own worn dress uniform, not caring one pin if the captain would be impressed with it or not, but he realized that Langley's mind was on the ladies who would dine with them. He said, "I see nae sense in hauling females on this ship. It's nae guid practice."

"Haven't you heard why they're on board, Angus? Scuttlebutt is that the daughter got into a torrid romance in New York with some rotter, and Captain Rommey hauled her aboard to break the thing off."

"It'll come to nae guid," Burns warned.

Langley stopped and spoke to a thick-chested sailor who was passing. "You've got all the new men out, Whitefield?"

"Yes, sir—'cept him I told you 'bout." Enoch Whitefield was a slight man of thirty. He was the best gunner in the fleet, some said, and was so effective with new hands that Langley often ordered him to take charge of them until they got their heads straight.

"What's wrong with him? Can't be drunk this long!"

"No, sir. He mighta been drunk, but he got some kind of bad bust in the head. Left side's all swelled up. My guess is he tried to fight it out with the press gang and they laid into 'im with a club. Thing is, he got hit right on top of a right fresh cut—a bad one all stitched up."

"One of the pressed men?" Burns asked.

Whitefield nodded his head.

Burns grunted dourly, "I've nae confidence in any o' that breed!"

Langley hesitated, then stated, "I'll have the doctor take a look at him, Whitefield."

"Yes, sir," Whitefield returned, saying no more, but both officers caught the sudden flash of mistrust that flickered in the gunner's eyes. None of the crew wanted anything to do with the ship's surgeon; for that matter, neither did either of the officers, but it would not do to let a seaman hear them say so.

"We'd best hurry, Lieutenant Langley," Burns urged. "Captain Rommey's nae a man to keep waitin'."

"Certainly!" As the two men hurried along toward the stern, both of them were searching the ship surreptitiously. The *Neptune* had been refitted in Southampton, brought to America by a skeleton crew—only the officers and a few experienced hands on board. The blockade that stretched along the eastern coast was thin—not nearly tight enough to pin the rebellious Colonists inside, and King George chose to ignore the fact that England had other commitments for the Royal Navy. The Naval Office was sending out anything that would float, and the abysmal conditions which the average seaman lived under in the fighting ships of England enticed few men to join the navy. The long, drawn-out wars had bled the service white, and both officers knew, as they carefully noted the hands, that it would not be an easy task to whip the crew into fighting trim.

The ship itself, the *Neptune*, was much more impressive than her crew. One hundred and thirty feet long on her gun deck, and built of good English oak, she was the picture of a shipbuilder's art. She had cost nearly fourteen thousand pounds, and being a frigate, was well worth it. Frigates were meant for speed and hit-and-run fighting. They were fast enough to catch any fighting ship, and the *Neptune's* thirty-two guns gave her power enough to take on any vessel except a ship of the line.

The two lieutenants moved swiftly toward the poop deck, descending the steep steps quickly to the great cabin. Langley knocked firmly on the oak door. "Come in!" the captain's voice sounded. Langley opened the door and stepped inside, closely followed by Burns.

Captain William Rommey was standing by the stern windows, his feet firmly planted against the ship's motion. He was a bulky man in his early fifties, square of face and blunt of feature. His mouth was very wide, but thin and pressed together in a habitual expression of suppressed anger. There was a pugnacious air about him, his heavy chin thrusting forward, his body constantly shifting as if seeking to move against a foe, the restless pale blue eyes now falling on the two officers, searching them as for some unconfessed fault.

"Sit down, gentlemen," he rasped, motioning with his hand. "I was about to send a search party for you." He ignored their apology and moved to the table. "The food is probably cold," he complained.

The great cabin was the most ornate area of the *Neptune*. The large stern windows rose almost to the ceiling, allowing the reddish gleams of the sinking sun to filter through, tinting everything with a warm rosy glow. The bench seat around the stern was covered with rich green leather; Rommey's desk, made out of finely carved mahogany, stood against the starboard bulkhead; and a French-made post bed occupied the space on the port side. Beside the bed was a large walnut bookcase filled to overflowing with expensive leather-bound books; the captain was a great reader. The large table had been extended in order to accommodate the party, and except for the two sixteen-pound guns extending from their ports into the cabin, it looked very much like a fine room in a mansion on shore.

It was typical of the two men as they seated themselves at the table that Langley began to talk while Burns sat silently, examining the faces of the others. He gave only a glance to Dr. Erich Mann, a burly German of fifty with a bald head, a round face, and small piggish eyes; there was nothing there to interest Burns. He noted, not for the first time, the butcher's hands that were unsteady now—the result of too much wine. Sooner or later, Burns knew, Mann would inform them all that it was his last voyage, that he would leave the ship and take up a private practice so that he could live like a gentleman. But the private practice, they all realized, would never be, for he was an incompetent, drunken boor, and only men who were helpless—such as seamen in the navy—would let him treat them.

Robert Baxter, the debonair captain of marines, was a different story. He was highly intelligent, shoulders always squared, and his uniforms molded around his limbs like wax. He spoke in short, clipped sentences. His marines were his whole life, although he hardly ever seemed to utter much in the way of orders. His massive sergeant, Potter, took care of the close contact with the men.

Burns had little respect for Captain Baxter, for the marine was an atheist, and the Scot thought that any man who held such a view was mentally defective. He gave a quick glance at the three midshipmen, a hulking, bully-faced seventeen-year-old named Rackam, a sharp-featured individual named Symmes, and one small, undersized lad named Arthur Pink. Pink was going to be a problem, Burns realized, for he was not only sickly but totally unfit for life at sea. His relatives no doubt had shuffled him off to the navy to get rid of him.

That left the two women—and the captain's wife, though highly decorative, was not a matter for much speculation. She was an attractive woman of about fifty, with a gorgeous head of auburn hair, a pair of beautiful eyes—bright but unintelligent—and a languid manner that never seemed to change. She had the incredible ability to sew for eight hours at a stretch (Angus had discovered on the voyage from England), and he wondered at the vacuity of mind that could concentrate on the trivial for such periods. She had long ago lost any force of influence (if she ever had any) with her husband and her daughter. To Burns, she seemed like an attractive life-sized doll.

If Captain Rommey's wife was insipid, his daughter lived as a sharp contrast—for Blanche Rommey was a heady article, indeed! Even the dour Burns could not keep from being somewhat overwhelmed by the girl, and he let his eyes rest on her as she carried on a spirited conversation with Langley over a play they had seen in London.

Tall, with a beautiful figure, Blanche Rommey was one of the most *alive* human beings Burns had ever seen. Her face was not pretty, but it was highly mobile, and her eyes moved constantly— huge eyes, almond-shaped, and blue as the sea off the coast appears at times. Her mouth was well shaped, but too wide and full for real beauty, and her high cheekbones were just a shade too high for the perfect proportion. She was, Burns realized, *overdone* somehow, in a way that was compelling and made mere beauty of no moment.

Even though the slight second lieutenant had very limited experiences with women, he discerned immediately something predatory about the girl. She was conscious of men, interested in them, and had no doubt for a long time drawn many with her almost overwhelming feminine presence. Langley was flattered by her attention, but Burns knew instinctively that Blanche Rommey was not really interested in the lieutenant. It was simply impossible for her to do other than to fix her attention on the most available man in her sphere, as she was doing now—but if a more interesting or challenging one walked through the door, poor Langley would be dropped at once like a toy no longer desirable.

"Better enjoy this fresh meat," Rommey offered as the steward placed platters of fresh beef and a saddle of ham on the table. "After it's gone we may be eating salt pork until we get sick of it."

Baxter looked up and asked languidly, "We'll not be in touch with the mainland, then?" He cut a geometrically perfect square of beef, examined it, then greedily stuck it into his mouth. "I rather expected we'd be a part of the American blockade."

"We'll be doing a little more than that," Rommey grunted, then looked up with a smile on his thin lips, adding, "Better get your gun crews trained as quickly as possible."

"I thought we were at peace with the world—except for these rebels," Blanche commented. "Whom do you intend to fight?"

Rommey grinned at her and then shot a quick look at his officers. There was a rebuke in his manner as he growled, "I rather expected my first officer would ask that question."

"I didn't want to be impertinent, sir," Langley said quickly, his face reddening at the reprimand.

"I don't expect my officers to stand on ceremony when there's a matter of tactics involved, Mr. Langley." This remark made the face of the first lieutenant grow even more rosy, for he knew—as did Burns—that Captain Rommey was not at all satisfied that his second in command had the aggressive character required of the first lieutenant of a fighting ship. Burns had some of the same apprehension, for he had noted, even in the short time they had served together, that Langley tended to lean more on the judgment of others and was reluctant to drive the crew. It was only a sign, but in the midst of battle when the heavens were falling, one wanted to know that the first lieutenant was capable of instant and sometimes even reckless decisions.

Burns spoke up hurriedly in an attempt to give Langley time to regain his composure. "If it's action right away, sir, we'd be hard put to hold our own. The gun crews are raw, as ye weel know."

"Of course, Lieutenant Burns. We have some time to shake them down, make seamen out of them. I doubt if we'll go into action tomorrow, but sooner or later we'll have to whip the Frenchies again."

"I thought that was taken care of in the war, Father," Blanche queried. She referred to the Seven Years War, which had ended in 1763. "I thought Admiral Hawke sank the entire French fleet."

"Would God he had!" Rommey said. He took a huge bite of beef, chewed it thoughtfully, and then began to give a lecture— which was his way. "Hawke did defeat the French. I commanded the *Dominant* in that action, you remember? By Harry, we put them to rout!" He slammed the table and his eyes glowed with the memory, but then he grimaced and added, "We had our chance, and we made the Frenchies renounce to England all Canada and the Ohio Valley, and we routed the Dons out of business in the War of Spanish Succession."

"Well, who's left to fight, then?" Blanche asked impudently. She smiled across the table, her blue eyes catching the lights of the candles, giving her a feline look. "You can't mean to fight the red Indians, can you?"

Langley spoke up, attempting to regain some ground with his captain. "I suppose you think we'll have to fight the French again, sir?"

"Blast it! Of *course* we'll have to put them down again!" Rommey's craggy face grew grim, and he almost tipped the wine glasses as he threw his hands up in disgust. "Our intelligence tells us that the French have eighty first-class ships of the line, and Spain has sixty more. England has only a hundred fifty, and they're scattered all over the world from Calcutta to Jamaica, not to mention our fleet in the blockade."

Burns added quietly, "And the Frenchies have been longin' fer revenge after the trouncin' they got in '63."

"Right you are, sir—and this insurrection is just the opportunity they've been looking for." Rommey gritted his teeth. "It may not come for a time—but sooner or later we'll be forced to take the French on again. When that time comes, I want the *Neptune* to be the best fighting ship carrying the British flag—the *best!*"

"Ach! It will not be easy, my Captain." Dr. Mann belched and took a tremendous draught of wine, then wiped his mouth with his napkin and nodded. "Make a silk purse out of a sow's ear, you cannot—and these pressed men will not make a crew. The press gang must have scraped bottom—the scourings of the earth! Half of them have the pox, all of them are drunks, and there's not a drop of honorable blood in the lot!"

Baxter nodded slightly. "Not far wrong. Can't expect to make a well-trained fighting crew out of that material." Baxter could afford to be critical, for his marines were all volunteers, but the remark displeased Rommey.

"Captain Baxter, the Royal Navy has utilized the press for more years than you have lived—and we shall continue in the tradition!" He shot a command at the surgeon, "Dr. Mann, it is your responsibility to get these men fit for duty!"

"But, sir—!"

Ignoring him, Rommey directed his remarks to his officers, smoldering impatience in his snapping eyes. "You are officers in His Majesty's Royal Navy, and you will take these men—no matter what methods you must use—and make fighting men out of them.

I will accept no excuses from them—or from you!"

The lieutenants knew enough not to argue, but Dr. Mann had taken on too much port, and was rash enough to say, "But, my Captain, I cannot work miracles! There is one of the pressed men who was hauled aboard unconscious—is still not awake. His face is scarred from a drunken brawl, I'd guess, and he's got a concussion. What can I do with him?"

Rommey paused, letting a silence build up. Finally he stood to his feet, his bulk blotting out the light from the stern windows, and addressed the men in a cold, hard voice. "I will make myself plain this one time. We have on this ship a certain number of shot for our guns. We have so many pounds of powder. We have water and food in casks. And we have a certain number of seamen. All of these are expendable." His eyes were fixed on Langley, and he added, "Use up the powder, the shot, the food, the water—and use up the men, Lieutenant Langley. Do you understand?"

Langley swallowed, his face losing its color, then nodded slightly and answered in a low voice, "Yes, sir, I understand."

The deadly seriousness of Rommey fell heavily on the guests, and the meal was finished with little talk. Excusing themselves as soon as it was polite, the two lieutenants left, both drawing sighs of relief as they came up on deck.

Burns took a deep breath of cold air. "Weel, Clarence, I feel like a schoolboy who's had his bottom whacked by a stern schoolmaster."

"Too right, Angus!" Langley swore and slapped the rail, shaking his head apprehensively. "It's not going to be a tea party."

"Captain Rommey's a hard man, but he's fair enough—which is more than ye can say aboot others I could name."

"We'll lose some of the men if we drive them too hard."

"It's God's will." Angus put his hand on the taller man's arm, something he'd never done before, and smiled. "We're all in God's hands, Langley—the crew, me, you. Even Captain William Rommey is just as much under God's rod as that poor lad below who may never wake up. Think o' it like that."

Langley felt a lift of his spirit. "I'm glad you're aboard, Angus. Can't say I agree with your gloomy theology—but you're a comfort." Then the two went below and dreamed their private dreams as the ship was driven by a sharp wind toward a warmer world.

★ ★ ★ ★

The clear morning brought a promise of the warmth that lay to the south, and the wind held firm. Captain Rommey stood motionless on the forecastle watching his officers and men work the ship.

Each mast had its own division of seamen, from the swift-footed topmen to the older, less agile hands that worked the braces and halyards from the deck. As the calls shrilled and the men poured up on deck through every hatch and companion, it seemed incredible that *Neptune*'s hull could contain so many. The deck swarmed with figures of seamen and marines formed into compact groups, each being checked by leather-lunged petty officers against their various lists and watch-bills.

Like the mass of seamen and marines, the officers, too, were at their stations. Langley stood beside the captain on the forecastle, the foremast his responsibility. Burns commanded the upper gun deck and the ship's mainmast, which was her real strength, with all the spars, cordage, canvas and miles of rigging that gave life to the hull beneath. Lattrimer, the third lieutenant, kept close watch on the crew managing the mizzenmast.

"Hands aloft! Loose tops'ls!" Langley cried with all his might through a trumpet. "Loose the heads'ls!"

Released to the wind, the canvas erupted and flapped in wild confusion; while spread along the swaying yards like monkeys, the topmen fought for the right moment to bring it under control.

Burns called, "Man your braces. Bosun, take that man's name!"

"Aye, sir!"

Take that man's name. It was a cry often repeated, for the old hands were few and the new men were many. The bosun ran around the deck like a madman constantly, using his starter, a thick rope with a knot on one end. It fell on the backs of the pressed men most often—for they were totally confused by the mass of ropes and the billowing sails above.

Burns felt a pity for them that the captain did not, for the lieutenant's sensitive spirit could empathize with the utter bewilderment they had been thrown into.

"Will they ever learn, Lieutenant?"

Burns turned to find Blanche Rommey standing behind him. She was dressed in a fine dress of blue satin that brought out the color of her eyes and clearly outlined her figure as the whipping wind pressed the thin cloth against her body. She was watching with interest as the bosun drew a cry from a thin lad on whom he was slashing viciously with his starter. There was, Burns saw, no real compassion in the girl's face. She was no doubt accustomed to the hard life of seamen, but it was the first actual sight she'd had of it.

"Aye, in time, most o' them will, Miss Rommey."

She came to stand beside him, and at her request, he explained the basic structure of the sails and spars. She was listening intently when a movement to her left caused her to turn. "What's the matter with that man?" she asked.

Burns followed her gaze and saw Enoch Whitefield and another seaman placing the limp form of a man on an unoccupied section of the deck. "That's one of the pressed men—the one Dr. Mann spoke of last night." He checked the progress of the men, then added, "I believe I'll see how he is, if you'll excuse me."

She ignored his implied order to remain at the rail and followed him as he went to where Whitefield was bracing the man against the rail in a sitting position.

"Has he come around yet, Whitefield?"

"No, sir."

"What a frightful scar!" The captain's daughter had moved to stand over the unconscious man, and was staring down at him with interest. "Except for that, he'd be very nice looking."

Burns glanced at the man and saw that she spoke the truth. The man was naked from the waist up, wearing only a pair of patched canvas breeches. He was not over five ten, but the muscles of his arms and chest were hard and well defined. His dark hair, dirty and uncombed, would lie neatly, Burns could tell, if it were clean. Clean-cut features were marred by a livid, half-healed scar that ran from his lower jaw to disappear into his hair. The wound had been stitched and was puckered, drawing the left side of his mouth up slightly and pulling his left eye into a squint.

"He ain't no weaklin', sir," Whitefield voiced thoughtfully, looking at the dark face. "Look at them forearms! I ain't never seen such. He's got smallish hands, but mighty strong, I'd venture!"

"Will he die?" the girl asked, staring down at the man.

"Mebby so, miss." Whitefield was a simple man, and added only, "It's in the great God's hands now."

"Blanche—" She turned to see her father who had approached and was staring at her, displeasure in his eyes. "It would be best if you did not come in contact with the deckhands."

A stubborn light leaped into the girl's eyes, and she retorted instantly, "Father, you have put me on this ship against my will. Now you are telling me that I must not speak with those in the world you've consigned me to."

"These men are not your sort. They're dangerous."

She laughed and glanced down at the unconscious man. "I very much doubt if he's any great danger to me."

His daughter was, Captain Rommey saw clearly, ready to make a scene right there on the deck. He'd had several with her in the process of separating her from a dissolute French nobleman, and desired no more—especially not in front of his crew. Rommey was not a man to deceive himself, and he realized that while he could command a ship of the line with eight hundred souls aboard, he was totally unequipped to handle this fiery daughter of his.

"Lieutenant Burns, my daughter is your responsibility. See that she is watched at all times." He felt like a coward as he whirled and left the deck.

"Miss Rommey, your father's point is weel taken." Burns bit his lip and gestured at the man at his feet. "This one seems harmless enough right now—but if he was to come to himself, I wouldna trust ye alone with him for one second."

Blanche Rommey was a strong-willed young woman, and the rebellious fury that had burned in her since her father had snatched her almost bodily from her affair with Jean D'amont still rankled. She looked down at the still figure at her feet, then deliberately took her delicate silk handkerchief and wiped the grime from his face.

"I wouldna do that if I were ye, miss," Burns warned nervously.

She looked up at him with a challenging smile in her eyes, saying sharply, "But you're not me, Lieutenant Burns!" She brushed the dark hair back from the unconscious man's wide forehead and then murmured so quietly that Burns barely heard her words: "And nobody else is me!"

She'll nurse the fellow to spite her father, Burns thought, and he caught a brief smile on Whitefield's lips, and quickly turned away, happy to deal with spars and sails instead of a beautiful, rebellious captain's daughter who had no place on board the *Neptune* in the first place.

CHAPTER EIGHT

ABLE SEAMAN HAWKE

★　★　★　★

"You don't give a hang about the man!"

Captain Rommey had attempted for two days to ignore what every man on the *Neptune* was fully aware of—that his daughter had disrupted the entire ship. There are no secrets on a frigate. A ship of war manned for active service is the most crowded place in the world—more crowded than the most run-down tenement in London's Cheapside. Every square foot of the vessel was spoken for, planned for, and even now as Rommey stood on the deck, he had to lower his voice to keep from being overheard as he spoke to Blanche, who sat beside the still figure of the injured man.

Forward there were groups of men yarning, men skylarking; there were solitary men who had each preempted a square yard of deck for himself and sat, cross-legged, with tools and materials, doing embroidery or whittling at models, oblivious to the tumult about them. Similarly aft on the crowded quarterdeck the groups of officers strolled and chatted, avoiding the other groups without conscious effort.

Blanche had had the injured seaman brought up out of the stuffy crew's quarters below, as she had done on the previous two days. The wind had grown balmier, and Whitefield had rigged a hammock on the port deck aft of the mizzenmast; there he had gotten well acquainted with his captain's willful daughter as they had sat beside the man. He admired her spirit, but realized clearly that the same impetuous impulse that had been the means of caring for the helpless man would be just as likely to lead her into less noble causes.

The two of them had been idly talking when Captain Rommey appeared unexpectedly, and Whitefield, wily enough to see a storm cloud in the face of Blanche's father, hastily slipped away. Rommey, towering over the girl, said with obvious displeasure, "You don't give a hang about this man!"

"Neither do you, Father," Blanche retorted sharply. She threw her head back, her eyes flashing. His daughter took a perverse delight, he saw, in taking him on in the matter, and added defiantly, "Perhaps you're right. He's just a common sailor. But you pulled me out of the only life I cared for—now I have to do something to entertain myself."

He bit his lip, pondering how to answer her. Finally giving up, his mouth drawn in displeasure, he said sternly, "The whole ship is rumbling about this thing. It's not good for discipline!" He waited for her to answer, but saw that she intended no such thing. Her rebellious disrespect flooded him with anger, for he was a man who could brook no opposition. Now he could only add, "You're doing this to spite me, Blanche. Or maybe you're playing dolls again."

His words stung her, and she stood up to face him, her features hard and her voice brittle. "What does *that* mean?"

"It means that you've always liked to play god with people. Even when you were a child, you had to rule the other children you played with. And as an older child, you learned you were smarter than most girls, and better looking, so you did as you pleased. Later when you became a woman, you played with men— just as you'd played with your dolls—pulling them to pieces when you got bored with them."

"Oh, Father, that's *wonderful* coming from *you!*" He knew her, and his words had cut deep—so deep that her face for all its rich color was a trifle pale. "You've done nothing all your life but rule people—and now you're saying that I'm the one who's spoiled!"

He looked around uneasily, for her voice had risen, and he realized that she did not care a pin if every seaman on deck heard her—but *he* cared, for he was jealous of his dignity and knew well that a captain must be aloof from his men. He shook his head and turned, saying only, "I'll be glad to get you to the Indies!"

She glared at his broad back as he wheeled and marched away toward the forecastle deck; then as quickly as it had arisen, her anger faded and she laughed aloud at herself. It was typical of the girl to shrug off anger so easily, for her emotions were quick rather than deep. Her father, she realized wryly, was right, and it was part of her charm that she was able to see a weakness in herself as readily as she could in another.

Curiously, she moved beside the gently swaying hammock, and with a gesture made easy by the practice of the last two days, lifted the battered head of the sailor and spooned some thin soup between his lips. She held his head, not missing the finely structured bones, the broad forehead, the high-bridged English nose, the small, neat ears, and the wide mouth, firmly molded and somehow a little stubborn even when relaxed. She paused before giving him more soup, and thought, *I wonder if I'd be doing this if he weren't so good-looking?* She smiled disdainfully and admitted, *Of course not! If he were homely, I'd never come near him.*

Blanche Rommey was a fickle, changeable, spoiled girl—but she had the rare gift of being honest with herself, and she knew that her father had been entirely correct in his evaluation of her motives—that she was doing it just to spite him and to play god.

She was furious with him for interfering with her life and bored to tears with the ship. She was not a girl given to books; her very being was the essence of action, and tending the sick man was just one handy way of burning up the energy that seethed inside her—and had the additional benefit of irritating her father!

Forward on the deck, as he emerged from the hold, Whitefield had been stopped by Oscar Grimes, the cooper. Grimes was shaped like a spider with a huge torso supported on thin legs, and his abnormally long arms, thin and sinewy, completed the illusion. His head was small, covered with a thatch of stiff black hair, and he had a pair of small, beady eyes, black as tar. Most of the crew were rough in their ways, but Grimes had the kind of evil in him that fascinated normal men. Repulsive as he was, in person as well as in mind, he drew a segment of the crew by the very power of his warped spirit.

"Wait up there, Whitefield," he called in an oily voice, and with a simian gesture reached out and caught the gunner by the arm. "Wot's this agoin' on?" he queried, nodding his head toward the spot where Blanche was tending her patient. Leering slyly, he added, "If that gel is that hot to 'ave a man—why, I reckon I can accommodate 'er!"

Whitefield was a small man and seemed dwarfed by Grimes's

powerful bulk, but there was something in his light blue eyes that made the cooper hurriedly remove his hand. "You just fly right at it, Grimes," he said menacingly. "Touch one hair on that woman's head, and you'll be hangin' from the yard arm by sundown—and feedin' the fish by dark."

His words angered Grimes, and the cooper's neck swelled; however, he well knew that Whitefield spoke no more than simple truth. In spite of that, he raised his voice as the gunner walked away, "All right, holy man—but I've got me ways! Oh, I've got me ways!"

Whitefield walked up to the hammock, looked down at the still face, and asked, "Any change, miss?"

"No, Whitefield."

"Aye—well, if you'd like to rest a bit, I'm off for four hours."

"Nothing to do on this awful ship!"

"Not much, miss—not for a lady like yourself." As he spoke his eyes caught sight of a large bird gracefully flying back toward the coast on powerful wings.

"What sort of bird is that?" she asked, following his gaze.

"Frigate bird, miss."

"Looks like an eagle. What do they eat?"

"Oh, pretty much what all sea birds eat—but they *are* different. They don't bother with doing much fishin' themselves, you see."

She looked at him with a puzzled light in her eyes before turning back to the bird. "How do they get their food?"

"Take it away from them what does work for it," Whitefield answered. "Like—a pelican will dive and get himself a nice fish; afterward he'll likely rise up and head off with it. But Mr. Frigate Bird, why, he's been asailin' round up there just waitin' like—and finally he says, 'Why, there's my supper, right in Mr. Pelican's beak!' So down he dives—and it's a fair sight, Miss Rommey, to see a frigate in a dive! So he hits Mr. Pelican and knocks 'im loose from the fish—and there's his supper!"

Blanche stared intently at the disappearing bird. "That," she said with a quick grin at Whitefield, "is the kind of bird I'd want to be if I had to be a bird."

He chuckled and nodded, pulling at a lock of his hair. "I thought you was a bit in that way—if you'll pardon me for sayin' so, miss." He waved his arm around and added, "That's why they call this kind of ship a *frigate*, you see? Light, fast, strong, and got enough guns to throw plenty of iron. She sees a ship filled up with good things, hits like a lightning bolt, and *bam*! She's got the goods and the poor old merchant ship ain't got no more than the pelican!"

She laughed, and although Whitefield would never have felt comfortable speaking freely with the captain, this girl had a natural quality that won his confidence. She was curious about everything, and for over an hour he kept her entertained with yarns of the sea. Her eyes glowed as he related some of the stories of sea fights between the great ships of the line, her desire for action and activity drawn to the excitement of that part of life.

Eventually she grew sleepy, and put her head back against the wooden bulkhead. He sat there quietly, finally pulled a small book out of his pocket and began reading. He looked up with a start when she said, "You read the Bible a lot, don't you, Whitefield?"

"Why, yes, miss. It's 'bout all the books I do read, you might say."

"Are you any relation to the Methodist preacher—what's his name?"

"That'd be my cousin George, miss."

"Of course." Blanche acknowledged, looking curiously at the sailor before responding. "Your kinsman, he's set the whole world buzzing! He's the talk of the court, you know. I was at a ball given by the Countess of Huntington, and *everyone* was there. The actor, David Garrick? Well, he said that he'd give anything to have a voice like Rev. Whitefield." She laughed and added, "I remember he said that Whitefield could make a congregation weep by pronouncing the word *Mesopotamia!*"

"I reckon the gentleman ain't far wrong, miss. George is a powerful man of the Word."

"Tell me about him."

Whitefield was reluctant, thinking that this wealthy girl would scoff at his simple beliefs, but she did not. She was, on the contrary, as fascinated by the phenomena of the enormous successes of the outdoor preaching of Whitefield and the Wesleys as she had been with the habits of the frigate bird.

Finally, she remarked, "Some people really dislike him, Whitefield—especially the clergy, I understand. Why is that?"

"Well, that's because he insists that people have to be born again."

"Born again?"

"Yes, miss." He opened his Bible and read her the opening lines of the third chapter of John, concluding with the words, 'Ye must be born again.' " He looked at her earnestly, saying, "You see, Miss Rommey, most people in the Established church of England thinks that if a man behaves himself, don't do no big sin, is good to his family and attends services—why, he's all right in the sight of the Lord."

"Well—isn't he?" Blanche asked instantly.

"Not according to what the Lord Jesus said," Whitefield shrugged. He explained in his rough way what it meant to have a change on the *inside*, but he saw at once that the girl had no concept of the matter.

She was just beginning to argue when a slight noise caused her to look at the man in the hammock, and she leaped to her feet, crying out, "Whitefield! Look, he's waking up!"

"Glory to God!" Whitefield exclaimed, breaking into a broad smile. "So he is!"

They stood there staring down, watching in anticipation as the eyelids seemed to flutter, then slowly opened, revealing a pair of murky eyes. They closed almost at once, but Whitefield moved to shade them. "Come, lad—open your eyes now." And once again the eyes opened. At first there was no expression in them, but as the two waited with bated breath, the gaze shifted, focusing on something to the left, later coming back to stare up at the face of Whitefield, who was leaning over the side of the hammock.

They were strange eyes, Whitefield decided. There was a bright intelligence behind them, giving them life, but there was something else—something the gunner could not identify. *Poor lad is terrible confused*, he thought, and he said in a mild, soothing voice, "Don't be too quick now, lad. Just lie easy till you gets your bearings."

Blanche moved closer, and immediately the eyes turned, taking her in. But there was no response on seeing her. He lay there considering her face, then looked back to Whitefield. They both waited for him to speak, but he seemed either unable or unwilling to open his lips.

"Are you all right?" Blanche asked. Once again his eyes shifted to look up at her, but as before there was no sign of recognition and no attempt to speak.

The wind was whistling through the shrouds, and the noise of the men's voices was like a hum of distant bees. Both Whitefield and Blanche unconsciously leaned forward to hear what the man would say—but he remained mute. Finally Blanche gave the sailor a puzzled look, somewhat fearful, and whispered, "Whitefield—something's *wrong*!"

He did not answer at once, but considered the eyes focusing on him. "Well, Miss Rommey, he's come a long way. You have to remember, this is all new to the lad. He was on shore, maybe in a cold, dark place, and now he wakes up in this warm sun on a ship. Let's not rush the poor chap."

"Water . . . !" They both jumped at the sound of the man's hoarse voice, rusty with disuse, but Blanche whirled and poured a cup of fresh water from the jug beside the hammock. She lifted his head and held it while he drank thirstily. When he stopped, she let his head fall back, holding it gently. "Do you feel better?" she asked.

He looked at her, slowly nodded, closed his eyes again and relaxed so completely that it frightened her. "Whitefield—he's dead!"

"Not a bit of it, miss," the sailor assured her. "Just went to sleep right sudden-like. Ain't uncommon in such cases. Men that's been wounded bad, they fall off like that—especially at first. But he'll wake up soon, and it's hungry he'll be."

"He looked at us so strangely," she murmured, looking down at the still face. "Do you think he'll be all right?"

"Oh, I should think so," Whitefield responded. "I been afraid he'd go out without waking up at all."

"You mean—die?"

"Yes, miss."

The thought troubled her, and she shivered slightly. "I've never seen anyone die. It would frighten me, I think."

"Takes most of us that way," he shrugged. "I'll be glad to talk to the lad—see if he's ready to meet the good Lord."

She stared at him, offering hurriedly, "We'll take turns watching him, Whitefield. I'll nap a little so when you go on duty I can sit with him."

"Yes, miss."

For the next forty-eight hours neither Blanche nor Whitefield slept a great deal. There was something a little frightening about the way the sick man would wake up, stare at them with a directness that was disconcerting, and after a time fall back into sleep as fast as a rock falling to the ground. It was as if he came from death, stared at them briefly, then descended back into a nameless cavern of unknowing. Always they tried to talk to him, but never did either one break through; the eyes would watch for a span, and, as though pulled by an invisible force, soon return to that dark place.

It was on the twenty-fourth, a Sunday morning, when he spoke for the second time. Most of the men slept late or came up on deck for their usual recreation or personal work, but Whitefield and half a dozen other hands held a service on the afterdeck. The sick man had been brought up and placed in the hammock. During the singing, which lasted for about ten minutes, Blanche had listened and watched everything with great interest, for she had never met anyone like the gunner. He was a simple man, truly religious—with the variety of religion called *enthusiastic*—that is, emotional to an abnormal degree. To be labeled an "enthusiast" was pretty much the same as being called a madman or a fanatic. With the exception of a handful of nobility, such as the Countess of Huntington, most Methodists and other varieties of "enthusiasts" came from the poorer class.

There was, however, something genuine about Whitefield, and as little inclined as Blanche herself was to becoming religious, she had a sharp ear for the counterfeit. She was convinced that if Whitefield was a fanatic, he was as gentle and honest a man as she had rarely met. So it was that she listened carefully as he spoke after the song service was finished.

But before the simple "sermon" had gotten well under way, she was startled when the words "Where is this?" came to her. She whirled around and saw immediately that this time something was different. The somber eyes were fixed on her, but now they held an awareness that was unmistakable. As if to prove that he was himself, he said slowly, "I don't—know this place."

She responded quickly, placing a hand on his head in an act of reassurance. "Don't be frightened—you're going to be all right."

The commotion had halted the service as everyone watched intently.

For a moment the man looked out at the fleecy clouds drifting across the azure sky, then brought his gaze back to her and asked again in a voice that was clear and distinct, "Where is this—place?"

"You're on the King's ship—*Neptune*. My father is the captain—Captain William Rommey."

He stared at her perplexed, trying to comprehend. As if thinking action would help, he tried to get up. She helped him into a sitting position, and as she did so, the swinging of the hammock confused him. He grabbed wildly at her, flinging his arms around her neck, and only by grabbing him around his waist did she manage to keep the man from crashing to the deck. "Be careful!" she panted, struggling with his weight. "You've been hurt. Here, lean against this wall."

He clung to her as she swung him around, setting him carefully against the bulkhead. Leaning back he took a deep breath, looked around, and murmured, "I—feel very queer."

"You've been very ill—don't try to do too much."

She was holding on to his hands, noting his strength even in his weakened condition. The white shirt that Whitefield had loaned him was thin as silk as a result of many washings, and she was very much aware that his torso was taut, swelling with a set of rippling muscles—not massive, but like a cat, lithe and elastic.

By now the man leaning against the outer bulkhead was surrounded by the other men. Whitefield asked Blanche, "Is he well?"

"I think so."

Whitefield stepped in front of the man, peered sharply into his eyes, and said exuberantly, "Well, bless God, you're out of it, are you? I'm glad to see you up and well."

The man stared at him, saying simply, "Thank you—but I'm not very clear on—"

"Don't be havin' to know everything," the gunner responded. "First thing is to get some real food down your gullet!" He helped the man down the stairs, and closely followed by Blanche, led the way to the kitchen where the cook, a fat Dutchman named Hans Boerner, used two of the few eggs left, and some of the bacon and fresh bread to make a meal. The man devoured it wolfishly, washing the food down with a cup of coffee.

"That was . . . good." There was a very slight hesitation in his speech, noticeable to both his listeners, as if he were learning a new language. He reached up and touched the side of his head, now only slightly swollen. "That hurts," he remarked quietly, a puzzled look on his face.

"It was a pretty hard lick you got, I'd venture," Whitefield replied. "Now, I expect you maybe have some questions—but first, what's your name, lad?"

"My name?"

"Sure. We have to know how to call you," Whitefield smiled. "My name is Whitefield—and this is Miss Blanche Rommey—our captain's daughter. Now, what's your name, lad?"

He stared at them, and his brow wrinkled with a sudden strain.

He bit his full lower lip, confused. Finally he shook his head slowly, saying in a voice that was thready with panic, "I—I can't seem to remember."

Blanche and Whitefield looked at each other questioningly. "Well," she assured him, "you've been badly hurt. Don't be afraid. It'll come in a little while. But maybe you remember where you came from. Where in America?"

"I don't—seem to know that, either," he answered, the hesitation in his voice now much more noticeable. He rose suddenly, grabbed at his temples, and tried to take a couple steps, but Whitefield caught him.

"Now, don't fret! It'll all come back."

"I don't . . . know much . . . about anything," he whispered. There was fear and confusion in his eyes, and he implored them, "Tell me . . . how did I . . . get here?"

The next half hour was unpleasant for all of them. The man was on the verge of panic, and Blanche and Whitefield had all they could do to keep him calm. It was fortunate that he tired quickly, going to sleep almost at once as Whitefield put him in a hammock next to his own.

Blanche had gone back on deck where Whitefield now found her standing at the rail, waiting for him. "He's asleep," he said, "but I fear the lad is not right."

"He seems not to be. What if he—what if he doesn't ever remember, Whitefield?"

"That would be bad indeed, miss." He shook his head. "Don't know as I ever heard of a man who didn't know who he was. Be a little like bein' a livin' dead man, wouldn't it now?"

The thought frightened her. "Keep me informed as to how he is, will you?"

"Yes, miss."

★　★　★　★

Three days later the captain questioned Burns about the injured man.

"Lieutenant Burns, about this man who doesn't know who he is—give me some facts."

Burns shrugged. "Weel, sir, I canna tell ye much." He had been expecting the captain's question, for as second lieutenant, he was responsible for the muster book, and therefore was expected to know the condition of the crew. But he spoke with even more caution than his Scottish reticence provided.

"Speak up, man!"

"Weel, sir, physically, the man is in guid condition. It's only been three days since he came out of the coma—and he's fit so far as his body goes—but his mind—?"

"Claims he doesn't know his name, is that it?"

"Yes, sir, and I think he's tellin' the truth. I've had a talk with him, Captain, and it's no act. Matter of fact, sir, the thing frightens him—as it would any man."

Captain Rommey stared at his feet as the silence ran on. Finally he looked up, perplexity marking his square face. "Well, we'll have to use the fellow, Lieutenant. Put him to work."

"Aye, sir. I've put him in Whitefield's care. He's a steady man, and he tells me the man's quite able—a quick learner."

"All right. Use him."

"Aye, sir, but what shall I put down in the muster book?"

"Put down—oh, you mean a name."

"We must have that, Captain."

"Of course." There was little humor in Rommey, but something caught at his mind and brought a light into his frosty eyes. "Little like naming a baby, isn't it, Burns? Well, I've named a few ships, but never a baby. Let me see . . ." he pondered. Shortly he exclaimed, "I've got it! You know the Hebrews had a genius for naming their babies, Burns. Like Jacob. Name means *deceiver*—and he didn't miss it far, did he now?"

"No, sir."

"Well, I need seamen—so I'm going to name this infant of ours after the best seaman I ever knew."

Burns grinned, knowing the captain's idol. "Admiral Hawke, that'd be, sir?"

"Of course! Name the fellow that—*Hawke*!"

"Aye, sir—and the first name?"

"Blast the first name! *Hawke*—that's good enough for the fellow—probably too good!"

"Aye, sir. I'll put it in the book. Hawke, able seaman."

CHAPTER NINE

I'D LET THE DEVIL HIMSELF MAN THE GUNS!

★ ★ ★ ★

Neptune's bell struck two double strokes. It was six o'clock in the evening, and the first dogwatch had come to an end in the gathering darkness.

"Sunset, sir," reported Burns.

"I see that," Captain Rommey answered, biting off his words.

"Six o'clock exactly. The equinox, sir. Now we'll have a westerly gale, or I'll miss my guess."

"I would not be opposed to a breeze, Mr. Burns. And I do believe the wind's freshening and the sea's getting up a bit, sir."

Burns shifted his feet and said uncomfortably, "We're vurry short o' water, Captain."

"Put the men on a pint a day."

"Yes, sir."

Rommey glanced at the small officer, noting the unhappy light in his eyes. "It won't kill them," he barked. The captain was not a man to explain his actions. And it wasn't as if he didn't know that the entire crew was rebellious and unhappy with the water shortage. Every man on board was aware that the *Neptune* could make port in five days, and they resented the captain's stubborn refusal to do what seemed reasonable.

Rommey thought back over the past five weeks, musing as to how he might have done differently, but nothing came to him. He thought of the first day the pressed men had been forced out on deck, naked and shivering, to rid themselves of vermin.

Their heads were shaved to the bare skin, accentuating the prison pallor many of them still wore. They had been driven by Thompson, the captain of the forecastle, to the wash-deck pump, fright making them shiver as much as cold. Most of them had never had a bath before, and Thompson's blood-curdling remarks terrified them: "Perhaps we'll make sailors of you, but if we don't, overside with a shot at your feet! Come on with the pump there! Let's see the color of your hides, jailbirds! When the cat gets at you, we see the color o' your backbones, too!"

Rommey had watched, and contrary to the opinion of most on the ship, he took no pleasure in seeing the pain or discomfort of these men. The shearing and the bath were necessary if the ship was to be kept clear of fleas and bugs and lice which would make life miserable.

The next day had brought one of those sudden, violent storms that seem to rise out of nowhere, ripping the seas to tatters, seemingly possessed with a demonic desire to destroy ships. It had been, in Rommey's judgment, a miracle that the *Neptune* had not gone to the bottom, for the new hands had been worthless. Only extraordinary courage on the part of the few old hands had saved them.

It had not saved their water or their food, however. The planking had been sprung, flooding the compartment containing fresh food and water, spoiling everything. There was one other compartment, very small, which held a few casks of fresh water and some staples, and it was on this that the crew had lived for three weeks.

Both his lieutenants had been surprised when he had not made straight for the Indies, but there had been a method to his seeming madness. *The men have got to be made into good seamen*, he'd thought stubbornly. *If they get thirsty enough—that may do it.* Such was his plan, and he was assisted by a lull following the storm that had becalmed the ship, preventing them from making any headway no matter what the captain decided.

The days had grown to weeks, and the water and food dwindled down so that rations were cut three times. But there had been no letup of drill! From dawn to dark the men ran up the lines and worked the sails at the commands of the officers. Below decks the gun crews labored harder than miners, running the heavy guns out, firing them, then doing it again. Every day, hour after hour, the drills were repeated as the *Neptune* drifted with slack sails across a windless glassy sea, which grew hotter and hotter as the days wore on.

Uncomfortable with the situation, Rommey was now anxious for someone to approve his action. "We've had a hard cruise, Mr. Burns," he acknowledged, "and I know the men are unhappy."

"Aye, sir."

Rommey looked up, smote his meaty hands together, saying brusquely, "It's hard to make first-rate seamen out of pressed men. Easy ways won't do."

Burns turned to stare at the captain, for he realized it was a plea for some sort of understanding. *Weel, now,* he thought in surprise, *the man is actually human!* Aloud he said only, "That's the sea, sir. You had to give them a little pride."

Now it was Rommey's turn to be surprised, for he had not thought the second lieutenant had that sort of discernment. Realizing that he had mistaken the Scot's reticence for a lack of intelligence, he smiled briefly. "I'm glad you see that, Mr. Burns."

"They got a bit o' it, sir—but if I may make a suggestion?"

"Of course."

"Weel, I don't think we'll get much more out o' them just now. They're landsmen, sir, an' not toughened up. But if we could make for port, get some fresh food an' water, why, I think we might see a better spirit."

"I agree. We'll set all sail and make for port. You may give the orders as soon as the wind picks up. I'll have Lieutenant Langley plot the course."

"Aye, sir." Burns was somewhat embarrassed, for he was a poor navigator, though excellent in every other aspect of seamanship. He spoke up hurriedly to cover his shame. "The men will have a heart for it."

"How's that man doing—Hawke?"

"Not bad, Captain. He's vurry strong an' healthy. Whitefield say's he's a first-class hand with the gun."

"Keep an eye on him," Rommey suggested, then left the deck to Burns. He thought sourly as he went wearily to his cabin: *And if you don't have time to keep an eye on him, Burns, my daughter will take care of the duty!*

The captain was not wrong, for at the same time that he was speaking with Burns on the forecastle deck, Blanche and Hawke were sitting at the small table in the galley. The men were in their hammocks, exhausted from the day's taxing drill, and Hans, the cook, had watched the pair furtively as he made dough for bread. He was a gossip, as most ship's cooks were, but the couple spoke so quietly that he was unable to hear. As he finally left the galley and went to bed, he was thinking up ways to improve on the telling of the thing—the captain's daughter and the strange man called Hawke who didn't even have his own name. He licked his lips and thought of how he could report their being alone in the galley, sitting *very* close indeed . . . and so his fertile imagination built on the incident until he dropped off to sleep.

Blanche looked up as the cook left. "I think he suspects us."

"Suspects us of what?"

The question took the girl off guard—as Hawke's remarks often did, and she colored slightly, an unusual thing for Blanche Rommey!

"Why, he suspects us of—of being—" She broke off, unable to meet his steady, inquiring gaze. "You know, Hawke."

"No."

The stark simplicity of his remark and the clear, dark eyes looking directly into hers made her give an uncertain laugh. "You are a difficult man to talk to!"

"I am?"

"Yes. Any other man in the world would have known *exactly* what the cook suspects. But you really don't know, do you?"

"No."

"No!" she mocked him, then leaned forward and tapped her finger against her chin, studying him as if he were some exotic specimen. She had done that a great deal for the past three weeks, and there was still an excitement in it that she could not explain. He was an enigma to her, of course, as he was to all, even to himself, and she was fascinated by what she was constantly finding out about him.

Things he didn't know himself came to light as they sat for hours in the dimly lit galley. She'd discovered that he knew the names of the newest fashions, exotic foods, a little about French dances and manners, though he spoke no French. He was not a common man, she had discovered quickly.

He had grown well and strong, she saw, staring at him directly. His face was reddish with a slight sunburn, which was evening out to a golden tan. The work he'd done with the ropes and the tackle of the ship had roughened his hands, but they were well-shaped, not the hands of a laboring man.

"What would Hans be suspicious of, Miss Rommey?" he asked when she did not respond.

"Oh, Hawke, he's thinking it's not right for a man and a woman to be alone like this."

"Why not?"

"Because they might—do things they shouldn't," she answered with some discomfort in her face.

"What things?"

Impulsively she shook her heavy hair in an extremely feminine gesture, and quickly put her hand on his arm and squeezed it, feeling the steely muscle beneath the thin cotton shirt. "Why, most men would try to kiss me if they were here alone with me."

He thought about that, and she watched his face carefully, wondering at the openness in his eyes. That, she knew, was what fascinated her. She had tried to explain the man's innocent behavior to her mother in answer to the charge that she was spending too much time with a deckhand. "Oh, Mother, he's not a deckhand—he's not anything. At least, no one *knows* what he is. He doesn't know himself. He's like a baby, really. Most people put on a mask, try to be somebody else. But Hawke doesn't even know enough to do that. He's the only person I'm aware of who doesn't have anything to cover up—or who doesn't *know* anything he has to hide."

Her mother had been totally bewildered, but now as Blanche sat there with her hand on his arm, she knew that part of the thrill of being with Hawke was his extreme attractiveness, and part of it was the excitement of discovery—finding out who he was. But, at the same time, she knew that once she had found out his identity, he would not be nearly so interesting.

She looked at him, a glint in her eyes. "We've talked about so many things, but we've never talked about women."

He flashed her a smile and said with the trace of humor that sometimes burst from him, "I don't know anything about women—just about you. You're the only woman I know, Miss Rommey."

"Now that's fascinating! All men say the same thing!"

"What do they say?"

"Oh, they all say 'I love only you!' "

"And they don't mean it?"

"No. Certainly not."

"Why do they say it then?"

"Why—!"

She halted, and he said frankly, "You're the only woman I love."

She gasped and then shook her head. "You are a danger, Hawke. It would be unsafe to let you go into society."

"A danger?"

"Yes. Either you'd charm the ladies out of their virtue with your point-blank simplicity—or you'd get snared by some hussy— or you'd marry a widow with six children because you felt sorry for her!" The last amused her and she laughed until the tears ran down her face.

Hawke rarely laughed, but he smiled as he watched her. His body had healed, but he felt incomplete, and for this reason said practically nothing to anyone but Blanche and Whitefield. Those two he felt safe with, for they never probed at him unkindly as a few of the crew had tried to do.

He sat there relaxed, trusting the woman, and submitting to her questions, for they were kind. Finally she rose and he got up with her. "I hate to go to bed. I always hate to go to bed."

"Why is that?"

"Oh, I don't know," she shrugged. "Afraid I'll miss something."

"But nothing happens at night. Everybody's asleep."

She could never get used to the absolute simplicity of his mind, and she smiled, coming closer to him. "I know," she stated, hating to leave. The ship swayed slightly, bringing her mind back to why she was on board. "Wind is picking up. Father told me we'll be in the Indies in a few days with a good breeze."

"Will you be glad?"

"No. It'll be boring." She stirred restlessly, and added, "I won't be able to see you. The ship will sail in a few days." She waited for him to ask where, and when he didn't, she questioned, "Don't you want to know where you're going?"

"No. Places are all alike to me," he answered quietly.

"One of them isn't! Your home."

"I—can't remember it."

A thought struck her and she voiced it, looking carefully at him. "You may be married."

He shrugged his shoulders, and then replied with one of his small smiles, "I don't *feel* married."

The statement pleased her, but there was a light of speculation in her eyes. The ship was still except for the creaking of timbers, and impulsively she turned fully to him and asked a little breathlessly, "Do you know what a kiss is?"

"Yes."

She looked at him, then put her hands up and drew his head down, kissing him full on the mouth. She held him there, and was not displeased to feel his arms go around her waist. But as he pulled her closer she drew away. Looking at him with a smile, she remarked, "You are very proficient in that area, Hawke. I think you must have had practice."

He stood there, a look of sadness in his eyes. "I can't say, Miss Rommey."

The hurt she saw pulled at her and she was sorry she had teased him. "Forgive me, Hawke. My father says I like to play with people as if they were toys. I hope you don't think I've done that with you."

"No. If you hadn't helped me, I couldn't have borne it."

"What's it *like*? Can you tell me?" All of a sudden she found herself filled with compassion, a rare emotion for Blanche, and she waited expectantly.

"It's—like being in a large room with all sorts of objects. I see them and I know what they're for—but I don't know how I know. And when I'm alone, in my hammock, I have bad dreams—or not dreams, really, but thoughts that come as I lie there in the darkness."

He paused and she whispered, "What do you dream?"

"Faces—all sorts of faces. People I don't know—but who seem to know me. And sometimes it's—scenes, like in a play. I seem to be in the play and I'm doing things—sometimes just simple things like eating a meal with someone. Sometimes doing something I don't even understand—that seems to make no sense."

He had grown pale, and she realized that beneath the even demeanor of Hawke, there was a frightening void, and she longed to comfort him. "It'll come to you, Hawke," she murmured, putting her arms around him. This time she did not kiss him, but held him as he stood there with an emptiness in his eyes. Then she drew back and said, "Good night. I'll see you in the morning."

"Good night, Miss Rommey."

After she had left, he went to the crew's quarters. A single candle threw a feeble yellow beam over the swaying hammocks, and he slipped quietly into his, not knowing that more than one set of eyes marked his progress. He lay there quietly, and for once slipped into a deep sleep, not awakening until the sun piped all hands up.

Whitefield had already risen and was gone, but a few of the hands still there spoke to Hawke as they began to pull their clothes on and stow their hammocks. As he left the cabin, he was abruptly caught by a strong hand and whirled about to look into the face of a tall, strongly built man with jet black hair and eyes to match—Dion Sullivan, an Irishman. He was the carpenter and also part of a gun crew. Hawke had been aware that the man was considered a bully. Sullivan had whipped one man badly, one of the new pressed men; and most of the crew suffered his bluster, fearing his powerful fists. He was a crony of the cooper, Grimes, and Hawke saw that the spider-like man was standing beside Sullivan, an ugly gleam in his beady eyes.

"Well, looky wot we got, Mates," Sullivan yelled. "A real ladies' man, that's what we got!" He did not notice that Pickens, a foretopman, had slipped out of the door. The Irishman continued holding Hawke in an iron grip, an unpleasant smile on his lips. "Now, wot I says is, when a fellow has himself a woman friend as purty as that there captain's daughter, why he owes it to his mates to give some details! Now that ain't askin' too much, is it?"

"Too right, Sullivan!" Grimes moved to block the way when Hawke would have pushed by the Irishman. "You've been cuddlin' up to that gel fer weeks now. Come on, wot's it like, eh?"

Hawke stared at the pair, confused, and several servile followers of Grimes began to join in, yelping like dogs.

Hawke pulled free from Sullivan's grip—and the ease with which he did it both surprised and angered the carpenter. "I have to be at my station," he said quietly, and would have gone through the door but Sullivan caught a wink from Grimes. He made a leap and threw a blow that caught the smaller man between the shoulder blades with such force that Hawke was driven against the bulkhead with a crash. Sullivan cried, "You ain't learned 'ow to act to yer betters, lubber!"

He threw a punch that caught Hawke high on the forehead and knocked him to the floor. A small protest went up from one or two of the hands, but Grimes cried, "Shut yer face!" and Sullivan pulled the smaller man to his feet and began to strike him in the face and body with hard, driving blows. Hawke held his hands up to protect his face, but made no attempt to strike back, which pleased and infuriated Sullivan.

"Look at the rat!" he cried with a twisted grin. "Won't even put his hands up!"

He began to strike again, but at that moment Whitefield came flying through the door with a marlin spike in his hand. He took a swing and knocked Sullivan to the floor with one fierce blow, dropping the spike in the process. Quick as a flash Grimes reached out one arm, plucked the spike, and proceeded to beat Whitefield to the deck with it. Grimes would have killed him, but Lieutenant Langley shot in, shouting, "Blast you, Grimes! Drop that spike!"

That was the end of the fight, but it was not the end of the matter itself. Langley was in a fit of rage, and he reported to the captain instantly. Rommey stared at him and said, "I'll have the lot flogged!"

Immediately Langley lost his anger, saying, "Oh no, sir, that would be too severe!"

Burns had come along with the first lieutenant, and he agreed. "It would nae be a guid thing to blow this up, Captain. The men will fight, an' that's all there is to it."

Rommey was angry, but allowed himself to be pacified. He said impatiently, "Well, take care of it. If it happens again, we'll see what a taste of the cat will do." Then he had a thought. "One of them was Hawke?"

"Yes, sir."

"I'll see the man in my cabin."

As the two officers walked away, Langley told Burns, "I'll work the tallow off Grimes and Sullivan. You send Hawke to the captain."

Ten minutes later Rommey opened the door at the sound of a knock, and found the seaman there. "Seaman Hawke reporting, sir," he stated, well schooled by Whitefield.

"Yes." Rommey beckoned impatiently and went back to sit at his desk. He stared at the sailor with a hard glance, noting the livid bruises on his face. When there was no response, he continued. "I understand there was a fight and you were involved, Hawke."

"Yes, sir."

Captain Rommey waited for an excuse, but none came, so he probed further. "I'm aware of your misfortune, Hawke, and am inclined to believe that you are innocent." He waited to be thanked, but Hawke simply stood there, his eyes alert but revealing nothing.

"I want to ask you—"

The door suddenly opened and Rommey turned angrily to find

Blanche coming in with an innocent look on her face. "I'm sorry to interrupt, Father, but Mother wants me to get a book for her."

He knew instantly that was a lie, for his wife read practically nothing. She had come, he knew, because she was fascinated by the man Hawke. Going to the bookcase, she looked over the books, took one, then stood there. "Good morning, Hawke," she nodded.

"I would appreciate it if you would take the book to your mother, Blanche. I need to talk to this man."

"Perhaps I can help." She sat down, settled herself firmly and added with a disarming smile, "Hawke and I have spent some time together, and I believe I understand more of his problem than anyone else."

She would not be budged by anything less than a charge of gun powder, Rommey saw. And not willing to give her the satisfaction of an argument, he gave in. "Very well. Stay if you must, but remain silent!"

"Certainly, Father. Anything you say."

He gritted his teeth at the over-sweet reply and turned to ask, "You remember nothing, Hawke—not even your name?"

"No, sir."

Puzzled, Rommey began to inquire further, asking technical questions about ships and the sea. Hawke answered them slowly and with great care, and finally Rommey stated, "You can answer all my questions about the tackle of ships—except for arms, and you even know a smattering of that."

"I've learned all that from Whitefield, sir," Hawke responded. "He's taught me that since I . . . . came on the ship."

"I see," Rommey nodded slowly. "That means, of course, that you've done considerable sailing—but not on a warship."

"Yes, sir. That's what Whitefield decided."

Captain Rommey caught a smile on Blanche's face and flushed, for he knew what she was thinking: *A lowly seaman—but he found out as much as the captain!* It flustered him, and he continued his inquiry but could find no pattern.

Finally he remarked, "Well, Hawke, I don't know what you *were*—but I know what you are now. You're a seaman aboard the frigate *Neptune*, and I will expect you to do your duty."

"Yes, sir. I'll do my best."

Rommey was caught off guard by the quick, respectful answer, and he turned and walked to the window. He stood there silently staring out. After a few minutes he spoke as he continued to gaze at the waves and the sky. "England is on the brink of a war, and it is ships like this one that will save her. It always comes to that—the navy is England's strength."

He began to pace the floor, forgetting momentarily the pair who were watching. His next words were intense. "The politicians and the merchants and the public—they all want peace. Good for business!" he snorted. "But they'll not get peace. Never! Then when war comes, they start to cry for the soldier and the sailor!" He shrugged and went on, "We'd all like peace, but when war comes, what good is a man of peace? That's when we need men of war. Let me see, there's a blasted good line about that . . ." He paused and tugged at his ear, staring at his books. "What is it? Something about a tiger! Imitate a tiger? No, that's not right. What *is* it?"

Suddenly Hawke quoted:

> In peace there's nothing so becomes a man
> As modest stillness and humility.
> But when the blast of war blows in our ears,
> Then imitate the action of the tiger.

Captain Rommey stared dumbfounded at Hawke, shot a startled glance at Blanche, then back to Hawke. "Do you know that line? Who said it?"

Hawke closed his eyes, thought for a moment, his brow wrinkled. "I believe," he replied, "it was Henry V, wasn't it, Captain?"

"By Harry, that's the piece!" Amazed, he burst into laughter, saying, "A scholar in our midst! And I need gunners!"

Immediately a thought struck him, and his eyes gleamed. He wheeled, walked to the large table that was covered with a nautical map, and picked up a scrap of paper and a quill. After scribbling something on it, Rommey extended the paper to Hawke, who took it and read it.

"Do you recognize what that is?"

"I suppose, sir, they are two positions."

"Exactly! The first is our present position. The other is our destination." He hesitated, looking at him intently. "Do you think you can take those two figures and plot a course on that map?"

Hawke bit his lip, stared at the paper, shrugged slightly and answered, "I can try, sir."

"Do it then!"

Hawke walked to the table and surveyed the project. He seemed to forget the captain and Blanche as he pored over the figures and the map. Finally he picked up the dividers, moved them across the map, then looked at the paper again. He checked his figures carefully, using some of the tools on the table. After several movements and rechecking, he put a mark on the map, traced a line, and stepped back. "I believe that's right, sir."

Rommey came over, stared at the map for a long time, and without looking up, said, "You may go, Hawke."

Blanche, fascinated by this unusual man, watched him leave. As soon as the door closed, she rushed over to stand beside her father. "Is it correct?"

"Yes," he said in a strange tone.

"What's the matter, Father?" She saw he was troubled, the cloud of anguish evident in his eyes, and for the first time in weeks Blanche felt a compassion toward him.

"What's the matter? I'll tell you what's wrong," he said quietly. "There are only two men who can navigate this ship—myself and Langley. And three times in my life I've known of ships that lost their captain and first mates in action. A ship without a navigator is a piece of wreckage, Blanche."

"But—!"

"And now I have a man who can navigate this vessel—and he doesn't even know his name! Can you imagine what they'd say at home if I put a man like that in any sort of position of responsibility?"

She stood there appraising him. "You would never let a common seaman chart a course."

He stared at her, then declared slowly, "Daughter, this is a fighting ship and I am a fighting man. That's all either of us is good for. And if fighting comes, and if it means victory—I'd let the devil himself man the guns of the *Neptune*!"

CHAPTER TEN

THE BLADE

★ ★ ★ ★

The frigid cold of the North Atlantic and the American shore was only a faint memory now to the crew of the *Neptune* as they sailed toward the Indies. The blazing June sun beat down like a fist on the crew as they sought the small islands of shade on the deck, and the southern breeze baked the lips dry and turned the pallid hides of the pressed men to a rich copper.

Whitefield glanced to where Hawke was sitting with his back against the bulkhead, his eyes half shut as he stared across the rolling troughs of green topped with sparkling white caps of spray. The young man was a source of never-ending wonder to the gunner, who had kept close watch on him since the trouble with Sullivan and Grimes—and the thought of that time prompted him to speak.

"Hawke?"

"Yes?"

"You ain't never said a word about that pair—" He waved a hand toward the stern where the two sat in the middle of a small group laughing loudly. "I been waitin' for you to complain about the way they beat you up—but you ain't said not one word."

"Nothing to say about it, Enoch." Hawke did not even shift his gaze, but suddenly his eyes opened and he said in excitement, "Look—what's that?"

"What? Oh, them's flyin' fish." Enoch watched carefully, and as usual tried to make some sort of connection with the remark. "You never seen flyin' fish?"

"No—at least, I don't think so."

"You ain't never been in these waters, then." He pondered that, chewing on his lower lip. But he was a stubborn man, and he went on doggedly, "Now, it ain't in a natural man to take a beatin' like you took from that pair an' not get mad."

Hawke took his eyes off the fish and considered the older man with a glint of amusement. "Why do you think that is, Enoch?"

"Well, I've been ponderin' on it—and it come to me that you might be a Christian man. The Bible teaches us to turn the other cheek, and that's just what you done, Hawke. And besides, you know more 'bout the Scripture than a sinner would know."

Whitefield was a single-minded man, eager to see all men embrace Jesus Christ; in that he was much like his cousin, George Whitefield. Hawke had been aware of the gunner's fervent desire, and had listened carefully to Enoch's preaching as well as to their conversations.

But he now shook his head, saying quietly, "I don't know what I am, Enoch. From what you've told me, a Christian has some feelings—but I'm just a blank. Maybe I had parents who read the Bible—or perhaps I attended a school where it was read aloud. And as for not wanting to get revenge on Sullivan and Grimes, it could be that I'm a coward."

The answer did not satisfy Whitefield, but he said no more. For the next hour they sat there quietly, Enoch from time to time relating some of his life to the young man. They were disturbed by the crowd on the stern who came milling to the mizzenmast with loud cries.

"They're tormentin' young Jones again," Whitefield said in disgust. He got to his feet, spat over the rail, and then shook his head, saying, "Why can't they leave the poor boy alone? He's sick. A fool could see that!"

Will Jones was one of the pressed men and, unfortunately, one of those human beings who is constitutionally unfit for life at sea. He had been seasick since the day he was brought aboard, unable to keep down any food, much less the unpalatable, rough fare served on a warship. He was nothing but skin and bones, his clothes flapping about him in the breeze as he was pulled roughly along by Sullivan toward the mast.

"Bully boy!" Whitefield said. "Ain't happy unless he's makin' some poor devil weaker than himself miserable! He'd 'ave been after you, Hawke, if Lieutenant Burns hadn't put the fear of the cat in him."

That, Hawke realized, was true. Burns had stood looking up into the face of the hulking Sullivan and in his quiet Scottish burr, had informed the sailor that if he laid one hand on Hawke, he would kiss the Gunner's Daughter—an expression that meant he would be tied over a cannon and flogged.

Since that hour Sullivan had not touched Hawke, but there was a burning hatred in his eyes, and now, as he held fast to the unfortunate Jones, his eyes were fixed on Whitefield and Hawke, addressing his words more to them than to the trembling sailor in his grasp.

"See here, Jones," he snarled loudly, "I've had enough of your play actin'! You ain't done nothin' but lay around and let these good men do your work. Now you climb them shrouds or I'll make you wish you had!"

Hawke saw that young Jones's thin face trembled as he looked up to the top of the towering mizzenmast; and bloodless as he was, his pallor seemed to wash to an even paler hue. "I—I can't do it!" he whispered. "Never could bear high places."

"Never could bear high places!" Sullivan mocked the boy with a grin, then gave him a shake that made the thin frame tremble violently. He held up his large fist in front of Jones's eyes. "I'm tellin' you, boy," he warned; "you climb that mast, or I'll bust you up!"

Pickens, one of the foretopmen, protested, "Sullivan, he's not lying. He tried once, and we had to pry his fingers loose. Some men is like that—can't stand no height."

"Shut your mouth, Pickens! I say he's a whining quitter and I aim to cure him right now."

"Let the boy alone." Whitefield left his place and came to stand beside Jones. "I don't remember nobody makin' you an officer on this ship."

"The officers expect us to make sailors out of these lubbers, Whitefield, and you can't deny it!"

There was some truth in that, and Enoch could only say, "They do expect that—but this boy is sick."

Hawke did not miss the look that passed between Sullivan and Grimes, and he realized instantly that this scene was directed at him. Then, when Sullivan spoke again, he was certain of it.

"Every man on this ship knows you're a great one for taking care of strays, Whitefield—like that one there." Sullivan gave a nod at Hawke, adding with a sneer, "You sold Burns a bill of goods on that dummy, didn't you?"

"He does his work!"

"He's a bleedin' coward, that's wot he is!" Sullivan said. "Won't fight like a man! Well, I can't touch your stray cat—not till I catch him ashore—but I can build a fire under this one!"

Hawke had been standing with his back to a bulkhead, watching as he always did. He was not touched by the plight of Jones, for he had seen much suffering on the part of the landsmen who'd been roughly handled on the *Neptune*. But he was disturbed by the troubled face of Whitefield. The gunner had become his touchstone with the world, and it was only through Enoch's constant attention that Hawke had been able to keep his mind off the sinister darkness—the frightening void that lay behind him. He saw Enoch's helplessness, and suddenly without knowing why, he stated quietly, "The boy's pretty small game for you, Sullivan."

Instantly the big Irishman swung his head, his eyes fixed on Hawke. "Well, well—another country heard from!" His eyes gleamed and he jabbed a thumb toward Hawke, saying, "And it's yourself who's takin' this lubber's part, *Mister* Hawke—who can't even do his own fightin'?"

"Let him alone. I'll fight you if that'll make you happy."

The challenge came so quickly that Sullivan's jaw dropped, and he retorted, "Well, that's what I'd like—"

"Don't do it, Mate!" Grimes, his ungainly body a blot on the bright sunlight, moved forward and put a restraining hand on Sullivan's arm. "Burns would 'ave you cut to rags." Then he smiled craftily and suggested with a sly look toward Hawke, "But just make a friendly wager with the man."

"What sort o' bet?" Whitefield broke in.

"Oh, a fair show, Enoch!" Grimes offered, lifting his hand in a mock oath. "Like, mebby, if Hawke can beat Sullivan to the crow's nest, why, Jones will 'ave no more trouble."

"And if I lose?" Hawke asked.

"I'd say six months' wages to my friend here would be fair."

"What?" Whitefield was enraged. "Why, Sullivan's a first-rate foretopman, and—"

"I'll take the bet." Hawke spoke almost with indifference, and moved toward the shrouds, the network of rope that formed a weblike ladder to the tops of the masts.

A shout went up from the men who loved any sort of contest, and Whitefield asked nervously, "Hawke, have you ever climbed a mizzenmast?"

"Why, I have no idea, Enoch." A trace of amusement was on the lean face of the younger man, and he added, "I suppose we'll find out in a few minutes."

Enoch could do nothing, but stood there helplessly as the two men took station on opposite sides of the ship, Hawke on the starboard and Sullivan to port. "You give the signal, Whitefield," Grimes grinned. "Just so all is fair and square. And we'll all be the judge of who's the winner!"

Enoch was sick at heart, for he knew that Sullivan, for all his bulk, was agile as a monkey. He was by far the best and fastest in climbing up the shrouds; and there was no hope, he felt, for Hawke. Just the way the two men stood revealed the difference, for Sullivan was crouched, his hands clutching the shrouds, while Hawke had one hand lightly, as if for balance, on one of the horizontal strands, and was looking bored with the whole affair.

"Go!" Whitefield shouted, and a cry went up from the deck, mostly cheers for Sullivan. The big man moved with practiced speed, not one wasted motion as he sped upward. *No man can beat him—he's too good!* Enoch thought. But he kept his eyes fixed on the smaller man—and what he saw made him shout with glee!

Hawke did not move as quickly at first as Sullivan. He seemed to fumble slightly as he climbed hand over hand, and his feet had to search for the horizontals. But then he seemed to take wing, and he flew up the web of ropes with a rapidity that not a one of them had ever seen. The cheering stopped abruptly, and Grimes alone raised his voice to yell, "Sullivan! Don't let the blackguard do you in!"

Sullivan paused long enough to look across at his counterpart and nearly fell off the shrouds as he saw the flying figure of Hawke come even with him, then leave him behind even as he watched. He cursed and drove himself upward with all his might, but a cry from the deck caught him; and ten feet from the top he looked up to see Hawke standing there looking down at him with a slight smile.

"Looks like you're getting old, Sullivan," he remarked, then grabbed a loose rope and slid down, almost falling to the deck before catching himself in time to step lightly onto the oak planks.

Whitefield pounded him on the back, exclaiming, "You did it! By the grace of the good Lord, you did it!" Looking up he yelled to the stunned foretopman, who was staring in rage at Hawke, "Mind you, keep your end, Sullivan. I can't abide a gambler—but a welcher is something the ship won't stand!"

Jones moved over to Whitefield and Hawke as the crowd broke up. Tears filled his eyes. "I—I can't say how . . ."

He paused, and Hawke put a brown hand on his shoulder, reassuring him. "Why, it was nothing, Will."

Jones looked at him, but could only say to Enoch as the other walked away, "He's a Christian man—ain't he, Enoch?"

"Will," Whitefield agreed slowly, "it's looking more like that all the time."

A fighting ship is a small cosmos, a microcosm of the world. And as in the world, news can travel with incredible speed. By nightfall every man on the ship knew the story. The crew was bored, for life at sea is monotonous, and any juicy tidbit was chewed over and over until every morsel was extracted.

The officers had heard a little, but at the captain's table that night, they got the full story from Burns, who'd gotten it out of Whitefield. When Burns finished, they all looked at Rommey expectantly, but he said only, "We'll need all the foretopmen we can muster—especially in light of our new orders."

A hum of excitement went around the room. That morning they had sighted a sail which proved to be HMS *Centaur*, a sixteen-gun sloop fresh out of England. Rommey had gone on board and returned later with a waterproof pouch which everyone had identified as a container from Flag Command in London.

Now there was satisfaction in the craggy face of the captain, and he nodded with a smile. "We have been given some time to get the crew toughened up and the ship smoothed out. Now we can do the job *Neptune* was built for."

"Action, sir?" Langley asked.

"Yes, Langley. Action!" He rose and pointed to a map tacked to the bulkhead. "We now know that the rebels are sending their ships along these lanes—both privateers and merchant ships."

"But the winds aren't favorable in those latitudes, Captain!" Burns protested. Then the truth dawned and he smiled. "Weel, of course! That's the reason they're there!"

"Exactly! Now that we know where the scoundrels are, we'll bag them," Rommey said fiercely. Then he added, "We'll head for home at once. On our return voyage and while we're provisioning the ship, Captain Baxter, I want you to train the seamen in small arms."

"Small arms, Captain?" Baxter gave a languid look around the room and asked, "May I ask for what purpose, sir?"

"I think it not unlikely that we'll have to board an enemy ship, and it's not impossible that we might make a raid on a port city. Your marines are well trained—but we may need to fill out our numbers with men who can handle a musket and a blade."

"If you wish, sir—but they're a scrub lot."

"Do the best you can, Captain."

During this exchange Burns had been watching Langley, and saw what he expected—disappointment. The tall lieutenant had fallen hopelessly in love with Blanche Rommey, and the thought of not seeing her turned him to putty! Burns shook his head in despair, for he had watched the one-sided courtship closely. The captain had installed his wife and daughter in a fine mansion twenty miles in the interior of Jamaica. After each short venture to sea in the *Neptune*, Rommey had gone there, usually accompanied by Langley and Burns.

Mrs. Rommey was satisfied—as she would have been in any place. She did her embroidery, went for rides through the countryside, and made infrequent trips to the port city. She seemed not to grieve when her husband left, not happy when he returned. She was, Burns had thought, the closest thing to a vegetable he'd ever seen.

But Blanche Rommey was a different story. She was almost out of her mind with boredom. Her quick spirit and impulsive nature were the worst possible combination to fit her for living in a secluded rural paradise, and she had been so hungry for company and excitement that she had practically forced Burns to take her to a party at a plantation over fifteen miles away.

He thought of it as he sat at the table looking at Clarence Langley, and felt very sorry for the man. Blanche had flirted with every man she saw at the party, even with Burns himself on the way home. When the Scot had cut that short by mentioning Langley, she had laughed and said lightly, "Clarence? He's a dear—but such a *stick*!"

Burns had tried to warn his friend, but given up in despair, for the tall lieutenant was deaf to his words. The meeting broke up, and Langley went to set the new course. "Lieutenant Burns, a word," Captain Rommey requested, catching him as the other left.

"I have a rather *unusual* order; that's the best word I can apply to it," he hesitated.

"Yes, sir?"

"We will be taking prizes, almost certainly, when we get into the lanes."

"I've nae doot we will." All the crew would share in the prize money, and Burns was as thrifty as his ancestors in far-off Scotland.

"There is a problem," Rommey frowned. "The prizemaster I put on board to take the captured ship to port must be able to navigate."

Burns flushed and shook his head. "Sir, I'm embarrassed to say I canna!"

"No time for that now, Burns. It's a weakness, but there are worse things in a King's officer. I have a plan I believe will work— but it's so unusual, I'm not going to order you to do it. You'll have to volunteer."

Burns was mystified, for this captain was not the sort to avoid giving orders. "I'll do anything to help, sir."

"I thought you would. Now, I trust that soon we'll be getting some new midshipmen who *can* navigate, but until we do, you'll have to learn. When we make port, I'm leaving Langley in charge of provisioning the ship. It will take about a week. I want you to learn to navigate during that time. You'll have no other duties— and I have a teacher in mind."

"Yes, sir?"

"This man Hawke, he's an excellent navigator." Rommey shrugged and gave a slight grimace, but went on. "I know he's only a seaman, and you're an officer. But he's all we've got. Will you let him teach you?"

"Why, I'll nae make any promises, but I'll do my best, Captain Rommey."

Rommey smiled and put his large hand on Burns's thin shoulder. "I knew you'd take it like that," he beamed. "Some officers have too confounded much pride, but I'd take instruction from Lucifer if it would make a better seaman of me!"

The next morning every hand knew that he would have shore leave, and the officers were careful to mention the rich possibility of prize money. "Just one fat merchant ship, men," they promised, "and you can retire for life."

After that Captain Baxter had no problem getting the men to

drill. Sergeant Potter drilled the hands in the use of the musket, and reported to Baxter, "Captain, they'd do more damage if they throwed rocks at the enemy! Never seen such rotten shots."

"Well, we thought it would be that way, didn't we, Sergeant?" Baxter smiled. "In the morning I'll find out if there's a good blade in the lot of them. Which I most sincerely doubt."

The exercise the next day was no better than Baxter had anticipated. Most of the ship's crew had never had a sword in their hands, and only three showed any skill. Most of them hacked away as if they were threshing wheat, but Baxter said to Potter after about half of the crew had been tested, "Sir, I reckon we may have six men who are fair. Sullivan is the best, in my judgment."

"Quite so, Sergeant. He's had some training. I'll try a bout with him."

Captain Baxter loved the sword. It was the only thing that ever caused him to drop his languid air and come alive. He had been a student of the foil, the saber, the cutlass, and every other form of blade for years, and his reputation was formidable among those who knew the art.

It had been boring to watch the heavy-handed crew hacking away, but when he squared away with Sullivan and saw that the big man was no amateur, he allowed a smile of excitement to crease his thin lips. "Have at me, Sullivan!" he cried out.

"Sir! These blades ain't got no buttons!"

It was the custom to blunt the tips of the foils for use in practice, but Baxter waved his free hand, saying, "Oh, I think it'll be safe enough."

Sullivan grinned and began advancing, his left foot extended in a long stretch behind him, his right knee bent at a sharp angle, his left hand well back. He came in quickly, so quickly and so skillfully that Baxter was taken aback, in fact, and was hard put to keep himself from getting embarrassed. But he was very good, and soon he controlled the bout. He did not have to exert all his skill, and he did not want to discourage the best prospect among the crew, so finally he called a halt. "Very good, Sullivan! Very good, indeed! If we had twenty like you, I'd not hesitate to tackle a ship of the line."

The drill continued until the last day, and Baxter had Potter pair the men off for practice. "Don't let them cut each other to bits, Sergeant," he warned. "And you might use Sullivan to help with the more clumsy fellows."

The last drill was at sunset, and most of the crew gathered either to participate or to watch. Baxter and Potter had grown tired of the routine, but were forced to stay and watch. They were paying little attention, so when Sullivan called Hawke out of the crowd they paid no heed.

"You there, Hawke," Sullivan called out. "I ain't seen you in the drill. Give him that blade, Atkins, and let's see what he's got."

Immediately the entire crew sensed that a drama was about to unfold. The officers were not paying attention and everyone knew that Sullivan was smarting under his defeat at the hands of Hawke. Several men had received minor wounds at the sword drill, and it would be easy for Sullivan to stab Hawke—and then protest that it was an accident. Who would there be to say differently? Surely not the officers.

Sullivan had waited for the right time, but had despaired. Always either Burns or Langley was in charge of the deck, or else Whitefield was present. But now Burns was far aft drilling some boat crews, and neither Whitefield nor the first lieutenant were in sight, so he had grabbed at the chance.

Hawke came forward slowly, taking the foil from Atkins, and he saw the cruel gleam in Sullivan's eye; this was not to be a drill! He slowly lifted the blade as Sullivan came forward with a grunt of pleasure, and the blades rang with a silver sound on the salt air.

Sullivan came in dancing, his blade flashing like liquid lightning, and there was no pretense of a "drill." He lunged with all his force, directing his blade straight at the heart of his opponent—but he did not succeed.

Hawke had known the moment the hilt of the sword nestled in his hand earlier that day that this was not a new thing. Now, after some fresh practice he felt like a *natural* as he picked the tip of Sullivan's blade out of the air with the tip of his own foil, directing it to one side with an ease he knew was born of a thousand hours of practice.

I've done this before, he thought as Sullivan recovered, his face red with murderous desire. *I've stood and faced men and I've felt my blood run down—and I've seen them fall to the ground pierced to the heart.*

And he could have killed Sullivan, he knew. For the man, for all his skill, seemed slow and clumsy. Hawke moved little, standing in one spot for the most part, parrying the thrusts of the other with ease, refusing to drive his own blade home.

Captain Baxter heard the rapid clashing blades and saw in one experienced glance that Sullivan was in the hands of a master. *Why, that fellow could have killed him half a dozen times!* he thought. Then he hurried forward, calling out, "Good enough for now!"

Sullivan was gasping for breath and his eyes were filled with astonishment and rage. "Sir, just let me have—!"

"Oh, you've done too much, Sullivan." Baxter reached out and took the blade from the Irishman, and moved to stand before the man with the scar. "I see you've done a little along this line before, Seaman Hawke."

"I couldn't say, Captain."

The even tenor of Hawke's voice and the bland look in his eyes stirred the captain's temper. He was not at all certain that the fellow was really all he claimed, and in any case he was anxious for a good bout.

"Well, let's see how good you are," he said, and raising his blade he began to advance toward Hawke. They circled one another, for Baxter had seen enough of the man to be cautious. He tried a feint, and to his chagrin, it was parried; for one instant he saw the tip of Hawke's blade poised and knew that he was helpless to prevent the thrust. But the thrust did not come, and a smile on Hawke's face caused Baxter's face to redden. *This one is no beginner,* he thought, and tightened his guard, taking no chances.

The crew saw two men, both light as a breeze on their feet, both quick as a striking snake with their hands. They circled slowly, but their blades rang and clashed so rapidly that it was impossible to follow the motion. Captain Rommey had come up out of his cabin and stood on the forecastle watching the contest with an inscrutable expression on his craggy face.

On and on it went, and suddenly Baxter realized that his opponent was *playing* with him! The dark face of the man was not triumphant—if anything, he looked slightly *bored!*

Desperately the marine tried to break Hawke's composure, driving at him like a madman, but always the flashing tip of the sword caught his own and parried it with ease.

Finally, Baxter stepped back, lowered his foil and stared at the man in front of him. It was almost dark, and the deep-set eyes of Hawke were hidden by the shadows of his brow and high cheekbones. He was not smiling now, and for one instant a sadness pulled his lips into a hard line—and at that moment Captain Baxter knew that Hawke was indeed a man without a past.

"You are a fine swordsman, Seaman Hawke," Baxter told the

man quietly. "I never saw one finer."

The compliment slid off the other man, and he said only, "Yes, sir. May I go now?"

"Certainly." Baxter watched him go to stand alone peering out over the rail into the gathering darkness, then said, "Drill is over, Sergeant. Dismiss the men." Looking up, the captain saw Rommey staring down from the forecastle, and he went to stand beside him. "Well, sir, what did you make of that?"

Rommey shook his head. "Another surprise from the man from nowhere, eh, Baxter?" He shook his head slowly. "He's educated, knows the world, handles a sword like a demon out of the pit—I don't know *what* the fellow is! A broken-down gentleman, perhaps?"

"I didn't get the 'broken down' part," Baxter replied with a rueful expression. "What are you going to do with him?"

Rommey looked at Hawke, who was still standing alone at the rail. "Do with him, Baxter? Why, I'll *use* him—just as I use you and myself and every other soul on this vessel. He may not have a past," he added grimly, "but I'll see to it he has a future!"

CHAPTER ELEVEN

BEAT TO QUARTERS!

★ ★ ★ ★

"I canna learn this blasted book!" Lieutenant Burns was a mild man, but his struggles with math had almost destroyed his patience. He stood up abruptly and threw the thick book he had been poring over against the wall. "Blast!" he cried in despair, pulling his sandy hair as if to remove it from his head. "I can do anything on the *Neptune* as weel as any man—but this—this accursed navigation—"

Hawke rose from his chair and walked over to pick up the book. Bringing it back to the small desk where the two of them had been seated, he said evenly, "Let's just go over it one more time, sir." He began to go over the problem, pointing from time to time at a large map stretched out on a table, and was pleased to see the officer stop glaring at him and come back to resume his seat.

Hawke could sympathize with Burns, for he realized that there was some part of the canny Scot's brain that was almost impervious to anything mathematical. For nearly a week the two had met to study at Captain Rommey's house, and the seaman had patiently gone over the fundamentals of the science of navigation, wondering at how difficult it was for Burns. Time after time the lieutenant had given up, but Hawke had sat there calmly, then continued his instruction as if nothing had happened.

Burns had become so distracted with his slow progress that he had allowed his temper to boil over, at time fastening fury on Hawke, but the seaman had never shown the least reaction. And now a light of respect came to the eyes of the Scot, and he laughed aloud. "Hawke—I dinna see how ye've put up with me! I know how tedious it is to drill a banana-fingered deckhand—but it's worse to work with a slow-witted lieutenant." He nodded, and added sincerely, "I thank ye for your patience, Seaman Hawke."

"Why, you're not slow-witted, sir." Hawke gave the other a rare smile. He had learned to respect the tenacity of the man who sat there; for many, he knew, would have given up. "It's just not your strong point. You're a fine sailor."

Burns's face flushed at the compliment, and he wondered at it, for he had never cared particularly what the crew thought of him. But his feeling for Hawke was different, and he was kept from forming a more personal tie only by the vast gulf that had to exist between officer and common seaman.

"Weel, that's guid of ye to say so, Hawke." He looked up as a clock chimed somewhere in the distance, and closed the book, saying, "It's time for dinner."

"Yes, sir. Tomorrow at the same time?"

"I don't rightly know. We may sail tomorrow—Langley tells me the *Neptune*'s fully provisioned." He walked to the wall, plucked up his coat, and slipping it on, remarked thoughtfully, "This partying every night is a bit much for a simple lad like myself. I'll be glad to put to sea."

He referred to the nightly festivities that went on at the house, for Blanche Rommey had made it a point to have a formal dinner each night, with dancing and cards after the meal. Since Burns neither danced nor played cards, he had gone to fill out the number, but had returned to his room as soon as possible.

Burns left, saying, "Better be ready, Hawke, in case we pull out early."

"Yes, sir." He picked up the books and shoved them into a small leather case; next, he took down the map and folded it carefully, placing it with the books. Closing the case, he put it on a mahogany table beside the bed and left the room.

Passing down the wide hall, he heard the sound of music— the small orchestra of native musicians. He smiled slightly, then turned left and passed out of the house into the warm night air. The mosquitoes made a whining harmony, and he brushed them away automatically with each step. He followed a stone path beside the house, down a line of *flagrante* plants rich with perfumed blossoms to a long, low stone building in a grove of mango trees.

Most of the building was taken up with a blacksmith shop, and he found Whitefield at the forge. He had been working for most of the week making spare parts for the ship, and when not instructing Burns, Hawke had watched and even helped a little.

"What's that you're making, Enoch?"

"Vent fittings."

Hawke came over to look more closely at a row of tapered cast-iron plugs laid out neatly beside the forge. Picking one up, he turned it over. "These go in the vent hole?"

"Right." Enoch gave him an approving glance and nodded, "You've picked up a heap 'bout gunnery in a short time, Hawke."

Hawke shrugged and asked, "How many of these do you need?"

"Well—a gun ain't worth spit without one, is it, now? So I thinks we better have fifty at least."

"Show me how."

"Right, lad."

Enoch had found Hawke to be a quick learner, and in less than an hour he had gone through the process. "If you think you can carry on, I'd like to get some sleep."

"Seems simple enough—and I'm not sleepy. Lieutenant says we may sail tomorrow."

"Figured we might. Don't worry if you don't do all them vent fittings, Hawke. We probably got enough."

After he left, Hawke worked steadily at the forge. It was not a demanding task, but he was getting little exercise and as a result could not sleep well. As he methodically filed the fittings, time slipped away. It was quiet in the forge, the silence broken only by the sounds of horses stomping the ground outside and the faint sound of music drifting across on the night air from the big house.

He realized after some time that his fingers were aching, and also that he was thirsty. There was an *olla* of water hanging on the wall, but he thought of the cold spring that fed the house, and left the smithy to get a drink.

The water was cold, and he sipped it slowly, thinking of what Whitefield had told him about water on ship. *In a few weeks, the water will be getting thick. Bless me! I've seen it so thick and green with stuff it wouldn't hardly pour!* The thought ran through his mind, and he lowered his head to drink, savoring the coldness and flavor of it.

He made his way back to the shop, and was startled when a

voice caught at him as he reached the door.

"Well, Hawke . . . ?"

He turned quickly, peering into the darkness, and relaxed when Blanche Rommey moved toward him. She was wearing a white dress, cut low in the neck, which set off her dark hair. "Hello, Miss Rommey," he said.

She stepped up beside him, saying, "I'm tired of that hot stuffy room." There was a husky quality in her voice, and she laughed as she took his arm, saying, "Let's walk a little."

He knew instinctively that it was not the right thing to do, but she gave him little choice. He found himself walking along the paved walk, listening as she spoke of trivial things. The sweet odor of frangipani was strong, but some scent that she was wearing mixed with it, stirring his senses.

They came to a low wall with a gate, and he stopped. "I don't think we should go outside the compound, Miss Rommey."

"What are you afraid of, Hawke?" she smiled. "Me?"

"No—snakes," he said evenly. "There's one kind here they call a Five-stepper."

"A Five-stepper?"

"Yes, because if one of them bites you, you have five steps to get help before the venom kills you."

She took a quick look at the ground, stepping closer to him involuntarily. "I don't like snakes." She took his arm, pressing against him as they walked back toward the shop. The sky was velvet black with icy points of stars, and she looked up and wondered aloud, "Look how bright that star is! I wonder what name it has?"

He looked up casually and said without thinking, "That's Sirius—the Dog Star."

She paused, stared at him, then shook her head. There was a smile on her rich, full lips. "I wonder how you know that, Hawke?"

"Common star—Sirius."

"Perhaps." She suddenly drew him to a halt, and all of the thoughts she had had of him the past days flashed across her mind. She had enjoyed the nightly parties, but the men had been insipid: a seventeen-year-old son of a planter on the neighboring property (with bad teeth and little charm); two cousins in the military, one aggressive, the other timid (both equally boorish); several cousins of the owner of the plantation (who thought of little but planting sugar cane); and one aging diplomat who fancied himself a ladies' man. Lieutenant Langley had come twice, and had done everything but throw himself at her feet. She had allowed him to follow her, but his fumbling attempts to pay compliments were so awkward that it was tedious to her.

She had thought often of Hawke, and now as he stood there, she saw he was better looking than she remembered. He had filled out, and there was a regularity in his features that was entirely masculine, but the long lashes and contoured features would have been effeminate in a man with less vigor. He was saved from this, Blanche saw, by the strength of his neck and the direct look in his large eyes, and by the scar on his cheek.

Suddenly she reached up and touched the scar on the side of his face. "I wonder where you got that?"

The touch of her hand on his cheek ran along his nerves, and he was intensely aware of her womanly figure revealed in the dress. "Probably my just deserts," he said.

"Do you remember any more?"

"Nothing." The pressure of her hand remained, but he did not know how to react, so he stood motionless.

The silence ran on. Finally Blanche spoke in an enticing voice. "You are a very attractive man, Hawke." Turning to him she whispered, "Have you thought about the time you kissed me?"

"Yes."

"So have I!" And then she lifted her face and came into his arms. There was a heavy silence over the earth, broken by the cry of a night bird, and as he lowered his head and met her full lips, softer than down, he did not *think* at all. Her body came against him, and there was only that moment, only a time of coming together, and he pulled her roughly into his arms with a hunger that suddenly came from a depth that he did not know.

She did not draw back, but gave him her kiss freely. She had been kissed many times, but always before, she had been in command of the moment; now she found that she was helpless in his arms, like a swimmer caught by a rip tide, and the thought flashed through her: *He can do anything with me!*

This shocked her, for she was a proud woman, and the sense that he was the stronger made her draw back abruptly.

He released her at once, saying shortly, "You'd better go back to the party, Miss Rommey."

She was breathing raggedly, and bit her lower lip. "Yes . . . I suppose so." Pausing for a moment, she continued. "You'll be leaving tomorrow. My father told us so at dinner." She waited for him to speak, and when he did not, she asked coyly, "Will you think of me?"

Anger suddenly rose up in Hawke's chest, and he took her by the arms and held her pinioned. His hands were frighteningly strong, but his eyes and voice had a paralyzing effect on her. "You like to play with men. I have no family, no wife, no country—and no God, as far as I can tell." His voice grew rough, and he released her so quickly that she staggered. "Don't play with me, Blanche!"

He turned to go, but she caught his arm, pulling him around. The moonlight changed the tears in her eyes to silver as she whispered brokenly, "I—don't want to do that, Hawke! Forgive me!"

Knowing instinctively that her pride had been hurt as perhaps never before, his anger receded. He shook his head, and a smile came to his lips touched by the depth of sadness in his eyes.

"It was my fault. But it won't happen again. I'm a common sailor, Blanche, and for you to think of me any differently would be wrong. So—I thank you for taking care of me—but this can't happen again."

He turned and walked away, and she slowly moved along the line of flowers toward the house. The scene had left her trembling and empty, but there was a stubborn and rebellious streak that ran deep in Blanche Rommey, and she thought, *No, he's not a common seaman. I don't know what he is—but he's not a common man—in any way!*

★　★　★　★

The sultry heat of summer gave way to the cool breezes of winter, bringing refreshment to the crew of the *Neptune*—at least to those not stricken by the virulent attack of fever that had fallen on the ship.

It was mid-January, and for six months Captain Rommey had been highly satisfied with the crew and the ship. They had taken three heavily laden American merchant ships, and even had a slight taste of combat with a fast frigate that had refused to be fully engaged. "Fine training exercise for the men!" Rommey had smiled grimly. "Not enough to bloody them, but a taste of powder and the sound of the guns. Now—we're ready for *real* action!"

But then on the second of February, Jenson, one of the lower deckhands, had fallen to a bone-cracking fever, and in five days, a quarter of the crew was down. Dr. Mann's treatment was the same as for every other illness—purging and bleeding. His brutal methods almost destroyed those he treated, and many of the crew dragged around sick to keep out of his hands.

Langley nervously approached Captain Rommey on the poop deck, saying, "Captain, wouldn't it be wise to put about? I mean, we don't have enough men to fight an engagement."

Rommey's frosty eyes considered the young lieutenant briefly; then he shook his head. "We're able to handle any rebels that come our way."

There was no room for argument, so Langley moved aft and said moodily to Burns, who was staring off in the hazy distance, "Captain won't hear of going back to port—so I pray God we don't run into an enemy frigate!"

"That's as God wills, Clarence." The dour Calvinism of the reply angered Langley, and he turned and left the deck. Two hours later when the lookout cried, "Deck! Sail off port bow!" Langley had a premonition, and he yelled, "What ship?"

"Sloop, sir! Twenty-four guns!"

Ordinarily the *Neptune* would be able to take care of such an adversary with ease, but with so many men ill, there would be little difference in the firepower of the two ships, and the sloop had the advantage of being faster and far more maneuverable.

"Beat to quarter!" Captain Rommey called the order loudly, and two small marine drummers ran to the larboard gangway, pulling on their black shakos and fumbling with their sticks. They beat a tattoo, their faces tight with concentration, and men poured up from below. The marines hurried aft and aloft to the tops, their uniforms shining like blood in the sunlight, with Captain Baxter in the lead.

Below deck Burns had the guns run out, and then walked along the larboard guns, his heart filled with doubt as he saw the pickup crews. At one gun a man stared without comprehension as a captain put a rope into his hand. Burns tried to instill some courage in the crew, calling out, "Men, we are going to engage that ship. Do nae hurry—just take your time and obey orders, and all will be well."

Hawke crouched beside his gun, sweating freely in spite of the breeze blowing through the open port. He saw the sloop, rebel flag flying, making a turn and his heart pumped against his ribs like the beating of a drum. It was like one of his nightmares with every detail clear and stark, but he was not afraid.

The men he had been given were pallid with fear, so he said easily, "Well, lads, we'll give the rebels a lesson, eh? Come, Harry, see to the slow match—quickly now!" He gave them something to do, keeping their minds off the ship that drew ever closer; and his eyes met those of Whitefield, who gave him a nod and a wink.

Topside Rommey was waiting until the last moment to set his sail, for if he timed it right, the smaller ship would come under his guns for one brief moment sooner than the sloop could bring her own guns to bear. "It has to be just right, Langley," he insisted, then watched the closing ship carefully. Finally he shouted, "Stand by to go about!"

The mizzen yard was squeaking and the helmsman, Spence, cried out, "Ready, sir!"

"Put the helm down!"

The order came from Rommey. Up forward the headsail sheets had already been released, and as the wheel went over and the great hull began to swing very slowly into the wind, Langley urged the men at the braces to even greater efforts as they strained back, their eyes on the yards above them.

Sails boomed and swelled, and as the ship continued to swing, Rommey commanded, "Off tacks and sheets!"

This was the moment, they all knew, and there was a tangle of flapping sails and jerking shrouds—and then they saw it! "Captain! There's not enough men to handle the sail!" Langley called out in horror. The ship fell back, helpless in the water as the fore-topmen struggled like madmen to set the sail.

"She'll blow us out of the water!" Langley moaned.

"Order the marines to open fire!" the captain ordered, disgusted with Langley's fright. "Get more men on those sails!"

Below deck, Burns felt the ship fall back and knew what to expect. He stood near Whitefield and their eyes met. "For what we are about to receive," Burns said so quietly that only the gunner could hear him, "may we be duly grateful!"

Looking out the port, Hawke realized that in the next few moments he might be dead. He took a deep breath, studied the sloop, then said, "Lads, we'll have to let them have first shot—but our turn will come!"

Suddenly the hull shuddered beneath his feet and splintering woodwork flew in every direction. The air quivered and shook with the crash of guns and the nerve-jarring scream of cannon balls as they whipped through the smoke like beings from hell.

The scream of passing shot mingled with closer, more unearthly sounds as flying splinters ripped into the packed gunners and bathed the smooth deck with scarlet. In the midst of this, men ran blindly, hopelessly trying to escape. Midshipman Symmes, who was in charge of gun number seven, fell to the floor clawing at it as if he could burrow into it and hide. Burns hurried to him immediately and kicked him hard, screaming, "Get up, you coward!" and lashed at him with a cane until he resumed his position with wild, mad eyes.

Hawke saw splashes of blood and gristle on the bulkhead, and as he turned he realized that one of the guns had been upended and its crew annihilated. One man lay legless, a handspike still gripped and ready.

Panic ran through the gun deck, and only the will of Lieutenant Burns and a few old hands like Whitefield kept the men at their stations.

Another broadside like that, Burns thought, *and we're done!* He waited, knowing that only if the ship regained the wind could they avoid the hail of metal that would sweep them to bloody death. Slowly he felt the ship tilt and he shouted, "She's comin' about; get ready to fire!"

But just at that moment, a ball came screaming across the water and flew right through a gunport. The shot struck a deck support, which broke its powerful flight—but a splinter went whirring through the air, striking Lieutenant Burns in the back.

He fell to the floor with a cry—panic, until now held in check, spilling over. Helplessly, he writhed on the deck, pain driving him half mad. Still he struggled to regain his feet, for he saw the crews leaving their guns, running mindlessly toward the hatch.

If we don't return their fire, they'll blow us out of the water! he thought—and he called on his God to help.

Hawke knew nothing about tactics—but even in the midst of the screaming shot and the terror-stricken men, he saw clearly through the port that the sloop was coming back to finish them off. He felt also the ship lift beneath his feet, and quick as flash, he knew that if the *Neptune* could get off a broadside, they would not be lost.

But how? He leaped to his feet, and was almost knocked down by the blind, stampeding crew. Then he saw Enoch and three other gun captains fighting to keep the men away from the hatch—but it was a losing battle, he realized instantly. The crew was clawing blindly, deaf to any orders; only a miracle would turn them.

Suddenly Hawke caught sight of Burns writhing on the floor, bathed in his own blood, but struggling to get to his feet. Without a logical process of thought, Hawke sprang to his side, and Burns looked up with a plea in his eyes. With a sudden gesture, Hawke ripped the man's sword from his side, and with a piercing cry threw himself into the fray.

He was a madman among madmen—but there was more fury in his madness than they could face. Like a screaming banshee, he ran along the line of men who were forcing Whitefield and the other gunners to the wall, and he slashed them with a blade that was a mere flash of silver in the smoke-filled air. "Back to those guns!" he screamed. There was no man able to face that blade—so they fell back, one, then another; and finally, as Whitefield and the others grabbed their weapons, the tide turned.

From where he lay, Burns watched in awe, and as the men were driven back to the guns, he looked up and breathed a faint prayer, "Thank ye, God!"

Back and forth down the line, Hawke shouted, pushing men into position, cursing and slashing with his sword. "Load!" he screamed. "Look, the captain's got us moving! All we have to do is let her have a belly full, lads! Fire! Fire! Bring your guns to bear!"

Topside, Captain Rommey was staring at the sloop as she took the full brunt of the heavy guns. He had been expecting nothing but death and disaster. After the terrible pounding the ship had taken, he had scarcely dared hope that his men could return the fire—but now he saw the sloop riddled by the heavy shot, and the crew gave a shout as she suddenly turned and fled.

"Not a victory, perhaps," he said quietly to himself. "But we'll fight another day."

"I'm going below," he announced to Langley. "Handle the ship."

He hurried to the gun deck, swept the scene quickly, then went to where the hands were pulling Lieutenant Burns to a sitting position.

"How bad is it, Burns?"

"Painful, sir—but it'll nae be the death o' me."

"You did well, sir!" the captain expressed with thankfulness, kneeling beside the wounded man. "You saved the ship."

"No, sir," Burns objected through white lips. "I was doon on the deck. It was Seaman Hawke who rallied the men. We'd ha' been gone if he hadna taken over when I went doon."

"I see." Slowly Captain Rommey rose, his eyes fixed on Hawke, who was trying to stop the flow of blood from a wounded man. "He did that, did he?"

"Aye, sir, he did." Burns was gritting his teeth against the pain, but he nodded across the gun deck, adding, "Midshipman Symmes is dead, sir."

"Let's get you to the surgeon, Burns," Rommey said. "And I'll see to it that he does a good job—or I'll keelhaul the butcher!" He did exactly that, standing right behind Mann, who was so nervous he did the best job of his life, extracting the splinter from Burns's back.

Then Rommey left, and when the battle damage was being repaired, he sent for Hawke. He was seated at his desk staring out the stern windows when the man came in.

"Yes, sir?"

Rommey stood up and came to stand before Hawke, saying, "Burns told me how you rose higher than your duty during the action. I commend you."

"Why—"

"And I have a daring scheme to propose to you. I intend to make you midshipman, effective at once. You are old for that rank, but I'll give you a brevet commission as an ensign, or even as a junior lieutenant, depending on how rapidly you advance. I *must* have a navigator, and now that Lieutenant Burns is out of action for an indeterminate period, I need a man who can stand watch." He paused and studied Hawke's face. "Well, what do you think?"

Hawke's face did not change, though a light leaped into his eyes. He considered the face of the captain, then slowly smiled. "Sir, I think you'll be letting yourself in for a great deal of trouble. I'm not an officer."

"How do you know?"

"Why . . . !"

"You're a man who isn't anything—which means really, you can *be* anything." The stern features of Rommey softened, and he said warmly, "I'm aware that this is an unusual action—but we are in an unusual situation, Hawke. I *must* have help to sail this ship, and there's precious little help coming from the Admiralty! So—I'll use what I can lay my hands on, and let the Lords of the Admiralty whistle up a dead tree! Now, will you be my officer?"

Hawke stared at the tall captain, doubt in his even features.

Finally he nodded. "I'll do my best, Captain."

"Fine! Fine!" Rommey beamed. "It'll be a shock to the crew—but you'll just have to make them like it! Now, we have to get you a uniform, Midshipman Hawke—and then we have to let my officers know they have help."

The new midshipman smiled, and reminded his superior, "I'm an American, Captain. Have you thought of that? What if my memory comes back? You'll have a rebel for an officer."

"Blast it, no!" Captain Rommey growled. "You're too good a chap to be one of those wild-eyed fanatics! I'll wager when you recall who you are, you'll be delighted to find yourself a good, safe servant of King George!"

"Well, sir, I'm your man for now. God knows what I'll be in the future."

"We all must say that, sir," Rommey stated soberly, then turned to his work as the newest ensign in the Royal Navy left the cabin.

CHAPTER TWELVE

THE LIEUTENANT

★ ★ ★ ★

Accustomed as he was to being in command, it was a rare thing for Captain William Rommey to feel intimidated—but as he passed under the massive arch of the Admiralty House and asked a rigid guard in full dress for directions to Admiral Hood's office, he had to clear his throat to make the request.

"Down the hall, sir," the guard replied sternly. "The big double doors to your left."

Rommey almost thanked the man, but bit off the words. Wheeling quickly, he made his way down the marbled floors and found another secretary, a lieutenant with a pinched face and skin that had not seen the open sea for some time. "Can I help you, Captain?" he asked languidly.

"Captain William Rommey to see Admiral Hood!"

"Oh, yes, Captain. The admiral is expecting you."

The quick change in the fop's manner made Rommey feel better. He followed him inside and found the grizzled Hood turning from his huge window, and the admiral's warm handshake made him feel even more relieved.

"Well, now, Rommey, it's been a long time!" He motioned at a chair, and the two seated themselves in the glare of the May sunlight that flooded through the high-arched windows. "Let's see—I believe it was on the old *Dominant*, was it not—back in '64?"

"Yes, sir." Rommey gave the older man an admiring glance. Hood might be aging, but there was still that quick intelligence in his smallish brown eyes. "I was a midshipman under you in that fight with the *Fleur de Rose*."

"Ah, by gad—that *was* a hot one!" Hood laughed with delight and slapped his thigh. "You made a name for yourself that day, Rommey! Gad, sir, you did!"

The captain shifted uneasily, but as the admiral went on reminiscing about the old days, he felt a twinge of relief. He hated to ask favors, but that was exactly what he had come for.

His opportunity came quickly, for Hood soon asked, "Well, Captain, what is it? I know you've been in for refitting. Let's see, didn't I sign an order for you to put back to sea duty this week? I know you must want something—everybody does who comes through that door."

"Well—yes, sir."

Hood laughed again, and waved a hand in the air. "Gad, sir! You're a breath of fresh air! Most fellows come in here wanting something and they're too sly to come out with it! I like a man like you, Rommey! Now, what is it?"

Rommey cleared his throat and then pulled a paper from his pocket and handed it to the admiral. "This is what I want in writing, Admiral Hood, but I can put it very plainly in just a few words if you'll permit me."

"What is it? A bigger ship?"

"No, sir, I'm happy with my command."

"I've read your reports. Good work you've done with the *Neptune* in the Indies. How long have you been there?"

"Almost two years, sir. I set up my family in a house in Jamaica but have brought my wife and daughter back to England for a visit."

"Yes, I'd heard you had been forced to get your daughter out of the hands of some Frenchman. The Lords of Admiralty have been most pleased with your work—especially with the prizes you've taken. Every American ship you take puts that much of a crimp in this rebellion!"

"How does the matter look to you, Admiral?"

"Why, very well. That bumpkin Washington lost at Brandywine and Germantown—and I heard that their best general, Benedict Arnold, came to his senses and joined our side." The admiral took a pinch of snuff from a silver case on his desk, sniffed it, then sneezed. "As long as we control the sea—there's no way those clods can win, Rommey. And since they have no navy, they have no hope of winning at sea."

"But everyone knows the French are getting a fleet ready to send to that area."

"Well, let them! I hope they do, sir! Then we can wipe out the Frogs and the blasted rebels at one blow!"

"I must say, though, that some of the rebels have done very well—fitting out ships with guns—privateers."

"Oh, some of them are good seamen, of course—come from good English stock." Then the admiral laughed and tapped the captain on the knee, adding, "But that's what we have you and a few others down there for—to keep the blasted privateers from getting at our merchant ships. A few more like that fellow John Paul Jones, and we'd be in trouble!" Glancing quickly at the clock on the wall, he returned to the business at hand, asking, "Well, Rommey, what is it? You've done a magnificent job, and—within reason—I think I can meet with you on any reasonable request."

Rommey took a deep breath and began. "Well, sir, two years ago last December, we took some pressed men onto the *Neptune*, and one of them was injured. He recovered, but the injury had done something to his mind."

"Crazy?"

"No, sir, but he can't remember anything of his past—not even his name. . . ."

Rommey had thought his speech out, and he saw that the admiral was caught by it. He related how rapidly Hawke had been able to learn, and after being appointed midshipman, had made amazing progress.

"I've made a report, Admiral, of his progress, and I can only say that in all my years at sea, I've never known a man so fitted for command as Midshipman Hawke."

"You gave him a good name, Captain," Hood mused. He looked up with a sharp glance. "I suppose you want him promoted—is that it?"

"Yes, sir." Now that it was out, Rommey expelled his breath and hurried on. "It's a little—personal, sir." He tried to find some way to put the matter, then shrugged, saying bluntly, "My daughter fancies herself in love with the man—that's why I'm here."

"I can't promote a man to please your daughter!" Hood exploded.

"Of course not!" The tone of his commanding officer ruffled Rommey's nerves, and he shot back, "I would not have him on my ship on that basis, sir; but he has mastered the ship—and in action he's proven himself a cool man under fire." He stopped abruptly, rising to his feet, his face tinged with pink. "I'll not bother you about this matter any longer, sir."

"Now, Rommey!" The admiral got up at once and there was a smile of reconciliation on his broad face as he took the arm of the younger man. "You always did go off half-cocked! Not too good for an officer—but on the other hand, most of the good ones do have some temper. Now, sit down, and let me read this report."

As the admiral read through the report, Rommey stared at the fresh blooms on the plum tree outside the window, wondering if he was doing the right thing. *If it is, it'll be the first time I ever did the right thing where Blanche is concerned,* he thought grimly. He'd hinted to the girl about seeking a commission for Hawke, and she'd given him no peace. He thought she'd grow tired of Hawke as she had of others, but during the two years that had passed, she and Hawke had spent practically all the time together that shore leave permitted.

Finally Admiral Hood looked up and gave a shrug. "I have no problem with giving the man a commission, Rommey. From your report, he's a far sight better than most!" Then he tilted his head and looked at him searchingly. "Would you have the man for a son-in-law?"

Captain Rommey made a helpless gesture with his hands, got to his feet, and walked to the window. "With a daughter like mine, sir," he remarked, "I'll pretty well have to have what she gives me. But this man—he's better by far than any she's ever been interested in before."

"I dare say—but there's the matter of your family. You know nothing of the fellow. What sort of blood will he put in your family line? That's not a trifle, is it now?"

Rommey had thought of that many times, so he said evenly, "I think the man is of good stock, sir. Beyond that I can't say. But I *will* say that's he's fine officer material—and we need all we can get."

"Very well, I'll have his commission drawn up."

"Thank you, sir. I am in your debt."

Hood called the vapid lieutenant in and in a few minutes, he was handing the document to the captain, saying, "I don't know if I'm doing you a favor or not, Rommey—but I trust so. Keep me posted, will you?"

"Yes, sir—and thank you."

"You can thank me best by capturing those rebel privateers—" He had a sudden thought and snapped his fingers. "What's the name of the one that did the *Safire* in six months ago?"

"*The Gallant Lady*," Rommey said, a grim line settling along his jaw.

"That's the one. I wouldn't have thought a sloop could take a man like Crafton." The admiral shook his head. "That ship—she's made quite a name for herself."

"She's taken more prizes than the rest of the rebels put together, sir."

"Well, I trust you'll put a stop to that, Rommey!"

Captain Rommey slapped his thigh suddenly, and there was a cold, frosty light in his eyes as he answered, "I think I can promise you *that*, sir! It'll be my first order of business. That ship has got to be stopped—and the *Neptune* is just the ship that can do it!"

He left the Admiralty and walked along the busy street, paying little heed to the mass of people streaming along the way. He was a seaman, and the land for him was a place to stay until he could get back on the ocean—a man's proper place.

The sight of the *Neptune* brought a lift to his spirits, and he stood long enough to admire the clean lines, the new canvas, and the glitter of new brass. Even more than that which he could see, he was pleased with the bottom of the ship, for she had been coated with sheets of thin copper held in place by copper nails. This kept out the teredo, or shipworm, and the gribble, creatures that bored into the oak of the hull—and it had the added advantage of preventing barnacle growth, thereby increasing the speed of the ship. "Ought to get eleven knots out of her!" he gloated as he moved to the dock where his gig was waiting.

He spent the afternoon going over the ship, driving his officers with determination. The purser, the quartermaster, the master gunner, the carpenter, the sailmaker, the boatswain were all summoned to his cabin. Mercilessly he picked their reports apart, until one by one they left with pale faces. Rommey knew he was too hard, but he knew also that battles often were won or lost before a ship weighed anchor, and he was determined that a matter of too-little powder would not be the element that spelled defeat for the *Neptune*!

Finally he rose from his desk, saying, "Mr. Langley, I'm going ashore. We'll weigh anchor at dawn."

"Aye, aye, Captain."

There was a miserable look on Langley's face, and it irritated Rommey. *Won't he ever get over his blasted puppy love for Blanche?* he asked himself, then said harshly, "I'll spend the night on shore."

"What about Midshipman Hawke, sir?"

Rommey shook his head, knowing that his first lieutenant was jealous of Hawke and the relationship he had with Blanche.

"You get the ship ready, Mr. Langley—I'll see to *Lieutenant* Hawke!"

"Lieutenant—!"

"You heard correctly, Mr. Langley. You may pass the word that Mr. Hawke is now third lieutenant on this ship."

"Aye, aye, sir."

He won't like it, Rommey thought as he climbed into the gig. *But Burns will—and so will the men.* That was one thing that had encouraged him to seek a commission for Hawke. The men trusted him—and not because he was soft, either. Some men had that quality, Rommey well knew. He himself ruled by stern force, but he knew a few choice officers whom men would follow blindly with a loyalty that was not easily put into words. *Hawke—he's got it, whatever it is,* he mused. *And I intend to use it!*

By the time he reached the large mansion, the home of a friend who had prevailed upon him to stay during his time in England, where Blanche was enjoying a final party, it was dark. The house was lit up with hundreds of lanterns, and when he entered the large ballroom, he had to adjust his eyes to the brilliance of the huge chandeliers that threw golden gleams over the room. The ballroom was crowded with the cream of London society, but he had no eye for the vivid greens, reds, and blues of the ladies' gowns, nor for the bare shoulders and creamy arms that rose out of them.

Finally he found Blanche standing at a long table covered with crystal goblets and golden plates piled high with morsels of exotic food. He paused suddenly, taken aback by her appearance. She was wearing a low-cut crimson dress; around her neck a single flashing diamond was suspended by a golden chain. Her hair was down, cascading over her smooth shoulders, and the yellow beams of the candles made her blue eyes glow. He wondered, not for the first time, where she got her good looks, then tossed the thought away and moved toward the table.

Hawke, he saw, was there too, a slight smile on his face. *His white and blue uniform sets him off well,* Rommey thought. Usually

Hawke was alert, but the party had dulled his senses, or so it seemed. He looked up and saw Rommey, leaned over and spoke quietly to Blanche.

"Father, you're late! Let me get you some wine."

"Well, just one." His daughter's attitude, he realized, had mellowed toward him, and he wondered how much that was due to her desire to get a commission for Hawke. She was, he knew, determined to get her own way—and since he was that way himself, he could not exactly fault her.

"Come out of this blasted noise," he said, and a look of anticipation leaped into Blanche's eyes. He turned and led the two through a pair of French doors into a garden, and when he closed the doors, the sound of the party was muted.

When he turned to look at them, he stared at Hawke and wondered again if he was being a fool—but it was too late to alter his course. "I've been to the Admiralty, Hawke."

He waited for the other to reply, but Hawke merely waited. It was one of the things the captain liked about the man: he could keep his tongue still.

Blanche, however, could not, and she asked nervously, "Yes, Father?"

Reaching inside his coat, Rommey pulled the commission free and extended it to Hawke who took it, asking quietly, "What is this, Captain?"

"Your commission." Rommey experienced a thrill of pleasure, and grinned as shock leaped into Hawke's face. "Well! For *once*, by heaven, you're taken off guard!"

"Yes, sir—I am!"

"Oh, Hawke!" Blanche cried, taking his arm and staring at the document. "I can't believe it!"

"You ought to," Rommey grinned. "You moved heaven and earth to get me to go after it!"

She laughed in delight, and there was no shame in her. "You wanted to do it—but were just too stubborn."

"As to that, you're probably right," he said ruefully. "But how do you feel about it, *Lieutenant* Hawke?"

There was one sign that gave Hawke away, Blanche had learned: when he was troubled—or pleased—he would touch the scar that ran down his cheek. He did so now, but there was a pleased light in his eyes as he looked at the captain. "I'm very glad, of course." Then a shadow fell on his face as he spoke. "I have no other life other than the one you've made for me, Captain Rommey. I'll serve you the best I can."

"I know you'll do that, Lieutenant Hawke. Now I must go. I'm spending the night at the inn. Take my gig. We'll weigh anchor at dawn, so get a good night's sleep."

"Aye, sir—and thank you."

After her father left the terrace, Blanche took Hawke's arm and shook it fiercely. "Is *that* all you can say? You're an old stick, that's what you are!"

"I'm very happy, Blanche."

"Ah, you're afraid to show how you feel—that's your trouble! You've got a career, Hawke! If you can't shout, why, dance with me!"

She fell into his arms, and they began to dance across the paved surface, and soon he was grinning at her. "You just want me to be a lieutenant because you're ashamed to be seen at your parties with a midshipman."

"That's it," she laughed. "And I won't be happy long with a mere lieutenant. A post captain—that's what you've got to be, Hawke!"

"Why not an admiral?"

"Why not? Shoot for the stars!"

He laughed, and she joined him, saying, "It's taken a long time to make you laugh, Hawke. I've invested two years of my life in you."

He paused, shook his head, and asked, "Why did you bother, Blanche? You could have anybody."

"Oh, I want—"

"You want something *different*," he finished more soberly. "I'm just a freak, you know, Blanche."

"Don't say that!"

His face looked thin in the faint light of the lanterns, and he said quietly, "You think it's romantic having a man who doesn't have a past. But it's not a game, Blanche."

She bit her lip, sobered for once, and then she put her arms around his neck and looked up into his face. "I'm not playing games, Hawke," she whispered. "I want you!"

The air was quiet, and he could hear the sound of cowbells far off on the night air. Holding her, he thought of the past two years, and realized that she had come to be the center of his world. His life with men on the *Neptune* was half of his world—and she was the rest of it.

"When I try to think of life without you," he murmured, looking into her eyes, "I can never do it. If it weren't for you, Blanche, I'd not have made it."

She pulled his head down and kissed him, and was shocked at the emotion running through herself. But she had long known that he was one of the most physically desirable men she had ever known.

"You don't need a past, sweet!" she whispered. "We've got a future—and that's all that counts!"

The rest of the night was like a dream to Hawke. They went back into the ballroom and continued drinking wine, Hawke trying to keep pace with Blanche. When they left the ballroom, it was very late, and he was so dizzy from the wine, he could scarcely give directions to Blanche's home to the cab driver.

He fumbled his way up the stairs, and then she said, "Come inside—just for a moment! You'll be gone for so long!"

It was much later when he left her room and walked all the way to the wharf where the captain's gig was still waiting. The crew of the small boat had been drinking, but he paid no heed. He got out of the boat and made his report to the officer on watch.

"Midshipman Hawke returning to duty, sir."

Burns grinned at him, returned his salute. "Not *Midshipman*, I think!" Then he turned and when they were below deck, he added, "Congratulations, man! Ye'll be a bonny officer."

"Thanks, Angus," he said faintly.

Burns looked at him more closely, and sniffed his breath. "Ah! A bit of the grape, eh? Weel, ye do deserve it."

"I—I think I'll get a bit of air before I turn in," Hawke replied. He left and made his way to the stern, and for a long time stood there staring at the myriad lights of London as they winked across the velvet blackness of the night.

Finally he shook his head, turned, and went below, thinking of the future. That night he dreamed of Blanche and her long black hair spread out like a fan on a linen pillow—and the dream frightened him, bringing him upright in his hammock. He could not remember being afraid, but now he was—and he did not know why.

He had not felt his alien past so keenly before. For long hours, until the first rays of dawn thrust red and gold fingerlike beams across his face, he lay there, and then the boatswain's whistle shrilled, and he got up to face his new world.

CHAPTER THIRTEEN

A NEW LADY

★ ★ ★ ★

"Why is it every time you two get together you fight like wild-cats?"

William Alden looked over his foaming glass of ale toward Charity and Daniel Greene with a mixture of humor and irritation in his sharp blue eyes. Taking a pull at the brew, he added mischievously, his voice rusty, "And I allus thought that you Quaker fellers was set against fightin'. Sure don't seem like it, Friend Daniel. Here you jump into this fight against King George with both feet. Then like that ain't enough action, you get engaged to this girl of mine—and you fight with her worse than with the Redcoats."

"She'd drive an angel to pick a fight, Mr. Alden, and *you* know it better than anyone else!" Dan retorted sharply, dropping the characteristic "thee," as he often did since his association with the Aldens. Greene's square face was ruddy with irritation, and there was a trace of real anger in him when he nodded at Charity and added, "If thee had been brought up with the Friends, thee would have a better idea of how to act like a lady."

"If I don't suit you, Dan, you'd better take your ring back."

"No! Don't say that!" She was, he saw, pulling at the thick band of gold that had been his mother's, and he went to her quickly. Holding her hands tightly he prevented her from pulling the ring from her finger, and shook his head sadly. "Why am I always the one to have to beg? And this time I'm *right*, Charity—even thy father says so."

"Oh, Dan, we've been over it a hundred times!" Charity pulled away from his grip and walked to the window. She stared out at the delicate cherry blossoms beginning to fall from the tree outside, and said nothing, but there was a stubbornness in the straight set of her back. Finally she sighed and turned to face them. As she began to speak, Dan was caught again by the beauty of her face, and thought back to the last two years and his struggle to keep from falling in love with her. He had not wanted it, for there was a reserve in Charity that he could not break down. He knew she did not love him as he did her, but he had gone after her with the same dogged persistence that marked everything he did. But even though she had finally (after six months hard pursuit on his part) agreed to be engaged, Charity seemed to be more distant than ever. Not that she didn't show flashes of affection, but more often she seemed to hold him off at arms' length.

He listened to her words, but he was asking himself silently, *Does she really love me?* And he was so afraid of the answer that he buried the thought and paid closer heed to her words.

". . . so we've done well because we've been able to outsail any ship the British have. But we've missed a dozen rich prizes because the *Lady* doesn't have the guns to take any ship except merchantmen. But if we sell the *Lady* and get a ship with bigger guns, don't you see? Why, we could hit the convoys and take what we pleased!"

Her father stared at her doubtfully. "Sell the *Lady*?" he murmured, then shook his head. "You're talking about a whole new thing, daughter. We can sail a ship—but engage an enemy warship? Why, we'd be lost!"

"Not if we got a good crew—and there are plenty of sailors just begging for a berth. A lot of them served on a ship of the line or one of the king's frigates."

"Thee would have us buy a frigate?" Dan asked sharply, unbelief in his face. "It takes *hundreds* of men for a ship like that. Why, even a brig would be—"

"Oh, Dan, a brig would be no good for a privateer!" Charity's green eyes lit up as she began to speak rapidly. It was an idea which had come to her months earlier, and now that she had shared it with her father and Dan, she was eloquent in her plea. "Look, if you use a schooner, she'll crush like an eggshell if you try to lay her alongside a heavy ship in any kind of sea. They're too delicate!

And if a British sloop of war ever takes out after the *Lady* and the topmast carries away, you know we'd be lost."

"Why can't we put heavier cannon on the *Lady*?" Dan asked.

"She's not made for fighting, but for freighting," Charity returned. "Look, what we need is a smaller craft, a sloop. Then we can use fewer men. You can come down on some lordly merchantman and blow him out of the water. You can tack three times to anybody else's once—and the heavier British ships won't waste time chasing you because they know they'd never catch you."

William Alden rubbed his chin and studied the face of his daughter. He had become a rabid Patriot in the years since his son's death at Valley Forge. Every prize they took from the hated British and consigned to the struggling forces of Washington seemed to be a taste of revenge, and for the first time he began to think that Charity's scheme was not as wild as it had seemed at first.

"Well, I'd do 'bout anything to put a crimp in the Britishers. What sort of ship are you thinking of?" he asked cautiously.

Charity hesitated slightly, and there was just a touch of a blush on her tanned cheeks. "Well, Father, actually, I've already found the ship."

"What!" Dan looked at her in consternation, and then shook his head in despair, but said no more.

"Last month she came through and took on supply. A good fast sloop, bigger than most—about ninety tons. Thirty or forty can fight her as well as a hundred and twenty could fight a brig. But she's already armed with enough guns—and there's plenty of room for a fair load of prisoners and for the prize cargo. And there's not a British-built vessel of any size whatever that can catch her."

"Where's she located?"

"Twenty miles south, Father, in Portleigh Harbor—and I know we can get her cheap. The captain's name is Benteen, and he's afraid he'll lose the ship in this war."

"Tomlison offered me six thousand for the *Lady* last week. He'd go to seven, I reckon."

Charity laughed out loud, pleasure spreading over her face. "Let's go take a look, Father. You'll not be able to say *no* to this one."

Then she went to Dan and put her arm through his, and looking up with a glint of affection in her eyes, urged engagingly, "Come on, Friend Daniel, wipe that frown off your face. You may like my plan better when you hear what I've got planned for you."

"I can't wait," he said grumpily, and stalked off, his pride injured. But later that day when they were on their way to see the ship, he brought the matter up. They were alone in the buggy, Charity's father having gone off on other business. The air was sweet with blossoms and the smell of new grass. Taking off his coat and putting it behind the seat, he looked at the warm blue sky and the rich greenery of the landscape.

"Not much like our buggy ride from Valley Forge, is it, Charity?"

"No." She bit her lip and shook her head, sending her auburn hair cascading like waves in the sun. "I don't like to think about that winter. I thought they'd all die in that place."

"They didn't, though." He smiled at her and added, "Christmas Winslow came through it."

The thought of the fat baby drove the gloom away, and she replied happily, "He's the prettiest thing I ever saw!"

"I've seen one thing prettier," Dan said quickly. He slipped his arm around her and drew her close. She did not resist, but when he kissed her, though her lips were warm and soft, there was something in her that held back. He quickly released her and said hurriedly to cover up his disappointment, "I guess Christmas is about the only high point right now."

"Things aren't going well for Washington, are they?"

That was putting it mildly, for though Washington and his ragtag continentals had lived through the winter of 1778 at Valley Forge, they had been on the run ever since. Clinton, the British general, had attempted to move his army from Philadelphia to New York, and in the battle of Monmouth, the Revolution had nearly gone to pieces. Washington's most trusted general, Charles Lee, had broken and commanded a retreat, and only the dramatic appearance of Washington had saved the day. He had dismissed Lee (which was, in Dan's mind, a move long overdue), and all that year the British had chased the Americans around like foxhounds on the scent.

Late that year a French fleet had come to help, but through a series of misfortunes had given up and left for the West Indies. Washington had almost wept, Dan had told Charity, for the general was convinced that only when they could cut the British off from their navy was there any hope of winning the war.

"It hurt the general when Arnold turned traitor, didn't it, Dan?" Charity remarked.

"Like to have killed him! He was the best we had, Charity."
He studied the landscape, then shook his head. "Never know what
went on in that man's mind. I reckon it was pride. He was sharp,
intelligent, but they never gave him any good posts."

"Are we going to make it?"

He looked at her in surprise. "God knows, Charity. I sure
don't."

They said no more, for the cause they loved was at the lowest
ebb. Finally they pulled into the small harbor and Charity cried,
"There she is!"

He looked up to see a tall-masted ship standing off shore, and
drove down to the landing. He gave a one-eyed fisherman a coin
to take them out, and soon Charity was talking animately with
Captain Thomas Benteen, a tall man with a thick mop of black hair.

Dan ran his eye over the ship while Charity went right at the
bargaining. "Don't think you'll be able to get much of a price for
your vessel, Captain," she expressed with a shrug. "She's too slow
for a privateer."

Benteen snorted and slapped the rail with his hand. "Not fast
enough! Why, she'll do thirteen knots!"

"Not likely!"

The casual treatment of his boast angered the tall man, and he
exploded, "Listen to me! This ship is staunch and she's gentle, but
she's fast. She can do better than ten knots for twenty-four hours
on end, and she ain't never been pushed. This ship is sweet as a
nut and sound as a bell . . . !"

Dan left and wandered around the ship. He had made three
short cruises on the *Lady* and liked the sea. There had been little to
do with the army, and Washington had suggested, "Chaplain, the
best favor you can do for me right now—besides your prayers, of
course—is to do anything you can to get guns, food, and supplies.
That young woman is doing more with the *Lady* than the whole
Congress of the United States." He had clamped his lips shut suddenly, for as everyone knew, he considered himself a servant of
Congress and would permit no one to criticize it. And this despite
the fact that in actuality Congress did practically nothing to help
the starving troops.

He returned from his walk around the deck in time to see
Charity and Benteen shaking hands. "You got yourself a sweet
ship, missy," Benteen was saying, and he looked sadly around the
deck. "I'll never get a better!"

"My father will have to agree, Captain," Charity stated. "But he will!"

For over two hours Dan followed Charity around the ship, taking pleasure in her delight. She poked into every cranny and climbed the spars. Finally he said, "Thee is like a child with a new toy." Then he added ruefully, "Wish thee were as proud of me as of this ship!"

She laughed and took his hand. "You'll love her just as much, Dan."

"Not me. I'm a landsman."

She looked at him soberly, saying, "I want you to do something. I'm not sure if you'll like it."

"What?"

"I want you to join Father and me permanently on the *Lady*." She cut off his startled protest by putting her hands across his lips. "Just listen for one minute. You're not a sailor, Dan, but we need someone we can trust. We're going to be taking thousands of dollars of prize cargo aboard, and it'll be a temptation to some of the crew. You're a strong man, Dan, and I'd feel safer if you'd come with me."

A warmth spread through Dan, and he was pleased with her request. It was the only time she'd ever asked for help, and he replied joyously, "Why, I'd be happy to come, Charity, but I'd feel out of place. I hardly know the mizzenmast from the jib."

"But you know guns," she said quickly. "We're going to arm this vessel until we can take on anything smaller than a frigate, and a good master gunner is hard to find."

He was attracted at once, for he had spent months with Henry Knox's command, the artillery. Much of that time he had helped them train, learning much about ordnance. He was tired of inactivity, so all day long as they drove back to town, he allowed her to persuade him. Finally that night after supper, he told her, "All right, I'll go see if my uncle will let me transfer. And if he will, I'll get the best gunners in Knox's artillery to teach me all they know about cannon."

"Oh, Dan, won't it be wonderful!" Her green eyes glowed, catching the lantern light, and she for the first time threw herself in his arms. "We'll get fitted out as soon as we can, and then look out, King George!"

He was suddenly speechless, for the rich curves of her body pressed against him was unnerving. He smiled warmly, saying hopefully, "Maybe we'll make the first voyage a honeymoon trip?"

She looked up, returning his smile. "Maybe so. You get the new *Lady* ready to fight, and I might just think about it!"

★ ★ ★ ★

"I still don't see why we have to have them here for dinner, Charles!"

Dorcas Winslow had made the same complaint steadily for a week, ever since her husband had told her that he had invited his brother Adam and the rest of the family for a meal. Now as she looked over the glittering white cloth covered with silver plates and polished crystal glasses, she made one final protest.

"What possessed you to do this?" she demanded, staring at him with displeasure. She was an attractive woman, a little over-weight, but with fine features and beautiful hair. There was, to be sure, a selfish cast to her face, and it was accented now. It had been a long time since Charles had deliberately ignored her wishes, and she was angry.

Charles glanced at her, weighing his words. "I think it's wise, Dorcas."

"But *why*?"

"Because we're Loyalists. You seem to have forgotten that." He lifted his gaze and considered the room. "If it weren't for Adam, we'd be in a shack or a prison somewhere—like most of our friends. I don't think you'd like that, Dorcas."

Charles had become a silent man since the loss of his son. His sickness had ended, or at least he had overcome it. As the months passed, Dorcas kept waiting for him to become more lively, but even as his health improved, there was a sadness in his counte-nance, and she could not remember too well the smiling, carefree man she had married. He had gone back to his business, leaving early and coming in rather late, so the house was not a happy place.

"Is—is there something you haven't told me, Charles?" Dorcas lifted a hand to her throat as a sudden spasm of dread gripped her. When the rebels had taken the city, she had nearly gone mad with fear, seeing her best friends torn from their homes and either shipped to England or cast out of their homes to make their way as best they could. She now was caught by that anxiety and came to grasp her husband's arm. "Are we in danger?"

"Why, certainly, we are!" Charles stated with a mild surprise. His broad lips turned upward in a smile, and he added, "We are enemies of this government, Dorcas, in name at least. We've been living on the razor's edge. Only Adam has kept us safe."

There was a sudden sound that made Dorcas give a nervous twitch, and he said, "They're here—and I think you'd be wise to make yourself pleasant to my family."

"Yes, Charles, of course," she assured him, and she was able to compose herself as they made their way to the spacious foyer. Charles was at her side, and she smiled graciously at the guests.

"Adam, you're looking well—and you are looking beautiful, Molly."

Dorcas thought how unlike they were, these two half brothers. Adam was thickset and dark, while Charles had the tall figure and blonde good looks of the Winslow clan. But Molly fit perfectly with her husband, and Dorcas spoke quickly to her, "How nice of you to come."

Molly Winslow was English by birth, with fine facial features. Her ash-blonde hair and gray eyes gave her a youthful look, and she said, "Thank you, Dorcas. We really came just to force you to see our grandson."

Dorcas looked up at the tall figure of Nathan and his wife Julie, and a pang went through her as a thought of Paul forced itself into her mind. Nathan and Paul were almost exactly the same age, and though they did not favor each other physically, there was something about Winslow men that could not be hidden.

To conceal the bitter thought that her own son was gone and this one lived, she looked at the baby Julie held and exclaimed, "What a beautiful child! What's his name?"

Julie held the baby to the light. "His name is Christmas. He was born on Christmas night at Valley Forge, Mrs. Winslow."

"Well, that's a fine name—and a fine boy." Charles Winslow moved to see the child clearly, and Adam, standing to one side, saw what the others missed. He loved his brother, despite the differences they had had in the past, and he knew him well. As Charles looked down on the fat baby and put out a finger for the child to seize, a sudden twitch ran across his lips, and Adam understood that the grief over Paul, his only son, was burning in him like a live coal.

Charles turned away blindly, saying in a husky voice, "Come, let's go eat, Adam—and all of you."

"Well, there's more of us than you invited, Charles," Adam began, then hesitated. Charles paused and turned to see a young couple who had been standing at the door.

Daniel Greene stepped forward and said, "I tried to talk Major Winslow out of bringing us, but—"

"I know about that, Reverend," Charles said with a sudden smile at his brother. "He's a hard man to say no to."

Charity was feeling terribly uncomfortable. Daniel had taken her to see the baby, and Adam had simply swept them along. "We've not had an invitation from my brother for a long time, and I want you to go with us."

"But, Major," Daniel had protested, "thee knows about the trouble I had with their son. It would be very uncomfortable."

Adam had simply overruled. "I want you to come." Molly had remained quiet, but Adam had told her when they were alone, "I'm afraid for Charles and Dorcas. Paul is dead, and they're not accepting it. I hope there's no bitterness in them against Daniel, but if there is, I want them both to face up to it—because a bitterness that isn't voiced eats at a man like a cancer."

But now Charity's eyes met those of Dorcas Winslow, and both of them were speechless. Each was thinking of their last meeting. Besides this, Charity's thoughts went back to the traumatic scene she'd had with their son, and the memory of it was suddenly raw and fresh.

Dorcas, however, merely said, "We're happy to have you all. I'm sorry our daughter Anne is away. Come in, please."

The moment of discomfort was broken as they made their way down the hall, and Dorcas busied herself seating the guests. She paused only when Charles's mother, Martha, a small, arthritic figure, came into the dining room, walking carefully, as if she were terribly afraid that her fragile bones would break.

"Why, Martha, how are you?" Adam went to her at once, and Charity gazed with interest at the sight. She had learned enough of the Winslow family history to know that the relationship between the two had not always been so pleasant. Martha Jakes had married Miles Winslow, and Adam, Miles's son by another woman, had not been a favorite. She had managed to sway her husband's favor from Adam to the son born to her and Miles, so that Charles had been the favorite.

But there was no trace of rancor in Adam Winslow, though the woman who had mistreated him so shamefully was now sickly and at his mercy. He must have sensed that it was gall to her to know that she was safe only because he made it possible. He took her thin hand carefully, and put the other on her frail shoulder, saying,

"It's good to see you again, Martha."

How different these Winslows are! Charity thought as she watched. *I've heard that Charles was a bounder in his youth, and his son was a rotter—but there is such gentleness in Adam and Nathan. There must be a streak of wildness in the Winslow breed!*

The old woman ducked her head, thinking perhaps of the hard treatment she'd inflicted on Adam when she was younger and he was helpless; and when she raised her face, a trace of tears glinted in her faded eyes. "Thank you, Adam. That's—that's like you."

Charles did not miss this, and laid his hand on Adam's burly shoulder. "It is like you, Adam." Then a flash of rare humor struck him and he laughed. "You and Mother weren't quite so friendly when you and I blew father's black Winslow chickens to bits—along with her prize rug! Remember that awful cannon you made?"

The memory brought a smile to Adam's broad face, and he replied ruefully, "I've never forgotten it. Father was so proud of those chickens."

"Well, never mind," Charles laughed. "They survived—or some of them did—we're having their offspring for supper! Come along now."

The meal went well after that, and Charity sat quietly beside Daniel, eating the delicious food, but not missing a word. Adam did most of the talking, mostly about the boyhood he had shared with Charles.

There was something in Charles's face that puzzled Charity. He was a handsome man, thin from sickness, and his face hollowed from the illness that had almost destroyed him. He was, she saw, toying with his food, thinking of other things. Finally he said, "I remember when you and Molly came back from Whitefield's meeting, Adam. You'd been converted." He paused and asked quietly, "Have you changed your mind?"

"In what way, Charles?"

"Well, so many are carried away with these 'revivals,' but after it's over the people don't seem to have been changed."

Adam reached over and took Molly's hand as he asked, "How about you, Molly? Are you still a servant of the Lord?"

Molly answered simply, "Ever since that moment when we took Christ as Savior and Lord, we've wanted nothing else, Charles."

The simplicity of the answer and the light in the eyes of the couple seemed to fascinate Charles, and he stared long at them, saying at last, "I see that you are happy."

Adam longed to speak a word to his brother about his soul, but it didn't seem the right time, so he refrained from saying anything. But he felt Molly squeeze his hand and knew that she would be praying for Charles. She was an intercessor of power, awesome in her efforts when she called on God for someone.

The rest of the meal was pleasant, and the visit in the long drawing room was equally so. But just before they left, a casual remark brought a sense of discomfort to the group.

They had carefully avoided any talk of politics, for the Tory in Charles and the Patriot in Adam would never mix. But a chance remark by Daniel in response to something Charles said brought the comfortable atmosphere to an end.

"How are things with you—in the chaplain business, I mean?" Charles asked Daniel. "Are the soldiers very religious?"

"Well, sir, I'm not with the army any longer. My uncle, General Greene, has assigned me to a new duty."

"What is that?" Charles asked.

"Why, my fiancee and her father are owners of a privateer—*The Gallant Lady.* I'm first mate and master gunner." Ordinarily Daniel Greene was a perceptive man, but he was so full of the past few months on the *Lady* that he did not see the flicker of warning in Adam Winslow's eyes. He said with some excitement, "We've made six voyages in as many months, and we've taken more prizes than we thought possible, Mr. Winslow!"

As he spoke of the sea with all the enthusiasm of a newcomer to an art, he did not see that Charles Winslow's lips were trembling, nor catch the warning shake of his head. Dorcas, too, was visibly shaken. Finally he paused, and realized from the awkward silence in the room that something was wrong.

Charles spoke slowly. "Paul was very fond of the sea. If he'd not died, I think he would have made a most able sailor." Then he turned and said in a whisper, "I'm not feeling well—pray excuse me, Adam—all of you—good of you to come . . ."

As he left the room, the guests felt a sudden urge to take their leave. They made their exits as quickly as possible, and as soon as they were clear of the house, Daniel said to Adam, "I'm awfully sorry, Major! I never once thought—"

"It's not your fault, Dan." He put his hand in a kindly fashion on the young man's arm, adding, "Don't fret."

Later on, Nathan brought up the subject, saying, "I know Uncle Charles wouldn't think so—but it's best that Paul died. He was marked for a bad end."

Charity had been strongly affected by the evening. She wrote in her diary that night:

> I feel so strange tonight. I wish we hadn't gone to Paul Winslow's house. It's like a ghost come back. I remember all the nightmares I had after I struck him and cut his cheek—and then when he disappeared, it was as though I was somehow responsible! But I'm not! I'm not!
>
> How sad they were, Charles and his wife. To lose an only son when you're too old to have another! He was bad, but if he'd lived, maybe he could have become better. Nathan says not, but you never know.
>
> Oh, God, don't let me dream of that time anymore! Let him stay in his grave—Paul Winslow!

But that night, she dreamed again of Paul Winslow seizing her. In the dream she moved in slow motion, cutting his cheek open so that the blood ran in crimson rivulets down his maimed cheek. Suddenly her eyes flew open, and she found herself screaming, "Don't! Don't come back!" as she woke up, drenched with sweat and so terrified that she could hardly breathe. Filled with fright, fists clenched, she sat straight up in bed waiting for dawn.

CHAPTER FOURTEEN

THE PRIVATEER

★ ★ ★ ★

A sea gull, wheeling motionless upwind, suddenly flapped its wings until it hovered stationary, and screamed raucously as it made a swooping dive at the wake of the ship below. Daniel followed it with his eyes from his perch high on the mizzenmast, smiling as he thought how he'd overcome his fear of heights. *Only six months ago,* he thought as he swept the horizon automatically, *I was hanging on to these shrouds until my knuckles were white!*

A fragment of something arrested his gaze, and he instantly whipped the heavy brass telescope up and peered intently across the glittering green waters. He adjusted instinctively to the roll of the *Lady*, and after one quick look called out, "Deck! Sail off port bow!"

He slipped the telescope under his belt and slid down the ratlines as easily as a squirrel. When his feet touched the deck, he handed the telescope to a young sailor, "Thad, get aloft and keep an eye on that ship."

Thad Alden nodded curtly, and his "aye, sir" was barely audible. Dan twisted his head and framed a sharp rebuke, but changed his mind as he watched the slender youth climb upward. He shrugged and tried to forget, but he knew that sooner or later he would have to rebuke the boy. Ever since Dan had come aboard as First Mate, young Alden had been sullen. He was totally in love with Charity, had been since he was thirteen years old, and his bitter hostility was obvious to the crew. Charity had tried to soften his attitude, but he had stubbornly refused to change.

"Maynard, I'll have the guns manned."

"Aye, sir!" Giles Maynard, a husky Frenchman, began to call out orders, and soon the deck was a beehive of activity. The powder monkeys scurried below deck to bring the linen bags of powder topside, while the gun crews freed the guns from the tackle that held them firmly in place.

Dan looked fondly at the twin rows of guns and remembered the long arguments he had had with some of the crew who served as gunners on the King's warships. He'd spent as much time as possible with General Knox's men, especially a tall gunner named Ericson, captain of a gun crew on the *Victory*. Ericson had listened carefully as Dan explained the plan to arm a new privateer, and had given him some revolutionary advice.

"It ain't never been tried that I knows of," Ericson had said. "But was I in your place, I'd use long guns."

"Long guns?" Dan had questioned in a puzzled voice. "I'm afraid of long guns. Their pivots are too high and they weigh too much. They'd make us too slow and heavy."

"Not if you mount 'em on carriages."

"What about carronades?"

"'Course you got to have 'em—but they're for close work. They're fat guns and can sweep a deck, right enough—but you got to remember that other ship's goin' to have carronades as well. What they won't likely have is long guns. You can stand off and take shots at them till you break them up, then get close and finish what's left with the carronades."

Ericson had convinced Dan, and he had spent weeks searching for long eighteens, traversing pieces, and ten eighteen-pound carronades. He moved across the deck now, pleased with the result of his labors, for port and starboard bristled with ominous cannon, and the crews that manned them were sharp and quick in their movements.

"What's away, Dan?" Captain Alden had popped out off the quarter deck and was staring eagerly around the horizon.

"Sail in sight, Captain. Too far to make her out."

Charity cleared the ladder, and as she hurried across the deck to stand beside them, Dan thought once again how impossible it had seemed for a woman to live on a fighting ship—but she had made it possible.

"We're about out of room, Dan." She raised up on her toes to see more clearly through the lines, the brisk wind molding her clothing to the slim lines of her body as she stretched. There had been one scene six months earlier, when Dan had tried to convince her to wear a dress. She had stared at him in surprise, then laughed. "I can't go up the mast in a party dress, can I now?"

She wore a pair of dark blue linen trousers, a red and white cotton shirt, and her hair tied in place with a bright red kerchief. The men, of course, had been slow to adjust to having a pretty, young woman on board, and several of them had taken liberties with their language in speaking to her—but that didn't last long. Dan had simply waited for an example—a hulking brute named Olsen. When the Swede had made a crude remark to Charity in Dan's hearing, he reprimanded, "Olsen, I could have you under the cat for that—but maybe you'd like to face me man-to-man."

Olsen had grinned in anticipation. "Why, I'll take you up on that, mate."

It had been a simple matter; the Swede, for all his strength, was awkward. Dan had let the man wear himself out swinging, then stepped in and with a crashing blow to the sailor's blunt jaw had driven him across the deck. It had taken six more knockdowns, for the man had the stamina of an ox, but finally his face was a bloody mask and he lay there an inert mass. There had been no more incidents, and if the men chose to sneak a look, they did it secretively.

"Looks like a brig," Captain Alden decided after the three had watched carefully. "Lying low in the water—like she's loaded."

"We'll have to go back if she is," Charity advised. "Three fat prizes! Not bad for a month's cruise!"

When they were close enough to make out details, Dan reported, "She's got twelve guns—five on a side and two in the stern."

"Probably carronade as well," Charity added.

The men, eager for prize money, were shouting, "Take her! Take her!"

Captain Alden asked, "You think like I do, Charity?"

"Take her!" Charity responded, and Dan turned and called out, "Double-shot the long guns!"

As they drew nearer, they could clearly see that the ports were open and the guns manned. She was flying a British flag and ran on silently, a beautiful, high-sided ship, her mass of sails ruddy in the sun. A cloud of smoke puffed from her stern and a spout of water shot into the air two hundred yards ahead of the *Lady* well off line.

"That's a twenty-four-pounder!" Dan said quickly. "We can outrange her and take her from here." It was exactly the sort of action he had fitted the *Lady* for, and they had taken nine rich prizes in the same fashion over the past months. "Open fire!"

Lige Smith sighted his long eighteen. The deck jerked, the gun roared, and white smoke covered the deck briefly. There was a distant crackle, like a dog crunching a stick between his jaws. A small cabin on the British ship seemed to fly apart into a million splinters. Almost before the smoke was cleared, the gun was ready. The gun crew moved with what seemed to be leisurely movements, but actually with precision beyond the ability of most gun crews.

"Caught her that time!" Captain Alden yelled. A star-shaped patch of white splinters appeared at the ship's waterline.

It was suicide to resist, and the ship dipped its flag in a surrender sign. It was a matter of minutes until Captain Alden and Dan were aboard. She was the ship *Blue Cloud*, James Tennant, master, from St. Thomas to the Indies, 518 tons and laden with a wealth of cargo.

"I should have stayed with the convoy another day," Tennant mourned. His remark caused Alden and Greene to exchange a quick glance. *Good luck for us and bad for the British*, Dan thought with a surge of pleasure.

"Well," Dan responded carelessly, "we'd have got you in the end. It's probably a small convoy and weakly guarded—like most we find in these waters."

"Not so little—and not so weakly guarded!" Tennant shot back. "Twenty-two sail and guarded by a frigate!"

Dan stared at him, then shrugged. There was no way for the *Lady* to take on a ship of that size, so he gave the orders, and the hard work of shifting the cargo to the smaller ship began. By late afternoon Charity informed him, "No room for any more, Dan. We're stuffed with cargo."

"Hate to sink that ship," Dan commented. "She'd bring forty thousand back home."

"Maybe next time we can bring prize crews," she mused.

"Maybe." Dan gave the order, and Lige blew a hole in the bottom of the ship. She sank quickly, and Dan looked away soberly. "Could be us, Charity."

"No. God's with us, Dan. We'll be all right."

There was a feast for everyone that night, even the prisoners who were stacked together into two small cabins. The enemy ship had been filled with galley stores, and the crew ate as few of them ever had.

In the great cabin, Malloy, the steward, served the captain's table with a liberal hand. The table was small, just large enough for Captain Alden, Charity, Dan, Middles, Conrad, and Lester. Rufus Middles was a fat man who served as sailmaker, but had considerable medical experience—having been apprenticed to a physician at one time. Laurence Conrad, the coxswain, was a tall, thin man, almost cadaverous. He was an incurable pessimist outwardly. Miles Lester was an older man, pushing sixty. But he had the bright eyes and indefatigable stamina of a much younger man.

All of them waded through a dozen courses—a huge joint of beef, chicken, kidney pie, steaming hot vegetables, plum duff and fruit washed down with rough, dry Cape Town wine and topped up with port. The captain did not drink, nor did Dan or Charity, but the others imbibed freely.

Finally they all leaned back, and Lester stated contentedly, "Well, man and boy, I've been aboard ships—but never a meal like that!" He took out a battered briar pipe, and soon the cabin was fragrant with the blue smoke rising from the bowl. "I suppose it's back home, eh, Captain?"

"Well, I suppose . . ."

"I think we might have a nibble at the convoy the captain of that Britisher told us about," Dan suggested.

Conrad stared at him in surprise, his thick eyebrows rising. "Whatever for, Greene? We're loaded to the waterline now!"

"That's right," Middles agreed. His fat face was sweaty in the lamplight, and he was so full of food he groaned as he leaned forward. "We get this ship back and we're all rich. I say set sail right now."

"A few days won't make any difference," Dan argued. "We might be able to pick off a stray."

"And do *what* with her?" Conrad's frown grew stronger and he demanded suddenly, "Didn't that captain say there was a frigate guarding the convoy?"

"Well, he did say that—"

"Then we don't need to be hanging around these waters!"

"I agree with Conrad, Dan. That frigate can throw enough iron to blow the *Lady* out of the water." Lester's wise old eyes were blue as a summer sky, and his wealth of experience commanded everyone's respect.

Charity looked at Dan. "What's your thinking?"

There was a pause as the big Quaker thought about his words. He was quick in action, but there was a characteristic way that came from his Quaker background—a slowness, perhaps the result of many hours sitting in "Meeting" waiting until the Inner Light fell on one of the Friends. Charity had heard him say that it was not unusual for a group to sit stock-still for two hours in absolute silence until one of the number heard from God.

The cabin was quiet as he paused, the silence broken only by the creaking of the timbers and the faint cry of a seaman calling out the watch change topside. Finally he spoke. "Maybe it's a great thing to be rich—though it's not something I've given much thought to. I guess the winter I spent at Valley Forge changed me."

Charity added, "I can understand that, Dan. I'll never forget the sight of bloodstains in the snow from the bleeding feet of those men."

He glanced at her and smiled, then said, "I didn't join this rebellion to get rich."

Middles shot back aggressively, "You're not the only Patriot on this ship, Dan. All of us believe in the cause—but look at it this way, the sooner we get home and unload, the sooner we can go back to sea and strip the bones of King George!"

"I'll drink to that!" Conrad cried, and downed another tankard of pale wine. "We've got nothing to gain nosing around that convoy."

"Every time a British ship is lost," Dan alleged stubbornly, "it's good for us and bad for them. If we do it enough, the British will have to quit. Their ships are scattered all over the world—and if we can make this fight cost them too much, why, they'll leave us alone."

"Not likely, Mr. Greene," Conrad commented gloomily. "Washington is hanging on by a thread—why, I've heard he doesn't have twenty thousand men in the whole Army! And the British blockade has us strangled!"

"God will not desert us, Laurence," Dan encouraged gently.

Laurence Conrad had no more religion than a cat—or so he made his claim. Throwing up his hands he said in exasperation, "Oh, it always comes to that, doesn't it, Friend Dan? No matter how big a mess we make of things, God will see us through!"

"Not a bad way of thinking, Laurence," Miles Lester said quietly, and he gave Dan a smile. "I don't see as how it can hurt to look around a bit. If we run into that frigate, the *Lady* can sail out of range while the British are tryin' to trim their jib!"

Some would have argued, but Captain Alden made the decision. "Just a day or two—then back to Boston." He arose and this was the signal for the party to disperse. Conrad glared at Dan as he left, muttering something about presumption, but the others accepted the captain's decision without comment.

"Come on deck with me, Charity," Dan requested. He left the hot cabin and led her up the ladder to the deck. They made their way to the sharp bow and stood there in the moonlight enjoying the breeze.

The sky was so blue that it seemed purple, and the stars glittered like burning ice—a million points of light scattered like jewels across the curving horizon.

"Makes me feel pretty small, that sky," he remarked. "Reminds me of what God promised Abraham—that his seed would be as the stars of the sky." He looked upward, awestruck. "God is a great maker, isn't He, Charity?"

"Yes. He is," she whispered.

He smiled at her, saying, "Remember what God asked Job when He spoke to him out of the whirlwind? 'Canst thou bind the sweet influences of Pleiades, or loose the bands of Orion? Canst thou bring forth Massaroth in his season? Or canst thou guide Arcturus with his sons?' "

His deep voice stirred something within her, but it was not a comfortable feeling. His walk with God disturbed her, somehow. She stared at him and suddenly asked, "Dan, you love God, don't you? I mean, more than anything else, you love God!"

"Why, certainly!" The question took him off guard, and he looked at her, leaning forward to see her face. She was, he saw, disturbed, and he asked, "Why does thee ask that, Charity?"

She stirred unhappily and did not answer immediately. A star fell off the starboard bow, and she watched as it traced a line of light down the sides of the north. "It's not like that with me, Dan. You don't seem to need anything but God—and that's not the way I am. I know it's what I *ought* to feel—but I just *don't*."

He stood there, making a large shape in the darkness, his face lit by the silver light that flooded the deck. Her words disturbed him, but he had known that she felt something like this. For months they had been together on the small ship, and they had stood many times at the same rail, talking of everything under the sun. She was a creature of moods, he had long known. But he also had discerned that the mood covered a dark side of her character, a part of herself that she kept carefully hidden. It was as if she would let him into her lighter moods, but put a large KEEP OUT sign over that part of her life that lay deepest in her soul.

He put his hand on hers as it lay on the rail, saying, "Why, thee does love God, Charity."

"Not like you do, Dan. You've got to realize that. There's something in you, and in Julie and Nathan—and his parents, too—that's different." She struggled to find words for her thoughts, and turned quickly to face him, her face tense and strained. "I don't think any of you know what it's like for the rest of us."

"The rest of you?"

"Yes—those who just have *some* religion—enough to get by, I suppose." She laughed shortly and said, "That sounds terrible! But it's the truth—and it's why I'd make a rotten wife for you, Dan."

"No such thing—!"

She cut him off with a wave of her hand. "You know it's the truth, but you're *stubborn*. You need a girl who's as much in love with God as you are—and I'm not that girl, Dan."

He shook his head, saying, "Thee is not talking sense, Charity!"

"*Thee* is a stubborn fool, Daniel Greene!" She struck him angrily on the chest, and there were tears in her eyes. "If it were any other man, you'd tell him quick enough, 'Get rid of that flighty girl and find yourself a woman who loves God like you do!' That's what you'd tell him, isn't it? *Isn't it?*"

A rare streak of anger ran through him, and he grabbed her suddenly and held her tightly, ignoring her protest and struggle. He lowered his head and kissed her, and though at first she struggled to free herself, gradually she ceased and they stood there under the stars, in each other's arms. For months he had been capping his desire with a steely brand of discipline. Day after day he had watched her; many times he had taken her arm or she had brushed against him, and often the physical desire raged in his flesh. He was not a man to take advantage of a woman, and he had bent over backward to avoid any hint of pressure, despite their engagement.

Now he forgot that, and he held her pinioned in his arms, savoring the softness of her lips and the intense femininity of her body. The slow roll of the ship matched the waves of longing that seemed to rise from deep inside his heart, and he realized that she was not struggling any longer.

Charity was taken off guard; she was so accustomed to the iron control of Daniel the Quaker that she had not sensed the fierce strength of Daniel the man. As he held her in his arms, she found herself responding to his kiss, pulling him closer and surrendering to the magnetic power of his nearness. There was a drumming in her ears, and she was trembling.

Abruptly she pulled away and looked up at him. "What does that prove, Dan?"

"It proves I love thee."

"No! It proves you're a man and I'm a woman. You find me attractive and want to make love to me. And I know you can tell from the way I kissed you that I also find you attractive. But that's nothing."

"Nothing, Charity?" He shook his head and steadied himself. The kiss had shaken him, and he waited as the ship rolled before he went on. "Thee is making too much of this. It was just a kiss. That's part of marriage—a good part, I think. God made them male and female. It's got to be that way."

"Yes—but it's *more* than that, isn't it? We can't spend the next fifty years kissing, can we?" She laughed as he blinked at her outspokenness. "Didn't think I could shock you, Dan! But it's true. Marriage is more than bodies coming together. It's minds and souls and spirits!"

"Thee is right, Charity."

"And we're right back to it. The most important thing in you, Daniel Greene, is God. And you need a woman who's the same way."

He was a stubborn man, awesomely so, she realized. His wide face seemed to settle in determination. "Thee will change, Charity. Thee is young."

She saw that everything she had said made no difference to him, so she reminded him, with a little streak of cruelty, "You were in love with Julie, weren't you, Dan?"

He reddened, for it was the truth. Nathan's wife had been his first love. He had told Charity of it, feeling that it was her right to know, and now he could only say, "I—I thought I was."

"And now you think you're in love with me," she stated quietly. Shaking her hair free, Charity turned to face the horizon, her voice weary as she added, "I don't think we can make it, Dan. I'm afraid it's not going to work. It's not your fault—it's mine."

He did not touch her, but replied calmly, "We'll see, Charity. There's no hurry."

They stood there looking at the stars, the silence of the skies a contrast to the turbulent scene below. The conversation had disturbed them both, and when they parted, there was only a brief word. For a long time Dan lay in his bunk trying to pray, but the heavens seemed like brass. Finally he said huskily, "Lord, I want that girl, but it's as Thee thinks best." He rolled over, feeling miserable and unable to sleep until the motion of the ship finally lulled him into a dream-filled slumber.

Charity fared no better, perhaps worse. She went to sleep but was gripped by an evil and frightening dream. She woke up with a cry caught in her throat, and the terror of it was so great that she rose from her bed and sat in a chair until the first streaks of dawn began to lighten the sky.

The Gallant Lady probed the green billows silently all night. Underneath her hull, millions of sea creatures stirred, while overhead a myriad of stars glittered. The crew slept, except for the watch, and the elderly helmsman, a worn sailor named Hobbes, who thought not of the stars in their courses, but of the leftover plum duff he would have for breakfast. He kept the ship on course and thought of food; such was the simplicity of his soul, and there were those on board the ship who would have traded much to have had his serenity!

CHAPTER FIFTEEN

HAWKE'S BAG

★ ★ ★ ★

Twenty-seven days out of London, the *Neptune* had been making painfully slow progress under light winds, breezes often falling to the merest zephyr, a whisper in the slack, sullen sails. Langley had done all he could, which was little enough: he had set every stitch of canvas available—skysails, studding sails below and aloft, and the seldom-used light moonrakers. He ordered the pumps to be played on the lower sails as far as they could reach and water manhandled aloft to wet the canvas above, and he edged the frigate a few miles north in the hope of finding new winds. In the ship's quieter moments, he had thought of asking Angus to pray for wind, but that would have been *too* much, he decided.

The crew watched him carefully, for they well knew that if the breeze failed entirely, they would have to man the small boats and tow the ship by brute force—a man-killing chore they all dreaded.

The frigate had been in the vanguard of the convoy, and had sighted no other vessels since leaving England. All the officers hated the convoy duty, for it was a slow monotonous task, as they were tied to the speed of the slowest vessel. Not that it mattered much, since the winds were almost nothing, in any case!

The days had merged into one another with little to note their passing in the unvarying routine of a warship at sea, except for the occasional small landmark, a bloody accident during gun practice, or a rare meal of fresh beef—fresh from the barrel, of course. Watch followed watch, four hours on and four hours off, the hands vary-

ing their night watches with a two-hour spell in the dog-watches
in order for one watch not to suffer continually the detested middle
watch. The routine of the day never changed: holystoning, breakfast, dinner, grog, quarters, grog, supper, sleep. In between came
gun practice, painting, shot cleaning, punishment, boat drill, clothing inspections—and on fine evenings, singing, dancing and skylarking on the forecastle.

On one of these nights as the *Neptune* inched her way through
a sea as smooth and unbroken as glass, Blanche Rommey joined
the three lieutenants as they stood on the poop deck and watched
the antics of the crew below. All three of them turned, but Angus
alone saw the pain that leaped into the eyes of Langley as she
appeared, clad in an emerald green dress, her hair falling over her
bare shoulders. *Still sick with love of her, poor lad!* he thought. *Better
if Mann could cut out that hopeless love like he lops off a leg or an arm!*

He shot a quick glance at Hawke, not surprised to see that the
trim officer only smiled at his bride-to-be. *I'd be pleased to know what
goes on in that brain of his—he doesn't act much like a man in love, that's
certain! It's her that has to do all the lovemaking! A whole month together
on this ship, and he acts like he's on parade before the Queen!*

The wily Scotsman had watched the third lieutenant and the
captain's daughter no less than did the others on the ship. Hawke
had been a target for every eye ever since he had been commissioned an officer; this was not strange, for an officer of any rank in
the King's Navy was a demigod to those who lived below the salt.
Every man in one way or another would be at his mercy, and all of
them had suffered enough under cruel officers to be avidly interested in how this new lieutenant would behave.

But Hawke had not been an easy man for the crew to figure
out; he was unlike any other officer they had ever seen. He was,
they soon discovered, not unfair, and they all gave a collective sigh
of relief when, after finding Will Jones asleep on the late watch,
Hawke punished him by cutting off his grog for a week.

"He could've had you torn to bits with the cat, Jones," Spinner
had told him. Then he grinned broadly. "We ain't got no worries
over this 'un, mates! He's too bleedin' easy!"

But the next week when Spinner himself carelessly brought a
bag of black powder into the vicinity of a lighted quick match, he
had suddenly found himself grasped and thrown backward into
the bulkhead with such force that he could not breathe for a few
moments. He got to his feet, his beady eyes blazing with rebellion,

an evidence to the crew that he was not cowed by Hawke. But then the husky sailor looked into the raging eyes of Hawke, and something he saw there made him shut his mouth at once.

"I've heard you think I'm an easy man, Spinner. We'll see if you think so tomorrow."

At punishment the next day, all hands were fully expecting that Spinner would get a taste of the cat, and the officers expected no less than three dozen lashes. But Captain Rommey put the option into the hands of Hawke himself: "Punishment will be assigned by Lieutenant Hawke."

Spinner watched fearfully as Hawke motioned to Lattimore, the husky sailmaker, who handed him a small object. It was, Angus saw, a canvas bag with straps. "Put those two shot into the bag, Spinner." Every eye was on the gunner as he picked up the two thirty-two-pound round shot that Lattimore had placed by the rail and put them into the bag. "Now, put that bag on your back," Hawke commanded.

"On—on me *back*, sir?" Spinner stared into the ebony eyes of the officer, swallowed at what he saw, then obeyed. There were two straps for the arms; he struggled into the knapsack-like bag, and the dead weight of sixty-four pounds pulled him backward, so that he could keep himself upright only with an effort.

He stood there with fear in his face, thinking perhaps that he was going to be thrown overboard—a thought which flashed through the mind of Angus Burns as well!

"Now, climb the mizzenmast," Hawke commanded in a hard voice, "all the way to the crow's nest—then back to the deck at once!"

Spinner licked his lips and cast a fearful glance up at the towering mast. He was a gunner, not a foretopman, and had seldom been aloft since his youth. Even then he had been uncomfortable, and his years spent in the small, confined world of the lower gun deck had made any work higher than the deck unwelcome. The empty spaces of sky and the thin lines that he slowly began to climb were alien to him, and the crew saw his fear as they watched him grasp a line and pull himself slowly upward. He was a strong man, but the dead weight of the shot pulled at his shoulders, throwing him off balance, dragging him away from the safety of the lines, and only by grasping the ropes with all his strength was there any hope. There was no relief, Angus saw, from the intense pressure of the weight that threatened at each laborious step to pluck him off the shrouds and send him plunging to the deck below.

By the time he was halfway up the mast, the sound of his ragged breathing was audible to the crew. Every man saw him look down once, saw his face turn pale at the sight of the deck below. They heard the gurgling cry of fear that rose to his lips and for one moment it seemed he would faint and fall, but he recovered and began his creeping progress until he reached the platform. He gave a glad cry of relief and fell into the safety of the small structure. His joy was cut short by a loud command from Hawke below.

"Now—down with you!"

Spinner had no choice but to begin the painful descent to the deck. It was no better going down, for there was still the weight jerking him back.

Something about the punishment frightened the crew. They were accustomed to a world of order, for there is no more rigid order than on a ship of war. All is by count and by routine, and seldom is that order broken. The seamen may have suffered under the rigid discipline of the navy, but even if they did not realize it themselves, they were "comfortable" under its rule.

Now the order was broken, and the crew to a man was touched with something akin to fear. If Spinner had been raked with three dozen lashes of the cat, it would have been hard—however, they were accustomed to that. But there was something frightening in Spinner's white face, his eyes bulging with fear—and his terror communicated itself to the sailors who stared at him as his feet touched the deck.

"Now, back to the top," Hawke barked, adding, "Mr. Rackam, you will see to it that this man carries those shot to the lookout and back."

Rackam looked at the stern face of Hawke, swallowed and asked in a strained voice, "How long, sir?"

"Until I give the command—or until he falls and kills himself."

The words struck against the minds of the crew, and one look at the dark face of Lieutenant Hawke gave them no assurance. Later Pickins, the foretopman, said in awe to Sullivan, "Did you see his face, Sullivan? Like stone it is, and he wouldn't have no more cared if Spinner was mashed to jam on the deck than if he'd squashed a fly!"

"All hands dismissed from punishment." Hawke nodded and turned to his duties, his face a mask of stony indifference for the rest of the morning. He was the only man on the ship who seemed to be unaware of the drama of Spinner's punishment. All morning long the gunner toiled to the top of the mizzenmast, then back to the deck. As time dragged on, the sun rose in a fierce blast of heat, and the weights seemed to grow heavier. By eleven o'clock Spinner had lost count of the journeys he had made, but he was paralyzed with a fear that was worse than anything he had ever known. In battle there was the sound and fury to take a man's mind off the idea of death, but the silence as he went up and down like a crippled beetle made every second a painful reminder that if he relaxed his grip one time, he was a dead man.

His hands, tough as they were, soon were bleeding, rubbed raw by the ropes, and the sun burned his lips and the sweat blinded him so that he had to grope for the lines overhead. Once he asked in a croaking voice for water, but when Rackam relayed his request, Hawke replied indifferently, "He can have water when he's learned to be a seaman."

Captain Rommey and Blanche had been watching the drama, and when Hawke came into the great cabin to report that one of the convoy had gotten out of position, Blanche was there. Rommey heard the report, nodded, then as Hawke turned to leave, cleared his throat and said with a touch of hesitation, "Lieutenant—I must say that your method of punishment is—well, *unorthodox!*"

A flash of humor appeared in Hawke's eyes, and he commented, "I suppose so—but they get so accustomed to the cat that it's lost some of its usefulness. They'll remember this for a little while, I believe."

"But—what if he falls?" Blanche asked uneasily. She was staring at his face intently; this was a side of his nature she had not seen, and she was baffled.

"He'll die."

"That's a little stringent for a small offense, surely!" Rommey protested.

Hawke's lips were wide and mobile, and now the corners of them turned up as he answered, "Well, sir, I remember what Queen Elizabeth once said in such a case as this."

"Queen Elizabeth?"

"Yes, sir. One of her admirals had been accused of treason and was scheduled to be executed the next day. One of the Queen's counselors tried to get her to pardon the man—it seems the evidence against him was very weak. But she refused. She said, 'It's good to have an admiral executed from time to time as an example to the rest of them.' "

The humor left his eyes and there was a steely quality in his voice as he continued. "I may never have the love of these men, but I'll have obedience—or I'll tear the hearts out of them!"

Rommey stared at him, wonder in his eyes. "Obedience is required, of course. You are dismissed, Hawke."

When the door closed behind him, Rommey turned to his daughter. "What do you make of that, Blanche? The man's got ice water in his veins!"

Blanche shook her head, biting her lip nervously. "He's—he's like two men, Father. One man is quiet and gentle. That's the man we've seen. Now we see that it's not that simple. He's got a cruel streak as well—but which of us doesn't have some of that?"

"Yes—but what *other* side will we see of him?" Rommey asked. Then he did something most unusual. He went to her, put his hands on her shoulders and when she looked up at him in surprise, there was a gentleness in his eyes that she had not seen in a long time—not since she had been a child and he would take her onto his lap on rare occasions.

"I know we've been hard on each other—my fault, I think. I've not been gentle. But I care for you—and that's why I ask, Are you *certain* this is the man you want? You can never really know him, can you?"

She shook her head, a far-off look in her eyes. Reaching up, she touched his cheek, saying softly, "No—but I have to have him." She slipped away, and for a long time Rommey stared out of the window, seeing nothing, but filled with the most profound sense of futility he had ever known. He was a hard, demanding man, and fully aware that he had taken his naval habits into his family life. Now he was grieved that he had not spent more time with his daughter—but it was too late. He struck the bulkhead a terrific blow with his fist and slumped down at his desk, defeat graphically written across his face, cursing the moment the battered form of the pressed man without a memory had been brought on board!

By noon there were bets being made in the crew's quarters as to how long it would be until Spinner fell to his death. "That Hawke, why, he's goin' to let the poor blighter die just to show us wot the rest of us can expect from 'im!" Grimes scowled.

"I didn't think he was so bad—up till now," Sullivan responded moodily.

"Bad—you'll think *bad* by the time this voyage is over!" Grimes screwed up his face, spat on the floor, bitterness spilling over.

"Don't make no mistake 'bout this one, lad. He's a bad 'un! Oh, he's been nice as a kidney pie up to now—but nobody crossed him. And now he's an officer—that's the point! Oh, he's a killer, no doubt of it! Ain't I seed enough of that breed!"

"Right you are, Grimes!" Teller, an undersized dwarf of a man, nodded sagely. "Did yer see his face? 'Let him go till he dies!' That's wot he said! Oh, he'll be the death of poor Spinner—just to teach the rest of us a lesson!"

"Spinner won't last till one, is wot I says, and I'll bet on it," Grimes predicted—and soon there were bets made all over the ship on the hour of Spinner's death.

Looking down from the quarterdeck, Langley remarked to Burns, "Like a flock of buzzards! Look at them!" He waved his hand toward the crew, who were all staring skyward as Spinner groped his way up the mast, leaving red bloodstains as he moved. He was moving so slowly now that each step seemed to take forever. When he almost fell off the ropes at the deckward part of his journey, Hawke suddenly appeared and said, "That will do, Spinner. I believe it's your watch."

Spinner fell to the deck limply, the shot in the knapsack making a *clunk* as they struck the oak boards. Rackam took one look at Hawke's face, reached down, and began hauling the exhausted gunner to his feet.

"I trust you'll keep yourself out of trouble from now on, Spinner," Hawke told him in a voice that was a quiet threat. "If I have any problem with you at all, I will have two shot added to your load and you'll carry them for twenty-four hours up the mast."

"No—no, sir! Mr. Hawke!" Spinner gasped and trembled in every joint. Fear sprang his mouth open, terror coursing through him as though the devil himself had appeared. "No trouble, sir—I swear it!"

That had been the end of it, but from that day, Angus reflected as he looked at Hawke's pleasant face, there had been no trouble at all from the crew. The term *Hawke's Bag* had become a symbol of dread, for all the third lieutenant had to say was, "Perhaps you'd like to carry my bag for a time?" and the hardest man on the crew was instantly turned to jelly! There was not a man among them who wouldn't rather fall into the hands of any officer on board than into disfavor with the slender black-eyed Hawke.

★　★　★　★

Now, however, there was a mildness in Hawke's eyes as he spoke. "They're having a good time, aren't they?"

Angus glanced down at the figures of the crew below, detecting at the same time a trace of envy in Hawke's face. "Weel, more power to 'em," Angus growled. "This convoy duty is drivin' me mad! If I could get doon on the lower deck there, and dance a hornpipe like Jenkins there, it might cheer me up a bit."

"It is boring, this duty," Blanche agreed. She smiled brightly and suggested, "When we get to New York, let's have the biggest ball that place has ever seen! I know enough pretty girls to satisfy you two." Taking the arms of Burns and Langley, she teased, "You two can't wind up crusty old bachelors smelling like dirty socks!"

"Weel, now," Angus nodded, "I'll take the party, but like the man once said about marriage, 'Many that set sail on the sea o' matrimony wish they'd missed the boat!' "

"You're just too *stingy*, you old Scot!" Blanche taunted. "And you've got too much religion, too. Why, you wouldn't know what to *do* with a pretty girl!"

"Probably read psalms to her," Hawke agreed with a grin.

"I'd not be so sure o' that—but in any case, it would do neither o' ye harm to read a bit of a psalm now and then."

Blanche was still holding Burns's arm, so Hawke pulled her away, saying lightly, "If you can't appreciate the merchandise, don't handle the goods, Angus!" Then he did something that surprised the three of them. He had never shown any affection for Blanche publicly, but now he put his arm around her and drew her close. Looking into her face with a smile that made him look much younger, he scolded, "You've got *me* going to the altar, woman—now don't torment the rest of the crew!"

She responded at once to his caress, leaning against him. "I'm not sure of you yet! I've seen too many hunters counting the fox as caught only to see him go to cover."

"No—I'm a lost man," he sighed, his lean, tanned face relaxed, almost playful. It was a side of him that Burns and Langley had never seen, and Blanche but rarely. She knew, as they did not, that beneath his stern face lay a lively spirit, playful almost, when he would permit it to be seen.

"I'll go check the course," Langley blurted out, leaving them abruptly, a bitter expression in his blue eyes. Angus and Blanche exchanged a quick glance, for they had spoken of Langley's jealousy—not being able to adjust to her engagement.

"Not much need for that—not with this calm," Hawke remarked, staring at Langley's retreating form. "We couldn't drift off course even if we tried."

"Not quite right, I'm afraid," Angus shook his head glumly. "The *Blue Cloud* managed to get herself lost. I'm a bit worried aboot that one."

"You think a privateer got her?" Hawke asked quickly. His whole manner changed, for in their cruise before going back to England for refitting, he had savored the action they had found. Rommey had been delighted to find that if his first lieutenant was somewhat slow, this third was a fire-eater. He had said as much to the other officers and to Blanche.

"That young fellow is *exactly* like his namesake, Admiral Hawke! He rocks along with that bored manner of his. But let a cannon fire and he's a savage out for blood—loves action like most men love women!"

Now that love of action leaped into Hawke's eyes, and Angus laughed, "Oh, don't get your hopes up! I doubt there's a Yankee within a hundred miles. The *Cloud* just fell behind. Helmsman probably went to sleep from boredom, I expect."

"She should have caught up by now," Hawke argued, his mind probing the possibilities. He had, they both had noted, a determination that would put a bulldog to shame.

"I expect Angus is right," Blanche smiled. "Come—let's join the fun. You're not on duty." Raising her voice she yelled down, "Morgan! Let's have some fiddle music!"

The tiny Welshman, one of the ship's most agile foretopmen as well as an excellent fiddler, caught the words and waved his fiddle at her with a broad grin. "Right you are, miss!" Soon the sprightly music of Ireland floated over the still air.

"Dance with me," she commanded, and with a laugh Hawke took her in his arms, and in the tiny space on the poop deck they moved gracefully in the steps of a dance.

"A praying knee and a dancing foot don't grow on the same leg," Angus lectured sternly, but there was a smile on his face, and he said, "I'm on late watch, so I'll leave ye two to your courtin'."

After he had gone, they seemed to be alone—a rare thing on a crowded ship of war. The crew below could not see them, and it was too dark for the lone lookout to view much of the deck. Blanche moved closer to Hawke, pressing her body close. "You're the best dancer I've ever seen. I wonder where you learned so well?"

She often voiced questions like this, but he never referred to his loss of memory. He only replied lightly, "Probably at the French palace."

"I'd hate to see you exposed to those French girls—they're such predatory evils!" Laughing happily, she looked up into his face. "That's the pot calling the kettle black!" Raising her hand, she stroked the scar on his cheek, wondering for the hundredth time how he had come by it, then murmured, "It's going to be exciting being married to you. Any other man would have lots of memories about other women—but you'll only know me! I'm so selfish, aren't I?"

"Yes—just the way I like you," he responded. "You're what you are, and I take all of you—the bitter with the sweet. If it hadn't been for you, God knows what I'd have become. I'm so grateful to you!"

She stirred uncomfortably, saying sharply, "I don't want your gratitude—I want love! Sometimes I think you don't really love me at all—that I'm just a stranger who helped you out of trouble—that you're marrying me just to show your gratitude."

"Nonsense!"

"Is it?" she whispered, clutching him closer. "Kiss me!" she demanded. "Show me how much you love me!"

She had done this before, and as his lips fell on hers, he sensed again the possessive streak in her nature. Little as he knew about women, he realized that she was no humble girl submitting meekly to a caress. She met him with passion and a hunger that was greedy, pulling at him until he finally drew back, saying, "You have all of me there is, Blanche."

He shook his head and the moonlight made silver highlights on his dark face, throwing his eyes into ebony shadows. "That may sound like a good thing to a woman—but you have to remember there's not much to me. I can only bring you those things I've learned in the past few years. You're marrying a cripple, Blanche, and I've told you before, you should consider that. It's not fair to you—and it might not be enough."

"You're what I want—what I need!" Her voice was intense, and she clung to him in the warm darkness. Looking out past her head as she stood there in his arms, Hawke heard the sound of Morgan's fiddle and gazed at the bright stars. She was headstrong, this woman, and he knew that it was the novelty of his condition that had drawn her. It was not that he did not feel strongly for her; that was inevitable in view of the circumstances. But he had strong doubts about the love between them, for with only his limited knowledge, he realized with a keen insight that she would be a difficult woman to live with—demanding, possessive, and headstrong. She was, to offset that, beautiful, wealthy, and witty. Whether it would be enough—that he could not fathom.

He drew back and smiled at her. "Your father said once, 'Blanche likes to make things—dolls when she was young, and *people* now. Don't let her make you into something you don't want to be, Hawke!' I think he was right."

"I love you and you love me! That's all that counts!" she argued adamantly, and pulled his head down once more.

Well, it won't be a boring marriage—not with this one! he thought as they kissed again.

CHAPTER SIXTEEN

CAPTURED!

★ ★ ★ ★

"Deck! Deck! Sail—three points off the stern!"

Captain Rommey had been shaving, but the urgency of the lookout's call caused him to drop his razor; he charged out of his cabin, raced up the ladder, and emerged on deck heedless of the flecks of lather clinging to his face. The bright morning sun blinded him, and he moved close to Langley, who was staring over the stern toward the north. "What is it, Langley?"

"Can't say, sir—the convoy has drifted so far. But I thought I heard something just before the lookout sighted sail."

"Heard what?"

"Well, it was faint—but it could have been gunfire."

"Gunfire! And you didn't call me?" Rommey's face was red with anger and his blue eyes flashed. "You should have known better!"

"W-well, sir, it could have been thunder . . ."

A distant sound suddenly came to their ears. Rommey lifted his head and a blistering curse fell from his lips. "Well, *that's* not thunder! That's ship's cannon! Put the ship about at once!"

"Yes, sir—but there's so little wind we'll have to tack—"

"I don't give a farthing *how* you do it, Lieutenant—just *do* it!"

The deck was soon swarming with seamen, but the vessel itself could not be hurried. Slowly as the faint breeze caught the sail, she began to swing about, and Angus said to Hawke as the two of them stood in the bow, "Makes a man want to get out and push, don't it now?"

Hawke was staring intently across the sea, narrowing his eyes against the brilliant rays of the sun. "The convoy must be spread out over twenty miles! I'll bet my life there's a Yankee privateer nibbling away at the stragglers!"

"Probably that's it," Angus agreed. "Captain warned 'em to stay close, but they're a heedless lot. Looks like some of 'em will pay for it."

"Well, that fellow can't do much without a wind."

"More than *we* can. These privateers are the fastest things in the water. And with enough sail for a ship of the line! We're weighted doon with a crew of five hundred men, cannon, shot, supplies. She'll make twice our speed."

"Yes—but if we could get in range, we could blow her out of the water."

"Not much chance o' that unless the captain's a fool—and most of them aren't. They're a crafty lot. As soon as they spot us, they'll turn tail and run for cover."

★ ★ ★ ★

The captain of the privateer was getting that exact advice. *The Gallant Lady* had encountered the convoy at dawn, and Daniel had shouted immediately, "Man the guns! They're out there like sitting ducks!"

At once the ship became a beehive of activity, but as the guns were run out and the ship was manned for action, Laurence Conrad hurried to where Dan stood beside Captain Alden to protest. "This is foolishness! We'll risk this ship for nothing!"

"There's no danger, Laurence," Dan replied easily. "Look—those merchant ships are loaded, and they're not armed. We can make a run right through the middle of them and punch the bottoms out of a lot of them with the long guns."

"And what about that frigate?" Conrad demanded.

"Why, in this calm she can't even move much faster than those fat merchant ships! We can walk away from her!"

"I don't like it," Conrad muttered gloomily. Then he shrugged his thin shoulders. "Well, there's one good thing, if you get us all killed in this crazy mess, we won't have to worry about getting caught by the British and sent to Dartmoor!"

"That's the cheerful way to look at it, Laurence," Dan laughed. "But there's no risk."

And for the rest of the morning his words were so accurate that the crew was convinced, and even Conrad, though he continued to prophesy awful messages of doom, seemed assured. The *Lady* moved steadily under the slight breeze, and by ten o'clock they were within range of a three-masted brig. "Look at them scurry around!" Rufus Middles cried gleefully. "They know what's coming!"

Charity had come to stand beside Dan, and she asked worriedly as he ordered the guns loaded, "Are we going to give them a chance to surrender?"

"What would we do with them?" Dan shrugged. "We don't have room for any prisoners, much less cargo. "

"But won't they drown?"

"No, they'll have plenty of time to get their boats off, and the other ships will pick them up." Then he gave the order, "Fire as you bear, Smith!"

Lige Smith grinned toothlessly and stated, "Like shootin' fish in a barrel, it is!"

It seemed like a merciless thing, and Charity couldn't bear watching the onslaught. Smith could not miss, and he put six shots just below the waterline of the ship that bore the name of *Portsmouth Belle* on her bow. She was already beginning to settle low in the water as Dan ordered, "That'll do her, Lige. Let me take that schooner."

Dan moved to his favorite long eighteen, and as they skimmed slowly and relentlessly across the smooth water, he hulled a schooner that was so loaded she could only waddle along in the light breeze. One of the shots went high and blasted the gun crew to bits. Charity could see the broken parts of flesh flying through the air, and the sight of a man's leg striking the mast made her turn away sick.

They had sunk four ships and were moving on when the lookout hailed, "Deck, there's a frigate bearing down, two points off starboard bow!"

"Time to get away," Captain Alden advised, and began to consider the direction.

"Wait a minute, Captain," Dan urged. He had seen an opening in the convoy and pointed to it. "If we go through that gap, we can get a couple more ships on our way."

"But that course will bring us almost within range of the frigate!" Charity protested. "Let's just put about and get out of here!"

"Wind's in the south, Charity," he reminded her. "We'll have to tack anyway. If we cut through like I say, we'll come a mite close, but she can't catch us. We'll get a couple more ships, and then we'll show them our stern."

Captain Alden opened his mouth to object, but Dan added, "It'll be striking a blow for Curtis." He saw that the words had power with Alden, so he exhorted, "Your boy died for this cause, Captain. Let's do it for him."

"That's not fair, Dan!" Charity cried, but her father's eyes had grown stern, and he nodded.

"We'll do it for Curtis," he agreed, and gave the order to turn.

As the *Lady* heeled and headed into the gap, every eye was fixed on the frigate—still far off in the distance but headed straight for them. A silence fell over the deck as the crew realized that they would pass close to the guns of the warship, and Laurence gave a melancholy sigh. "Well, I've often wondered what it would be like to look down the cannon of one of the King's ships—now God has blessed me with the opportunity. Let us be duly grateful for the bounties of the Almighty!"

★ ★ ★ ★

Rommey had watched helplessly as the privateer had destroyed the merchant ships, and his failure to drive his ship to the rescue enraged him. He had gone to stand beside the three lieutenants who were staring with loathing at the scene.

"Shall I have the guns run out, sir?" Langley asked.

"What for? We'll never get close enough to get a shot. They wouldn't be such fools."

At that instant, Hawke saw a movement that the others missed, and he yelled, "Look, she's putting about, sir!"

"What?"

Hawke's sharp eyes had taken in the maneuver of the privateer, and he reported hurriedly, "Sir, she's not going to run south—there's no breeze at all that way. She's going to cut through the convoy—see there? She's heeling around." Then his eyes blazed, and he cried out in excitement, "Sir, we'll have one chance—she'll *have* to pass fairly close to us on that course. Let me make a try for her with the bow chaser."

"That would be too long a shot," Langley argued. He had seen that the third lieutenant had done what *he* should have done, and it enraged him. "It would take a miracle!"

Captain Rommey snorted, "Well, we'll have a miracle then!" A glitter of excitement rose in his eyes, and he smiled. "You man the bow chaser, Mr. Hawke—and take Mr. Burns along to pray. That ought to cover God and man!"

The remark was taken seriously only by Burns, who said, "It'll do nae harm to invoke the favor of Jehovah. David prayed that God would help him destroy his enemies."

The others stared at him, Hawke in particular, fascinated by the religion of the dour Scotsman, but he grinned and agreed. "You pray and I'll shoot, then, Angus!"

It was a full two hours before Angus called excitedly, "There! I can read her name—*The Gallant Lady*." He was watching the trim privateer as she glided between the merchant ships, and he added thoughtfully, "Beautiful craft. Be a shame to sink her."

"I don't have your mercy, I'm afraid," Hawke remarked. He was bending over his bow chaser, lining the gun up with the enemy ship. "I'll sink her with every man if I can."

"Weel, now, that's a man o' war speakin'—but I doot ye'll get the chance. Look, she's tackin' now. Ye'll not get more than five or six shots at her, I'm thinkin'."

"One is all it takes. I've put a double charge in the gun, and a single shot. Ought to be in range in a few minutes."

"One hole in her wouldn't do it, though," Angus surmised, shaking his head. "Even if ye hit her with two or three o' them six-pound shot, they could plug the holes and pump the hull dry before we could catch up with 'em."

"That's right enough," Hawke agreed. "But you just ask that God of yours to let me place one shot where I want it—and then we'll see."

Every member of the *Neptune*'s crew was on deck, the gun crews gathered about their weapons, all watching the progress of the enemy ship.

"Do ye think the wind's going to hold?" asked Angus. "Looks like the sun's swallowing it."

"Can't say, but if we can get in a good shot, we'll have a chance of coming up to her. Ready to fire," he ordered, and there was a long moment as he waited for the slow roll of the ship. At the extreme point when the bow was lifted free from the white foam, he yelled, "Fire!"

The gun exploded almost before his words died, and the gun was driven backward, coming to an abrupt halt as she hit the end of her harness. All eyes tried to trace the flight of the ball, but under the force of the double charge, no one could spot it.

"Didn't see the ball hit," Angus said, but Hawke was yelling at the crew, who were toiling like demons.

"Load your powder!"

The cartridge slid down the barrel.

"Rammers—first wads!"

The wad was rammed down on top of the cartridge.

"Load roundshot!"

The ball rang and rumbled its way down the barrel.

"Second wads!"

The rammer damped the wad hard onto the ball.

"Run out the gun!"

The men clapped on to the side tackles and ran the gun down the slight slope of the deck, hauling it hard up against the ship's side, the black-painted muzzle jutting out over the green water.

"Handspikemen—train hard forward!"

The crowbar dug in and levered, inching the gun rapidly around until the muzzle was pointing as far forward as possible.

"Adjust your quoins—minimum depression!"

The gun muzzle rose as the wedge slipped into place. The gun captain, in this case the burly Dion Sullivan, crouched over his flintlock, waiting for the final order.

"Fire!"

The lanyard jerked, the spark flew, the muzzle belched flame and smoke and thunder, and the gun hurled backward, brought up sharply by the breechings.

This time Angus thought he caught a glimpse of a thin black line against the sky, and then he shouted, "Close miss! Too long by half a cable."

Hawke cried out the commands and the next shot was seen by all, falling too far by a cable.

"Ye're overshooting!" Angus yelled. "Lower the gun."

"Mind your praying! I'll take care of this gun!" There was a flaming light of battle in Hawke's eyes, and he once again cried out "Fire!" The thunder of the gun had not died away before a cry went up from the crew.

"You got her main mast!" Angus screamed and did a war dance on the deck. "Hit her again!"

Sure enough, the mainsail of *The Gallant Lady* was snapped off as if sheared by an invisible axe halfway up. The mainsail and the royals fell directly against the foremast, tearing down the top gallants and bringing a mass of wreckage down onto the deck.

"We've got a chance now!" Captain Rommey had come to stand close to the stern gun, and his eyes were alight with pleasure. "Good work, Mr. Hawke. I'll mention this in my dispatches."

"Thank you, Captain. Keep up firing, of course?"

"Of course. If you can keep up the pressure, we'll be close enough to swing about and give her a broadside—that'll take care of her!"

But that was not accomplished so easily. The crew of the privateer cleared the deck quickly; and even stripped of part of her sails, she was able to keep her distance from the *Neptune*.

Slowly the two ships moved through the water, and the first success of the warship was not repeated. The *Lady* presented a small target, and even though the six-pound shot came close, no more hits were repeated.

Angus was watching the fleeing ship through the brass telescope, and he cried out, "She's got stern chasers—look like eighteen-pounders to me! I think we're in for it!"

He had no sooner spoken than clouds of smoke rose from the stern of the *Lady*, and then they heard the roar of the stern chasers. Instantly there was a terrific crash midship, and Hawke looked around to see a section of the ship disappear. Bodies and parts of them splintered through the air. Lattimore received the full impact and lay still on the deck.

Confusion reigned, but Langley ran to the scene, and soon had the wounded carried below. Almost at once, another large shell struck the superstructure of the small cabin containing storage just below the poop deck. No one was hurt, but Angus yelled, "We can't stand up to that kind of pounding! She's got good gunners, sir! She can pound us to pieces with those long eighteens!"

"I thought we had her—but you may be right, Burns."

"We'll take that ship! As long as we can fire this gun, I won't quit!" Captain Rommey was startled, for Hawke's face was blazing with anger.

"We can't risk our ship, Hawke!"

"Hell loves a quitter, sir!" Hawke shot back, a fierce light in his eyes. "We came to destroy this ship, sir! Isn't that what the admiral said? I say we do it! Let's show those Yankees what Englishmen can stand!"

Rommey stared at him, then smiled and nodded, "I stand rebuked. Continue firing, Mr. Hawke."

For two hours the duel continued, the breeze tantalizing the British. It rose and fell, and the shots from the *Lady* fell, too, sending shrapnel whirring through the air. Bresington, a huge Swede, was crossing the deck of the *Neptune* when one of the shots exploded on the side of the ship, driving a splinter the size of his arm through his back, knocking him forward and killing him instantly.

There were other casualties, and the crew stayed away from the deck unless compelled by orders. By some miracle, none of the shots hit the bow chaser, and all the crew were awed by the way Hawke stood there giving commands as calmly as if he were in a living room at home. More than once he heard the *whizz* of a shot close to his ear, and he was amazed to see the crew fall flat. "What are you doing?" he demanded. "Get back to your guns. I'm ashamed of you!"

"The man has no more nerves than a brass statue," Rommey muttered to Burns. "I think he lost his fear the same way he lost his memory."

Ten minutes later a shell did strike one of the crew, a tall Cornishman named Wells. He was bringing up a round shot when a missile from the *Lady* hit him with such force that he fell to his death without a sound.

The crew flinched, and Hawke saw them ready to bolt. He knew at once that if they left, he'd never get a crew to stand exposed to the stern chaser. He spotted Captain Baxter immaculately dressed in his red uniform, and cried out, "Captain Baxter! Take the name of the next man who dies without permission!"

The crew stared at him unbelievingly, and then Sullivan laughed wryly. "Sink me! That's a good one!" Then the rest of the crew joined him, and they got off another shot as the body of Wells was carried away and the deck was covered with sand to soak up the blood.

"That's the way the good ones are," Rommey commented as he watched. "They can rise to any crisis and the men know they're not afraid. All the great fighters have been like that. I think you've seen the birth of a legend, Mr. Burns—Look! Got his rudder!"

Burns looked and saw the rudder of the *Lady* dangling by a cable, and the ship veered helplessly to one side. "We've got her, sir! She can't get away now."

Hawke came charging down the deck, pulled up before the captain and demanded, "Permission to fire broadside, sir!"

"Permission granted," Rommey answered. "I'll have the ship put about, and if she doesn't lower her colors, sweep her decks with the carronades. We can take her as a prize, I think. Have the guns loaded with chain."

"Aye, sir!"

Angus looked at the reeling ship, and said, "She'd better surrender. I hate to think of what a broadside with chain will do to those on that deck."

"It's their option, Mr. Burns. If I had God's ear as you do, I think I'd ask Him to give that captain enough sense to surrender!"

★ ★ ★ ★

Ever since the main mast had fallen, the crew of the *Lady* had been hard put to avoid panic. Captain Alden had shown no fear, and it helped the crew to see the old man standing straight and tall on the deck as unconcerned as if he were in his own garden at home. Dan Greene looked up from where he labored over his guns long enough to say with a grin, "Well, Captain, we're in a fight!"

"Blast the suckers out of the water, Daniel!" Alden cried. He shook his fist at the *Neptune* and shouted, "Come on, you blasted cowards."

Dan shook his head later and remarked, "Captain, I wouldn't say they're cowards exactly. They're standing up to our fire better than most. But unless they get more of our sail, we'll make it. Once it's dark, we can shake them off. Maybe we can get a little more sail on, do you reckon? Every yard helps."

Alden went off to see about jury-rigging a jib, and Charity came to stand beside Dan. Surprised, he shouted, "Charity, get below!"

"No! I'll stay here with you and Father." She ignored him as he begged her to leave, and after he got off the next shot, she asked, "Are they going to get us, Dan?"

"I pray not." He stared out across the water, then shook his head. "This is my fault. But I pray God will deliver us."

"And there are men on that ship praying that God will put us in their hands." She stared at him bitterly, bright anger in her eyes as she stormed, "I don't understand your God, Dan. I never will!"

He stared at her unhappily, and she turned and stalked off. He wanted to run after her, to explain. For now that would have to wait. She was angry with him for getting them into the danger, and rightly so, but he had no thought of being taken.

It was only when the shot from the warship knocked the rudder off that he knew they were lost. He felt the shot hit; then when the ship heeled to starboard, he knew it was over.

He walked slowly toward where Alden was standing beside Hobbes, the ancient helmsman. "We've got to surrender, Captain Alden."

"Surrender the *Lady*? Never!"

"No choice. Look, she's swinging around to give us a broadside."

Alden looked, but had no idea of what that meant. "Get to your guns, Daniel."

Greene stared at him, amazement in his face. "Sir, we can't stand a broadside from a frigate! Why, a ship of the line couldn't stand that!"

Alden seemed dazed. He shook his head stubbornly. "We'll fight her! Get to your guns!"

Dan saw that the old man had cracked. He turned and stated numbly, "I'll lower our colors, Captain."

He left the cabin and heard Alden shouting, but could not make out the words. Suddenly just as he approached the mast and was prepared to haul the colors down to indicate surrender, he was seized and thrown to the deck. He fought, but Olsen and three other husky members of the crew held him down. Olsen had never forgotten the whipping he'd taken, and now he laughed in delight as he pinioned Greene to the deck.

"Let me up, you fools!" Dan shouted. "They'll blow us out of the water!"

But Olsen only laughed. "Let's see how strong you are now, Mr. Greene!" he taunted.

Fear rose in Dan's heart, for he knew that as soon as the frigate made her turn, she would throw enough metal at them to blow the *Lady* to bits.

But he could not free himself. He thought mostly of Charity, and struggled frantically to break the hold. Others were giving the orders to man the guns, and he caught a glimpse of the port deck, lined with gunners. It seemed that every hand was on deck, not knowing they were about to be hit with a hail of iron.

Some of the guns fired, but then he heard Laurence Conrad cry clearly, "Look out! She's coming to bear!" He paused and then added, "For what we are about to receive—"

He never finished, for there was a terrific thunder of guns, and the *Lady* reeled under the blow. The air was full of sounds, and

cision; so they waited un
and came to stand before

"I'll have a prize crev
not badly damaged, I und
don't suppose you gentl
prize money?" He smiled
are problems, of course."

"We're undermanne
quickly. "Can't spare mai

"It's always that way
thing. The problem, of co
to New York, and that's
be a difficult job at best
before the *Lady* is repaire
you go, Mr. Burns, but—

"No, sir," Burns int
tion."

"Yes, I thought so,"
Langley, of course—so, I
ter."

"Yes, sir."

"You can fight it out
you can take with you—
make the decisions. I sug
a wind rising. Be good t

"How long do I hav

"Take today. Get su
stores to repair the ship
in New York some few c
all."

"Sir," Burns spoke
aboot Miss Alden."

"Who? Oh, is she th

"Aye, sir. Well, is sl

Rommey's square f
chin with a forefinger.
member of the crew of
here, will it, Burns?"

"I don't believe so, (
the prisoners and had s
of the late captain, and

Greene knew as he lay powerless on the deck that the *whirring* noise was six-foot lengths of chain that swept the deck of the ship like a scythe. The men who held him down were knocked off him as if with a giant fist, and as Dan sprang to his feet, he saw that Olsen had been cut almost in half.

A deadly silence followed, strange and eerie after the crash of the guns—and then the cries of the wounded and dying began. It tore against Dan's nerves, but he hurdled the bodies that lay squirming on deck and ran for the cabin. The sides of it, he saw, had been blasted away, and he flung himself through the door in an agony of fear. He saw the mangled body of Hobbes huddled against the bulkhead, and in the middle of the deck William Alden lay holding on to his stomach. He had taken the wound that spilled his life, and he was staring at the wound with eyes that were already beginning to cloud.

"Father! Father!" Charity came flying through the door, falling beside the dying man, weeping and pulling at him. "Don't die! Please don't die!"

He lifted one hand, and the blood ran like a stream to the deck. Touching her hair, he waited until she lifted her head. When he spoke his voice was weak. "Daughter, you have been my joy—but now it's time for me to leave. God will keep you—for I go to Him— I go to my Beloved!"

She shook in every joint, and her hands plucked at him. "Don't leave me!" she cried.

His face was pale as death, but he took his other arm and threw it around her. Then the strength drained out of him, and he managed to say only, "I—will wait for you—your mother and I—we'll be—"

Then he fell back, and she flung herself across him in a paroxysm of grief.

Dan Greene stood there silently. He had killed her father as surely as if he had put a gun to his head, and his heart was dark with hopeless grief.

He heard the sounds of the warship's boats arriving a little later, but when a British lieutenant entered and commanded, "Take him away, and see that this lady has proper treatment," he did not say a word, but turned and left the cabin without a backward look. His eyes were blurred, but he did not know if it was for the crew, for William Alden, for Charity, or for himself that he wept.

AN OL

Captain Rommey
of the great cabin and t
captain had given then
and to care for the wo
chair and went to stan

"I'll have full repo
I want to know what c

"Captain," Langle
prisoners on board, ta
Mary Ann. She's got a
can carry that many pe

"Very good. We c
vilians on this ship. W
Oh, *The Gallant Lady*."

Langley shifted u
face as he answered, '
the broadside hit. Tho
badly hurt. I had Dr.
of them will make it."

"The captain was
"Yes, sir. His dau
"I see." Rommey t
hands clasped behind
acteristic behavior, the

energetic note in his voice as he made his plea: "She's lost her father—and, of course, the ship was all the family had for a livelihood. And her people are strong on family plots, Captain. She's been beggin' me to see that her father's body gets back to America."

"That's impossible!" Rommey snorted.

"Not really, sir," Burns responded quickly. "There's plenty o' alcohol on board. I could have the body sealed in a barrel full of spirits, and it would be preserved."

Rommey stared at the Scot in a mood close to anger, pausing to consider his absurd suggestion. "This must be a very pretty young lady, Mr. Burns," he allowed with a slight smile. "You wouldn't do as much for a homely woman."

"Perhaps, not, sir," Burns nodded, "but it would nae be to my credit to behave in such a fashion. The young woman is vurry attractive—but I trust my motive is somewhat more humane than that."

Rommey stared at him, shrugged, and continued. "Very well, Mr. Burns. If you will take care of the details, I will arrange to insure that Miss Alden is listed as a passenger, not as a crew member."

"Thank ye, sir. 'The quality o' mercy is not strained,' as the bard says."

Rommey snorted. "I'm not interested in your blasted poetry, Mr. Burns, and I want every man of that crew who's able to walk sent as a prisoner to Dartmoor—no exceptions, you hear me?" Rommey appeared to be apprehensive that someone would interpret his act of mercy to Charity Alden as a weakness, so he scowled at them sternly, adding, "Put them in that hellhole, Mr. Burns, every man jack of them!"

"Yes, sir. They're under lock and key—but there's not more than fifteen of them."

"You are dismissed!"

The three officers filed out, and it took the combined efforts of all of them to get the job done by dark. It was no minor matter to get the material for repairs shifted from the *Neptune* to the *Lady*, but the business of the prize crew brought Langley and Hawke into a bitter altercation, as the captain had known it would. Langley contested every choice that the other made, and Hawke deliberately set his sights too high, knowing he'd have to settle for less.

In the end, they were forced to hand Burns their lists, and he agreed to pick the prize crew. "On the condition," he demanded, staring at them sternly, "that my decision is final. No hard feelings toward me if ye don't agree. Both of ye are my friends, and no matter *what* I put on the list, neither of ye will like it!"

He was correct, but Hawke was secretly pleased when he heard the names—especially with Rhys Morgan, the best foretopman on the ship. He was not so pleased when Burns named Oscar Grimes—but he saw a twinkle in the Scotsman's gray eyes and knew he had done it to placate Langley. He was not sorry to hear the name of Dion Sullivan, for despite his differences with the man, he needed strong hands and good seamen. He received only fifteen men, but one of them was Robert Graves—a fine carpenter who could oversee the repair of the *Lady*. Once again, this was balanced by the addition of Spinner—but Hawke knew that the gunner was in such fear of him he'd cause no trouble.

The crew worked furiously all day, and it was not until after dark that Hawke came to the captain's cabin, having been summoned by the steward. He knocked, and when the captain called out "Come in!" he entered to find a table set and Blanche and her father sitting in the golden light of the lanterns.

"Come in, Mr. Hawke!" Rommey indicated a chair with a place set on the white tablecloth, and as Hawke took his seat, he said, "Better enjoy this meal, my boy. I've approved the list for your prize crew—and there's not a cook on it. You'll be eating poorly until you arrive at port."

"You're probably right, sir," Hawke smiled. "I don't suppose you could part with Hans for the rest of the voyage?"

"On no account! I'll part with any other man before I give up my cook!" Rommey responded. "Well, pitch in, Hawke, and you too, Blanche!"

It was the most ornate meal Hawke could remember, consisting of a large fish, beef-and-kidneys, a magnificent kidney pie, even some fresh vegetables. In addition there was a ragout of pork and a dish of brawn with dark specks, which the captain identified as truffles. For dessert, they were served a pudding rich with raisins and currants, jellies of two colors—all washed down by an ocean of fine wines.

Finally, Rommey pushed his chair back and stared at Hawke with an odd smile on his blunt face. "Now that you are hopelessly full and unable to argue, I must tell you, Lieutenant Hawke, that I have brought you here under false pretenses."

"Sir?"

"You don't see Mr. Langley or Mr. Burns here eating like a

king, do you? No. That's because I want you to do something for me."

"Why, sir, you are my captain."

"I'm also your future father-in-law, and as such I think it wise that you get a good look at the woman you are marrying."

Hawke glanced across the table at Blanche, who was looking smug as a cat who'd just eaten the canary. "She looks very beautiful, sir."

"That's on the *outside*, Hawke—but you are now to learn what a devious piece of baggage my daughter is." The captain leaned back and passed a hand over his forehead, made a slight groan, then slapped the table with his hand. "Sink me! A man must partly give up being a man to live with women!" Shaking his head, he went on, "Well, let's have it out, my boy. When Blanche heard that you were taking the *Lady* into port as a prize crew, she came to inform me that she was going along as a passenger instead of aboard the *Neptune*."

"Now, Father, I simply came to ask if I might have your permission," Blanche remonstrated demurely, but the dancing light in her eyes confessed that her father had pretty well stated the truth.

"There it is!" Rommey spread his hands. "Had her mother not taken passage to New York on a faster vessel, she would no doubt refuse Blanche's request. But what chance does a mere man have against this one? And you'll fare no better, I warn you, Hawke!"

Hawke smiled at the captain, reached his hand across to Blanche, and replied, "I am warned, sir—and I'll take the risk."

"Done you in!" Rommey grinned. "Well, I must tell you, my boy, that your engagement was somewhat of a concern to me. However, I must also say that it's brought a father and daughter closer together than they ever were!"

"I'm glad of that—but what about—" Hawke hesitated. How could he say it delicately? "Well, there might be talk—gossip, you know? I mean your daughter and I alone . . . ?"

"Oh, she's been quite able to take care of *that*, Hawke!"

"It's simple, sweet—I will share the cabin with the captain's daughter. I mean, after all, the poor girl needs a woman at this time!"

"I'm sure your concern does you credit, Daughter," Rommey acknowledged dryly. "But you'll have it your own way. I don't know how I'll explain all this to your mother—with any sort of luck, the *Lady* won't be too far behind the convoy. Now, you'd better get aboard the *Lady*—both of you. I'd planned to get under way at dawn, so I'll say goodbye now."

"Have a safe voyage, Father!" Blanche rose and went to put her arms around his neck, an act which pleased him greatly. He stood there with one arm around her, and put his hand out to the young lieutenant. He made a massive shape in the lamplight, and the years of rough living had toughened his features, but there was real affection in his face as he said, "I am entrusting you with a prize ship—but here is the real prize, my boy." He patted Blanche's arm and gave it to Hawke.

"I'll take great care—and thank you, sir—for everything!"

"All right—off with you!"

He did not follow them, but in thirty minutes, they were in the captain's gig on their way to the *Lady*. "Are you happy with your passenger?" she asked as they moved across the velvety waters.

"It's the best surprise you could have given me," he returned, and the answer contented her. She loved adventure, and this was, to her, an opportunity for an idyllic voyage with her sweetheart. *I hope it takes a month to repair the ship!* she thought as she snuggled close beside him in the darkness.

★ ★ ★ ★

Charity rose from her bed stiffly. Her face felt drawn and tight, for she had wept until she had finally drifted off into sleep. But it had been a troubled sleep, filled with phantoms, and more than once she had almost awakened with her body twitching in terror. She seemed to hear over and over the sound of the thunderous broadside that had killed the crew, and she looked wildly around, not knowing where she was.

Startled by a knock, she stared at the door in terror. Lieutenant Burns had been gentle, but he had been forced to tell her that she might be treated as a prisoner of war; and fear of what could happen grabbed at her as she stood there helplessly.

"Miss Alden! We must come in!"

It was a woman's voice, and that confused Charity, but she wiped her tear-stained face as the door opened. It was a young woman dressed in a stylish gray dress, flanked by a muscular seaman with a large trunk on his shoulder. She came straight up to the startled girl and put her hand out, a smile on her lovely face, "Miss Alden, my name is Blanche Rommey." She turned and spoke to the seaman. "Put the trunk there." When he had put it down with a grunt, she gave him a coin, saying, "That's all."

"Thankee, miss!" He knuckled his forehead, grinned shyly, and left the room, closing the door behind him.

Blanche removed her cloak, tossed it onto one of the two beds, then came to stand before the girl, whose face was pale and tear-streaked. "This is very painful for you, Miss Alden," Blanche said quietly. She had not expected such a young woman, nor one who was obviously very pretty in spite of her swollen features. But there was a vulnerable air about the girl that made her reach her hand out impulsively and say, "I'm so very sorry about your father."

She had not intended to say that—in fact, she had not given a moment's thought to the woman on the privateer. She was not given to such compassion, but now that she saw the squared shoulders and the quivering underlip of the girl, she was moved. Blanche Rommey was a selfish creature, but she had sympathy for anyone in such a predicament—though it would have to be added that she would have been just as moved at the sight of a wounded puppy!

"What—what are you doing here?" Charity asked.

"I'm afraid you'll have to put up with me for the rest of the voyage—but I have good news. Lieutenant Burns told you that there was a possibility you might go to prison, I believe?"

"Yes . . . ?"

"Well, my father is Captain Rommey of the *Neptune*. And I'm very glad to tell you that he has made arrangements for you to be treated as a passenger."

"That's very kind of him . . . and my father?"

"He'll be buried in your cemetery—Lieutenant Burns is making all the arrangements. Does that make you feel any better?"

"Oh, yes! I'm—I'm very thankful, Miss Rommey."

"You had quite a champion in Lieutenant Burns. He was very determined. Not many lieutenants can move my father in that way."

"He was very kind."

Blanche nodded, adding, "I must tell you, I come with a double purpose." She hesitated, looked at the other girl, and smiled slightly. "My fiance has been appointed prizemaster of this ship. I asked my father to let me come with him—and he only agreed because there was another woman on board."

"Where will we go?"

"To New York. I am sorry about the loss of your ship. But I

suppose privateers look on that sort of thing as an occupational hazard."

"Yes, of course."

There was such sadness in Charity's face that Blanche went on quickly. "It will be a short voyage—and I'll see to it that you have no problems. There'll be no lock on the door or anything like that. And you'll take your meals at the captain's table—that's my future husband, Lieutenant Hawke." She hesitated. The girl looked so vulnerable. "Is there any way I can make this easier for you—may I call you Charity?—anything at all?"

Charity bit her lip. "What about the crew? I—I know that most of them were killed."

"I'm afraid so. The severely wounded are on board the *Neptune*. Those that were not are in the hold under guard. I'll get the names of the survivors for you."

"What will happen to them?"

"They'll be sent to a prison until the rebellion is over—Dartmoor, I believe." She gave Charity a close look, asking intuitively, "Is there one of them you'd like to see? Perhaps a relative? I'm sure I can arrange a visit."

Charity licked her lips and murmured quietly, "I was engaged to one of them—Daniel Greene. But he was the cause of all this— my father's death!" Her youthful face grew tense and she shook her head. "I hope I never see him again as long as I live!"

Blanche felt a sudden surge of inner pity for the girl. She herself had led a sheltered life, lacking nothing, never a tragedy. Now she looked into the eyes of the girl before her and felt a shame at her lack of compassion. *I must do what I can*, she thought. Going to her, she put her arm around Charity and said, "We'll talk about it later. There's going to be lots of time for that. But now, do you mind too much having to share your quarters with me?"

"No, of course not, Miss Rommey."

"Well, maybe you'll help me unpack. Perhaps tomorrow morning you can show me the galley and cook a breakfast. I understand there's no cook, so I hope you've more experience along those lines than I!"

It was a strange night for Charity; she was very conscious of the British woman in the bed so close to her, but she managed to get through the ordeal with some sleep. They rose late, not wanting to interfere with the crew's meal, and dressed. Charity led her to the galley where she cooked a fine breakfast of battered eggs and toast. The two of them sat down, and finally Charity ate a little. Afterward they went up on deck where the repairs on the ship were already under way, a mass of tangled cordage, ripped sails, and splintered timbers being removed by the crew.

"That's my fiance," Blanche told her, pointing to the bow where Hawke, surrounded by workmen, was supervising the repair of the outer jib. "But," she went on, "I can see we're going to be in the way up here." She glanced up nervously as Sullivan cut away a top yard, letting it fall to the deck with a crash, and said quickly, "We'd better get below. You can meet Captain Hawke at dinner tonight."

They went below, but Charity had a thought, and asked as they went down the ladder, "Some of the crew are still aboard—those who weren't badly hurt?"

"I heard so."

"We were a close ship, Miss Rommey. I know all these men—they're old friends, most of them. I wonder, could I go see if they need any help? Bandages or medicine?" Charity said, knowing that Dan might be among them, but refusing to let her anger stop her from helping the others.

"Why, of course, Charity." Blanche felt that it would be much better if the American girl had something to do other than dwell on her misfortune, so she added, "I'll go with you. Maybe I can help get what they need."

"I suppose they're in the hold?" Charity inquired. "It's this way." The young women descended to the lowest deck, finding there two of Captain Baxter's marines guarding the door.

"We'd like to see the prisoners," Blanche stated.

"Why, I'm sorry, Miss Rommey, but we can't let you do that—not without permission from the captain."

"Oh, very well. I'll go get an order. You may as well wait here, Charity." She made her way to the deck and threaded the cluttered passageway to where Hawke was working. "Oh, Captain! I need you," she called.

He raised his head, came to where she stood, and grinned down at her. "I'm not a captain, Blanche. Just a lowly lieutenant."

"Well, give me a note and sign it 'Captain Hawke.' "

"A note?"

"Charity Alden, the captain's daughter—she wants to visit the prisoners."

"I'm not sure about that!"

"Oh, it's all right," Blanche promised and reached up to straighten his collar. "She's a poor creature, and it'll give her something to do." She smiled at him coyly. "*Please*—and I'll give you a reward when we're alone!"

He flushed, and gave in. "Oh, all right. You write it and I'll sign it—or you might as well sign it yourself, I suppose."

"Oh, that wouldn't be right!" she giggled as she went off to find paper and ink. After getting his signature, she returned to the hold and handed the paper to the marine, who looked at it carefully, then unlocked the door. "You want us to go in with you, Miss Rommey?"

"I don't think we're in any danger," Blanche shrugged. "Go in, Charity."

The room they entered was a low-ceilinged affair, lit by several lanterns. It had been filled with supplies, but most of them had been removed to make quarters for the prisoners. The lanterns swung with the motion of the ship, casting a series of yellow waves of light over the makeshift bunks on which the men were lying. It was close, and there was the smell of waste and sweat, strong and harsh in the nostrils of the two women.

"Charity—!" Dan had risen from one of the bunks and stood before her, his eyes filled with pain. "I—I'm glad thee has come—"

"I came to see if I could help with the wounded." Even to Blanche's ears the words sounded flat, even angry, and they struck against Dan Greene like lethal blows.

He stared at her silently, his wide shoulders sagging in despair, and he responded simply, "That is kind." He stood back, and a voice suddenly rose from the side.

"Charity! Charity!"

She turned and strained her eyes in the dim light, then moved to stand beside a bunk. "Thad!" She knelt quickly and took the hands of young Alden. "Are you badly hurt, Thad?"

"Ah, not so bad," he answered, but his voice was reedy and thin. She looked closer and could see the pallor on his face even in the dim light.

"What is it?"

Rufus Middles appeared, and his round face gleamed with sweat in the yellow lamplight. "Got a splinter in his side, Miss Charity. He ought to have gone to the *Neptune* with the others that was bad wounded—but he begged so hard to stay, the Scotsman let him do it."

"Can't you take it out, Rufus—the splinter, I mean?"

He rubbed his cheeks, thought on it, then said slowly, "I tell you the truth, Miss Alden, just like I done told the boy here, it's a bad 'un. Got to do a heap o' cuttin'—and I warn you, he might bleed to death."

"But—it's got to come out!" Charity took Middles' beefy arm and insisted. "I'll help you, Rufus!"

He hesitated, saying, "Well, it's up to Thad. It's his life."

"Do it!" Thad gasped. "If you'll help, Charity, it'll be all right."

Charity turned to Blanche. "Can you get us a place where we can treat this boy?"

Blanche was overcome by the stench of the hold, and she croaked, "Yes! I'll see to it—I'll get everything ready—instruments as well." She turned and almost ran out of the room. Charity knelt beside Thad again, taking her handkerchief and wiping his brow. "It'll be all right, Thad—you'll see!"

"God sent you, Charity!" he cried, and he held on to her hand, his eyes bright with fever. She felt the feeble grasp, and tried to pray, but could not. Then she looked up and saw Dan sitting on his bunk with his back against the wall, his head bowed, the picture of grief—but she felt nothing. *He killed my father!* was her only thought, and though the rest of the crew spoke gladly to her, Dan did not lift his head, not even when a seaman came and carried Thad to the makeshift surgery. Even afterward, when Charity came back, drained and sick from the bloody operation, Greene was still sitting in the same position, with head bowed.

Blanche was shocked at the pallor of Charity's face when she saw her later during the day, and she was relieved that the girl seemed to crave solitude. "I feel so sorry for her," she said as she sat with Hawke under the shade of the afterdeck. "She's lost everything—even the man she loves. She blames him, somehow, for her father's death."

"Too bad!" he murmured. "War is like that."

"I want you to be nice to her," Blanche requested. Then she smiled archly and added, "Not *too* nice—because she's a very pretty girl! But I've asked her to eat with us. You clean up and I'll manage to get something fit to eat."

He agreed, and she spent most of the afternoon locating a sailor named Harrison who admitted having had some experience as a cook's helper, so the two of them worked the rest of the day preparing the evening meal. For Harrison it was an easier job than moving heavy timbers, and for Blanche it was fun—something different.

It was growing dark when she went to her cabin and found

Charity sitting in a chair, staring at the wall. "Come now, Charity!" Blanche cried out gaily. "We're having dinner with the best-looking man in the King's service. We must look our grandest!"

"I—I'd rather not, Miss Rommey."

Blanche went over and pulled her up. "I know you've had a hard time—but it will be good for you. Come now, I insist!"

Under Blanche's prodding, Charity put on a dress, a green one with white trim, and let Blanche fuss with her hair. "My, what fine hair! Beautiful!" She stood back and looked at Charity, then smiled gaily, "It's a good thing I'm not a jealous woman—or you'd do without supper tonight! Come now, we'll be late."

Reluctantly Charity allowed herself to be pulled out the door and up to the captain's cabin. It had occurred to Blanche that Charity might be saddened at seeing her father's room, but there was no choice. "She's got to start facing reality," she had said to Hawke.

When the two entered, there was no one inside but Harrison, who was wearing a white coat, acting as steward. "Captain will be here soon," he informed them. "Said for you two to wait."

"Well, I'll teach him better manners than this—after we're married," Blanche laughed. "You sit there, Charity, and I'll take this seat."

As they waited for Hawke, Blanche did most of the talking, telling her about her fiance, and Charity responded with a smile at her enthusiasm.

The door swung open and Hawke entered. He was wearing a blue uniform with white facings. His brass buttons glittered like gold in the bright lamplight, and his hair was neatly drawn back, tied with a blue ribbon. *Heavens!* Blanche thought with a burst of pride, *he is a handsome man!*

Hawke stepped to the table and smiled, his teeth chalk white against his dark tan. The scar on his lower jaw stood out like a white line, and his eyes were kind as he bowed and apologized, "I'm sorry to be late. This is Miss Alden, I believe?"

He paused, waiting for a reply, but Charity was staring at him, her eyes full of fear. Hawke was taken aback. He glanced at Blanche, who was openly puzzled.

"Charity—are you all right?" Blanche asked, concern etching her face.

Instead of answering, Charity abruptly rose to her feet, her face pale. She was trembling, they both saw. She quickly put her hands together, trying hard to control the shaking.

She sees me as the man who killed her father! Hawke thought, and a glance at Blanche confirmed his thought. He started to speak, saying, "I must apologize, Miss Alden. This is too much—"

"Winslow!" The name leaped to Charity's lips, and she threw her hands out in a helpless motion, her throat constricted. The dreams she had of this man—the dreadful nightmares that had come a hundred times to fill her with terror—came rushing back and she raised her voice and cried out, "Paul Winslow! What are you doing here! You're *dead!*"

The last word was a scream, and she fell back in her chair and put her face in her hands, weeping hysterically.

Hawke paled, and he and Blanche stared at each other, speechless. Then slowly, Blanche went over to the weeping girl. She was afraid, but she knew the time had come for something that could be a tragedy for her. She slowly pulled the girl's hands from her face, saying, "Do you know this man?"

Charity stared at him, shivered and whispered, "Know him? Of course I know him!"

"You—you may be mistaking him for another man," Blanche whispered, almost in a plea. "You can't be *sure!*"

Charity pushed Blanche away, stood straight and pointed at the man whose face had gone pale beneath his tan.

"There's no mistake!" Charity seemed to weave and she began to back toward the door, fearfully, as if afraid they would attack her. She reached the door, then turned. They were both staring at her, and there was an expression in the dark eyes of the man who stood before her that would have brought pity to her heart if it had been any other man.

"Not know him? *I put that scar on his face!*"

She turned and with a sob left the room. They heard her feet as she fled down the corridor, and then they stood silently.

Finally he spoke, his voice heavy with foreboding. "Well, my dear, we don't have to wonder about me anymore, do we?" He dropped his head, standing there like a statue. After a while he lifted his eyes, and a bitter smile touched his mobile lips.

"Paul Winslow—I wonder what sort of fellow I'll turn out to be? It seems we'll know pretty soon, doesn't it?"

They stood there like strangers, and she felt an ominous fear that he had gone far, far away—and that the man she knew as Hawke would never come to her again!

CHAPTER EIGHTEEN

HERO—OR VILLAIN?

★ ★ ★ ★

When Blanche left her cabin just after dawn, she nearly stumbled as the ship took a slow roll that threw her off balance. Twice as she made her way to the deck, she saved herself from being thrown against the bulkhead by sheer effort alone. Stepping out on deck, she saw at once that the sky was no longer blue, but was like a lead-colored bowl pressed over the sea, colorless and somehow ominous. The sea itself was different, for though there were no whitecaps, the surface was flowing with long undulations that slowly picked the ship up, then dropped it into the troughs.

The repair work was still going on, and Blanche sensed an urgency in the men as they drove themselves at a frantic pace. Hawke was standing beside the rail on the quarterdeck taking a sight with a sexton, and she hurried to his side. He turned quickly at the sound of her footsteps, his questioning eyes searching hers. Without waiting for him to speak, she began. "You look like you didn't sleep a wink," noting the dark circles.

"I got a few winks," he shrugged. "But you look worn out. I guess you didn't rest much, either." He turned his eyes skyward, then back at her. "I almost came to your cabin to question the girl— but she was in a bad state. I thought maybe she'd talk to you."

"Not a word!" Blanche drew her mouth together in anger. "I told her how you'd lost your memory—but she didn't believe it! Then I tried to get something out of her, and she just turned her face to the wall."

"She said nothing at all?"

"Well—she did tell me—"

"What?" He saw that she was uneasy, and understood the reason. "She obviously hates me. What did she say?"

"Oh, only that I'd be sorry if I married you. I thought all night about it, and I think the girl has lost her mind." There was a defiant stubbornness in Blanche's chin and she added, "The strain of losing her father has driven her too far."

Hawke smiled and shook his head. "I'm afraid that's wishful thinking. We can't ignore this, Blanche." He looked up quickly, lifting his eyes to the mainsail. It was furled, but a sharp gust of wind caught the loose ropes, causing them to whip around the mast sharply.

Seeing the uneasiness in his face, she asked, "What's the matter?"

"I think we're in for a blow—maybe a bad one. And if it hits before we get the rigging repaired, it could wipe us out." He stared at the sky steadily, shaking his head. "I can't leave the deck for long, but I'll get the working crews going. After that we'd better have a talk with the girl."

She stayed where she was, watching as he moved along the deck, giving orders calmly, answering questions and pointing from time to time at the rigging as he explained. There was an air of quiet command about him, and she'd been around the navy long enough to see that he was a natural leader. Finally he returned and took her arm, "Let's go below."

They made their way to the cabin, and Blanche opened the door and entered, followed by Hawke. Charity was standing with her back against the wall, her eyes hard and defiant. Hawke immediately began to speak, his voice quiet and even. "Miss Alden, I'm sorry to intrude on you, but I don't have much choice. . . ."

As he stood there explaining how he'd come aboard the *Neptune*, battered and without a trace of memory, Charity searched his face. He *was* different, tanned and lean, though his face was the same, and the white scar that traced its way along his cheek was like a flag. *He's better looking than ever*, she thought briefly, but she was caught in a rush of memories, not only of the terrible scene when she'd slashed his cheek, but of the countless nightmares that had haunted her ever since. Furthermore, there was the knowledge that he was the enemy who had killed her father and stolen her ship—this burned in her as well, and she remained silent, challenging him with cold eyes, her face pale as old ivory.

Finally he finished. "So you see, Miss Alden, it's been a difficult time." He bit his lip and the firm gaze wavered slightly. "It's been an ordeal that you probably can't understand: not knowing what you are is terrible."

Charity almost weakened, but once again the hatred that had taken possession of her raged within and she shook her head stubbornly.

"I think she made the whole thing up!" Blanche glared at Charity, adding venomously, "You probably heard of Lieutenant Hawke's problem and decided to get revenge for the death of your father. I think you're lying!"

"Do you?" Charity's eyes flashed in anger, and she lifted her head high. "I can prove what I say easily enough. All you have to do is send for Daniel Greene. I haven't said a word to him—but he'll know you as soon as he lays eyes on you!"

Hawke stared at her, then nodded, "Very well, we'll see." He stepped to the door and called loudly, "Sergeant! Sergeant!" He waited until a red-coated marine appeared and stood to attention. "Go to the hold and bring the prisoner Daniel Greene to this cabin—immediately!"

"Aye, sir!"

An oppressive silence pervaded the room as Hawke shut the door, and the three stood there stoically. Charity remained against the wall, waiting silently. Blanche bit her lip nervously as she looked at Hawke's expressionless face. It was a painful time; the only sound that broke the silence was the creaking of timbers as the ship rolled slowly with the swells. Finally they heard footsteps, and soon a knock on the door.

"Bring the prisoner in, Sergeant," Hawke called out. He walked toward the far bulkhead, pausing deliberately, keeping his back toward the door as it swung open. "Remain outside, Sergeant," he ordered. He waited until the door closed, then wheeled to face the prisoner.

Dan had been in the darkness of the hold so long that the light of day was painful, and he was forced to squint. As his eyes adjusted, he surveyed the scene quickly: Charity against the wall, the woman across from her who'd come with her to the hold, and an officer in a blue uniform, who now spoke. "Do you know me, Greene?" Captain Hawke asked sharply.

Greene batted his eyes, focused on the man's face, and as the truth dawned, his eyes widened with shock. "Winslow! Paul Winslow!"

"Does that satisfy you?" Charity snapped. She saw the befuddled look on Dan's face, and explained hurriedly, "He claims to have lost his memory."

Greene looked back into the dark eyes that were regarding him intently, and inquired soberly, "Is that true?"

"Yes. I can remember nothing that happened before I was brought aboard the frigate *Neptune* about two years ago. I was carried there by a press gang," he added, "and I had an injury to my head. Evidently it did more damage inside than out, because until Miss Alden called my name, I had no idea who I was."

Dan waited, listening carefully to the words. He glanced at Charity, shifted his gaze back to Winslow, and finally said, "Well, I can tell you that your name is Paul Winslow." He hesitated slightly before asking, "Don't you remember me at all?"

"No."

The monosyllable fell flat, and Dan shrugged. "Well, we were not friends, Winslow. As a matter of fact, we were enemies. I might as well tell you that we were scheduled to meet in an affair of honor."

"An affair of honor? What was the quarrel?"

Dan shook his head, but Charity spoke up. "*I* was the cause! You had dishonored me, Winslow."

He stared at her, his eyes expressionless. She was waiting for him to apologize, but he said nothing for what seemed like an eternity. When he did speak, it was not of her.

"Who am I, Greene? Will you tell me about my family?"

Dan was taken aback. He had never heard of such a thing, and his first thought was that Charity was right: the man was playing a role. He studied the face of the officer, and finally asked quietly, "Are you telling me the truth? You don't know who you are?"

"I do not."

Dan Greene was a perceptive man, and he could see nothing in the steady gaze that suggested Winslow was lying—and he had been doing some rapid calculations with dates. "I believe you—"

"Well, *I* don't!" Charity broke out.

"But, Charity," Dan protested, "remember how he disappeared? It was in March when we went to the Winslows'. That was two years ago—and they told us Paul had disappeared."

"But they said he'd been murdered and his body thrown into

the sea! Mr. Winslow said he *couldn't* have been pressed—he said he'd had it checked!"

"Obviously, whoever checked was not successful," Dan shrugged. "Was it in March when you were brought on board?" he questioned, turning to Winslow.

"It was the third day of March," Blanche declared. "That was the day my mother and I boarded ship to go to the West Indies— and I was there when Hawke—" She broke off abruptly, an odd look in her eyes. "Or should I say *Paul*? Anyway, I was there when he came out of his coma. He couldn't remember a thing about his past. I've been with him for these two years—and he's not lying."

For a moment the cabin was still, then Dan said in a subdued voice, "Well, I think it's obvious that you were injured and lost your memory. I'm sorry for it. Would you like to ask questions?"

Paul Winslow's eyes grew warm at Greene's willing spirit and he replied hastily, "Well, of course, I still want to know about myself. I mean, am I a criminal?"

"You're the son of Charles and Dorcas Winslow. They are a well-to-do American couple living in Boston. You have one sister, a girl of sixteen named Anne. Your people are Loyalists, but your father's brother is an officer in the Continental Army—Major Adam Winslow."

"A tangled web," Paul murmured. "And what about me, Mr. Greene? What was I?"

"A drunk, a brawler, and a lecher!" All three turned toward Charity, who, though she had not raised her voice, spoke with such anger that Dan shook his head in silent protest. She went on, "Your uncle Adam and your cousin Nathan, his son, are the finest men in America. But your father allowed his brother to save him from what the rest of the Tories got, and your parents have no more gratitude than a pair of vipers!"

"That's not quite true, Charity," Dan argued. "And you are being unfair to Paul as well."

"You defend him?" Charity scoffed.

"We're all weak, frail vessels, Charity," Greene remonstrated. "Thee has lost that quality that makes people love thee. Charity is your name, but thee has lost that quality," Dan finished softly, lapsing into the Quaker use of "you."

"How can you babble about love, Dan? Have you forgotten what he did to me? He didn't care if his own family died in that frozen waste of Valley Forge while he tried to ruin me when I sought his help. And now he's joined our enemies—and he was one of those who killed my crew—and my father!"

Blanche ignored the tears that gathered in Charity's eyes and declared hotly, "He is an officer in the King's service! It's his duty to fight the enemies of his country!" Then she said in a different tone, a guarded voice that was devoid of emotion but which all knew held the question most real to her, "What about—Paul Winslow? What did he—do to you? Were you lovers?"

"Lovers? Not likely!" Charity brushed the tears from her eyes and told the story that had led to the scene in the inn, and ended by saying, "I slashed at him with that candle snuffer, and it cut his face! There's the scar! And I wish it had cut his heart in two instead of his face!"

Dan interrupted her outrage, saying, "I think perhaps it might be better if you didn't press Charity too hard. She's not herself. I'll answer any questions I can, Winslow."

"I agree—and I'm in your debt, Mr. Greene." There was an enigmatic look in his eyes, and he added, "As long as we're on this ship, I will be Lieutenant Hawke. You can understand that."

"Yes, of course," Dan nodded.

"We're in for some bad weather, Greene. If we don't get this ship rigged and refitted, she may turn belly up. I don't know that there's a precedent, but I have an offer for you. If you will give me your parole, I'll set you and the others free to work the ship—with the understanding that you will still have the status of prisoners. Will you do it?"

"Yes! I'll do anything to get out into the air—and I think you are right. We're going to need every hand on board to weather this one. I feel it in my bones!"

"Talk to your men. I'll take your parole and theirs as well."

"Aye—Lieutenant Hawke!"

Hawke left the room with Greene, and the two women studied each other. Finally Blanche's shoulders sagged and she went to sit on her bed. "I know you hate all of us—but what you've heard is the truth. I love him, and I know he's not like you say."

Charity did not answer for a moment, but when she did, there was an unhappiness in her and she murmured softly, "I'm sorry about all of this, Miss Rommey. It was—it was such a shock—seeing him! I've—I've never gotten over that scene! The horrible dreams I've had—over and over!"

Blanche Rommey looked up in surprise, and her features softened. She had not thought for one second that the girl was truthful in her concept of Hawke, but now she intuitively knew that there was no reason why the man she had come to know would have been incapable of such things. She nodded slowly, "I suppose I let myself in for this when I fell in love with him. We always knew his memory might come back, or that we might run into someone who knew him. My worst fear was that he'd have a wife!"

Charity looked at the other perplexed. "Are you still going to marry him? Now that you know who he is?"

"He's still Hawke, Charity. You can *tell* him that he's Paul Winslow—but the man that fell in love with me is another man. Don't you see that?"

Charity replied wearily, "I don't know. I don't know—or even care—about anything anymore!"

But neither Charity nor anyone else aboard the *Lady* had any time or emotion to spend over personal grief, for by nightfall the ship was rolling like a chip in a white-water mountain stream. If the prisoners had not been released and allowed to work, the ship would have rolled over during the night. As it was, they managed to get enough sail on her to make a run before the wind, and that was what finally saved them.

All night they fought the raging seas that rose and fell like white-crested mountains, the force of the waves repeatedly striking the battered ship with terrific blows. "It's like gettin' hit with the fist of a giant!" Dan exclaimed, wiping the water from his face as he struggled to get a little more sail on the yards.

"Sure if that giant don't get tired pretty soon," little Rhys Morgan sputtered as a wave took him square in the face, "we'll be kindlin' wood by mornin'!"

While the crew worked around the clock, Charity nursed the wounded men. Thad was recovering, but the rolling of the ship made him sick, and she had to stay by him for long hours, holding him in the bed and trying to ladle broth down his throat.

When she wasn't tending the wounded, she was in the galley. Cooking was not a simple thing, for the galley was a constantly tilting platform, so that just to keep a fire going was a feat that called for all her ingenuity! Harrison helped some, but his skill was needed topside to work the ship, so Charity worked long hours to keep hot food and coffee for the crew.

Dan came from time to time to grab a quick bite, but there was a strange wall between them. He said nothing, but thanked her for the food; and on the second day when it seemed that nothing could save them, she was momentarily filled with shame at the way she had treated him. He had eaten a chunk of bread, washed it down with scalding black coffee, and murmured quietly, "That was good, Charity. Thanks."

That was all, but his steady gaze was a rebuke to her. She tried to shake it off, but the memories came quickly, and she thought of his kindness, and what a true gentleman he had always been. With shame she remembered how he had loved her father. Again she tried to shake off the thoughts, but the shame grew greater. Finally, she grabbed a covered pan, put some hot beef in it and headed for the deck, intending to take it to him. But she never made it.

When she stepped out on deck, the howling wind smote her with a terrific force, filling her with fear. But she saw Dan crouched over, working one of the jibs in the bow, and started toward him. She was halfway there when the ship suddenly nosed down and she lost her balance. A huge wave broke amidships, and she felt herself lifted high and thrown toward the open sea.

She opened her mouth to scream, but the water rushed in, and she knew she was lost. Just as she was even with the rail, staring down into the trough of raging water, a hand caught her wrist, and her entire body seemed to snap as her progress was checked. She grabbed wildly at the arm that held her, and clung like death to the man who had caught her. He had anchored himself to one of the davits, but the water was sucking with such force that his grip was loosening. She stared at his hand, watching the knuckles grow white—then she saw his fingers straightening out as he was inexorably pulled by the force of the waves.

"You can't hold me! Let me go—save yourself!" she screamed, but the hand tightened on the wood, splaying out the fingers with effort.

Charity saw another wave sweeping down the deck, headed for them, and knew that he could not hold on. She bent her head back to shout for him to let her go—and found herself looking into the eyes of Paul Winslow! The shock was so great that she was speechless, but he forced his head forward and shouted above the roar of the wind and water: "Hang on, Charity! Don't give up!"

"No—let me go!"

He shook his head stubbornly, and then in the midst of the storm, with death pulling them into its watery maw, he suddenly grinned. He put his lips against her ear and shouted, "Well, maybe

I'm not the fellow you talked about—he sure wouldn't have done this! Look out—here it comes!"

The world was water, and Charity gagged as the brine went down her throat. She clung to the hand that held her, thinking, *This is death*—but it was not, for the crashing of the water abated, and she heard the moan of the wind again.

"Better get below." She looked into a pair of somber eyes, and then she felt him lift her onto the deck. She staggered at first, and then he was gone before she could say a word.

Dan had seen the incident, and he came running along the deck. "Is thee all right, Charity?" He grabbed her in a hug and said in a joyful voice, "The good Lord was with thee!"

She waited until he released her; then a tremulous smile touched her lips. "I guess so, Dan—but it looked like Paul Winslow to me."

She left the deck, and he stood there staring after her. Throwing a glance at the form of the lieutenant, he muttered, "Well, you can't be *both*; which are you—Paul Winslow, the villain, or Lieutenant Hawke, the hero?" He grinned ruefully, saying softly, "I guess you are like all the rest of us—a little of both!"

★　★　★　★

"I don't think that's the same sea, sweet! It's so calm."

Hawke and Blanche were standing at the stern rail, looking back over the glistening wake of the *Lady*. Diamond-like flakes of foam were spread out in a large V, catching the light of a moon round and bright as a silver sovereign.

"It's the same sea—just in a different mood," he murmured. They both thought of the rolling seas that had nearly sent the ship to the bottom ten days earlier, and the placid, mirror-like surface of the water beneath them was so peaceful it did seem impossible that such waves could have driven them miles off course.

"Listen—that's Morgan's fiddle!" she exclaimed, and the plaintive sounds of the music came drifting to them on the slight breeze. The crew were all gathered around the mainmast enjoying the steady progress of the ship and content with the delicious supper they had just indulged in.

"The crew did very well," Hawke remarked. "Greene and his men saved us, of course."

Blanche responded instantly, "You would have managed."

"No. They knew the ship, what she could do. We'd all be

feeding the sharks if it weren't for them. It was a close call. I hope your father's all right—but then the *Neptune*'s weathered worse storms."

Blanche stroked his arm, thinking of the events of the past few days. "You've spent a lot of time with Greene and Charity since the storm," she commented, an edge to her voice.

He looked at her in surprise, discerning a sharpness that he could not explain. "Why, of course. I want to know all I can about my people."

"They didn't know them that well."

"Not my parents—but did you know that Dan and my cousin Nathan were in love with the same woman? She turned Dan down, but he and Nathan are great friends."

"And now he's lost another woman," Blanche laughed. "He's not lucky in love."

"Oh, I think Charity will come around. She thought at first that Dan had refused to surrender, but one of her crew—a fellow named Conrad—saw the whole thing. It was actually her own father who gave the order. Conrad told her, and it's made a difference."

Blanche was unhappy, but could not explain it to herself or to him. Ever since the name *Paul Winslow* had jumped out at them, she had felt a vague uneasiness that continued to grow. It had bothered her to see the three of them talking so often—probably because she felt left out and wasn't sure how he would handle the new identity. Now she broached the question. "What will you do? About your family, I mean? Will you go see them?"

"Not likely," he admitted. "I'm a sailor of the King, and if I left my ship and went to Boston, I could be arrested for treason. That's if I went in disguise and got caught. If I didn't conceal who I was, I'd be arrested by the Yankees and thrown in a prison as an enemy of the Colonies."

She shrugged, saying, "This stupid rebellion will be over soon. My father says it can't last much longer."

"Dan thinks it will. He says that if Washington ever cuts the British Army off from the support of the navy, it'll be over."

"But that's exactly what *won't* happen!" she argued. "You're an Englishman, Hawke. You can't even remember America—and your family is loyal to the King."

"That's true."

His admission did nothing to change her feelings of unrest,

and she announced petulantly, "I'm going to bed. It's getting late."

"Good night." He made no attempt to kiss her, so she turned and left, her back rigid with disappointment.

For twenty minutes he remained there, enjoying the music that floated up to him. He was about to retire for the night when he saw Charity leave the small group gathered around Morgan and move toward the stern. She did not see him, and would have gone down the ladder had he not spoken. "Beautiful music, isn't it?"

She glanced up, hesitated, then came to stand beside him at the rail. There was an uncertainty in her attitude, but her voice was decisive. "We've had several chances to talk—but never alone. I—I want to tell you that I'll never forget what you did during the storm."

"Anyone would have done the same."

"No, that's not right. I wouldn't have, I don't think." Her face was turned to him, and he was struck with the pale beauty of her features. Her eyes were light in the moonlight, and the curves of her cheeks were smooth and chaste. She had, he noted, a chin that was a trifle pronounced, a reflection of her character! But she was a beautiful young woman. She went on quietly. "You almost went over with me, trying to save me. Most men would have let go—but you didn't, Paul, and I'll never forget it."

He stared at her, then said pensively, "*Paul*—it's odd, but when you say that name it—I don't know. It tugs at me somehow in a way I can't understand. It seems—*right* somehow."

"You remember it!"

"Oh, nothing like that. It's just a vague thing—like some odor you know you've encountered—but when you smell it, you can't remember just where." After a pause he laughed, saying, "I'd ask you to tell me more about myself—but it's all bad."

She moved along the deck, and the two of them stared out over the wake. She was bothered by the man, and had been since he had saved her life. Before that night it was easy to hate him. But the following days found her being fretful, uncertain. Now standing by the rail, she spoke what was in her heart.

"I don't know you, Paul. The man I hated and had nightmares over is dead. You're not the same at all."

For a long time they stood there, talking quietly, and finally he blurted out in a voice of bitter resignation, "I'm the nobody man, Charity. I can't be Hawke—and I can't be Winslow. I'm a dead man who won't stay buried!"

Instantly she was filled with a great pity for him. Never before had she known what it was like to be locked in time with no past, and it made her want to reach out to comfort this man she'd hurt so deeply. Without thinking, she put her hand on his arm, and when he turned in surprise to face her, she whispered, "Paul—don't be bitter! Please don't!"

Her face was only inches away from his, and he could see that she was weeping. Tears glittered like diamonds on her lashes, and the sudden rush of sympathy shook him as never before. He had no notion of doing such a thing, but impulsively he leaned forward and kissed her. She moved against him, and the salt of her tears was on his lips.

Charity was swept with emotion, and his lips on hers made her shake like the wind that had battered the *Lady*! She seemed to lose all her strength, and she clung to him as she had the night when only his arm kept her from being pulled to a watery grave.

They were both shocked when a voice spoke mockingly, "Well, I see that you two are having another 'talk'!"

Charity pulled back, confused, and saw Blanche, who had come out of the hatchway and was regarding them with a twisted smile on her lips. She did not say another word, but turned and dashed down the ladder into the darkness.

And before she could answer, he whirled and left her alone on the deck, confused and swept with a painful feeling that she'd not be able to forget the moment—not ever!

CHAPTER NINETEEN

TELL HIM WE LOVE HIM!

★ ★ ★ ★

The blazing sun of August faded into a pale specter as September brought winds with a taste of fall and a hint of winter. *The Gallant Lady* forged steadily through the gray sea, making for New York with all speed.

Since the night that Paul Winslow had kissed her, Charity had found herself living in a state of restless confusion. Although she had tried her best to apologize to Blanche the following day, there was a strain between the two women. She wanted to talk to Dan—but even after she had asked his forgiveness for unjustly blaming him for her father's death, she could sense a definite wall when she saw him. She felt isolated, cut off, and the future looked empty, dull, without any hope of pleasure or satisfaction. The *Lady* had been her life, and now that both her father and the ship were gone, her heart was heavy when she tried to plan the next steps in her life.

Thad was the beneficiary of this time of her confusion, for she spent much time nursing him back to health. She tried as best she could to lay to rest his youthful love for her, but she had only partial success.

While she was changing Thad's bandages one afternoon, she had her first encounter with Paul Winslow since that fateful night. Charity had just pulled the old bandages free and was carefully sponging the wound when a shadow fell over Thad, and she looked up with a start to see Paul looking down at her.

"How's the patient doing?" he asked.

"Oh—he's doing well—no sign of gangrene."

"From all reports, you've done a fine job with these men," he remarked. When she didn't comment, he continued. "I'd like to have a word with you when you're finished here."

She glanced at him sharply, wanting to refuse, but heard herself saying, "I'll be finished soon."

"Captain?" Thad spoke urgently as the officer turned. "What's going to happen to us—the crew, I mean?"

Winslow looked down at the boy, regret in his eyes. "I'm afraid you'll be sent to Dartmoor. It's a naval prison for captured enemies of England."

"We been hearin' it's nothin' but a grave, Captain. Word we've had is that nine men out of ten just die there."

Winslow shook his head. "I wish I could tell you more—but I know little about the place. It *does* have a bad reputation—but I guess all prisons do."

The boy's eyes gleamed with anger, and he spat out fiercely, "Well, they ain't goin' to do me in, I tell you flat! I'm bustin' out of there!"

"Don't do that, boy!" Winslow shook his head sternly. "It's a bad place with lots of sickness, and men die—but from what I've heard the escape rate is nonexistent. Every man who's tried to escape has been caught—and most of them killed by the guards. Try to be patient. This war can't last long."

"Easy for you to say!"

"I'll see you on deck," Winslow nodded at Charity, and left the cabin.

After she finished the bandaging, Charity promised, "I'll bring you something to eat later, Thad. Try to sleep."

She left the hold and went up on deck, where she saw Winslow standing on the poop deck looking out over the bow. When she climbed the steps he turned, saying, "I'm sorry about your crew. It's one of the most terrible aspects of war—prisons. There are no good ones, I believe."

"What did you want to see me about?"

He seemed uncertain, and took off his bicorn, twisting the hat around nervously, staring at the object as if it held a particular interest. The brisk wind ruffled his crisp black hair, causing a rebellious lock to fall across his forehead. Finally he lifted his gaze and said quietly, "I want to apologize for my behavior. It was unpardonable."

His frank approach and the directness of his gaze pleased her, but at the thought of his kiss, she felt her cheeks flush. Quickly she ducked her head and turned to look out across the sea to compose herself. "It was not altogether your fault, Paul," she murmured.

"I must risk contradicting a lady—for I know that in this case you are mistaken. Am I forgiven?"

"Well . . ." She shifted her eyes to meet his, and the beginning of a smile touched her full lips. "You are forgiven as far as *I* am concerned, but—"

He grinned ruefully, and came to lean on the rail beside her. "Blanche? You needn't mention *that*! I've already discovered that a woman scorned is a fearful sight!"

"She'll forgive you. She loves you very much."

He didn't answer directly, but traced an intricate design in the encrusted salt coating the rail. When he looked up, he asked hesitantly, "Would you do something for me?"

"Why—I'm not sure," she answered.

"Let me ask—afterward you can feel free to refuse—and no hard feelings." He brushed the salt off his hands, and as he began to speak, she saw that he was tense. "I'm in a difficult position, you see. I'm an officer in His Majesty's Navy—and if I am apprehended by the authorities—the American authorities, that is—I'll be arrested. But I would like very much to contact my family."

"How can I help, Paul?"

"You could go see them, Charity," he responded instantly. "Tell them about me. They think I'm dead, so it'll be a shock. However, the truth may be even a worse shock, don't you see?"

"I don't understand."

"Well, I've thought about it a lot, and it seems to me that when my family hears I'm alive, they'll all rejoice—at least I would *hope* so! But they need to be told that they're not getting their son back again—because I'm not the same man. It's going to be terrible for them, Charity!"

She stared at him, nodding her head slowly. "I hadn't thought of that."

"You agree—to go, I mean?" He spoke faster, seeing that she was not convinced. "I know you have to bury your father, of course, but after that, if you could go to Boston and speak with them, I would be so grateful! You know what I'm like—as contrasted with what I evidently was before, and they need to be aware that the Paul Winslow they knew really is dead."

A small column of smoke was rising from the galley, and she smelled the acrid scent of coal burning. It got in her eyes and she blinked to clear them before she answered. "I'll go to Boston, Paul."

"You will?" He involuntarily took her hands, then dropped them instantly, saying, "I suppose *that* won't do! But it's like you, Charity. You seem born to take care of helpless creatures like Thad and me."

"It's no trouble," she assured him, and bit her lip. A sadness touched her green eyes, and she stated evenly, "I don't have anything else to do."

"That's my fault, too, isn't it?"

"No. We knew there was a risk of losing the ship," she answered. "Don't blame yourself. Now, what do you want me to say to your family?"

"Tell them what I am," he began slowly, his brow furrowed in thought. "And tell them that I think it best that we don't meet at all. I have another life now, and it will never be possible for me to be what I was."

"I'll try."

He nodded, a look of relief etching his face. "I'll do the best I can for the crew—but it's out of my hands. There may be a way to help make life there easier. I'll see what I can do."

"Dartmoor is a hell, they say." Charity's lips trembled, a sadness touching her eyes at the fate of her crew. "Most of them will die there." She turned hastily, and left him standing on the deck.

For the next two days she kept to herself, but she noticed that Blanche was almost always at Paul's side. *She'll fight for him!* she thought; and try as she could, she could see no happiness for the family of Charles Winslow.

★ ★ ★ ★

Twelve days after *The Gallant Lady* dropped anchor in New York harbor, Charity found herself for the fourth time in her life standing at the door of Charles Winslow's house feeling totally unsure of herself. The first time, she'd come seeking help for Nathan and his wife; the second time she'd come with Dan to apologize; the third time she'd been with Dan and the Winslows; but this time she was even more apprehensive.

She knocked on the door, and while she waited, she thought

of the events of the days since the docking of the ship. She had left the *Lady* with tears, for she'd said her goodbyes to the crew. Dan and the rest would be placed on an English warship and taken to Dartmoor the following day, and they all knew it was the last time they'd ever meet—at least for most of them.

She'd fallen into Dan's arms, grief and shame engulfing her. She knew she did not love him—at least not in the way a woman must love the man she marries—but he looked so alone standing there! "Dan—I'm so sorry!"

"Thee mustn't weep," he had encouraged steadily. "Let me see a smile. It'll have to do me for a time—that's better! Now, I'm believing the good Lord that somehow I'll see this country again— and thee must pray with me."

"My prayers aren't worth a farthing!" she had sobbed. "I don't know God! I'm not even sure I believe in Him!"

"Well, He believes in *thee*—and that's enough." Then it was time to leave, and he had smiled, saying, "Thee has my love, Charity."

The parting had been hard, and just as difficult had been her coming home to Boston to an empty house. She had not realized how much her father had filled the home, had made it happy and full of life. But now it was a burden on her to stay there, and she knew she could not live in the place alone for long.

She thought of the funeral, when the members of the church had gathered around the stark grave, and Pastor Johnson had spoken the old words about resurrection. She had stood there, her mind locked, frozen; when the black casket was lowered into the red clay, she had fainted for the first time in her life.

That had been two days ago, and during all that time she had tried to steel herself to keep her promise to Paul. As the door began to swing open, she had the absurd inclination to whirl and flee— but it was too late. Cory, the same house slave that had told her where to find Paul the first time she'd come, asked, "Yas'um? What can I do fo' you?" And when she recognized Charity, her obsidianal eyes filled with hatred.

"I would like to see Mr. Winslow."

"Mistuh Winslow—he not well."

"Mrs. Winslow? I *must* see one of them!"

"I go see—you wants to come in?"

Charity entered and stood there waiting. The morning sun fell in gold bars through the heavy glass in the door, but it was unable to dispel the depressing silence in the house. Cory came back after what seemed like a long time and said, "You kin come dis way."

Charity followed the servant down the wide hall, glancing in at the dining room where she'd been entertained on her last visit, but Cory led her past that, around a corner, and finally indicated a door.

"You kin go in, dey say."

Charity pushed the door open and found herself in a study that had been converted, it seemed, into a bedroom. Charles Winslow was seated in a leather chair with his right foot on a low stool. His wife was standing across the room, her eyes fixed on the visitor, a hostile expression on her face.

"You must forgive me, Miss Alden," Charles apologized. "This gout has laid me low. I'm bound to this chair, you see."

"I'm sorry to hear of it, sir," Charity responded. She hesitated, not knowing how to begin and it showed on her face.

"Is there something wrong, Miss Alden?" Charles asked. "You seem disturbed."

"Well, I have news for you—but I'm not sure how to go about it. Is the rest of your family here? It's something that concerns all of you."

"Why, yes, they're here. I can't imagine what—"

Charity burst out, "Perhaps it's better if I tell you—and you can break the news to them."

"Break the news?" Dorcas frowned, coming forward. "That sounds ominous. What news could you possibly have that would be of interest to us?" A thought struck her, and she asked quickly, "Does it have to do with my husband's family?"

"Oh, Lord!" Charles moaned. "It's Adam—he's been killed!"

"No! No! It's not about Major Winslow at all!" Charity wet her lips and tried again. "Perhaps I'd better tell you where I've been for the past few months."

"I understand from my brother you've been at sea—in your ship."

"Yes, that's true. And we had bad fortune. . . ."

She began slowly, telling how they'd encountered the convoy, and finally how they'd been captured. Then she said, "The captain of the *Neptune* put a prize crew aboard, and the prizemaster was a young lieutenant named Hawke."

Winslow noted that Charity was gripping her hands so tightly they were white. "Well, my dear, I don't believe I recognize that name."

Charity swallowed, and went on. "You don't know that name, Mr. Winslow, but you know the man. He is your son—Paul Winslow!"

A cry broke from the lips of Dorcas Winslow, and her face drained of color. "No! It can't be so!"

Winslow's countenance was white, but he admonished, "Sit down, Dorcas, before you fall." He waited until she sank into a chair, her eyes fixed on Charity, before he spoke. "I don't understand you, Miss Alden. Our son an English naval officer? You must be mistaken."

Charity protested strongly, "No, sir, I'm not mistaken. He . . . still has the scar from the blow I gave him." She flushed at that, but forced herself to be calm. "It was a shock for me to see him—so I can't begin to understand what it must be for you."

"But—how did it happen? Why hasn't he come back to us?"

Charity looked at Paul's mother. She had never seen the woman behave with anything less than iron control—but that was gone now. Her face was twitching, tears running unheeded down her cheeks.

"I must tell you something," Charity hurriedly went on. "Paul is alive. He was brought on board the *Neptune* by a press gang; he'd been badly injured—and not just in body. . . ."

The couple hung on her words as she related how Paul had completely lost his memory. Then under their questions, she told the rest of it—how he'd become an officer and was engaged to the daughter of a British captain.

"But, why didn't he come here?" Charles asked when she was finished. "You told him about us, so he *knows* we're his family."

"Yes, but he's a British officer. If he were caught here, he'd be arrested."

"Of course," Winslow nodded. He put his head in his hands, his voice breaking as he cried, "And I *can't* go to him—not with this foot!"

"Miss Alden, you must go back and persuade him to come!" Dorcas Winslow had risen and come to stand beside Charity. She held out trembling hands. "I must see him! Oh, God! I must have my son!"

Charles, too, voiced his opinion, but was more reasonable. "I realize it would be dangerous, but a thought has come to me. If

Paul comes here and sees all of us—might it not jar his memory? I mean, he's not seen anything familiar. But if he were here with us . . . ?"

"I don't know about that, Mr. Winslow."

"Will you try? He can wear his old clothes—and he'll have his papers! We can send it all. He'll just be Paul Winslow on a journey home from New York."

"Please do this for us!" Dorcas sobbed. "I know he'll remember us when we get him here!"

Charity was not certain he would, but she only said, "I'll do what I can. But he'll have to make the decision."

"I'll get his things!" Dorcas dashed out the door eagerly, her face alive with hope.

"Tell me more about Paul, please, Miss Alden," Charles begged quietly, and he sat there intently as she told him how he behaved, including how he had saved her life. He listened avidly, and his sharp eye did not miss the warmth that came into the girl's face as she spoke of his son.

Finally when she halted, he responded, his penetrating eyes fixed on hers, "I believe you are telling me that my son is a better man now than he was before." He ignored her protest, and continued thoughtfully. "Paul was a spoiled child. He had too much, and that was my fault. It would be good to believe that we could have the best of all possible worlds."

She grasped at his meaning. "You mean, have his memory return, but not lose this—this better spirit?"

"You are quick, Charity." He put his hand on hers. "Tell him we love him. Tell him we want him home! This is his place. He is a part of the House of Winslow!"

"I'll—I'll tell him, Mr. Winslow, but it may not work out. Things don't, for the most part."

She had told him of the death of her father and the loss of their ship, and now the doubt and fear showed in her smooth face.

Winslow felt her grief, and he spoke earnestly. "You know my brother and his family. They are all devout believers. Not like me. I'm a nominal church member." His lips twisted sadly, and he shook his head in disgust. "I heard a preacher once say, 'God deliver us from half-baked Christians!' Well, that's what I am—but I have always known that God is much larger than my thought of Him, for I've seen it in Adam and Molly. Nathan and his wife are probably the same."

"They are! When my brother died at Valley Forge, I'd have died with grief if they hadn't helped me with their faith!"

"Yes, I know. They have *something*, don't they? Well, I'm an impious man—but I am convinced that God didn't save my son, then put you in his way, then get him back to this country *by accident*! No, Charity, God is in this! Now, you go tell my son to come, and we'll see God do the rest of it—give him his memory back and restore him to his family and his place!"

CHAPTER TWENTY

THE TRAP

★ ★ ★ ★

Charity made the trip to New York quickly, but filled with apprehension. She had no desire to get involved with the family of Charles Winslow, yet there seemed to be no way out of taking the message. *I'll tell him what they said—and after that I'll pull out of the whole thing,* she promised herself as she got off the coach and made her way to the dock.

The sight of *The Gallant Lady* in the repair yard saddened her, and she forced herself not to think of how much the ship had meant to her. Paul had been aboard waiting when she had left for Boston, but the dockmaster told her that he had gone back on board the *Neptune*, anchored a half mile away. She made her way to that section of the harbor and waited until the captain's gig came ashore, and she saw Lieutenant Burns stepping out onto the dock.

She approached him as he walked away from the gig. "Lieutenant Burns?"

He turned at once and touched his hat. "Yes, miss?—why, it's you—Miss Alden!" His homely face lit up with a smile and he strode to her at once, adding, "I'm glad to see ye, miss."

"Thank you, Lieutenant." She offered her hand, saying, "I never had an opportunity to thank you for your thoughtfulness— and I do so now. You were so kind when I lost my father!"

"Nothin' at all, Miss Alden," he protested. "I only wish I could have done more."

"Would you be able to do me a small service?"

"Anything, Miss Alden!"

"I need to have a word with Lieutenant Hawke. Would there be any way you could get a message to him?"

"Certainly there is!" he nodded vigorously. "I'll be goin' right back to the ship as soon as I make one call in town. Just tell me where you'll be, and I'll tell Mr. Hawke."

"I'll be at the Eagle Inn—right over there."

"Shouldna be over a couple o' hours, miss. Captain Rommey's been generous with us aboot shore leave. We'll be shippin' out in a week, so he thought we might like to see a little o' America. Weel, I'll hurry on now—the Eagle, is it?"

"Yes, and thank you so very much!"

The officer scurried off, and for the next hour Charity walked along the beach, noting that the harbor was a forest of masts—most of them English warships. The fleet of England was the mightiest in the world, and she wondered how the tiny nation seeking a birth could ever survive matched against such a force.

She was several hundred yards down the beach when she saw Burns return, get in the gig, and set out for the warship. Less than an hour later, the gig pulled away from the *Neptune* and she saw Winslow in the prow looking landward. She hurried toward the dock and waited with mixed emotions as she saw him step out on the dock. There were eight men pulling the oars, and after catching her eye, Winslow turned to his men, ordering, "Those of you with overnight leave better not get so drunk you can't get back to the ship tomorrow—or you'll find yourself carrying my bag up the mast." He waited for the "aye" that came rather reluctantly from the men, then turned and walked toward her.

"Lookee, there, Sullivan! Blimey! If 'e ain't gone and got hisself another dolly!" Oscar Grimes kept his beady black eyes fixed on the couple as he got out of the gig. His stiff black hair was pasted down with grease, and he was dressed in his "town" clothing.

"He's a ladies man, right enough," the hulking Irishman agreed, staring avidly at the figure of the woman. "But I ain't got no doubts about findin' meself one that good, Grimes. Let's get to the liquor and the gals!"

Ordinarily Grimes would have joined Sullivan at the fleshpots, but he was a man capable of storing up hatred like a miser stores his gold. He had never forgotten how Hawke had treated him and his friend Sullivan; in fact, the memory had grown over the months until now there was a hatred like a fiery coal in the brutal mind of the seaman. Very rarely can a common seaman find any way to revenge himself on an officer, but an idea had leaped into his mind.

"You go on, Sullivan," he suggested, a crafty smile twisting his lips. "I got me another sort of pleasure in mind."

Sullivan stared at him, shifted his gaze to the officer and the girl, who were headed toward one of the inns, and grinned. "Oscar," he told him, "you ain't hard to figure out. You're gonna get some goodies on Hawke—then see that the captain's daughter gets wind of it, right?"

"I dunno—but I'll find some way to get some of me own back on him, blast 'is eyes!"

Sullivan shrugged his heavy shoulders. "You can get burned playin' with fire—but I know it won't do no good to talk to you when you see a chance to do him dirty. I'm out of it!"

Grimes scowled at him, turned abruptly, and followed Hawke and the woman. He kept well back out of sight, and when they entered an inn with a picture of an eagle on the sign, he found a spot down the street where he could remain invisible, yet see the door. "Guess they'll be goin' upstairs for their fun," he muttered. "But I'll get the goods on 'em!"

He was surprised when, twenty minutes later, Hawke came out alone and headed for the dock. "Wot's this?" he scowled. He watched to see if the woman came out, but she did not. Baffled, he kept Hawke in sight and saw him walk rapidly to the wharf and leap into the gig. He grew angry with frustration, for the situation seemed to offer no possibilities for revenge. He skulked about the street, still waiting for the woman to come out. He got a drink from a bar and took it outside to continue his watch, but finally gave it up and started to find Sullivan.

At that moment he looked across the harbor and saw the *Neptune*'s gig making for shore again with Hawke in the bow. He hid himself as he watched the officer come in sight—and saw that he was carrying a bag. He entered the inn and did not come out again.

"I'll bet the blighter went and got leave!" Grimes mused out loud. Slowly a grin split his face. "He's movin' ashore, sure as Sunday, to be with that gal. Now I'll git 'im for sure!" He was prepared for a long wait, but it was a pleasure for him to think about the damage he could do the officer. He was so caught up with his plans to ruin Hawke that when a man came out of the Eagle an hour later, he almost missed it. Only when the woman came out did he cast a startled glance at the man—and his mind reeled when he saw that the well-dressed civilian was Hawke.

"Wot's this?" he gasped. "Wot's 'e up to out of 'is uniform?"

He followed the couple as they made their way out of the harbor to a red barn-like building located on what seemed to be a main road. Grimes couldn't read, but he asked a man who was passing by, "Wot place is that, do yer say?"

"That's the coach station" was the answer. "Coaches out of New York all leave from here. You pay for your seat in there."

Grimes stared at the building uncertainly, noting that the pair had entered. But they were out almost at once and went to a small inn facing the red building. "Well, wot they up to? Leavin' town?" A light burned in his beady eyes, and he snapped his fingers. "Blimey! He's gonna take that little wench away from here—get away from where he's known!"

He was certain this was the way of it, but he was stymied as to what to do next. Finally he moved carefully down the street and entered the coach station. An elderly man with silver hair looked up from the desk. "You need a seat?"

"Why, no—not fer meself—see, wot I need is to find out if a man has already been here—and bought a seat."

"What's his name?"

"Why—that's the trouble!" Grimes was thinking fast, and he was a quick-witted fellow. "Me captain told me to check the station and see if one of our officers had already left—but I forgot 'is bleedin' name!"

The old man shook his head. "No naval officers have bought seats today."

"Well—maybe 'e wouldn't be wearing 'is uniform, seeing as 'e was on leave."

The clerk thought, then shook his head. "There are only five people on the coach that leaves for Boston—and there's no other coach until tomorrow. There's a woman with two small children and one couple—a man and a woman."

"Was the man a dandy sort of fellow—sort of dark and well set up?"

"Why, yes, he was. Said his name was Paul Winslow. You could find him down the street, I think. The coach will leave in an hour."

Grimes nodded and headed out the door, muttering, "Now— I dunno wot to do with this. Why would 'e change 'is name? Just to cover up 'is tracks, I reckon—but how the devil can I get the proof on 'im? They won't never take my word against 'is—not likely!"

His mind raced, and he stood there baffled. Just as he was ready to give it up, he remembered something he had heard one of the officers say: *If there's trouble with the men on shore, it'll be handled by the commandant's office—a Major Locke. He's Army—but he takes care of discipline problems—sort of a policeman.*

Grimes scurried off quickly, and by the simple expedient of asking an army officer, discovered the location of Major Locke's office. He went in with his hat in his hand, more than a little frightened at what he was about to do, but the hatred he had for Hawke kept him going.

He told a sergeant in an outer office that he had secret information for the major, which was evidently a common thing. He was taken to a larger office, and soon the English officer—a smallish man with a thin moustache and penetrating gray eyes—had pumped him dry.

"So this Lieutenant Hawke is now going by the name of Paul Winslow?"

"Aye, sir, and I gotter say 'e ain't never been no *regular* officer, if you know wot I mean!"

Locke listened, and although Grimes had no way of knowing, the principal job of the officer was not the discipline of unruly troops so much as secret service operations. The English were in the midst of an enemy people, and the Americans had developed an effective method of obtaining and passing along military information. It was, Locke had learned, not so much a formal organization as a loosely joined group who were as hard to pin down as running water.

He listened as Grimes spoke of how Hawke had come aboard, and thought with a shock, *What a clever way to get one of their men inside our service!* He rejected the idea at once as being too complicated and totally unrealistic, but he was determined to run the matter down.

"I'll see about this, Grimes. I can find you on the *Neptune*? Well, you keep what you've told me quiet—and that's an order."

"Right, sir. I was just doin' me duty!"

Locke waved the man out impatiently, and as soon as he was gone, called out, "Sergeant, get Mackley in here at once." He leaned back in his chair, staring at the wall until a nondescript man in civilian clothes came and stood before him. "I have something for you, John. Probably not worth much, but I don't think we can ignore it." He gave the details as he had gotten them from Grimes, and ordered, "Get going. The Boston coach leaves in less than an hour. Find out about this fellow."

"Take him in, sir? Might be a bit touchy, you know. I mean Boston is packed with rebels."

Locke frowned. "You're right, of course—but take McCoy with you, out of uniform, of course. The two of you should be able to get the fellow out of Boston. Use your judgment, John. These blasted Americans know every move we make before *we* do. If the man's a spy, he's in a position to do us tremendous damage—an officer on board one of His Majesty's ships! Think of it!"

"I'll be on the coach." Mackley turned and hurried out of the room. The major went to the window and saw him moving rapidly along the streets. "He'll be a clever fellow if he gets by Mackley!" he muttered with satisfaction.

★ ★ ★ ★

Hawke had been expecting a message from Charity, but when he got inside the Eagle Inn, he was taken aback by her proposal. He listened carefully while she told in detail of her meeting with his family, but shook his head at once when she told of their plea for him to come to Boston.

"That would be too dangerous," he replied immediately.

"But not if you went as Paul Winslow," she urged. "I've brought your clothes and plenty of papers. After all, you *are* Paul Winslow, so if we're stopped, what can they say?"

He hesitated, shaking his head doubtfully, "The ship will be leaving soon. I might not be able to get back—besides, I'm not sure it's the best thing—I mean, for my family."

"They love you—that's what your father told me to tell you." She studied his face, not missing the longing in his dark eyes, and she put her hand on his arm. "Do this one thing for them, Paul. You'll never be at peace until you do!"

He smiled at her, saying quickly, "You know me too well, Charity. For that is what's been on my mind." He thought rapidly, then replied, "I'll have to go back to the ship and get leave. You wait here, and I'll see if it's possible."

He had gone back and, as he expected, he found Captain Rommey willing to grant his request—but somewhat surprised. Blanche was not there, having gone to the country house to be with her mother, where they stayed when the ship was anchored in America. "You'll go by and check with her, of course?"

"I have a short trip to make, sir, but as soon as I return, I'll make my apologies."

"Well, take ten days," Rommey suggested. "You deserve it, Hawke. I feel we'll be having some hard service when we ship out again—perhaps we won't touch shore until this mess is over in America."

"Goodbye, sir, and thank you."

He had hurried back to the inn, changed clothes, and a few hours later, Winslow and Charity were on the Boston coach. It was a fast journey, and the coach was crowded. A burly man propped himself upright and went to sleep at once. A young woman with two children who were difficult to handle furnished some diversion. Charity, seeing her dilemma, took over as playmate for the two girls, allowing the exhausted mother to rest.

A small man, who gave his name as Samuel Wilkins, said little at first, but as the trip went on, he and Paul talked from time to time. At one of the stops for the night, they were forced to share a bed in a very dirty inn, and Wilkins remarked with a smile, "Not much your habit, Mr. Winslow. I can see you're used to better accommodations."

Before he thought, Paul answered, "On the contrary, this is not bad at all. It's about ten times as large as my cabin aboard ship."

He bit his tongue, but Wilkins did not react; and when Winslow added, "Oh, well, when we travel on a ship, we all have to take small space," he breathed a sigh of relief. He determined to say nothing more to the man, and managed to keep to his vow.

They got to Boston in the late afternoon and Winslow stepped down, giving a hand to the young mother and to Charity. Wilkins left immediately, and Charity and Paul rented a buggy from the stable that served as coach station. As he drove the team along the road that led out of town, she observed, "You drive well; you've done it before."

He looked at her and shrugged. "Yes, it's familiar—but I guess most men can drive a team."

They didn't speak again, except when Charity gave him directions. He was in a concentrated study, thinking of the strangeness of his position and wondering what the next hour would bring.

Finally they drew up in front of the big house, and he looked carefully at it, noting the huge pillars and the ornate structure. He said nothing, but got down and helped Charity out of the buggy. He tied the reins to a post, turned and took her arm, and they walked to the door. But before he knocked, he faced her and said, "Charity, no matter what turn my life takes, I want you to know how much you've meant to me."

She stared at him, her heart beating faster as he reached out and took her hands in his. "Oh, Paul—I've done nothing!"

"Not true," he murmured. He shook his head and gave her a fond look, and there was a quality in his voice—gentle and longing—that he'd never used with her. "You can't know what it's been like—being what I am. No past at all. No friend to think of from the old days. But you've helped to fill that gap. We *are* friends— aren't we, Charity?"

"Oh yes, Paul!" she responded quickly and squeezed his hands. She felt such compassion for him at that moment, yet she realized it was not altogether pity, for her heart would not race so madly if that were all. She tried to speak, but could not. Instead, she reached up, pulled his head down and kissed him. Then she gave a short laugh and dashed the tears from her eyes. "Now, don't you dare say *that* kiss was your fault, Paul Winslow! And you just remember, no matter what happens, we'll not lose each other!"

His eyes were moist as he lifted the knocker on the door. When it opened, he was confronted with a small, thin black woman who stared at him with eyes that widened like moons in her dark face. Her jaw dropped and she cried out, "Lord God! It's Mistuh Paul!"

She swayed for a moment, then whirled and ran down the hall, crying out, "Mistuh Charles! Mistuh Charles! It's you boy! He's done come back from the grave!"

Paul was unnerved by the scene, and he gave Charity a nervous smile. "I guess this *is* the right place!"

Soon the woman came back, saying breathlessly, "Go on to the study, Mistuh Paul—you folks is dere!"

Charity felt her arm gripped so tightly that it was painful, and looking up she saw Paul's ashen face. The strain made him compress his lips until they were a thin line, with beads of perspiration across his brow.

"Do you remember the way to the study, Paul?" she asked.

"No! I can't even *think*, Charity!"

"It's this way." She led him down the hall and Cory reached out and touched his arm as they passed, whispering, "Thank you, Jesus! Thank you, Jesus!"

The door was open, and Charity heard Paul take a deep breath as they went through it. She got a quick glimpse of the family—all looking as if they were posing for a portrait. Charles sat in his chair with his foot raised, his eyes wide; Dorcas stood by his side with her mouth twitching; Martha sat on the edge of a hard-backed chair, her dim eyes peering at the man who stood before them. And Anne, grown into a young woman with the Winslow look, stared at her brother silently.

"My boy!" Charles cried brokenly, "you're alive!"

He held out his hands and Paul moved across the room to take them. He may have intended to shake hands, but Charles gave a sob and reached up and pulled him down into an embrace. Charity saw that the cold formalism was broken; Charles Winslow was a man who prided himself on never showing emotion, but now his face was twisted as if in pain, though she knew it was joy. Tears ran down his cheeks and his eyes were tightly shut. He kept saying, "Thank God! Thank God! You're alive!"

Then he released his grip, and Paul straightened up in time to catch his mother, who fell against him, weeping, and she was soon joined by Anne and Martha. Paul stood like a statue, not knowing what to do with his hands. But Charles, wiping his eyes, saw his embarrassment.

"Dorcas, let the boy alone—and you, too, Anne and Mother!" He spoke roughly to cover the emotion that had welled up in him. Gazing up at Paul, he tried to smile as he said, "Well, sir, Charity has told us of your affliction. You must forgive us—because though you don't remember us, we remember you."

"I understand," Paul replied. He looked into the face of his father, then to his mother, his sister, and grandmother. "Somehow I feel as if I'm being very unfair—not knowing you."

"No, you mustn't think that!" Charles protested. "It's been horrible for you, Paul, but certainly not your fault." Turning to his wife, he sputtered, "Well, don't just stand there! Give the boy a chair, Dorcas—and one for Charity."

There was a bustle as the chairs were brought and everyone was seated. An awkward silence fell on the room as they stared speechless at Paul. He laughed lightly, attempting to break the stilted atmosphere. "I feel like a prize exhibit at the county fair, sir!"

"I don't wonder!" Charles exclaimed. "But let me look at you. You're so brown. And I've never seen you looking fitter!"

"You look so handsome, Paul!" Anne burst out in wonder. "I

wish I could see you in your uniform!"

"That will have to come later, Annie," Charles stated gently. Then he turned back to his son, feasting his eyes on him hungrily—as if he could never get enough of the sight of him. "Now, tell us everything! You can't think how we've grieved over you—and now you're here! I don't ever intend to doubt the mercies of the Almighty again!"

With a certain trepidation, Paul spoke, telling them of his recovery. They all listened avidly—drinking in the details, exclaiming over some of his trials and smiling in appreciation over the tale of his rise from seaman to lieutenant.

Finally he stopped and uttered, with a short laugh, "I can't tell you how strange I feel."

"Do you recognize anything at all, son?" Dorcas asked quietly. "Any of us? Anything at all?"

He looked at her, saying carefully, "It's so hard to tell. I—I seem to feel *different*. But this is so strange and bizarre—it could be that."

He seemed despondent, and Charles broke in hastily, "You're tired. Why don't you rest, and we'll have a good dinner—and you must stay, too, Charity!"

She protested, but he overrode her and held his hand out. When she rose to take it, he pulled her down and kissed her, saying with a twinkle in his eye, "I'm getting to be as emotional as a Methodist! But I just don't feel responsible—everything is so bright!"

At that moment there was a knock on the door and Cory stepped in with an angry expression on her face. She was stuttering with rage, trying to say something, but was roughly pushed aside by a short man, who was followed by a burly man in a black coat.

"Who the devil are you?" Charles demanded. "What are you doing in my house?"

"Mr. Charles Winslow?"

"That is my name!"

"My name is John Mackley. I am an officer of His Majesty's forces. My superior is Major Charles Locke."

The room had grown ominously quiet, and suddenly Paul cried, "Why, I know this man—his name is Wilkins!"

"That is not my real name—just as your real name is not Hawke." He stared at Paul coldly. "You needn't deny it—for we have proof that you are indeed Paul Winslow. He is your son, is he not, Mr. Winslow?"

"I won't answer any of your questions! Get out of this house!"

"I am leaving—but I am taking him with me." He turned to Paul and announced, "In the name of our Royal Sovereign, I arrest you, Paul Winslow."

"On what charges?" Charles broke in.

"On the charge of high treason."

A deadly silence fell, and then Mackley declared, "I'll have to ask you to come, Winslow."

"You can't take him!" Charles protested loudly. "This is Boston, not New York. You have no authority here!"

"This is my authority, Mr. Winslow." Mackley drew a pistol from beneath his coat, and the other man did as well. "We have a carriage outside, and if you try to stop us—or have us stopped—the first bullet will go into this young man's brain." He glanced at the large man, and added quietly, "See to that, will you, McCoy?"

"I'll shoot him at the first sign of trouble, sir."

Charles started to protest, his face pale, but Paul stepped forward, "No use, sir. I'll have to go."

"Well, try not to worry," Charles said quickly. "It's all a mistake. We'll get lawyers—"

"It will be a military court, sir," Mackley interrupted. "No civilians will be admitted to the court martial. Put the irons on him, McCoy."

He spoke sharply and McCoy drew a set of heavy manacles from his coat and fastened them on Paul's wrists. Paul looked at the others, saying sadly, "I'm sorry I've caused you such trouble—twice now."

As they left, led by Mackley, Dorcas collapsed on the chair, trembling in every limb—and weeping helplessly. "It's my fault! I never should have asked him to come! Charles, we must *do* something!"

Her husband replied quietly, "We must try—but I know these courts, and the way things are now in this country, he doesn't have a chance."

"Will they . . . hang him, Father?" Anne asked weakly.

He did not answer, his body slumped in the chair, his face a picture of abject fear and hopelessness—his son alive, and now facing certain death! Charity looked at him with compassion and murmured gently, "I'll go now. Call on me if I can help."

Charles stared at her blindly, and whispered hoarsely, "Only God can help, Charity! Only God!"

The next day, Charles had himself carried to a large coach that had been fitted with a bed. He had asked Charity alone to go with him, insisting that his family stay at home. His lips were white with pain as the carriage bumped over the road, but he uttered no word of complaint.

A week later he returned, weak and grim, and was helped back into the house by two servants. They put him in the study, and as soon as they were gone, Dorcas asked, "What happened?"

Anne was there, and Martha, the old woman looking as grieved as the rest of them. Paul had been her prize, and now he was gone. She sat rigid, her eyes fixed on her son.

"It's not death," Charles explained, but when they all gave a glad cry, he held up his hand. "No, listen to me—it's not death. Captain Rommey saved him—so they say. I wasn't there, but we heard that it was the captain's plea that kept the court from handing down the death penalty."

Burns had sat in on the court, and he had sought Charity and Charles out to give them the verdict. "He's nae goin' to die—but it's prison for life."

"Dartmoor?" Charity whispered.

"Yes, I'm afraid so." Burns bit his lip, and there was real grief in his eyes. "They're wrong! Wrong! There's nae treason in him! But he is an American who put on a British uniform—and that's all the court could see."

"Can we go to him?" Charles asked.

"No, sir—they say not. Some of the members of the court are still screaming. Your son will get to Dartmoor with a bad recommendation, I fear." Then he added, "But God is still merciful. I am goin' to pray that somehow this will nae be the end o'it."

Now sitting before his family, it was all Charles could do to hold back the tears, but he was a Winslow. He said adamantly, "We will not give up. We'll spend every penny, pull every string! I will have my son back again!"

Dorcas stared at her husband, for she had never seen him so determined. Neither had his mother. Martha Winslow had always known that Charles was not a man of character—that was why she had hated her stepson Adam. Now she said quietly, "God keep you strong, son!"

Dorcas stared at her husband incredulously, and then Charles drew himself up and repeated quietly but with an intensity that had never manifested itself in his life: "I will have my son back again!"

CHAPTER TWENTY-ONE

THE GATHERING OF THE CLAN

★ ★ ★ ★

"Get up! Get up!" The guard's voice echoed in the filthy hold of the frigate *Mantigo*. Paul gathered his belongings and joined the line of prisoners that waited for the door to open. The voyage from New York to Plymouth had been slow, for the ship was old. He had not complained, but others who had found the moldy ship's biscuit and rotten beef uneatable were chastised.

A short, muscular seaman with tattoos everywhere but his face laughed gruffly at them. "Yer don't like this grub? Wait till yer gets to Dartmoor! This'll look like a piece of cake! Why, a fine, prime rat goes for ten shillin's, and no lack of bidders!"

They were taken to the berth deck, then put ashore in a drizzle of cold October rain that seemed to freeze the marrow of Paul's bones. In spite of the early hour as they passed through the town, they found themselves surrounded by drunken sailors out of grog shops, old women carrying jugs of ale and baskets full of cakes, fried eels and boiled sheep's heads. Devon farmers in corduroy breeches and red vests that dropped halfway down their fat thighs stared at the ragged prisoners, colorless from the lack of sun.

The escort was a troop of Devonshire militiamen. As they left the city the wind roared down the abrupt roadways, and rain began to soak their tattered garments. It beat the road into a brown river of mud that sucked at their feet; and when one of the prisoners fell, he was prodded to his feet, shivering in every joint.

All morning they plodded, laboring up range after range of the rolling hills until finally, just when Paul was about ready to drop, they came to a long hill. Its top was lost in fog and rain, and there were massive granite-like knobs jutting out, as if God had stuck it together as an afterthought.

He caught the word "Dartmoor," and asked one of the round-faced militiamen, "Is this Dartmoor?"

"Aye, Dartmoor" was the answer. They crawled like blind insects upward until finally late in the afternoon they came to a halt; there below was a circular mass of granite, a sort of giant millstone. Paul stared down at it, then lurched drunkenly down the slope, a mud-caked scarecrow, not caring much whether he lived or died.

Prodded by the militiamen, the bedraggled group entered the huge gate and was immediately surrounded by guards with muskets. Soon the troop escort from Devon was on its way back to the coast, and a florid-faced, hook-nosed man with tiny eyes and a cruel mouth came to look at the prisoners. After a quick glance he snorted, "What's Snyder thinkin' of to send me a hundred prisoners—and me with nine thousand crammed in like sardines? Well, give them hammocks, blankets and mattresses. Oh, mess equipment, too, and spun yarn for slingin' their hammocks."

After receiving their gear, they stumbled forward, pushed by the sharp bayonets of the guards. Paul expected Dartmoor to be a warren of small cells, but suddenly he was pushed into an enormous room, with colonnades of slender posts extending from floor to ceiling along the length of it. Everywhere men were squatting around kettles in groups of six—eating, drinking, laughing, and shouting. Among them were flickering candles whose beams seemed to make their garments and faces appear yellow.

The newcomers were pushed into the room, most of them falling instantly to the floor, exhausted. Even as they fell, Paul saw the old prisoners begin to creep toward them, and a skeleton of a man began to go through the pockets of one of the new arrivals. *Got to stay on my feet!* he thought. *If I go down, they'll take all I have.* He had a knapsack stuffed with food and trading items, given to him by Burns the last time they'd met.

"Hang on to this, Hawke," Burns warned, calling him by his old name. "Ye'll need it in Dartmoor—and do nae give up on God!"

The words echoed in Paul's mind, but as he staggered around the hellish room, he almost thought that God had given up on *him*. But just when he was about to collapse, he felt a hand on his arm. He whirled around to fight off an attack—and found himself looking into the face of Daniel Greene!

"I've been looking for thee, Friend Paul," he greeted with a smile that gleamed in the semidarkness. "We got word of the trial—and I figured they'd send thee here."

"Dan? You're here?" Paul's mind was blurred, and the words came from his lips in a slur.

"Here, come with me—thee is about past going."

He took Paul's arm with a powerful hand and steered him to a stone stairway, then into a room filled with faces. He recognized some of the men—Thad Alden and Laurence Conrad among them. Weeding their way through the mass of humanity, Dan finally pushed Paul into a corner where he fell onto a straw-stuffed mattress and passed into unconsciousness.

It was no lighter when he awoke. He rubbed his eyes, trying to get his bearings. Fear gripped his confused mind as he began to remember. He sat up quickly and heard a voice. "Well, sir, you've finally come out of it. I thought you were waiting for the general resurrection of the dead!"

Paul squinted in the dimness and found the long face of Laurence Conrad peering at him. The tall man was even more cadaverous than Winslow remembered. "Have some grub," he offered, and then with his usual mixture of pessimism and cheer, remarked, "If it don't kill you, boy, it'll keep you alive for a time."

Paul found he was ravenous, and gobbled down the food without inquiring into the contents. He drank tepid water from a stone jug, taking huge gulps before setting it down. Ashamed at his crude manners, he said, "Well, thanks for the food, Laurence. I guess I was pretty hungry."

"Might as well get used to that," Laurence stated. "You'll spend most of your time trying to find grub." He nodded at the knapsack. "I kept an eye on your kit—and you'd better do the same."

Paul looked around and asked, "All of you in here—you're from *The Gallant Lady*?"

"Most of us—the rest are from our part of America. We don't trust each other much—but we don't trust anybody else at all."

"Well, if you hadn't helped me, that food would have been gone—so it belongs to the crew—all of you. And I'd like to be a part of it—if the men will have me."

Conrad stared at him with a peculiar intensity. Then he shook his head and remarked dryly, "Just when I convince myself that mankind is no blasted good—totally depraved—somebody like you has to come along and ruin my theology."

Dan Greene came over to the corner and sat down beside Conrad. "Well, thee is among the living again," he nodded to Paul.

"Maybe, but he's not in his right mind," Laurence answered with a shrug. "He just donated all his goods to our little group."

Greene gave Paul a thoughtful look. "Well, two is better than one—and a threefold cord is not easily broken." He slapped Paul on the shoulder, saying, "I'm sorry thee is here—but in this place no man can live without friends."

Paul was embarrassed, and replied nonchalantly, "Why, it's nothing. I'm grateful to you." He picked up the bag and hefted it. "There's gold in here—courtesy of Angus Burns."

"Gold! Good Lord!" Laurence exclaimed in a low voice. "Don't say a word to anybody, man!"

Paul looked at him strangely and asked, "Gold is rare here?"

"It'll get you anything you want," Conrad divulged. "Even a woman, so they say."

"Not anything, Laurence," Greene broke in. "It won't get you freedom."

Paul gave him a searching look. "I—I'd hoped it would help make an escape possible."

Conrad and Greene exchanged quick glances and Greene commented, "We wondered how long it'd take before thee got to that."

"We all get to that point, Winslow," Conrad explained. "But it won't pay to dwell on the subject. Nobody gets out of here alive."

"Nobody? Not even one or two?"

Greene stared at Paul and shook his head. "Well, there were a couple of cases—or so I'm told. But they all had one thing in common."

Paul waited for him to finish, and when he hesitated, Winslow inquired, "What did they have in common, Dan?"

Greene bit his lip and shrugged his shoulders. "They all had plenty of help from the outside—wealthy friends who were willing to pay any price to get them sprung. Which leaves all of us out, Paul."

"You have any relatives with a fortune they'd like to throw away on your worthless carcass, Winslow?" Conrad regarded the younger man with interest. "Your newfound father—he's got money, hasn't he?"

Paul thought of Charles Winslow, but he shook his head. "No."

He knew that as a Tory, the Americans would have frozen Winslow's assets, if not actually seizing them. "No, there's nobody out there who'd be able to redeem me."

Greene and Conrad heard the sadness beneath his steady tone, and Conrad said softly, dropping a friendly hand on Paul's shoulder, "Well, the good part of it is, my boy, if we die in this place, we won't have to go out and fight another war with the lousy British for our freedom, will we now?"

Greene was more sober, and urged, "It's no good thinking about freedom, Paul. I've found that out in the short time I've been here. The old-timers have lots of stories about men that go crazy thinking all the time about getting out. The way to beat this thing is just to ride with it. This war will end, and then they'll let us go."

"Not me," Paul informed them. "My sentence is for life—the penalty for treason." He stood up and looked around at the mass of men in the cell and remarked, "The rest of you have a chance of getting out of here. I have none. So I won't be able to stop thinking about escape."

"God help you, my boy," Conrad nodded sadly. "For nobody else will."

Winslow stood up and surveyed the cell, then walked to the end and gazed out on the massive room that held the rest of the prisoners, noting the thin, mean, pock-marked faces. There were ugly features, gray-looking even in the yellow light of the candles, and gaunt. All wore yellow rags and some nothing but a piece of cloth twisted around their loins.

He came back to stand before his two friends, and stated quietly, "I may go to hell when I die—but I'll die before I spend the rest of my life in this hell on earth." His lean face grew utterly serious and he added, "There's nobody out there who can help me—so I'll have to do it myself."

★　★　★　★

Paul had no way of determining that a small group across the sea had already come together, bent on getting him out of Dartmoor. Originally they had not met with the purpose of getting him free, but rather to ease another Winslow out of the world.

Charity had been drawn into the world of Charles Winslow's family almost against her will. She discovered that her own life was empty, and after several days of cleaning the old house on the sea, she welcomed a message from Charles: "My mother is ill. Could you help Anne and Dorcas with her?"

She had gone at once, and found her services almost hysterically welcomed. It was obvious that Martha Winslow was dying, and neither of the women knew what to do—in fact, they were both stricken with fear at the coming event. They had almost grabbed at Charity when she arrived, and from that time both of them depended on her desperately.

After two days, Charles came into his mother's room where Charity was sitting beside her, reading the Bible aloud. He sat down, his foot much better but still tender; and when she paused, he waved her on. She was reading in the Gospels, and his gaze never left her face. When she finally put the Bible on the table, he remarked, "You've been a blessing, Charity. I was afraid for Dorcas and Anne. They have no experience in this sort of thing. You're so calm. How did you learn to handle sickness and death?"

She bit her lip and answered quietly, "At Valley Forge. I don't like to think about that time. Every day—almost every *hour*—men died, most of them just boys. I never got used to it, but I learned to last through it."

Charles put his hand on his mother's and murmured, "She's going to die, isn't she?"

"I think so, Charles." The elderly woman had been ill for a long time, but a week earlier she'd been found unconscious on her bedroom floor, struck down by a stroke, they assumed.

"I've sent for Adam. He should be here any time." He looked at the Bible and asked, "Do you read the Bible to her often? She doesn't hear you, does she?"

"I don't really know, but when my brother Curtis was dying at Valley Forge, Julie would read to him for hours as he lay in a coma. When he woke up, I think it had somehow been . . . heard. It sounds odd, but Julie said there's a verse that reads: 'The *entrance* of thy word giveth light.' She told me that just *hearing* the Bible is a good thing. I hope so."

"All my brother's family are godly people—as you are, Charity." A painful light touched his eyes and he whispered, "I wish now I'd been more attentive to such things."

"It's not too late," Charity encouraged, adding hastily, "No, I'm not a Christian, Charles. When my father died, I cursed God. I'm not like Julie. But like you, I wish I were."

They sat silently for a long time, listening to the faint, labored breathing of Martha, punctuated by the sound of the ticking of a clock on the mantel. Finally Charles rose. "She keeps asking for Adam, have you noticed? Every time she regains consciousness, she asks for him."

"Yes. I hope he comes soon, Charles. I don't think she can last long."

Adam did come, early the next morning. His wife Molly was with him, and so were Nathan and Julie. There was a quiet meeting in the parlor, and all of them embraced Charity exactly as they did Anne. It did funny things to her heart and made her eyes sting with tears. She had no family, but somehow they had made her a part of theirs. Julie saw her tears and plopped Christmas down in Charity's lap. "There! You take care of this fat wad! He's almost worn me down." Julie was expecting again, and for the next two days Charity became a key member of the Winslow family. She helped Cory with the food and beds, she tended to Christmas, who was into everything that wasn't tied down, and she cared for Martha.

She found herself talking to Julie a great deal, for she still remembered the strength of the young woman when Curtis had died. She told her about Dan, and as she did so, a queer look came into Julie's eyes. Finally she said, "Charity, you're filled with guilt because you can't marry Dan. Well, so was *I*!" She touched her cheek and her eyes were cloudy for the first time since Charity had known her. "I loved Dan—but he would never have had all of me. Nathan had that—and if you can't give a man all of yourself, you're cheating on him even before you marry."

"But it's my fault he's in prison. If he hadn't met me, he'd never have been on that ship!"

"No, he'd probably be in a shallow grave at Princeton or Cowpens or any one of a dozen spots where our men have died. Charity, you can't blame yourself, for you can't know what God had in mind. Maybe He had Daniel on the *Lady* to keep him from getting blinded or torn apart in some battle. You don't know. All you can know is, God is good."

"I wish I believed that!"

"You will believe it someday. God has told me."

The calm statement hit her like a blow, and she got up and left the room. It angered her, somehow, when people talked in such terms, and she avoided Julie for the rest of the day.

It was almost midnight when Martha woke up for the last time. Charity was asleep in her chair, and she heard a voice calling, "Adam! Oh, Adam!" Charity sat up with a start to see the elderly woman staring open-eyed at the ceiling, her hands grasping at the counterpane.

She leaped to her feet and ran down the hall. Adam and Charles were talking quietly in front of the fire when she burst into the room, crying, "She's awake—she's calling for you, Major!"

"Go get the others, Charity," Adam urged. "Get them all."

The men walked rapidly down the hall, while Charity summoned Dorcas, Julie, Molly, and Anne from their beds. They threw on robes and hurried to the big bedchamber where Martha lay.

She was resting in Charles's arms. Adam was kneeling beside the bed, his face close to hers. Charity saw her lips move, and she heard Martha saying, ". . . was never fair to you, Adam—never!" Her voice was weak and thready, but her eyes were brighter than Charity had ever seen them.

"Don't fret, Martha," Adam assured quietly. He took her hand in both of his, and she grasped with the other until he caught that one as well.

"No, I hated you. I was jealous—wanted Charles to be first with Miles. And I made him hurt you—you know I did."

Adam pulled one hand free and removed a white handkerchief. He gently wiped the tears from her withered cheeks, remarking, "It came out all right, Martha. You must remember. Father and I became very close."

She sobbed, "Yes—and I hated that, too—I was so hateful!" She continued to weep softly. As Charity watched the scene before her, her throat ached under the strain. She wanted to run, for the old grandmother's guilt was terrible.

Finally Adam said, "Martha, you must listen to me—just lie there, and let me talk to you. . . ."

He began to speak of his own youth, and how unhappy he'd been. He told her how he'd felt left out, and then how he'd found God.

"I didn't see how God could forgive me, Martha. But Molly will tell you—she was there. I heard about Jesus and how He loved me in spite of my ways. And I called on Him—and Martha, He heard me! He forgave me! That was such a wonderful time—I can't explain how it was—but mostly it was like Bunyan's Pilgrim. I had a load of guilt that was wearing me out, but when I called on the Lord, it rolled away—and it's been gone ever since!"

She was watching him quietly, and there was a strange look in her old eyes. "Martha," he went on, "how could I not forgive *you*—

when God forgave *me*? I forgive you, dear Martha—but I want you to know more than that. Wouldn't you like to know God's forgiveness—wouldn't you like to meet Him with not a single sin or flaw in your heart?"

"Adam—I can't!"

"Yes, you must! Now, I'm going to pray, Martha, and you must pray, too, but only one prayer. Just tell God you're guilty. He knows you are. Tell Him you're not able to help yourself. He knows that, too. Then ask Him to forgive you—and ask it in the name of Jesus—He always hears that prayer. . . ."

Adam began to pray, and as he prayed Charity began to sob. She tried to stop, forcing her fist against her lips, but she could not hold it back. Through her sobs, she heard Martha Winslow calling on God in a feeble voice; then it became stronger. She heard Adam and Molly praising God. Soon she felt an arm around her, and she turned to see through her tears that Julie was there. She began to shake so violently that she could not stand, but slipped to the floor. She did not even wonder what the others might think, for something was moving inside her—a power she had never known before.

She was weeping and moaning, striking her hands against the floor. Julie touched her gently, saying, "It's your time, Charity. Remember what Curtis said? *I'll be waiting on you!* God is calling you right now. Martha has heard and answered. Now it's your turn."

Charity was filled with fear, but there was a longing such as she had never known, and she cried out, "Oh, my God, my God! Forgive me! In the name of Jesus! Help me!"

She continued to sob, but there was a difference. The fear left, and she was filled with a peace that seemed to flow over her. She felt light and free, and she knew that never again would she have the terrible emptiness and fear that had preyed on her.

As Charity rose to her feet, Nathan and Julie embraced her, both of them weeping. She saw Charles and Adam as they looked down at Martha—who had slipped away.

Charles stammered, "I—I'm glad you were here, Adam. She needed you."

"She went to meet God, Charles. I know it!"

"Yes, I know it, too." Charles brushed away the tears streaming down his face. "She was at peace—for the first time, I think. See how rested she looks—she's looked so tired for a long time."

They all left the room subdued, their hearts filled with the wonder of God's working in their lives. But the affairs surrounding death had to be carried out, so in a short while Charity prepared the body, while the rest went about the other duties.

The funeral was held the next day, with the pastor preaching a sermon. Afterward the family returned to the house that now somehow seemed so empty.

After the funeral, they were all seated around the living room and Charles announced, "I have something to say to all of you." Immediately there was a hush, and he looked around with determination in his thin face. "Mother is gone, but my son is in a prison. I want to tell all of you that until he's free, nothing else matters to me."

"Why, Charles, there's nothing to be done, is there?" Dorcas asked.

"Yes, there is and I'm going to do it. Maybe it might surprise you, Adam, but I've been reading the Scriptures myself a little bit." He smiled at his brother as he continued. "I even know a verse you may have missed."

"That's possible, Charles," Adam replied. "What's the verse?"

"It's in Ecclesiastes, chapter 10, verse 19, I believe. It says, 'Money answereth all things.' "

Adam looked curiously at him, as they all did, then asked, "I don't recall it. Does it say something to you?"

"It says that Dartmoor is like any other prison on this planet. It's run by men, and men can be bought. It's simple. I'm going to get Paul out of Dartmoor if it costs every cent I've got. If I need more, I'll steal it."

Adam shook his head. "Don't do that—steal, I mean. Your assets are frozen by the Congress until you lose your Tory ways—"

"I just lost them!" Charles interrupted. "I don't blame England for all our problems, but for whatever reason, I'm an American. I know people won't believe me, but it's the truth."

Adam stared at him, nodding slowly. "Well, *I* believe you, Charles—and I can drop a word here and there. I think we can get your property released."

This meant he himself would speak to Washington, and that was all it would take. Charles bit his lip, but said only, "I thank you, Adam."

"Nonsense!" Adam cried cheerily. "The boy's a Winslow, isn't he? Of course, we'll have him out of that place. But you can't go to

England. In the first place, you're not able—and in the second place you'd be under suspicion from the minute you set foot within a hundred miles of Dartmoor. And I can't go—nor Nathan. This war seems to be winding up to a climax, and we have to be here."

Charles looked at him, a haggard expression on his face. "I know—but *somebody* has to go!"

The room was quiet, and then without the slightest intention of doing so, Charity stated flatly, "I'm going!"

They all stared at her, and she reddened, but held her head high. "I was going anyway—to try to get Dan out of that place. I might as well get two as one."

"But, Charity, you're only a woman," Anne protested.

"I was only a woman when I was captain of a privateer, Anne, and I did that job all right. I'm going to sell my house and use the money to get Dan and Paul out."

Adam started to argue, but Julie interrupted him. "She will do it, Adam. The Lord said to me last night, 'I will deliver these men from prison—but not by the hand of man.' I didn't understand it at the time, but now I do. It'll be by the hand of a woman!"

Charles argued, "Charity! What could you do?"

"I don't know, but I'm going."

"And you're going as a Christian, aren't you, Charity?" Julie asked.

"Yes. I have given my life to God," Charity declared. Lifting her head high, she went on. "I'm only a weak woman, but God will go with me."

Charles snapped his fingers and leaped to his feet. "Of course! Adam—William! She can stay with William!"

Adam looked startled; then a smile broke across his wide lips. "That's right! His church is very close to Dartmoor!"

"Who is William?" Charity inquired, confused by this sudden burst of enthusiasm.

"William is Adam's older brother," Julie explained. "He is a Methodist minister in England, and very fond of Adam."

"He'll be risking everything, Charles," Dorcas warned.

"He'll do it! I know he will!" Charles assured, his face was alight with excitement. "Adam, how soon can you get something done about the property? I want Charity to start right away."

"I'll get on it—and I think with a little 'encouragement' in the right place, things will go pretty fast."

"I'm leaving this week," Charity added. "I can sell my house tomorrow, I know for a fact. I've already had offers."

"I can't let you do that," Charles protested.

"You can't stop me, Charles Winslow!" Charity was startled at her own boldness, but laughed, "Now you know the worst about me—I'm a stubborn female, bound to have her own way!"

"I think, Charity," Adam told her, "your way is God's way. And I want us all to pray right now for God's angels to go before you, and that our men will be delivered by the same hand that delivered two other men long ago from a jail in Asia—Paul and Silas."

"But that was in the old days!" Anne protested.

"He's the same God—yesterday, today, and forever! Now, let's pray to that God!"

As they all joined hands, Charity felt a moment of fear. But as Major Winslow bombarded heaven, the fear fled like a beaten dog, and she was convinced that God was going to England with her!

CHAPTER TWENTY-TWO

ESCAPE

★ ★ ★ ★

Paul adjusted to the rigors of Dartmoor quickly, primarily as a result of those in his mess. There were six men, including Dan, Laurence Conrad, Thad Alden, Rufus Middles, and Miles Johnson, the white-haired ex-master of the *Lady*. The sixth man was introduced to the group by Paul himself, about whom he wrote in the journal he began keeping from the first day.

Dec. 25, 1780

Christmas Day—and my third month in Dartmoor. My beard is long and full of lice, I'm down to no more than a hundred and thirty pounds, and the Christmas dinner was a chunk of cold beef, stringy and well on its way to being spoiled, washed down by a cup of flat ale—but that's nothing!

Dan and the others have been my salvation—for since I've come here, more than one of the prisoners who came with me have given up and died. They were sick when they came and never had a chance. Our mess is a little band of brothers— reminds me of the words of Henry V in Shakespeare's play: "We few, we happy few, we band of brothers!" If it hadn't been for these men, I would have been swallowed up by now, for the survivors here become beasts of prey, vultures that swarm over the weak and destroy them.

So, I'm thankful for our mess—and it grieved me when Lige Smith died last week. He was wounded when we took the *Lady*, and despite all Lester could do, the wounds worsened and he died. All the men in the mess except Laurence Conrad and I are Christians, and they took it better than us—the unbelievers. Before we took Lige's body to the guards, there was a "funeral" service, and it was like nothing I'd ever seen. Dan did the talking, and he was smiling through his tears—they all were!—and it was like saying, "We'll see you soon, Lige!"

Well, it almost sank me. I was so depressed that I could hardly eat—but yesterday, a miracle happened. (I'll have to learn to believe in miracles if I stay with this group of Christians long!) I was amazed to see Enoch Whitefield brought in with a new group of prisoners. He was just the same as ever, calm as you please. He'd left the *Neptune* and gone to be with his cousin, the famous preacher, George Whitefield. Then he'd signed on an American ship, which had been captured by the British—so here he was. I was so glad to see the poor fellow, and so sad that he was in this place, but he said, "Why, it's God's will, sir!" I proposed him as a candidate for the vacancy, and all the men were glad. Conrad had to be opposed, just to keep his status as resident cynic. "He'll want to have all of us falling to the ground like those Methodist enthusiasts. Oh, for a group of sound atheists for me to have fellowship with!"

But Conrad's a fraud. He's fascinated by these men who can have joy in their God, even in this hellish place—just as I am!

I have tried all I know to find a way out of this place. My only ray of hope was one of the guards. When he saw my gold, he made me all kinds of promises and took the money—but I never saw him again. Conrad says I was a fool, and he's right. Now I have nothing—no money at all. It's hard not to give in. All I want to do is die—better that than this place for the rest of my life!

Paul wrote the last words, closed the small notebook, then leaned forward and put his head on his knees. He was sitting alone in a corner of the large room, in the cobwebby hours of the morning. The din of a thousand voices had not yet begun—only the groans and cries from dreams came to him as he sat there. He tried to pray—something he'd been doing for weeks, without much result—and he had no sense of God. He had observed that when Dan or Enoch prayed, a smile would come to their faces, and it was like they were lifted out of the dark and squalor of Dartmoor, lifted to a place of light and music and pleasure. They could pray like that for hours, and he longed to know what it was that could make the horrors of Dartmoor grow dim.

Now as he tried to pray, he did not have a similar experience, but something came to his mind—something so different that it frightened him.

It was the face of a woman, a beautiful face. He was half asleep but totally conscious of himself. He could smell the stench of the prison, feel the dank cold air, hear the bedlam of voices that was beginning to sound—but for a few seconds in his mind a scene unrolled.

He was at a ball, and the woman in his dream was there. She was outside on a terrace kissing a man, a very tall man with blonde hair and eyes bluer than any he'd ever seen. He felt a rage in him in the dream, and he saw himself going out on the terrace, seething with anger. The woman had fair skin, rich brown hair, and her clear hazel eyes were unafraid as he rushed out to meet the two. The blue eyes of the tall man were angry, and suddenly there was a violence of some sort—and then the memory faded.

By the good Lord! Paul cried out, coming back to the present with a jerk. *I remember! I remember it!* He sat there with his heart beating, his eyes hazy with tears, for it was beyond all doubt a scene from the shadows of his past. He did not know who the man and woman were, but it was *something!*

He was still sitting in the same position when Dan came in, and he immediately told him about the experience. "I don't know who they were," he ended, "But, Dan, I *remember!*"

Dan smiled at him and said gently, "I know who they are, Paul. The man is your cousin, Nathan Winslow—and the woman is Abigail Howland. You two both courted her. Nathan himself told me about that scene. He'd had too much wine, and the two of you nearly had a brawl over the Howland girl."

"It was so *real*, Dan!"

"Praise the Lord, I believe it's a beginning, Paul. I've been praying about your loss of memory, and God's going to give you back your mind and your memory."

★ ★ ★ ★

His words had been prophetic, for in the next three weeks, all through January, flashes of scenes, bits of memory, a parade of faces came to him. He'd be almost asleep, or eating or listening to the talk of his messmates, and some face would leap into his mind clear as a painting. He told no one except Dan, but the hope of regaining his memory revived his anticipation of escape.

He threw himself into the work of making soup bones into small pieces that would serve as planks for the fashioning of ship models to be sold. After whittling at this project for a while, he realized it would take six months, and at that rate he knew he'd never make enough money to bribe anyone; so he tried plaiting straw into baskets and boxes, but despaired. One day when Enoch stopped to talk to him, Paul grumbled, "We'll never buy our way out of this place! It'll have to be something else. Maybe we can get together and break out by force."

"It's been tried—and every man was killed," Enoch informed him. "Just pray, my boy. God has you here for a purpose."

"He has me here to be eaten alive by these pesky lice?" Paul had a bitter smile on his face as he spoke, but then added, "You're beginning to sound like Angus Burns with his confounded Calvinism!"

"Well," Enoch leaned forward to stir the soup he was brewing, "the lieutenant is a pretty fair Bible scholar. I remember once in Savannah a couple of years back, my cousin George was preachin' to 'bout twenty thousand people out in the open. He read a scripture from Romans—let's see, it goes like this: *And we know that all things work together for good to them that love God, to them who are the called according to His purpose.* 'Course, I can't say it like George, but I believe it like he does."

"Why, Enoch, that doesn't make sense!" Paul cried in exasperation. "How could a good God let us wallow in this place?"

"He let Joseph stay in a jail that was probably 'bout as bad as this one! Did that prove he didn't love Joseph? No, sir! It proved He *did* love him. 'Cause later on, Joseph faced his brothers—who'd done him 'bout as wrong as they could—and he said, 'You thought evil against me, but God meant it unto good.' Why, if it was the goodness of God that put Joseph in that prison, and if he hadn't gone through all that, he would never have been able to save 'is people from the famine."

Paul stared at him, and replied quietly, "I'd like to believe that, Enoch. It'd be a little easier to be in this place if I thought there was a purpose in it."

From that time on, Paul listened more and more to the words of the Bible, for each day Dan or Enoch would read aloud to the group. He borrowed the worn black Bible and pored over it, trying to find the secret, but day passed into day with nothing changed.

Winter wore on, and his hopes at times grew as cold and barren as the prison he was in. Only the flashes of memory that kept recurring and the encouragement of his friends kept him alive.

And then, one day late in the afternoon—though afternoon meant nothing inside the dark prison—he was walking aimlessly through the babbling crowd, looking at the wares brought in by the vendors that were permitted in from time to time. He had no money, but it was something to do, and he found himself confronted by a short, fat man with a handful of chestnuts. "Hey, buy some fresh chestnuts! Cheap!"

"No money," Paul shrugged, and would have turned away, but his arm was caught in a steely grasp, and he stared at the vendor who closed one eye in a wink. He held up a small sack and there was, Paul saw, a slip of paper protruding out of it.

Paul's heart lurched, and he stared at the man, who grinned and murmured under his breath, "Pretend to give me some money."

With his hands trembling, Paul reached into his ragged coat and pretended to bring out some coins and give them to the man. The vendor handed him the bag and whirled away without a word.

Paul left the crowded area at once, and getting to his own smaller area, opened the note and read:

> Be selling something in the market one week from today—Jan. 22.

He stared at the words, then with his heart racing, he folded the note carefully and put it in his pocket. He leaned his head against the wall and cried out to himself, *Dear God! Somebody cares!*

For a week he waited impatiently, saying nothing to anyone, but on the twenty-second he was in the market with a few baskets he'd woven out of straw. They were poorly done, and none of the buyers that came in from the villages for the sale looked more than once, but he kept moving, his eyes searching for the fat man who'd given him the note. When, after hours, he did not see him, his heart sank.

He was about to leave the market area when he heard a voice at his elbow: "Let me see your baskets."

He turned quickly—and found Charity Alden looking at him, her greenish eyes gleaming in the flickering candlelight.

"Charity!" he breathed. "Good Lord, what—!"

"No time, Paul," she answered softly. "Show me the baskets while we talk." She spoke quietly, and there was an assurance in her manner that brooked no argument. "You'll walk out of here in three days—you and crew of the *Lady*."

His head was spinning, and he responded, "How can we do that? It's impossible!"

She gave him a smile, confident and fearless. "With God all things are possible. Just be ready. Have the crew come to the east gate. They'll be taken out as a work party. When you get outside the prison, watch for a wagon with a canvas top. The guards have been bribed. They'll put you in the wagons; then they'll disappear."

He stared at her, and would have asked more, but she said hurriedly, "I can't stay—someone might suspect. Remember—three days!"

She took one of the baskets, gave him a coin, and left, threading her way through the milling crowd.

Paul walked back to the inner cell, his mind humming. He wanted to shout, but keeping a tight grip on himself, he said nothing until late that night. The prison went to sleep, and for a long time he listened as Dan read the Scripture. Finally, when the Bible was tucked away and the men were turning to their hammocks, he whispered, "Come close. I have news."

They stopped, moved in close, and he began, his voice barely audible. "We're getting out of this place in three days." Seeing the unbelief in their eyes, he pulled the note out of his pocket and showed it to them.

"That's Charity's writing!" Dan uttered excitedly, keeping his voice low.

"Yes—and somehow she's paid the guards off. We've got to be ready. The agreement is for six of us. Members of the crew of *The Gallant Lady* are paid for."

"Why, that's not me," Enoch returned quietly.

"Yes, you're one of us," Paul reassured. "You'll be going along in Lige's place." He stared at Enoch, saying, "I guess God took Lige home so you could make the escape with us. All things work together for good. That's what the Book says, didn't you tell me?"

There was a sudden burst of smiles on the men's faces, and Paul cautioned them, "Don't act any differently. Only the guards on the outer gate who take the work patrols out are bought. If one soul in this place gets wind of what's going on, it'll be over. Everybody in Dartmoor will be lined up to make the break."

"Paul's right! We've got to act as though we were in here for the rest of our lives."

"I promise to be as miserable as ever," Laurence Conrad predicted, but his eyes were gleaming. "If this comes off, Winslow, I fail to see how I can remain an atheist—because only the hand of God can open the locks of Dartmoor!"

★ ★ ★ ★

The air was cold as the tall man and the girl left the house and got into a wagon pulled by a sturdy pair of roan horses. A large brown canvas covered the top, raised by steel hoops. It looked no different from many such vehicles used by merchants to haul their wares from the country to the port of Plymouth. The man helped the girl onto the high seat, climbed aboard, and gave the horses a slap with the reins. They broke into a brisk walk.

Charity said nothing for a time, but she was so nervous her hands twisted in her lap, and finally the man noticed it. "You don't have to worry, Charity. It'll be all right."

She looked at him, and the sight of his smile reassured her. She had instantly seen the Winslow look in William the first time she stepped inside the little house where he lived with his wife and five children. He was taller and more fair than Adam, but the family resemblance was there. He favored Nathan more, but when he'd read the long letter she had brought from Adam, he had smiled and set her fears at rest by saying, "We believe God for the deliverance of our men."

She had spent the next weeks with his family, posing as a distant relative from America. She'd been amazed to find that the congregation of the Methodist church where William was pastor was passionately opposed to the American war. It was not a popular war anywhere in the country, she was to discover, and William had encouraged her. "If Washington can hold out, America will win. The people here are angry at the whole thing. They'll quit if they can find a way."

Working out a plan to free the crew had been a matter of many meetings with many people. Charity had sold her house, and Charles had sent her what seemed to be an enormous amount of money—but getting it into the right hands was the problem.

William had proposed, "We'll ask God for wisdom—and I think I know a thing or two that might help." Charity never was sure how he did it, but she found herself at a luncheon in an inn in Plymouth with a man named Thomas White. He was some sort of official at Dartmoor—she never learned his exact position—and after the meal the conversation drifted to Dartmoor. William finally mentioned casually, "I understand there's no way for the prisoners to escape, Thomas."

"Quite impossible!" White shrugged. "And if they did, where would they go? There's no place to hide; we'd have them back in a few hours—or dead, more than likely. The guards are really callous. Just as soon kill a man as look at him."

They talked about that for a time, and then William commented, "Miss Alden here is quite saddened. Some of her people are in your charge at Dartmoor."

"Oh?" White suddenly stared at her with fresh interest. At William's direction, she had purchased expensive clothing just for the meeting and she felt the man's eyes on the diamond necklace that had been bought for an enormous price in London. "How is that, may I ask, Miss Alden?"

She told him of the *Lady*, and he listened carefully as she ended by saying, "I intend to buy a new ship, and I'll miss my crew." She looked carefully at the massive ruby ring that glowed on her finger and gave a little laugh. "It'll cost a fortune to train a new crew—and I was so fond of them. As a matter of fact, Mr. White, one of the men is my fiance. I am sick over it." Then she sighed and said in the saddest tone she could muster, "If it were only a matter of *money*, there would be no problem!"

White did not take his gaze from her, and replied, "How sad! We'll all be glad when this war is over. I as much as anyone." Then he sipped his coffee and remarked without emphasis, "I would be glad to do anything I can for you, Miss Alden. Let me know if I can be of any service."

After Charity and William had bidden their farewells and were on their way home, William chuckled and repeated White's statement, "I would be glad to do anything I can for you." He laughed aloud and put his arm around Charity, saying, "In translation, that means *I am for sale! How much will you give me to let them go?*"

And that had been the key. There had been many meetings, much bargaining, for White had to buy off others and at the same time protect himself. It would have taken the assets of Lloyds to give him what he demanded, but Charity, for all her tender appearance, proved to be a hard bargainer.

Finally the deal had been made. Half the price was in White's hand, the rest with William, to be paid when he received a letter from Charity saying they were safe in America.

Now as they headed for the prison, Charity wished it were over. "There are so many things that could go wrong!" she worried to William.

"O ye of little faith," he chided her. Then he asked, "You are engaged to this man Greene?"

"Well—we had an understanding once . . ."

He turned to stare at her, for they had grown close. She had told him much of her life, and he struggled to put into words what he wanted to say to her. They would not meet again after the escape, and he wished to make something clear. "Charity, you have said more than you meant about Paul Winslow."

"Paul?"

"Yes, my nephew." William thought hard, then spoke frankly. "I think you've grown attached to him without being aware of it— and I want to warn you about him."

"What about Paul?"

"The Winslows are a good family—but there are some bad seeds—and I fear that Paul is one of them." He talked about how the young man had been nothing but grief to his parents; and he ended by saying, "I am happy that you have found the Lord, Charity—but don't make the mistake of getting involved with a man like Paul. He would ruin your life."

Then he changed the subject, but his warning had not left Charity, and for days she thought about it, never easy in her mind, for she trusted the judgment of William greatly.

They reached a side road not far from Dartmoor about noon, and waited anxiously until late afternoon. Both of them were nervous, but at three o'clock William exclaimed suddenly, "There they come!"

A line of prisoners dressed in faded yellow uniforms appeared, and she counted six of them, with only two guards. William advised her urgently, "Be ready to leave."

The guards were on horseback, and as the line came forward, the two men watched the wagon intently. Not a word was uttered until they got even with where Charity and William were waiting, and then one of them ordered the men, "Here they are! Get in there!" As the six men scrambled inside with wild haste, the guards whirled their horses and dashed down the road at full speed.

"Let's go!" William yelled, whipping the horses and driving like fury. As soon as the wagon began moving, Charity pulled back the canvas and jumped into the back with cries of joy. "We made it! Oh, I was so worried something would go wrong!" The crew members of *The Gallant Lady* closest to Charity threw aside all restraint toward their captain and embraced her, joining their tears with hers.

The happy reunion was an emotional time for all of them. Even Laurence Conrad made no attempt to staunch the tears, and there was none of his usual cynicism as he embraced Charity and murmured with fervor, "God bless you, girl!"

Only Paul and Dan held back, and she had to turn to them, holding out her hands. They each took one, and stood there staring, unable to express what was in their hearts. Finally she said, "Let's go home!" and then whirled and left, saying, "Get out of those clothes! You'll find new ones in the chest."

As the men changed into new clothes, Dan remarked, "I was worried a bit about getting back across the ocean, Paul—but with a woman like that—what's a little thing like the Atlantic?"

And Paul Winslow responded with utter and complete sincerity: "Amen."

★ ★ ★ ★

Two months passed before they could leave England, for the men had to be hidden until the uproar over their escape died down. Then they had to obtain passage to America, and that was not a simple matter.

But on the third of March, Paul Winslow walked up the steps to his home, entered and announced to Charles Winslow, who stood there staring at him: "Father—I'm home! You brought me out of it as no one else could have." He turned and took his mother in his arms, and then the three of them wept.

CHAPTER TWENTY-THREE

CHARITY HAS A PLAN

★ ★ ★ ★

Spring had come early to Boston, the freezing winds of January turning almost warm by the first of April. The fruit trees were deceived by the bright sun and the life-giving breezes, and all around the country the brown hills were spotted with white and pink blossoms of wild plum and pear.

Since his return to his father's house, Paul had done little but stay indoors. It was a strain on him, for he still had only flashes of memory, but he was conscious that he was needed there. His mother clung to him, and he had grown very close to his father. The two spent long evenings together in front of a fire. Charles did most of the talking, and to Paul it was fascinating, for the Winslow name went back to the *Mayflower* and even further. One evening Charles had handed him a book richly bound in red leather, saying, "This is my favorite book—your great-great grandfather's journal." He held the book, running his hands over the smooth cover, and looked up with a warm light in his blue eyes. "Gilbert Winslow was his name. I never knew him, of course, but his granddaughter Rachel stayed at our house a great deal while I was growing up. Adam was her favorite, which didn't always make me happy. But I never forgot her stories of how her great-grandpa had left England to come to this land on the *Mayflower*."

Charles stopped and looked intently at his son, then smiled and remarked, "You have something of him in you, Paul."

"I do?"

"Yes. Gilbert Winslow was the best swordsman in England in his day, or close to it. I believe you got that gift from him. Adam has his sword, and you'll want to see it. It's a fine piece of craftsmanship, and you'd appreciate it. Ought to be in a museum, but then perhaps not. Maybe Gilbert would like it better if one of his seed carried it."

"I—I'd like to see it."

"I'll tell Adam to bring it next time he comes." Charles hesitated, then said, "Take the book, Paul. Read it, for it's got the heart of this new country in it. He lived for a long time, and he saw something here that's haunted me. Adam sees it better than I— he's broken with England and is an American."

"I've wondered what to do—but I have no decision to make, really," Paul stated slowly. He took the book, opened it and read a few lines. "I'm a traitor to the English. I've got no choice now but to be an American."

Charles nodded. "You are right, and you know, Paul . . . I'm glad of it!" He slapped the desk, saying, "By the Lord, I'm going to do the same! Here's one Tory who'll never be an Englishman again!"

"Major Winslow will be happy."

"Yes, he will. I'm not so sure about Dorcas—but from the latest signs in Anne, she's not going to be far behind me."

Paul looked at him, and a smile touched his lips. "You mean that crush she's developed on Dan Greene. . . ?"

"Just that." Charles shook his head. "Of all the men in the world she'd be attracted to, that Quaker is the one I'd put last."

"He's a fine looking fellow, Father. Strong as a bull—and he's not only smart, he's as good a man as you'd want for a son-in-law—if it comes to that."

They thought about it—how Greene had come to stay with them when the crew had gotten back from England. He had spent much time with all of them, but Anne at the age of seventeen was captivated by him. Greene never noticed, for to him Anne was a child.

He found out different quickly enough when they were taken to a ball one evening. Charles had asked him to watch out for Anne, and he'd agreed. But when she'd come down the hall wearing a pale green dress that set off her red hair and molded itself to her fully developed young body, he had gazed at her speechless. She had left her arms and shoulders bare, and as she stood looking up at him, smiling and taking his arm, he had almost stuttered when he said, "Thee—thee does look beautiful, Anne. I never knew—" He broke off quickly, but she finished it for him with a teasing tone.

"Thee did not know I was a woman, did thee, Friend Greene?" Anne was a natural mimic, and he had to smile at how she used the Quaker words. They sounded strange dropping from her full rounded lips, and he had been very conscious of her womanhood from that day.

Anne had approached Charity with all the blunt manner of youth. "Are you in love with Dan, Charity?"

Charity had stared at her, a slow smile forming on her lips. "No. He thought he was in love with me—but he wasn't really." A touch of humor surfaced in her eyes, and she asked innocently, "Why are you asking, Anne?"

"Oh! I—I just wondered." Anne's face turned pink. "You're too quick for me, Charity," she laughed. "But isn't he *something*?"

"He's not very showy, Anne," Charity had warned her. "He's a Quaker, and his religion is very important to him."

"I know. We've been talking about that." The girl had paused and a look of wonder came into her eyes. "I didn't know people could *enjoy* being Christians—the way he does."

Charles and Paul had watched this relationship grow, and now Charles remarked with a smile, "Looks like this house is going to be turned upside down, Paul. From Tory to Patriot, and from Anglican to Quaker—or maybe even worse. Adam will make shouting Methodists out of us if he has his way!"

★　★　★　★

Paul had read Gilbert Winslow's journal, then read it again, and one warm afternoon, he spoke of it to Charity. She had come to spend time with Anne, and he had encountered her as she was walking across the yard from the barn with a basket of eggs in her hand.

"Breakfast, Charity?" He took the basket, saying, "Look up there—the first of the purple martins. They're early."

As she lifted her head she saw a pair of bluish birds circling the house. "Purple martins. I've seen them but didn't know their names."

"I built that house up there—see, on that pole?"

She studied him for a moment. "You're remembering a lot, aren't you, Paul?"

"Well, more all the time. I met a fellow in town last week whose face was familiar, and I remembered that when I was just a boy he came to our house and plowed our garden. His name was Tom Tillis and he loved to sing folk songs. I remembered that—but other things just aren't there."

"It'll come, don't worry."

He sat down and pointed to the seat, "Rest for a minute, Charity. You work all the time." He looked at her as she sat close to him on the small bench, then said, "I've been reading my ancestor's book. He came over on the *Mayflower*."

"Yes. I've read it. It's a wonderful book."

" 'He was a man, all for all. I shall not look upon his like again.' " He flushed and wrinkled his brow. "I can remember lines from Shakespeare, but can't tell you what my first teacher's name was! Anyway, they don't make men like that anymore."

"Oh yes, I think so."

"Name *one*!"

"All right," she responded with a saucy light in her green eyes. "Adam Winslow."

He thought about Adam, smiled, and nodded. "You have me there. He's some man! My father thinks there's nobody like him."

She traced the design in the pattern of her dress for a moment, then looked up at him and said with a rush, "You could be like him, Paul—if you wanted to."

"Me?" He stared at her incredulously, threw back his head, and laughed. "I thought you were a bright girl, Charity—but that's crazy!"

"No, it's not." She had bathed that morning, and he caught faint whiffs of lavender as she moved; her skin was almost translucent in the sun. He had never seen such lashes, long and thick, shading eyes that were sometimes blue-green like the sea. She put her hand on his arm, and if she did not notice it, *he* did, and his arm tingled under her touch.

"You could be anything you wanted to, Paul. Look what you did on the *Neptune*. You rose from a battered pressed man to become an officer in the Royal Navy. Why, some men try for years and never manage that!"

He looked at her unbelievingly, still conscious of her touch, and stated flatly, "I didn't have any choice."

"Well, you have a choice now, Paul Winslow!" She snatched her hand away, adding, "You could do as much for America as you did for England—but you won't!"

"I won't *what*?" he asked, taken aback by her flash of anger. He didn't understand her reaction, but he saw that her face was pink with indignation.

"You won't be an American—because of Blanche Rommey!" She was sorry the moment the words slipped out, and a wave of scarlet touched her neck and crept into her cheeks. "Oh, Paul! I had no right to say that!"

He grinned at her, saying ruefully, "You do have a temper, Charity! But you're wrong."

"You don't love her?" The question leaped to her lips, and she waited for his reply, a shade of doubt in her eyes.

"Why, it's not that easy, Charity," Paul returned. He stripped a splinter from the wooden bench, bent it into a U, then dropped it. "It's not like I am only one man, is it? Blanche fell in love with Lieutenant Hawke—and now I'm just half of that man. I'm half Paul Winslow. Why, I'm a traitor to her country, Charity! How do you think she'll feel about that?"

"If she loves you, it won't matter," she answered warmly. "A woman doesn't fall in love with a man's politics!"

He smiled. "It would be a little awkward, wouldn't it, for the daughter of a British captain to be in love with a traitor? Play havoc with the social life, I'd venture."

"Oh, hang the social life—and you take care of your own love affairs!" Charity snapped. "Anyway, I really have wanted to ask you something."

"Ask away."

"What are you going to do, Paul? I mean, are you going to work or what?"

"Don't know. I could work with father—or I could join the Army. I'm no soldier, but I could learn."

"Why, you'd be wasted as a soldier!" Charity protested. "You're a sailor, and that's what you should be doing."

"Not much in that line available, Charity. No warships looking for lieutenants as far as I know."

Charity bit her lower lip and leaned closer to him. He breathed the lavender again and gazed at her curiously. She was being very secretive, and he was sure there was no one within a mile to listen.

"Would you go to sea again—if you could get on an American privateer?"

Startled, his eyes searched hers, for it had occurred to him.

"I'd go like a shot—but do you know of a ship?"

She moved closer, the pressure of her firm body pressing against him. He almost asked why she was getting so close, but decided against it. He liked lavender.

"I know of one. It would be a little trouble to get her, but she's the best there is."

"I thought you always said *The Gallant Lady* was the best."

"Yes—that's what I'm talking about!" she explained excitedly, her hand gripping his arm.

"But—Charity!" he protested, "she's in the hands of the British!"

"She's in the harbor in New York right now, Paul." She spoke softly as if there were spies hanging from the boughs of the huge cherry tree ten feet away: "Paul—we can take that ship!"

He was not sure he'd heard her. "Take her how, Charity?"

"We can get a crew, sneak on board some night, and sail her out of the harbor."

The humor of it struck him, and he laughed out loud. "Why, sure we can! There are only about ten ships of the line, no telling how many frigates under the British flag there to stop us—not to mention most of Howe's army running all over the streets of New York. Charity, it's the wildest thing I ever heard of."

"That's why it can be done, Paul." Her eyes were wider than he'd ever seen them, and they seemed to set off sparks. "Do you think they *expect* someone to steal a whole ship? They're watching everything else in the Colonies—*but they're not watching that ship!*"

He stared at her, not knowing whether to laugh or just walk off and leave her. He opened his mouth to tell her how ridiculous the idea was, but instead, the thought of the *Lady* flashed into his mind. With a frown he reached up and stroked his chin, and after a long silence he voiced his thoughts. "I remember how it was when we tied up there. The harbor is busy enough by day—but at night it's a ghost place."

"It could be done, Paul. I know it could!"

Her excitement was contagious, and he began to think out loud: "We'd need to get a good crew—some hearty fellows who aren't afraid to take a chance. We could filter into the city a few at a time. Then we could go out in small boats after dark and take the ship."

"We can get plenty of men—all we need," she added. "And when we get clear of the harbor—"

"Wait a minute!" he interrupted. "You're not going—and that's final!"

Anger lit her eyes, and she jumped to her feet and challenged him with clenched teeth. "I'd like to see you try and stop me!"

He was on his feet, and before he thought he grabbed her shoulders and cried, "You may think you're a man, Charity Alden, but this time you're going to act like a lady. You'll stay ashore—ow!"

She had lifted her hand and given him a crack on the cheek; without meaning to, purely as a reflex action, he slapped her full in the face. The blow was far from his full strength, but it drove her head back and she stumbled, falling to the ground with her cheek glowing red from the force of the blow.

"Oh, Lord!" he cried out, and in horror he stooped and put his arms around her. She was sitting there with a blank expression, not hurt so much as shocked, but when she saw his agony and grief, she knew the day was hers. Ordinarily she would have given him another slap across the face, but a streak of feminine wisdom ran deep in Charity despite her mannish ways. She let her body relax, and with no trouble at all began to sob softly, and as he frantically muttered his apologies, she allowed herself to fall on his shoulders, holding tightly to him.

Paul was dumbfounded. He had hit plenty of hard-headed sailors, but the sight of Charity's head being driven back under his blow was frightening, and he continued to pat her shoulder as she lay in his arms sobbing as though her heart would break.

Carefully, as if she were made of fine crystal, he pulled her to her feet and whispered, "Oh, Charity—I'm so sorry . . . !"

She made the most of it, clinging to him with both arms and pressing her face against his shoulder. He began to be uncomfortably aware that he was holding a beautiful woman in his arms, and soon he could do nothing but stand there thinking of her soft beauty.

"Charity—please don't cry!"

She looked up and the soft, damp eyes smote him like a blow. "Paul," she begged, "don't be mean to me—please don't!"

Her lips were inches from his, and he lost all consciousness of the world. Only she was real, this desirable young woman who was melting in his arms. He said huskily, "Charity, I—I . . ." Then one of them moved; he never knew which, and it didn't seem to matter. Her lips were soft as down, and he felt her hands on his neck pulling him closer. Time seemed to stop, and all he knew was the fragrance of her and the soft vulnerable figure pressed against him.

"Paul! Oh, Paul!" she whispered as they parted.

His eyes searched hers. "Are you all right?"

"Yes." She dropped her head, and then asked quietly, "You won't leave me behind, will you, Paul? When you go for the ship?"

"No," he assured. "We'll go together." They turned and walked down the path talking of the ship, but her heart was crying, *He can't love Blanche! Not if he kisses me like that!*

He was thinking of how he was going to explain taking her along on a dangerous exploit, and not once did he stop to realize that he had never consciously made the decision even to try the thing. It was fortunate for Charity that he had no memory of affairs with women, for the old Paul Winslow would have laughed at those tears, seeing them at once as a weapon a woman uses to get her way.

But he was not sorry, and as they walked along the fresh blooming boughs of the apple orchard, he was more aware of her soft hand in his than of the plans they made to capture *The Gallant Lady.*

★ ★ ★ ★

It took three days to convince Charles that the plan to take the *Lady* was worth the risk. It took another week to collect the men for the venture, but Dan Greene and the old crew knew every seafaring man in Boston—and more important, they knew which of them could be trusted. Dan was in and out of the house constantly, with Anne like a shadow, staying as close as possible.

Charity and Paul were inseparable, Charles noted, and mentioned it to Dan one day. "That is a remarkable young woman," he commented. "She's been good for Paul. Look at them!"

Dan glanced to where the pair were sitting at a table. Charity was arguing, her arms flailing, and Paul was watching her quietly, with his head moving from side to side. "They fight all the time, Charles. I hate to think what would happen if he married her!"

"They're both strong people—and if they don't kill each other, I think it might work out. But of course, he has a fiancee, I understand."

Plans for taking the ship continued. Then one day Charles disappeared, telling no one where he was going. He came back in a few days with a strange smile on his face. He called for a meeting, and the leaders of the venture gathered in his living room.

"How would you like to be farmers?" he asked with a droll smile.

"Farmers?" Laurence Conrad frowned. "They grub around in the dirt and grow things, don't they? Not for me!"

"What's in that devious mind of yours?" Paul inquired.

"I thought it over, and I decided that to take the ship by force in the harbor was too great a risk. So I came up with a different plan."

"What does thee propose?" Dan asked.

"I propose that the entire crew go as passengers on the *Jupiter*—that's the *Lady*'s new name."

"Passengers!" Paul was staring at his father with bewilderment. "Passengers to *where*—and for *what*?"

Charles Winslow's face had a light of excitement clearly evident to everyone, and he looked much younger than he had the first time Charity had seen him. The lines had faded and his voice was clear as he continued. "I've been to New York and done a little ground work. The *Jupiter* was sold to a man named Whitaker. He's taking a load of cannon and powder to Admiral Hood's squadron in the West Indies."

"What's Hood doing there?" Dan inquired.

"I talked to Adam, and he told me that the French Admiral de Grass is out there with a large force—nearly thirty ships of the line. Washington has asked him to come and pin the British down at Yorktown. If the French Navy can hold the sea, Washington can take Yorktown and force Cornwallis to surrender—and it'll be the end of the war!"

"Glory to God!" Enoch exclaimed. "But it'll be hard for de Grass to get through Hood. That man is a hawk!"

"So Adam said. Well, the *Jupiter* leaves in a week for the Indies. Adam talked to General Washington, and His Excellency said—and I quote: 'If those men could take the ship and make it to the Indies, they could be the eyes of de Grass. Poor fellow has no fast ships like an American schooner!' "

"Washington said that?" Paul's voice was filled with wonder. Then he looked around and declared fiercely, "By heaven, we'll take that ship or die!"

"But not in New York Harbor," Charles stated. "Here's what must be done—I met the master of the *Jupiter* and I told him that I was starting a farming venture in sugar in the Indies. I asked him if he could take my crew of planters when he went. He said no at first, that it was against the custom for naval ships to haul passengers. But he somehow discovered that it was a custom which had lost its importance—when I waved more money at him than he'd ever seen!"

"Mr. Winslow—you can't afford that!" Charity protested.

"Well, no—but then I don't expect the good captain will keep it long," Charles smiled. "Because when we seize the ship—just before we get to the Indies—I'll get a refund from him."

"By Harry—it'll work!" Conrad exclaimed, and the room buzzed with excited talk.

"I never thought of you as a schemer, Mr. Winslow," Charity told him. "But you've come up with a real plan."

Charles Winslow ducked his head, and then raised it slowly. Both Paul and Charity could see by the stiffness in his patrician features how he was struggling with his emotions.

"All the Winslows have fought for this land. I've been the only one who hasn't—but if I could do this one thing, I could think of myself as a *real* Winslow—and an American!"

"I'm very proud of my father, sir!"

Charles took the hand that Paul held out, and his eyes were suddenly blinded. He whispered, "I have something for you."

Paul and Charity followed him to his study, and he picked up a sword that was on his desk. He handed it carefully to Paul.

"It's the sword of Gilbert Winslow, Paul. Adam said that you're the Winslow who can use it best."

Paul took the shining blade, lifted it, and made a pass. "Beautiful!" he breathed.

"It's been red with the blood of our enemies, Paul."

A firmness tightened Paul's jaw, and his eyes were bright as he declared, "I may die with this sword, sir, but I'll never dishonor it!"

Charles's eyes misted as he murmured wistfully, "I wish your grandfather were here—my father, Miles. He would think better of me—but that's the past. Now, let's make ready for this thing as best we can!"

CHAPTER TWENTY-FOUR

CAPTAIN WINSLOW

★ ★ ★ ★

Over a hundred men dressed as farmers were standing on the dock on the morning of March 15. Captain Whitaker came ashore and looked at them with distaste. They all wore rough clothing, and had bags and chests piled high beside them. Whitaker spotted Charles Winslow standing at the back of the crowd and made his way through the milling crowd, a frown on his face.

"Ah, Captain Whitaker, here you are!"

"Look here, Winslow, you've got more men here than we agreed on."

"Why, there may be a few more, but all the more profit for you, eh, Captain?"

Whitaker opened his mouth to argue, but when Winslow tossed him a soft, heavy leather bag, he clamped his teeth immediately. "Well, all right—but no more!" he warned. Then he turned and yelled, "Stevens! Get the passengers stowed away—on the double!"

"What time do you sail, Captain?" Winslow asked.

"Dawn tomorrow—and if any of your blasted peasants ain't on board, they get left!"

Winslow replied cheerfully, "Oh, you needn't bother about that. My men are all anxious to get to their work—isn't that right, men?"

A chorus of assent rose from the pseudo-farmers crowded around, and Whitaker grunted and moved away.

"I wish I were going with you, Paul, but your mother wouldn't hear of it," Charles said wistfully. Then he nodded toward Charity, who was moving among the crew, laughing at something Conrad had said. "I still think it's a mistake to let Charity go—but she's hard to deny."

"She's that, all right. I'm too big a coward, but I've told Miles Lester that when the action starts, his one job is to get her below and sit on her if he has to!" An odd look leaped into Paul's face, and he added, "There's something I have to do before we leave, Father. I'll be back in plenty of time."

Charles stared at his son knowingly before he replied, "If you must do it—whatever it is, Paul—that's all there is to it. I'll be here when you return."

Paul nodded, and turning quickly, moved across the dock and disappeared into the teeming crowd that swarmed the harbor. Charity saw Paul leave and came up to Charles, inquiring, "Where's Paul going?"

"Oh, he had something in town to take care of."

Charity fixed her eyes on him, a strange look in her eyes. She said nothing, but there was a stiffness in her shoulders as she whirled around and went back to the crew.

It took many trips for the small boat to get all the men on board, but finally as dark was falling over the gray sea, Dan reported to Winslow, "Well, Charles—they're all on board."

"I hope none of them drops his bag. If one of those sailors gets a look at the weapons and the uniforms those men have stored, it'd be all we need." The men's bags and chests did not contain farming tools as Winslow had told Captain Whitaker. They were stuffed with pistols, cutlasses, muskets, bayonets, dirks and a variety of other weapons. And Paul had insisted on the uniforms. "We're not pirates but seamen of the Continental Navy, and when we take the ship, it'll be in that uniform." Adam had obtained the commission for the men, naming Paul as captain and Dan Greene as lieutenant.

"No fear," Dan shrugged. He looked around quizzically. "I haven't seen Paul all afternoon. Did you send him on some duty?"

"No—he had some personal business."

Dan looked at him searchingly, but said only, "I'd better get aboard." He put his thick hand out and smiled. "Thee is as good a man as Adam Winslow, Charles!"

Charles waved his hand in denial. "Oh, that's not so, Daniel!" He smiled and added, "If I didn't know you for a man without guile, I'd think you were trying to butter me up. I expected to have to listen to you asking for Anne's hand in marriage. What's holding you up?"

Dan's broad face burned, and he answered quickly, "Oh, she's too young for me, as I've told her, Charles."

"You're twenty-seven and she's seventeen."

"Well, it's not that, really. I'm not a rich man, and she's used to fine things."

"That's not it, either, is it now?" Charles took Greene's arm firmly. "I used to dream of a rich man marrying Anne, but I've had some sense beaten into me lately, thank God. Now I want more than anything else for Anne to have a man who's honest and good. And you're the finest example I've found."

Greene regarded Charles Winslow for a moment, then said huskily, "Thee is kind to say that—"

"It's the girl's religion, isn't it, Dan?"

"Well, sir, it is." Dan's lips turned up in a rueful smile. "I've courted two women, and both of them have turned me down. I'll be pretty slow to declare myself to any woman. Anne is a beautiful woman, and any man likes that—but the woman I marry will have to love God."

"I honor you for that, my boy," Charles replied seriously. "And it's true that Anne has little religion. But that's my fault. She has a warm and loving heart, and if I'd been wiser in my own ways before God, she'd be different." He paused momentarily. "I think she's in love with you—and it's my notion that with a little help from you and other real Christians, Anne will find your God."

Dan smiled at him, and remarked, "I think thee is hard on the track of God, Charles."

"It's the other way around, I think. I feel like God is on *my* trail—and I have the joyful sense that He's about got me cornered!"

The night passed slowly, but Dan did not go to his bunk. There was too much to think about. He leaned on the rail of the ship and looked at the thin clouds sliding across the sky, masking the yellow moon. *I wonder what will come of this desperate venture*, he mused.

"Dan—" Charity interrupted his thoughts as she joined him on the deck. For a long time they stood there watching the stars and talking about unimportant matters. She was, he discerned, tense and restless. She was always an active girl, but the nervous movements of her hands and the abrupt starts and stops of her speech told him she was not herself.

About an hour after she joined him, they heard a hail from the port side, and Dan looked down to see a small boat making for the *Jupiter*. "It's Paul," he told her, turning back.

They waited until the boat was alongside and saw Paul leap over the rail. "Paul," Dan called. "Over here."

There was a hesitation in Paul that neither one missed. For a moment Charity thought he would turn away, but instead he came toward them. His eyes were shaded by the cap he wore, hiding any information they might glean. "You two still up?" was all he offered.

"Couldn't sleep," Dan stated.

"Everything go all right?"

"Fine." Dan hesitated, then said, "I was worried about thee. If thee hadn't made it back, the whole affair would probably fail."

Both Dan and Charity were waiting for him to explain his errand, but he only replied, "Oh, there was no danger of that," and turned to go. "I guess I'll turn in. Whom am I bunking with, Dan?"

"With me and Enoch. I'll show you."

"All right." His eyes fell on Charity. "It's late. You must be tired."

"I am, a little. Good night."

She left without another word, and Dan led the way to the small section of the crew's quarters where he and Paul strung their hammocks. Some of the *Jupiter*'s crew were already occupying the quarters, so there was no possibility for talk. Dan fell asleep thinking, *He is surely behaving in a strange way!*

Paul lay awake for a long time, immobile in his hammock, thoughts running through his mind that left no mark on his face. He stared blindly at the deck overhead, oblivious to the watch sounding the calls that night.

In the morning the crew ate in shifts. There was no room for all the sailors to eat at once, not to mention the passengers, so in the days that followed, life consisted of shifting from one section of the ship to the other, eating and moving out of the small cabin so that others could come in and have their turn.

Usually some of the ship's crew were close, so meetings between Dan and Paul and the other passengers had to be rare. Charity seemed to keep to herself, and Paul found himself missing her, but there was little opportunity for a meeting.

Day followed day, and everyone became more edgy with the strain of the situation. Finally Conrad growled, "If I have to talk about potatoes or beans one more time to fool these dolts, I'll die."

"Don't you like vegetables, Conrad?" Paul asked with a twinkle in his eye.

Conrad drew himself up to his full height and answered solemnly, "I ate a pea once!" As everyone burst into laughter, he stalked off, offended at their rudeness.

The one completely happy person aboard was Thad Alden. He found Charity willing to talk to him more than she ever had. They spent time together in the bow of the ship, talking about the days back in Boston before the war. Charity should have known better, but she didn't notice how her attention brought the lad into a state of blissful joy.

She was scarcely listening to him one day when he inquired, "You figure a man like me could ever get married and have a family, Miss Charity?"

She was half asleep from the warmth of the tropic sun, and answered, "You, Thad? Why, a girl would be lucky to have a fine man like you for a husband." She almost named Lucy Gambell, knowing that the girl, daughter of a local butcher, was wildly in love with Thad. But she didn't, and she failed to see the flush that came to his face.

"Thank you, Charity."

★ ★ ★ ★

On Sunday the thirty-first, the group met for church on deck, the only place large enough. Dan preached, and the rest congregated around him. Charity felt someone squeeze in between her and Laurence. She looked up to see that it was Paul. He smiled at her, and asked, "Room for one more sinner?"

"Why, I think so."

She sat there so disturbed that she was unable to concentrate on the sermon, but when she glanced at Paul, he was listening intently. After the service was over and they got to their feet, he said, "Come to the stern. I want to talk to you."

She followed him, and by some miracle there was no one at the rail. He was silent at first, just gazing across the shattered water that the ship sent boiling in its wake. Finally he asked quietly, "Charity, are you angry with me?"

"Why—no."

"You've not said ten words to me on this voyage."

She bit her lip, shrugged, and replied evasively, "I . . . I suppose I'm a little bit afraid."

He searched her face, trying to read beneath that facade. "You've been so distant. I . . . I've missed you."

She looked at him, startled, and fingered her bodice nervously. "I didn't think you would."

He saw that she was unhappy, so he hurried on. "Charity, we take the ship day after tomorrow."

"Paul!"

"And I want you to promise me something."

She smiled, the sadness leaving her. "I know. You want me to hide until it's over."

"That's it. You see, I'm very fond of you, Charity. If anything happened to you, I'd—"

She waited for his next words, and prompted him. "You'd what, Paul?"

He searched for an answer, then turned his dark eyes on her. "I don't know what it would be like—not having you." He reached out and stroked the rail nervously. Suddenly he blurted out, "I don't have much to think about, Charity. My memory's coming back—but it's very limited. I have a few items stored there—a few people. But if you were to be taken away, it would be like having the sun disappear!"

She dropped her head, feeling a mixture of joy and hope at his words. She heard the hissing of the water and the flapping of sails, but there was an ease in her heart, a diminishing of the weight she had felt since they had left New York.

"I'll stay out of danger, Paul, if that's what you want."

"I thought I'd have to beat you again." She looked through the darkness to see him smiling in the old way.

"I'll be glad when it's over. Keep yourself safe."

"I will," he promised as he turned and disappeared down the deck.

★ ★ ★ ★

It had been decided to seize the ship just before dawn. That was when the majority of the crew were asleep. Paul met with Enoch, Dan, and Conrad at dusk. "We've been over this a dozen times, but remember, if we can get the marines disarmed, that'll be the best we can hope for. I'll take that detail—oh, and be certain the men wear their uniforms. Enoch, you take care of the watch, and Dan, you take the captain and the officers. All right?"

"It'll be a piece of cake," Conrad yawned.

Dan stared at him, shrugged, and said, "It ought to be."

The night slipped by, and finally Paul whispered quietly, "All right—it's time."

He had tried to time the attack so that no one element of the crew would be able to unify against them. His was the hardest job, for the marines were tough, and he gripped his sword tightly in one hand and saw that the others had only cutlasses. Those taking the crew would have muskets, but the marines would have to be hit hard and swiftly.

He stopped the group of ten men that he had chosen, and murmured softly, "All right. They're not expecting us. They'll be asleep, so when—"

He gave a start, for a musket had gone off midships, and the explosion rocked the night air. Cursing the fool that had thrown them all in danger, he yelled, "Come on—they'll be armed in a minute."

It was too late, he saw, for the door of the marines' cabin burst open, and the deck was filled with the figures of marines half dressed but carrying muskets and sabers. "Cut them down!" Paul screamed. A musket exploded almost in his face, and he heard a scream and a body hit the deck. He cut the marine down with one stroke of his blade, but was nearly skewered on a bayonet that he avoided only by twisting his body to the side in a violent movement. He was too close to use his sword, so he pulled the pistol from his belt and fired it straight into the staring face of the startled marine. The man fell at Paul's feet.

As he cut down another marine who came at him with a wild swing of his saber, he heard the sounds of gunfire and yelling from forward and from below. The crew of the *Jupiter* came swarming up the ladders, and soon the deck was a bloody tangle of men, screaming and slashing at one other. The rising sun cast reddish beams the deck, and Paul saw Dan and a small group besieged and fighting like madmen at the foot of the mizzenmast.

He lost track of time, and once he was knocked to the deck by a blow of a musket barrel, and came to his feet blinded by the blood that ran into his eyes. He wiped his eyes free with his sleeve and yelled, "Come on—we've got them now!"

He had no idea if the men would follow, but as he went charging across the deck, he heard the pounding of feet behind him, and his group struck the knot of men that was about to annihilate Dan's small team. It was knife, club, bayonet, and saber now—all the muskets and pistols had been fired.

The clash of steel was a ringing chorus that sounded over the screams of battle. Paul was all over the deck, lifting Conrad up where he'd fallen beneath the attack of a burly sailor, directing a counterattack at the stern where Middles and Lester were cutting their way through a wall of flesh. He saw Middles lift his sword, but a seaman with only a dirk leaped under it and cut Middles' throat. For one terrible moment the man stood there, trying to yell, then fell to the deck grabbing his throat and died as Paul watched, helpless to aid the man.

Others went down, and as Paul raced across the deck, he saw Captain Whitaker with his first lieutenant driving his remaining men toward the center of the fray. *If I don't break up that charge—we're whipped!* Paul thought. He yelled at Dan, "Look! We've got to get those officers—then the crew will quit!"

The two of them hurdled side by side over the bodies of the dead and dying, and Whitaker looked up to meet them, his face livid with rage. He lifted his pistol and fired—and Dan went down on the deck. Paul lunged at the captain, who was trying to draw his sword—but it would not come free. The lieutenant leaped forward and caught Paul's blade on his own sword, giving the captain time to draw. The two officers lunged at Paul, and he parried both flickering blades and took one step backward.

"Get him, Stevens! He's the leader!"

They pressed him, and he kept his feet by a miracle, for the deck was slippery with blood. Both of the men were good swordsmen, and they divided so that he could not keep his eye on them at the same time.

He knew it was a matter of time until he was caught, for they were playing him just right. One would lunge while the other waited; then when Paul's blade was engaged, the other would strike. Three times they maneuvered him into position, and only by fighting like a madman did he escape.

Finally their lethal thrusts came as he knew they would. The lieutenant pulled his blade to the right, and he saw the captain to his left driving forward at his unprotected side! He expected to feel the steel driving through his body—but instead he heard a cry and someone fell against him.

He looked down to see Thad Alden, who had come to his aid,

the blade of Captain Whitaker buried in his stomach almost to the hilt. Thad looked up at Paul with unbelieving eyes and whispered hoarsely, "Please!"

The eyes of the lieutenant were fixed on the boy, gaping at the captain's blade trapped in Alden's body. Quicker than a striking cobra, Paul ran the lieutenant through the throat and even as he fell to the deck kicking and gagging, Paul whirled to face the captain.

Whitaker saw Paul's red blade, and his eyes bulged as he saw the merciless face of Winslow, but he could not move fast enough, and instantly the blade that had killed his lieutenant was buried in his chest. He touched it almost delicately with one hand; then a dullness came to his eyes and he fell backward, dead before he hit the deck.

There was a shout, and Paul heard men crying for quarter. Looking around he saw that it was over. He dropped his sword and knelt to lift Alden's head. The boy opened his mouth to speak and was gagged by a rush of crimson blood. Paul wiped the blood from the boy's lips and Thad moaned, "Now I never—won't never be able to—marry Miss Charity—take care of—" Unable to finish, he died in Paul's arms.

Winslow rose to his feet sick at heart, but then he saw Dan getting up, holding his head where the ball had creased it. The big man was smiling, and he came and threw his arms around Paul, saying, "God has been good to us, Paul."

Paul looked around at the dead men and those that would soon die but who now were crying out with pain. He bowed his head, filled with sadness. Then he looked at Dan and cried, "Why do men treat each other worse than beasts?"

Dan shook his head, compassion filling in his eyes. "Why, God's not finished with us yet, Paul. One day we'll study war no more."

"I wish I never had to lift my hand against another human being!"

"Why, thee *should* feel like that. Don't thee suppose that Gilbert Winslow and all thy people felt the same? We're weak vessels, Winslow, but God will see us through."

Winslow nodded, and began tending the wounded and the dying. Charity came running up and stopped short as she saw his bloodstained garments and bloody head.

"I feel like something out of the sewer, Charity," he groaned, and a wave of fatigue and horror gripped him. "Thad is dead. He died with your name on his lips." She gave a cry and fell down to touch the forehead of the boy, and when she looked up Paul had moved away and was speaking to the crew.

All morning the cries of the wounded sounded as the surgeon tried to sew them together, and by noon the warship *Jupiter* of the Royal Navy was *The Gallant Lady* once again, under the command of Paul Winslow, Captain.

CHAPTER TWENTY-FIVE

ADMIRAL DE GRASS

★ ★ ★ ★

Lieutenant General de Armees Navales, Le Comte de Grass, Commander in Chief of His Most Christian Majesty's naval forces in the West Indies, paced the high poop of his flagship, swinging at anchor in Port Royal bay. Fore and aft, he paced, taffrail to quarterdeck.

He had fought in thirty campaigns, this man, and for more than forty-five years he had served French kings. In the American war for independence he had already taken part in eight engagements. His thoughts turned longingly toward home—the Chateau de Tilly, near Versailles. He yearned to feel the rich earth of France underfoot, treading his family estate instead of hard oak decks. His love for home and France was written in his will; no matter in what part of the world or on what sea he might expire, his heart was to be sent to repose eternally in the chapel of his chateau.

But short of death, the count knew that months must pass, perhaps years, before he would see home and family again. There was much to be done for his king on this side of the Atlantic, and he had done little. Rodney and Hood, the English admirals, had checkmated every attempt he had made to bottle up the American coast.

His second in command called from the wheel, "Ship is arriving, monsieur."

The count moved to starboard and saw a fleet three-masted ship that could only be American-built skimming over the water.

As he admired the way she seemed to glide in the peculiar fashion of her type, he mentally added up his triumphs since arriving in the West Indies with his fleet two months before. He had attacked St. Lucia, where the English fleet was a constant threat to French ships, and had driven Hood farther north. He had captured the island of Tobago, but had been repulsed at Barbados, one of England's richest and largest naval supply bases.

All in all, it had been a stalemate—a duel of the minds, a threat of fleets. Thrust and parry and thrust again. He had not succeeded, but M. de Grass well knew the final test was still to come. The war for American independence would be decided not by armies but by ships. The sea lanes along the American coast would be decisive. If he could gain control of those water routes, the war would soon be won. Yet he dared not leave the West Indies until Rodney's fleet had been drawn away.

He said, "I will speak with the captain of that American schooner." Going below, de Grass spent the next two hours poring over maps, as he did every day. So engrossed was he that he did not hear the steward enter, and he looked up with a start when he heard the man say, "Sir, the American captain—he is here."

"Bring him in, Pierre."

He straightened up stiffly, and moved in front of the map table to meet the three Americans who came through the door. He greeted them politely, surprised to see that one of them was an attractive young woman dressed in a man's trousers. *Ah, who can tell with these wild Americans?* the count thought, but he said only, "Welcome to my ship. I am Count de Grass." His English was flawless, and the richness of his French accent gave a fluid motion to the language that invested it with life and interest.

"I am Captain Paul Winslow, Continental Navy, and this is my first lieutenant, Mr. Daniel Greene." The trim young captain introduced the third member. "And may I present Miss Charity Alden."

"We have so few ladies out here, it is indeed a pleasure to have you, Mademoiselle Alden." He moved forward and took the hand she extended, then bent to kiss it.

The gesture brought a blush to Charity's face, and she said in a flustered tone, "Oh, thank you, sir!" The count was a handsome man, over six feet tall, powerfully built, yet moving with agility and grace. His advanced years were evident only in his graying hair, drawn back from wide temples and gathered by a ribbon at the back of his neck. His eyes beneath heavy brows seemed aware of everything; a patrician nose marked his noble lineage.

"Are you attached to any commander, Captain?" de Grass asked, motioning them to take their places around the large oak table.

"Well, sir, we are in a rather peculiar position." Paul spoke quickly of the way they had recaptured *The Gallant Lady*, and the count was properly impressed.

"Indeed, you have done well!" he exclaimed. "I have never heard of such a thing in all my years in the navy." He gave Charity a warm smile and said, "I take it that the ship will be in your name as the original owner?"

"I . . . I'm not certain, Your Excellency," she answered. "Captain Winslow's uncle, a major with General Washington, persuaded the general to give us a commission. If we could recapture *The Gallant Lady*, she was to be under the authority of the naval forces of the United States until the end of the war. He also gave Paul Winslow a commission as captain."

"Ah, and what were his intentions—General Washington?" the count asked, his face intent. "I have had a recent communication from His Excellency—and he is very insistent on our plans."

"General Washington sent us word through Major Adam Winslow that we were to come to you as soon as possible, to be of any aid we could," Paul spoke up.

"Good! I have no ship as fast as yours. You will be my eyes, Captain! If we are to be of service to your country, we must somehow slip through the fingers of the English admiral and strike the British fleet off your coast. That is what General Washington urges. He thinks the time is ripe—but it will not be easy."

"You will take your fleet to America, sir?" Charity asked.

"My fleet needs to be in three places at once," the count replied. "To escort the trade home, to go to the American coast to aid Rochambeau, and to protect our West Indies while the British fleet remains."

"My uncle thinks that Rodney will take his fleet from here to reinforce the British blockade. And he says if that happens, there's not much hope of winning the war."

"Yes, that is what General Washington warns me of in his dispatch." A frustrated look came to the count's eyes. "I must decide," he stated slowly, "for this is one of those times when history hangs in the balance. Most of the time, history is slow, seeming not to move at all, or if things do happen, they have little impact.

But every now and then, there comes a moment of destiny, and the decision rocks empires. I think we are now at such a time—and what happens now will change the nature of America—and of the world."

"I agree, sir," Greene replied. "If this war is lost, England will rule North America. That would be the end of France as a world power, as you well know—and it would mean that America would remain forever a minor colony instead of becoming a powerful nation."

Count de Grass smiled at him. "Lieutenant, you have said it well. So, I would have you be at my call at all times. I must find a time when Rodney is looking the other way—and when that moment comes, we will drive across the sea at full speed. I will need your ship desperately."

"It will be our pleasure to serve you, sir."

The count rose and the others followed. He went with them onto the deck, saying as he walked, "I will give orders for your ship to be supplied, and if you need men, I will have them transferred to your ship. I want you to be battle ready as soon as possible."

They left the ship and returned to the *Lady*, where they brought the crew up-to-date on their new assignment. There was a meeting with the nucleus of the original crew—Miles Lester, Laurence Conrad, who would be the second lieutenant, and Benjamin Smith, the new master gunner. They met in the captain's cabin, and as Paul outlined the plan, speaking swiftly and moving with authority, Dan leaned forward and whispered to Charity, "He's a born leader!"

They all received their assignments, and Paul continued. "We'll take on all the powder and shot we can carry. Smith, you'll get some new hands, experienced men, and I'm expecting you to hit with those guns like they were Kentucky long rifles!"

Ben Smith, a wiry brown man of few words, spit on the floor before he thought, wiped his mouth with embarrassment, then said, "I'll shoot the eyes out of them Britishers, Cap'n!"

"We'll go out every day for firing practice, and I want you to get the crew so sharp they can spin the *Lady* around like a shake of a duck's tail! We'll likely run up against ships with more fire power, but if we're ready, they'll never be able to get a shot at us. Anything else?"

"I think we ought to investigate Port Royal's social life, Captain," Conrad spoke up. "I mean, if we're going up against the whole British fleet, why, we ought to have a fling first, don't you agree?"

Winslow's white teeth gleamed as he smiled at the lean form of Conrad, and he nodded. "Shore leave for everyone—but in shifts. I want the ship manned and ready for action twenty-four hours a day. One third of the crew can ruin themselves at a time."

Conrad let out a long sigh. "Well, then, here I go to the flesh-pots to get drunk again." He shook his head mournfully, and added, "And do I dread it!"

★   ★   ★   ★

There are few spots on planet earth more beautiful than the West Indies in spring, and for the next two weeks the crew of the *Lady* had the most pleasant time of their lives. The fitting of the ship was not difficult, but the training was hard, though brief. Captain Winslow was a hard-eyed slave-driver during morning drills, pushing the men with a single-minded determination; but when the ship returned to her slip in the afternoon, a third of the crew piled off and eagerly headed for downtown Port Royal.

Dan and Charity found time to explore the town, though Paul refused to leave the ship until everything was to his liking. It was a time of relaxing pleasure to stroll along the narrow streets, which appeared to have had no preconceived plan as they wound through the ancient city. The two also spent time shopping and watching the pageant.

One afternoon when they had stopped for a fruit drink, Dan asked suddenly, "Does thee think Paul has changed?"

She sipped the sweet drink, shrugged, and thought for a moment. Her skin was already a golden color from the southern sun's rays, and very becoming to her. "Oh, I suppose—but it's just the responsibility."

He studied her profile a while and smiled. He was such a big man that the cup of juice looked fragile in his large hands. He rolled the drink around, took a sip, then commented solemnly, "We have changed, too. How long is it since we were engaged? Now look at us."

"Poor Dan!" she comforted teasingly, and her teeth gleamed against the tan as she added, "Be glad you didn't get me, Dan. I'll be a frightful wife. Bossy and mean!"

"Not true!" he protested.

"Anne will be perfect for you—if you can convert her."

He blinked at her in surprise, and she laughed at him and shook his shoulder. "You think I'm blind as well as stubborn? She's so much in love with you she can't see straight!"

"I—I don't want to rush into a marriage, Charity. Once bit, twice shy, as they say."

"Oh, you're still sensitive over getting passed over by Julie—and by me," she shrugged. "Does a man no harm to get rejected a few times, Dan. Makes him humble."

"It's not much pleasure. Makes me feel like a fool."

She got up and pulled at him until he arose. "Come on, let's walk. Maybe I'll make you buy me a parrot."

As they left the crowded street and walked along the white beach, she had a thought, and asked him, "Did you ever hear the old tale about how lovers find each other?"

"Not in the Bible, is it?" he grinned. "Then I don't know it."

"Well, it seems that when God created the world, He made a creature, a beautiful creature and it was both male and female. But this creature did something very wrong, so God tore it into two parts and threw it into the world. Now there were many of these creatures, but all of them had been torn in half, just like you tear a sheet of paper in half, you see?"

"Not really."

"Why, when you tear a paper in half, only the other half of that paper will really fit, you simpleton! So the male half and the female half of this creature spent their lives searching through the whole world to find each other."

"So they could fit properly together again?"

"Of course! So in this world every man has to search for the one woman that's a perfect fit for him—and the woman does the same. And I think that Anne Winslow is the one you're looking for, Dan. Neither Julie nor I would really 'fit' you."

"And who is the other half of *thee*, Charity?" Dan asked quietly, pulling her to a stop and looking at her intently.

She was taken off guard, and to her extreme disgust, tears gathered in her eyes. He put his arm around her, murmuring softly, "I think that thee does know the answer to that."

She sobbed against his shoulder, her words muffled as she uttered, "I do love him so, Dan!"

He held her until she finally pulled herself away, then handed her a large white handkerchief. "It's clean," he remarked.

"What are we going to do, Dan?" she moaned. "We've both

given our lives to God—though I'm just a baby at such things—
and we can't marry anyone who's not going after the Lord."

"Why, we must ask God to change them," he replied. "He is
able to do exceeding abundantly above all we ask or think."

"Well, I can *think* a lot," she spouted, a tremulous smile touching her lips. "But it's a big order—even for God."

They got back to the ship to find Paul bright-eyed with excitement. "Where've you been? Never mind—I've got a word from de
Grass!"

"We're pulling out?" Dan asked, his eyes shining.

"Not right now, not today—but soon. Here's what he told me
this afternoon. He's let word get to Rodney that he's sick, that he's
going to take the fleet back to France. And he's even giving a farewell ball to make them swallow the bait."

"Then what?"

"After the ball when Rodney is lulled to sleep, de Grass will
slip away, but not to France. Our fleets will go to drive the British
fleet away from the coast, and then Washington can move on Yorktown to whip Cornwallis."

"It will work!" Dan agreed instantly. "Always before, when we
whipped the British, they'd back up to that fleet, and we couldn't
do a thing. With the French there, Cornwallis won't have anyplace
to hide."

"Get your best dress ready, Charity," Paul laughed happily.
"I'm taking you to a ball, and we have to make the English spies
think it's the real thing!"

"I don't have a dress!"

"Well, *get* one!" he commanded. "I'm not taking you to a fancy
ball in those breeches, and that's final!"

"Aye, Captain Winslow!" She snapped to attention and gave
him a mock salute. "I'll be in uniform when you come to take me
to the ball."

The secret was guarded so carefully that even the men in the
fleet were persuaded that the armada would sail for France. The
ball was the talk of the whole island, and everybody with any pre-
tension to social standing wrangled an invitation.

On the evening of the ball, Paul put on his uniform: snowy
white breeches and a blue coat with one epaulette on his right
shoulder. He wore Gilbert Winslow's sword at his side, and his
long black hair was tied back with a white ribbon.

He went on deck, and saw that the gig was ready. Just as he

was about to ask where Charity was, she came up the ladder. He stared at her as if she were an alien creature from another planet.

She had managed to have a dress made by a woman on the island who sewed, and it had not turned out quite as she expected. The woman had spoken little English; she had done a beautiful job, but she was accustomed to making dresses for her own people— who wore their dresses cut much lower than was usual in Boston.

Charity had picked up the dress the day of the ball, and had not tried it on until she got back to her cabin. She slipped it on, then stood aghast, staring into the mirror. It was a beautiful dress, made of some frothy material she did not know, with ribbons of green interwoven through the hems of the white cloth. It fit perfectly—but she gave a gasp when she saw how low the seamstress had cut the neckline. She quickly gave a tug to lift it higher, but it was useless, for the dress fit like a glove.

"I can't go like this!' she wailed, and stood there staring at herself. "He'll think I'm a—a *hussy!*"

But it was only an hour before the gig left—so finally she set her jaw and declared through clenched teeth, "I'm going to that ball if I have to go stark naked!"

And when Paul Winslow looked at her as she came up to him on the deck, he batted his eyes, for he had never seen anything more beautiful!

She stood there challenging him defiantly with her large green eyes and said, "Well—are we going, or are you just going to stand there staring at me?" Despite her words, her face was red, and she pulled a thin shawl around her shoulders.

"You look ravishing, Charity," he replied, taking her hand and leading her to the gig. The boat was full, and Dan took one look at her, then smiled broadly, though he said only, "Well, thee is all dressed up for the party, I see."

The ball was held at the great ballroom of Government House. It was a grand affair, with light from a thousand candles flashing on gold sword hilts, setting aglow the decorations of noble and distinguished officers. The Count de Grass, with the wife of the governor on his arm, led the grand march, the blue, white and gold of uniforms making a splash of color.

"I've never seen such a beautiful sight!" Charity murmured, clutching Paul's arm tightly. She looked carefully at the beautifully gowned ladies, their white shoulders and bosoms bathed in soft loveliness from the golden light of the candles, and felt less conspicuous in her own dress.

The evening sped by, and she found herself in Paul's arms, gliding across the floor. He held her loosely, but she was conscious of his strong arms around her. She danced with other officers, and when he came to her and suggested, "Let's get a breath of air," she was ready.

They stepped outside, moving away from the palace until they came to an open garden. The music and the sound of voices were muted as she stood beside a fountain with him.

He said nothing for such a long time that she began to get nervous. But then he looked at her and said, "I remember a time like this, Charity. It was the first thing from my past that came to me—and now it's all as clear as if it happened yesterday! I can remember all of it!" His voice rose with excitement, and he took her hands unconsciously as he cried, "All of it! Not just bits and pieces!"

"Tell me, Paul!" she begged.

"Why, I was in love with Abigail and so was Nathan—but both of us were fools, though we didn't know it. And it was at a ball like this that Nathan took her out to a garden and I followed them. I was ready to kill both of them." He shook his head in wonder as he continued. "I betrayed Nathan to the British, and he was almost executed. What a fool I was!"

She asked quietly, "Do you remember—about us, Paul?"

He stared at her, then nodded grimly. "Some of it I do. I remember you coming into the inn looking for help for Julie—and I remember getting drunk and taking you upstairs."

She reached up slowly and touched the scar on his face. "Do— do you remember when I gave you this?"

He put his hand on hers and shook his head. "No, thank God. I was too drunk, I suppose—and that's *one* memory I never want to come back. What a swine I am!"

She left her hand on his face and shook her head swiftly. "No! You've changed, Paul. Your father spoke to me about it. He said you *did* die in some ways—that the man you were doesn't exist. And he's so proud of you—and so am I!"

"Are you, Charity?" he whispered, his face pale in the silver moonlight. "Are you fond of me?"

"Yes!" she whispered, letting him take her in his arms and press his lips to hers. It was not a demanding kiss, but gentle and sweet.

When he lifted his head he said evenly, "I want to marry you."

She stared at him and stammered, "But—what about Blanche?"

"What about her?"

"Why, you're going to marry her."

"No. I went to her before we left New York. You do remember I left to go into the city?"

"I—I believe I do remember something about it."

He laughed and squeezed her in a delightful fashion. "Oh, Charity, you didn't speak to me for days! You were jealous, weren't you?"

"Of course I was!" Her eyes flashed and she pulled back from him. "And what did you two have to say? Was it a loving reunion?"

"Not exactly," he said dryly. "I managed to sneak out to their summer place and send a message inside. She sent a note back. Would you like to see it?" He pulled a slip of paper from his pocket.

She took it from him and held it to the yellow light shining from the windows of the house.

You are a traitor to your country! it stated in large letters. *If you don't leave at once, I'll notify my father and you will be shot as you deserve!*

"So much for my hopes," he sighed. He took the paper, tore it to shreds and tossed it into the air, saying, "Now that is settled—will you marry me?"

She longed to throw herself into his arms, but she shook her head. "I want to, Paul. I love you so much! But something has happened to me."

"Can you tell me about it?"

"It was when your grandmother died. I called on God—and He came into my life." She peered up at him, her eyes filled with tears, and said, "I belong to God, Paul—and the man I marry will have to belong to Him, too."

He stood there, his face lean and his eyes fixed on her. Finally he said, "I seem to be running into God at every turn. All I can say is, I can't go to God just to please you. That would be wrong—but I tell you this, Charity, everything I've seen that's good in this world has been in the form of one of God's people. I want that goodness in my own soul."

She touched his cheek gently, and then whispered, "You will find God, Paul! You will find Him!" And her eyes were filled with faith as they turned to go inside.

CHAPTER TWENTY-SIX

THE DUEL

★　★　★　★

The plan of de Grass to pull Hood's eyes away from the French fleet was a success—or so it seemed from the reports of the informants who brought news to the count. He waited for two weeks, and was gratified to learn that Hood's squadron had moved away from their position toward the north. De Grass acted immediately, issuing orders that the entire fleet move out. The fleet set sail two days later, and according to the count's orders, took a course that would lead to France rather than America.

"He's a wily old fox," Dan remarked to Charity as they stood with Paul on the *Lady's* deck admiring the fleet. They had taken station off the flagship, and had a clear view of the white sails of the warships as they followed in order. "I think we've fooled Hood—which is a pretty hard trick to bring off!"

"What happens now, Paul?" Charity asked.

"Oh, we'll fake him out on this course for a day or two, then turn and make a drive for the coast. There are just a few British warships there now, and this fleet will drive them off, bottle up the army—then Washington will move in and have Cornwallis in the palm of his hand. And that'll be the end of the war. But," he went on thoughtfully, "if we run into trouble, remember your promise to stay below. I'll need every man I've got."

Two days later, de Grass ordered a change of course exactly as Paul had predicted, and for the next four days every square yard of canvas was put on the yards, for surprise was the essence of the scheme. If word of the attack got out, Hood or Rodney would race to meet the French fleet and parry the blow.

On a bright Sunday morning Dan hurried into Paul's cabin with a message. "Signal from flagship, Captain. You're to report to the admiral aboard his flagship at once. I've had the gig put out for you."

Paul wiped the lather from his face, threw on his clothes, and was soon in the gig headed for the flagship. He climbed on deck, and was escorted at once to de Grass' cabin.

"Captain Winslow reporting, sir."

"Winslow—you made good time." The count's face was tense and he told Paul hurriedly, "We're in trouble, I fear. Our lookout spotted a ship up ahead just at dusk. He got only a glimpse, but she was there this morning—a frigate, he thinks."

Winslow saw the danger at once. "You think she's a British ship?" That was what they had feared most—the fleet being spotted and a report made, alerting the English forces.

"It has to be," the count concluded gloomily. He struck his hands together and cried in anger, "It will destroy our plan!"

"We'll have to capture or sink that ship, sir!"

De Grass stared at Winslow with a set jaw. "It's our only hope—but she's a frigate. We have only ships of the line. None of my ships could catch her—" He paused and seemed to be weighing the quality of the young captain as in a balance. He studied the dark eyes, the firm mouth, the air of determination, then added, "No ship—except yours, Captain Winslow."

A fire leaped into the eyes of Paul Winslow, and he said instantly, "We'll do it, Admiral!"

"Think of it, Winslow!" The count came close and looked down into the face of his officer. "She carries three times your guns, as you well know. Her crew will be well trained, and I don't know of an instance of a sloop defeating a frigate in a close action duel."

"We've got to try, sir," Winslow urged. "If that ship gets away, I think it will mean America loses the war."

De Grass nodded slowly, his eyes moody. "I believe you may be right. Washington can't hold the army together much longer. We're his last hope. You know the odds, my boy. Are you certain you want to attempt it?"

"We must do it, Admiral—there's no other choice!"

"Then go, Captain!" De Grass' French blood got the better of him, and he impulsively threw his arms around Winslow, giving him a mighty hug, and then to the younger man's shock and amazement, kissed him soundly on the cheek! The admiral stood back, smiled and apologized, "Forgive me, Captain. We French are so emotional!"

"Oh—that's all right, sir," Paul answered as he turned to leave. "I'd better get back—and, sir, it's an honor to serve with you!"

"Captain Winslow, the honor is mine! Now, God go with you!"

Paul drove the oarsmen of the gig as if they were galley slaves, and as they sent the craft skimming back toward the *Lady*, he kept his eyes fixed on the horizon where the English ship was lurking. He knew that as soon as the English captain was convinced a French fleet was making for America, he'd drive his ship toward the coast to give the warning.

He hit the deck running and shouting commands. "Lieutenant Greene! I want every inch of canvas at once! Change course three degrees south. All officers in my cabin immediately!"

He hurried to the cabin, followed by the officers as they rushed to his command. He gave them the news, then the ultimatum. "We've got to stop that ship! I don't have to tell you what that means—and I don't know how we're going to do it. But it means the war, I think."

"She's a frigate, Captain," Laurence Conrad stated grimly. "One broadside and she'll blow us out of the water."

"Then we'll have to be certain she doesn't get a good shot at us, Lieutenant! The only plan I've got is to use the qualities built into this ship. We can sail rings around that frigate—and thank God for the long eighteens! We can keep up a running fire and maybe knock her sticks off—dismantle her. If we can slow her down, it'll give de Grass time."

There was an air of uncertainty in the faces of most of the men, a fact Paul knew he could not change. *If I could only speak better—somehow convince them that we have a chance!* he thought, but nothing came and he stood there watching their doubt grow.

"I'm not afraid." Charity suddenly spoke up, and every eye turned to her. She was attired in old blue breeches and the red-and-white checked shirt she wore as her uniform aboard ship. Her heavy mane of auburn hair was bound with a white silk scarf, framing her tanned face and enormous eyes. Her countenance was set, confident, even content.

"My brother died at Valley Forge. My father died on the deck of this ship, and some of your comrades with him. We've all shed our tears for the fallen—but that's not enough!" Her voice rose and she searched them with her gaze. "It's not enough! If our country goes down and becomes a rag for England to wipe her feet on, my father and my brother and your family and friends will all have died—for *nothing*! I say we may go down, but I'd rather go down fighting than run like a whipped dog and let the British put a chain around my neck."

"I says the same, miss!" Ben Smith, the master gunner, had been brought to the meeting by Dan, and he nodded his head with grim determination. "I was born in Devon, and I done my share below decks in England's ships—but I ain't no Englishman. I'm an American. Let's send that there ship to the bottom!"

The air of the cabin was altered immediately, and Paul, seeing their sudden shift, asked, "We're all agreed, then? Good! Now, to your stations—but first, Dan, it might be well for you to offer a prayer."

Dan looked with surprise into the face of the captain, but saw there only an honest light in the dark eyes. He bowed his head and prayed, "Thou art our God—and we are thy people. I know, Lord God, thou hast some of thy children on the ship we'll soon do battle with. We are but weak, foolish men. We have no way to know the mind of our God—but we fight to make a land where the songs of Zion will be sung, where the Gospel of Jesus will be preached, where we can raise our children in the fear of a holy God. We remember the words of thy servant David: 'He teacheth my hands to war, so that a bow of steel is broken by mine arms.' Lord of Hosts, teach all of us to war—and break the bow of steel. Set thy people free—in the name of Jesus Christ."

"Amen," Paul Winslow murmured, and his eyes were fixed on Dan as if the words had somehow gone deep into his spirit. He did not move, and they all saw that he was stirred by the prayer. Then he shook his shoulders, saying quietly, "Take your stations. Tell the crew the situation. They need to know how important this mission is. God be with us!"

The Gallant Lady, carrying full sail, seemed to shoot out of her station, and as she passed the flagship, the signalman, Simmes, called, "Signal from flag, sir." He stared at the pennants and read them to Winslow with a smile. "Little David—slay your Goliath!" He shrugged when Captain Winslow gave him an unbelieving look. "That's what the flags say, sir!"

"Signal *Thank you—and Amen*."

The *Lady* ran before a breeze all morning, and at noon, when all that could be seen of de Grass' squadron were the top gallants of the ships, Dan Greene spotted the frigate. "Sail! Two points off port bow!"

"Where does she bear, Lieutenant?" Winslow shouted from the deck.

Dan peered through the glass, then answered, "She's turning, sir—I think she's spotted us!"

"Stay where you are, Lieutenant. Keep me posted."

In two hours of hard sailing, with the masts bending under the weight of full sail, Paul could see the enemy ship for himself. He was standing beside Blake, the helmsman, when Greene came to his side. There was, Paul saw, an odd look on his face. "What's wrong, Mr. Greene?"

"Well, sir, that ship there—"

When he hesitated, Paul asked impatiently, "Spit it out, man!"

"Well, sir—she's the *Neptune*!"

His words caught Paul off guard, and he could not say a word. The *Neptune*! His mind raced as he thought of what that meant. He had been prepared to do battle—but he had never once thought that he might be directing the deadly fire of his guns against men he knew well! He thought of Captain Rommey, blunt and hard, but who had been almost a father to him—and Burns, that dour Scot who had been his friend—and even Langley, who had been jealous of him, but fair. To fire on them? And the crew! He knew most of them, and soon he would be sending the shot that would mangle them, leave them dead and crippled.

It's not fair, God! he cried out in his mind, and he tried desperately to find a loophole. *I'll let Daniel command,* he thought, but one look at the honest face of the big man told him that was hopeless. He was the only man capable of fighting the ship. *Go back and let de Grass appoint another captain!* But it was far too late for that, he realized in despair.

He turned and walked to the rail, motioning Dan to follow. When they were out of Simmes's hearing, Paul asked, "You know what's eating at me, Dan?"

"Those men are your friends," he nodded. "You are facing the choice of killing men who aren't faceless anymore."

"What can I do?"

Dan stared at the tortured face of the man he'd learned to love. He wanted to put his arm around Paul Winslow, but discipline had to be observed. He answered quietly, "Some things a man must face alone, Paul. This is your Gethsemane—and you only can make the decision."

"I can't do it, Dan! I can't!"

Dan Greene forgot the eyes of the crew. He put his big hand on Paul Winslow's shoulder, and with tremendous compassion in his warm brown eyes, said, "One thing is good—the old Paul Winslow is gone—for he would never have hesitated to do this. I think God has you about whipped, Paul. His grace will see you through and bring you in. Into His house."

Paul slowly nodded, saying in a heavy tone, "Thanks, Dan." He looked up and his eyes were bright with pain as he spoke. "We'll be engaging in an hour. Get the gun crews ready."

"Aye, sir."

A sudden thought struck him, and he lifted his head to glance at the *Neptune*. "Dan—for all Rommey knows, this is still a British ship!"

"Why—I suppose so."

"Quick—run up the British flag! This may be our chance."

Dan saw it at once. "Get in close and blast them? It may work—if they don't blow us up first!"

"I'm hoping that Rommey won't think of that. Get those colors up! Have the gunners rake the decks with the carronades and hit their gun ports with the eighteens!"

"Aye, sir! And I guess you might say that the Good Lord is answering my prayer—teaching our hands to war!"

★   ★   ★   ★

Lieutenant Burns turned to Captain Rommey, who had come on deck to take command. "Sir, that ship that's been shadowin' us, weel, I don't know what it means—but she's the *Jupiter*!"

Rommey's eyes grew large and he took the glass from Burns with an impatient air. "Impossible!" he snorted. The captain froze for a moment, then lowered the glass, his eyes puzzled as he muttered, "It *is* the *Jupiter*! Now what the devil . . . ?"

The two of them watched as the ship grew larger, coming closer by the second. "I can't fathom it, Burns! What is she doing out here? I heard she was being used to take supplies to Admiral Hood." He stared at the English flag on the *Jupiter* and pondered. "Perhaps she's got dispatches for us."

"Perhaps, sir." Burns's voice was doubtful, and then as the

ship drew closer and tacked to come broadside to the *Neptune*, he yelled, "Sir! Her guns are run out! Look! She's pullin' doon the British flag and flyin' the Yankee flag!"

Instantly Rommey bellowed, "Change course! Full about! Beat to quarters!"

The two officers remained in position, stoically willing the frigate to wheel out of range of the guns that threatened them from the sloop, but it was hopeless. "She's goin' to give us a broadside, sir! I'll get to my guns."

"Do the best you can, Lieutenant." Burns disappeared and Rommey stood there listening to the sound of men scrambling and guns being run out, but his attention was on *The Gallant Lady*. He saw that she bore that name on her bow, and she was close enough now to see the officers at their deck stations.

He had never felt so helpless! Ordinarily, he would have laughed at the idea of fighting a single-ship action with a sloop of war. But this was different! Two things ate at him. He remembered the guns aboard the ship, and what Burns had said in his report. "Sir, she's nae such a big ship—but Lord, the guns on her deck! Why, I don't doot she could sink a ship of the line if she got in the first broadside!"

He remembered saying to the Scot with a smile of disbelief. "And do you think a ship of the line would let her get close enough for that? Why, any captain would have her blown out of the water before she could get off a shot!"

But I let her come alongside without a thought! Rommey beat his fist against the rail, and then gripped it with all his might as he heard the lower ports open and some of the guns put in position. *Too late! It's going to be too late!* The deck of the enemy ship was visible now, and it seemed to bristle with guns. His practiced eye could see no flaw in the arrangement, and he thought, *Those big eighteens are aimed low to knock out our guns and hole us below our water line—and those carronades—Lord, how many are there?—will kill every man on deck! They can't miss!*

Then the two ships were even, and the air was filled with the mighty roar of cannon. The *Neptune* reeled beneath the shock, and Rommey fell to the deck. The fall probably saved his life, for the helmsman, who was directly behind him, was transformed into a mass of raw flesh by the whirring chains that ripped up the wheel even as it killed the man.

The air was full of death, as canisters of grape—small musket balls in cans that exploded—sent a deadly hail of fire over the deck, cutting the crew down as with a scythe!

Rommey struggled to his feet and looked around in despair. Most of the men were either lying still in death, or were twisting on the deck in their own blood, and the ship was helpless. One of the eighteens had struck the foremast dead center, and it had fallen back into the mainmast, killing several men as the heavy yards crashed to the deck. The ship was reeling like a drunken man, for the wheel was gone and the rudder flapped and thrashed in the water.

Rommey began to cry out orders, rallying the crew. "Baxter, get the marines to the tops! Have them pick off the gunners of that ship! Lieutenant Rogers, rig a line to the rudder—get us some control. She's turning to give us another broadside!"

He would not have believed a ship could turn so quickly, but he saw that the American captain was doing just what he himself would have done—seeing the terrible damage the first broadside had caused, he was driving the sloop around and in a few minutes would be in position to deliver another!

Down in the lower gun deck, Burns was misled. He heard someone cry, "Here she comes again!" and he thought the enemy would come to his starboard. There were too few gunners left alive to man both batteries, so he commanded at once, "All gunners, man starboard guns!" The men obeyed, but then as the guns were run out, Dion Sullivan, captain of number-three gun, rose up with wild eyes. "Mr. Burns! She's comin' on the port!"

Burns stood there, his mind reeling. He dropped to stare out one of the ports—and there she was, *The Gallant Lady*! She was beginning her run, and before he could even reverse his orders, the bow guns fired and he saw the first two gun crews blown to bits by the explosions! He began to weep as once again the *Neptune* shook beneath the hail of heavy metal. "God! Our enemies have triumphed!" he whispered, and tears ran down his cheeks. After the broadside had shattered the lower deck, there was a babble of cries, and then he heard a command: "All hands on deck to repel boarders!"

When he got to the deck, fighting his way through the press, he reached the forecastle deck, and saw the captain staring at the enemy ship that had completed her turn and was gliding in, her decks lined with boarders.

"We must not lose the ship, Mr. Burns," Captain Rommey told

him quietly. His face was pale, but calm. And he added, "We've been outdone—but we have more men than that sloop. We must win the battle on this deck!"

"I doot, sir," Burns replied, "that we have more men." He stared about the deck and thought of the carnage below. "But we'll nae give up, sir!"

"Look at the enemy. That's their captain getting ready to lead the boarding party. Do you recognize him, Mr. Burns?"

Burns followed the direction of Rommey's hand and breathed a name. *"Hawke! It's Hawke!"*

"Yes!" the captain hissed. He looked at Burns and asked, "Do you still believe in predestination, Angus? Did God put that man on this ship so we could save him and train him—in order that he would one day be the instrument of our destruction?"

Burns did not answer, for his mind was blank. "Shall I command the deck defense, sir?"

"Yes. We must not lose! If that fleet gets to the coast, we will have lost America—so have no mercy, Mr. Burns! Save that for later!"

★　★　★　★

As the two ships converged, Paul stood beside the rail, his sword drawn. The crew had gone wild as the *Lady* had shot the larger ship to pieces without taking a single blow. Several men had gone down, the victims of the marines firing from the tops of the *Neptune*, but a murderous blast with the carronades had ripped through the tops, shredding men and sails alike.

"Ready!" Winslow yelled, and there was an answering cry as the men waved their swords in the air. He looked at the deck of the *Neptune*, and it gave him a queer feeling, for he knew every inch of it. Now it seemed to be carpeted with dead men—dead and wounded. He looked midships where Angus Burns and Captain Rommey were ready to direct the battle on the deck, and almost parallel with him, he saw Langley. Suddenly their eyes met, and Langley's jaw dropped, for he had not known until that second who was in command. Then his mild eyes blazed with fury and he screamed, "Ready, men! Kill them all!"

Paul saw two of the marines in the tops drop like red fruit from the foretop, their screams lost in the battle cry that came from both crews. Beside him, a young seaman named Trent took the full impact of a musket ball. The sound, like someone thumping a ripe fruit, went through Paul like fire. Then they were on top of the enemy.

"*Ready, lads!*"

He watched the sea rising and breaking against the *Lady*, the pressure mounting against her yards.

"*Now!*"

He gripped the rail as the helm went over and the bows started to pull toward the enemy. Sunlight flashed on the sloop's quarter-deck, and then her side exploded in a crash of musket fire, blowing great gaps in the crew of the *Lady*.

Winslow almost fell as the man next to him crashed against him, killed by a musket ball. He dragged himself up, and threw himself over the side. Paul waved his sword above his head and ran toward the deck where Rommey and Burns were waiting. *If we can take them prisoner, it'll be over*, he thought.

"*This way!*" he screamed, and then he was in the thick of battle. The steel of the English was ready, and Winslow crossed swords with a petty officer and then slipped on the deck, the breath driven from his body as he pitched headlong across the other man. He felt the man jerk and kick, and saw the awful agony in his eyes as Whitefield pulled him away. "Be watchful, sir!' he cried out. "We can't lose you!"

The deck was so packed with fighting men that it was almost impossible to move; but somehow he made his way to the ladder that was already crowded with men—some of them English, some American. He glanced up and met the eyes of Captain Rommey— but at the same moment he was struck by a blow in the back and turned to put his blade through the chest of a wild-eyed seaman.

The fight raged from stern to bow, and there was no quarter asked and none given. He saw Dan Greene duck under a blow of Langley's sword, and then leap onto the man like a tiger, the two of them rolling on the blood-spattered deck. Benjamin Smith was killed, fighting beside Winslow. He was run through by a bayonet, and the marine who killed him died instantly, shot in the right eye by Conrad, who was fighting like a madman.

It could not go on long with such intensity, Winslow knew, and the issue was in doubt. *Got to get the captain!* he thought desperately. With a gargantuan effort he scrambled up the ladder and found himself in a fight with the small group that had ringed Rommey.

Angus Burns saw him instantly, and came at him with his saber lifted high. The Scotsman knew he had no chance—not against Hawke's sword! He had seen the dark American play with the best swordsmen on the *Neptune* as if they were children. Nevertheless he threw himself between the two captains in a wild attempt to save Rommey!

Paul could have killed him with a single thrust—but he could not do it. He avoided the wild slash of Burns; then pulling his heavy pistol from his belt, he struck the man on the head. Burns went down like a dead man, and someone yelled, "Sir! Behind you!"

He whirled to see that a lieutenant with battle-crazed eyes was lifting a pistol, and there was no time to duck. He was frozen to the deck, expecting at any moment to feel the pain of death—and then a form was in front of him, and he recognized Enoch Whitefield's face. There was an explosion and he felt the man's body jolt, then go limp.

"Enoch!" he screamed, and struggling to his feet, saw that Conrad had cut the officer down. Dan Greene was there, blood all over his chest. He had a sword, and seeing his captain down, he had leaped forward and Captain Rommey had parried his thrust. Their blades rang like bells, but even as Winslow got to his feet, he saw Dan's strong blow drive Rommey's sword upward. Then with another slash, he drove the blade out of Rommey's hand.

The rage of battle was on Dan's face, the tears streaming down his cheeks. His mild expression was gone, and there was madness in his eyes.

Rommey stood there helpless but with no sign of fear in his eyes as the American drew back his blade, and he knew he was a dead man.

Then, as Greene's blade leaped forward, it was deflected, for Paul Winslow had made a lightning-like move with his sword; and Greene's blow went to Rommey's left, doing no harm.

There was a single instant when the eyes of Rommey and Winslow met. The older man was bitter, and in the agony of defeat, for one moment he wished more than anything else to destroy this man who had been like his son. Then he nodded and the light in his eyes dimmed.

"The ship is yours, Captain," he said quietly. Rommey shouted to his crew, "All hands, *Neptune*, surrender!" He stooped, retrieved his sword, and tendered it to Winslow.

"Keep your sword, sir." Winslow shook his head, saying, "I didn't think it would come to this, sir." Then he turned and knelt down on the deck over Whitefield.

"Enoch!" His voice cracked and he shook his head helplessly.

"Sir?" Whitefield was breathing, but his lips were flecked with blood and his eyes were glazed with death. "I—I'm proud you're safe—sir!"

"Whitefield! You shouldn't have done it! You're dying for me!"

The eyes of the sailor opened, and he smiled. His voice was so faint that Winslow had to lean forward to hear it.

"Sir—I'm not—the only one—who died for you! Jesus did!"

Winslow felt his eyes fill up, and he nodded, unable to speak.

"Sir—would you—like to take Him? He's come for me—but it'd please Him—and me, too, if'd you'd ask Him to be—your savior. Would you—do it, sir?"

Winslow's heart suddenly broke and he whispered, "Oh, God! I ask you to forgive me! Jesus, save me!"

At the words Whitefield gave a glad cry, and he reached up to touch the face of his captain. "Sir—it's happy—I am—"

And then he slipped away, slumping in Winslow's arms. Paul Winslow knelt on the bloody deck, holding the body of his friend. And looking up to heaven, he said, "I'll serve you all my life, Jesus!"

CHAPTER TWENTY-SEVEN

IT'S GOD'S WILL

★ ★ ★ ★

The damage done to both ships had been considerable, though the *Neptune* had suffered the most. More than a dozen balls had punched holes below the water line, so for several days it took every effort to keep her pumped out. Finally the damage to the hull was repaired, but there was not an available spar to replace the foremast, so Winslow commanded Greene to go aboard as prize captain.

"You'll just have to keep her afloat the best you can," he said as the two of them met on the deck of the *Lady*. The battle and the loss of many men had etched lines in both their faces. But for Winslow it was worse, for he had stood at the rail to bury his own dead, and then beside Captain Rommey as the still forms of the *Neptune*'s crew slid into the deep.

"Aye, sir." Dan paused for a moment before asking hesitatingly, "What will happen to the prisoners?"

"Prison for most—but I expect Captain Rommey will be exchanged."

"His career is over. He'll never live it down, a frigate being defeated by a sloop!" Greene's eyes were bright with admiration, and he added, "It was tremendous, sir! Nothing like it ever!"

Winslow allowed himself to smile, saying, "It was—but the credit goes to the crew—and to you." His face darkened, and he groaned, "Poor Langley! He was a good officer." Langley had gone down under Greene's sword, and though he had not been a close friend, he was part of Winslow's life, and the loss saddened him.

"Aye, sir. But think of it as a thing that had to be done."

"It's still hard." He forced himself to smile, then said, "Well, off with you, Lieutenant! Make the best speed you can and we'll lag along behind."

"Aye, sir."

"And tell Captain Rommey I'm expecting him and his officers to dinner tonight."

Actually, Paul had been wondering if he should issue such an invitation. He had slept badly, riddled with guilt as he thought of the captain. The officer had done him nothing but good, and it cut him sharply to know that he had engineered Rommey's downfall.

All day he walked the deck silently, speaking only to issue necessary orders, apprehensive over the meeting with Rommey and Burns. He made a trip to the hospital area, thankful that it was not in the same condition he'd found it after the battle—*that* had been a scene from hell itself!

Lanterns had revealed a seaman named Cates strapped and writhing like a sacrifice on an altar, his leg already half amputated by Rafe Morgan, the ship's surgeon. The latter's face was devoid of expression as his fingers worked busily with the glittering saw. His assistants were using all their strength to restrain the struggling victim and pin his spread-eagled body on top of the platform of sea chests, which sufficed as an operating table. The man had rolled his eyes with each nerve-searing thrust of the saw, and had bitten into the leather strap between his teeth until he passed out from the excruciating pain.

It had taken more out of Winslow to stand there and share that agony than it had to tackle the *Neptune*, but he knew such was part of his duty.

He had been sickened by the sight all around him, as the other wounded had awaited their turn, some propped on their elbows as if unable to tear their eyes from the gruesome spectacle. Others lay moaning and sobbing in the shadows, their lives ebbing away, and thereby spared the agony of knife and saw. The air had been thick with the stench of blood and rum, the latter being the only way of numbing the victim's senses before his turn came.

He had gone around to each man, speaking a word of encouragement, and was surprised to find Charity in a corner of the room putting a bandage on the stump of a young man's leg. The heat was terrible; he saw that she did not have on a dry thread, and her face was worn with strain.

"Don't do this, Charity," he said thickly. "It's not a job for a woman."

"It's a job for who will do it," she retorted, her pugnacious air forcing him to nod and smile grimly.

"If you won't obey the captain's orders, then the captain will have to join you." He had stripped off his coat and all day they had borne the burden of the pain and death that lay heavy in the small room.

They had been drawn closer than they'd ever been, and now as he entered the surgery, he was pleased to see that it was different. Charity had put the surgeon to rout, demanding fresh air for all the men, so that a place had been made for them on deck where they could soak up the life-giving sunshine. She had commandeered the galley, seeing that the wounded men got the best of the food, and even now as Paul entered, she was bathing the chest of a boy not over sixteen who had lost his left arm.

The boy's name, Winslow knew, was Tommy Hooks, one of the lads from Boston. He'd been a powder monkey and one of the most cheerful members of the *Lady*'s crew, scampering up the rigging very much like a real monkey. Now he lay with his face turned to the wall.

" . . . won't have to worry, Tommy," Charity was saying. "You'll be able to get a place on a ship. There are lots of jobs for a bright young fellow like you."

"With only one hand?" he retorted bitterly, and turned his head to look at her. "Wot could I do, Miss Charity?"

"You can serve on the next ship I get, that's what!" she promised. "I'll need a quartermaster, and you're quick with figures and write a good hand."

"Would—would you really take me, miss?"

She laughed at him, and slapped his chest sharply. "You know what I think? I don't think you're worried about a job. You're worried about what the girls will think!"

His face grew red, and he mumbled, "Aw—who cares what they think?" He swallowed hard and asked timidly, "Do you think they'll mind much?"

She picked up the towel she'd been using, put it in the basin, then bent over and whispered so that Winslow barely caught it.

"Tommy, I'm a woman, and I'm in love!"

"Are you, miss?"

"Yes! And my sweetheart's got a wound, too. Not his hand—

but he's got one. And I'll tell you a secret—I don't mind a bit. As a matter of fact, I'm so crazy in love with him, I wouldn't care if he had both his arms cut off! And neither will the girls. When that arm heals, you'll get a shiny steel hook, and when you go to church with your new white uniform on, and the girls see that hook, they'll start whispering, like girls do! And one of them will say, 'That's Tommy Hooks, the one who fought on *The Gallant Lady!* He lost his hand—see that hook! He's a hero!' And then they'll fairly jostle each other to get to sit next to you! Oh, won't you be something, though!"

Winslow saw the boy swallow; then with his face working to keep back the tears, he had suddenly seized Charity's hand and kissed it.

"Oh, getting a little practice, are you, Tommy?" She had laughed, and as she turned Winslow saw the worship in the boy's eyes.

"Why, Captain!" she exclaimed, "how are you today?"

"First rate," he smiled. "Are you about ready to leave?" he asked Charity.

"In a few minutes."

After they left the cabin, they walked to the rail and stood looking down at the waves lapping against the ship.

"I heard what you said to Tommy," Paul began, breaking the silence.

"About the girls? Well, he needs some encouragement."

"Not about that—though that was wonderful—but the way you handled it. You always know just what to say to the men to make them forget their loss. But that wasn't what I meant."

"Why, what did you hear?"

"I heard you tell him about your sweetheart—the one with the scar that you—how did you put it. Let me see . . ." He put his finger on the scar on his cheek and said, as if he was having trouble remembering, "I think it's something like: *I'm so crazy in love with him, I wouldn't care if he had both his arms cut off!*"

Charity stared at him and her face flushed a fiery red. "You—you had no business eavesdropping!"

"That's one of my minor sins," he replied, taking her hand in his. Then he sobered. "Charity, do you love me?"

She looked at him quietly, finally whispering, "You know I do, Paul!"

"I love you, too. And I'll say as much for you as you said for me—nothing can change what I feel for you. If you lost your beauty, I'd still love that girl that's inside."

They stood there looking into each other's eyes, searching, probing the depths. After a while, he dropped her hand and leaned on the rail. "I want to tell you something. It's about Enoch."

He told her how the man had died, and how it had made him call out to God. "It's been different since then, Charity," he concluded. His eyes were happy and he added, "I'm not what I ought to be—and I'm not what I'm going to be; but I'm not the man I used to be—that Paul Winslow has died somewhere."

"Paul! I'm so happy!" She forgot all about protocol, and there in the bright sunlight, threw her arms around him and kissed him soundly. Then she drew back, her face rosy. "There! That's the kind of woman I am—no propriety at all! Will I make a captain's wife?"

"I hope you never change!" he smiled. "And you have to marry me, because I've got to go home and tell my family I've become a shouting Methodist! It will shame Mother frightfully."

She laughed at his rueful face. "Oh, Paul, it won't be hard. She's been worried about Anne marrying Dan and dressing up in gray and becoming a quiet Quaker woman. Now she'll be so busy trying to keep you from acting like an enthusiast, she'll have no time to worry about Anne!"

"I hope so. Father—I think he'll come around. He's been hit on all sides with the Gospel."

"So the House of Winslow is coming to the Lord!"

"Yes."

They stood silently for a moment, each lost in thought. Paul was the first to speak as he remembered his invitation for the evening meal. "Rommey and Burns are coming to supper tonight. I want you to be there to help me. I feel terrible about them. I owe both a great debt, but look what I've done to them."

She agreed, and that night she took all the strain out of the meeting.

When they were all seated, she looked across the table at Angus and said, "I have a treat for you, Lieutenant Burns. We have a cook who comes from your country—and he's made a special dish for you."

"For me? What is it?"

"You'll have to wait and see," Charity replied. Then she turned to Rommey. "Captain Rommey, I'll be blunt with you."

"Oh?" Her manner amused him, and despite the gloom that

shadowed his eyes, he smiled. "What form is this bluntness to take?"

"A personal remark." Charity told him frankly, mystifying him further. "I have stolen the heart of your prospective son-in- law," she stated calmly.

Paul, who had taken a sip of wine, suddenly choked on it, shocked at her words. "Charity!" he exclaimed, "for heaven's sake!"

She gave him an impatient look, saying, "Oh, Paul, did you think we'd manage to get married without his finding out about it? Be sensible."

"I don't know what to say to you," Rommey returned, wonder in his eyes.

"Well, I know what to say to you. You're a man of sense, Captain, and I tell you to your face that Blanche and Paul would have been perfectly miserable if they had married—and I suspect that you've been aware of that."

Rommey nodded. "I have thought it would be difficult. She's a willful girl—and Mr. Winslow has proven to be quite a rugged type. It would have been like fire and gunpowder."

"Of course it would!" Charity declared emphatically.

Rommey smiled at her and remarked, "I must say, however, that the same problem seems to be in your future, Miss Alden; for you are a very *forceful* young lady yourself."

"Yes, but Paul loves me—and when two people love each other as we do, they'll make a marriage work."

At that moment the door opened and a small, sandy-haired man brought a dish in and with a single glance went straight to where Lieutenant Burns sat. He put the bowl down and said, "Sir, I trust you'll find this a bit of home."

"Haggis!" Burns nearly shouted when he lifted the lid. He looked up with his eyes gleaming and a huge smile. "Oh, man, how did you do it?"

"It's a bit of what we brought from the Indies, sir."

"What is it?" Winslow asked.

"It's a dish made from a sheep's head, Captain," Angus explained happily. "Would ye care for a leetle bite?"

"No!" Paul responded quickly, restraining a shudder. "I wouldn't want to deprive you, Mr. Burns!"

The cook brought food for the rest and the supper went well, and just before Charity left, she reached out and shook hands with

Captain Rommey. An impish light touched her green eyes, and she said, "I couldn't give you a sheep's head to make peace with you, Captain; but I think I deserve your thanks for taking Paul off your hands."

"Well . . . thank you, Miss Alden," he answered. "Perhaps you're right— and I can tell you that Blanche is such a nationalist, she'd never marry an American. But it will be a comfort to me in prison to know that I won't have to adjust myself to a Yankee son-in-law."

She stared at him, saying soberly, "I do have one gift for you, sir—but you can't have it until we land. Then I think you'll feel better."

"No man feels better about prison—but I am grateful for your kindness, Miss Alden. Captain Paul Winslow is a lucky man!"

"What gift are you going to give the captain?" Paul asked as soon as they were alone.

"I'll let you know when we're almost home," she promised. Then she put her arms around him and kissed him thoroughly. "And I know what I want for a wedding present."

"Something expensive?" he smiled. "I'm a poor officer."

"You'll find out when we get home."

He teased her for several days, but she would never tell him. Finally they were on deck one evening and he said, "We'll be home tomorrow or the day after. Tell me what you want for a wedding present."

So she told him.

Two days later the ships reached the coast, and to Dan Greene's surprise, he received a written order from his captain.

Lieutenant Greene:
    See to the docking of the *Neptune*—I will take *The Gallant Lady* for a short cruise to the north. Have Captain Rommey and Lieutenant Burns sent to *The Gallant Lady*.

Greene obeyed, but as the *Lady* sailed away, he scratched his head, wondering, "What's that woman doing to Paul now?"

Rommey and Burns were soon standing on the deck of the *Lady*. They looked up to see Charity and Paul coming across the deck.

"Captain, it's time for you to have your present."

"Indeed?" Rommey asked politely. The dark future of a prison had dimmed his eyes, and he could not say more.

"I hope you appreciate your gift, Captain," Paul said with a smile. "It's what Charity asked for her wedding present."

"Her wedding present? How could that—?"

Charity looked earnestly at Rommey, stating quietly, "I want a *whole* husband, Captain. Paul was so consumed with guilt over you and Mr. Burns that I don't think I could have stood living with it—nor could he."

"He did nothing wrong, Miss Alden."

"Perhaps not—but he has grieved over what he feels was a wrong. So I asked him for something for a very selfish reason. I want a whole man, not one who's eating himself alive over guilt."

Rommey looked puzzled. He shook his head, saying, "I don't understand."

"Why, I asked him for your freedom, Captain—and he agreed."

Both men stared at her. "But he can't do that!" Rommey exclaimed. "He has no authority!"

"But he's not English! He's an American!"

"What difference does that make?"

"You English have traditions that are hundreds of years old," she answered simply. "There's a rule for everything. But in America, why, we're *making* our traditions right now. So, Paul has said that both of you can go free."

"Well, not *quite* free," Paul broke in quickly. "I want your paroles—that you'll not serve against America again."

Burns replied instantly, "That's very generous, Captain." He gave a half-sour look at his superior and remarked, "Now that the French have broken the blockade, there won't *be* any action against America in a short time."

Rommey nodded slowly. He walked to the rail, stared out at the coast line, saying nothing for a long time. A gull was crying in the wind, and the sails flapped in the brisk breeze.

Finally he turned and there was relief on his stern face. "Mr. Burns is right. You have won." Then he went to Charity and reached for her hands. "You are a lovely woman—and Mr. Paul Winslow will have his hands full with you. But I am in your debt." He looked up at the sails, then shook his head with a light of gratitude in his eyes. "Miss Alden—this is a very fine ship. But to me *you* will always be the gallant lady!"

He stepped back, and Angus took her hands. "It's a bonny girl ye are! And that man is nae deservin' o' ye." The haggis seemed to have thickened the burr of his speech, and there was a fond light in his eyes as he took Paul's hand. "I'm not going to over-thank you, Paul."

"I hope not. It was Charity's gift."

"I beg to differ." Angus Burns lifted his head and said, "It was God's will! As ye should nae be forgettin', Mr. Paul Winslow!"

"I'll remember, Angus."

Burns shook his head and looked at them, a canny light in his eyes. "The trouble the guid Lord went to—just to make America free! Every man carryin' a musket, and here He has to knock you on the head and have the British make a fine officer out o' ye—so that ye can save the day for Washington!" He lifted his hands and exclaimed, "Marvelous are His ways—but the guid Lord has found a strong man of war in ye, Paul Winslow. God bless ye both!"

They got into a small boat that Winslow had made available to put them on board a British ship anchored off shore, and Angus shouted as the boat moved away from *The Gallant Lady*: "It was God's will! Remember!"

The two of them watched until the small craft was out of sight, and then Charity questioned him anxiously, "Paul, will you be in trouble? for letting prisoners go, I mean?"

"A fine time you picked to think of that!"

"You won't be. Adam will tell His Excellency, and that will fix it."

He stared at her and shook his head. "It's a good thing you're such a beauty! At least I'll have something to look at when I get home after all the trouble you're going to get me into."

She smiled and asked demurely, "Am I beautiful? You must tell me more often—every day!"

"I'll be too busy winning the war!"

"Will it last long?" she wondered.

"There's no way for England to win now." He put his arm around her and they looked at the shore. "It took a French Navy to pull the English out—but our country is going to be all right. And we won't be just a loose collection of colonies. One nation will arise, Charity. And our children will be *Americans*—not Englishmen!"

She lifted her face to gaze at him, her eyes shining. "And we'll be a part of it? Together?"

"Together, Charity—on the Lord's side," he murmured, kissing her softly. Then they turned and looked again at the land—at America that was to come.

The
Indentured
Heart

★ ★ ★ ★ THE HOUSE OF WINSLOW / BOOK 3 ★ ★ ★ ★

THE INDENTURED HEART

★

GILBERT MORRIS

BETHANY HOUSE PUBLISHERS
MINNEAPOLIS, MINNESOTA 55438

Cover illustration by Dan Thornberg
Bethany House Publishers staff artist.

Published by Bethany House Publishers
A Ministry of Bethany Fellowship, Inc.
6820 Auto Club Road, Minneapolis, Minnesota 55438

Printed in the United States of America

Library of Congress Cataloging-in-Publication Data

Morris, Gilbert.
    The indentured heart.

    (The House of Winslow ; #3)
    I. Title. II. Series: Morris, Gilbert. House of
Winslow ; 3.
PS3563.08742I5   1988   813'.54   87-34128
ISBN 1-55661-003-3 (pbk.)

This book is for my favorite Cajuns in all the
world—the Neals.
There may be more generous, hospitable people on
this planet—
but I have not found them yet.

KENNY   OPAL

ANDY   JAMIE

THE HOUSE OF WINSLOW SERIES

GILBERT MORRIS spent ten years as a pastor before becoming Professor of English at Ouachita Baptist University in Arkansas and earning a Ph.D. at the University of Arkansas. During the summers of 1984 and 1985 he did postgraduate work at the University of London and is presently the Chairman of General Education at a Christian college in Louisiana. A prolific writer, he has had over 25 scholarly articles and 200 poems published in various periodicals, and over the past years has had more than 20 novels published. His family includes three grown children, and he and his wife live in Baton Rouge, Louisiana.

GILBERT MORRIS spent ten years as a pastor before becoming Professor of English at Ouachita Baptist University in Arkansas and earning a Ph.D. at the University of Arkansas. During the summers of 1984 and 1985 he did postgraduate work at the University of London and is presently the Chairman of General Education at a Christian college in Louisiana. A prolific writer, he has had over 25 scholarly articles and 200 poems published in various periodicals, and over the past years has had more than 20 novels published. His family includes three grown children, and he and his wife live in Baton Rouge, Louisiana.

CONTENTS

PART THREE
VIRGINIA

PART ONE

BOSTON

★ ★ ★ ★

1740–1745

THE

HOUSE

OF

WINSLOW

Martha Jakes
(1702–   )

|

1727 ———————● Charles Winslow
(1728–   )

|

Miles Winslow
(1675–   )

|

1715 ———————● William Winslow
(1720–   )

|

● Mercy Winslow
(1724–   )

Anne Hawthorne
(1690–1727)

● Adam Winslow
(1727–   )

Gilbert Winslow
(1600–1692)

|

1622 ———————● Matthew Winslow
(1642–1730)

|

Humility Cooper
(1600–1660)

|

1660 ———————

Lydia Carbonne
(1643–1737)

Rachel Winslow
(1661–   )

|

1692 ———————● Saul Howland
(1708–   )

|

Robert Howland
(1658–1715)

CHAPTER ONE

THE PRINTER AND THE PREACHER

★ ★ ★ ★

Adam Winslow never forgot the momentous events of his thirteenth birthday—the first, his meeting with Benjamin Franklin.

Adam had arrived at his special birthday that morning, and thus had been permitted to make the trip from Boston to Philadelphia with his father. But even these august matters faded; in the years that followed, he always remembered that the famous statesmen had, on that late afternoon in 1740, flirted with his sister Mercy in a most forward manner!

Not that it was unusual for men to find his sister attractive— far from it. Adam had grown accustomed to finding the front yard cluttered with young men on Sunday afternoons, drawn by the bright blue eyes, fair hair, and trim figure of Mercy Winslow. But even at that age, he had heard enough of the famous Franklin to be amazed when the portly printer bowed low over his sister's hand, kissed it with a flourish, never letting his eyes wander too far away from her even when he talked business with Miles Winslow.

They had arrived in Philadelphia at dusk after a schooner trip from Boston to New York, and a two-day buggy ride over rough roads. Adam had missed little of the scenes along the way.

Sitting in the back seat of the buggy with Mercy, he had listened to his father talk to William, his twenty-year-old brother. And when they pulled into the crowded streets of Philadelphia, he sat straight up, taking it all in.

Miles Winslow drove the matched bays against a flood of traffic, which all seemed to be headed west. He was a good driver, but it took all his skill to thread the buggy through the mass of pedestrians, horses, and carriages until he arrived at a two-story frame building.

"What's that sign read, William?" he asked wearily.

William Winslow stepped out of the buggy, peered upward in the fading light, then turned and said, "Benjamin Franklin, Printer."

"Hope he's not gone home yet," Miles said, then added, "Mercy, you and Adam come with us." William helped his sister down as Adam scrambled out; then the four of them stepped onto the wooden sidewalk, pushing their way through the crowd. Miles shoved the door open, giving a grunt of approval when he found it unlocked.

The four entered, and Adam's nose twitched at the exotic aroma of ink and paper. A large press was rumbling, operated by a skinny apprentice who gave them no attention at all. Finally a man wearing an ink-stained apron came out of an inner office. He was middle-aged, somewhat portly, and his hair had receded, leaving a large bald dome over his small close-set eyes.

"Yes?" he said with a nervous smile. "Can I help you, sir?"

"Looking for the printer—Franklin," Miles stated.

"At your service, Mister—?"

"I'm Miles Winslow, Mr. Franklin. I wrote you a letter about printing my grandfather's journal."

"Of course! Of course!" Franklin exclaimed. He appraised the two tall men, both over six feet, noting the bright blue eyes and the blond hair with just a touch of red in the lamplight. The older of the two was in his sixties, the younger about twenty. The girl, he saw immediately, was a beauty, with the same fair hair and astonishing blue eyes. But the young boy was quite different—small and very dark. "I believe it'll be an excellent production, Mr. Winslow, excellent!" He looked at the large clock on the wall and shook his head. "It's a little late, but come into my office for a moment."

"This is my son, William, my daughter, Mercy, and my younger son, Adam."

Franklin acknowledged William with a handshake, Adam with a pat on the head, then turned his attention to Mercy. With a smile he bent over her hand, kissed it, and said, "You are most welcome, Mistress Winslow—you grace our poor city!"

William saw Adam staring at the printer, and when he caught his eye, gave a sly wink, then shook his head. Miles gave Franklin a dour look, but Mercy seemed to enjoy the attention, for she smiled and said, "You are gallant, Mr. Franklin."

He held her hand a moment longer than necessary, then wheeled and led the way into the small office in back of the shop. It was cluttered with books and manuscripts of every sort, piled up on the floor and stuffed into every crevice.

"Do you have the manuscript with you, sir?" Franklin asked, glancing through the door at the clock, obviously anxious to leave.

"It's in the buggy," Miles said, then asked with some irritation, "What's going on, Mr. Franklin? I never saw such a mob as that one out there. Is there a public hanging or some other choice entertainment?"

Franklin laughed aloud, with a twinkle illuminating his brown eyes. "Nothing quite so exciting as that, I'm afraid—" Then he gave a shrug, saying, "Only a preacher come to town."

"A preacher!" William's head lifted sharply, and he asked quickly, "What preacher would draw that kind of crowd, Mr. Franklin?"

"None of your home-grown variety, I assure you, sir! No, this is a British minister. Been making quite a stir in England—quite a stir. Name is George Whitefield."

Miles gave a snort and shook his head in disgust. "I've heard of the fellow. All mixed up with the enthusiasts!"

"I'd like to hear him, Father," William said. "You say he's preaching tonight, Mr. Franklin?"

"Yes, I'm going to hear him myself." Pulling off his inky apron, he added, "Why don't you come along, Mr. Winslow—

and we can talk business tomorrow?"

Miles started to shake his head, but William insisted, "We can't miss this, Father. He's set England on her heels, and he's likely to shake up the Colonies the same way."

"Quite so, sir!" Franklin slipped into a brown coat and quickly took Mercy by the arm. With a smile he held firmly to her, piloted the group out of the shop and turned them west. As they made their way down the crowded street, he explained how Whitefield had landed at Newport a short time earlier. He had made a tour of the coastal cities, and his reputation had drawn thousands.

"Never heard anything like him!" Franklin professed, with a wave of his hand.

"Then you are a Christian, sir?" William asked directly, a keen light in his eyes.

The question seemed to take the famous printer off guard, for he faltered slightly, but then threw his head back and said hurriedly, "Why, I am a believer in a divine power, Mr. Winslow!" Then he changed the subject by pointing at a large building directly in front of them. "There is Rev. Whitefield's pulpit this evening—the courthouse steps!"

"He's going to preach *there*?" Miles asked incredulously. "Aren't there any *churches* in Philadelphia?"

"A great number of them, sir," Franklin nodded. "But many of them are closed to Mr. Whitefield due to his rather harsh remarks about the clergy—and in any case, none of them would hold this crowd!"

He waved a hand at the shifting mass of people that stretched from the courthouse steps way down the streets. Nearly every house showed lights in its upper story, and by the flickering lanterns hanging from the walls, Adam could see people hanging out of most of the windows. Franklin crowded them in as close as they could get, and it was fortunate they were with him, for the people made way, so that he was able to find them a place beside the large landing. William, seeing Adam struggling to peer over the level of the porch, picked him up and stood him up on the ledge.

Just as he did so, a massive door opened and three men

walked out, one of them wearing a clerical robe. "That's White-field," Franklin said.

William stared at the minister curiously, for he had heard much of his work in England from a friend at Yale who had been at Oxford with Whitefield and the Wesleys. John and Charles Wesley had been the founders of a small prayer group called by their opponents "The Holy Club." Wesley had simply smiled and adopted the name, and the small band had grown dramatically. The group had been so methodical in their spiritual discipline that their foes had tacked another name on them—"Methodists"—and this name too had been accepted by the Wesleys.

George Whitefield had joined the group at a tender age, and after an awesome spiritual struggle had found a new experience with God. He had gone forth to proclaim his new birth and to call for a turning away from old dead forms. His preaching had shaken England, producing many devoted disciples for the young man—and almost as many critics. When the doors to the churches had been closed to him, he had gone to the fields, preaching in the open air to thousands. The mention of his name had become a magnetic force strong enough to draw massive crowds in any place he chose to speak.

Now he had come to America, and, if Franklin spoke truly, Whitefield was on his way to turning the Colonies upside down as he had the mother country. William realized his father was opposed to the revival methods that had appeared in the Colonies in the early 1730s, but William was eager for a breath of life to touch the churches, so he looked at Whitefield with tremendous interest.

He saw a neat, undersized man, with a boyish look—a stripling of twenty-five with a pallid face. He was youthful, almost angelic; William could hardly believe that such a youth could shake the nation of England. He had dark eyes, one of them with a noticeable squint, and he looked out over the crowd with such calm assurance that a thrill shot through William.

Then he spoke, and such a voice! There was not a sound from the thousands who stood there, no scuffling or whispering. The voice was like a bell, and although Whitefield was speaking almost in a conversational tone, that organ-like voice carried clearly across the night air, down the streets, every syllable sharp and definite.

For over an hour he spoke, and the crowd stood there, rooted and motionless as statues. His text was "Come unto me, and be ye saved, all ye ends of the earth." The voice carried authority, comfort, command, pleading—and William felt, as he was certain that everyone else in that massive crowd felt, that George Whitefield was speaking to *him* directly!

Whitefield preached the riches of God's mercy; then in closing, he lifted his head and called out, raising that magnificent voice to such a pitch that it seemed as though it would touch the clouds floating high overhead: "Father Abraham, whom have you in heaven? Any Episcopalians?"

"No!" he cried, answering his own question in a thunderous voice.

"Any Presbyterians?"

"No!"

"Any Independents or Seceders, New Sides or Old Sides?"

"No!"

"Any Methodists?"

"No!"

"Whom have you, then, Father Abraham?"

"We don't know those names here! All who are here are *Christians*—believers in Christ, men who have overcome by the blood of the Lamb and the word of their testimonies."

Then he threw his arms up and cried out in a voice that seemed to rend heaven and earth and run through the crowd like a bolt of lightning: "Come unto Him, all ye that labor and are heavy laden—and *He* will give you rest!"

And that was the *second* event that Adam Winslow never forgot about that day—not only did Benjamin Franklin flirt with his sister, but for the first time in his life, as George Whitefield cried out those last words, Adam wanted to know God.

William felt the tremor run through his brother's small frame, and after Whitefield turned and left and the crowd began to melt away, William held on to Adam a moment, asking, "Did you like the sermon, Adam?"

The dark blue eyes of the boy touched his with what appeared to be a pleading look; then a curtain seemed to fall over them like a hood, and he shrugged and said, "It was all right, William."

The tall man stared at his brother, regret mirrored in his face as he put him back on the ground. "We'll talk about it later, all right?"

"If you want to."

But that time never came. William watched for a proper time, but the vulnerable air he had seemed to see, if it existed at all, was hidden beneath a shell the boy assumed. He mentioned it to Mercy, who bit her lip and said, "I've been worried about him for a long time, William. He's so—so *hard*! You've seen it, haven't you?"

"Yes. He shuts himself off from the rest of us." He gave her a quick hug and said, "We'll find a way to get at him, Mercy."

But the next day was very busy. They spent a large part of the morning wandering around the streets of the city; then they went to the print shop where Miles and Franklin worked out the details of the printing job.

"Your grandfather was a Firstcomer, I believe you said, Mr. Winslow?" the printer asked, turning the pages of the thick notebook handbound between brown leather covers.

"He and his brother, Edward, were on the *Mayflower*, and my grandmother as well—Humility Cooper her name was."

"Winslow—Winslow? I've read Mr. Bradford's book, of course. I call to mind Edward Winslow; he was an officer in Cromwell's court, if I'm not mistaken—but I don't recall anyone named Gilbert."

"Well, Edward is quite well known," Miles said. "My grandfather lived to be nearly a hundred. He died at 92, and I remember him very well."

"Ninety-two! Remarkable!" Franklin exclaimed. "How did he die?"

A flash of anger ignited Miles' eyes. "If you want the truth of it, he was a victim of the Salem witchcraft trials!" he answered harshly.

"He was executed in that monstrous affair?"

"Not executed—but he was so weakened by the exposure in prison that he never recovered. My whole family was named—my father, my mother, and my sister Rachel. She's still living in Boston. It was God's mercy that they didn't all die in that affair!"

Franklin was reading a page from the book as Miles spoke of the Salem trials, and he got so lost in it that he finally looked up with a start, his eyes gleaming with interest. "My word, sir! This is a *treasure*! I'm honored that you have chosen to trust me with such a task—quite honored! It will sell very well!"

Miles bit his lip, then shrugged, saying, "Well, Mr. Franklin, I wouldn't mind making a bit of money, of course, but that's not why I want it printed." The printer stared at the tall man seated before him, for Winslow seemed to be at a loss for words. Finally he said in a defiant tone, "We've lost something along the way, sir, and that's why I think it's a book that should be read."

"Lost something, Mr. Winslow?"

"Yes!" Miles Winslow slammed his fist down so hard on the oak table in front of him that they all started. "Those people on the *Mayflower* left England—left all they had really, and they risked their lives for a dream. Almost *half* of them died the first year! Died like flies, they did, and why did they do it? Because they had a dream, sir, and we've lost that vision!"

"You think this generation needs regeneration, I take it, Mr. Winslow?" the printer asked quickly.

"All most people care about these days is making money and building fine houses!" Miles Winslow snorted in contempt, and for the next ten minutes he railed at the younger generation, leaving no doubt in Franklin's mind that there was precious little hope for any of the upstarts in charge of the New World. His children had heard it all before, but there was a force in Miles that struck William afresh, and he found himself caught up with it all.

"What you're saying, Father," he said, "is that we need a revival. Get the people back to God."

Miles nodded, then shot a quick look at his son. "Well, we need that—but not the sort that your Whitefields will bring." That set him off again, so that for the next ten minutes he went on about the sad state to which the world had come.

Franklin, William noticed, found it possible to talk about vellum and printing styles (after Miles finally finished his tirade) while at the same time paying close attention to Mercy. The printer hovered over her, finding more than one opportunity to pat her shoulder and pay her effusive compliments.

"The man's a born womanizer!" Miles said in disgust as he and William left the shop after all the arrangements were completed.

"Oh, I think he's just practicing, sir," William said with a faint smile.

"A man his age with a wife has no business *practicing* that sort of thing!"

"I agree. It's strange, Father, but beneath those smooth manners and for all his interest in Whitefield, I have the impression that the man has no feeling at all about God."

"In that you're right, I dare say," Miles nodded. "He's a clever man—interested in how things work, you know? And I think he's just interested in Whitefield as some sort of freak."

"Yes, I think you've hit it." William stared at his father and shook his head, saying, "I wish I could see into the hearts of men as clearly as you, Father. It's a gift every preacher ought to have."

Miles looked fondly at his son, pride in his fine clear eyes; then his smile turned bitter. "I've not always been so wise about people."

They had been to the harbor to see a ship owner, and now they came back to Franklin's shop. Going inside they found Mercy and Adam in the owner's office. Franklin got up at once and said cheerily, "I've just heard that Whitefield will be preaching in a large field just outside of town. I think we've agreed on the printing job—suppose we go hear the good man?"

"I've heard him!" Miles growled.

"That's like saying, 'I've already seen a sunrise!' " Franklin laughed. "Come along, Winslow; it'll do us both good." He turned suddenly and put his hand on Adam's shoulder, saying with a smile, "I don't suppose I could persuade you to leave this good fellow here with me, could I?"

"Leave my son here?" Miles stared in amazement at Franklin.

Franklin laughed and held up his hand. "Only jesting—but I tell you, sir, if I could have this one in my shop for a year, you'd see a thing or two! Look at this, Winslow!" He turned and picked up a handsome rifle with silver insets in the stock and pointed at the matchlock. "See that? It's a new approach to the art of musket making. I designed that new matchlock system myself."

"Looks complicated," Miles said.

"So it is. I had it all apart, and while your daughter and I were talking, that boy of yours put it together in no time!"

"Adam is very good with his hands," Miles shrugged. He did not say so, but he was disappointed that his younger son was not as good with books as his other children. Being good with the hands was not a trait Miles Winslow valued. He did not notice that Adam's eyes dropped when he said this, but William and Mercy exchanged glances.

Franklin's sharp eyes caught the byplay as well, and he gave Adam's shoulder another pat, saying warmly, "Well, my boy, if you ever need a profession, come to me and I think we can work something out!"

Adam looked up quickly, and seeing the kindness in the eyes of the printer, ducked his head and muttered, "Thank you, Mr. Franklin."

William reached out and ruffled the boy's hair, saying fondly, "Well, now, don't suppose there are many thirteen-year-old boys who get an offer from a great man like Mr. Franklin! Wouldn't be surprised if you don't outshine us all, brother!"

Miles looked at the clock and said sharply, "If we must get preached at by this Britisher, I suppose we'd better get at it." It was not an unkind remark, but it seemed suddenly to William that his father had cut short Adam's little moment of triumph— as if he did not like to hear the boy praised. *I must be mistaken,* he said to himself, for he knew no man on earth kinder than his father.

Franklin joined them in their buggy, directing them to the large saucer-shaped field about a quarter of a mile from town. Whitefield was at one end of it, standing on a stone outcropping waiting for the crowd to gather.

He began his message, and William was amazed to discover that though they were hundreds of feet away, he could hear as if he were standing right next to the man! "Amazing, isn't it?" Franklin whispered. "I measured this field once, the first time he spoke, and by calculation, I discovered he could be heard by thirty thousand people!"

Whitefield spoke first of a work for orphans he was trying to establish in Georgia, and after a brief but moving plea, an offering was taken. After it was over, William heard Franklin grunt, and turning he saw that the rotund printer had a crestfallen look on his round face. Then he laughed and shook his head. "Amazing! Just amazing! I was determined to put a shilling in the box—"

"How much *did* you put?" Mercy asked with a smile.

Ruefully Franklin patted his pocket, saying, "Four gold sovereigns—all I had!"

"You'd better be careful, Mr. Franklin!" she smiled archly. "A little more Whitefield and you may become an enthusiast!"

"I dare say!" Franklin replied. The whole matter seemed to amuse him considerably, and he smiled at his own weakness.

Then the preacher began speaking of hell and the punishment of the damned, and he was so graphic that little cries began to go up from some of the listeners. Directly in front of the Winslows there were two young women, both attractive and well dressed. One of them looked back and saw William, and her eyes took in his handsome features and tall athletic form. Franklin's hand closed on Mercy's arm as the young woman looked back again at William.

As Whitefield's words grew stronger, thundering like a storm over the open field, suddenly a man close to the front seemed to fall in a faint. Mercy gasped; then a woman not ten feet in front of them gave a piercing scream, her body arching as she fell to the ground senseless.

"What utter foolishness!" Miles said between clenched teeth. He turned to go, but just as he did, the young woman in front of them suddenly screamed and began swaying backward. William leaped forward and caught her as she folded up; carefully he eased her to the ground, and as he did so, Mercy felt

Franklin's hand squeezing her arm, and she saw that there was a wry smile on his lips. "The pretty ones always manage to hold off until a handsome young chap is there to break their fall," he murmured so quietly that only she heard it.

Mercy looked at the young woman William was supporting. She seemed to be breathing deeply in some grip of agitation, and Mercy whispered, "You think she's a fake?"

"I never judge people, my dear," Franklin said piously, but there was a smile in his small eyes as he looked down at the pair.

Adam had not missed any of this, but as he looked around, he saw that many were not being "caught" by anybody. Some were on the ground crying, tears pouring down their faces, and many were on their knees holding their hands up to heaven. The boy took his eyes off them and looked at the minister, listening to his words.

"God is angry with the wicked every day!" Whitefield called out, his boyish face stern. "His bow is bent! He will in no wise spare the guilty, and hell gapes for those who will not heed His Word!"

Adam felt lightheaded, and there was a cry somewhere deep inside, but he clamped his lips together and stared stonily at the preacher until the sermon was over.

It ended with a different note, for Whitefield, after holding the crowd over the pit of hell, suddenly changed his tone. Holding his hands toward them, he cried out, "This is a faithful saying, and worthy of all acceptation, that Christ Jesus died to save sinners, of whom I am chief!"

Strangely enough, as he left the themes of hell and judgment and began to speak of God's love, more people were moved to tears than ever!

Miles said suddenly, "Come—enough of this!" And they had no choice but to follow him as he picked his way through the crowd, stepping over some who were on the ground weeping.

William carefully put the young woman's head down on the grass, and her eyelids suddenly opened. "Thank you, sir!" she said sweetly, and her hand plucked at his sleeve.

"You're—quite welcome, I'm sure!" he managed to say, then

rose and followed the others to the buggy.

On the way back, Miles spoke harshly of the wild scene, and then he said, "Surely *you* don't believe in this sort of thing, Franklin?"

For once the face of Franklin was utterly serious. He thought about it, then said evenly, "I am not a religious man—but I am, I believe, an honest one. And I must in all fairness say that it is wonderful to see the change made in the manners of some of our inhabitants. From being thoughtless or indifferent about religion, it seems as if all the world here is growing religious, so that one cannot walk through the town in an evening without hearing psalms sung by different families in every street." He paused and added gently, "Some of it is, I fear, not genuine. But I cannot deny that many lives have been changed for the better as a result of Mr. Whitefield's preaching."

Miles was silent for a few moments, then shook his head. "All well and good, sir, but it could be done as well in a church!"

"Ah, I fear that you cannot put new wine in old bottles," Franklin said with a shrug. "You may discover something about that, William, in your new charge."

William had told the printer that he was on his way to pastor the church at Amherst, east of Boston, and he nodded thoughtfully. "Yes, Mr. Franklin, I may indeed. Mr. Whitefield says that many of our clergy preach an unknown and unfelt Christ. If he is right, we shall soon see."

"You would not have that man in your church, William?" Miles turned to stare at his son, alarm in his eyes. "Why, he will divide the people!"

William Winslow turned to look at his father, but he did not answer for a moment. He seemed almost to have forgotten the question as he watched a red-tailed hawk rise up from the warped branch of a dead tree. Finally he took a deep breath, then looked back at his father. "If this thing is not of God, it will die—but if it *is* of God, I will not fight against it!"

Sitting in the back, Adam listened to his brother and his father, and he was afraid, for never had he heard *anyone* stand up to his father!

Then he felt an arm go around his shoulders, and he looked up to see Mercy looking at him with a gentle expression in her eyes. She said nothing, nor did he, but as they rolled along, he was very glad that she had put her arm around him.

CHAPTER TWO

THE WINSLOW CLAN

★　★　★　★

The Winslows arrived in Boston on Saturday, their ship dropping anchor in the late afternoon. The pulsing trade of the busy city was symbolized by the forest of masts in the harbor, for the invention of the Yankee Schooner in 1713 by Captain Andrew Robinson had brought faster travel and a boom in commerce. Masts were the product that linked the great American forests with the ocean, tying the New England colonies to the rest of the world. A good mast 100 feet high could bring as much as ninety pounds sterling on the market after it had been cut in deep snow, dragged behind oxen from a forest, then floated downriver to a shipyard.

"Good to be home!" Miles grunted, leading the group down the gangplank. He paid no attention to the tangle of sloops, schooners, whalers and fishing ketches, but Adam's dark eyes were everywhere, taking in the scene and reveling in the smell of fish. He gazed at the sedan chairs and brightly painted wagons of red, yellow, and blue along the streets, and the signs of taverns and shops fascinated him.

"I'll miss all this, I suppose," William murmured, gazing out the carriage window at the busy marketplace. "Amherst is quite a tame little village."

"I wish we were *all* going with you!" Miles said sharply, giving a contemptuous wave of his hand at the busy streets. "Be better off to get away from this Babylon of a town! For two pence I'd sell out and move to the backside of Virginia!"

Mercy caught the sudden look William shot at her, and shook her head slightly. They both had realized long ago that their father would never leave Boston—not as long as Martha lived. *He'd really like to do it!* William thought, caught suddenly by the sadness in his father's eyes. *Just sell out and go to the wilderness—but it's too late for him.* The happiest days of his father's life had been those years when he'd accompanied his own father, Matthew Winslow, on long trips to the west, establishing the fur business that had prospered the family. Miles had loved the woods, the lost trails and the cathedral-like quiet of the timbered woods. *He used to talk about that all the time—and how he'd do it again someday,* William thought. *But that was when Mother was alive—he's given up on all that now. Martha's burned all his dreams!*

It was almost dark when they pulled up in front of the large white house, a salt-box style with two stories in front, and the roof sloping down sharply in the rear over the kitchen and storage rooms. The ground floor was composed of four rooms—parlor, dining room, library and kitchen. Above, on the second floor, there were four bedrooms with sloping ceilings. Below was a cellar for storage, and just behind the kitchen, with a door opening into it was the woodshed—a dark, roomy place in which a whole winter's supply of wood for heating and cooking might be kept.

The town had not yet caught up with the house, which stood alone beside the dirt road surrounded by large locust and poplar trees. Behind the house was a garden, an orchard of pear trees, a stable, and a press for making cider. A dovecote and a dozen beehives were just behind the garden.

"I see Rachel's here," Miles remarked, waving toward the buggy drawn up underneath a large oak. The sourness that had marked him earlier was replaced at once by a smile, for his sister was a treasure to him. He pulled the team to a halt and got out of the buggy quickly. A short, strong-looking black man neatly dressed in brown homespun came running out of the stable, a smile lightening his dark face.

"You home, Mist' Winslow?" He took the reins and added, "Miss Rachel here!"

"Put the team up, Sampson," Miles said. "Did Saul and Esther come with my sister?"

"Yas, they's here, Mist' Winslow—come early dis mornin'. And Rev. Chauncy, he here, too."

Miles led them around to the front of the house.

"You're late, Miles," Martha Winslow said sourly. She was an imposing woman, somewhat heavy in figure, but her face was sharp-featured. Her brown hair revealed no sign of the white that marked her husband's, and her slate-gray eyes flashed with displeasure. She had a thin, hawkish nose, and her lips were rather thin and narrow, a small mouth for such a large woman.

"Ship was late," Miles explained with a shrug. The two made no gesture of affection, and he looked over her shoulder toward the parlor. "Rachel's here?"

"We're waiting for you in the dining room; the food's getting cold."

Miles moved past her and gave a nod at the others, saying, "Hello Saul—Esther." Martha gave a sharp look at Adam, who was slowly moving indoors, and said sharply, "You're not eating with those filthy hands, Adam! Go wash!"

As he scurried toward the kitchen, Mercy and William followed their stepmother into the dining room where their father was embracing a woman with pure silver hair, saying, "You're looking more beautiful than ever, Rachel!"

William could not help noticing that his father was much more like a loving husband with his sister than with his wife, and he saw the bitter twist of Martha Winslow's small mouth as she took in the scene. "Sit down, Miles," she said sharply. "The food is cold."

Miles stepped back, his fond glance resting on the face of Rachel Howland. She was eighty years old, but her back was straight as a ramrod, and her eyes, bright blue, unfaded by the years. She was wearing a simple gown of blue silk that matched her eyes, and somehow it made Martha's ornate dress look cheap and overdone.

"I've missed you, Miles," Rachel said quietly. "How was the trip?"

"Fine! Franklin will do us a good job, I think." He felt the pressure of his wife's eyes then, and moved to shake hands with the short, portly man dressed in a somber suit, who had risen. "Pastor Chauncy, I'm glad to see you."

"You're just in time, Miles—I was about to eat your dinner!" Charles Chauncy was thirty-seven years old, and as pastor of First Church, Boston, was one of the most influential men in the colony. The office of the minister, while not as prestigious as it had been in the days of Bradford, was still a potent force in the political as well as the theological arenas of the day.

They all sat down, and as the food was served, Miles gave them a report of their dealings with Franklin. Even Chauncy was impressed with this, for the printer was one of the best known men in the Colonies. "It will be an edifying work, Miles," the preacher said, pausing between bites long enough to comment. "Your grandfather and the others on that ship were a different breed of men—yes, sir, a wonderful group."

"We heard Mr. Whitefield while we were there." William's face was smooth, and he looked very innocent as he added, "He preached most powerfully, Rev. Chauncy."

"No doubt!" Chauncy's face turned red, for he had gone on record from his pulpit condemning Whitefield and the revival that had swept the Colonies in the early thirties as spurious, and more than once had come close to consigning the whole thing to the devil. "I suppose people were wallowing all over the ground—as usual?"

"Tell us about it, William," Saul Howland said with interest. He was Rachel's only son, and along with his sister, Esther, constituted the only family that Robert Howland had left at his death. Saul was a thick-bodied man of medium height, with his father's heavy features, while Esther looked much like her mother. Saul was thirty-two, a rising businessman, much sought after by the mothers of Boston with marriageable daughters. Neither of them, to Rachel's quiet sorrow, was devout in his Christian commitment. They were worldly and ambitious, though they attended church more or less regularly.

Miles said brusquely, "Oh, it was the usual sort of affair, Pastor—preaching in the open field to a mob of the lower classes. Of course, the man is an orator—never heard a better voice!"

"It's his theology I'm worried about!" Rev. Chauncy snapped. "He's made a name for himself in England by attacking the clergy, and I have no doubt he'll try the same tactic here!"

"Oh, he's already done that," William said cheerfully. He helped himself to a slice of boiled beef, cut off a bite and put it in his mouth. Chewing comfortably he went on. "Mr. Whitefield has let it be known that at Harvard—and I quote—'Its light has become darkness'!"

"Why, the man's a heretic!" Chauncy sputtered. "He'll not preach in Boston!"

"I understand from Mr. Franklin—who's quite an admirer of Mr. Whitefield, by the way—that we will be honored by a visit in the not too distant future." He sighed sadly, adding, "I'll not be able to hear him, for I'll be at my church by then."

"Why do you dislike the man so, Reverend?" Esther asked curiously. She had no interest in theology, but everyone was talking about the sensation of Whitefield's preaching, and she longed to see the spectacle.

"Why, the man says that most of the clergy do not even know Christ! And he insists that everyone in the church must have what he calls *a new birth*! Makes little of baptism, good works, communion!" He gave William Winslow a sharp look, then said pugnaciously, "Your church is very close to Northampton—you'll be seeing something of Rev. Jonathan Edwards?"

"Why, I trust so," William nodded.

"He's an able man." The words were not unkind, but there were marks of anger on Chauncy's face, and he suddenly burst out, "*He's* responsible for the whole thing! It was in his church back in '32 that the whole miserable business of *revival* had its start."

"He's quite a scholar, Pastor," Miles said evenly. "None better in the Colonies, I hear."

"Oh, as to that, Edwards is quite brilliant—but he has some wrong ideas. I suspect he's an enthusiast."

The word *enthusiast* was much used at the time, and never with a good connotation. England in the eighteenth century was immersed in the age of reason, and any expression of emotion was frowned upon as being *enthusiastic*. In the course of the Wesleys' work in England, some followers had gone too far; every movement had some of these, of course. But now, simply to name a man such in religious circles was enough to classify him as an irresponsible character incapable of reason and on the brink of lunacy.

Men like Rev. Chauncy had forced the Wesleys and White-field out of the churches into the streets. They saw the revival as a threat to their offices, and were contemptuous of the emotional content of religion.

"Nothing but a bunch of hysterical women!" Chauncy summed it all up, then took a huge draught of ale from the silver tankard beside his plate. "Troublemakers, William—have nothing to do with Edwards if you can help it!"

Suddenly Martha Winslow interrupted the minister, saying shrilly, "Adam—let me see those hands!"

Every eye turned toward the boy, who was shoveling his food into his mouth methodically, paying little heed to the table talk. As he felt the weight of so many eyes, a flush darkened his tanned face, and putting his knife down, he slipped to the floor and moved reluctantly around the table to where Martha stood to her feet glaring at him.

She snatched one of the boy's hands, peered at it, then cried, "Filthy! You won't eat at my table with hands like that. Go wash again, and then you may go to bed! Why can't you ever be clean like your brother Charles?"

Adam cast a look at the young boy sitting next to Rachel, and said nothing. His stepmother took that as an act of sullen rebellion, and twisting him around, propelled him toward the door with a strong hand. "If you go to bed with those black hands, I'll have the hide off your back!" she said, giving Adam a nudge out toward the kitchen.

"I think it's tar on his hands, Mother," Charles said with a smile. "Soap and water won't take it off."

Charles Winslow, Miles' only child by Martha, looked very

much like all Winslow males—which is to say, he was very handsome. One year younger than Adam, he was already taller, and his thick shock of reddish-blond hair and bright blue eyes drew attention everywhere he went.

"Maybe you'd better go help him with a little turpentine, Charles," Rachel suggested with a smile.

"Yes, ma'am, I will."

William watched his father, who did not take his eyes off Charles; he shook his head almost imperceptibly, then looked up quickly to see that Rachel had seen and understood. She had talked to him once about his father, and he had never forgotten it. He had been fourteen years old and had made some remark to his aunt about how strict his parents were on Adam.

She had put her hands on his shoulders and looked into his eyes, saying, "William, you are very sensitive. I am going to tell you something about your parents. I want you to remember it and I want you to say nothing to anyone. Do you understand?"

"Yes, I promise," he had said.

"Your father," his aunt had confided, "loved your mother to distraction. He worshiped her, William—maybe too much! And when Adam was born and she died bearing him—why, I hate to say it, for I love your father—but he blamed Adam for her death."

"But that's not fair!" William had protested.

"People are not always *fair*—even good men like your father! But there's more. He was so lonely after your mother died that he made a mistake. He married your stepmother. She is not a woman who can make your father happy, and as soon as she found out that he would never love any woman in this world but your mother, why, she became bitter. I can't exactly blame her—but it has made your father unhappy—and since you and Mercy are both too old to whip, she takes her unhappiness out on poor Adam."

"I know. She beats him all the time, Aunt Rachel."

Rachel had taken his hands then and looked up at him, for he was already taller than she. There was a break in her voice and sorrow in her eyes as she said, "Adam needs your help and your prayers, William. He isn't quick with books as most Winslow men have been. He looks much like my mother, Lydia—your grandmother—and that endears him to me—but not to Miles, I fear. Help him, William!"

William looked at his aunt, and saw a fierce compassion. He nodded to her, making a silent promise to do his best for the boy.

Charles found Adam in the kitchen scrubbing listlessly at his blackened hands with a sliver of lye soap. "You'll never get that stuff off with water," he commented. He went to a shelf and pulled down a brown glass bottle, pulled the cork out, sniffed it, then said, "Try this turpentine."

"All right." Adam seldom questioned anything that his younger brother said, and he obediently cupped his hands. He was not surprised to see the pungent liquid cut into the dark stains. "That's what it took, Charles," he said. "I wonder I didn't think of it."

"Where'd you get all that tar on you?"

"On the ship. The sailors let me help them tar the ends of the ropes. I wish you could have been there. You feeling better?"

"I'm all right. Tell me about the trip." Charles sat down and listened as Adam, in his slow manner of speaking, told him about everything. Scrubbing methodically at his hands, he told about the voyage and the events in Philadelphia. Charles pulled a stool up close and said nothing, for he had hated to miss the trip. His mother said that he had a cold, but he was certain that she just wanted to keep him at home with her.

Adam was slow of speech, but he told a story strangely well for a boy with a reputation for being mentally slow. Sometimes he had to search for words, but he made it come alive for Charles—the pushing, pulling crowds who listened to White-field, the smells of unwashed bodies, the crying of the women, and the solid *clunk* of a head striking the earth as a man fell down under the spell of the preaching.

"Sounds like fun," Charles smiled. "Tell me some more." He looked at Adam's hands and said, "That's good enough. Why didn't you think of turpentine yourself, Adam? You've used it before."

"Don't know. Just didn't think."

Charles was irritated. "You're so good at some things—and so dumb at others! If Mother had beat me as much as she has you, I'd think of ways to get out of it. That's the difference between you and me, Adam. Why, Mother's thrashed you a dozen times for coming to the table with dirty hands, and here you do it again! I take better care of myself than that!"

Adam looked ashamed and mumbled, "I just got to thinking and forgot, Charles." Then he looked up and said humbly, "You don't ever forget anything, do you? Wish I wasn't so dumb!"

Charles shrugged, saying, "You're smart enough in everything except books—and learning how to watch out for yourself. All you have to do, Adam, is find out what people want and give it to 'em. Then when you get big enough, you can tell 'em to jump in the river! Now, tell me some more about the trip."

The adults had moved to the parlor, and the talk soon turned to business. Saul was saying, "Uncle Miles, you ought to get out of the fur trade. I know your father made a lot of money, but it can't last."

"I'm doing all right," Miles grunted. He stretched his legs out and said, "Rachel, this boy of yours may get rich, but tell him to leave me alone."

Saul shook his head. "You've not looked at it in the right light, Uncle Miles. Sooner or later you're going to go broke—and Mother is your partner."

"Why should we quit the fur trade? They're still buying furs in England, aren't they?"

Saul had a didactic streak in him; he loved to inform people. He leaned against the fireplace and began a lecture on the fur trade. The fur trade was based on beaver, he informed them. By the 1600s fashion had decreed that men should wear large hats of felt, and beaver fur was the best. The skin itself was not used, but the short underfur, the so-called "beaver wool," was stripped from the skin and formed into a hat by the felting process. And by the end of the 1600s New France was exporting about 150,000 skins a year, while New England sent only about 8,000.

"And there's your problem, Uncle Miles," Saul concluded with a wave of his hand. "Beaver and all kinds of fur are getting more scarce all the time."

"Then we'll send our trappers farther west," Miles said.

"Ah, but you won't be able to do that—because France won't permit it. We've just had two wars over that territory in the Ohio River Basin—and mark my words, we're about to have another!"

"I don't believe it," Miles said in a bored tone.

"You'll see! Martha, you'd better talk to your husband. In a few years you'll be broke if he doesn't change his profession."

"I've already talked to him," Martha said, shooting a dour glance at Miles. "We ought to get into the plantation business— tobacco, perhaps."

"We have to have slaves for that," Miles objected.

"What's wrong with that?" Martha shot back. "In Virginia the Hugers, the Lees, the Washingtons—they all have slaves, and I think they're good churchmen, are they not, Pastor?"

"Yes, indeed!" Chauncy nodded. "Leaders in the community."

"Tobacco is a bad thing." William rarely said much about business, but he felt strongly about this one matter. "It just about ruined most people in Jamestown! It's a one-crop system and it makes the ground worthless. If you want to farm, don't go to tobacco. And you don't have to go to Virginia. There's good land right here in our own colony."

They argued about the matter for an hour; then Rachel suddenly got up and stretched her back. "Well, if you want to get out of the fur business, Miles, and go to farming, it's all right with me." She turned a smile on her brother and went to pat his arm fondly. "It's all going to burn anyway, isn't it?"

Miles laughed and hugged her, saying, "Yes! That's what Grandfather would have said. He didn't give a bent pin for anything in this world—had all his treasures in heaven, didn't he, Rachel?"

"But God prospers the righteous, Miles," Martha reminded him sharply. "Being poor is no virtue, is it, Pastor?"

"I shall preach on that very subject next Sunday, Mrs. Winslow!" the rotund preacher said with a smile. "Miles, you be there and take some good spiritual advice—and listen to your nephew. He's a sound man—though he is somewhat lax in his church attendance," he added with mock severity. Then he made his thanks and departed.

Rachel, Saul, and Esther left soon after, but Rachel went off first to find Adam before she left. She said goodbye to him and to Charles, giving them both a gold coin. She kissed them both, then said, "Adam, you come to stay with me soon, you hear? I have lots of things that need fixing, and you're the man to do it! All right?"

After she left, Charles said enviously, "Aunt Rachel sure does think a lot of you. Wish she liked me half as much!"

Adam stared at him in amazement. "Why, she likes you as much as she does me!"

"No, she don't," Charles said regretfully. He looked at the gold coin and added, "You can get more of these out of her, Adam. If you'd just learn to butter her up, why, she'd give you 'bout anything you asked for!"

The idea had never occurred to Adam, and he stared at the coin in his own hand, pondering the thought. Then he shook his head, saying, "No, she doesn't like me more than you."

Charles looked at the dark face of his brother with disgust. "You *are* dumb, Adam! You gotta learn to watch people and when they can do you some good, why you gotta play up to 'em! It's the only way to get what you want, see?"

Three days later, William left to go to his new charge in Amherst, but his departure was marred by a rare scene with his father.

He had packed his clothes and Sampson was loading the trunk into the buggy when he heard his father's voice raised in anger. Descending the stairs, he saw Adam standing in front of the older Winslow, who was holding a heavy crop in his right hand.

Miles was saying, "You have been nothing but a lazy drone with your books, boy, and I'll not have it! There's never been such a thing as a stupid Winslow, but you seem to be just that! Now, you did not do this Latin—why not?"

Adam's answer was slow, and William's heart went out to him. "I—I can't do Latin very well, sir—"

"Nonsense!" William caught a glimpse of his father's face, and he saw it was swollen with rage—something quite unusual.

"You shall learn what it means to work, and I've had enough of your loafing at the forge and in the shop! Do you hear me?"

"Yes, sir."

The very submission of the boy seemed to anger Miles even more, and he grabbed his arm, whirled him around and began to strike him viciously across the back with the crop, breathing heavily with each stroke.

William hurried down the steps and through the front door, his face pale and his lips drawn. He took ten paces across the yard, then his eyes met those of Sampson. The black man did not say a word, but every time the whip fell, his eyes seemed to blink.

William stood there, listening; then suddenly he whirled and dashed into the house and into the parlor. He grabbed his father's wrist and held it in a strong grip, saying, "Sir! That's enough!"

"What's that?"

Miles stared at his eldest son's face, not a foot from his own. He would have been no more shocked if the roof had fallen, for William had never once in all his life challenged his father's authority. But he did so now, and Miles grew suddenly furious. He pulled to free his arm, but it was held in a steely viselike grasp, and he was shocked again.

He knew, of course, that he was getting on in years, and William was a strong young man. But now as he stood there, helpless in the unyielding grip of his son, he knew what it was to grow old—and it angered him even more.

"Sir! You are my son!"

William did not raise his voice, but it carried a steely note, a toughness that Miles had heard in that of the boy's great-grandfather, Gilbert Winslow—a voice he had heard and admired.

"So is *this* your son, Father—and you are beating him as if he were a slave!"

Miles bit his lip, and his own face lost its angry glow. "I— was simply chastising the boy, William."

"You were beating him as if he were a grown man, sir, and I must say, for the first time in my life, I do not admire my father!"

"William. . . !"

Miles' lips suddenly trembled, and he looked down at Adam's face, taking in the pinched lips and the misery in the dark eyes, so unlike his own, and he was ashamed. Those dark eyes suddenly brought back the memory of his mother—Lydia Carbonne, and he bit his lips. She had been a cheery woman, dark with French blood, and beautiful enough to win the heart of his father, Matthew. He thought of her dark beauty and looked down, seeing something of it in the face of this undersized, silent son of his, and he turned away from both his sons, his eyes suddenly blinded by tears.

William at once put his hand on his father's shoulder and said, "Try to remember—he's only a boy. And he's *different*, Father. But he's a good boy!"

Miles stood there for a long moment; then he said without turning, "You were right to stop me, William. I—I will be more thoughtful."

"I'm sure you will," William replied, then added, "you've been a wonderful father, sir, and this affair does not mean that I admire and love you any less."

Miles wheeled and caught at the hand William put out to him. Gripping it strongly, he said, "I *will* do better, William!" Then he turned to look down at Adam, saying, "I was wrong, Adam, very wrong."

Adam turned slowly. He had not flinched when the whip was falling, but he seemed to be hurt by hearing this, and he muttered only, "No, I didn't do the work—I'm sorry to be so stupid."

William nodded at his father over Adam's head, approval in his eyes. He smiled and said, "You two must learn to pull together!"

"We will try, won't we, son?" Miles said, tentatively putting his hand on Adam's shoulder. "We'll try!"

Adam said nothing, but there was a light in his dark eyes as he turned to look at the hand on his shoulder.

William said quickly, "Well, I must go!" He wheeled and made his way out, but turning at the door, he took one more look at the pair, the tall man with his hand on the small boy's shoulder, and he smiled as he left.

Sampson was waiting at the buggy, holding the reins, and there was a strange expression in his face. He did something he'd never done in all his life—he put out his huge black hand, and William took it without thinking. Then the black face broke into a smile, and he said, "I thank you, Mist' William!"

"For what, Sampson?" William asked in astonishment.

The black man nodded, gave a powerful squeeze to the other's hand, then said, "Jes' fo' being whut you is!"

As William rode away, he wondered at the scene, for it seemed little short of miraculous to him that his father could change so abruptly—but he had prayed much and, being a simple man of faith, he said fervently, "Thank you, Lord—and let Father know the joy of making a man out of Adam!"

CHAPTER THREE

DISGRACED!

★ ★ ★ ★

Miles was indulging himself in feeding his flock of black banty chickens on a crisp September morning. He had purchased the original pair at the dock from a dark-skinned woman arriving on a schooner, and since she spoke no English, he had no idea of the origin of the birds. Their shiny ebony color had caught his eye, and he had been pleased to find that they bred well and that their flesh was far more tender and delicious than the tough speckled variety he used for his table meat.

"Chick—chick—chick," he called, and as he tossed a handful of grain to the ground, the small, noisy birds came running to him. As they pecked at the grain, he counted them, and was delighted to see that there were still eighteen hens and six jaunty roosters with brilliant red combs. He nodded to himself, deciding that it would not be too risky to have one of the plump roosters for supper. He knew of six nests containing the tiny greenish eggs, and if a skunk or a blood-thirsty weasel did not get loose, and if no other natural disaster occurred, it seemed as though God would prosper the flock so that he could not only have enough of the succulent dish for his own table but develop the species for sale as well.

"Black Winslows!" he said with a smile. "Now that would

be something—to have this breed all over the country with the Winslow name!" He tossed another handful of grain and glanced across the yard. A steady thumping sound had started, and he saw Adam driving dust from a multi-colored carpet hanging on a line. "Be careful with that thing, Adam," he called out. "You know your mother treasures that carpet more than her assurance of heaven!"

Adam looked up, smiled and called out, "Yes, sir. I'll be careful."

We're doing a little better, thank God! Miles thought with some satisfaction. Ever since William had spoken so strongly to him, he had been very careful with the boy. He had noticed for the first time that though Adam was slow with books, he was a worker, never stopping until the job was done. Miles had been forced to take note also that Charles, for all his intelligence, was the opposite; he gave short attention to his chores, half-doing them and avoiding them as much as possible. This discovery had precipitated a family quarrel, for when he had caned Charles for neglecting his work, Martha had interfered with a burst of anger more fierce than he had ever seen in her. An armed truce was now in force that made meals most unpleasant, and Miles was forced to notice how merciless and strict his wife was with Adam.

As he threw the last of the corn to the chickens, a horseman galloped down the road and, seeing him, pulled his small roan up and dismounted. "Sampson!" Miles called out to his slave as he went to meet the visitor, "Tell Clara I'll have one of these Black Winslows for supper."

"Black Winslows?" the tall black man asked, scratching his head. "Wat in de world is dat, Mist' Winslow?"

"Black Winslow—that's what I'm naming these chickens."

Sampson suddenly laughed and nodded, "Yessuh—I tell her—but I thought *I* was de onliest black Winslow round dis' place!" The thought tickled him, and he went off chuckling at his wit.

"Hello, Henry. Come in and we'll have some tea."

"Can't do it, Miles." The man who stepped forward to take Winslow's hand was very short, but wide as a church door. He had a round red face and when he took off his hat to wipe his brow, he exposed a vast expanse of skull, having only a thin fringe of reddish hair around his ears. "You see this article 'bout George Whitefield in the *Boston Newsletter*?"

"No—but I can guess what it says." Taking the paper from Henry Whaley, his closest neighbor, Miles read the item:

> Last Thursday Evening the Rev'd Whitefield arrived from Rhode Island, being met on the Road and conducted to Town by several Gentlemen. The next day in the Forenoon he attended prayers in the King's Chapel, and in the afternoon preach'd to a vast Congregation in the Rev'd Dr. Coleman's Meeting House. So great and unruly was the crowd that what should have been a prayerful congregation was in fact a turbulent mob. When Rev'd Whitefield was advised that five persons had killed themselves in illadvised leaps from the gallery, he decided the Commons might be safer, and there he spoke to a multitude numbering twenty thousand.

Miles shoved the paper back at Whaley in disgust. "I can't believe people will go out after such things!" He lifted his voice and called out, "Adam, that's enough! You're going to put a hole in that thing. You can go down to Farmer's and pick up those hinges for me."

Adam tossed the beater down and ran out of the yard, leaving the two men talking. Ned Farmer's blacksmith shop was a mile and a half away, on the road toward town, but it was his favorite spot in all the world, so he sped away before his father had second thoughts. His sturdy legs pumped steadily and he stopped only once to get a drink from a cold spring that bubbled out of the ground. As he bent over, his coal-black hair fell over his eyes, and he tossed it back with a sudden motion of his head. He hated his black hair and dark skin, and had cut his hair clean to the skull when he was only five. The fair hair and the skin of the rest of his family made his own dark color stand out so that he felt like an outsider.

Ned Farmer was pumping the handle of the bellows as Adam entered the low building that housed the forge. He was a squat man with huge arms and a pair of soft brown eyes peering out of a square, brown face. "Ah, now, here's me helper!"

he grinned. "Give us a hand, will you now, Adam?"

With a quick nod, Adam took the handle, and with practiced, even strokes forced air onto the coals till they glowed yellow, then red, and finally when they were almost white, Farmer took a pair of tongs, plucked a long glowing strip of metal, and carrying it to the anvil began to hammer it with mighty strokes that sent a shower of sparks across the shop.

Adam left the bellows, and getting so close that some of the hot sparks landed in his hair, he watched intently as the blacksmith flattened out the glowing iron. Then he took it up with the tongs and plunged it into a barrel of water, making a sizzling sound and causing steam to rise.

"Well, now, I'd guess your father wants them hinges, don't he?"

"Yes, that's what he sent me for—but can I do some work first, Mr. Farmer?"

"Well, just a bit, maybe. Get them tongs and fish one of them small strips—but let me soften them a bit." As Farmer pumped the bellows he watched the face of Adam Winslow with affection. He'd never seen a lad so anxious to work with iron! Since his father had brought him to the forge as a very young lad, he'd spent every free moment with the blacksmith, and now the boy knew more about metal craft than most men. Farmer's own son had shown no interest in the trade, and now he thought, *Too bad he's not my boy—I'd make a fine smith out of him! He's got the knack.*

Without being told, Adam drew a strip of white-hot metal from the coals, picked up Farmer's smallest hammer and began to beat it with even strokes. The hammer was too big for him, but the smith noted that he held the piece firmly and the hammer fell evenly—not too hard, not too easy—on the metal, and when the piece hardened, Farmer picked it up with the tongs and said, "That's a good job."

Adam's face flushed with pleasure, and Farmer wondered that the son of a wealthy merchant could be so pleased with the praise of a humble workman like himself. He had no idea how little of that sort of thing the boy got at home.

Adam stayed as long as he dared, helping the blacksmith,

and if Miles had heard how freely he talked, he would have been amazed, for at home the boy was taciturn. When Farmer mentioned going to hear the preacher Whitefield, Adam related his experience in Philadelphia, and the large man took it all in. Finally he said, "I never heered nothing like it, Adam! Never! To tell the truth, I allus believed I was a fair sort of man. Good to my family, honest with people." He ran his hand over his face, and shaking his head, he grinned and said, "Well, Mister Whitefield knocked all *that* outta me! Just a no-good sinner, that's what I am—or was!"

Adam stared at him. "What did you do, Mr. Farmer?"

The blacksmith looked embarrassed and bit his heavy underlip before he answered. "Well, I don't rightly know, boy, but when that man told me to repent and throw myself on God's mercy, I done it!" He looked up with wonder in simple dark eyes and said, "I tell you, I called out, and it was like I got hit right between the eyes with a sixteen-pound sledge!"

"You fell down?"

"Right enough, I did!" Farmer shook his head slowly, and then he added, "I been in church all me life, man and boy, but I tell you when I called on God, it was the *first* time I ever really had any notion that He was *real*—and I ain't been the same since!"

Adam was taking it all in with wide open eyes, and he said, "Mr. Farmer, when I saw all those people falling down in Philadelphia—I thought it was put on. But if you say it's real, then I guess it is."

The muscular hand of the smith fell on Adam's shoulder, and tears appeared in his eyes. "It is real, boy! I don't rightly understand it, but since that time, it's been like Jesus Christ hisself has been right beside me—just as real to me as you are!"

Ned Farmer was not an emotional man, Adam knew, and he saw that he was embarrassed by his own display, so Adam smiled and said quickly, "I'm glad for you, Mr. Farmer."

"Well, here's the hinges, Adam."

The boy took them; then his eyes fell on a pipe sticking up out of a barrel of junk. "What's that, Mr. Farmer?"

"That? Oh, Squire Mason had me make him some of them—

got something to do with a new-fangled way of farming—I dunno' what."

Adam went to the barrel and pulled out the pipe, which was about thirty inches long and nearly two inches in diameter. He stared at it, his brow wrinkled in thought, and then said, "Could you put an end on this, Mr. Farmer—and put a hole in it?"

Farmer laughed out loud, then asked, "What in the world you got in that brain of yours, Adam? You going to be an inventor like that Mr. Franklin?"

Adam said evasively, "Oh, just an idea."

Ned Farmer was somewhat of a tinker and an inventor himself, so he chuckled and took the pipe from Adam. "Let's see, seal up the end? Why, that's no trouble—I'll show you." He made an end for the pipe, and showed the boy how to attach it, then asked, "A hole in it?"

"Yes, right there—just a little hole."

In no time, the job was done, and Farmer cooled it in the barrel, then handed it over, saying, "Can you carry this thing and the hinges, Adam?"

"Oh, sure—and thanks a lot, Mr. Farmer."

"Let me have a look at the great invention when it's all done, boy, and don't forget your poor old friends when it makes you rich and famous!" he called out as Adam sailed out the door and headed for home. He shook his head as he went back to his work. *Sure will be the ruination of a good blacksmith to make a scholar out of that one!*

"What's that thing?"

Charles had come into the small building used as a combination shop and storage house to find Adam busily working at something on the work table. There was an injured look in Charles's eye, and for some reason he blamed his brother for the thrashing he'd gotten from his father. Adam glanced at him, then shrugged, "Oh, just an idea I had."

Charles peered at the iron tube that Adam had wedged fast into the top of the workbench. "You're always wasting your time making stuff," he grunted. "What's this supposed to be?"

Adam shifted his feet, reluctant to speak, but when he saw

that Charles was not going to leave, he said, "Well, it's a cannon."

"A what?"

"A cannon." Adam's dark eyes glowed, and he began to explain the mechanism to Charles. "Look, a musket is nothing but a tube with one end plugged up. Well, I saw this piece of pipe at the blacksmith shop, and Mr. Farmer let me have it."

Charles gave a disdainful sniff. "You can't make a cannon!" Although he surpassed his older brother in many ways, he had no head for mechanical things, and it irritated him to be outdone. "That things's just an old piece of pipe, and you're making believe like you always do."

Adam shook his head stubbornly, insisting, "Well, it ain't a *real* cannon, but it'll shoot. Look, when they shot the cannons off over at the fort, I watched 'em. All they do is put some black gunpowder down inside; then they put the cannon ball on top of that."

Charles tried not to be impressed with Adam's knowledge. "Oh, sure, but how do they make it go *off?*"

Adam smiled, and said, "I watched them and they stuck a flame down in a hole in the back—and there's the hole we put in this cannon, me and Mr. Farmer." He pointed to the small hole in the rear of the pipe, and his eyes lit up. He grinned and said, "This cannon would make the biggest noise you ever heard, Charles!"

"Well—" Charles tried to find something nasty to say, and finally blurted out, "You don't know that! It's just an ol' piece of pipe!"

"Is not!"

"Well, if you're so smart with your dumb old pipe, why don'cha shoot it off then?"

" 'Cause I don't have no gunpowder," Adam shot back. "If I just had some black powder, you'd see something!"

Charles suddenly grinned "I'll get you plenty of powder," he yelled. "I know where Father keeps it—and I'll get some of his musket balls, too!"

Adam was shocked. "You better not! You know he told us not to fool with his guns and stuff!"

"How's he going to know?" Charles shrugged. He was still angry with Adam, and he turned, saying "I'll get the powder then you'll see your old pipe is nothing at all!"

Adam was afraid, and he hoped that Charles would change his mind—but he knew his brother too well for that. In five minutes Charles came out of the house carrying something in his hands. He entered the shop, dumped a powderhorn and a leather pouch containing musket balls on the table.

"There, Big Mouth!" he grinned. "Now, let's see your big ol' cannon do something!"

Adam shook his head, looking down at the powder and balls. "I can't use these, Charles. Father would—"

Charles snorted and struck Adam on the shoulder. "You're not only *dumb*, you're a *fake*, too! All this stuff about inventin' things—you can't really do any of it!"

Adam's dark eyes suddenly lit with a rare flash of anger, and he snapped, "You're a liar."

"Well, prove it!"

"I will!"

Adam grabbed the pipe and began strapping it to a section of round wood about six inches thick and two feet long. As he tightened the leather thongs, Charles asked, "What's that?"

"You don't think I'm gonna *hold* this cannon and shoot it, do you? I gotta have a gun carriage."

He finished lashing the pipe down, then picked up the unit with a grunt. "Bring the powder and balls," he commanded.

Charles obeyed, and followed him out the door. Adam struggled as far as the tree line that was beside the house, a hundred-yard strip of oak and poplar separating the pasture from the house. "We gotta get away from the house," he grunted. "It's going to make a big noise!"

"What you gonna shoot at?" Charles asked. He forgot his irritation and began to enter into the spirit of the adventure. "Let's have a target." He looked around, and spotted a large section of the light gray canvas covering up some equipment next to the carriage house. "I'll get us something."

He ran to get the piece, and by the time he got back, Adam had dug a trench in the loamy soil with a stick and had planted the log which served as a mount for the "cannon." "Stretch it across those saplings, Charles," he called out, his face intent. "No, farther back than that!"

Charles retreated into the stand of trees and put the canvas across several small saplings, then came back. "Let's load 'er up, Adam!" he urged.

"Sure! Look, I'll tilt it back and you pour powder in." He took the pipe in both hands and lifted the end into the air. Charles took the powder horn and dumped the entire contents down the pipe. "Wait a minute—that's too much!"

Charles grinned at him. "Thought this was a *real* cannon, Adam!" He took the leather sack and emptied the contents down the tube and said, "That ought to do it."

Adam said with a worried look, "That's a lot of powder, Charles!"

"You scared to shoot it?" Charles jibed. "Then *I'll* do it!"

They argued about who was going to touch it off, all the while maneuvering the piece to aim at the canvas target. Finally, they were satisfied, and then Charles said with a sudden blank look, "How are we gonna shoot it? You have to have fire."

"Sure, you do," acknowledged Adam. "I'll go get a spark from the kitchen stove." He darted across the yard, scattering the black chickens as he ran. There was always fire in the kitchen stove, and he went into the wood room and brought out a large pine splinter. Raking the coals back, he stuck the splinter into the stove and it burst into flame almost at once.

He left the house and made his way across the yard, shielding the flame with his free hand. When he got back to the trees, he looked down at the cannon, and suddenly he said, "We better not do this, Charles."

"You scared?" Charles taunted.

"Well, a little bit. You put so much powder in, it could just blow up and kill us—and besides, if Father finds out we've used his powder, why, *he'll* kill us!"

Charles snorted, "You trying to back out, Adam?"

Adam moved behind the cannon. "All right! One of us will need to put his foot on top to keep it from kicking up, and one of us has to shove this fire down the hole."

"I—I'll—put my foot on it," Charles decided, but his face was a little pale. He gingerly put his foot on top of the pipe and looked at Adam. "Well, go on—do it!"

Adam didn't want to do it—yet at the same time, he did. He almost threw the splinter down and stamped it out, but the pale sneer on Charles's face told him that he'd never hear the last of it. Carefully he moved to one side, knelt, and held the tiny flame over the hole. Then with a sudden burst of desperation, he thrust the splinter into the hole.

There was a short sizzling sound; then the cannon bucked wildly, skipping out from under Charles's foot! The explosion deafened both of them temporarily, and they fell backwards with their eyes shut tightly.

A stillness followed, and Adam rolled to his feet, followed by Charles, and he yelled, "Look at the target!"

The canvas had been blown almost off the saplings, but they could see at once that it was riddled by dozens of holes.

"What a cannon!" Charles yelled back, and the two of them started running toward the tattered canvas. Picking it up, they looked at the holes, counting them. "Boy, we sure got us a good cannon here!" Charles cried excitedly.

Adam started to reply, but suddenly there was a cry from the house. Both boys wheeled around, and they saw their parents running out of the back door, closely followed by Sampson and the household servants.

Charles gasped. "We hit the house! Come on, Adam! We gotta get away from here!"

Charles took off running into the woods, but Adam stood fixed to the spot. It never occurred to him to run, and with his heart beating in his chest for fear, he stepped out of the woods and made his way toward the house.

The musket balls had plowed through the canvas, a few of them had lodged in the trees on the edge of the tree line, but most of them had swept the yard.

As Adam slowly walked across the yard, he saw his father standing in the midst of a dozen dead black chickens. A few others were flopping all over the yard uttering plaintive clucks.

Adam could not bear the look of sorrow and anger on his

father's face, and lifted his eyes to the house, where he saw that one of the expensive glass windows, which had been shipped all the way from England, was shattered, and there were round holes all along the sides of the house.

Then he saw his stepmother standing beside the rug she'd inherited from her grandmother. She stood there staring in disbelief and shock at the holes that let the sunshine through in tiny bars.

Adam heard his father's voice calling his name in anger, and the fear in him was so strong it robbed him of his strength. He stood there with his face down, pale as a ghost, and he knew that his father was standing over him, yelling.

He looked up once and saw his father's face twisted into an ugly mask; not being able to look at him, he shifted his gaze away. He saw his stepmother, her lips like a knife, take one look at the rug, then stoop to pick up something. She straightened up, strode over to his father, and raised her arm, revealing the carpet beater in her hand. It was a heavy piece of rawhide, blunt and dry, with sharp edges where it had aged.

Martha Winslow drew her arm back, and Adam saw his father's head twist, heard him cry out, but it was too late. She was a big woman, strong and quick. The beater whistled through the air; then he felt something like fire and ice together. For a second, it did not hurt, but then the agony tore through him. His hand leaped to his face, and he felt the raw flesh on his cheek and neck.

"Martha! No!" Miles cried out in shock. He ripped the beater from her hand and threw it as far as he could. Then he knelt beside the boy and said with a trembling voice, "Let me see, Adam."

He lifted Adam's hands away, and then he stopped breathing—as though he'd been kicked in the stomach by a mule. He rose and cried, "Sampson, get the buggy hitched—quick!"

"Yessuh!"

Adam knew that he was badly hurt, but he did not cry. In a few minutes he heard his father say, "You drive, Sampson— I'll hold him. Whip them up—to Dr. Stone's!"

Then he heard his stepmother's voice, but Miles snapped

coldly, "Get your hands off this buggy! Whip them up, Sampson!" The servant obeyed and the buggy leaped forward.

Adam remembered one thing about that wild ride, and it was not the pain in his face. It was the first—and last—time in his life that his father ever held him in his arms!

A month later Miles took Adam aside and told him he'd be leaving. They were in the parlor, and Miles saw that the stitches had done fairly well, but Dr. Stone had said, "He'll always have a scar, Mr. Winslow." His manner had been harsh, for he was sure, Miles realized, that *he* had struck the boy.

Now looking down, he saw that the puckered marks of the scar, which ran along the boy's lower cheek on the jawbone and continued across the neck, would always be a symbol of his own failure.

Martha and he had been farther apart than ever, and he had seen that it would be impossible to have Adam at home. Martha hated him and would make life unbearable.

"Adam, I've decided to send you away."

Adam looked up quickly, despair in his eyes, but he said nothing. He had said practically nothing for a month. When Charles's part in the business had come out, he'd said, "It wasn't his fault. If I hadn't made the cannon, it wouldn't have happened."

"I know things have been hard for you, but I think you'll like your headmaster." He waited for Adam to ask who it would be. When there was no response, he said, "It'll be William."

Adam's head shot up and some of the bleak despair left his face. "I'm going to live with William?"

"I thought you'd like that," Miles grinned. Then he sobered, "You'll study with him—and you'll study Latin with Mr. Jonathan Edwards—in return for which you'll chop his wood."

"I'm to stay there always?"

Miles put his hands on the sturdy shoulders, and his voice was gentle as he tried to explain, "There's no happiness for you in this house." *For any of us!* he nearly added, but did not. "William has a nice house and a housekeeper. He tells me there's a workshop and a good blacksmith who likes boys. I—I haven't been as good a father as I should, Adam." He paused and with an effort went on. "You are not a bookish boy—but you have a genius. Despite all the bad things about the cannon—you *made* it—and I'm very proud to have a son who is gifted in that way!"

Squeezing the boy's shoulders lightly, he spoke softly, "I'll take you tomorrow. Say goodbye to Charles—and to your mother."

Adam saw his father had trouble saying all this, and he whispered, "I—I'll miss you, Father!"

After the boy left, Miles cursed himself. *Why didn't I hold him when I said goodbye? Why didn't I?*

CHAPTER FOUR

A LITTLE LATIN

★　★　★　★

"Well, Adam, it's time for your first Latin lesson with Rev. Edwards."

Adam's first two weeks with William at Amherst had gone quickly. Although he had missed his sister, Mercy, he had adjusted to his new life far better than his brother had expected. But as the two sat at the breakfast table eating the fried ham and scrambled eggs that the housekeeper, Mrs. Little, had set before them, a cloud fell across the boy's face.

"Do I *have* to, William? Can't you teach me?"

"No, I can't. In the first place, Rev. Edwards is the best Latin scholar in the country, and in the second place the arrangement is already made for you to chop his wood in exchange for his teaching. But I've got a surprise for you that ought to make the whole thing much easier. You eat all that breakfast, and you can have it."

William watched Adam surreptitiously, wondering not for the first time if they had done the right thing by the boy. He had been shocked and angered when Miles had brought Adam to him a month earlier, the scars on his face and neck red and not fully healed. It had been hard for his father to put his feelings into words, but William had seen the resentment in his stepmother years earlier, and when Miles had pleaded with him to take the boy, he had agreed at once.

And it had worked well—indeed, he had never seen Adam so cheerful. The scar on his face was still red and angry, but there was a peace in the boy's face that had been missing.

"We're going to be two old bachelors, Adam," William had told the boy after Miles had driven away. "We've got this big old house, and you've got a room all your own. We have Mrs. Little to cook for us and clean up after us. Mr. Little, her husband, is a fine blacksmith—even makes rifles—and he'll be glad to have you help him. We'll get a dog and hunt a bit. We'll also catch some fish out of the stream down the road. Why, it's going to be fun!"

Well, it's been good for the boy, William thought as Adam finished his breakfast. *He was wound tight as a spring when he got here—but he's lost a lot of that. I think being around Edwards and his children will do more for him than anything else—maybe help get that defensive set out of his back!*

"I'm all finished," Adam said.

"Right! Now, let's get to that surprise!"

He put on his coat and led Adam outside to the barn. Opening the door, he commanded, "Now, close your eyes and don't open them until I tell you!"

He threw the door open, went inside and drove out his own horse and the small reddish mare he'd bought from Samuel Sinclair. Then he stepped outside, saying, "All right, you can look now."

Adam opened his eyes, and when he saw the horse, he looked wildly at his brother and whispered, "That's—that's not for *me*, is it, William?"

"Well, I can't ride *two* horses, can I? It's yours, Adam—and happy birthday. Remember your last birthday in Philadelphia?"

Adam nodded and reached his hand out, and the red mare came slowly toward him, then licked his palm. Adam did not look at his brother, and there was a break in his voice as he said, "Thank you, William!"

"Man ought to have his own horse, Adam." William knew how to please a boy, and soon the two of them were saddled and riding down the road headed for Northampton. It gave the man a great deal of pleasure to watch his younger brother as they tried out all the mare's gaits along the way.

It was only an hour's ride to Edwards' parish, a busy village with six hundred parishioners living in the area around the church, a fine frame building with a high turreted roof. Going past it, William led the way to a simple foursquare house bounded by a slab fence. Most of the houses in the village were unpainted, but the minister's was a chaste white with red trim and jaunty green shutters.

The pair dismounted, tied their horses to a post, and as they walked onto the porch, the door opened and a man stepped outside. "Well, William, you're here early."

"Your newest scholar can't wait to get started, Reverend. This is my younger brother, Adam. Adam, this is Rev. Jonathan Edwards, your new Latin teacher."

"Good morning, young man!" Edwards stepped forward and put his hand out, gripping Adam's hand firmly. "You are *most* welcome!" His piercing eyes took in the boy; then he laughed and said, "I suspect you'll not mind that monstrous woodpile out back so much as conjugating Latin verbs!"

"He's a hard worker, sir," William stated. "But if your Latin lessons are as hard for Adam as your theology lessons are for *me*—why, I pity him! I couldn't make head nor tail of this book you gave me!"

Edwards laughed and said, "Well, well, we have time this morning to spend on that old demon of Antinomianism! Let me introduce Master Adam to his woodpile and you to the writings of Mr. Sewell."

He stepped off the porch and led them around the house, pausing to wave a thin hand at a pile of logs strewn over the ground. A set of cross trestles for holding them, several rusty saws scattered on the ground, and a variety of wedges and mauls completed the picture. "There's your wood—and I trust you will take better care of the equipment than *I* do," Edwards remarked. "Suppose you spend the morning on this while I read with your brother. Then this afternoon, I'll see what sort of scholar you are."

The two men left, and Adam picked up the saw and felt the teeth. Finding it to be dull, he walked over to the small shed a few feet away from the house. Tools were strewn everywhere in a careless fashion, and he spent an hour sharpening the saw with a rusty file. He did the same for an ax and for the two splitting mauls. Then he spent the rest of the morning cutting the logs into short sections.

Adam liked to cut wood. It gave him pleasure to run a sharp saw across the log and feel it bite down; soon he had cut a stack of two-foot-long logs. Splitting was even more enjoyable. The air was cool, and the beech he split divided as splinterless as a cloven rock. He had the gift of letting his mind go as he worked, his hands and body operating with machine-like precision while he thought of pleasant things—mostly that day of his new horse and what fine things they were going to do.

The hours sped by, but he had no sense of the passage of time, and it startled him when he heard a voice say, "Oh, my word! Look at the wood that young man has cut!"

He turned quickly to see Rev. Edwards and William standing there watching. They had been watching for some time, Edwards fascinated by the easy way Adam split the wood. He was an indifferent woodsplitter himself, and it was a mystery to him how the boy never seemed to strain, but the ax always fell exactly where he wanted it to.

"I told you he was a worker," William smiled. "And if you have anything broken, he's likely to be able to fix it for you—a real gift with his hands, sir."

"Plenty of that around here, William," Edwards sighed. "I'm not very good in that way. Well, let's wash up, Adam. Mrs. Edwards has fixed us a nice lunch."

A small porch was attached to the rear of the house, where they washed their hands before going through the oak door into the long room that served as a kitchen. "They're waiting for us. I fear we're a little late." Edwards led the pair into a low-ceilinged room with a large window on the long outside wall letting a stream of golden light fall on the white tablecloth that graced the rectangular table.

"I'm sorry to be late, my dear," Edwards said at once. He

walked to a place at the end of the table and introduced Adam. "This is my newest scholar, Mr. Adam Winslow."

William pushed Adam into a chair to his right and the boy gazed in amazement at what appeared to be a sea of girls! Actually, there were only six, including the beautiful woman sitting to Edwards' right, but every eye was fixed on him, and he ducked his head and felt his face burn. He knew that made the fresh scar stand out starkly, making the situation worse.

"You are very welcome, Adam," the lady greeted quickly, seeing the boy's embarrassment. "But you'll have to pardon our daughters for staring. Girls, tell our guest your names and how old you are."

"I'm Sarah—age twelve," the largest girl said at once.

"And I'm Jerusha—ten."

"Esther—nine years old."

"Mary. I'm six years old—how did you get that scar on your face?"

"Mary!" her mother reprimanded sharply, "I've told you not to ask questions. You may leave the table!"

Adam's hand reached up and covered the scar with an instinctive motion, and a quick anger shot through him. But when he saw tears form in Mary's eyes as she slipped to the floor, he said impulsively, "Oh, don't make her go, please! I—had an accident, but it's better now."

"Very handsome of you, sir!" Edwards interposed quickly. "You'll soon discover that Mary is somewhat impulsive, Adam! Now that's Lucy, age three and here you see young Timothy, age two—the only boy among this troop of females!"

"He'll be spoiled by all these older sisters, Rev. Edwards," William said.

"No doubt! I was the only boy in my family. Had *ten* sisters and they all spoiled me." Then without a pause Edwards suddenly offered up a blessing over the food, and they began at once to eat.

"I can tell you, Mr. Winslow," Sarah Edwards stated as she passed the fresh hot bread, "those sisters of his did spoil him. He's not gotten completely over it to this day!"

"My sisters were all tall, and Father used to say he had sixty feet of daughters!" Edwards remarked, then turned to listen to what Jerusha had to tell him.

It was a strange meal for Adam, for while the children never interrupted the adults, they were encouraged to take part in the conversation. He picked at his food, and once when Edwards made a little joke, with the last line in Latin, even Mary laughed! It made him feel stupid, and he wished he could go back and split more wood.

After the meal, however, Edwards asked, "Now, sir, would you go with me to my study? We'll see if your brain is as strong as those sturdy arms of yours!"

Adam gave a despairing look at William, who threw him an encouraging smile, and followed the minister out of the dining room into a small study down a narrow hall. The walls were lined with books, and the single large desk that took up most of the room was piled high with neatly organized papers.

"Sit there, Adam, and read me a little of this."

Adam took the book gingerly and opened it. His heart sank when he saw that it was a book he'd never seen, and for one moment his mind went completely blank—he could not have read one word of it if it meant to save his soul.

Edwards' penetrating eyes searched the boy's face, and he said quickly, "You know, before we start, I have a book here that I have not read myself, but it's just the sort of thing a handy young fellow like you would probably like. Let me get it." Standing to his feet, he reached up and pulled down a plainly bound reddish book, opened it then shook his head. "I never can quite grasp how these things work, Adam. Perhaps you can give me a clue."

He put the book down in front of the boy, and Adam saw on the opened page a very fine mechanical drawing of a pistol. He picked it up eagerly, never dreaming that William had told Edwards of his interest in such things, and said excitedly, "Oh, this is a good drawing, sir! Look, this is the frizzen, and this part here is the pan. . . !" He kept his eyes glued on the book, his finger tracing the lines, while Edwards' kind, luminous eyes watched carefully.

"So that's the way it works, Reverend," he finished at last.

"My, you're so quick at that sort of thing! And you've made even a poor mechanical mind such as mine understand it! Well, let me show you how this page of Latin can be almost as easy for you as that drawing."

Then with easy patience, Edwards drew the boy's attention back to the book, and soon Adam found that he *did* remember some of it, and by the end of an hour, he was doing better than he had dreamed. He did not understand how much that was due to the skill of the tall man in front of him, who said at last, "Why, you did very well, Adam! Very well, indeed!" He got up, and smiled, leading Adam to the door. "You need a great deal of work—but then I've got a great deal of wood, so by the time the woodpile is gone, you'll be reading Tacitus like a scholar!"

"I—I never thought I'd—" Adam broke off and the minister finished his sentence.

"You never thought you'd like Latin? Well, you'll find a great deal to like in this world, my boy. It's a great world the Lord has made for us to study, and I can see you're not going to let much get by you!"

When they stepped back into the main part of the house, they were met by a conspiracy. Mrs. Edwards put her hand on Adam's shoulder as she spoke to her husband. "No more wood-cutting today! The girls have to have a ride on Adam's new mare." Then she put her arm around the startled boy, who had never been hugged by anyone except Rachel and Mercy, and she said warmly, "Happy birthday, Adam!"

"Birthday, is it?" Edwards smiled. "I didn't know that! How old are you?"

"Fourteen, sir."

"Well, many happy returns—but you are trapped, sir, trapped! No escaping these women—so go give them a ride. The wood can wait for another time."

Adam went outside, and William asked, "How did he do?"

"Oh, very well for a beginning—but his heart is in science."

"Yes, and Father could never understand that. I appreciate your interest in the boy." He hesitated, then taking a plunge, told Edwards the problems Adam had at home.

Edwards frowned, then remarked, "Usually, it's best for a

boy to be at home, but this is an exception. He will be better off here."

Outside, the object of their conversation was besieged, every young Edwards claiming the right to ride the mare first. Finally Mary said, "Me first, Adam! You stood up for me at dinner, so you have to let me ride first!"

Adam stared at her bewildered, but he was to learn very quickly that Mary Edwards had a gift with words, and that she was quite likely to get her way even if her logic was sometimes a little fuzzy.

He lifted her on, swung up behind her, and the mare moved obediently down the road. "What's his name?" Mary asked.

Adam laughed suddenly. "It's not a he—and she doesn't have a name. I just got her this morning."

Mary turned around and stared at him in astonishment. "You've got to give this poor horse a name, Adam."

"There's no hurry."

"Yes, there is! And I'm going to help you—I can think of lots of names!"

"I don't need help to name my own horse!"

"Yes, I can think of better names than you can," she cried out, and then she began kicking her heels against the mare's sides, calling out, "Faster! Faster!" She was not satisfied until they galloped at a fast clip down the road.

All afternoon he took the Edwards' children on short rides, and in doing so he learned their names—and he found out that they were all very intelligent. But it was a fine time for him as well as for them, and when William came up and said, "Time to go home, Adam," he was surprised at how quickly the afternoon had gone.

The Edwardses lined up to bid them goodbye, and Mary scurried over to Adam and threw her arms around his neck, pulling him down to whisper in his ear.

"Her name is Abishag!" she said fiercely. Then she kissed his cheek and murmured, "I'm sorry you got hurt."

They left, and the arrangement was made that Adam would ride over three times a week for his lesson and to chop wood.

"How'd you like the family?" William asked on the way home.

"All right."

William was accustomed to his brother's taciturn ways, but he saw the glow on Adam's face. "You'll have to think of a name for your mare," he remarked carelessly.

They said nothing until they were almost home, and then as they slipped to the ground, Adam reached up and stroked the mare's velvety nose.

"Her name is Abishag!"

William's eyes blinked in surprise, and then he smiled and went over to pat the mare's neck. "Well, one thing about a name like that—you won't find any other horses with that title!"

CHAPTER FIVE

A FAMILY AFFAIR

★ ★ ★ ★

"Adam, how long will it take you to get ready to go to Boston?"

"Boston?" Adam was sighting down the barrel of a long rifle, carefully bringing the tiny silver bead into the lowest spot of the rear notch until it was aimed on the eye of one of Little's fine cows, a quarter of a mile away. He snapped the trigger, grunted with satisfaction, then glanced over at William, who had come into the blacksmith shop late in the afternoon. "You're all excited about something," he remarked, taking in his brother's flushed face and bright eyes.

"I've got a letter from Father." He extracted a rumpled sheet from his pocket, smoothed it out and read: *I've agreed on a price with Hunter. Bring Adam to Boston with you and the papers will be ready. You can have your own way, I suppose, about Oxford.*

Adam wrapped the rifle in a piece of soft leather, then turned to face William. There was something slow and methodical in his movements, and though he lacked three inches of his brother's height, there was a thickness and breadth in his torso that William lacked. His chest swelled against the homespun shirt, deep and very broad, and there was a suggestion of power in every move he made. His thighs were heavy and his thick wrists and forearms swelled the sleeves of his shirt—the product of three years at the forge swinging a ten-pound hammer.

"What's this all about, William?" His voice was quiet, his words slow and even. "I don't want to leave right now—need to work on this breech mechanism some more."

"Oh, you'd never be ready to leave this smoky forge!" William gave a half laugh, then sobered, saying, "Two things, Adam. First of all, Father's going to buy the Hunter place, and I suspect he wants you to have a hand working it."

"I'd rather be a blacksmith, William—and I don't know all that much about farming."

"You can learn, can't you? And I've been wanting to go to Oxford to do some study for years. So now Father's agreed to finance me for a year. Come on, Adam, let's get ready so we can leave early in the morning. I'm packing all the things I'll need at Oxford, and that'll include a trunk of books."

He turned and Adam followed him out, but there was a stubborn look on his square face. As they mounted up and started for the house, he thought about the letter, but he said nothing until late that night after William's things were packed.

When everything was ready, he stated, "I'll go with you to Boston, but I don't like the idea of working on that farm."

William considered Adam's sturdy form, and after a moment replied, "It could be a good thing for you."

"I don't want to be a farmer, William. I want to be a blacksmith."

William stared at him, then smiled. "You've changed a great deal in the last three years, Adam. You've done well studying with Mr. Edwards, and Little says you've got the best hands of any man he ever saw for work at the forge—and I guess you've become a pretty stubborn young man as well."

Adam shifted uncomfortably. "I don't want to be quarrelsome; I think I can be good at making things, but not much good at farming."

William shrugged and said, "Well, you can explain it to Father, not me."

The next morning they pulled out early, the buggy piled high with William's luggage. "I've got to take this box of books to Edwards, Adam."

They pulled up in front of the house, and William left Adam in the buggy while he took the books inside. As he went in, Mary came sailing out like a whirlwind. She swarmed up the side of the buggy and began chattering at once like a magpie.

"Why didn't you come last Wednesday like you said, Adam? I waited all day, and then I had to try to go find those eggs all by myself—and I *did* find them, too!—all except the woodpecker. Let's go get that one now, Adam! I know right where it is. . . !"

He smiled down at her, marveling how her tiny ten-year-old frame could hold so much energy—and how that head could hold so much knowledge. She had attached herself to him like a leech since the first day three years ago when she had named his mare, and he realized that her talkative way and unbridled curiosity had been good for him, especially in the first months at Amherst.

As she chatted on, he watched her mobile face and intent eyes, startled somewhat to think of how many of his memories were connected with her.

She had led him through a thousand paths in the woods around Northampton seeking birds' eggs for her collection—she chattering like a squirrel to his silence. Many times he had spent the night at her home, sitting at the feet of her father, leaning against her as Edwards told Bible stories. Every time he attended church at Northampton or went with William to a nearby church where Edwards preached, Mary always wedged herself beside him.

He thought suddenly of his first real fight, a bloody, awkward brawl with a tall, rawboned youth named Landon. He had made Mary cry, and the two of them had fought until neither of them could stand!

He had been with Mary that morning in Enfield when her father had preached a sermon with the frightening title, "Sinners in the Hands of an Angry God," and Mary had clung to him with fear as many of the hearers fell to the floor shaking with terror! He had been badly shaken himself, he thought with a sudden grin, but he had not let her see it.

"I can't go with you today, Mary," he interrupted her steady flow of words. "I'm going to Boston with William."

"Boston? Why? When are you coming back?"

"Don't know," he answered. Looking up, he saw William hurrying out of the house. "I guess I won't be gone too long. Maybe I'll be back day after tomorrow. Then we'll get that egg from that redheaded woodpecker. Jump down now!"

She threw her arms around him, delivered a moist kiss on his cheek, then hopped down like a grasshopper, calling after them as Adam whipped the team into a trot, "I'll see you Friday! Don't be late!"

William looked at Adam with amusement. "That child dotes on you, but you shouldn't have told her you'd see her Friday."

"Why not?"

"Well, Father's business may take longer than you think."

Adam gave a rare smile, his teeth bright against his heavy tan. The long white scar across his face and neck puckered slightly with the movement of his jaw. "Won't take long for me to say what I've got to say, William. How long does it take to say 'No thank you'?" He touched the team with his whip, leaned back and shook his head, saying, "You'll be on your way to England Friday—and I'll be hunting a woodpecker egg!"

"When was the last time you were home, Adam? Last year?"

Adam had drawn the buggy up in front of the house and was getting out as William asked the question. He thought quickly, then said, "No, it's been nearly two years."

"So long as that?" William shook his head, and as they mounted the steps, he murmured, "That's too long, Adam. Father's getting on—we're going to have to come home more often."

Adam could have replied that he had not been invited, but he said nothing. He stood there as William knocked, and when the door opened, the sight of his father shocked him.

"Come in, come in!" Miles took them both by the hand, and to Adam the bones felt thin and brittle as the bones of a bird. His father had lost much weight, and his stoop was so pronounced now that he was little more than Adam's height. There were brown spots on his face, his cheeks were sunken, and his rheumy eyes gave the picture of a man in bad health. *He's sixty-*

nine years old, Adam thought, and he could only say briefly, "How are you, Father?" so great was the shock; the last two years had changed Winslow from a healthy man to a sick one with the smell of death about him.

"William! Come in here—and don't waste any of your preaching on me!" Charles stepped forward, his eyes sparkling, and after shaking William's hand, he turned to Adam. His eyes narrowed, and then he smiled. "Why, you've become a man, brother! Look at those hands!" he grinned. "Strong as vises, I'd say!" But he seemed glad to see Adam and gave him a hearty shake.

"Hello, Charles."

"Adam—It's been a long time."

Adam looked into the eyes of Martha Winslow, seeing that she was not changed. Indeed, she looked stronger, if anything, as if somehow she had drawn all the health and strength out of her husband for her own use. Her eyes, he saw, suddenly fixed on the white scar that ran along his jaw and he smiled, saying, "Hello. You're looking well."

"Thank you," she replied quietly. "Come in and sit down, both of you. You must be tired."

"I'll send Sampson after Rachel and Saul," Miles said. "They're required for this business." He left the room, and William remarked quietly, "He doesn't look well."

"He was bad a month ago—ague, I think it was," Martha nodded. "He hasn't been able to get his strength back." She turned, saying, "Come into the kitchen. I've got something for you to eat."

As they ate, Charles sat across from them, full of the news of Boston. "Did you know I'd been working with Saul, Adam?"

"William told me. Do you like business, Charles?"

"Yes!" Charles looked far older than his sixteen years, and as he spoke it was clear that he was intoxicated with the world of finance. His blue eyes flashed and his hands cut through the air with eloquent gestures as he told a story of how he had, with the help of Saul, been able to pull off a very successful deal in furs from Canada. Adam understood little of it, and he was depressed to think how much Charles knew and how little he had learned since he had left home.

They had just finished eating and had risen when they heard voices. Rachel came to greet them. "Adam! You've grown so much!"

"Not so tall as Charles, Aunt Rachel," he smiled. She looked more fragile than he remembered her, and the lines around her eyes were etched more deeply, but there was still a vitality about her that was missing in his father.

Saul advanced, gave Adam a critical look, then remarked with a smile, "You look strong as a bull, Adam. It's good to see you."

He made his reply to his cousin and to Esther; then Miles entered, saying, "Let's go into the parlor. I've got a lot to say."

Adam followed them into the parlor and sat near the window on a straight-backed chair as his father took a stand beside the tiger-striped oak table in the center of the wall and looked around the room. His voice sounded a little weak, but it grew stronger as he spoke.

"It's good to see you—all of you. It's been a long time since the Winslows have been together—and I regret it. A family is the best thing on earth next to God, isn't it? And we've wasted some time."

He paused, then shook his head almost imperceptibly. Looking across the room he continued: "William, this meeting is for you and for Adam. The rest of us have done a lot of thinking and considerable planning. I've called us all together so that we can agree on which direction the family business ought to go. Saul's been talking a lot about making some changes, and perhaps we ought to listen to him. Saul?"

Saul looked around but did not stand up as he said, "We've done very well, I think, for the past few years. Uncle Miles did a fine job of getting the fur business established. But these are new times, and if we survive, we're going to have to adjust."

"What sort of changes do you have in mind, Saul?" William asked.

There was a line of concentration around Saul Howland's eyes. He had always been a serious man, and was so much older than his cousins that they had always looked upon him as the businessman in the family. Now he stated carefully, "Basically, we ought to guard our interest in the fur trade by expanding as much as possible into the Ohio River Valley—but there's a danger in that. The fur is plentiful, but the French are going to give problems."

"You think there'll be a war?" William asked.

"Yes, I do, but nobody can say how soon. Fur's a good business, so we need to keep our interests going. But we must diversify." He turned suddenly and smiled at Charles, saying, "Charles has been a godsend! I've never seen a young fellow who caught on to business so quickly. Tell them about the ideas we've been working on, will you, Charles?"

It was clear that Saul was grooming his cousin for leadership in the family, and Charles was equal to it. He stood up and said easily, "Of course, these are all Saul's ideas, but they make sense. What we plan to do is buy land and develop it. There's no way that the price of land can go *down*, and we can protect ourselves against any reverses in the fur trade." He went on smoothly, speaking with a confident grace, and Adam was amazed at how his brother had matured.

Charles drew out a map, pinned it to the wall, and pointed at several spots that had been considered. Finally he said, "There are two plots that Saul and I think will be safe and profitable. The first one is here in Virginia." He pointed to a spot on the map, saying, "It's cheap land because it's not really developed, and we can get it for almost nothing. The owner's in trouble and has to sell." Then he moved the pointer to a spot east of Boston. He gave a wide smile, looking at Adam. "Adam, you ought to be interested in this—as a matter of fact, you've probably been over most of it hunting, from what William has told me."

"That's the Hunter place?" Adam asked. "It's pretty run down, Charles. Gone back to woods—and a lot of it's in timber."

"You know it, do you, Adam?" Miles asked, giving his son a sharp look.

"Yes, sir. Everybody knows the place."

"Well, William is going to Oxford," Miles told them, then smiled briefly, adding, "Nobody expects you to be a businessman, William, and I'm glad that we've got a Winslow preaching the Gospel. Edward would have been very proud of you—and

Grandfather Gilbert, too." He paused as some memory rose out of the past, swept across his mind; then he shook his shoulders and stated decisively, "Adam, Charles is going to go to Virginia and start our work there, and we would like you to learn to operate the Hunter place."

Adam grew still, always awkward when called upon to say anything in public. He knew that what he was going to say would sound ungrateful, and yet he could think of no way to agree.

"I—I'm not cut out for farming," he said, then hastened to add, "I've seen enough of that life to know that you have to have a gift for it—and you have to like it."

Martha's lips tightened, and she snapped in a waspish tone, "You ought to be *grateful* for the opportunity—but you always were an unthoughtful boy!"

Saul silenced her with a look, and answered, with just a trace of displeasure in his voice, "It's a trade, Adam. A man can learn it, as he could anything else."

"I think, Saul," Rachel said quietly, "that Adam is right. We don't want a man there whose heart's not in it. He would please neither us nor himself."

"But, Adam, you have to have a profession," Charles argued. "And we're not talking about just being a farm laborer; it will be the family business—*your* business, actually. You can get rich if you work at it."

Adam felt the pressure growing and he looked around, seeking assurance, but even William offered no encouragement. He said, "I want to be a blacksmith," he stated firmly. "It's what I'm good at."

"You can do that, too, Adam," Miles affirmed. He looked across the room at Adam, and there was a plea in his tired old eyes. He knew that he had failed with this strange dark son of his, and he knew that he had little time to rectify the mistake. "I ask you to do this thing, Adam, for the family, of course—but it's really *you* I'm thinking of."

It touched Adam suddenly, this plea coming from his father who had never asked him for anything. They had not been close, but now he saw that his father was reaching out for some way to help, and doing so in the only way he knew. And he longed to agree, but he could only say, "Father, it wouldn't be good for me *or* for the family if I did this."

The pressure grew, and for fifteen minutes Adam was urged to follow the line pointed out by Saul. Martha finally sniffed and said loudly, anger rising in her voice, "Well, I'd think there'd be a *little* gratitude in you, Adam! After all, it isn't as though you had a great deal of talent! Heaven knows we've all worried about what would happen to you if you had to take care of yourself!"

Then Rachel stood up, her thin face drawn with anger. "All of you, be quiet!" Esther and Saul looked at her with shock, and even Martha blinked. Rachel rarely raised her voice, but when she did, it was like a storm cloud, and there were none in the family who cared to confront her when she was roused.

Going over to Adam, she put one hand on his shoulder, raised his face with the other. Her eyes were bright with indignation as she spoke, "Adam, do what you want to do!" She leaned over and kissed him, and her kiss burned like fire on his face.

Then she stood up and stared down at him. "Let me suggest this—and you tell me to mind my own business if you don't like it, all right?"

He smiled suddenly and said, "All right, Aunt Rachel."

"Most of the farming today is done with tools that haven't changed since Gilbert Winslow got off the *Mayflower*, isn't that right? Well, why don't you make better ones, Adam?"

He stared at her in bewilderment. "Me? Make better farming tools?"

"Well, as I remember it, you've spent most of your life making things—the cannon, for example?" She laughed as his face burned with shame, but she cried out, "What's the matter? The thing worked, didn't it?" Suddenly Miles laughed loudly—a rare thing, indeed. "Certainly it worked! Nearly wiped out a whole species—the Black Winslow Banty!"

William joined his father in laughter, then suddenly stood up, his face alive with excitement. "Why, of course! Why didn't I think of it? You can do more good that way than doing the work yourself, Adam. I'll bet you've got a dozen ideas right now about how to make a better harrow or a new way to cut brush quicker with some kind of a new blade? Isn't that right?"

Adam suddenly was filled with excitement. "Why, I can do that!"

A murmur of pleasure ran around the room; Miles stepped over and put his arm around Adam, an act that embarrassed both of them, and stated, "That's it! We'll get a good overseer—and you can oversee *him*—and *make* all the inventions you want!"

"And keep on with the gunmaking, too," Charles laughed. "When a war comes, there's nothing like a munitions-maker to make a family rich!"

They all laughed, and for the first time in his memory, Adam felt like a member in good standing of the Winslow clan!

A week later, William and Adam stood at the rail of the schooner *Rosebud*, watching the coast of America grow dim. Adam had gone back to get his clothes. His assignment was to go to England, to spend three months studying the most advanced methods of farming, and visit as many manufacturers of farming equipment as possible in that time.

Now William remarked, "Well, brother, life is odd, eh?" He laughed and clapped Adam on the shoulder, adding, "You thought you'd be looking for a woodpecker egg—but here you are on the high seas—a businessman!"

Adam rubbed his jaw ruefully. "Mary will never forgive me, William! When I went back to get my clothes, she gave me fits for leaving her!"

"She's a bright girl," William smiled. "But it'll only be a short time, and she'll have you back again. Charles will have the house ready for you and an overseer hired. He's a brilliant young man, that brother of ours!" Then he squeezed Adam's muscular arm and laughed, "But I'll bet he can't bend a horseshoe or make guns like you!" He looked at his brother and added gently, "I know you're a little afraid of all this new responsibility—but you can do it, Adam. In this New World we don't have a long time to be children—girls are married at fifteen, and boys, not much older. It's a new land, and we've got to grow up in a hurry." He would have said more, but finally he merely smiled and put his arm around Adam's shoulder.

The land dropped out of sight, and the two walked slowly around the ship, coming to the bow. Standing there peering into the misty distance, Adam mused, "It's a long way to England, isn't it, William?" Then he leaned on the rail and murmured, "Mary told me to get her something pretty in London. Wonder if she'd like a doll?"

"As smart as that one is, you'd do better to get a set of reference books!" William laughed.

"No, a doll would be nice," Adam decided with a gentle smile on his broad lips. The two stood close together staring across the deep waters, each seeing a vision of his own.

CHAPTER SIX

MOLLY

★ ★ ★ ★

"I hate to abandon you like this, Adam," William told his brother for the third time, a worried look on his face. He stood blocking the door of the coach. The driver had already called down twice for him to get in. He bit his lip nervously, looked around at the hustling mass of humanity that filled the Cheapside Street, then grabbed Adam's arm. "I *must* go to Oxford— but this is a wicked city, and a country lad like you could be easily taken in!"

"Get on the coach, William!" Adam grinned. "Every night since we've been here you've kept me awake warning me about the dangers of this iniquitous place. I promised to trust no one— *especially* handsome females with painted faces!" He laughed aloud at the alarmed look on his brother's countenance, then gave him an affectionate slap on the shoulder. "On with you! I'll be in no danger. I'll be looking at farms and factories; there'll be no tricksters or fancy women in *those* places!"

"Be you goin' or not?" the driver yelled, leaning over the edge of the coach, his yellow face wrinkled with impatience. "Either get yerself in—or get out of the way!"

"You have my address!" William yelled, as he piled in and the coach rolled off. "Write often, Adam—and don't forget to go to church!"

Adam waved, then turned and made his way down the busy streets. He had been afraid of the city at first; it was so big and boisterous, but as he threaded a path through the vendors that cluttered the walks and spilled over into the narrow street, he was seized by a spirit of freedom that was intoxicating. There was no one to tell him what to do, and for the first time in his life he was responsible to no one except himself.

They had disembarked from the *Rosebud* four days earlier after a fast crossing, and had found a room for Adam in a two-story half-timbered house near the center of the city. That same day they had gone to the bank, Lloyds of London, and presented the letter of credit. The funds were in two parts—one sum for William to draw on for his expenses at Oxford for the year, the other for Adam.

"I feel strange with all this money, William," he had said as they left Lloyds. "Three hundred pounds! That's a fortune!"

"It won't seem like it if you buy all that new-fangled farm equipment, though. Saul expects you to get good value for that cash."

The plan had been laid out for Adam. He was to buy as much equipment as he could and have it shipped to the two plantations, but there had been objections from Esther and Martha about his ability to handle money. Miles had raised his head and spoken with a tone of finality: "Adam must learn to handle business, and there'll be no more said about it!"

As Adam made his way to the first of the factories he planned to visit, he felt again the warmth that had flooded him at that moment. He had not known until then how much he had longed for the approval of his father. Now dodging carts and coaches that thundered down the street, he vowed he would not let his family down. He passed by men, women, and children—some dressed in the sooty rags of chimney sweeps, others arrayed in the gold and gaudy satin of the aristocracy. Porters sweated under their burdens, chapmen darted from shop to shop, and tradesmen scurried around like ants pulling at Adam's coat as he fought his way through the human tide that flowed and ebbed on the street.

He found the factory on the edge of the city, and the owner

was not too busy to show him around. It came as something of a shock to Adam to see the primitive methods used in the production of the equipment, and he thought with a start: *Why, I could do as well as this—better!* But he only looked, made notes, and thanked the owner.

Adam visited two other factories that day, finding one of them to be quite advanced. He stayed until late afternoon, making drawings, and by the time he made his way back to Cheapside, he was hungry. He went in to a small, smoky inn called "The Eagle" for a meal. He had eaten with William, and devoured a steak and kidney pie with gusto.

As he left The Eagle and started back to his room, a voice startled him—a tiny, thin voice that came from his left.

"Sir? Will ye buy a handkerchief—only five bob!"

A young girl not more than ten or eleven years old stepped out from the overhanging shadow of an apartment. She held out a fragment of white cloth, but he shook his head, saying, "I don't need any handkerchiefs, Missy, thank you." Already hardened to the infinite pleas of vendors and beggars, he would have passed on, but she took a quick step forward. There was a note of panic in her small voice as she pleaded, "Oh, please, won't yer tyke a bit of fancy work to yer lady, sir? Yer can 'ave it fer four bob!"

He looked down at her, intending to shake her off, but paused when he saw the fatigue in her face. She had large eyes that looked gray in the fading light, and the smudges under the lower lids made them look larger. Her face was thin, her lips drawn with either pain or fatigue, and the finely-etched planes of her face with high cheekbones and a sweeping jawline did not seem to go with the ragged clothes that hung on her thin body. Most of the young beggars had faces blunted by ignorance and eyes dulled by the monotonous life of poverty they led; this girl, for all her rags, had something that was delicate and sensitive.

"I don't have a lady, Missy," Adam said gently; then suddenly she reminded him of Mary Edwards back in America, and he put forth his hand to pat her head the way he had often done with children.

"Don't—!" the girl cried. Dropping the handkerchief, she

threw her hand up over her face, cowering back against the wall.

Adam stood there staring at her, then an anger flared up inside and he bent to pick up the handkerchief. It was a finely done piece of work, now stained where it had touched the filthy sidewalk. He looked at her, then reaching into his pocket, he drew out a coin and held it out, "I'll take the piece, Missy."

She dropped her arm, swallowed convulsively, then stepped forward to take the coin. "I—I ain't got no change—"

"You can keep it, Missy." He looked at it, then lifted his eyes to her face. There was a sudden relief in her features, and he suspected that she had saved herself from a beating by the sale. "Did you make this? It's very fine."

"Oh, me mother made it, mostly—but she's a' teachin' me."

Darkness was falling fast, so that he had to lean forward and strain to see her features. "It's getting dark, Missy. You'd better get home."

"Yes, sir, I be goin' now." She looked around at the man now made faceless by the dark, and asked in a tiny voice, "Sir, be yer goin' down ter 'auberk?"

Adam's rooming house was in Hauberk, and he nodded. "Come along." As she fell into step beside him, he adjusted his steps to suit her. Glancing down at her as they walked, he wondered that such a small girl was allowed to roam the streets of a city. "How old are you, Missy?"

"Ten, sir."

"My name is Adam Winslow. What do they call you?"

"I'm Molly."

He found out that she had two brothers and three sisters, and lived in a run-down section filled mostly with the very poor. When he asked her what her father did, she said with a shrug, "Oh, he's a bricklayer—only there ain't no work nowadays."

They left the main business district, then coming to a side street that led off from Adam's street, she said, "I live down here aways. Thank you, sir."

"Oh, I'll see you home, Molly," Adam replied quickly. She did not protest, and led him down a street that degenerated quickly into a gin lane. The houses were decayed, held up in some cases by long poles. Derelicts stumbled along, bleary-eyed and loose-lipped. Several times along the way, men dressed in rags shambled out of the shadows and approached Adam, eying him slyly. They did not miss, however, the strong, muscular figure nor the direct stare in his dark eyes, and offered nothing more than a plea for money, which he denied.

He wondered grimly what could protect a child like the one beside him, and he realized with a shock that his little world in Amherst where children were safe on the streets lay thousands of miles away. London was a world of predators, feeding on strangers—or on one another when there were no other victims.

"There's me 'ous, Mr. Winslow," Molly said. The two-story house she led him to faced the street and, like the others, was in a state of decay. A strong smell of garbage and sewage rose from the trench in the middle of the cobblestoned street. A single lantern cast feeble yellow beams over several young children playing in the front. A woman who was leaning against the wall straightened up as the two approached, calling out "Molly?" in a thin voice.

"Aye, Ma, it's me," the child answered. Adam paused in the street, and heard Molly say, "This 'ere gentulman, Mr. Winslow, 'e bought the nice lace, Ma. And 'e lives in 'auberk, so 'e let me walk with 'im."

"Why, thank you, sir," the woman said. "It's late for a little one, and that's a fact."

"Glad to be of help," Adam replied. He touched his hat, a gesture that brought a sudden quick look from the woman, as if she had forgotten such manners existed. He turned to go, but she stalled him, "Mr. Winslow? I—I wonder if you be needin' any cleaning done—or like your clothes done up nice and clean?"

"Why. . ." Adam paused, then before he could answer, he was interrupted by a raspy voice.

"Wot's this now!" A thick-bodied man, tall and hulking in the dim light had come up from somewhere down the street to take a stand behind Adam. He had a loose-jawed face with piggish little eyes, and there was something threatening in the way he stood there, his arms held out from his sides and his massive fists clenched.

"Tom! This is Mr. Winslow—he just bought one of my pieces from Molly—and I was just askin' him if he had any cleanin' to be done!"

The woman's voice was threaded with fear. Her hands twitched nervously on the shawl she held as she stepped forward to put herself between her husband and Adam.

The man paused, relaxed his fists, and a loose smile spread across his face. "Oh, yer bought somethin', is it? Well, let's 'ave the cash!" Molly held out the coin, which he took. Holding it up to the light and grunting with satisfaction, he slipped it into the pocket of his vest. "Now, that's 'andsome of yer, sir."

"Not at all," Adam shrugged. "It's very fine work."

"Ah, yer ain't from 'ere, then? America, I tyke it? Burns is me name, Mr. Winslow—Thomas Burns. And be yer 'ere fer long?"

"Three months, more or less."

"Aw, now, Mr. Winslow, 'ow is the brick business in the Colonies, do yer say?"

"Very good. Quite a bit of construction in Boston."

"Do yer tell me that?" Burns said in surprise. "It's been in me 'ead to try me luck over the waters. This 'ere place is dead, it is! Nothin' fer an honest workman!"

He laughed and came forward to stand toward Adam; he was of average height, but massive as a draft horse. The gin on his breath was a raw stench in Adam's nostrils as Burns said, "Well, I got me some business, Mr. Winslow. Yer let me little woman do yer cleanin', yer see? And later me and you can talk some more about workin' in the Colonies, yer hear me now?"

Adam took the huge paw the man held out, and instantly found his hand collapsed beneath the power of Burns' grip! He caught his breath, leaned forward against the pain of it—then tightened his own grip. Burns was peering at him out of a pair of muddy eyes, and Adam realized it was an old trick with the man—but he closed his hand and Burns' mouth sagged open as Adam began to exert power. The sinews of his forearms and fingers had been transformed into flesh as hard as the iron they had wrought on the forge, and Burns was out of condition. Slowly the balance shifted, and Burns, instead of crushing

Adam's hand, found his own caught in a viselike grip that was paralyzing his nerves. Pain began to run up his arm, and he wrenched his hand away with a mighty effort, then stood there glaring down at Adam.

"Be glad to talk to you any time, Burns," Adam offered without a sign of exertion in his face. "Mrs. Burns, my room is with Mrs. Havelock—next to the green grocers. I won't have much cleaning, but you're welcome to do what there is."

"I'll be by every Tuesday, sir," Mrs. Burns said.

Adam said goodnight, turned and made his way home. He went to bed at once, but could not go to sleep. Too much was happening, and he lay awake thinking of the factories and the machinery he had seen, trying to plan ways to improve the equipment.

Finally he dropped off to sleep, but tossed fitfully, dreaming of the events of the day. Several times he seemed to see a pair of enormous gray eyes and hear a reedy voice saying, "Oh, please, sir, won't yer tyke a bit uv fancy work to yer lady, sir?" Finally he woke up, remembering how Molly Burns had flinched from him; he thought of the massive hands of Thomas Burns leaving their marks on the child, and anger ran so strongly through him, he could not sleep for a long time.

11 November, 1744
Dear Father,

I have seen in the past three months practically every factory in central England that makes any sort of farming equipment, and have made up a list of such machinery along with the prices for your consideration. There have not been very many, but there are a great number of gunsmiths, and I must confess that I have spent much time there!

I have not missed a single Sabbath going to church, but I must say that the preaching here is frightful! I know you are opposed to Mr. Whitefield and the Revival, but if you had to sit through one of the sermons delivered by Church of England pastors, you would perhaps change your mind.

I have made few friends here and am looking forward to arriving home. I have taken passage on a small freighter, and should arrive home by the first of the year.

Your devoted son—Adam

Adam sat back in his chair, arched his back, and thought how difficult it was for him to write to his family—and how easy it was for him to write to Mary. He took a fresh sheet, and with a sudden laugh thought, *I'm about on her level, I suppose! I wonder if I'll ever be able to talk to adults?* He began the letter, which, unlike the one to his father, ran several pages. The mails were so slow that he never expected answers; thus his letters amounted to a journal. He had included descriptions of the vivid side of London life for Mary, and had taken pleasure in letting his experiences reshape themselves on paper for her eyes. He was unaware of how he used the child for a sounding board, a confidant on whom he could try out his ideas—one to whom he could speak freely with no reservations.

He wrote steadily for over an hour, then put the quill down and leaned back to read the letter. He was surprised to discover (not for the first time!) how much of his thoughts were taken up by the Burns family. The week following his first meeting with Molly, he had told Mary in an earlier letter, she had come to his door for his washing. He had invited her in, then while gathering up his scarce wardrobe for washing, he had encouraged her to talk. She had been more open than on the street, and it ended by their having tea together. Then he had told her stories of America, which she delighted to hear.

She was, he discovered, quite ignorant, but not stupid. Her questions were sharp, and a voracious appetite for learning lay beneath the surface. He had read to her from some of his books, and her face was a picture of contentment and delight as she sat there in his straight-backed chair drinking it all in.

He put some of his feeling about the family into his letter to Mary:

> I have told you quite a bit about the Burns family. I know all the names of the children by now. Molly is your age, but you would find her quite ignorant. She cannot read a word, but she delights in books. I wish she could spend some time in your company, Mary, for she is a warmhearted and loving child who could do well if she had the opportunity.
>
> Alas, there is no chance for that! Her mother is a good woman, but worn out with work and dominated by her hus-

band. I can say nothing good about *that* one, for he is a brute who lives on the labors of his wife and children. Worse, he mistreats them frightfully!

I have seen the bruises on Mrs. Burns and on the children, and pray that I will never be present to witness the thing! I had an awful battle once with a man who was mistreating his dog, and I do not think I could stand to see a woman or a child beaten!

Keep me in your prayers, and remember me to your parents and your dear sisters and to Timothy. I long to see you, and when I return the first of the year, I will expect to go egg-hunting with you, though the snow be five feet deep!

Your friend and admirer, Adam Winslow

William's black robe billowed in the cutting December wind, making him look like a monstrous bat fluttering across the grounds of Oxford. He broke into a run, casting off his dignity, and reached the relative warmth of the vine-covered three-story building where his quarters were. Climbing to the top story, he shoved his way into the room, then stopped dead-still. A fire snapped in the fireplace and Adam stood there beside it, his face a patchwork of blue bruises and half-healed cuts.

"Adam! What in the world happened to you?"

"I was in a fight." Adam smiled but that was painful, for one of the cuts ran from his cheek right across the right corner of his lips, so he said with a grimace, "You were right about London, William. It's a dangerous place."

"Sit down, and I'll make some tea while you tell me about it." William nudged his brother into a chair and picked up the brass kettle. "Was it highwaymen—or what?"

"It was a monster named Tom Burns!"

William paused, shooting a quick look at Adam. "The father of the girl you've taken under your wing?"

"The same." Adam leaned back and there was a fire in his dark blue eyes that matched the glow of the coals in the grate. "I've told you he mistreated his family? Well, up until two days ago I'd only seen the bruises on Mrs. Burns and on the children. But I stopped by there on my way home last Tuesday, and that's when it all happened."

"He was cruel to his wife?"

"He knocked her against the wall with his fist, the rotter!" Adam stormed between clenched teeth, his face contorted with the memory. "He was drunk, of course, as he usually is. Up till then he'd behaved himself around me. But he'd lost some money gambling, and I was just leaving when he came roaring in, demanding more from his poor wife! When she gave him the few small coins she had, he doubled up his fist and struck her in the face, cursing her for not having more!"

"That must have been hard for you, Adam," William remarked. He listened intently, saying little as his brother went on. There was, however, a deep anxiety in him, for he knew that any Colonial that got into trouble with a citizen of England was in danger of prosecution. He handed Adam a cup of tea, then sat back waiting for the rage that filled the young man to pass. "What happened then?"

"Well, I saw red—so I started to leave, but then he took Molly by the arm and started shaking her so hard I thought her neck would break! I grabbed him and pulled him away—but he almost knocked my head off, William!" Adam touched the cut on his mouth and said, "It's a wonder I've got a tooth left in my head! The man's a bull! He knocked me right out the front door, then came roaring out to finish me off!"

"I would guess you went at it with him?"

"Well, I really think he would have killed me, William. Fights in that part of town turn into kicking matches, and I reckon he'd have kicked my head off if I hadn't fought him."

"He's a big man, you say?"

"Tremendous—not tall, but strong, you know, and very slow! Quite out of condition, and I began to give him a few belts in his belly; that slowed him down! But it was a brawl, William! Lasted over half an hour, and we cut each other to ribbons!"

"What about the law? Did anyone fetch a sheriff?"

Adam laughed shortly. "That's not their style, William! No, everybody on the street came to watch, but no law."

William sipped his tea, then asked, "Well, I take it you didn't agree to be friends after it was over?"

"He didn't agree to anything!" Adam's face showed a grim

pleasure, and he even chuckled. "It's hard to *agree* when you've been beaten unconscious! I was just about as bad off, to tell the truth, but I staggered home and had to stay in bed all day, I was so stove-in! You ought to see what my ribs look like!"

"Well, what's next?" William asked.

Adam slammed the cup down, then stared his brother in the face. "I can't tell you—because you'd tell me not to do it!"

After a long period when William reasoned with Adam, he finally discovered that Mrs. Burns had come to his room in terror. She had told him that her husband could not move from his bed, so badly was he beaten, but he had sworn that he would beat her and Molly to death when he was able to get up. And she had asked Adam to take the girl away!

"Take her where?" William asked sharply.

"Anywhere so long as that monster can't find her!"

"That's kidnapping, Adam—a hanging offense!" William snapped. "Get it out of your mind!"

"Well, I can't do *nothing*, can I?"

William put his cup down and said quietly, "I'll go back to London with you. We'll see. I have a few connections here at Oxford—influential men. Maybe they can help. But what a man does inside his house is pretty hard to regulate, Adam. There's no law against a man beating his wife and children."

Adam's eyes were hard, harder than William had ever seen them. It was not the gentle boy that William had grown up with who stood there glaring into the fire! No, this was someone he had never seen before, and it sent a streak of apprehension tingling along his nerves as he saw that Adam was not going to be talked out of this. He breathed a quick prayer, then said, "We'll do something, Adam. God won't let us down!"

But God did let him down, or so Adam thought bleakly two weeks later. His ship was due to sail in less than five days, and he had spent most of that time trying to work something out for Burns. He had let the paper work on the machinery go, spending all his time either going around to lawyers with William, or hanging around the street where the Burnses lived, trying to keep some sort of watch over the family.

But nothing had come of it. William had said in despair, "Adam, there are some things in this world that we just can't change, and this is one of them. You'll just have to accept it!"

William had gone to see a judge who was a son of one of the dons at Oxford, hoping that perhaps he could offer a solution, but not having any real hope.

Adam walked around the streets, ignoring the biting cold, and finally, he set his jaw and stalked up the door of the Burnses' house. Mrs. Burns' eyes widened as she opened the door, and she tried to keep him out, "Go 'way, Mr. Winslow! You'll just make him worse!"

"I've got to talk to him! There'll be no trouble! I think I can help."

She opened the door, a weak futility on her thin face, then led him to the small room off the rear of the main room. All of the children were in the large room, huddled beside a small fire kindled in the grate, and he smiled at Molly as he passed.

When Tom Burns looked up from where he lay in the bed, a light blazed in his dull eyes, and he sat up with a groan and a curse, but Adam cut him off sharply. "Shut your foul mouth, Burns!" he snapped and when he moved close, Burns' huge bulk shrank back in sudden fear.

"You leave me be, Winslow! I'll have the law on yer!"

Adam picked up a chair, placed it firmly beside the bed, then sat down in it, staring straight into Burns' face. "How would you like to have a large sum of money, Burns?"

The question caught the big man off guard, but at once a crafty light leaped into his muddy eyes. "Well, I guess yer see you wus in the wrong!" He rubbed his hands together with satisfaction and began to say, "Now, I figure—"

"Shut up!" Adam snapped. "I will make you an offer, and I will make it only one time. If you don't agree at once, I will walk out of here and you'll never see a penny. I won't bargain, you hear me?"

"Wot's yer offer, then?" Burns asked sullenly.

"Two hundred pounds cash."

It was practically all the money Adam had, and it would be a direct violation of his trust. He dared not think what Saul and

Charles would say, but he had no other choice.

"Why, that ain't enough—"

Adam got up instantly and made rapid strides to the door. Burns saw a fortune slipping through his hands, more money than he'd ever seen, and he cried out loudly, "Wait now, don't go runnin' off, Winslow!"

"Yes or no—which is it?"

Burns saw the square jaw of Winslow set firmly, and the light in those cobalt blue eyes told him there would be no bargaining. "Well, yes."

Adam came back and sat down. "Now, this is the way you will get the money, and once again, I will not bargain! I will give you one hundred pounds in cash. I will leave the other one hundred pounds with a reliable party in this city. You may do what you please with the first hundred, but the second hundred will be closely supervised by a man I will choose. He will see to it that the money is doled out over a period of time for food and clothing for your family. He will be certain that it is spent for that and not on gin for you. That is the bargain. Do you agree?"

Burns could hardly bear the thought of his family spending money for food when he could use it for gin, but he saw that he had no choice. "All right, I agree."

Mrs. Burns said suddenly, "He'll beat the girl, Mr. Winslow!"

"Shut yer mouth!" Burns screamed. "I'll show yer—"

"You see?" she said in a rare defiance. "He'll have to let us have the food, but he'll beat me and Molly. You'll have to take her away or he'll kill her."

"I intend to do just that. Burns, in exchange for the two hundred pounds, you will sign a paper—"

"Wot kind o' paper?" Burns' eyes squinted in suspicion.

"A paper saying that for ten years Molly is a bound girl," Adam stated.

"Wot's that mean?"

"It means that for ten years she'll be under an obligation to serve me, but at the end of that time, she's free." Adam realized that Molly would have to be protected until she was grown.

"Take her to America, Mr. Winslow!" Mrs. Burns cried, tears

making a track down her cheeks. "She ain't got no show here! Maybe she can be somebody over there!"

The room was small, but when Adam raised his voice and called the girl, Molly came at once into the room, her eyes enormous in her pale face.

"Molly, would you like to go to America?"

She stared at him, and after casting a furtive glance at her father, she whispered, "Will I belong to you?"

"No!" Adam said sharply. "You'll belong to nobody! For ten years I'll be responsible for you; then you'll be old enough to make up your mind what to do. But until then, you'll work in the house for my family—and you'll learn to read and write."

That brought her head up, and a light came into her fine gray eyes. "Yes, sir, I'll go with you! And what is it I'll be?"

"A bound girl, Molly. That means a servant, but one who can't quit for a certain length of time." He rose and went to her, putting his hand on her thin shoulder. "You can't leave me for ten years—so be sure you want to do it."

Molly Burns looked around the small, dirty room, stared at her father, who was glaring at her with resentment, then looked up at Adam.

"I'll be your bound girl, Mr. Adam—for always!"

The *East Wind*, a three-masted schooner, swayed with the swell of the outgoing tide as Adam led Mrs. Burns and Molly up the gangplank. As they stepped onto the deck, a rattling of chains followed the bosun's shout: "Weigh anchor! Hearty, now!" There was a patter of bare feet on the wooden deck as topmen began to pour out of the depths of the ship to take station for setting sail.

"You'll have to be quick, I'm afraid," Adam said. He could barely see the worn face of Mrs. Burns in the heavy morning fog, for she wore a shawl over her head and kept her face averted. "I'll wait over there by the ladder."

Molly watched him go, and the strangeness of the ship frightened her. She put out her arms, and as her mother put her thin arms around her, holding her fast in a way she had seldom done, great sobs welled up in her throat, and she cried with her face buried against her mother's bosom, "Ma! I don't want to go! I'm afraid!"

The words seemed to rive the heart of Mrs. Burns, and her thin body trembled, but she said, "It's what you must do, Molly." She held the frail body of the child close, and heroically choked back the sobs that rose to her own throat. "Mr. Winslow, why, he's going to take such good care of you! He'll be so kind to you, Molly!"

"But I'll miss you, Mama! I won't have *anyone*!"

"Oh, but you'll have Mr. Winslow, and ain't he told us about his good brothers and sisters who'll take you for their own? And just think, Molly, in no time you'll be comin' back here for a visit—and you'll be wearing new clothes. Mr. Winslow says you'll learn to write too—and it'll be grand!"

She knew in her heart that it would not be—at least the part about Molly coming back. Such travel was expensive, and she was well aware that this was the last time on earth that she would ever hold her child to her breast. The tears burned her eyes, and she had to struggle to keep the agony out of her voice, but she squeezed Molly hard, then dashed the blinding tears from her eyes, saying, "Well, now, I'll have to go—but we'll be writing, won't we now?"

"Mama! Don't leave me!"

They stood there, holding each other until a cry came from the bosun, "All visitors ashore!"

Then Adam came to stand beside them and with a subdued tone, said, "It's time, I'm afraid."

Mrs. Burns slowly released her daughter, but Molly wildly threw her arms around the woman, crying, "Mama! Mama! Don't leave me!"

"Take her, Mr. Winslow!" she cried out. "Take her!"

Adam's own eyes were moist as he reached out and un-wound the thin arms of Molly from her mother. For a terrible moment he felt that this was all wrong—that he had interfered in a matter that would lead to a tragic end.

But it was too late now, so he pulled Molly away, and Mrs. Burns gave one final cry. "My baby! God help my baby!" After kissing the girl, she turned and ran blindly across the deck to the ladder, where a sailor helped her down.

Molly struggled wildly, crying out, "Let me go! Let me go!" But then as her mother's form disappeared into the fog, she threw her arms around Adam's neck and, shutting her eyes, held on with all her might.

The bosun called out, "Set sail! Set topsails—set the gallants! Set sail for the voyage."

Holding the child tightly, Adam whispered in her ear: "Don't cry, Molly! Please don't cry! We're setting sail for a new world—and I'll take care of you always—I promise!"

"Will you, Mr. Adam? Will you?"

She moved her head back, and as he looked into her tear-stained face, into the clear gray eyes, she said, as if it were a vow to God made on the altar: "I will take care of you, Molly—always!"

As she clung to him, the ship moved under them, heading out to sea—to a new world.

CHAPTER SEVEN

THE HOUSE OF WINSLOW

★ ★ ★ ★

"Mist' Adam! Look at you now, all back from 'cross de watuh!"

Sampson was waiting at the wharf as Adam stepped out of the dory that brought him ashore from the freighter. His teeth shone in the black expanse of his broad, black face as he reached out and lifted Molly out and placed her down carefully, saying, "And whut's dis you done brought home wif you, Mist' Adam?"

"This is Molly Burns, Sampson." He saw the girl looking up at the large black man with fear in her eyes, and leaping out, he said, "This is one of my best friends, Molly. His name is Sampson." He looked at the buggy and stated, "I didn't expect you to be here."

"Oh, Mist' Miles he been chompin' at de bit fo you to git home! We heard that yo' ship was sighted yesterday, so he sent me go fetch you."

They made several trips getting the luggage to the buggy before Adam lifted Molly into the seat, then sat down beside her. As Sampson clucked to the team and they started up at a brisk trot, he asked about the family, but hardly listened as Sampson rambled on.

What am I going to tell them? What will they say? he asked himself, as he had every day since he'd signed the papers with Burns and forked over the money in his trust. It had seemed so right then, and home and the family so far away, but now as they progressed steadily through Boston and turned down the pike toward home, a blind panic overwhelmed him.

"Is anybody at home, Sampson?"

"Oh yas. I went by and tol' yo' aunt—so I reckon de whole bunch is waitin' fo you, Mist' Adam. I guess you feels mighty big, goin' over de watuh and bein' a big businessman! Yo' father is sho proud, I tells you! He talk about you jes' about every day you been gone—says you gonna be a big plantuh and make lots of new stuff. He proud as I ever see him!"

Adam's heart sank lower and as Sampson rattled on, telling how everyone was looking forward to his return, misery settled down on him like a heavy cloud. As they came in sight of the house, he had one wild impulse to grab the lines from Sampson and drive the team in the opposite direction, but he knew he could do no such thing.

Sampson drove the team into the yard, but Adam said, "Sampson, pull into the barn."

"What I do dat fo?"

"I want to go in alone. You stay with Molly in the barn for a little while." Sampson obeyed, and Adam jumped down, saying with a smile he didn't feel, "Molly, I want to talk a little to the family. You don't mind staying out here with Sampson for a little?"

Molly took a long look at the black man, who smiled and patted her hand, saying, "Why, me and Miss Molly, we do fine, Mist' Adam! Won't we, now?"

She evidently found some assurance in his kind face, for she smiled and said, "All right, Mr. Adam."

"I won't be long." He went around to the front steps, and when he walked up onto the porch, the front door opened and his father stepped out to greet him with a smile.

"Welcome home, Adam!" he said smiling broadly as he took Adam's hand in both of his. Pulling him into the house, Miles urged him down the hall, and then almost pushed him into the parlor, saying, "Well, here he is!"

Except for the absence of William, all the family was there, and for one brief moment, Adam experienced a striking feeling that he had been in this place, doing this same thing before. Then he was met by his aunt who hugged him, as did Mercy. Saul and Charles both gave him a hearty handshake, and even Esther seemed glad to see him. Only Martha did not advance; she stood against the wall, giving him a nod and saying briefly, "I'm glad you had a safe journey, Adam."

There was a bustle as everyone tried to talk; then Saul said loudly, "Quiet, everyone! I can't hear myself think—and poor Adam is quite overcome with all this attention."

"Right you are, Saul," Miles smiled. "Sit down, Adam, and we'll fill you in on what's been going on here."

"Yes," Charles agreed, "and then we can hear what great things you've been doing to boost the family fortune."

For the next half hour Adam sat listening while they rehearsed the details of business that had taken place over the past three months. Basically, the news was that everything had gone very well. The plantation in Virginia had been purchased, and Charles was going to go and begin operations in a month. "I'll have one of Saul's best managers to go with me," Charles smiled. "Really to keep me out of trouble, I suppose."

Rachel said, "The house in the Northampton property has been made ready." She looked tired, but there was a gleam of excitement in her eyes as she told Adam the details of the matter. A good manager had been found, and he would be able to teach Adam the business of running a plantation very quickly.

The talk ran on briskly, everyone excited, and all too soon for Adam, Miles said, "Well, so much for our news, son. Now, let's hear what you've been doing."

"Right!" Saul agreed. "We have to make arrangements to get the equipment moved. It came with you, I suppose?"

Adam cleared his throat, which was suddenly dry as dust. Looking around the circle of smiling, expectant faces, he could think of nothing to say. Somehow he had thought that when he faced his family, he'd be able to explain his conduct in a satisfactory way. Looking around, however, his heart sank, and he knew there was no way that he would ever make them understand.

He had only one hope, so he began to speak, going into great detail about the equipment he'd seen in England, explaining at great length how primitive most of it was. He took so long at this that Saul and Charles gave each other an impatient look; even his father began tapping his foot against the floor as he did when he grew restless.

Finally Adam stood up and said desperately, "You know, sometimes plans change. I mean, we start out to do something, and then when circumstances jump out at us, why, we have to act differently, you see?"

"What are you trying to say, Adam?" Miles asked, staring at him strangely.

Charles expelled a deep breath and said, "You've been up to something, Adam! What is it?"

Adam's face burned, and he saw no encouragement except in Rachel's eyes, and even she looked tense. He replied finally, "I—I've had to make a few—adjustments, you might say—to what we planned."

"What sort of adjustments?" Martha's voice shot out. "You haven't lost that money gambling or something like that, have you?"

"Adam would never do that!" Mercy said instantly. She had been seated to Adam's left, out of his line of vision, and now she came to stand beside him. Placing her hand on his arm, she looked up into his face with trust shining out of her eyes. "Tell me what it is, Adam. I know you did what you thought was right."

That faint encouragement drove Adam to action. "I've got to go outside and bring something in. I'll be right back!"

He left the room at a run and cleared the porch in one jump. Entering the barn, he called out, "Molly! Come inside with me!"

She came to his side, and he grabbed his brown leather case with one hand, took her small hand with the other, then made his way back. "Don't be afraid, Molly," he said, although his own heart was beating fast.

"I won't be if you stay close," she said. Then she asked, "Is something wrong, Mr. Adam?"

"Just a little family problem." He opened the door, led her

down the hall, and into the parlor.

"Adam!" Miles stood to his feet with a gasp, his eyes locked on the child.

"Father, will you sit down and listen for a few minutes? Then I'll answer all your questions." Adam was relieved to see him sit down, but there was doubt in almost every face. He said, "Molly, sit right there, will you?" When she went over hesitantly, Mercy moved over and pulled her down onto the couch with a smile.

Adam opened the brown case, and pulling the papers out, selected one. He went to the oak table, spread it out, and said, "I want you all to see this."

They gathered around and stared down at a beautifully executed drawing of some machine with a great many intricate parts. "Why, that's a very good plan, Adam!" Rachel exclaimed. "I don't know what in the world it is, but the drawing is so good. Who drew it?"

Adam replied quietly, "I did. I've taken a few drawing lessons from a builder at Amherst. It's a machine designed to plow between rows. See, you can do four rows at a time instead of just one."

"Was this one of the machines you saw in a factory?" Saul demanded.

"Well, it's *like* one they had," Adam shrugged. "I made a drawing, but the one there only did two rows, so I drew this one. If you hitch a second team, you can double the number of rows—get finished in half the time; the labor is the same."

"How much did this machine cost?" Charles asked.

"They wanted fifty pounds."

"Fifty pounds! That's a lot of money!" Saul shook his head. "We'll do better with four plows and four slaves."

"I don't know about that, Saul," Rachel remarked. "You can hire one good white man pretty cheaply. What else do you have there?"

"Well, there's this automatic churn." He found another drawing and laid it out. "Instead of sitting there jogging a plunger up and down, you put five or six urns in a row and with this overhead arm, you can agitate all of them at the same time.

You could even hook it up to wind power and do the job with no human labor at all."

"How do you know it will work?" Martha demanded. "Have you ever seen one of the things?"

Adam stared at her. "Why, no, but why wouldn't it work? Just look at the drawing."

"I'd like to know what you have actually bought with the money we sent with you!" she stated grimly. "All these pictures are very pretty, but none of them will get a crop in the ground!"

"How about it, Adam?" Saul interjected quickly. "You're covering something up—and I'd guess it has something to do with that girl."

Adam saw that he couldn't hide it any longer, so he said, "I have a list here of machinery that could be used—and the total of it was over a thousand pounds." A mutter went up at that figure, and he said loudly, "I added up what it would cost to *make* those tools—and it comes to a little over two hundred and fifty pounds."

"Why, you're not saying you can make these things yourself, are you, son?"

Adam nodded and his square face was stubborn in the lamplight. "Yes, that's what I'm saying. Give me time, and I can make all of them—and most of them better. And we can even make them to sell. There's money to be made in that."

"I want to know what you did with the money you took with you." Martha's face was adamant, and she looked around adding, "I think he's lost it or thrown it away."

Rachel came to stand beside Adam, saying quietly, "Who is this child, Adam?"

He went over to stand beside Molly, and as she rose, he explained the whole thing. When he was finished, Martha's face was livid! "You spent our money on that ragpicker!"

"Martha!" Rachel spoke sharply. "Watch your tongue!"

"This is my house and I'll say what I please, Rachel! I knew you'd stand up for him, but I'm telling you what I've said all along, and that is that he's a fool!"

Miles looked totally defeated, his face gray with strain and disappointment. Adam's heart grew sick as he looked at his father, and he could say nothing.

A frightful argument ensued, raging for over an hour. Saul, Esther, Charles, and Martha argued bitterly against Rachel and Mercy. Miles said little, but sat down in a chair, his head slumped over his chest.

Finally Adam shouted, "Listen to me!" His tone startled them, and with a pale face he said, "You'll get the money back. I can get a good job at a forge in Philadelphia. Mr. Franklin will help me."

"We need it now!" Charles growled.

"Yes, it'll take you years to earn that much," Saul spat out in disgust. "I suppose we can put the girl out to work somewhere—try to get some of the money back."

Adam stared at him, then looked around the room. Finally he said quietly, "You know, I've never been much good for anything. Never did well at books. The rest of you are all good at things. But I've always been proud to be a Winslow. I always had that, even though I wasn't much myself." He started to say more, but changed his mind. He reached down and took Molly's hand. "Tonight I'm ashamed to be a part of such a grabbing, selfish bunch of heathens!"

He started for the door, but suddenly Miles called out, "Wait!"

Adam paused, turned to look at his father, who had risen and was staring at Molly with a strange look in his old eyes. He was quiet for so long that they could all hear quite clearly the tick of the clock in the hall. Finally he began to speak, his voice reedy at first, but growing stronger.

"I was just thinking of my grandfather. Remember him, Rachel?"

"Yes!"

"He told us so many times about the poor, half-starved crowd that stumbled off the *Mayflower*! None of them rich. All poor, but all hungry for a new way of life. I was thinking about that poor boy that died in his arms just as the ship came in sight of the new land. What was his name, Rachel?"

"William Butten," Rachel said quietly. "Yes, I've heard that story."

"Yes, poor boy! Risked everything to see a new world—then died without setting foot on it." Miles spoke softly, but his words held them all in place; even Martha could not move, so intense was he. "Grandfather told it so well! How the sky was gray as ashes, and the cold wind swept the deck. There were only a few harsh cries from the gulls. And just before William died, John Bradford stood up on the deck and cried out with a loud voice—like an Old Testament prophet, Grandfather always said!—and he had the words memorized: 'One day our children will say, "Our fathers were Englishmen who came over this great ocean and were ready to perish in the wilderness. But they knew they were pilgrims, and he saved them!" ' "

"That's what he said!" Rachel whispered.

"Well, I'm glad he's not here tonight—to see what his descendants have become!" Miles struck his thigh with a thin hand and rose to his feet. "God help us, we've become so money hungry, we can't spare a few pounds for a poor child to have a new life in this country! If we've come to that, I'm ready to die and get out of it all!"

"I think we can spare the money, Miles," Rachel said softly. Her blue eyes were bright and there was a defiance in her voice that made Saul drop his head. "Don't you think it would be good to support Adam in his generous gesture, Saul?" she prodded.

He swallowed, and his voice sounded hoarse as he nodded. "Of course, Mother! I—I wasn't thinking."

"Charles?"

Charles towered over Rachel, but his face suddenly looked weak; speechless, he only nodded.

"Martha, what about you? If you feel you must have the money, I will pay the entire sum into your hand to do with as you will."

Martha stood there stiffly, her face gray, every bone in her body stubbornly resisting Rachel. She cast a baleful look at Adam, but one glance around the room told her that she had no choice. As gracefully as she could, she nodded and said, "I will agree to stand with the family."

"I thought you might!" Rachel said, irony like a silver blade in her words. "I need not ask you, Mercy, so we all say to you, my nephew Adam—" She turned and went to him, reached up and kissed him on his cheek, then said, "Well done! A real son of Gilbert and Humility, Firstcomers!"

Adam could not believe what was happening! He stood there, unable to speak; then Rachel put her arms around Molly, smiling tenderly at the child. "Molly, you are far from home, but I hope you will let us be a family to you. Would you do that?"

Molly had been shrinking into a little ball, frightened by all the arguments and harsh words. She stared up at the beautiful lady in silks, and seeing something in her face, nodded. Rachel stooped down and looked into her eyes. "I'm very much afraid you're going to have to kiss your new aunt, Molly!" And the child, frightened and confused, felt safe and secure for the first time as Rachel Howland enfolded her.

The arguments and accusations seemed to fade in the light of that which was good and compassionate. Slowly the family members left, some only too happy to get away—especially Saul and Esther. Charles did not leave, of course, but after saying a few words to Saul, he went to his room, chastened and somewhat sullen.

Miles and Mercy stayed for only a brief time. "Would you like to leave the child here with us, Adam?" Miles asked.

Adam felt the alarm in Molly's eyes, but said quickly, "No, I think I can persuade the Edwards family to have her, Father. She'll learn a lot from those children."

Miles seemed relieved, and added, "That sounds like a good plan. And your ideas, son, are good!" He stared at Adam, shook his head and then gave a half laugh. "We Winslows have a devil of a time with our sons! Your great-great-grandfather tried to make a minister out of Gilbert, and it was nearly the ruination of him! I've been stupid about you, thinking only about a bookish sort of way to get ahead, but I see this gift for making things that God has put in you—it's real, son, and if I live long enough, I expect to hear much good of you."

Adam could only nod, and then Mercy said, "Molly, why don't you sleep with me tonight? I've got this big bed and we can warm as toast!"

As she led the child away, Molly turned and ran back to Adam. Looking up at him, she asked uneasily, "Am I still your bound girl, Mr. Adam?"

Adam smiled down at her, touched her smooth cheek. "Of course, you are! You have to put up with me for ten years, child!"

She smiled and said quickly, "I don't mind! Really, I don't!" Then she turned and followed Mercy out of the room.

"A sweet child, Adam!" Miles remarked quietly. "I'm proud that you fought for her. It's what a Winslow man should do—and what my father and his father would have done!"

"It's what *my* father did, too!" Adam said quickly. "If you hadn't jumped to my aid tonight, why, I don't know what I would have done, sir!"

Miles' old eyes suddenly dimmed with tears and he turned hastily away. "Do you think that, Adam?" he asked tightly, not trusting his voice. "Why, that makes me feel very proud—very proud, indeed!"

Adam reached out and, hesitating, put his strong hand on his father's thin shoulder, and felt it tremble beneath his touch. He said quietly, "Why, you're all Winslow, sir! I am very proud to be your son—and a small part of the House of Winslow!"

Miles Winslow stood there for a moment, savoring the feel of his son's hand on his shoulder, and then he said in an unsteady voice, "God bless you, my boy! God bless you in all your ways!"

Then he pulled away suddenly and left the room, and Adam stood there alone. Finally he looked at the crest on the wall over the sword that Gilbert Winslow had carried off the *Mayflower*. He touched the keen blade, then stared at the coat of arms: a mailed fist clenched against a diagonal stripe of blue on white, and the single word *fidelis*—"faithful"—at the base.

He stared at the shield for a long time, then turned and walked away, thinking mostly about Gilbert Winslow, the First-comer. As he walked, he pulled back his shoulders and raised his head with pride.

Upstairs as Molly lay under the heavy comforter that smelled like lavender, she asked suddenly, "Miss Mercy, do yer think I can learn ter read?"

"I'm sure you can!"

There was a long silence, and then Molly asked another question: "Miss Mercy, Mr. Adam likes me now, but will 'e like me when I'm growed up?"

Mercy laughed quietly but said quite seriously, "Yes, dear, I think he'll like you very much indeed!"

Sleepily the voice came one more time.

"That's good—'cause I like 'im better than anybody!" And then Molly Burns, the bound girl with the indentured heart, dropped off into a deep sleep.

CHAPTER EIGHT

"HOW MUCH TROUBLE CAN ONE SMALL GIRL BE?"

★ ★ ★ ★

"There's your new home, Molly." Adam pointed with his buggy whip to the two-story frame house that seemed to nestle in a grove of blackjack oaks beside a large, open field. When the child didn't answer, he looked down and saw that she had fallen asleep. She had a firm grasp on his coat with one hand. *Poor child!* he thought. *She had little enough in London, but at least she wasn't among strangers!*

He drove up to the front of the house, and when he said "Whoa!" to the team, Molly stirred, then sat straight up, staring out at the house. "Is this 'ere the 'ouse, Mr. Adam?" she asked.

"Yep. Come on, let's see our new home." He jumped to the ground and as he picked her up and set her down, he thought, *She's so tiny—I'll have to see she gets lots to eat.*

"Let's see our new home, Molly." As she took his hand quickly, he looked down at her with a smile. "I've never seen the place inside either."

She stared up at him solemnly, then said, "Ain't it funny t' 'ave a 'ouse you ain't never seen?"

"Well, Aunt Rachel said she made sure it was fixed up nice,

and there's got to be a couple here somewhere—the overseer and his wife. Doesn't seem to be anybody here, though."

They walked up to the door, and when nobody answered his knock, he opened the door and led Molly inside. They found themselves in the middle of a wide hallway with a set of stairs to one side leading to the second floor, a door to the left, which they found led to a large parlor, and at the end of the hall a massive kitchen and larder.

They went upstairs and he saw with satisfaction that beds were made and there was firewood by the small fireplaces, which two of the bedrooms had. He grinned at her and said, "Which bedroom do you want? This one?"

She stared at him wide-eyed, then her gaze swept the room in doubt. It was a small room, not more than ten feet square, and the ceiling sloped sharply toward the outer wall. The only furniture was a small bed, a washstand, and a small trunk, but there were plenty of wooden pegs in the wall for hanging clothing and a red rug lay beside the bed. She stared up at him, her gray eyes filled with awe. "Aw, Mr. Adam, this ain't *mine*?"

He laughed, glad to see that she was happy. She had been very quiet on the voyage home, so quiet that he became anxious about her, doubts about the wisdom of his decision filling his mind. And it had not helped when Charles had stared at him with pity in his light blue eyes, thrown up his hands in disbelief and said, "Adam! Only *you* would do a thing like this—bring home a girl practically off the streets! Why, you don't have the faintest idea of what to *do* with her, do you now?"

The truth in Charles's words had disturbed Adam, but now as he saw her mobile features light up with pleasure, he felt somewhat better. "Of course, it's yours, Molly! Now I'll bring the trunks in, and we'll get unpacked. Then we'll go see the minister, Rev. Edwards."

As they went downstairs, they heard the back door slam. "That must be the overseer," Adam said, but it was a woman who emerged from the kitchen. "Mrs. Stuart?"

"Yes, I'm Beth Stuart," she nodded. She was a large woman in her thirties with glossy brown hair and sharp eyes. He also noted that her left hand was deformed, bent into a permanent fist. "Mr. Winslow?"

"Yes, and this is Molly Burns."

"Ah, yes." A light appeared in Mrs. Stuart's eyes as she looked at the girl; then she nodded at Adam. "Seth and me have the place all ready. We been expecting you."

The front door opened and a short, skinny man with a red face and a thick mop of sandy hair staggered through the door with a large trunk. "This is my husband, Seth. Mr. Winslow and Molly Burns."

Seth Stuart dropped the trunk with an alarming crash, came forward to shake Adam's hand. He was older than his wife, in his late forties, and his grip was almost as powerful as Adam's own.

"Weel, now, Mr. Winslow, I dinna expect ye today, but welcome hame!" He had a Scottish accent and his merry blue eyes looked down at the child. "Molly Burns, is it? A gude Scottish girl ye are indeed!"

"Molly is going to be your helper, Mrs. Stuart," Adam said. "While your husband and I are taking care of the outside work, you and Molly will take care of the inside. I think you'll find Molly a good hard worker." Saul had hired the Stuarts, and from the looks of them, Adam decided, he could not have done much better.

"I know we'll be good friends, Molly," Mrs. Stuart said, going to the child and putting her hand on her shoulder. "I've never had a little girl of my own. Maybe we can teach each other some things, all right?"

Molly looked up at her, and the reserve that was a part of her character lasted only a second, then she smiled and said, "I wants to learn 'ow t' work, Ma'am." She had been tense, her lips tight, for the whole journey had been a nightmare for her in some ways. To leave her home with a man she scarcely knew had been frightening! She had not had much joy in her hovel of a home in London, but fear had lain in her heart ever since Adam had taken her on board the ship. She had slept little, eaten little, and even the warmth of Rachel and Mercy had done little to give her heart any peace.

But Beth Stuart's kind face encouraged her, and when the large woman said, "I'll help you get settled, Molly," she went upstairs with something like a light heart for the first time since she'd left England.

"Your wife is good with the child," Adam remarked as they went out to get the luggage.

"Aye, we never had any of our own," the overseer said sadly. "It'll be good for her to have a young one to fuss over."

Adam shared a few of the details of Molly's hard life with Stuart, and added quietly, "I want to see the child get a good start—a good education and everything."

"The gude Lord bless ye fer it, Mr. Winslow." He nodded and said with satisfaction, "It's glad I am to be workin' for a Christian man!"

Adam cleared his throat nervously and said, "Well, my family are Christian, but I guess I'm not much of anything myself."

"Do tell me!" Stuart said in surprise. "I thought you studied under Rev. Edwards."

"Well, a little Latin, Seth." Adam changed the subject and asked about the farm, and after they unloaded the luggage, they left Mrs. Stuart and Molly to unpack while they walked over the property. The scrawny Scot had been there only a month, but he knew all six hundred acres of it—not only the cleared fields, but the springs, the timber and even where the best hunting could be had!

"Seth," Adam said finally, as they made their way back to the house, "I might as well tell you now that I'm no farmer. I guess you know more about it than I ever will."

"I'd not be too quick to say that. . . !"

"This is mostly my family's idea, and if it works, it'll be your doing. We might as well understand each other right now." They paused, and Stuart saw that his young employer's dark blue eyes were about as intense as any he'd seen. "You do the farming, and I do the rest of it. Mostly I'll be working on machines and keeping things up in that way."

"Weel, if you can do that, we'll maybe make a farm of this place, Mister Adam!" Stuart had been apprehensive about the whole matter, and had said often to his wife, "We may be movin' on, lass. If the new owner's not a man of sense, we'll have to leave." Now he saw that Adam Winslow was his kind of man, and his intelligent eyes warmed in a smile. He stuck his hand out, saying, "It's no going to be easy, mind you, for the place is run down something fierce! But give us a few good years and some willin' hands, and we'll make this farm something to notice!"

Inside the house, Mrs. Stuart had helped Molly fix up her small bedroom, noting how scanty the child's wardrobe was, and making a firm resolution to remedy that. Then she had led the way to the kitchen and was pleased that as she prepared a noon meal for the men, the girl was anxious to help and quick to learn.

Beth had noticed that Molly got more nervous as noon approached, but said nothing. Then, as she expected, the girl spoke out her fear. "Ma'am, Mr. Adam, 'e says I gotta go to the minister's 'ouse to learn me letters."

"Well, now, that's fine, isn't it? Everybody in the parish speaks well of Mr. Edwards."

Molly's brow knitted, and she picked at her blouse nervously; when she looked up there was fear in her clear gray eyes. "I don't wanna go there."

"Why not, Molly?"

She ducked her head and said nothing. Then she finally looked up, there were tears in her eyes. "I—I'm *stupid*—and they're all so smart—" She bit her lip and then said with anger, "And that 'un called *Mary* is the wust!"

"How do you know that, child?"

"Cause Mr. Adam, 'e's allus gabbin' about her, 'e is!"

Mrs. Stuart knew little about Molly's past except what few facts she had learned from the brief history the child had given her while they were working. She had sharp eyes, however, and it was obvious to her that Molly Burns had fastened on to Adam Winslow, and this "Mary" was clearly seen as a threat.

She started to speak, then heard the men approaching, so she said only, "Now, you just wait, Molly! Mr. Adam is very proud of you, and I hear that the Edwards children are very nice."

There was time for no more, but there was a rebellious set to Molly's posture. Adam said while they were eating, "We've got plenty of time to go over to Rev. Edwards this afternoon, Molly. I know you must be tired, but I want you to meet them. I'm sure you and the girls will be great friends—especially Mary!"

Mrs. Stuart gave her head a quick shake and thought, *Don't do that, Mister!* But she saw that Winslow was smiling happily and had not the slightest concept of how desperately the English child clung to him. *He's a good young man,* she thought, *but he's a bit thick where it comes to young girls!*

Adam talked happily as they covered the four miles from their new home to the Edwardses' house, not noticing that Molly sat stiffly beside him, saying almost nothing. Finally he pulled up in front of the house, and the two of them got out of the buggy.

They were halfway up the walk when the front door swung open and a young girl about her own age came sailing out. She was crying out Adam's name and he dropped Molly's hand and stepped forward to catch her in his arms. He spun her around laughing, and said, "Well, I guess you really *did* miss me, didn't you, Mary?"

Molly drew back as he put her down, and as the two of them chattered away, she felt very lonely. Then several other girls came out to greet Adam, but the one called Mary did not turn loose of him, holding on to his hand as if she owned him!

"Welcome home, Adam!" A tall man and a beautiful woman came out, and they both shook his hand.

The entire family swarmed around Adam, all talking and laughing, Molly drew farther back, wanting to run to the buggy.

"Well, who is this young lady?" The tall man separated himself from the group and came to stand before her. There was a kind light in his eyes as he put his hand out, saying, "I'm Rev. Edwards, child."

"Oh, this is Molly Burns, Rev. Edwards!" Adam moved to come to where they stood, but Mary held tightly to his hand, so he stood there and explained. "She's come all the way from England, and I've told her so much about you and your family."

"Why, we're so glad to have you, Molly," Edwards said.

"Come inside and we'll let you try to learn the names of this mob!"

One of the older girls, who looked about fourteen, came up and smiled. "I'm Jerusha, Molly. You come on and tell us all about England." Molly looked up and saw that there was a gentle look on the girl's face, so she let herself be led inside.

They went into the parlor, and for the next hour Molly's head swam, for she had never been around such a group of talkers in her entire life. They wanted to know all about her, but she was too shy to talk, so she listened while they chattered.

She looked around several times for Adam, but at first he was off in the next room talking to Mr. and Mrs. Edwards. Then when they came back, Mary pulled him off and made him sit down in a chair and was right up in his face talking as fast as she could.

Finally, they went in and sat down at a big table, Mr. and Mrs. Edwards on one end, and the children opposite each other. Molly sat next to Jerusha, whom she had trusted at first sight. She heard the names of Esther, Lucy, Timothy, Susanna—and Mary, of course, but her head was swimming with all the talk.

Adam sat across from her between Mary and Mrs. Edwards. He smiled at Molly, asking, "Isn't this nice, Molly?"

She forced herself to nod, but she had wanted him to sit by her, and she blurted out, "Oh, yas, Mr. Adam, but this 'ere 'ous ain't nowhere as big as ours!"

Mary stared at her, then covered her mouth with her hand and laughed merrily. "She talks so *funny*! Is that the way everyone talks where you come from, Molly?"

"Mary!" Mrs. Edwards looked displeased. She turned and gave the visitor a smile. "Mary is very rude at times, Molly. You must forgive her."

That incident served to seal Molly's lips; she would have allowed herself to be torn to pieces rather than be made fun of again. Jerusha and her parents saw the tears form in her eyes, though Adam did not.

After they left the table and the children all went into the parlor, Mrs. Edwards detained the young man long enough to say firmly, "Adam, you split wood very well." He stared at her blankly. Then she smiled and said, "That child is very frightened, and you must be very careful. She's far more fragile than a log of oak. Didn't you see how frightened she was at the table?"

"Frightened?"

"Yes! You left her and talked with others and then you didn't sit beside her. She's very much afraid—as anyone would be in her situation."

Adam's face flushed, and he said, "I—I guess I wasn't thinking. I'll be more careful."

She stared at him with apprehension in her fine eyes. "Adam, I don't think you have any idea of what you've done. Oh, it was noble of you, from what you've told us, and I honor you for it. But it's so much more than having a *servant*! She's a bound girl for ten years, but she's a small girl who's very much afraid. And her future is in your hands, Adam. You've taken upon yourself the responsibility of her life—do you understand what an awesome thing that is?"

Adam Winslow stood there twisting his hands, his eyes suddenly cast down. He shook his head slowly. Then he looked up and there was sadness in his dark blue eyes. "I'm always doing some fool thing! Guess this is just another one, Mrs. Edwards— I must have been an idiot to think I could help the girl!"

She touched his cheek, looking at him with a soft light in her eyes as she shook her head. "No, you did what very few men would have done, and I'm very proud of you, Adam. But you must always remember that from now on *you are Molly's family!*"

He stared at her, swallowed hard, then nodded. "Yes, Mrs. Edwards. I—I'll remember that."

"We'll help you, of course. But I must warn you of one thing."

"Yes, Ma'am?"

"Mary is very possessive, Adam! She is the brightest of our children—but not the kindest. That's Jerusha. Do you understand what I'm saying?"

Adam looked blank, then said bluntly, "No, I don't."

"Men!" Mrs. Edwards snorted. "Well, let me make it plain for you: Molly needs you—but you've let Mary monopolize you ever since you've been in this place. You're a big toy to her. All she has to do is snap her fingers and you jump. Well, that may have been all right before, but you must be more careful now."

"You mean, my first responsibility is to Molly?"

"Exactly! Now, it will all work out, but you must be careful, Adam!"

She said no more, but Adam was downcast. He said little, but he saw that Molly was unhappy, so half an hour later, he said, "We must be getting back."

"Why don't you let Molly come over on a regular basis and begin her schooling with the girls?" Edwards asked.

Jerusha saw the fear in the child's face and went to her at once. "Why, that'll be fun!" she said, putting her arm around the girl. "You will come, won't you, Molly?"

It was a kind and tactful thing to do, and Molly nodded, saying, "Yes, if you'll 'elp me, miss."

"We all will!" Jerusha said gently, and Mary added, "Why, I'll teach you better than anybody, Molly!"

They left then, and Adam tried to find out what was going on in Molly's mind, but she answered his questions shortly. Finally he said, "Molly, I'm sorry if you didn't have a good time."

She bent her head and he was startled to see a tear run down her cheek. "Oh, Molly, you mustn't do that!" he said in dismay. Stopping the team, he turned to her, and in an awkward display of affection, he put his arm around her, saying, "Molly, I know I'm thoughtless sometimes, but you mustn't be angry with me. It's just that—well, I've never had anyone to—to take care of, so I don't know how to go about it." He felt her shoulders shaking, so he sat there helplessly, not knowing what to do or say— wishing that he'd left her in London, wishing that someone else could step in and take over, but knowing there was no one else.

Finally he said huskily, "I know I neglected you today. I shouldn't have left you alone. But I want you to know one thing—look up at me!"

He pulled her face up, appalled to see her small defenseless features contorted with grief. She had her eyes shut tightly, and was biting her lip to hold the sobs back.

"Molly," he said quietly, holding her fast with one arm, "I

want you to know that I love you very much—and as long as I live I'll take care of you. That's all I can say!"

She opened her eyes suddenly, and he saw the fear that had been in them all day replaced by a sudden flash of joy. She smiled tremulously and whispered, "Will yer now? Will yer truly allus take care o' me?"

"Yes!"

Molly Burns—bound girl—did not say anything, but he saw that his promise had driven away the despair that had filled her. She nodded once, then grabbed him in a wild embrace, the first time she'd ever done such a thing. And as she held on to him, Adam Winslow thought, *God help me if I ever let this child down!*

As they sat there holding one another, Adam realized that it was not the child that was "bound"—*he* was the who was bound by his promise!

Ten years! he thought wryly. *Some of those who came over on the Mayflower were bound for that long—I guess I can do it, too. After all, how much trouble can one small girl be?*

PART TWO

NORTHAMPTON

★ ★ ★ ★

1745–1750

CHAPTER NINE

A Brooch of Silver

★　★　★　★

A sudden movement caught Molly's eye, and she held the goosequill pen off the sheet of paper, glancing out of the single window of her bedroom at the antics of a pair of purple martins. As they sailed acrobatically to a landing at the birdhouse, a smile turned the corners of her wide mouth up. It was the third time she'd watched a family of the connubial birds raise a family, and she suddenly remembered how Adam had built the birdhouse and set it outside her window during her first lonely months at Winslow House. She cast an involuntary glance at the forge, noting the smoke pouring out of the chimney, and her eyes softened at the memory of Adam sitting beside her for hours as the birds had come that first March. He'd held her in his lap, pointing out the antics of the martins, and a warmth filled her as she thought of how he'd drawn her out of her solitude during those days.

She sighed, lowered her eyes and, noting that her pen was dull, she cleaned it with a small cloth, trimmed it with a silver-handled knife Adam had made for her for that purpose. A small stack of papers was neatly stacked on the desk beside her, with *Molly Burns—Her Journal* written across the first sheet in a careful childish hand. Dipping the pen in a bottle of ink, she began writing in an even hand across the sheet:

28 May, 1747

Yesterday Adam's brother, Rev. William Winslow, preached instead of Rev. Edwards. I liked his sermon very much, and afterwards he came home with us to take dinner. Mrs. Stuart and I cooked a good meal. I made some blackberry tarts and he liked them as much as Adam. He asked me how old I was, and when I said *thirteen years old*, he seemed much surprised, and said many nice things, like "My! what a fine young lady Molly has grown into during the last two years!" He is so handsome—much taller than my master, I'm afraid, and Jerusha says that every young woman in his parish is dying to marry him!

The sow gave birth to fourteen pigs yesterday, so with the two new calves, we will have plenty of meat. The garden is much better than last year! The new kind of tomatoes are already so big the stalks are bending double, and the potatoes are doing well.

I am very excited about meeting Miss Jerusha's young man. We are going to the Edwards' house this afternoon for supper. It is Mary's birthday, and I made her blue blouse out of the silk that Adam had bought at Boston last month. Mrs. Stuart helped me, but I did very well, Adam said.

I hear Mrs. Stuart calling me, and must end this writing, which I do with a prayer of thanksgiving to God for bringing me to this place. When at times I wake up at night after one of my bad dreams, almost crying out with fear as I do when I dream of my childhood at home, how wonderful it is to suddenly know that I am here at Winslow, with Seth and Beth almost like parents—and of course with my master, Adam Winslow, who has shown nothing but kindness for these two years!

Beth Stuart had been calling urgently. Molly blotted the sheet, carefully added it to the others, then slipped the journal into the lower drawer of the small chest beside her bed.

"I'm coming!" she called out, then ran out of her room and down the stairs.

"Molly, I've been calling you for ten minutes!" Mrs. Stuart said sternly. "If you're going to get Mr. Adam to that party, you'll have to go drag him out of that shop right now!" She spoke harshly enough, but there was a light in her eyes that betrayed her affection for the girl, who was not in the least frightened by her frown. The Scotswoman had been a mother indeed for the past two years, showering her with love such as she had never known, and teaching her many skills—cooking, washing, canning, sewing, and a dozen other arts of the country housekeeper.

"I'll get him—but will you finish hemming my new dress, please?" Molly did not wait for an answer, but patting Mrs. Stuart fondly on the shoulder, skipped out of the back door and ran lightly to the large wooden building a hundred yards east of the main house.

Pushing the door open, she entered and saw Adam standing with his back to her at the wooden workbench. He did not hear her enter, and when she said, "Mr. Adam. . . !" he gave a sudden start, and wheeled to meet her with a frown on his dark face.

"Molly! Don't sneak up on a man like that!" He turned and swept something into a soft leather bag, then blew out the large lamp that served as a light for the fine work he did. Turning again to face her, he saw that he had driven the smile from her face. He smiled at once, saying, "I didn't mean to speak so rough." He was rewarded at once as her face lit up, and he thought as he had many times, *This child is so sensitive! Have to remember to be gentle.* He put his arm across her shoulders, grinned and said, "It's hard to live with a grumpy old blacksmith, Molly, but you and Mrs. Stuart will make something out of me yet!"

"It's time to get ready, Mr. Adam," she said, pulling at his arm. "You've got to wash and shave and I've pressed your best suit—you hurry up now!"

He allowed her to pull him through the door, and as they made their way across the yard spotted with Black Winslow chickens, he marveled at how she had changed since the first day they set foot at Winslow House—the name that had gotten attached to the farm. She had grown taller, of course, so that now at thirteen she was almost as tall as Mrs. Stuart. He thought suddenly of how much she was like the young colt that frolicked in the pasture across from the house—leggy, awkward, but with the grace that all young things seem to have. *First thing you know,* he thought with a sudden grin at her, *the place will be cluttered up with a herd of young fellows wanting to court her!*

"You wash, now, and don't forget your neck!" Molly gave a warning shake of her finger at him, then left him at the pump, saying, "I'll have the hot water and your razor as soon as you're finished."

He washed his upper body, then his face, then stuck his head under the pump. As he worked up a lather with the heavy square of lye soap, he thought of how the girl had lost her early fears. She had been as shy as one of the wild kittens at the barn for the first few months. *Now she bosses me around like I was the bound servant*, he thought as he dried his thick black hair on the towel she'd left. *Mostly Beth's doing—she and Seth have been a god-send for the child!*

He went inside and found the water and his razor and soap waiting. He shaved carefully, then turned and noted his clothes carefully laid out on the bed. He put on linen undergarments, the brown homespun breeches, then the fine white shirt, the buff-colored coat, and finally the fine leather boots he'd bought on his last trip to Boston.

He took a small bag from the pocket of his work clothes, put it in his inside coat pocket, then left the room, calling out, "Molly—are you ready?"

"Yes, I'm coming!"

He met Mrs. Stuart at the bottom of the stairs and said, "We may be late getting home, Beth. You and Seth don't have to wait up." Hearing light footfalls on the stair, he turned; seeing Molly he said, "My word! How nice you look!"

Beth Stuart saw the rosy glow that rose to Molly's neck and cheeks at Adam's words, and she was gratified to think that the hours she and the girl had spent on the dress had not been wasted.

"Thank you, Mr. Adam," Molly murmured breathlessly. Her clear eyes were blue-gray—Adam could never decide which—but the dark blue material of her dress brought out the blue. Her ash-colored hair was combed back into a single heavy strand, and was so thick and heavy it seemed almost to pull her head back. Her figure was only beginning to fill out—just a hint of womanly fullness in her straight carriage. She wore no jewelry, but the bright yellow ribbon that held her hair, and another at the high neckline of the silk dress, added a touch of color to her attire.

Seth had brought the buggy to the front, and as they got in, he gave a spare smile, saying, "Weel, now, I'm thinkin' there's a little vanity in your dress—but ye'll no be the worse for such, maybe." He helped Molly into the seat, gave her a steady smile and said, "Ye watch this one, Molly girl! That Jerusha Edwards may set her cap for your master!"

She laughed and said as Adam released the brake and they pulled out, "No fear there! Miss Jerusha's got herself a minister— she'll not be after a blacksmith like Mr. Adam!"

They drove out of the yard, and Molly felt very grown-up as they made their way along the road, the buggy sending a cloud of dust high in the air behind them. She had been going to study at Jonathan Edwards' house for nearly two years, but this was the first time she'd gone almost as a guest. She realized, of course, that she was expected to help with the serving, but all of the other girls would be doing that as well. She sat beside Adam, brushing the fine dust of the road off her dress, and more than once she stole a look at the man beside her. *He's not as handsome as William*, she thought, then looked at his square jaw, the dark blue eyes that were now mild, but could set off sparks when he had one of his fits of fierce anger. She thought contentedly, *He may not be handsome, but he's strong and he's good!*

"Looks like you'll be losing your teacher, Molly," Adam said mildly. "I look to see Mr. Brainerd carry her off pretty soon. You'll be pretty sad, I reckon."

Jerusha Edwards was being courted at the age of sixteen by Rev. David Brainerd. Molly had been closer to her than anyone in the world except for Mrs. Stuart, and she gave Adam a sorrowful look. "Are they really going to get married, Mr. Adam?"

"I think so." Adam gave the girl a look, and added gently, "She's young, Molly, but lots of girls no older than Jerusha have families. And Mr. Brainerd is a good man—a famous one, too."

"I know."

Jerusha had met David Brainerd a year earlier, and after

Molly's lessons, she had spoken in glowing terms of the young minister who had attracted her. He had left Yale after a stormy career to become an evangelist to the Indians, and in a short time, every church in America was buzzing with his activities. He had walked into the woods at the forks of the Delaware River with no training, not speaking a word of the Indian language. Not a few had told him he would perish in the wilderness—that he would either die of starvation or be butchered by the fierce tribes that still made that area their home. Instead, he had encountered a young Indian with the unpronounceable name of John Wauwaupequuaunt, who happened to know English, having been raised by a minister in Longmeadow, Massachusetts.

From that time on, Brainerd had driven himself, ignoring the frightful hardships of the wilderness, and his success with the savages had sped about the Colonies. He had emerged from his labors with the Indians only long enough to preach on a tour. On his engagement at Northampton, he had met Jerusha Edwards. Their courtship had been swift as lightning, stunning the Edwardses and everyone else.

"I wish she wouldn't do it," Molly said wistfully. "I think he's too old."

Adam cast a quick glance at her, then said gently, "Why, he's only twenty-six or so." Then he laughed and threw his arm around her, giving her a rough hug. "I keep forgetting what a child you are, Molly! Guess folks as old as Mr. Brainerd and me seem old as the hills to you!"

"*You* don't seem old!" she said instantly, then flushed and looked away, adding, "He's so thin, though, and looks sickly."

Adam nodded. "You're right there, Molly. Mr. and Mrs. Edwards are real worried about that. Mr. Edwards told me that the man's spent too much time exposed to all kinds of weather—and he wasn't too strong anyway." Shaking his head, he said a few moments later, "I don't see how they can make it. Marriage is hard enough, and I can't see him draggin' Miss Jerusha into the wilds. That'd be hard enough on a strong man, but for a woman . . . !"

They talked little on the rest of the journey, and it was mid-afternoon when they pulled up in front of the Edwards' house.

Several buggies were drawn up at the hitching rail, and Adam said, "Looks like Judge Dwight is here—and most everybody else!"

They dismounted, and the younger children came in a rush to greet them. "Molly!" Susanna Edwards cried, pulling at the girl's dress. "You come and play with us!" She was six, the youngest of the Edwardses' girls, and a favorite of Molly.

"I have to go help with the food, Susanna," Molly said, giving her a pat on the head. "We'll play later."

"Adam!" A huge young man stepped out of the house, coming down the steps to meet them with a smile on his broad face. He stood six feet four and weighed 250 pounds. He stood over them, dwarfing Adam, but there was a mildness in his hazel eyes. "Been waiting for you. You want to take a look at the spring on my buggy? The stubborn thing won't stay together!"

Adam smiled up at the genial giant, nodded and said, "Sure." The two were acquaintances, though not close friends. Everyone in the area knew Timothy Dwight, the strongest man; and Adam Winslow was almost as well known for his genius for making things work. "You go on in, Molly," he added.

"You look real nice, Molly," young Dwight smiled down at her. Then they turned and walked toward the buggies, and Molly went up the steps and into the house.

She was met by Mrs. Edwards, who gave her a relieved look. "Oh, Molly—what a relief! We're absolutely *buried* in here." She gave Molly a quick squeeze and smiled. "I have to talk with Mrs. Dwight and the others. Would you help Jerusha and Esther with the food?"

"Yes, Mrs. Edwards," Molly smiled. She went quickly to the kitchen, which was a beehive of activity. Jerusha and Esther welcomed her with cries of relief. Molly felt as much at home in this kitchen as she did at Winslow House, and though the others were older, she had an efficiency about her that soon made itself felt. For two and a half hours she worked with the other girls, Mrs. Edwards popping in to check on the progress of the meal, and finally at four o'clock, Esther said with relief, "I think it's all ready. I'll go tell Mother to get everybody seated."

There were too many guests by far to seat them all, even in

such a large dining room. The children and the younger people were herded into the parlor, while the Edwardses and their guests ate around the large dining room table. Molly, wearing a white apron over her dress, served the adults. Carrying in the large platter of sliced beef, she saw the Edwardses seated at the head of the table. To their left was the guest of honor, David Brainerd, and seated beside him was Jerusha. Across from them sat Judge Dwight, a large man with a florid face, and his wife, a thickset woman with silver hair. Their son Timothy sat beside his mother, and Adam beside him. Two other ministers and their wives from nearby parishes completed the table with one exception—Mary Edwards, the only child present, who sat beside Adam.

Molly was surprised, but not greatly. Mary was the one child who seemed to be able to manipulate her parents. And after all, it *was* her birthday. She was looking even prettier than usual in a beautiful white dress with green ribbons at the shoulders, and her glossy brown hair gleamed in the candlelight. She caught Molly's eye, gave her a saucy wink, then turned to pull at Adam's arm, drawing him away from a conversation he was having with young Dwight.

The meal lasted a long time, for it was far more of a social event than Molly was accustomed to. At Winslow House they sat down and ate steadily, then got up and went to the parlor to talk. That night the meal went on for an hour and a half, with over six courses, then coffee or tea with cakes as the talk rolled on and on. Molly was in and out of the room constantly, or else standing beside the wall ready to carry a plate away or fill a glass, so she heard it all.

She was most interested in David Brainerd, and she noticed that he ate practically nothing, merely picking at his food. Jerusha would lean close and urge him to eat, and he would give her a smile, but did not eat enough for a child. He was a slight young man, with a thin face and very fine hands. Molly noticed as she bent over him to pour tea that his fingers were bony, and there were two red spots on his cheeks—not a healthy red, but feverish and sickly.

He did take part in the conversation after sitting silently for the first thirty minutes. He had a high voice, not strong at all, as most ministers, but as he spoke of his love for the Indians and made little of his own hardships, Molly warmed toward him.

Judge Dwight said when Brainerd had finished, "Ah, Reverend, would that a little of your good spirit were abroad in our Colonies!" He shook his heavy head sadly, then continued. "There's a coldness among us spiritually that makes the physical cold of the wilderness seem as nothing!"

"The Revival has lost its fire," one of the older ministers said sadly. He looked at his host and said, "Brother Edwards, you must be heartsick over the lukewarm condition in our churches, are you not?"

Edwards nodded sadly, and there was a fatigue in his face that had not been there, Molly noticed, when she had first come to Northampton. "Yes, it is tragic to see a revival fade—and I must admit that we are in decline."

"I remember back in the early thirties," Judge Dwight stated. "My, it was nothing to see a whole congregation falling to its face before God, convicted of sin and ready to repent. Now we seem to be frozen."

"Well, there are exceptions, of course," Edwards returned, "and we must not give up hope, Judge. The Spirit of God will move when His people respond."

Timothy Dwight picked up a large tankard that looked like a toy in his huge hand, emptied it, then remarked, "Well, it seems to me there are more church members busy fighting their pastor than fighting the devil."

"Timothy!" his mother admonished instantly with a warning look.

"Oh, it's no secret that many of my church members are unhappy with their pastor, Mrs. Dwight," Edwards said with a faint smile.

"The sermons you preach against the Half-way Covenant have made you no friends," Adam said. The Half-way Covenant was a compromise agreement that allowed the children of church members to become a part of the church without a conversion experience of their own. Edwards had taken a strong stand against it, insisting that every individual must have a conversion experience.

"When Jesus said, 'Ye must be born again,' " Edwards smiled at Adam, "that eliminated any other options."

Judge Dwight looked uncomfortable, shifted in his seat, then said bluntly, "Rev. Edwards, you know that I stand with you on this issue, but many of our churches do not. And your controversy with Charles Chauncy has hurt you."

"Charles Chauncy is a good man, but not at all sound," Edwards stated without anger. "He believes that some of the unfortunate cases of emotional excesses of the Revival prove that the entire move was not of God. I must demonstrate that despite these errors, the awakening was a move of God. If he wins people to his way of thinking, Judge, we will never see God move in a mighty way among His people."

Molly listened carefully, for she was aware of the opposition Edwards was facing. It had gotten so bad, Jerusha had told her, that many church members refused to speak to the pastor or to any of his family. Her heart ached, for she loved the Edwards family dearly, and she had seen the strain grow as the situation worsened.

Finally the talk dwindled, and just as Molly waited for them to get up and go to the parlor so she could clear the dishes away, Rev. Edwards got to his feet. His tall frame seemed even taller in the flickering light of the lamps. There was an expectant expression on his face as he spoke, "We must not forget the dual purpose of our coming together, friends. We have said little about our guest, but Mrs. Edwards and I would like to express our joy in the coming marriage of our daughter Jerusha to Mr. David Brainerd."

There was a time of congratulations and toasts, during which Jerusha blushed and Mr. Brainerd nodded his thanks with a smile.

"Now, it only remains that we owe our youngest guest a happy birthday," Edwards said with a smile. "Mary, on your thirteenth birthday, we wish you many returns!"

Again applause and laughter ran around the room, and Mary rose to her feet, poised and beautiful, to open the gifts that were placed before her. The children all crowded in from the parlor as Mary began opening the presents, making a witty comment about each.

She's so beautiful! Molly thought, hanging back in the shadows. Mary had always been the brightest of the children, the natural leader. She had been cordially kind to Molly most of the time, although there had been moments when she ran roughshod over the English girl. The most obvious of these times had involved Adam, for Mary felt she had first claim on him, and Adam had not always been careful to keep his promises to Molly when Mary had other plans.

Finally, after all the packages had been opened and Mary had thanked everyone, Adam rose and suddenly said, "Here's one more, Mary—a small one made by a very clumsy blacksmith."

Molly recognized the leather pouch; it was the one he had had in the shop! Mary took it, pulled the drawstring, and let something fall out into her open palm.

Every eye was on it, and Molly saw the girl's eyes open wide as she held something that glittered brightly in the candlelight.

"Adam!" Mary whispered. "It's the most beautiful thing I've ever seen!"

She held it up to her throat, and they saw that it was a beautifully designed silver brooch with a red stone in the center. It was in the shape of a star, and the silver was worked so delicately that it seemed to be spun of silver thread.

"I got the stone from a peddler," Adam explained, as he stood there enjoying the look on Mary's face. "He claimed it was a blood ruby."

Mary turned and threw her arms around his neck. She was a tiny girl, much smaller than Molly, and looked as delicate as the brooch. Adam laughed and caught her to himself, hugging her joyously.

Molly suddenly whirled and left the room, her eyes smarting with tears. She pushed her way through the crowd, ran to the back door, and almost fell down the steps as she sought the darkness of the outdoors.

She walked blindly along the path that went to the pond, biting her lip to keep from sobbing. How long she walked she never remembered, but when she came back, Jerusha met her.

"I've been waiting for you, Molly," she said, then took the younger girl in her arms. She said nothing, but held her quietly as the child sobbed, giving way to the tears that could not be held back any longer.

Finally Molly drew back, ashamed, and wiped her face with a handkerchief. "I—I'm sorry, Jerusha. I don't know what's wrong with me."

Jerusha smiled strangely; then she said, "You're growing up, Molly," adding quietly, "Mary is sweet, but she's careless of others' feelings. And Adam is not tactful."

"I don't care what he does!" Molly snapped quickly. "I'm just a bound girl to him—just a servant!"

She whirled and raced away from Jerusha, who stood there for a long time staring into the darkness. Then she sighed and went into the house.

CHAPTER TEN

TRIP TO BOSTON

★ ★ ★ ★

"Adam, will you be going to Boston this week?"

"Why, yes, I will, Brother Edwards. My father sent word for me to come, so I figured to go right away." Adam noted the strain etched on the pastor's face, and asked tentatively, "Is there anything I can do for you while I'm there?"

"Actually, it's a little more than that I'm asking—perhaps it will be more than you'd care to do."

Adam's tanned face lit up and he said strongly, "No, I owe you more than I can repay, Brother Edwards. You and your family have been so good to Molly that I'm beholden."

"Why, that's been no burden, Adam. As a matter of fact, it was Molly who told Jerusha you were going." He hesitated, and there was a stoop to his shoulders as if he bore a burden. Adam knew of the opposition Edwards had been having in his church, and he thought at first that the request had something to do with that; however, it was something quite different.

"David Brainerd is quite ill, Adam," he said heavily. "I've been concerned about him for some time, so I asked Dr. Mather to stop in and see him earlier this week."

"What did he say?"

"He—could not give him any encouragement." Adam

stared at Edwards, knowing that this was more serious than any of them had thought.

Edwards suddenly gave Adam a peculiar look. "I can see that bothers you, Adam."

"Why—of course, sir!"

The minister bit his lower lip—something Adam knew he did only when he was struggling with a knotty problem. He looked directly at Adam again and said, "It bothers you, my boy, because you are not ready to meet God."

That blunt announcement caught Adam off guard. He reddened deeply, unable to answer. Edwards was the kindest man he knew, and unlike many of the hell-fire-and-damnation preachers that abounded in the country, he seldom spoke so plainly. Perhaps it troubled him as well as Adam, for he went on quickly. "I'm sorry to be so direct, Adam, but I think you must know by this time how Mrs. Edwards and I feel about you. We couldn't think more of you if you were our own son—but I feel that I've done you an injustice by not speaking on the matter long ago."

Adam's flush deepened, and he stared at his feet. Finally, he lifted his eyes to meet those of Edwards', saying, "You think I'm not a Christian, sir?"

Edwards said simply, "Ye must be born again." He put his hand on Adam's shoulder and added, "I would be very glad if you could tell me that you are indeed a new creature in Christ. Can you say that, my boy?"

Adam struggled with his thoughts, but finally whispered, "No, sir, I can't say that."

"I was afraid not—but that could change! You have heard the Gospel for quite some time. Do you believe the Word of God? Well, I feel certain that you do."

"Yes, sir!"

"Then you know what God requires—repentance, faith toward God in His Son the Lord Jesus. All that remains is for you to obey the scripture. The trouble in my church is tied to this. I say that men must have a personal experience with God—they must be born again, as the Scriptures clearly state. Would you like to call upon the Lord, Adam?"

With all his heart, Adam longed to say *yes* but there was something blocking this impulse. He stood there, torn between the desire to do exactly what Edwards asked—and the fear that rose up in him like a black cloud.

Finally he said sadly, "I—I can't do that, sir."

Edwards did not press the point. He said only, "I have faith that you will find Christ as your Lord very soon, Adam. I'll pray for that!"

"Mr. Brainerd—he's going to die, then?"

"We all must do that, Adam," Edwards said with a shake of his head, "but David is in critical danger. He insists on going to Boston to wind up his affairs. He feels he must put his missionary work in good hands, so that if he does pass away, the work will go on. Jerusha wants to go with him, and Mrs. Edwards and I have agreed. But it's out of the question for a young woman to make a trip like that alone with a man. It's asking a great deal, but would you be willing to take them? He says he can get the business done in two or three days."

"I'll be glad to." Adam shook his head sadly. "Wish I could do more." A streak of fatalism flashed in his dark blue eyes, and he stared off into the distance, thinking about Brainerd. "Not much anyone can do when something like this hits, is there, Pastor?"

"No, there isn't—but you'll give us some comfort if you watch out for David and Jerusha, Adam." He put his hand on the younger man's shoulder, and there was a warmth in his eyes as he said before he turned to leave, "Take Molly with you. She'll be a help to Jerusha."

Two days later Adam drove slowly along the road to Boston with Molly on the front seat beside him while Brainerd and Jerusha sat in the back. When he had told Molly that she was going to Boston with him, her face had glowed with pleasure, but he had felt it best to tell her the truth, that Brainerd was dying. She had stared at him; then tears had risen to her eyes. "Poor Jerusha! She loves him so much!" she had said quietly.

They had stopped overnight twice, and Adam was glad that Molly had come. She was cheerful and a great help to Jerusha. Brainerd was frail in body and had a bad cough, but he smiled often and his calm acceptance of the dark shadow that had risen to touch his life made a deep impression on Adam.

The last day of their journey, Brainerd had looked out at the wildflowers that crowded the fields outside of Boston and said with a smile at Jerusha, "God appears excellent, doesn't He?" Adam had actually turned around and the serenity on the sick man's face was genuine. "His ways are full of peace."

Adam felt a touch on his arm, and glancing down he saw Molly looking up at him. A smile trembled on her lips, and her gray eyes were moist—the first sign of grief she had allowed to escape on the three-day trip. Dropping his hand to her shoulder, he gave it a squeeze and whispered so quietly that the two in back could not hear, "Miss Jerusha's got herself quite a man, Molly!"

They arrived in Boston at midday and deposited the couple at the home of one of his friends. "Stay as long as you like, Mr. Brainerd," Adam had said after he carried the luggage in and stood there at the door with Molly. "I'm in no hurry at all."

"You have been an angel in disguise, Mr. Winslow," Brainerd said with a smile. "Jerusha and I are in your debt."

"An angel?" A quick flash of humor swept across Adam's face, and he shook his head in wonder. "I've been called lots of things, sir, but no one ever put *that* one on me! Send word to my father's house when you're ready."

Jerusha kissed Molly goodbye, and Adam turned the horses toward the outskirts. The two of them said little as they made their way through the city and down the dirt road. Finally, just before they arrived at the house, Molly said in a quiet voice, "Mr. Adam?"

"Yes, Molly?"

"You said Mr. Brainerd is going to die?"

"I think he is," Adam answered slowly.

"He's not afraid, is he?" Molly turned to look up at him, her thin face tense with strain. "I'd be afraid if I was going to die— wouldn't you, Mr. Adam?"

The simple question caught Adam off guard, and he dropped his head as he tried to find an answer. Her own honesty prevented him from making a quick, easy answer. He suddenly realized that with one simple question, she had released something he'd kept buried deep in his spirit—a fear that he'd kept caged within, like a dangerous animal locked in a dark place. Now Molly had loosed the beast. He remembered when Jonathan Edwards had preached about sinners being held over the pit of hell, like loathsome spiders, how he had quaked inwardly with a fear that stripped away every thought but terror. He had almost fallen to the ground, as so many others had done that night. Now he suddenly realized that the fear that had eaten at his heart that night had not vanished over the years. He had only managed to muffle it by shoving the issue into a dark corner of his mind.

"I'd be afraid, too, Molly," he said slowly.

"But you go to church all the time—and you aren't bad!"

They were at the front of the house now, and as they pulled up to the iron ring driven into a huge oak, Adam shook his head, saying only, "I guess it takes more than that to satisfy God, Molly. And David Brainerd, he's sure got something inside him that most folks don't have!"

Not wanting to continue the conversation, he jumped to the ground then helped her down. "You can talk about it to Rev. Edwards, Molly—" his broad mouth grew hard, and he said as they went to the porch, "And that's what I ought to do, too!"

They were met at the door by Charles, who grabbed at Adam and pulled him roughly inside. His bright blue eyes sparkled and he grinned as he cried, "You Indian, you! Come into the house—and you, too, young lady!" Laughing, he leaned down and gave her a kiss on the cheek, then laughed louder at her rosy confusion. "I never miss a chance to kiss a pretty lady, Molly. And you're growing up to be a beauty!"

Adam allowed himself to be pulled into the parlor, saying little. He saw at once that Charles had grown into a different man, for there was an ease and assurance in him that many men twice his age lacked. He spoke easily of his travels, of meeting important men; and large sums of money seemed small when he talked about them. He was wearing expensive clothes, and a large diamond flashed as he cut the air with his hand to emphasize a point.

He was charming in a way that Adam knew he could never emulate. There was an easy grace in every move, and as Charles hovered over them, pouring tea into bone china cups, he radiated charm. He let just enough drop in his narration of the venture in Virginia to let it be known that he had become a full-fledged member of Saul Howland's firm. When he spoke of Winslow House at Northampton, he somehow made the high praise he gave to Adam for his efforts there seem—not unimportant, exactly, but at best a minor side issue.

Finally he pulled a gold watch out of his waistcoat pocket, glanced at it, then said in surprise, "I've kept you too long! I'm beginning to talk like a woman!" He got up, and nodded at the study. "Better go and see Father."

"How is he, Charles?"

"Well, not very well, I'm afraid." Charles bit his lip in a worried fashion, shaking his head sadly. "His rheumatism is bad right now, you know. Mother does her best, and Aunt Rachel helps out when she can. We've had to move him from upstairs and make a bedroom out of the study. Look, I must go now, but we'll have plenty of time to talk. You'll be here for several days, won't you?" He acknowledged Adam's nod, then smiling down at Molly, he left the house.

"I've got to go see my father, Molly," Adam said. "Come with me." He guided her to the door leading off the hall, knocked softly, then opened it as his father's voice called out, "Come in!"

Miles was sitting up in bed with a large book on his knees. A smile of pleasure crossed his lips as he looked up at his visitors. "Adam! Come in, my boy, come in—and you too—Molly, is it?"

"How are you, sir?"

"Why, you can see I'm sentenced to this bed!" Miles' face was drawn with pain, but then his old eyes sparkled and he said, "I'm like an old bear chained to a log, Adam! Terrible patient! Snap at everyone."

Adam sat down in the chair beside his father's bed, hiding the shock he felt at seeing his condition. Age had fallen with a heavy hand on his father: the once strong, upright frame was shrunken into a smallish bundle of bones. The eyes were sunk back in the sockets, and the skin was dry and fragile—parched like old paper.

"Tell me about your place, Adam," Miles urged. He pulled himself up with an effort, and for the next hour Adam told him of the progress at Northampton. Realizing how hungry his father was for talk, he went into great detail on the innovations that Seth Stuart had made, then spoke of the work he'd done at the forge. It was pathetic to see how greedy the old man was to hear of a work that he'd never see.

Finally, Adam ran down, then grinned. "I'm getting to be quite a talker, Father! But what we've done is pretty small compared to what's happening in Virginia. When Charles was leaving, he told me what great things were happening there."

"Hmmm, I suppose so," Miles shrugged. "But all that's speculation, Adam. Could all vanish like a vapor. If the French decide to flow into the Ohio Valley, we'll lose our shirts. Now, your place, why, it's *real*! Never be worth a penny less—probably a lot more. I'm proud of you, Adam. Rachel and I both are; you've done a fine job!"

Adam's tanned cheeks flushed at his father's praise. He ducked his head, muttering, "Why, that's kind of you, sir! Most kind!"

"No, it's not kind!" Miles snorted. "Just plain truth. We'll have a meeting now that you're here. The family has to go on, Adam, and I'll not be around to see to it."

"Sir—!"

"Don't be foolish, son." Miles gave an impatient shake of his head, his voice suddenly strong. "I'm old, Adam. I've had a good life—a good life! God has blessed me, and I'm thankful to Him." Suddenly he reached out and said, "The one thing I'm most grateful for, I think, is that you and I have come closer. We have, haven't we, son?"

Adam's throat tightened, and as he took his father's thin hand, he could only nod, saying in a choked voice, "Yes, sir— we have!"

The two looked into each other's eyes, and suddenly Molly (who had been quietly watching them) saw that despite the many differences in the two men—they were somehow *alike*. Not in appearance, she thought, but there was the same look in their faces.

Then Miles seemed embarrassed. He touched the book he was holding, saying quickly, as though to get away from the emotion that had risen to engulf them so unexpectedly, "I've been reading Grandfather's journal quite a bit. You must have it, Adam! Here, I've got this one for you—best leather Franklin could find in the Colonies."

"Thank you, sir," Adam murmured, taking the book. "I've read some of it."

"It's more than a book, Adam. It's a life, and it makes most of us look pretty small. The Winslows have had some pretty good men, if I have to say so myself!" The old eyes grew warm with humor, and then a light of speculation glowed as he peered at this son who was so unlike him. "I have not been a good father to you, but I have a feeling that you're going to be the best of us, son!"

"Oh, sir, not me!" Adam flushed, and said uneasily, "Charles—he's the one who'll make us all proud."

Miles said nothing, then lifted his head, but as he was about to speak the door opened, and his wife came in.

"Adam, I'm sorry I wasn't here to meet you." His step-mother looked no older than the last time he'd seen her, but there was still a hard-edged expression around her thin lips, though her words were civil enough. "Charles told me you were here. I've made up the south room for you, and your servant can have the little room off the back porch."

It made Adam uncomfortable, the way she said *your servant*, referring to Molly. Technically it was true, of course, but he was so accustomed to treating her like a young sister or cousin that he never thought of her as a bound girl. He glanced quickly at Molly, noting her pale face, but she said nothing.

"Why, that's kind of you, ma'am," he acknowledged, "but I thought we'd impose on Aunt Rachel." He made up a story quickly, not wanting his father disturbed over the arrangements: "I'll be doing quite a bit of business in town, and it'll be more convenient to stay there. And I wanted Molly to spend some time with her, too."

"As you will, Adam." She looked at Miles, who had missed none of this, and said, "Charles told me you want the family to meet tonight?"

"Yes."

"I wish you'd tell me these things, Miles," she said evenly, and there was an edge in her voice that gave Adam a hint of what his father had to put up with. *The old witch!* he thought.

"Sorry, Martha," Miles said quietly. There was something about the helpless manner in which this strong man lay that cut Adam to the heart.

"I'll take Molly over to Aunt Rachel's, sir." He got up and Molly followed him out of the room.

They drove back to town, and when they arrived at Rachel's house, she greeted them warmly. "Of course you can stay here! You're always welcome. We just rattle around in this big old barn of a house." She showed them to their rooms, and when Adam left to conduct some business, she took Molly into her own bedroom and talked with her for over an hour.

At first Molly was withdrawn, but Rachel was adept at drawing people out, and finally the girl spoke freely. She talked about the Edwards and the Stuarts, of the way she'd learned to read and of the life on the farm. She found herself telling of her life in London—the first time she'd shared it with anyone—and most of all she told Rachel of Adam.

Rachel sat listening, her heart going out to the young girl, who so obviously leaned on her nephew body and soul. Finally Molly seemed to realize how much of her secret self she had allowed to let slip, and she reddened and grew silent.

Rachel did not attempt to touch her, much as she longed to draw her into her arms. She merely said, "You've done well, Molly. I know Adam is very proud of you—as we all are." The praise drew the color into the girl's fine gray eyes, and she drew herself up, giving a rare smile. "Now," Rachel exclaimed, "let me tell you all about Adam when he was a boy! Did he ever tell you about blowing up almost a whole flock of his father's pet chickens. . . ?"

They all assembled in the parlor. Miles was sitting in the large chair, looking around at his family. There had been much talk of Virginia, the fur trade, the danger of French invasion. Adam had given a brief report on the farm in Northampton, with a touch of heat in the discussion between Saul and Miles concerning some future developments. Saul wanted to spread out, buy more land in Virginia. "This country is filled up, Miles!" he exclaimed. "Can't make a profit unless there's room to grow."

"You can lose your shirt, though!" Miles snapped.

"But, sir, don't you think it's important to move with the times?" Charles spread his hands eloquently, a smooth persuasion in his whole manner, one which most had found difficult to deny. "After all, Adam's farm can never get much larger— while those tracts on the Ohio, why, they'll be worth a fortune someday!"

"We've not seen any great profit yet, Charles," Rachel said quietly. "Your expenses, as a matter of fact, have been so high lately that it has set the project back considerably."

Charles suddenly turned pale, and Adam saw a streak of raw anger flash in his eyes; however, he mastered it, saying smoothly, "You're correct, Aunt Rachel. I stand rebuked, but let's look to the future."

Adam looked at the faces around the room, and realized suddenly that tension was in the building. Charles, he sensed, had done something that had disturbed the rest of them, but they did not speak of it again.

Finally Miles said, "Some fools wait until they die to let their family know what they intend to do with their property—but I'm not one of them!"

His words cast a silence over the room, and he grinned, adding, "Well, *that* got your attention, didn't it! But, there'll be no surprises in my will." He looked at his wife, who was staring at him suddenly with suspicion, and said, "It's a man's duty to see to his wife, and I have done that. William, because of his position in the church, will receive a cash endowment rather than property. Mercy will be given a generous trust fund and a suitable dowry. The rest of the property will be evenly divided between my other two sons."

Adam glanced at the faces around the room, and even as shock ran through him he thought, *Charles is shocked—he expected more!* But the face of his brother was a smooth mask. Charles smiled easily, saying, "Why, that's just as it should be, eh, Adam?"

"Yes, it is!" Rachel said strongly. She nodded at her brother, saying, "I approve, Miles. You always did have good judgment."

Then suddenly it was over. After the goodbyes Adam drove his aunt back to her house. It was quiet, and the cries of the owls sounded ghostly as he guided the buggy down the road.

"What did Charles do, Aunt Rachel?" Adam asked finally.

"Nothing very admirable." Rachel paused for so long that Adam thought she was finished, but then she added wearily, "Charles didn't show much originality in sowing his wild oats, Adam. Gambling, drinking—and a very large sum went to a young woman who was quite expert in such things!"

Adam stared ahead, unable to accept what he was hearing. Finally he shook his head, asking, "Does Father know all this?"

"I'm afraid so."

"It's a wonder it didn't kill him! Charles has always been his fondest hope."

"It did nearly kill him—but it made him look more closely at his other son, so it wasn't all bad."

"I'm afraid they don't like it—my getting a half interest."

"No. And I want to warn you, be very careful in your dealings with Charles, and with Saul, too! My son is a good man, but he bends things to get his own way."

"No, you're wrong about that, Aunt Rachel. I trust them to do the right thing."

"Well, let *me* be a little suspicious," Rachel said firmly. Then she changed the subject. "I like your Molly. She's going to be a beautiful woman. And she's bright, too."

"She's all of that!" Adam was glad she liked Molly, and he went on recounting the girl's good points the rest of the way home.

When Rachel repeated some of those things to Molly the next day, it brought a glow to her cheeks.

"But, he'll always think of me as a bound girl," she said with a droop in her shoulders. "And he likes small girls—like Mary Edwards—not a big old thing like me!"

"Adam Winslow is a man, and therefore sometimes quite blind!" Rachel said pertly. Then she smiled and patted Molly on the cheek, and her eyes looked amazingly young in her withered face as she whispered, "One day, Molly, he'll open his eyes and see what I see!"

When Adam got home that night, he was taken aback when Rachel said with no warning whatsoever: "Adam Winslow—you can make pretty things, but you're blind as a bat!" She stalked off, her back rigid, and Adam stood there staring at her helplessly.

"I think Aunt Rachel's getting old," he said finally.

CHAPTER ELEVEN

A VALENTINE FOR MOLLY

★ ★ ★ ★

For a week Adam and Molly stayed with Rachel, and during that time the girl learned more about the Winslows than Adam himself knew. When Martha was called away to visit her sister in Philadelphia, Rachel came to the country to take care of Miles. Adam was gone a good deal of the time working with a gunsmith named Simms, but Molly accompanied Rachel. There were plenty of servants to do the menial work, so Rachel spent a great deal of time in the sick man's room.

Miles and Rachel had not been together much in recent years, and with Martha gone, they enjoyed going back over the old days. When Rachel left Molly there alone, Miles often asked her to read from Gilbert Winslow's journal, and all through the long afternoons she lived the adventure of Gilbert Winslow and his odyssey on the *Mayflower*.

Miles lay there watching Molly's eyes widen as she read of his grandfather's duel with Lord Roth, his romance with Lady Cecily North, and his adventures with the intrepid band that planted Plymouth so long ago. "Was Lady North *really* in love with your grandfather, Mr. Winslow?" she asked breathlessly.

"I think she must have been, Molly. She sailed all the way from England to America to find him."

"And then he fell in love with a poor girl and married her?"

Miles smiled at her. "Sounds like a fairy tale, doesn't it, Molly? But my father told me many times how his mother—who was Humility Cooper, you know—told him she never had a thought that Gilbert would turn from a wealthy and beautiful woman to marry her."

Molly looked down at the book, then lifted her eyes. She was, Miles reflected, a strange child—not at all like other children her age. Part of it was her background, but even beyond that, he saw in her something of the maturity and quiet beauty that the Scottish women frequently have. "You're happy here, child?" he asked suddenly.

"Oh, yes!"

"What do you want to do—I mean, when your period of indenture is over and you'll be free?"

A startled look crossed her face, and he realized that the question had taken her off guard. "Why, I don't think about it, Mr. Winslow. It's not for a long time."

He smiled suddenly, thinking of what an eternity that was to her—and how short it was to him! "It'll be here sooner than you think, Molly. Now, read some more." He lay back on his pillow, and she picked up the story of the Winslow clan again— she, intent on the words, while the old man watched her face.

Word came from Jerusha that they were ready to return home, and on Sunday the 19th of July, Adam and Molly picked the pair up and started their journey. They made slow time, only about sixteen miles most days, and by the time they reached the Edwards' house, Brainerd was so weak that Adam had to practically carry him in.

The sick man was unable to climb the stairs, so the Edwards' maid had prepared a bedroom downstairs. Adam shook off the profuse thanks of Sarah and Jonathan Edwards, saying only, "It was nothing." Then he looked at Mrs. Edwards, who was pregnant again, noting that her face was pale with strain. A thought came to him, and he asked, "Maybe Molly could stay and help with things. You wouldn't mind, would you, Molly?"

Mrs. Edwards' face brightened, but she said, "It would be asking a great deal of Molly. . ."

"Oh, I don't mind—really I don't!" Molly said at once. She had looked forward to going home with Adam, but her heart was touched by Jerusha's pale face. She said only, "Would you bring my things, Mr. Adam?"

"Of course I will—and I'm mighty proud of you, Molly," Adam said, and the light of approval in his dark eyes brought a flush to Molly's face.

8 October, 1747

I have not written here in so long! The last three months have been dreadful. Mr. Brainerd has gotten weaker day by day, and all of us cry when we are alone. I heard the doctor tell Mr. Edwards that Mr. Brainerd won't live a week longer.

Last night Jerusha was sitting with him, and I was beside her. He'd been unconscious for a long time; then he opened his eyes and said, "Dear Jerusha, are you willing to part with me?" And she couldn't do anything but cry, so he said, "I'm willing to part with you, though if I thought I couldn't see you in heaven, I couldn't bear it."

I couldn't stand it, so I ran out and cried. Then this morning, he called all the children in and said, "When you see my grave, children, remember that there lies the man who wants to see all of you in heaven."

9 October, 1747

Mr. Brainerd died today. He said goodbye to every one of us, even me. And then he raised up and looked around with a smile and said, "It is another thing to die than people think!" And then he put his head back and closed his eyes.

12 October, 1747

Mr. Adam brought me home after the funeral. The church was full, and Mr. Edwards preached on "True saints, when absent from the body are present with the Lord."

Miss Jerusha cried when I left, and when we got home Adam said, "This place has been lonesome without you." And he gave me a hug and kissed me on the cheek. And I don't know why, but as I write this, I can't see to write for crying. Not for Mr. Brainerd, but for some reason I can't even say.

The shock of David Brainerd's death passed away for people, as such things do, but the Edwards family did not get off so lightly. Jerusha had worn herself down caring for him, and in the weeks that followed she began to develop severe symptoms. Winter was bitter that year: in January she got drenched in a freezing winter rain, and the next day took to her bed.

Adam brought the bad news to Molly and the Stuarts one Friday evening. He had come in after dark, stomped the frozen ice and snow from his boots, then gone to stand by the fireplace.

Molly brought him a tankard of hot cider and asked at once, "Did you go by Mr. Edwards'?"

"Yes, and Jerusha is sick." He took a sip of the scalding drink, made a face, then shook his head. "I didn't see her, but Pastor Edwards was real worried."

"And Mrs. Edwards with a baby coming on!" Mrs. Stuart said. She set a plate on the table, piled it high with ham and eggs for Adam. "I don't see how they make it, Mr. Winslow! Nothing but trouble. First, that fine young man, and now their own daughter."

"God's been gude to them, tho'—" Seth said, puffing at his pipe. "Most families lose a child, or more than that. And they got ten leetle ones, all alive!"

"Maybe I better go help nurse Miss Jerusha," Molly said. "There's not much work around here."

Adam took a bite of ham and stared at her. "If you feel like you ought to do it, Molly, it'll be fine with me."

She nodded and said, "I can help a lot. Esther's the only one who's any help to Mrs. Edwards."

"Except for Mary, of course," Adam added. He did not see the sudden frown on Molly's face, and it was gone by the time she looked up. "I'll take you over tomorrow—and I can cut some more wood for the pastor."

The next day Molly packed and came down wearing her warmest clothes. Mrs. Stuart was in the kitchen, and Molly said, "Let me help with breakfast."

"It's ready. Go down to the shop and get Mr. Winslow."

Molly walked across the packed snow to the shop, opened the door, and saw that Adam was not there. He had been, however, for a fire was glowing on the forge. She went over to hold her hands over the burning coals, and as she stood there soaking up the warmth, she saw a small box on the workbench. Adam was always showing her things he made in the shop, and she opened it curiously, then she caught her breath—for a flash of gold picked up the light of the forge, glowing dully in the darkness!

She pulled out a gold necklace, marveling at the tiny links and at the delicate round pendulum, not more than an inch in diameter, but marvelously worked to look like tiny strands of golden cords. It was a beautifully done piece, and she stood there gazing at it when she heard footsteps. She quickly put the necklace inside the box, closed it, then moved to the door.

"Molly?" Adam stepped inside, and seeing her, said, "I was in the barn hitching up the team. Let's eat breakfast."

"All right."

They ate and were soon on their way down the hard-packed, icy road. Adam had made special shoes for the horses and converted a small buggy to a sleigh by pulling off the wheels and putting steel runners under it. As they raced along, Adam grinned at her. "Beats any ride I've ever had!"

"Oh, yes! I wish we could ride like this all the time."

"It would be hard to do in August, wouldn't it—without snow." He glanced at Molly and said suddenly, "I'm proud of you for helping the Edwardses."

"Oh, I don't do much."

"I don't agree. Means a lot to them." The runners hissed as the sleigh raced along, and they were soon at the house. As he pulled up, he said, "Won't be long 'til Valentine's Day, will it, Molly?"

"Well, this is January 15, isn't it? Just about a month."

He helped her down, then held on to her shoulders and said, "Well, you've got a real surprise coming, Molly."

She stared at him, and his eyes were gleaming. "What kind of surprise?"

He laughed and said, "No need to pester me. You'll just have to wait—and don't go poking around in the shop looking for it, you hear?"

"I—I won't, Adam. I promise!" Molly's heart was swelling, and a joy such as she had seldom known came to her at the thought that he would give her such a gift.

He cut wood all day while she helped with Jerusha, and

when he left that afternoon, he smiled and said, "Now, don't forget about Valentine's Day!"

As he drove off, Mary came to stand beside Molly. She watched as Adam waved, then drove down the road. "What was that about Valentine's Day, Molly?"

"Oh, nothing," Molly said. "He always gets me something on Valentine's Day."

"Really?" Mary said nothing more, but she could not disguise the envy in her voice as she added, "I'll bet he'll get me something, too! Something nicer than my silver brooch!"

Molly only said, "He probably will, Mary." Then she went up to sit with Jerusha. But all day long, she thought about Adam's promise, and it made her smile when she thought of the delicate golden necklace.

She stayed with the Edwardses for a week; then Jerusha seemed to be getting better, so Adam brought her home. He said nothing more about Valentine's Day, but the next day while he was out hunting with Seth, she went to the shop and found the box on a shelf. Carefully she drew out the necklace, then carried it to the door so she could see it clearly. It was even more beautiful than she remembered! Carefully she put it around her neck, and it made her feel somehow *precious* in a way she couldn't explain. Then she carefully replaced it, and did not look at it again.

On the 8th of February Adam suddenly spoke of his promise for the first time. They were eating supper when he said, "There's going to be a little Valentine's Day party at the Edwardses on Friday; we'll go over there. Mrs. Edwards thinks maybe Miss Jerusha will be able to sit up for a little of it."

The days seemed to drag by for Molly, and finally on Thursday he took her to the Edwardses to help cook for the party. "See you tomorrow, Molly." He winked and was gone.

She worked hard all that day, not only cooking but helping catch up with the washing and ironing. She was tired when dark fell, but she went to sit with Jerusha.

"My Molly!" the sick girl said with a wan smile. She coughed with a hollow sound, and Molly got her a glass of water. "Tell me all you've been doing, dear," she said. "I get lonesome for news lying here all the time."

Molly never intended to tell anyone about the necklace, but she let it slip before she thought. As soon as she realized what she had done, she gasped, "I—I didn't mean to tell *anybody* about it!"

Jerusha had large dark smudges under her eyes, and there was an ominous leanness in her cheeks, but she smiled and said, "It means a great deal to you, doesn't it, Molly?"

"He's been so good to me—but he's never given me any-thing—anything just for *me*!"

Jerusha had known for a long time that Molly was in love with Adam Winslow as only a very young girl can fall in love with an older man. She had thought, *It will pass as she gets older.* Now she said, "I'm glad for you, Molly." Then fatigue washed over her and she drifted off to sleep in that sudden fashion that had come to alarm them all.

If telling Jerusha was a mistake, Molly made a more serious one the next morning. She and Mary and Esther were making little cakes in the kitchen, and Mary had been chattering on about the party. She had a new dress and had been describing it to them for the third time. Molly was only half listening, her mind on the necklace. Then she heard Mary saying, "I've got my silver brooch to wear—it's too bad you don't have a nice piece of jew-elry to wear, Molly. I'll let you wear my brooch sometime!"

"I don't need it! Mr. Adam is giving me a gold necklace of my very own!"

Mary and Esther stared at her, and Mary at once began trying to discover more, but Molly set her lips and would say nothing. Finally, Mary sniffed and said, "You're just making that up, Molly Burns! Adam wouldn't give a servant a gold necklace!"

Had it been possible for her to leave, Molly would have fled, but there was no way. She kept as far away from Mary as pos-sible, and she knew that the girl had told others what she had said.

When Adam came that afternoon, Timothy Dwight was with him. The two had been replacing a timber in the church, and they both got washed up just in time to join the party.

It was a simple party with just a few young people who lived closeby. They played a few games, sang songs, and spent the evening enjoying one another's company.

Jerusha was brought in when it was time to exchange valentines. It worried Molly to see how sick she looked. She went and sat beside her, and saw that her face was flushed with fever. "You need to be in bed, Miss Jerusha!" she whispered.

"I'll go as soon as you get your necklace," Jerusha smiled. "I couldn't miss that!"

It was a loud time, squealing and laughing, and finally when they all had their valentines, Adam said, "I've got a valentine here for every Edwards on the place!" He began to hand out small items he had made—such as a pair of tiny tongs for Sarah Edwards, a spoon for Jerusha, small toys for the younger children. He had pewter cups for Mary and Esther, and there was a broad smile on his lips as he passed these gifts out.

Finally, he looked around and said, "Well, that's all, I guess."

"What about Molly?" Mary said loudly. She smiled saucily around and added, "You didn't give her anything."

Molly wanted to fall through the floor, and she shrank into the chair, wishing that she were anywhere else in the world!

Adam looked surprised, then shrugged. "Well, as a matter of fact, I *do* have something for Molly, but it's outside in the sleigh. I'll go get it."

While he was gone Esther said in a whisper, "See, Mary? He did get her a necklace!"

Mary said nothing but her eyes went to the package that Adam had in his hand when he came back. He came to stand in front of Molly, and smiled as he said, "Well, here's your valentine, Molly. And if there's another like it in the country, I'll eat my boots!"

Molly stared at the package he placed in her hands, and could not say a word. It was much too large for the necklace. *Maybe it's in a larger box,* she thought. As she unwrapped the paper, she felt Jerusha bending close to see what it was.

Then she pulled out a black metal container of some sort and stared at it. It was a round pan about a foot in diameter with a sturdy metal clasp on the side. She stared at it, and he reached down and said, "It opens like this," and he lifted the top.

There was a silence, and Molly could not lift her eyes. Finally Mary asked loudly, "Well, what in the world *is* it?"

Adam smiled. "We've all gone to bed with our feet freezing. But Molly won't have any more cold feet, because she's got the first footwarmer ever made!"

"A—a *footwarmer*?" Molly whispered.

Adam did not see the distressed look on her face. He was so pleased that he took the pan from her and held it up, saying, "Look, you put hot coals in here when it's time to go to bed. There's a frame with it that goes under the bed. You put the footwarmer on it, and you've got nice warm feet no matter how cold it gets!" Then he looked at Molly, who still had not lifted her head, and he said, "Well, didn't I tell you you'd get a valentine like you never dreamed of?"

Mary laughed. "Well, it's very nice—but it'd be hard to wear it around your neck."

"Around your neck?" Adam asked. "That's not what it's for, Mary. It's to keep your feet warm. Do you like it, Molly?"

Molly sat there, and suddenly the room seemed very quiet. She raised her head slowly and he saw that there were tears in her eyes. "Thank you, Mr. Adam. It's—very nice."

He stood there, aware that something was terribly wrong, but having no idea what it was. Then Jerusha said, "I'm very tired. Would you help me to bed, Molly?"

Molly's eyes were filled with tears, but she instantly got up and led Jerusha out of the room. When Jerusha was in bed, she reached out and took Molly's hand. "Try not to feel too bad. He was thinking of a way to make things easier for you."

"I know." There was a dead sound to Molly's voice. She had dried her tears, and she said, "I'll stay with you tonight."

"No, you must go home. Come tomorrow—and don't be angry—"

She dropped off into a restless sleep, her face flushed from the high fever. Her mother came in, looked down and said, "We shouldn't have let her get up, but she wanted to so much!"

"I want to stay with her, Mrs. Edwards!"

Mrs. Edwards had heard from Esther about the necklace,

and she went and put her arms around Molly. "If you want to," she said quietly.

"I'll go tell Mr. Adam." Molly slipped away and found Adam standing beside the door, his face pale. "I'd better stay with Jerusha, if you don't mind."

"Molly, Mary told me about the necklace. I—I never thought—!"

"It's all right. I should have known better." There was something different in Molly's voice, and her lips were thin as she said, "It wasn't your fault. I'm stupid!"

"Don't say that! I—I just didn't think, Molly. I made it for Aunt Rachel, but you can have it—!"

"I don't want it. Bound girls ought to have better sense than to expect gold necklaces from their masters!"

"Molly, don't—!"

He reached out to touch her, but she pulled back, her face pale as paper. "I won't make a mistake like that again, Mr. Winslow."

She turned and walked away without another word, and Adam suddenly left the house just as quietly.

Jerusha died early the next morning, hemorrhaging without warning. It was a difficult time for Molly, but she forever looked back on that night as the time she left childhood behind.

19 February, 1747
   I have tried to pray, but nothing happens. When Mrs. Edwards told me that Jerusha was dead, I died, too.
   I can't love God, even though I try!
   Why did she have to die? Or Mr. Brainerd?
   Adam brought me home, and he tries to tell me about how sorry he is about the necklace. It doesn't matter. I don't care!
   One thing I promise! I'm a bound girl, and I'll never forget that—not as long as I'm his! Never!

CHAPTER TWELVE

CHARLES FINDS A WOMAN

★ ★ ★ ★

Fall came late in '49, the soft grasses stubbornly keeping their emerald color all through September. The leaves, ordinarily trodden under foot by the end of the month, still clung tenaciously to the oaks, and the winds, though cool, did not bite and freeze the fingers. Even in October the brooks were not skimmed with ice, and the morning sun warmed the earth by noon.

Molly caught the first trumpet of fall on the morning of the 15th as she was sitting at her small desk writing in her journal. At this time of day, the house was quiet, so Molly had formed the habit of spending the early hours of the morning writing. But now her journal had thickened. Suddenly a sharp breeze swept through the window, scattering some of the loose pages. Picking them up, she glanced at the date, then let her eyes run down the page.

It was the page she had written two years earlier on the day of Jerusha's funeral, and although time had blurred the sharp pain and bitterness, her lips grew soft as she thought of her friend. Then she read the last comment on the page: *One thing I promise! I'm a bound girl, and I'll never forget that—not as long as I'm his! Never!*

She leaned over, shut the window, then got up and slipped

out of the flannel nightgown, thinking of that time of her life—
something which she rarely did. *I was thirteen years old when I said
that—now I'm fifteen*, she thought as she pulled a gray cotton
dress from a peg and slipped into it. The fact that it was too small
made her realize how rapidly her figure had developed the past
year. She and Beth Stuart could not seem to keep up with her
wardrobe. *Fifteen—and he still thinks I'm a child!*

She looked down at herself, not at all happy that she was
five feet nine—taller than any girl she knew and only an inch
shorter than Adam. A year earlier she had begun to stoop trying
to disguise her height, but Beth had railed at her: "Sit up straight,
girl—you look like a worm all bent over! God's given you a tall,
strong body, and you go creeping around like a cowering slave!"

She had been bullied into a good carriage, but now she
thought rebelliously, *Why couldn't I be small and dainty instead of a
giant?* Then she stooped and peered into the small mirror on her
desk.

What others saw was a face with rather high cheekbones,
the planes sweeping down to a firm jaw totally feminine for all
its strength. The eyes were calm, a strange blue-gray color, large
and wide spaced. Thick black lashes curled over them, and the
brows arched gently under a smooth broad forehead. Her lips
were full with a hint of stubbornness, yet soft and red, and when
she smiled, a dimple appeared on her left cheek, making her
look almost saucy. When she let her thick ash-blond hair down,
it cascaded down her back like a smooth waterfall, but usually
she wore it up in a crown of braids that framed her face.

She went downstairs and cooked breakfast. As she was taking the bread out of the oven Adam came in. "Winter's in the
air—maybe snow," he said.

He sat down and she put a bowl of hominy and a pitcher of
cider in front of him. "Charles should be in this afternoon," he
said, pouring a stream of dark molasses over the hominy. He
waited until she sat down; then they bowed their heads and he
said briefly, "Lord, we thank thee for this food, and ask you to
grant thy mercy over us this day in Jesus' name."

"Is he going to stay long?"

"No, I don't suppose." He took a pull at the tankard of cider she had put in front of him, looked at it and said, "That's a good cider, Molly." Then he shrugged, saying mildly, "Charles doesn't stay anywhere long, I guess. He's been all over Virginia, even went to England last year, according to Aunt Rachel."

"Did he say why he's coming?" Molly cut a thick slice of fragrant bread, adding a thick layer of yellow butter. "He's never come before."

"I think he wants to see that we're making money—or maybe why we're not making more."

She was suddenly indignant, and her sharp white teeth snapped off a morsel of bread; then she said, "This is the best farm in the colony! And that new plow of yours has made a good profit, Adam!"

He looked across the table, grinned at her, but only said, "I guess this operation is pretty small potatoes to Saul and Charles. They've been buying land like crazy in Virginia. Can't think what he'd want to tell me, though. He and Saul are the businessmen, and I'm just a plain blacksmith."

Molly started to deny his statement, but she had learned long ago that while there was no man more confident in working with metal, Adam Winslow saw his brother and his cousin as being superior to him in every way. It infuriated her that he put himself down so, but she only shrugged and watched him finish his breakfast.

He was twenty-two years old, and looked much the same as he had the first time she'd seen him. Among the Winslows, where all the men were uncommonly tall, he seemed small, not over five ten, but the years at the forge and on the farm had molded him into a solid shape. He did not look large, but she had seen him without his shirt, washing at the pump, and the swelling chest, the heavy muscles of the shoulders and arms, and the massive development of the muscles in his back made other men look frail. In a land of strong men, only one man was his superior—Timothy Dwight. But Dwight's strength was massive and ponderous, like a heavy draft horse, while Adam's was quick as a cat.

I wish he wouldn't feel so inferior around Charles, she thought, then gave it up as she always had in the past. Only once had she mentioned this to anyone. Mrs. Stuart had listened while Molly burst out, complaining how Adam always saw Charles as being better at things. Beth Stuart had shocked her when she'd smiled and said, "You don't like that, Molly, but I can tell you something—you do exactly the same thing with Mary Edwards!"

The memory disturbed Molly. She rose and began to clear the table. "We'll put him in the downstairs bedroom—oh, yes, we're invited to the Lindons' day after tomorrow. A last fling for Tom, I think."

"I'm not sure if Charles will want to go to such a small party," Adam said doubtfully.

"Well, let him stay at home and stare at himself in the mirror then, because I've already told them we'd be there!"

He grinned at her, amused at the fiery response. "You don't like Charles, and you don't even know him, Molly. And you better watch that temper of yours. What if the preacher heard you?"

She ignored him, and later that day when Charles got off his horse and came inside, she greeted him with a smooth countenance. He filled the doorway, his eyes alive and dancing, and after greeting Adam with a bear hug, he turned to her, and with a startled expression he said, "This isn't *Molly*?! Why, you're not a snub-nosed little brat anymore—let me see!"

"She's grown up a bit, Charles, hasn't she?" Adam grinned.

Charles was looking at Molly strangely; she felt uncomfortable, yet at the same time it pleased her. He was, she decided, the best looking man she'd ever seen, even more handsome than she remembered him. He had filled out a little, and his eyes, blue as cornflowers, seemed to look right inside her. There was a boldness in his manner that was lacking in Adam, and she knew instinctively that he had had much experience with women. He reached out to take her hand, and she saw the sharpness of his expression, heard the smooth ease in his voice as he said, "Miss Burns, I'm glad to meet you. Always a pleasure to see a young woman blossom into a beauty."

"Enough of that, Charles!" Adam laughed. "Don't give her any ideas along that line. I've warned her about your worldly ways."

"Ah, too bad!—but how do you know I haven't repented, Adam? I assure you that my feeling for Molly is strictly honorable." He still held her hand and added with a wide smile, "Just think of me as a big brother, Molly. Come to me with all your troubles."

"I'm afraid that'd be like putting the fox to guard the chickens!" Adam said wryly. They all three smiled, and Molly saw at once that Adam was incapable of believing any wrong of this flamboyant brother of his.

They spent a good afternoon, sitting around the kitchen table, with Charles telling them tall tales of Virginia. Adam and Molly sat drinking in the talk, for the man was a born storyteller. He made the dark forests and the painted savages come alive, and finally he said, "It's not so much my world as yours, Adam. I've liked seeing it, but I'm a city man. You'd do well there, as much as you like the out-of-doors."

Adam was stirred. "I don't guess I'll ever find out, Charles. Someone has to mind this place."

"I suppose, but as much as you know about guns, you'd make a place for yourself. All Virginians are sportsmen, and they'll swap their sisters for a good rifle—pardon the loose talk, Molly! There's a family named Washington close by, and they're good enough farmers, but they live to hunt. Ride to the hounds, of course, but the youngest son, George, he loves a good gun. Wish you could come and see the country there."

"I'd like to."

Later that day, Charles brought out a leather case and extracted a sheaf of papers. "We've managed to get an option on a large tract over the mountains, Adam. I couldn't believe the price!" he exclaimed. "Saul and I are spread a little thin, but you know how it is—you have to take opportunities when they open up. Saul's figured out a way to keep what we have, get a loan on some of it, and buy this section. It's really pretty involved— but we can't lose. It's all tied up with the general estate, so all of us have to sign it."

"What did Father and Aunt Rachel say?" Adam asked. He felt uncomfortable dealing with papers and lawyers, and wished that he'd gone to Boston so that his father could explain it all.

"Oh, you know how they are, Adam," Charles shrugged. "Getting on, I'm afraid, and old people are all conservative. Took a lot of talk, but Saul finally got his mother sold, and she talked to Father, so that's all right. They've already signed, and so have I. Your signature is all we need—but we've got to move fast or The Hudson Bay Company may get wind of it; then it'd be a lost cause!"

Adam stared at the papers, then nodded. "Well, if they signed, I guess I will, too."

"It's going to make us all a pile of money, brother!" Charles said. He took the papers after Adam had signed his name, and put them back into the case with an air of satisfaction. "Now, maybe you'd like to show me the place. Rachel thinks you've done something unique here."

For the rest of that day, and all the next morning, Adam and his brother walked over the entire farm and Charles showed a quick intelligence that went beyond his indolent manner. He commended Seth Stuart for his work in managing the crops, but he was most interested in what Adam was doing at the forge.

"This is fantastic, Adam!" For the past few years Adam had been experimenting with muskets, and Charles was holding his brother's latest effort. It was something of a cross between the old style musket and the Kentucky hunting rifle. "This is beautifully balanced; is it accurate?"

"Well, I hate to brag, but it'll do very well against most competition," Adam shrugged. "You know how the old flintlocks are—the Brown Bess that English soldiers use. Anything over fifty yards and you might as well forget it! The soldiers just aim in the general direction and blaze away. They don't even have a front sight! But they're easy and quick to load and the powder and ball aren't too critical—just about anything will work. Now the Kentucky rifle, why a good marksman will knock a squirrel out of a tree at a hundred paces—but the balls have to be specially made, and so does the powder, and they take three times as long to load—so massed troops can't use them."

"And what's this you've done?" Charles sighted down the gleaming barrel of the rifle.

"Well, I'm trying to find a weapon that's got the best of both the rifle and the musket. Quick and easy to load, but accurate. This is better, but the powder and shot is still critical." He hesitated, then said, "I've got an idea, Charles, but it's still just that."

"Well, Adam, after seeing this piece of work, I'm convinced you can do anything! What's the idea?"

Adam faltered, taken off guard by the praise, but he said, "Well, the obvious answer is a breech-loading mechanism, of course. Lots of men have tried, but nobody's hit the answer yet."

Charles's wedge-shaped face was alive with excitement. "You think you're on to it? Adam, if you could get that thing made, why, it'd be worth millions! Every army in the world would sell their souls for it! Why. . . !"

Adam laughed, and held up his hand in protest. "Hold on now—it's just an idea, Charles!"

"You work on that, you hear me? Why, the Winslow rifle will make our name famous!"

Adam laughed suddenly. "Remember how we blew up Father's chickens with my first gun? This may turn out like that!"

Charles threw back his head and roared. "And I ran away like a rat and left you to take the blame, didn't I, Adam?" he said finally. "You must have hated me for that!"

"Why, no!" Adam's open face showed surprise, and he added, "I couldn't fault you for anything, Charles."

The remark moved the tall young man, yet he seemed disturbed. "You're too trusting, Adam. You've got to learn to be a little more careful about people."

"You're not people," Adam smiled. "You're my brother."

Charles stared at the smaller man, and there was a light of wonder in his face. Finally he shook his head, saying, "I shall have to watch out for you, brother!" Then his face changed and he said, "Saul will be interested in your rifle, but now tell me about yourself."

"Myself?"

"Yes, not the farm or the forge, but *you*. Are you in love?"

"In love?"

"Confound it, don't be such an echo! You must have done *something* all these years besides grow turnips and make rifles. Come on, now, tell old Brother Charles all about it!"

There was a light of expectation in the face of Charles Winslow, and Adam was speechless. He opened his mouth, closed it, then finally said, "Well, I haven't had much time for such things, I guess."

Charles studied him, and there was a sharp light in his eyes. "But I think there's somebody special, right?"

"Why, she doesn't really know how I feel. . ."

"Why not?"

Adam flushed, and biting his full lower lip, he cleared his throat, saying, "Charles, I've never told anyone about this. There's only one woman I've ever felt anything for, but it's not easy. She's very young, and I've been like a big brother to her."

"The best thing in the world!" Charles grinned. "Why, all you've got to do is let her know that you're *not* her brother!"

"But she's only fifteen years old, and she's the daughter of the best friend I've got in the world."

"Well, who is this paragon of youthful beauty?"

"Mary Edwards!"

"Ah! The plot thickens!" Charles stroked his chin. "The famous preacher, I take it?"

"Yes."

"Well, I don't care if she is a preacher's daughter, she's just like any other woman! See here, I've got to give you some help in this business!"

"Oh, I don't think—!"

"When will you see her again? Soon?"

"As a matter of fact, Molly says we're invited to a party at some neighbors, and Mary will be there. But I didn't think you'd want to go, Charles. It's really a rural affair."

"Lead me to it!" Charles laughed. "Country matters are what I crave. And by the time I get you fully instructed, you innocent young Hercules, Fair Mary will fall into your arms helpless with young adoring love!"

Over thirty young people had gathered to celebrate the coming wedding of young Tom Lindon and his bride-to-be, and with the older guests, well over fifty people were present. They were hard-working people, these children of the Pilgrims, and they delighted in donning brightly colored clothes and having a time of relaxation.

Molly had drawn an exclamation from Charles as she came down the stairs in a new dress that she'd been saving for a special occasion. It was a simple blue-gray gown with a cluster of red ribbon at the high neck and sleeves and a wide red sash. It showed off her maturing young figure well. "Good heavens!" Charles breathed, taking her hand, "let me look at you!" He made her turn around, and there was a flush on her creamy complexion when he kissed her hand and said quietly, "You look very beautiful, Molly—very beautiful, indeed!"

Adam, taken aback by Charles's attention, said nothing, but he stole several glances at Molly as they went out to the carriage. He was quiet on the way to the Lindons', but Charles kept the conversation flowing, eliciting a giggle from Molly several times as he described some of the amusing happenings at parties he'd attended in Virginia.

They arrived at the Lindons' late, and Charles was immediately the center of attention. There was an exotic air about him, and his stunning good looks and fine dress would have marked him if his elegant manners had not.

Adam introduced him to the senior Lindons, then to the guests of honor, and he won the bride's favor by saying fervently to young Tom Lindon, "Zounds, Mr. Lindon, I'd advise you to keep this beautiful creature away from the city! She'd cause a stampede there, I vow it!"

Timothy Dwight came in a little late with Mary Edwards, and Adam whispered, "That's Mary!"

"Who's the elephant with her?" Charles grinned. "I hope you don't have to fight it out with him for her fair hand!" Then he looked at Mary, who was elegant in a green silk dress with white brocade, and said, "Well, she's a beauty, old boy!"

On being introduced, he kissed Mary's hand and said, "Miss Edwards, I'm honored. Your father is a man I cannot presume to praise too much. Would you object, sir, if I stole this lovely creature for a time? I've read every book her father has written! He's quite an idol of mine, you know."

As Charles walked off with Mary by his side, not at all disturbed by the thundering lie he'd just uttered, Timothy looked at Adam with a smile and said, "Well, I'm glad his charm doesn't run in the family, Adam."

Adam looked up at young Dwight, and realized that there was more in his words than the others around knew. For the last few months the two of them had been bumping into each other constantly, usually at the Edwardses, often at church or at functions like this. Adam was so accustomed to having Mary claim his attention, as she had done for years, that he only now realized, although nothing was said, that he and Dwight were engaged in some sort of rivalry.

Now staring at Timothy, Adam knew that the big man's constant attention to Mary had awakened him, making him realize that he no longer felt like a brother to her—not in any way!

Timothy read Adam's expression and said, "It's taken me a year to get Mary's eyes off you. Matter of fact, I almost gave up! Worst case of a girlhood love I ever saw!" He smiled as Adam gave him an incredulous look. "Oh, you're too dumb to know it, Adam, but everybody else did!"

"In love with me?"

Timothy laid a heavy hand on Adam's shoulder, the weight of it enormous. "Too late, old man. I've managed to cut you out pretty well, but if you were a man who knew women—as that dandy of a brother obviously does!—why, I'd have had no show at all!"

Adam felt as though he'd been kicked in the stomach by one of his mules! His mind reeled as Timothy walked off, and his thoughts tumbled wildly. *Mary in love with me? But I've never even kissed her! Never really courted her!*

For the next hour Adam was stunned. He was still able to function, but his movements were automatic and his thoughts were fragmented. He managed to play some of the simple games that the young people engaged in out in the yard, but he could not have told you a thing that happened. *Mary in love with me!* The idea shook him, but despite his confusion, he did notice one thing: Dwight was never far from Mary, and the smile she gave him was not that of a little girl, but of a woman aware that she was being pursued!

Adam Winslow was a slow-moving, easy-going sort. He smiled and was amiable in most things. But from time to time, he fixed his eye on something and, with every ounce of determination in his spirit, said, *I'll have that or die trying!*

The thick cords of muscles in his solid jaw suddenly bunched up, and his eyes narrowed to slits of royal dark blue. He stood there like a cat watching a bird, getting ready to pounce! Then he forced himself to relax, but there was something in his face that Molly saw at once—for she knew him well enough to recognize the tenacious look he had when his mind was made up.

He said little, but he began moving closer to Mary, and she recognized at a glance what was happening. Her bright eyes flashed, and all afternoon, young and inexperienced as she was, she managed to play them off against one another.

Charles had been drinking cider with Molly, and he said, "That young woman is a menace, Molly! Look how clever she is with those two!"

"Mary's clever enough," Molly answered. "She's always been able to get anything she wanted."

Charles stared at her in surprise, for there was an edge in the girl's voice. "You don't like Mary, do you, Molly?"

"Yes, I do. She's a fine girl, Charles, but she's hard on people. She's so much smarter than the rest of the world, she can get what she wants without trying. That would be bad enough in a plain woman, but she's beautiful as well—and that could be terrible."

He stared at her, a sudden flash of approval in his eyes. "You're a very observant young woman, Molly. I like that." Then he stared at the trio across the yard and said, "My word, he's huge! No man could stand up to him in a fight! I hope Adam's got sense enough to know that—but then, Adam never had any sense! He'd tackle a grizzly bear if he got mad enough!"

"I wish we'd go home," Molly said suddenly.

"Why? The party's just started!"

"These parties are pretty much the same, Charles. Sooner or later the young men will start having contests. Running, jumping, wrestling—that sort of thing." She looked up at him, and bit her lip, murmuring, "I've never seen Adam so aggressive! He usually stands on the outside and just smiles—but look at him now!"

Charles saw what she meant. Adam and Timothy were both practically hovering over Mary, looking for all the world as if they wanted nothing better than to fall on each other.

"I don't think wild horses could drag him away," Charles said. He looked at Molly and said tentatively, "Adam and I have not been very close, but he confided in me yesterday. He told me he was in love with Mary."

"He has been for a long time." There was no emotion in Molly's voice. She said it as if it were not very interesting, but he saw her lips were pressed tightly together, the small blue vein in her forehead pounding.

"Well, let's hope they don't lock horns! That fellow's a bull!"

But they did. Just as Molly indicated, the young men soon began to engage in athletic contests, and as always it turned into a tournament, each of them determined to prove to the young women how strong or fast they were.

It began with a shooting match, and Charles took part in that himself. They blazed away at a target, moving farther and farther back. They were all good shots, but soon it became evident that young Dwight and Tom Lindon were the best. Charles was eliminated, and then Dwight hit dead center, while Lindon missed.

"What about you, Adam?" Timothy asked with a challenging smile. Adam had taken no part, although several had urged him.

Now he saw that it had become a personal thing, but still he shook his head. "I guess not today."

Mary smiled and said, "Oh, I wish you would, Adam."

He lifted his head and smiled, "You want me to, Mary?" He looked at Dwight with a strange smile, then said, "I'll take a shot."

He got the rifle that Charles had admired, and came to stand beside Dwight. "You can set the distance, I guess."

Timothy looked somewhat uneasy. "That's a new rifle, isn't it, Adam? Well, I guess we can set the target back a little." He waved the young man back who was setting the white piece of board onto a tree. "That's a hundred yards. Suit you, Adam?"

"Fine."

Timothy shot first, kneeling and taking careful aim, the flint-lock steady in his huge hands. He took a long sight, then finally fired. The young man ran over, looked at the target, then yelled, "Almost a miss. Touched the outside corner!"

It was a good shot, considering the distance, and Dwight smiled, "Your turn."

Adam swept the rifle up and pulled the trigger. There was no appreciable pause between the time the gun rose and fired. The young man looked, then yelled, "Dead center!"

A sudden cheer went up from the crowd, and Mary joined in the applause. Adam's face reddened, and he should have stopped there, but he had been stung by Dwight's attitude. "Move back!" he called, and twice more he waved the man back. "Right there."

"Nobody can hit that mark!" Lindon exclaimed. "That's over two hundred yards."

Adam had reloaded, and now asked, "You want to shoot first, Dwight?"

The big man looked at the distant mark and shook his head. "You're showing off, Adam. Tom is right."

Adam raised the rifle, and this time he steadied his piece. It was, they all saw, as steady as if it were fixed in rock. Adam fired, and the call came back: "A hit—to the right."

Mary ran over and took Adam's arm, her face a picture of delight. "Adam, I never knew you could shoot like that!"

Molly said loudly, "He made that gun, Mary. Why wouldn't he be able to hit with it?"

The young men instantly crowded around, demanding to see the rifle, and Adam, for the first time, was the center of attention.

"Dwight's not happy," Charles said quietly to Molly. "I'd guess he'll try to top that shot."

And he was right. For a while there were foot races, but neither Adam nor Dwight entered into that, both of them far too heavy to challenge the striplings.

Then someone cried out, "Let's toss the stone!" They chose a stone that weighed about fifteen pounds, a round one, slapped smooth in a stream, and the young men took turns seeing who could heave it the farthest.

Adam and Timothy were deliberately placed last. Everyone in the crowd realized that Adam was tremendously strong, but young Dwight's strength was proverbial. Everyone in the village knew of the time when as a very young man he had crept up to a farmer who was driving a yoke of oxen hitched to a cart. Timothy had tiptoed up behind the cart, yanked the oxen to a halt, then held them as the farmer urged them on, their hooves skidding and scrambling as the young giant held them in place.

As Adam picked up the stone, hefting it in one hand to catch the balance, the crowd held its breath. He crouched and sent it sailing twenty feet past the best attempt.

Then Timothy walked over, and just the way he picked up the stone in his huge hands, as if it *had* no weight, brought a whisper from the crowd, and Adam bit his lip. He came back to the mark, turned ponderously, then sent the stone flying through the air! It went far beyond Adam's mark. Everyone gasped.

Every eye turned to Adam, and there was an eager light in their eyes, for the thing was turning out to be a personal contest between the two men. It happened often that two young men would pursue the same girl, and most of them realized that Adam and Dwight were actually competing for Mary Edwards.

Adam glanced at the stone, shrugged, and smiled briefly, "No man in the world can beat *that*, Timothy."

"I hope that's all of it—they're even," Charles muttered, but it was not to be.

"No, they'll wrestle," Molly said grimly. "They always do. But Timothy never has. He said once he was afraid he'd hurt someone."

"Adam has more sense!" Charles protested.

"No. He doesn't!"

Molly's bitter words were prophetic, for when all the others had wrestled, someone cried out, "Timothy, what about you and Adam?"

"No, it wouldn't be fair," Dwight answered.

Adam's face burned at the implication, and he said at once, "I'll take a fall with you, Timothy."

A cry of excitement went up and a circle formed instantly around the two men.

To Charles it was incredible. He stared at the bulky form of Timothy Dwight—six foot four and 250 pounds of hard muscle. Then he looked with apprehension at his brother. Adam had taken off his boots and was circling his huge opponent; he looked small. Charles had laid his hand on Adam's shoulder once and been amazed at the thick sinews, but he still had no hope. *A bullet in the brain! That's what would stop that big ox!* he thought.

Everyone saw at once that Dwight's tactics were simple. He could not hope to match Adam's quickness, but if he got one hand on the smaller man, the contest was over; no human could pull free from a grip such as his!

Twice Adam feinted, and twice Dwight was faked out of position. Both times Adam could have gotten a hold, but he knew full well that if he missed, he would be as helpless as a baby in Timothy's hands.

Then as Adam moved close, Dwight's hand shot out, but he caught only the fabric of Adam's shirt. It tore away like paper, and the crowd drew a sudden breath, for none of them had ever seen such a man as Adam. His body was smooth with muscle, tapering from a trim waist to enormous pectoral muscles, and with every move, the tremendous power of his arms was revealed.

It could not last long, and it didn't. Adam moved to his left, drawing Timothy after him, and as the large man went for him, he shifted, agile as a cat. He reached out and jerked Dwight even more off balance, and for one second, the giant's back was to him. Adam leaped high, whipping his arms around Dwight's throat, and locking his powerful legs around his waist.

A cry went up, and Molly saw that Adam's eyes were blazing, and she put her hand to her mouth.

Dwight tried desperately to reach back and get his hands on Adam, but the smaller man ducked his head and clung like a burr. His right forearm was pressed against Dwight's windpipe, and his left locked that arm in place.

Dwight's face grew red as his air supply was cut off, and a terrible whistling noise came from his tortured throat. Charles suddenly ran to the pair and pulled at Adam's arms, but they were like iron bands. "Adam! You're killing him! Let go!"

Adam did not relax and Charles saw madness in his eyes. He reached out grabbing Adam's thick hair and pulling his head back, at the same time yelling in his ear, "You're a Winslow, idiot—not a murderer!"

The words got to Adam, and he loosed his grip at once, and stood there, a dazed look on his face. He stared at Dwight, who was gagging and trying to get his breath; then his face turned deathly pale. He went over and stood looking up at the big man, saying, "Timothy, I—I didn't mean to. . . !"

Dwight glared down at him for a second; then the inherent good nature of the man took over. He forced a grin, slapped Adam on the shoulder nearly driving him into the ground, and said in a raspy tone, "Well, Adam, you'll have to admit one thing—it's been the most *interesting* party we've ever had in our whole lives, ain't it now?"

Molly saw Mary Edwards smile and come up to stand between the two men, and she turned and went into the house. Charles followed her and as they went inside, he said, "Well, they didn't actually kill each other that time for her—but it's not too late, is it?" There was no one in the parlor, and he suddenly stopped. Putting a hand on Molly's arm, he swung her around, and before she could think, he drew her close and kissed her firmly on the lips!

He released her at once, and she stood there gaping at him.

He laughed at her and said, "It won't kill you, one little kiss, Molly. And if those two fools had any sense, they'd be fighting over you instead of that little mouse!"

He had thought little of the kiss, but when he looked at her, he was taken aback by the flashing anger in her eyes. She was pale, but her voice was steady as she said, "Mr. Winslow, don't you *ever* do a thing like that again—not ever!"

And as she whirled and left the room, he took a deep breath, shocked to discover that her anger had shaken him!

CHAPTER THIRTEEN

"THE BEST OF THE WINSLOWS!"

★ ★ ★ ★

Charles went back to Boston, telling Adam before he left, "You can beat Dwight out, Adam. These preacher's daughters are pretty hotblooded! Grab her, kiss her soundly, and she'll wilt in your arms."

Adam had smiled, but had done no such thing. During the three months since Charles's visit, he had worn a path to Mary's door, but he usually found Timothy there, so the two of them spent most of the time trying to wait each other out. Neither of them referred to the wrestling match, but Mary did from time to time. She delighted in the contests, encouraging both of them, but seeming to favor neither.

Once her father came and sat with them, on one of the rare occasions when Timothy was not there. He had a sober look on his long face, and Adam's heart sank, for he was fully ready to hear Rev. Edwards tell him to leave his daughter alone. But that was not what was on the minister's mind.

"Adam, I'm afraid you've not been helped by your friendship with us."

"Sir?"

"We've become very unpopular in this place, as you've noticed."

"Why, there are some malcontents, Brother Edwards," Adam said quickly. "But they'll come around."

Edwards sighed, and he looked suddenly old and worn in the yellow candlelight. "I fear not. My stand on the new birth has alienated many of them."

"Not a single person has joined the church in three years!" Mary said indignantly. "They're jealous of Father's fame. All they want is someone to visit them. They don't understand that it's an honor that he gets calls to preach all over America!"

"I'm not a very good pastor, my dear," her father sighed. "I can't seem to make small talk." Then he smiled and said, "If we have to leave this place, Adam, you'll be one we'll miss the most."

"Leave? Why, it can't come to that!"

Edwards shook his head sadly. "It may, my boy. There is much dissatisfaction with me in the church."

"Father's been so worried," Mary said tearfully after her father left. "With ten children and a new baby, you can see why."

A proposal leaped to Adam's lips, but before he could speak, Mrs. Edwards came in with Elizabeth, the new addition, and the moment passed.

Adam stayed long hours at the forge, working on the rifle, but his temper grew short. It leaped out when people spoke harshly of Rev. Edwards, and when he offered to thrash the next man he heard speak critically of the pastor, everyone was careful to keep quiet about the matter when he was around.

His bad temper flared out at home. For the first time, he was short with the Stuarts, even with Molly. Seth had endured one of his rare outbursts, then said, "Weel, now, Mr. Winslow, I think you're yellin' at the wrong man. I dinna' think ye'll go too far wrong if ye look in the mirror. Ye'll see there whose t' blame for your troubles."

Adam had stared at him, then stomped off with his eyes smoldering.

Molly came in for her part of his wrath one Tuesday evening. A young farmer named Robert Wells had been stopping by the place quite often. His father owned a large tract of land, but it was mostly the son who operated it. He and Seth were good friends, and often they exchanged ideas, but lately he had come over several times in the evening and talked. The kitchen was the warmest room, so all of them sat around the table.

He was there when Adam came through the door with a glum look on his face. He'd had another failure with the breech mechanism, and his bad temper was obvious to everyone but Wells.

For several hours the young man sat there, talking some to Seth and speaking at times to Adam, who only grunted. He and Molly were reading some book that Adam had never heard of, and they grew animated, laughing at their wildly differing interpretations of some of the poems. Beth Stuart sat near the fire sewing, her face expressing pleasure in the visit.

Finally she and Seth went to their quarters; Adam expected Wells to go, but he did not, for he and Molly were sitting together on the bench, laughing at one of the poems. Time ran on, and Adam grew more irritable until finally he stood up and said, "Well, it's late. We'd all best get to bed."

Robert jumped to his feet, his face red with embarrassment. "Oh, I—I'd forgotten the time! Sorry, Mr. Winslow!"

Molly walked with him to the door, handing him his heavy coat, and saying, "It's been a wonderful evening, Robert. I hope you'll come again."

Wells gave a quick glance at Adam, who was shifting impatiently, and muttered, "Why—I'd like to! I'll be more careful of the time in the future, Mr. Winslow."

He left and Adam went over and latched the door. "I thought he'd never leave! Why can't he talk business with Seth at a decent hour?"

Molly wheeled to face him, her face rigid with anger. There was a tremble in her voice as she said, "He didn't come to see Seth—he came to see me!"

Adam stared at her stupidly. "You?"

"Yes, Mr. Winslow—me!" She was on the verge of tears, but her eyes were flashing as she stood facing him. "Is it completely incredible to you that a young man would want to come to see me?"

Adam stared at her, but he was still uncertain of what she

was saying. "Wells was here to *see* you? You mean *calling* on you?"

"Yes!"

Adam's anger flared out. "Well, he can't do it!"

"Why not?"

"You're too young, that's why not!"

"I'm as old as Mary Edwards!"

He floundered, trying to find an answer and, knowing he was making a fool out of himself, finally blurted out, "Well—I'm the master here, and *I* tell you he can't come hanging around you any more!"

"That's it! You're afraid of losing your bound girl! You're afraid Robert will pay off my indenture and you won't have a slave anymore!"

He grabbed her by the shoulders and shouted, "That's a lie, Molly Burns!"

His grip was so strong she winced, but she looked straight into his eyes. "You're hurting me—why don't you go ahead and beat me, Mr. Winslow? That's what people do with bound girls!"

He dropped his hands as if they had been burned, and for a long moment the air was charged with the violence of the scene that had exploded without warning. Then he said with an effort, "Molly, I never think of you like that—never!" Then, perhaps because he knew himself to have been unkind, he could say no more. Wheeling quickly, he left the room, leaving her standing there in the silence; as soon as he was gone, she gave a small cry, then collapsed at the table, her face in her hands, weeping as if her heart would break, crying, "Adam! Oh—Adam!"

The next day he was gone when she got up, and for three days she watched the road to no avail. She asked Seth, and his only reply was, "He took his gun and went on a hunt. May be a good thing for him, too."

When he did return, he came to her at once and said, "Molly, I'm sorry about Wells. See him as much as you want."

He stayed late at the forge every night for a week, and as she listened to the clanging of his hammer all day long, she felt cut off, but did not know how to mend the situation.

On Saturday morning, Adam and Seth were standing in

front of the house when a messenger came riding up on a lathered horse. "That's Henry Caldwell," Adam said to Seth. "He works for my cousin in Boston."

"Must be bad news to wear a horse out like that," Seth said dolefully.

Adam felt the same, and said quickly, "What's wrong, Henry?"

"Your father's taken bad, Mr. Adam. You'd best come at once."

Adam stared at him, then said, "You rest your horse, Henry. I'll leave at once." Then he called out, "Seth, saddle the bay for me!"

He ran into the house and met Molly, who asked, "What's wrong?"

"Father—he's dying, I think!"

"Oh, Adam!" She put her hand on his arm, and her lips trembled as she said, "Let me go with you!"

"No, it'll be too hard."

"I won't complain," she said quickly. "Please, Adam!"

He stared at her, then smiled briefly. "All right; we'll have to take the buggy. Get your things!"

She scurried off and fifteen minutes later Adam sent the team off at a hard gallop. "Me and Beth, we'll be praying for you!" Seth called out.

The horses played out halfway there, and Adam changed teams at a smalltown blacksmith shop. "Keep them 'til I get back with yours, but I don't know when that'll be," he told the owner.

They pulled into Boston a little after midnight, and Adam drove straight to the house, which was lit up. Several buggies were tied at the post, and Adam hurried up the steps.

He was met by Rachel, who looked almost dead herself. "You made good time, Adam," she said as she put her arms out. Adam held her close. She was nothing but skin and bones, but she clung to his neck with a fierce grip. She finally released him and reached out to embrace the girl. "Molly, I'm so glad you came! Miles has spoken of you so often these last days!"

"How is he, Rachel?" Adam asked.

She stared at him, her dark eyes sunk deep in the sockets.

"I think he's only holding on by a thread, Adam." She smiled as she added, "He always was a stubborn man, you know, and he told me yesterday, 'I won't go 'til I see my son—you can bet on it!' "

Charles came out of the parlor with his mother behind him, and said tersely, "Better go in, Adam. He could go any time—and he wants to see you."

Adam nodded but did not fail to notice the bitter look he received from Martha. He started down the hall, then turned and said, "Molly, come with me."

She nodded to Charles and followed Rachel and Adam down the wide hall and into the same room where she'd read to the dying man from Gilbert Winslow's journal. The room was dim, only one lamp burning on the table, and the sound of Miles' breathing was raspy and erratic.

Rachel walked to his side, bent over and said clearly, "Miles—Miles?"

He stirred, moving his head from side to side, then slowly his eyes opened. "Adam?"

"He's right here, Miles."

As she moved back, Adam stepped forward and saw the recognition in the old eyes. A smile touched the shrunken lips, and he whispered, "You cut it pretty fine, boy. I didn't know if I could wait . . . who's that with you?"

"It's me—Molly!"

He reached out and she took his hand. He held it tightly, then smiled, "We had quite some times, didn't we, Molly?"

"Yes, sir. I—I've never forgotten a word!" She leaned forward and kissed his hand.

Feeling her hot tears on his hand, he reached out and touched her head with his other and said, "You remember how my grandmother kept on believing?"

"I—I remember." She hoped he wouldn't say more, for he referred, she knew, to how Humility Cooper had believed for a husband named Winslow.

"You must always believe, Molly," he whispered. "You have a gift for that, you know!" Then he seemed to catch his breath and a look of pain raked across his face. "Adam?"

"Yes, sir?"

Miles released Molly's hand and took Adam's. The dying man's grip was surprisingly firm; he said, "Rachel?" and she moved to the other side of the bed to take his other hand. He lay there quietly, then said, "Rachel, you remember how all of you were in jail at Salem? All of you—Father and Mother and Grandfather?"

"I remember, Miles." Rachel leaned over and brushed her brother's long hair from his forehead. "You used to bring us food every day. And you and Robert would cheer us up. You never let us down."

Miles whispered, "I always felt bad that I wasn't in there with you. I would have been if I could."

"No, you kept us going. I remember Grandfather said once, 'We'd all be dead if it weren't for Miles.' "

"He said that? You never told me."

"He was always very proud of you—we all were."

Miles smiled then, and the tension left his drawn face. He held on to their hands and seemed to sleep. Finally his chest rose and he strained for breath.

"Miles!" Rachel cried, and stared at Adam. "He's going!"

But the eyes of the old man suddenly opened, and he said in a firmer tone than they'd heard: "Yes, I'm going—it's time!" He turned his face to Adam, and stared at him open-eyed. His chest heaved and he blinked, but then he opened his eyes and gasped, "Adam, my son! I have loved—have loved you greatly— these last years!"

"And I have loved you!" Adam said, tears flowing down his face.

"Have you? Have you? Then I am happy! For you—" he coughed and half rose in bed, and his grip tightened—"you are—the best of—our house!" he gasped. "The best of the Winslows. . . !"

He expelled his breath, closed his eyes, and then his head fell back. Adam lowered it to the pillow and stared at Rachel.

"He's gone, Adam," she whispered. She put her brother's hand to her cheek and whispered, "He's gathered to his fathers!"

The room was silent. Adam heard only the labored sound

of his own breathing and Molly's sobbing.

Then he looked at Rachel and said, "Aunt Rachel—I feel so alone!"

She nodded, her old face shrunken and tired. "He was so much of my world," she whispered as she placed his hand down carefully. "Somehow the world seems empty to me without him!" Then she said softly, "Goodbye, Miles. . . .I won't be long!"

They turned and left the room, but Adam paused for one last look. He heard again the words he did not himself believe: *You are the best of the Winslows!*

His lips formed the words, *I'll try to be!*, and then he left the room.

CHAPTER FOURTEEN

BROTHERLY LOVE

★ ★ ★ ★

"Weel, it's a fair pleasure, Wife, to get oot of the house and fight weeds." Seth Stuart straightened up, gazed down the row of beans he'd hoed, then glanced at the house. "It's my guess what we're adoin' to these blasted weeds is what Adam would love to do to young Mister Robert Wells!"

"You think they're tellin' him about getting married?" Beth gave a troubled glance at the house, then shook her head sorrowfully. "She told me last night that Robert had worn her patience down and she'd agreed just to make him hush."

"She don't love him?"

"Not a bit of it! But she's sure that Mary Edwards will be mistress of this house soon—and she'd marry any man rather than stay here under the same roof." She chopped viciously at a weed, missed, and cut a thick bean stalk down. "Oh, it'll be a good match, I suppose. And Adam Winslow's been enough to drive a saint crazy these last six months! Since his father died he's done nothing but run around in circles after that girl!"

"Weel, I guess he'll let Molly go—and sorry I am for it."

Inside the house Molly looked out the window to see Robert come riding down the road. He'd gotten off his horse with a bound, and there was a determination in his face that made her wish she had never agreed to marry him.

She turned to Adam and said, "Robert is coming."

He looked up at her, and the restraint that had built up between them was like a wall. He stared at her bleakly; then when the knock came, he moved across the room and opened the door.

"Mr. Winslow." Wells stepped inside, saw Molly standing there twisting her apron nervously. "I need to speak with you."

"Come in, then." Adam stepped back, and the young man went over to stand beside Molly.

"I'll not take much of your time." He nodded at the silent girl, and there was defiance in his voice as he said, "I suppose Molly's told you about us?"

"No."

The blank look in Adam's eyes and the single monosyllable offered no encouragement, so Wells said bluntly, "Well, I want to marry her. I'll pay whatever is owing on her paper, so that's no problem."

Adam did not speak, but turned his dark eyes on Molly. She met his gaze defiantly, but there was a tremor in her lips and a vulnerable expression in her eyes.

"Is this what you want, Molly?"

"I think it would be best."

"That's not what I asked." He wanted to beg her not to throw herself away on a man she didn't love, but he had no right to interfere. "Do you love him, Molly?" was all he could ask, and the words came hard. This girl was precious to him in a way that was somehow confusing. He could never quite think of her as a woman ready for a man, despite the full erect figure and the quick mind behind the calm blue-gray eyes. His mind carried a memory of a tiny frightened child, dirty and thin, that he'd held in his arms long ago. For years he'd protected her, loved her—so much that this beautiful woman who stood staring at him still evoked the sharp memory of that child.

She hesitated slightly before she spoke. "Robert and I have agreed, Mr. Winslow," she said evenly. "You know his reputation in this place. He's a good, hard-working man, and he's offered to make me his wife. I'm most grateful for your many kindnesses." Her voice trembled slightly, but she pressed her lips together and added. "I'm sure you'll be able to replace me without any trouble."

Adam's lips were dry, and he longed to find some way to deny their request, but there was nothing he could say except, "There'll be no money in this, Wells. I've never considered Molly in any other light than as a dear sister. I—I wish God's blessing on you and your marriage."

Molly's eyes burned and she said quickly, "Thank you."

Wells nodded, relief in his voice. "Thank you, Mr. Winslow! You may be sure I'll be very good to her!" He put his hand out to take Adam's.

Adam shook his hand, then said, "I suppose you two have plans. I have a lot of work, so you'll pardon me."

As Adam left the room, Robert turned quickly and put his arms around Molly, kissing her fervently. It was not the first time, of course, for he was passionately in love with her, but she was not responsive to his kiss, so he released her at once. He stepped back and asked quietly, "When will it be, Molly?"

"I'll—think on it, Robert." She mustered up a smile and said, "You get on now. Come back tonight and I'll have some of that apple tart you like so much."

The Stuarts had been watching the house furtively, and as Adam left, his back straight as a ramrod as he stalked to the shop, Seth said, "Adam's not happy." Then a few moments later when Robert Wells came out and rode off down the road, he added, "Aye, woman! It's likely things won't be too happy around here. Hate to see it come—it's been a bonny place up to now."

Stuart's words were prophetic, for from that time on there was an air of unhappiness in the Winslow House. Adam continued his single-minded pursuit of Mary Edwards, never coming to blows with Timothy Dwight, but both of them working at their courtship with desperate intensity.

Robert came almost every night, often to eat, and when Adam was there, he made every attempt to be a good host. He talked to the young man of farming, hunting, politics; everything, in fact, except what Wells wanted to talk about—his marriage to Molly Burns.

The weeks went by until finally Timothy Dwight came striding up to Adam, his cheerful face marked with strain. "Adam, I'm sick of all this business!" He groaned and shook his massive head. "I thought courtship was supposed to be *fun*—and it's making a wreck out of me!"

Adam smiled up at the big man. He had perversely grown more fond of Dwight during the tiring struggle for Mary's favor, and he knew the feeling was mutual. "Well, I guess sooner or later one of us will up and die, Timothy." He scowled then, and shook his head. "I agree with you, though. You got any ideas?"

"Well, not a wrestling match!" They exchanged grins remembering the last match. "But I've had enough, Adam!" Dwight's face grew serious. "I'm going to tell Mary tonight I want to marry her. I think you ought to do the same thing. Then we can both stand back, and the whole thing's in her lap."

Adam stared at him. "I think you've got a good idea, Timothy," he replied, smiling. "You know what I've been thinking? I've thought that if there'd been only *one* of us—and I mean *either one*—Mary would have been married by now. What time are you going over?"

"Thought I'd drop over early, maybe about six."

"I'll be there at eight."

They suddenly grinned and shook hands. "One way or the other, Adam, one of us is going to get hurt—but if Mary chooses you, I'll not be able to hate you like I would nearly any other man!"

"Same here, Timothy."

They parted, and at eight o'clock Adam seated himself in the large parlor of the Edwards' house. Mary started to speak brightly of a quilting party she'd been to that afternoon, and Adam asked bluntly, "Dwight came over earlier, did he?"

"Why—yes, as a matter of fact. . . !"

"He have anything important to say, Mary?"

Her face flushed, and for one of the few times he'd known her, she was confused. She started to speak; then her lips trembled and she stumbled as she said, "Well—Adam—he said that. . ."

Adam smiled at her and nodded. "Yes, well, I've come to

say the same thing he did. I love you, Mary. I want to marry you, but I can't keep up this game we've been playing anymore."

"Game?"

He was suddenly impatient with her, and reaching out, he pulled her close and kissed her firmly. She tried to resist, but he ignored her struggles. Finally, he released her and said, "Me or Timothy, Mary. You can't marry *both* of us!"

Wide-eyed, she looked at him, breathing hard. His kiss had stirred her, and she whispered, "Why, Adam, you're angry!"

"A little bit, Mary," he confessed. Then he took her hand and said quietly, his eyes warm as he looked at her. "Mary, I know a young girl has to have a time of courting. But it's gone too far! Why, the whole country's laughing at me and Timothy, and your parents are embarrassed. It's hurt me to see them having to endure this farce."

She sat there and tears welled up in her eyes. She was a girl of deep feelings, although she seldom let them show. She was so bright and full of fun that things came easily to her, and now these two strong men who wanted her had offered themselves honestly. "I know I've been frivolous, Adam, with you and Timothy. I love you both, of course. But Timothy said the same thing—the time's past for this."

"He's a fine man, Mary—none finer!" Adam stood up suddenly, saying, "I love you, Mary, but you'll have to choose."

She stood up, and there was no foolishness in her as she looked at him. Reaching up to place her hands on his broad shoulders, she whispered, "I—I know I don't deserve to have two men love me, not men like you and Timothy." Her eyes filled with tears, a rare thing for this girl!—and she said, "There'll be one happy person come out of this thing, Adam."

"Just one?"

"Yes, because no matter which one of you I marry, I'll grieve for the other!"

Timothy and Adam proposed in early June, but as July and August went by, Mary said nothing definite. Both Timothy and Adam shrugged and stayed away from her to a great extent, knowing that sooner or later she would make a choice. Both of them yearned for it, yet dreaded it.

Molly and Robert went on much as before, though at times he grew impatient with her. She refused to name a date, and once when he pressed her, she looked at him and said calmly, "Would you rather we called it off, Robert?" Her readiness frightened him, so he fought down his impatience and said no more about it.

A letter from Saul came in September, so confusing that Adam could not make head nor tail of it. It was an involved matter of business that required Adam's signature, and since Rachel had agreed to the deal, he signed it and mailed it back.

Scarcely a week later, Molly came to the forge to get him. "Charles is here."

"Charles?" Adam stared at her, and saw something in her face. "What's wrong, Molly?"

She hesitated, then tears filled her eyes. "It's—Rachel."

He put down the hammer he was holding on the anvil, then looked at her. "Is she dead?"

"Yes!" Then her face broke and tears flowed down her cheeks. She turned from him, bringing out a handkerchief and trying to stem the flow.

He stood there, tense, feeling as if life had been drained from him. A great emptiness filled his heart. Unable to believe what he was hearing, he finally murmered, "She was very good to me. Never gave me anything but love." He pulled off his apron and stated calmly, "We'll have to go right away for the funeral."

"She's—already buried, Adam."

He stared at her, then said, "I'll talk to Charles."

He found his brother in the parlor, and went straight up to him with a blunt question, "Why didn't you come and get me for the funeral?"

Charles looked startled. He was weary, and it was the first time Adam had ever spoken to him with such obvious displeasure. He licked his lips, then said in a conciliatory voice, "Adam, there wasn't time!"

"It's not that far to Boston!"

"No, but she died of some sort of plague," Charles said

quickly. "Nobody knows exactly what it is, but it's all over the city. There's a new law—bodies have to be buried within twenty-four hours."

Adam relaxed, and he shook his head. "Sorry to be so sharp, Charles—but she meant a lot to me."

"Yes, I know. I wanted to come, but there was just no way."

"Did she suffer much?"

"No, thank God! She was taken on Monday and the terrible thing works so fast that by Wednesday it was over." He put his hand on Adam's shoulder. "Her last words—she spoke of you."

"Of me?"

"I was with her. She'd been unconscious, but before that she'd said goodbye to everyone—Saul, and Esther and me. Then she woke up and she said, 'Tell Adam that Miles was right!' "

You're the best of the Winslows. That was what she was saying, and she'd managed to pass it along without offending her family.

Adam blinked, then said, "I'll miss her, Charles."

"Yes. You were always her favorite."

They stood there in the grip of that paralyzing helplessness that comes with death—struggling to say that which can never be said, to express that which can never be framed in words. Charles sensed that Adam did not want to talk about Rachel, so he excused himself as soon as he could.

All afternoon Adam walked through the woods, seeing little, but going over and over old memories. He startled a mule deer and watched as it went sailing smoothly over logs in a motion that was as much like flight as any animal ever achieves, but this time the movement did not provoke the admiration it usually did. He could almost hear Rachel's voice telling the tales of Matthew Winslow, of his fight to the death with an Indian to save her life. She had not been a dramatic woman in her Christian life, but as he looked back, he realized that her iron-ribbed convictions to her God were part of what he had loved. She had never wavered, and now he thought of all the times she'd spoken so confidently of this very time—for her belief that she would see Gilbert and Lydia and Matthew again was unshakable.

It made his own intellectual acceptance of faith look scanty and foolish, and he wondered how she and others had come to such belief. Finally, he looked up, overtaken by dark, and made his way back to the house.

Molly met him at the door, and he tried to eat, but could only nibble at his food. Charles sat there, watching him furtively, but said little. Finally they went to bed, but Adam lay there most of the night thinking of his aunt.

The next morning Charles said, "I have to talk to you, Adam." He hesitated, and there was a lack of assurance in him that puzzled Adam. "I know it's a bad time. . ."

"It's all right." Adam got up and led the way to the parlor. He stood beside the window, but Charles paced back and forth, his face strained and his voice higher than usual.

"Adam, it's an awful time to come to you with this, but there's no way it can be put off!"

"What's the matter, Charles? Bad news?"

"No!" Charles paused abruptly, and said the word so quickly that Adam at once knew he was not honest. "Well, Adam, to tell the truth, *you* may think so, but somehow I've got to show you it isn't."

Adam stared at him curiously. "Why don't you just tell me what it is and let me decide if it's bad or not."

Charles paused, bit his lip, then shrugged and said uneasily, "I wish Saul were here, Adam! This thing is so complicated that I'm not sure I understand it myself. And I wish that we'd got it all settled before Rachel died! You'd have believed her!"

"And I'm not going to believe you?"

"I'm hoping you will, Adam! I really am!" The tall man began pacing again, and said, "I wish we'd been closer, you and I. Oh, it's my fault, I suppose—or maybe it was inevitable, with Mother feeling like she does." He halted abruptly and rushed on hurriedly, "I—I didn't mean that like it sounded, Adam!"

"I've never been Martha's favorite, Charles," Adam said. "That's no secret. Look, what's the matter? Something gone wrong with the business? Come on, let's have it!"

"All right, here it is. . ." Charles stated, a bead of perspiration rising on his upper lip. Then he said in a rush: "Adam, the whole picture has changed—everything! The fur trade has picked up so much in the last year that Saul and I *had* to increase that side of the business. And that meant that we had to have money, so we shifted as many of the assets as we could to get the cash."

Adam said doubtfully, "But that's pretty risky, isn't it? I mean, what if the French invade the Ohio Valley? Where does that leave us?"

"England will never let that happen, Adam. Look at the map, and what do you see? We're pinned in here along the coast right up against the Appalachian Mountains. The whole continent lies over those mountains, and if you think King George is going to let the French have it, you're just not thinking!"

"Well, we haven't done much so far," Adam argued. "We've had two wars over that territory, and there's another around the corner."

"And we'll win this time!" Charles' face gleamed with excitement. "France may keep Canada, but never in a million years will the Crown let this New World go! Not if she has to fight a full-scale war for it! And if that comes, whoever owns that land in the Ohio Valley will control the country!"

"I don't know politics, Charles," Adam shrugged.

"You've got to see it, Adam! A whole new world over those mountains, and it's ours for the taking!"

Adam grinned at him and remarked, "You're trying hard to sell me, Charles. You must want something from me pretty bad. Well, you're going to *have* to tell me sooner or later what it is."

"Adam," Charles stated quietly, "it took all of it. That's what it cost to get in on this thing."

Adam looked at him, doubt in his eyes. "All of what?"

Charles took a deep breath, then answered quietly, "I mean we had to liquidate everything; Adam—we had to sell this place, too."

"This place?" Adam stared at him. "You can't sell this place, Charles. It's part of the general estate. We'd all have to agree and sign."

"You *did* sign, Adam."

Then it finally dawned on Adam, and he said slowly, but with a growing rage beginning to swell up in his chest, "Those papers you brought last time you were here, and that letter from Saul? That was what I signed?"

Charles saw for the first time the dangerous light in his brother's dark eyes, and said hastily, "It—it all happened so *fast*, Adam! Why, we had no idea at the time that we'd ever sell this place—or anything else—but when the thing came up, we had no choice!"

"Rachel knew about this?"

"Y-yes."

"You're a liar, Charles," Adam stated with a deceptive calm. "You lied to her, too, didn't you? You and Saul arranged this, and you knew we wouldn't be in favor of it. So you lied and got our names by fraud."

"I tell you, Adam, there wasn't time—!"

"How long does it take to get here from Boston, two days? And was Aunt Rachel all that far away? You're lying again, Charles!"

The easy assurance of Charles Winslow had fled, and he wished with all his heart that Saul had come, or that they'd put the thing in a letter as he'd suggested. But Saul had said, "You'll have to face him sooner or later, Charles. Might as well meet him head-on with it."

Now staring at Adam's face, Charles tried vainly to make the thing look better, but the more he talked the worse it sounded even to him.

Finally Adam said, "I want an answer from you right now—and don't beat around the bush. Father left his property equally divided between the two of us. What do I have and what do you have?"

"Why, it's not that simple, Adam!"

"Nothing is ever simple to a crook, Charles! You sold this place that I've poured my life into—what do I have to show for it?"

"Don't worry, Adam," Charles said swiftly. "We got a good price, and you've got one of the finest tracts of land in Virginia."

Adam stared at him. "A plantation?"

"N-no, not exactly!"

"It's just a patch of wilderness land, isn't it? That's what you've sold this place for?"

Charles said, "Well, it's wild land, but—!"

Then with a cat-like spring, Adam was on him! He caught his brother by the throat, and though Charles was much taller and a strong man, the iron hands of Adam Winslow held him as though he were a child.

"You're a thief!" Adam roared, his dark face contorted with rage. He ignored the gurgling sounds that emerged from Charles's throat, and his voice rose as he shouted, "Liar! I trusted you! And you stole this place. . . !"

Charles's tongue was protruding, his face a dark crimson. His hand beat ineffectually at his brother, but the room was exploding into flakes of light.

Adam was cursing him, blinded by rage, and then he heard a voice scream, "Adam! Let him go!" He felt small hands beating on his back and pulling at his hands, and he suddenly saw Molly standing there crying.

He loosed his grip, and Charles slumped to the floor, his oxygen-starved lungs gulping in air in great swallows.

"What is it, Adam?" Molly asked. When he didn't answer, she took his arm and moved in front of him so she could see his face. "What's he done?"

Adam took a deep breath and forced himself to relax. He looked down at his brother, who was slowly pulling himself up. Reaching down, he plucked him off the floor, stood him up, and said quietly, "He's robbed me of my inheritance, Molly." Then his lips twisted in a parody of a smile and he added, "Brotherly love, he'd call it."

"No!" Charles gasped. He put out a hand to touch Adam, and he tried to explain. "It's still yours, Adam! More than ever!"

Adam stared at him, and Charles saw a door close inside his brother. "I'll never believe you again," he said quietly, then he turned and walked from the room.

"Molly! You've got to talk to him!" Charles groaned. "He's gone crazy!"

"Did you take this place from him?" she asked abruptly, and he found it as difficult to face her as it had been to look at his brother.

"Molly—Molly, it was a matter of business! We did it for his good as much as ours. Adam needed us! He hasn't got the head for this sort of thing!"

Molly stared at him, contempt in her eyes. "No, he's not as smart as you are, Charles. He's so simple-minded he believed in you, trusted you. I heard you tell him once, 'You've got to learn to look out for yourself, Adam!' Well, he didn't listen to you, did he, Charles? He didn't look out for himself—so his own family destroys him!"

"It's not *like* that!" he tried to reason. Taking his handkerchief out of his pocket, he wiped his face using the time to regain his composure. Finally he calmed down. "Molly, this place is gone, but nobody has *stolen* it from Adam! I—I see now that we should have come to him, but there's nothing to be done about that now. But he can have *ten* places like this in Virginia!"

She looked up at him and studied his face. Finally she said, "Are you telling me the truth, Charles? With you I can't tell."

"I know I'm no good," he said quietly, then smiled at the look on her face. "You think *I* don't know that, Molly? Adam, he's the one who's like Gilbert and Edward and Father!" A look of pain touched his light blue eyes, and he whispered softly, "I've wished a thousand times that I didn't just *look* like a Winslow—but that I *acted* like one!"

Molly felt a sudden touch of pity for this tall, strong man, for she had not seen this side of him. "I—I believe you, Charles—and maybe you're not as bad as you think."

He straightened his shoulders, smiled wryly, then said, "Let us pray that I am not—but in any case, as much as Adam hates us—and as much wrong as we've done him—he's got a great opportunity. He was made for Virginia, Molly! And you've got to see he doesn't let his hatred for Saul and me let him miss out on it!"

Molly looked away from him, thinking of Adam; then she sighed and replied, "I'll not be a help, Charles. He's going to marry Mary Edwards."

The thin veneer of sophistication that covered the cynicism in Charles suddenly slipped, and he stated with a grin, "Not likely she'll marry a man who has no big farm here. She'll go for that other fellow!"

Molly thought about Mary, and Adam's pursuit. "No," she returned, shaking her head, "I don't think so—but I'll certainly pray in that direction!"

"Well, I trust your prayers work. But just in case they don't, here's what we've planned."

For the next hour Molly listened as Charles explained to her how it was going to be.

CHAPTER FIFTEEN

"AND THE WALLS CAME TUMBLING DOWN!"

★ ★ ★ ★

The mood of New Englanders is delicately hinged to the weather; nowhere else is winter so trying, the mud season so endless, spring so giddy, summer so brief, fall so glorious. Tuned to the caprices of weather, New Englanders' moods swing as the climate does. Perhaps that was why Jonathan Edwards was hounded by the Northampton church in 1750.

The whole year had been one of spooky extremes. The winter was unusually severe. Mill River had frozen over by early October. The town was smothered by six feet of snow that lingered monotonously for months. The gray weeks dragged out, chill rains slanted over stubble fields, maples gauntly swayed in the harsh winds.

To make matters worse, Edwards grated on his people in a campaign against taverns—an old struggle that he fanned into new fury. He intimidated people, quite unintentionally, with his intelligence. He tried to be less awesome, but it was difficult.

The antagonism against him increased, and finally two hundred parish members signed a petition for his dismissal. The council was dominated by a man named Joseph Hawley, who read a diatribe against the pastor, and the council voted 8 to 7 to dismiss Jonathan Edwards.

Adam Winslow had scoffed all along at the idea that his friend would be voted out, and when he got the bad news it was coupled with a second blow.

He heard of it early in the morning, and late that afternoon he rode over to the Edwards' and went directly to the pastor.

Edwards was calm, his face was pale, but it was obvious to Adam that the man was deeply hurt. He listened quietly as Adam raged against those who had raised their hands against him; then when the storm ceased, Edwards said mildly, "It's not the end of the world, Adam."

"But—what will you do?"

A smile broke across Edwards' face, and he said with a look of wonder on his face, "Judge Dwight has offered to share half his income with me—if I will start a new work with those who did not agree with the decision to release me."

"Good!"

"No, it would be divisive. It wouldn't do at all."

"Then what? Where will you go?"

"I'm not sure. God is not finished with me, I'm sure. I may become a teacher at a college. Write some books, perhaps."

He was so calm that Adam marveled, but he was still angry enough to say, "I despise those cowards who fought against you!"

"You mustn't say that, Adam! Jesus said, 'If you have aught against any, the Father will not forgive you.' "

Adam said no more to Edwards, but as he left, Mary was waiting for him. She took him off to the small parlor, and he told her of his anger. He did not notice that she was saying nothing, nor did he see that she was nervously twisting her handkerchief into a rag.

Finally he ran down, and started to rise, saying, "Well, it will come out all right somehow."

"Adam. . . !"

There was such a strain in her face that he sat back down, thinking that she wanted to talk more about her family's disaster. She sat there, looking very small in the large chair. Finally she bit her lip and said, "Adam—I've got something to tell you."

He stared at her, noting that she looked more miserable than he'd ever seen her. Suddenly he knew.

"It's Timothy, isn't it, Mary? You wouldn't look so miserable if I were the one."

"Oh, Adam!" she cried out, throwing herself at him and clinging to him as she had done when she was ten years old. Sobs racked her body, until finally she had no more tears. Drawing back she mopped at her eyes, then said pitifully, "How could I do this to you? I've loved you all my life!"

Adam felt nothing, but he knew the pain and loneliness would come later. He was not in the least angry, and discovered to his surprise that he had known all along it would be this way. He patted her shoulder, saying, "You must never grieve about this, Mary. It wouldn't be fair to Timothy."

That set her off again, but he said firmly, "Come now, I want to see you smile. I may have lost a wife, but I've still got a friend, haven't I?"

She could not stop crying, so he left. He was so much in shock that he got a mile down the road before he realized that he'd forgotten his horse. Going back, he mounted and went straight to Judge Dwight's house. There was a determination to finish the matter as much as possible, so he was glad to find Timothy at home.

There was a look of alarm on the big man's face as he opened the door, but Adam said, "I haven't got a gun, Timothy. I just came to wish you well."

Dwight stood there, his vast body filling the room, a sad look on his good-natured face. He looked at Adam, and a heaviness filled his voice as he said, "I wish it hadn't come to this, Adam."

Adam mustered up a grin, and put his hand out. It was swallowed by Dwight's huge fist. "You're the one for her, Timothy. I just told her I couldn't afford to lose a friend like her—and that goes for you, too. All right?"

"Adam—I guess you know. . ." He tried to put his feelings in words, and finally said, "Looks like the world is breaking up for you. I know you're taking it hard about losing your place—

and it hurts about Brother Edwards—and now this."

"It's been a bad month, Timothy," Adam agreed. "Guess I feel like the folks inside Jericho when the walls started falling down."

Timothy Dwight stared at him, started to say something, then seemed to change his mind. "I started to give you some good advice, maybe quote some scripture. But that's apt to get on a man's nerves, ain't it, Adam? Never could stand to hear somebody preaching at me about trusting God when *I* was hurtin' and *he* wasn't!"

Adam grinned, and turned to go. "Got to get back. All the best to you and Mary."

"Wait," Timothy said quickly. "You got to move off your place? Where you goin'? You can get a place close around here, Adam. Everybody knows what a good man you are."

"They know Seth Stuart has made that place a farm," Adam shrugged. "I'm just a blacksmith."

"But what you going to do? Where you goin', Adam?"

Adam considered the question, then looked up at Dwight and said directly, "Why, I'm going to get drunk, Timothy."

He wheeled and left, and Timothy Dwight sighed and said under his breath, "Well, under the circumstances, I'd say that's not a bad idea, Adam!"

Adam had not been serious about drinking. He had just used it as an excuse to get away from Dwight. He rode back home, and for the next two days he kept to himself.

On Wednesday the final straw came. A man drove up to the front yard, talked to Molly, then came to find Adam at the shop. "Hello," he said as he entered. He held out his hand, a big man with buck teeth and a shock of black hair that fell over this eyes. "Name's Royal Taylor. You're Winslow?"

Adam took the man's hand, nodded, then asked, "You're the new owner?"

"Sure am. Just stopped by to see what your thinkin' is on this thing."

"My thinking?"

"Why, yes." Taylor seemed surprised. "Didn't your cousin tell you what I said?"

"No. I haven't talked to him."

"Well, I been talkin' around, did some before I bought the place and some after. Winslow, everybody I talked to said what a good thing you made of this place." Taylor took off his hat and pushed his hair back. "I got to have me a man, see? I won't be here much, and I told your cousin to ask you to think on it."

"Stay on here?"

"Sure! Why not? I ain't a hard man to get along with. I reckon we can agree on the money."

Adam leaned against the forge, his face still, while Taylor waited. Finally Adam shook his head. "I'm grateful for your offer, Mr. Taylor, but I'll be moving on."

Taylor did not protest. He stared at the young man, then said, "Sorry to hear it. Been sort of countin' on it."

"You don't need me," Adam said quickly. "Seth Stuart is the one you've got to have, Mr. Taylor. I do the forge work, but Seth—he's the farmer. You ask around, then talk to him. Folks around here will tell you he's a good man."

"Sure," Taylor nodded. "I already heard that. Guess I'll talk to him." He put out his hand and said, "You stay around here long as you like, Winslow, you hear?"

"Mighty nice of you—but I'll be moving on soon. You'll find Stuart in the east pasture, I think."

All that day Adam walked around the farm, avoiding Stuart, who was taking the new owner on a tour. He had several jobs started on the forge, but knew that he'd never finish any of them. All day he roamed, and every foot of the farm brought some sort of memory: here he had to pull the ox out of the mud hole; there was the thicket where he'd shot a panther eating the carcass of the colt; there was the deep hole in the creek where he'd caught his big catfish.

It was long after dark when he returned, and the lamp was still burning in the kitchen. He looked around, then went to the cabinet and pulled out the jug of whiskey. Everybody kept whiskey; even preachers sometimes took their pay in it. He sat down, poured a generous amount into a cup, and stared off into space.

He thought about his father, then drained the cup. Filling it to the brim, he thought about Rachel, then drained it again. He was not a drinking man, and the powerful liquor went to his head. He sat there thinking of his life, and somehow it didn't add up. He'd come to nothing.

How long he sat there, he could not have said, but the jug was half drained and his head was swimming when he heard a voice say, "Adam?"

It was a hard job just lifting his head, and he had to blink his eyes and strain to see clearly. "Molly—zat you, Molly?"

He concentrated on focusing his eyes, and when he saw her face, he blinked and said, "Late—you'sh be in bed." He knew that his tongue was thick, so he pronounced every syllable carefully, the way a drunk will do. "I—am—having myself—a—party." He was proud of having said the words right, and grinned at her.

"Yes, I see you are." She sat down across the table and put her chin in her hands.

"Wouldja lika drink?" he asked, peering at her owlishly.

"No, thank you."

"Everybody—Molly—gotta' believe—in something, right?"

"That's right, Adam."

He peered at her, then said solemnly, "Right—I believe—I'll have a drink!"

She said quietly, "Maybe you've had enough."

He considered her words thoughtfully, then said, "No, I doan think—so."

She watched him try to pour, but he missed the cup. The clear liquor ran onto the table then to the floor. He sat there staring at it, and she got up and mopped it up with a cloth from a rack.

She came to his side of the table and asked, "Mary chose Timothy, didn't she, Adam?"

Adam slammed the jug on the table and asked pugnaciously, "Well—why not! He's—good man! Make—her good—husband."

The room was whirling and he suddenly felt very sick. He got up to head for the door, but the room reeled, and he fell headlong to the floor. The jug broke as it fell, and as he started to throw up, he was aware that someone was holding his head, trying to help him.

When he opened his eyes, he knew that he'd been asleep. A shaft of sunlight hit him a blow that made his head pound. His mouth was dry as dust, and he had the most terrible taste in his mouth he could remember. He was still on the floor, but a blanket was over him, and somehow a pillow was under his head. He threw the cover back, sat up, and almost cried out, so great was the pain that struck him in the back of his head.

"You might want to wash up and change clothes."

He squinted up, and there was Molly looking down at him. He got to his feet, holding on to the wall, and then he ducked his head and went to the porch. He stripped off his stained shirt, washed in the basin, then put on the clean shirt she hung on the peg beside the washstand.

He walked slowly back into the kitchen and she had a cup of cold tea poured for him. He took it, stared at her, then drank it down. It felt good in his parched mouth, but made his stomach roll.

"You'll feel better after awhile."

He stared at her, then tried to smile. "That's good. I'd hate to think I'd feel this bad the rest of my life."

"You'd better try to eat something."

He shuddered at the thought, but when she fixed him a soft boiled egg, he ate it and to his surprise felt better.

"Sorry to be so much trouble."

"You had it coming," she said. "Most men would have been drunk long before this."

"I hate drunks," he said quietly.

"You're not a drunk," she insisted. "You *got* drunk, but you're not a drunk."

He sipped at the cold tea and said, "Mary's going to marry Timothy."

"I know. You told me."

"I did?" He tried to remember, but couldn't. Then he said, "I'm leaving, Molly. But you can stay here."

"I'm leaving, too."

He stared at her. "You can't leave! Your time's not up."

"You going to have me put in jail?"

"Of course not!" He looked at her, and his head hurt. "Where you going?"

"I don't know—where are *you* going?" she shot back, then smiled at his confused look. "I want to talk to you, Adam—about Charles."

"I don't want to hear it!"

"Will you get that mulish expression off your face?" she said sharply. "You're acting like a child!"

He shuffled his feet, and looked into her eyes. "What do you know about all this?"

"I know a lot more than *you* do, Adam Winslow," she said pertly. "You were so set on feeling sorry for yourself that you went off pouting. Well, I want to tell you what you'd have heard if you'd been sensible enough to listen to Charles."

"He's a crook—and so is Saul!"

"I guess they come close, but now that you've finally come to see that, you can take care of yourself."

He stared at her, then stated humbly, "You knew it all along—so did Aunt Rachel. I was just too dumb to see it!"

"Not *dumb!*" Molly said sharply. "You—are—not—dumb! Can't you accept that? You *trusted* your family, and that's not dumb. But it would be if you didn't keep your eyes open from now on."

He sat there admiring her. She was wearing an old robe he'd seen a thousand times, but there was a light in her clear eyes and he could not bear the thought of not seeing her. "All right. Tell me what Charles said."

"Charles said there's a man named Tom Cresap, an old man that all the Indians trust in the Ohio Valley. He came to some of the richest men in Virginia and said he'd get the Indians to trade with them and nobody else—so ten of them formed the Ohio Company of Virginia. One of them is a man called John Hanbury, a rich London merchant who markets the furs, and he's a good friend of the King!"

"How do we fit into all this?" Adam asked.

"Why, Charles has been making friends in Virginia, and some of them are in the company—there's Lawrence and Austin

Washington and George Fairfax, the richest man in Virginia. Anyway, they petitioned the King for 200,000 acres of land on the south bank of the Ohio and they offered to build a fort at their own expense. They had to agree to settle at least 100 families on that land within seven years, and then they'd get another 300,000 acres."

"That's 500,000 acres of land!" Adam exclaimed.

"And some of it will be yours," Molly said. "Saul and Charles used the money from this place—and their own money—to get into the company. So you've really sold this place to become part owner of the Ohio Company of Virginia."

He sat there, trying to take it all in. He had determined never to believe Charles again, but everyone knew the Washingtons and Thomas Fairfax. Those men would not be involved in a crooked deal.

"You've got to go to Virginia, Adam," Molly prodded him.

"Me? Go to Virginia?"

"It's your kind of place—a man's world, Adam," she stated firmly, a wistful smile on her lips. "You can't stay here—this world is lost. This place, and—and Mary." She faltered at that, but he did not flinch. "You've got to go!"

As Adam sat there considering the possibilities, the thing grew on him. Northampton was gone, as Molly insisted. A new world—a big new world, with big challenges awaited him. He could not think of a single reason why he should not go.

Then he looked at her and said, "I can't go and leave you here. When will you marry Wells?"

"Not ever."

He stared at her stupidly, then shook his head. "I don't understand you, Molly."

"I told Robert yesterday I wasn't going to marry him." She smiled and added, "He wasn't too surprised. It's been wrong from the beginning—and he was starting to see that."

His mouth was open, and he stared at her, then laughed. "I can't keep up with you, Molly Burns!" Then he asked, "What are you going to do?"

"I'm still bound to you, Adam," she said quietly.

"You'd come with me—to Virginia?"

She nodded and a smile touched her lips. "I think you have to take me. You can't just run off and leave a bound girl behind." She knew it irked him to hear her speak of the indenture.

But this time Adam held his hand out, and she looked up at him questioningly, then placed hers in his.

"It'll be beautiful in Virginia in the spring, won't it, Molly?"

She suddenly felt her eyes burn, and her hand trembled in his, but she smiled up at him.

"Oh, yes, Adam! I know it will!"

VIRGINIA

★ ★ ★ ★

1751–1755

CHAPTER SIXTEEN

A BALL AT MOUNT VERNON

★ ★ ★ ★

After four years in the backwoods of Virginia, Philadelphia looked huge to Molly. She smiled at Adam's excitement as he pointed out buildings he remembered; then she thought of the letter in her pocket. "Adam, can we post this letter to Mother?"

"Sure—let me have it."

As he took it and stopped the team long enough to run into a small office, she thought over what she had said to her mother:

14 March, 1754

Dear Mother,

I know I have not written as I should, especially since you have been in poor health. Please forgive me! It is impossible to tell you how life is here—how it has been for the last three years since we left New England and came to Virginia. As I told you when last I wrote, Mr. Winslow has prospered in his trade of making guns. He has a small shop in a small village, and one helper, who with his wife lives with us.

I am well, very well. Virginia is very different from England. It is rather wild, with large tracts of woods like nothing in England. Our lives have been very simple. We work, we go to church, we visit neighbors.

One problem occurred some time back. Some of the women in the village said it was wrong for a woman full grown—can you believe that I am grown up, Mother?—to live with an unmarried man. But the pastor of the local church, Rev. Terry, is very understanding. He shut the gossips down by pointing out that Mr. and Mrs. Tanner live in the house and are adequate protectors. He is very fond of Mr. Winslow.

I must close, for we leave in the morning for Philadelphia—the longest journey I've made since we moved here three years ago.

I suppose you remember me as a little girl—and I still remember you with love. You asked in your last letter if I would marry—and you hinted at the possibility of marrying Mr. Winslow. My time of indenture will be up soon, and I will marry, I suppose. But Mr. Winslow gave his heart to another young woman, and when it did not work out, I think he resigned himself to remaining single.

I enclose a small gift. Use it for yourself and for the children.

Your loving daughter,
Molly Burns

She sat with thoughts of sadness over how her mother had endured such hardness. It had been easier after Tom Burns had died, and Molly had been generous with her—for Adam insisted on helping. But London seemed far away, and she thought of her mother and brothers and sisters like characters in a book she had read rather than as real people.

Adam came back soon, mounted the wagon, and they continued down the busy street.

"Look, Molly!" There was excitement in his eyes as he pulled the team to a halt in front of a plain white building, and he pointed up to a sign that read: BENJAMIN FRANKLIN, PRINTER. "He's still here."

"Do you think he'll remember you, Adam?" Molly asked.

"Why, I don't reckon so. That was—let's see, this is 1754 and I was only thirteen, so that'd be—why, it's been fourteen years ago!" He shook his head, then got out and helped her down. "No, Mr. Franklin's now a famous man; I don't think he'd remember me."

He led her into the shop and was surprised to see that very little was changed. He had remembered it as being much larger, and now there were at least five men working a series of presses that lined the walls instead of the single one that had stood in the middle of the floor.

"Help you?" a tall man asked, leaving his press to come and stand before them.

"Is Mr. Franklin in?" Adam asked.

"Yes, but somebody's with him. He ought to be able to see you before too long."

"We'll wait."

The tall man eyed the long rifle case that Adam carried easily under his arm, and said, "Don't guess that thing's loaded?"

"No."

Reassured, the printer went back to his press, and the pair stood there watching the work for ten minutes. The door to the inner office swung open and two men walked out talking. Adam recognized Franklin at once, for the man was little changed. Indeed, except for a larger girth and a hairline that had crept upward, the famous man looked almost the same as he had at their last meeting.

He stopped abruptly, took a look at the pair, and there was a puzzled look in his small brown eyes. He stepped forward saying, "I know you, sir—but the name is gone."

"Why, I'm surprised you remember me, Mr. Franklin. It's been a long time ago—fourteen years. I'm Adam Winslow, and you printed a book for my father—"

"Of course!" Franklin slapped his high forehead with his palm, and a smile spread over his round face. "The journal of Gilbert Winslow, your great-grandfather—why, it's one of the finest pieces of work ever put out in my shop! And your father, how is he?"

"Gone, Mr. Franklin. He died five years ago."

"Ah, well, I'm sorry, my boy!" Franklin shook his head, and put his hand out impulsively.

"I think he got as much comfort out of your book as anything," Adam said. "He was very proud of it."

"Well, now, I'm very happy—very happy!" Franklin nodded his head and there was a smile on his thin lips. "So much of the work I do is ephemeral—much of it not worth a great deal, you know. But *Winslow's Journal* was the first book I was really proud of—and still am! Not only a first-class piece of printing, but the subject matter—oh, my word!"

"May I meet your friend, Benjamin?" Franklin's companion, spoke up suddenly. The moon-faced man dressed in buff broadcloth declared, "I always said that was the best thing you ever put out of this shop. I've read it many times."

"Why, that's so! This is Adam Winslow—great-grandson of Gilbert Winslow. This is Mr. Paul Revere."

"Gilbert was my great-grandfather," Adam said, shaking the hand Revere offered.

"And you have another beautiful young lady with you, I see," Franklin said. He smiled at Molly and added, "The last time, I recall, your lovely sister was with you."

"This is Miss Molly Burns—Mr. Franklin and Mr. Revere," Adam returned. He was always a little awkward introducing Molly, so he said quickly, "I remember we went to hear Mr. Whitefield."

Franklin was admiring Molly with a steady glance, but he looked back at Adam and smiled broadly. "Why, so we did! Twice, if I remember correctly."

Revere seemed amused by the reference. "People can't really understand your fascination with that preacher, Ben. Every time he comes to America, he practically lives with you. You sure he's not made a convert out of you?"

Franklin sighed regretfully. "Unfortunately, not, Paul. I'm still just a seeker after the Lord. But—there is *something* about that man—there really is!" He shrugged and changed the subject quickly. "Well, Mr. Winslow, can I help you in any way?"

"I came to Philadelphia to get some advice on a new type of rifle I'm working on, Mr. Franklin, and I remembered that you were interested in inventions."

Revere threw up his hands, exclaiming, "Heaven help us, Mr. Winslow! You've touched on his madness! If there's one thing Ben dotes on more than politics, it's some hare-brained invention—the wilder the better." He snorted impatiently and added, "Why, right now he's working on some fool thing that'll bring a fire right into the middle of the room without even a fireplace! He'll burn the town down before he's finished!"

Franklin shook his head, and reached out for the rifle. "You're a fine one to talk! Why, you spend half your time tinkering at that shop of yours."

The two men argued mildly as Franklin pulled the rifle out of the soft leather case. But when both men began to examine it, they gave cries of approval. "Why, this is fine work!" Revere said instantly, then added, "But what's this part here?"

"That's the new firing mechanism I've been working on," Adam answered.

Franklin looked at the part Revere was pointing to. "Come back into my office, Winslow," he said, "I want to examine this more closely. Goodbye, Revere."

"I'm dismissed, you see!" The other man laughed and added as he shook hands with Adam, "He's afraid I'll steal your idea—and he may be right. But you'd better keep your eyes open—and you, too, Miss Burns." He lowered his voice so that Franklin, who had walked away toward the office, could not hear. "An invention—a pretty woman—those are Ben Franklin's weaknesses!" Then he winked and left the shop.

Adam led Molly into Franklin's office, and for the next hour she listened as the two talked about frizzens, pans, priming, and other matters. At first Adam was in such awe of Franklin that he said little, but soon he forgot himself and argued loudly over the design of the mechanism.

Finally, Franklin looked up and said, "Why, Miss Burns! We've quite neglected you!" He shook off her denial, adding vigorously, "You must be bored to death with all this technical talk."

"Why, no, Mr. Franklin, I'm not."

"Mr. Winslow, would you mind stepping over to the inn and getting us a pot of tea? I'll entertain Miss Burns."

Adam left and Franklin looked closely at the girl, taking in the clear gray-blue eyes, the golden tan that no woman of fashion would have, the strong hands and erect carriage. He had been conscious of her beauty, but now he began to speak with her, and he was quite adept at the business, his questions seeming quite artless.

Soon, however, she found herself telling the printer all about herself—and Adam. He had asked where they lived, and she hesitated, then said, "Well, we moved from Boston to the Ohio Valley in 1751. Mr. Winslow has a large tract of land there."

Franklin stared at her. "But—that's not a very safe place, or so I understand. And you were with him?"

"Oh, yes." She saw a question flicker in his eyes and knew what he was wondering. "I'm indentured to Mr. Winslow. My time will be up in another year."

"I see," Franklin said simply, "I'm sure that'll be a happy day for you."

Molly had grown accustomed to people being curious as to her rather unusual relationship with Adam, but her face grew warm under the scrutiny of Franklin. "I—I suppose it will. I don't think of it." Then she said quickly to change the subject, "We're living in Virginia now."

"Virginia?"

"Yes, a little town near the Potomac River, Woodbridge."

"I know Woodbridge. It's not far from Alexandria."

"Adam's brother Charles has a large plantation close to there—the family business. Their cousin is Saul Howland—you may have heard of him?"

"The businessman from Boston? Yes, a very shrewd man, so I hear. And what do you do in Virginia?"

"Why, I work." Molly looked up in surprise, and then she added quickly, "Adam's going to have a shop in town. That's all he wants to do, Mr. Franklin—work on guns. For the last few years he's been so busy with the fur business he had to put it off, but then he finally told his brother that he was going to quit— so that's when Mr. Howland and Mr. Winslow agreed that Adam should start a shop close to the Virginia property."

Adam came in just then, bearing a pot of steaming tea. Franklin took the teapot and insisted on serving them. As they drank the beverage, the printer remarked, "I think your new matchlock will not work—not as it is, Mr. Winslow. But it has promise."

Adam flushed with pleasure and replied, "That's my own thinking. I thought you might be interested in doing some work on it yourself."

"I've no time, unfortunately—too many irons in the fire as it is!" Franklin shook his head, but there was a steady light of interest in his eyes. "You and I both know that the answer is in breech-loading rifles—but nobody's been able to come up with a workable model, not yet."

"It's got to come—but if I could just perfect this firing mechanism—why, any army in the world would jump at it."

"Yes, and do you know. . . ?" He paused and seemed struck by a new thought. "Miss Burns was telling me you're going to settle down in Woodbridge?"

"Yes, sir."

"I know some people there who might be of help to you. I had a very good friend, a Mr. Lawrence Washington, who died a little over a year ago. He was very interested in the Ohio land where you've just been."

"Yes, he was one of the founders of the Ohio Company, so my brother Charles tells me."

"Ah, yes. Well, his brother, a young chap named George, has taken over for Lawrence—and I believe you ought to talk with him."

"Why is that, sir?"

"Because he will be very interested in your views on the land in the Ohio Valley, for one thing. He's been there himself. He and a man named Van Braam took a message to the French to clear out of the land claimed by the Crown."

Adam smiled grimly. "You know how much good that did? The French are dug into that country and nothing short of a war is going to put them out!"

Franklin sipped at his tea, staring at Adam, then nodded. "That's *exactly* the sort of view that Washington needs to hear, my boy! He feels the same way himself, so I hear, but the politicians are blind to the situation."

"They won't be when the French turn the Indians loose to butcher the settlers there."

"You think they'll do that! Surely not, Mr. Winslow—I mean, they *are* civilized—the French, that is!"

"They've already done it," Adam shrugged. "That's why I took Molly and cleared out. The Iroquois are champing at the bit! You don't hear about it here, but every month some helpless settler and his family are butchered!"

Franklin nodded. "Yes, you must see Washington. Not only to pass this word along about the French in the Ohio Valley; he'll be interested in this rifle as well. He's a lieutenant colonel in the Virginia militia, and his brother Lawrence often told me how fascinated he was with small arms and cannon."

Molly spoke up suddenly, "Adam, don't you remember that name?"

"What name, Molly?"

"Why, George Washington. Charles mentioned him in his last letter—no, it was the one before last. He said his plantation was called Mount Vernon."

"That's Washington's home, all right," Franklin confirmed. "A fine place, so they say."

"I can't remember," Adam said thoughtfully.

"It's at his home that the ball is going to be."

Adam snapped his fingers, saying, "That's right, Molly!" He smiled at Franklin, adding with a twinkle in his dark blue eyes, "I came to Philadelphia to see somebody about my rifle—but Molly came to buy a dress. My brother tells me we're going to go to a ball, and it's at Mt. Vernon. I'd forgotten."

"You'll be moving in high society," Franklin smiled. "Along with the Hugers and the Lees, the Washingtons are at the top of the ladder."

"Maybe you could suggest a place to get a fancy dress for Miss Burns?" Adam asked.

"And a suit for you, Adam," Molly added quickly. "You can't go to a ball wearing those buckskins."

"I think we can find you something suitable," Franklin offered with a smile. "Philadelphia has quite a few shops, and a beautiful young lady such as Miss Burns will have no trouble." He nodded to Adam, saying, "You tell Washington about those Indians—and make him look at your rifle."

"Don't see myself taking a rifle to a fancy ball, Mr. Franklin," Adam grinned. "Just the thought of *goin'* is pretty scary after being out in the woods for so long. But I want Molly to go. She's not had many fancy things, and I want to see her all dressed up in silks myself!"

Franklin did not miss the expression that swept across the young woman's face as Winslow spoke, but he only nodded and said, "It will be quite good for both of you—that ball at Mount Vernon!"

"You say this brother of yours has been living with the savages, Charles? Can't see how he'll fit into a ball!"

Lord Stirling leaned back against the rich leather of the seat, pulled a snowy white handkerchief from his pocket, and flicked away a spot of dust from his sleeve. He was a big man, slightly corpulent, with large bold eyes in a florid face. He had the air of one who was accustomed to being obeyed, but he appeared indolent as he turned his eyes to the tobacco field they were passing through.

"I dare say you're right, Henry," Charles shrugged. "My brother never was much for things of this sort. A diamond in the rough, you might say." He cast a glance at the large man beside him and added, "He'll be useful, I think."

"How could a bumpkin be useful? Seems he'd be quite out of place and a bore. Don't suppose he's shaved or had a bath for years?"

Charles laughed. "Oh, he'll be presentable, never fear. But he knows that Ohio country like a book—and we've got to convince the others to come into the Ohio Company."

"You've been at me for a month about the blasted company, Winslow!" Stirling complained. "I'm not sure it's going to be as profitable as you say."

"Then I'll have to do a better job of selling you on the thing, Henry!" Winslow laughed. "You made a fortune in the slave trade—now I want to see you make another in the fur business."

"And make you a bundle of money at the same time?"

"Of course!" Charles Winslow shrugged and replied, "I've never lied to you about that. You wouldn't believe me for a second if I told you I was only out to serve you. We're two of a kind, Henry—get rich and stay that way!"

Stirling suddenly threw his head back and roared with

laughter, his large teeth gleaming in his wide mouth. "Now I believe *that!*" he cried. "So we'll have this rural brother of yours to entice the Lees and the other rich fish into the company, eh?"

"Adam may not look like much—but he's spent the last four years working among the fur traders and the Indians out in the wildest part of that country. He knows every inch of it, and somehow he's gained the confidence of some big chiefs—Indians, you know."

"All very well, but you should have sent your man to clean him up—dress him like a gentleman!"

"Oh, I told him to go by a shop in Philadelphia and buy some good clothes."

"It'll have to do, I suppose."

Stirling leaned back and looked over the small town that they were entering. He said nothing until the driver pulled up and asked a passer-by where the gunsmith's shop was located, then moved on down the street.

"I hope he's ready," Stirling grumbled as they pulled up in front of a neat frame building with the sign GUNSMITH over the door.

Charles swung down, saying, "He just moved in three days ago, but I sent word yesterday we'd pick him up early today." He moved to the door and entered without knocking. Inside he saw a room about twelve feet wide and at least twenty feet long. There were weapons of all kinds hanging from pegs, and several large workbenches were covered with parts of rifles, muskets and pistols. A burly man with a shock of thick black hair beginning to go silver stood up and asked, "Yes, sir? Can I serve you?"

"I'm looking for Adam Winslow."

"Ah, yes, sir, I'll just call him for you." He moved to the back of the shop, called through the door, "Mr. Winslow? Can you come to the front?" He came back to stand beside his bench, and said with a smile, "You'd be Mr. Winslow's brother?"

"Yes."

"I'm James Tanner, Mr. Winslow. Your cousin, Mr. Howland, hired me to come and help Mr. Adam. Me and my wife live here with Mr. Winslow." He looked at the back door, then added, "He's a fine gunmaker, sir. But then you know all about that."

Charles nodded and started to speak, but Adam came into the room. "Why, Adam, I wasn't expecting you to look so—"

"Civilized, Charles?" Adam laughed. He was wearing a plain suit of brown, with a white linen shirt and a light blue waistcoat. His muscular figure gave the simple attire a certain air, Charles saw, and he was relieved that he would not be embarrassed over his brother's dress.

"You look very well, Adam," Charles said with a smile. "Are you ready?"

"Let me call Molly."

"Molly?"

There was such surprise in Charles's voice that Adam stared at him. "Yes, she's going with me."

"But—she's a servant!"

Adam settled in his tracks and the familiar stubborn look came to his jaw. Charles knew there was no need to argue, and he smiled, saying, "I'd forgotten about Molly, to tell the truth. Does she look presentable?"

Adam said nothing, but went to the stairs to the left and called loudly, "Molly! Come on—it's time to go!"

She must have been waiting, for they heard her light footsteps as she came down the stairs. Charles looked up and almost gasped.

"Why, Molly—you look lovelier than ever!"

She was wearing a gown made of a light blue material, with lace at the bosom and around the hem. Her ash-blond hair was lighter than he remembered, and her lips fuller. She smiled suddenly at him, and there was little left of the teenaged girl he'd seen in Boston. This was a woman of twenty, with all the fullness of figure and mystery of expression he had rarely seen.

"I'm glad to see you again, Mr. Winslow," she returned, her voice lower than most women's, with a vibrant tone that suggested great power.

"Well," Charles said finally with a smile, "you have grown up—which I believe I told you the last time we met, didn't I, Molly?"

"Yes, you did. You're looking very well."

"Now, shall we go?"

As they came out of the building, Henry Stirling took one look at Molly and quickly limped out of the carriage. The indolence that had kept him half asleep in Charles's presence vanished. As he took Molly's hand and kissed it, there was an alertness about him—a predatory air that he could not quite conceal.

He greeted Adam with a word, then insisted on seating Molly in the frontward facing seat, sitting down beside her and waving the Winslow men to the other seat with a laugh. All the way to Mount Vernon he kept the conversation going, and Adam noticed that Stirling sat closer to Molly than was absolutely necessary.

Charles noticed as well, and he engaged Adam in conversation about business. He told him, in effect, that there were some wealthy planters who were not yet investors in the Ohio Company, but were interested. "We're expecting you to convince them it's a good proposition, Adam."

"Do they know there's going to be a war?" Adam asked.

"Why, no—and neither do you!" Charles said in alarm. "Don't say anything about that, Adam!"

He was so alarmed that Adam stared at him. He said nothing, but as Charles continued to urge him to give a good report to the potential investors, it became clear that he'd been brought in to sell them on the idea. The idea depressed him. For the past few years, he'd lived on the cutting edge of life—one day at a time, all he could be sure of. It had been a simple matter—just stay alive—and now he was being drawn into a complex world of business that he had no taste for—and he hated it.

But it was too late, so he followed the two men and Molly inside when they arrived at the magnificent mansion with the large white pillars in front. When they went inside, Adam had an impulse to flee, for there was an opulent air to the house that was unlike anything he'd ever seen. Everything was rich and gilded, and the dress of the men and women made him feel like a poor relation.

Molly caught a glimpse of his face and knew at once that he was miserable. But Lord Stirling pulled her into the large ballroom and, with the assurance born of much dealing with women, led her onto the floor and began to dance.

It was a strange evening for both of them. Adam lurked on the outskirts of the ballroom, feeling totally out of place. Charles stayed with him briefly, then went off to his own devices. Adam watched Molly, who was like a stranger to him. He was accustomed to seeing her in simple cotton dresses, and this girl in silk, who moved with such grace in the complexities of the dance, was not his Molly at all.

She saw him from time to time, his dark face in the shadows along the walls, but there was no opportunity to go to him. Stirling monopolized her time, and she had seen enough of men to recognize that he was in full pursuit of her. Even though her experience was limited to the rural scenes, men are men, no matter what the station, and she saw the same hot desire in his eyes that she had seen in the eyes of the hunters of the Ohio Valley.

The hours sped by and Adam was almost ready to leave and walk home when Charles touched his arm, saying, "Come with me!"

He led the way to a door at the end of the large room, then as they went down a broad hall, whispered, "Be careful what you say to Washington, Adam. He's a fox!"

They went into a room that seemed small after the large ballroom, but was actually fifteen feet long and almost as wide. There was a long table around which seven men were seated. The man at the end stood up as they entered, and Charles said, "This is my brother, Adam. Adam, I want you to meet Colonel Washington."

"Happy to have you, Mr. Winslow," Washington returned. "Won't you join us?" There was a rawboned look of power about him—blunt features, including a broad nose and heavy forehead. His pale blue eyes looked inquiringly at the young man. "Your brother tells me you've just spent several years in the Ohio Valley."

"Yes, Colonel. In the fur trade."

"Ah, we would be most interested in your thinking on how things are going in that area."

Washington leaned back, and Adam, feeling very uncomfortable, began to speak. He had not gotten far before Washington began to ask him specific questions, and that made things much easier. He found out at once that the colonel knew the area well.

Finally, one of the other men asked, "What about trouble with the French? If we sink our money into this venture, can we expect peace from them?"

Adam felt Charles's intense gaze on him, urging him to deny any possibility of trouble, but he was looking into Washington's face. There was such a power in the colonel's gaze that it could be felt, and he heard himself saying simply, "There will be trouble with the French until the Crown of England settles the matter of who owns the land."

Washington slapped the table so hard that the rest of them jumped. "Exactly what I've been trying to make the House of Burgesses understand!" He smiled at Adam and said, "I'm very happy that you have settled in our area, young man. Would it be possible for me to enlist you under my command in the militia?"

Adam stared at him. "Why, I'm no soldier, Colonel Washington!"

"But you know the Ohio Valley—and you know guns." Washington nodded at Adam's surprise, and added, "Your brother has told us much of your efforts to come up with a superior firing system for the musket. I would very much like to see your work. But I would more like to see you in my company. Can I count on you, Mr. Winslow?"

Adam felt the power of the man, as did the others in the room, and as many others would feel it in the days to come. It was almost perceptible, a tangible thing, the force of George Washington, and Adam found himself assenting.

"Why, I'd be proud to serve under you, Colonel!" When Washington took his hand, he knew at once that something had come into his life—something new and different.

Much, much later, he and Molly were deposited by Stirling and Charles at the shop. James and Hope Tanner were still up as Adam and Molly entered, and Adam thought—not for the first time—how their presence in the house made it possible for Molly to stay there. A young woman living alone with an unmarried man would be impossible otherwise! They got up, said good night, and he turned to her.

"Molly?"

"Yes?"

The candle guttered and threw a golden gleam over her face, and her eyes looked enormous as she faced him.

"You—looked very lovely. I didn't know you could dance like that!"

"Robert taught me years ago. Although he wasn't very good at it, I learned the steps. It just seems to come naturally to me."

"Everybody was watching you. You were quite popular."

"I was disappointed."

"Disappointed?"

"I thought you'd come dance with me—at least once."

"Me?" He seemed shocked at the thought. "Why, Molly, I'd have been a poor show—with all the fine gentlemen in their fancy clothes."

"I—I wish you had come," she whispered. She was standing so close that he could smell the faint odor of the violets she wore, and it made him suddenly nervous.

"Well if I'd known that—maybe I'd have come."

"Will you dance with me the next time?"

He nodded, and suddenly his throat seemed tight. At a loss for words he simply said, "Go to bed, Molly."

"Good night, Adam." She went up the stairs without another word, and for a long time he stood there, in a trance, thinking of her. Then he smiled and shook his head. "Me dance with her! Now wouldn't that be a sight!" He turned and went to bed.

CHAPTER SEVENTEEN

THE BULLETS WHISTLE

★ ★ ★ ★

Molly put down her quill, rubbed her eyes, and picked up her journal to read the entry she had just made. Her fingers, she noticed, were trembling and the lines across the page wavered in a manner quite unlike her usual even script.

April 2, 1754
Woodbridge
Adam left this morning with Lieutenant Colonel Washington. They are part of the force to drive the French out of the Ohio Valley. I was so proud that Washington made Adam his aide! But they are too weak a force, Adam says (and the colonel agrees), to push the enemy out. I pray that he will be safe!
I am glad that Adam is gone, for he was so angry with Lord Stirling that there would have been trouble. Oh, what can I do? I have avoided Stirling, have told him I do not care for his company, but he forces himself on me. I have tried for the past few months to hide this from Adam, but two days ago he came home and found Lord Stirling here—and my face was flushed, for he had been—well, he had been no gentleman! It hurt me, for Adam thought I had been encouraging his attentions—that I was kissing him, when in fact I had just managed to pull myself away from him.
Charles is no help. He *encourages* the man, telling me that

I must be *nice* to him, for he can help with the family business—that's his answer!

Somehow I must free myself of his attentions—I must! My heart pounds even now as I think of how he forces himself on me as if I were a common girl!

And Adam—I cannot bear for him to believe I like the man—yet if I told him the truth, he would beat him. And for a common man to strike a member of the nobility would be a tragedy!

What can I do? Lord, help your servant!

"You're impatient, Adam," Washington said quietly. He had come up to stand beside Adam, who was looking over Great Meadows—an open plot of land in the midst of the forest lush with grass for horses and cattle.

"Well, I guess I'm guilty, Colonel," Adam nodded ruefully. "We've been on the march for two months almost, and we've only been within striking distance of the enemy once."

"I know." Washington looked westward to the gap in the woods that marked the road they'd hewed out, and there was a frown on his heavy features. "If we could have followed the first plan, we'd have been there by now, but when Colonel Fry got lost, we had no choice but to hack our way through." He looked down at Adam with a smile and added, "At least you can tell your grandchildren you had a part in building the first road west—for that's about what this is!"

"We could have taken a party of riflemen through the woods, Colonel."

"I think now that's what we should have done," Washington admitted. "By this time we've been seen by enough enemy scouts to carry the word to the French at Fort Duquesne. They'll be waiting for us."

Adam pulled a weed, bit it off, then asked sharply, "We going on, Colonel—anyway?"

"Yes! You see that hill?" Great Meadows was about 200 to 400 yards wide and two and a half miles long. At a point about 100 yards from a forested hill on one side and 150 yards from another on the other side was a rise. "I've marked off an outline there. We're going to build a fort."

"A fort? Why, that'll take even *more* time, sir!"

"I know—but we may need it, Adam. If we get over-whelmed, we can't run all the way back to Virginia, can we?" A smile touched Washington's firm lips, and he put his hand on Adam's shoulder—an unusual action for him, but he had grown to trust the young scout during the past two months. "We'll call it—Fort Necessity."

Building the fort was not such a big job, for all the men were expert axmen. They simply dug a trench three feet deep, placed logs twelve to fifteen feet long upright in it, and then packed the dirt around it. Loopholes were cut through the logs, and in less than a week, Fort Necessity stood ready for action.

"Wouldn't take but one cannon to knock it down, Colonel," Adam said as the two men stood inspecting it early one morning.

"No, but we could hold it against any massed infantry at-tack—and there are no cannon in this part of the world." Washington turned to see an Indian runner emerge from the trees on the western side of the clearing.

The Indian approached one of the soldiers, who waved an arm to where Washington stood with Adam, then ran at once to the rise. "Colonel Washington?"

"Yes."

"I am Silverheels. Message from Davidson."

Washington took the leather pouch the runner had handed him, pulled out a parchment and scanned it. He looked at Adam, his pale blue eyes alive with excitement. "You won't be bored anymore, Mr. Winslow! Get the men out!"

Forty men left Fort Necessity—with the colonel after less than an hour. As they made their way through the thick woods, Washington said little, but as heavy rain set in, he told the men to rest. "The message was from a man who was with me last December, Winslow. He tells me that an expedition of French-men are on their way to attack. But I don't think we'll wait for that."

"Do you know where they are, sir?"

"The messenger will lead us to their camp."

"How big a force do they have, Colonel?"

"Davidson wasn't sure—but it could be over a hundred."

Adam surveyed their unit, rubbed his chin, and said, "We'll be outnumbered."

"We'll have the advantage of surprise, though—and if we wait for the other men, we'll let them get away!"

Adam smiled at the tall man, for he had learned much about this aristocrat over the past two months. They were facing an enemy that outnumbered them two to one, and Washington was afraid they would "get away." At a time when other men would be thinking of retreat, this soldier feared only the loss of an opportunity to do battle. In years to come, Adam was to think often of this moment, but as they stood there in the dripping rain, he could only think, *He's going to get some of us killed—but he'll be right in the middle of it too.*

It was a bedraggled, hungry lot who saw the sun rise. They marched single file with Washington, who was following Silverheels. The guide led them to a depressed glen, rimmed with rock that concealed the French army. "A perfect hiding place!" Washington whispered to Adam as they circled the camp. Breakfast fires were burning, but the dense overhanging foliage absorbed their reflections.

Colonel Washington glanced around, saw that his men were in position, then yelled, "Attack! Attack!"

The French threw down their eating utensils, grabbed guns, and made a dash for the protection of the rocks. The French commander fell in the attack, but Washington did not rush the makeshift fort because the French put up a furious fight.

Adam loaded and fired again and again; he heard for the first time the cries of the wounded and dying. He fired and saw a shadowy figure drop; then as he stood up to reload, a ball whistled by his head and he heard a *thunk*. Turning around he saw a soldier named Jake Kilrain still standing, but mortally wounded, a musket ball in his forehead. Suddenly the man fell like a tree, slowly, his unbending body slamming into the ground. Adam's heart went out to the wounded but there was no time to tend them. The battle was fierce and he wondered if he would survive.

"Cut them off!" yelled Washington as he walked from tree to tree, ignoring the vicious whistling musket balls. He signaled a sergeant with a small squad to fill in a breach where the enemy was running to escape.

The battle lasted about fifteen minutes, though it seemed much longer to Adam! Finally a cry went up asking for quarter, and Washington bellowed out, "Hold your fire! They're surrendering!"

A tense moment passed, but the French rose slowly, hands over their heads, and their officer, Captain La Force, came forward to stand before Washington. "We will fight no more," he said with tears of anger in his eyes. "You have win these fight— but you nevair get back to your country!"

There was celebrating in the camp that night. Colonel Washington and his small force remained at Fort Necessity to search the forest for signs of the enemy, for they were certain that some of the French troops had escaped to Fort Duquesne with word of their defeat.

A week later, Silverheels departed on a scouting trip and came back at twilight with one of the braves from his own tribe. Washington listened carefully as the Indian spoke, then to Silverheels' translation: "He says that the French with many Indians have left Fort Duquesne—he says they have heard how you beat La Force and they vow to kill all of you."

The colonel believed the report and drove the men to strengthen the fort. The water had become contaminated and dysentery spread through the camp, but a construction crew never had greater incentive to work. Every now and then a man would drop out because of illness.

In the center of the fort was a stockade 57 feet in diameter, loopholed for rifles and muskets. Within the stockade was a hut 14 feet square, roofed over with shakes, which offered protection to the most seriously ill and the dangerously small supply of powder.

The scouts kept them posted as they built, and finally Washington told Adam, "They'll be here tomorrow."

That night it rained, and day broke to reveal the first signs of three French columns advancing on the fort. Their Indian allies had put aside their blankets and came naked in the rain.

"There's too many of them," declared the colonel. Adam

stared at Washington, not believing his ears. He knew the colonel was stating the truth, but he never once considered that the tall Virginian would agree. "There are too many for us, but it won't be very glorious if we don't fight, will it?"

"No, sir."

Washington watched the approaching ranks and said evenly, "I don't think they want to die any more than we do. If we put up a show of force, I think they'll allow us to surrender—then they can go back claiming victory."

That, to Adam's surprise, was exactly what happened. He wondered afterward how Washington could *know* such things, but at the time he simply obeyed orders.

The French and Indians advanced, flanking the fort. Washington drew his men into the palisade, stationing them in the trenches, and the battle continued through the afternoon.

Heavy clouds gathered and the rain began, making steady firing impossible. Water soaked into the guns, and the flint sparks only hissed in the wet powder. When that happened, it was necessary to draw out the wet charge with a ramrod fitted with a screw.

"I wish that new gunlock of yours was finished, Winslow," Washington remarked once as Adam's piece misfired. "But at least they're having the same trouble we are."

As darkness fell, the French commander called out, "Voulez-vous parler?" "Do you want to negotiate?" Washington's interpreter met with the French officer and returned after a while with articles of surrender. The French had won, but Washington was allowed to leave on the condition that he and his men would return home.

The next morning the sun was high in the sky when the English, with the wounded supported by able-bodied soldiers, marched out with drums beating and colors flying. As they left Fort Necessity, Washington looked back, and said to Adam, "Though war is terrible, there is something strange about being in the thick of it, Winslow."

"Yes, sir?"

Washington was not a talkative man, and Adam saw that he was trying to find words for something. There was a strange look on his face, and finally he smiled and looked into Adam's dark eyes.

"Those bullets whistling around our heads—" he paused, his eyes lighting up with wonder. Then he finished, saying slowly, "Even when one is in danger of death, there's something quite charming in that sound!"

The morning sun crested the tall elms that shaded the shop as Adam slipped from the back of the leggy gelding that had carried him from camp. He had marched back with the army to Williamsburg, but after two days in camp, had gone to Washington, saying, "Sir, if you don't have any use for me, I'd like to get home."

The Virginian had smiled, shaken his hand and said, "Certainly, Winslow. I'll be leaving myself shortly. Take one of my horses. You can return it to Mount Vernon later."

Adam walked across the plank walk, and was surprised to find the door closed, even more so to discover it bolted. "James! James!" he called out. "Where are you?"

At first there was no answer, but soon he heard footsteps, and then Hope Tanner, James's wife, asked, "Is that you, sir?"

"Yes, it's me, Hope."

The door opened and he went inside, asking at once, "Is James sick, Hope?"

She hesitated, then shook her head, saying, "No, Adam, he's in jail."

He stared at her in disbelief. "Jail! What for?"

Hope Tanner was a middle-aged woman, steady and firm, but there was trouble in her eyes and she twisted the cloth she held in her hands nervously. "Well, sir, it's bad news for you, I'm thinking."

Startled, Adam thought immediately of Molly. "Where is Molly? Is she sick? Is she—" He started to say *dead*, but said instead, "Is she all right?"

"She's not sick, Adam. But she's not here."

Adam stared at her, then cried out, "For God's sake, Hope! Tell me what's happened!"

"Well, you maybe didn't know, Adam, but that English lord,

he's been after Molly real hard."

"I—I knew he was interested in her," Adam hesitated. "And I thought she liked him."

"Never!" Hope cried out indignantly. "She never did! It was him, the dog!"

Adam grew tense, and then he asked directly, "What happened, Hope? Let's have it all."

"Well, he kept coming here, bothering her, Adam. Kept pestering her to go off with him, but she wouldn't do that. Then last Wednesday, me and James went to church, but Molly stayed here alone. When we got home, we seen his carriage in front of the shop, and then we heard her crying out! Like she was hurt or scared!"

She bit her lip, then forced herself to go on. "We run in and he had her pinned up against the wall, pawing at her. Her dress was torn and she was fightin' to get away from him, but he was too strong for her—the beast!"

Adam's temples throbbed, he felt lightheaded, as he always did just before rage came. He listened carefully, his fists clenched as Hope said tearfully, "James jumped at him and when Stirling hit him in the face, James knocked him down, then he picked him up and threw him out of the shop!"

"And next James was arrested for assaulting Lord Stirling, is that it?"

"They come the next day and took him, Adam," she nodded. "I knew he'd come again, so I sent Molly to stay with my sister over close to Alexandria. She didn't want to go, but I couldn't protect her here."

"Thank God you and James were here, Hope!" Adam said fervently. He went over and put his arm around her shoulders. "Don't worry about James; they can't hold him."

"But, Adam—"

"Is Stirling still at my brother's house, do you know?"

"Yes, but he's been here every day to try to get me to tell where Molly is."

"You stay here, Hope."

She watched carefully as he walked over to the wall and took down a small pistol. It was a twin-barreled over-and-under flintlock with a tap action. He loaded it, saying nothing, but there was something frightening about his intensity, and Hope said as he put the pistol in his belt and headed for the door, "I—I'll pray for you, Adam."

He shot her a look from under his narrowed brows, his dark blue eyes frosty and cold. "Pray for his soul, Hope—for he's a dead man!"

He left the shop, mounted, and turned the horse's head toward his brother's plantation. The rage that had fallen on him in the battles at Washington's side had no comparison to the frozen hatred that seemed to eat away at his heart. Not for one moment did he consider the consequences that would follow if he killed Stirling, and if he had any cries from his conscience, he stifled them.

He arrived at the house at dusk, and the short, fat slave who took his horse recognized him immediately. "Mist' Winslow!" he cried out, taking the reins of Adam's mount. "You done been gone a long time!"

"Is Lord Stirling inside, Jim?" Adam asked.

The black face suddenly lost its toothy smile, and Jim swallowed, for he saw something on the white man's face that frightened him. "Yessuh! The gentulmens is playing cards in de den."

Adam walked around the carriage in front of the door, then paused and stared at it. His lips curved slightly in a smile, and he reached out and plucked the buggy whip from its holder, then walked to the front door. He went in, almost running over Minnie, the house slave who had come to admit him. She took one look at his face, then wheeled and left as quickly as she could without a word.

The den was a large room off the hall, and as Adam went toward it, he heard the sound of laughter. He paused outside the door, listening for a moment, then pushed it open and entered.

The five men seated around the table looked up at him, and a silence fell on the room. Charles was seated next to Lord Stirling, and across from him was John Franklin, a wealthy planter. Next to Franklin sat Lawrence Carter, a member of the House of Burgesses, and to his right was a lean man with a pale face that Adam had never seen.

The table was covered with cards, and each of the men had a glass at his hand. Tobacco smoke was thick in the air, and the sudden silence was heavy as Adam stood there, the whip in his hand.

Charles turned pale, but tried to carry the thing off. "Why, Adam, you're back!" He rose to his feet, forcing a smile. "I believe most of you know my brother, Adam—he's just returned from serving with Colonel Washington."

Adam paid no heed to his brother. He was staring at Henry Stirling. The large man had been slumped in his chair, but now he came slowly to a rigid position, for there was death in the eyes of the man who stood framed in the doorway.

Charles tried again, saying, "Adam, sit down and join us. We must hear all about the battle! You're quite a hero around here, you know!"

His words fell flat, and there was a ghastly silence broken only by the sound of a slave out in the yard singing a song about Moses and the Lamb.

"Stirling, you're a dog!"

Adam's deliberate words cut across the nobleman's nerves, and he jumped to his feet, his face livid. "I won't be insulted by you, Winslow!"

Adam's dark blue eyes were unwavering, and his voice grew quiet and menacing. "I didn't come to insult you, Stirling—"

"You'd better retract!" Stirling cried out in rage, striking the table angrily.

Adam raised his own voice, his words cutting like a knife. "I didn't come to insult you—I came to horsewhip you!" He cut the air suddenly with the whip, filling the room with the loud *whishing* sound.

Charles jumped forward, crying out, "Adam! You've gone crazy!"

"Stand still, Charles!" Adam said, not taking his eyes away from the Englishman. "I have a few 'brotherly' remarks to make to you later, but not now."

"Can't you do something, Winslow?" the thin, pale man said loudly. "I can't believe you'd let your guest—especially an honored guest such as Lord Stirling—be insulted!"

"Adam, just let me explain—!"

"I'll do the explaining." Adam bit off the words and swept the room with disdain. "This 'distinguished guest' of yours has assaulted a young woman in my care. He forced himself on her, and when a friend of mine intervened to save her, he had him put in jail."

"I'll see the fellow sent to Botany Bay for life!" Stirling cried. "He'll be taught a lesson."

"He'll be out of jail tonight—or you'll be cut to ribbons right now."

"I won't—!"

Adam suddenly flicked the whip across the table, the tip catching the end of Stirling's cigar, snatching it from his fingers and flinging it across the room.

"Stirling, you can have your choice." Adam's steady voice was almost a whisper. "Either you give your word in front of these men that James Tanner will be out of jail tomorrow—or I'll open you up like hot butter!"

Stirling turned pale. He licked his thick lips, then running his eyes around the room, suddenly stood up. He made a dash for the end of the room, and Adam let him go, seeing what he was attempting.

There was a musket on the wall, a Brown Bess, such as the British soldier used, with a bayonet gleaming on its end.

"We'll see who does what, Winslow!" Stirling yelled venomously as he lifted the rifle high, then lunged across the floor, thrusting the blade at Adam's belly.

Adam waited on the balls of his feet. As the naked steel shot toward his unprotected midsection, he reached out with the whip and forced the blade to one side. With his free hand he whipped a sudden blow into Stirling's stomach. The rifle clattered to the floor, and the big man fell, holding his stomach and gagging.

A movement to his left caught Adam's eye, and he turned to see the tall man pulling at a pistol that was in a coat hanging from the back of his chair. He came out with it, but the fire in his eyes died as he looked down the barrel of the pistol that had seemed to jump into the hand of Adam Winslow.

"Either use that, or drop it!" Adam commanded, and stood there waiting.

The thin man had the pistol almost lifted. Just a little move of the wrist and he would have it dead center, but he could not do it. There was something frightening in the smile on Adam Winslow's lips, and he let the pistol drop hurriedly, his face suddenly ashen.

"Second thoughts are usually best," Adam said quietly, then turned to look at Stirling, who was struggling to his feet. He waited until the man was upright, his face pale as paper, and then he said, "I won't ask you again. You have five seconds to decide if you'll have Tanner out of jail—or if you'll have a horse-whipping. Which shall it be?"

"He'll do it, Henry!" Charles cried out loudly. "He'd do it if he knew he'd die for it two minutes later!"

Stirling took one long look at Adam, then slowly, with hatred freezing his face, nodded once.

Adam said, "These men see that you have agreed." He put the pistol back in his belt, tossed the whip on the floor, then wheeled and went to the door. He paused and looked back at Stirling, saying, "If you don't keep your word—you can ask my brother what will happen."

Then he turned and was gone.

There was not a sound in the room, but Charles said in a whisper, "I can't answer for him, Henry! I know he's my brother, and I'm sorry for it all—but I have to tell you, if you've got any idea of not keeping your word, forget it!"

"Why, I'd have him locked up, Stirling!" the lean man cried.

"It wouldn't help, Ralph," Charles said, shaking his head with a bitter smile. "He'd dig out somehow, Henry, and you'd never have a night's sleep—because you know Adam would get you."

"I'll kill him for this, Charles!" Stirling whispered, and there was an insane gleam in his protruding eyes.

"No doubt you'll try, Henry," Charles shrugged. "But you're too shrewd to do it head-on." He slowly put a cigar between his lips and his hand trembled as he lifted a candle to light it. As the blue smoke rose, he said bitterly, "Let it rest, Henry. For now. He'd kill you out of hand—and I need you." Then he said quietly, "Shall we continue the game?"

CHAPTER EIGHTEEN

"I WANT TO BELONG TO YOU!"

★ ★ ★ ★

"General Braddock, this is Adam Winslow—he served with me at Fort Necessity."

Major General Edward Braddock, a foot shorter than Washington with more fat than muscle in his bulk, peered at Adam from his shaggy brows, his small eyes suspicious. The powdered wig under his winged hat and the uniform blazing with bright decorations and embroidering seemed garish in the plain room where the three men stood.

The stubborn Englishman's nose flared in disdain. "You mean when you were *defeated* at Fort Necessity, before you had even reached your objective."

Washington refused to be humbled. "As you please, General. But you have asked me to be your aide, and it's my duty to tell you that Adam Winslow knows the terrain as well as the Indian scouts; we'll need his kind to guide us."

Braddock grunted and snapped with some irritation, "You mean you need *us*, Washington! Orthodox war, that's what I intend! No games, no hiding behind trees and jumping out at the enemy like children!" The bulldog of a man looked up with his eyes hard as marble. "Put him in uniform if you please—but I want only men who respect my authority!"

He nodded shortly, then left the room, and Washington shook his head, smiling grimly. "I never said he was an *easy* man to deal with, Winslow, but he is one of the most experienced soldiers in the British army. He's a long-time career officer. At the Battle of Culloden he broke the enemy with his headlong charges, much to the satisfaction of the Duke of Cumberland."

"Well, sir, if he tries to charge massed troops into a thick woods bristling with sharpshooters and Indians, it'll be a different story."

Washington bit his lip, then shrugged, saying only, "I have no authority, you understand?"

"A shame it is, too, Colonel!"

After the battle at Fort Necessity, Washington had been awarded thanks by the House of Burgesses for negotiating a surrender that allowed him to bring his troops home. He had been offered a command by Governor Dinwiddie, but the English government had issued an order that officers holding the King's commission should rank above provincial officers. The degradation of being outranked by every whipper-snapper who might hold a royal commission by virtue of being the illegitimate son of some nobleman's cast-off mistress had been more than Washington's temper could bear. He rejected the offer.

But when on February 20 of 1755 Braddock had arrived with two regiments to make a fresh attack on the French, he had decided that the young soldier's experience would be valuable; he had offered him a place on the staff with the rank of lieutenant colonel, where he would be subject only to the orders of the general. Washington had accepted.

Adam had known of this, and resented the treatment of the tall soldier whom he had learned to admire. "Why did you agree to serve under Braddock, sir? He obviously despises all soldiers who aren't regulars in the British army."

"I want to learn," Washington rubbed his chin, and there was a determined light in his eyes as he stared at Adam. "These are the picked troops of England. They have been unbeatable on the Continent. Braddock says they'll sweep the French out of the west—and he must have his chance."

"Yes, sir." Adam pondered a thought, then asked, "You

want me to go with you, Colonel?"

"It would be a personal favor. You will be my aide, not a regular." The tall man smiled and said, "Maybe we can get some of our own back on the French, eh, Winslow? Can I count on you?"

Adam warmed at the thought of serving with Washington, but hesitated. "When will the army move, sir? I need to make a trip to Boston right away. My family is in the fur business, and I've got to freight last year's pelts to our warehouse there—and then I'd be willing."

"You've got plenty of time for *that*! This army doesn't know the meaning of *hurry*! It's been almost a year since our battle, and it'll be another month at least before this army takes a step!"

"With your permission, then, I'll make my trip, and report back to you for duty as soon as possible."

"Fine—fine!" Washington gave one of his rare smiles and asked, "Still working on that rifle of yours?"

"Well, actually, that's why I'm stopping by Philadelphia on my way back, Colonel. I've made some progress, but Mr. Franklin says he has a new idea."

"Benjamin Franklin? Well, tell him I sent my regards," Washington replied. "If we could get a weapon that was accurate, that could be loaded in less time and fitted with a bayonet, we'd be a force to be reckoned with!"

"It's just a matter of time, Colonel."

"Ah, but that's just what we don't have—time! Those Frenchies will be settled so thick in the Ohio Valley in a year or two that we'll never get them out."

"You think there'll be another war, sir?"

Washington smiled grimly. "We're already in it! Remember Fort Necessity? Those bullets we heard whistling around our ears? Now we're going back. And I tell you if we fail, it'll take a miracle of the Almighty to root those scoundrels out!"

Adam asked curiously, "You believe in miracles, Colonel Washington?"

The man's features broke into a smile, and he murmured as he turned to leave the room, "There are precedents!" He turned to smile strangely at Adam. "There are, indeed, precedents!"

Molly never forgot that trip to Boston, for despite Adam's mild objections, she insisted on accompanying him. She gave several reasons, but did not mention the chief one—that she did not want to be left alone anywhere near Henry Stirling.

Months had passed since Adam's humiliation of the nobleman, and on the surface the affair seemed to have been forgotten. Adam of necessity had to go to Charles's home, and it was impossible to avoid Stirling. There had been no way for the man to avoid having Tanner set free, and he nodded and spoke whenever he met Adam, but there was a coldness in his watchful eyes.

"Watch out fer 'im, Mr. Winslow!" James Tanner counseled. "I had me a mule once who'd behave 'imself a whole year jes to get the chance to kick me once!"

Charles had come to Molly once after the incident and pleaded, "Molly, he's not a bad man—just spoiled, you know? Try to get on with him." Charles had suddenly looked haggard, his handsome face tense. "I—I haven't been careful enough, perhaps, in some ways."

"You owe him a great deal of money, Charles?" Molly had asked.

"Oh, I'll get it back when the company starts producing—but until then, I'm tied to the man. He won't bother you again, Molly, so if you could just try to keep things—well, smooth, you see?"

She had seen no profit in offending Stirling, though the thought of his hands on her made her flesh creep. But Adam had been her strength; she had subconsciously made him so, and when he had announced that he was going to be gone for several weeks on a trip to Boston, she had felt a streak of fear at the thought of being at Stirling's mercy—so she had asked if she could join him for the trip.

It turned out to be a wonderful trip, spring setting the frozen brooks free to gurgle in their beds, and the fruit trees shimmering pink and white dresses in the distance. The air was crisp and clean, and after the hard winter both of them relaxed in a way they had not since the days back at Northampton.

They avoided the inns along the way, preferring to camp out beside the trail. Every night they would stop early beside a stream or a spring, bring out the cooking gear and feast on game that Adam killed along the way.

On the last night before they arrived in Boston, they pulled off from the main road farther than usual. Adam shot a buck in a stand of oak and hickory half a mile to the east, and since there was plenty of dead wood and a creek, they made camp early. He skinned and dressed the deer, and by the time Molly had made a fire and they had cooked a choice cut, the sun was down.

"It may be a little cold tonight," he said, staring into the fire. "If you get cold in the wagon, just pull up another bale of beaver pelts."

Molly stood up, stretched, and said lazily, "It's so cozy in there, Adam!" She sat down across the fire, picked up a stick and began to poke the coals, sending up tendrils of smoke. "I wish Boston were another hundred miles away!"

Adam laughed. "So do I, Molly!" He lifted his head and watched as an owl sailed silently across the open field to their right and dropped making a sudden tiny scuffle in the grass. "It'll be strange seeing the house again."

"I think about your father a lot—and Rachel." Molly dropped the stick and watched it begin to glow in the coals. She leaned her cheek on her knee, and by the firelight her eyes seemed large and her lips looked soft as memories stirred through her. "I—I miss them, Adam," she sighed.

"So do I. They were—different." There was a hesitation in his speech and somehow he could not frame his thought. Finally he said, "They were godly people, Molly. I envy them that."

They had not talked much of religion since those days at Northampton, and now she asked, "You were bitter, weren't you, Adam—I mean about the way the church treated Rev. Edwards?"

"Yes! I still am, I guess. It wasn't fair!"

"Nothing much is."

He looked up swiftly, for in all the years he had known her, there had been few times when she had spoken so sadly. He tried to weigh her tone, her words, then asked, "Are you unhappy, Molly?"

She stood up and there was a restlessness in her as she took a few steps away from the fire, then came back to stand over the blaze. "No, I'm not."

He rose and she turned from him, but he reached out and pulled her around, trying to read her expression. A golden wash of light from the fire tinted her smooth cheeks, and her eyes were enormous. "You don't worry about being indentured, do you, Molly? You know that's never *meant* anything."

Suddenly her lips quivered, and he saw tears form in her eyes. She had been thinking of how he had come to her that first time—long ago in England. For years she had struggled to bury the memories of the filth and poverty, the mistreatment she had suffered at the brutal hands of her father. Each time those thoughts rose in her like ghastly phantoms, she had learned to force them deep down—yet all the time she was aware that somewhere they lurked in her spirit.

The last year had been difficult in a way she could not understand. Her thoughts had often been confused, wandering back across the years like ghosts seeking freedom from a dread yet uncertain bondage. Often she had been wrenched from sleep drenched in perspiration with a scream rising to her lips, terrified of something she could never quite understand. Sometimes it was a dream of sinking into some dark pool; she would thrash out wildly, seeking for something solid to grasp, something to keep her from sliding helplessly into the depths.

She had been restless in mind, and her body was changing in some subtle way, so that she was often swept with a vague emptiness—more like a longing—but she could not have said what she sought.

Now here in the darkness broken by the flickering fire below and the cold silver points of brilliant stars, she stood close to Adam in a silence that became almost palpable. All these things seemed to converge, causing her throat to constrict, her breathing to quicken, and her heart to trill like the voice of a small bird.

His face was only inches away from hers as he bent forward, striving to see what troubled her. His dark eyes were warmed by the reflection of the yellow tongues of fire, and every plane of his face was familiar to her in a way that no other had ever been.

Perhaps it was the cathedral-like silence of the forest that seemed to breathe gently, stirring her heart like the tender green leaves high overhead. Perhaps it was the sudden rising of the old fears that loomed like dusky phantoms, but died as she saw the kindness in his face. She remembered how he had come to her years ago, and warmth suddenly filled her as she recalled he had held her in his arms and soothed away the fears, murmuring softly into her ear.

Perhaps it was the long loneliness she had known for years, having no one, of walking alone with her guard held high while her heart cried out for someone to walk beside her—for Adam!

He leaned toward her and asked again, "Molly, you don't worry about being a bound girl? You—you have never *belonged* to me!"

Without volition, her hands rose, and she placed them on both his cheeks, gently caressing the scar that ran the length of his face. She whispered the thought that must have been kept guarded for a long time, but now passed her lips almost like a prayer:

"But—Adam—I *want* to belong to you!"

The words startled him, and his eyes suddenly opened wide. He was caught by the same spell that had caused her to speak, and there was a roaring in his ears as he searched her face, taking in the smooth cheeks brushed now by the thick curling lashes. His arms encircled. Suddenly her lips were under his; in a gesture as unrehearsed as her utterance of trust, he kissed her softly, warmly.

For her, it was like coming into a port after a wild storm. The fears that lay beneath her mind were now no more, for his arms were holding her tightly. Standing there, so secure, so safe, a sudden gust of joy swept through her.

For Adam the kiss was like nothing he had ever known. He had kissed women, but in Molly's response there was a sense of trust—complete and without reservation. She leaned against him, and though her woman's figure stirred him, somehow, for one fleeting moment, she was the small child that he had comforted so long ago.

Molly never knew how that kiss ended, nor did she remember who pulled back. But finally his arms dropped and she took a step back.

"Molly! I—I've never felt like this!" He seemed embarrassed, and uttered a strange half-laugh, saying, "Don't be afraid. I just—lost my head for a minute." Then he bit his lip and smiled, adding in a voice of wonder, "You've grown into a beautiful woman, Molly! I hadn't realized how pretty you are until . . ."

She smiled at his rising color, and said quietly, "I'm not afraid, Adam. How could I ever be afraid of you?"

His head rose and he looked into her face, then relaxed. "I'm glad of that!" He seemed awkward and uncertain of himself, and it was as if he were the small child and she the adult. Finally he said, "Guess I'll take a walk before I turn in."

It was his way of giving her time alone, and she watched him move across the tree line and disappear like a wraith in the silver moonlight. She made her preparations for bed, washing her face and hands in the cold waters of the brook, then climbed into the wagon and lay down. She could see the silver points made by the stars through the rear of the wagon, and for the first time in many years she was not afraid of the darkness. She remembered the firm warmth of his lips, and raised her hand to touch her own mouth. Finally she smiled enigmatically, but she did not sleep until after what seemed to be a long time, she heard him come back to the fire. She listened as he unrolled his blanket, and then she smiled and went easily into a dreamless sleep.

CHAPTER NINETEEN

"YE MUST BE BORN AGAIN!"

★ ★ ★ ★

The trip to Boston was uneventful, but the scene beside the fire had marked both Adam and Molly. She had gotten up at dawn lighthearted, singing cheerfully as she made breakfast. Adam, on the contrary, seemed subdued, and more than once he let his gaze rest on her face, a puzzled expression in his dark eyes.

Although neither of them mentioned the kiss, the moment was a sharp memory to both of them. Once she turned suddenly and caught him looking at her, and as his face burned with embarrassment, she laughed and said, "Why in the world have you been staring at me?"

He gave the reins a twitch, thought about it, then shrugged his massive shoulders. "Don't rightly know, Molly. Guess I ought to know by this time that you've grown up—but it keeps sneaking up on me." It was as close as he would ever come to mentioning the kiss, and he added, "If anybody had tried to tell me the dirty little girl I bought a handkerchief from in London would turn out like—like you have, I'd not have believed it."

Her eyes dropped with pleasure, but she said only, "That was a long time ago, Adam."

They pulled in to the warehouse in Boston, only to discover

that Saul was out of town, so the next day they headed home. The weather held firm, and they made good time, arriving at Philadelphia at midday on Thursday. Adam drove straight to Franklin's shop, but the master of his shop shook his head, saying, "Mr. Franklin's gone to France. Won't be back for two months." He had wiped his hands on his blackened apron, cocked his head and added with a sly grin, "He wanted to stay and hear Preacher Whitefield, but he likes them French gals a leetle better'n hearing a sermon."

"George Whitefield is here?" Adam asked.

"Been here nigh on to a week—and like always, he's got the whole town buzzin'! Ain't no church big enough to hold the crowds, so he's out in a big field the militia uses for drillin' soldiers."

Adam thanked the man, then went back to the wagon and told Molly what he'd learned. "Sure am sorry to miss Franklin," he added ruefully.

"Could we go hear Mister Whitefield, Adam?"

He looked up in surprise, then smiled, "Why not? Soon as we get back, I'll be leaving with the army. Why don't we walk around town, get something to eat, then go to the meeting?"

"Oh, that would be so nice!"

Adam drove to a modest hotel, took two rooms, and after cleaning the dust of the trail off, they walked around town for a few hours. There was a holiday air about Philadelphia that infected them, and when they saw a theater with a sign that offered the latest drama direct from London, Adam bought two tickets, and they went in, feeling rather guilty. Neither of them had ever been to a theater, and the play was a melodrama with singing, romancing, duels, and a happy ending. Sitting there in the darkness, Molly became so tense when the heroine was threatened by a fate worse than death that she unconsciously reached out and gripped Adam's arm.

He looked over to see her large eyes fixed, her teeth biting her full lower lip in an agony of suspense. She was leaning forward, completely absorbed in the action on the stage, not at all conscious that she was holding his arm tightly.

Finally, when the rather exaggerated heroine was saved by

a tall actor wearing a blond wig, Molly leaned back and expelled her breath. Turning to Adam she cried, "Oh, I was *so* afraid he'd be too late!" Then she noticed she was clutching his arm, and a rosy tint spread over her neck and cheeks. She dropped her eyes and pulled her hand back quickly. Noticing her confusion, he laughed, saying teasingly, "You only bruised me slightly!"

After the performance and dinner, they still had an hour, so the two walked along the boardwalks looking into the windows at the new fashions. He offered her his arm, and as she slipped her hand under it, she felt a sense of delight and security. Other couples were walking together, and she watched them, wondering how they had met and if they loved each other. Not once did she see a man who seemed as attractive to her as Adam, plainly dressed though he was.

He was aware of her hand on his arm, and like her, felt a strange sense of delight in walking with her. When they turned and left the central section of town to walk to the drill field, she suddenly looked at him trustingly, "Adam, do you ever think of Mary?"

Giving her a startled glance, he considered her question. "Well, I got a letter from Rev. Edwards last week," he said casually. "Mary and Dwight had a son last month. Named him Timothy, too. They're doing fine, Rev. Edwards says." He took a few more steps, then asked, "Why'd you ask about Mary?"

"Oh, I don't know." The crowd grew as they moved off the boardwalk and took a wide path to the large field that was already beginning to fill up. "You were very much in love with her. I guess you always will be."

"Why, I guess not, Molly." Adam was struck with a thought that seemed to disturb him. He bit his lip and his brow wrinkled as it did when he was intent. She thought he would say no more, but finally, he spoke.

"I wanted her pretty bad—and for a long time it hurt to think about her. But now that's all gone. I just think of her as Timothy's wife, a nice girl I knew a long time ago."

She considered that, then said timidly, "I thought love was supposed to last forever."

"Maybe it does in stage plays—or maybe it really does,"

Adam mused. "Most likely, all it proves is that I never really loved her at all."

At his answer she gave him a swift look, trying to discern his expression, then she smiled and said, "I'm glad you feel that way, Adam. It'd be hard going through all your life loving somebody you could never have, wouldn't it?"

They had become a part of a river of people that came from every section of the town and merged into one stream, already packing the area around a platform at one end of the field. Adam spotted a small rise over to the left where a large oak spread its branches, and taking her arm, he guided her through the crowd. "This is about as close as we're going to get, I reckon."

For the next half-hour they watched the crowd grow until a sea of humanity surrounded the platform. There seemed to be no single type of hearer; many who wore silks and sported diamonds rubbed shoulders with laborers wearing rough clothes. Age was not a factor, either, for though there were many young people with rosy cheeks, there were more with white-hair, and leaning on canes.

The sun was warm, but not uncomfortably so. Finally there was a stir in the crowd over to the left, and someone shouted, "There he is!"

A small group of men were making their way through the massed spectators toward the platform. Adam recognized Whitefield at once as the group mounted the wooden structure. He was heavier than the other men, leaning somewhat to corpulence, but he mounted the platform gingerly and waved his hand to the crowd.

"He looks older," Adam commented, "but not bad for a man who's preached as hard as he has for all these years." Since Adam had heard Whitefield preach, the man had crossed the Atlantic back and forth a dozen times. He had preached before the King, and the Countess of Huntington had introduced him to the nobility of England. David Garrick, the greatest living actor, had said, "I'd give a fortune to have his voice! He can make people cry by saying *Mesopotamia!*"

Whitefield had toured both America and England so many times that he'd lost count, making both enemies and admirers in the process. His remark, "Harvard's light has become darkness," had closed the doors of that school as well as Yale to him. He'd also been refused the pulpits of some of the most prestigious churches in the country, having said that an unconverted ministry was ruining the land.

Yet none of these things had succeeded in dampening the enthusiasm of the common people. No matter where the preacher went, people came by the thousands to stand in the open air to hear him proclaim the gospel of Jesus. Adam marveled at it, trying, as he studied the crowd, to account for such a thing. "I can't understand it, Molly," he said finally. "What has the man got to make people come out in mobs like this?"

"Brother Edwards always said he had the anointing of God, didn't he?"

"I'd forgotten that," Adam mused. "Look, I think it's going to start."

A tall, thin man with a booming voice prayed a long prayer. Then a short, heavy man with full whiskers stepped forward and for nearly an hour led the crowd in singing. They sang psalm after psalm, filling the air with music from the lips of twenty thousand people singing at the top of their lungs.

Finally the singing came to an end, and Whitefield stepped forward. He was bareheaded and wore a black robe. Whitefield knelt immediately and began to pray, looking rather ordinary as he prayed aloud, beseeching God to look down from heaven. He ended his prayer, but did not rise. For a long time he knelt there in profound silence—but it was not a dead silence, for Adam began to feel the same intensity he remembered from the last time he'd heard Whitefield speak. And now there began to be heard from various parts of the crowd, a few cries as people began to weep. A tall, broad-shouldered man just to Adam's right bowed his knees suddenly and began to sob, and farther down a woman raised her hands and with tears running down her cheeks began to cry out, "God have mercy! God have mercy!"

There was something electric about the way emotions were charged, even before Whitefield rose, but when he did stand and begin to speak, at once the power of God began to sweep over individuals.

As he began his address, clouds broke and the afternoon sun streamed down. He laid a solid doctrinal foundation by reading the story of Jesus and the man called Nicodemus, but as he read from the third chapter of John, clouds broke the sun's rays, with alternating bars of light and shade falling on the audience. Suddenly he stretched his arm out, crying in a bell-like tone that carried to the edge of the great crowd: "See that emblem of human life! It passed for a moment and concealed the brightness of heaven from our view. But it is gone! And where will you be, my hearers, when your lives are passed away like that dark cloud?"

"Oh, my dear friends, I see thousands here with their eyes fixed on this poor unworthy preacher. In a few days we shall all meet at the judgment seat of Christ—every eye will behold the *Judge*! With a voice whose call you must abide and answer, He will inquire whether on earth you strove to enter in at the strait gate. Whether your hearts were *absorbed* in Him."

By now the sun had gone behind another cloud, and the sky grew dark; in the distance the rumble of thunder sounded. "My blood runs cold when I think how many of you will seek to enter in and shall not be able. Oh, what plea can you make before the Judge of the whole earth?"

He began to rebuke them for sin, but soon he was on his favorite theme—the new birth. "You were born once of the flesh—but except a man be born again, he cannot see the kingdom of God!" he shouted. "But I have been a good man, you say." He lifted his voice and thundered louder than the rumbling in the distance, "Except a man be born again, he cannot see the kingdom of God!"

And then he began to tear down their excuses—that they had been members of the church, that they had taken communion, been baptized. That they had done no one ill, and on and on. To each of these Whitefield reiterated sternly, "Except a man be born again, he cannot see the kingdom of God!"

The storm was almost overhead. The preacher stood in the eerie light of a thundercloud about to break. "Oh, sinner! By all your hopes of happiness I beseech you to repent. Let not the wrath of God be awakened! Let not the fires of eternity be kindled against you!"

Forked lightning scored the sky. "See there! It is a glance from the angry eye of Jehovah!" He lifted his finger, then paused. Tension hovered at the breaking point, and then came a tremendous crash as thunder pealed and reverberated. As it died away, the preacher's deep voice came from the semidarkness. "It was the voice of the Almighty as He passed by in His anger!"

Adam had expected to hear a powerful sermon, had been prepared to be impressed by Whitefield's oratory. He had heard many sermons, and he had been stirred by many of them—not the least by "Sinners in the Hands of an Angry God" by his friend Jonathan Edwards.

But something was happening to him that he had not counted on.

It had begun when Whitefield had knelt and prayed. That simple act had struck some deep chord in Adam's heart. His knees suddenly felt very weak, and a lightheadedness seized him. He had attempted to shake the feeling off, but as the sermon progressed, he was more and more aware that something akin to fear was rising up in his spirit.

Adam Winslow was not a man who had known a great deal of fear. He had been in danger of death for several years in the Ohio River country, and that had been something he'd learned to control. But now he could not control the trembling of his hands as Whitefield continued to describe the plight of the lost, and his lips were so dry that he could not swallow.

Once he tore his eyes away from the preacher to look at Molly, and he saw that her face was pale, that her hands were twisting her handkerchief into a knot, and that she was beginning to moan.

We've got to get out of here! he thought wildly. But his feet seemed rooted to the ground, and besides that, no matter how disturbing the words of Whitefield were, he could not tear his gaze away from the man!

The sky grew darker than ever, and then Whitefield cried out, his voice like a trumpet: "Oh, will you die? Will you perish? Will you make His blood and His cross as nothing? Why will you trample underfoot the Son of God and do despite unto holy things?"

Then he cried out, "Come to Jesus! Let His blood wash you from your sin and guilt. Ye must be born again!"

He began to move his arm, repeating, "Ye must be born again!"

Adam saw the finger of Whitefield moving relentlessly across the crowd, and then it pointed to him! He felt as if all the air had been drained from his lungs, and he began to pant for breath. Then a great fear, such as he had never felt, grasped him, and the strength left him. He felt himself falling, and as he fell, he cried out, "Oh, God! Help me, for Jesus' sake!"

When he hit the ground there was no sensation of shock, and he felt almost as if he were out of his own body. There was no awareness of the ground, nor did he have any care for those around him. He lay there praying and calling on God for mercy, but he had no sense of time. The voice of Whitefield seemed to come from very far away. He was conscious that many were calling on God in tears and groans, but he was shut off, insulated from it all.

Finally there came a change, and he seemed to come back to the world, as if he had been locked in a dark room and had stepped back into the world of light. He was shocked to discover that he was lying flat on his stomach, his face pressed against the grass. He got to his feet and looked around. Molly was staring at him, her cheeks stained with tears, her eyes large with fear.

He looked at her and tried to smile, but he could not. She came close and put her hand tentatively on his arm, whispering softly, "Adam? Are you—all right?"

He nodded, conscious that he was totally exhausted, so tired he could hardly stand. But he knew also there was something in him that had not been there earlier. He stood with his head bowed, his arms hanging limply by his side, and examined his feelings.

The one thing he was most aware of was that he had a sense of complete and utter restfulness, and he marveled at how he seemed to be totally at ease, almost as if his spirit were floating. He smiled at her and said quietly and with wonder in his voice, "Yes—I'm all right, Molly."

Then he said more strongly, "You know what? I'm more all right than I've ever been in all my life!"

Molly's eyes opened wide and she held on to his arm. She saw something in his face that moved her, and she asked quietly, "Adam, are you born again?"

Adam Winslow looked up to where the skies were beginning to clear, then back to her. He smiled, but his voice was not completely steady as he said almost in a whisper, "I think so, Molly. For the first time in my life, I'm not afraid to think about meeting Jesus Christ."

Then a look of amazement touched his eyes, and he threw his head back and said in wonder as he looked up at the skies, "You know, I'm even looking *forward* to seeing Him! Now, isn't that a strange thing? For a man to actually *want* to see God?" He looked back to her and asked suddenly, "Well, do you think I've lost my mind, Molly?"

She threw her arms around him. He heard her say in a muffled voice as she buried her face against him, "No! I think you've just begun to find out what you are, Adam Winslow!"

Then she leaned back, tears gleaming in her eyes. As they turned to go, she said the one thing that he wanted most to hear, "You know, your father and Aunt Rachel—they must be very proud of you!"

"You think so?"

"Oh, yes! We'll write William and Mercy, too. Think how happy they'll be."

His mind reached out and images of the kind faces of those two swam before him, and he whispered, "They will, won't they, Molly? They really will!"

CHAPTER TWENTY

DEATH AT MONONGAHELA

★ ★ ★ ★

Adam knew as soon as he took one look at Charles that something was wrong, but he had no time to listen to him carefully, for Braddock's expedition against Fort Duquesne was pulling out of Will's Creek even as his brother came riding up.

"Adam—I've got to talk to you!" Charles pulled his horse to a halt, his face tense under his wide-brimmed hat. A big cannon pulled by a span of heavy draft horses lumbered forward, forcing him to pull his mount over to the side of the narrow road, and Adam followed him to where he dismounted under a spreading elm tree.

"I can't talk now, Charles," Adam said impatiently. "Whatever it is will have to wait until we get back."

"I've been trying to catch up with you for a week!" Charles complained. "Where've you been?"

"Trying to help Washington get this army started—and it's a miracle that we're on our way as it is!"

Neither Adam nor Washington could believe the complications that had arisen to delay the expedition—but it was Braddock's fault, for he insisted on a force that was unwieldy, massive, and awkward. He had an army consisting of 1,445 regulars fit for duty, 262 men in 3 independent colonial companies,

30 sailors to assist with block and tackle in hauling the cannon over the mountains, and 449 Virginia, North Carolina, and Maryland troops, as well as a small detachment of gunners.

The artillery train consisted of ten 6- and 12-pounder guns, 4 big howitzers, and 14 small mortars. The heaviest piece weighed well over half a ton, not counting its carriage, a discouraging object to haul over mountains where no road existed. In addition to the guns themselves, shot and shell had to be carried, as well as powder. There was, moreover, a host of necessary artillery supplies that must be taken, about 269 separate items, many of them in several sizes, ranging from a small derrick down to candles and carpet tacks. Food had to be supplied for more than 2,000 men for at least a month and food for the horses, for there would be little or no natural feed in deep woods. No horse could maintain its strength on leaves alone, but part of the time they were to be reduced to that. All this meant many wagons, and only by the aid of Benjamin Franklin, who produced 150 heavy wagons, was the expedition made possible.

"How we'll ever get this train through to our objective, I can't see!" Washington had protested, but he had thrown his energies into the project, and Adam had been hard driven to keep up with the colonel.

Now Adam said impatiently to Charles, "I've been busy—say it quick, whatever it is."

Charles's handsome face was thinner than usual, and he seemed nervous. Finally he said, "We've had some backsets in the business, Adam. I've been wanting to talk to you about it."

"You and Uncle Saul will have to take care of it," Adam said, and then he heard his name called. Looking up the road, now clogged with wagons and marching men, he saw Colonel Washington hailing him. "I've got to go, Charles. You'll have to take care of the problem." Then he paused and asked quickly, "You never wanted my advice before. What's different about this time?"

"Well, to tell you the truth, it's Stirling."

"Stirling? What about him?"

"We've borrowed a lot of money from him, and—well, he's getting anxious."

Adam stared at him, then said with a harsh line around his mouth, "Get free from the man, Charles! And I don't say that because I've had trouble with him. He's not good for us. How deep are we into his debt?"

"Too far," Charles admitted grimly. "He's in a position to make it hard on us if he wants to force it."

Adam stared at him, then shook his head, and swung up into the saddle. "We'll talk about it when I get back. We better go see Saul—find a way to get Stirling out of our hair. Stall him off until I get back."

"But, Adam. . . !" Charles called. But there was no time, and Adam had only a final glimpse of his brother as the young soldier caught up with Washington and the train rounded a turn in the narrow road that had been hacked through the woods by Washington's force a year ago.

"Winslow, ride on ahead," Washington said urgently. "I've tried to get the general to put out scouts and flankers, but he laughed at me."

"You're not expecting an attack this early, are you, Colonel?"

Washington's face was flushed; he had been fighting a fever for several days. He hated sickness, in himself most of all, and now he shook his head, impatient with his weakness. "No, but we'll have to send a crew ahead to clear the road. It gets much narrower up ahead, you remember. Go take a look, then come back and I'll try to get General Braddock to send the axmen ahead to do the clearing."

"Yes, sir!"

Adam wheeled his horse around and rode past the lumbering wagons at a fast gallop. It was hot, and he knew that by noon the soldiers in their wool uniforms designed for the cool climates of Europe would be staggering under the heat, and that the overloaded wagons would pull the strength of the horses down to a walk.

Soon he was far in advance of the army and entering the silent thick forest. The contrast was a pleasure. He had been in the midst of noise and confusion for the past month, and the solitude of the woods had a healing effect on his spirit.

He searched the trees constantly, his head moving from side

to side, but it was with the automatic watchfulness he had learned during his years in the Ohio Valley. He noted soon that Washington had been right, for the road narrowed down to a rutted track not six feet wide—enough for troops to pass, but not nearly enough for the wagons. He kept on for the rest of the morning, then turned his mount back, his head filled with thoughts of the past few weeks.

Since the afternoon Adam had fallen to the ground under the influence of Whitefield's preaching, he had been strangely peaceful. The next morning after his experience, he'd gotten up half expecting that the whole thing would have faded. He'd known enough converts to shout and profess salvation, only to fall away once the excitement was over. Jonathan Edwards had been clear enough on that, for he had insisted strongly that the test of the new birth was not an emotional experience but a new walk with God. "It's not how high a man jumps, Adam," the preacher had said to him once. "It's how straight he runs after he hits the ground! The one mark of the new birth is this: *A new birth will always make a man love Jesus more!"*

And that had been the essence of the days that followed. Adam had been consumed with a hunger for the Bible, and the person of the Lord Jesus Christ had been a reality in his spirit.

Molly had noticed it instantly. "You're different, Adam," she had said when they got back to Virginia. "You were never a hard man, but now there's something new in you!"

He turned and searched her face intently. "You found Christ, too, didn't you, Molly?"

"Yes," she said, and there was a fullness in her smile that reflected a joy in her spirit. "It's so *different*, isn't it, Adam— being saved? Jesus was always just someone in a story to me— but now He's my best friend!"

Adam had stared at her, then a smile had touched his broad lips, and his eyes warmed as he said, "We've got lots to talk about, haven't we, Molly?"

But there had been no time, for as soon as they reached home, he found an urgent message from Washington instructing him to come to Alexandria at once. He had thrown a few things together and said a quick goodbye to Molly. "You'll be all right with James and Hope until I get back."

"Be careful!" she had said nervously. "If anything happened to you, I'd—"

He had smiled at her, a thought coming to him. "You know, you're not going to be a bound girl much longer. What is it, two more months?"

She had stared at him, wondering what was on his mind, and then she'd shrugged, saying, "I don't ever think about it."

"Well, it's something we'll talk about when I get back. I have a thought or two about your future." He'd said nothing more than that, but her head had lifted, and her fine gray eyes had warmed.

Now riding back down the road toward the army, Adam wished he'd told her what was on his mind. "Why in the name of heaven didn't I kiss her—tell her I love her?" he said aloud in disgust. He had thought of it, but one fact had kept him from speaking: he might not get back—or it could be he'd return as a hopeless cripple. Such things happened in war, he knew, and he didn't want her to be the victim of that.

I wonder how long I've been in love with her? he mused as he picked his way along the rutted road. All the way back to camp, he thought what it would be like when he returned home.

But the only time he had to think of Molly for the next few weeks was at night after he'd eaten and lain down on the ground, wrapped in his blanket. The days were filled with work, and the expedition advanced slowly, ponderously through the primeval forest. The soldiers, all wearing swords, left the weapons behind, as well as some of their other heavy gear. The work involved was incredible. The road had to be hacked out, rock ledges drilled and blasted, swamps corduroyed and streams bridged.

The expedition advanced slowly. Small parties of French and Indians continually hampered their progress, entering into skirmishes with the flank guards Braddock had put out at Washington's insistence.

Finally Braddock realized that the rate of advance was far too slow, and a council of senior officers was held; the decision was made to detach a part of the force, lightly equipped, to proceed forward as rapidly as possible, with the remainder, and most of the wagons, to follow at a slower pace under the command of Colonel Dunbar, the officer next in seniority to Braddock.

On the morning of July 9 the advance army was on the south bank of Turtle Creek, which flows into the Monongahela. The scouts urged a crossing by marching to the main channel, which because of drought would be easily fordable.

At the first crossing, Washington, who had been riding on a bed in a wagon, ordered one of his horses brought up and saddled, with a pillow placed on the saddle. The fever had left him, but he was still weak from twenty days of illness.

Adam rode close beside him, worried about the officer, but said nothing. He did point to where the British were crossing the river. The red-coated regulars splashed into the stream, relishing the cool water on that hot July day. The river was so low that it exposed a pebbly beach a quarter of a mile wide. Here Braddock paraded his army with unfurled guidons, drums beating, and trumpets blaring.

"I suppose General Braddock thinks this will impress the enemy," Washington said. "But I don't think it'll have much effect on their marksmanship."

"No, I'd much rather we sent out more scouts," Adam admitted. He bit his lip, shook his head and asked, "Did you talk to General Braddock about the attack—I mean what we spoke of last night?"

"About letting the men take cover if we're attacked? I tried, but he only said, 'There'll be no hiding behind trees!' "

"He's a fool, sir!" Adam exclaimed angrily. "Look at those troops! Why, it'd be impossible for a marksman to miss them!" The brilliant scarlet coats and the high red mitre caps stood out like a flame against the green woods, and Adam shook his head, saying, "If they jump us, we're finished!"

Washington did not answer, but when Braddock led the line of troops into a small thicket lined on both sides with towering trees and intensely thick ground cover, he said, "I don't like this ground!"

He had no sooner spoken than a ragged volley of shots rang

out, and red-coated troopers fell writhing to the ground. "It's a trap!" Washington shouted, and spurring his horse, he drove forward past the line of soldiers to pull up to Braddock. "Sir! There's a walnut grove back there—we can pull back and see the enemy."

Braddock stared at him as if he were insane. "Retreat from this rabble? No, sir! You may now see how the British soldier handles an enemy!" Galloping ahead he ordered Colonel Burton to bring his troops forward, then rode to find the Virginia troops had taken to the trees and the Pennsylvania axmen were doing the same. Some of Gage's men had taken cover also, and Adam saw Braddock's face turn scarlet with rage. Drawing his sword he galloped up and began beating his own men away from the trees, crying out, "Forward! Charge!"

The troops moved forward, but the firing from the bushes became more intense. "Sir, this is the main body!" Washington cried loudly.

"Nonsense! It's just a few skirmishers!" Braddock scoffed. He gave a command, and the British fired into the forest. Their musket balls cut leaves from the trees and splintered saplings, but the enemy was firmly entrenched behind the huge trees. They knew, of course, that the British having once fired would have to reload, so they came zigzagging through the trees like phantoms, firing at will, felling the redcoats like stalks of grain before a scythe.

Suddenly the general's horse reared as a musket ball struck its flanks, dumping Braddock unceremoniously to the side. He mounted again and screamed, "Forward! Charge the enemy!"

The massive force was marching in ranks, officers on horseback, drums beating the cadence. A wall of red filled the entire road as the men walked shoulder to shoulder. Behind them were the others, the entire flying column, the militia and the Virginia blues—all walking into a twelve-foot-wide trap, with walls of trees and underbrush on either side of them.

The woods blazed with musket shots. Bullets hailed from the unsecured heights. Within minutes the outer columns were decimated. Every bullet seemed to find a target. The officers ordered their men to face the right and march in formation into the woods despite the fact that there was no target in sight.

The cries of dying men were everywhere, creating a madness that broke the spirit of the troops.

"Hold your positions!"

It was Braddock's last command, for before he could shout again, a bullet knocked him from his saddle. The shot smashed his elbow and punctured his lungs. He fell to the ground, and a groan went up from the soldiers. Some of them began to run, turning to meet a wall of their own kind marching into the narrow passage.

Mob hysteria took hold, and the road became the landscape of a nightmare. Fallen men were trampled by heavy black boots. Faces contorted with a continuum of emotions, from terror to determination to rage. Commands were ignored; few could even be heard above the curses, bellows, and whines.

It was then that Washington cried out: "Retreat!" He had had two horses shot out from under him, but there was no sign of fear on his stern face. The army fell back in total disarray. They ran like rabbits, and as they fell back, Adam saw the Indians come out of the woods, scalping, looting, and mutilating the dead and wounded, their elated whoops blending with the cries of the living victims.

Braddock had been put in a litter, bleeding from his lungs, as the army fell back. The Virginians and the Pennsylvanians brought up the rear, and it was only the firm hand of George Washington that saved them, Adam knew. He was a marvel, organizing the retreat, sending for help from the troops they'd left behind, taking care of the wounded—he was everywhere at once. Adam was at his side, carrying his orders to this officer and that, and he thought, *We'd all die if it weren't for him!*

The count was sickening. Of the 1,451 who had crossed the river at noon, 456 were left dead and a dozen taken prisoner. Of those who escaped, 421 were wounded. This left only 562 unharmed, and it was likely that no more than twenty of the enemy were killed, if that many.

The next day at noon they met Dunbar and the rear guard, but it was too late for Braddock. He died later that night. The last thing he said was, "Next time we will know how to deal with them."

He was buried, then every wagon and every horse was marched over his grave to conceal it, lest the Indians should dig it up for its graying scalp and resplendent uniform.

Dunbar took command, and before retreating, ordered all stores destroyed, including 150 wagons, many of them valuable. The remnants of the army that had marched out so proudly made its way back to Virginia at a crawl.

Washington and Adam rode together, and only once did the colonel comment on the tragic affair. He repeated to Adam Braddock's last words: *Next time we'll know how to deal with them.* Then he said grimly, "I have learned something, Winslow, and I trust that you have also. European tactics will never win a victory in this country!"

They arrived home, and Adam prepared to ride to Woodbridge, but a message from Charles was waiting for him at Alexandria. It was given to him by one of the house slaves, stating only, "Come here as soon as you can. Urgent!"

"Your master wants me now?" he asked the slave, whose name was Junius.

"Yessuh. He say doan go home 'til you see him."

"All right, let's go."

He found Washington, told him of the message, then asked for permission.

"Of course!" Washington said instantly, and a smile lighted his stern face and he put his hand out. "I am in your debt, Adam Winslow—indeed I am! Come to see me at Mount Vernon. We'll hunt a fox and you can show me your new gun again."

A warmth filled Adam as he shook Washington's hand, a warmth that stayed with him until he got to Charles's plantation. He dismounted wearily, made his way across the yard and up the steps. As Charles came out to meet him, Adam saw immediately that he had been drinking heavily.

"Glad you're home, Adam," Charles mumbled. He stood there swaying slightly; there was a hollowness in his cheeks, and dark shadows underscored his eyes.

"What's wrong, Charles?" Adam asked sharply.

"It's bad news, I'm afraid.

"Business?"

"Well—yes, but not like you think." Charles seemed embarrassed, and he rubbed his face with his palm, then held his hand out in a helpless gesture. In a panic-stricken voice he hurriedly said, "I know you'll blame me, Adam—but it's not my fault!"

"Spit it out, man!" Adam snapped. "I've got to get home."

"Molly's not there!"

Adam stared at Charles, fear gripping him. "What does that mean? Where is she?"

"Well, you remember I told you that Stirling was pressing us on the loans?"

"Yes? Did he call them?"

Charles shifted his feet and could not meet Adam's eyes. "Yes, he called some of them—but Saul and I sold off some land and managed to save most of the important things, but—he had a lien on the gunshop."

"He took that, too?" Adam asked, but was relieved. "Well, it's just a place. We can find another. Did you bring Molly here?"

"No, she's not here, Adam."

Adam lost his patience. "*Where* is she, then?"

"Stirling has her, Adam!"

A chilling silence fell between them. Charles's eyes were filled with shame as he tried to explain. "He—took over the shop, and since she was an indentured servant, he claimed her, too. I tried to stop him—really I did, Adam!"

Adam stared at him. "I guess you didn't try too hard, Charles. But he can't make it stick."

"No, not legally—but he *has* her, Adam! He took her by force a week ago. And he left you a message."

"What was it?"

"He said if you came to his place, he'd kill you!" Charles held out his hands impotently, and added bitterly, "I got the lawyers on it, but what good does that do? You know the kind of man he is, Adam!"

"I know, all right." Adam stared at Charles, then asked quietly, his voice steady, "Do you know where he's holed up?"

"Yes. He's in the house on that tract of land you liked on the Mohawk River—the one we got from Cartwright. It's on the bluff by the old Indian burial ground."

Adam turned and ran to his horse. Charles shouted after him, "Adam! He's not alone there! He's hired a bunch of Indians to guard the place. It'll be like trying to get into a fortress!"

Adam ignored him, and for a long moment Charles watched him ride down the road, and then ran across the yard yelling at the top of his lungs, "Junius! Junius! Saddle my horse!"

CHAPTER TWENTY-ONE

CAPTURE THE CASTLE

★ ★ ★ ★

Summer heat lay like a blanket in the Hudson River valley as Adam led Charles along the eastern foothills of the Appalachians, draining the strength of the horses so quickly that they had to exchange mounts three times before they reached the spot where the Mohawk joins the Hudson. The Green Mountains lay east, and Lake Ontario was directly west.

Charles had managed to stay in the saddle only by dogged determination, for Adam had ridden twenty hours at a stretch, stopping only long enough to eat and rest the horses. Now as they turned west, the younger man called out, "Adam! Wait a minute!"

Adam pulled his horse to a halt, turned in the saddle, his face grim. "What is it?"

Charles drew close, straightening up in the saddle to get the kink out of his back. He groaned wearily, saying, "Adam, we've got to rest these horses or they'll break down on us!"

"They'll make it."

"No they won't!" Charles argued. "Look at this animal— he's windbroke already. Be a miracle if he gets there at all." He looked at the three horses Adam was leading, and added, "Why don't I dump this nag and ride a fresh one?"

"Because these horses are our ticket out of this place, Charles. When we get Molly back, we've still got to get away, and if Stirling has any good Indians hired, we'll need all the speed we can get." He looked at Charles's mount, then at his own, and shook his head. "You're right, though. These two are about finished."

"How far do you think we have to go, Adam?"

"Maybe thirty miles—but there's a settler I know about five miles from here. We'll trade these two animals for fresh mounts."

He spoke to his horse, and as they proceeded at a slower pace, Charles was silent. He had thought he'd known this dark half-brother of his, but since he'd given him the news about Molly, the easygoing mildness in Adam's makeup had disappeared. *I don't know this man*, Charles thought as they plodded along. *He's like an Indian now—and I'm glad he's not on my trail!*

They reached the cabin of Adam's friend, found nobody home, and took fresh mounts—a tall buckskin for Charles and a powerful gelding for Adam. They made a quick meal of some cold beef in the smokehouse, then, after Adam left a note explaining the situation, they plunged immediately along the overgrown trail that followed the twisting banks of the Mohawk.

It was late afternoon the following day when Adam finally pulled up and slipped from the saddle. "The house is only three miles from here. We'll eat and sleep until dark."

"Will it be all right to make a fire?" Charles asked.

"Better not. My guess is that Stirling will be expecting me, and he'll probably have those Iroquois fanned out as scouts."

They had a quick meal, and when they finished, Adam lay down with his head on his saddle and closed his eyes. Charles stared at him, and said heatedly, "Well, are you going to let me in on the plan? After all, I'm all the help you have!"

Adam's eyes opened, and he rolled over on his side to look at his brother. His dark blue eyes were intent, and there was a sudden break in the austere hard cast that had been on his face for days. A smile suddenly broke across his broad lips, and he mused, "I've been wondering about that, Charles." He studied Charles's wedge-shaped face and added, "Didn't expect it of you, to be honest. You can get hurt—I guess you know that?"

"You think I'm an idiot?" Charles snapped. "We can both get killed—probably will. It'd be just my luck!" He picked up a dead stick, slapped his palm with it, then suddenly broke it in two and threw the pieces aside. Glaring at Adam he said with a streak of irritation in his voice, "I don't know what I'm doing out here. Looking out for my own skin—that's been my way. Why'd you get me into this?"

Adam considered the face of his brother, and after a long pause he said, "You fooled me, Charles. I never figured you to risk your scalp for anybody—least of all me."

Charles stared at him, a baffled look in his bright blue eyes. "We Winslows haven't been all that close, have we? Guess I've been jealous of you."

"Why—!" Adam sat up, astonishment in his face as he replied, "That's crazy, Charles! You're the bright one of the family—always have been."

Charles nodded, but there was a disgust in his face as he said slowly, "A man can get too smart, Adam. Like this mess we're in now. I wasn't very smart to let this happen, was I? Guess that's why I'm sitting here waiting for a bunch of Iroquois to swoop down and butcher me. It was my fault—and I always liked Molly."

"We'll get her."

There was confidence in Adam's voice, and Charles stared at him, incredulous. "You're sure of that, aren't you? Wish I had as much confidence."

"I'm praying about it, Charles," Adam said quietly.

"Oh? You've prayed about it, and that settles it?" Charles shook his head in disgust. "Can't believe that prayer's going to get her away from Henry."

"We'll do our part, but God's going to help us!"

Charles stared at Adam, his face a curious mixture of disgust and longing. "Well—you'll have to do the praying, brother. But do you also have a *plan*—something we can actually *do*?"

Adam nodded and sat up. Picking up a stick, he drew a curving line in the dust, saying, "Here's the river—and right about here is where the house is." He drew an X beside the wavy line, and said quickly, "The house is built up on a high bluff overlooking the river—must be a hundred feet or more—and it's plenty steep, Charles. I always liked the location. It's like a fort, see? The house is in a sort of projection with steep gullies on both sides—so there's only one way for anybody attacking the place to hit."

"Just one way?"

"Right! The place is practically impregnable, because there's an open space in front, a high wall closing off the house, just like a fort."

Charles looked at the lines in the dust, then up at Adam. "So, how in the world are we going to take a place like that?"

"I've been thinking about it—and there's one way. They'll be watching the front like hawks, but nobody will be watching the bluff because nobody's ever climbed it—that I know of."

"But—can you climb it?"

Adam clamped his lips shut and shrugged his heavy shoulders. "I don't know."

Charles licked his lips, then asked nervously, "You don't know if you can even *get* to the house?"

"No." Adam suddenly smiled, and added, "And I can't carry a musket with me. Just a knife. Even if I could take a rifle, I wouldn't dare use it. It'd wake everybody up, and we'd never get away."

"You don't know where Molly is," Charles protested. "But even if you can find her, how'll you get out? They'll be watching the gate, won't they?"

"Sure. We'll have to come back the same way I go up—down the bluff."

"Why, you can't climb down a thing like that in the dark! And even if you could, Molly couldn't!"

"We'll jump for it—it's the only way." Adam smiled grimly at Charles's expression, then said, "Here's the way we'll do it: I'll climb up the bluff after dark, find Molly, bring her to the bluff. We'll signal and jump for it. You'll be waiting there with the horses, and we get away as quick as we can."

"It's insane!"

"There's no other way, but if you want out, I won't fault

you for it, Charles." Adam shrugged and said, "Even if I get Molly out of there, those Indians are going to be on our trail— and you know what they'll do to us if they catch us!"

A soft breeze lifted Charles's fair hair. The fear lurking in his face gripped him as he sat there contemplating their chances. Adam said no more, but he could sense that inside his brother there was a war. Charles had never been a coward, but the odds for success in this case were small. Both of them knew that, and while Adam was set like flint, Charles was struggling against a lifetime of selfish indulgence. He yearned to get on a horse and ride away, and for a moment, Adam expected him to do just that.

"All right, Adam—I'll do it!" he exploded in despair. "But if you get me killed, I'll never forgive you for it!"

Adam laughed and got to his feet. "Thanks, Charles," he said gratefully; then he put his hand out awkwardly, and when his brother took it, he stated matter-of-factly, "We Winslows are a pretty tough breed, brother—and although God's on our side, we've got one little asset that might make a difference."

He stepped to one of the horses, pulled a rifle from the pack, then fished a leather pouch out of a pocket. Returning to Charles's side he said, "This is our secret weapon. I want you to learn how to use it."

Charles watched as Adam took out a handful of paper cylinders, then asked, "What are those?"

"Cartridges for these rifles," Adam answered. He held a rifle up, moved a lever and put one of the cylinders into the breech of the rifle, then pulled a plate over it. "Ready to fire," he announced with a smile at the expression on his brother's face. "It's what you've been after me to make for years—a breech-loading rifle."

Charles took it, staring admiringly at the new type of mechanism, and listening carefully as Adam pointed out how it worked. "How long does it take to load up?" he asked.

"Maybe five or ten seconds."

Charles stared at him, then looked down at the weapon. "Why, we'll be rich!"

"If we're not dead," Adam replied with a shrug. "There's

just one thing—I haven't got it all perfected. Usually it works, but sometimes it fails. But even when it does, it's quicker to throw a faulty cartridge out and re-load than to load down the muzzle with powder and ball."

Charles looked at the weapon, then up at Adam, respect in his eyes. "Well, it's plain that *I'm* not the smart Winslow!"

"We'll argue about that when we get back to Virginia. Now, let me drill you in how to load this thing. If we get rushed, I want you to load and let me shoot."

Charles learned quickly, for the process was simple. Then he lay down and just before he dropped off to sleep he asked aloud, "I wonder how much we can get for a Winslow rifle?"

"Lord Stirling, he say you come now!"

The speaker was a statuesque Indian woman, not more than twenty-five years old. She was wearing an expensive dress made in a London shop, and the delicate bows and ribbons set off her primitive beauty. Molly knew her by the name of Alice, and though she had tried, she had been unable to break through the woman's reserve. She had been introduced by Stirling with a smirk as his "housekeeper," but Molly had discerned instantly that she had been his Indian "wife." Such things were common enough on the frontier, and trappers sometimes married such women legally.

Stirling, of course, had no thoughts of doing that but Alice had no way of knowing this; it accounted for the sharp glint of hatred in her ebony eyes as she stared at Molly, saying again, "Lord Stirling say you come!"

Molly tried again to talk to the woman, for Alice was her only hope of escape. "Alice—remember what we talked about yesterday?"

Momentarily hope glowed in the woman's face, then faded as she said with a fatalistic shrug, "You no get away from this place. When he tired of you—then you go."

"But you could get me a horse—I could get away after dark—"

"You think you outride one of my people? No. You stay here."

"Alice, you could hire one of your braves to take me home! He'd be well paid, and then you'd have Lord Stirling all to yourself."

A flash of hatred ran across Alice's face, but the stolid look fell over her features. "You come now."

Molly suppressed an urge to beg and plead with the Indian, but knowing it would be useless, she followed her down the hall to the dining room.

"Ah—just in time for supper!" Henry Stirling came from the window that looked out across the river and put his hands on Molly's shoulders. She tried not to show fear, but he saw it in her face, and it made him laugh. He turned to the woman, saying, "Alice, bring the food in—and you can go to bed early tonight."

Alice shot a quick glance at Molly, hatred in her agate eyes, but she merely nodded and left the room.

Molly walked quickly to the window, looking out in the falling darkness. The view was magnificent, for the dining room projected over the bluff. The river far below was barely visible, catching the last gleams of the dying sun, and throwing up myriad points of light. The land fell away, the valley green and lush, running to the low-lying hills far to the south.

She had no eye for the beauty, however, and the fear that had been her constant companion since Stirling had brought her to this place rose in her throat. As he came to stand behind her, she forced herself to stand very still, for she had learned that any sign of fear not only pleased him, but aroused him to passion as well.

When he had first brought her into the house, he had said, "You'll have your own room, Molly, and I'll give you a little time before we get better acquainted."

He had, in some sort, been faithful to that, not so much as a matter of courtesy, but because he had been away on some sort of business—to look at land, she learned later. She had slept little, staying awake and trying vainly to think of some way of escape, but there was none. The Indian woman, Alice, had been her one hope, but it had become apparent that she knew all too well what Stirling would do to her if she helped arrange an escape.

As the days went by, Stirling returned—to begin a heavy-handed courtship of Molly. He was a vain man, accustomed to easy conquests, and it seemed to be something of a shock to him when Molly failed to respond to his advances. He even went so far as to hint of marriage, but this ploy was so absurd that Molly could not hide her disdain.

On one occasion, after a dinner such as was planned for this evening, he had drunk several bottles of wine, and in a drunken stupor had come after her. She had fought clear of him, and was saved only because he had fallen down drunk.

As Molly stared blindly out of the window, her mind was racing, for there was something in his manner that caused fear to mount and grip her heart. This night was different. Her hands were trembling; as she turned to face him, she saw the intent in his eyes.

"Now, let's have a nice meal, and then we'll have time for some good talk, my dear!" Stirling said. He turned to the table, pulled out a chair, and when she was seated, took his own seat. A bottle of wine was on the table, and he poured two full glasses, handed one to her and urged, "Drink up, Molly." When she hesitated, he commanded with a trace of anger, "Drink it, I say!"

She sipped the wine, and as the meal was served by Alice and a black servant, she realized that he was trying to get her drunk—not the first time he'd attempted such a thing.

The meal went on for a long time. Candles were lit as darkness fell, and there were many courses. Stirling had brought his cook from England, and he pointed out the virtues of the various dishes. As Molly picked at her food, sick with fear, he told her tales of his life in England.

Finally the dishes were all taken away, and Stirling said to the housekeeper, "Alice, you may go to bed—and tell the rest of the servants they won't be needed tonight."

"Yes, Lord Stirling."

As the door closed behind Alice, and Stirling turned to her, Molly was possessed with such a fear that she wanted to run to the door and flee, but she knew that such a course would only give him a warped pleasure.

She could see in his eyes the hunger for her that he did not bother to conceal, and when he came over and put his hands on her under the pretense of guiding her to the sofa beside the wall, she did what she had done ever since she had been made captive: she prayed to God for deliverance.

For the next two hours she did little but try to think of God's promises—and she found that the many scriptures she'd heard Jonathan Edwards quote both in his pulpit and in his home to his own family came to her mind. One especially was so clear that she seemed to hear it spoken in his clear, high voice: *I looked on my right hand, and beheld, but there was no man that would know me: refuge failed me; no man cared for my soul. I cried unto thee, O Lord: I said, Thou art my portion in the land of the living. Attend unto my cry; for I am brought very low: deliver me from my persecutors, for they are stronger than I. Bring my soul out of prison, that I may praise thy name.*

She held on to the verse, repeating it with all her heart; soon it was obvious that, indeed, only God could help, for after several crude attempts at flattery, he cast away all decency and began to paw at her.

"Please!—don't do that!" she begged, but he merely laughed and pulled her closer.

Molly pulled free, leaped to her feet, and made a blind dash for the door, but he caught her and held her fast. Then holding her with one arm, he took her face with his other hand and kissed her again and again.

Struggling helplessly, Molly's mind was paralyzed with fear, and when he lifted his face to smile at her, she cried out, "God, save me!"

"No, God isn't going to save you, Molly," he laughed. "I've waited long enough—and nobody's going to save you—so you might as well be nice to me!"

"Turn her loose, Stirling!"

The voice came so unexpectedly that Stirling uttered a cry of shock and alarm. He loosed his hold on Molly, whirling to see Adam Winslow standing in the doorway!

"What. . . !" Stirling tried to speak, but his mind was not able to comprehend the situation. He had felt so secure with the guards fanned out across the front of his house that the last thing in the world he expected to see was his enemy facing him in such a manner.

"How did you get in here?" he demanded, and took one step to the side toward the wall where a brace of pistols were mounted.

Adam leaped forward like a tiger, a knife suddenly in his right hand. He fell on Stirling, driving the larger man back against the wall. With one hand grabbing a fistful of hair, he pulled Stirling's head back and laid the keen edge of the knife against it. "You make one sound, Stirling, and I'll cut your throat out!"

"Adam!" Molly stood there staring at him, her eyes large with shock. Then she suddenly smiled and said, "I knew you'd come!"

Stirling risked saying, "You'll never get away from here, Winslow! There are twenty braves out there!"

Adam made his mistake then, for he turned to look at Molly, to speak to her, and as he did, Stirling moved suddenly with a speed surprising in a big man. He knocked Adam's knife hand away with one arm, then struck Adam in the chest with a powerful right—a blow that drove the smaller man back across the room.

Stirling wheeled, and in one smooth motion, ripped one of the pistols off the wall. He aimed it and fired at Adam point blank!

Molly screamed, but the shot narrowly missed, clipping a lock from Adam's hair as he drove forward, and in that split second he could have driven the knife into Stirling's heart—but something made him reverse the weapon and he struck the Englishman in the temple with the weighted handle.

Stirling went down in a crumpled heap, and Adam wheeled and caught Molly's hand. "Let's get out of here!"

He did not go to the door, but pulled her to the window. Throwing it open, he said, "We're going to have to jump for the river, Molly!"

He leaped to the ground, reached up his arms and caught her, then in two steps they were standing on the brink of the bluff. It was a dark night, and neither of them could see more than a few feet. He swiftly turned to her, put his arms around her, and asked, "Molly, will you trust me? It's a leap in the dark— but God will be with us."

"I—I'll always trust you, Adam," she murmured, pulling his face down to kiss him. When she drew back, she said, "I can't swim, Adam."

He took her hand and said quietly, "Hang on to me, Molly!"

Then together, they leaped off into the darkness, plummeting toward the water far below, and as they fell, Molly cried out, "Lord, Thou art my refuge!"

CHAPTER TWENTY-TWO

DEATH IN THE AFTERNOON

★ ★ ★ ★

Charles had never considered himself a coward, but the long wait in the darkness beside the river had drawn his nerves tight. For the first thirty minutes after Adam had waded into the river and disappeared in the inky darkness of the night, he had strained his ears for any noise coming from the house high above, but there was no sound save the gurgle of the water. As another fifteen minutes had passed, he had stared up, craning his neck to see the dim, yellow lights that glowed from the windows.

Suddenly there was a splashing to his left, and fear struck him like a blow! He whirled and almost fired the rifle, but loosed his finger when he saw a large buck come out of the river and disappear into the thickets downstream from where he stood.

"Devil take it!" he swore, relaxing his cramped fingers and rubbing his stiff neck. He rolled his head, forcing himself to relax, then moved back from the stream to check the horses. Coming back to the shelving bank of the Mohawk, he thought again of what would happen if the Iroquois caught them—scalped alive, burning splinters under the fingernails, gunpowder in raw wounds set on fire. . . !

"Why doesn't he hurry up!" he muttered under his breath—

then realized that Adam was taking the most dangerous end of the business. He forced himself to stand still, listening to the river and dreading to hear the sound of shots above. *I must be crazy,* he thought—*risking my scalp like this! Here I am, the Winslow who's always looked out for his own—and now I'm risking my life for a girl I hardly know.* He wiped the cold sweat off his brow, moved back a few feet to get a better view of the lights above, and suddenly smiled in the darkness. *Maybe I'm getting religion— that'd make Adam happy, I guess.* But he knew himself too well for that, and being a man not given to introspection, he finally gave up and stood there waiting for Adam's return.

Ten minutes later he heard a sound that brought his heart up into his throat—a single muffled explosion that came from high up the bluff, so low he barely caught it. "Oh, Lord! He's caught!" he thought with agonizing fear, and he almost ran for the horses—but forced himself to wait. *Five minutes! I'll wait that long!*

But it was less than two minutes later when he heard the sound of a loud splash, and he ran forward to the edge of the water, straining his eyes in the darkness. "Adam! Adam!" he cried out quickly. "Is that you?"

He held his rifle ready, but almost instantly he heard Adam call out, "Charles—here we are!"

Charles waded knee-deep into the water, and out of the darkness Adam appeared, supporting Molly with one hand. They stumbled to the bank and Molly said, "Thank God!"

"Amen to that!" Adam said huskily. "Are you all right?"

"I—swallowed some water, but—"

"Let's get out of here!" Charles interrupted. "What was that shot? Never mind—it woke up everybody in the place, no doubt!"

"You're right about that," Adam said. "We've got a mighty short lead, Charles—they'll be down on us in minutes."

He ran to the horses, and as he helped Molly mount a bay mare, he said, "They won't have their horses. They'll scramble down the bluff somehow, and then they'll have to go back and get mounted. We've got to put as much distance as we can between us and here before they get that done."

The two men swung into the saddle, and Adam turned his horse toward the river, saying, "We'll make it a little harder on them. Make sure your horses don't touch the bank!"

The river was shallow at the edge and he led them for over a mile along the edge, then pulled his horse to a halt. "I know this old trail—and I guess they do, too. But maybe it'll take them a few hours to think of it."

"I can't see a thing, Adam!" Charles complained fretfully.

"You don't have to. Molly, your horse will follow mine, and Charles, you stay in the rear. There're some low branches, so keep your head down. By dawn, I want to be far away from this spot."

He drove his horse out of the river, and the others followed blindly. It was a hard ride, for although Adam sometimes warned them "Low limb!" sometimes he did not, and both Molly and Charles had scratches from the branches that clawed their faces.

Some time before dawn they came out of the thick woods, relieved at seeing the open country after riding the Indian trail. At dawn they stopped and rested the horses. Adam pulled some cold beef out of a saddle bag, and they ate hungrily. After they finished, he said, "Molly, I want to show you how to load this rifle." For the next thirty minutes he went over the procedure, then said, "That's good! I hope we get clear, but if we don't I want you and Charles to load for me."

"You think we got a chance, Adam?" Charles asked doubtfully. "I keep expecting those Iroquois to jump us at any minute."

"I think we're all right for now. It'll take a while for them to get organized—and then maybe they'll have to hunt for our trail for a time—but they'll kill their horses to get us."

"Well, I'm going to sleep," Charles said defiantly. He threw himself down on the ground, and was asleep almost at once.

Adam moved out of the glade where they'd tied the horses, and took a position on a small rise that commanded a view of the west country. "You better get some sleep too, Molly," Adam said.

"What about you?"

"I'll keep watch—you never can tell."

"No," she said softly, and then she smiled and came to stand beside him. Her ash-blond hair hung to her waist, and there was a gentleness on her lips as she put her hand on his arm and repeated his words: "You never can tell." Then she smiled suddenly and added, "I prayed you'd come, Adam!"

"Did—did he hurt you, Molly?"

He dreaded to hear her reply, but there was a glad light in her blue eyes, and she shook her head quickly. "No—there was nothing like that." Then she bit her lip and added, "But if you hadn't come—!"

He reached out and placed his hand on her cheek, marveling at its smoothness. The glade was quiet, disturbed only by the sound of small birds and the rustling of green leaves overhead. His hand was rough on her face, but she reached out and covered it with her own, holding it against her cheek.

She was so tall that she had to look up only slightly to gaze into his face, and as they stood there in the silence, both of them felt a strange peace. "Funny," he whispered, "here we are just a moment away from being attacked by Indians, and all I can think of is your eyes."

"My eyes?"

"Yes." He put his other hand on her face and stood there with her face cupped between his palms. Looking into her eyes, he grinned, saying, "I'll never be able to say what color your eyes are! Sometimes they're blue—sometimes gray, sometimes both."

She leaned forward to whisper, "And what color are they, Adam?"

"I'll tell you, Molly, they're just the color that every woman's eyes ought to be."

"That's—the nicest thing you ever said to me, Adam," she whispered.

"Molly, I was so afraid when I found out you were taken! And you know what I thought over and over again while Charles and I were on the way to get you?"

"What?"

"If anything happens to Molly, I'm a dead man!" Putting his arms around her protectively, he said, "I don't know what's going to happen—but whether we get out of this or not, I want to tell you something." He pulled her closer and her arms slipped around his neck as he said quietly, "I love you, Molly Burns! As much as God will let a man love a woman—I love you!"

Then he kissed her and felt a deep stirring; as he held her close, she was aware of the strength of his muscular body. It was for both of them a promise of a love that had not been—but which lay waiting to blossom, to enrich their lives with more than passion.

She stood still in his arms, then pulled her head back and whispered, "I love you, Adam. I—I think I always have, ever since I was a little girl."

He shook his head, and there was a wonder in his dark eyes. "I'll never forget the first time I saw you on that street in London!" He laughed, saying, "If anybody had told me that one day I'd marry that ragged, scared little girl, I'd have thought he was crazy!"

"Marry?"

"Why, that's what people in love do, Molly!" Then he kissed her again and said, "You go sleep while you can, my love. We're not out of this yet."

"All right—but I'm not afraid," she replied, then laughed softly. "I've got too much invested in you, Adam Winslow, to lose you just when I've got you ready to marry me!"

She laughed at his startled expression, then whirled and went back to the shelter of the glade. Adam watched her go, and then turned to face the tree line, and his face grew hard, for he knew, as the others did not, how pitifully slim their chances were. While they slept his mind worked steadily, trying to come up with some trick, some way to avoid the Iroquois, but nothing came to him. He knew once the Indians found their trail, they would sweep forward at top speed, killing their mounts if need be to catch up with them.

There was no fort near enough to seek shelter, and those few settlers in the area offered no protection; they'd be destroyed if he went near their homesteads.

We've got to ride like Satan himself is after us—which is pretty much the case! he thought ruefully, then settled down to watch while the others slept.

Four hours later, he awakened them, saying, "Time to ride."

He kept the pace steady, not so fast that the horses would break down, but swift enough so that by four that afternoon, Molly and Charles were exhausted and the horses were beginning to stumble. The sun was setting when he pulled into a small grove and they all dismounted. "We might as well have a fire and a good hot meal," Adam decided.

Charles asked in surprise, "Won't it be seen?"

"No—not by anyone who counts." Adam spoke shortly, and there was no more talk until they had built a small fire and made a hot meal of beef and coffee.

After they had eaten, Molly studied Adam's face as he gazed into the fire. There was something stubborn about his features. Finally she asked quietly, "Something's wrong, isn't it, Adam?"

He tossed the dregs of his coffee into the fire, looked up at her and nodded, "They'll catch up with us tomorrow."

"How can you tell?" Charles asked quickly.

"I saw them late this afternoon—dust from a big party. Who else would be coming at us that fast?"

"Can't we hide—or outrun them?" Charles asked anxiously.

"Not either," Adam shrugged. "I figure we'll have to be ready for them by tomorrow afternoon."

Molly stared at him, her hand going to her throat in a sudden gesture. "Adam. . . ?"

Adam Winslow was not, in appearance, a flamboyant man; Charles had received that from Miles. But there was a steady strength in him as he sat there looking at them across the fire. His eyes were deep wells, reflecting the firelight, but there was a fearlessness in the man that leaped out, and as he said, "I think we'll make it," Molly and Charles both felt a gush of relief. The fear that had risen in them seemed to flow away—such was the strength of Adam in that hour.

"What will we do?" Charles inquired.

"We'll have to catch them in a spot where their numbers won't mean so much," Adam said. "I know this country—came through it many times with a load of beaver pelts. There's a spot up ahead—maybe ten miles, and if we can get there before they catch up with us, I think we've got a good chance."

"How'll you fight that many, Adam?" Molly wondered.

"I've been thinking on it—and it goes against the grain, what we'll have to do." He picked up a stick, motioned them to his side, and drew a crude map in the dust. "There's a break in the mountains up ahead, a pass that just cuts right through the peaks. It saves lots of climbing, because it's easy to get through— flat and about fifty yards wide. Now, if we get through that pass and set up behind some rocks, we can be sure that bunch is going to come right through after us. Then we wait until they're close enough so we can't miss—but just far enough away so they can't charge easy. If we can do it just right, we'll get enough of them right off, so the rest of them won't be too ready to follow."

"You mean—they'd quit?" Charles asked.

"Sure. Indians do that. They don't have any pride about it— and they don't have any shame when they decide not to fight. They just say their charms aren't right—and off they go. That's why they're no good as troops. You can't count on them to stand fast and take a beating."

Charles stared at him, apprehension in his light blue eyes. "Sounds like a good way to commit suicide to me! If there's a big bunch, they'll swarm us!"

Adam looked at his brother, then stated quietly, "Guess I'll have to admit that if the Lord isn't with us, we can't make it, Charles. But you know there's a line in the Bible, in the Book of Esther. The Jews are about to get slaughtered, and the only one who can save them is a woman named Esther. And it's pretty clear that if she won't help, they're all going to die. So her uncle says to her, 'You have come to the kingdom for such a time as this.' Well, I've been working on these breech-loading rifles most of my life." He smiled and remarked wryly, "Guess they were made for such a time as this. If they work, we'll be able to knock them off quick enough to break up the charge. If they don't work—"

"They will!" Molly nodded fiercely, her eyes bright with purpose. "I know they will, Adam."

Charles stared at them, and then a nervous smile touched his thin lips. "Well, I guess tomorrow will tell the story on the House of Winslow, won't it? You and I, we're almost all that's left of our name. All that Gilbert Winslow started ends here if those guns don't work."

Adam stared at him, then replied quietly, "I suppose that's so—but there's another verse I like pretty well—'Some trust in chariots, some in horses, but I will remember the name of the Lord my God!' If we get out of this, Charles, it'll be God, and not my guns!" He smiled, and to Charles's surprise pulled Molly into his arms and kissed her. Then he laughed and said, "You never saw a man kiss his bride-to-be, Charles?" Then he sobered and said, "We'd better get some rest; we sure won't have any tomorrow!"

Dawn had not broken when he roused them, and they rode hard all morning. By noon the horses were beginning to falter, but this time Adam gave them little rest. "Whip them up!" he cried out to the others. "If we don't make it to the pass, they'll be dinner for the Indians anyway!"

By the time they got to the foothills of the mountains, Adam's mount was so lame that he was forced to go afoot, leading the animal. It was two in the afternoon when he led them into a narrow gap that they had not noticed, saying with relief in his voice, "We made it!"

"Thank God!" Charles said fervently, then laughed a little. "Guess this trip will make a Christian out of me yet!"

Adam smiled at him, saying, "I hope so." Then he turned and led his horse through the pass, which grew wider as they proceeded.

Finally they came to a long straight stretch at least a quarter of a mile long with walls on both sides so steep that no trees were rooted there. At the end of the straight stretch, the pass veered to their left, and Adam instructed, "Put the animals behind there where they won't be seen."

They secured the animals; then Adam continued, "Get all four of the rifles—and all the cartridges." When they had the weapons, he led them back to an outcropping of rock three feet high and not over ten feet wide that lay almost in the middle of the pass.

"You get on my right, Molly," Adam said. "Charles, take the left."

"Why don't I shoot, too?" Charles asked as they waited. "I'm not a bad shot, you know."

"It's going to be close, Charles. We can't afford even *one* miss, and I've been at this a long time," Adam replied. He bit his lip, and then shook his head. "I don't like what's got to be done. It'll be like murder—those first few shots!"

Charles stared at his brother in astonishment. "Why, that's not sensible, Adam! They're out to kill us all!"

"I know," Adam answered. "It's like a war. But I don't like to kill a man—not even an Indian who's trying to take my scalp." Then he managed a smile and said, "Oh, don't worry, Charles— I've already fought this out. Guess every Christian has to settle it for himself, and I'm going to do what I have to do to save our lives."

They said no more, and as it grew hot, they drank sparingly out of the canteens. It was a little after two when Adam stated quietly, "There they are."

Charles and Molly had been sitting down; now they scrambled up and peered over the rock. "There's a lot of them, Adam!" Charles exclaimed.

"And Stirling is with them," Adam said grimly. "I didn't expect that. He hates me more than I thought." Then he asked sharply, "You've got all the rifles loaded? All right, you two stay down. I'll let them get another hundred feet; then I'll kill the first man."

Molly shivered at the coldness of the phrase, but she knew there was no alternative. "Will you—will you shoot Stirling?"

Adam hesitated before he said, "No—not him first. Then he whispered, "They're almost here—don't get up. Load as fast as you can, but don't get so fast you get jerky. Try to think of it as just a job that is a little tricky, but can be done if you're careful."

Then he raised up, put the barrel of his rifle on the rock, and put the sight right on the broad chest of the Indian riding beside Henry Stirling. He did not allow himself to think, but pulled the trigger. As the Indian was knocked backward to the dust, he handed the rifle to Molly, and took a quick sight on another Indian. Their horses were plunging, and he could hear their cries of alarm, but he put a ball through the body of another Indian, and exchanged weapons with Charles. A horse reared as he fired, taking the bullet he had sent at the rider, but with the fourth rifle he knocked another brave from his horse with a bullet through his head.

The whole thing had taken less than fifteen seconds, and there were three dead Iroquois on the ground!

Molly had loaded the rifle in her hands, and he took it, his face like flint. He noted as he sent the shot home that Stirling was standing in his stirrups, his face red with anger, and he drove his horse forward. For one moment Adam hoped that the Indians would refuse to follow, but after a moment's indecision they screamed and came after him.

"Here they come!" he said quickly. "They think we've got to reload!"

Then the action unfolded—and Adam never forgot that explosion of death in the afternoon!

The red bodies of the Indians made perfect targets, and one by one he knocked them from their saddles. Only twice did a rifle misfire, and he was careful to hit the leaders so that those that followed would see their fellows die. Once he let his aim fall on Henry Stirling, and almost blew the man out of the saddle. But for some unfathomable reason, he could not kill the man— though it would have been wise.

"I don't think they're going to stop the charge!" Adam said as he exchanged a weapon with Molly. "I'm not going to let them have you alive! I love you too much!"

"All right!" she replied with a steady voice. Then she handed him the rifle and added, "I love you, Adam!"

He touched her cheek, then rose, knowing he could not miss, so close were the remaining Indians, and a tall, thin brave took a bullet in his throat and fell to the ground trying to scream.

It was the one thing that turned the tide, for as he fell, Adam saw the mark on his chest that identified him as the war chief of his tribe. With his death, his medicine was gone, and the Indians swerved right and left, leaning to the sides of their mounts to avoid the fire of their enemy.

"They've stopped!" Adam yelled, then saw at once that Stirling had not even noticed that he was alone—or if he had seen the flight of his allies, he was too filled with battle madness to care.

Adam threw up his rifle, took a bead on the broad chest, pulled the trigger—and the weapon misfired!

As he reached for the rifle that Charles was handing him, Stirling reached the outcropping of stone, pulled his lathered horse around in a tight circle and was suddenly at Adam's left!

"Now, Winslow!" Stirling cried, aiming the weapon directly at Adam, "I'm going to kill you!"

The man stood out clearly in Adam's sight, so clearly that he could even see his trigger finger whiten as he applied pressure. The muzzle of the pistol loomed large, and he knew there was no chance for a miss at such a short distance.

He wanted to say goodbye to Molly and to Charles, and there was a great regret in him, for all the things he'd never see, for all the times he'd never have, but he was not afraid.

Charles had not had time to reload the rifle in his hands, and as Stirling pointed the pistol at Adam, he had nothing to fight with. He did not make a decision, dared not think what he was doing. Stirling was too far for him to reach, so he did the only thing left to do—he threw his body in front of Adam. As the bullet meant for his brother struck him in the chest, he was driven back against Adam, who caught him as he fell.

Adam had no time to move but even as he saw Stirling pull another pistol from his belt, a shot rang out, and a small blue hole appeared in Stirling's forehead. The man fell dead from the saddle and landed in the dust as his horse shied away.

Adam whirled to see Molly, her face white as flour, dropping the rifle to the ground. She suddenly stared at him, horror in her eyes, then put her hands over her face, weeping.

Adam said instantly, "Molly! Stop that! Help me with Charles!"

She gave a sob, then came to kneel beside the two men. Charles's eyes were closed and there was blood high on his chest.

"Is—is he dead, Adam?"

"No. I think the bullet missed a lung," Adam said. His own

face was pale as he pulled Charles's shirt away from the wound and peered at it. He lifted his brother from the ground to examine his back. "The ball's still there. We've got to get it out."

"Oh, Adam, he'll be all right, won't he?"

He looked at her trembling lips, then laid Charles down and took her into his arms. "Yes, Molly, we're all going to be all right—thanks be to God!"

Charles opened his eyes suddenly and looked up at them, saying feebly, "If you can spare the time, lovers, I'd like to get this thing out of my chest."

His thin voice drew Adam and Molly back to reality. They knelt beside him and Adam took Charles's hand, as he said, "You saved my life, Charles. I guess I owe you my life now, don't I?"

Charles Winslow's thin lips turned upward in a smile that ignored the pain, and looking up in Adam's eyes, he whispered so faintly that they had to lean forward to understand his words: "I guess Father would have been pretty proud—of me—do you think so, Adam?"

"Very proud!" Adam agreed, smiling down at Charles and adding, "You saved the House of Winslow this day, brother!"

EPILOGUE

★ ★ ★ ★

Mrs. Edwards was busy trying to wash the ears of her grandson, so when someone knocked at the front door, she called out, "Jonathan! You'll have to see who's at the door!"

The old rambling house at the Indian reservation had been a haven for the Edwardses, for after the hectic days at Northampton the lazy Connecticut village of Stockbridge had been quiet and restful. Not the least of the attractions for Jonathan Edwards was the huge room he had appropriated for a study. Here he had written the books that were beginning to make him famous, and now as he came through the door, he carried a stack of books in his hands with papers sticking out as markers.

"I'll get it," he called out, and putting the books down on a chair, he went down the long, wide hall and opened the door. For one moment he stood struck dumb, for he had expected to see one of his Indian church members.

"Why! Bless my soul!" he exclaimed, and his long face lit up with a broad smile. "Adam—and Molly! Mother—here's someone for you to see—come quick!"

Jonathan Edwards was not an emotional man, but he stepped forward and embraced Adam, then Molly, all the while beaming and exclaiming, "Bless my soul! I can't believe it's really you!"

Mrs. Edwards came in with young Timothy in tow, asking, "Well, who is it—why, Adam, it's you! And Molly, look how pretty you are!"

They stood there in the wide hall, exclaiming over the young people. Finally Mrs. Edwards ushered them all into the parlor, still towing the boy at arm's length.

There was a babble of voices as Edwards told how they had learned to love the work among the Indians. Finally his wife looked at the child who was pounding on the floor with a stick apparently made for that purpose. "This is Timmy—Mary and Timothy's boy," she said, a hesitation in her voice. She was thinking of how devastated Adam had been when Mary had married Timothy, and she feared that it might arouse bad memories.

Instead, Adam laughed and picked up the boy, tossing him high in the air. "Well, thank God he looks like Mary!" he said with a crooked smile. "But he may be as big as his father! Are they here—Timothy and Mary?"

"Yes, they came two days ago to visit. They're out for a few minutes, but they'll be back soon."

Edwards asked curiously, "And what about you, Adam? What have you been doing?"

Adam gave an abbreviated account of his life since he'd left Northampton, ending by saying, "It's been a good time for me."

"And what brings you to Stockbridge?" Edwards asked with a smile. "It's not on the way to any place else, you know, so you must have come just for a visit."

"Well, not really," Adam said. "You remember that Molly was a bound girl, indentured to me for ten years?"

"Yes?"

"Well, Rev. Edwards, the time ran out on her indenture last month, and it disturbed me."

Edwards gave his wife a puzzled look, then asked in some confusion, "Well, that's the way those things go, Adam. You wouldn't want Molly to be a bound girl forever, would you?"

"As a matter of fact, Reverend, I *would*!"

"But, Adam—!"

"Yes, I'm determined not to let her go free!" Adam announced.

Mrs. Edwards suddenly laughed out loud, and came to Molly and kissed her, then did the same for Adam. Then she looked at her husband and said, "Jonathan Edwards, for all your big words and long books, you are the slowest man on the face of the earth!"

Edwards stared at her, then as Adam put his arm around Molly and smiled up at him, his face lit up. "Oh, my word! You're going to marry her!"

"I am indeed—and we want you to do the ceremony!"

"Why, my dear boy, certainly I will!"

When Timothy Dwight and Mary came in thirty minutes later, they were as surprised to see the couple as the Edwardses had been, and just as happy. When they heard the purpose of the visit, Mary sniffed and said, "Well, it certainly took you long enough, Adam Winslow! I could have told you this would happen years ago!"

"Would have saved us some trouble if you'd made it clear, Mary," Adam said with a straight face.

Dwight put his massive arm around Adam and laughed, "You are a lucky man, Adam!"

"When's the wedding to be?" Mary asked. "I can help you with your gown, Molly."

"You'd better do it fast," Molly smiled. "We want to be married now."

"Right now?" Edwards asked.

"If you will, Reverend." Adam looked down at his bride with a smile and said, "I've wasted too much time as it is!"

There was no little confusion for half an hour, but finally, Adam Winslow and Molly Burns stood before Jonathan Edwards and recited the ancient vows. There was quiet in the room despite the fact that all the Edwardses' children were there, and as Adam and Molly quietly promised to love each other in the sight of God as long as they lived, a sudden ray of sunlight came through one of the high windows, falling across their faces and forming a golden corona that seemed to Mrs. Edwards much like a crown. She looked at the couple and thought, *They are made to love each other*. They reached the end of the promises and Jonathan Edwards said, "You are now man and wife." Adam bent to kiss his new bride, but just before he did, he whispered so softly that only she heard it: "Now, Molly Winslow, you're my bound girl forever!" She whispered back, "And you're my very own—bound forever!" Then he kissed her, and they were one.

THE CAPTIVE BRIDE

THE CAPTIVE BRIDE

★

GILBERT MORRIS

BETHANY HOUSE PUBLISHERS
MINNEAPOLIS, MINNESOTA 55438

Cover illustration by Dan Thornberg.
Bethany House Publishers staff artist.

Published by Bethany House Publishers
A Ministry of Bethany Fellowship, Inc.
11300 Hampshire Avenue South
Minneapolis, Minnesota 55438

Printed in the United States of America

Library of Congress Cataloging-in-Publication Data

Morris, Gilbert.
    The captive bride.

    (The House of Winslow : bk. 2)
    Sequel to; The honorable impostor.
    I. Title. II. Series: Morris, Gilbert. House of Winslow : bk. 2
PS3563.08742C3   1987   813'.54   87-15782
ISBN 0–87123–978–7 (pbk.)

To Stacy Lee Smith

Who makes being a father
the easiest task in the world!

THE HOUSE OF WINSLOW SERIES

The Honorable Imposter
The Captive Bride
The Indentured Heart
The Gentle Rebel
The Saintly Buccaneer
The Holy Warrior
The Reluctant Bridegroom
The Last Confederate
The Dixie Widow
The Wounded Yankee
The Union Belle
The Final Adversary
The Crossed Sabres
The Valiant Gunman
The Gallant Outlaw

GILBERT MORRIS spent ten years as a pastor before becoming Professor of English at Ouachita Baptist University in Arkansas and earning a Ph.D. at the University of Arkansas. During the summers of 1984 and 1985 he did postgraduate work at the University of London and is presently the Chairman of General Education at a Christian college in Louisiana. A prolific writer, he has had over 25 scholarly articles and 200 poems published in various periodicals, and over the past years has had more than 20 novels published. His family includes three grown children, and he and his wife live in Baton Rouge, Louisiana.

CONTENTS

PART ONE

BEDFORD

★ ★ ★ ★

1659

CHAPTER ONE

POWER IN THE BLOOD

★　★　★　★

"Catherine, there he is—Matthew Winslow!"

The speaker, a short young woman with sharp features, grabbed at the arm of her companion. The pair had just turned off the narrow path that followed the curving coastline onto the main road leading up to the settlement.

Her companion, a tall, willowy girl of twenty, turned a pair of curious dark eyes on the horseman approaching from the other road. She wore a simple blue dress set off by a white collar, but its plain cut did not conceal her fine figure, and there was a boldness in her direct gaze that most young women of Plymouth did not possess.

"So that's the young dandy that's been interrupting your dreams, is it, Martha?"

"Catherine! If you ever breathe a word—!"

"Oh, don't worry," the tall girl laughed. "Your secret's safe with me." She gave the rider a closer look and tapped her chin slowly. With a light of speculation she murmured, "So this is the famous Matthew Winslow who's broken the hearts of half the young women in Plymouth!"

Martha suddenly giggled. "*Half?* Catherine, I don't think there's a maid in all Plymouth who hasn't set her cap for him!"

The taller girl gave an impatient shake of her head, and her lips tightened. "And his head is probably as big as that horse he's riding, I'd venture. Martha, he may be the answer to a maiden's prayer in this little place, but in Boston—"

"Shhh! Here he comes!" Martha gave a tug at Catherine's arm, then shook her head in wonder, saying in a whisper, "I knew he'd come! It's almost witchcraft the way he finds a pretty woman, Catherine—you could blindfold him, and he'd still know."

The two women had reached the dusty road that led up to the fort just as the object of their conversation arrived from the opposite direction. He looked up, saw the pair, then touched his horse with his spurs, driving the animal toward them. Wheeling the jet black stallion around, he dismounted with a motion so easy and fluid that he seemed to flow to the ground. The horse tried to throw his head up, but was held by an iron grip; the handsome rider swept his hat from his head, then bowed in a courtly gesture.

"A good day to you, Miss Martha."

His words were directed to the shorter of the two, but Catherine Brent knew instantly that she was the object of his attention. It irritated her, for she felt like a quarry of some sort—he the hunter and she the trophy he sought. As she heard Martha say, "This is my cousin, Catherine Brent, from Boston," she gave Matthew Winslow a direct stare.

Her eyes scrutinized the young man before her—tall, over six feet, with a shock of rich auburn hair. His face was bronzed, wedge-shaped, the wide mouth lifting at the corners as he smiled at her with a frank inspection. His ears were rather small, his nose straight, and there was a suggestion of tremendous strength in the corded neck and wide hands. He was wearing a red velvet coat and breeches, yellow waistcoat with ruby buttons, and shoes with gold buckles. The brown hat held under his arm, had a large yellow plume, and despite the summer heat he wore a cloak of dark maroon.

What a dandy—a fop! Catherine thought at first, but when she met his eyes, she was thrown off guard. He had the bluest eyes she had ever seen—blue as the sky overhead, blue as the cornflowers growing beside the road. But the power in those eyes made her feel as if his gaze had *touched* her physically!

"I trust your stay will be a long one, Miss Brent," he said in a deep, slightly husky voice.

In spite of herself, she felt her hand going out to him as he stepped forward and touched it with his lips. She suddenly hated herself for the thrill that swept through her. Snatching her hand back almost rudely, she said haughtily, "I fear there is little in this place to hold my attention, Mr. Winslow." *That ought to put him in his place,* she thought with some satisfaction.

He was not crushed, however. On the contrary, he smiled. "Plymouth is a small place, as you say." She felt the power of eyes laughing into hers. "But if you will permit me to call on you—and on Miss Martha, of course," he continued, "I would like to show you a side of Plymouth you've missed."

Catherine opened her mouth to say, "There's nothing in this town that attracts me in the least."

Instead, she said, "That would be very nice, Mr. Winslow."

She hated herself for that response, and had the impulse to reverse her words, but Martha broke in, saying, "You can come tonight if you like, Mr. Winslow."

He pulled his horse around, then swung into the saddle easily. "Nothing would please me better, but my uncle is arriving from England. I see his ship in the harbor there"—he motioned to a three-masted schooner at anchor in the bay—"and my parents will expect me to stay at home tonight and help welcome him." He wheeled the horse around and gave a sudden smile, calling out as he left, "I'll be there tomorrow!"

"Insolent puppy!" Catherine said waspishly. Somehow she felt he had bested her, and she found herself wishing for tomorrow. She'd put him in his place!

Martha looked at her friend and smiled. "I know what it is, Catherine. You think he's too proud, and you'll give him a taste of humility. That's it, isn't it?"

"Why—!"

"You think that hasn't been tried?" Martha glanced up the hill as the black stallion grew smaller, then shook her head with a smile of despair. "Isn't he the most handsome thing you ever saw—proud or not?"

"Well . . ." Catherine said grudgingly, "I will admit he's the most attractive minister I've ever seen."

"Oh, he'll never be a minister! That's his parents' idea, not his," Martha shrugged. "He's their only son—the last of the Winslow name, you see. His father, Reverend Gilbert Winslow, came over on the *Mayflower* and so did his mother. You know how it can be though, Catherine. Being a minister's son doesn't give a man a calling from the Lord."

Catherine tapped her chin thoughtfully, then said with a gleam in her eyes, "Well, I'm looking forward to Mr. Winslow's call tomorrow." She laughed suddenly and added, "Those blue eyes of his—they've got more of the devil in them than a minister ought to have."

Edward Winslow caught sight of Gilbert and Humility standing in the front ranks of the crowd and raised his hand in response to their greetings. The long journey from England had stiffened his joints, and the monotonous diet had stripped some flesh from his bones, but he was still portly as he stepped out of the *Fortune's* small boat to the shores of Plymouth. He took a few steps, then began to sway, the earth seeming to reel beneath his feet. Gilbert rushed forward and grabbed him in a firm embrace, steadying him.

"Careful, Brother Edward!" the younger man said with a grin. "If you stagger like that, our sharp-eyed elder will think you've been lifting the bottle a bit too much!" There was a light of affection in Gilbert Winslow's cornflower blue eyes, and since hugging among relatives was not common in the family, he took the opportunity to give his brother a rough hug under the pretense of holding him steady.

Edward Winslow felt a warm glow, as he always did on seeing this younger brother of his. In the past the two of them had been estranged, but since that epic journey on the *Mayflower* and the first terrible winter endured together in Plymouth Plantation, the two of them were extremely close. The long periods Edward had to spend in England in the service of the government were the harder to bear for his separation from Gilbert and his family.

Clapping Gilbert on the shoulder he said, "By heaven, it's good to set foot on solid ground!" Then he turned to Humility and put out his arms to embrace her. She, too, was his favorite, and he concealed his shock on seeing how poorly she looked. "Well, here's my favorite sister-in-law!" he said fondly, and as she came into his arms he noted that she had shrunk to almost nothing since he had sailed for England two years earlier. Her eyes were sunk back into her head, and there was only a faint trace of the rare beauty that had been the cause of several fights on board the *Mayflower*. Her complexion, which had always been radiant, was faded to a sallow color, and the once rich blonde hair was thin and dry, shot through with streaks of white. *Very sick—Gilbert kept it from me,* Edward thought as he looked down on Humility.

"Well, well, come along," Gilbert said quickly, noting the shocked look in Edward's eyes. "You must be starved after two months of biscuits packed with weevils, Edward. Humility began cooking as soon as the mast came in sight."

"Lead me to it!" Edward cried, and the two men linked arms and started up from the beach to the settlement that crowned the low hill. As they reached the first street that ran parallel to the shoreline, Edward paused, looking at the neat cottages, each on a good-sized lot. The cold fingers of winter had not yet touched the land, and the thick grass that would be dry and gray in another month glowed with an emerald sheen that almost hurt his eyes. Taking in the white-sided houses with neatly thatched roofs, some of them half-timbered just as in an English village, Edward murmured, "Doesn't look much like it did when Captain Jones put us off the old *Mayflower* the first time, does it, Gilbert?"

"No. That was—let me see—thirty-nine years ago, was it?" Gilbert shook his head and said ruefully, "You know what I said to Miles Standish that day, Edward? I said, 'Miles, this is as close to hell as I expect to find on this earth!' "

"What did Captain Standish say?"

"Oh, he swore a great oath—you know how Miles was in those days! Said it was a paradise on earth compared to some of the places he'd soldiered." Gilbert shook his head. "Poor old Miles. Been in his grave for twenty years now. I still miss him."

Humility joined the conversation, saying quietly, "I rejoice that he came to know the Lord before he was taken."

"That's true, sweetheart," Gilbert said, turning from Edward to gaze fondly down at her. There was, however, a sadness in his fine blue eyes as he shook his head and murmured, "Not too many of us left—the Firstcomers!"

"Well, *I'm* left, Brother!" Edward said heartily. "But if we don't get some of Humility's cooking inside this hollow stomach of mine, I can't speak for tomorrow!"

They made their way up the main street leading to the town, past the single street intersecting it. Houses lined both sides of the main street, each with a small, fenced-in garden, now mostly gone to seed. At the point where the two main streets intersected, four small cannons were mounted on swivels. Pigs roamed freely about the streets, serving both as the main meat diet of the colony and also as four-footed garbage collectors.

They passed the cross street and turned into a small house with a high-pitched thatched roof. It was sheathed with unpainted clapboard—short boards handmade by splitting a log lengthwise, then shaving it down to the proper shape with a drawknife. "Come in and let's hear what's happening in England, Edward," Gilbert urged.

The room they entered was dark, illuminated only by two small windows ten inches square, sealed with glass instead of the oiled paper used by many. Humility moved to a cavernous fireplace that took up half of one wall. It was three and a half feet deep, and so high that a tall man could walk around in it. The back was lined with rounded stones, and the inside studded with iron hooks, bars, and chains suspended from a wooden beam.

As Gilbert and Edward sat at the table talking, Humility took some of the goat's meat she had roasted on a spit and put it on hollowed-out wooden trenchers. She filled three large drinking cups with fresh milk and set out a sharp knife for each of them. Adding a wedge of cheese, she then pulled the loaf of bread baked in an outdoor iron-box communal oven close to the fire.

"All ready," she called, and the three of them took their places and bowed their heads. Gilbert prayed, "Thank you, gracious Lord, for this good food, and for the safe journey of our brother, in the name of Jesus Christ."

Edward reached out, cut a huge slice from the loaf with his knife, then laughed, "Gilbert, you have the shortest prayers of any minister in America! I trust your sermons are not so brief, or the congregation will feel led to seek another preacher who will give them their money's worth!"

Humility had gotten up to get salt and paused to lay her hand on Edward's shoulder. He could not help noticing how thin and frail it was as she said with a smile, "He is guilty, Brother Edward, I fear. A shame that the best preacher in Plymouth speaks no longer than an hour when others with nothing to say last for three or four!"

Gilbert sliced off a liberal portion of meat, held it impaled on the point of his knife, then said with a smile, "True. It all stems from an incident that occurred when I first began preaching. I heard someone say in a loud whisper, 'Is he done?' And then someone else said in a disgusted voice, 'Yes—but he's still preaching!' I think that made me choose to stop when I had nothing else to say." He shoved the portion of meat into his mouth and began to chew it slowly.

"A dangerous precedent!" Edward chuckled. "Now, tell me how it goes—I'm hungry for news."

As the two men sat there chewing the tough meat and washing it down first with milk, then with ale, the more common beverage, Humility leaned back against the wall and observed them. Though the Winslow blood was evident in both men, time and circumstance had sculptured them differently, and she was a little amused to see the variations.

Edward was sixty-five, six years older than Gilbert, and slightly taller. He was far heavier, his full face still red; the chestnut hair that had glowed in youth was still thick and only faintly tinged with gray. He had a smooth, good-natured face, a neatly trimmed moustache, and eyes of a penetrating blue. He was wearing a fine lawn collar turned out from his throat, tied beneath with a silk, red-tassled cord. A corduroy coat with a double row of silver buttons and silk breeches in the Dutch style completed his outfit. He had an air of authority, and his years of dealing with kings and later the Lord Protector, Oliver Cromwell, had given him a rather ponderous dignity.

Turning to look at her husband, Humility saw a man not greatly different in some ways than the young blade she had met forty years earlier. The face, to be sure, was somewhat lined, but the athletic movement was little slowed by time. He still had the broad, bronzed brow, and the face that tapered down to a jutting chin adorned with a small white scar was only slightly heavier than on the day they had met. Tall and muscular, he wore the plain, dark clothing of the Puritan minister, with pewter buttons and a broad, starched neckcloth folded over his shoulders.

He turned his head to smile at her, and her heart leaped, as it always did, and then a longing to be well again swept her. She had always been his equal physically, despite the burden of child-bearing. But now a stranger seeing them together for the first time might take her for his older sister. The memory of that time when she walked by his side, brimming with health (and beauty, so they said!), was more than Humility could bear. She rose and said, "You two will want to go visit the governor. I'll not go with you this time."

Edward got to his feet at once and said, "We should call, I suppose, but we'll be back soon. I'm anxious to see my nephew. He'll be here for supper?" His astute eyes did not miss the glance exchanged by the pair, and he said quickly. "Well, I've a month to see that young rascal—no matter."

Gilbert said, "Go lie down, dear. I'll take care of this when we come back. Don't argue—'Wives, be in obedience to your husbands' as the Book teacheth." He kissed her and then led the way out of the house and down the street toward the governor's house.

"How bad is it?" Edward asked at once. "What does Fuller say?"

Gilbert bit his lip and cast a glance over the iron-gray billows rolling ponderously over the docks below. "Bad enough, Edward. Sam said when she first fell ill, it was the result of too much bathing. He's always said that noxious vapors from winds and waters make bathing very dangerous." He smiled at the thought of Sam Fuller, their only physician since the *Mayflower* touched the New World. Then a gloomy light clouded his bright blue eyes and he said heavily, "But it's serious, Edward. She goes down every day! Whatever it is, it's draining her life before my eyes!"

Edward reached out and gripped his brother's arm, saying only, "God is able, Gilbert!"

"Yes, He is."

For the next three hours the two men went from house to house as Edward performed his duty to pass along the news from England. He had been governor of Plymouth, in addition to his offices for the Crown and later for Cromwell, so there was a certain amount of awe in the attitude of some. Others like John Billington, who had long resented Edward (or any other man of authority), and latecomers to the settlement, were less impressed.

Governor Bradford, of course, was pleased to see him, and they spent the bulk of the day with him. His house was larger than usual, more than twice as large as Gilbert's. Bradford was a compact man, and since the beginning had been the driving energy that kept Plymouth intact. After hearing some minor news he said, "Come, Brother Winslow, get to it. What will happen now that Cromwell is dead?"

"His son, Richard, sits in his place." Edward shifted uneasily, then added, "I fear him, Mr. Bradford. He is not a strong man, and the English have not lost their taste for monarchs."

Bradford's intelligent eyes searched the face of the other, and he nodded slowly. "My thinking exactly."

"You think Charles will be brought back?" Gilbert asked.

"His royal trunk has been packed for some time, Pastor Winslow," Bradford smiled grimly. "And if Charles sits on the throne of England, we all know what his thought will be concerning such men as ourselves."

"He will remember that it was the Puritan forces under Cromwell that beheaded his father and drove him to exile," Edward nodded. He looked sharply at Bradford and added, "It is well that we are here, with an ocean between us, is it not, Mr. Bradford?"

"Yes—but our brothers in England are not so protected," Bradford answered. He shook his head, and there was a sadness in his voice as he said, "I fear there will be a shaking soon in England."

They left the governor's house and made their way up the hill, speaking of the dangers that beset their brothers in England, and as they turned down the street and caught sight of Winslow's horse, he said, "Matthew is home." He added drily, "Most of us hitch up a steer or a dry cow to do our traveling—my son has some disdain for such primitive customs."

"I see what you mean, Gilbert," Edward responded, noting the horse tied to the fence in front of the house. "Where did he get the money for such a fine stallion?"

Gilbert shrugged and said as they passed through the gate, "Not from me. The price of that horse would pay my salary for six years. Matthew doesn't work, so he either stole it or he gambled for it." He put his hand on Edward's arm, saying in a low voice, "I felt it necessary to ascertain which, and I am pleased to report that it is the latter. It would have been disgraceful if a minister's son had stolen, would it not?"

Edward noted the edge of sarcasm in Gilbert's voice, and it saddened him. He had stood by grave after grave where the stillborn children of Gilbert and Humility were buried, and he knew the deep grief that had almost destroyed them both. When the last child had survived, they had poured themselves into the boy with such an intensity that Edward had always feared the result should the child have followed the others to an early grave. He had not been unaware, being a shrewd observer of human nature, that Matthew had been blessed with a strong body and cursed with a rebellious spirit.

Gilbert opened the door, and as Edward stepped inside and was greeted with a rush from his nephew, he thought for the ten thousandth time, *It's Gilbert at seventeen!* It was an eerie resemblance, for young Matthew had the same sharp features, the cornflower blue eyes that all Winslow men seem to have, he moved the same, had the same smooth gait of the natural athlete—balanced, almost sensual, with not a fraction of wasted motion as he crossed the floor.

"Uncle Edward!" *Even the same voice!* he thought, and the hard hand that crushed his was corded with muscle as were the arms and shoulders. "My word, it's good to have you back!"

"You're looking well, my boy." Edward smiled at the young man, "I haven't seen such fine clothing since I visited Bond Street in London."

There was some embarrassment in the young man's eyes as he said, "Well, Uncle, I suppose I am a bit of a peacock—but I've been to Boston, and they expect such things there."

"Some do," Gilbert said quietly. His brother saw the young man's face flush and the quick flare of resentment in his blue eyes.

Edward had not been a diplomat for nothing. He said with a laugh, "I remember your father wore an outfit much like this when he was a student at Cambridge. I believe Father took a rather dim view of it, eh, Gilbert?"

A startled look crossed Gilbert's face, and then he threw his head back and roared with laughter. "I haven't thought of that in forty years, Edward!" He threw a smile at Humility and said ruefully, "Father threatened to have me put in the stocks if I ever wore such a garb in his presence!"

"Father was a stern man," Edward said gently, and he saw the remark had its intended effect on his brother.

Gilbert nodded, and there was a softening of the lines around his mouth as he looked at his son. "He was that." He said no more, but the angry air that had filled the room faded, and young Matthew shot a grateful look at his uncle.

"Now, let's hear what you've been up to since I've been away. How's the Latin and the Greek? Still giving Mr. Littleton fits?"

"I'm bound to say," Gilbert said as he sat down beside Humility, "that it's rather the other way around." He gave a fond glance at the young man across the table and smiled. "I mean to say that Matthew has surpassed his teacher."

"And *that's* what I want to talk to you about, Uncle."

"Oh, not *now*, Matthew," Humility protested. "Your uncle is weary from his long voyage."

"Let the boy talk, Sister," Edward said easily. He leaned back in his chair and considered the eager face of the young man who at once began to pour out a plan he had obviously spent much time conceiving. In brief, he would either go to school in England or he would die!

Edward asked, when he could find a gap in the young man's flow of words, "You want to enter the church, Matthew?"

"No, the law!"

His uncle gave a quick look at Gilbert and Humility, and the disappointment on their faces was plain. He saw at once that this family, so precious to him, was on the razor edge of disaster. If the young man had his way, he would be embarking on a path odious to his parents; in addition, they would lose him forever—at least, Humility would! The study of law was a long, arduous process, and he knew in his heart that Humility would never live to see her son again if he left on such a mission.

"Mr. Shakespeare has given us many fine lines, my boy," Edward remarked slowly. "My favorite is not well known, but reflects my own views."

"What line is that, Uncle?"

"First we kill all the lawyers!" Edward remarked. "A sentiment I hold firm concord with after dealing with the breed for a lifetime and finding not enough honor for a squad in the whole profession!"

"The army then!" Matthew cried, his eyes piercing those of his uncle. "I'm not fit for the church, and the law, you say, isn't fit for me. Let me go for a soldier, Father!" He turned and held out one strong, square hand in a strange pleading gesture to Gilbert.

"Son, you can't mean that!" Gilbert protested, drawing nearer to Humility in an unconscious attempt to protect her, adding, "Your uncle will tell you it's impossible!"

"Why is it impossible?"

"Think, Matthew!" his uncle said intensely. "There *is* no army in England for you to serve in." His face grew stern and he slapped the wooden table with a sharp gesture. "The Model Army of Cromwell was the finest body of fighting men on earth—but Cromwell is dead, and there is no man alive who can rally those troops. Within a year—if God doesn't do something—Charles II will be the ruling monarch of England, and if you think the son of a Puritan minister could serve in *that* army, you're a simpleton!" He had half risen in anger, but it was not at the boy in front of him, but at the fate of the England he loved. Now he settled back and forced himself to be calm.

"Not the army, Matthew." It was a rare thing for a Winslow man to beg, but there was a pleading note in the older man's voice as he said, "Matthew, give the church a try. You're young and think you have to have excitement. Very natural in a young fellow such as yourself. Your father was much the same," he added with a smile.

"You've hit it, Uncle!" Matthew said at once. "I've heard stories all my life of you, Father! How you were the best swordsman in England, and how you fought duels and—"

"Son! Son!" Gilbert held up his hand and there was a horror on his face. "Don't call those days back! For heaven's sake, do you think I'm *proud* of them?" He shook his head, and let his head fall as he whispered, "I'd give my life to wipe out those wild days."

Humility put her arm around him and said, "Hush! I won't hear it, Gilbert. You were not evil. You used your sword, yes, but in every case it was to right a wrong."

"That's true, Brother," Edward added. He waved his hand at the young man in front of him, saying, "He has your blood, Gilbert, and perhaps some of the faults that Winslow men seem prone to."

"Are you saying he *should* go?" Gilbert asked in astonishment.

"No, certainly not! It's not my place to make such decisions for your family." Then Edward rose and said, "I find myself more weary than I thought. Would you mind if I took my rest a little early?"

"You're sleeping with me in the loft, Uncle," Matthew responded quickly. "I'll go make things ready."

As he skimmed the stairs with agility, Humility suddenly sobbed, and Gilbert put his arms around her. "He's going to leave us!" she said in a broken voice.

Edward looked at the couple, not knowing what to say. He averted his head, and his glance fell on a sword hanging from a peg driven into the wall. He stepped to the wall, removed the sword and held it in his hands. "I haven't seen this in some time," he remarked quietly. It was a rapier made by Clemens Hornn, once the greatest swordmaker in England. He stroked its shallow guard, gleaming like a closing flower carved in steel, then traced the blade down to the tapering, murderous point.

"The boy has your skill with this, Gilbert," he remarked quietly.

"Would God I'd never let him touch the thing! I would not teach him, as he begged me to do. But others did, and I allowed it—"

"You can't keep the boy locked up in a cage, Gilbert!"

"Yes, but—"

"Man, don't you remember *anything* about your youth?" Edward asked sharply. "You of all men ought to understand a little of the struggle the boy's going through!" He slapped the sword back on its peg, then turned and observed the pair with compassion, but with a severity in his face.

"You were forced into the church, remember? And what good did it do you, Gilbert? None! You gambled and ran after wenches day and night! And whom did you hate for it?"

Gilbert raised his head and said slowly, "You. I thought you talked Father into putting me into the church."

"And whom do you suppose Matthew will hate if *he* is forced to follow the same path?"

Gilbert's face was pale, but he said steadily, "Me, of course. Do you think I haven't thought of that?"

Humility drew out of Gilbert's embrace and stared at Edward. "You have a thought, don't you, Edward?"

"I fear," Edward shrugged, "there's no easy answer to this business—there never is! But you *must* see that it can't go on. Sooner or later the boy will go bad if he doesn't have some liberty."

"What—what sort of 'liberty' do you mean?" Humility asked.

"Not the law—and not the army!" He paused and began setting things in order in his mind, a custom they recognized. Finally he said, "Let him come to England with me—not to London, but to a small town where he'll be out of *some* temptation. I have a friend there, the pastor of the church. He was quite a worldly man at one time. Served as a Major in the Royalist Army for a time, and was pretty much of a gambler, a drunkard and a blasphemer. But that's different now. He's 'Holy Mr. Gifford' now."

"But—what would Matthew do there?"

"Study business, perhaps. At least that could be the excuse for his going. I have a man there who does very well in that way, and we could set Matthew under him. But I hope for better things."

"Such as?" Gilbert asked.

"Such as Matthew growing older. And under the influence of a man like John Gifford, he will, I pray, find his way. I dare hope you will receive him back a candidate for the ministry in a few years."

Gilbert glanced down at Humility with a strange look on his face, and Edward added at once, "As a matter of fact, it might be well for all of us to go. Why, it would be very good for you to go back to England—see old friends—"

"Gilbert could never leave his church, Edward," Humility said. She stood there, thin and worn, but there was a light in her eyes that reminded both men of the fire she had had in her youth. "We will pray," she added quietly. "God will give us His mind on this."

As Edward turned to mount the stairs, Gilbert asked, "What place is this—where Reverend Gifford lives?"

"Bedford."

"A small place?"

"Very small," Edward assured him. "Matthew will be bored, but he will be safe. Nothing ever happens in Bedford."

CHAPTER TWO

LYDIA

★ ★ ★ ★

The 200-ton *Fortune* rose and fell with the rolling waves under an iron-gray sky. The crew stood by to weigh anchor, waiting only for the couple who had come aboard to have a final word with young Matthew Winslow.

Gilbert held Humility in a firm grasp to steady her against the motion of the ship, and with the other he held to the rail. His bright blue eyes scanned the face of his son as if he sought to find in the handsome features some portent of the boy's future. He raised his voice against the rising wind, saying, "God guide you, my boy. God make His face to shine on you." The strong baritone softened to a lower pitch, and he held out his free hand to grasp that of his son, and he said, "Be faithful to God, Matthew! Never fail Him—never!"

Matthew nodded, marveling at the strength in his father's right hand, and he moved forward quickly to throw his free arm around his mother. As he bent to kiss her faded cheek, the thought that he might never see her again on earth swept through him, cutting his spirit more sharply than the stinging winds whipping across his face. He bit his lip and said impulsively, "Mother, if you ask me to stay . . ."

Humility raised her face to his, the dark blue of her eyes dominating her wasted face, and put one unsteady hand on his cheek. "You would never be happy here, son," she murmured so quietly that he had to lean forward to catch her words. Her hand lifted to push a lock of his reddish-blonde hair back from where it fell in his eyes. There was something so familiar in the gesture that the lump in his throat grew unbearable and his eyes stung with unshed tears.

"Only a year, Mother," he finally whispered, gathering her in his arms and fighting off the dismay her fragile form triggered in him. "Just a year!"

"Time to go," Gilbert said quietly. "The captain must catch the tide."

Humility pulled away from Matthew's grasp and looked up one last time. "Christians never say goodbye, son," she said, and touched his cheek once more. "Just until we meet again."

Then she turned and Gilbert handed her down the ladder into the boat, aided by a burly sailor. He started down, and when just his head and broad shoulders were visible he caught his son's eye, raised his hand in a curious gesture, as though he were flourishing a sword. A smile broke the austerity of his face, making him look very young in the clear sea air, and he called out loudly, "Be faithful, my boy! Be true to God—and to yourself!"

Then he was gone, and Matthew turned blindly and walked toward the forecastle. He heard the thumping sound as the sailors shoved the small boat off, but did not stop until he had found a place of solitude along the forward rail. The first mate cried out, "Weigh anchor!" and the rattle of the chains struck sharply on his ear. He bent over the rail, his lungs filling with the sharp briny air faintly mixed with the odors of land, the loamy smell of raw earth. "Hoist the mainsail!" came the cry of the mate, and slowly the ship heeled over, her prow turning away from the land.

As the sails slid up, the wind caught them, and filled them with puffs of air that cracked like whips. The riggings creaked, and suddenly the ship caught the breeze and lifted like a living thing to breast the waves, leaving the land behind.

"Give them a wave, boy!"

Matthew wheeled to face his uncle, who motioned toward the receding shore. "See? They're waving at us."

Matthew turned to see the small figures of his parents, still in the boat, both of them lifting their arms in a gesture that was sadder than anything he'd known all his days. But he lifted his arms and waved strongly, continuing until the small boat touched the shore. As it did the ship shifted and he could see the small craft no more.

"I'm a fool, Uncle Edward!" he said bitterly, his lips twisted into a grimace of pain. "What kind of man would leave his mother behind, sick as she is?"

"A *young* fool, I suppose," the older man said gently. He put his arm around Matthew's shoulders in a gesture of affection, which was unusual for him, and added, "Never grieve over past decisions, Matthew. There'll be no end of it if you do—and it never changes things."

His uncle's words stayed with Matthew in the three weeks that followed, as the *Fortune* nudged her way across the rutted surface of the gray Atlantic. For a few days he kept to his cabin, surfacing only to eat, then to stand beside the rail, his eyes fixed on the unseen land they were leaving far behind. He made a lonely figure, but his uncle was wise enough to let time heal the worst of the parting grief. Finally, since no emotion can be sustained forever at such a pitch, Matthew began to recover, and day by day as the ship drew closer to England, his spirit lightened.

He spent the days watching the sailors scamper like monkeys up the shrouds to trim the sails. He listened for hours to his uncle tell of the first voyage in the *Mayflower*, of the hardships of that terrible first year when half the colonists died. "We finally had to bury our dead at night—so the Indians wouldn't know how we had dwindled to nothing," he told his nephew one night as they stood at the stern watching the broken reflection of stars shatter like diamonds in the wake of the ship.

"I marvel any of you ever had the courage to go," Matthew said.

His uncle thought about it, then raised his fist and struck the rail with a sudden sharp blow. "We had to have God, Matthew!"

"I—I thought it was land and freedom."

"No! It was God that we hungered for!" The older man paused, then smiled gently in the silver moonlight. His eyes gleamed and he gave a small laugh. "We were all fools for God in those days!" Then he told more about how Matthew's father had found God, and had turned down a life of ease in the service of Lord North to become a poor preacher. "He could have married Cecily, Lord North's daughter," he added idly. "He was quite a ladies' man in those days." A thought struck him and he said slyly, "Like you, I suppose."

Matthew flushed and was glad for the covering darkness. He changed the subject quickly. "Tell me about Bedford."

For the rest of the trip the two talked a great deal, but after they landed at Southampton, made the trip by coach toward the north, Matthew's spirits were dashed by his first view of the small village his uncle indicated. "There it is, boy. That's Bedford."

"It's . . . small, isn't it?" Matthew said. Perhaps if he had not seen Southhampton first, he would have not been so disappointed. Bedford was composed of a scattering of half-timbered houses, all with thatched roofs. They followed only a very slight sort of plan, seeming to have been thrown like a group of dice to rest at random where they landed. The one road more or less connected many of the houses, but in the center of the village, Young Winslow saw, was a more structured look. "That's the Mote Hall," his uncle said, indicating a large two-story building with high-pitched gables crowning the over-hanging second stories. "Most of our large meetings take place there."

The coach stopped in front of a tavern with a large red lion on a sign, and they got out. "Let's have something to eat before we get you settled." Edward gave orders concerning their trunks, and they went inside the Red Lion where they were met by a snaggle-toothed man with a white apron tied around his prodigious stomach. "Mr. Winslow! Yer back again ter see us?"

"Just a brief visit for me, Williams, but my nephew here will be staying in your town for a time. Now, can you feed us?"

The question insulted the innkeeper and he sniffed, saying, "And did yer ever go hungry in the Red Lion, sir?"

"No, indeed not, Williams!" Master Winslow laughed, and the two sat down at a huge oak trestle table and talked until the meal was brought. After the ship's diet, the fresh meat and vegetables set before them were delicious. They were wolfing down portions of cold beef, chunks of fresh bread larded with fresh yellow butter, and boiled potatoes when a man entered the inn.

"Mr. Winslow, welcome back to Bedford!" He was only of average height, but held himself so straight that he seemed tall. His hair was brown, coming down low on his forehead, and his thick brows shaded intelligent brown eyes that held a quizzical look. He moved his head with quick, sharp movements that matched his words, a curious jerking as if his neck were caught in a tight collar and he was attempting to free it.

"Well, it's good to see you, Pastor." Winslow rose and the two gripped hands. "This is my nephew, Matthew—my brother Gilbert's son, from America." He watched as the two men shook hands, and added, "This is Pastor John Gifford, Matthew. You'll be a member of his congregation while you're here."

"I'm pleased to meet you, Pastor." Matthew liked the sharp-featured preacher at once and added, "I trust not to be an additional burden to your cares."

"Oh, I expect young men to be troublesome!" Gifford's eyes twinkled and he gave a slight wink at both men. "When I was your age I was studying for the gallows—but I trust you're a more settled young man than I was."

"Nay, that's past praying for, Pastor Gifford!" Edward laughed. "Fast horses, pretty women, and a duel now and then to put a little spice in the day—that's our boy!"

"Now, Uncle Edward!"

"All in jest, my boy!" Winslow laughed, holding up a hand. "Matthew will be living with Asa Goodman, an apprentice, to learn some of the world of business." He glanced out the door then added, "It's getting a little late, by the way. Will you walk with us as we go to Mr. Goodman's Pastor?"

"I can fill you in with the news on the way," Gifford agreed. The three men left the Red Lion and threaded their way through the maze of cottages in the dying light of the sun. Matthew listened as Gifford spoke somewhat gloomily of political conditions. When the pastor mentioned the possibility of the restoration of Charles to the throne, Edward broke in quickly, "It's coming, Pastor. We may as well get ready for tribulation."

They turned down a dirt lane and Gifford hailed a man sitting in front of a low-roofed cottage. "Ho, John, here's someone for you to meet!"

As the three men approached, the man arose, releasing the small children he had been holding in his lap. He was a tall, portly man, perhaps thirty years of age, Matthew judged, with broad shoulders and a full, round face. His eyes were not large, but had a penetrating quality, and Matthew felt that he was being carefully weighed in the balances as the large man gave him a direct stare.

"John, this is Matthew Winslow, Edward's nephew. Edward, this is Mr. John Bunyan—one of our more promising lights among the ministry."

"Why, I'll deny that, Mr. Winslow!" Bunyan said looking at Edward, a smile touching his full wide lips beneath a reddish moustache. "I'm just a tinker with a longing to speak of Christ." Bunyan had one of those clear tenor voices that carry over long distances without losing any clarity, and there was some sort of magnetism in the man, Matthew saw—a quality he had observed in Governor John Bradford of Plymouth. It had nothing to do with attractiveness, for neither man was particularly well favored. Neither was it a quality of voice, for though both men spoke clearly, they did not thunder as some men felt compelled to do to exert their authority. Whatever it was, Matthew knew that both men had that indefinable quality of leadership; men would listen to them and be led by them.

"John's become quite a traveler since you left, Edward," Gifford said. "He's been preaching all over the country—and with very good response."

The praise bothered Bunyan and he shifted uncomfortably. "Well, if Charles comes back as king, we'll none of us be doing much preaching, will we now?"

"Too true, John," Edward said heavily. "He'll clamp down on our churches—especially men like Pastor Gifford here."

"Perhaps you could come to America, Pastor Gifford," Matthew suggested. "And you, too, Mr. Bunyan."

"We can't *all* leave England!" Gifford snapped. His quick eyes flashed fire and he jerked his head in a series of quick motions as he added, "I was on the Royalist side in the war against the Crown—but this time it'll be different."

"There'll be no new war, Gifford," Edward said at once with a shake of his head. "The English *want* a king—demand one, in fact. And no matter what Charles promises—and I've heard that he's promised no revenge against those who executed his father—there's a host in France who fled the country one jump ahead of Cromwell. And it's *their* turn now, mark my words!"

There was a sense of gloom in the older men that galled Matthew, but he said nothing. He had come to England to find an escape from the boredom and monotony of Plymouth, and it appeared as if he was jumping into a very hot fire. Excitement and adventure were on the horizon, and these friends of his uncle spoke as if Doomsday had been announced!

"Well, you must come with me on some of my preaching engagements, Mr. Winslow." Bunyan interrupted Matthew's thoughts with a nod and a wide smile. "You won't hear much in the way of a preacher, but you'll see some very fine countryside and meet some choice saints."

"I will indeed, Mr. Bunyan," Matthew answered.

"Come, we must go," Edward urged. "Good night, Mr. Bunyan."

As the three men walked away, Gifford stated, "He's a rare one, John Bunyan. Born to preach!"

"Aye, I'm sure he is," Edward agreed. "But he'd better stick to mending pots and pans if Charles comes back."

"John? He'll not do that!" Pastor Gifford shook his head and indicated a house set off in a clump of towering yew trees. "There's Asa Goodman's house." He was silent until they reached the steps, then added quietly, "No, Bunyan is just the sort of man that the Royalists will hunt down. He's a man the people listen to. He's got a gift of moving people—just what the King will be dead set against!"

Winslow knocked on the door, and it was answered at once by a short man with weak eyes who peered at them suspiciously, then as he recognized them, cried out, "Why, it's *you*, Mr. Winslow. Come in! Come in!"

The three men entered, and Matthew made the acquaintance of Asa Goodman, his wife, Ruth, and their two daughters, Chastity and Faith, ages sixteen and eighteen respectively. He was shown to his room, a small one on the second floor, containing little other than a bed, a desk and a washstand. As they came down, he saw his uncle making for the door, but he stopped long enough to say, "I must make another call, Matthew. Mr. Goodman will lay out your duties." He left with Pastor Gifford, and Matthew spent the next hour explaining to Ruth Goodman that he had just eaten and could not hold another bite.

As he sat at the table, sandwiched between Chastity and Faith, he told them about America, but had great difficulty convincing them that elephants were really not a danger to the population. All the family had been reading travel books, and they hung on his every word as he told them of the Indians; the girls were especially avid for blood-curdling stories about their savagery. Matthew knew of none, but they were so pitifully anxious that he invented several to satisfy them.

He escaped to his room as early as possible; removing a small book from his pocket, he sat down at the desk and dipped a pen into an ink bottle, then began writing:

The year of our Lord, 1659, 6 August, Bedford.

My first night in Bedford, and I have purposed to keep this journal a record of my new life—and to be as brutally honest as a man can be!

My poor mother! Shall I never see her face again? I fear not. And I shall carry the picture of her face that last time on the *Fortune* to my grave! How much capacity we have to hurt the ones we truly love!

If there is such a price then, to my leaving home and parents, I resolve to make it worth the candle! The future is a book whose pages I may not read, save one at a time. The times are troubled. Fear is already in the air. Bunyan, Gifford, my uncle—all are like men standing on the brink of an awful chasm, blindfolded, not knowing what lies before them, but convinced it is a dark day for England—for the Puritans, at least!

And what will *I* do? Little enough, I suppose. Perhaps I will be a dry and dusty man of business like Asa Goodman. At any rate, I am here, and it is an adventure—I will not be bored to death!

But Matthew was, in fact, terribly bored after the excitement of living in a new land wore off—which was about one month. Bedford was, he admitted ruefully, much the same as Plymouth. He soon learned his duties with Asa Goodman, and since his uncle had left for London two days after depositing him in the small village, there was no one to talk to. Oh, Goodman was not a hard driver, but he had no thought of anything except business. Pastor Gifford was a man of wit, but he was a busy man, ranging far in his pastoral duties. He enjoyed the meetings on Sunday, thinking Gifford the best preacher he'd heard, by far, but the days grew long and the nights grew lonely.

He wrote a bitter note in his journal:

> I might as well have stayed in Plymouth! When Uncle Edward returns, I will make him send me to London or somewhere else on some sort of business. I will be bored out of my head with this place if nothing turns up this week! Please, God, Give me *something* to do in this place!

The day after this plaintive prayer, Matthew sought out John Bunyan in desperation. "Take me with you next week when you go to preach!"

Bunyan gave him an understanding look, then nodded. "Bored with it, are you, Mr. Winslow? Well, it's a small village. Nothing exciting now. Let's see, I go to Elstow next Sabbath. It's my old home, and there's a goodly congregation with no real pastor. Would you like to go there?"

"Yes! Tell me the time and the place, and I'm your man, Bunyan!"

The tall tinker laughed and punched Winslow on the arm, "Well, you might be a help. Can you sing?"

"I'll do my best," Matthew grinned. "Anything for a little variety."

"Be here at dawn next Sabbath, lad," Bunyan nodded. "And be in much prayer for the service, you mind?"

That was on Thursday, and it was with a spirit of release that Matthew met Bunyan as first light began to bathe the little village. "Come now, we go long shanks!" Bunyan said with a smile, and the two set out at a fast pace for Elstow, which lay only eight miles from Bedford. As they walked, Bunyan spoke quickly, sharing with the younger man some of his early history. He had been a terrible sinner as a young man, had served in Cromwell's Model Army, and after the war had been converted to Christ by John Gifford's preaching, then had begun preaching himself a few years earlier.

The sun was bright as the two men entered the small village of Elstow, and Bunyan greeted everyone they met, leading Matthew to a large barn-like structure on the north side of town. To

Matthew's surprise, the place was full. He found himself a seat on one of the backless benches, and for the next three hours, listened spellbound to this mender of pots preach the most powerful sermon he'd ever heard in his life!

It was a strange sermon, and at first he could not tell why it seemed so different. Finally he realized that it was the strange quality of imagination that linked the Scriptures and the message together. Bunyan had the gift of the storyteller, and he employed it in a masterful manner, yet so simply that even the small children that sat there through it all must have understood it.

And it was when he spoke of Jesus—mostly as "the Man"— that Matthew was most moved, for Bunyan had such a love for Jesus Christ that it communicated itself to his hearers. Matthew had never heard such poetic figures, and such plain devotion in a preacher!

He was carried away with it, and when Bunyan called a halt at noon, he moved forward to stand with him. Twisting his head to look at the preacher he felt his foot step on a soft object, then heard a faint cry of pain.

"Oh—pardon me!"

Then he found himself looking into the eyes of the most beautiful woman he'd ever seen!

She was not tall, her black curls not reaching far above his shoulders, and the tear-filled eyes so black that the pupil could hardly be discerned. She bit her lower lip, and swayed helplessly, so that he took her arm without a thought, saying, "Oh, what a clumsy oaf I am! Here, let me help you to a chair."

"It's . . . all right." Her voice was low and husky and there was a trace of an accent which seemed to Matthew quite charming. She tentatively tried her foot, winced, then said, "Perhaps I'd better sit down."

"Let me help you!" As Matthew guided her through the crowd, he could not help noticing that in spite of the drab gray gown she wore, she had a splendid figure. He helped her ease herself down onto a bench, then stood there feeling like a fool. "I say, can I get you anything?"

"No, it will be quite all right." She looked up at him and he thought that he had never seen such coloring! Her lips were like crimson petals against her pale skin, and the enormous eyes and arched brows were bewitching. She suddenly laughed and said, "Don't be so silly! You only stepped on my foot."

He let out his breath in relief, then shook his head. "It's such a small foot, my lady, and mine are so large."

She smiled and shook her head. "I'm all right—oh, here comes my aunt." As she pronounced her words with a distinct French accent, Matthew turned to meet the woman who came to stand beside them.

"Are you all right, Lydia?"

"Yes. I just twisted my ankle, Aunt," she said, turning her large dark eyes on Matthew, who quickly explained, "My fault completely. I'm so clumsy!"

Then John Bunyan appeared, saying, "Ah, have you met?"

"No."

"This is Miss Smith and her niece, Lydia Carbonne. This is Matthew Winslow. I believe you are acquainted with his uncle, are you not?"

The mention of his uncle softened the rather severe look on Miss Smith's face, and she nodded. "Of course." She gave Matthew a direct look and said, "You resemble him greatly."

"Oh, all the Winslows look alike," Matthew remarked with a shrug.

"There are refreshments outside," Bunyan offered. "Will you join me?"

He led them all outside where tables were set up and soon filled with cold cuts and fresh bread. Bunyan and Miss Smith were soon in conversation, and Matthew found himself sitting by the niece, who was eating with a healthy appetite.

"You'd better fortify yourself, Mr. Winslow," she said with an arch smile. "Pastor Bunyan hasn't really begun yet. We'll have the second half of the sermon after lunch."

Matthew Winslow could have been eating sawdust instead of cold beef! He was gazing into the blackest eyes he'd ever seen, and it took all his powers to keep his mind on the conversation with Lydia.

Realizing he was staring at her like a fool, he took himself in hand and began asking her about her background. He learned that she was an orphan, her mother and father (French, of course!), having died in a plague. She had then been taken in by her spinster aunt, Martha Smith. The sermon interrupted the conversation, and he was forced to content himself with glimpses of her beautiful face and form as Bunyan preached.

All too soon it was over, but Bunyan might have preached on the gray beard of Daniel's Billy Goat for all Matthew knew!

One thing he *did* know, however—he was invited to tea the following week at Miss Smith's!

On his way back to Bedford, Matthew was like a drunk man. His jovial mood didn't entirely fool the tall preacher, who gave him a quiet smile as they arrived at the street where Matthew turned to go to the Goodmans'.

"It was a fine sermon, Mr. Bunyan," Matthew said warmly, shaking his hand.

"What did you think of the second part?" Bunyan asked with a straight face. "Was it as interesting doctrinally as the first?"

"Why . . ." Matthew saw the faint smile on Bunyan's lips, and returned it. "Why, as to that," he said, "it was true enough—and the congregation was very fine."

"Yes, she was, wasn't she?" Bunyan stated. Then he laughed. "You'd best sit on the front row next Sabbath, Brother Winslow. I can't compete with a beautiful woman like Miss Lydia Carbonne!"

Matthew flushed, but finally grinned. "You have sharp eyes, Mr. John Bunyan."

Bunyan clapped him on the shoulder and said, "I was young myself once, you know!"

That night Matthew's journal recorded one line:

Lydia—Lydia—Lydia—Lydia—oh, Lydia Carbonne!

CHAPTER THREE

A YOUNG MAN'S FANCY

★ ★ ★ ★

"Lydia, you must stop seeing this man at once!"

From where she sat in front of a small table brushing her hair, Lydia Carbonne looked up defiantly at the tall figure of her guardian. Her full lips compressed and a rebellious light smoldered in her dark eyes. She had heard this statement in one form or another for the past two months from Martha Smith. At first she had submitted with a sigh, but now she shook her head, causing the mass of raven-dark ringlets to sweep her shoulders.

"There's nothing wrong with seeing Matthew Winslow."

"There's something wrong with a young girl making a spectacle of herself over a man in public!"

"That's not true! He walks me to the meetings, he comes here to tea, sometimes we walk together—is that what you call making a spectacle of myself?"

Miss Smith stared at her niece in despair. "You're every bit as stubborn as your mother!" She shook her head and wondered for the thousandth time how her sister Mary could have been so foolish as to marry a Frenchman. Her mind flew back to another time, another place, when she had faced the mother of this fiery young woman in precisely the same way.

In this same room, less than a year after the death of their father, Mary Smith had met a dashing young foreigner, Andre Carbonne, had fallen in love with him, and agreed to marry him.

Their mother had been a woman of no force, prostrated by the death of her husband, so the lot fell to Martha to do her best to stop the match.

"He's not even of your faith," she had said in horror to Mary. "Your children, God forbid, will be brought up as idol worshipers!"

"Not all Christians are outside the Catholic church!" her sister had shot back, and from that instant Martha Smith knew there would be no hope of changing the girl's mind. "We're going to be married and live in Dover, Martha. We love each other, and I must have him!"

Now, twenty years later, Martha Smith had the eerie feeling that her sister Mary, dead along with her husband and buried in the soil of France, somehow stood before her. *She's Mary come back again!* she thought helplessly. *The same beauty—and the same rebelliousness—like the sin of witchcraft!* The thought shocked her, and she said quickly, "You don't know this man. He's a stranger to us."

"I *do* know him, Aunt Martha," Lydia shot back at once. She gave one more pull through her luxurious hair with an ivory comb, rose and came to stand by the older woman. Placing a hand on her aunt's arm, she modified her voice and said quietly, "Don't be afraid. I know it broke your heart when mother married out of the faith. It—it was hard on her, too, you know—to be cut off from her family."

"It was her choice, Lydia."

"I know, I know, but she had to follow the man she loved. Can't you see that?"

"Oh, Lydia, it's just that I'm afraid for you!" Martha Smith had never married, and this girl had been the daughter she'd never had. Now she was losing her, and fear filled her at the thought that tragedy might strike her down. "Will Howard wants to marry you, and I'd hoped you'd make a match of it with him."

"I don't love him, Aunt. I never could."

The statement left no room for argument, and Martha Smith stood there looking at Lydia, and finally asked the question she had not dared to ask before: "Are you going to marry this man?"

"If he asks me, I'll marry him."

Yes, the same as Mary! Martha Smith thought instantly. *Mary stood in this very room, and she looked me right in the eye and said the same thing. "I'll marry Andre if he asks me."*

"Will you talk with Pastor Gifford about this? Will you at least do that for me?"

Lydia smiled and suddenly pulled her aunt's head down and kissed her cheek. "Of course I will. And you may have nothing to worry about, Aunt Martha. He may never ask me." A thought struck her, and she smiled, adding, "Matthew is spending so much time with John Bunyan these days, he may forget me entirely!"

The object of their conversation was, as a matter of fact, sitting in the Bunyan cottage at that very moment, engaged in conversation with the head of the house on the very subject of matrimony. It was not, however, Matthew's marriage that they spoke of, but Bunyan's.

A light rain was falling, so instead of sitting outside the front door on a stool as he worked, Bunyan was seated at the table putting a series of small rivets in a utensil made of pewter. He held it up to the light and then looked across the table at Matthew and asked, "Some tea, my boy?" He glanced across the room where his daughter Mary was seated on a stool sewing. "Mary, would you brew a little tea for Brother Winslow and me?"

"Yes, Father." Matthew turned to watch as the girl rose, moved unerringly across the room to where the teapot sat on a table and began making the tea. Her blindness was a source of constant sorrow to Bunyan, Matthew knew, though the big man seldom mentioned it. But now there was a veiled grief in his eyes as he watched her.

"She's like her mother, Matthew. I wish you could have known her." All four of Bunyan's children were by his first wife who had died in childbirth. "She was a godly woman, indeed," he went on, tapping the head of a rivet carefully, then holding it up again to the light.

"I suppose you had a hard time, as most newly married couples do," Matthew remarked.

"Hard? Why, I suppose it was," Bunyan remarked. "I had nothing, but she had a marvelous dowry which she brought to our marriage."

"Indeed?"

"Yes, Matthew. I became a wealthy man with that dowry."
His lively eyes twinkled and he rose to go to a bookcase nailed
to the wall. Taking down two books, he returned to the table
and placed them carefully before his guest. "There it is."

Matthew picked up the worn volumes and read the titles
aloud: *The Plain Man's Pathway to Heaven* by Arthur Dent and
The Practice of Piety by Lewis Bayly. I don't know these books,
John."

"Well, they're solid gold, my boy, solid gold!" Bunyan
smiled. "You know I found the Lord in a most unusual way."
He touched Matthew's arm, adding with a smile, "Perhaps I've
told you the story before—but *I* want to hear it again."

"How was it, John?"

"Why, I was in the army, you know, and we were about as
holy as soldiers ever get. You can thank Cromwell for that! Sermons every day, and God help the poor devil who cursed and
used the name of the Good Lord in vain! He'd be tied over a
cannon and whipped until he was raw! But it paid off, my boy."
His eyes grew dreamy as he leaned on his hands across the table,
thinking of the past. "We went into battle singing hymns of
praise to God. I think that frightened the enemy as much as our
guns! Well, anyway, I was mustered out and went home to Elstow. There I found Sarah, married her and we set up housekeeping. But I was a wild fellow, Matthew, aye, a very wild
fellow!"

"What form did this devilment take, John?"

"Oh, playing stupid games like tip-cat on the Sabbath, ringing the church bell at odd times, midnight and such, and the
worst was my filthy tongue. Oh, I was one for cursing in those
days! But then one day I was walking along the street in Elstow
and there were three or four poor women sitting beside a door
into a room, talking about the things of God. I thought they
spoke as if joy did make them speak; they spoke with such a
pleasantness of Scripture language and with such appearance of
grace in all they said that they were to me as if they had found
a new world!"

"A new world, John?"

"Aye, nothing less than that!" Bunyan shook his head, marveling at it all, then went on in a low voice. "I knew nothing of Jesus Christ—except what little I'd heard in sermons. They spoke of Him as a dear friend whose company they shared. Well, I had to have that, Matthew, I had to! So I was drawn to their company, these poor women, into the fellowhship of which they were a part. It was like a voyage to a new world, indeed, and when I met Mr. Gifford a few months later, I was so hungry to find God that I moved my family here to Bedford, just to sit at his feet. And I've never regretted it."

"He's a fine preacher."

"A man of God indeed." They spoke of the preacher until Mary brought them two large cups, filled them with tea, and allowed herself to be drawn into Bunyan's lap as he drank the steaming beverage. "Good to your poor old father, you are, sweetheart!" he exclaimed, giving her a hug. "And what a helper to her mother—I tell you, she's a marvel, Master Winslow!"

"I know." Matthew watched as the two sat there, Bunyan holding the child close, her blind eyes turned up to his seeing ones.

The two of them sat there listening to Bunyan's talk until Elizabeth came in carrying an empty basket on her arm. "Still preaching at the poor boy, Husband?" she said with a smile. Elizabeth Bunyan was a tall full-bodied woman of twenty-three with the rosy cheeks and clear eyes of the Saxon blood. Her hands were roughened with work, but she had a natural winsomeness which Matthew admired. She had married Bunyan, taking on the care of his four small children, when she could have made a much better match.

Bunyan rose at once, embraced her and said, "Now you sit down here and let me spoil you!" She smiled and obeyed. He brought cakes and tea to her, leaving a trail as he went. Matthew was amused to see that the tinker, so exact and careful in his work with metal, was so careless in his service.

She told him of the poor people she'd seen that afternoon, and he shook his head sadly over each case. It was a pleasant scene, and Matthew, for all his desire to wade into action in the wide world, thoroughly enjoyed soaking in the atmosphere of the family group. The smaller children came in, clinging to either the father or the mother, and Matthew reached out and pulled

Mary to his lap, laughing at her protests that she was too big.

Finally, the children left to play, except for Mary, who helped her mother prepare the evening meal. "Looks like the rain has stopped," Bunyan observed. "Let's take a walk before supper."

They walked around the village streets, and Bunyan observed slyly as the neighbors all greeted young Winslow along with himself, "You've become quite a fixture here, Matthew. How long has it been since you came—two months?"

"About that."

Bunyan said suddenly, turning to face Matthew, "You're completely taken with the Carbonne girl."

"Well, she's a charming young woman—"

"Faw!" Bunyan snorted. "Don't you think I have eyes? Even Mary, who can't see a thing, asked me when you two were getting married."

Matthew stopped suddenly, then turned to lean against a rock wall that encircled a snug cottage. He pulled a piece of moss from between two smooth stones, stroked its silky texture, then tossed it to the ground. "I didn't come to England to get married, John. I came to find—" He paused and once again he plucked a shred of the emerald green moss and seemed to be lost in thought as he stroked it with the tip of his finger. "To tell the truth, Brother Bunyan, I don't know *what* it was I came to find. I thought maybe it was adventure—for I've always wanted that! But these last few days in this place have made me uncertain."

Bunyan nodded sagely and said, "I know, boy, I know. Didn't I run off when I was only a lad to fight in the war? And there's some of that in you. You'll not be a man content to rust unburnished, I tell you! But war—that's not the answer." He shook his head and looked up as a swallow sailed gracefully to land in the chimney of the house beyond the wall. "No, men tire of that. But there's another kind of action, the warfare of the spirit. Jesus calls us to arms, you know. He urges us to put on the whole armor of God, to train as athletes for the race. Being a Christian isn't a soft, easy life—especially in this poor country of ours, in the year of our Lord 1659."

Matthew tossed the shred of moss to the ground and looked at Bunyan with excitement in his bright blue eyes. "I think I'd like to be part of that struggle, John."

Bunyan took in the lean form, the eager wedge-shaped face turned toward him, and then he shook his head sadly. "It won't be easy, you know. I don't think we can win this war. Some of us won't die in our beds—and some will go to prison or be driven beyond the sea."

"I'm not afraid of that!"

"No, not now, perhaps. But I tell you flat out, Matthew Winslow, the only ones who will survive this coming darkness will be those to whom the Lord Jesus Christ is a living reality! Can you say that's true of you?"

Matthew dropped his head, and there was a silence on the air so profound that he could hear the far-off cry of a curlew. The silence ran on, broken only by the tinkle of bells on a few sheep in a distant meadow.

When he raised his head, there was a mixture of sadness and desire in his face. "No, John," he said slowly, "I can't say that. I've been watching the people here, and I confess to you— as I have to Pastor Gifford—Christ is not formed in my heart. Not *yet*! But I'm willing to throw myself into this battle you say is coming."

Bunyan straightened his back and looked carefully into the eyes of young Winslow. He liked what he saw but was not ready to say more than, "It's a beginning, Matthew. God will guide you—and as I said, you'll not be a dusty man of business! The spirit in you, why, it's far too strong for that!"

"I—I've been confused about just about everything, John, but one thing I'm sure of is that I want to marry Lydia Carbonne."

Bunyan stared at the young man, then shook his head. "Be sure of yourself, Matthew." He held up his hand to cut off the protest that leaped to Matthew's lips. "In the first place, you're young and have no profession. Now, I hear that you may do well in business, so Asa Goodman says. But that's not enough for a marriage."

"But I love Lydia!"

"There is one thing that few people know about Lydia, Matthew, not even her aunt suspects it."

"What is that, John?"

"She seems flighty, not at all serious about her religion, but I tell you she *is*! Even her aunt mistakes her; being so much opposed to her mother's marriage, she chooses to think that the French strain has corrupted the English piety. Tell the truth now, son, do you not think the young woman to be somewhat frivolous—though very beautiful?"

"Yes, I suppose so, but—"

"You are mistaken, and you will find out that there is a will of steel in her makeup. I have had more than one talk with her about her commitment to the Lord Jesus Christ, and I tell you she will not be happy with a husband who is less of a Christian than she is."

"And you think I am not enough of a Christian to be her husband?"

Bunyan smiled and put his large hand on the young man's arm. There was a mixture of love and judgment in his direct gaze. Then he said, his voice low but firm, "I think you have not found yourself yet, my boy—and you have not found your God. I travail much in prayer for you." Then he slapped the broad shoulder of the young man, saying with encouragement, "You will find your way! Now, let us go inside."

The two went into the cottage, but for once Matthew had little appetite for Elizabeth's good cooking. He played with his food, then after supper spent some time with the children. Finally he left, thanking the Bunyans for their hospitality. When he went up to his room, he picked up his journal and struggled to put down on paper what was happening to him.

October 3, 1659. Bedford.

This country is in a fever! There is no government, and the talk is all of the restoration of Charles to the throne. Pastor Gifford says it will come within a month, and each Sabbath he exhorts the congregation to prepare their souls for the terrible times he says will come then.

And what will *I* do? Run home like a cur with his tail between his legs? Deny the faith and join the Church of England? It would be so easy!

And what of Lydia? I have not let myself think of it, but here in this room on this night, I set it down so that it will give me strength and purpose to stand when the tribulation comes: By my soul, I love this woman. *You are young—you don't really know yet—you have no profession!* They will say this, and more.

And what is my answer? I love this woman. That is my

answer, and I know that even if she does not love me, I will go to my grave with her image in my heart. Yea, though I never see her again in this world, she has spoiled for me the image of all other women—no, not the *image*—the *reality*!

What will I do then? I will do this one thing. I will take my courage all rolled up like a ball, and I will go to her and I will say, *Lydia Carbonne, I love you with all my heart. I want you to share my life, my bed, my heart for all time on this earth.*

She will probably say no. That is *her* decision. Mine is made—to offer her my name and my strong right arm—and my heart—so help me God!

Slowly Matthew closed the journal, cleaned the tip of the quill, and placed it on the desktop. His face was slightly pale, and as he knelt beside his narrow bed, instead of the rather ritualistic prayer that usually closed his day, he lifted up his face and for a long time waited for some answer. Finally he got into bed and lay there staring at the low ceiling.

Lydia thereafter said of Matthew's proposal, "It was the most *unusual* proposal any man ever made or any girl ever received!"

The scene was the small chapel in Elstow. The audience was the congregation of Separatists gathered for the customary Sabbath morning sermon. Since the church had no pastor, John Bunyan had been asked to bring the sermon, and he had just started his seventh major point when Matthew Winslow came in, his face pale as paper. Ordinarily he took a seat at the rear of the church, but on this occasion he swept the congregation with a swift glance, and finding Lydia sitting in the second row with her aunt, walked steadily across the pegged wooden floor and plunked himself down firmly beside her.

Lydia was startled, for the Elstow congregation held to the old ways, men seated on one side, women on the other. Her large eyes flew open as Matthew sat down beside her, and she felt her aunt stirring angrily on her other side.

Matthew leaned forward and said something in a faint whisper which she did not understand, primarily due to the fact that Brother Bunyan was preaching about hell, and it was the usual custom to raise the volume considerably when the subject was under consideration.

He leaned forward until one of her black tresses touched his cheek as he whispered into her ear, but at the exact moment he repeated himself, Bunyan slapped the desk in front of him and gave a resounding roar.

Lydia was confused, having no concept as to what urgency could warrant such behavior on the young man's part. She turned from him, only to have her arm firmly grasped, pulling her back to face him again. This time he raised his voice so that she understood him *very* clearly!

Indeed, every living soul in the congregation heard him, for just as he raised his voice, Brother Bunyan suddenly stopped speaking. And into that sudden and absolute silence that fell over the church, Matthew Winslow said in a clear, urgent voice: "I said, *will you marry me, Lydia?*"

The loud question drew a sudden gasp from Lydia's aunt, and she jerked around, causing her large Bible to drop to the floor with a *thud*! A hum swept through the room, and John Bunyan, who had heard the guns of war with more aplomb, stood there behind the sacred desk staring at the couple.

Lydia was stunned. The silence that followed seemed to roar in her ears as she became conscious of the stares burning into her from all sides. Her lips parted and she wondered if she had heard him correctly. Surely no man would be so forward as to propose to a young woman under such circumstances!

But apparently Matthew Winslow was exactly such a man, for he seemed totally unaware of the gaping audience, and said again, "Lydia, I love you and want you to marry me!"

She stared at him, her face flushed, tears of vexation filling her eyes. "No!" she snapped indignantly, and with a suddenness that caught everyone off guard, she rose and rushed out of the church, leaving Matthew staring into the angry eyes of her enraged aunt.

Turning from the irate woman, and without a glance at either preacher or congregation, he dashed out, his heels drumming rapidly on the wood floor.

As the door slammed behind Matthew, Pastor Bunyan looked with startled eyes at his congregation, took a deep breath and then continued as though nothing had happened. "Hell," he stated firmly, "was created for the devil and his angels—not for men!" He cast one furtive look at the door where the pair had escaped and added enigmatically, "God made other things for men—such as marriage." But his attempt to recapture the attention of his flock was hopeless.

Outside, Lydia ran along the narrow street, crying with humiliation, stumbling over the cobblestones. As she turned the corner onto the lane where she lived with her aunt, strong hands grabbed her from behind.

"Let me go!" she cried, trying to free herself from the iron embrace. "I hate you, Matthew Winslow!"

But he just stood there holding her as she beat her fists against his chest, tears running down her cheeks. Finally she stopped and, in a gesture of surrender and helplessness, fell against his broad chest, moaning, "What will I do? What will I do?"

Placing his hand under her chin, he drew her face upward. She had never seemed so beautiful to him.

"Why did you do such a thing to me?" she cried.

Pulling her close, he said passionately, "Because I love you! And I'll have you, Lydia, or die in the attempt!"

She gasped at his boldness, but had no time to do anything else, for he suddenly bent his head and kissed her intensely. Then as his kisses grew gentle, she found her arms going around his neck. How long they stood there or who drew back first she never knew, but when they looked at each other in breathless wonder, she whispered, "I love you, Matthew Winslow! I'll never love anyone else!"

She took a deep breath and released it. One hand went up to touch his cheek tenderly; then she smiled with trembling lips and murmured, "I never knew love could be like this."

"Nor I," Matthew responded quietly. "But it's only the beginning, sweetheart!" he said triumphantly. "Only the beginning! Why, we've got a whole lifetime to love each other!"

Then she said something that startled him, so unexpected it was. "And we can love God together, can't we, Matthew?"

He thought at once of Bunyan's comment: *She will not be happy with a man who is less of a Christian than she is.* He might have given thought to that if he had not been so in love, but he merely smiled and said, "Yes, of course we will!"

They turned and walked back toward the church with a choir of small birds singing an echo of the joy that had filled their hearts.

CHAPTER FOUR

HE THAT FINDETH A WIFE ...

★ ★ ★ ★

Edward Winslow felt the weight of his years as he climbed heavily out of the dusty coach in front of the Mote Hall. He moved stiffly down the narrow lane that led to Pastor Gifford's cottage, speaking briefly to those who greeted him. The brilliant May sunshine painted the thatched roofs of the village with gold, but he had no eye for the beauty of the lush countryside that day.

I'm like an old dog looking for a place to die, he thought wearily, then paused abruptly, for he had been a man of great zest, and the discovery that he had given up swept over him. He stood stock-still in the middle of the street, unaware of the white-washed houses of Bedford or the noisy flock of geese crossing the village green like a snowy cloud. He suddenly remembered the day he had stood on the deck of the *Mayflower*, just off Southampton, with Pastor Robinson—now dead. That day with the small band of believers, they had looked their last at England and turned to face the unseen land across the sea. A lump rose in his throat as thoughts of them—Standish, Alden, Mullins, Bradford, and Captain Christopher Jones! *All gone now—and I'm not far behind*.

"Mr. Winslow!" A voice caught at him, interrupting his reminiscing. As he turned he saw Pastor Gifford approaching from the square with his nephew. "You're two days late," Gifford said as he came to take Winslow's hand. "We've been concerned."

"Every coach was full for two days after the King arrived from France." He shook his head sadly. "I'd have been most happy to leave earlier."

"Come, Uncle," Matthew said quickly, noting his evident fatigue. "These coach rides are enough to make a man take to his bed. I'll accompany you to Pastor Gifford's house. You can tell us the news on the way."

"I think I will take a little rest, Matthew," his uncle nodded. He allowed himself to be led along the street by Matthew's gentle pressure. He said little as they made their way past the first group of cottages north of the Mote Hall, but gave a sigh of relief as they came to the small cottage of the pastor.

"Wife!" Gifford called out as they crossed the threshold, "We have a guest."

Gifford's wife Sarah, a short, heavy-set woman of fifty, turned from the massive fireplace, her face lighting up at the sight of the older man. "Ah now, I've been cooking for you for two days! Sit you down, and you can have these meat pies I've had to fight my husband and your nephew for!"

"Yes, sit down, Edward," Gifford urged, pulling a heavy chair back from the table. "Sit you down, too," he said to the younger Winslow. "You can lie down after you've eaten, Edward, but first, tell us about the event."

"Charles is king of England—and that's the whole of it," Winslow said heavily. He reached into his inner pocket, fumbled around briefly, then pulled a letter out. "A letter from your father."

As Matthew opened the letter, he heard Pastor Gifford saying, "Well, we knew it was coming, didn't we?"

"Yes, we knew it." Winslow leaned forward, placed his brow on his fist and closed his eyes. "Aye, we *knew* it, John— but I don't think any of us really have any idea of what it's going to be like."

"In that you are probably right," Gifford said slowly. "It'll be a dark night of the soul for our people."

As the two older men spoke of the new order and the problems it would bring to their small world, Matthew read the brief lines:

4 March 1660

My son Matthew,

Your request that we travel to England to meet your new bride is, of course, quite out of the question. I fear you do not yet understand how ill your mother is. She is almost completely bedfast now, and I must stay at home to take care of her, except for those times when the neighbors sit with her.

I do not even dare go to preach overnight at any of the churches, for fear she will be gone when I return. She is quite ready to go home to the Lord. This morning when one of the good ladies asked her if she had any fear, she roused up, and her eyes had the same fire they had when I first saw her, and she said right smartly, "Afraid? How could I be afraid to go to Him whom I have loved and longed for these fifty years!"

She had memorized your letters word for word and only wishes that she might have seen your bride. But what has meant the most to her—and to me, my son!—is the portion of the last letter where you indicated your intention to pursue the Lord. That, along with the word from your uncle in which he speaks of your interest in preaching along with good Master Bunyan, have been the joy of her heart, and mine also.

When we parted, Matthew, I said, "Be true to God and to yourself." I can add nothing to that, except that your mother and I have great faith now in you, and that if we do not meet again on this earth, we will be reunited in a better Kingdom!

Gilbert Winslow

Matthew blinked rapidly, his eyes burning as he read the lines, and he bit his lip as he folded the letter and stored it in his pocket. He had been over-hasty in his marriage, he knew, and the guilt of it bore heavily on him. The original plan had been for a trip to Plymouth with Lydia so she might meet his parents, then marry there. But there had been such objections from Martha Smith over Lydia making such a voyage in an unmarried state that they had given up on the idea. "We'll go to America soon, dear," Lydia had said, knowing something of the pain he felt. But the trip was long and expensive. So the five months of their marriage had served only to increase the pain Matthew felt over his parents.

He shook off the thought and heard his uncle speaking of the restoration of Charles to the throne. "The whole country is one big ball, John. You should have seen the excitement when Charles came ashore day before last! He came in a barge with two dukes. Mr. Pepys was with him, and the captain of the brigantine steered. There was also Mr. Mansell and a dog the king loves—and many others from his nest in France. A large crowd was there to meet him, including General Monk, who fell on him with all imaginable love and respect, thousands of horsemen it seemed, and noblemen of all sorts. The mayor of the town presented him his white staff, the badge of his place, which the King gave him again." He gave a short laugh and a sardonic light came into his eyes. "You'll like this, John, the mayor gave him a very rich Bible, which he took and said, holding it up, 'This is what I love more than anything else in the world!' "

"You don't think he meant it?" Matthew asked.

"Meant it? Him, with his fancy French whores in his cabin on the ship he'd just left?" Winslow shook his head violently and struck the table with a clenched fist. "The man's an actor, I tell you! Now it pleases him to play the benevolent monarch, forgiving his enemies—but mark my word, within months the gallows in England will bear the weight of those who were closest to Cromwell."

"What about you, Edward?" Gifford asked quickly.

"I would not be at all surprised to find myself among those pinpointed by Charles."

"But—you won't stay here, will you, Uncle?" Matthew asked.

"Stay here? Of course I'll stay here! I've not so much life in front of me that I'd sell out what I've lived for just to have a few more hours on this earth!"

"That's very well for you, Edward," Gifford nodded. "But I think for your nephew it might be best to return to Plymouth."

"I agree," the old man said.

"Well, I don't!" The face of young Winslow flushed and there was a stubbornness in the set of his chin that brought a sudden image of Gilbert Winslow to the older man. He watched as Matthew got to his feet and paced the confines of the small room in agitation, his trim figure alive with nervous energy. "What sort of man do you take me for? A coward?"

"Now, Matthew, there's no question of that," Gifford soothed. He had grown accustomed to the quick, impulsive shifts in the young man's behavior, so now he reasoned with him carefully. "First of all, this isn't your home. What happens here isn't your battle—except perhaps in prayer. Secondly, you are not alone now. If you were single, that might be a different story, but as Mr. Bacon has said, 'He that hath wife and children hath given hostages to fortune.' You must consider Lydia. And thirdly, you must have been under constant burden concerning your mother. You must see that going back to Plymouth would be the wise thing to do."

"Perhaps so, but you forget one thing," Matthew responded quickly. "You and I have had long talks, have we not, about my preaching? Am I to leave that, too? And don't tell me there's preaching to be done at Plymouth, Pastor Gifford! I will quote you one scripture, and you tell me how I may without peril to my soul ignore it: 'He that putteth his hand to the plow and turneth back, is not fit for the kingdom of God!' "

Pastor Gifford gaped open-mouthed at the fiery ardor of young Winslow. Then he gave a short laugh and threw up his hands. "I leave him to you, Edward!"

"Well, that's no good, either," Edward smiled, and for that moment the lines of his face softened and he looked much like the young man before him. "The Winslows have always been fool-stubborn, and I see this one is no different. His father is that way himself—and so am I, I suppose."

Matthew stood there, so tall that his head almost brushed the rough beam over his head. He smiled down at Gifford. "It would be so much easier if it were a real war with swords and pikes, wouldn't it? Just go out slashing and hacking—then you either killed or got killed. But this isn't like that, is it?"

"No, our weapons are not carnal, but mighty to God to the pulling down of strongholds," Gifford stated emphatically. "And it's a mighty stronghold that lies before us—the realm of England will be set to crush every Puritan and Separatist to powder, and very soon."

There was a silence as Gifford's wife came to the table with trenchers full of meat. "Well," the younger man said, "Lydia is expecting me." He took his uncle's hand. "You'll come to our house for supper tomorrow night, will you, sir?"

"Done!"

"Good day, then. I'll read the book by Mr. Hooker before our study tomorrow, Pastor."

He left the room hurriedly, and as the two men began to eat, Edward asked, "What's your judgment, John, on that young man?"

Gifford chewed a morsel of meat slowly, swallowed, then said, "He's either going to be a great man—" He paused, then with a shrug of his narrow shoulders, finished by saying, "He's got the raw material, Edward, but the crucible we're all going to be in soon will test him out."

"It would kill Gilbert and Humility if he failed," Edward remarked with sadness in his old eyes. "He's all that's left of the House of Winslow, isn't he? If he goes down, it'll be like there never were any of us."

"No! He won't go down!" Pastor Gifford said suddenly, his usually mild expression twisted to an explosive anger. "This king may think to wipe us out, but he shall not do it, not by all that's holy! You and I have fought, but we are old. It'll be young men like your nephew who'll have to stand in the gap this time!"

"Amen!" Edward Winslow agreed loudly. Then he looked at the door and said in a prayerful whisper, "Amen!"

The tiny house on the edge of town was like a doll's house, having only one room for cooking, dining, eating, and studying, and one small room no more than eight feet square for sleeping. It had been used by one of the deacons, Matthew Prince, as a storage shed for his blacksmithing equipment, but he had agreed to rent it to the newlyweds very cheaply.

It had been a delightful game for the pair, cleaning out the rooms, finding a few pieces of furniture and fitting them into every possible location. They set up housekeeping with a wedding gift from Edward Winslow, a small bag of gold sovereigns. "If it hadn't been for your uncle Edward, we'd be roosting on a tree!" Lydia had laughed once as they tried to put a sideboard along a wall that was only two inches longer than the massive piece of oak furniture.

He had dropped the end he was struggling with, picked her up in his arms and covered her face with kisses, crying out, "I'd rather have a woman like you roosting in a tree than any other in a castle!"

"Matthew!" she had cried, but there was a look of intense

satisfaction in her dark eyes as she pretended to pout. She had always been a romantic girl—far too much so for her aunt's tastes. Perhaps it was the French blood. In any case, she had somehow been able to maintain a balance between an inner life alive with imagination and the rigid creed and austere practices of the Pilgrim way. She had learned while very young to act out little dramas she made up only when alone, but even when she ceased to pantomime such things, she kept up a lively imagination.

Those little dramas had been buried deep inside, but she had learned almost at once that the man she had married was at *least* as romantic as she, although he denied it vehemently.

To outsiders, Matthew and Lydia seemed a rather conventional young married couple. She tended her tiny house, sewed, cooked, and sat demurely by her tall, handsome husband through the four-hour sermons, and he went faithfully to work with the dusty books of Asa Goodman, looking as solemn as a deacon.

But when they were alone in their snug cottage, their behavior would have been a scandal to the neighbors, not to mention the deacons and pastors! They both had playful minds, and their verbal give-and-take, puns and jokes that would have been meaningless to anyone else, was a source of constant delight to both of them.

Even now as he walked to the door and stepped inside, his heart beat a little faster at the thought of her. She met him at once, throwing her arms around him and pulling his head down for a kiss. They stood there for a long moment, savoring each other. Then he stepped back and pulled the letter from his pocket. "Uncle Edward is back. He brought a letter from Father."

She read it quickly, then looked up with apprehension. "It sounds very serious."

"I think it is. Father isn't given to idle words."

She bit her lower lip, then said quietly, "You feel very bad, don't you?"

"I . . . wish we could have gone home." Then seeing her face grow tense, he took her in his arms and added, "Now, don't you fret, Princess. It just couldn't be."

"Do you think we should go now?"

He released her and sat down on the single bench in the room. "Uncle Edward and Pastor Gifford say we should go. Not just because of Mother's illness, but they think there's going to be hard times for all of us."

She nodded and sat down next to him. Taking his hand in hers, she spoke softly. "And what do you say, dear?"

He shook his head stubbornly, an expression she had learned to recognize. "I say we stay here. Where in America is there a man like Pastor Gifford or John Bunyan to sit under?"

"All right, we stay!" she cried out; then she jumped up and ran to the fireplace. "Oh, I've burned the potatoes!"

He laughed and rose to go to her side. "Forget the potatoes! Here I'm trying to make the most important decision of our lives, and you're worried about burned potatoes!"

"And you'll be screaming like a madman when I put them in front of you for supper!" she laughed.

"Madman I may be, but not over burned potatoes—just you," he returned, grabbing her and whirling her around the room.

"Oh, Princess," he said, holding her tightly, "I didn't know love could be so wonderful." He looked into her glowing face and kissed her tenderly. "My love, I—"

"Good day, Brother Winslow."

Matthew loosed his grip on Lydia so suddenly that she almost slipped to the floor, then both of them stood there with their faces flaming, staring at John Bunyan and Elizabeth, who had come up to the front door.

"Oh—" Matthew stammered. "Why, Brother Bunyan, come in—we were just—just—"

Lydia pushed at the mass of ringlets that had fallen wildly over her shoulders and moved toward Elizabeth. "Come in. Matthew and I were just discussing our future!"

"It's a joy to see young love. I hope you're enjoying each other like this when you've been married as long as some of us!" He put his arm around his wife and smiled down at her. Then he asked, "Well, Matthew, will you be going with me tomorrow to preach at Hinton?"

"Of course."

"Good!" Bunyan gave the young man a smile. "I think you

might say a few words this time, Matthew."

"You mean—preach?"

Bunyan smiled at his expression. "You have to begin, don't you? We all do. Come, Elizabeth, we must go."

"He's a wonderful man," Lydia murmured, watching them walk away. "So simple."

"Yes, but he's a deep one," Matthew mused. He stared after the departing pair. "Four children! And expecting another! Elizabeth's first—and he may be in jail or deported. How can he face up to that?"

Lydia took his arm and said quietly, "We must pray, Matthew. And we must cling very close together. You know what I fear most?"

"What?"

"Not jail or persecution, but that we'll be somehow divided."

"How could that be, Princess?" he asked gently. "I would never leave you."

She stood there staring out at the disappearing forms of the Bunyans and seemed to be struck by something in their figures. "I don't know how, but it's what I fear. Don't let it happen, Matthew!" she cried, throwing herself into his arms.

"Never!" Matthew stated, smoothing her hair. "Let the world fall, you and I will stay together."

She put her head back and looked up at him with a tremulous smile. "That's all I want, Matthew. It's not too much to ask, is it? We may miss out on the world, but we can ask God to give us that one thing, can't we? Is that too selfish to ask Him for—to let us stay together as long as we're on this earth?"

"No, not too much."

He led her back inside the small, dark cottage and pulled the door, shutting out the outside world with all its clamor and demands. And as it closed with a firm sound, he found himself wishing that it could be as easy as this always—just leave the world, find a snug hiding place with the one you love, and shut the door.

But as he turned to her uplifted face, he felt a wave of fatalism grip him. A cloud crossed the sun, cutting off the bright rays and leaving her a vague and indistinct shadow as she stood before him.

CHAPTER FIVE

THE SKY IS FALLING!

★　★　★　★

Justice Twisten lived in the largest house in Bedford, a sprawling two-story half-timbered affair, with five large chimneys rising high above the eaves. Plumes of white smoke rolled out of them, caught by the sharp September wind and twisted into a braided column against the iron-gray sky. Summer's emerald green lay buried under a dull covering of dead leaves that crunched briskly under the feet of the three men marching down the long lane from the main road.

John Bunyan glanced at his companions, then lifted his gaze to the house which lay in the circle of a serpentine drive. "I wish your uncle were here with us, Matthew. He's used to talking with lawyers and government people."

"There's not much even he could do this time, John, even if he were able to come," Pastor Gifford responded. "I have no hope of any mercy from Twisten. He's always hated our faith."

Bunyan scraped the mud off his feet on the brick steps and grimaced as he gave the brass knocker a loud blow. "No, I suppose that's true. How is he, do you know, Matthew?"

"Very poorly." Anger flew across Matthew's face as he thought of his uncle jammed into a common jail in London. "He has weak lungs and that cold cell could be the death of him." The Winslow blood flared up and he struck the moss-covered bricks with a clenched fist. "Curse them! An old man like that who's served his country all his life!"

"But they'll never forget he served Cromwell," Pastor Gifford reminded them. "I hear the jails are packed with Fifth-Monarchy men and Separatists, but—" He broke off as the door opened and he announced, "We are called to see Justice Twisten."

"He's waiting for you," the tall, thin man who answered the door said. He led them across a large open room, down a broad corridor lined with a series of portraits of stern-faced men. "In here, please."

The three men stepped into a large book-lined study, dominated by a massive desk behind which sat Justice Simon Twisten. He was a large, portly man with a neck of a bull, his small eyes buried in the folds of fat lining his face. He offered no greeting.

Pastor Gifford waited for a moment, then seeing that the man was not going to speak, said, "You sent for us, Justice Twisten?"

Still he waited, the antagonism in his piggish eyes gleaming; then he said abruptly, "You know why you've been sent for, Gifford. We'll have no discussion!" His high voice rose, incongruous in such a bulky form, and his fat face flushed as he added, "You are lawbreakers, and I'll have none of it in this country."

"Sir, if I might—"

"None of your smooth talk, I said! You have been told of the Conventicle Act, and you can spare me your pleas for mercy. The law is plain; it forbids the assembly of more than five people for any religious gathering." He glared at Bunyan and spat out maliciously, "You, John Bunyan, are a known felon!"

"I am no felon!"

"Quiet!" Twisten roared. He heaved his bulk out of the chair and stood there, massive and dangerous, "You have been preaching at night to groups of people—we have information on this. And I warn you, Bunyan, if you are apprehended, you are subject to the full weight of the law!"

"Surely, Justice Twisten," Gifford objected, "you would not classify a few simple preachers with murderers and thieves!"

"The law, Gifford, the law does the classifying!" Twisten shot back as he leaned forward like a huge bear, resting his fists on the desk and glaring at the three of them.

"The same law that throws an old man like my uncle in jail with common murderers?" Matthew raised his voice and took a step toward the justice in a move so unexpected that Twisten straightened up and stepped backward, alarm on his face. "You call that *law*? I call it cowardly tyranny!"

"Matthew!" Gifford warned, taking a firm grip on the young man's arm, but he was too late.

Twisten wheeled and moved across the room surprisingly fast for such a big man. He threw open the door and shouted, "Matthew Winslow, is it? You will join your famous uncle the moment I hear one word of your defying the Act! Now get out, all of you! I called you here to tell you that I am set against you! You had your way with the true servants of the King while that traitor Cromwell lived—now we'll see who will bend their necks to the Royal Monarch, King Charles the Second! Get out!"

Matthew made to move toward the justice, but his arms were pinned at once by Gifford and Bunyan. As they struggled to get him outside the door, he cried out with a ringing voice, "You godless dog! Put me in the jail! I'll stay there until the moss grows up to my eyes before I'll give in to you!"

He was still raging as they cleared the front door.

"You young fool! What good did that do?" Bunyan said roughly as he jerked the young man so hard his neck popped.

"You expect me to stand there and listen to that—!"

"Shut your mouth!" Bunyan interrupted fiercely. As soon as they were clear of the drive and back on the main road, he released Matthew and turned to walk rapidly toward the center of town, Gifford joining him.

Matthew stood transfixed, then hurried to catch up with the two men who ignored him, speaking quietly only to each other.

"No hope for mercy from Twisten, just as I said," Pastor Gifford said despondently. He gave a quick sideways glance at the burly tinker beside him. "What will you do, John?"

"What God tells me to do!"

"But you know the end of that—I mean, if you are apprehended preaching, you'll be deported, maybe for life!"

Bunyan did not look at Gifford. His eyes were fixed on the horizon where small groups of scudding clouds broke the monotony of the gray sky. He seemed to be lost in thought and it was not until they were abreast the field where the lane turned to his cottage that he stopped and turned his eyes on Gifford and Winslow.

"I'm afraid, Pastor."

"*You*—afraid?" Matthew asked in surprise. Never had a man seemed so filled with total dedication as John Bunyan, and he could not believe what the tall preacher was saying.

"Yes, I'm afraid," Bunyan said simply. He smiled slightly, and his eyes were fixed on Winslow. "You've often told me what a good imagination I have, Matthew."

"Yes?"

"Well, I do have more of that than most men, but it's a curse—at least in this case." He brushed his hand across his face in an odd gesture, as if he were attempting to brush away invisible cobwebs. When he lowered his hand there was a vulnerability in his strong face that Matthew had never seen before. "Every night I have this dream—always the same. I'm in a cell, a dirty, dank cell with filth everywhere. And in the dream I've been there so long I can't remember when I came there, and there's no end to it! Every night is an eternity stretching out to the crack of doom—but that's not the worst!"

"What is it, John?" Gifford asked quietly.

"It's my family—my wife and children." Bunyan brushed his hand across his eyes, and when he looked up Matthew saw they were filled with tears. "I hear them outside the cell, crying—especially Mary—oh, the thought of my blind one, what she may endure, breaks my heart to pieces!"

His companions stood there helplessly. Gifford glanced quickly at Matthew as if to say, *I've never seen this side of John Bunyan.* Then he said gently, "It's asking too much—for a man with a family. Let the younger men do the front-line fighting, John."

"Stop preaching?"

"Just for a while."

"No! Never. I spoke too quickly against you, Matthew," he said with a faint smile. "I like what you told the justice! What was it you said?" He searched for it, then said, " 'I'll stay there *until moss grows up to my eyes.*' " He smiled and clapped Winslow on the back with a hearty blow. "That's what you said—and it's what I feel."

"But your family?" Gifford protested. "What about them?"

"God will be the father of the fatherless!" Bunyan exclaimed. He seemed to have shaken off the weight that had fallen on him. Squaring his shoulders, he looked fearlessly back toward Twisten's house. "God will not forsake us. We are in His hand, and if it will be to His glory to be put in a cell, then by the grace of God that is what I will do!"

"Amen!" Matthew cried. "And we will go to lower Samsell tomorrow just as we planned?"

"Yes! Meet me at five. The people there will gather at the river, and we'll preach in the dark if we have to!"

"I would not go if I were you, John," Gifford spoke up. "Twisten is no fool. He'll have you watched."

"Well—perhaps that's so." He thought of it, then said, "Scripture says that a wise man looketh well to his going. We will leave after dark, Matthew. That way we can be sure no one is following us. I'm sure no one in the congregation will betray us."

"I'll be there!" Matthew exclaimed, afire with excitement. He waved quickly and ran off to tell Lydia.

"He's a firebrand, isn't he, John?" Gifford said with a fond glance at the young man.

"He's that. We could have used him in the Model Army. But this is going to be a different kind of war. If it were a matter of swords and gunpowder, Matthew would be the ideal warrior. That kind of hardship he could take. There'd be plenty of danger and excitement—which is what he's after. But his zeal is for adventures not for God. And this struggle is going to be different. Can he take persecution of another sort—jail, deportment, malice from high places?"

Gifford shook his head. "That would not be his strength, John. Until he truly comes to a personal faith, he won't be able to stand under it. We must try to keep him clear of it."

"We can try, but he's young—and he's got a cause. A holy war." Bunyan turned and said, "All of us are going to bear scars from this, Pastor! I pray young Winslow finds faith enough to support him!" The two men fell into silence and made their separate ways home.

Lydia was caught off guard when Matthew came rushing in, his eyes blazing with excitement. She had been scrubbing the tiny floor of their single room when he burst through the door, crying out, "Lydia! Come here!"

He seated her at the table and began pacing back and forth as he told her of the encounter with Justice Twisten and of the determination he had formed to join in the struggle against the tyranny of the crown. She smiled briefly, amused at the boyish quality of his excitement, but when he repeated Bunyan's words, she sobered and raised a hand to interrupt him.

"But, Matthew, you really aren't a preacher—not yet."

"Oh, I will be soon enough," he said carelessly. "Sooner or later I'll be accepted, and until that happens I can go with Bunyan. Oh, we're going tomorrow to Lower Samsell. I forgot to tell you. And we'll have to go after dark—to shake off the sheriff's men." His eyes glowed at the thought, and he laughed aloud and pulled her to her feet.

Lydia hesitated, then asked quietly, "Matthew, why are you doing this?"

He paused, arrested by the question, "Why—for honor, I suppose. Someone must stand against the tyranny of the King!"

"And for God?"

"Yes, I suppose; for God as well!" Catching her in his strong arms, he whirled her like a child. "Come on, you King's men! Try and catch us!"

She had sensed this reckless spirit in him from the first, and it had been part of his charm. There was something of the wild hawk in this spirit, something daring, and she loved that part of him.

But a cloud fell over her face, and she said as he lowered her to the floor, "But, it's very dangerous! Sooner or later. . . ?"

He caught her hand up and kissed the palm. He looked so young as he stood there smiling down into her face. There was no cloud in his bright blue eyes. He was excited with the sheer adventure—much like at a game of chance or a closely fought contest with swords.

Suddenly a fear shot through her, and she caught at him blindly, throwing her arms around his waist and holding on so tightly that he stopped short in surprise.

"Why—what's this?" he asked. "You're not afraid, are you, Princess?"

"For you I am," she whispered, her voice trembling.

"Why, you mustn't be afraid," he soothed, holding her close. "I can take care of myself."

He sounded so sure, so happy, and she drew back, dashing the tears away that had risen to her eyes. "God will have to do that," she said with a serious look. She knew that his commitment to God was not as strong as her own, and this troubled her. Always when she had thought about marriage she had thought of a man stronger than she, and in some ways he was. But his experience with God was superficial; despite the capacity she sensed in him for a devout life of service, he had never been tested, never given himself to the arduous struggle of finding God in anything other than the ordinary ways.

But she had. Bunyan's analysis had been accurate, for despite her appearance (her beauty caused some to think she was not at all spiritual!) and her rather flighty behavior at times, she had gone through a time that had brought her close to God. When her parents had died, she had been distraught, almost slipping off into derangement. No one knew how close she had come to losing her mind, but in that time of crisis, she had learned to pray—and to be obedient to the still small voice of the Holy Spirit.

The strange people called the "Quakers" had risen about this time, led by George Fox, and all over England they had suffered persecution for their outlandish behavior. John Bunyan felt called to speak out against them, and was writing a book exposing what he perceived as doctrinal errors—one of them being a doctrine of "The Inner Light."

Although Lydia had no deep theological views, she had experienced something of the "inner light." It had come suddenly, but only after long periods of desperate prayer. She had eaten little and would not have consciously called it "fasting," but the experience came after several days of eating nothing.

She had been alone in her room, lying across her bed, exhausted by weeping and fear, and she cried out aloud, "Oh, God, I'm so afraid! Help me, please help me!"

And then she experienced something so different from anything she had ever known. She never forgot it, and it controlled much of her life from that moment on.

Her poor, exhausted body suddenly seemed to be filled with light, accompanied by a sense of warmth that ran along her entire frame! The fatigue and the stomachache that had plagued her immediately faded, and she felt warm and safe. Mostly *safe*, for that was her need. She had felt so alone!

For a long time—she never knew how long—she lay there resting in the warmth and sense of security. Then there came something into her mind that she could not understand. It was not a voice, and she heard nothing with her ears, but the words were there—deep inside, as if carved into her mind.

Child, do you love me? Would you let me into your heart? Would you let me be in you forever?

With all her heart, Lydia yearned for love, for comfort and safety. She stretched her hands up as if reaching for her lost father's comforting arms and cried out, "Yes! Oh, yes, come into my heart!"

And at that moment someone came in. She could never explain it, nor did she ever try to. But it was like a door opened and someone came into the room, bringing health, joy, and peace inside!

She began to thank this Guest whose name she didn't know, lifting her small voice in praise. As she prayed, the presence of a mighty power filled her spirit, and she whispered, "Jesus, is it you?"

And in her heart there came an answer that swelled and grew until she could hardly bear it.

Yes! I am now in you, child!

She had lain there for a long time, knowing she was now different. Though she didn't immediately share this experience with anyone, one thing she quickly discovered: when she had troubles or fears, she could pray, and almost at once she was conscious of the presence of the Lord Jesus!

She longed to tell Matthew of this experience, but had not been able to do it. Now, looking into his bright-blue eyes, loving him with all her heart, she knew that he knew nothing of this kind of walk with God—and that frightened her.

"Let's pray, Matthew," she said quietly.

He looked at her in surprise. "You do the praying, Princess," he laughed, "and I'll do the rest." Then he began talking excitedly of the coming trip to Samsell, but failed to see the disappointment on her face.

He left the next night at dusk, and as he grabbed her in his arms and kissed her, his eyes gleamed with excitement. "Wait up for me, Princess!" he whispered, kissing her fervently. "I'll play the hare to these hounds of Twisten, and when I return, we'll celebrate!"

"I'll pray for you," she said, fighting the fear that threatened to fill her.

"Yes, you pray," he said with a broad grin. Then he was gone.

She went back and sat down, her heart heavy. She knew it would be hours before he came back, perhaps near dawn, but she was so burdened she fell on her knees and began praying with all her heart for him.

She prayed until she was worn out, then fell asleep on the hard floor, one arm under her in a cramped position. When the loud knock came at daybreak, she aroused slowly, confused and heavy-eyed from sleep.

"Lydia! Lydia, wake up!"

She struggled to her feet, almost falling because of her numbed legs, and threw open the door. There stood Pastor Gifford—alone. She took one look at his face, then said quickly, "They've been taken, haven't they?"

"Yes, both of them."

"I'll get my cloak."

As she went slowly toward the small jail that sat perched on a bridge over the small stream, she listened quietly as Gifford told her how Bunyan and Matthew had been arrested and charged with breaking the law.

She heard little of what he said, but she knew that never again would life be as simple as it had been when the sun had touched her face through the window that morning. The jail, which she had seen so often, suddenly seemed ominous, and a quick fear shot through her as they approached. But she called out, "God, be my helper!" And as always, the peace came.

Matthew will have to learn to pray! she thought as she followed Pastor Gifford inside.

CHAPTER SIX

BEDFORD JAIL

★ ★ ★ ★

"Elizabeth?" Lydia knocked at the door of the Bunyan cottage and stood there shivering in the cutting November wind. She held a steaming iron pot by the handles, her hands almost numb from the icy cold that had fallen like a physical blow on the countryside.

The door swung open and she stumbled stiff-legged into the room toward the small fire that flickered in the fireplace. "Mary, is your mother here?"

The blind eyes of the child swung toward her unerringly, and she said, "Yes, but she's in bed, Mrs. Winslow. She's sick again."

A look of alarm crossed Lydia's face, and she said, "Well, I've brought a pot of good strong beef broth. Why don't you set the table while I go talk to her."

"Oh, that smells good!" Mary shoved by the other children who had swarmed in close, looking like a miniature adult as she began setting the bowls on the table. As Lydia moved to the door that led to the sleeping room, she thought, *Mary's too young for such things. She's never had a childhood.* It disturbed her that the Separatists treated their children like adults. Her French father had been openly affectionate, and her mother had bent to his ways. The result had been a happy life while they lived, and a cruel shock when she had been taken into the strict world of her aunt.

She moved in the dark sleeping chamber to the high bed and found Elizabeth on her back holding her stomach, her back arched rigidly. Leaning over she put her hand on the suffering woman's forehead, whispering gently, "Elizabeth?"

The sick woman's eyes opened slowly, and she moved to get up, saying feebly, "Oh, I—must have dozed off, Lydia." Her face contorted suddenly with pain. "I must take John something to eat."

"No, you rest," Lydia said, pressing her firmly back into the bed. "I've made enough broth for all of us. I'll take a big pot of it to John and Matthew. And I want you to eat all you can when you get up."

Elizabeth caught Lydia's hand and held it to her face, saying softly, "I don't know what I would have done without you, Lydia!" She shook her head slowly, then said, "I want so much to have this baby—but it seems that everything's gone wrong!"

"I know—but we must trust God." Lydia pulled up the covers and tucked Elizabeth in carefully. She turned to leave, then paused and bit her lip. "I want to ask you something—don't answer if you think it's silly."

"It won't be silly, dear!"

"Well, I've thought so much about my marriage," she said slowly. "We were too hasty, Matthew and I. We should have waited at least until we could have seen his parents! I wanted to, but Matthew was so insistent!" She traced the design of the quilt that covered Elizabeth, then asked with some hesitation. "I—I've been wondering, Elizabeth, about you and John, I mean—?"

"Why did I marry a man older than I with four children?"

"Yes!"

The lines of pain that etched Elizabeth's face seemed to grow faint as she smiled, making her look younger. "You wouldn't believe how I fought against it, Lydia! All my life I'd had this dream of marrying some young man with a future; we'd have our own little house, and he'd be successful; then we'd have a baby—and then perhaps one or two more in time." She laughed then, and brushed her hair from her forehead. "Then came John

Bunyan, with all his awkward ways and his four squalling children—one of them blind! What a time I had when I knew God wanted me to marry him and be the mother of his children!"

"How did you know that, Elizabeth?" Lydia interrupted quickly.

"How? Why, I can't say, Lydia. I didn't hear a *voice* or anything like that—but I *knew*!" She smiled and asked, "Do you think I'd have married him in his condition if God hadn't told me to? No, somehow God let me know that my service for Him was to be tied up with John Bunyan, and that's been my life." She looked up at Lydia and asked, "You've been having doubts, haven't you, dear?"

Lydia nodded slowly. "We married so quickly, and I thought that we had the same thoughts—but the last three months that Matthew's been in jail have been—hard!"

"It would be hard for any man to endure that prison."

"Of course, but it's doing something to Matthew!" she said sadly. "Your husband is different. He's been a soldier, and he's had a hard life in many ways. But Matthew—why, he's never had a trial in his whole life, Elizabeth!"

"But he's so young!"

"Yes, that's just *it*!" Lydia shook her head in agitation and the problems she had struggled with overflowed as she said, "Maybe he's *too* young for all this—and maybe we married too fast. I don't know, but I can see him getting—he's becoming bitter, Elizabeth! You must have seen it!"

"Yes, I have. And so has John. We've talked about it many times."

"Last week he got so upset he—he blamed God for all the trouble!" Lydia's voice trembled and Elizabeth reached up and took her hand again. "He cursed and said that God was either asleep or didn't care what happened to men! Oh, he caught himself, apologized to me. But it was his heart speaking—and I'm afraid! What's going to happen to him, Elizabeth? To *us*?"

Elizabeth asked quietly, "What was it you said to me a few moments ago, Lydia? *We must trust God*. You will have to believe for Matthew until he can believe for himself. He must make it through this trial, for if he falls away now, he may never be God's man!"

Elizabeth's voice had grown strong and her grip bit into Lydia's arm. "We must pray that at the trial, they'll be set free."

"Yes, that's been my prayer," Lydia murmured. Then she said, "You *must* rest, Elizabeth—I'll take the food to the prison."

"Come back and tell me how they are—and don't tell John I'm ill. Tell him I'll be in tomorrow."

"All right."

Lydia returned to the large room, filled a smaller pewter pot with broth, wrapped a fresh loaf of brown bread in a cloth, and set out for the prison. It was not a great distance, but the sharp winds stung her unprotected face and hands like needles. There was a bite of sleet or snow in the air, and she shivered violently as she hurried along the frozen ground.

Bedford was not noted for much, but its jail was the equal of any in England for a town that size. It sat beside the small river that touched the edge of town, a large two-story structure—three, counting the lower floor. The third floor held the rooms for Paul Cobb, the jailer, and his family. The first floor had one small compartment immediately inside the door, and was separated from the rest of the space by solid iron bars. The lower floor, or basement, was used for prisoners as well, but it was so damp, being on practically the same level as the river, that only when the first floor was filled was it used.

Fortunately, the number of prisoners had been low since the beginning of winter, so the twenty or so prisoners were kept in the more comfortable section of the prison. "Comfortable" was a relative term, since there was no fire of any sort to take the chill off the prisoners. They wore all the clothing they could get, and moved around like huge, fat bears in the confined space of their common cell.

Two single windows set high in the wall let in light and air as well as snow and rain, and one set of double windows—heavily barred, of course—was set low enough in the wall so that by standing on tiptoe or on one of the few rough benches a prisoner could get a view of town—or from the other side, a view of the river.

In early fall, this was pleasant enough, and there was keen competition for the space. But during the winter the freezing winds piled sleet and snow several inches deep inside the cell.

Everyone slept in every thread they could put on, and under all the bedclothes they could lay hands on. The bare stone floor, covered by a few wisps of straw, grew more evil-smelling day by day.

Paul Cobb, a thick-set, balding man, came down the stairs at Lydia's call, and as he opened the door, he growled, "Ye'd best be sayin' a word to thot hoosband 'o yours, Lydia Winslow." He pulled the massive door open and added as Lydia stepped through, "He had quite a row with old Jamison last night! I had to step in and keep him from wipin' up the floor wif the old man! Ye'd best have a word with him, I thinks." He shut the door and called out, "Winslow, here's yer wife—maybe she can talk some sense into yer head!"

Lydia caught sight of Matthew at once, but he made no move to come to her. He was standing at one of the windows, staring moodily out at the brown river that purled around the town, and after one glance at her, he turned his back.

John Bunyan caught Matthew's action with one quick glance and tried to cover it by approaching her quickly, saying, "Well, well, what have we here? Do I smell beef soup?" He began busily helping her set the small table, keeping up a steady line of small talk. "Elizabeth didn't come? Oh, well, tomorrow, then—my, look at this fresh bread, Matthew!" He broke the loaf open and smelled it eagerly. "Ah! Now *that's* the way bread should be baked, I tell you! And look at this cheese? Where have you been hiding that, I ask you?"

Lydia let him busy himself with the food, and she stepped over to where Matthew was staring stolidly out the window. She took his arm and stood there, saying nothing until he finally turned and said, "Bloody cold today!"

"Yes. I'll bring another blanket tomorrow—or maybe I can bring it later today."

"No matter," he shrugged. "We'll be out of this hole the day after the trial."

Bunyan looked up sharply at that, then shrugged and went back to slicing the bread and cheese. "Come and have a bite of this, Matthew," he said cheerily.

"I'm not hungry."

"Oh, you have to eat!" Lydia urged, and she pulled at his

arm, forcing him to approach the table. "I put some thyme in this broth—just the way you like it." She ladeled out some of the hot stew into his bowl and set it in front of him. He shrugged, took up a spoon and began to eat indifferently.

Bunyan ignored that, and bowed his head. "Thank you, gracious God, for this good food, in the name of our precious Savior. Amen."

Matthew had the grace to look embarrassed, then grinned and said, "I'm losing all my manners in this place. Pardon me, John."

Bunyan smiled and gave him a clap on the shoulder. Then he looked across the room and said quietly, "Maybe you ought to ask Mr. Jamison to have a bit of this fine stew, eh, my boy?"

Matthew gave him a sharp look, anger suddenly scoring his face. "That old buzzard? He's lucky I didn't pound him into the floor last night!"

Bunyan rebuked him at once, saying, "Matthew, he's old and alone in the world. You're young and strong and you have friends. Can't you be a little charitable?"

Matthew bit his lip, then got up and put some stew into an extra bowl. He walked over to where a very tall old man sat hunched up against the wall, his face buried in his arms.

"Here, Jamison," he said, "have a bit of this good stew. It'll warm you up."

The old man looked up, and when he saw who it was, he spat on the floor and buried his face again.

"Well, that's what you get for being a Christian in this place!" Matthew snapped as he came back and sat down. "Can't blame the old man much. I'm about to go batty in this place! Be glad when the trial is over and we can get out of here. When will the trial come, John?"

"No way of telling. I'm hoping Justice Twisten will schedule it in a week or two, but he's vindictive enough to stretch it out till the crack of doom." He bit his lip and shook his head. "I want to be there when Elizabeth has her baby. The first baby is always harder on the mother, I think." He gave a shake of his heavy shoulders, rose and smiled. "I'll let you two have a little privacy, such as there is."

"Have some of this cheese, Matthew," Lydia urged as Bunyan moved across the room to speak to Jamison. "You're so thin!"

He took a piece of the cheese, bit into it and chewed slowly. "I can't stand this place much longer, Lydia." He spoke quietly, but there was a thick despair in his tone and she was appalled at the hollow look in his face, the fear that leaped out of his eyes.

"It's a time of testing," she whispered softly. Putting her arm around him, she moved as close to him as the narrow bench would permit. She yearned to draw his head to her breast and comfort him as she did the smallest Bunyan child, but it would have been improper in view of the prisoners. "We're going to get through this, you and I. Remember the scripture, 'Whom the Lord loveth, he chasteneth'? This will make our marriage stronger than ever!"

He stared at her as if she were speaking a language foreign to him; then a shiver ran through his thin frame. "I could stand anything, Lydia, I think—except these walls." He gave a look that was almost wild at the massive stones that hemmed them in, and again a violent tremor shook his shoulders and she tightened her hold. "It's not the cold or the stench of this place, though God knows it's miserable enough! It's not even being cut off from *you*. Oh, God, I could be happy in poverty—even in sickness, I think—if only I didn't have to be caged up like a dog!"

His voice rose higher so that several of the prisoners looked their way, and Lydia gave him a sudden hard grasp and said fiercely, "I know! I know, dearest! But it's only for a little while!" She hesitated, then drew his head down so that her lips were close to his ear and whispered something so softly that he missed it.

"What's that? I can't hear you."

She pulled his head yet closer, and her breath was warm and soft as she murmured with gladness in her voice, "You must be brave, Husband, because you're going to have a family!"

He sat there stock-still, as though he had not heard her, then slowly he turned and looked down into her eyes, which were brimming with tears—tears of joy.

"A—baby?"

"Yes!"

He moved his lips but no sound came; only his eyes reflected his deep shock. Finally he smiled wanly, put his arm around her and kissed her, ignoring the guffaws from several of the prisoners. "A son!" he said, and there was more life in his voice than she had heard in weeks.

"Or a daughter."

"Of course—it could be a girl!" He sat there, and despite the abysmal surroundings—the stench and the frigid blasts of air that cut to the bone, the stares of the ragged prisoners and the gray, blank walls—Lydia's heart sang, for it was the time she'd prayed for. Never during their short marriage had she felt in perfect harmony with Matthew—not until now. They had laughed much and their minds were equal, and no couple, she was sure, could have been more fulfilled by the vibrant love they had shared.

But she had always known there was a part of him she had not been able to enter—just as there was a part of her she longed to have him know, but he could not find it. Deep down she was aware that it was their walk with God—that private place, like a deeply hidden grotto where the spirit leaves the noisy world and meets with the living Lord—it was that element which she had not been able to share with Matthew. And deep within there was the lurking fear that the two of them, for all their bonds of body and mind, were strangers. Matthew lacked something, and while she dreaded being judgmental, she sensed a shallowness in his walk with God that kept them apart.

But this moment had been one of total intimacy of spirit, and her heart cried out for him as he sat there holding her. *This is marriage*, she thought happily.

But then he suddenly gave a start, looked around the cell with wild eyes, and when he turned to face her, there was something distraught in his eyes—a fear that was mastering the joy that had flashed out when he had heard of her condition.

"I've got to get out of here, Lydia!" he gasped, and with a moan he put his head in his hands. "How can I live with you having a baby—while I'm cooped up like a dog?"

She put her arm around him and whispered fiercely, "We are God's children, dearest—He will never forsake us!"

But it was as if she had not spoken, for he sat there with his face buried in his arms, and nothing she could say would bring him out of it.

Finally she arose and said, "I must go to Elizabeth. She's having a difficult time with this baby."

Matthew raised his head and looked at Bunyan. Suddenly he motioned for the preacher to come, and Bunyan rose and stepped to where they stood. "John, Lydia is going to have a child!"

Bunyan's broad face beamed and he said heartily, "Is she now? Well, that's fine—fine!"

"No—not with me in prison! And Elizabeth—she's having a hard time, Lydia says. John, we've got to get out of this place!"

Bunyan asked quietly, "Elizabeth is worse?"

"She's not well, I'm afraid."

He stood there, a strong shape in the gray light that filtered feebly through the high window. His form seemed to be made of the same material as the walls—enduring, tough, and impervious to time or hard wear. But his face was not so, for as the light caught it, though his eyes, hidden in the hollow sockets of his face, evidenced deep pain, his features held such an expression of pain and sorrow that Lydia wanted to weep.

Matthew stood there waiting for his reply, but when it came, it was not what he expected.

"We must be faithful to God, my boy. 'He that loveth husband or wife more than me is not worthy to be my disciple.' Those are hard words, but our Savior speaks. You and I can bear the suffering to our own bodies, and Satan knows this well enough! He will not attack us there, but where we are weak. And that is—that is our wives and our little ones!"

Matthew stared at him, then shook his head. "He that does not provide for his own is worse than a heathen," he quoted. "Does God expect us to let our loved ones suffer, those whom we've vowed to protect?"

"He is the Father of the fatherless, and we must be faithful to His word. He will care for Elizabeth and my little ones—and He will take care of your dear wife and the little one to come."

Matthew stared at him, then turned with a bitter light in his blue eyes. "God is unfair!" he said through clenched teeth, then wheeled and stalked stiff-legged to the window he'd occupied earlier, staring out at the gray river that rolled heavily by the prison.

"He'll be better," Bunyan whispered to Lydia as she stood there with tears in her eyes. "He's young in the faith, and I was no stronger at his age. Pray! Pray for him!"

Lydia was so full of fear she could not answer, but finally said, "Yes, John, I'll take care of Elizabeth—perhaps she'll be strong enough to come tomorrow."

She went home, walking slowly with her head down, impervious to the icy bite of the wind. A deadly spirit of fear more potent than winter's blast was sweeping through her heart, and the tears that she could not contain rolled down her pale cheeks.

She tried to pray, but the words would not come. So she walked beside the cold river, the dead brown grasses of summer breaking beneath her feet, and her heart rose up to God. She did not know what it was that she brought to God, but as the urgent cries of her soul ascended, somehow the presence of God came down, and the fear that had pierced her fled and she knew a peace in her spirit such as she had never known!

For many days this was her strength. Day after day rolled by, turning into weeks, then months, and there was no trial. Everything in her world was shaken. Elizabeth grew worse, so much worse that Lydia moved into the Bunyan house and with Mary's help did all the housework. She was a comfort to Elizabeth, spending hours reading the Word of God, and the children came to look on her as a second mother.

She made the short journey to the jail daily, for the state did not furnish food for the prisoners. This made the chore even more demanding, for neither she nor John Bunyan could bear to see those prisoners who had no family nor friends starve; therefore, she brought as much extra food as she could.

Matthew's condition worsened almost daily. He lost weight at such an alarming rate that she feared for his life. His lungs were affected by the biting cold, and he developed a cough that disturbed them all. But even worse was the awful depression that gripped him. He spoke little, and seemed not to hear what she said most of the time.

Her walks along the river grew longer, and she prayed fervently; prayer built her up, edified her spirit, and enabled her to carry the heavy burden.

Snow came, and on the second day when the earth was

muffled with white, Lydia left the Bunyan cottage and started for the jail. The heavy pot of soup dragged at her arm, and walking was difficult in the six-inch blanket of snow that covered the earth.

She had turned the corner onto the main road that led to the jail, and as she lifted her eyes, what she saw sent a shock running through her so violent that she almost dropped the heavy iron pot.

"Matthew!" she cried out, struggling to run toward him, crying out his name, filled with wonder that he was free.

Finally she set the pot down and ran toward him, her eyes so blinded with tears that she could barely see the tall figure so familiar to her. She fell into his arms and he caught her with a powerful grip.

"Matthew! Oh, my dear!" she cried out, holding to him as if she would never let him go.

Then she heard the familiar voice—but at the same time strangely different, "Well, daughter, I am here. . . !"

She looked up, drawing back at once from his embrace. She saw a wedge-shaped face with wide lips, cornflower blue eyes such as she loved in Matthew—but it was not her husband!

He said, "I've just come from my son, Lydia. We have much to pray about, you and I." Then he smiled, and she saw the same courage and strength in the father's eyes that she had fallen in love with in Matthew. "But first, will you allow me to have a father's embrace? For you are my daughter now!"

She gave a cry and fell into Gilbert Winslow's strong arms as a battered ship comes out of a wild tearing storm into the peace and safety of a calm harbor!

CHAPTER SEVEN

THE TRIAL

★ ★ ★ ★

"She slipped away with the tide," Gilbert Winslow said slowly. "Just as she had lived trusting in the Lord God, so she endured her going hence." He sat relaxed in front of the cheerful fire that threw leaping figures on the walls of the small cottage. There was a quietness and peace in his voice that took away the sting of the news that Matthew's mother was dead. He leaned forward to pick up the heavy iron poker, and Lydia's eyes stung as she recognized in her father-in-law the easy grace and strength that she loved in Matthew.

"It must have been terribly hard on you, Mr. Winslow."

"Hard?" He looked at her with a starboard twist of his head, just as she'd seen in Matthew a thousand times, then smiled and shook his head. "No, child, not hard. What was hard was watching her in pain from day to day. That last night the pain left, and we both knew it was time. She'd always loved to watch the tide go out, so I picked her up and carried her to a clearing on the hill—the same spot where I'd asked her to marry me forty years ago. It was dawn, and just as the morning light came to turn the sea red, and the tide began ebbing from the shore, she turned to me, put her arms around my neck, and whispered, 'You've been a good husband to me on this earth, Gilbert—but I must go now to my heavenly Bridegroom!' And then she put her head on my shoulder—and she left to be with Him!"

Sitting with her feet tucked beneath her, Lydia could not

keep her eyes off her father-in-law. *He looks far more like Matthew's older brother than his father!* she thought suddenly. As he went on speaking quietly, she drew the brightly colored quilt around her like a cocoon, her eyes never leaving his face. *Matthew is so much like him—but there's something different*, she thought. It was not long until she discovered what that difference was. Gilbert's face was Matthew's, but it had been refined by hardship to a countenance of sharp planes and fine lines that contrasted strongly with the soft, handsome features of the son.

"I—I'm glad you've come, Mr. Winslow," she said when he paused. "Matthew has been a good husband, but he's changed since he went to prison."

Gilbert smiled at the first confession, then shook his head at the second. "He's been like a wild hawk all his life, Lydia. He'll dare anything, but you can't cage a wild creature without killing his spirit, I think."

"It's killing him, that prison." She threw the quilt back, got up and bent to pick up the heavy kettle. As she poured a cup of steaming water for his tea, she said steadily, "What do you think will happen to him?"

"If he stays in prison?" He took the tea, sipped it carefully, then looked at her over the lip of the heavy cup. "He may not survive it. I hardly *knew* him, Lydia!" he exclaimed. "He's very ill, as you know. That cough is bad—down deep in his lungs, and prison fever is quick and deadly as a serpent!"

She stared at him, hesitated, then asked the question aloud that she'd never dared to frame to anyone. "Do you think he should give in to the Crown? You realize he and Brother Bunyan can leave anytime they agree to obey the new law?"

"I know." Gilbert turned the cup in his hands, seeming to find something fascinating in the plain surface. He sat comfortably in the chair, a strong figure even in repose. She had heard both from Winslow's son and his brother how he had the daring of a buccaneer in his youth; how he had been forced to choose between a place of prominence as the husband of Cecily North, daughter of Lord North, the beautiful aristocrat who had followed him across the Atlantic, and the simple Pilgrim maiden, Humility Cooper. He had been a swordsman with few peers, a lover of some repute, and would have risen in the world—but threw it all away to embrace the hard life of a poor minister on the rocky shores of Plymouth.

She saw that strength in his hands, in his face, and in every line of his tall figure, and suddenly she thought, *This is what I want for a husband! This is what I thought Matthew was like!*

He looked at her sharply, and said in answer to her question, "If he gives in to the Crown, he'll live—but what will he have left? A man who lets a king—or anyone else!—direct his soul may be alive physically, but he's dead to the best that's in him!"

"I'm afraid for him. I'm afraid for myself, for Mr. Bunyan, and for his poor wife and children!"

He rose and came to stand by her. Taking her hands in his he looked down on her for a long moment, then said gently, "Never take counsel of your fears, Lydia. I would be afraid, too, for Matthew is the last of his family—the last of the House of Winslow."

She smiled tremulously and said shyly, but with a note of triumph in her voice, "No, this child will have the Winslow name."

"Ah!" A tender smile crossed Gilbert's broad lips, and he embraced her, and the tender kiss he placed on her forehead broke down all restraint. It was as if she had known him all her life, and she leaned against him, clinging to him in her need as she had clung to her own father years ago.

"I'm glad you're here," she said again. "It gives me faith, and I know you can help Matthew."

He shook his head, saying only, "I trust that is so—but in one sense and in some things, a man must make his own way. We will try and we will pray, but my son must choose for himself."

"I know—but he has such faith in you—and so do I!" She laughed awkwardly and added, "Here you are fresh off the ship, and I dump all my care onto you the first time we meet!"

He said at once, "You're not a weak woman, Lydia. No, indeed! You know that thought that came to me, not five minutes after we met? *Here is a woman as strong as my Humility!* I never thought to hear myself say it," he smiled.

She was embarrassed by the compliment, but warmed all the same by his approval. "I must go to Mrs. Bunyan's. Would you go with me, to pray for her?"

"Of course!"

The two of them made their way through the falling snow, and Mr. Winslow became an instant success with the small Bunyans. He knew all sorts of games it seemed, and he thought nothing of roughing with the little ones. Elizabeth felt well enough to sit in a chair by the fireplace, and she watched in amazement while the tall minister got down on his hands and knees with the children. "He's an unusual man, isn't he? He loves children, that's plain," she whispered to Lydia.

When the children were in bed, he spent a long time reading the Bible to Lydia and Elizabeth; the Book of Hebrews, the eleventh chapter, and the ancient promises seemed to fill the small room with warmth. Finally he closed the book and prayed for Elizabeth and for her husband warmly and fervently.

After he had left, the strength of his presence lingered somehow, and Elizabeth smiled at Lydia, saying, "He's got a strength in him, that man has! John will love him!"

"Who wouldn't?" Lydia responded softly. "He's the kind of man—"

She broke off and Elizabeth finished, "The kind of man you saw in Matthew? Yes, and it's there, my dear. Blood will tell, and there's enough of his father's blood in Matthew Winslow to win his battle!"

During the weeks that followed, Lydia thought often of Elizabeth's words. But there seemed to be little to merit hope that Matthew would justify the thought. She saw no improvement in him; indeed, the news of his mother's death came as such a blow to him that even the strong encouragement Gilbert offered was offset.

Gilbert's presence was more of a blessing to John Bunyan, it seemed, than to his own son. The two men became fast friends at once, and Winslow spent most of his time at the prison studying the Scripture with Bunyan. Gilbert was captivated by the man's vivid imagination, and often when Mary came to visit, he sat there listening to Bunyan's stories as intently as she. "You ought to write a book, John!" he often said.

"I'm no book writer!"

"You're the best teller of tales I've ever heard," Winslow insisted. "That one about the chap named Pilgrim—it's almost like reading the Bible, in a way! Think what it would mean if Christian parents had a story about a man who leaves his home and fights his way through difficulties to get to heaven!"

"They have the Bible," Bunyan shrugged.

"But, Father, your stories make the Bible easier to understand," Mary protested.

"There you have it, John," Winslow laughed. "Wisdom from the lips of babes, eh, Matthew?"

"Yes, I suppose so." Matthew sat on a pile of straw, picking at it listlessly. There was no life in his voice.

Bunyan and Winslow exchanged glances, but said nothing. They had spoken quietly about the young man when Matthew was out of hearing, and agreed that if he gave in to the Crown's new law, he would live, but would be forever scarred in his spirit.

Bunyan picked up the story of Pilgrim and had gotten the hero into a terrible predicament when Paul Cobb opened the door of the cell and Pastor Gifford rushed in, his eyes filled with excitement.

"Twisten—he's set a date for the trial!"

"*When?*" Matthew wheeled from where he stood and leaped to the pastor's side, showing more animation than they had seen in weeks.

"A month from now, less a day!"

"Thank God!" Matthew cried out, tears gathering in his eyes.

"Yes, thank God," Bunyan said; then he added carefully, "Now we must pray for a verdict in our favor."

Matthew stared at him, then declared defiantly, "God will not leave us here to rot!" He shook his head and laughed for the first time since Gilbert had come to Bedford. "It's going to be all right! You'll see!"

When Lydia came later that day, she was taken off guard by the difference in Matthew. He embraced her, swinging her around in a circle in the old way, crying, "It's over, Lydia! It's over!"

"Matthew, be careful," she cried out breathlessly. "You'll get your cough started again!"

"Devil take the cough!" he grinned. "Let me get a breath of free air and that cough will leave one way or another!" He carried on wildly all the time she was there. The activity did start his cough again, and she had to force him to lie down before he strangled. The two red spots which had shown in his cheeks a week earlier reappeared, and she knew his fever was up.

That night when Gilbert came by to pray for Elizabeth, she said, "He's better, isn't he?"

"Yes, I suppose." There was a caution in Gilbert's voice, and he added soberly, "But it will go hard with him if the verdict isn't favorable."

"Do—do you think that it will be bad—the verdict?"

"It's a bad time, Lydia. The tide is against us. I have to go to London to see my brother in two days. I'll find out something from him. He's in prison, but he still has powerful friends, and some of them may help."

After Gilbert left, Lydia made the mistake of mentioning his words to Matthew, and he grabbed at the chance eagerly. "Why, of course! Uncle Edward will help us!"

"He's unable to help himself, lad," Bunyan said quickly.

"You never have a cheerful word, do you John?" Bunyan's efforts to prepare the young man for the possibility of bad news from the trial had not worked; on the contrary, they had driven a wedge between the two that had given grief to the Bunyans as well as to Lydia.

"John is just—"

"I know what John is doing!" Matthew snapped at her. "You're a fine help, all of you! Where's your faith? We're supposed to believe God, aren't we? Well, that's what I'm doing—and the rest of you are digging my grave with your unbelief—!" He broke off into a paroxysm of coughing and fought Lydia as she attempted to help him. "Leave me alone, you doubters!" he gasped and withdrew into the farthest corner of the cell.

He apologized the following day, but there was a constraint in him, and he had little to say to either of them. The only subject that he cared about was the trial—that and the return of Gilbert with good news.

Lydia was at the jail the afternoon Gilbert came back. Bunyan was standing on a bench, speaking out the window to a small group who had formed the habit of coming from time to time to hear him preach.

Gilbert saw them as he approached, and he paused to listen as the strong voice of Bunyan carried easily on the cold air. The shivering listeners stood there, shifting from one frozen foot to another, beating their hands together to get the cold blood stirring, but none left until he prayed a final prayer and called out a cheery "God bless you!"

Cobb said as he entered, "Well, sir, here you are, ain't you now? I hopes it's good news you be bringin' to the lad. He's lived for little else!"

Matthew saw his father enter and came to him at once. "Father, what did Uncle Edward say? Will he help us?"

Gilbert pulled off his cloak slowly, not taking his eyes from Matthew's face. There was something in his eyes that held the young man speechless. Finally he said, "Your uncle is dead, my boy. Gone to be with his Lord."

Matthew jerked as though he had been struck; his face twisted and he dropped his head, turning blindly toward the wall.

Lydia ran to him, and Bunyan said quietly, "I'm sorry to hear it, Gilbert. He was a godly man."

"Yes." Gilbert sat down and Bunyan joined him. "He's better off, John. He was very ill, and there was little hope of any sort of life for him. I think they would have executed him if he had lived until the next sitting of the court."

"No, surely not!" Bunyan said, shocked at the thought.

Gilbert leaned back against the wall, saying in a tired voice. "They executed Major-General Harrison last Friday. I was there."

"I can't believe it," Bunyan said. "He was such a good man."

"But close to Cromwell—as was Edward. It was Edward who asked me to go. I'll never forget it. He came to his death as cheerful as any man could do in that condition. He made a brief speech giving glory to God, making no reference to the shameful manner in which he was being treated by his enemies. After he was taken down, his head and his heart were removed and shown to the people—amidst great shouts of joy, John! How beastly these people can be! That's why I cannot grieve over Edward. He was spared that. I was with him when he died. He was anxious to go."

The shock of his uncle's death hit hard at Matthew, causing him to speak only of the trial. Two days before the date which Justice Twisten had set, Lydia sat beside her husband, listening as he spoke eagerly of the day he would be set free.

Finally he stooped, and she said, "I found something you might like, Matthew."

"What is it?"

"Oh, it's just a poem. Your father showed it to me last night. A man he knew as a boy wrote it, and it's become famous."

"A poem? What does it say?" Matthew asked listlessly.

"It was written to a young woman by a man named Lovelace. It's just the last verse that I thought you might like." She took out a slip of paper and read it softly:

> "Stone walls do not a prison make,
> Nor iron bars a cage.
> Minds innocent and quiet take
> That for a hermitage.
> If I have freedom in my love
> And in my soul am free,
> Angels alone that soar above
> Enjoy such liberty!"

She smiled up at him, saying with a smile, "Stone walls do not a prison make, nor iron bars a cage."

He stared at her soberly, then shook his head. "That's pretty poetry, but it's not life."

She sat there and for the first time she asked what had been in her heart for weeks, "Matthew, what if—what if things don't go well?"

"What?" he asked angrily. "What are you talking about?"

"I've prayed so *hard*," she said, taking his arm. "But even if you and John *did* have to stay here for a little while longer, it'll be—"

"It's not going to be that way!" he interrupted with a wild look around at the walls. "Lydia, I'll *die* in this place! God won't let it happen!"

She changed the subject quickly, but her heart was filled with foreboding as she went home, and she knew that Gilbert felt the same.

The hours crawled slowly by, but at last the day came for the trial. Every square inch of space was filled in the large hall used for trials, and in spite of the freezing cold, those who could not get inside thronged the outside.

Justice Twisten sat on a raised platform, his beefy face stony as the case proceeded. "What is the charge against these men?"

A reedy-voiced clerk named Jacob Tillage read from a large sheet: "John Bunyan and Matthew Winslow, both of Bedford, are charged with a violation of the King's law, being upholders and maintainers of unlawful assemblies and Conventicles, and for not conforming to the National Worship of the Church of England."

A great hulking fellow named Ryeson was the deputy who had arrested the two, and he gave a long, rambling testimony as to how he had followed the two and found them addressing a group of people.

"Were they armed, any of them?" Justice Twisten demanded.

"Sir?"

"Were they armed, I say!"

"No, sir, they didn't have naught but Bibles!"

"Very well."

The testimony droned on and finally the justice said, "John Bunyan, you may rise and give your defense."

Bunyan was pale from his stay inside, but he spoke firmly and eloquently. A duel soon developed between him and the justice, and it terminated in Twisten shouting, "You will heed the laws of England or I will either see you hanged or you will be harried out of this land!"

"I will in all civil laws be obedient to my king—whom God knows I respect and pray for—but I will obey the voice of that King who is immortal when there is a conflict between the two!"

"You stand convicted by your own mouth!" Twisten cried out, getting to his feet in his anger. "You have not denied that you and Winslow were engaged in breaking the King's law. On the basis of your own testimony and on the evidence presented to this court, I sentence you to perpetual imprisonment!"

A hum went over the court and he looked around the crowded room, adding, "Do not waste your pity on these men. They may leave prison at any moment—at any moment, that is, when they agree to obey the law."

Bunyan suddenly raised his voice and cried out loudly, "I will preach the gospel until the moss grows up to my eyes!"

"Be it on your head then," Twisten said, staring at the two men. "You will stay in Bedford Jail until you promise to do your preaching within the limits set by the King! Bailiff, take these two men back to their cells! This court is dismissed."

CHAPTER EIGHT

END OF A MAN

★ ★ ★ ★

"Will you go tell him, Gilbert?" Lydia asked wearily. She leaned her arm against the wall, placed her forehead on it, and bit her lip to keep back the tears. "It's going to kill him, you know—he's lived for this new baby."

"Too bad! Too bad!" Gilbert shook his head. He picked up his heavy coat and said as he pulled it on, "Yes, I'll go. You'll stay with Elizabeth?"

"Yes." She straightened up and tried to put a little cheer into her voice. "At least Elizabeth is all right. She can have other children, the doctor said. Tell John that."

"All right."

"And tell Matthew—" She broke off suddenly and stared at the tall man so much like her husband. A question leaped to her lips, and she suppressed it, then seemed to be in fear of something. Finally she asked, "I don't know what to tell him. Have you noticed anything—different—about the way he is?"

Winslow nodded slowly. "His mind is troubled. I worry about that more than his health."

"Yesterday he talked so wildly I couldn't make sense of it. He talked about dying. I think he's given up hope."

Gilbert nodded slowly. "He's sick in body, but we must pray even more for his spirit, Lydia."

Winslow left the cottage and made his way along the muddy

road, dodging puddles as he went. The first breath of spring had come, melting the snow and stirring the life that lay buried in the frozen ground. He looked at a tiny crocus shouldering a chip inside, vibrant with color against the dull winter earth, and thought of the dead child that all of them mourned. "Too bad!" he murmured again.

Cobb admitted him into the cell, and he went at once to where Bunyan and Matthew sat together on a bench. Bunyan rose at once, and there was a prophetic look on his heavy features. He waited until Gilbert drew near, then he searched his face, and said quietly, "Elizabeth's lost the baby."

Gilbert nodded. "Yes. I'm sorry, John."

"Is she all right?"

"The doctor says she's fine. She can have other children."

"Praise God!" Bunyan breathed heavily, then went over to stare out of the window, alone in his grief.

Gilbert sat down by Matthew, noting that he looked more worn and haggard than ever. The cough had gotten worse, too, but the mental state troubled Gilbert more. "It's getting warmer, son. Spring is on the way."

Matthew shrugged, saying only, "I suppose I should have known it would happen."

Gilbert did not understand him. "What's that, son?"

"I knew the baby would die."

"It's a shame—but you mustn't worry about Lydia. She's very healthy."

Matthew looked at his father out of haggard eyes, sunk deep in his skull. He bore little resemblance to the vigorous young man he had been before his imprisonment. When he spoke, his voice was dead and lifeless as his eyes. "I can't believe anything anymore."

"You don't mean that, son," Gilbert said quietly. He put his hand on the young man's shoulder and there was an urgency in his eyes and in his voice as he spoke. "You've had a bad knock, but these things will pass . . ."

Matthew listened as his father spoke, but there was a sullen set to his shoulders, and finally he said, "Didn't you hear Justice Twisten? 'Perpetual imprisonment' was the term. You know as well as I that there's no way out of this hole, unless—"

"Don't even *think* that way!" Gilbert said quickly. "I know you're sick and despondent and there's the baby on the way. But if you give up now, you'll never be a man again."

"And if I don't get out of here, I'll be dead!" Matthew snapped, a madness glowing in his eyes. Then he took a deep breath and said, "I've decided what I'm going to do, Father— and I know you and John will disapprove. You think it's terrible for a man to give in, but it's different with me."

"How is it different?"

"Why, you must see that John is a preacher—that's what he's going to do. But I'm not."

"You were preaching the gospel, Bunyan tells me—and you told me yourself that you felt God's hand on your life."

"Well, I did say that, but many young fellows take a try at preaching and find out it's just a notion."

"Matthew, don't—"

"Don't tell me what to do!" Matthew cried, and his voice turned Bunyan from the window. He watched carefully, then came over to stand beside them. "I couldn't help overhearing." His fine eyes were filled with compassion and he said, "Don't make a decision now. Wait until you've had time to pray about it."

Matthew stared at them and a wild look came into his eyes, a look of madness, and Gilbert saw how close his son was to losing his mind. He said at once, "I'll leave now, son. You try to calm yourself and I'll come back tomorrow. We'll think of something."

He bade goodbye to Bunyan, begging him with his eyes to look after Matthew. He did not go to the cottage but walked along a little-traveled road, seeking God with desperation. Bunyan had spoken to him of his son's preoccupation with death, and it frightened him more than anything that had ever come to him. He prayed until finally he looked up and saw that the sun was setting, then turned his steps toward the Bunyan cottage.

Lydia was busy with the children, and he took over some of the chores so she could be with Elizabeth. It was late by the time the children were in bed and Elizabeth was asleep, but he sat beside her, telling her about his visit with Matthew.

She sat there staring at the glowing coals in the fireplace, then said, "I'm so tired of it all, I can't even think."

"I know. I—I'm not sure it's right, Lydia." The strain had etched new lines on Gilbert's face, and he shook his head in despair. "If it were my life, I'd know what to do—but who can decide a thing like this for another?"

That was as far as they got, and he trudged on home wearily. He did not expect to sleep, but he did by some miracle. He had missed much sleep, and slept far past his usual early time for arising. A loud knocking at the door awoke him, and he saw in one startled glance that the sun was high in the sky.

"Gilbert! Wake up!"

He staggered to the door groggy with sleep, threw the door open to find Lydia there with fear in her eyes. "He's gone!" was all she could say. Then sobs rose to her throat and she fell against him, weeping with abandon.

"Matthew?" he demanded.

He had to wait until she could collect herself. Finally she drew back and wiped her eyes. "Yes! He sent for Justice Twisten yesterday and agreed to obey the new law—so the justice released him."

"Did he tell you this—Matthew, I mean?"

"No! I haven't seen him—but when I got home from the Bunyan's yesterday, his clothes were all gone, and I found this note."

Gilbert took the scrap of paper she thrust at him and read it quickly: "Lydia, I'm going away. Please try to forget me—and God forgive me!"

It was written in a wavering hand and was not even signed.

"He was almost mad yesterday," Gilbert said, biting his lip, trying to think what to do. "And I think he was delirious with fever."

"Where could he have gone?" Lydia moaned.

"Well, he can't have gone far," Gilbert said quickly. "Don't worry, we'll find him, Lydia."

But that was not the case, for after getting the word out to all the village, the best they could discover was that he was not in Bedford. Everyone knew him well from his connection with Bunyan, and it was not until the following day, after a sleepless night, that Gilbert came to the Bunyan cottage to meet Lydia.

"You've found him?" Lydia cried, seeing no gloom on Gilbert's face as he had worn since the previous day.

"No—but the coach driver came back through—the one that drives the London stage. He didn't make the trip all the way through this time, but he has said that a man of Matthew's description got on here in Bedford and was still on the coach headed for London yesterday."

"London! Why would he go there?"

"I fear he's making for the coast to get a ship out of the country." Gilbert took her arm and squeezed it tightly. "I'll go at once. Surely I'll be able to find him! All I have to do is check the ships about to depart."

"You must find him, Gilbert! He's out of his mind—I'll go with you . . ."

"No, you stay here in case we're wrong and he comes back," Gilbert said. "I'll not go on a coach; that'd be too slow. I've already bought a fast horse, and I'll be in London almost by the time the coach gets there. God willing, I may even overtake it!"

"Yes, hurry! And I'll pray," Lydia said. She touched her body unconsciously, and he knew she was thinking of the child that was to come. "God is still in control!"

"Amen!" he said; he embraced her, then hurried away, his mind whirling with plans.

The hours crawled by for the next week, and although Lydia knew with her mind that the distance was too great for Gilbert to go and return in such a short time, she spent hours looking south down the Great Road. She ate nothing, but fasted and prayed until her face grew pale with strain. Bunyan urged her to eat: "God knows the intent of your heart," he said gently. "You must think of the child."

On the sixth day, Pastor Gifford brought a note direct from the coach. It was from Gilbert: "I have looked day and night with no success. But do not despair. It may be that he left the coach and went on to a coastal town. I go to Southampton, which is the most likely place for a man to take a ship for other lands." He urged Lydia to keep her trust in God, and promised to write as soon as he found any trace of Matthew.

Three weeks later Lydia looked up the lane and saw Gilbert walking slowly toward her cottage. There was something in his air that brought a great fear into her heart, and she rose to her feet slowly. His face was very thin, and it bore the unmistakable marks of grief as he walked up to her side and said at once, "Lydia, my dear . . ."

She saw that he could not finish, and she said dully, "He's dead, isn't he?"

"Yes." Gilbert's lips tightened, and he took her in his arms. "You must be mother and father now to the little one." He drew back and there was a fierce intensity scored across his strong features.

"What happened, Gilbert?" she asked quietly. "I want to know all of it."

"There's little to tell, child," he said wearily. "I found no trace of him until a week ago. I had gone to Southampton first and found nothing. One of the men I met there was a ship's carpenter named Lyle. He was waiting for his ship to be refitted. It took longer than he thought, and he came to Portsmouth where his family lives. I ran into him by accident, and he remembered me at once."

"Had he seen Matthew?" Lydia asked eagerly.

Gilbert nodded slowly. "Yes. Lyle knew him from my description, and he told Matthew about my inquiry."

"What?"

Gilbert shook his head, his eyes cloudy with grief. "Lyle reported that Matthew said, 'There's no one in this world who'd want to find me now!' "

"But what happened?"

"Lyle told me he took passage on a trading schooner *Intrepid*, Captain George Milton's ship." He took Lydia's hand and said softly, "My dear, the *Intrepid* went down with all hands in a hurricane two weeks ago."

"Could—could there be a mistake?" Lydia's eyes pleaded with him, but Gilbert shook his head firmly.

"I went to Southampton and talked to the owners. Another ship, *West Wind*, was in the same storm. She saw the *Intrepid* go down, but there was no way they could help. He's gone, my dear!"

She looked up at him with horror and pain in her dark eyes. "Are you certain?"

"It would be torment to live on false hope, Lydia, much as I would like to offer some hope. I questioned the quartermaster who fitted out the ship, and he remembered Matthew well. He signed on and left with the ship."

Lydia shut her eyes and suddenly began to sway. Gilbert helped her to a bench in front of the cottage and sat down beside her, waiting until she had wept her heart out. Then he said, "I want to tell you what I think God has said, Lydia, concerning you and the child . . ."

The salt spray bit Lydia's lips as she stood on the deck of the *New Hope*, a two-masted schooner, watching England fade as the ship plowed into the green-gray seas.

"I know, child," Gilbert said quickly. "It's hard on the heart, leaving your home—but the New World will be a better place for you—and for my grandson."

That had been his plan, and Lydia was anxious to go—to find a new life for herself and her baby. The only relative she had in England was her aunt, and she had grown to love Gilbert Winslow as a father. He had no blood kin of his own, and this loss drew them together more than anything else.

Now she expressed one flickering moment of doubt. "Gilbert, is it right—my going to Plymouth?"

He looked down at her, and she thought with a sharp pain in her heart, *I'll never forget Matthew—not as long as his father is alive!*

He put his strong arm around her and smiled. "It's only a little while before we *really* go home, Lydia. But until that day comes, you and my grandchild need a place and a people." He paused and looked westward, almost as if he could see Plymouth with his keen blue eyes.

Then he looked down at her and said quietly, "The last of the House of Winslow, Lydia—that's the precious burden you're carrying!"

And then he led her to the jutting prow of the *New Hope*, where they looked out to the open seas to the future together.

PART TWO

PLYMOUTH

★ ★ ★ ★

1675

CHAPTER NINE

RACHEL

★   ★   ★   ★

The wedding day was clear and bright on the morning of April 2, 1675. Rachel Winslow smiled to herself as she peered into the polished mirror, murmuring, "Fourteen years old this day—an old woman you're getting to be!"

She tossed the mirror on the bed with a typical careless gesture, and left her small upstairs bedroom in a rush. Her mother looked up from the table where she was kneading dough, saying, "One would think you were the bride, the trouble you take prettying yourself up!"

The words sounded harsh, but there was little of that quality in Lydia Winslow. Plymouth folks had come to take almost for granted her numerous charities, and the daughter who came over to smile at her did not seem in the least alarmed. She reached out and tucked a raven black tress of her mother's hair under the kerchief she wore and said carelessly, "I want to look nice for Joshua, Mother. He's probably going to come by and ask me to marry him again." Lydia did not miss the saucy look in Rachel's hazel eyes, and she shook her head.

"And you'll turn him away as usual. You may be sorry for that one day, Rachel. He'd be a good husband."

"Country's full of good husband material," Rachel responded cheerfully. "Full of groundhogs and all kinds of other pesky varmints, too, but I don't have to take up with any of them."

Lydia stared at her, knowing she ought to be outraged and shocked, but as usual she threw up her hands and laughed. "You are a silly girl!" she said with affection.

"Grandfather says I've got more brains than the whole New England Confederation," Rachel stated with a demure look.

"Your grandfather is a wise man—except where you're concerned, and in that area he hasn't a grain of sense!"

"He says you're the most beautiful woman in the Colonies. I guess he's just prejudiced about you, too, Mother."

"Indeed he is. Now, get out of here, you goose! Go help that poor girl who's going to look as plain as an old shoe when she stands up next to you!" Then she flung one last comment at Rachel as the girl was leaving: "But homely as she is, she's marrying today—and that's more than I can say for you!"

Rachel laughed and ran lightly down the road that sloped past Governor Bradford's house toward the harbor, and took a right. She found Mercy Doolittle, the bride, inside the bungalow where she lived with her parents and five other children.

"Oh, it's you, Rachel!" Mercy's mother exclaimed. She handed the comb to Rachel, saying, "See if you can do anything with Mercy's hair—I'll go help with the cooking!"

"Well, the big day is here, girl," she said, pulling the comb through Mercy's hair with such force that the poor girl cried out. "Be still, now! This is your last day of freedom, and that husband of yours will give you worse if you don't mind him."

"Oh, Praise God and me, we'll do fine."

Rachel smiled at the name of the bridegroom—Praise God Pittman. "It'll be hard for you to have a fight with him, won't it, Mercy? I mean, how can you scream with anger and yell 'Praise God!' at the same time?"

Mercy was a tall, homely girl, rawboned and awkward, but her good humor and kindness redeemed her for everyone—especially Praise God, who could not be convinced that she was not as lovely as a rose. The stocky, muscular man of twenty-two was a blacksmith and a tinker, had been known to drink a little too much on occasion, and his reputation as somewhat of a ladies' man persisted in spite of his denials. In any case, the two were satisfied with one another and as Mercy put it, "So long as we suit each other, why, let others keep their noses out!"

Her one beauty was her hair, and as Lydia combed it into a shining fall of reddish gold, she asked curiously, "Mercy, are you afraid?"

"Afraid? Of what?"

"Why, of marriage," Rachel answered. "Won't it be hard to do everything Praise God tells you?"

Mercy pulled away, turned and stared at her friend, and a smile touched her lips. "Why, it would be for *you*, I'm thinking, you bein' so smart and all. But most women don't have a very strong mind." This was commonly believed among most of the colonists, and Mercy elaborated on the doctrine. "Why, I heard tell of a lass once, and her father taught her all sorts of readin' and writin'. Well, one day she goes mad and strangles her daughter, she did! Them at court said 'twas the learnin' of readin' and writin' as done it, destroyed the brain, it not bein' so strong as a man's brain."

"I see," Rachel smiled wryly.

Mercy reached out and touched the cheek of the dark-haired girl, saying with a smile, "You'll not take to a man orderin' you around, will you, Rachel Winslow. Lord help the poor fellow who tries to get *that* job done!"

"No hurry about me," Rachel said; then she laughed and urged, "You'd better get your finery on, Mercy, or Praise God will have to wait for his bride—and he's not a man to wait for a woman long, is he now?"

She had just finished helping Mercy put on her wedding dress, a bodice dyed blue for constancy and an orange skirt. Some who came from England had the idea that the Separatists at Plymouth wore only black or gray, but that was only for meetings on Sabbath; most of them loved bright colors and decked themselves out with finery on every other occasion.

They heard the sound of singing and Rachel cried, "There they come!" Soon the air was filled with the sound of song, and they went outside to be greeted by the marriage party. There were at least forty of them, every young person who could get free, for marriage was not a church matter to the Separatists, just as Christmas was not recognized as a religious holiday.

They proceeded to the large open space in front of the Common House, where the civil wedding was performed by Judge Haskell. A long prayer by Gilbert Winslow completed the ceremony.

"Now, for the cake!" Judge Haskell cried out, and he took up a large plain cake in his hands, and parted it by breaking it gently over Mercy's head. He tossed it out to the crowd in fragments, and there was a wild scramble, for it was considered a fine thing to gather up a piece of bridecake and put it under your pillow and dream of whom you were to wed.

As Rachel picked up a small piece, she heard a voice in her ear say, "Why settle for a dream, Rachel, when you can have the real man?"

She turned with a smile to face a tall fair-faced man with dark blue eyes in his large round face. "Why, David, is this a proposal?"

He laughed at her and there was admiration in his face, but caution, too. "Well, you've got enough poor devils wandering around moonstruck without adding me to the bedlamites."

"I thought you'd back out, David Morris! You're no man!"

He stood there laughing at her, drinking in her fresh beauty and her wit, but like others, he wondered if it was quite *right* for a woman to be so witty. *Well enough for a man to have sharp wit, but would it be wearing to have a wife who was so sharp?* He admired her, but she saw the same reservation she'd seen in other men, and since she had no idea of marrying David Morris, it gave her pleasure to keep him off balance.

Noticing her grandfather standing close, listening to their conversation, she left young Morris to take his arm. She pulled him away, saying, "Let's go eat while the food's hot."

"You give these young men a time, Rachel," he said with a smile.

"You've spoiled me, Grandfather," she laughed up at him. "When I find a man as handsome and as witty as you, I'll submit at once!" She looked at him with a smile, half-serious, for he was still a fine-looking man at the age of 75. The auburn hair had some silver in it, but was still thick and smooth over his neck, and the lines in his angular face only made it look stronger than ever. His wide-set bright blue eyes, undimmed by age, gleamed from under bushy brows. He moved easily, his tall frame still strong enough to walk most young men into the ground.

"You'll have to settle for what you can get, girl," he jibed with a sudden smile that made him look much younger. "You're pretty enough, but you've scared most of the suitors off with your pert tongue."

"If they're afraid of a woman's tongue, they won't do for me!" she retorted.

He could never argue with her for long, this beautiful granddaughter of his. He had been the first to hold her after she was born, the only grandchild he'd have on this earth, and although he'd hoped for a grandson to carry on the family name, he had lost his heart to the red, squalling bit of humanity—part French, part English, and for fourteen years he had made her his chief interest in life, taking second place only to his loyalty to God.

They came to the great table laden with roast venison, roast turkey, fricasse of chicken, beef hash, boiled fish, stuffed cod, pigeons, boiled eels, Indian pudding, succotash, roast goose stuffed with chestnuts, pumpkin pies, apple tarts and to wash it all down, beer, cider, claret, flip, brandy, and sack posset.

As they ate Gilbert said, "I'm going to the Indian camp tomorrow."

"Oh, take me with you!"

He grinned at her and said, "Who wants to make a hard journey to a dirty old Indian camp filled with fleas?" He laughed at the color which had risen to her cheeks. "You couldn't intend to stop by and see Jude Alden, I don't suppose?"

"Why, I suppose, since it's on the way . . ."

He smiled at her, knowing her as well in some ways as he knew himself. "You little minx! Think I don't read that devious little head of yours?"

"Can I go, Grandfather?"

"I suppose. Someday you're going to ask me for something I won't give you!"

She smiled up at him, and he said impulsively, "You're very much like your father—when you smile, I see him in my mind's eye as clearly as I see you."

Her eyes opened wide, and she stared at the old man, for

he almost never mentioned her father. "Do I really look like him, Grandfather?"

"Not so much as you look like your mother—which is God's blessing!" he added, and as always Rachel marveled that the only bitterness she had ever seen in Gilbert Winslow found its object in his son, Matthew. She had heard the whole story of his short marriage to her mother and his death. When her mother had first told her of her father's sad end, she had cried for days, then ended up hating him. She never reasoned it out that she despised him for being a coward, or for depriving her of a normal family. Inside she kept her feelings buried, but it always shocked her to see her grandfather subject to any fault, and now she stood there marveling at this one flaw in his otherwise perfect character.

He said hastily, "Be ready early, child, it's a long trip."

He left, and all afternoon during the dances and festivities, Rachel could not help thinking of her father—even as Praise God carried Mercy over the threshold as the sun was going down. As the custom was, the rosy-faced couple sat in bed dressed in their shifts, and the young people took turns standing at the foot of the bed throwing socks over their shoulders. The belief was that if a sock thrown by a girl hit the bride, or one thrown by a boy hit the groom, it was a sign of a speedy marriage.

When Rachel threw a sock that hit Mercy square in the face, a scream went up, and she ran from the room with her hands over her ears to shut out the rather crude jokes that always accompanied such a feat.

She made her escape from the crowd and walked along the rocky beach. Soon she passed beyond the large rock where it was said the first of the Pilgrims set foot when alighting from the *Mayflower*.

Weary of the wild singing and loud merry-making, she let the quiet of the isolated beach flow over her. The crashing of the surf punctuated the silence and the cry of the gulls melded with them. She loved this coast, this beach, and for a long time she made her way aimlessly, picking up a shell to examine its intricate whorls, then tossing it back to the sandy beach.

You're very like your father sometimes. The words of her grandfather came back to her, and she tried again to imagine what he had been like. There was no portrait at all, of course. Few people had such things, for they were expensive. The one portrait her grandfather had was a beautiful oil painting of his brother Edward, the older brother he'd been so close to. Rachel's mother had told her once that her father had looked very much like Gilbert and his brother. "All Winslow men look alike, they say. But you take after me."

She thought then of her mother, who spoke of her father in a general way, but Rachel could never get beneath the impenetrable surface of Lydia Winslow's manner—in this one matter. Once Rachel remembered saying in exasperation, "Mother, you never tell me anything *important* about my father. Just little things!"

She thought of that conversation as she climbed the hill that led to the house she shared with her mother and grandfather, and her powerful gift of imagination brought it back to her as clearly as if it were painted on a canvas before her. She saw her mother's smooth face suddenly break in some minute way, and her eyes dropped. Finally she said with just a suggestion of a tremor in her voice, "We had so *little* time, Rachel! Just a few months, and then he was—gone."

"Did he love you?" Rachel heard her young voice piping back to the present.

Her mother looked up, her eyes moist as she whispered, "Oh, yes, child, yes! He loved me at first—but later . . ." She had suddenly straightened up and said in a tone almost harsh, "He's gone Rachel, and it grieves me to speak of it."

Rachel reached the house, a new "salt box" that Gilbert Winslow built when a chimney fire destroyed the tiny house he had built in 1622, when he and Humility had first been married. She passed through the front door into a short entrance hall; to the left was a combined kitchen and dining room, but she turned right into the common room where she found her mother entertaining Mr. Oliver Bradford, the grandson of the famous governor, John Bradford.

"Well, did you get the young folks married, Rachel?" he asked, getting up as she entered. He was a robust man of 46, slightly less than medium height, with brown hair cut short and warm brown eyes. He had always been partial to Rachel, and since the death of his wife, her willingness to spend time with his young children had made him value her even more.

"Oh, they're tied together forever, Mr. Bradford," she smiled. "Happy as larks and poor as church mice!"

"Ah, but Praise God is so much in love, he'd never notice a thing," Lydia laughed. She was dressed in black, as she always was, but the sober garb only seemed to set off her beauty. Her cheeks were as rosy as a girl's, as were her full lips. Many young women were put to despair when they took in her slender, rounded figure, for at the age of 32, time seemed not to have touched her. Her grandfather had said once, "Rachel, if I didn't know better, I'd think your mother was a witch! It's *unearthly* how she simply refuses to get old—why, she looks exactly the same as she did before you were born!"

Indeed, the dark beauty of Lydia Winslow had drawn men to her for years, but she had never shown the slightest interest in marriage. When Deacon Charles Milton had courted her in vain, Gilbert had said, "Well, Charles has looks, money, charm, and is a godly man, Lydia. If *he* won't do, who will?"

His daughter-in-law had only smiled at him, and gone to carry food to a hungry family. The church had become her life, and though many had said that an unmarried man like Gilbert Winslow would have trouble with her, she had spiked those guns by being a handmaiden of the Lord in a way that nobody could fault.

"Did you manage to give the bride a touch with the sock?" Bradford asked with a smile.

"Yes, but I'm waiting for a man like you or my grandfather to come along," Rachel shot back. Glancing slyly at her mother, she asked innocently, "Did you two settle anything?"

Oliver Bradford had been slow in making his decision. It had been over a year since his wife died, but his sudden frequent calls on Lydia Winslow had been a little too obvious. Everyone in the settlement knew he had made up his mind to marry Lydia Winslow.

His sharp-featured face flushed, and he answered, "We— have talked somewhat, but your mother is reluctant." He rose, suddenly uncomfortable, and took his leave. Lydia followed him to the door, and they said a few words that Rachel could not catch.

When Lydia returned, she said, "You shouldn't tease people, Rachel."

"Why don't you marry him, Mother?" Rachel asked suddenly. She came to look closely into Lydia's face, and then, seeing a trace of confusion, she added a question she had wondered about for years. "I've wondered why you never married—but then, everybody has. Is it because you're still in love with my father?"

"No!" Lydia answered brusquely. "No, that would be foolish, Rachel. I shall never marry because I believe that God has called me to live a single life."

"Don't you need a man, Mother?" she asked, then flushed suddenly and stammered, "I—I mean . . ."

Lydia threw back her head and laughed, and it made a merry sound in the room. "That's one of the few times I've ever seen you blush, Rachel!" She put her arm around the young woman, a younger edition of herself, and laughing, added, "I thought you were much too grown up and 'advanced' to be embarrassed by a reference to what the deacons call 'the intimacies of the connubial bed'!" Then she saw that the girl was really stricken, and she stopped laughing, saying softly, "Most women do need a man, just as a man needs a woman, Rachel. But Paul says, 'The unmarried woman careth for the things of the Lord, that she may be holy in body and spirit.' That is what I will do, Rachel—and it is not hard, for we have such a loving Bridegroom!"

Her mother had always had such a close and intimate walk with God that Rachel had learned more from just being around her than from all the sermons she'd heard in church. Lydia Winslow could pray and God would answer. Rachel had learned when she was just toddling that when she scraped her knee or injured herself, she could run to her mother, and as she prayed and rubbed the injury, the pain went away. She never called it "healing"; indeed, she never called it anything; she just did it. Rachel had come to take her mother's faith for granted, and never questioned her about it.

"Well, Mother, what about me?" Rachel asked suddenly. "I'm going with Grandfather to the Indian Village, and you know I don't give a pin about that. I'm thinking a lot of Jude."

She had always been an honest girl, and as Lydia looked into her eyes, she was thankful that her daughter had confidence enough in her to speak her heart.

"He's getting to be quite prosperous, I hear. How much land does he own now?"

"I don't know. I told him once he just wanted *all* the land that joins his, and he got embarrassed. But I don't care about land, Mother."

"What *do* you care about, Rachel?" Lydia asked quietly.

Rachel stood there in surprise. The question had caught her off guard and it went through her quick mind. Finally she said, "I don't know, but I want to do *something*!"

Lydia Winslow bit her lip, then said slowly, "That's your father, Rachel. He was exactly like that."

"Am I like him, Mother?"

"You have some of my French impulsiveness, but it's not that I fear."

"What then?"

Lydia gazed at her daughter steadily. "It's the Winslow blood. Your grandfather may seem to you the most steady man in the world, but when he was your age, he was *wild*! And my Matthew had the same restlessness. It sometimes skips a generation, Gilbert tells me, but you have it, Rachel—and that's why I've wanted to see you marry early."

"So I'll have a husband to keep me from running wild?"

"You laugh at that, but I've seen it happen. Your father was for me all that I could ever desire—but the Winslow blood was strong, and—I lost him. I can't lose you, Rachel! Not you, too!"

Rachel suddenly found her mother's arms around her, holding to her fiercely as if to protect her from some sudden danger.

Finally Lydia drew back and said gently, "Well, I've wanted to say these things to you for a long time. Now you think I'm just a nervous old woman worried about her only chick."

"No." Rachel stared at her mother, and for the first time in her life, she saw her as a woman—not a mother, just as a woman, and it saddened her.

CHAPTER TEN

KING PHILIP

★　★　★　★

Rachel left the house when the east was barely tinged with the red light of dawn, and was delighted to discover John Sassamon standing beside her grandfather, his bronzed Indian features a welcome sight. "John! You're back!" She ran to greet him, and in an uncharacteristic move he embraced her. It was a rare gesture; women and men who were not related never embraced, but it was even more unusual for an Indian to show such feeling for a white woman.

But John Sassamon was not a typical Indian by any means. He had been reared in a community of Christian Indians at Natick, fifteen miles west of Boston, and had studied at Harvard. Then in a crisis of identity, perhaps, he had rejoined his native Indians in the wilderness. He served as an aide to Philip Metacomet, the son of Massasoit.

Philip had treasured the young man, and had broken into one of his legendary fits of fury when John had been led by the Spirit of God to return to Natick, where he was given the task of instructing young Indian converts.

Rachel had practically grown up with him, for he had been assigned to study under Gilbert Winslow, and the two of them had been a sturdy pair, accompanying the tall minister as he made his pastoral calls. They had sat together through the eternity-long sermons and studied the same books together, but her fondest memories were their times in the woods. He had made an Indian out of her, teaching her the forest arts of tracking, hunting, and a thousand other facts of the wilderness. She had cried for days when he left to go to Harvard, and beneath his stolid features she had seen that he was saddened, too.

Now he stood there, embarrassed at their embrace, but with a glow of joy in his ebony eyes as he said, "You are a woman, *Nahteeah*." She laughed as she heard his pet name for her, "little deer."

Gilbert said, "You two can renew your acquaintance as we travel. We've got a long day's journey." The road to Middleborough, some fifteen miles southwest of Plymouth, was good enough for the cart pulled by one of Gilbert's two horses, but past there they would have to ride or walk through Indian trails too narrow for any vehicle.

Rachel walked behind with John as Gilbert drove the cart, and after giving him all the news on what his old friends at Plymouth had been doing, she asked, "What are you going to do now that you're through at Harvard, John?"

"My people at Nemasket have prospered in the Lord, Nahteeah," he smiled. "I go to be their pastor."

"How wonderful!" Rachel exclaimed. "That's not so far. We'll get to see each other often."

"That will be good, Nahteeah. I have missed you." He laughed and said, "Do you remember when you were twelve years old and fell in love with me?"

Rachel laughed in delight at the reference. "I tried to get you to run off with me, didn't I? And you said, 'I can't marry you because I'm going to be a preacher!' "

"What a pompous boy I was!" The memory warmed them; then John gave her a look and said with a peculiar tone in his voice, "You haven't chosen a husband yet, Mr. Winslow tells me. You are fourteen now, and one of our maids would be disgraced if she got to be so old without getting a husband."

Rachel looked away from him, glancing up at a squirrel chattering angrily at the travelers for disturbing his peace. Then she said with a trace of embarrassment, "There's plenty of time."

"Is Jude Alden still courting you?"

The question disturbed her, and she said shortly, "I see him sometimes."

"He does not love my people, Nahteeah," John said quietly. "If you marry him, we could never speak to each other like this."

"He's a good man! If I did marry him, I would change his mind."

John gave her a sardonic smile, saying briefly, "That is the talk of a foolish woman, Nahteeah. If a woman cannot change a man's ways before marriage when he is warm and eager to please her, how can she do it when he has captured her and has no need to satisfy her any longer?"

The statement troubled Rachel, and she changed the subject, but all the way to Middleborough she had turbulent thoughts about what John Sassamon had said. She had long been aware of Jude's hatred for the Indians, but, despite her close friendship with Sassamon, had tried to ignore his attitude. His prejudice left no room for distinction between friendly and hostile Indians—all red men were "savages" to him. Such a perception was not rare on the frontier, although there had not been an Indian war since the war against the Pequots in 1637. But three tribes—the Nipmuck of Massachusetts, the Narragansett in the Bay area, and the Wampanoag led by Philip in Plymouth— were growing restive under the increasing pressure of white civilization. Living on the frontier was like living on a powder keg, for if war with the Indians did come, there was no protection, no militia or army to keep the tribes at bay.

All morning they kept to a steady pace, stopping only briefly at noon to eat a simple meal of cold beef and bread washed down with cold water from a clear brook. They rested for less than an hour, then continued their journey, but this time Rachel rode in the cart and the two men walked in front. She listened as they talked over the matters of the ministry, and presently they spoke of the low spiritual state of Plymouth.

"You young people must get tired of hearing old men say that the church here isn't what it was in our day," Gilbert said. "But it's true. Oh, there are little fires of true godliness breaking out in places, but I can't help remembering the first years here."

"Why is it so, Brother Winslow? Why has the fire died down in the people?"

Winslow thought about the question, and finally said, "It's partly the easy living, John. People are born in town situations instead of having to wrest a life out of the wilderness. This generation has never known desperate need. They grow up never knowing what it means to be imprisoned merely because they love God enough to put Him first—like John Bunyan. They don't know what it's like to have no land and no work and no say in how they are governed. It did something to us, John—the first-comers, I mean—to live for weeks in wet misery on the open seas, then living in tents or holes in the ground, while cold and sickness ticked us off one by one. I remember one month that first year when we had to bury our dead by night so Indians wouldn't know how our ranks had thinned! We ate ground nuts or grubbed for mussels to stay alive—and all for the sake of a vision of a Promised Land!"

John nodded. "I have often heard you say, Mister Winslow, 'God hears only desperate men!' "

Winslow shrugged, and his step was as strong as it had been at dawn, causing Rachel to marvel again at her grandfather's youthful body. "I fear the only way God will get the attention of our people, John, is for them to become desperate—as we were at the first."

"You think good times ruin the church?"

"Rev. Cotton Mather believes that. He said in a sermon last month, 'Religion begat prosperity, and the daughter devoured the mother.' And he's not alone, for Daniel Gookin showed me a letter from Judge Sewall, and the wise judge said, 'Prosperity is too fulsome a diet for any man—unless seasoned with some grains of adversity.' "

They passed through Middleborough that afternoon, and leaving the cart with a friend, proceeded on foot to Philip's camp. It was growing late in the day when they walked into the collection of rude huts, made for the most part of saplings tied together with vines. The smell of cooking fires was in the air, and they were greeted at once by Philip, sachem of the Wampanoags.

"You have come," he said, advancing to meet them. He held his hands palms up in the traditional Indian greeting, showing that he had no weapons. "We eat first, then talk."

They sat down in a circle inside his tent, which smelled strongly of fish, dog, and unwashed bodies, and Rachel made a show of eating. The food was some sort of stew in a great iron pot, and the guest simply reached in, pulled out a piece of meat or vegetable and ate it with the fingers. She avoided the meat, knowing the Indians' weakness for young dog. She had many times seen a squaw knock a puppy on the head, dress it in a few deft movements and throw it into just such a pot; although she had eaten such food, it never appealed to her.

Philip was not physically impressive. He was small, and his slight frame was covered with stringy muscles. A large nose dominated his face, and he had a small mouth which he kept tightly shut. But he had not risen to be sachem over his tribe because of his appearance, but simply because he was by far the most intelligent of all his people. Perhaps *crafty* was a better word; as Rachel studied the small Indian who was talking to her grandfather, she was struck again with the glittering eyes that illumined his face. She had always been somewhat afraid of the man, and now she felt a chill as he spoke angrily, making violent gestures with his hands.

"You come like locusts, you white men," he said staring hypnotically at the visitors. "Soon the People will have no place to put their feet. You talk about Great God in the sky, but is He only the white man's God? Does He not make the People as well?"

"He is the God of all men, King Philip," Winslow answered quietly.

"Then does He let one of His children rob the other? The Wampanoag fathers are not so cruel to their sons! He is cruel, this Jesus God!"

John Sassamon spoke up then in his clear baritone voice. "No, Jesus is not unjust. He died for the sins of all men, red and white. He longs for all His children to walk in love with one another."

Philip shot a malevolent glance at the young man, and fairly spat out his next words: "The white man robs us, takes our land and pushes us into the sea! How can you call this love? You have forsaken the People, and can see only the white man's way!"

Philip's thinly veiled hatred of Christianity, especially of the Christian missionaries who were pulling away some of his best warriors, was no secret. To Philip, John Sassamon was a turncoat of the vilest sort, and from that moment, he turned from the young Indian, ignoring him completely.

"You have been paid for your land, King Philip," Winslow said, but he knew the words were meaningless to the man. Indians never understood ownership of land in the English sense. Their idea of signing a deed to real estate, usually in return for a specified number of axes, kettles, matchcoats, or mackinaws, was to share it with the palefaces, not to move out; they regarded the price as rent, to be repeated every so often.

Philip listened sullenly as Winslow pleaded with him, stating the case for the white man in the fairest terms, but finally when all was said, it was obvious that the smoldering hatred in Philip was not quenched.

"We must go before it gets too dark to travel," Winslow said, and they took their leave of the surly chief, to hurry along the trail.

"We'll not get back to Middleborough by dark," John remarked.

"No, but we can stay the night with Alden," Winslow said.

They walked as fast as Rachel could go for two hours, but the sun was behind the low range of hills to the south when they turned off the trail to Jude Alden's farm. He was not expecting them, but when they came into the clearing cut out of the large oaks where his snug house was set, he came out at Winslow's hail.

"Mr. Winslow—" he said, then peering behind caught sight of the two behind him. "Well, Rachel, this is a surprise."

He did not acknowledge John. Rachel went up to him and said, "Hello, Jude. Can you take in three tired travelers tonight? You remember John Sassamon."

Alden hesitated, glaring at the Indian, then nodded. "Of course! Come in and we'll have some tea and a little bite of food."

They filed into the small house, and he put his musket down and busied himself with the food. He talked steadily, mostly with Winslow, but he was very conscious of his other two guests.

He could not disguise his suspicion of Sassamon, and Rachel was grieved to see the covert glance of distrust he gave the Indian who stood silently with his back against the wall.

But he was most aware, she saw with some pleasure, of her.

He listened to her grandfather, even made replies, but he could not keep his eyes off her. Rachel was accustomed to attention from young men, but as he poured the tea and they sat down to eat, she felt a sudden pride that he was so captivated by her.

"God, we thank you for this food—Amen!" Jude said quickly, and they were all caught off guard by the brevity of it.

Gilbert laughed and said as he cut a slice of beef from the large portion in the platter, "That's your grandfather speaking there, Jude." He referred to John Alden who had courted and won Priscilla Mullins on board the *Mayflower*. "He was a devout man, but had no time for long prayers—or sermons, either! I recall he said once to Governor Bradford's face after a three-hour sermon, which was not one of the governor's *best*: 'Yer pardon, Governor, fer goin' to sleep, but yer should take note of the oyster.' Well, Bradford stared at him, completely mystified, and finally he asked, 'The oyster? Why the oyster?' And John looked him right in the eye and said, 'Because, sir, the beast knows when to open—and *when to shut*!' "

Jude laughed louder than the others and said, "I believe it of him, Mr. Winslow. I miss him very much."

"So do I, Jude," Winslow said quietly. He traced a figure on the table with his finger, then looked up and said, "They were a goodly people, the Firstcomers."

"Yourself, too, Mr. Winslow," Alden nodded at once.

"No, I was the black sheep, John." Gilbert Winslow shook his head sadly. "I could tell you some of my sinful past that would curl your hair, if I so chose."

"I've always wanted curly hair, Grandfather," Rachel piped up suddenly. "Please tell us about those times."

Winslow seldom spoke of his part in the settlement of Plymouth, but he did that night. He did not spare himself, for he had not been aboard the *Mayflower* voluntarily, but was fleeing from the King's Justice. He told them how he had entered the service of Lord North, fleeing the life of a ministerial student at Cambridge to pursue fame and fortune with one of England's most powerful lords. He told of Lady Cecily North, the beautiful aristocrat he had fallen in love with, and Rachel longed to ask him more about her, but was afraid to interrupt.

"I joined Bradford and the Pilgrims in Holland with one idea in my mind," Gilbert said with a sad look in his fine eyes. "I was to ferret out William Brewster, one of the founders of the congregation, so I became a spy."

"A spy, sir? I can hardly believe it!" Alden exclaimed.

"Then you do not know the depravity of the human heart," Winslow smiled. "But there is a worse thing; I gained the love of a pure young woman in the group in order to get myself into the inner circle."

He went on to tell how when the choice had to be made, he had fought a duel with Lady North's admirer, Lord Roth, and had killed him in a duel to protect the young woman and the congregation.

"So I fled England on the same ship with the congregation, but I hated God!"

"What happened then, Grandfather?"

Winslow spoke slowly, seeming to live over the days when they had fought for survival, with what they called simply the general sickness, killing over half their number the first winter. He told how he had been profoundly influenced by the sacrificial lives of Bradford and others, and how he had finally found Jesus Christ as his Savior in a blinding blizzard, as God revealed himself.

"Tell about the young woman, about Grandmother," Rachel insisted.

Gilbert Winslow leaned forward, put his chin on his folded hands, and thought. Finally he said, "She was the loveliest thing on God's earth." Then he turned his head and there were tears in his eyes as he said, "You are very much like her, Rachel. Very much. Oh, you don't *look* like her at all, but her spirit has come to you." He hesitated so long they thought he was finished; then he said quietly, "All that was good about your father came from her—his generosity, his sympathy with the downtrodden, his wit—and all that was wrong came from me—from the Winslow blood!"

"No! I don't believe that!" Rachel reached over and took his hands in hers, gripping them fiercely. "You mustn't say that!"

The candle was guttering in the pewter holder as he finished, and he looked around in shock. "I can't believe it! I've never told some of this to a soul!"

"I'm glad you did!" Rachel said, putting her arms around him. "It's wonderful to have a hero for a grandfather!"

He laughed in embarrassment and got up, "Well the 'hero' is dead on his feet. Shall I sleep in the loft, Jude?"

"Yes. Rachel can have the bedroom. But there's only room for two in the loft—" he turned a hostile eye toward Sassamon.

"I will sleep in the barn," the Indian replied impassively.

Jude hesitated, then continued blandly, "I've got to see to the new calf first. Just a few hours old, and can hardly eat."

Rachel glanced from Jude to Sassamon, whose face betrayed no hint of anger at Jude's rudeness. She hesitated, as if making a decision, then turned back to Jude.

"Let me go with you, Jude!" she pleaded, just as he'd known she would. She loved all animals, especially baby ones, and she skipped over to go outside the door, calling back, "You sleep well, Gilbert Winslow; I want to hear more about this Lady Cecily North!"

She heard her grandfather's loud laugh as they stepped outside and took the path that led to the small hay shed fifty feet from the house. He opened the door and held the candle high so that she could see.

"Oh, what a darling!" she cried, and ran at once to stroke the tiny calf wobbling across the straw. "How beautiful!"

Jude Alden put the candle on a stool, and came to stand over her. "Yes," he said with a smile. "A darling—and very beautiful."

She felt her cheeks grow warm, and confusion swept her. Alden reached down and pulled her to her feet, and she felt his strong arms go around her. As he pulled her close, she whispered, "No—Jude!"

But he said again, "You are very beautiful, Rachel—more so all the time!" She was intensely aware of his male strength as he tightened his arms, pressing her even more closely to his chest. "I think about you all the time, you know. Stuck out here by myself in this wilderness! Every night I go to sleep thinking of you."

She began to tremble, filled with a fear of wrongdoing, but at the same time dizzy with the raging emotion that had suddenly risen in her. She lifted her head, and in the flickering light of the candle, he saw her lips frame his name: *Jude!* She felt her arms go around his neck, and she wondered at her boldness, but it was almost as if it were another, and not she herself, who was responding to his kiss.

He released her slowly, and as she slipped from his arms, he said, "I've never known a woman like you, Rachel."

She waited for him to say more, but he did not. Suddenly she remembered what she had heard said of him, that he was something of a ladies' man, and the thought shamed her. "I'd better go inside, Jude," she said quietly.

Then he said, "Have you ever thought of marrying, Rachel?"

She stared at him, then said, "Every girl thinks of that." Then the quick sense of humor came to her and she quipped, "You'd better ask Betsy Small, Jude. Her father's got a big farm he's going to give for her dowry—big enough that you won't mind her being so thin!"

He smiled but said at once, "I've got a bad reputation, haven't I, Rachel? About women and about being ambitious."

"There is talk—about both."

"About the first," Alden said easily, "I must confess that I've been lax—but that's over. About the second, I plead guilty. I see nothing wrong in having things. What's wrong with that?"

"It depends on how you prosper—and what you do with the money when you get it."

"I'll spend it," he smiled. "You think I'd enjoy sitting around *counting* it? No, I'll work hard for a few more years, then I'll live the good life—travel, go places, meet people!"

He had touched on a longing that she had never let another soul know of—her desire to travel, but she did not let a flicker of this yearning show in her eyes.

Then he said, "What about you, Rachel? What do you want?"

She bit her lip, then shrugged and said, "I don't know, Jude. I suppose I'm trying to find out."

He looked at her in the darkness and said, "Maybe we can help each other to find our way, Rachel."

"Maybe, Jude." She turned and they walked out into the night; then she went to her room and tossed fitfully on the straw mattress.

The next morning they left early and on the way home, Gilbert said to her out of John's hearing, "You decide on Jude?"

She stared at him, then laughed. "I wouldn't put it past you to climb out of the upstairs window and creep on your hands and knees to eavesdrop on us."

"I would if I thought it would help you," he said simply.

She took his hand and squeezed it, saying, "Tell me about Cecily North." Then she added with an odd smile, "I don't know about Jude. I'll tell you as soon as I know."

CHAPTER ELEVEN

OUT OF THE PAST

★　★　★　★

Lydia said nothing to Rachel, but for several days after her return from the Indian village, she was aware that something was troubling the girl. Finally when she and Gilbert were alone in the church after a service, she approached him about it.

"You haven't said much about your trip to see King Philip," she said as they sat down on one of the benches. "Were you discouraged about him?"

"Yes. He's sour, and sooner or later he's going to give trouble."

"Rachel's been very quiet since you came back."

"Oh, that's a different matter," he said. "She's all tangled up about what to do with young Alden. They had some sort of meeting out in the barn, and she's been all het up ever since."

"In the barn!"

He laughed and patted her shoulder. "Now, don't get your feathers ruffled, Lydia. She told me some of it, and there's nothing to worry about. They're just circling around trying to decide whether to make a match of it or not."

She shook her head. "I wish she would marry him, Gilbert."

He shrugged and bit his lip. "I'm not so sure I agree. He's a good match, I suppose—he's got land, and he's a hard worker, but his walk with God isn't much. Pretty much of a Sunday man. And he's got a rather unchristian attitude about this Indian issue.

Snubs John Sassamon dreadfully. I'd like to see Rachel get a man who puts God first."

They talked for a long time that night, and it was on the following Wednesday that Sassamon came by. It was late afternoon, and they did not hear his step. A knock at the door startled them all as they sat reading in the front room.

"Who can that be?" Gilbert muttered, as he went to answer it. "Well, John, come in!"

Sassamon entered and said, "Hello, Mr. Winslow—and how are you, Mrs. Winslow?"

"Hello, John," Lydia smiled. "Come in, come in."

"No, I have to go see the governor right away." He hesitated, then said, "I would like for you to go with me, Mr. Winslow. He may not believe what I have to tell him."

Gilbert looked hard at him, then at Lydia and Rachel. "What's the trouble, John?"

He shifted his weight from one foot to the other, then burst out, "It's Philip, sir!"

"What about him?"

"He's organizing for war against you!"

"I knew it!" Winslow cried. "The fool! He'll set the frontier on fire!"

"Will you come with me to see Governor Bradford?"

"Yes, of course, but is it certain, John?" He pulled his coat from a peg and was shrugging into it. "How did you find out?"

"My brother, Matthew, has been to see me. He says that he was there when Philip came to his village. Philip promises that if the tribes all rise up together, the settlers will be wiped out and the land will be back in the hands of the People!"

"Come along!" Gilbert barked, plunging out the door. "I don't know if we can convince the governor or not, but we'd better!"

Rachel and Lydia stayed up until midnight, waiting for them to come back. They had talked fearfully about the possibilities of a war, but it was late and they were sitting quietly, busy with their thoughts, when Rachel suddenly said, "I kissed Jude Alden in the barn, Mother."

Lydia almost laughed out loud at the confession; it was much like those times when as a small child Rachel would think over some small misdeed for a long time, then come marching in to look her straight in the eye and announce it boldly.

"Did you now?"

"Are you angry?"

"No, I don't think so," Lydia said with a smile. "Did you think I would be?"

"Oh, I suppose not. But it made me feel a little wicked, Mother." She turned her clear hazel eyes on Lydia. "How do you know you're in love with a man?"

"Why . . ." Lydia was caught off guard. She finally cleared her throat and said, "I don't think there's any rule about that, Rachel. You just have to be sure you want to spend your life with him and that you respect him."

But that was not enough for Rachel, and she asked insistently, "But how did you know you were in love with my father?"

Lydia was trapped, and the pulse in her throat beat more rapidly as she said at last, "I can't put it into words, Rachel. You'll just have to—to—"

Rachel was staring at her mother, disappointed that there was no simple answer coming. Just as she was about to pursue the subject, they heard voices, and they got up as Gilbert and John entered.

"What did he say?" Lydia asked at once.

"The governor can't believe that it's so serious as John says," Gilbert shrugged. "He wants John to keep an eye on the situation and let us know if there's any danger."

John was angry, and Rachel saw it. "There's danger right now!" he said grimly. "When Philip attacks, he won't send any announcement, I tell you!"

"I'll work on it, John," Gilbert said, and he put a restraining hand on the young man's shoulder. "Governor Bradford is getting on, but I may be able to bring him around."

John shrugged. "It will have to be that way, I suppose. But be quick, Mr. Winslow."

"You'll stay the night," Lydia said and she went to get some cover for John. She gave it to him, and she went to bed, saying, "I'll make you a big breakfast before you go home tomorrow."

"We will pray about it, won't we, John?" Gilbert said, and

gave the young man a firm embrace before he went to his own room.

Before she left, Rachel said, "Be careful, John. Philip hates you. If he thought for one second that you were talking to us about this, he'd cut your throat."

"You're right about that. I'll be very careful." He turned to go with the blanket in his arms, then paused and said, "You're very special in my heart, Nahteeah. I treasure the memory of our childhood days here more than anything else."

She stared at him, for he had always been reticent about his feelings. "I feel that way, too, John. But there'll be more good days to come."

"I hope so, Nahteeah," he said, then turned and left silently as a shadow.

He was gone when they got up the next day, and Gilbert said ruefully, "He's in a bad place, Lydia. I fear for the Praying Indians, converted to Christianity. They're going to be in the middle if a war breaks out. Both sides will hate them."

"We'll have to see that they don't," Lydia said, and as they spoke, Rachel felt a chill of fear, for there had been something fatalistic in John's eyes as he had left her the previous night.

Then she felt the two watching her, and Gilbert said, "It'll be bad for Jude, too. He's right in the middle of Philip's territory." He said nothing more, and the weight on her heart kept her subdued for the next few weeks.

Lydia awoke and glanced carelessly at the calendar, little thinking that the date—April 10—would be any different from another day. She rose, dressed, and spent the first hour with her Bible, praying quietly while kneeling beside her bed. Then she hurried to the kitchen and put some bread in glowing coals left from the night's baking, and by the time she had sliced the loaf, Gilbert and Rachel entered and sat down.

When the simple fare was on the table, Gilbert said, "I must go to see Mrs. Hewitt over at Langley. She's not doing well. Would you like to go with me, Lydia?"

"No, I'll go later in the week, Gilbert. You tell her I'll make her some of that good strong rabbit broth she likes so well."

"All right. I think I'll stay overnight. Be back by noon tomorrow." They bowed their heads and ate quickly. "What are you going to do today, Rachel?"

"I'll help Mother this morning. Maybe I'll go to see Mercy this afternoon."

Winslow gave her a sharp look, for she had been subdued, but he said nothing. After the meal he left, and the two women spent all morning cleaning house.

It was almost noon when Rachel glanced out the window and said, "Why, there's Grandfather! I wonder why he came back?"

Lydia looked up in surprise from where she sat at the table sewing. "I can't imagine. Maybe he changed his mind."

Rachel stepped to the door and opened it. "What brought you back—?"

The words were cut off as if a noose had tightened around her neck. The man who stood there was not her grandfather—but so like him she was speechless!

He stood there, his bright blue eyes searching her face calmly, and he had the same wedge-shaped face, the same broad cheekbones and wide mouth as Gilbert Winslow—only this man was in the prime of life.

Lydia looked up to see why Rachel had broken off, and when she saw the two standing there, a fear ran through her. She rose and went quickly to the door. "What's wrong, Gilbert?"

She had no doubt that it was her father-in-law, for he had the same tall frame, and the shape of his head was so like Gilbert's that it never entered her mind as she stepped forward that it was anyone but him.

Rachel stepped to one side, her eyes fixed on the man. He took one step forward and said, "Hello, Lydia."

He stepped out of the brilliant sunshine and Lydia saw his features clearly for the first time. Her hand flew to her mouth and she felt terribly sick. She heard her heart pounding fast and hard, and the room seemed to sway. She closed her eyes and almost fell, but Rachel caught her, crying out, "Mother!" and she backed away from the door until the edge of the table caught her.

There was a sudden silence, and the three of them seemed to be frozen in place—or like a picture painted on a canvas. Lydia knew that as long as she lived she would see that scene: the brilliant

April sun streaming through the windows highlighting myriads of dust motes that swarmed madly as if to escape the shaft of light— Rachel, pale as old ivory, staring at the tall man who had stepped inside and stood looking at her across the small room.

"I've—come back. Lydia."

She tried to speak, but her mouth was so dry she had to lick her lips. When she finally found her voice, the sound was harsh and brittle, cutting the intense silence.

"I—we thought—you were—dead!"

Rachel gave a small cry, and Lydia saw the fear scoring her pale face. She moved quickly to stand beside the girl. Rachel placed an arm around her mother as if to steady her, but she herself was faint and dizzy with shock.

Matthew, too, was trembling, his ruddy face, burned with the sun, gray with strain. But he swallowed hard, his words coming slowly. "You need to sit down, both of you." He grabbed a chair in each hand and shoved them toward the two women, saying, "Please—sit down, Lydia!"

Lydia sat down heavily, for the shock of his appearance had robbed her of strength. She had seen a man almost sever his foot with an ax, and she had had the same lightheaded feeling as the scarlet blood had pumped out on the white snow. She closed her eyes and tried to pray, but nothing came. Her thoughts rolled wildly through her mind, but as she sat there, her breathing became more even, and she could feel her racing pulse slow to a normal rate.

She opened her eyes, took a deep breath, and carefully looked at her husband's face, repeating, "We thought you were dead."

"I thought of sending you word that I was coming, but I had no one to send."

Lydia stared at him; then she looked up at Rachel. "This is your father, Rachel."

The two looked at each other, and neither spoke. Finally he said, "You are beautiful—" He broke off, bit his lip and said, "I'd like to sit down myself, if you don't mind."

He stood there, and for all the strength he radiated, a vulnerability filled his face—a slight movement in his broad lips, just a trace of uncertainty in his clear blue eyes. Certainly not the brash Matthew Winslow Lydia had known. He did not move, but stood there as if he expected to be ordered out of the house.

Lydia nodded. "Of course." She watched as he pulled the third chair from the table and sat down. There was something eerie about him, for he was not the eighteen-year-old she had pictured in her mind for years, but a heavier man, stronger, with an assurance and steadiness in his gaze that was foreign to her memories of him as a youth. There was an air of authority in him, as if he were accustomed to being obeyed, yet his face bore a look of simple humility. His hands were brown and corded with muscle, and as he moved there was a suggestion of tremendous power, ready to leap into action at an instant's notice. He had a white scar that began over his right eyebrow and disappeared into his thick hair, and another on the side of his neck shaped like a fishhook.

He was dressed in knee breeches and boots, a waistcoat of dark red velvet, and a dark-brown coat of fustian with silver buttons. His shirt was of white linen; he held a felt hat with a wide brim and high crown. There was nothing to mark him as to profession, but the clothes, though not new, had been expensive.

He let the silence run on as the women stared at him, enduring it quietly, and not taking his own eyes off them.

"I know it's a shock, my walking in like this." He hesitated then said very quietly, "You can't know how I've longed to see you all these years, Lydia."

"But—we thought you were dead!"

He stared at her, then nodded. "I suppose that would be natural enough, not hearing from me all this time. But I couldn't write!"

Lydia twisted her hands together, trying to conceal the trembling, but the anger in her voice betrayed her as she said, "You let me think all these years that you were lost at sea!"

"Lost at sea?" he exclaimed, lifting his head. "Why would you think that?"

She stared at him in disbelief, and her lips grew pale as she pressed them together. "You left on that whaling ship—I've forgotten its name—but it went down with all hands!"

His mouth dropped open, and he tried to speak, but the words would not come. Finally he swallowed and said, "As God is my witness, Lydia! I never once *thought*! Why, I was signed to go on the *Intrepid*—but at the last moment I changed my mind and took a berth aboard a schooner headed for Africa. I never knew—not until this minute—that the whaling vessel sank!" He got to his feet and began to pace nervously back and forth, twisting his head to one side in a familiar motion that Rachel had seen in Gilbert Winslow a thousand times.

"By all that's holy, I never thought of such a thing—not once!" He shook his head, then said, "I was almost mad, Lydia, in that prison, you must remember how my mind was going."

"I—remember," she said slowly, her eyes cold as steel.

"That day, the day I sent for the justice, I was in a fever, maybe you remember that, too? It seemed to burn what little will I had out of my soul! So when I signed the paper promising to never preach again, I was numb. I think I went mad. I remember Bunyan trying to talk to me, but it was like—it was like I was under water, in a way. I was moving slowly, and I couldn't see through the haze."

"Why didn't you come home?" Lydia demanded, and such pain filled her eyes that he bit his lip and looked away. "Oh, why didn't you just come home, Matthew?"

"I wanted to, Lydia—and that was where I started. But I was out of my mind. I—I knew you and Father would never understand what I had done! I suppose if I had been rational, I might have done it, but all I could think of was the shame of it! So I wandered around for a while, and then the idea just came to me—to leave the country and get away from it all."

He stopped, finding it difficult to explain. Pulling a handkerchief from his pocket, he wiped the perspiration from his brow. "That's what I did, Lydia," he began again in a hoarse voice. "I went to the house, got my clothes and some money—then I got on the coach and left Bedford. Couldn't bear seeing you."

Breathing heavily, Lydia waited for him to continue, but he said nothing more. Finally she asked, "And then? Where have you been all these years?"

As he turned to face her, she saw something in his eyes she did not recognize. He hesitated, then answered quietly, "I can't tell you now. You would not be proud of my life for the past fourteen years, Lydia."

Anger suddenly coursed through her and she got to her feet.

"And that's your explanation for deserting your wife and child?"

He flinched, but faced her blazing eyes steadily. "If there were a reason for my behavior, Lydia, don't you suppose I'd give it? But I have none." He straightened his heavy shoulders and implored, "I've come to ask for your forgiveness, Lydia—and for yours, daughter—but don't ask me to account for my life! Forgive me—that's my only request."

Lydia stared at him for several minutes, and then she began to tremble violently. Rachel watched, dumbfounded, for she had never seen her mother lose control.

"Forgive you!" Lydia spat out. "Just like that, Matthew Winslow, you expect to walk back into our lives and take up where you left off fourteen years ago?"

Winslow's head jerked as if he had been physically struck. "I can understand, Lydia—"

"Understand? You understand nothing!" she interrupted. "Once I thought you dead, I was free from the anguish of your desertion. I could go on with life, forgive your memory, give myself to God. But here you are again, and—"

Lydia stopped short, her face flushed. She breathed deeply once or twice, fought for control, then finished in a whisper, "Sin it may be, Matthew, but I cannot pretend to forgive you when my heart cannot accept you. I—I can't think clearly—"

He got up at once. "I don't wonder." He picked up his hat and stood, a tall shape against the sun that caught him in a yellow beam. He started to speak, then shrugged. Rachel saw a dark look of fatalism cloud his eyes. He looked at the two women and asked, "Where is my father?"

"He's gone to Langley," Rachel said. "He'll be back tomorrow at noon."

"I'll be on board the *Carrington*, just offshore," he stated. "If he will see me, tell him to send word."

"I'll tell him. . ." She paused, not knowing how to address him.

He gave her a slight smile and said, "You are indeed lovely, Rachel."

Then he wheeled and left without another word. Rachel watched him walk rapidly down the street until he was out of sight. She turned to look at Lydia, and said, "Mother—I can't believe it!"

Lydia whispered, "Nor I, child." She walked over to the door and stood looking down the street. Then she turned, her shoulders sagging, and she began to weep.

"Mother! Are you all right?" Rachel ran to her mother and held her close. For a long time great sobs racked her mother's body. Finally she took a deep breath, wiped her eyes, and pulled away.

"I must go to Gilbert," she said numbly.

"I'll go with you!"

"Rachel—would you mind if I went alone?"

Rachel sensed that there was a need in her mother that only Gilbert Winslow could meet, so she said, "Of course. You'll have to hurry to get there before dark."

Ten minutes later Lydia stood at the door and in an unexpected move embraced Rachel, then said, "How do you feel, Rachel? I won't leave you if . . ."

"I'm fine, Mother, really. It's just so strange—to have a father."

Lydia glared at Rachel. "You don't have a father. Matthew Winslow gave up all rights to that name when he ran away fourteen years ago!"

"I suppose so—but it's different." Rachel shook her head. "No matter *what* he's done, he's *real*."

Lydia bit her lip and said gently, "Rachel, I have done my grieving over your father. To me he died before you were born. Now he comes back and begs for forgiveness. I hardly know how to forgive him. But I will not let him hurt me again—nor *you!*"

"Yes, Mother," Rachel said quietly. "You must hurry; it'll be dark by the time you get there."

"We'll be home early in the morning."

Rachel watched her mother until she was out of sight, then stood there, uncertain and filled with such emotion that she could not be still. She threw on a coat, and all afternoon she walked the shore, looking often at the ship that lay offshore, thinking of the tall man who had appeared out of the past.

"My father." She said the title aloud as she continued to look at the vessel until darkness began to descend. The fog soon swallowed the ship, making it invisible, so she turned and walked slowly back to the cottage, filled with an emotion she could not identify—a mixture of hope, joy—and fear!

CHAPTER TWELVE

A NEW MAN

★ ★ ★ ★

Rachel slept no more than the barn owl that kept calling all night. For three hours she tossed about on her bed, then finally rose and dressed. Her mind was confused, filled with wild thoughts and an emotion she could not define. She had long ago accepted the fact that she had no father, but for him suddenly to appear made her somehow angry. *He could have come home before this!* she thought as she waited for Gilbert and Lydia to arrive. *If he had loved me and my mother, he would have come!*

By the time she heard the footsteps approaching the house, the hurt and bitterness had taken a firm hold of her mind. She opened the door, and saw at a glance that neither of them had slept. Gilbert's face was pinched in a way she had never seen it, for he was a cheerful man, never gloomy; but now he looked old and worn as he came to embrace her. "You look tired, Rachel," he said quietly.

"I didn't sleep much. You two didn't either, from the looks of you. I've got some tea ready." She sat them down and as she poured the tea, she said, "It's hard for me—but much worse for both of you."

Gilbert took the tea, stirred it slowly with his spoon, then tried to smile. "I feel very guilty, you know. Here is my only son come back from the grave, and I've not been giving God the glory."

Lydia sat down wearily, looked out the window where the morning sun was beginning to warm the earth. She shook her head and said, "Matthew is alive—not dead, and I feel so—so . . ."

Gilbert gazed at her steadily and said, "It will take a while, my dear." He sipped his tea, adding, "I've sent word for him to come as soon as he can."

"But—what are you going to say to him?" Rachel asked, frustration mirroring her usually cheery face. Her full lips narrowed under the pressure, as she continued. "He can't expect to just step back into our lives as if nothing happened! I can't just smile at him and say, 'Father, I'm so glad you're home,' can I?"

Gilbert stared at his cup, then looked up at her. "I hardly think he expects that, Rachel. But I know what you mean." Nervously he bit his lip, then added, "Let's wait until we talk to him before we try to make any decisions or form any judgments."

The next hour was a strain as each tried to occupy himself. But none mentioned Matthew's name. Then as Lydia looked out the window she cried, "Here he comes!" They all stiffened. Following the knock at the door, Gilbert moved stiffly forward, then pulled it open and stepped back.

Matthew took two steps into the room, paused, then meeting Gilbert's gaze, said quietly, "Hello, Father."

The two women did not move nor speak, for they were caught by the tension that filled the room. Both of them looked at Gilbert's face, now masking his emotions.

Gilbert Winslow was not a man to hide his feelings; that was one of his charms. His expressive features reflected his moods, for he had not formed the habit of concealing his emotions. When he was angry, his bright eyes blazed with a fury that most men could not match, and when he was filled with joy, the light on his face made all who saw him glad.

But now his impassive face revealed no emotion. "Matthew," he began, "this is a glad day for me. Welcome home." The words were cordial, perhaps, but they were spoken in a careful, guarded tone, with little warmth.

Matthew's face, bronzed with an eastern sun, had been tense, but Lydia had seen the sudden light of expectancy that had lurked in his eyes and on his lips. At his father's words, his face had gone still, and he bit his lip, nodding slightly. "Thank you, sir."

It was all so formal, painfully so, that Lydia said quickly, "Come in and sit down."

"Thank you." He moved toward the table, sat down and folded his hands on the table. Gilbert sat down opposite him, but the two women remained standing.

Gilbert looked his son in the face and said, "You're looking well." Then he suddenly struck the table and cried, "Matthew, why—!"

"Father, wait!" Matthew implored, twisting his head to one side. The memory of that mannerism raked hard across Gilbert's nerves, and he knew for a long time he would be seeing and hearing things he had forgotten.

Matthew suddenly smiled, and though it was a bitter-sweet expression, his tone revealed no malice. "Let me put your minds at ease—all three of you. You're all in a state of shock—and you're all angry with me—" He held up his hand as Gilbert started to speak, and raised his voice as he said, "How could it be otherwise? You are angry, Father, because I ran away from duty. Lydia, how could you not be bitter with a man who deserted you? And you, Rachel, how can you possibly accept a stranger as a father—a man who's never done one thing for you that a real father would have done?"

The words struck all three of them like musket balls. Gilbert finally spoke, his voice edged with agitation and a trace of wonder. "You have picked up some discernment along the way." This time a smile touched the corners of his mouth and he said, "In my case you are correct—but I will expect that as we spend time together, I will be able to overcome this attitude."

Looking intently at each one, Matthew said quietly, "You need have no fear that I've come to move into your lives." At his words a look of surprise swept across Lydia's face, but he did not see it. "It took me two years to convince myself even to come back. I was ashamed, of course, and I had decided that whatever else I did, the one thing I would not be guilty of was inflicting *more* pain on you."

"What changed your mind—Matthew?" Lydia asked. She

seemed to have trouble pronouncing his name, but the shock of his presence was lessening, and the tense lines on her face had softened.

He hesitated, then gave a smile tinged with embarrassment. "I'll tell you—but it sounds so weak, I'd not expect you to believe it."

"I'd like to hear whatever part of your life you will tell us, Matthew," Gilbert encouraged him. "Lydia informs me it's your opinion we would be shocked by some of it—but I think we deserve to know *something*! You owe us that, I think."

Matthew bit his lip, then shrugged, saying, "Certainly. Father, if you want to know, I'll tell you." He got up and began to pace the floor, and his gait, his every movement brought back to Lydia and Gilbert the young man they had last seen fourteen years earlier.

"As I told Lydia, I was delirious when I left the jail, and you remember that my mind was in bad shape at that time. The ship was bound for Africa, but for most of that long voyage, I was so ill they kept me in the hold, pretty much expecting me to die. Perhaps you don't know this, but England and Spain are in stiff competition with one sort of merchandise—black slaves from Africa. Well, the *Eagle* made a good haul, but she was overtaken by a Spanish man-of-war and impounded as contraband. They kept the ship and the slaves, and every man on board was tried and found guilty of smuggling!"

Matthew gave them a curious look, then said, "I was in a Spanish prison for nearly six years—which is as close to hell on earth as you'll find on this planet!"

"I've heard something of it," Gilbert responded. "It's a miracle you're alive at all, from what's said of such places."

"I wouldn't be if I hadn't escaped. There was a prisoner named Rolfe, Isaac Rolfe. He'd been a soldier, a pirate, and just about everything else—but he got us out of that prison!"

"What did you do then?" Rachel asked suddenly. She had been watching her father pace the floor, and there was a burning desire to know all about him.

"Why, I joined with Rolfe," he shrugged. "And for the next six years we did all manner of things that men in our condition do to stay alive. We called ourselves 'soldiers of fortune'—which was a fancy way of saying we would fight on any side for any cause if there was enough gold in it for us." He paused and his brow furrowed as he thought; then he added, "I must have been in half a dozen armies, and most of the time I didn't even ask what the war was about."

"There are worse things than being a soldier," Lydia said.

"Yes, there are, and I managed to discover one," Matthew said bitterly. "Trading in human flesh—that was my next fine profession! I joined with Rolfe to buy a schooner and we made the trip to Africa time after time, but it never failed to make me sick. We packed them in so thickly on the ship they had to sleep hugging each other, like spoons pressed together. And when the plague would break out in the hold, they'd die like flies! We've thrown them over the side by the dozens—women, nursing mothers, babies—!"

He walked to the window and leaned on the sill, staring out at the green grass and the swaying hills. He stood there so long that he seemed to have forgotten them. Finally Gilbert gave a quick glance at Lydia and cleared his throat. "What happened then?"

"What? Oh, I took it as long as I could—" Matthew turned and looked at them with an odd light in his blue eyes. "Finally I sold my share of the ship to Rolfe and cleared out. I had enough money so that I could go anywhere, and for a few months I just wandered around, looking for something—but I couldn't find any peace."

He smiled at Gilbert and said, "Here's the part you won't believe. It sounds too much like a bad story. You see, ever since those days in that Spanish prison, something you told me once kept coming back. You may not remember it—but I've never forgotten. On the day that Uncle Edward and I were leaving for England, you and mother were there. It was the last time I ever saw her."

"I remember very well," Gilbert said quietly.

"Do you remember that you started down the ladder, and you called out to me: *'Be faithful to God, Matthew—never fail Him! Be true to God—and to yourself'* ?"

"Yes, I said that."

"Well, those words came to me all the years I was in prison, and even while I was serving the devil in the wars and in the slave trade. But when I finally cut all my ties with Rolfe and was alone with nothing to do, those words got even stronger. I tell you, it was like losing my mind—the way they kept ringing in my ears! So then—and here's what I find hard to say to you . . ."

He seemed so embarrassed that Gilbert said, "Go on. Let us hear it, son!"

Matthew nodded, then continued in a quiet voice charged with emotion. "I went back to England with no purpose, but one day I suddenly decided to go back to Bedford. It was like a dream when I got there, seeing the little house where we lived, Lydia—and the jail, of course! I found out Pastor Gifford had gone on, but you know about John Bunyan?"

"Yes." Gilbert smiled for the first time. "He's become quite a famous preacher since his release three years ago. In great demand all over England. And he and Elizabeth have two children of their own now!"

"Yes, I know," Matthew said. "I stayed with them for six months. He hasn't changed, John hasn't. The years in prison just made him pure gold! But now I have to tell you both—I was a lost sinner when I went to stay with the Bunyans, but through their love and kindness—I found Christ as my Savior." The confession seemed very difficult for him, and he laughed shortly. "I told you it would sound like a bad piece of fiction. Sinner gets converted and runs for his father's house—after ruining the lives of the three people he loves most." Matthew got up, wheeled and started for the door. He paused, turned and added roughly, "I won't trouble you, you may be sure of that!"

His departure was so sudden that they were stunned. Gilbert called out, "Wait—!" But he was gone.

"I—I don't understand, Gilbert," Lydia said in bewilderment. "Why should he be so—so *ashamed* to tell us he's become a Christian?"

"It sounds too easy for him, I think," Gilbert said slowly, rubbing his chin thoughtfully. "I can see how he feels, can't you? He behaved shamefully, and now his pride won't let him believe that all he has to do is ask forgiveness."

"But—is it real? His conversion, I mean?"

Gilbert turned to look at Rachel, then answered, "I don't

know, but in a way, it's just as well he feels this way. It will give us all time to think, to try and sort this out."

"But, what will he do?" Lydia asked.

"I think," Gilbert murmured softly, "he'll spend a lot of time *showing* us that he's found God—instead of *telling* us!"

Matthew's words on leaving—*I won't trouble you, you may be sure of that!*—were followed so strictly that for the next month it was almost as if his sudden appearance had been a dream! He did not return to the Winslow house, and they had to learn of his movements from others.

"The gentleman with your name, Pastor Winslow, he's your relation, is he?" Martin Tillotson asked one day as Gilbert stopped by the single inn in Plymouth. Tillotson was new to the town, a small, polite man, very regular in his church attendance. He smiled and said, "I could see the resemblance between the two of you—a fine looking man he is, too, like yourself, if I may say so."

"Yes, Brother Tillotson," Gilbert said quickly. "He's my son. How did you happen to meet him?"

"Why, he took a room here last week, Pastor—but he's been gone since that first day. Said he'd not be in much. He didn't mention his business."

Gilbert didn't take the broad hint, for not knowing himself what Matthew was doing, he could not very well answer the innkeeper. He repeated the conversation to Lydia and Rachel. They too were perplexed.

"Why did he come here if he was intending to leave so soon?" Rachel asked sharply. "Everyone knows about it. Mercy asked me right out, 'Is that *really* your father living at the inn?' And what was I to say? The whole thing makes me feel so— awkward!"

All three of them felt that way the next Sabbath Day, when Matthew walked in and took a back seat in the small church. It was a small town, and every stranger was subjected to minute examination, but Matthew's appearance sent a hum of whispering around the congregation, and several members were in danger of dislocating their necks trying to swivel around and catch a glimpse of the visitor.

Lydia's cheeks burned. Rachel turned to her mother and

whispered, "We can't *bear* this, Mother!"

Gilbert took in the avid interest, noting the embarrassment on the faces of Rachel and Lydia. His own face was paler than usual, but he rose and called the congregation to order as if nothing had happened. They sang and several members gave interpretations of scriptures; then Gilbert preached for an hour.

No one dared to turn and stare at Matthew during the sermon, except Mrs. Lawson, who would have stared at the archangel Michael. But if the eyes of the congregation were not directed at their visitor, their interest surely was.

Gilbert concluded the sermon, but instead of closing with a final prayer, he said in a steady voice, "We have a guest in our congregation this morning, my son, Matthew. Some of you who have been here for a long time will remember him. He was presumed to be dead for many years—but God in His mercy preserved him. I ask you to welcome him back, and to join his wife and his daughter in thanking God for His tender mercies."

Then he prayed, and afterward several of Matthew's old friends approached him eagerly. Matthew's teacher, in his eighties, but with eyes as sharp as a bird's, greeted the tall man, so unlike the small boy he had known. "Thank God, my boy! I thank God!" he exclaimed, giving him a hearty grip of the hand. "I've never forgotten you, never! It cut me like a knife when the word of your death came, and for all these years I've had fond memories of those days when you came to my house—such a bright little chap!" Then he suddenly reached out and embraced Matthew, weeping and patting him on the arm.

Matthew looked over the old man's head at Gilbert, his eyes misty as he said, "Why, that's good of you, Mr. Morrison—and just like you! I've thought of you often."

Others came, and those who had moved to Plymouth after his presumed death came to be introduced.

It was a strange moment for Matthew, who stood there receiving the greetings of old friends and others, feeling like an imposter. But it would not have been quite so difficult if Mrs. Lawson had not raised her voice, saying loudly, "Well, now, Lydia Winslow! What will it be like to have a husband again after all these years?"

Lydia flinched slightly at the impertinent question, but she managed to smile. "I rejoice with all of you," she said noncommittally, "that God has seen fit to preserve my husband."

Then the awkward moment passed, and the crowd began to leave. Gilbert walked over immediately and said, "I'm glad you came, son."

"We—expected you to come back," Lydia said with some hesitation.

Matthew gave her a direct look, then shook his head. "As I said, Lydia, I'll not be a trouble to you."

Rachel had moved to stand beside Lydia. "Well, you can't just *ignore* us!" she said sharply.

Matthew smiled at her. "Rachel, I realize how awkward it is—especially for your mother—but I'm leaving Plymouth today, so people will have to just *wonder* about our family."

"Leaving!" Lydia said quickly. "But—where are you going?"

"I was going to stop by and tell you about it before I left, but—"

"Come and have a bite with us," Gilbert said quickly. "It will look odd if you don't—and besides, I want to hear your plans."

They ate cold beef and bread, their usual Sabbath noonday meal, and Matthew related his plan. "There's a big market for beaver in England. I'm going into the trading business. As a matter of fact, I brought a wagon load of trade goods with me from England. I'll be gone for a few weeks; then when I get a shipment, I'll come back and put them on a ship here at Plymouth."

All three of them realized it was more than a business venture; he was taking himself out of Plymouth to remove some of the pressure from the three of them. "Matthew," Gilbert said, "you don't have to do this on our account—"

"It will be best, I think," Matthew broke in, "if I'm gone for a time. Give people time to get used to the idea of my being back." Then he added simply, "I'll have to go permanently, sooner or later, you know. There's no other way."

These weeks since Matthew's sudden appearance had not been easy on anyone. All three had wondered how he could fit into their lives. It would not do for him to remain at the inn, separated from his wife and daughter. In Plymouth that was simply not done, and in any case, it would have put an intolerable strain on all of them.

Breaking the awkward silence, Matthew stated, "I'll call when I get back in a few weeks."

He left, and although the village had not stopped speculating about the strange and sudden appearance, by the middle of June most of them had given up trying to ferret the truth of the affair from the family.

Lydia lost weight, Rachel noted, and was much quieter than usual as she went about her work at home and tended to the many charities she pursued. Rachel wanted to speak about her father to Gilbert and her mother, but they seemed engaged in some sort of inner journey and would only say, "We must continue to pray about it," when she brought the subject up.

On the last of June John Sassamon suddenly appeared, full of news. Arriving at the cottage, his first words to Rachel were, "I've been with your father!"

Rachel eagerly pumped the young Indian for information, and discovered that her father had gone to John's village. The two had met and become fast friends; Sassamon could not speak highly enough of Matthew.

"He is a good man, Nahteeah! As good as his father!" That was high praise, indeed, from the Indian! He went on to add, "He is the most honest trader my people have ever met, but the other traders are very angry with Mr. Matthew because he gives a fair price and does not rob the People! And he is as good as an Indian in the woods, Nahteeah! I have traveled with him and he can stalk the deer better than I!"

Rachel hung on his words, and Sassamon asked suddenly, "What is wrong between Mr. Matthew and you, Rachel?"

"Why, nothing, John!"

"That is the first lie you have told me in a long time!"

She bit her lip, ashamed to be dishonest with him, then said, "It is an old thing, John. My father did a bad thing years ago, and it still lies between us, I suppose."

"That is bad—for he is a good Christian," Sassamon said vigorously. "I am disappointed for the first time with Pastor Winslow. He should thank God he has such a good son—and you and your mother—you have a good husband and father."

Rachel had no answer, and John said, "I must go to Governor Bradford now."

"Is it bad news again, John?"

"Not good! Philip is trying to get the other tribes more unhappy with white men. And he is having success." Sassamon shifted his feet. "I think it will come soon," he added.

"You must be very careful, John," Rachel continued. "He will kill you if he even suspects you are talking to the authorities."

He shrugged, "Do not worry about me, Nahteeah." Then he smiled, saying earnestly, "You must learn to love your father."

Then he was gone as quickly as he had come. His visit left Rachel so shaken she could not concentrate on her work. She went to the beach, walking the rocky shores and thinking, wondering if John was right. "But I don't hate my father," she protested to herself. Even as she spoke the words, she knew she was being dishonest. *I've never forgiven him for deserting me and mother!* she admitted.

She walked home slowly, unhappy with herself. When she arrived, her mother had come back, so she went to where she was sitting outside in the sun. "Mother, I've got to tell you something."

"What is it, Rachel?"

Rachel hesitated, then said with a vigorous gesture of her head, "I—I can't feel right about my father!" she said. "No matter how hard I try, I still can't—can't—"

"You can't forgive him, Rachel, is that it?"

"Yes—but I *want* to, Mother! Why is it so hard?"

Lydia shook her head, and looked out at the sea before she said with bitterness in her voice, "I'm having the same trouble, Rachel. And it's pride—nothing more. We've been hurt, and we won't be satisfied until *he* suffers as we have!"

Rachel looked at her mother in amazement, for she had never known of Lydia bearing a grudge. "But, Mother—surely *you* don't feel that way!"

Lydia suddenly put her fist to her mouth, pressing hard, and Rachel knew that she was stemming a sob that had risen to her throat. "Yes! I feel that way—and God forgive me! But He won't, Rachel, because the Bible says that if we won't forgive those who've wronged us, God will not forgive us!"

Rachel said slowly, "I want to forgive him—but I just *can't!*"

Lydia stared at her daughter and then before she rose to go into the house, she said slowly, "We're finding out something about ourselves, aren't we, Rachel? God blesses us with a miracle—and we throw it back in His face! I wonder how we will pray when we need God? And I wonder if He'll say, 'I gave you a blessing and you rejected it—now you provide your own miracles!' "

Rachel watched her mother go inside. The rest of the afternoon she went slowly about her work, mechanically and duly, unable to forget her mother's words. *Whom would I call on if I needed a miracle?*, she wondered.

And there was no answer except the slight breeze that stirred the trees and the far-off cry of a curlew.

CHAPTER THIRTEEN

DEATH IN THE WINTER

★　★　★　★

Jude Alden was a contented man. He leaned against the rail fence and gazed off into the distance, savoring the knowledge that every blade of grass and every tree as far as the eye could see belonged to him. He glanced down at Rachel, then raised his arm and indicated a low rise of hills off in the distance. "There's where the new plot begins—see? There—by that line of timber off to the left."

"How many acres did you say?"

"Over three hundred in the whole tract." Jude chuckled deep in his chest, and a broad smile crossed his lips as he said, "Old Taylor thought he'd do me in on the swap—but I knew if I held out, he'd get greedy and make a snatch for that worthless piece I traded for this. I let word get out that the new road to the north was going to go through my place—and I made sure that Taylor thought I *didn't* know it. Why, it was enough to make a dog laugh, Rachel, the way he came up so innocent and offered to trade me this place! It was like taking candy away from a baby, I tell you!"

Rachel looked up with an uneasy smile at Alden as they walked back along the trail to his house. She was sure her grandfather would never approve of his methods. Besides, she could never understand the pleasure he got in trading, and now she asked curiously, "Doesn't your conscience ever hurt, Jude? I mean, you traded the old man a worthless piece of rocky ground for one of the best farms in the area."

He stared at her in surprise, and the blank look on his face showed that he had never once considered such a thing a moral issue. He studied how to explain it to her, his sharp-featured face expressive. "Why, I'd not treat a widow or an orphan this way—but if a man wants to do some trading with me, he'd best watch out for himself. It's just a game, you see, Rachel? I try to best him and he tries to best me—and that's the fun of it!"

She thought about it, but her own sense of right and wrong was too limited to render judgment, so she shrugged and said, "Well, you own it, Jude—all this land. But I can enjoy the trees— and the birds sound just as sweet to me with their singing as they do to you."

He said little more as they made their way back to the cabin. Finally he smiled and said, "Now, you're a woman, Rachel, and not able to think about business like a man. And that's all right with me. I don't want a wife to do the trading in the family."

"What do you want from a wife, Jude?" she asked mischievously. She was amused to see his jaw drop and a look of confusion sweep across his regular features.

He suddenly stopped, pulled her around and kissed her resoundingly. His lips were cold in the December chill, and the bulky clothes they both wore hindered him. "I guess I want a wife for *that* for one thing!" he laughed, then kissed her again, holding her soft form tightly until she pulled away.

"Come on, I'll race you back to the house!" She took off running, and was so light and fleet of foot that he did not catch up to her until they turned into the clearing where his house sat. She stopped suddenly and was not even breathing hard as she said, "You've got company." She lifted her hand to shield her eyes from the bright winter sun and bit her lip, adding, "It's my father and John Sassamon."

He gave her an odd look. Then as they walked across the open field he said, "Nobody in Plymouth understands about your family, Rachel." She didn't answer and he went on, "Your father came out of nowhere eight months ago. He doesn't live with you and your mother. He runs all over the country with those savages, and I suppose he's made a fortune in beaver by this time. But—you never say a word about him."

"It's a family problem, Jude." Rachel shrugged and added only, "There was a falling out years ago, between him and my mother."

Jude shook his head. "I don't like to say anything about your family, Rachel, but it'd be a tragedy if your mother took him back."

"Why do you say that?" She lowered her voice, for they were less than a hundred feet away from the house. "My grandfather says he's a changed man."

"Changed from *what?*" Jude asked instantly. "This country is on the verge of an Indian war, Rachel. Philip is a madman! And your father spends all his time with the Indians."

"It's the Praying Indians he's with most, Jude. He's working with Reverend Eliot a great deal."

"Praying Indians!" Jude muttered. "When the trouble comes, there'll just be one kind of Indian! You'll see. And your friend Sassamon will be right with them!"

Rachel had argued this with Jude many times, but it was hopeless; Alden, like many of the settlers who lived in the wilderness areas, had no confidence in any Indian.

Sassamon stepped forward, saying, "Hello, Rachel."

She took his hand and gave him a warm smile. "This is a surprise, John. Hello, Father. You're looking thin." She took his hand also, and thought about the many months it had taken for her to do a simple thing like calling Matthew Winslow "father." He had been to their house exactly four times over the past eight months, never staying the night anywhere except in the inn. It was always something like an armed truce, and none of them had been able to feel very comfortable, though outwardly they appeared to be.

"We're like a bunch of porcupines!" Gilbert had exclaimed in disgust one evening after Matthew left the house. "We just seem to be full of spines that keep poking somebody else in tender places!"

"Well," Lydia said, "it's not as bad as it was. We can sit down and talk now, at least."

"That's just, *wonderful*, isn't it?" Gilbert had growled. "I'm actually able to sit down and *talk* with my own son!"

For the first time in her life, Rachel had flared up at her grandfather. "Well, you're as bad as she is! He comes here and sits and you talk about nothing but some idiotic sermon! It wouldn't kill you to *bend* a little and say a kind word to the poor man, would it?"

Gilbert and Lydia had stared at her, and finally Gilbert had said resentfully, "Maybe you're right, Rachel, but there's some deep wounds in our past. Scars that don't heal all at once. But what about you? I don't notice as how you're sitting on his lap, and if you said one warm kind thing to Matthew tonight, I missed it!"

Lydia had stopped the quarrel, saying, "We're all guilty, Gilbert. The next time he comes, I—I'll be more—gentle."

Now, standing there in the cold air, that scene flashed back to Rachel, and she made herself smile at Matthew. "We've been disappointed that you've not been back to the house."

Matthew's face changed suddenly, and a warmth appeared in his bright blue eyes. "Why, thank you, Rachel. I've thought of you every day."

Jude said, "Where you headed, Mr. Winslow?"

"John and I thought we'd make a sweep around the north country. Maybe find a few beaver streams we can trap in, in the spring."

Jude frowned. "I'd be careful if I were you. You know how jealous Philip is of his territory."

"Philip won't mind if we take a few beaver, Alden," Matthew said easily. "Indians don't mind sharing things."

Jude grew defensive then, for Winslow was actually saying that settlers such as himself made the Indians go on the warpath. "Well, I been hearing that the tribes are restless. You hear about the attack on that farm in Bennington?"

"Bunch of wild young boys drunk on whiskey," John Sassamon answered. "They weren't Wampanoags, either." He turned and said, "I'll be back this way in three days, Mr. Winslow. Where can we meet?"

"Why, right here, if Alden doesn't mind."

"Of course." There was not a great deal of warmth in Jude's voice, but he could not refuse with Rachel standing there.

"Rachel and her grandfather are here for a visit. You'll be welcome."

"Lydia didn't come?" Matthew asked Rachel.

"Oh, yes. She and Grandfather are over at Pageville. There's a little church there having a struggle and they visit when they can to try to help out."

"You'll stay for supper, Mr. Winslow?" Jude asked.

"Yes, please do, Father," Rachel said quickly. There had been a cold formality in Jude's voice, and she had seen Matthew start to shake his head. He was surprised at her insistence. "Why, I think I will."

John was not included in the invitation, but as he left, he whispered to Rachel. "That's my good girl! You honor your father and you'll live a long time, like the scripture says!" He started to leave, then paused and said so softly she almost missed it, "God love you, Nahteeah—you've been a good sister to this Indian!" Then he left on silent steps and disappeared into the line of trees to the east of the house.

Rachel spent most of the afternoon cooking, and to her surprise, Jude and her father walked around the farm talking, apparently content with each other's company. Jude was making an attempt, she saw, to get to know her father, and it gave her a warm feeling to see it.

Gilbert and Lydia got back just as the sun, white as if frozen by the raw winter wind, slipped behind the tall oaks. They came inside the house and as they took off their heavy coats, Rachel said, "Did you know Father is here?"

Lydia stopped abruptly, turned and said quickly, "No, where is he?"

"Jude's been running him all over the farm." She laughed ruefully, adding, "You'd think Father was interested in *buying* it, the way he's looked at it."

Gilbert came to stand before the fireplace, holding his hands out to the flickering blaze. There was a wry light in his eyes and he said, "Matthew wouldn't be interested in this farm—maybe in the man who owns it?"

Rachel flushed slightly, then said, "Mother, will you help me set the food out? They went up to see a tract of land that Jude is interested in. Said he wanted to know what Father thought of it."

By the time the table was set, the two men walked in. Rachel did not miss the way her father's face changed at the sight of Lydia and his father. She could not say exactly what it was, but there was a certain sadness in his face that she had gradually come to notice. It was not gloom or despair, and few would even discern it, but now as she watched him enter, she saw his whole expression subtly alter. As his eyes fell on Lydia, she saw a longing in his face and a soft smile on his lips. *He still loves her*, she thought. Then her attention turned to Jude.

Jude's face was flushed from the long walk, and he spoke briskly, saying, "Look at that food!" He moved to the table, shook his head and said, "I haven't had a home-cooked meal like this since the last time you were here."

"Hello, Matthew," Gilbert said, coming to take his hand. "You've been away for a long time."

"Yes," Lydia said quickly, coming to stand beside Gilbert. "We expected you back before this."

"I've been on some pretty far trails since I was in Plymouth." He hesitated, then added, "You're both looking well."

Rachel interrupted, "We can talk while we eat—everything's getting cold."

They all sat down and spent the most relaxed time any of them had had since Matthew's return. Time had blunted the initial shock, so they were not constantly ill at ease just being with him. It helped to have the presence of Jude, making it necessary to speak of ordinary things in a normal fashion.

Jude kept the conversation going, and as the two women kept the food coming and the cups filled, he told Gilbert how he'd been increasing his holdings. "Land will never be so cheap as it is now, Rev. Winslow!" he exclaimed. "Now's the time to buy up every inch of ground you can, because this country will be worth a great deal of money in the years to come."

The rest of them listened, saying little, and finally the meal ended. As the women cleaned the table and put the dishes away, the men sat around talking idly of local matters. Rachel came and sat off to one side, joined by her mother.

Gilbert had been telling of the church close by. Then he turned to Matthew. "Deacon Lattimore tells me you've been quite an encouragement to him, son."

"Why, I've done little enough," Matthew protested.

"Lattimore would disagree," his father smiled. "He thinks you're quite a Bible scholar. Told us over and over how much he's appreciated your visits. And I didn't know how much you'd done to help with the Indian mission schools."

"Oh, John is responsible for most of that. I've just been able to help a bit with the cost."

Gilbert saw that his son was embarrassed, so he merely smiled and said, "God will bless your work, I'm sure."

At last Matthew went to sleep in the barn, and Gilbert and Lydia retired. Jude and Rachel sat before the fire talking for a while.

Jude had been put in a mellow mood by the quiet evening, and he talked of things he hoped to do—not business matters, but of things he'd never shared with her. His face grew dreamy, more relaxed than she'd ever seen him, and he moved his hands expansively as he spoke of travel, of going to England, even to Germany, someday. For a long time she sat there, her feet curled under her, her head resting on her palms as she listened intently. Several times he said *we* when speaking of journeys and plans, and she smiled quietly, thinking of how carefully he'd avoided any direct talk such as that for a long time.

He got up to poke up the fire, then came to sit beside her; she said in a whisper, "I love it when you talk like that, Jude!"

She made a lovely picture as she sat there, the golden firelight catching fire in her eyes, her lips slightly parted. His blood was stirred, and he lowered his head and kissed her, then put his arms around her, holding her close.

She allowed this, even went so far as to put her hand on his neck, her heart beating faster. Then just as she was drawing back from the increasing pressure of his lips, whispering, "Jude, we mustn't—" the front door suddenly opened, and Matthew entered, saying, "Alden—there's some kind of—"

Jude and Rachel pulled away so rapidly that she nearly fell off the bench. Her hair fell in disarray and there was a look of guilt in the way they came to their feet, staring at Matthew who stopped suddenly, the words broken off abruptly.

He stared at them, and for the first time in her life, Rachel saw the Winslow anger she'd heard about since she was a child.

Her father's light eyes blazed like blue fire, and he actually took a step forward so suddenly that Jude stepped backward and raised his hands!

"Don't!" Rachel cried, taking a step forward, and it was well she did, for it brought her father's eyes to her, and she saw his wrath turn to sorrow as he looked at her. Then he pulled himself together and said, "There's some sort of animal after the stock, Alden—a bear, I think."

Jude, welcoming the break in Matthew's mood, leaped to pull a musket from the wall, crying, "I'll take care of him."

He left the room at a dead run, and Matthew turned without a word to leave, but Rachel said sharply, "Wait!"

"Yes, Rachel?"

She was suddenly angry through and through, and she did not realize it was at herself instead of her father. She threw her head back and it was his turn to see some of the Winslow wrath, this time in the French blackness of his daughter's eyes!

"I resent what you think!" she said in a tense voice that quivered with rage.

"I—said nothing," Matthew answered. He stood there, a tall shape in the flickering light of the candle, the sharp planes of his face bolder in relief.

She struck out at him; it was not the embarrassment of the moment that drove her to a rage, but the buried resentment and anger at what she had felt from the moment of his return. His act of betrayal fourteen years ago struck the fire that blazed out at Matthew as she stood there.

"You're so *holy*, aren't you?" she cried. "The father looking so offended that his precious daughter is kissing a man!" Tears then flooded her eyes, and she dashed them away angrily, saying bitterly, "Well, what gives you the right to think *anything*? Where were you when I was growing up—when all the other children had fathers—and I—didn't!" Her voice began to break as sobs rose to her lips, and she took two steps that brought her up to him, staring up into his face with an anger she had never shown to a living soul. "Why did you have to come back?" she cried. Then she raised her hand and struck him in the face twice, each time crying out as if he had struck her!

He stood there, the burning imprint of her hand on his

cheeks. His eyes held no anger—only a deep, profound sadness. He let the silence run on, so that the sound of a log breaking in the fire sounded very loud. Then he said so quietly that she almost missed it for her sobbing.

"I can't blame you for feeling that way, Rachel," he said. He hesitated, then added, "I never should have come to this place."

She turned blindly and ran to her room, not hearing the door close. For a long time she cried bitterly, until there was nothing in her but emptiness. Finally she got up and undressed and went to bed. As she pulled the covers over her, she thought of the sadness in his face—that face so much like Gilbert's from whom she'd never had an unkind word, and her throat ached with the pain of it all.

Tomorrow! Tomorrow I'll make it right with him, she thought. All night she lay there, longing for the dawn.

But he was gone, and Jude, not meeting her eyes, said, "He just left."

Rachel waited until she had a chance to speak with Lydia alone, and when she had told the whole story, her eyes filling with tears, Lydia took her in her arms. "You'll have a chance to tell him you were wrong." She hesitated, then added, "I have to tell him some things, too—many things."

Rachel and Lydia waited anxiously for Matthew to make one of his rare visits, but he did not come back to Plymouth. Two weeks passed, and the winter scored the land, closing the trails to travel. They did not speak of him, but he was not far from their thoughts. Lydia vacillated between a longing to recapture those lost years and feelings of bitterness that would spring up, locking her in a vise of unforgiveness.

The weeks ran on into February. Then the settlement was shaken with a violence such as it had not known in years.

Rachel and Gilbert were on their way to take food to a widow with three small children. They had just turned to go past the cannon on the square when they saw a crowd milling around near the Common House, making so much noise that Gilbert said, "Must be trouble."

He led her in that direction, and they were met by Jake Mason, whose face was blazing with anger, red despite the freezing wind. "They killed 'im, they did!"

"Killed who, Mason?" Gilbert demanded quickly.

"Why, that young Indian—" Mason stopped at once, cast a quick look at Rachel, and said in embarrassment, "It's bad news fer you, Miss Rachel!"

"For me?" Rachel thought with a blinding stab of fear that it might be her father.

"It's the young Indian lad, you know? John Sassamon. Murdered, he is!"

Rachel gave a sharp cry and followed Gilbert, who pushed his way through the crowd until they came to stand before a sled drawn by two large horses. The driver was a man he knew slightly, Samuel Holt, a deacon of the church at Lenton, one of the magistrates of the town. He said at once, "We have much trouble, Pastor Winslow!"

"What happened, Mr. Holt?" Gilbert asked.

"Why, one of our young men found the body of Sassamon nigh onto a week ago. John Wingfield found him, and it was strange! John and two others was passing by a frozen pond near Middleborough and they noticed something out on the surface of the pond. It looked like a man's hat, and they found a musket close by. Well, a man's not likely to leave them things in the dead of winter, so John took another look. And then he saw it!" Holt shivered a little, and went on, his words being devoured by the crowd.

"Right there under the ice was a face! They ran to get an ax, and they chopped the body out, and it was John Sassamon!"

Gilbert felt the shock run through Rachel, and he held her with one arm, asking, "He drowned, then, and the pond froze over him?"

"Well, so we thought, but Sassamon was an Indian. He wouldn't have been fool enough to cross the ice before it was hard. We took a look and seen a swelling on the side of his head, which could have come from a blow—but then we found out his neck was broken! Now a man falling into a pond, he's not likely to do that, is he now, Pastor?"

"Not likely."

"No, indeed!" Holt said vigorously. "We began to think the lad had been murdered, and it made to look like an accident."

"No way to prove that, is there, Mr. Holt?"

The magistrate had the audience in his hand, and he savored the moment. "Not for most, I'm thinking. Be sure your sin will find you out.' " He nodded as a few of his hearers muttered *amens*.

"What? You did discover something?" Gilbert asked.

"Yes, Reverend, we did—and it was like this: An Indian who'd been on the outs with King Philip seen the whole thing! And he come to me and when he told his story, we arrested three men for the murder. And we had a trial—well, we had *two* trials, as a matter of fact, to be sure. One was made up of settlers and the other of Indians as can be trusted."

"What was your finding?"

"Guilty as charged—and sentenced to be hung, all three of them!" Holt stared at the crowd and said solemnly, "And hear this, if you please—Philip was in a rage, and all three of the men denied it. They stood on the gallows and swore they was innocent." Holt again paused, and despite the cold, his brow was beaded with sweat, and he pulled out a large handkerchief and mopped his forehead with a trembling hand before he went on.

"We hung two of them, but the rope broke under the last one, and he came to himself! He confessed that all three of them had done the deed, and he swore Philip put 'em all up to it! Well, we hung him again and the rope *didn't* break that time!"

A babble of questions rose up, but Gilbert's voice rang strong and clear. "What about Philip?"

Holt stared at him, licked his lips, then shook his head.

"That's what I've come to tell you," he said. "Philip is on the warpath, and we got to organize—because when that red devil breaks loose, there's not a man, woman, or helpless child in this part of the world who's got a chance to live!"

CHAPTER FOURTEEN

THE WINTER IS PAST

★ ★ ★ ★

Spring melted the icy covering of the land early, freeing the rivers by early March. It was one of the fairest springs that Rachel remembered, but she could not rejoice in it. The memory of her last words to her father came to her day and night: *Why did you come back?* She avoided his presence whenever possible.

Lydia observed Rachel's reaction. In turn she saw what Rachel's rejection was doing to Matthew. It made her ashamed of her own resistance to him, suppressing the happy memories of their life together, but she could not seem to break out of her resentment. As long as she had thought him dead, she could manage to forgive him. But he was alive! And no matter what changes had come about in his life, she could not get past her own deep bitterness. She longed to speak to her strong-willed daughter, but could not find a way. How could she help Rachel forgive when she herself could not?

June came, and Rachel grew restless. She walked the shores of the sea and followed the nearby paths through the woods, and she threw herself into the work of the church with an energy that both Gilbert and Lydia recognized.

Relief at last offered itself in the form of a trip to Swansea, a village only a few miles from Jude's farm. Mercy and Praise God Pittman had moved from Plymouth in the fall, and the stocky young husband dropped by unexpectedly to ask a favor.

"It's time for the baby—and Mercy is asking for you to come and be with her," he said to Rachel. " 'Course there's some older married women there—but she's partial to you, Miss Rachel."

Rachel said instantly, "Of course, I'll come."

"But there's talk about the Indians, Praise God," Lydia said. "Why don't you bring Mercy here to have her baby?"

"I tried, but she says she wants me around. I told her I'd beat her into submission," he joked, grinning, broadly, "but she knows she's safe enough 'till the little 'un comes!"

Lydia resisted the idea, for the settlement swarmed with talk about the possibility of Indian raids, but Rachel got around her by getting Gilbert to agree. She had always been able to sway him, and when she put the request in the form of an opportunity to perform a Christian charity, he could hardly refuse.

"You're a fool where that girl is concerned, Gilbert!" Lydia said angrily. "War could break out at any time, and you know it!"

Gilbert felt the rebuke keenly, but he had given his word, so when he and Lydia said goodbye to Rachel as she left with Praise God, he could only make one last plea. "Wait until next week, Rachel, and I'll go with you myself."

She laughed and kissed him, her eyes bright with excitement. "Where's your faith, Reverend Winslow? God's still in control, isn't He?" She ran to Lydia, gave her a tremendous hug, whispering, "Don't you worry now, Mother. Who knows, maybe you'll get a son-in-law out of this trip!"

She left with Pittman, and when they were out of sight, Lydia stood there staring, her dark eyes filled with apprehension. "She's been very unhappy lately, Gilbert."

"And so have you, Lydia," he answered, looking intently down into her face. He made a restless movement with his shoulders, then said tightly, "The Lord has been very quiet to me lately—and after all these years of sweet harmony with Him, that's very painful. I—I feel rebuked by the way I've treated Matthew, Lydia. I had a dream about it last week."

"A dream?"

"Yes, I dreamed I was going into a beautiful house, and somehow I knew it was the house of God. I went through a door and there was a beautiful light, so powerful I couldn't bear to look at it, but I yearned to go closer, for I knew it was my Beloved! So I tried to go closer, but out of the light came a voice, and it said, 'You are my son, but I will not accept you until you have been made pure!' " Gilbert stared at her, and there was such pain in his honest eyes that she wanted to weep. Then he added, "It doesn't take a Daniel to give the interpretation, Lydia. I've been saying that to my own son ever since he came back."

"You haven't been unkind, Gilbert—"

"Not *unkind!*" he cried out. "God in heaven! *Not unkind*—is that all I can be to my son who comes back from the dead? What if the father in the story of the Prodigal had been only that—*not unkind!* Lydia, I should have brought forth the best robe and put a ring on his finger! I should have shouted from the rooftop, *This my son was dead, and is alive again—he was lost, and is found!*"

Gilbert's eyes were blinded with tears, and he wheeled, stumbling away, his shoulders shaking with grief.

Lydia was overwhelmed, and she sought the quiet of her bedroom, fell on her knees, and prayed as she had never prayed before. All day she stayed there, unconscious of the passage of time. The sun reached its zenith, then began its fall; and still she called out to God. Sometimes her cries were out of the Bible, "Help, Lord, for thy servant perisheth!" Her grief often struck her dumb and she simply lay on her face saying nothing; then a prayer would rise up in her very innermost being, as she called out, the absolute certainty that she was in the presence of God flooded her spirit.

Darkness came, and still she prayed. On into the night as the stars came out to make icy dots of light on a velvety sky, she waited for something. She seemed to be tied to the diurnal movement of the earth itself, and as the night covered the earth, so her spirit seemed to be covered by a terrible darkness. She remembered when her child was born, the pain and grief, and all night long she struggled to give birth to something in her spirit.

By dawn her strength was gone. She lay spent and drained on the floor, her hair wet with perspiration and her limbs trembling with weakness. She could not cry any longer, and as the ebony sky outside blushed into pale crimson, the room suddenly seemed to catch some of that light. Lydia did not lift her head, but she felt her heart strangely warmed, and her spirit became calm.

She felt as the disciples must have felt as the stormy, raging seas that filled their ears with blasts of sound suddenly fell silent and only a hush remained.

For a long time she lay there, drinking in the silence, knowing that she was in the presence of the Lord God of all the earth. Then a message came, beginning as a whisper far away, but swelling louder until it filled her heart:

> Rise up, my love, my fair one, and come away. For, lo, the winter is past, the rain is over and gone; the flowers appear on the earth; the time of the singing of birds is come, and the voice of the turtle is heard again in our land.

Never did Lydia forget that voice, nor did she forget the commandment that followed, for after the words of Solomon's Song echoed sweetly in her heart, there followed a time which she knew she could never speak of on earth. Some things are too sacred for words. When she finally rose from the floor, her limbs were cramped with pain, but her heart was filled with a peace such as she had not known existed.

All week long she walked with God, shut in with a holy presence, and the light on her face told Gilbert that she had passed out of her crucible.

He was made sure of this when on Wednesday of the following week, he came home late in the afternoon to say, "Matthew came in today with a load of beaver pelts."

She looked up suddenly from the garment she was sewing, and said quietly, "Gilbert, I want you to go to Matthew. Tell him I want to see him."

He stared at her, caught off guard by her sudden announcement. "You mean—now?"

"Yes."

He slowly got to his feet, a question in his eyes, but he said nothing. He had learned over the years that when his dark-eyed daughter-in-law made up her mind, there was nothing to do but stand aside.

"I'll go at once, Lydia," he said, and left at a fast gait. She sat there holding the cloth for a while, her eyes fixed on nothing. Then she took a deep breath and said, "Amen."

Thirty minutes later she heard his footsteps on the walk.

Her heart quickened and she stood up. Then he was at the door knocking.

"Come in, Matthew," she said quietly, trying to suppress her emotions.

He opened the door to see her standing beside the table, and as always, her dark loveliness caught at him powerfully. He stepped inside, closing the door, then stood there waiting for her word. "You wanted to see me, Lydia?"

Her oval face was framed by a halo of dark curls, and the smooth planes of her features made her dark eyes seem enormous. Her full red lips trembled slightly, then she nodded. "Matthew, I want to ask you—to forgive me."

He stared at her, noting that she was trying to maintain her composure. "Why, Lydia, I don't think—"

"Please—" she whispered softly, "don't say anything! Ever since you came back, I've been—terrible!" Tears welled up in her eyes and she let them run down her cheeks unheeded. "I've been so filled up with bitterness and hurt pride that God has had to break me! And it's not only that I've been unjust, but I've made Rachel feel the same—and that's what's breaking my heart!"

Matthew stood there quietly enough, but his emotions were chaotic. He shook his head, and wonder touched his eyes as he said, "Lydia, you have nothing to reproach yourself for."

"But I do!" she cried out, and she raised her hands and came to him so suddenly that he caught her in his strong arms. She looked up into his face, and slowly she said, "I am your wife, Matthew—if you want me!"

A great roaring seemed to fill his head, stirring memories he thought had died long ago. She put her hands on his neck, and as she drew his head down, she suddenly cried out, "I love you, Matthew!"

He kissed her gently at first; then exulting in her courageous offer of herself, he finally lifted his head and whispered huskily, "I've never stopped loving you—Princess!"

The use of the old name ran through Lydia, and she laughed softly. "You haven't forgotten?"

"Forgotten?" he said with a smile. "I've lived on those scraps of memories from our love."

She pulled closer to him, and pressing her face against his chest, she said, "No more! Thank God, we can start over—and we'll make better memories than any you've ever dreamed, Husband!"

Gilbert had waited at the inn for Matthew to come back, but when nine o'clock came, he gave an odd smile and glanced toward the hill where his house stood. Getting to his feet, he said to the innkeeper, "Brother Tillotson, I have a strong impression that my son will not be using his room tonight, so I believe I'll use his bed." He started up the stairs, then paused and called back with a gleeful note in his voice, "I don't think my son will be requiring the use of this room anymore. I believe he's found more suitable accommodations!"

CHAPTER FIFTEEN

CAPTIVE!

★ ★ ★ ★

For two days after Rachel arrived at Swansea, she managed to forget her woes, giving all her time to Mercy, who was having a difficult time of it. The baby was not due for three months, but as healthy as Mercy had been, she was so ill she could eat little and had grown so weak that Rachel had to attend to her constantly.

Praise God left to go back to Plymouth for a load of tools, and Jude came the next day. He found Rachel churning butter, and came to her at once.

"Jude, I was hoping you'd come!" she said, and rose to greet him. He embraced her and gave her a quick kiss. Then she pushed him away with a smile, saying, "That will have to wait. How long can you stay?"

"Just until tomorrow," he said, and then a worried look crossed his face. "You shouldn't be here, Rachel—and neither should Mercy. The savages around here are stirring up trouble, and when it comes, nobody will be safe—not man, woman, or child."

She laughed and squeezed his arm playfully, "Oh, you're getting to be a regular prophet of doom! Besides, all Indians aren't 'savages,' as you call them. Sit down and tell me what you've been doing."

They had a pleasant day together, and that night they sat

up long after Mercy went to bed, talking and laughing. He finally got up, and as she walked with him to the door, he suddenly stopped, turned and said earnestly, "I want to marry you, Rachel."

She stopped, taken aback by the suddenness of it. For one moment she stood there, then she said quietly, "All right, Jude."

He took her in his arms, kissed her more gently than ever, and said, "I love you very much, Rachel! Very much!"

Then he released her and walked out of the room quickly, as if he did not trust himself. Rachel stood there, leaning against the wall, thinking how different life would be shortly, then she went to bed and slept a dreamless sleep.

The next morning she arose and was fixing some gruel for Mercy when she heard the first cries. Puzzled by the voices, she put the skillet down and started for the door. When she opened it she saw a wagon loaded with women and small children careen wildly around the big oak tree in the yard. A bearded man leaped from the driver's seat, and seeing Rachel, yelled at her, "Get these women into the house!"

"Indians are coming!" a young woman carrying a baby answered, looking over her shoulder. "They're killing everything in their path!"

Rachel's heart turned to ice, and she deposited the child in the house. Running back to get another, she saw Jude running from the barn with his musket. "Is it Indians, Isaac?" he yelled.

"They'll be here in thirty minutes, Jude," the man answered, his face grim. "They wiped out the Hendersons and the Potters and God knows how many more! My boys is coming—there they are now—but we'll be hard put to it, Jude!"

"We'll have to fort up in the house," Jude nodded. He turned and saw Rachel, then came to her. His face was pale and set as he said, "Do what you can to help the women and children!"

"I can shoot, Jude!" Rachel cried. "Grandfather taught me that."

"Good," the older man nodded. "We'll need everyone who can fire a gun. I got a load of ammunition and some extra muskets in the wagon!"

Two boys aged about fifteen came running up, completely

winded, and their father, whose name was Trowbridge, said, "John, I want you and Luke to load every musket we got. Come on, now, we got precious little time!"

They all began hauling the muskets and ammunition inside the house, and for the next fifteen minutes Jude and Trowbridge organized their little force as well as they could. There were four women, all of whom could load a musket, each situated so the shooters could reach the freshly loaded firearms easily.

"They'll be here soon," Trowbridge said. He looked around at his wife and children, then said, "Let us give ourselves into the hands of God." They all bowed their heads and he prayed a short prayer, then said urgently, "Me and my boys will take the downstairs, Jude. You two take the upstairs. You ought to be able to keep 'em off up there, but they'll be trying to pot you first."

"Come on, Rachel!" Jude said, climbing up the ladder leading to the loft, when he placed her at one of the small windows. "They'll have to cross that clearing to get to the house, and we can stop that—at least until it's dark."

"Do we have any chance at all, Jude?" she asked quietly.

He came to her, put his arm around her and they stood there in the quiet. "I don't know, Rachel," he said softly. "I been told all my life that God is able to do anything. Maybe He can get us out of this but I have to tell you, it's a mighty small chance."

"I thought so."

"I—I'm glad I asked you to marry me last night, Rachel," he said. "You know what I thought about all night?"

"What, Jude?"

"I thought, *That Rachel—she'll make a better man out of me!*"

He kissed her quickly, and she said, "I hope we have a life together, but if we don't—at least we found each other."

Just then a shot rang out; he wheeled and, picking up his musket, laid it on the sill and aimed carefully, then fired. "That's *one* redskin who won't do us any harm!"

Rachel picked up a musket and laid it carefully on the sill. Her heart was pounding, and she wondered if she could send a man to death. Just then she saw an Indian painted in various hues running for the house, a rifle in one hand and a hatchet in the other. At his belt were several bloody scalps, and without hesitation she drew a bead on his chest and felled him with one carefully placed shot.

Before she had a chance to feel sick, another Indian approached from the far side, and she snatched up another loaded musket and hurried her shot. His leg was knocked from under him as he fell, badly wounded.

A loud volley of shots erupted from the first floor, and both Rachel and Jude emptied their muskets, then loaded them quickly as the Indians withdrew. But they were not gone, and their hideous screams of rage cut through the morning air.

For over an hour there was no sign of an attack, but then a sudden burst of musket fire riddled the house, sounding like gravel as it struck. Every pane of glass was shattered; a sliver of it sliced Rachel's cheek, but she was unaware of it until she felt the blood running down her face, and even then had no time to do more than wipe it with her sleeve.

As the shots continued to rake the house, driving them away from the windows, there was another rush, and this time three of the Indians managed to reach the house. They threw their weight against the stout oak door; when it refused to budge they moved to try the windows, but were cut down at once by Trowbridge and his sons.

Again there was a lull. Rachel eased her head around the facing of the window. From a shelter of gum trees, a blazing arrow flew in an arc and fell to the ground a few feet from the house. "Get ready to run for it! They'll get the roof sure!" Jude shouted.

He was right, for despite their attempts to drive the archers back and disturb their aim, an arrow sailed high, and landed with a *thud* in the roof.

The dry thatch caught at once, and within minutes Rachel and Jude were forced to climb down the ladder, blinded by the thick smoke.

"We'll have to take the fight outside, Jude!" Trowbridge shouted over the roar of the blaze. "We'll burn to death in this cabin!"

Suddenly the roof began to collapse, and wisps of blazing thatch fell past them to the floor.

"I'll go first and you come after me, Jude!"

Trowbridge threw the door open and started to run out, but an arrow hit him in the chest. He dropped his musket to pull at the shaft, but another caught him in the throat and he fell to the floor lifeless.

"Everybody out!" Jude shouted, and they all made a rush at the door. Rachel ran to Mercy who was struggling to get to her feet, and by the time she helped her to the door and stepped outside, the butchery was in full sway.

One burly Indian had seized John Trowbridge with one hand and even as Rachel watched, he drew his war club up and killed the boy with one blow to the head. The other boy was trying to protect his mother from two warriors who were pulling at her, and one of them slashed him across the throat with a long knife, leaving him dead.

The other Indian then turned to the woman who was on her knees clutching a small baby to her breast. She turned her face up, and cried out, "Please—don't kill my baby!" But the Indian gave a howl and killed them both.

Screams of agony and fear scored the air. Suddenly a shout louder than the rest rang out: "Rachel! Look out!"

Rachel whirled to see a tall, muscular Indian with red paint smeared all over his body running for her, a hatchet raised high.

Jude came through the surging bodies to her right, and the Indian took his eyes off Rachel and Mercy. He swerved to meet Jude's charge, making a wild sweeping blow with his hatchet. Jude parried it on the barrel of his musket, then swung the heavy butt around, catching the Indian with a blow that crushed his skull.

"Rachel!" Jude yelled and turned to her; even as he turned, a bulky form on his left appeared—a short Indian with a heavy war club raised high. Jude caught a glimpse of him, but he was too late. The heavy head of the club struck him in the temple, and he dropped to the earth dead.

As the short Indian swung around and raised his club to strike Mercy, Rachel instinctively did what she would never have dreamed of. She leaped in front of the woman who had fallen to the ground and faced the savage without a sign of fear.

"In the name of Jesus Christ!" she cried out in a voice that carried like a trumpet over the bloody yard, "I command you to leave this woman alone!"

The Indians stopped short, looking around to see who was calling out. They saw a young white woman standing over her friend. The most fierce warrior of their tribe held a club over her—and she was not afraid.

But it was more than that. She had called on the name of her God, and although none of them were Christians, they were superstitious, and there was magic in what they were seeing.

The short brave who had killed Jude was called Fox. He was not only the most valiant warrior among them, he was also as shrewd as his name suggested. He stood there, aware that the others were watching, and his Indian sense of drama overtook him. He gave a scream and raised his club, whirling it over his head and giving every impression of a man intent on killing.

But the white girl did not move—did not even blink. She said again more quietly this time, "In the name of Jesus, I *command* you to leave us alone!"

Fox let the club fall to his side, and stood there staring at the girl. He was not as impressed with her God as he was with her courage. He had a contempt for most Christians, having seen enough greed in some of them to convince him that their religion was a sham. But one or two had been different, and he was curious.

The blood lust had died down, and he suddenly said in broken English, "We take this one."

A heavy-set Indian leaped forward to grab her arm, but Rachel drew back and knelt beside Mercy. She looked straight at Fox and said, "You are a *woman* if you hurt this mother!" The word she used was one that John Sassamon had taught her when they were children. It meant a womanish man, one who would rather be with squaws than with warriors, and it was a deadly insult. "If you ever want to rile an Indian," John had said, "just call him that!"

She had heard that Indians conceal a peculiar sense of humor under their impassive faces, and now she saw it. Something about the young girl telling Fox he was womanish tickled their fancy. They began to laugh wildly, like small boys, and it was a sight that Rachel would carry to her grave—those brutal killers smeared with the gore of children and women slapping their hands on their sides and screaming with laughter, taking up the word that she had used on Fox.

Fox himself would have killed a man instantly for such an insult, but the very weakness of Rachel, and the absolute fearlessness of her demeanor somehow cooled his blood; it was the kind of joke an Indian could understand.

He said something she didn't understand, and two Indians, still laughing, came forward. *They are going to kill both of us*, she thought, but they did not. They helped Mercy to her feet, and then marched both women toward their camp, being especially careful with the pregnant woman. Fox came back to the rear of the war party and walked along with Rachel, looking at her from time to time with curiosity. Finally he said, "You not afraid to die?"

"No." For the first time in her life, Rachel realized it was true. Something had happened back there when she had called upon the name of Christ. Suddenly she was aware of a presence with her—perhaps the presence her mother had so often spoken of, the peace that settled on her when she prayed. Rachel had scarcely had time to pray, but she knew—amazingly—that she was not afraid.

"Fox not afraid either." He looked back toward the light from the burning house. "The man I kill—your man?"

She almost broke down then, thinking of Jude's broken body lying on the ground, but drew herself up straight and said calmly, "He was going to be." Then she looked at Fox and said, "Now he is with Jesus Christ."

He met her gaze for a moment, then said, "Your God, Jesus Christ, he not save your people."

She replied at once, "He saved me, Fox."

He nodded, admiration lighting his black eyes. But he said only, "Yes—for now His medicine is strong for you. We will see."

He looked ahead, saying, "We camp here. You take care of woman."

Mercy was almost unconscious, but she was alive. Rachel washed her face with water from the river, and later they ate some of the half-raw meat that one of the Indians didn't want. He tossed it to Rachel as he would have to a dog. Her pride rose up, but she instantly thought, *Do what you have to do to keep Mercy and yourself alive!* She almost forced the meat down Mercy's throat, saying, "Eat! It may be the last for a long time."

They slept a few hours, then Fox prodded Rachel with his foot, saying with a gleam in his beady eyes, "Up—see if you can keep up with Woman." He had taken up her name "Woman" to jibe at her insult. "What is your name?"

She stared at him. "Nahteeah."

He blinked and said, "Who calls you that?"

"My brother—John Sassamon."

He looked at her in a different way, and she had no way of knowing that Fox had hated Sassmon for leaving the old ways for the white man's God, but he had come to admire him for his honesty and willingness to suffer for what he believed.

"We go now," Fox said, but he made the pace easier so that the pregnant woman would not die. In the days that followed, he came often to speak with the two women, and his influence kept them alive.

They arrived the next day at a larger camp, and for several days they rested. Rachel had been afraid that the shock would kill Mercy, but miraculously she seemed to thrive on the scanty diet and the hard conditions. She had one fixed thought in her mind. Every day she would say, "Praise God will find us, Rachel—don't fear!"

Rachel was not at all certain, for the Indians were on the move constantly. Philip was in the camp from time to time, and there were long war talks; then he would ride off again. Soon after, the band would move and raid another group of settlers or a small village, then move as far away from the scene of the raid as possible.

Often Fox would come and sit with Rachel, and in some strange way the two grew into a strange intimacy. He often argued with her about religion, telling her that Jesus was too weak, but she never let him see a doubt. "Jesus has me here for a purpose, Fox," she would say. Once she added to this, "Maybe to show *you* the way to the true God."

He rocked back and forth with silent glee, finally saying, "You want me to be a Woman, like you say first time? Fox a man—Jesus men weak."

She never lost her temper, and he was impressed at the way she accepted the frightful hardships of camp life without a word of complaint. He also was waiting for her to beg for release, but she never said a word.

She worked hard all day, doing her share of the work, and the Indian women, who had been cruel at first, came to marvel at her patience. At first she could do nothing that they did with ease, but by the end of two weeks, she could keep a pace nearly equal with theirs, and they let her alone.

At night she prayed—she and Mercy together; then for long nights she prayed as sleep came and enveloped her. She had dreams of Jude for a while, but she was far too weary to grieve.

She lost track of time, knowing it had been weeks after Jude's death. Then one day Fox came to see her with some news. "We leave this place soon—maybe two days." He waited for her to ask where they would go, but she said nothing. "Maybe you think white men come—take you home? No, we go far away— to Nipmuck people, very far away." He waited for her to speak, then grew angry. "You die with us! Never go home!" She stared at him and said evenly, "Fox, my God has a million angels in His tribe. He could send *one* of them, and you would be helpless against him."

Fox reached out and grabbed her long hair, the first time he had touched her, and said angrily, "No one Jesus man can kill Fox!" He let her go then, and shook his head. "We leave soon."

For the first time, Rachel's faith wavered, and she wept in the darkness. And for the first time as she prayed, there seemed to be no answer. As she rose the next morning and left the old campsite headed for the north, Fox saw her face, and he smiled and said, "Now you see that Jesus God is weak!"

CHAPTER SIXTEEN

"GOD IS STILL IN CONTROL!"

★ ★ ★ ★

News of Philip's raid swept through the country. They heard almost daily of new massacres after Swansea—Dartmough, Taunton, Middleborough and Sudbury. Fifty men were massacred in Lancaster, and forty homes were put to the torch in Groton. The Indians were set to move with Philip as their head, and New England was totally unprepared—strategically, mentally, and spiritually. A company of ill-trained militia would blunder out to be cut to pieces by an Indian ambush, and no one knew what to do.

When the news of the raid of Swansea came, Matthew and Gilbert were stunned. Praise God came riding in wildly, trying to raise a party to go to the rescue.

"They got my Mercy—and your girl, Master Winslow," he moaned bitterly. "God forgive me for leavin' her!"

"Are you sure they're alive, Pittman?" Matthew asked harshly.

"I helped bury everybody, and we followed their heathenish trail," he nodded. "They left the horse alive, at least, and I'm goin' to git my woman back if I have to go alone!"

"I'll be with you in an hour, Praise God," Matthew said. "We have to go tell Rachel's mother; then we'll be leaving."

As they hurried to the house, Gilbert said, "We'll have to raise a militia, Matthew."

He said nothing, but when they went inside the house he went to Lydia and took her in his arms. "The Indians have raided Swansea—and Rachel and Mercy are captives." He looked into her eyes and said, "I'll bring them back, Lydia. Do you believe that?"

The shock weakened her, but she looked up into his strong face, trembling and whispered finally, "If you say so, Matthew. I'll wait for you."

There was no time for long partings, but as Matthew gathered his musket and dressed in old leather clothing used on the trail, Gilbert argued with him.

"You can't go alone, son. Let me go to the governor. He'll *have* to act now!"

Matthew picked up a bedroll and started for the door, then turned and looked at Gilbert. They were so much alike, yet now there was a hardness in his son that the old man had never seen. Always *he* had been the strength of the family, and now he saw that his time was past. "What can you do, Matthew?"

The blue eyes glowed with the light of battle, and Matthew said, "Militia will never catch up with Philip's band or any other Indians. But there's one bunch who can catch them!"

Gilbert asked blankly, "Why, who can do that?"

"The Praying Indians!" Matthew smiled grimly. "I'll pick up a group of them and we'll find out where the women are. It may take a year, but I don't think so. Some of the Praying Indians have family who haven't come over, but they hear things."

Gilbert nodded, then said, "That may *find* them, but how do you plan to get them out of the camp?"

Matthew dropped his bedroll, walked to the wall and reached up. He pulled down Gilbert's sword, the one he'd used to fight Lord Roth and the mutineers who took over the *Mayflower*. He pulled it out of the sheath, held it up, and looked along the line of light that gleamed on the cold steel.

"I'd like to borrow this, Father," he said quietly.

Gilbert smiled, his eyes burning with a longing to go along. But knowing that he would be far too slow, he said, "Take it, my boy—and God go with you."

Matthew suddenly knelt before his father and huskily said, "Give me your blessing, Father!"

Gilbert Winslow prayed over this son, the last of the House of Winslow—and then Matthew rose and was gone.

The Praying Indians had learned to trust Matthew, but they were slow to respond to his call. "We are but a few, and Philip has the largest army of Indians ever seen since the beginning," James Bearclaw said.

"God will provide a way, James. He has preserved the lives of the two women, and I know that He will help us. Will you go if I promise there will be no battle—not for you?"

After discussion with the others, finally James said, "We will find the women—but you must take them yourself."

"A bargain!" Matthew smiled, and later he told Pittman, "We have a chance, Praise God."

"How we gonna do it, Matthew? The two of us against all them savages?"

"Not by might, nor by power—but by my Spirit!" Winslow quoted. "Let's find them first, then we'll see."

It took only four days to get wind of the camp. One of James Bearclaw's relatives, a young man named Rookna, brought word, and James came immediately to Winslow and Pittman.

"We know where they are, but the band is moving soon. Rookna says they are going to the Nipmuck band, and you'll never find them if they get there!"

"Take us to the place!" Matthew said, and in two hours they were on their way toward the west. They traveled hard all night and at dawn, one of the scouts came back with a word. "They are not two miles away, in a little canyon. Not very many warriors—but Fox is there."

"Did you see the women?" Matthew demanded.

"Yes. They are there."

Winslow gave some instructions and they moved out silently. Praise God asked nervously, "I don't think it's going to work, Matthew. This Fox, he's not stupid, is he?"

"No—but he's proud, and that's what we've got to play on. You just keep your hammer down on that musket. We'll have to win by something other than muskets if we win this one, Praise God!"

Rachel was walking down the path toward the rear of the band when she heard the shout; she looked up to see Fox and the other warriors spanning out with their weapons drawn.

"What is it, Rachel?" Mercy asked.

"I don't know. Let's get closer."

They approached the head of the canyon they'd been walking through, and Fox gave them a savage look and waved them to a halt. He looked up at the sides of the cliff on his right, and then to the left. A thick growth of oak covered the lips of the canyon, and he could see nothing.

Then a voice came from somewhere, a ghostly voice that floated on the morning air.

Fox—you are a Woman! It was the same insult that Rachel had offered to him, but this was no frail girl that called so strongly!

"Come down—and you will see what Fox is!" the stocky Indian shouted.

There was no answer for a moment, then suddenly an Indian called out something, and Fox whirled to see a man standing on the edge of the canyon wall—a white man.

Instantly, Fox gave a command and several of his men leaped to go after the intruder, but halted abruptly when a volley rang out, plowing the dust at their feet!

Fox stared at the dust, then raised his eyes to the man on the wall of the canyon. "What you want, white man?"

"I want the two women, Fox!"

Rachel suddenly gasped, and shielding her eyes she stared at the man and breathed a word: "Father!"

Fox whipped his gaze around, then stared back at the man. "I have the women. We will have you, too, white man."

Again a shot rang out, and the dust kicked up at Fox's foot, not two inches away. He jerked the foot back involuntarily and then scowled.

"That shot could have been in your head, Fox," Matthew shouted down at the Indian.

"I am not afraid to die!"

"I say you are!" Winslow challenged. "You are a Woman, Fox, and all your men are cowards, able only to fight women and children!"

A yell of rage went up, and Fox raised his hand for silence. "We soon see who is coward!"

"I will prove you are a Woman." Matthew said, "Choose your four best warriors, give them a blade, and I will fight them by myself!"

Instantly a cry went up, and Fox knew he had no choice. He was leader as long as the others knew he was not afraid. If he did not take up this challenge, he would be challenged by every warrior in the band.

"Come down, big wind!" he said. "You will not say anything for long."

The silence was broken only by the far-off cry of a bird. Rachel's pulse quickened, beating like a hammer.

Matthew disappeared, then in a moment came walking out of a group of trees a hundred yards down the road. He carried no musket, but there was a sword in his hand that flashed in the sun like silver fire. He wore no hat, his auburn hair catching the sunlight.

Every eye was on the tall man as he walked easily along the trail, as blithely as if there were no band of armed savages lined up against him.

"Fox, I give you good day," he said, and then he smiled and nodded at Rachel. "You are all right?"

Rachel caught her breath, answering quietly, "Yes, we have been well treated."

Matthew nodded, then said, "Fox, you have been good to my people, and it hurts me to destroy your warriors. Give me the women and we will part like men."

It was a good try, and Fox smiled briefly. "That not what you say. Are you liar like other white men?"

Winslow suddenly whipped the blade through the air. It made a whistling sound and the suddenness of it startled the Indians. "This is a magic blade, Fox. It was my father's blade, and he has used it to destroy our enemies. It is not like other blades, and I do not like to see young men die like sheep. But you are the leader. I wait for your men."

He turned, took five steps, then wheeled, with the sword held high over his head.

Fox asked, "Who kills this man for our People?"

Every single warrior cried out, but Fox was cautious. He saw something in the white man he did not like, and he wanted no mistakes, so he named four names—all of them tested warriors, not a beginner in the group.

The four men yelled and tossed all their weapons to the ground except for their knives, then began to advance on Winslow, who did not move except to lower his sword, leveling it at the group.

As they approached one of them spoke, and they began to spread out as Matthew had known they would. It was what he himself would have done, had he been one of them. And it was the problem he had pondered night after night, for this plan had been born of desperation—the only thing he could think of with even a slight chance of success.

He had no plan except to have no plan. The only thing he had in his favor was that these men had never seen a swordsman in action. They had no concept of the speed with which he could lower a blade and send it home, faster almost than a striking serpent.

But not if they were behind him, and not if they threw their knives. But knife-throwing was not an art that Indians practiced.

Now, like wolves, they began to circle, and the scene drew a sob that Rachel had to choke off. Her father looked so alone out there! The savages who moved like cats to encircle him were strong, quick and totally devoid of fear, she knew well. How could he hope to win? *And he came for me—after all my hatred!* her heart cried out, and she uttered a mighty silent prayer to God for him!

Now was the time, Winslow knew; the two braves on his flanks were almost out of his line of vision, while the other two before him stood three feet apart, their weapons ready if he turned to face either one.

Always do the unexpected! The words had been spoken years ago by the master who taught him his lessons with the sword. *The best swordsman in the world—if he gets rattled—can be taken!*

He did the one thing that could be done. Ignoring the two Indians who were moving to flank him, and paying no heed at all to the man on the left, he suddenly lowered his blade and with his right toe lunged his entire body toward the large Indian on his right!

The distance was critical, for if his enemy was too far away the sword would never touch him, and he would stand at full stretch, helpless. If the man were too close, the sword might catch in his flesh, and he would be cut to pieces trying to get the blade free.

Now the power flowed through his leg, and with the speed of a lifetime of practice the tip of his blade leaped through the air with all the force of his body behind it! The Indian was leaning forward balanced on the tips of his toes, tilting forward, and he could not believe that the white man was moving at him. Desperately he tried to reverse his feet, but it was too late!

The stroke brought the sword into his body, penetrating the heart—then it was withdrawn as Winslow whipped his blade back, stained crimson and shouted, "You see, Fox! The blade is magic!"

The man he had run through dropped his knife, and stared down at the small puncture on his breast in disbelief. He looked across at Matthew and tried to say something, suddenly dropped to the ground—dead.

Matthew saw that the savage on his left was paying no heed to him, and he did what he never would have done if the lives of the two women had not been at stake. He shouted and lunged with the same speed. The man had time to get his knife up, but the tip of Matthew's blade rasped over it, entered the fleshy side of the brave who grabbed his wound and gasped. But he was made of strong stuff, for he threw himself at Winslow, who had no choice but to strike the final blow.

But as the second Indian fell, he knew that he had turned his back too long, and even though he made a wild lunge to his left, he felt a line of fire run along his back as a blade ripped through his flesh. A cry of victory went up from the Indians as he went down, and he knew that both men would be on him like animals.

He had time only to roll over on his back before the sweaty body of one Indian fell on him. By catching the man's forearm with his left arm, Matthew managed to divert the knife thrust that would have driven straight to his head.

The sword was useless at close range, so he dropped it and with a mighty lunge of his body, threw the Indian off, and rolled to his feet just in time to see a shape to his left. He had no time at all to think, but simply reached out and grabbed for whatever part of the man he could get. The flesh was slippery but his hands closed on a muscular arm and with all his might he whipped the man around in a giant swinging motion and released him.

As the savage went flying through the air, Matthew reached down with one motion and picked up his sword, fell to his left in time to avoid the wicked slash that would have slit his throat, found an opening, and drove the blade into the body of the Indian who was off balance.

As the Indian went down, Matthew whirled to find his last opponent rushing in, blade out before him. But suddenly he stopped short when he realized that his three companions were on the ground, dead or dying.

Winslow could have killed him where he stood, but he lowered his blade, and in the silence that suddenly fell on the scene, he looked at Fox and said, "There is no need for this man to die, Fox. He has proven that he is no coward."

The man cried out and ran toward Matthew's blade in a suicidal rush, but Fox shouted to him, and he stopped.

Fox stood there staring at the tall white man, then looked at the men on the ground. Matthew knew that if this small Indian gave the word, he would die with an arrow in his heart, but he did not move nor speak.

The Fox said, "Take the women."

Rachel came forward half-supporting Mercy, and Fox gave her one look. He moved closer to her and said in a voice only she and Mercy heard.

"This Jesus man is strong. Few more like Him—maybe Fox become Jesus man, too!"

Then he said, "You go now." For a long time he stood there watching Matthew and the two women as they faded away into the woods.

They did not speak until Praise God and James suddenly appeared, and as Mercy wept in her husband's arms, Rachel turned to her father.

He was smiling at her. Suddenly she threw herself into his arms—and it was like coming home! For a long time they stood there. Finally he kissed her cheek and said, "Your mother has forgiven me and we're together now."

She smiled through her tears and nodded. "Forgive me, Father, for being so—"

He put his hand on her lips and said, "I've found a daughter now—and we must start from this day."

"Yes!" she cried. Great joy filled her heart as she said, "Oh, Father—let's go to Mother now."

Three days later Lydia heard the sound of steps on the porch.

"Mother! I'm back! Father brought me back!"

As Lydia held the girl in her arms, she looked over at her husband and said with a smile, "I knew he would." Then she held out her free arm and as Matthew came to her, she added with misty eyes, "These Winslow men—they do what they say!"

PART THREE

SALEM

★ ★ ★ ★

1691

CHAPTER SEVENTEEN

A NEW MINISTER

★ ★ ★ ★

Miles Winslow raised himself high in the stirrups and, shading his eyes from the brilliance of the midday April sun, stared down the road, then yanked his hat off, exposing a thick shock of yellow hair. "There they are, Howland!" he yelped, and spurred his startled bay into a hard run toward a small clapboard house.

His companion, though, only shook his head and continued the steady pace of his horse. Not an impulsive man, he looked with amused tolerance as he watched young Winslow pull his horse down, spring to the ground with the ease of a natural rider, and throw his arms around the pair who stood outside the neat white fence that enclosed the house.

Not very dignified for Harvard's newest scholar, Robert Howland thought. *A minister ought to be a little more restrained.* Howland was a solidly built man with heavy shoulders and a muscular neck. His square face and strong chin revealed a stubborn streak, which he tried unsuccessfully to curb. His light-gray eyes were wide set deep beneath a broad forehead. His light-brown hair was cut short, and his features were more durable than esthetic. He looked, in fact, more like a strong, active gentleman squire than an intellectual scholar.

He came up to the fence, swung easily from his saddle, then waited patiently while young Winslow finished greeting the couple. There was in Howland a strange mixture of deliberate thought and a sort of ponderous behavior, which covered a quickness of mind and easily stirred emotions kept carefully in check.

"Come, now, Robert," young Miles said, turning the attention of the couple toward the visitor. "This is my father and mother—and this is my friend and teacher, Rev. Robert Howland."

"It's a pleasure to welcome you to Salem, sir," Matthew Winslow said warmly, and the hand he gave in greeting was as hard and strong as Howland's own. "We've heard nothing but your name since Miles arrived at Harvard."

Howland took in Winslow's strong figure with approval. He had heard of Miles' father by reputation, and the man's appearance was impressive. He was six feet tall with the strong, athletic figure of a man in his late forties. He was an older edition of Miles, the resemblance between the two so sharp that it caught Howland off guard. They both had the same sharp features, the light hair with the trace of reddish gold when the sun caught it, as it did now, the broad mouth and bright blue eyes that revealed the Winslow blood.

"I'm happy to meet you, Mr. Winslow—and you, ma'am," Howland said in a deep, prideful voice that would shake the rafters had he cared to lift it. He nodded to the beautiful woman who looked small in the presence of the three large men. She still appeared too young to be the mother of a sixteen-year-old son.

"Come inside, Rev. Howland," Lydia Winslow said. There was a trace of coquetry in her voice and in her black eyes. Her dark beauty and expressive features still bore evidence of the French blood of her father.

They entered the house, and for the next hour sat around the oak table, where Howland discovered the source of his young pupil's wit and intelligence. He had "discovered" Miles three years earlier when the young man had come to Harvard at the age of thirteen. In their first meeting he had been astounded at the breadth of Miles' scholarship and at the same time warmly approving of the modest charm of the young fellow. For three years he had nurtured the boy, who had become known at the school as "Howland's Student," for the older man had been jealous of the lad, not trusting other instructors to do the finishing he felt necessary.

Ordinarily this sort of monopoly would have been forbidden, but Robert Howland himself was on a special footing at Harvard. He was a close friend of Cotton Mather, and such prestige was enough to permit Howland to do pretty much as he pleased. In all fairness, it was not his friendship with the titular head of the Puritan world, but his own brilliance that had made him a legend at the school. Cotton Mather had graduated from Harvard at the age of fourteen, but he had said often, "I got an early start, and Robert Howland got a late one—but if we had begun together, I have no doubt he would have eclipsed my record."

Sitting there at ease as he had rarely been on a first visit, Howland noted that Matthew's intelligence and his wife's ready wit and charm were combined in their son.

"I'm surprised you'd think of leaving your position with Harvard to pastor a small church, Rev. Howland," Matthew said at last.

"It was a difficult decision," Howland admitted. "But I've grown too bookish over the last few years. The Lord has instructed me to go out where the harvest is white. Except for the time I've preached for Rev. Mather, I've been rather tied to my desk."

"Aye, a man needs to be with the people," Winslow nodded. "My father says that there are too many people at universities who have more degrees than they have temperature!"

"Matthew!" Lydia said sharply, "you shouldn't say such things to Reverend Howland."

"Oh, Father can say anything!" Winslow laughed. "He's ninety-one, you know, and he never was noted for his tact."

"I've been anxious to meet him, sir," Howland smiled. "Miles says he has more brains than all of Harvard combined."

Matthew threw back his head and reached over to pound his son on the shoulder, "Son! You've got no more tact than any other of us bull-headed Winslows! Imagine telling your teacher a thing like that!"

"It's good to see a young man who honors his parents, Mr.

Winslow," Howland remarked, smiling at the young man.

They talked a little longer and then Miles looked out the bay window and jumped to his feet. "There's Grandfather and Rachel!" he yelped and dashed out the door. Howland heard him talking excitedly and was amused at how the young man, who had gone to great effort to be dignified at Harvard, had now reverted almost to a wild, puppyish excitement in the presence of his family.

As they entered the cabin, Miles said, "This is my grandfather—and this is Robert Howland, sir!"

Howland looked at Gilbert Winslow, and was in some awe of the man, for this one, after all, was the last living member of the Firstcomers—that intrepid band of Pilgrims who had come on the *Mayflower* so many years ago!

"I'm honored, Mr. Winslow. I believe you knew my grandfather, John Howland?" the minister said at once, and the hand that gripped his was still strong and without a tremble despite the years.

"John Howland!" The old man stared at him. "I did, indeed, and a fine man he was, too! Your servant, sir. My grandson speaks highly of you."

Time had taken a fraction from his height, so that he was slightly beneath his son and grandson, but he still stood straight as a pine sapling. The cornflower blue eyes were undimmed, and the tapering face was browned by the sun. His voice was not strong as it had once been, but there was no tremor as he spoke in a thin, clear tone, and his movement, if not swift as those of his tall descendants, was sure and still graceful.

"Reverend Howland is going to be pastor at Littleton, Father," Matthew said.

"They need a man of God there," Gilbert snorted. "The last one they had had no more backbone than an oyster!" He shot a glance at Howland and said, "My grandson tells me you know the Word, sir. I trust you will preach it undiluted—put the fire back in hell and the fear of God in those half-baked, lukewarm, imitations of Christians in that church!"

Miles laughed in delight, and gave Howland a sly wink. "Don't beat around the bush, Grandfather! Just come right out and say what you think about Brother Howland's new charge!"

"Now you behave yourself, Gilbert Winslow!" Lydia commanded, giving his arm an affectionate squeeze. "I think Reverend Howland can be trusted to take care of his church without your help."

Gilbert had opened his mouth to continue, but at Lydia's words he shut it. Giving her a quick smile, he said, "Still trying to make a gentleman out of me, Lydia? You should know by now how hopeless that is!"

"Reverend, this is my daughter, Rachel," Matthew said, and Howland, who had looked to one side to speak with Gilbert Winslow, turned to face the woman who had entered and was standing quietly beside her father.

"This is Reverend Robert Howland, Rachel—the teacher Miles has been talking about for so long."

"Welcome to Salem, Reverend Howland."

"I'm—very happy to meet you, Miss Winslow."

Howland had stammered slightly, for although Miles had talked almost constantly about his older sister, he had never once mentioned the fact that she was a strikingly beautiful woman. *Why didn't the young pup tell me she was so lovely!* he thought with some irritation. He was a man who didn't like to be surprised, and it bothered him that he had been struck so forcibly with her beauty that he had stammered like a callow youth. At the age of thirty-three, he was fairly hardened to the good looks of young women. Being one of the most eligible bachelors in the country, he had discovered, brought out the worst in most people. Almost everyone had a sister, a niece, or some girl who would make the *perfect* wife for him, and he had long ago thrown up a wall of defense against such ploys.

But this woman shook that hardness, for she was without a doubt the most attractive woman he had ever seen, he admitted grudgingly. He gave her a hard stare, hoping to find some flaw, but was unable to do so.

She was, he knew, thirty years old, but no one with eyes would have taken her for such. *Why, she looks no more than twenty!* Howland thought suddenly. He took in the creamy smooth cheeks, like pale ivory, highlighted by a pair of almond-shaped eyes, hazel except for times when there was a greenish glint which gave her a saucy look. Her hair was black, and it curled rebelliously from under the white cap that perched atop her head. The simple gray homespun dress did not conceal the smoothly rounded form, and there was an intensely womanly air about her, despite the direct look and almost militant posture.

"You'll be staying with us tonight," Miles said slyly. He had not missed the startled look that Howland had given his sister, and it delighted him that the self-assured minister was put off stride for a change.

"I don't want to be troublesome," Howland replied quickly.

"No trouble, sir," Gilbert Winslow offered, "I want to talk to you about a few matters."

"Look to yourself, Reverend" Lydia laughed. "The Winslows show no mercy where theology is concerned."

"And this one is the worst," Matthew stated, going to Rachel and putting his arm around her.

"Got more scripture in her than most of these fools who call themselves ministers have these days," Gilbert nodded. "We'll look for you at supper—all of you."

He turned and left, and Rachel said with a smile, "I'll look forward to seeing you this evening, Reverend Howland." She followed her grandfather through the door, and the minister saw that they were chattering like two school children as they headed down the street.

"I hope you won't be offended at my father, sir," Matthew apologized. "He speaks his mind a little bluntly."

"I've heard so much about him from Miles that I'm rather intimidated," Howland answered. "He's quite an institution, isn't he?"

"We weren't sure how he would take the move here from Plymouth," Matthew remarked. "But my business was here in Salem, and Reverend Findley died soon after we moved; Father practically pastored the church for years—with Rachel's help."

Miles nodded at Howland, adding with a smile, "She's the best minister in the whole colony, according to Grandfather. And I don't much doubt it." He shook his head in admiration and warned Howland with a grin, "Don't get into a theological argument with her, I warn you. Aside from yourself, she knows the Scripture better than anybody I know."

"Can preach a better sermon, too!" Matthew vowed.

" 'Course she calls it *teaching*—but I tell you, Reverend, when she speaks to a congregation, it's a thing to hear!"

Howland frowned. "I rejoice that she knows the word, but the Scripture says, 'Let the women keep silence in the church,' you remember."

"I'm afraid Rachel has too much Winslow in her," Matthew returned ruefully. He scratched his head, then shrugged his shoulders. "Miles is right, though, and I'd advise you to steer clear of her. She has a way of being more logical than you'd think for a woman so attractive."

"That's what does it, Father," Miles decided. "She's so pretty that men don't think she has any intelligence—or else they get all nervous because she's a beautiful woman. Anyway, I've seen some pretty fair Bible scholars get put flat on their backs—theologically speaking, of course!—and never knew what hit them!"

"You two hush!" Lydia interrupted, then continued, more quietly but with force, "Rachel is a handmaiden of the Lord, Reverend Howland. She'll never marry, so she says, because she can serve God better in the unmarried state, as the Apostle Paul puts it. And you'll not find a woman in these parts—or a man either—who serves God so faithfully."

"That's true," her husband nodded. "The poor bless her, and her prayers for the sick—" He shook his head in wonder and finished, "Well, you'll admire her, as we all do, but she is a problem for some of our ministers."

Howland nodded. "Miles has told me of his sister's good works, and I know you praise God for such a daughter. It will be my pleasure to become better acquainted with her."

Robert Howland got better acquainted with Rachel Winslow that evening, but it did not improve his disposition.

The meal had been excellent, and he had enjoyed listening to Gilbert Winslow tell of the voyage on the *Mayflower*. It was almost as if a witness had stepped forward from the Scripture, for the Firstcomers were, of course, the heroes of the church in America, and to hear the old man say things like: ". . . so Standish said to me. . . !" or "Then I went to Governor Bradford and told him it had to be so!" These demigods—or so they seemed to Howland—had been Winslow's friends; he had known them intimately, and it was a wonder to hear it.

Finally Gilbert Winslow said, "It was a grand crew, and I would to God that some of their spirit would come on this generation!"

"Oh, I think we have a goodly number of dedicated Christians in our own day," Howland said. "It's a common mistake to think that people in earlier times were more spiritual than in our own days."

"Do you really think that, Mr. Howland?" Rachel had said little all evening, but now she faced him directly across the table where they sat drinking tea, her hazel eyes gleaming, with a pronounced tilt to her chin as she shook her head. "You have been leading a sheltered life at Harvard."

Howland flushed, for he was not accustomed to being challenged—especially by a woman. "I think we are not so bad as many say, Miss Winslow."

"I think we are *worse*, sir!" She did not raise her voice, but there was no weakness at all in her tone or her look as she began to speak directly to the tall minister. "Our Fathers gave up everything they had in the world, risked death and the loss of all things for the privilege of worshiping God. And what are men risking today? Nothing!"

"Well, really, Miss Winslow, from a theological point of view, we are not in such bad condition. We have more members in our churches now—"

"More members, yes!" Rachel said instantly. "But what of the *quality*? You are aware of the Half-Way covenant, I trust?"

"Certainly! But—"

"A covenant straight from the pit!" she said directly, and Howland blinked at her bluntness. The Half-Way Covenant had been approved in 1657 by the Ministerial Convention in an attempt to settle a question that was both theological and social. Only members of the church could vote in the Bay Colony, and when the children of the first settlers grew to maturity, they were thought to be saints because they shared the covenant with their parents. But then *their* children came along, and most of them had no conversion experience of their own. The church was in a dilemma; if these unregenerate people were admitted to the church, it meant that no man needed to be converted—but on the other hand, they could not vote if they were not admitted. A solution had been reached in the Half-Way Covenant, which permitted the children of members to belong to the church without a conversion experience.

Howland replied with some fervor, "Certainly, that covenant is not the best answer, and Rev. Mather opposed it, but we must work within the framework of the entire church, Miss Winslow."

"The church, sir," she debated, "is the bride of Jesus Christ, and no man nor any group can by agreeing together soil her garments!"

"You oversimplify!" he answered hotly.

"Jesus said, 'Ye must be born again.' Are you going to say that the Savior 'oversimplified' the conditions for salvation?" she challenged.

"Well—of course I'd not say that—"

"Then the Half-Way Covenant is wrong?"

Never had Howland felt so ill at ease, and the fact that he was confused as much by her enormous eyes as by her use of scripture and logic did little to make him feel any better. "I think you would need to do much research and study before you can draw that conclusion, Miss Rachel!" he said lamely.

"The conclusion is simple, sir," Rachel insisted, ignoring her mother, who was trying to signal for her to stop. "Either men are saved by good intentions and moral living—or they are saved by grace through the blood of the Lord Jesus!" She suddenly reached over and plucked up a Bible, placing it before Howland. "Show it to me in the Word of God, sir, and I'll believe it!"

"I tell you, ma'am, it's not so easy as that!" Howland's resonant voice rose, filling the room, and his face was red.

Suddenly the tension that had risen so unexpectedly was broken as Gilbert Winslow slapped the table and laughed. "By my head, Robert! You're your grandfather all over again! He was a dear fellow, John was. I knew him in England, you know, before we came to Plymouth."

Howland stared at him, his quarrel with Rachel forgotten. "I never knew anyone who knew him, sir."

"Well, I did, my boy!" The old man smiled at the memory.

"As a matter of fact, you wouldn't be here right now if it weren't for me."

"Sir?"

"Why, your grandfather went up on deck one night, and somehow managed to fall overboard. He caught a rope, though, and hung on for dear life. I came topside and heard him calling, so I got some help and we hauled him on board."

"I've not heard of that!"

"Mr. Bradford tells of it in his history," Gilbert said. "And he was much like yourself—in a physical way, though no scholar. A strong man—a strong man! Once when the general sickness cut us down in that first winter, it was just myself, Miles Standish, John Bradford and your grandfather who were able to stand up. John and I dug many a grave—and he never once complained, he didn't! A good strong man and a faithful companion he was," Gilbert said softly, and then wistfully, "And I miss him to this day."

The old man's words brought a peace to the room, and soon they left, after Howland promised to return the next day to visit with Gilbert. As they were walking back to the house, Miles said slyly, "I told you not to underestimate Rachel."

"I'll remember that," Howland said shortly. "She needs a husband with a strong hand, I think."

Miles thought about that. "Well," he noted, "if there's any man on this earth any stronger than my sister, I'd like to meet him. There's been quite a list of candidates—wanting to marry her, I mean. But none of them measure up."

Howland did not answer, but he thought wryly, *What the woman needs is a good beating.* But he realized at the same time that his own admiration for her beauty would make such a thing difficult, so he put the whole matter of Rachel Winslow out of his mind.

CHAPTER EIGHTEEN

A BROTHERLY KISS

★ ★ ★ ★

"Robert, all this talk of witches—what do you make of it?"

"The devil, sir, is not dead—and he will find an entrance if God's people do not keep the door blocked."

The duties of his church kept Howland close to his village as a rule, but his one recreation in the two months since leaving Harvard had been angling with Gilbert Winslow. The young man had found that being a pastor required a certain amount of practical experience that no knowledge of Latin or Greek would solve, and he came at least once a week to fish with the aging man in the stream that wound its way through Salem.

They sat under a huge chestnut tree and said little until Winslow broke the silence with his question about witchcraft. He was not, however, satisfied with the answer, for he shook his head and said, "I mislike it, Robert. There's something about the subject makes people behave stupidly. Why, would you believe that fool Putnam woman has spread the rumor that she lost all her children in childbirth because Rebecca Nurse put a curse on her? And if there ever was a shrew it's Ann Putnam, and if there ever was a saint, it's Rebecca Nurse!"

"Aye, there will always be ignorance, Mr. Winslow, but Rev. Cotton Mather's book *Relating to Witchcraft* documents the acts of witches well. It's all there, the invisible world, all your incubi and succubi—all your witches and wizards of night and day.

'Thou shalt not suffer a witch to live,' as the Scripture says."

The soft May breeze blew a lock of silver hair across Gilbert's eyes, and he brushed it back. "No good will come of it. What's needed is a dose of good old-time religion. *That* would purge all the silly notions people have of trying to live for God on Sundays and for the devil the other six days."

A laugh broke from Howland's deep chest, and he pulled his cane pole up and began to wind up the line. "Things are always so simple with you, sir! No grays—just black or white, right or wrong."

"Well, I'm an old man now, son," Winslow remarked with a smile as he took his own line in. "When I was your age I was just about like you, running around trying to split hairs on matters. But the closer I get to home, the more I see that living is not very complicated. Jesus said, 'Whosoever cometh not after me and forsaketh all he hath cannot be my disciple,' and that's fairly simple—'all that he hath.' "

Howland reached down and scooped up the stringer of fish they had caught. Then as they walked along the side of the bubbling stream, he mused thoughtfully, "But yours was a different world, wasn't it? Things are much more complicated now than when you came to Plymouth."

"Men are born, they love, they die—and someplace along the way they either meet Jesus Christ and follow Him, or they don't."

"You sound like Rachel," Howland chuckled. "Or I suppose she sounds like *you*. All you Winslows are pretty much alike, aren't you?"

"A stubborn breed, Robert!" Gilbert smiled. They made their way back to his house, and Rachel met them at the door, smiling at the pair.

"More fish to clean?" she asked, shaking her head. "Put them in the back and I'll clean them when I return. I've got to go over to Elizabeth Crowley's with some food."

"I'll clean the fish," Gilbert said, taking the string from Howland. "You go with Rachel, Robert—then come back and we'll have these fellows for supper."

"Why, I'm not sure . . ."

"Oh, come along, Reverend," Rachel urged; then she gave

a little giggle, which surprised him. "I promise not to bite your head off or argue about scripture."

Howland had steered clear of Rachel since their disagreement on his first night, but now took the heavy basket of food she handed him, and they made their way through the village, talking about unimportant things.

Finally he said, "I've been wanting to apologize to you, Miss Winslow, for my sharp words."

She turned to look at him and smiled. "I'm too straightforward, I know that. Forgive me, please."

Then the air was cleared and he told her of his church and the problems until they came to a small unpainted clapboard house on the edge of the village.

Four children were playing in the yard, but they all came running when they saw her, calling her name and pulling at her clothing. It made a pretty sight, Howland decided, and he wondered—not for the first time—why she had never married.

She gave each of the children a piece of honeycomb from the basket, then led him inside. "Elizabeth?" she announced. A small, worn-looking woman came to the door and paused at seeing the tall form of the minister.

"This is Reverend Howland, from Littleton, Elizabeth. Reverend Howland, this is Mrs. Crowley."

"How d'you, sir?" the woman said in a small voice, then turned to say, "Jamie is took bad, Miss Rachel!"

"Let's see," Rachel stated, and the three of them entered the room where a small boy, not more than four or five, was lying on a bed almost hidden by the covers. His face was red, and he was breathing roughly and unevenly.

Rachel sat down beside the boy, started to speak, then turned as if she had just remembered something. "Reverend Howland, will you pray for Jamie?"

"Why, surely." Howland stepped forward and prayed briefly, then stepped back, his duty done. "I trust the Lord will be merciful on your boy, Mrs. Crowley," he murmured quietly. It always made him feel inadequate, praying for the sick, and he had done little enough of it at Harvard. As the pastor of a flock, it was different, however, and it was one of the things that drove him to talk with Gilbert Winslow.

"Please, Miss Rachel," Mrs. Crowley whispered, "won't you say a prayer, too?"

"If you like, Elizabeth." She reached into a pocket and pulled out a small object. Howland leaned over and saw that it was a small vial. Opening it, she put a drop of oil on her finger, closed the vial, then replaced it. Softly she touched the boy's forehead with the oil, and then put her hand on his head. For a long while she said nothing at all, then she said, so softly that he barely caught the words, "Lord, what is your will for Jamie?"

Howland was mystified! He stood there staring, and the silence was so heavy it almost had substance as she continued to wait. The boy did not move and she did not speak again—for what seemed like a very long time. Then he saw her head nod, as if she were agreeing with something someone had said. "Lord, we ask you to heal this child."

The boy's eyes fluttered open. He focused on her and said in a tiny voice, "Hullo, Miss Rachel."

She stooped and gave him a kiss. "Hello, Jamie."

"I've been sick."

"Yes, but you'll be fine now." Rachel rose and there was a peaceful look on her smooth face as she moved past Howland. "I'd not let him stay under that heavy cover, Elizabeth. And don't let him have anything very heavy to eat until tomorrow."

"Bless you, Miss Rachel!" Mrs. Crowley cried out, wiping her eyes with her apron. "God bless you—and you, too, sir," she added as they left the house.

They made their way along the street, everyone they met greeting Rachel by name and nodding to Howland. He waited for her to say something about Jamie, but she did not.

Finally he said, "You think the child is—no longer sick?"

"Jamie?" she asked in surprise, looking up at him. "Oh, yes, he's fine." Then she asked, "Why do you ask?"

"Well—" He gave an embarrassed grin, and despite his manner, which was sometimes heavy, she saw that he had humor. "I suppose that I've had so little success in praying for the sick that it startled me the way you prayed—so *positively*!" He looked down at her, thinking how clear her eyes were, and confessed, "I'd not be able to do that! What if he didn't get well? What would people think?"

"I don't mind what people think, Reverend Howland," she returned firmly. "God didn't call me to be popular, but to do His will. And the instant you start doubting God's word, you're *already* a failure, aren't you?"

He thought about her words, then shook his head. "Well, doubt comes to me, I confess. Don't you ever wonder if your prayers will be answered?"

"God has never refused to answer my prayer."

He stopped short and stared at her in disbelief. An elderly couple passed, stopping to turn around and stare at them standing there in the middle of the street. "God has answered every one of your prayers?" he asked, doubt threading his speech. "I never heard anyone say so."

She looked up at him, the smooth countenance calm and possessed. Her full lips turned up in a smile and she seemed amused by his doubt. "Didn't you teach the eleventh chapter of Mark at Harvard?"

"Why, of course!"

She began to quote it, and her voice was filled with a certainty that held him still.

> "Jesus answering saith unto them, Have faith in God. For verily I say unto you, That whosoever shall say unto this mountain, be thou removed and be thou cast into the sea; and shall not doubt in his heart, but shall believe that those things which he saith shall come to pass, he shall have whatsoever he saith. Therefore, I say unto you, What things soever ye desire, when you pray, believe that ye received them, and ye shall have them."

He stared at her, then said, "But—surely that's symbolic?"

"I try to think the Lord Jesus meant exactly what He said."

He shook his head, saying nothing. They began to walk. Finally he broke the silence. "I've never known anyone who says that God answers *all* their prayers."

"Yes, you have!" He stared in surprise at her certainty, and she laughed. "You know my Grandfather."

"He says that, too?"

"Yes, and my mother."

"I can't believe it!"

"Reverend Howland—"

"Please, call me Robert!"

"I like that name!" she smiled at his invitation. "Well, Robert, I don't know if I can explain or not, but I'll try. Years ago," she began, a distant look filling her dark eyes, "I watched Mother as she prayed, and I saw how God always seemed to answer her. But I hadn't experienced that power for myself. It took a crisis—a desperate situation—to bring me to the realization of my own need for Christ and His power to meet my needs."

"A crisis?" Howland's expression intensified as he became drawn into the drama of Rachel's story.

"Yes. I was caught in the middle of an Indian raid on a small village near Plymouth. Someone I cared a great deal about was—" She paused, groping for words.

"Go on," Howland encouraged gently.

Rachel took a deep breath. "Well, in the midst of all the shouting and burning and bloodshed, something happened inside of me. I called out to the Lord, and He answered—really answered—and miraculously saved me and a friend from certain death."

Howland let out a long, low whistle.

"We were held captive by the Indians for some time, but in some ways I was less captive than I had been all my life. I had been adhering to a 'form of godliness,' as the scripture says, without experiencing its power. At last I knew Christ's presence for the first time, and saw Him answer my prayers. Before then my faith—if you could call it that—had been a secondhand experience from my mother."

"Is that why you're so set against the Half-Way Covenant?" Robert grinned, remembering their last spirited encounter.

Rachel laughed lightly. "Let's not get into *that* again! Let's just say that afterward, I knew Jesus Christ for myself. And since that time He has always answered my prayers."

"But how?" Howland was still mystified.

"Grandfather taught me to pray, and the one thing that makes him different in his praying is that he never asks God to do anything unless he's sure it's God's will."

"I don't quite understand," Howland frowned. "How can he always know God's will? God may choose not to reveal it."

"Then he waits until God *does* choose to speak. So that's the way I pray. When we were with Jamie, I was asking God to reveal His will."

"And God *told* you it was His will to heal the boy?" Howland was skeptical, as he always was of those who had visions and personal words from God, always prefacing their remarks with *God told me to say* . . .

She did not answer immediately. Her face was still as she thought how best to tell him how it was with her. "I don't *hear* God, not as I hear you," she admitted. "But there is a spirit in man, isn't there? And didn't the Lord Jesus tell us that His Holy Spirit would teach us all things?"

"Well, yes, but I don't think that means—concrete things."

"Why not?" she asked simply. "Don't you think Jesus is interested in the things we do? Doesn't He care about Jamie more than you or I ever could?"

"Yes, God cares, but—"

"He said, 'My sheep *hear my voice*,' didn't He?"

All this was making Robert Howland very nervous, and he sought for a way to change the topic, but she did not notice his agitation.

"I asked God if it was His will to heal Jamie—and in my spirit I felt that He said *yes*. So I simply prayed for what God already wanted to do. And he is healed."

Her eyes filled with tears, and she whispered, "Praise the Lord, for His mercies are everlasting!"

All this was a far different thing from studying a dusty book on the subject *Praying for the Sick*, and Howland was certain that the woman was a victim of rank emotionalism. He had been carried away by the charm of the family; now he suddenly resolved to spend less time in their company.

But he was committed to the fish supper, so he went with her to the home of the local pastor, Reverend Samuel Parris. Parris lived in a small brick house in the center of the village. As they approached the house, a black woman opened the door. "Hello, Tituba," Rachel said. "Is Reverend Parris at home?"

"Yes, he with Miss Betty."

At that moment a thin man with close-set eyes and a harried expression entered the hall. He was followed by two young women, both pale and agitated. Catching sight of the two visitors, he stopped abruptly, gave a sharp look at the two young women, saying, "Abigail, you and Susanna run on now—but come back this afternoon."

"Yes, sir," one of them said, a very pretty brunette with a sly look. "Come along, Susanna." The two of them left, and Rachel introduced the men.

"Reverend Parris, this is Reverend Robert Howland, the new pastor at Littleton. Reverend Samuel Parris."

"I welcome you, sir," Parris said quickly. He had a nervous tic in his left eye. "I trust you will have a fruitful ministry in your new field—but you must watch yourself! These people can be untrustworthy, sir!"

"Why, I think I have been treated quite fairly, Reverend Parris," Howland answered, a little shocked that a minister would be so outspoken in his criticism of his church members to a stranger.

"They have been most unjust! Why, would you believe that they have forced me to cut my own wood, sir, when our agreement was that the church would provide wood for me!"

Howland soon learned that there was a running warfare between Parris and his membership. Most of them, including the Winslows, were sick to death of his constant harping on the wrongs done him.

"I heard that your Betty is sick," Rachel said, changing the subject.

"Sick? Who told you that?" Parris snapped, as if accused of a crime. Then he sniffed and calmed himself. "Why, she has a cold, nothing more."

"Would you like us to pray with her?" Rachel asked gently.

"Not at all necessary!" Parris answered quickly. "Perhaps I could make you some tea?"

"Oh no, I have several calls to make," Rachel informed him. "I wanted you to meet Reverend Howland since you will be brothers in the ministry."

"We must have a visit when you're more settled," Parris stated. As he talked the tic in his eye grew more pronounced, so he placed his hand over it in a habitual gesture.

"Your servant, sir," Howland said, and shook the frail hand

of the minister. After they were out of the house, Robert said diffidently, "Reverend Parris seems upset."

"He is, isn't he? He's a very nervous man, Robert. He's never been happy here. He thinks he's being wasted in a small village like this."

" A minister's life is usually hard, don't you think, Rachel?"

"Why, I don't agree," she returned in surprise. She walked along for a few steps, then added, "What's hard is not knowing the grace of God. If Jesus Christ is with me, how can anything be hard?"

Robert suddenly felt a great admiration for this woman, and he took her by the arm without realizing it, saying, "You have a wonderful spirit, Rachel!"

She flushed, then laughed, "Oh, let's hurry, Robert. I wouldn't put it past Gilbert Winslow to cook those fish and eat them—every one!"

It was a delightful evening for all three of them. After they ate the delicious supper, it was too late, both Gilbert and Rachel decided, for Robert to walk back home. "We have a spare room, a Prophet's Room, we call it," Rachel smiled. "You'll be good company for Grandfather."

They sat around the table until eight o'clock, and Robert kept the old man telling tales of the first days. Finally, Winslow yawned. "I must be getting old! Getting so I can't stay up till midnight." Then he smiled and for the first time there was a little weariness in his voice and a slight tremble in his hand, as he said, "You've given me a fine evening, my boy! I hope you'll come again—very often. You're *very* like your grandfather, John!"

He went to his room and Howland said, "It's so hard for me to remember he's ninety-one years old, Rachel!"

"I know," she said quietly. "He's the strongest man I've ever known, Robert. I shall—miss him."

Howland started, then said, "He's not ill, I trust?"

"No, thank God—but it's time soon for him to go to his Lord. That's what he lives for. And I will rejoice when that time comes, but I'll be . . ."

She got up abruptly and walked out into the warm summer night, and he followed her. She leaned against the side of the house, and he came to stand close beside her.

She said nothing and neither did he. *It is strange,* he thought, *that we don't have to talk.*

"You know, Rachel," he said finally, "you're the only woman I know who can stand a thirty-second silence."

She turned and looked at him, and he saw with a shock that there were tears in her eyes. He had never seen one trace of weakness in her, and he was moved. Suddenly he took her hand and held it tightly, saying, "You were going to say, before we came outside, that you'll be lonely when he's gone?"

"I suppose so."

He looked down at her, and she seemed very small, very vulnerable in the soft moonlight. At last he asked her directly what he had often wondered. "Why have you never married, Rachel? Have you never been in love?"

"Once—I was," she whispered. "At least, I thought I was. But then he died, and I promised God I'd serve Him always."

Howland prided himself on his control. He lived by a code of iron discipline, never yielding to the weakness of the flesh. Years before, he had put all idea of marriage out of his mind, at least until God gave him freedom to seek a wife.

But as he stood there holding Rachel's hand, he was suddenly conscious of her upturned face and was filled with a strange feeling of weakness, causing his hand to tremble.

Feeling the tremor in his hand, she looked up in surprise, her large eyes luminous in the moonlight. "Why, you're trembling, Robert!" she exclaimed. Without intending to do it, she reached up and touched his cheek, and a tear rolled down her cheek, making a silver track on her face. "You mustn't be sorry for me," she said.

But it was deep compassion and the suddenness of the emotion that shook him. He was a man who kept his emotion, as well as anything else, under strict control, but her hand on his cheek released something that had been bound up in him for years.

He took her shoulders, then lowered his head and kissed her soft lips, tasting the salt of her tears.

Rachel had not been unaware of Howland as a man, and his kiss swept through her with a power she found difficult to repress. He put his arms around her and held her gently. Though there was pity and compassion in his caress, there was more. She had stirred something deep within him, and he found his heart reaching out to her.

Like Howland, Rachel had kept this part of life tightly locked, but suddenly the door was flung open, and she was conscious only of his strong arms around her, holding her closer, his lips on hers.

Then she gasped and drew back. Immediately, he dropped his arms, embarrassed. They stared at each other, neither able to speak. Finally Howland said, "I—I must be—"

He could not finish, and Rachel moved to wipe the tears from her face. "Don't be upset, Robert—it's not your fault."

He was shocked beyond reason, and stammered as he said, "I—can't believe that I've acted in such a fashion!"

She gave him a strange smile. "You have a large heart, Robert. And you keep it well caged! But I think I have just seen what a compassionate man you are underneath all that bluster!"

He shook his head. "I'm glad you can think of it like that, Rachel."

"You were just sorry for me—that's all." Then she moved away from him, and as she came to the door, she turned and said, "It was a brotherly kiss, Robert. Good night."

He watched her go inside, and then he walked for a long time beneath the stars, and finally returned to the house. The last thing he thought of before he finally went to sleep was her words: *It was a brotherly kiss*—nothing more!

CHAPTER NINETEEN

THE HUNT IS ON

★ ★ ★ ★

"Robert—come in, come in! Where in the world have you been hiding?"

Grabbing Howland's arm, Miles literally pulled him into the house and began to berate him for his neglect. Howland's face broke into a smile; his affection for the young man dissolved the sober look in his student's face. Robert rode out the storm of words, thinking not so much of what Miles was saying, but of the strange state of mind which had dominated him since his last visit to Salem.

He was not a man given to excessive introspection, but that short interlude with Rachel had impressed him so much that no matter how he tried to put it out of his mind, the scene kept returning. For years he had been on his guard against anything that would be a hindrance to his ministry—and the most obvious handicap, in his judgment, was marriage. Fending off potential brides had become almost second nature to him, but something was different in this case. He could not put his finger on it, nor could he forget. Their last meeting nagged at him, pulling his mind in two ways at once, and for a month his work, his study in the Word, and his sleep had suffered. Finally that very morning, he had set his jaw after another fitful night, and started for Salem. He had no plan of action, but he knew he had to face Rachel, if only to see if his vivid memory of her was a figment of his imagination.

"Are your parents at home?" he finally asked, breaking into Miles' running monologue.

"Why, no, they're not, Robert—and you barely caught me." His face revealed a sudden concern and he said earnestly, "I'm glad you've come—things are in a ferment here. I swear the whole town's gone insane!"

"What's happening?"

"Why, it's this fool witchcraft business!" Miles said in disgust. "Some silly women accused a poor old woman—Bridget Bishop—of being a witch, and the trial is on right now. Come on, it's already started, and you may be of some help."

"I hardly see how," Howland protested, but he allowed himself to be drawn along. There had been much talk of witchcraft in his own village, and he was curious to see how the business was handled in Salem.

They made their way to the largest building in Salem, a two-story structure of red brick, and found a crowd pressing around the outside, excitedly talking and staring through the open windows.

"We'll never get in there!" Howland said, but Miles pulled his arm, and they were admitted by an elderly man who nodded at the youth and opened the door just wide enough for them to slip through.

The door they passed through was in the back of the large room, so few people saw them enter. As they took places along the wall, standing with the others who had missed out on the bench seats, Robert saw the Winslow family sitting together close to the front on one of the benches that was at right angles to the room, facing the raised platform where several elderly men sat at a long table—magistrates, he suspected, and judges for the hearing.

Rachel looked his way, and as their eyes met, he had the strange feeling that she had been as restless as he, for she bit her lower lip in agitation, then nodded and turned back to the scene before her.

An old woman, plainly dressed and so upset that she could not speak without a break in her voice, stood on a smaller platform with a small rail built around it, waist high. She must have been at least sixty-five or seventy years old, and from her speech and actions, Howland judged her to be of humble origins and not especially intelligent.

"And you have heard witness after witness testify that you appeared to them in a horrid shape," one of the judges said sternly. He was a tall, thin man with a long face and staring eyes. "John Cook swears that you appeared to him five years ago, that you struck him on the head, and that on that same day you walked into the room where he was and an apple strangely flew out of his hand into the lap of his mother, six or eight feet from him. What say you to that, Bridget Bishop?"

"Oh, I ain't never hit his mother with no apple—please God, I never once hit 'im."

"He has sworn that you did! Are you calling Master Cook a liar?"

"Oh no, sir!" The old woman trembled so violently with fear that she swayed back and forth. "Please God, sir, Mr. Cook—he was angry with me over the business with the suckling pigs, but I never done 'im no hurt!"

"What is this about pigs?" Every head turned to see Matthew Winslow stand up and face the court.

"Mr. Winslow! We will take care that all the evidence is heard! You are not a judge in this hearing!"

Winslow suddenly raised an arm, pointing it like a rapier at the long-faced man who had gone livid with rage. "Thomas Carlew, you have permitted a dozen witnesses to testify of some ridiculous incident going back ten years, while at the same time you are *deaf* to any suggestion that these people may be as silly as they sound!"

An angry hum went over the room, and Miles whispered to Howland, "Father's all stirred up, isn't he? Look at how mad the witnesses are."

Howland saw that many were boiling with anger at Winslow, and he thought, *Winslow is making trouble for himself!*

There was a heated argument about whether or not the defendant should be allowed to amplify her statement on the pigs, but the direct attacks of Winslow prevailed, and the old woman said, "Please, sir, it was only that Master Cook bought six suckling pigs from me, and four of 'em died—so he come and wanted his money back—and said they was cursed. Only I didn't have none of it—so he said I was a thief and a witch." She began crying, and Matthew turned to a sallow-faced man in the front row.

"Mr. Cook, you are a prejudiced witness—your testimony is worthless."

Cook jumped up and began to scream at Winslow, but the judge said loudly, "Sit down, Mr. Cook! And you, too, Matthew Winslow! Or I will have you put out of this room!"

Winslow stared at him, then said loudly, "You are a disgrace to your office, Jacob Sneed!" He swept his arm over the entire courtroom and cried out, "In God's name, can't you see what a farce this hearing is? Not one trace of *evidence*! Nothing but a bunch of sniveling, silly, witless *gossips* determined to have a Roman holiday with one poor, unfortunate woman! God help you all!"

The room broke into a roar, some being in sympathy with Winslow, but most of the crowd angry at the interruption. Justice Sneed finally quieted the crowd enough to say, "You will leave this room, Matthew Winslow—before I fine you for contempt of court!"

Winslow rose to his feet with fire in his eyes as he called out in ringing tones, "There are not words enough in the world, not brains enough in your heads, to describe the contempt I feel for this—I will not say *court*, for it is none! For this pack of dogs without a single trace of Christian love! I wash my hands of you!"

He stepped to the aisle, and Lydia, Rachel, and Gilbert followed him as he stalked toward the door, his face a mask of outrage. As the party left the room, Miles and Howland joined them. Outside the crowd milled around them, some angry, some saying, "Well done, sir!"

A burly man with a pock-marked face planted himself before Matthew, a sneer on his lips as he said, "Ye had yer say, Winslow, now I'll have mine!" He gave a quick look around and was satisfied to see that he had the crowd's attention. "Now wot about it, Winslow? Ye called me own brother a liar, did ye?"

Matthew lifted his head and looked coldly at his accuser. Something in Matthew's eyes made the heavy-set man blink and take a sudden step backward. "Rufus Cook, your brother is a liar, as is well known in this community. You are a liar and a thief, which I am perfectly willing to prove either in a court of law—or right now with fists, knives, guns, or any weapon you care to name!"

A silence fell over the yard, for Winslow's youthful reputation as a fighter of terrible proportions had not been greatly dimmed.

Rufus Cook backed down quickly. "Aw, yer so good an pure, all you Winslows! But lemme' tell ye, there's talk about the lot of ye, there is! The girl there, why, the hull town knows there's something that ain't natural about the way folks git well when she goes to 'em. And if a body can make somebody *well*, why, they can cast a spell and make 'em sick, can't they now?"

A sinister mutter went over the crowd, and Cook nodded savagely, "And that wife of yers, she prays strange. Some say in some kinda language that ain't good English!—and wot we wants to know is—wot sort of words is it, Winslow—mebbe' the Lord's prayer backwards, could it be, now?"

Matthew's arm moved so quickly that it was difficult to see. His fist shot out, catching Cook in the face with a solid *thunk*! The force of the blow drove the burly man backward, and he fell on his back in the dust. Then Winslow reached down, grabbed his coat and yanked him to his feet. He ignored the blood streaming from Cook's nose, and in a deadly voice said, "You open your mouth about my family one more time, Rufus Cook, and this community will not be bothered with your worthless presence any longer!"

He shoved the man away, and the crowd parted to let the family through. None of them spoke until they were out of sight of the square. "They're mad!" Miles said bitterly.

"They surely won't convict the old woman on such evidence!" Rachel said.

"They might," her father said heavily. "We must have help with this. I shouldn't have struck Rufus Cook!" He shook his head and gave Robert an apologetic smile. "You have any ideas about this, Reverend?"

"I think you must go to Reverend Parris," Howland instructed. "He may not be your idea of a good pastor—but he *is* in a position to do some good."

"Yes, that's true." Gilbert said suddenly. "The man has not much of the Spirit of the Lord, but as pastor, he has authority to disperse those idiots!"

"I wonder why he wasn't at the trial, Matthew," Lydia said.

"His daughter is sick, I believe," Rachel spoke up. "Perhaps he didn't want to leave her."

"Well, I don't like the sound of *that*," Matthew grunted. "In a matter this important, the pastor should be on the scene. We'll wait until the hearing is over; then we'll have a talk with Reverend Parris."

It was a long wait, and Howland felt somewhat awkward being there, but when he mentioned leaving, Matthew objected. "No, you must go with us, Robert! Parris may listen to a fellow minister—for he surely won't pay much heed to *me*."

The morning went by, and Lydia prepared a small lunch. No one was hungry and though the hearing was not far from their thought, they talked mostly of other things. After lunch, Gilbert lay down to take a nap, and Miles left on an errand for his father. When Matthew and Lydia also disappeared, Howland was disconcerted to find himself alone with Rachel.

As he sat at the table sipping tea, she came and seated herself across from him. "You look tired, Robert," she remarked. "I suspect you've been working hard."

He shrugged, started to agree, then a sudden streak of honesty overtook him. "No, I've been troubled about the last time I was here, Rachel." He caught her look of surprise and laughed shortly, adding, "I take it that you haven't been upset?"

Rachel stared at him, a slight color rising in her cheeks—making her even more attractive, he thought. "I've thought of you," she said quietly.

The silence ran on, making the ticking of the clock on the mantel seem very loud. She put her hand on her throat in a feminine gesture, and her eyes found his; for several seconds they looked at each other.

Then she said, "We're alike, aren't we, Robert? I mean, both of us have chosen to give our lives to God. And we've both been very careful to build a high wall around our hearts. I saw it in you the first time we met." She smiled at the memory. "It was like a large sign a man would put on his door: *KEEP OUT—NO LOVE ALLOWED!*"

Howland's face changed, for her words had put his life into sharp focus; he had never thought of it in that way, but now he said, "Why, in that you're right! I do want to give God my life, but I never made a vow about it."

"Nor I!" she admitted, then bit her lip and a sadness filled her hazel eyes as she said, "When I lost the man I was going to marry, I thought life was over—in that way. So I turned to God, and since that day, I've tried to think of nothing but serving Him."

He got up and paced nervously around the room, pausing to look out the window. Finally he came to stand before her, looking at her with troubled eyes. "I find myself thinking of you constantly," he said, then added, "I can't forget your kiss."

She rose in agitation, and he caught her before she could turn away. "Robert!" she protested, but he held her fast, and she found her heart beating furiously as they stood there.

"I may be in love with you, Rachel," he said quietly.

"You—mustn't be!" she cried. "This is no time to talk of that, not with all the trouble," she finished bruskly.

"If a man's in love," he said roughly, "the time to talk about it is when he has the woman in his arms—like now." He kissed her again, ignoring her effort to release herself.

She never knew which of them broke away first, for she was lost in the wonder of it. But when he lifted his head and stepped back, she said swiftly, "This can't be! It's too—quick! What would you say to one of the young people in our church who did what we've been doing?"

"We're not children, Rachel," Howland answered. "I know one thing, and that is that I feel about you as I've never felt toward any other woman! If it's not love, I don't know *what* it is. But answer me this, how do *you* feel?"

She was caught between two desires, both of them strong, and she could not answer immediately. He waited as he watched the struggle reflected in her face. Finally she sighed and said, "I must pray! It's no small thing, is it, to put your heart in the hands of another human being!"

He smiled as he took her hands. "This is the testing time, Rachel. You say God's never refused you anything? Then the matter is simple. You must ask Him if it is His will for me to come into your life."

"I will," she said quietly. "But this time, I don't think God is going to shout the answer from the housetop. I think the answer will be like the treasure hid in a field. Robert, I think we're going to have to give all we have to find God in *this* matter!"

Lydia was not ignorant of what was going on between her daughter and Robert. As they were on their way to the pastor's house, Lydia looked questioningly at Robert, but said nothing. There was a light in her dark eyes, though, that made him feel uncomfortable, like a small boy caught with his fingers in the honey jar. To avoid any misunderstanding, he resolved to make his feelings known to Rachel's parents as soon as possible.

Their visit with Parris was brief, almost abrupt, for the pastor was so agitated that he found it difficult to speak. His red-rimmed eyes indicated he hadn't slept in days. When Matthew told him why they had come, Parris cried out, "Oh, I cannot put myself against the court! No, not after what has happened here, in my own home!"

"Why, Pastor, what's the trouble?" Winslow asked in surprise.

The slight man began to moan in distress. Finally he made an attempt to compose himself and began. "I must—must tell you," he said with some pain, "the devil has raised his head—in my own house!"

"What do you mean?" Winslow cried.

"My daughter Betty and my niece Susanna have been attacked by the devil! Betty is in a trance, and her cousin informed me that the two of them have been afflicted by my servant Tituba and two others! Oh, it's worse than you can even think! They have been dancing in the forest, naked! And Abigail Williams—she is involved—and God knows who else! The devil is loose among us, I tell you!"

"Brother! Calm yourself!" Matthew commanded. He stared at the distraught minister and said, "You must be mistaken!"

"Would God I were!" Parris moaned. "But they have confessed, and I have sent for help from Boston. Reverend Hale is on his way, or so I trust."

"John Hale, of Beverly?" Howland asked instantly.

"Why, I believe so," Parris nodded. "Do you know him, Reverend Howland?"

"Yes. He was at Harvard last year."

"He is the most knowledgeable man in the matter of witches in the country—except for Cotton Mather, of course."

"We have not come to that, surely! Sending for *experts* on witches!" Winslow exclaimed. "We are godly men! Surely we can find the truth of this business!"

Parris pressed his lips together stubbornly. "My daughter is in a trance, sir! We must root out the devil—even if he takes the form of a faithful member of the church!"

"That's the danger, Parris!" Matthew cried. "If you had been at the hearing, you might have seen a sample of this smelling out of witches! John Cook points at a poor old woman he's hated for years over a trivial matter and cries out, 'She's a witch!' And others begin to get caught up in the thing, so that before you can bat an eye everyone is anxious to be a part of the hunt!"

"Mr. Winslow, I refuse to discuss the matter!" Parris shouted. "Reverend Hale will find the devil who's taken our people by craft—and then we will deal with him!"

Winslow nodded, "We will see what this man has to say, but we are in danger of losing ourselves in this thing, I tell you!"

They left and the door slammed behind them.

"What sort of man is this fellow Hale?" Matthew asked as they made their way back to the house.

"He's not a bad man, Matthew," Howland said slowly, "but he's obsessed with his subject! Spends all his time reading about witches and studying the invisible world. Now, Reverend Mather is interested in this subject, as you know, but there is no—no *balance* in Hale! He sees a demon behind every bush! But he's a fair man, and one who loves God."

"It's a sad thing—a sad thing, indeed!" Gilbert shook his head and added as they proceeded along the way. "In the old days, on the *Mayflower*, we helped each other, and during the first years, we clung together like children—now Christians seek the life of their fellow believers!" He said nothing until they got to the house, and then he stopped and looked over the village, shook his head and said, "I've lived too long, I think!"

"No, don't say that!" Rachel cried quickly. "We'll see this through, Grandfather!"

"It's a time of darkness, child," he said quietly. "And there'll be many of us who'll get swallowed in this wave of evil!" His prophetic tone sent a chill through Howland, and he left for home depressed as he had rarely been.

CHAPTER TWENTY

BRIDGET

★ ★ ★ ★

Reverend John Hale was a man of forty, small in stature, but filled with zeal for his task. He'd been at Salem only a few hours when, to his complete satisfaction, he found the hoofprint of the devil.

Howland was present when Hale located the problem of Reverend Parris's daughter Betty. Hale had been reluctant to allow Howland's presence, but he could find no good excuse for excluding the young favorite of Cotton Mather.

The small room was crowded. Joining Hale, Parris, and Howland were the West Indian servant, Tituba, Parris's niece, Susanna, and Abigail Williams.

Hale began by saying, "We must be precise in this matter, for the devil is subtle. But we will have him out!"

For over an hour there was a long interrogation of the girls, and the truth, though slow in coming, finally surfaced. Susanna Walcott was so nervous during the first part of the interview that she could hardly speak, while Abigail Williams defended herself angrily. It was Susanna who finally began to weep, crying out, "Yes, we were dancing! And there was a bowl of soup with something awful in it, but Abigail made me drink it!"

Howland happened to be looking directly at Abigail Williams as the younger girl cried out, and he saw an instant change go over her face. She had been sullen and angry, but in the flicker of an eye she assumed an expression of grief and sorrow! *She's acting!* he thought in astonishment, and immediately she began to cry out and gave every evidence of honest grief.

"It was Tituba!" she moaned. "She put blood in the soup and said she'd kill us all if we didn't drink it!"

Hale turned his guns on the black woman, and in no time she was broken down, confessing all that he put in her mind. An air of hysteria came into her voice as she began to scream, "I saw Mistress Mason with the devil! I saw Bridget Bishop with the devil!"

Instantly Abigail began to screech, "I want the light of God! I want the love of God. I saw John Proctor with the devil! I saw Mistress Osburn with the devil."

Betty Parris suddenly began to cry, and she too began to accuse various people. Finally Hale led the men out and said instantly, "We have it now!"

"Sir, what you have is a group of hysterical women!" Howland stated sharply.

Howland's statement offended Hale, and he countered. "I'll brook no opposition, sir! You may be a favorite at Harvard through your friendship with Mr. Mather—but that avails nothing here!"

Howland tried to reason with the man, but he was finally convinced that other means would have to be found. Leaving the house, Robert went directly to see Matthew Winslow.

Winslow and his father listened carefully, then both of them exploded with anger. "That fool!" Matthew cried. "Can't he see that those girls are play-acting?"

"I saw it," Howland admitted. "But Hale is a man on a holy quest, at least in his own mind."

"We'll have to fight it!" Matthew told them bitterly. "And what will happen to the gospel while we are wasting our time with this abomination?"

"Winslow, you must be careful," Howland warned. "This is going to get worse—I've seen it before. I know you want to help, but when things like this are just beginning, they're like a forest fire, and nobody can stop it!"

"But—what would you have me do?"

"Wait, that's all!" Howland spoke earnestly, but he saw the

stubborn lines in Matthew's face, and knew that it was hopeless.

"I played the coward once, Robert," Matthew said with a glance at his father. "I was in Bedford Jail with John Bunyan, you know, and I let my God down—but it'll not happen this time!"

Howland shrugged. "I thought it might be that way, Matthew."

For three weeks, all through the month of May, Salem was a battleground. Denouncing a neighbor for witchcraft became so common that no one could be sure who would be in jail next.

The Winslows and a few others stood against the witch hunt, denouncing the whole thing as a godless affair but their resistance had little effect, for as Howland said, it was like a forest fire, gaining ground each day.

On the seventh of June the blow fell. Howland was with the Winslows, for he had practically given up his own parish work to support them in their efforts. They were all sitting around the table when someone knocked on the door.

"Must be William Gates come about the new shipment," Matthew decided. He got up and opened the door, only to find a company of men, six in all. Instantly he knew their purpose.

Marshall Herrick, a man in his early thirties, held out a paper and said harshly, "I have a warrant for you, Matthew Winslow."

"Matthew!" Lydia rose and came to stand beside her husband.

"Don't fret, Lydia. I'll be back to you by dark—"

"The warrant is for both of you," Herrick interrupted.

Matthew turned pale, and Lydia, fearing his temper, said quickly, "I'll get my coat—don't be upset, dear!"

Matthew set his teeth and bowed his head. *Oh, God!* he cried inwardly, *not again!* The horrors of the Bedford jail flashed into his mind with sickening impact. Finally he exhaled and said, "All right."

Herrick looked relieved and said, "I'll have to ask you to put these chains on, Mr. Winslow—and your wife."

"Chains!" Winslow looked aghast at the irons. Seeing the flash of fire in his eyes, the men in the door readied themselves for violence, but once again, he managed to control himself.

"Miles, take care of your sister," he said, and stood there as they put the irons on his wrists.

"Is there no warrant for me, Marshall?" Rachel asked.

"Well—you've been named," Herrick admitted, "but as yet there ain't no warrant."

"And none for me either?" Gilbert said. Then he lifted his head and said fiercely, "There *will* be one, by heaven! I'll see to that soon enough!"

Rachel went to his side and put her arm around him. The two stood in stunned silence as they watched the group disappear down the lane.

Breaking the heavy stillness, Howland said, "I know this is a blow, but you mustn't despair. This madness can't go on forever!"

"It doesn't have to go on forever, Robert," Gilbert stated. "Just long enough to get people hanged."

"It won't come to that, I tell you!" Howland insisted. "At the worst, some people will have to stay in jail for a few weeks—they wouldn't *dare* execute anyone!"

"In England last year they executed over three hundred people for witchcraft," Rachel added quietly.

"This isn't England!" The thought of it made Howland angry, and he cried out loudly, "There's got to be a way out of this!"

But day after day went by, and matters grew worse. Over a hundred people were in jail by the middle of June. Finally a special tribunal of judges—all prominent men, arrived in Salem to take charge of the trials.

"Now they'll bring some reason into this business!" Howland said. "Samuel Sewall is a just man, I know for certain."

But it was Judge Hawthorn and Deputy Governor Danforth who dominated the legal scene, and their first action was to sentence Bridget Bishop to hang!

Rachel and Miles were visiting their parents in the common cell when the news came. They had brought hot food as usual, but the cell was so crowded that they had difficulty finding space.

Miles was haggard, looking worse than his father, and he ate nothing. "Do you know what's happening now—about confessing, I mean?"

"What's that, son?" Matthew asked.

"Why, they've all gone crazy, Father!" Miles said huskily. "They tried Mistress Raymond, and she confessed to being a witch—"

"What! Why, the woman's silly enough, but no more a witch than I am!" Matthew said in a shocked voice.

"Was she sentenced to die?" Lydia asked quickly.

"Sentenced!" Miles snorted grimly. "She was set free—after she confessed her own guilt and repented of it. She accused Giles Cory of witchcraft, so now Giles is arrested and the Raymond woman is free."

"But—that's monstrous!" Matthew's voice shook, and he stared at Miles in disbelief.

"And three more have 'confessed,' " Miles said bitterly. "All you have to do now is name somebody else as a witch and you're dismissed."

They were still talking about it half an hour later when Howland came in, his face pale as he picked his way through the crowd. He said not one word, but stood there looking at them with an expression in his gray eyes that they could not read.

"What is it, Robert?" Rachel asked, taking his arm.

He looked at Matthew and said as though his voice were trapped, "Your father—he's been named, and they've gone to arrest him."

"God have mercy on them!" Matthew hissed. "I'll have none of it!"

"There's more." Howland face was grim. "Bridget Bishop—she'll be executed tomorrow at dawn."

"No! That's impossible!" Lydia breathed.

"You can hear the hammers if you go to that window," Howland said. "They're building the gallows now."

They waited silently, and in less than an hour, the door clanged open and Gilbert Winslow entered. He saw them at once, and came over to say, "I feel better now. Somehow I felt like a traitor to the family being outside."

Matthew stared at his father, shaking his head in unbelief. "From the *Mayflower* to this place!"

"God's still on His throne, son," Gilbert smiled. He seated himself comfortably and picked up a piece of cake that Rachel had brought. "Now let the devil do his worst—for my Lord Jesus has His foot on the slimy fellow's neck!"

Miles struggled to keep his composure, then looked at Howland, asking, "Robert, can't you do *anything*? You must know somebody who can help us!"

"I'll leave tonight, Miles," Howland said. "I've written Cotton Mather twice, but have received no answer. I can't believe he's gotten the letters, so I'll hunt him down, and he'd better do something about this, or I'll know the reason why!"

"Robert—don't go until tomorrow. Bridget needs you."

The two of them had visited the old woman every day, taking food and trying to cheer her spirits. She had come to lean on them, and Howland nodded. "Yes, of course, Rachel. Perhaps we'd better go now."

They left the common cell, and found armed guards had been placed around the small building where the convicted prisoners were kept. One of the guards knew them, but said, "You can't see the Bishop woman without permission from one of the judges."

Howland and Rachel went to the courtroom, which was mostly empty. The judges, they were told, were eating before the next session, so Howland went to the door at the back of the large room and knocked on it sharply.

It opened and the Deputy Governor Danforth stood there with an irritated expression. "What is it, man? Can't you let us have a moment's peace?"

"I don't think you'll ever have much peace of any sort, Danforth," Howland said, staring at him directly.

Danforth was a tall man, accustomed to having his own way in all things. Anger flared in his pale eyes as he demanded, "What does that mean—and what do you want?"

Howland stepped closer, causing Danforth to retreat, a move that bruised his pride. "I mean that none of you will have any peace, sentencing senile old women to die!" He saw his words strike against the man, but gave him no quarter. "And I've come for a pass to see the innocent woman you've condemned to die."

"Who are you?" Danforth shouted. "Do you dare insult this court!"

"I'm Reverend Robert Howland." Howland began to raise his voice. "Declare me for a witch, if you will, but I *will* see Bridget Bishop."

Samuel Sewall, a small man with a pale face and distressed look in his eyes, had been sitting at the table nibbling at a piece of bread. Rising suddenly he came running over to say, "I know this man, Danforth—let me take care of this!"

Danforth glared at Howland, but said no more as Sewall and Robert stepped outside.

"Robert, control yourself!" Sewall warned.

"But, Reverend Sewall, how can you—"

"You'll do no good by getting yourself arrested, will you now?" Sewall fished through his pocket, but finding no paper, he called out to a guard, "You there! Take this man to Bridget Bishop—pass him and this young lady through at once, you hear me?"

"Thank you, sir," Howland said; then he looked Sewall straight in the eye and said, "I'm going to Cotton Mather. It's too late for that poor woman, but I intend to pull your house down around your head—if I can!"

Sewall closed his eyes in distress and implored, "Go at once, Robert! Would God *someone* would call a halt to this thing!" He said no more, but turned and went back into the other room.

Howland and Rachel followed the guard to the small building and were passed through on his word. They found the old woman sitting down on a small bench. As they approached, she stared at them with a fearful look in her face; then hope came into her faded eyes.

"You won't let 'em hurt me, will you, dear?" She clung to Rachel, weeping. For the rest of the day they stayed with her. In the evening Robert left but Rachel stayed with her all night, quoting scriptures to her. When Howland returned at dawn, both of the women were exhausted.

"We have only ten minutes," Howland murmured quietly. "Is she—"

"She's ready to be with her Lord," Rachel said. She leaned over and whispered, "Bridget, wake up. The Lord is near unto you."

Howland never forgot that time. This old woman, who had

been on the verge of insanity when he left, opened her eyes and looked at him with a quietness she'd never shown him.

She sat up and asked Rachel, "Is it time now?"

"Yes. In a few minutes you will be with Him who loves you more than you can ever know! Will you think of Him as you go to the end?"

Bridget took a deep breath, closed her eyes and said, "I wisht it were over—and I were with 'im now!"

They sat there quietly as Rachel quoted a chapter from the Gospel of John, and then there was a knock at the door. They all rose, and when the door opened and Bridget saw the deputy governor and the hangman with the black hood, Howland was afraid that she would break down, but she did not.

"I'm ready," she said quietly, and without another word, moved to the door. As the crowd made way for her, Rachel went with her, the two holding hands like schoolgirls.

There was a thick silence in the dawn air, and despite the crowd that had gathered at the foot of the rudely built gallows, there was no speech heard.

Howland followed the two women, his throat aching. When they arrived at the foot of the gallows, Rachel kissed Bridget and whispered, "Goodbye, sister! Greet the precious Savior for me!"

Bridget's step was firm as she climbed the steps. As the black hood settled over her head, she said nothing. Her eyes were open and there was a smile on her wrinkled lips as the hood slid down. Then the noose followed.

The hangman stepped back, put his hand on the lever and looked to the deputy governor for a sign.

Just as the sign was given, from beneath the black cloth came a strong voice, crying out, "He is here! I see Him!"

Then the trap fell, and it was over.

CHAPTER TWENTY-ONE

A TIME TO DIE

★ ★ ★ ★

Howland had expected to return to Salem within a week, but it was near the end of August before he entered the village, his nerves frayed and his eyes red-rimmed from the loss of sleep. He went at once to the jail. As he dismounted, the guard exclaimed, "Why, Reverend Howland, I didn't know you was back!"

Howland nodded. When the door opened he went at once to Matthew, who was standing at the window. Lydia and Gilbert were lying on a rude pallet at his feet. Matthew was so engrossed, he did not hear Howland approach.

"Matthew—" Howland said quietly. When the tall man turned from the window, he looked ten years older than he had a month before. His hair was unkempt and he had lost weight. He had lines on his face that hadn't been there before, but his eyes brightened as he saw his friend.

"Robert—you've come back!"

His voice awakened Lydia, and he stooped to help her to her feet. She, too, looked exhausted and ill. She tried to smile, but her voice was not strong. "Have you seen Rachel?"

"No, I came straight here."

Seeing him hesitate, Matthew tried to smile. "I know you have no good news, Robert. From your letters we really didn't hope too much."

Howland said wearily, "Mather was gone, and it took me three weeks to catch up with him. Then when I did find him, he refused to interfere."

"I never thought he would," Matthew shook his head. "They all hang together, don't they?" Then he tried to laugh, adding, "I shouldn't have used that figure—*hang together*—it's a forbidden word."

"How many—?"

"Have they executed?" Matthew finished when Howland could not complete his statement. "Why, it's difficult to keep count. There were five in July and six in August—that makes eleven, doesn't it?"

"Robert," Lydia said quickly, "you must talk to Rachel and Miles—at once! They are denouncing the court in public, by name. It's just a matter of time until they are arrested if they don't stop. I wish they'd go away until—"

"You know they won't do that, Lydia!"

Gilbert was stirring, and he was so stiff from the hard floor that Matthew and Lydia had to help him to his feet. He started to speak, but a spasm of coughing cut off his words. It frightened Howland to see how thin the old man had grown. His face was sallow, unhealthy, and filled with pain.

Howland looked at Matthew with a question in his face, and received a warning shake of the head. It was obvious that Gilbert was very ill. Howland said, "I failed, but I'm not giving up."

Gilbert Winslow stood up carefully as if he were afraid his brittle bones would snap with the strain. Though Gilbert had little strength in his body, he held his head high and his gaze steady. His spirit was strong and unchanged. "Well, Robert, we're still here, you see." A grin touched his tough old lips, and he coughed hard; then he went on, "They haven't killed me yet—and even if they do, they won't kill me but once!"

Matthew smiled, then turned to Howland. "See if you can get better quarters for Father, will you, Robert?"

"I'll try," Howland promised. "Maybe Sewall will help."

"Go to Rachel first," Lydia pleaded. "Try to talk to her, Robert!"

"Yes, I'll do my best—but this stubborn Winslow blood is a hard force to oppose, you know!" He smiled at them, then left at once.

Rachel was at the house when Robert stopped by. Surprised, her eyes opened wide when she saw him. Without a word, he took her in his arms and held her. She clung to him for the first time with complete abandonment, and finally she pulled his head down and kissed him.

He stared at her in amazement, then said, "Well! You know how to welcome a man back!"

She flushed, and then laughed shortly. She had lost weight, as had he, and there was the same strain in her face that he'd seen in her parents. "Did you talk to Reverend Mather?" she asked, looking up into his face.

"Yes—and he refuses to do a thing." Howland answered slowly. "I begged and threatened, but nothing would move him. We'll have to find another way."

Rachel turned and walked to the window. She stood there for a long time and he came to stand beside her. A pair of bluebirds were building a home in a knothole of the oak tree, and they made a vivid patch of blue as they streaked back and forth carrying straws and small twigs.

"Robert—maybe there *is* no other way," she said, continuing to look out the window. "This may be one of those times we have to stand and die. There are times like that, aren't there?"

He put his hand on her shoulder, and the smell of her hair was sweet as he stood there. "I suppose so—but we can't *know* if it is. We have to fight as though it were not. Then, when we've done all the arm of flesh can do, we leave it to God."

She turned and looked up to him, and there was such a trust in her face that his heart was overwhelmed. He could not fail her! "No matter what happens, Robert, at least I found you!" she murmured.

He started to reply, but even as she spoke, her eyes flew open wide, and she gave a short cry, her hand flying to her lips. She whirled and leaned against the wall, her shoulders shaking with grief.

"Rachel! What is it?"

She would not answer nor turn at first, but finally he pulled her around. "I—I said the same thing to Jude Alden—and that same day—he died!"

He put his arms around her and let her cry; then finally, when she stopped, he said, "I have something to say to you, Rachel. Something you may not understand."

"I'll believe you, Robert Howland, even if I can't understand you!"

"Will you now?"

"Truly!"

He smiled down at her, and then grew sober. "We must pray— pray as we've never prayed before. But there are things that can be *done*, Rachel. And I have to try *something*—I must! Now, in the days to come, you may see me do some things that will seem— unusual. Right now, I can't say what they will be, but I believe that God has put me in this place, at this time, for a purpose. And that purpose may be to help your family. I intend to do it, but it won't be easy, and it won't be—respectable, I fear."

She stared at him in bewilderment, then whispered, "I—I don't understand you, Robert."

"You will understand less in the days to come—but I want you to try to remember this—" He took her in his arms and kissed her with almost a finality in his manner. "Can you re- member that I love you, and will love you until the day they put a stone over my head?"

"Yes, if you say so, Robert!"

He stroked her hair, then stepped back. "Try to talk to Miles. See if you can keep him out of this. Now, I must go."

He left the house, and she stood there waiting for him to turn and wave as he often did, but he walked straight on. The set of his strong shoulders looked like someone squaring off to do battle. What the battle would be, she did not know. She did know, however, and smiled to herself as she thought of it, that he loved her—and that was enough!

August passed away, and as September rolled over the vil- lage, the executions continued—twenty-one in all. Still the jail remained crowded, for no matter how many died, there were always more accused and arrested.

The steamy heat inside the jail, together with the constant dust from the floor and the straw used for bedding, irritated the lungs of all the prisoners. Coughing was so constant that they ceased to notice it. Sickness swept through the cells, and by the first of September, six had died of illness; others were past help, even if they had been freed.

The trials went on slowly, and as prisoners were condemned to die, they were taken from the larger cell and placed in the smaller one. Here there was no overcrowding, for the gallows continued to snuff out the lives as soon as they were transferred to the smaller unit.

Rachel and Miles worked steadily, not only to keep their own family from suffering, but to provide as much as they could for those in prison who had nobody to help. Rachel functioned as both nurse and cook from sunup to long past dark until she was worn almost to a razor's edge.

"Daughter, you must rest," Matthew pleaded with her one night. She had helped wash some of the sick women, and afterward when she came as usual to sit with her parents and grandfather, she fell asleep leaning against him.

She straightened up at once, laughed shortly, and said, "Oh, I'm fine. Just a little tired."

Giles Cory, another prisoner, had attached himself to the Winslows. He was a hearty man of eighty, or had been until the prison had eaten away at his strength. He feared for his wife, who also was charged, and he spent much time discussing the problem of his property with Matthew. "If they convict me, Mr. Winslow, they'll take my property, and my children and grandchildren will starve," he had said. Indeed, Matthew could give him little comfort, for such might well be the case not just with Giles but with all of them.

Gilbert was growing much worse, his cough by this time becoming chronic. Had he subsisted on jail food, he would have been dead. He was sitting with his back propped against the wall when he looked up at Rachel and asked, "Where has your young man been, Rachel? He's been gone—what, a week or more?"

Rachel looked slightly confused, then said, "I—I think he's been very busy with his church, Grandfather."

"The big minister?" Giles asked. "He be in court most of the time, so they say. John Proctor say he do sit there with his book out, writing down what the judges say."

"I didn't know Robert was doing that," Matthew muttered.

"Aye, and it make Judge Hawthorn cry out in open court at him, so John said." He laughed and added, "The judge asked the minister what he wrote, and the minister said he knew that God was keeping a record for judgment day—but *he* was keeping one fer when the world found out about these trials!"

Lydia looked at Rachel and asked quietly, "Did Robert tell you what he was doing?"

"No." Rachel got up and said, "I haven't seen him for a week." Then she left and Matthew stared after her.

"Something is wrong there," he mused quietly.

"Yes. She's been hurt." Lydia looked out the window and watched her daughter walk past the gallows with shoulders slumped and defeated. Her own heart was heavy, for although she had little hope for herself or Matthew, she spent most of her time praying that Rachel and Miles would survive. She was shocked to suddenly realize how much she had depended on Howland to help.

Abigail Williams left the courtroom, and as was always true, the tension had built up in her. She was there every day, and many times over the past months she had been called back to testify. She was a beautiful girl with a sense of drama in her blood. Since childhood she had made up scenes and acted them out when she was alone; now the action was real, and she was intoxicated with it.

She lived with an elderly woman named Mistress Taylor, who paid absolutely no attention to her activities. Until the trials had begun, Abigail had worked out, cleaning houses for people. Now she did nothing but sit in court and afterward talk about the trials to Susanna and one or two other girls.

She turned down the street, unaware of the tall man coming from across the way. Suddenly she ran into him and would have fallen if he had not caught her and held her up.

"Careful!" a deep voice cautioned. Startled, she looked up into the face of Robert Howland. "Sorry to be so clumsy, Miss Abigail."

She was very conscious of his hand on her arm and countered with a smile, "Why, it's my own fault, Reverend Howland. I'm always running into things and stepping into holes."

"Are you going this way? So am I." He fell into step beside her, saying, "I've been wanting to speak to you, Miss Abigail."

She had expected anything but that, for she had kept up with his attachment to the Winslow family as closely as the rest of the small village. She said suspiciously, "To me? I think your friends, the Winslows, would not like that, sir!"

"No." He sighed and remarked, "They are to be pitied, don't you think?"

She thought about that, then answered, "I thought you held

that they weren't witches at all!"

"Oh, that was my position *at first*, as it was with most of the poor wretches," Howland said.

Abigail listened to him talk, and something about the big minister excited her. He was, she had always felt, the most attractive man she'd seen, and now to be walking with him triggered her active imagination. She began to see him calling on her, taking her to the courtroom, while everyone gawked at the two of them.

By the time they got to her house, she knew at least one thing about Howland—he was a man who appreciated a *woman*. She was a beautiful girl and had been aware of male attention since she was fifteen years old. She knew admiration when she saw it—as she did in Howland's glances at her.

"Why don't you come in and have a cup of tea," she smiled up into his face boldly.

"Why, that would be very nice," he said in surprise. "Perhaps you could tell me a little more about your experiences with these frightful witches," he added. "I've really no experience, and to hear the *real* thing would be most helpful—though I can't expect an attractive young woman such as yourself to dwell much on these things."

"I don't mind," Abigail smiled, as he led him into her house.

From that day Howland no longer sat on the front seat taking notes, but seated himself farther to the back. It did not escape the attention of the village that he walked Abigail to and from the court each day, and as often as not had tea with her. It was all respectable, for old Mistress Taylor was always present. But if they had considered that the old woman went to bed at seven, and Howland rarely left until ten or later, there might have been even more talk than there was.

There was little said in the common jail, at least by the Winslows, though the other prisoners picked up the gossip from their relatives and friends.

Howland did visit his friends from time to time, but there was a constraint between them that made his visits very painful, so he came no more after the first of October.

Matthew said only one brief word to Lydia, and spoke to no other: "I have never been so deceived in a human being." Lydia only pressed his arm and said nothing.

Miles was not so tactful. He heard the rumor that his friend had taken up with Abigail, but he refused to believe it at first. Finally he had confronted Howland with it, and when Robert said only, "That is the way it is, Miles. I'm sorry for your family," he had stared at the man in disbelief.

"I can't believe you mean that, Robert!" he said, with color filling his cheeks. He had loved this man, more than anyone outside his family. After admiring him, trusting him, now to see him cast off his ties with the family for Abigail Williams, the central figure of the trials, was more than his spirit could bear.

"What about my sister?" he gritted between his teeth.

"That's none of your business."

Miles drew himself up, his face pale. "You are a scoundrel, Howland!" he cried, drawing back his hand and delivering a ringing blow to the older man's face.

Howland did not move. Looking steadily at his friend, he said only, "Leave it there, Miles. I will not fight you."

Miles wheeled and walked blindly away, his youthful face twisted into a mask of grief and disbelief.

Miles had little time to grieve, for two days later, Rachel was named and arrested. Her accuser was a slatternly woman whom Rachel had often helped, taking food to her four ragged children, nursing her when her drunken husband beat her, and going to her when she had the pox and no one would come to her cabin for any price. The woman herself had been accused of casting spells, but she had endured the jail for only a week before she began to scream. In her fear she had accused six or seven women, including Rachel.

Rachel was brought to the jail, with the few things she could carry. Miles had followed close behind, silently suffering as one by one his loved ones were arrested. Lydia took one look at her, and for the first time in all the dreary weeks broke down. She turned her face to Matthew's chest, her thin body racked with dry sobs. Tenderly he held the frail, sobbing form, willing his strength into her. He remembered those last months in Bedford Jail when he had turned from her, refusing to be comforted. Now, in a small way, he could repay her.

Rachel smiled as she looked at them. "Well, I'll not have to go home every night now, will I?" she said cheerily. "But Miles is all right, and we'll soon be out of this place." Even as she said it, she wondered at the dismal future.

Gilbert sat on a bench, his face gaunt, but a fiery light burning in his faded blue eyes. "I wish your grandmother could see you, girl! She'd have been so proud!"

Three days later, five more prisoners were hanged, and the next day the Winslows went to trial—all except Rachel. She, they said, would be allowed time to repent of her wickedness. They were taken into the crowded courtroom, dirty and sick from the long imprisonment, and it went as they feared. One after another, a line of accusers rose up, but there was no defense against their enemies. There was no *evidence*, so there could be no refutation.

"The accusers are always right," Matthew said wearily after the mockery of a trial was over. The end had come when Danforth had said, "Confess your guilt! Point out those who are your companions in this vile witchcraft! Do this—and you will be set free."

"Suppose I confess that I am guilty and repent," Matthew asked at one point, "but am not willing to incriminate others?"

"Then you have not repented!" Judge Hawthorn said with heavy illogic. "A true Christian will always side against the devil—you will identify those who are witches or you will die!"

Each of them was asked to recant, and each, of course, refused. They were pronounced guilty and sentenced to be hanged.

"There was never any hope, you know," Matthew said quietly as they entered their dark quarters. "Not one soul has been found innocent since this farce started."

They fared a little better physically, since there were beds and more space. But day by day the trap of the gallows fell, and it was only a matter of time before they too would make the last walk to their deaths.

Howland had disappeared, they were told. "I hope I never look on his face again, the traitor!" Miles cried bitterly.

Rachel said nothing at all. Two days later, the jailer came with the announcement: "Your turn tomorrow, Rachel Winslow!"

She was so exhausted that her only reaction was to thank God that it would soon be over!

CHAPTER TWENTY-TWO

THE TRIAL OF RACHEL WINSLOW

★ ★ ★ ★

Morning came in a feeble gleam of light that filtered through the small window. Rachel stood looking out, but she saw nothing, for though her eyes were opened, her mind was in another place.

She turned quickly, startled when the key turned in the latch, and Martin Plummer, the young jailer, came in with their food. "Here's your breakfast, Miss," he said. He was twenty, and had no sympathy for the court; now he said apologetically, "No eggs this morning, Miss."

"Thank you, Martin," Rachel said with a faint smile.

Matthew and Lydia arose, and then, moving very slowly, Gilbert pulled himself up and sat on the side of his bed looking very ill.

As they sat down to eat, Rachel noticed that the young jailer did not move to go. He stood there shifting from one foot to the other, and she asked, "Is something wrong, Martin?"

He bit his lip and shook his head with an abrupt and angry motion. "It's—Mr. Cory!"

"Giles?" Matthew asked, lifting his head. "What is it, young man?"

Martin licked his lips and mumbled, "He's—he's dead, sir. Died last night."

The prisoners looked at each other, and Gilbert spoke up in

a rusty voice, "They didn't hang him at night, did they?"

"No, sir, they didn't. They didn't hang him at all."

They waited for him to continue and finally he cleared his throat and said, "They pressed him!"

"Pressed him? What's that, in heaven's name?" Matthew asked.

"Why, you see sir, Mr. Cory, he wouldn't say aye nor nay to his indictment—because he knowed if he denied the charge, they'd hang him and sell his property. So he said nothing and died under the law—so his sons will have his farm."

"What does that mean?" Rachel asked.

"Why, it's the law, Miss! He couldn't be condemned a wizard without he answer the indictment, don't you see?"

"And they did what, boy?" Gilbert asked, his eyes fixed on the young jailer.

"They pressed him, sir," Martin said.

"Press? Press how?"

"They put great stones on his chest until he'd plead aye or nay."

Gilbert stared at Martin, then said softly, "And he said nothing, did he?"

Martin licked his lips and then lifted his head. "He said, 'More weight!' That's all they got from Mr. Giles Cory!"

"He was a fearsome man, Giles Cory!" Gilbert said slowly, his face lit with an awed expression.

"I'll have to come and get you in an hour, Miss," Martin said. "The rest of you are to come as well, by order of the court."

"We'll be ready, Martin."

After the jailer left they ate a little, all except Gilbert—he could only drink a little liquid from the pitcher.

"I hope Miles will not come to the courtroom," Rachel remarked.

"He'll be there," Matthew nodded. He looked around the room and said, "This room is a lot better than Bedford Jail!" His face grew thoughtful. "I've thought so often of Bunyan these days. Eleven years in that foul den, and he could have walked out at any time."

"He was a fearful man, too," Gilbert smiled. "Gone to be

with the Lord now, but his book about the Pilgrim—it's all over the world, I reckon."

Matthew looked at Lydia and then at Rachel. "I can't see any reason in all this," he said in a defeated voice. "It seems so—useless!"

"All things work together for good to those that love the Lord," Lydia said softly, renewed courage in her voice. She came to stand beside Matthew, placing her hands on his shoulders. "We've had so many good years, and our God is good—no matter what!"

They talked quietly for a time, and when the hour was almost up, Gilbert suddenly said, "Rachel, I'm thinking about Howland."

Rachel stood perfectly still. "Yes, Grandfather?"

Laboriously the old man got to his feet and came over to stand beside her. He took her hand in his and stared at it for a long time, so long that she thought he had forgotten what he intended to say. Then he said quietly, "There was a time in my life when everything I did looked wrong—to everyone."

He said nothing more, but she knew that he was trying to tell her something that he had not words for. Finally she said, "You think he's a good man, Grandfather?"

"What do you think, girl?"

She stared in his eyes, and now it was her turn to be silent. Finally she said slowly, "I thought he loved me—and I know I loved him."

"Rachel," he said steadily, "never take counsel of your fears! If you love a man, then stick with him, and don't doubt if the world is falling!"

Rachel's eyes opened wide, and she blinked and nodded, "All right, Grandfather!"

Then the door opened and Martin said, "The court's in session. Come with me, please."

They followed the guards into the courtroom, and despite the early hour, all seats were filled, and as usual, the windows were filled with the faces of the observers.

The judges sat in their places, and Rachel went forward to the chair indicated by Martin, while the others sat on one of the side benches. Rachel sat down and was slightly surprised to find that she had no fear at all. She was thinking of Gilbert's words about Robert Howland, and it took an effort of her will to bring her mind back when Judge Hawthorn read the charges.

"You have been charged, Rachel Winslow, with using familiar spirits, with using unholy arts, with calling forth the dead, and with casting spells. The witnesses have sworn under oath that you have done these things, and we will now proceed to hear the charges from these witnesses in open court."

For the next hour testimony was taken from five witnesses, and Rachel made no response to any of them. Her immobility aroused the ire of Danforth, who interrupted the testimony to say, "You do not appear to know your peril, girl!"

"I am in none, sir, from this court."

"We have the power to hang you!"

"I do not fear him that is able to kill the body, but him that is able to cast both soul and body into hell," Rachel said calmly.

Samuel Sewall broke in to say, "Miss Winslow, we have heard testimony after testimony of your many good works—"

"For which of these do you condemn me?" she shot back.

"For being a witch!" Hawthorn cried.

At that moment Rachel heard the front door slam, and instantly there was a babble of excited whispers. She turned and saw Robert Howland walking down the aisle in the company of a small elderly man.

She heard a noise from the judge's bench and turned to see all of the judges rising from their seats, their faces white as a sheet.

Howland came to the front of the courtroom, looked around for a seat, then said to two men who were staring at the elderly man, "You two stand by the wall," and when they popped up and scooted away like rabbits, he said, "You may have this seat, sir."

The man, in his seventies at least, nodded and sat down. Howland sat down beside him, and both men looked at the court expectantly.

Judge Hawthorn looked as if he were having some sort of attack. His face was ashen and beads of moisture suddenly appeared on his brow. When he spoke his voice trembled slightly.

"Reverend Mather. . . ?" he said tentatively, then cleared

his throat and asked, "Is—would you like to sit with the judges?"

"No, I would not. Get on with the trial."

"But, really, sir, it would be more fitting if you would join us."

Rachel heard the name *Increase Mather* and looked quickly at the small man. She had never seen the man, but he was the unofficial monarch of the Puritan world, ruling from his pulpit in Old North Church in Boston. His son, Cotton, was the rising star, but it was well known that the son honored the father. There was simply no one in the New World like Increase Mather; he was the American equivalent of the Archbishop of Canterbury— or even the Pope, some had said. In any case, his very presence was enough to freeze the judges in Salem, and it was with some effort that Hawthorn managed to say, "We have two more testimonies, do we not?"

"Yes, sir," the bailiff nodded. "Sarah Marsh will come forward."

This was the woman who had first called out Rachel's name, and was a poor witness for the court. She began crying as soon as she laid eyes on Rachel, and when Hawthorn finally said, "You saw this woman use black arts to heal your child?"

"She came—and she put something on his head—and she prayed—and he got well!"

"Ah, and was it blood she put on his head, Mistress Marsh?" Hawthorn demanded with some assurance.

"No—it was just oil—that's all!"

"You can swear to that?"

"Oh, I seen it, 'cause I asked her, and she let me see—it was just olive oil!"

Hawthorn kept badgering the woman for thirty minutes. She would repeat anything he told her, but there was no substance in her testimony.

"Call the next witness!" he said in disgust. For the benefit of the distinguished guest, he announced loudly, "Fortunately there are more vocal witnesses to show this woman for what she is. Call Susanna Walcott!"

"Susanna Walcott—come forward," the bailiff called, and the girl came forward, looking miserable. She sat down and looked at the floor.

"Susanna Walcott, did you see this woman with the devil?" Hawthorn asked.

"Yes, sir."

"Tell this court about it."

"Well, I was in bed, and she flew in through the window, and there was this awful *thing* with her—the devil, it was! And she tried to get me to sign the book he had, and when I wouldn't do it, she pinched me until I was blue!"

She said all this in a rote fashion, as though she had it memorized, but it satisfied Hawthorn, and he asked for more details.

Susanna opened her mouth, but it was not her voice that began to cry out. "I saw Rachel Winslow with the devil!"

The voice was clear, and every eye in the court swung to where a young woman named Sarah Good was standing up, looking at the ceiling. She began to sway from side to side, and again she cried out, "I saw Rachel Winslow with the devil!"

Several other young girls began to take up the chant, calling out that they had seen certain people with the devil. It had happened often in the court, and Hawthorn stood there looking satisfied.

Finally he said, "The devil is revealed! Rachel Winslow, you stand accused! The evidence is that you are a worker of iniquity and a servant of the Evil One."

He would have said more, but suddenly Sarah Good's voice rose again. This time she came out of her seat and moved in a ghostlike fashion down the aisle. Then she held out her finger and cried in a piercing voice, "I saw Judge Hawthorn in the forest! He was drinking from the devil's cup!"

A deathly silence fell on the room. Not a soul stirred, and then Sarah Good cried even louder, "Judge Hawthorn is the Black Man—he came to me in my room—he made me sign his book! He is the Black Man!"

Hawthorn's face was the color of old putty, and his voice mute. He sat in his chair as the girl continued to cry out terrible accusations against him—things no decent girl would even *know* about!

Then, as before, others began to take up the chant. It was the young girls who had cried out before, and older women, too, and some men. But this time they were crying out, "I saw Governor Danforth with the devil!" "I saw Samuel Sewall with Satan!" One of them began to cry out that she had seen the governor of the colony with the devil!

Then a young girl, no more than fourteen screamed out, "I seen Cotton Mather with the devil! I seen Increase Mather with the devil!"

A gasp went up from the crowd, for Howland's companion had risen. He walked to the front platform and stood there staring at the judges. He said nothing but let the silence build up, and then he said in a silky voice, "You gentlemen are accused of witchcraft, I believe."

"But this is ridiculous!" Hawthorn sputtered. "These witnesses are lying!"

"Have they accused other people?" Mather asked, still not raising his voice.

"Why, I believe they may have—one or two—"

"Have some of those who were accused been executed, Judge Hawthorn?"

A mutter swept through the room. Hawthorn sat as though paralyzed, unable to speak.

"Yes, they have," Judge Sewall answered quietly.

Increase Mather stared at the judges, then said with no emotion whatsoever, "I declare this court dismissed—and I will meet with the judges immediately in private."

He turned and walked to the door in the rear, and the judges followed him with ashen faces.

Not a soul moved to leave, but there was a rising tide of talk, and for thirty minutes the courtroom buzzed like a beehive. Then the door opened and Reverend Mather walked out, his face set like a flint. He was followed by the judges. This time they did not mount the platform but stood there staring out at the crowd.

Increase Mather looked out over the people, his face still, but with a light in his dark eyes that revealed the smoldering anger he kept carefully under control.

"People of Salem, I have received testimony that the so-called 'evidence' used by this court to prosecute defendants is of an illegal nature." A gasp went up from the crowd, but he ignored it, and continued. "I hereby dismiss this court, and de-

clare that all prisoners be set free pending further investigation."
He paused again and looked down at the judges. "The judges
of this court are relieved of their offices and will report to Boston
at once. They will remain there until a full and complete report
of these trials has been made by the authorities."

He said no more, but stalked out of the courtroom, closely
followed by the sulking judges, who walked with their heads
down.

Howland got up and walked over to where Rachel stood
speechless. "You're free, Rachel," he said. "Let me take you
home."

She turned to face him but couldn't make herself heard because the crowd was coming alive with an accelerated wave of
emotion. She raised her voice to cry, "Yes, take me home, Robert!" She looked over at her family who were watching them
with unbelievable, joyous shock in their faces. "Take us all
home!"

Gilbert was too weak to walk, so they got a carriage, in which
he, Matthew, and Lydia rode. Since it was not far to the house,
the rest of them walked. Neither Rachel nor Miles could say a
word to Howland. They walked in silence. Rachel looked up at
a crow clutching the denuded branch of a peach tree, croaking
in a gutteral tone as they passed. She breathed deeply, drinking
in the fall air, crisp and keen with the bite of winter in it. Oh,
the joy of being alive and free. *I'll never take anything for granted
again!* she thought.

It was a moment to be treasured when they all entered the
house. Matthew and Lydia stood there, holding Gilbert upright,
looking around as if they'd never seen the room before.

"I never thought I'd see this room again!" Matthew exclaimed as he assisted his father to a chair. Then with a sudden
motion, he turned to Howland. "Robert, you're a wonderful
actor!" Overwhelmed by the magnitude of Robert's service, Matthew wrapped his arms around Howland's shoulders, tears
coursing down his cheeks. He was joined by Miles and then
Lydia. Gratitude radiating from her eyes, Lydia took his hand
and kissed it.

"Oh, come now, you don't have to do *that!*" Howland protested.

Rachel came and stood before him while the rest watched silently. "Robert, you warned me I wouldn't understand—and you were right. I—doubted you. Forgive me! But you have an advocate here—Grandfather told me never to doubt—and from that moment, I didn't!"

"You make too much of it!" Howland said, embarrassed and humbled by their response.

"I want to know what happened. Tell us everything!" Rachel urged, pulling him to a chair. As the rest of them sat down, looking at him eagerly, he began.

"Why, it's simple—at least it seems so now," Howland stated with a smile. "I'd seen Abigail Williams before—you remember, when we went to Parris's house the first day I came to Salem with Miles. And later I saw her when Reverend Hale examined Parris's daughter. One thing I didn't miss—as soon as it was evident that she was going to be found out, the girl put on an act. It was a good act, but I saw her when she thought nobody was looking!"

"She fooled almost everyone else," Rachel remarked.

"I knew she was lying," Howland nodded. "And I knew Cotton Mather was *not* going to do anything about it. The idea came to me that there was only one man more powerful than Cotton Mather—and that was his father!"

"Did you know him?" Edward asked.

"No, but I knew he'd not interfere in anything his son refused to touch. They're very close. So I put the two things together—Increase Mather could do something to stop the trials, but he had to be convinced. Abigail knew the trials were false, but she wouldn't admit it."

"That's why you started seeing her!" Miles cried. "What a fool I was!"

"We all were," Lydia said quietly. "But we have a lifetime to make it up to you, Robert."

Rachel had a frown on her face, and she gave Howland a peculiar look. "I wonder *how* you got that girl to help you, Robert? She's very clever."

Howland's lips lifted in a wry smile, and he answered grimly, "I used the only thing in the world that would have made her admit she'd been a fraud—money."

"You paid her to admit her guilt?" Matthew said, incredulous.

"It was all I could think of. If I'd tried to threaten her, she'd have laughed at me. So I kept on seeing her, and little by little she let her guard down."

"But wasn't she afraid of what would happen to her if people found out she'd been lying?" Rachel asked. "And wouldn't she be put in jail for lying in court?"

Howland lifted his hand in a gesture of disgust. "That young woman doesn't care what anyone thinks of her—not really. And as for being in trouble with the law, they'll have to catch her first."

"She's left Salem?" Lydia asked quickly.

"Never to return, I'd venture." He gave a shrug and added, "She's one shrewd vixen, I can tell you! When I told her I wanted her to tell her story to Increase Mather, she upped the price high enough so that she can go anywhere she likes and live like a queen."

"You don't have that kind of money, Robert," Matthew broke in quickly. "I'll pay the fee."

"You may have to, Matthew," Howland smiled. "I don't have any money myself, so I had to borrow up to my neck to get the price."

Lydia, sitting near Matthew, shook her head in disbelief. "I can't believe that girl was so wicked."

"She sent men and women to their deaths!" Matthew sighed with aching heart. "Poor old Giles and Bridget and John Proctor—and all the others—dead in vain!"

"But God sent us a deliverer!" Lydia cried out. "Our friend and deliverer—Robert Howland—"

"Could you add to that—*son-in-law*, please?" Howland interrupted. Going to Rachel, he put his arm around her.

A glad cry went up as they all welcomed their new son and brother.

Gilbert looked at Robert, tears in his eyes. "My boy," he said quietly, "you're very like your grandfather! Very like!" He wiped his eyes, then said with a sudden laugh, "I'm very glad I fished John out of the sea! He's given me a good return, he has! A new limb to the family tree of Winslow!"

CHAPTER TWENTY-THREE

TAKE ME HOME!

★ ★ ★ ★

The winter that year was mild, but for Gilbert Winslow it was a time of sickness. He could not shake the cough he had contracted in jail, and by March he was unable to walk without assistance.

"He'll be better in the spring," Lydia said hopefully to Rachel. "The winter air keeps him down."

Rachel did not reply, for she saw it was more than physical weakness—it was weariness of the spirit. He was weak and unable to eat, but the trials had drained him of something.

"He's not fighting as he once did," she said worriedly to her father. "He's low in spirit."

"I've seen it, Rachel," Matthew agreed. He stared at her and then sighed. "He's had more life than most. We'll miss him—you'll miss him more than anyone, I think."

She said no more, but by spring he still had not improved. The doctor visited him but was noncommittal. He knew as well as the fiery old man did—he was wearing out.

Then one night in May as Rachel sat reading, she saw her grandfather sit up and try to walk. He began to lean and before she could get to him, he fell to the floor. His breathing was irregular, his face ashen. She ran quickly to get a neighbor to run for the doctor and the family.

When they arrived, they tenderly lifted him into bed. He

did not move, and the doctor decided Gilbert had suffered some sort of stroke. For three days he lay there without opening his eyes.

Howland arrived as soon as he could and stayed with the family night and day. None of them expected Gilbert to regain consciousness, but he did. Early one morning, while Rachel watched by his bedside, he opened his eyes and said, "Rachel?"

She began to weep, and he smiled and said weakly, "Now, this is not the time for that, is it?"

She left him only long enough to call the family.

Gilbert lay there looking at them. "I take it you're surprised to see me back with you?"

Matthew took his hand. "You gave us quite a scare."

"I'm about to give you another one!"

Matthew stared at him, puzzled. "How is that, Father?"

Gilbert smiled. He looked so much like both Matthew and Miles that Rachel almost cried. "I want to go for a little ride," he said.

"A ride!" Matthew cried in astonishment. "Why, when you get better—"

"I mean *now*, son," he affirmed. "And not a short one, either."

They all looked at one another. Then he continued. "Oh, I'm not out of my mind. But it's a small request—just one ride."

Rachel knelt down and took his hand. "Where do you want to go, Grandfather? I'll take you anywhere!"

"There's my good girl!" he breathed. He closed his eyes and they thought he'd gone to sleep, but he opened them and said, "Take me to Plymouth—to the sea—where Humility is buried."

Matthew started to protest, but Lydia squeezed his arm. He stared down at his father for a time, then said quietly, "I'll get a carriage ready."

Robert and Miles went with him, and in less than an hour they had taken a seat out of a carriage, built a framework, and placed a mattress in it.

By the time Matthew came to the house, the women had dressed Gilbert. "Are you ready, Father?" Matthew asked.

"Take me home, son," he said with his eyes closed.

Matthew went to him, and with easy strength picked his

father up as he would a small child. As he did, Gilbert opened his eyes and smiled. "Once I carried you, my boy—now it's your turn!"

Matthew did not answer, but carried him out, placed him carefully in the carriage, then said, "We'll go slowly."

Miles had obtained another carriage, and they all got in and started out with no more ceremony than if they had been going across town.

They had to stop often, and the inns were not of the best, but Gilbert got no worse. He never complained, and much of the time at night the family would gather around and he would listen as they talked. He said little himself, but from time to time he would mention something that had happened long ago.

They came to Plymouth at midday, and he said, "Take me to the sea, Matthew."

They skirted the town, coming in from the seaward side. When they arrived, Gilbert cried, "Help me up!" As Matthew raised him, he gazed at the rolling waves of the ocean, the scudding white clouds, and then turned his eyes upward toward the village on the hill, soaking in the memories, etching them on his mind.

"Now, let it come," he whispered.

Matthew found a house for rent, and all of them set up temporary housekeeping. It was a quiet, holy time, for as the days went by, they saw Gilbert's face grow more and more peaceful.

On the fourth day after their arrival, just before sunset, Gilbert called with urgency in his weak voice, "Rachel—Matthew?"

"Yes! What is it?" Rachel ran to his bedside.

"It's time to go home," he told her simply, a high expectancy in his eyes. Turning to Matthew he urged, "Take me to the sea, son; the tide is going out."

"All right, Father. Rachel, go tell the others."

Though they had prepared for this day, sadness tugged at their hearts, knowing this might be the final parting. After gently placing his father in the carriage with his head in Rachel's lap, Matthew drove the carriage, while the others followed in another.

"Go to the hill where she is, son," Gilbert directed.

Matthew drove to the high hill overlooking the harbor, and stopped the horses beside an iron fence that enclosed a few worn stone markers.

Carefully he picked up his father and carried him to the plot. The others followed close behind. He stopped at a special marker, holding his father's thin form in his strong arms as the others crowded around them.

Gilbert opened his eyes and looked down at the stone that said, *Humility Cooper Winslow—She hath done what she could.*

He said nothing, but there was a smile on his face. "Put me down here for a moment, son."

Matthew gently placed him on the marble bench and sat beside him. As Gilbert lifted his eyes again to the sea, he said quietly, "There's where we landed that first time. What a crew we were—God-hungry and afraid of nothing—Bradford and Standish and Howland—good old John Alden and his Priscilla!"

Raising his voice, he continued. "This land is like no other—and you are Winslows! You must never do other than serve the Lord Christ with all your hearts—but you will live in this land—a land that offers—freedom—"

He paused and lifted his head as if he'd heard someone call his name, and he smiled and whispered, "Yes!" He opened his eyes and looked around, taking in each of them. "I am proud—of all of you! God—is—good—"

Then he gave a little gasp and his head fell forward. "Father!" Matthew cried, but he knew, as they all did, that Gilbert Winslow had gone to his true home! Rachel stared at the face she'd loved all her life. "Goodbye—for a little while!" she whispered as she kissed his brow.

For sometime they knelt there with heads bowed, tears flowing; then they got up and Matthew carried his father back to the carriage.

The next day, they had a little ceremony and once again, Gilbert Winslow lay beside his beloved Humility.

Rachel walked blindly away from the small plot, wanting to be alone. For hours she walked the shores, thinking of all the times she'd spent there as a girl with her grandfather; how he'd been both grandfather and father to her those years she thought her father dead. The pure joy of living and love for the Lord he had instilled in her. He had given her so much. She would miss him. But as the day wore on, a peace fell on her, and she felt the presence of the Lord. It was as though His loving hand reached down and touched that deep ache within, filling her with joy.

"Rachel?"

She turned to see Robert standing by an outcropping of stone. With a cry of joy she ran to him, falling into his protective arms.

"Are you all right?" he asked gently as he held her close.

She squeezed his hard muscular body with all her strength, then threw her head back. There were tears in her eyes, but she dashed them away. "Yes, I'm all right—as long as you love me!"

He crushed her to him, kissing her tears away.

"Rachel Winslow," he said simply, "if you're all right as long as I love you, why, you have nothing to worry about! I'm never going to let you go!"

She kissed him again, then said with a smile of victory:

"Take me home, Robert! Take me home!"

THE HONORABLE IMPOSTER

★ ★ ★ ★ THE HOUSE OF WINSLOW / BOOK 1 ★ ★ ★ ★

THE HONORABLE IMPOSTER

★

GILBERT MORRIS

BETHANY HOUSE PUBLISHERS
MINNEAPOLIS, MINNESOTA 55438

Cover illustration by Dan Thornberg,
Bethany House Publishers staff artist.

Copyright © 1986
Gilbert Morris
All Rights Reserved

Published by Bethany House Publishers
A Ministry of Bethany Fellowship, Inc.
6820 Auto Club Road, Minneapolis, Minnesota 55438

Printed in the United States of America

Library of Congress Cataloging-in-Publication Data

Morris, Gilbert.
    The honorable imposter.

    (The House of Winslow)
    I. Title. II. Series: Morris, Gilbert. House of Winslow ; bk. 1.
PS3563.08742H6   1987   813'.54   86-31065
ISBN 0-87123-933-7

To Johnnie
We have saved the best
till last

GILBERT MORRIS spent ten years as a pastor before becoming Professor of English at Ouachita Baptist University in Arkansas and earning a Ph.D. at the University of Arkansas. During the summers of 1984 and 1985 he did postgraduate work at the University of London and is presently the Chairman of General Education at a Christian college in Louisiana. A prolific writer, he has had over 25 scholarly articles and 200 poems published in various periodicals, and over the past years has had 16 novels published. His family includes three grown children, and he and his wife live in Baton Rouge, Louisiana.

CONTENTS

PART THREE

THE NEW WORLD

PART ONE

ENGLAND

★ ★ ★ ★

CHAPTER ONE

THE MASQUERADE

★ ★ ★ ★

"What! Not ready *yet*?"

Lord Henry North burst into his daughter's lavishly adorned chamber like the brusque February wind that furrowed the Thames and drove the beating waves against the stones of his ancestral home. His outburst made little impression on Cecily North. She gave a quick smiling glance at her father as he stomped in, shaking the snow from his ermine cape, then calmly continued gazing at her reflection in the silver hand mirror. A diminutive maidservant stroked her hair with an ivory comb studded with amethysts and jade.

"We needn't hurry, Father. They won't begin without us."

Only three or four men in England could have taken so little heed of Sir Henry North. At the age of forty-five, he stood high on the pyramid of English culture. Except for the Lord Chancellor, the Lord of Lancaster, and King James the First of England, there was none to question his ways—and *none* who would answer him so casually as this beautiful daughter of his.

His eyes suddenly flashed at Cecily's careless answer, and he strode across the room to her. Taking her smooth bare shoulder with a surprisingly strong grip, he said, "You need a beating, my girl!"

"No doubt I do—and so do you, Father." Then she turned to him, taking his hand in hers and giving him a quick smile.

"We are both too proud for our own good. But then—who's to give us the whipping? There's the rub."

Lord North could not conceal the quick grin that leaped to his lips. The hard grasp on her shoulder softened to a caress, and he grunted, "Know me too well, you do! You should have been a boy."

A touch of regret tinged his voice, and Cecily reached up with her free hand to cover his. No one knew better than she that the one vacuum in her father's life was the lack of a son, and she got up and gave him a quick kiss, saying, "Never mind, Father. If Mother has her way, you'll have a son-in-law soon. Then you can make of him what you will."

North held on to her, staring at her and wondering that she knew him so well. He saw a woman of twenty with hair black and sleek as a raven, highlighted by bold black eyes able to meet any man's glance. Her full red lips needed none of the paint which ladies of the English court had imported from France. They were almost pouting, and smooth as silk. Her complexion, like his own, was olive and flawless. She was not tall, but the full curves of her body made men forget her stature; she had the full-bodied figure of her mother—in the eyes of many, the most beautiful woman in the court.

"A son-in-law?" North released his grip and picked up her white fur mantle from the table, casting it around her shoulders. "I've lost out on the cattle show. Which hunk of prize young nobility has your mother been parading in front of you this time? Young Wentworth?"

"No, Father, that was last month. He fell below the required standards," Cecily laughed. "I think when Mother found out that there was a bar sinister on his mother's side, she threw him to the wolves—along with all the others. Really, Father, I think Mother would marry me off to Lord Findlay—if he could stand up long enough to get through the ceremony!"

"Well—perhaps it's not so bad as *that*." Lord Findlay, nearly ninety, was an enormously wealthy earl of Scotland. "But I must say that Wentworth was the *best* she's dredged up so far."

"He's a cup of cold tea," Cecily shrugged. "Why don't you ever nominate a candidate for the office of son-in-law, Father?"

He was suddenly serious, and there was a faint light of

anger in his eyes. But he said only, "Cecily, your mother and I have disagreed on so many things—but most of all on this. I want you to have a husband who will have three assets—courage, wit, and loyalty."

"What about titles and money?"

"I can give him all he needs along those lines," Lord North shrugged. "But I've seen enough of this marrying a girl off to a scarecrow made of sticks for a fancy title and a few sovereigns. I want your husband to be—the son I wanted. Then—then I can be at ease."

She turned to the door and shot him an arched look, "Well, there's always Lord Roth. *He* has enough gold to satisfy even Mother."

He gave her a quick look and said, "Yes, he has. And enough courage and wit to satisfy me. But what about you, Cecily? Does the Lord Simon Roth have enough to satisfy *you*?"

For one brief moment, Cecily let the habitual smile slip from her face, and she said soberly, "I don't know, Father. I just don't *know*."

He took her arm and led her to the door. "Well," he said gently, "perhaps at the ball tonight you may find out. It's revealing, what a man is in his own castle. Maybe you can look beneath that smooth surface Simon covers everything with."

"Yes, that may be." Then Cecily smiled at him. "He'd do for all of us, wouldn't he, Father? Enough money for Mother, enough courage and strength to suit you—and enough of a *man* for me."

As they went down the stair to meet Lady North, Cecily heard her father say so softly that she almost missed the words, "Strength, money, a title—but what about the *man*?"

Cecily did not answer, but said instead, "Mother, you look beautiful!"

"Thank you, Cecily."

Lady North had heard those words so many times that they slid easily off her smooth face. She was more beautiful than her own daughter, this woman. Even now at the age of thirty-five, the smooth skin, the flawless figure set off by the low-cut gown, the hair without a touch of white, the sleek complexion that put to shame younger women—all was totally admirable.

"We'll be late, Cecily," Lady North said. "But you will be worth the wait for the guests."

"Thank you, Mother," Cecily answered with a rather cold smile. "I suppose it will be the same party, after all."

"Who else would you expect?" Lord North asked. "The nobility doesn't grow a great deal from day to day. Now, the barque is waiting. Let's be on our way before this snow gets worse."

The home of Lord North was on the Thames, and he kept a barque for transport on the river; designed by Henry the Eighth, it was manned by a crew of twelve oarsmen who could send the vessel up or down the Thames as fast as the best carriage. The royal symbol, a lion, was still affixed to the prow, a circumstance that prompted the rather rare wit of the Sovereign, King James. He had once remarked to the court, "North has all the money in the realm—and all that's left is the Crown itself."

"Not so, Your Majesty," North had protested with a wry smile. "As long as I have the money, you may keep the crown!"

Not many dared jest so easily with this dour king. He had grown up with a sour breed of Scottish churchmen who had taken most of the humor out of him, but it was a mark of the royal favor that he had merely laughed at North's jest.

The journey from the palace of Lord North to that of Lord Simon Roth took less than two hours, but it was bitter cold, and the family shivered in spite of the thick furs.

Finally, after what seemed like hours, Lord North pulled the curtain aside and peered out into the swirling drifts. "I think we're about to land. That looks like Simon's palace."

"Good! I'm about to turn into a block of ice!" Cecily said with chattering teeth. "And after all this, I suppose it'll be just another boring affair."

"Not *quite* the same, Cecily," Lady North smiled. She seemed to be impervious to the cold. "Remember, this may be *your* home someday."

Cecily shot her a quick glance and then looked toward her father. Then she said wryly, "Then *Simon* is the next hot-blooded stallion we must consider?"

"You are crude, Cecily," Lady North shrugged without a trace of anger. "Try to be more civil to Lord Roth."

"And to the parson," Lord North added suddenly as he helped Cecily up onto the pier.

"Parson?" Cecily asked suddenly. "What parson?"

"I forgot to mention that a relative of mine—a distant relative—will be one of the guests tonight," Lord North grinned. His face was fixed with the cold, but there was a grim humor in his dark eyes as he handed his wife up to stand on the wharf beside his daughter. "I would appreciate it if you both would be hospitable to him."

As they hurried along the paved walk toward the towering palace of Lord Roth, Lady North asked, "What parson is this, Henry? You haven't mentioned him to me."

"Just a poor relation," Lord North said with chattering teeth. "A son of old Henry Winslow—a younger son, a distant cousin of mine, I might add. I'm thinking of employing him."

Lady North thought about that, then as a footman opened the door to the palace, murmured, "Beware of poor relations, Husband. They can do you no good."

"Must we be concerned only with those who can do us good?" Lord North asked with a humorous look in his eye. He led the two women into a hallway, and they took off their wet cloaks and proceeded down toward a large set of double doors. "Can we not do some good for a worthy relation?"

Lady North did not even acknowledge his question, but Cecily asked pertly, "What possible good can a *parson* do you?"

They had reached the double doors which a footman opened to reveal a large anteroom, and Lord Simon Roth walked toward them.

"He may be of more use than your average parson," Lord North murmured. "I hear he's an able man."

"He's probably a dried up, pinch-lipped piece of dust!" Cecily said, then put a smile on to meet the man who was reaching out to take her hand.

Lord Simon Roth looked a great deal as an English nobleman ought to look, Lord North acknowledged. He took in the tall figure—spare, to be sure, but muscular and youthful despite his thirty-seven years. There was a hawk-like quickness in the brow as well as in the lean face that bent over his daughter's hand. *I should have looked like that*, Lord North thought regretfully.

"Welcome," Lord Roth murmured to Cecily as he touched her hand with his thin lips. "I hope you will feel at home."

"Perhaps I shall," Cecily answered, giving her dark and piercing eyes into his gaze. Both of them knew that he was proffering more than a casual visit, and there was a light in Lady North's face as she nodded slightly at her husband.

"You ladies will want to dress, will you not?" Simon said. "Henry and I have a little business. We will meet you in the ballroom."

"Thank you." Cecily followed the maid who led them down a hall, across a spacious anteroom and up a flight of winding steps. Then, they went down another carpeted hall and finally arrived at a room so large and spacious that it might have served as a ballroom for a lesser lord. It was flanked by a row of tall windows with real glass that let the dim light through quite effectively and illuminated the rich walnut tones of the cupboards, tables and chairs, as well as the massive bed that dominated the room.

Cecily took in the ornate decorations, the tapestries and silver and gold plate that gave a touch of color to the room, then shrugged. "Simon has built quite a place here."

"None in England like it," Lady North agreed, looking at the rich furnishings. "And it may be yours, of course."

"Oh? You're really thinking of Simon now?"

"Of course." Lady North cast a smooth glance at Cecily. "He's the most powerful man in the kingdom—next to your father—or will be, with the proper guidance."

"I see. And what about Wentworth and the others?"

"Not at all possible!"

"No, I can see that," Cecily agreed wryly. "But Simon—he has all the qualifications for a son-in-law?"

"Certainly!" Lady North said. Her smooth composure was broken by a faint surprise. "Surely you must have known that he was the only choice? The others were merely preliminary."

"Of course!"

"Well, now that it's settled—"

"But is it settled?" Cecily asked quickly. "What about Father?"

"Oh, Simon has enough *dash* even for *him*," Lady North said impatiently.

"Oh—and what about *me*?" Cecily asked suddenly. She

picked up the dress the servant was holding up for her approval, then added, "Marriage is a *little* more than money and a title, Mother!"

Lady North seemed to freeze. Her cold face focused on her daughter, and she said almost in a whisper, "No—it is *not*, Cecily! You are engaging in some sort of romantic dream—a poetic fancy—" Her nose wrinkled slightly as if she had smelled a fetid odor. "Your *private* affairs I will not inquire into, but your duty to marry within the realm where fate has placed you, *that* I must see to."

Cecily gazed into her mother's cold eyes and said almost in a whisper, "That is *your* way, Mother. It is not *mine!*"

For a long instant they stared at one another—mother and daughter, so alike, yet separated by a great gulf in mind and passion. Finally Lady North nodded slowly and said, "You will have your own way, Cecily; your father has spoiled you. But in the end, you will do as I have done. You will consider what is best for your own destiny. Have your fling, but do not make the tragic mistake of throwing yourself away for some romantic dream. You are your father's daughter—and he is a romantic fool. I cannot help *that*. But you are *my* daughter as well. I know you do not love me, but it is my way you must follow if you are to survive. So—be cautious!"

"Yes—as you were, Mother," Cecily said, and allowed the maid to dress her for the masquerade.

But as the maid draped her with the ornately bejeweled gown and tried the black mask over her face, she thought bitterly, *I don't need this to hide what I am!*

Then she followed her mother down to the ballroom to join the merrymakers—all adorned, and all masked.

CHAPTER TWO

A PARSON AT THE BALL

★ ★ ★ ★

"Not longing for the days of Good Queen Bess, are you, my dear?"

Cecily turned from the large painting she had been staring at to meet the gaze of Lord Roth. He wore an elaborate doublet buttoned up the side with gleaming pearl buttons. The complicated embroidery on his sleeves alone must have commanded the work of a seamstress for weeks. A black mask hid his face, but there was no mistaking the bold eyes that gleamed at her through the eye slits.

"Yes, I think so, Lord Roth." Cecily held her own mask of Dutch lace away from her face carelessly. "There were men in those days—look at them."

The large painting portrayed a wedding, with Queen Elizabeth carried in a canopied litter borne by courtiers. There was a festive air of celebration gleaming from the painting, and Cecily pointed out the famous men close to the queen.

"See, there's the Lord High Admiral—and there's Edward Somerset, the Earl of Worcester. What a *man* he was! Then I think this must be Lord Hundson, holding his rapier, as usual! I don't know this one, however."

"That's Henry Brook." Roth smiled wolfishly and let his mask fall. "You would have liked him, I think. He had a great deal of that dash and spirit you profess to admire."

"Oh? What happened to him?"

"He was beheaded for treason by Queen Elizabeth, who had first raised him to power." The glittering eyes of Lord Simon held a gleam of humor as he added, "The usual fate of adventurers such as you find so admirable, Cecily."

"You do not find such men necessary, my Lord?"

"No. This is the year of our Lord 1620—not the age of Elizabeth. When she died in 1603, I am pleased to think that the romantic crew she lavished with her praise also went out of style."

"Like Sir Francis Drake—and Hawkins, not to mention Raleigh and the Earl of Essex?"

Lord Roth threw his head back and laughed in genuine amusement. He took her hand boldly and kissed it, then leaned very close to whisper, "I can see I have touched unholy hands to your list of sainted heroes, Cecily! I beg your pardon—though all those men would be out of place in our world."

"The world of King James the First." Cecily gave a sour smile. She waved her fan around the large room and said languidly, "You imitate his horrid taste, Lord Simon. His Majesty thinks that if only one spends enough, the result will be beauty. Father says he will ruin the kingdom if he keeps emptying the coffers on his ridiculous attempts to rival the Roman emperors."

Simon shrugged and glanced around the large ballroom. "Guilty, my Lady, I must confess. It seems to infect us all—the rash and foolish habits of our Most Sovereign Majesty."

They both gazed now at the room, which in itself was larger than many small palaces. Massive walls of stone held up the fan-arching of the ceiling, and on each side huge fireplaces blazed, six of them, and each held logs up to eight feet long. The flickering flames, aided by a great many candles, threw light up among the shadows, and the flash of gilt was everywhere. The rushes on the floor served to deaden the sound of dancers who moved back and forth across the room in the latest Italian steps, and the colors of the costumes almost dazzled the eye—red, green, yellow, all mingled and flashed as the dancers wove intricate patterns in the ever-changing firelight.

Lord Roth drew his gaze from the milling scene of dancers, servants, musicians, jugglers, and a group of Kempe dancers accompanied by three men with taborers and pipes, to draw closer to Cecily.

"It *is* rather *busy*, isn't it? Perhaps we should find a quieter place?"

With an arch smile, she put her mask up and said, "No, Lord Simon, that would be too *romantic*! And you have already informed me that such romance holds no interest for you."

He gave her a sly glance. "I shall hope to convince you otherwise, Cecily. Would you care to try one of those new Italian dances? They are certainly *romantic* enough, even for you!"

She nodded, and they began to move back and forth in the intricate patterns of the newly imported dance that had been accepted by the court of England. There was a seductive quality in the ritual; as Cecily played her role, she felt as if she were the quarry and Lord Simon the aggressive male who must sooner or later corner her and have the way of the flesh.

"Perhaps now that you have finished putting the Wentworth whelp through his paces, you may be more attentive to genuine prospects?"

Despite herself Cecily reacted strongly, throwing her head back to look up at her partner, her eyes growing enormous as she swept his dark saturnine features. Then she attempted to cover up her surprise by murmuring in a bored tone, "I presume you refer to yourself, Lord Roth?"

"You're not surprised at that, surely," he said, holding her even more closely. "Your mother must have pointed out my eligibility to you long ago."

"My mother will not select my husband—nor will my father."

Suddenly Lord Roth drew her through a narrow opening into a small room set in one side of the vast hall, evidently made for storage. In the flickering light of the candles he kissed her, his hard lips pressing against hers, trapping her within the confines of his iron grasp.

Cecily was shaken by his rough passion, but attempted to cover her feelings. She laughed and ducked away from his embrace, saying, "Come, let us dance again!"

As they moved smoothly through the intricate steps past the spectators lining the walls, many eyes were fixed on them—

but none more intently than two men who stood behind one of the long tables filled with food. Lord North watched his daughter with a slight frown on his face, but his companion had happier thoughts.

"They make quite a pair, don't they, Henry?"

Lord North cast a quick glance at the huge form of Bishop Charles Laud. His massive physique swelled out his robe. As the bishop tore at a huge drumstick dripping with fat, North thought, *Laud looks even less like a bishop than I look like a royal duke.* But he only nodded and said quietly, "Yes—quite impressive."

"Money is always impressive, Henry." Bishop Laud paused to wash the meat down with a tremendous draught of wine, wiped his lips, and looked directly at the smaller man. "And power—that's impressive, too. Simon has both, of course, and I suppose you and Lady North will approve of his suit for Cecily's fair hand."

"You would approve, Bishop?"

"Approve? Certainly! He has money and power. You have that, and family as well. What else is there?"

North saw a slightly confused look in Laud's eyes, and he said, "There are those who say that Simon's rise was built on rather unsavory practices. Wouldn't you, as a churchman, object to that?"

"Oh, we'll take care of *that*!" Laud laughed, picking up a hummingbird pie topped with curls of crisp bread shavings. "That's what the church is for, Henry—to wipe out the sins of the successful."

"I stand corrected," Henry North smiled. "I had thought it was a little more complicated than that—from what I've read in the Scripture. And from what the Reverend John Donne puts forth from his pulpit at St. Paul's."

A frown slipped across the heavy face of the bishop, and he shrugged his beefy shoulders restlessly. "Oh, Donne! He's a fanatic! Not much better than those rag-tag Puritans!"

"The Brownists, you mean?" North asked idly. He referred to the followers of Troublechurch Browne, a minister who had filled the land with his idea that all true Christians should separate from the Church of England.

"Yes! And all the rest of them!" Laud's face, usually lit up with good humor, was suddenly ugly, and Sir Henry saw that beneath the sleek, smooth facade of Bishop Laud's cultivated manners lurked a carnivore. "The King has seen the danger of such heresy at last."

"Yes, hanging Penry and Greenwood was a rather strict pronouncement, I thought."

"They won't be the *last!*" Laud snapped. "It was Penry who wrote those scurrilous articles signed 'Martin Mar-prelate,' which attacked the holy Church of England. It must be *stopped*, Henry! It must!" North had heard all this before. His thoughts went to his daughter and Sir Simon Roth—and he was not happy.

As the tapers burned out and were replaced by the servants, Cecily began to grow bored. Simon excused himself, and for over two hours Cecily danced with practically every man of her rank in the room. Finally she sat down with one of her few close friends, Mary Stanhope, daughter of the Earl, and they waved the young men off and talked idly of the ball and other matters.

Cecily yawned and said, "Let's go to our room and talk, Mary. I've never been so bored in my life."

Mary smiled and turned her well-shaped head to one side. She was pretty, but boasted no such beauty as her friend. "Bored with all these men falling at your feet? You're spoiled, Cecily."

"No. They're milksops. Not a red-blooded man in the room."

"Now that Lord Roth is gone?"

"He doesn't have red blood, Mary. Ice water flows through his veins." She said this quickly, but was aware that a flush was touching her cheeks as she remembered his kiss.

Mary caught it, and laughed delightedly. "I can see you don't mean that!" Then she looked up and said, "But—the crop of men isn't much tonight, I'm afraid." Then she paused and added, "Except for *him*, of course."

Cecily followed the direction of Mary's gaze and saw a man dressed in a uniform which bespoke the military, but which she could not recognize. "Who is he? I haven't seen him before," she said.

"He came in about thirty minutes ago," Mary whispered. "He's been watching all the ladies ever since. I think he's trying to decide which one to honor with his presence. My! Look how tall he is! And that hair!"

"Probably cross-eyed and gap-toothed behind that mask," Cecily shrugged.

"Look Cecily! He's coming this way! I think he's chosen *you*! Do you feel honored?"

"I feel he's an insolent puppy who needs to be brought to heel," Cecily smiled slowly behind her fan. "It's a task I delight in."

"I don't know, Cecily," Mary whispered quickly. "He doesn't look like a puppy."

"Watch!" Cecily hissed. "We'll teach him to beg."

"Lady, will you take pity on a poor stranger? I will be lost forever if you refuse to dance with me!"

The voice was low and husky, and the eyes that peered behind the mask were the bluest she'd ever seen—blue as a cornflower. There was a humorous light in them that mocked at the humility of the words, for there was nothing humble in his figure. Tall and lean, like the rapier he wore at his side, there was an athletic smoothness to his bow as there had been to his walk. The mask he wore was thin, not concealing the wedge-shaped face that began with a broad bronze brow and tapered down to a jutting chin bearing a small white scar. The scar drew attention to his wide mouth; a crooked smile exposed perfect even teeth that gleamed in the light of the fires.

Cecily took in the square, well-shaped hands, the strong wrists and shapely arms, the legs set off by the tight-fitting doublet and hose, then said languidly, "A lost soul? Then you must find a priest. There is one over there—Bishop Laud. I'm sure he will help you to find your way."

"Ah, Lady, the bishop can only save a soul; it is not my soul that is lost but my heart."

"Indeed? Then you need a surgeon. I recommend Mr. Deverreaux. He knows all about hearts and their problems."

The wide mouth turned upward in a quick smile, and the blue eyes sparkled gaily as he said, "Not so, fair Lady. He would find nothing wrong with my heart, could he take it out and examine it. For it is not what is in my heart that brings me to death, but what is not there—your lovely self, Lady."

It was the language of courtly love, usually innocent enough. Cecily had seen a performance of *Romeo and Juliet*, and the word play between the two young lovers was light, clever, often stinging. She was quick-witted enough to play the game well, and as for the young man who stood before her, she realized his wit was as keen as his eyes were bright.

Finally she said, "It is my Christian duty to take pity on those who are in pain. Perhaps the dance will restore your health. But your soul will still need the attention of a parson."

Then began a very strange time for Cecily North. For the first time in her life she found a man who could match her wit; indeed, sometimes his words flowed so smoothly she found herself trapped in some of the cunning conceits he laid for her. The ease with which he led her through the dance made the exercise so natural that their conversation—filled with barbed jests and clever innuendoes—was not at all impeded.

Then he said, in that peculiar husky voice that had the unusual effect of sending a shiver along her nerves, "Lady, time is on the wing. Let us not do as yonder tapers and burn ourselves out with nothing to show for all our brilliance."

He had skillfully guided her into the same tiny niche where Lord Roth had led her earlier. *If he had it built for this sort of thing,* she thought with a wary smile, *he ought to keep it locked when he was not in residence.* How the red-haired man had found it she couldn't guess, but she was intrigued by his flow of words and wit as well as by his attractive form.

"What are you suggesting, sir? Surely you are too much of a philosopher to suggest that physical gratification is more important than matters of the soul."

He stepped closer to her and asked, "Do you know Mr. Herrick?"

"No. Is he a minister or a philosopher?"

"A poet, who says better than I what I am feeling this moment—" As he began to quote the poem, Cecily found herself leaning toward him of her own free will. Perhaps she had taken too much wine, or perhaps she was just bored—but as he spoke, that husky voice drew her close to him.

Gather ye rosebuds while ye may,
Old time is still a-flying:

And this same flower that smiles to-day,
To-morrow will be dying.

That age is best which is the first,
When youth and blood are warmer;
But being spent, the worse and worst
Times, still succeed the former.

Then be not coy, but use your time;
And while ye may, go marry:
For having lost but once your prime,
You may for ever tarry.

Then he kissed her—but the encounter was not at all like the one earlier that evening. Simon had held her with his iron arm and battered her lips with force. This time, Cecily was lost in a moment of surrender she could not explain. The room was warm; she had tasted the wine more freely than usual; she was weary—but none of this explained how she suddenly leaned forward and lifted her lips to the stranger who promptly took her in arms that, despite their corded muscle, caressed her rather than bound her. Her own arms seemed to rise of their own accord until she was pressing his head closer and her body closer to his. Cecily had been kissed many times, but never had she given herself like this. The music faded and there was a ringing in her ears, like far-off music heard over water.

"I trust I'm not intruding!"

Cecily pulled back from the man in sudden confusion. The tall form of Lord Roth stood in the opening; his face was pale, and a wild light glowed in his pale eyes.

"I—I—" For once in her life, Cecily North had no quip, no reply; not a single word came to her lips.

"I think this is our dance, is it not, my Lady?" the stranger said suddenly, and she found herself practically pushed through the opening. The red-haired man brushed abruptly past Lord Roth and led her to the floor. He led her through the steps and her head was quickly cleared as she took a glance around the room.

What was I thinking of! she asked herself. Quickly she looked up at her partner to see if he was laughing at her. If there had been one trace of humor, she would have left him at once, but his gaze was sober and he smiled faintly with a lift of one eyebrow. "We must compare poets, my Lady. I'm sure you know a great many."

She felt a quick surge of gratitude as he managed to take the sting out of the moment. Quickly she cast a look toward the wall and saw her father standing with Bishop Laud and another man.

Anxious to speak of something trivial she smiled and said, "There's the parson."

"The parson?"

"Oh, yes. My father said that he had invited one of our poor relations here. I think he's going to make him an object of charity—create some sort of post to keep him from starving. He looks like a parson, doesn't he?"

Her partner took his look at the three men and nodded.

"Most decidedly, a holy man," he nodded, a merry look in his cornflower blue eyes. "He looks sour and unhappy. Quite right. All parsons should look exactly like that."

"Come, I'll introduce you to my father—and to my poor relation."

The three men were watching them carefully, and there was a slight smile on the faces of Laud and her father. The smaller man, who was wearing a common garment, rather the worse for wear, was peering at them also, but narrowly as if he were weak in the eyes.

"Well, now, you've danced the evening away, Lady Cecily," the bishop laughed. "You look quite ravishing."

"Bishops aren't supposed to notice such things, are they?" Cecily smiled, then turned to her father. "May I introduce you to my partner, Father? Except that we have not met. At a masquerade introductions are necessary sooner or later." She glanced at the poorly dressed man beside her father. "I take it this is our cousin, the parson?"

All three men looked a little confused; then her father said, "This is Mr. Tiddle. He serves me in the court from time to time."

"Oh, a lawyer." Cecily looked at him, then shrugged. "I take it you are not insulted to be taken for a parson, Mr. Tiddle?"

"Not at all, Lady Cecily." Tiddle shook his head.

"Your spiritual condition should be considerably better now than at the beginning of the ball," Lord North said with a quick smile at Cecily.

Cecily stared at him and wondered if he *too* had seen the tall man kissing her! "Why, how could that be at a dance, Father? This is no place to practice one's devotion—even if the bishop does attend."

"Perhaps not, but your partner must have given you good counsel, Daughter. That's his business." He took one step forward and put his hand out to the red-haired man. "How are you, Mr. Winslow? I trust you've been quoting holy writ to my daughter as a good parson should."

"I doubt it very much, Henry," Laud laughed loudly; he, too, offered his hand to the man. "Winslow here had a devilish bad reputation at Cambridge. The most *worldly* parson in the whole university, it's said. Well, Lady Cecily, has our parson been effective in saving your soul?"

Slowly Cecily turned to look up at the face of Gilbert Winslow, who removed his mask and was trying not to smile. For a long moment they exchanged glances, somewhat like the clash of rapiers as they searched for weakness; Cecily, especially, tried to cover up her confusion by throwing up a guard.

"I have certainly been highly edified by Parson Winslow's company," she said carefully. "He was just telling me that life is brief—and that all of us must not neglect to use what time we have in the best possible manner. Isn't that so, Mr. Winslow?"

"I doubt that Reverend Donne himself could put it more clearly, Lady Cecily," Gilbert said. His words were smooth, but there was a mocking light in his amazing blue eyes as he continued innocently, "I trust that we will have many opportunities to exchange views on such matters—now that I am the hired drudge of your father."

Cecily's cheeks burned as she remembered his words about the parson, but she made herself smile, and said, "Mr. Winslow, you may depend on it. I will give careful heed to what you have said."

"Then this poor parson is amply rewarded, Lady Cecily. My greatest joy is to pass along a little of what I value most to those I meet from time to time."

This was a new sensation for Cecily North—to be outwitted, especially by a parson! She made herself smile and curtsy, saying before she left, "I shall look forward to your teaching, Mr. Winslow. The bishop is always encouraging me to attend to my religious duties more strictly. Now that you are here, it will be much more convenient. Good evening."

She left smoothly enough, but she knew that he was laughing at her behind that handsome countenance. That would change, however. He was a man, and no man had ever yet bested her. A smile crept over her face and she murmured, "The next time I'll be ready for our parson!"

CHAPTER THREE

TOURNAMENT OF STEEL

★ ★ ★ ★

Gilbert Winslow slept until the bright February sun pierced the window slit high on the wall, then a servant awakened him. "Sir, you are wanted by Lord Roth."

Quickly he dressed and made his way after the servant along several corridors, up two flights of stone steps, then passed through a set of massive oak doors, probably weighing a hundred stone each, set on hammered iron hinges.

"Well, well, Gilbert, come in!" Bishop Laud was sitting at a low table, perched on a substantial stool eating meat off a silver dish.

"Good morning, Bishop," he said, then nodded his head to Lord North who had turned from staring out a large window to watch him. "Good morning, my Lord." Lord Roth was sitting behind a massive table covered with manuscripts of all sorts, but the cold light in his eyes required only a nod from Gilbert, and a brief, "How do ye?" to which the nobleman did not respond except to turn his head to look at a map lying before him.

Lord North turned to Gilbert. "Sit down, Mr. Winslow. It's time you discover what I have in mind for you. I suppose you've wondered why I sent to Cambridge for you to come to a ball?"

"Yes," Gilbert said. "But for whatever reason, I must admit that the holiday has been a relief."

"You're not content at Cambridge?" Lord North asked.

Gilbert shrugged. "It's not a hard life."

"But you are not happy in your calling—the church, that is?"

"It—was not my choice, my Lord." North saw his firm lips grow suddenly harsh as he added, "My brother, Edward—it was his decision for me to enter the church."

"An able man, Edward Winslow," Laud put in. "He wanted to enter the church himself—but your father had other ideas."

Gilbert bit his lip, turned red, then suddenly smashed a hard fist into his palm, crying impatiently, "That's what Edward has let get out—that my father wanted *me* to go as a churchman—but it's a lie!"

"You think your brother has deceived you?" Lord North asked in surprise. "I have always thought of him as an honorable man. Just as I have thought of your father. You may as well know, Gilbert, I sent for you on your father's account—to offer you a post in return for a service he did for me."

Gilbert stood still, thoughts racing through his mind. He had wondered about this summons from one of the most powerful men in England and what it might mean for him; whatever Lord North's reasons, the words *offer you a post* sent a sudden explosion of release through him.

He shrugged and said more slowly, "Lord North, you know how impatient young men are. In many ways Edward has been a good brother to me. I have been a misfit at Cambridge, but that is not *his* fault. You may know, my Lord, I have had several experiences during the last year which have brought me to the attention of the authorities there."

"Yes," Laud said, trying to look severe. "I have heard of your escapades. According to a report you spend more time gaming, gambling, even chasing local wenches, than reading books of theology. I am shocked!"

"I cannot deny reports, Bishop—since I have been caught in the act," Gilbert grinned ruefully. "But in my own defense I will only say again, Cambridge and the church was the desire of Edward—or of my father, if what you say is true. I have tried to be that man—but it is not my nature, my Lord."

"That may well be," Lord North nodded. "And if that is so, then my offer of a post may be welcome to you. It is not an opportunity without merit, but it will entail your leaving Cambridge and learning to conduct yourself as a man of affairs in business. It will mean travel, and I suppose that will spell *adventure* to a young man such as yourself."

"Sir, I will do it!" Gilbert said, advancing toward Lord North with a light on his face. "I ask not what wages, how hard the work, I ask nothing, for to be set free from my life as it now is, that is a boon from heaven. I will serve you faithfully as well as I can—and I am in your debt eternally!"

"You change careers lightly, Winslow," Lord Roth said. He looked steadily across the table at the younger man and added to Laud and North, "I would think that a young man who can throw over one loyalty so easily would be a rather poor risk. Was there not some sort of vow, some commitment to the church to be made? What of your word there?"

Gilbert flushed and stood stubbornly, meeting the cynical glance of Lord Roth. His voice was even huskier than usual. "A hit, Lord Roth, I must confess. You have me, indeed. I can only say to Lord North, give me the opportunity to prove that when my heart is in the task—as it has *never* been at Cambridge—I will let them take this head from these shoulders before I will betray you!"

"I will have you, then," Lord North said quickly. He advanced and held his hand out, which Gilbert took and gave a hearty squeeze. "Now, we will work out details of your stewardship later in private, but while we are all here, we must make plans. All three of us are involved in an affair which will require your service."

Gilbert looked at the three men, and could not imagine any three more different spirits than North, Laud, and Roth, but he merely nodded and waited for Lord North to explain.

"Lord Roth and I have several trading interests in common, one of them in Holland. We are in need of a man who will give his attention to the venture, and it is for this that I have suggested you to Lord Roth. You will have my clerk, Tiddle, to assist you. He will know the details, but you will handle the affair as well as you can on your own authority. I will rely on Tiddle to keep you out of trouble, but you must learn to stand on your own feet as quickly as possible. Now, you are perhaps wondering about the presence of the bishop in this matter of business," Lord North said. "I will let him explain that to you, and I must tell you that if you take the post, I have promised the bishop he will have your full cooperation. That will be one of the terms of your employment with me."

Bishop Laud began to pace back and forth in front of the window. He had a high-pitched voice, which he ordinarily kept under control, but Gilbert noticed at once that the matter he spoke of angered him so greatly that he spoke shrilly.

"You know of the trouble the Separatists have given us, Winslow. You know it because your brother, Edward, is sympathetic toward that vile movement. I fear he has been drawn into their designs, and one benefit you may reap from this task I am going to require of you is the salvation of his soul—not to mention, possibly his *head*!"

"You're not serious, Bishop!" Gilbert protested. "Edward is no traitor."

"Perhaps not *now*, but others have been destroyed by listening to Troublechurch Brown and others of his ilk. We know that Edward Winslow has had close communication with one William Brewster, and that alone is enough to put him in jeopardy."

"William Brewster? I don't know him."

"If you *did*, you would not be standing here," Laud snapped. "He is a fugitive from justice, from the King's justice."

"What is his crime?"

"He is part of the Scrooby group, a troublesome pack of Separatists and Puritans who fled England ten years ago to escape their obligations to the English Church. They settled in Amsterdam, then moved to Leyden. Brewster was one of their leaders, and in 1617 he set up a press in Leyden." The bishop gave a short laugh and waved his hand toward Holland. "The press was located, poetically enough, on *Stincksteeg*—Stink Alley, in English! He avoided that name by adopting the address of his side door, which was located on Choir Alley—and that is the name of the press."

"What sort of things did he print?" Gilbert asked.

"Violent attacks on the Church of England. Especially one called "Perth Assembly," which our noble Sovereign King James read. He at once demanded that the guilty printer be found and brought to justice!"

"But he was not?"

"No, he escaped. Sir Dudley Carleton, the English Ambassador to Holland, was put in charge of the case. He found the press, and French wine barrels stuffed with seditious pamphlets. Brewster, however, had vanished, and is still at large."

Gilbert stared at the fat bishop. "But—what does this have to do with me?"

Laud stopped pacing the floor and smiled slyly at Gilbert. "Why, my dear young man, *you* are going to find William Brewster for us!"

"I! Why—I am not a sheriff!"

"You will be better to us than a sheriff," Laud said quickly and there was a grim ferocity on his face now. "No officer of the King will ever find the man. Those psalm-singers are too closely knit for that! But there is a way—and it is your employment with Lord North that makes it possible."

"The bishop came up with this idea after I informed him of your employment—and your first assignment," Lord North nodded. "I have a young clerk who is violently in love with a young woman who is a member of the Separatist group at Leyden. His name is John Howland; the young woman's name is Elizabeth Tilley. He has been involved in the Dutch venture in a very minor way from its beginning."

"Exactly! And he is, we think, a member of the church there, although he does not make that public to *me*!"

"He'd be a fool if he did, Laud," Simon grinned suddenly. "You'd have his head in a basket!"

"I would indeed!" Laud nodded vigorously. "But, here is the plan, Winslow. You will go to Leyden with Tiddle and Howland. You will join yourself to that same body and discover the whereabouts of Brewster."

Gilbert stared at the bishop and then at the other two men. North was watching him carefully, interest filling his round face, and Gilbert knew he had no choice but to accept the task.

"I see," he said finally. "I'm to be a spy."

"A spy?" Laud protested. "Perhaps. But this man Brewster is a traitor to English justice. Winslow, you will be doing your country, and your church, a service by turning the man over to the law. And, I might mention, there is a *very* large reward offered by the King himself for his capture. Enough to begin your new career with some dash and style!"

Winslow stood there, caught in a wave of passion. With all his soul he longed to enter the service of Lord North. But—to be a *spy*! It went against the grain, and there was a revulsion that stuck in his throat at the thought of worming his way into a group—then selling the victim for gain!

Lord North was watching him closely, and he murmured, "Gilbert, your father was a good friend to me. If you cannot with good conscience undertake this mission, we'll find another man. And someday I may be able to find other employment for you."

"No!" Gilbert shook his head, swallowed, and said strongly, "I will do it, Lord North. After all, the man is a criminal!"

Lord Roth laughed harshly, and got up, a sardonic sneer on his wolfish face. "And after all," he snapped as he passed through the door into the corridor, "there is money to be made from it!"

"Lord Roth will come around, lad," Lord North said, reaching up with a friendly slap on Gilbert's shoulder. A warm light filled his face. "You'll need to stay tonight. I want to meet with you and Tiddle; we'll give you a good background on the Dutch affair."

Late that evening the Great Hall was abandoned in favor of a small room for the evening meal. It was large enough for the thirty or so who sat around the long tables, with enough space left over for the traveling players to put on their show.

Gilbert could not decide if it were by chance or design that he sat directly across from Lady Cecily North. He had thought at first that Lord North wanted him to be close by so that he could talk more about the Dutch affair, but the nobleman had paid him no attention save a friendly word on the quality of the jugglers.

Cecily had not been as quiet. At first, to be sure, both of them were somewhat reserved, but as the meal progressed and ribald barbs of wit flew around the room, as the wines and ales began to loosen the tongues of most of the guests, she began to show a little more poise. He found it easy to tell her about his slight acquaintanceship with Ben Jonson (whom she admired greatly), and they were soon deep in conversation about that poet and others. Their tastes were a great deal the same, and both were naturally quick-witted. From time to time, Lord North and other guests who were close enough to hear their talk would listen, but a baffled expression soon revealed that such conversation was of no interest.

A faint gleam in Lord North's eyes revealed his pleasure in his daughter's quick wit and wide knowledge; he had educated her as fully as a woman could be taught in his day. He was even more interested in her response to the tall young man he had taken into his service. Looking at Gilbert, he traced the firm line of the determined jaw, the clear blue eyes and highly arched nose, thinking how much more he himself could have accomplished if he had been blessed with a more well-favored body. Not one to waste time mourning over impossible things, however, Lord North had long ago decided that since he would not have a son to pass his name and his fortune to, the next best thing was to find a man who could have the courage, determination, and wit to hold onto it—or even better, to enlarge it. As he watched Gilbert hold his daughter's attention as no other man had, he began to hope that he had found his man. *Too soon to tell*, he told himself. Nevertheless, Winslow was all he longed for in a son. No money, of course—but North had plenty of that, and if the young man proved himself worthy, and could carry Cecily along with him, what could hinder?

After the sumptuous meal Will Stanton cried out, "Well, let's have some excitement! Lord Roth, what say you to some fencing, eh? I volunteer to challenge you—*again!*"

"You are a stubborn fellow, Will," Simon smiled. But his face lightened as he looked at the foils on the wall behind him. "Shall we have a tournament, then?"

A cry went around the room, and the servants appeared to make ready a space for the swordsmen. Quickly they cleared one of the tables, and soon it was filled with rapiers, daggers, broadswords, masks and guards of all sorts.

"Lord Roth keeps an arsenal, Lord North," Gilbert murmured as they heaped the weapons high.

"Yes, it's his one interest—aside from getting richer," North said quietly. "He's one of the best swordsmen in England. He's already killed one man in a duel."

Gilbert watched as the two men chose two foils which were tipped to prevent injury, then set themselves for the contest. There was something deadly about Simon's attitude, even though it was only a fencing match. His eyes narrowed and there was a strange unholy light in his pale eyes as one of the men touched their blades and said, "Engage!"

The hall rang with the sound of steel on steel, and the spectators' cheers began to break the air. "Ah, that's the way, Will!" Waller cried out. "Keep it up! Keep it up!"

But although most of the crowd was cheering for the younger man, it was quite clear to Gilbert that there was no contest. Roth was simply toying contemptuously with his opponent. Several times he almost touched his chest with the tip of his foil, then let it pass so that he could play with young Stanton a little longer.

Then, suddenly, Gilbert saw Roth's face turn cold, and with a wild lunge he forced his younger opponent to the wall and drove the foil against his chest with such force that Stanton gasped with pain and Simon's foil bent nearly double.

"Oh! That's it for me, my Lord!" Will cried out, rubbing his chest. "I see I have a little practice in store before I challenge you again."

A laugh went up, and as Stanton put his weapon on the table, Gilbert found himself staring into the eyes of Lord Roth, and even before the older man spoke, he knew what was coming—and why!

"It's too bad, Mr. Winslow, that you are a man of the church. We might have an interesting match, you and I. Oh!"—Lord Roth pretended to be surprised—"well, you are wearing a sword! How odd for a parson! But surely it's not for use?" Lord Roth's lip curled and he looked up and down Winslow's tall figure, then said with contempt in his tone, "But I never knew a parson yet who could do anything well—anything but hide behind the skirts of the church."

Gilbert stood there in sudden silence, the red of his hair suddenly complemented by the crimson flush that touched his high cheekbones.

He knew it was a foolish thing even to consider. He was to be an employee of Lord Roth, at least for one very important venture. To alienate him would be stupid!

"My Lord, it would not be seemly for me to cross blades with you. I am afraid—"

"Yes, we can all see *that!*" Lord Roth laughed loudly, and slammed his foil down on the table. "Oh, do not be perturbed, Parson. I did not really expect to see a person such as yourself behave like a *gentleman!*"

This time there was no alternative. Gilbert turned pale, but his voice was steady as he said, "I was about to say, Lord Simon, that I was afraid—that you would be deceived if we were to have a match. My studies at Cambridge have been such a source of boredom to me that for the last year I have sought relaxation—in the art of fencing."

Suddenly Lord Roth laughed. "And which of the scholarly Dons gave you lessons, Winslow?"

"Monsieur Paul Dupree."

Lord Roth's face went still and he echoed quickly, "Paul Dupree? You have studied under him?"

"Yes, my Lord."

"Well, in *that* case, we must certainly have a bout!" Lord Roth picked up his foil and said, "Choose your weapon, Parson."

Gilbert peeled off his coat and gave his sleeves a turn up to the elbow. Picking up a thin-bladed rapier already tipped, he slipped his own sword off and turned to face his opponent. "I am ready, Lord Roth."

They touched blades and it could not be said that Simon Roth was a rash man. He knew the formidable reputation of Paul Dupree better than anyone else in the room, and any pupil of his was no novice.

Carefully they circled the room, and the fire threw huge contorted shadows on the masonry walls. Swaying back and forth, they moved catlike across the rushes, their feet making swishing noises, and ever the ring of steel sounded in the ear.

Gilbert knew that he had never faced such a master—except for Dupree, who was not quite *human!* Roth had a fencer's body—lean, muscular; his timing was exquisite.

There were no cheers, in fact, the only sound was the sliding feet of the fencers and the steel pinging out repeatedly. Once Gilbert almost failed to parry, and the button on his opponent's sword almost touched his breast, but he recovered and drove Simon back with a desperate show of physical strength.

It would have ended with a touch had things continued. But the button fell off the tip of Lord Roth's foil—and suddenly Gilbert backed away from a violent rush from the older man, managing to turn aside the needlepoint of Simon's foil by a series of minor miracles.

He had no chance to look into Roth's eyes, but the man *must* realize that he was playing with an uncovered tip! He must! Then, one quick glance during a moment's respite and he saw the catlike cruelty in his opponent's eyes. Roth knew—but he was going to keep on until he buried the blade in the heart of Gilbert Winslow.

It was relatively dark in the room, and by the faint blaze of fires, and in view of the fact that Lord Roth never let his sword stop, no one saw the condition of the foil. And of course, if Lord Roth killed him, he could look sad and astonished. "Poor fellow! I never *dreamed* the guard had fallen off!"

Desperately Gilbert gave ground, his sword arm tiring. Simon drove himself forward, thrusting, twisting, darting like a madman; then Gilbert felt the table strike the back of his legs!

Lord Roth must have seen it, must have maneuvered him into that position, for he lunged forward, ignoring the feeble parrying thrust that Gilbert managed to achieve. The next thrust, Gilbert knew, would go right through his heart! And as he saw the arm of Lord Roth draw back for it, he threw his arms over his head and did a violent and awkward backflip over the table! Dishes and goblets flew everywhere with a tremendous crash, and the top of his head struck the floor with a dull thud—but he was alive!

Several women screamed, and as he started to scramble to his feet, an inspiration struck Gilbert. If he got up, Lord Roth still had that naked point—and there was no doubt about his willingness to use it.

Instead of standing up—which was *exactly* what Lord Roth was expecting—Gilbert rolled under the table. There was Roth, poised and ready to skewer him across the table, and he had time only to catch a quick movement at his feet as Gilbert reached out and slapped Roth's sword wrist with all his strength!

Lord Roth's sword fell, and Gilbert quickly got to his feet. He said with scorn, "You've dropped your weapon, my Lord. Use mine."

He tossed his own blade to Roth, handle first, then in a single motion scooped up the fallen rapier and faced Lord Roth with the naked tip pointed right at his throat.

"Shall we continue, my Lord?" he asked, and Simon saw that he was bested.

Before he could speak, however, Lord North said loudly, "Wait, Gilbert! That sword—the point has been knocked off." He rushed forward and took it from Gilbert's hand. "Why, this could have been most tragic!"

"A good thing you noticed it, Lord North," Gilbert said, not taking his eyes off Lord Roth. "Someone could have gotten killed."

"I can't think how such a thing could happen," Lord Roth said, taking it from North. "They don't make these as well as they should." Then he laughed and said to Gilbert, "Well, Mr. Winslow, you do well—for a parson. Perhaps we can try it again at a later date?"

"At your pleasure, Lord Roth."

Gilbert stared at the man, knowing that he'd made a deadly enemy, and he cursed himself for his foolishness.

He was still angry at himself the next morning when he mounted his horse and rode out of the stable. All night long he'd tossed and turned, trying to think how he could have behaved with more wisdom.

"Gilbert—Gilbert Winslow!"

He pulled his horse up, and there, leaning out a glass window opened to the weather, was Cecily. She was more beautiful than he had thought. The snow on the sill and the white stone of the castle set off her dark beauty like a foil.

"Lady Cecily," he said with a rueful smile. "I must take my leave. Your father is my employer now, and I am his to command."

She laughed and leaned out a little farther. "So? But he is

mine to command! Didn't you know that? I can wind him around my little finger!"

"Him or any man," Gilbert smiled.

"Will you come back soon?"

"If you would have it so."

"You are a daring man, Gilbert Winslow; therefore, I dare you to come again. Come to see me, not my father. We have something more important to talk about than business," she smiled; then loosed a scarf and let the breeze carry it down to where he waited. He nudged his horse with his spurs, caught the snow-white fragment of lace, kissed it, then put it in his inside breast pocket.

"You will see me soon, my Lady Cecily—and the next time we meet, I trust I can think of a better name for you. *Cecily*— that's for parents, for friends. I must think of something much better."

"You'll steal it from some poet, Gilbert," she laughed, then turned quickly to look inside. "Someone is coming. Don't forget—I'll be waiting!"

As Gilbert rode toward London to meet with the lawyer, he thought himself a very fortunate fellow. His future now was secure! No more pettifogging little parson's life for him—no, indeed! With a man like Sir Henry North to favor him—and a woman like Cecily North to inspire him—to what could he *not* aspire?

If he could have seen, at that moment, the face of Lord Simon Roth, he might not have been so cocksure. Simon had not missed Winslow's leavetaking with Cecily, and for a long time his pale eyes remained fixed on the road where the young man had disappeared. Finally, he nodded as if to himself, and a strange smile of satisfaction appeared on his thin lips. "I think the parson must be seen to," he said softly.

CHAPTER FOUR

A MATTER OF HONOR

★　★　★　★

"You know London, do you, Mr. Winslow?"

Gilbert felt a sudden pull at his arm, and looked up just in time to avoid being flattened by a coach-and-four driven by a haughty driver in livery. "Well, I've not been in this part of the city." The lawyer nodded and plunged into the thick of the heavy traffic, skillfully threading his way between vehicles and pedestrians.

"This is Cheapside," Tiddle said out of the side of his mouth. "Our man lives not far from here. Step lively, Mr. Winslow! Our ship weighs anchor in three hours!"

"I think you'd best call me Gilbert—since we're to be together so much, Mr. Tiddle."

"Fair enough. I'm Lucas." He lowered his head and led Gilbert down the street almost at a lope. Carts and coaches made such a thundering it seemed as if all the world went on wheels. At every corner they encountered men, women, and children— some in the sooty rags of the chimney sweeps, others arrayed in the gold and gaudy satin of the aristocracy, gazing languidly out of their sedans borne by lackys with thick legs. Porters sweated under their burdens, chapmen darted from shop to shop, and tradesmen scurried around like ants, pulling at the coats of the two men who fought their way through the human tide that flowed and ebbed on the street.

"Watch yourself!" Tiddle said sharply, pulling Gilbert back just in time to avoid a deluge of slops that someone threw out of an upper window. "Nearly got you, lad! But now that the city's put the drain in the street, why every rain will wash away all this garbage." He waved his hand at the ditch about a foot wide and six inches deep in the center of the cobblestoned street. "That carries all the slops and garbage away quite nicely, you know? Wonder what a change modern improvements make, isn't it? Why, most cities just let the garbage and slops pile up—but not London! No, sir!" Tiddle paused in his admiration of the open sewer to wave his hand and say, "There. I think that's it."

Gilbert followed him up two flights of rickety wooden steps, then down a dark corridor. The lawyer knocked firmly on the oak door and at once it opened, as if the young man who stood before them had been waiting for their appearance.

"Mr. Tiddle, I saw you coming up the street." He was a husky fellow, perhaps twenty-five, with warm brown eyes set far apart under a pair of bushy brows. Turning his head to one side like a bird to stare at Gilbert, he asked, "Be this Mr. Winslow?"

"Yes," Tiddle said. "This is John Howland, Winslow. We must hurry. John, I suppose you're ready?"

"All packed," Howland said. He picked up a wooden chest bound in brass and followed the two men into the corridor, pausing only to fasten the massive padlock on the door.

"We'll take a coach," Tiddle said. "Wouldn't do for us to miss our ship." He gave Howland a sharp grin and said, "You've been away from that wench of yours so long I daresay you'd *swim* the Channel to get your hands on her, eh, John?"

The young man's tanned face grew rosy, and he answered, "You mustn't talk like that 'bout her, Mr. Tiddle; she' not one of your tavern wenches!"

Lucas laughed and slapped the husky young man on the shoulder. "I know she's not, John. I know." Then he glanced at Gilbert. "John's got himself a real preacher woman, Gilbert. Got him so holy he won't even *spit* on the Sabbath! But she's a good cook—and a fine figure, too! You *did* notice that, I trust?" He dug his elbow into Howland's ribs and gave a piercing whistle at a coach which stopped as if the horses had run into a wall.

Tiddle and Howland kept the conversation rolling as they threaded their way through the narrow, crooked streets of London. Gilbert had seen only a little of the city, but he felt a warm glow as he realized that before long he would know it as well as Tiddle.

Winslow had left the university with a sense of adventure rising in him. Tiddle met him at his office, and the next three days were spent learning the rudiments of the business affairs that would occupy him in Holland. They had packed and left to pick up Howland for the journey.

Tiddle was a talker and Gilbert was a listener. The lawyer was not impressive in appearance, but he had a mind like a razor. He was, after all, the most trusted advisor of the second most powerful man in all of England, and Gilbert wanted to gain his confidence.

Once Tiddle stopped abruptly in the middle of a complicated explanation and gave Winslow a straight look. "This is tedious, Gilbert—but you must learn it if you are to become the man Lord North desires." Then he grinned and peered up at Gilbert in his shortsighted fashion, adding, "And I do not mean a man of business!" He laughed aloud at Gilbert's blank look, then continued, "You may be aware that North is shopping for a son-in-law?"

"Well—I hardly think he need look my way," Gilbert said with a rueful laugh. "He's got the pack of English nobility to pick from!"

"He's already sorted through that crowd," Tiddle sniffed. "Nothing there for him. No, he's a man who'll pick his own raw material, pour money into the man he likes, and that'll be *it*!"

"Modesty forbids me to say how much I think I deserve such an honor, Lucas."

The shrewd eyes of the lawyer held a sly twinkle, and Lucas smiled as he said, "You may just do it, Gilbert. It wouldn't be the first time a young fellow such as yourself made his way to the top by way of a rich father-in-law." He paused and added, "I see that doesn't trouble you; but have you made up your mind as to this business with William Brewster?"

Gilbert shifted uncomfortably. "Well, I must admit it seems pretty raw. I'll be a spy no matter how you try to refine it."

"That's the way of it, I'm afraid. I'm thinking you may have too much religion for the world of business, Gilbert. You were preparing for the church at Cambridge, and the world is no church!"

"It's not that," Gilbert answered slowly. It was difficult for him to explain his distaste for the mission, but he felt he had to try. "I'm not really a churchman. That was my brother Edward's idea. And I would never have fit into that world in a million years! But—well, church or no church, Lucas—there *is* such a thing as honor! What I'm being asked to do is beneath a gentleman!"

"Oh." Tiddle stared at the young man as if he were scrutinizing a rare animal. He took a pinch of snuff, then said gently, but with a barb in his tone, "A gentleman, is it? If you'd seen as many 'gentlemen' as I have—selling their souls for a shilling, all ready to step on anyone who gets in their way—well, you might have to adjust your ideas somewhat."

"But there is such a thing as honor!"

"There's such a thing as doing the job Lord North has assigned to you! You will either do it or you may as well go back to Cambridge. It's not at all complicated, Gilbert." Tiddle lifted his hands in an abrupt gesture and spoke to the young man before him as he would have to a slow-witted apprentice. "You either pack your rather antique sense of honor away and do what you have to do—or you leave the world of business alone."

Gilbert bit his full lower lip and stared out the window. Finally he said, "All right, I'll do it."

"I thought you might," Tiddle nodded dryly. Gilbert felt as if he had parted with something that had been quite valuable, and the emptiness which he carried about in its place sobered him considerably. Tiddle patted the young man's broad shoulder. "Don't feel too bad, Gilbert. The loss of innocence is rather painful—but I assure you the time will come when you will cease even to think of it." He stared at Gilbert soberly, then shrugged and ended, "And the good news is that no man ever died from losing it."

Gilbert stared at Tiddle and finally gave a tight grin, saying in his husky voice, "Well, now that I've sold my soul, when may I expect to gain the whole world, Lucas?"

The lawyer laughed suddenly, but there was a note of sadness in his face as he looked at Gilbert. "Now that you have put the next world out of your plans, Gilbert, I think you will soon see your barns begin to fill up. I'm a little sad to see a young man like you sell his soul for a mess of pottage, though!" he jested to take away the sting.

"A mess of pottage!" Gilbert exclaimed, then grinned at Lucas. "Why, I'm getting a much higher price for my soul than that! I'm new in business, but even such a novice as I can drive a better bargain with the devil than a mess of pottage!"

Tiddle stared at Gilbert for a long time, then spoke so quietly that the young man almost missed it: "Well, I trust you will enjoy your bargain—but it may be more expensive than you think now, Gilbert Winslow!"

"There's Leyden just ahead, Gilbert," Lucas nodded out the carriage window. He turned to look at the young man slumped in the seat beside him and gave a wink in the direction of Howland sitting across from him. "Don't tell me you're still seasick, lad? Come now, you can't have anything left in your stomach—not after the way you heaved all the way across the Channel!"

Gilbert raised a hollow-eyed face the color of old ivory. The voyage had been a nightmare for him, for he had discovered with the first roll of the twenty-ton merchantman that he was no sailor.

By the time the ship touched at Amsterdam, Gilbert had long ceased to be afraid that he would die—he only wished he *could*! Howland had practically carried him off the ship and put him in a carriage, and he had been unconscious for most of the trip to Leyden. They had stopped for a meal at a small inn, and while his companions had wolfed down a huge meal of veal and cheese, Gilbert had managed to keep down a half pint of cold ale and a few swallows of fresh bread. Deciding he was going to live, he finally managed to sit up and take in the scenery that unrolled as they made their way toward Leyden—mostly flat fields silvered with winter's touch. Windmills everywhere turned their huge sails, and neat stone and clapboard houses dotted the fields. "We'll put you off at your brother's house," Tiddle said. "He's expecting you. I wrote to him myself."

"When will we . . ." Gilbert began, then glanced at Howland and bit off what he was about to ask. The husky young man with the innocent face was to be his key to opening the mystery of William Brewster, but the plan to infiltrate the church fellowship was to be between him and the lawyer.

Tiddle said quickly, "You have your visit out, Gilbert, and John here will be courting his young woman. Just make yourself at home." Lucas's face did not change, but at the words *make yourself at home*, a light touched his small bright eyes, and Gilbert nodded slightly, knowing that it was his role to become a familiar figure in the little community of Separatists.

When the coach finally pulled up in front of a snug little cottage set in the midst of a small grove of trees, Gilbert felt ill at ease. "We'd better hurry," Lucas said. As Howland got the baggage from the boot, he whispered to Gilbert, "Remember, we must be quick. Don't go too fast; your brother is no fool— and neither is Bradford. But the thing must be done quickly before the man gets away for good. I'll probably leave you here for two or three days." He got in the coach with Howland and they rolled away, leaving Gilbert feeling very much alone.

There was nothing to do but go on, so Winslow moved to the door. He had raised his hand to knock when the door opened, and he found himself face-to-face with his brother, who reached out and pulled him into the house.

"Gilbert! Why, you've grown into a fine man!"

Edward Winslow was in the prime of life, thirty-two years old. He had long red hair, a smooth, good-natured face, a neatly trimmed moustache and a powerful frame overlaid with a layer of fat. His eyes were the same cornflower blue as Gilbert's and seemed to look right into the soul of the person before him. He was wearing a fine lawn collar turned out from his throat, tied beneath a silk, red-tassled cord. A fine corduroy coat with a double row of silver buttons and silk breeches in the Dutch style completed his costume.

Gilbert took only a quick glance at his brother's dress; he was staring at his beaming face. For six years Gilbert had made this man the villain in his little drama. Now looking at his brother's face, he could not find the evil foe he had slain in his thoughts a thousand times.

"Elizabeth!" Edward called, and kept his arm around Gilbert's shoulders as he turned to a woman who came through the low doorway at the end of the hall. "Elizabeth, he's here! Gilbert's here!"

"I'm glad to see you, Gilbert," Elizabeth said, holding out a bony hand for him to clasp. "But you don't look well."

"I was seasick, Elizabeth," Gilbert stammered. His brother's wife was a frail woman, specter-thin and possessed of numerous ailments, real and imaginary. She was a startling contrast to her husband, who was blooming with vitality.

They took him into a large comfortable room with a huge fireplace, and for a time Elizabeth plied him with remedies for his ailments while Edward questioned him about his activities. When Elizabeth left it seemed to make the air a little freer, and both men breathed more easily. Edward once again clapped his younger brother on the shoulder and smiled warmly. "I hear you're changing careers."

It was a critical moment, for Gilbert realized that if he were to gain entrance into the Separatist fellowship it would have to be through Edward. Now he stammered as he tried to explain. "Well, Edward, I know you always thought that I should be in the church, but—"

"Just a moment, Gilbert," Edward said quickly. "Father wanted that, and I have tried to carry out his wishes—but it was never *my* design."

This put Gilbert at ease and he went on more smoothly with the speech he had planned. "I have tried to find my place in the Church of England, really I have. But, it's not for me, Edward. Let me explain. For the past two years I have grown to be more unhappy with the practices of the English Church. Now, there are many good men who serve as priests, and I have no quarrel with them if they are content. But I *cannot* in all honesty continue to follow what I believe to be unsound Christian practice!"

"I see."

Gilbert noted the quick look of interest Edward took in this, and worked himself up into a pitch of excitement, loathing himself for his pretense. "To be quite frank with you, I find the Church of England to be a huge mass of old and stinking works—a patch of popery and a puddle of corruption! The Lord has said, 'Come ye out from among them and be ye separate, and touch not the unclean thing!' " Gilbert had learned this speech by rote from the men at Cambridge who were known as "precise men" who advocated separation from the state church, and he hoped fervently that his face pictured the outrage that his words stated. He finished with the defiant words: "The true church must be restored to purity!"

Edward was staring at him with burning blue eyes. "You really mean that, Gilbert?"

"Yes!"

"Then I welcome you into the fellowship of those who are on just such a quest!"

There were tears in the eyes of Edward Winslow, and he threw his arms about Gilbert, saying huskily, "I have prayed for this, Gilbert! It was not our father's way—but it is the way of God!"

"You're not angry with me?"

"Angry? No! It is the way of courage, Gilbert. I welcome you into the ranks of God's warriors!"

"I—I will try to be faithful, Edward," Gilbert said, but there was a heavy weight on his spirit. This man, this brother—whom he had trained himself to hate—this was no hypocrite! If he was a true sample of the Brownists in Holland, the task he had vowed to accomplish would violate the very foundation of a truth held sacred! Gilbert remembered suddenly the words of Lucas Tiddle: *It may be more expensive than you think!*

Then he thought of Cecily and Lord North, their glittering world of excitement—and he smiled and took his brother by the hand. "I will join you, Edward!"

Edward Winslow's face was bright with a sudden happiness, and he gripped his younger brother's hand, saying, "I have prayed for you, Gilbert. Now that the Lord has opened your eyes, like the great Apostle Paul you must begin your race. We will go to the meeting tomorrow, and you will meet your companions on the quest. They will welcome you into the fellowship of saints and receive you as a brother beloved—as I do now!"

Gilbert Winslow had violated most of the Ten Commandments with enthusiasm. His life had been a careless affair insofar as doing *right* was concerned. He had defiled himself almost cheerfully, tasting of forbidden pleasure at will. But never had he felt the condemnation of spirit as he did now—holding his brother by the hand, committing himself to the society of those who had renounced the world to follow Christ. And as Edward embraced him again, he could almost hear the words *thirty pieces of silver*! They seemed to echo from heaven—or from hell. He resisted the impulse to put his hands over his ears to shut out the sound.

Instead, he stepped back and made himself smile. He said, "I trust I may prove myself worthy to be a part of God's band of saints, Edward."

He was thinking, *Thus I begin my new career! Gilbert Winslow—spy and hypocrite!*

CHAPTER FIVE

AT THE GREEN GATE

★ ★ ★ ★

Gilbert took a long drink from the pewter mug and slammed it down on the oak table, exclaiming, "I never thought it would be so easy to be a Judas!"

Tiddle leaned back in his chair and gave Gilbert a tight smile. He shook his head. "So, that *honor* of yours is bruised already, is it? Well, you'll have to be more of a Judas than that before you're of any use to us here in Leyden, Gilbert. You've been here three days and nothing you've found out is worth a farthing."

Gilbert shook his head stubbornly, took another drink of the dark red wine, then said, "Why, I don't see any problem—Edward has already accepted me as one of the *saints*. Doesn't appear to be too difficult to join this congregation."

Lucas shrugged his thin shoulders, pulled a large watch out of his vest pocket and stared at its face. Replacing it, he pulled his cloak around him and said, "I must hurry to catch the ship—but let me tell you this, young man—these aren't fools you're dealing with! I notice you haven't heard the name of William Brewster mentioned, have you?"

Gilbert shook his head. "Well, no, but that's only—"

"That's only because these people are not going to give the man up!" Tiddle got to his feet. "I'll be in London reporting to Lord North in two days. I'll tell him what we've accomplished, which is precious little!"

Lucas threw a coin down on the table, turned and left the inn without another word. When Gilbert followed him outside, he saw a frown on the face of the lawyer and was taken aback when Lucas said in a voice absolutely harsh, "This is the world of business, Gilbert Winslow! You'll do what you have to do to find this man Brewster. Lie, cheat, steal, deceive—whatever is necessary. That's what it will cost you to make your place with Lord North. You have my address—don't bother to write until you have something to say!"

Winslow stood there, struck dumb by the harshness of Tiddle's manner. Caught short by the savagery of the attack, for a moment he considered getting on the ship and going back to England, forgetting the whole thing. But it was too late for that! For better or for worse, he was committed to the world of business—and as he turned and made his way slowly down the cobblestone street toward the house of his brother, he pondered—not for the first time—the end of this strange business.

He forced himself to smile as Edward and Elizabeth came to meet him. "Am I very late?" he asked.

Edward took his arm and smiled, "Why, as it happens, we just have time to stop by Elder Bradford's house before the service if we hurry."

As they walked down the linden-shaded avenue he asked, "Did you get your lawyer friend off properly, Gilbert?"

Gilbert nodded and said with a sigh, "Yes. He left me here for a few days to finish some business. I trust I'll not be an inconvenience to you and Elizabeth."

"An inconvenience!" Edward flashed him a brilliant smile, struck him lightly on the arm and said with enthusiasm, "We'll have time to get acquainted, brother! And I'd have you know and be acquainted with your fellow saints. Come now and we'll have time to talk a little with Bradford and his wife."

They made their way to a poor section of town, passing through crowded quarters, the street cut by many winding lanes and alleys. At the end of the street they came to a small brick house covered with moss up to the eves and topped with dull red tiles. As they paused in front of the cobblestone walkway, a man and a woman came out and made their way down the sidewalk. Edward said, "Ah, William, we're not late I trust—

and Dorothy—you look well today! Let me make known to you a new seeker—this is my younger brother Gilbert, about whom I have often spoken. Gilbert, Elder William Bradford and his dear wife Dorothy."

William Bradford was a middle-aged man with a full beard and a large wart on his right cheek. He had the air of one impatient with those who were not quick and he pulled at his nose nervously, nodded shortly and said, "It is good to have you in Leyden, Brother Winslow. I trust your stay here will be profitable."

"We'd best hurry or the services will begin," Dorothy said. She was much younger than her husband, not at all the type of woman Gilbert expected in a Separatist. She was blonde, with large blue eyes; the frilly lace at her bodice reflected a taste for finery that clashed with the stern grays and blacks of the rest of her costume and with that of her husband. The fine planes of her face spoke of an aristocratic background, this also in contrast to her husband. His features were craggy, rough and deeply creased.

"Dorothy is right—we must hurry," Bradford said, leading them down the street and across a series of small intersections.

Whether deliberately or not, Gilbert could not tell, but Bradford fell into step beside him, leaving Dorothy to follow with Edward and Elizabeth. He commented briefly on Gilbert's arrival, asking several rather pointed questions about his business in Leyden, and there was a faintly suspicious light in his eyes as he glanced at the young man and asked, "You are, I understand, a member of the Established Church?"

At once Gilbert realized the snare that was laid. Edward had, of course, accepted him at face value as being an earnest seeker, but this man had no reason to trust him. Carefully Gilbert said, "That has been my history, Elder Bradford, but along with many others, I've had serious doubts of late concerning the integrity of the way I have been taught to follow."

Bradford's head swiveled and his eyes bored into Gilbert, his question sharp, "You intend, then, to leave the Established Church and become a Separatist?"

Fighting the impulse to blurt out a quick agreement, Gilbert allowed a note of regret to creep into his voice. "No, I cannot say that at this time. It's too soon. I have hopes that the Lord will give me a word of wisdom on this subject soon—but as for now I am, as my brother says, merely a seeker for the truth of the kingdom of God."

The sharp light in Bradford's eyes, Gilbert saw with relief, softened and he nodded, saying in a more genial tone, "As the Scripture says, 'Ye shall find me when ye shall search for me with all your heart'!"

"Amen!" said Gilbert and as they walked along, Bradford gave him a few details on the meeting place.

"For many years, we met in the homes of individuals. It was not until May of 1611 that we acquired a permanent place of worship—this is it up ahead. It's called the Kloksteeg—or Bell Alley, as we would say it. For a long time it was known as the *Groenepoort*, or Green Gate, and so it is still called by most of the natives here. It is a fine house, and it serves both as a meeting place and a parsonage for our pastor and his wife and three children."

"We're late," Bradford said. "Come and let us join in and afterward, my brother, you will have an opportunity to meet the congregation."

Nothing about the meeting that day suggested the Church of England to Gilbert. The first shock came when he discovered that the saints were not allowed to sit as they pleased in cozy little family groups. As they filed in, the men took their seats on the hard wooden benches to one side, the women sat apart across the aisle, while the children were placed off by themselves under the stern and restless eye of the deacons. Gilbert learned that this was known as "dignifying the meeting."

The saints prayed, and during the prayer the members of the congregation stood up, for kneeling was, as Gilbert learned later, an idolatrous Roman practice. After the opening prayer, which continued a little longer than an hour, a small, pale-faced man identified as Pastor Robinson took up a huge Bible and read aloud. He paused often for comment and exposition, and after this a psalm was sung without any instrumental music of any kind, nor did the congregation have musical notation of any kind to aid its singing. All tunes were sung from memory. Someone set the pitch, usually one of the deacons, then all lifted their voices together, with the men taking the lead in the simple melody. The saints evidently shared Calvin's aversion to any frills in a religious service.

After several hours of the singing came the sermon, preached not from a pulpit but a low dais supporting a simple wooden table. Here, in black clothes and black gloves, Robinson expounded his text with a quiet and moving eloquence, a deep human understanding, and a wealth of apt illustration.

When the sermon was concluded, the congregation sang another song, and the sacraments were then administered. Two men came forward to pass the collection plates, and the morning exercise ended about noon with a benediction.

Gilbert felt rather awkward, but he was led by Edward through a small garden behind the house where the congregation met to talk briefly before their noon meal. He was, of course, an object of curiosity to the congregation, and most of them gathered around to be introduced. Isaac Allerton, a thin man of about thirty-five, his wife Mary—a little younger—both bowed deeply and introduced their children—a young boy named Barth and a girl with the strange name of Remember. Standing beside them a couple named White, William and Susanna, whose son was dressed in black exactly like his father, although he was only five. He bore the unusual name of Resolved. Noticing that Gilbert was taken slightly aback by the unconventional names of the children, Bradford brought forth a slender woman with a dark olive complexion, accompanied by two small boys. A twinkle appeared in the elder's eye as he said, "This is Sister Mary Brewster, Gilbert—" and Gilbert looked up swiftly, recognizing this woman as the wife of the man he had been sent to ferret out. "And these are her two boys, Love and Wrastle."

A large, thick-bodied man with a black beard and a pockmarked face shouldered his way through the crowd surrounding Gilbert and said in a voice that thundered, "Well! So this is the young scholar we've heard so much about, is it, Edward?" His massive hand swallowed Gilbert's, and a solid thump on the shoulder shook the newcomer to his heels.

"Careful there, Deacon!" Edward laughed, and turned to say to Gilbert, "This is Samuel Fuller, one of our deacons."

"And a physician, sir!" Fuller's large eyes gleamed with

humor, and he stepped back to survey the visitor shrewdly. "Cambridge, is it now? Well, I'd spend some time with you, young master Winslow—to see if your stay there has left any brains in your head!"

Bradford smiled gently and with a shake of his head said, "Now don't wear the young man down, Samuel—he's not one of your patients, you know."

"Well he will be, soon or late!" Fuller smiled and said to Gilbert confidentially, "I'm not the best physician in the world— but my fees are reasonable, so come to me when you have an ailment for body or soul! Sam Fuller's your man!"

The burly physician seemed to have taken a liking to Gilbert, for he pulled him toward a table set with a light meal of round loaves of fresh bread, butter, cold cuts of several types and large containers of fresh milk. It was a time, evidently, of fellowship and of simple relaxation, and Gilbert allowed himself to be ushered to a stone bench in the garden while Fuller ran on with his mouth full, usually concerning the church—of which he was obviously very proud.

"Now, you'll not understand some of our ways, Winslow, but if you'll pay attention to the Holy Discipline, why you'll soon find your way!"

After listening for an hour to Fuller expounding the views and beliefs of the Brownists, they got up and went again into the house where Gilbert was introduced to "prophesying." Pastor Robinson chose a text, spoke on it briefly, and then opened the meeting for general discussion. Despite himself, Gilbert was impressed at the broad and deep knowledge of the Scripture possessed by most of the men and was likewise struck by the gentlemanly nature of their bearing.

By three o'clock Gilbert had dozed off several times, losing track of the sophisticated arguments that went around the room. But his attention had been attracted by two young women who sat well toward the front of the room on the women's side. The one closest to him was a small girl with brown hair and a pretty face. From the looks she exchanged with John Howland, who sat on the men's side across from her, Gilbert assumed this was the Elizabeth Tilley whose praises he had heard from the husky young man. The other young woman was hidden behind Elizabeth, but when the final "amen" was said and the congregation rose and filed out into the afternoon air, Gilbert made it a point to tell Edward that he would walk for a while around the town before returning to the cottage. Most of the congregation took time to stop by and say a friendly word of greeting, and out of the corner of his eye, he saw Howland and his young woman leaving through a gate to the north of the house, accompanied by the other young woman. Quickly he made his way through the gate and caught up with them as if by accident.

"Oh, there you are, Gilbert," Howland said with a broad smile. "I don't believe you've met these two members of our congregation. This is Elizabeth Tilley, and this is Humility Cooper. May I present my friend Gilbert Winslow."

Gilbert was taken slightly aback as the young woman turned her eyes upon him and said in a low voice, "How do you do, Mr. Winslow?" She was far more attractive than any of the other women of the congregation. And even the strict dark colors of her long black dress did not disguise her womanly figure. She had green eyes with a broad face and her coloring was glorious— red lips, bright cheeks, eyes very wide spaced and the whitest teeth he had ever seen. Her hair was tied up under her bonnet— as was the custom with all the women—but the blonde tresses that escaped had glints of red that caught the fading afternoon sunshine. A slight dimple appeared on her right cheek when she smiled at him, and she had honest frank eyes more like a man than a woman. She looked directly at him, and there was something bolder in her appearance and her appraisal of him than he had expected.

"I'm walking Elizabeth and Humility home, Gilbert," John Howland said. "Won't you walk with us for a way?"

"You're very kind, John," Gilbert said with a smile. He allowed Howland and Elizabeth to go on and the girl named Humility fell in beside him as they strolled down the street.

Gilbert Winslow had enjoyed some success with women, and he was prepared to begin his tactics by charming this girl with the strange name of Humility in his usual manner. But she looked at him and asked in a most serious manner, "The Spirit of God moved quite wonderfully among us this morning, did He not, Mr. Winslow?"

Gilbert's jaw dropped open, and for one moment his mind was totally blank. The girls he had known had had nothing to say about the Spirit of God, and he coughed slightly before he managed to answer, "Why—ah, yes, I think that is very true, Miss Cooper."

"And what was your opinion of Reverend Robinson's concept of sanctification?"

It was fortunate for Gilbert that at exactly this moment Howland turned and said, "This is the street where the Tilleys live, Gilbert." For Gilbert had nothing to say in response, and he was furious at himself at being taken off guard. *This is one of those holier-than-thou wenches who has forgotten how to be a woman!* He managed to stammer out a few words as they watched the young women go into the house; when they turned to head back toward the center of town, Howland did not notice Gilbert's discomfort. He was too busy singing the praises of Elizabeth and encouraging his friend to see all of her virtues.

After Gilbert put the matter of Humility Cooper aside, he began to listen more closely to John, and to lead him into a description of the members of the congregation. Howland was so simple that Winslow had some difficulty ascertaining the basic facts about the various individuals and their families. All the same, Gilbert noticed that not even Howland mentioned William Brewster. Gently he brought the young man's mind on the track by saying, "I don't remember meeting the dark lady's husband— what's her name? Oh, yes, Mrs. Brewster. Is she a widow?"

Howland looked disconcerted, bit his lip and said, "Oh, no, her husband is one of the elders of our congregation—Elder William Brewster."

"Oh? I don't believe I met him, did I, John?"

"No," Howland stuttered, and the words came slowly from his lips as he attempted to explain. "You see, Elder Brewster has been away. Humility and Henry are servants of Mr. Tilley, but the Brewsters are really like parents to them—especially to Humility."

With a little urging, Howland told the complete story without being aware in the least of his friend's interest. Gilbert knew from his earlier reports that the leadership at the Green Gate Assembly had been under close surveillance by spies of the crown from time to time. None of them had had any direct contact with William Brewster—that much was certain. But Brewster *had* to maintain some kind of communication with these people. *If this girl is that close to Brewster,* Gilbert thought suddenly, *how possible, even likely, it is that Brewster's contact with the leadership might be through her!* By the time Gilbert said goodbye to Howland and turned to go to Edward's cottage, a scheme was fully formed in his mind.

He hastened to the small upstairs room that had been allocated to him, threw himself down before a table, and with bold strokes wrote a letter to Lucas Tiddle. There was a cruelty of sorts on the broad lips of Gilbert Winslow as he set down the following words:

My dear Tiddle,

You left me under a cloud, suggesting that I would be rather useless so far as Lord North's mission is concerned. I must confess, my dear fellow, that I was both hurt at your rather pointed and barbed statements and somewhat fearful that they might prove to be true!

I write hastily to inform you that you may soon expect to hear from me very good news! I am no detective, and must confess that my talents for spying have not been developed by my earlier career—however, one discipline I have studied and pursued with alacrity, and that studying now stands me in good stead.

In a word, there is a member of this congregation, Humility Cooper, who is in the confidence of our friend Brewster. She appears to be quite an attractive girl, and perhaps intelligent, but I have taken dead aim upon Miss Cooper, and if she can withstand the wiles of this novice spy, she will be unique! Expect to hear from me by the next post more concerning the elusive Mr. Brewster and the decline and fall of Miss Humility Cooper!

Your most obedient servant,
Gilbert Winslow

CHAPTER SIX

HUMILITY

★ ★ ★ ★

Edward Tilley pushed his chair back from the table and looked around at his family—his wife Anne, his daughter Elizabeth, called "Bess," Humility Cooper, age eighteen, and Henry Sampson, age sixteen. Humility and Henry were his adopted children and served as servants in his household.

"Anne, be sure you have enough bread baked to last over the Sabbath," he said quietly, pushing back from the table. "I'd not like to run short as we did last week."

"I will see to it," Anne replied quickly.

"Papa, will it be all right if I go with the group to Bargsteen?" Bess asked. "All my friends are going, and I must let them know right away."

"I don't believe you should, Bess," Edward Tilley said thoughtfully. "We have heard some evil reports of the activities of young people who go on these trips."

A frown swept across Bess's pretty face and she said petulantly, "Oh, Papa, don't be so narrow-minded! Nothing wrong happens on these trips; I've told you that a hundred times!"

Anne Tilley looked nervously at her husband, nodded shortly and said, "I think it would all right, Husband. They are very nice boys and girls, and there's not much for Bess to do in the town."

Humility rose from the table and began collecting the dishes as the argument went on. When she got back from the kitchen, Mr. and Mrs. Tilley were gone, and Bess looked up with a mischievous smile on her rosy lips. "I think you ought to go with us this time to Bargsteen, Humility. You never go anywhere, and we'll have such fun!"

Humility gave her smile and said, "I'm too busy this time, Bess. Maybe later."

"Oh, all you ever do is read the Bible and talk with Pastor Robinson about it," Bess said in disgust.

She got up and began to help pick up the dishes and when they got into the kitchen with them Humility said, "I've got to go down to the harbor for a few minutes, Bess. Would you please mop the floors in the bedrooms for me?"

Bess gave her a sharp look and tapped her chin with her forefinger, then asked in a teasing voice, "Going to the harbor *again*? It seems everytime a ship comes in you have to run down to meet it." She laughed gaily and said, "You must have a sailor for a sweetheart, Humility! Or maybe more than one, from the way you meet all the ships."

Humility flushed slightly and shook her head. "Don't be silly, Bess. Will you do the bedrooms for me?"

"Oh, of course I'll do them," Bess said, "but you be careful about meeting those sailors—you know their reputation!" She gave Humility a playful pinch on the arm and said as she went from the room, "I've got to go down to the Millers and get that flour we're short of, but as soon as I get back you can go to the harbor—for *whatever* reasons you have!"

Bess made her way to the Millers which was only a few blocks away, got the flour, and was within a block of her house again when someone spoke to her from behind.

"Good morning, Miss Tilley."

Bess turned to see Gilbert Winslow smiling broadly. He seemed to tower over her, and as she leaned back to look up into his wedge-shaped face, her heart fluttered as it always did in the presence of a handsome man. "Why—good morning, Mr. Winslow! My, you're out early this morning."

Gilbert walked down the street with her and after exchanging pleasantries, he mentioned Humility's name, and immediately Bess turned her head and looked at him. "Well, you needn't waste your efforts pursuing Miss Cooper," she smiled. "She's a very virtuous girl and absolutely man proof!"

Gilbert laughed and said, "Come now, Miss Tilley, no beautiful woman is absolutely man proof—no one should know that better than *you*!" He began to flatter her, and before they had gone ten steps she was giggling at his remarks.

"Surely Miss Cooper must have many suitors?" he asked.

"Oh, no, not Humility! Though of course, I *have* been a little suspicious of her for the past few months."

Gilbert quickly asked, "Oh, she has been seeing someone, then?"

"No, not really," Bess shook her head. "But I have noticed that every time a ship comes into port, Humility doesn't waste any time getting down there."

"Oh, you think she has a sailor as a sweetheart?"

"No—no, not that—but I believe she is getting letters from someone abroad—probably England. As a matter-of-fact, I'm hurrying home now so she can go to the harbor."

Gilbert said hurriedly, "Well, here you are, but I must run, Miss Tilley. I'll see you again soon."

Gilbert walked rapidly down the street, took the first turn to the right, and paused, thinking hard. He had to gain a closer standing with Humility Cooper, but that task seemed almost impossible. Grown girls were watched so closely in this community of saints that is was rare for a strange young man to have access to any of them. But what he had heard from Bess, however, made him hopeful. If his guess was correct, and Brewster was getting information to the elders, this might be the lucky coincidence that would lead him to find the source.

He loitered around the neighborhood, always keeping out of sight of the Tilleys' front door, and within fifteen minutes Humility Cooper came out and headed directly toward the harbor, a twenty-minute walk. He kept well behind, although it was not likely that she would be suspicious. When she reached the wharf, he saw her stop a man, ask a question, and walk along the stone wharf until she came to a small two-masted schooner. Several sailors were on deck, and she called to one of them and then stood waiting. A portly man, obviously the captain, came down the gangplank, and Gilbert saw them nod to one another then carry on a short conversation. He handed her an envelope, which she placed in a small bag she was carrying, then nodded, and went back up the gangplank.

She did not come back toward him but took another route, and Gilbert said to himself as he followed her, *I'll bet my last farthing she heads right for the Reverend John Robinson!*

He would not have lost the bet, for in a few moments she went up to the door of the Green Gate and, without knocking, passed inside. Gilbert thought quickly, and without hesitation walked down the street, turned into the door, and knocked briskly.

He recognized the small woman who opened the door as the wife of Pastor Robinson, and said, "Good morning, Mrs. Robinson; may I see your husband, I wonder?"

She hesitated then said, "Come in, please. Someone is with him now, but I think he will be glad to see you."

She led him across a large open hallway. On the left he recognized the meeting room where services were held. They walked to the end of a long hall, and Mrs. Robinson tapped at a massive heavy door on the right.

"Yes, what is it?" Pastor Robinson himself opened the door, and from where he stood, Gilbert could see Humility standing near a large desk in front of some high bookcases. She gave him a startled look, but he kept his eyes fixed on the man in front of him.

"I'm sorry to intrude, Pastor Robinson. Perhaps I should come back later?"

"No, no, come right in, Mr. Winslow."

Robinson stepped back and nodded to his wife, who turned and left. Gilbert went in to stand in front of the desk, saying, "Why, it's Miss Cooper!"

Pastor Robinson said, "I think Miss Cooper was just leaving—"

Gilbert waved a hand hurriedly and said, "Oh, no! I only wanted to stop by and see if you could spare me a little time, Pastor."

"Time for what, Mr. Winslow?"

"Well, I have been much aware of late of my need for a deeper knowledge of the Word of God, and if you could be my mentor, I believe it would be a great blessing to me."

A willing smile crossed Pastor Robinson's face, and he said, "Why, certainly! Why don't we begin to meet on a regular basis—say, at three this afternoon? Perhaps that would be suitable?"

"Excellent!" Gilbert cried, and he shrugged slightly, saying, "I'm afraid you'll find me dreadfully stupid! My time at Cambridge seems to have been totally wasted!"

"Oh, I doubt that," Robinson said, "but I can recommend a list of books that we might begin with." He leaned over his desk, wrote rapidly across a sheet of paper with a goose quill pen, then handed it to Gilbert. "These will do to begin with—if you need to purchase them, I believe you'll find them at the bookshop down by the market."

Gilbert gave a negative shake of his head, "I'm afraid I don't know the place." He did, but he was hopeful that he could lure Humility Cooper away. He was totally successful.

Robinson nodded toward Humility. "Humility, would you be so kind as to show Mr. Winslow the bookshop? It isn't out of your way, I believe."

She gave Winslow a quick look, then said, "Of course, Pastor. If you're ready then, Mr. Winslow—?"

As Pastor Robinson led them out the door, he asked by way of parting, "Humility, are you going on the trip that Bess has been pestering me to death about—over to Bargsteen with that group of young people? I doubt her father will permit it."

Humility smiled and shook her head, "Oh, she's going, all right. Did you ever know Bess to fail at doing exactly what she wanted to do?"

The pastor shook his head. "I wish you'd go with them, Humility. I'd feel much better, and I'm sure your parents would also if you would accompany Bess."

"If you say so, I'll be glad to."

Immediately Gilbert said, as if in surprise, "Bargsteen—Bargsteen? Why I have to make a trip to Bargsteen! That's one of the cities I'll have to make a business trip to for Lord North."

"Why, perhaps you can serve two purposes, Mr. Winslow," Robinson said quickly. "If possible, perhaps you might go along with these young people as sort a companion and see to your business at the same time. They leave day after tomorrow—would that suit your purpose?"

Gilbert nodded and appeared to think about it. "Day after tomorrow—let me see—why, the very thing! It will work out admirably! And I'll have the opportunity to do some small service for the congregation—perhaps the first of many, Pastor Robinson."

"Fine, fine!" Pastor Robinson said. "Well then, Humility, if you'll show Mr. Winslow his way, he can get his books, and we'll begin to make a theologian out of him—and thank you very much, Humility."

"Come, Mr. Winslow, I'll show you the bookshop."

As he walked along the cobblestone streets toward the center of the village where the bookshop was located, Gilbert said, "You're looking lovely today, Humility."

His use of her first name made her cast a quick glance at him, but the pleased expression immediately changed to a frown. "Thank you, Mr. Winslow." She slightly emphasized the word *mister*, but Gilbert had seen the startled expression of pleasure.

"Mr. Winslow, I'm happy to hear that you're starting to study the Word of God with Pastor Robinson. I feel he is the most able minister in the whole world."

She had shown, Gilbert realized, a defense against men, and there was no quick way to penetrate it. He thought then of the trip proposed by the young people which he had agreed to participate in, and determined that he would break her resistance down one way or another on that trip. For the present he had another scheme, so he said when they got to the bookshop and she turned to leave, "Thank you very much, Humility, for your assistance. I'll see you again soon, the Lord willing."

He felt no guilt at the religious expressions he used, for he was convinced that Humility Cooper was playing one game—the game of being a Christian saint. He was simply playing another game in order to achieve his own ends. If he could find out from this girl the whereabouts of William Brewster, it would be simply a matter of winning a game—and he was better at his game than she was at hers.

"I'm glad you're going on this trip with the young people,

Mr. Winslow. Pastor Robinson tells me you're studying theology with him, and I'm quite pleased that you are choosing to do so."

William Bradford had drawn Gilbert aside on the morning of the departure for Bargsteen. Gilbert had been aware that there was a reservation in Bradford's manner, and he had gone out of his way larding the elder with scriptural quotations and pious talk on every occasion. Now he felt sure that he had gotten the confidence of the man, and he said modestly. "I do feel that God is speaking to me in an unusual way, Elder Bradford. I trust that I will be found worthy to join your congregation before too long."

Bradford shook his head and said, with more openness than he had shown in the past to Gilbert, "I fear, Mr. Winslow, that our congregation stands on precarious ground here in Leyden. We are here by the permission of the Dutch government, and as you know, Holland and Spain have erupted into open warfare several times already. There are two powerful forces struggling for control of this country, and if it comes to an open conflict—well, we still remember the horror of the Spanish Inquisition when it was introduced to this country in the 1570s."

Gilbert stared at him and asked, "You may have to flee for that reason, Elder Bradford?"

"Not only for that reason, for even if that situation never developed, we are troubled over the future of our children. You see, a new generation has grown up here without memories of England. The discipline of our congregation bears down hard on the spirits of the young. They watch their Dutch friends having entertainment on Sundays, while they are expected to spend the day listening to sermons. It is inevitable, I suppose, that young people will be attracted by the high-spirited traditions of Holland. You have seen, I'm sure, Mr. Winslow, the women of these parts give great liberty to their daughters. Sometimes they stay out until the gates of the city are locked, and the young men entertain them at inns all night or until they please to take rest. The young men and women go by horseback and in carriages to cities ten or twenty miles distance and there feast until late at night—and this they do without all suspicion of unchastity. That is why I am glad you are going on this excursion," Bradford said with a smile. "And I exhort you to take care of the virtue of our young women."

"You may trust me for that," Gilbert Winslow said with a straight face. "If there is anything in this world that interests me, it is the virtue of young women!" Then, lest Bradford should see any humor in his eyes, he asked quickly, "And this situation is so serious that you may move out of Leyden?"

"It is indeed; necessity forces most of our young people to labor in shops and mills. It is hard work, and they have no economic gain to look forward to in this country."

"But—where would you find a place for your people?"

Bradford stared at him for a moment, pursed his lips, and then said quietly, "The New World." He seemed to be lighted inside by the thought, and his eyes gleamed as he went on. "We are engaged now in such an investigation that may prove profitable." Then suddenly he stopped and looked straight at Gilbert, and the open manner disappeared from the elder as he said quickly, "This is all confidential, Mr. Winslow, and I urge you to say nothing of it."

"Why, of course not," Gilbert said at once. He filed the matter in his mind, knowing that it was the sort of information the authorities of England would be glad to have.

Later that morning, Gilbert and John Howland were packed into a carriage with several other young people as they made their way across the brilliant countryside. Bargsteen was a large village some ten miles from Leyden, and when they arrived, the village square was packed with people. Gilbert reached up and handed Humility down, an action which caught her unawares and brought a faint flush to her cheeks. She nodded to him and said in almost a whisper, "Thank you." And he held on to her hand a few seconds longer than absolutely necessary.

They all went to a large inn and were shown to their rooms, Gilbert sharing a common room with Howland and two Dutchmen, and Humility and Bess doing the same with some of the young women. They met together for a supper at the long table in the inn; after supper, just as darkness was beginning to fall, Gilbert noticed that Humility got up and walked out of the room through the large front door. Glancing around, he saw that no one was paying any attention, so he rose up and went after her. When he got outside, he saw that she was walking slowly, head down, toward the long canal that intersected the center of the marketplace. It was a narrow canal, no more than six feet across, spanned at frequent intersections by arching stone bridges. He let her get a few hundred yards from the inn and managed to come up quite close before he called out, "Humility."

She turned in surprise and said, "Oh, it's you, Gilbert." The use of his first name did not pass unheeded, and he stepped up beside her, noticing for the first time that she was taller than most women.

He said, "It's beautiful tonight, isn't it?" Then he added, "May I walk with you for a while?"

She hesitated then said, "Well, only for a little way—I must go in soon." He walked beside her, and the red flashing sun threw rippling streaks along the surface of the water in the canal below. The cool breezes of evening brushed against their faces. As they went farther from the center of town, a quietness spread out, and their voices seemed loud in the silence. Once he allowed his arm to brush against hers—apparently by accident and noted that she did not draw back. They spoke idly of the things that had occurred on the journey until finally they came to one of the arched bridges, and Gilbert said, "Let's cross this bridge and pretend it's London Bridge."

She smiled at him quickly and he recognized with a shock, *Why, she's beautiful!* Taken aback, he did not speak until they reached the crest of the bridge. They stood staring down at the rippling water beneath.

"I've never seen London Bridge." Humility took a tiny stone, threw it over the side, and watched as it hit the water and the circles spread to the sides of the tiny canal. "I suppose you've been there many times, Gilbert?"

"Oh, yes, I've been to London. I've been to many other places, too—but, I suppose places are about the same." He hesitated, then looked down at her and added softly, "People are born, they grow up, they fall in love—" Gilbert paused at this last word and watched her face carefully for any response. Finally, he smiled and went on, "—they marry, they die—and that's what life is, Humility." He looked at her face and asked gently, "Isn't that what you want with your own life, Humility?"

She looked up at him and said breathlessly, "Oh, I don't

know! I really don't know, Gilbert—" She bit her lip, shook her head, and there was a note of desperation in her voice as she went on quickly, "I've thought about—about love—and, and—" She seemed to have trouble with the word, but forced herself to go on. "I've never been able to get it straight in my mind how I can love God best and love a man at the same time." It seemed to shock her that she had said something like this so bluntly, and she gave a little gasp and started to draw back.

Gilbert Winslow was never a man to miss a golden opportunity like this. He drew her close with a smooth, practiced motion—not so recklessly that he would frighten her nor so gently that she could pull away. Her eyes opened wide as he pulled her into his embrace, and she seemed unable to move as his body pressed against hers. Her lips opened slightly in shock, and he strongly suspected that never before had Miss Humility Cooper ever felt as she was feeling at this moment. He lowered his head, and let his lips fall upon hers. They were lips soft by nature, and soft as a result of the surprise and shock that came to her as his arms met, closed around her.

At once a resistance stiffened her backbone, but as the warmth of Gilbert's lips touched hers, it seemed to spread like a fire through her veins; he felt her resistance melt, and she allowed him to pull her even closer. Humility's heart was beating fast; unconsciously, her arms raised and went behind the back of Gilbert's neck, and for one moment they stood there embracing, caught in the powerful magnetism between a woman and a man.

Then she drew back with a gasp, her eyes staring; her face, at first pale, took on a crimson flush starting at her throat and sweeping up over her face. She said in a stammering voice, "I— I can't—" Then she put both hands to her face and turned blindly away.

Gilbert instantly took her arm and said what he knew must be said. "Humility! Forgive me—I don't know what came over me!" He led her down the bridge and continued as she walked blindly down the lane. "I can't tell you how I regret such behavior! I've *never* treated a young woman in such a fashion in all my life!" This was true enough, for the young women Gilbert Winslow had kissed in such a fashion had never been let off so lightly, and he had to conceal a quick grin that swept across his features.

He continued apologizing all the way back to the inn; finally she stopped and turned to face him, her composure restored to some degree. Her eyes were still wide and her lips trembling, but she did not appear angry. She was, Gilbert perceived, shaken from her complacency, and he rejoiced to see it. Finally she said, "We were both wrong, Gilbert."

Gilbert shook his head, "There can be no wrong on your part! I have never known a young woman who has such depth of spirit; I must say the thought that came to me when I first saw you: a woman of virtue and of such beauty is a pearl of great price."

Humility touched her cheek with one hand, then, confused, turned away from him and went through the doorway, leaving Gilbert standing outside. He stood there for a few moments; then a broad smile flashed across his lips and he said under his breath, "*Well, Humility, my dear! Underneath that drab exterior and strict Puritan behavior lurks a tiger! I'm glad to discover it; and it will be my duty as well as my pleasure to tame the beast!*" As he followed her into the inn, he knew he had won the game.

CHAPTER SEVEN

THE INNER RING

★　★　★　★

"Oh, Gilbert, I'm so glad you returned in time for my birthday!"

Dorothy Bradford leaned forward, put her hand on Gilbert's arm, and swept the crowded room with excitement in her eyes. She was wearing a bright green dress full in the sleeves and trimmed with yellow silk. The other women, for the most part, wore bright colors also, and even some of the men were decked out in gay array. Gilbert had been surprised at first, thinking that the Separatists wore only black or dark gray; he soon discovered, however, that the more somber dress was only donned on the Sabbath—and on festive occasions they loved to wear brighter colors.

"My dear Sister Bradford," Gilbert said with a smile and a nod, "you did not think I would miss it, did you? After all, when a beautiful lady issues an invitation, it becomes, in effect, a royal command!"

Dorothy lowered her eyes, then looked up with a brilliant smile. "Oh, you're such a flirt, Gilbert! I don't see how Humility can put up with you!" She slapped his hand playfully, then looked up, saying, "Oh, here come the Tilleys—I must go speak to them." She turned to leave but paused for one moment to give him an arch look. "And now that Humility's here, I suppose none of the rest of us will be able to get your attention for one moment!"

Gilbert watched her go to greet the Tilleys, then made his way through the crowd toward where Humility stood. The hot June sun had warmed the Bradford house, and the heat from the packed bodies made a sweltering furnace of the large living room. As he approached Humility, he wiped the sweat from his brow, thinking how quickly he had entered into the life of the little fellowship. Only two weeks had elapsed since the trip to Bargsteen, but he had spent almost every day since in her company. The lifestyle of the Separatists was simple, composed primarily of work and services that lasted all day on Sunday, and from time to time a celebration such as this birthday supper for Dorothy Bradford. He had achieved the distinction of being accepted as Humility's suitor, so that they were spoken of together often. It was common to hear the phrase, "Gilbert and Humility," when plans were being made for such events. Pushing his way through the crowd, Gilbert smiled and thought: *Almost any time now Mr. Tilley is going to corner me and demand to know what my intentions are!* He reached out, took the hand that Humility extended to him, and raised it to his lips, delighted as always with the blush that rose to the girl's cheek when he made any gesture of affection. Her eyes dropped, and she hesitated as he held her hand a moment longer, then she murmured, "You— you shouldn't do that, Gilbert. It's—"

He laughed easily, his white teeth flashing against his ruddy skin, and said, "I can't think why not! Doesn't the Scripture say to greet one another with a holy kiss?"

"I'm not sure how *holy* your greeting is," Humility responded quickly, but there was a light of pleasure in her wide green eyes.

"Well, I suppose it's my fate to be forever misunderstood. As the Scriptures say, 'Man is born to trouble as the sparks fly upward.' " He took her by the arm and piloted her through the crowd toward the long table laden with food, saying cheerfully, "You aren't fasting, I trust? I'm practically starved to death! Let's try to get something into our stomachs before these gluttons devour it!"

They filled their pewter plates with coldcuts of beef, fish, mutton, and fresh vegetables of a bewildering variety, then found a tiny vacancy in one corner of the room. Sitting down, they ate and enjoyed the noisy hum that ran around the room. Gilbert looked around, thinking again of how mistaken he had been about the habits of the Separatists—not only in the matter of dress but in their character and social habits. Somehow he had formed the idea that all they did was sit around in dark clothes, looking mournful and trying to think of new ways to keep people from enjoying life. He had, however, soon discovered that though they worked terribly hard, when they got together on festive occasions, they put equal energy into that part of their lives. They loved to eat and to fellowship and not only the children, but the adults as well loved games of all kinds—a trait which gave some misgivings to the more sober leaders of the congregation.

He had discovered quickly, too, that the same energy with which they worked and played carried over into their services when they worshiped God. Accustomed as he was to the staid and formalized rituals of the Established Church, Gilbert had been taken aback at the emotional fervor with which the Brownists approached God on the Sabbath. There was a sense of excitement as they sang; he was shocked to find that they actually *believed* the words of the Psalms they sang with such gusto! He himself had long since failed to relate the words he sang in the services of the Established Church with anything having to do with real life! When he had heard the Green Gate congregation sing Psalm 150 for the first time, enthusiastically singing the words: *Praise ye the Lord! Let everything that hath breath praise the Lord!* the volume and pitch almost lifted Gilbert out of his seat. And all through the long sermons (which sometimes numbed his brain), an alertness illuminated the eyes of the hearers, and a little refrain of sound echoed the minister's words: "Amen! Yes, that is true! Bless the Lord!"

Gilbert Winslow's experience with formal religion had not been of this nature. These people looked forward with anticipation to celebration when they went into the house of God. Most Christians Gilbert had known left church with the feeling, *Well, now that's done—I can get on with the things that really matter!* But to the worshipers at the Green Gate, worshiping and serving

God seemed to be the things which *did* matter, and they went through the rest of their duties in order to get to this experience. It somehow made him feel uncomfortable, but try as he might to attribute their fervency to some sort of emotional disorder, when he sat in the service, looked about, and saw the pleasure written on the countenances of the worshipers, he felt himself out of step with some deep reality.

When Gilbert finally took his leave, he said goodbye to Dorothy, leaning forward to whisper in her ear, "Many happy returns, dear lady!" He gave her hand a squeeze, kissed it, then added, "Elder Bradford is a fortunate man indeed to have such a beautiful rose planted in his garden."

At first a wave of pleasure swept across Dorothy's face, then a cloud touched her eyes and she shook her head. "Thank you, Gilbert. It is nice to hear such things—though I suppose it's vanity that makes me like it. I fear that my beauty—such as it is—will not remain long in view of what's to come."

"What's to come?" Gilbert paused, looked down at her, and asked, "What could possibly take the bloom from those cheeks?"

"Why, if we make this terrible journey, if we live through it, there's little likelihood that neither I nor anyone else will have anything resembling beauty!" A mixture of anger and sorrow drew her lips down and she shook her head, adding, "Don't mind me, Gilbert. I know it must be done."

Gilbert wanted to press her, for this attitude was unusual. He suspected it had something to do with the proposed journey to the New World, and it was imperative that he find out anything he could about such a project. But he could not talk with the crowd around, so he took his leave from Dorothy, bade goodbye to Elder Bradford, arranged to meet Humility the next day for a walk, and left the house. Making his way along the cobblestone streets that twisted and wound through the city, he was greeted by a smallish boy on a path beside one of the canals. "Mr. Winslow, I've been waiting for you!"

"Oh, it's you, is it, Tink?" He looked down at the boy, fourteen years old and undersized. The boy had tow-colored hair that shot off in all directions almost covering a pair of jutting ears, and bright blue eyes. He had a large purplish birthmark on his right cheek that marred his face and ran down onto his neck.

Despite the smile in his face, there was something vulnerable about the lad.

During the long afternoons with nothing else to do, Gilbert had taken Tink strolling along the canals, catching the small, silver-scaled fish. The boy, who had been painfully shy at first, had opened up in the warmth of Gilbert's attention, and Gilbert had the impression that Tink communicated more with him than with anyone else, for he seldom saw him with the other young people his own age.

Now as Gilbert put his hand on Tink's shoulder and they walked toward the canal to find a favorite spot, Gilbert said, "Well, how was it today, Tink?"

"It was all right." Tink helped his father, a wool carter, and if he ever complained about the long hours or the arduous work, Gilbert had never heard him. The idea of using the boy as an informer somehow still lingered in Winslow's mind but it would be difficult now, for he had developed a genuine affection for the lad.

"Mr. Bradford says that in the New World it won't be hard to make a living like it is here," Tink said enthusiastically. "My father will have his farm like everyone else and they do say that the ground is so rich that the fruit falls off the trees all year round! Won't that be wonderful, Mr. Winslow—just to have apples— or even bananas—anytime you want one?"

Gilbert shrugged his shoulders and said, "That will be good, Tink, but is it all settled? I mean grown-ups talk a lot about things like this—about moving, about finding a new place and bettering themselves, but often it never happens."

Tink shook his head violently. "Oh, we're really going! I heard Mr. Carver tell my father that the ship to take us there has already been bought!"

Winslow saw that the boy was in deadly earnest about the journey to the New World. If the departure was to be soon, that meant to please Lord North he had to find Brewster at once. It made no sense to think that Brewster, one of the founders of the Green Gate congregation, would be left in England while the rest of the flock went to seek new homes. He would somehow make an attempt to get aboard one of the ships.

He was so deep in thought that when a man standing beneath a dimly flickering light at the intersection of the main street called his name, he did not hear. Tink caught his arm and said, "Mr. Winslow—I think he wants you."

Winslow came to himself with a start and turned to see a large burly man dressed in dark clothing approach. "Mr. Winslow, is it?"

"I'm Winslow—and who are you?"

The husky man stepped even closer and by the flickering light Gilbert saw that he had a broad face with one eye turned outward in such a fashion that it was difficult to keep from staring at it. He had huge hands, thick, broad, and short stubby fingers—butcher's hands, they seemed.

"May I have a word with you, Mr. Winslow?" The straight eye glanced quickly at the boy, and he added in a high tenor voice, "Alone, if it's all the same."

Curiosity touched Gilbert, and he said, "Run along, Tink. Here, take these fish and leave some of them with Mrs. Winslow for tomorrow—off with you, now!"

Tink took the string of fish, gave the stranger a quick glance, then nodded at Gilbert and turned to move off quickly down the darkening streets.

"What's your business?" Gilbert asked sharply. The man did not seem to be dangerous—but at the same time he was a stranger and there was a furtive air about him. Gilbert thought perhaps he was a beggar of some sort, but his clothes were not worn enough. A gold ring on one thick finger of his right hand and a gold watch chain gleamed dully in the light of the lantern.

"I'm Johnson." He nodded his heavy head quickly three times, searched the dark shadows with one eye suspiciously, turned back and said suddenly, "My business is the same as yours, Winslow—Brewster!"

Gilbert stared at him and said cautiously, "Brewster—which Brewster is that? I know no Brewster."

"You'd best know one and quick or your master will be displeased, Winslow!" Johnson winked his good eye, bared his large teeth in what passed for a grin, and again nodded sharply with a firm movement of his chin. "You've wasted too much time, and they're getting restless."

"Who is *they*?"

Johnson reached into the recesses of his coat, pulled out an envelope, and handed it to Gilbert. "It's all in here, Winslow. But I'll tell you what it says—it says that you're to be on that ship that came in this morning and report in person to Tiddle in London."

Opening the letter, Gilbert scanned it and saw that it was indeed a short note from the lawyer instructing him to return as soon as possible and give a report. Characteristically, the lawyer made no eloquent pleas, but phrased the request in blunt language, and signed his name simply—Tiddle.

Johnson said, "Ship weighs anchor tomorrow at three. Be sure you're on it, Winslow!"

"But I've got to stay here, Johnson! I've got to keep an eye on a girl that may lead us to Brewster."

Johnson nodded his head savagely, and winked his glaring eye. "Aye—I know the wench! You get to Tiddle and I'll watch her! If I have to, I'll break her neck to find out what we need to know!"

Gilbert reached out, and although Johnson was a massive man, he was jerked up on his toes by the powerful grip that gathered the front of his coat. "Keep your hands off her—you hear me!" Thrusting Johnson back, Gilbert turned and walked away, throwing over his shoulder the words, "I'll be at the ship when it leaves!"

As he walked swiftly toward Edward Winslow's house, Gilbert's mind swam and he tried to make some sense out of Tiddle's request. He did have some business affairs to report on, but there was an urgency in the lawyer's reply that seemed uncalled for. He somehow felt it had more to do with Brewster than with business.

It was not late when he got to the house, and as he entered, Edward greeted him, saying, "Come in here, Gilbert—we need a word with you."

Gilbert followed Edward into the dining room and saw that Bradford and Carver were seated at the carved oak table. "Why, good evening Mr. Bradford—Mr. Carver."

Edward moved to his chair, sat down, and motioned for Gilbert to do the same. There was an air of tension in the room, and Bradford's craggy features were set in lines of discouragement. Looking across the table, he said, "Mr. Winslow, we have decided to accept you into the fellowship of our congregation."

Gilbert's heart leaped—his mission was accomplished! He covered this exaltation by nodding his head and saying humbly, "I am honored, Elder Bradford. I trust that my devotion to the church will be proved by my faithfulness in service."

John Carver spoke up at once. He was in his sixties and his hair was a beautiful silver. There was a placid air in Carver that Gilbert had noted and envied, and now the older man said evenly, "You have heard, Gilbert, of the voyage to the New World, I suppose."

"Have you obtained a charter, Elder Bradford?" Gilbert inquired.

"Of sorts," Bradford admitted, nodding his head slowly. "At this very moment we have two men making the final arrangements for the voyage—Elder Robert Cushman has arranged for a ship called the *Mayflower* that is being fitted out even now in Southampton. Another ship has been purchased called the *Speedwell*, which will take our people from Leyden to Southampton."

Gilbert said, "It is a tremendous undertaking, gentlemen! I know that you have sought the will of God in the decision."

"Indeed we have, Gilbert!" Carver said, and his face lit up with a holy light. "And we have wondered if perhaps you could be of some service at this time to the congregation?"

Gilbert said at once, "Anything—anything at all."

"There is an urgent necessity for getting the mission underway," Edward said, striking the table with his fist. "This is the fourteenth of June and we must leave in July or we will come to the New World in the dead of winter."

"Do you plan to make a visit to England soon, Gilbert?" Carver asked.

"Why, yes, as a matter-of-fact—my business calls for me to return home tomorrow."

"Wonderful! Surely it is the hand of the Lord!" Carver cried out. "Could you perhaps go to Southampton and carry this message to Elder Cushman?"

Gilbert reached out and took the bulky envelope that Bradford held, looked at it, then said firmly, "It will be my pleasure to be of some small service. We weigh anchor tomorrow afternoon, and I should be able to convey the message instantly upon arrival." This agreement made all three men beam and when he left the room, a warmth and a friendliness shone in the face of Bradford that exceeded anything Gilbert had seen before.

Gilbert slept fitfully that night and was up early getting his few belongings packed. He spent the morning working on the reports of business that Tiddle would expect, then went shortly after noon to find Humility, only to discover that she was gone. He was disappointed, but there was nothing he could do but to take ship without saying goodbye.

As he walked up the gangplank that afternoon, Winslow heard his name being called. He turned to see Humility approaching the foot of the gangplank carrying a small box. When he turned and went quickly to meet her, she shoved the box at him, saying, "It's a lunch for you for your crossing, Gilbert. I'm sorry I missed you earlier today, but I thought you might like something to eat."

Gilbert laughed and tucked the box under his arm, then shrugged his shoulders. "Many thanks, Humility, but if I'm as sick as I was on the way over, all your efforts are for naught."

Humility looked up at him and smiled. "It will be different this time—I'll pray for you to have a good crossing."

Gilbert looked down and saw that her hands were trembling. "I'll miss you, Humility," he said gently. "Every foot that ship takes me away from Holland will be like a million miles."

He was speaking the language that he had learned to practice on young women, and as she had done often before, she caught him off guard. Looking up straight into his eyes, her lips trembling slightly, she said, "I'm learning to love you, Gilbert."

Gilbert Winslow's jaw dropped and he felt as if someone had struck him a solid blow in the pit of the stomach. Twice he tried to say *something*, but the words that came to his lips seemed silly and futile and unworthy. He looked down into Humility's sea-green eyes, noting the steadiness of her gaze, and the firmness of her lips now that she was under control, and he knew what it had cost this girl to say those words. She was not, he knew, a woman given to light language—what she said represented the very depths of her heart. Now as never before, he felt the heat of perfidy and despised himself thoroughly. But he said only, "And I'm beginning to love you, too, Humility."

"I'll pray for you that you won't be sick, and I'll pray for you to come back soon, and I'll—I'll pray for our life together." Humility did that which would have been impossible for her only a short time before. With a swift gesture, she reached up and pulled his head down, kissed him lightly on the lips. Then with a bright smile and tears in her eyes, she whirled, ran down the gangplank, down the street, and around the corner. Even as he stood there, Gilbert saw the burly form of Johnson suddenly appear and follow her, and the appearance suddenly brought all the sordid details of his life into focus.

As the ship crossed the channel, the waters grew rough, and the winds drove the ship hard—but so deep was he in thought that he took no notice. It was only when they came within sight of England that he suddenly stopped dead still, looked wildly back toward the land across the channel, and said out loud: "Why, I wasn't sick a bit this time!" And quite unreasonably, he was angry and ashamed.

CHAPTER EIGHT

BACK TO BABYLON

★ ★ ★ ★

Great skeins of tattered clouds were drifting raggedly across the horizon as Gilbert disembarked and made his way along the Southampton quay. He took little note of the fishermen unloading their catch of cod, stopping only long enough to ask of the ship he sought.

"*Mayflower*?" a barrel-shaped sailor pulling a small dinghy up on the beach scowled. He jabbed a stubby thumb at a ship sitting low in the green water, then asked, "Take 'ye aboard for a shilling?"

"Good enough." The price was high, but Gilbert had determined to have an interview as quickly as possible with Cushman, the elder from Green Gate.

The *Mayflower*, he judged, was not more than eighty feet long. Being a typical apple-cheeked boat, perhaps twenty-five feet across in the beam—only a little over three times as long as she was broad—she had a stubby, awkward appearance. She would have a crew of about twenty, he guessed, and being low in the waist, would certainly be a wet ship. Carrying the usual three masts, the fore and main were square-rigged in the simplest manner, while the short mizzenmast behind on the poop was rigged to fly a lateen sail. Built across the foredeck was a roomy forecastle, like a small house that had been forcibly jammed forward. A set of steps were rigged on the flat down the sloping side, which the outswelling curve of the ship caused to stand out from her several feet at the bottom.

The two crafts touched, and Gilbert said, "Wait for me! I'll not be long," then scrambled aboard. Swinging over the low bulwark, he stepped onto the deck. Three of the crew standing at the rail had been watching him, and the tallest of them—a thin blade of a man with sharp features and a huge beak of a nose, snapped querously, "What's yer business?"

"I'm looking for Mr. Cushman."

"Another one of them holy psalm-singers, Coffin," a thick-bodied tar grinned. He spat over the side through a large gap in his teeth, and added, "Looks like a proper parson, don 'e now?"

"Belay that, Daggot!" the man called Coffin snapped. He stared at Gilbert then said in a surly tone, "In the Great Cabin—up there."

"Better hold 'is hand, Coffin," Daggot jibed. "He might fall overboard!"

"No great loss if the whole pious bunch drownded," Coffin said with a glare at Gilbert. "Too many parsons in the world, I say."

Gilbert gave a curious look at the man, then shrugging, he made his way up a short stair to the poop deck and knocked firmly on the heavy oak door that led to the captain's cabin.

In response to Gilbert's knock, a voice called, "Come in!" The Captain's Cabin, or Great Cabin, was shaped to fit the rounded swell of the ship's side, and a row of windows along the stern allowed the last rays of the sun to light up the low-ceilinged room. A brass lantern hung from one of the ribs overhead, and there was a Spartan simplicity in the furniture—a single bed in one corner, two chairs and several stools ranked along one bulkhead. Pegs driven into the sides of the inward sweep of the ribs served as a wardrobe for shirts, oilskins, and various items such as a highly polished sextant and a broad-sword of the old style.

"Well? Have you got a tongue, man?" Gilbert took in the man, whom he took to be Captain Christopher Jones, sitting behind a mahogany desk—a solid, tightly built man in his early thirties. Bronzed to a ruddy color, he had a full head of brown hair, slightly curly. "Speak up, man!"

"My name's Winslow. I have business with Mr. Cushman."

"I'm Robert Cushman." A slight man dressed in brown broadcloth was standing beside the desk. He had a thin face, and a tic in his right eye drew up that side of his face from time to time. "You come from Leyden?"

"Yes."

"I don't believe we've met," Cushman said tentatively with a trace of suspicion in his thin face.

There was a tension in the room that Gilbert didn't understand, but he needed to assuage any doubts if he were to get any information. "I'm new to the Green Gate, Elder Cushman. But you know my brother, Edward, I think."

The name had the power to remove all doubt, and Cushman smiled at once, stepping forward to offer his hand. "Of course, of course. You'd be Mr. Gilbert Winslow. I've heard much from Edward about you! Come with me, Mr. Winslow," he said quickly, then walked to the door and stepped outside, closely followed by Gilbert. He walked with quick nervous steps to the far rail of the poop deck, then asked, "How are things progressing at home?"

"I have this letter from Mr. Bradford and Mr. Carver." Gilbert took the large envelope from his pocket, then watched while Cushman eagerly slit the seal, opened it, and read the contents with darting eyes.

"You know the contents of this?"

"No. I was coming to London on business and the elders asked me to bring it. It has to do with the voyage, I assume."

"Yes. In order to hire the ship to take us to the New World, we must have a full company. Mr. Thomas Weston has organized a group of Merchant Adventurers who will provide the funds for our venture, but he also insisted that the new colony be sufficient in number."

"Aren't there enough volunteers from the Leyden church?"

"Not half enough—and Mr. Weston has recruited a group to fill out our number."

"Are they of the Brownist persuasion?"

"Mr. Winslow, they're *nothing*! Many of them are poor—weavers, tanners, shopkeepers, and the like. But that's not the trouble. They have no faith! Most of them are members of the

Established Church—just what we are sailing across the ocean to escape from!" A wry smile creased Cushman's thin lips and he added, "Why, already there's a name for the two groups— saints and strangers!"

A smile touched Gilbert's lips, and he repeated the phrase. "Saints and strangers—I'd lay a gold angel to a lead shilling there'll be trouble between those two groups!"

"I do fear it, Mr. Winslow! But, let me ask, do you return to Leyden soon? I must send an answer as soon as possible."

Gilbert hesitated, then said, "I'll see it gets there, Mr. Cushman. But I'm pressed for time at the moment."

"It will take only a moment." Cushman scurried off to find writing material, and Gilbert spent twenty minutes struggling with his conscience, for he had decided to open the letter on the off chance that it might have valuable information concerning the whereabouts of Brewster.

He took the envelope which Cushman handed him, but when the thin man said, "God bless you, Mr. Winslow! I am grateful to God for your help in this matter!" a wave of shame swept through him. He mumbled goodbye hurriedly, and as the sailor oared him back to shore, he almost decided not to read the letter.

"Fie on it!" he said to himself angrily as he sat down in the small room he hired for the night. But after tossing and turning for two hours, he got up, lit the candle and read the letter. It said nothing of Brewster, being a plea from Cushman to make all haste possible in winding up the affairs at Leyden. The postscript added, *Mr. Gilbert Winslow is a welcome addition to our small fellowship. He will be one of the saints—not a stranger!*

Cecily pulled the dappled mare to a halt with a sharp tug on the bridle that brought the lathered animal to an instant halt. Slipping to the ground with a careless grace, she tossed the reins to a short stable boy who led the exhausted mare toward the stable. If anyone had ventured to suggest that she had been cruel to the animal, Cecily North would have been incredulous. "But it's *my* horse," she would probably have said.

A tall man was stepping out of a coach in front of the wide steps that led into the boxy mansion designed by Inigo Jones,

England's most sought-after architect. As she advanced, the man turned, and she called out, "Gilbert!" and a quick smile touched her lips as she ran forward to greet him.

"Cecily!" Gilbert took her hands, and her beauty caught him off guard, so much that he stood there staring at her, speechless. Finally he said, "You're lovely in the morning!"

"Morning! It's almost noon!"

"Well, you're even more beautiful at high noon!" he grinned.

"Come inside. I demand to know why you've stayed away so long. I warn you that I have an unerring ear for a romantic lie, so you may as well confess to all your indiscretions!"

As she pulled him into the stately foyer, he said, "I've thought about you since we parted."

"And you came only to see me, didn't you? Nothing to do with my father or business?"

Gilbert faltered slightly. "W-well, to be truthful . . ."

Cecily threw her head back and laughed. "Oh, you perfidious creature! Caught in the act! And I thought you were such a *romantic* suitor!"

"I trust to prove myself just so—but I do have to see Lord North at once."

"Tomorrow," Cecily said firmly. "Tonight you'll escort me to the Duke's ball!" She called loudly, "Thomas, show Mr. Winslow to the guest house and make certain he's taken care of."

"Cecily . . ."

"We'll leave at seven, Gilbert." She swept out of the room, and Gilbert followed the servant out of the house.

For the ball Gilbert wore clothes provided by his host: red velvet coat and breeches, yellow waistcoat with ruby buttons, and yellow hose above his shoes with gold buckles. The red hat with the large yellow plume was almost too much, but he shrugged and tucked it under his arm as he walked across the garden to meet Cecily.

Cecily achieved a triumph by choosing a simple gown ornamented with very small pink roses against vertical stripes of silver set off by sky blue. He took the scarlet cape lined with dark blue from her maid and as he slipped it over her smooth shoulders, said, "I didn't think it possible for anyone to outshine your beauty, Cecily, but I fear it has come to pass."

She shot him a smoky glance and asked in an icy tone, "And who has eclipsed my beauty, may I ask?"

Gilbert made an elaborate gesture with his plumed hat, sweeping it downward to indicate his elaborate dress, and said with a grimace, "Me! I feel like a tailor's ape, Cecily—fool of a coxcomb in ribbons and hose!"

Her lips curved into a smile, and she said, "You look well enough." She took in his lean athletic form, the slightly crooked smile and the coppertoned hair that framed the intensely masculine wedge-shaped face, and then added, "You are a beautiful man, Gilbert—you're most likely to charm the ladies of the court, I fear."

Gilbert was embarrassed at her comment on his appearance, but turned it off by saying with a rueful laugh, "Faugh! If your father finds me unsatisfactory for his service, I can always become a gigolo, can't I?"

The ball was a blaze of splendor that Gilbert could afterward remember as some sort of fantastic dream. He brushed shoulders with the demigods of British royalty, and was amazed—and somewhat shocked—to find out how strictly human they were. The Countess of Wentmore, fabled like Helen for her fabulous beauty, looked well enough at a distance of twenty feet under artificial light, but Gilbert was repelled to discover that she had apparently never discovered bathing. "Scratch me!" he exclaimed under his breath to Cecily. "But she smells like a hog in a ditch!"

Simon Roth turned from a group to stare at Gilbert, and Cecily quickly led him away.

"Why did you do that? Pull me away?" Gilbert asked.

"My dear, I didn't want another duel like the last time you met." She took the glass of wine he got for her and looked over it at him, her eyes catching the gold of the plate and the glare of the chandeliers. She took a sip, then murmured, "You know he hates you, don't you?"

"It's quite obvious. And there can only be one reason."

"Yes. He wants me." It sounded crass, but she shrugged and added, "He's always gotten what he wanted—and I suppose he'll get me, too."

"Do you love him?"

"No. But he's rich and attractive in a strange sort of way. Mother wants him for a son-in-law. Father wouldn't object."

Gilbert stared at her and said angrily, "You sound like love doesn't enter into it!"

"I don't think it does." Cecily reached up and touched his cheek, then said with a sad smile, "You are such an innocent man! You would be terribly shocked if you knew how rarely love is a factor in marriage."

"You're different, Cecily!"

She gave him a warm smile then, and pulled his arm close. Looking up at him she said quietly, "You think I am, don't you, Gilbert? Perhaps that's why I'm drawn to you—a penniless man with no title. But it's so *good* to find one man who's not blinded by money or my father's position!"

"You're woman enough for any man," Gilbert said, and would have pulled her into his arms in the center of the crowded room.

She laughed, bit her lip and drew back. There was the glimmer of tears in her eyes—the first Gilbert had seen, and in the softest voice he'd heard her use, she whispered, "Thank you, Gilbert. I—I'll treasure that!" Then she swept her hand across her eyes and with a laugh pulled him to the floor and made him dance with her.

The following day, Thomas handed him a letter. Cecily watched as he opened it, and the summons from Tiddle to be at Whitehall the next day was a cold shock.

"You have to go, don't you?" Cecily asked.

"I fear so."

She walked to the window and stared out, saying, "It will be lonely here without you."

"And even more lonely for me." He turned her around to face him, and said, "I'll come back."

"Will you?"

"I would always come back for you, Sweet."

He kissed her then, tenderly, yet she clung to him fiercely, like a lost child. Finally she drew back and said, "I'll have Smith drive you to London. What time must you be there?"

"As soon as possible, I fear. Tiddle urges all haste."

Cecily bit her lip and nodded, then they parted. Gilbert threw his things together, ignoring Thomas's attempts to help, and in half an hour was in the coach on his way to London. He did not see Cecily, and there was such confusion in his mind that he had to be spoken to twice by the coachman when they arrived.

He got out of the coach, gave the man a coin, and went inside the large inn Tiddle had mentioned. The clerk informed him that instructions had been given for him to occupy a room next to that of Lord North. "And I think—yes, there's a letter for you."

Gilbert took the letter, opened it, and read Tiddle's blunt script. "Come to Whitehall as soon as possible. The clerk will give you directions."

"Have these things put in my room, please; and can you tell me the way to Whitehall?"

"Well, sir, will you walk? It's not far."

"All right."

"You'll have to pass through a pretty bad section, sir," the clerk warned. "Perhaps a coach . . ."

"I'll walk; just tell me the way."

A high wind was whistling down the Strand from Charing Cross, driving the sooty drizzle from chimney pots. It endangered hats and flapped the curls of periwigs, then set the street signs dancing. Gilbert paid no heed, but passed through the half-deserted streets in the falling twilight.

Passing east along Pall Mall, he passed into a section the clerk had called Dead Man's Lane—one of the many old sections of London grown gray with age and mossy with time.

Darkness was filling the sky, and he was caught off guard when a voice said, "Would you pass by here, Mister Jackan-apes?"

Instantly a sense of danger scraped across Gilbert's nerves, as he saw a tall man blocking his way. He responded harshly, "The only pass I make will be through your rotten heart!" He drew his sword and whirled to face the man who had accosted him. He was lean, his tattered coat fastened tightly to his body with pewter buttons to the neck. He wore an old scabbard, but the sword in his hand was new, and there was a leer on his face as he crowed in a harsh voice, "I heard you fancied yourself as a good blade. But cock of the hectors am I, that can spit a running fowl through the neck, and am here to do quite as much for you!"

"Your health will remain good if you step aside," Gilbert smiled grimly.

Instead the man shouted, "God rot ye!" and lunged in quarte for his opponent's chest. Gilbert's hand swept to the left across his own chest knocking the thrust wide, yet so close to the body that the blades hissed together.

Twice more the blades darted and rattled, and then Gilbert did something that Paul Dupree had taught him. It was a secret *botte*, a sword trick. If a man fights closed-up, and ventures little more than a half-lunge, his antagonist comes to underestimate his reach. But if he draws his right-angled foot up close to the left foot, as Gilbert did, he has an incredibly long leg-lunge when he goes forward. His arm and sword, rigid as a rod together, seems far longer.

As his long-legged opponent launched his own thrust, Gilbert's blade tapped that of the other, then swiveled upward, and the extra distance he gained from the *botte* allowed Gilbert to stretch just far enough. The tip of his blade caught the man through the upper throat not far under the chin. It ripped up behind the teeth, crashed through the roof of his mouth and lodged in his brain. In the next instant Gilbert ripped the blade free; it came away in a gush of blood that spattered heavily on his hands and cuffs.

For half a second the long-legged form stood upright, hardly swaying. The gaunt corpse tried to take a step, but he was already dead. He fell full length, face down, and Gilbert asked bitterly, "Still cock of the hectors, are you?" Then Gilbert remembered his words: *I heard that you fancied yourself a good blade!* and he knew at once that the fine hand of Lord Roth lay behind the attempted murder!

Quickly he wiped his blade on the dead man's clothing, sheathed it, then hurried away before the watch came. Twenty minutes later he walked up the high steps of Whitehall palace, the London residence of King James, the royal majesty of England. Glancing down at the drying blood on his cuffs, he thought, *first a betrayer, now a manslayer!*

Winslow was aware that there was no way under heaven to prove that Roth had any connection with the attempt on his life, but he was in too deep to back out, so he marched up to the guards bearing silvery armor and said, "Mr. Gilbert Winslow of Leyden to see Lord North!"

CHAPTER NINE

AT WHITEHALL

★ ★ ★ ★

Gilbert spent the night in a small room after being unable to contact either Tiddle or Lord North. Rising at dawn, he found both men eating a sumptuous breakfast after which North led the way through the maze of rooms that made up the palace.

"We have an audience with the King in one hour," Lord North said. He led them through a tremendous ballroom with fully a thousand lights in chandeliers and iron-gilt holders.

Gilbert trailed along behind as North led them down several corridors to the southeastern corner of the hall into a shut-off space with a fireplace built in the very angle of the wall. Four high folding screens, of heavy leather with brass nailheads and thickened with three inches of padding, had been drawn around to form an intimate space in the large room. There were several Oriental chairs, draped and padded for comfort, and seated in two of them, Gilbert saw, were Lord Roth and Bishop Charles Laud.

"Ah, North, there you are . . ." the portly clergyman beamed. He waved a fat hand toward the chairs, saying in his rich baritone, "His Majesty will arrive shortly—but before he comes, perhaps we can have a brief report from Mr. Winslow, eh?"

"Have you discovered the whereabouts of Brewster, Gilbert?" Lord North asked quietly.

"I regret, sir, that I have not."

"No progress at all?" Tiddle rapped sharply. "You had enough time, it seems, to find out *something*."

Gilbert plunged ahead to explain how he had attained membership in the Green Gate assembly, and made the most of the fact that he had been entrusted with a message to Cushman. While he was trying to explain that Brewster would try to join the expedition to the New World, the door swung open, and James the First, dread sovereign of England, walked into the room.

As Gilbert joined the others in making a low bow, the King said, "No ceremony! No ceremony, if you please!" As he seated himself on one of the chairs, Gilbert took occasion to examine the ruler of England.

He was of middle stature, more corpulent in appearance than in reality, for he wore his clothes large and easy, the doublets quilted for stiletto protection, his breeches in great pleats and fully stuffed. There was something of a timorous disposition in his face, which no doubt explained his dagger-proof doublets, and his large eyes rolled over the men in front of him with a trace of suspicion. His beard was very thin, and as he began to speak, Gilbert noted that his tongue seemed too large for his mouth, which made his speech muffled. He took a cup of wine from one of his attendants, and seemingly had to wallow the liquid to the sides of his mouth in order to drink.

As Lord North replied briefly to a question, the king got up and walked in a circular manner, and Gilbert remembered having heard about the weak legs which some attributed to some sort of foul play on his youth, or even before he was born, for James had not been able even to stand before the age of seven.

"Enough of that, North!" James interrupted, and his eye fell on Gilbert. "Is this the spy?"

Hearing the matter stated so bluntly, Gilbert turned pale and North said quickly, "This is Mr. Gilbert Winslow, Your Majesty, a very accomplished gentleman who has generously agreed to interrupt his own career to help root out Your Majesty's enemies."

Roth said in a strident tone as if Lord North had not spoken, "Yes, this is the fellow I told you about, Sire. I believe I mentioned he left Cambridge after developing a distaste for the ministry."

A wave of anger shot through Gilbert, and he opened his mouth to make a defense, but Tiddle hurriedly said, "I must add to that, my Lord, that Mr. Winslow left the university in order to enter the service of Lord North under my care. He has made an excellent beginning, and will prove a useful subject to the crown."

"I believe you are acquainted with Mr. Winslow's brother, Edward?" North asked.

"Oh—Edward Winslow? Yes—yes—an able man!" James nodded rapidly, and the suspicion in his weak eyes faded. He sat back and asked, "Well, what has been done about this Brewster fellow? I'll have him drawn and quartered, d'ye heed me?"

Catching the slight nod from Lord North, Gilbert plunged again into his report which the King listened to carefully. A murmur of approval went around the circle as he ended by saying, "The Separatists will leave England soon, Sire; in fact, they *must* leave by August if they are to make landing in the New World before the dead of winter."

"What then, Winslow?" James snapped. "How does that bring Brewster into my hands?"

"Why, it is certain, my Lord, that he will make this journey," Gilbert answered. "He is the leader of the congregation—and besides, he must know that he will be apprehended sooner or later if he stays in England! I have made a close acquaintance with one of the Separatists. Brewster has written to this young woman often, and is sure to do so again. Sire, I must return at once to Leyden, for time is running out! Brewster will be contacted—he must be! They may wait until the last possible moment to attempt to get him aboard the ship, but that will work to our advantage."

"How is that?" the King asked.

"I am in the confidence of the leadership of the group at Leyden. They are aware that I know the country and that I travel freely. I will put it in their way to ask for my assistance. Be assured, Your Majesty, the moment I find the man, he is as good as in your hands!"

"That soundeth well, Winslow!" the king cried out and got

to his feet. Moving toward the door, he exclaimed, "I said at the beginning I'd *make* them conform or harry them out of the land! See to it, man, and ye'll not go unrewarded!" He left accompanied by the bishop, and a silence ran around the room after the door closed. Then Tiddle said, "You've not mentioned your adventure last night, Gilbert."

North nodded and there was a serious look on his face. "We got a report early this morning on your encounter in Dead Man's Lane. When they found you were connected with me," he added, "the authorities brought me the report—and left it in my hands."

"Otherwise you might be cooling your heels at Tyburn prison," Tiddle nodded grimly.

"It was a matter of self-defense—the witness made that clear," North mused. "A robbery, I take it—but the woman said she never saw anything like the way you dispatched the varlet."

"What then?"

"Murder—or an attempt at it." Gilbert carefully kept his eyes away from Lord Roth as he added, "The varlet knew me, my Lord. He made it clear that I was marked as a victim."

North had a puzzled look on his face. He glanced at Tiddle and said, "That makes things more difficult, I suppose?"

"Could be the Puritans saw through your masquerade, Winslow," Lord Roth remarked carelessly. He picked a piece of lint off his tunic and gave a thin smile. "Such things frequently happen to informers, I'm told."

Gilbert nodded slowly, locking eyes with Lord Roth, and finally he said, "Anything is possible, my Lord."

"Once again, Winslow, I must pay tribute to your blade," Roth said smoothly. "We must have another match soon."

"At your leisure, Lord Roth."

"Gilbert, you'd best get back to Leyden," North interrupted. If he caught the tension between Roth and his young friend, nothing of it showed in his smooth face. "The King's eye will be on you—and a success in this matter will open many doors for you."

"Yes, my Lord, I'll return at once."

Lord North said a hearty "Godspeed," and clapped Gilbert across the shoulders with a rare show of affection. Roth did not even glance at him as the two left the room.

"I'll go with ye to the ship, my boy," Tiddle said at once. "Get your things and I'll engage a carriage."

They left shortly, Tiddle going over detailed aspects of business that Gilbert would need to attend to in Holland.

"Your mind isn't on business, is it, Gilbert?" Tiddle asked suddenly. "I see you're still not easy in your mind—on this business of turning Brewster in."

"It's different from the duel in Dead Man's Lane," Gilbert said vehemently. "I'll lose no sleep over that one! But if William Brewster is like the others I've met, he's no criminal!"

"He is in the eyes of the King."

"Then the King is wrong!"

"Hush, man!" Tiddle said with a glance upward toward the driver. "D'ye not know men have gone to the Tower for saying less!"

Gilbert shrugged, then forced a smile. "I know you're a lawyer, Lucas, and accustomed to putting moral questions in neat little boxes. Well, I can't do that! To me Brewster is a human being—from what I hear, a fine one! I can't hand him over to torture and death because he printed a sermon that offended the King!"

Sadly Tiddle shook his head. "I fear it's like that. The world's a bad place for romantics and idealists, Gilbert. As I once told you, you must pack your sense of honor away, retaining only the name and join the rest of us who are busily selling our souls to the devil."

"This world or the next, eh, Lucas!" Gilbert sighed. Then he turned to face the lawyer. "Let me ask you, are you a Christian?"

"I am a member of the Established Church, Gilbert," Tiddle said evenly. "I pay my tithes, take communion when I am obliged to by the bishop, and do not give aid to dissenters. That is my religion. Having done those things, it is up to the Church of England to keep me out of hell!"

The coach rattled along, and Gilbert watched a high-flying falcon stoop to take a field sparrow in an explosion of feathers.

Finally he said heavily, "The world would be a much simpler place—if it weren't for God and all that."

"No doubt—but it's the only world we have, lad!" Tiddle echoed sadly.

CHAPTER TEN

HUMILITY FINDS A MAN

★ ★ ★ ★

Humility made her way along the canal, and if the water below was calm and glassy, her thoughts were not. Since the moment she had confessed her love for Gilbert Winslow, fierce restlessness had distracted her during the days and kept her tossing for hours after she went to bed.

"Daydreaming, are you, lass?"

She glanced up to see the burly form of Sam Fuller, and greeted him with a wan smile. "I suppose so."

His sharp black eyes took in her pale face and the fatigue that marred the wide-set green eyes. He picked up a pebble, tossed it in the water, and smiled at her, "I do a bit of daydreaming myself. Brain gets all messed about with cobwebs, eh?" He gestured at the widening gyre of the wave below, and said, "Now you take that bit of a circle there—perfect! Nothing out of line in it." He smiled sadly, saying, "But us human beings, why, we ain't so simple as that, I reckon."

"I—suppose not, Sam," Humility said slowly. She stared at the circle below, then tossed in another stone. It made a *plop* and a second circle radiated outward, crossing the line of the first. "Look—Sam!" she exclaimed. "If you throw one pebble in the water, you only have one circle—but if you throw two, the circles interrupt each other."

"I take it you're making some sort of comment on life,"

Fuller stated. "You seem to be saying, 'Just let me alone, and things will be smooth; don't let my life get all complicated with other people.' But you can't live like that, Humility."

"I thought I could, Sam," she murmured uncertainly. Biting her lower lip, she said, "I had my life all planned out. Since I was a little girl, Sam, I've thought never to marry, just serve God."

"But along comes young Gilbert Winslow, eh, lass?"

"Why—"

"Tut, Humility, no shame in it!" Fuller answered warmly, seeing the guilt in Humility's face. "The Apostle said that not everyone is fitted for a single life. And if I ever saw a young woman made for love, I'm looking at her now!"

"Oh, Sam—I'm so unhappy!"

Fuller had held her in his arms when she was barely able to walk, and now he put a fatherly arm around her and she grabbed at him blindly. He held her close for a long time, and when her tremors finally ceased he reached down and picked up a handful of pebbles. He threw one in, then another. "See how the two circles cross? I guess if those circles could talk, they'd complain about how they'd been confused. And look here—" He tossed a small handful of loose gravel into the water, and the concentric circles began to intersect and fragment. "Now that *is* confusing, eh, lass? But that's the way life is. We have our own little circles, all nice and neat. But there are other lives, too, and if we live with people we'll sooner or later have our little circles all interrupted—over and over by all kinds of relations—friends, lovers, husbands, wives, enemies—but there's this one thing, Humility. We serve a God who knows every little circle, and when our little lives get rocked and the pattern goes by the board, why, He's not at all confused!"

Humility watched the water until it cleared, then looked up and smiled at Fuller. "Thank you, Sam."

They turned and began to walk along the canal. "How does your young man feel about this, Humility?" Sam asked.

"Oh, I think he cares for me—but we've not talked about such things as marriage."

"Well, he seems like a fine young fellow," Fuller nodded, then added stridently, "I'll break the pup's neck if he tampers with your affection, I will!"

She laughed and squeezed his thick arm, saying, "I'll threaten him with that, Sam! Maybe a little push wouldn't be unscriptural!"

They said little as they wound their way through the crooked streets, but when they came to the intersection where Fuller left her, he patted her arm and said, "D'ye know the verse that says, 'He that findeth a wife, findeth a good thing, and obtains favor from the Lord'?"

"Yes."

"Well, lass, that could as well read, 'She that findeth a man—a husband, that is—findeth a good thing!' You take my meaning?"

"How could I help it?" Humility smiled at the burly man. "You're about as subtle as a broadaxe, Samuel Fuller!"

He gave her a wide smile, then said with a sudden sadness that darkened his cheerful face, "Marry a man that will make you smile, lass!"

Then he left her with a lurching walk down the cobble-stones.

Slowly she turned, and as she walked home she knew that until she had made up her mind about Gilbert Winslow, nothing in the world about her would have any significance.

When Gilbert returned two days later, Humility found his presence did nothing to settle the restless spirit she could not shake.

He caught her off guard, coming up behind her as she was hanging clothes to dry on the line. She was totally unaware of his presence when suddenly two strong arms reached around her waist and she was plucked up and whirled around like a child.

When he set her down, breathless and flaming with indignation, he laughed at her, embraced her and gave her a resounding kiss, daring her to be angry.

"You—you mustn't do that!" she protested, her smile threatening to break through the sternness she tried to assume.

"I promise not to," he said with his lopsided grin that made her feel strangely happy. "Not until the next time!"

She broke into laughter, put her hand on his cheek in a rare gesture of affection, and said, "You *are* a fool, Gilbert Winslow! The elders will have you up for discipline for this sort of thing!"

"If they try to clap every fellow in love with a beautiful girl in the stocks, they'll have to cut down the forest for new stocks!"

She looked up at him, her face almost translucent, and with a husky quality in her voice, she whispered, "*Are* you, Gilbert? In love with me?"

A dusky flush swept across Gilbert's high cheekbones; there was a slight hesitation, then he smiled warmly, put his hand on her cheek and said, "Can you doubt it? A man would have to be dead not to love a woman like you!"

She took a sudden deep breath, then nodded. It was hard for this girl who had kept her emotions under strict control to let them slip, to let the warmth and pure love she felt so deeply rise to her lips. Twice she tried to speak and failed; then she swallowed and said in a whisper, "Do you know what I'm thinking?"

"What, Sweet?"

"Of the scripture—The Song of Solomon." She looked full in his face and quoted the ancient script with a passion that leaped out at him like a living thing:

> Let him kiss me with the kisses of his mouth: for thy love is better than wine.
> My beloved is white and ruddy, the chiefest among ten thousand.
> His mouth is most sweet, yea, he is altogether lovely.
> He brought me to the banquet house, and his banner over me was love.
> My beloved is mine, and I am his.

Winslow stood there like a man in a trance. There was something so sensual in the words—yet something so *pure* in Humility's uplifted face and in her whole attitude that he could not speak.

"That's—that's very beautiful, Humility," he said finally. He dropped his hands, and she saw that the playful spirit had left his face.

"Gilbert—I embarrassed you!"

"No! It's just that—well, I'll have to get accustomed to a woman who makes love out of the Bible!"

"God made love," she said simply. "Male and female, created He them."

"And does He have one particular woman in mind for every man?"

"Of course!" she exclaimed, surprised that he asked. "Have you not ever read in the Scripture how God chose Rebekah as a wife for Isaac?"

"I see." Gilbert gazed into Humility's green eyes, flecked now with fragments of gold around the iris, and mused, "What if a man takes a notion for the wrong woman—one that God *didn't* intend for him?"

"Then—then it's terrible and very sad!" She glanced at him, and could not but think of how much he looked like his brother—who had, she felt, married the wrong woman.

"Gilbert, did you ever hear the old Persian myth about how marriage began?"

"I'm not really up on my Persian myths, to be truthful."

"Well, according to the story, God made a creature in the very beginning. But the creature did a very wicked thing, so God cut His creation right in two pieces and scattered the fragments out into the wide world."

"Pretty lonesome, I'd say," Gilbert mused. He was fascinated with the piquant animation that stirred her face as she spoke.

"Oh, yes! There were lots of the creatures in the world, all torn in two. One part of the creature—according to the story—was man, and the other part was woman, so you see what happened!"

"Well, not quite."

"Why, one of the man pieces had to search all over the world to find the piece that fit him—the woman who had been his other half. And none of the others would do—it had to be the very one!"

Gilbert stared at her, then said soberly, "That's pretty hard doctrine! One man—one woman. No substitutes."

"You don't think love is that way?"

He hesitated, then smiled, saying, "I hope so, Humility. It's a nice thought."

For the next few days they spent most of their waking moments together. Except for short visits on business to neighboring towns, Gilbert could be found either at Pastor Robinson's studying the Scripture or walking the countryside with Humility.

The closeness of community made for talk, some feeling that the affair was progressing much too rapidly. The silver-haired elder, John Carver, however, expressed what most felt about the couple when he said, "If we're going to make a new world, we'll need new blood—and Winslow blood is better than most."

Humility was happy, but from time to time grew restive—almost worried. Gilbert had spoken of love—and for her that meant marriage. But on that subject, Gilbert had said nothing.

Once when he had fallen into one of his moods—not angry but withdrawn—she said half joking, "You're so *quiet*, Gilbert! I believe you must be thinking about some girl you have in England."

"No!" Gilbert stated, then his face reddened and he forced a smile. "No, I'm just concerned about the future. Humility, are you going to the New World?"

"Why, of course!"

She waited, expecting him to state his declaration, but he said nothing. Finally she asked in a small voice, "Are—are you going?"

He hesitated, then stated, "It's such a big decision, Humility!"

"I'll be there," she said, then waited for his response. When it came she was disappointed.

"I haven't much time, have I?" was all he said.

On the next Sunday morning, Elder William Bradford's face was slightly pale as he preached the sermon. He was distinctly more subdued than usual, and after the last *amen* was spoken, he held his hand up and said, "I have something to say to you." The congregation, sensing the tension in his face, grew absolutely still. "The time is now here for us to leave this place. We will leave on the 22nd of July in the *Speedwell*."

There was a tumult in the room, and for the next hour Bradford and the other elders answered questions on the venture.

There was nothing but the voyage on the lips of everyone the next day, but for Humility there was something else.

Getting word that a certain ship had docked during the

night, she quietly slipped away and picked up a letter from a sailor, taking it directly to Pastor Robinson.

He broke the seal, scanned it quickly, then said, "Humility, can you find Mr. Bradford and ask him to come here? Then come back with him?"

She left, and was fortunate in finding Elder Bradford at home. When she told him her errand, he asked at once, "A letter from Brewster?"

"Yes."

"I'll come with you."

Bradford and Pastor Robinson secluded themselves at once, and Humility waited until after nearly an hour, the pastor called her.

She went into the study, and Robinson said without preamble, "We have a problem, Humility, and it may be that you can help us."

"I'll do anything. Is it about Mr. Brewster?"

"Yes, we must see to it that he makes his way to the dock at Southampton and gets aboard one of our vessels before we sail."

Bradford said heavily, his brow creased, "That would be difficult under any conditions—but we have word that the search for Elder Brewster has been stepped up. It will be very difficult to get through the lines to the coast."

"We think you might be the one to make the attempt, Humility."

"Me!" She was amazed and began to make excuse, but the pastor interrupted her.

"Not alone. That would be too dangerous. You don't know England well enough for such a mission. But if you had someone to help you, someone who *does* know England, and who has legitimate business—that would be different, would it not, Humility?"

"Why, yes, but whom would you mean?"

"Gilbert Winslow," Pastor Robinson said.

"Gilbert!"

"I've already sent for him," Robinson said. "Most of us are known to the searchers in England, but Gilbert is a businessman—in the service of Lord North—perhaps the most powerful man in England next to the King himself. No one would question him!"

"Just one word." Bradford faced Humility with a stern look on his gaunt face and stated, "I am against this move, but Pastor Robinson has convinced me that it is our best—nay, perhaps our *only* hope of getting our brother on the ship and to the New World."

There was a knock at the door, and he said, "That will be Gilbert now, I should think."

He opened the door and Gilbert entered with a wary look on his face.

"I must be direct, Mr. Winslow," William Bradford stated flatly, not taking his eyes from those of Winslow. "You are an alert young man; you must know pretty well what is happening in our community."

"The move to the New World? Certainly, sir, I am aware—"

"I ask if you are familiar with the name of William Brewster?"

Gilbert could not conceal the shock that ran along his nerves. Hesitating for an instant, he said with a slow nod, "I will not deceive you, Elder Bradford. I have been aware for some time—even before I came to Holland—of Mr. Brewster. It's common talk in England, I believe."

"Mr. Winslow, we have observed your conduct well, and Pastor Robinson indicates that you have a respect for the Word of God which does you credit. We feel that you have some intention—honorable, of course—for this young lady."

"Thank you, sir," Gilbert nodded. "If I may boast, I would say that any task you might care to set, I will undertake."

"Very well. We ask you to do a dangerous thing, Gilbert Winslow. We must get Elder Brewster out of his hiding place and to Southampton as quickly as possible. We think that you and Humility might be able to accomplish that." He frowned and added, "Ordinarily we would not permit an unmarried couple to make such a journey unchaperoned—but we face a crisis."

"I agree," Gilbert said, "but let me urge you to let me undertake this mission alone. It's too dangerous for a woman." He argued valiantly for ten minutes, but to no avail.

"Both of you must go," Bradford insisted stubbornly.

"Very well." Gilbert shook his head. "Where is Elder Brewster hidden?"

"We think it best that no one know that—or as few as possible," Bradford said smoothly.

Gilbert saw in a flash that he was on trial—and that it would require more doing than he had thought to do the job. But he said only, "A wise decision, Mr. Bradford. When do we leave?"

"As soon as possible. A ship is due in two days. Will that be satisfactory?"

"Perfectly."

Gilbert spent much time during the next two days sequestered with Bradford and Pastor Robinson, going over details. Not once did they allude to the location of the elder. Humility spent the time tying up that part of her life that had been spent in Leyden—saying goodbye to those who would remain, making plans to be reunited with those she would see again on the *Mayflower*.

Finally, after a tearful parting at the dock, they stood on board a three-masted schooner, headed for England.

They said little for the first few hours, but after the moon came up, they stood in the bow, watching the white waves break, flashing with a rich golden light. The tang of salt was in the breeze that whipped through their hair, and there was a hissing sound as the schooner slid through the water.

"Are you afraid?" Gilbert asked suddenly.

Humility turned to him and thought about his question. Her blonde hair billowed in strands like golden threads, and she smiled as she said, "Not of being caught and sent to gaol."

"Of what, then?"

"Of something happening to us."

He bit his lip, and asked quietly, "To us?"

"You remember about the Persian myth?"

"Yes."

"That's what I'm afraid of most, dear. That we'll be torn apart—and never find each other again." Then she leaned against him, saying, "I'm like that myth, Gilbert. If I got lost from you, I'd never have anybody—not anybody! I never wanted to marry, and I never expected to love anybody as I love you."

He stood there, staring into her eyes, and finally said, "Humility, I have to tell you something—"

She waited, then when he said nothing, she asked, "Yes, what is it, Gilbert?"

"Nothing. Things will be all right."

He pulled her into his arms to prevent her seeing the twitching of his face as he said the words.

"It will be all right," she murmured, pressing her face against his heart. "It will be fine—now that I've got you, Dear Heart!"

The ship faltered, changed course, and as the sails slipped and the masts creaked, a silence wrapped around the pair in the bow of the ship.

CHAPTER ELEVEN

A TRAITOR UNMASKED

★ ★ ★ ★

After getting ashore at Dartmouth, Humility and Gilbert caught the mail coach, then rolled along the Great North Road, huge plumes of dust rising like waves behind them. The fine grains of whitish dust coated them from head to foot, and even the water tasted dusty in the hot July weather.

They passed Cambridge on the left, and hours later the Boston Road flanked west, but they rolled steadily toward the north.

They changed teams three times, and shadows were growing long as the coach pulled into a quiet hamlet on the bank of the River Ryton, within sight of its junction with the Idle, both sluggish small streams in the watershed of the Humber which drains the moors and lands of the middle eastern counties.

"We leave the coach here," Humility said, catching Gilbert off guard.

"What place is this?"

"Scrooby."

Gilbert stared at the cluster of cottages and small houses. "He's not *here*! It's the first place they'd put a watch on!" He knew that because Tiddle had mentioned that the only wise thing Dudley Carleton had done was to set a man to keep close watch on Brewster's former home where he still had distant relatives.

"No, but we can get word of him," Humility said. She led

the way past a small parish church, well built of cut stone, and a great manor house of timber.

They went past the last lights of the small town, and for nearly half an hour groped their way along the stony road. Finally Humility said, "We go in here," moving toward a dim light set well off the road.

"Who's there? Stand and declare!"

Out of the small cottage, a huge man with a tremendous beard appeared, holding a flickering lantern high. He had a large cudgel in his fist, and he called again as the pair approached the house, "Who be ye?"

"It's me, Gabriel—Humility."

"Is it now!" the giant exclaimed, then leaned the club against the side of the house and took her shoulder with his free hand. He towered over her, but there was a warm smile on his craggy face as he said, "Well, now? Is it a ghost you are? Appearing like a spirit in the middle of the night?"

"This is Mr. Winslow, Gabriel."

Gilbert put his hand out and it was crushed in a fleshly vise. "Gabriel was Mr. Brewster's servant in the old days."

"Still am, Lady! And always will be!" He stepped back and urged them inside, saying at once when he put the lantern on the handmade table, "Ye'll want to see him, I take it?"

"As soon as possible," Humility nodded. "Tonight if we can."

"You stay close here tonight," Gabriel said at once. "Tomorrow old Simon will get word to Mr. Brewster—then he'll bring word back of what to do."

After a meal of bread and cold meats, Gabriel put Humility in the single small bedroom, and Gilbert slept on fragrant hay in the loft above the half-timbered cottage.

The sun was warm on his face when Gilbert woke up, and he hastily descended the small ladder into the house below.

"Good morning, Gilbert," Humility smiled. She came to him and lifted her face for a kiss, then went back to the small hearth where she was warming fresh bread and stirring a black pot hanging over the fire. "Try some of this porridge—straight from Scotland."

After cleaning the dishes, they wandered through the fields

and woods, taking pleasure in a staggering, newborn fawn crossing the path. As they went deeper into the woods, Humility took him to a small stream, and sitting on the green, mossy banks, they talked until the sun reached its zenith, then realized with a start that the whole morning had passed.

"I wish every day could be like this," Gilbert said suddenly. "Life gets so *complicated!*"

Humility, thinking of the time she'd stood on the bridge at Leyden watching the circles in the water ripple and clash, smiled and put her arm around him. "One day it will—when we get to the New World."

Gilbert started, then gave a rueful laugh. "I expect it will be a little more difficult than this."

"Even so, we'll be together!" she said. Since Gilbert had agreed to undertake the mission they were on, there had been no doubt in her mind that he was committed to the voyage, and the hardships did not frighten her. She was so complete in her happiness, she failed to notice the awkward silence that inevitably followed any reference she made to the exodus to America.

Gilbert had his mind made up to one thing, at least: he would turn Brewster over to the authorities, but he would keep Humility free of the business. Somehow he would pull her away before the actual arrest.

It was a little after one the next day when Gabriel returned, accompanied by a gnome of a man named Simon Lee.

"Simon will take you to the place," Gabriel said. "It's a goodly walk."

The "goodly walk" turned out to be a twelve-mile trek through brambles, bushes, and jagged paths that stabbed at the feet like dragon's teeth! Simon led them upward from the table land to the foothills south of Scrooby, the beginnings of Sherwood, until finally they crested a rise, and there in a valley below was a small stone house, and beyond, a large meadow spotted with sheep and goats.

"It's an abandoned sheep farm," Humility explained as they made their way down the winding path. "It was too far away from market, so it was abandoned years ago."

Fifteen minutes later they approached a man sitting on a large buff stone outcropping, and Gilbert got his first look at

William Brewster, fugitive from the King's justice.

He was of medium height, and had that healthy thinness that old men sometimes achieve. Over a broad forehead, mild eyes were set rather narrowly, and he had a full brown beard streaked with white. The hand he raised in greeting had the long fingers of an artist, and a stubborn set in his chin was the only evidence of the iron determination that lay like bedrock in his character.

"Daughter, it's good to see you," he said in a high-pitched, pleasant voice, then turned a pair of inquiring eyes on her companion and put out a thin hand, saying, "And this is Mr. Winslow. God bless you for your aid, sir."

Gilbert nodded, unable to reply, but Humility threw her arms around Brewster's neck, and cried out, "Oh, just think, soon we'll be in the New World."

Brewster gave Winslow a quick smile over her shoulder, saying, "Well, this old world isn't all that bad, actually."

Brewster took Gilbert by one arm and Humility by the other, turned them toward the cottage, saying, "I'm thankful you've come—both of you. I've been alone so much I talk to the hares—and even they go to sleep! Come, let's go to the cottage."

The next three days were a strange time for Gilbert. The mornings and afternoons were spent doing little but wandering the beautiful hills with Humility, while the nights provided good talk with Brewster. The old man had lived a great deal and had known many famous people. Gilbert had nearly fallen out of his chair when Brewster casually mentioned being rather close to the poets Spenser and Sir Philip Sidney. But that was nothing to what he felt when Brewster said, talking about the old days, ". . . They were not so good as they remember," he had mused. "Why, I remember once when Bess had a half dozen of her ministers cooling their heels in the tower at the same time. I recall it was at that time that Essex came to see my master, Mr. Davenport, and we were talking in the parlor—"

"You spoke with *Essex*?" Gilbert stared at him as if he had said he talked with Moses.

Brewster's eyes twinkled and he nodded, "Oh, yes, but he wasn't much—Robert wasn't. A tailor's dummy—beautiful to look at, but not enough sense for a nit!"

"But Elizabeth—Queen Elizabeth—you actually saw her?"

"Many times, lad—but she wasn't much to *see*," Brewster smiled. "She was getting pretty long in the tooth, but she'd bed down with anything that caught her fancy! And curse? Why, she would put the roughest sailor in the fleet to shame!"

Gilbert stared at the old man, then shaking his head in sad wonder, said, "You don't think about people like that having flaws—temper, or bad teeth."

"Ah, that's because you're a romantic at heart, lad!" Brewster chuckled. "You'll choose to think of something long ago rather than today, because time dulls the rough edges of things. And a true romantic will always think the land across the sea will be much more wonderful than Scrooby or London. It's only when he gets there and discovers that garbage and leaky roofs occur about as often in a far-off paradise as they do in England!"

Humility said, "Why, you seem to be saying that all of us who are going to the New World are romantics, Mr. Brewster!"

"Why, bless you, child," Brewster hooted with laughter. "Of *course* we are! Every pilgrim is!"

"I never thought of it that way," Gilbert mused.

"Rich, successful men don't become pioneers, Gilbert. They are settled down in this world with both feet. It's only those who have a dream who tear up and risk everything in a new world."

"I suppose that's why the Scripture says, 'Abraham looked for a city which hath foundations, whose builder and maker is God.' "

Brewster nodded approval. "Ye know your Bible, son. And you'll mind the verse in that same chapter that says all the pilgrims 'died in faith, not having received the promises, but having seen them far off, and were persuaded of them, and embraced them, and confessed that they were strangers and pilgrims on the earth.' "

"Not a happy prospect, is it?" Gilbert mused.

"Because they didn't get what they wanted?" Brewster demanded, and there was a fire in his fine old eyes. "Son, the most miserable man in creation is the man who has everything he wants! Ye've heard of Alexander who wept because he had no more world to conquer? Well, he deceived himself, because there was one world—more wonderful and rich than Greece or Persia—that he never conquered!"

"Which world, Elder Brewster?"

"Himself." The answer came quietly, but there was such fervor in Brewster's manner that he seemed young, and Gilbert had a sudden hope that he would have the spirit of William Brewster when he came to the end of his life.

Humility had not taken her eyes off Gilbert's face. Now she put her hand on his, and said gently, "Strangers and pilgrims on the earth." She smiled at him with a faith so steady it shook him, and added, "It's better, though, to be on the pilgrim way *with* someone, isn't it?"

Gilbert put on an evasive cheerfulness, and the moment passed.

As the days passed, Gilbert was drawn to the spirit of Brewster, and the idea of betraying the good old man grew increasingly repulsive.

On the third night the thing got the best of him. He was sitting beside Humility listening to Brewster read from the Scriptures, as he did each night. He was reading the account of the last hours in the life of Jesus, and when he came to the story of Judas, an icy fist seemed to seize Gilbert's heart: "The Son of man goeth as it is written of him; but woe unto that man by whom the Son of man is betrayed! It had been better for that man if he had not been born."

It would have been better for that man if he had not been born!

The words echoed in Gilbert's brain with an eerie cadence— an anthem straight out of the Pit!

He stared across the room, and the holiness etched on the face of William Brewster was an indictment of his own wretched soul—and one glance at Humility as she smiled at him with love and confidence was enough to fill him with a self-loathing such as he had never known!

"Gilbert, don't you feel well?" he heard Humility ask.

"You look pale as death, boy—are you ill?" Brewster asked.

Gilbert got up, averting his face and lurching toward the door. "I—I am a little sick—don't come—I'll get some air!"

He wandered blindly along the path, paying no heed to anything save the agony of guilt that had suddenly exploded within his soul. Finally he threw himself face down on a grassy knoll and bit his lip to hold back the cries that rose from within him, and there was such a power in the storm of emotion tearing at him that he was drenched in sweat and his hands were scratched from beating on the earth unconsciously.

How long he fought that battle he never knew, but finally he rolled over on his back, drained and empty, staring up at the sky. Then a decision came—like the return of an old friend who had been long on a journey; he felt his honor come back. He lay there, wondering why he had ever thought he could sell another human being for his own gain and hope to be a man.

Getting up, he looked to the sky and said, "I may never be lord of any land—but by my honor, there's *one* thing I'll rule over, and that's myself!"

The stars seemed friendly, and he made his way back to Brewster's cottage. He felt clean, refreshed, as if plunged into a pool of water that washed away all the stains the past had marked him with.

But he also felt a twinge of fear, thinking that he would lose his place, lose the main chance that had come to him in life if he did not deliver up Brewster. He laughed aloud, saying to the night, "Why, let it be, then! If Lord North turns me out for being an honorable man, why, he's none himself! If Cecily boots me out for refusing to be a man-seller, I'm best off without her! Let Tiddle prate on about how a man can do without honor—but I notice that he's none too happy for having sold his for a place!"

He found light still burning in the window as he burst through the door and said to Humility, who was sitting at the table with Brewster, "Well, I feel much better! Must have been that third chop you forced on me for supper, Elder Brewster."

He stopped abruptly and the smile left his lips as he saw that Humility's face was pale as a sheet of paper, and Brewster looked very disturbed.

"What's the matter? You have some evil tidings?"

"Why, I think not!" Gilbert whirled in time to see Lord Roth step from behind the door that had swung back to conceal him. There was a savage joy in his piercing eyes as he stepped forward, sword in hand, and said, "The tidings are good for the loyal subjects of King James—evil for traitors such as William Brewster—and those that are involved in his escape."

Gilbert stood like a man turned to stone. It was like a nightmare! Coming as it did on the heels of his decision to aid Brewster, he could not find any avenue of escape.

"Ah, you are speechless?" Roth stated with mock sadness. He whipped the foil in his hand through the air idly, then nodded to the pair at the table. "I salute you, Mr. Brewster. You have outwitted the law for quite a long time. As a matter-of-fact, if it had not been for the help of Mr. Gilbert Winslow, it is likely that you would have made your way to the New World after all."

"No!" Humility cried. She rose, hands at her breast, and the pain in her eyes was unbearable to Gilbert. She stepped to his side, and said in a voice strained to the breaking point, "He's lying! Tell me he's lying, Gilbert!"

The inside of his mouth was dry as toast, and the words stumbled to his lips, but he had to try!

"I—I did agree to help the law find Elder Brewster—that's true—but—"

"Oh, that's true enough, Lady," Roth said with an oily smile. "I see he's used you for his evil purposes—as he has used another lady!"

"Another lady?" Humility stared at Roth, then at Gilbert. "What lady?"

"Lady Cecily North, the daughter of Winslow's employer. He has led her to believe that his affections were due only to her." Roth shrugged and added with a show of sadness, "But that has been Mr. Winslow's downfall—by his own testimony. I hear he has been a womanizer of terrible proportion."

"Gilbert, is it true? Have you made love to this woman—all the time that we—"

"Humility!" Gilbert said hoarsely, "I know how you must feel—and I've been wrong! But just tonight, I decided that I couldn't go through with it! That's why I looked ill, and when I got alone, I took a close look and decided that I could not betray you!"

"Dear me!" Lord Roth sniffed. He gave Gilbert a sad shake of his head, saying, "I regret that you must resort to the final excuse of all evildoers! I never knew one who did not cry, 'I was just going to repent'!"

One look at Humility's face, and Gilbert knew that she hated him. His mind raced, and suddenly he saw his sword hanging from a peg on the wall. With a sudden leap, he pulled it from the scabbard and set himself on guard against the form of Lord Roth.

"You devil!" he whispered. "No matter what I've done, one thing is certain—you'll not take this man!"

Simon Roth did not seem alarmed at the threat of Gilbert's sword. He said easily, "Well, now we see, don't we? First you betray this woman, then you betray Brewster. Now you intend to betray your employer, the bishop, the law and the King of England. There's nothing in you of truth, is there, Winslow?"

The raw truth of Roth's speech raked across Gilbert's nerves, and he could have wept at the foolish decisions that had brought him to this time!

But he shook his head and said drily, "You mistake me in one thing at least, my Lord—and I will now prove to you by my sword that my honor may be tattered by my foolish choices— but there is enough remaining to stop *you!*"

Gilbert advanced to engage swords with the lean man in front of him, but to his surprise, Roth did not lift his blade. Instead, he called out, "Johnson!"

Aware suddenly that his back was to the bedroom door, Gilbert whirled to find the man he had encountered on the dock at Leyden framed in the doorway, in his hands a heavy blunderbuss, trained right on Gilbert's chest!

"We meet again, eh?" he said with a wide grin. "Thought we might."

"Well, well, we must get on with it," Roth said. "As you must have guessed, Johnson followed you and the woman here all the way from Leyden. Followed you here, also, then came to get me. So we'll have your head on a pike on London Bridge, I shouldn't wonder, Mr. Winslow. It'll look well enough—until the crows pick out those bright blue eyes!"

"We better chain this one 'till morning, Lord Roth," Johnson suggested.

"Quite so, Johnson. I believe you brought the irons?"

"Right enough! Here, you put yer arms behind yer back!" Johnson commanded, bringing a set of heavy manacles out of a roomy coat pocket.

He kept the blunderbuss trained carefully on Gilbert's middle, and there was no chance of avoiding being torn in two at that range. "Just drop the sword!"

Gilbert gave up hope then, and his sword clattered to the stones of the floor. Turning to face Lord Roth's triumphant gaze, he heard Johnson approach and felt the touch of the iron on his wrists.

"Don't grieve over Cecily too much, Winslow," Roth said. "I'll see that she gets the proper consolation. As a matter-of-fact, it—"

Roth's words were drowned out by a tremendous *bonging* sound almost in Gilbert's ear, and the weight of Johnson's body came crashing into his back. The blunderbuss hit the floor, exploding with a tremendous boom! The shot tore huge chunks of plaster from the wall next to Lord Roth, and the nobleman's face turned pale.

Gilbert whirled to find Elder William Brewster holding a large chamber pot made of solid brass in both hands and staring down at the still form of Johnson whose head was beginning to bleed from a large gash over his left ear.

Brewster looked a little stunned at his own action, but a gleam came into his mild eyes, and he said distinctly, "The Lord is a man of war!"

In a heartbeat Gilbert snatched up his sword, but barely in time, for Lord Roth recovered his senses in time to make a lunge that would have pierced the heart of Winslow had he been one fraction of a second slower!

They met in a fierce instant, hilts locked, their faces not six inches apart. They strained fiercely, then Gilbert thrust his opponent backward, sending him against the wall with a tremendous crash that rattled the dishes.

There was a silence, the two men frozen for one brief moment. Then Lord Roth said, "I had thought to see you hang, Winslow, but this way is better!"

"Lord Roth, look to yourself. One of us will be in the presence of God in a few seconds!"

Gilbert lifted his sword, the creation of master swordsmith Clemens Hornn, a gift from Paul Dupree. He stood sideways, right foot straight forward with knee bent, left foot sideways and a little behind him, creeping to the right leg. The rapier, so balanced to his hand that it seemed to carry its own weight, was as steady as if it were carved in stone.

The adversaries moved forward, the blades rang; then they disengaged and fell back. This was no tournament with buttoned foils; both men knew that one error would be fatal.

Time and time again, Roth's blade circled slowly, then like the strike of a snake it drove straight toward Gilbert's heart; each time Gilbert used just enough pressure on Roth's blade to deflect it.

Once Gilbert saw his opportunity, and made a lunge, but the long arm of Roth made it ineffective.

Roth was fencing according to all the rules, and Gilbert was caught off guard when suddenly, instead of lunging in a classic thrust, Roth bent to one side and slashed viciously at Gilbert's leg. A sudden pain ripped through Gilbert's thigh, and blood spattered the floor, making it slippery.

"A foretaste, Winslow!" Roth smiled. He wiped his sweating brow, and glanced at Brewster and Humility who were backed up against the outside wall, saying, "Just a moment more, and we can have our tea!"

Pain was running through Gilbert's leg, sending its message through live nerves. He knew at once that he was cut to the bone, and was aware that if he put his full weight on that wounded right leg, he would go down. Backing up slowly, parrying Roth's now frantic thrusts, he saw that his opponent knew as much and was bearing down with all his might to end the fight with one thrust. He need not fear Gilbert's blade, for the wounded leg meant that he could not thrust at all.

Then Gilbert felt the wall against his back, and saw instantly that Roth was uncoiling that long body of his ready for the final thrust that would pin his helpless opponent to the wall!

Throw the rule book away, Mon Ami! The words rang in Gilbert's mind—words he had heard a hundred times from his master Dupree: *When you are losing, what good are rules?*

As Roth gathered himself into a coil of muscle, Gilbert knew that the last thrust was coming. Then Gilbert did what he had never done—what he had never seen done, and what he had never heard of; and he did it smoothly as though he had practiced it every day of his life.

As Roth's blade drove toward him, Gilbert's left hand flashed out, grasped the tip of the flat sword. It was pure chance that his finger's closed on it, for no man is fast enough to achieve that sort of reaction on purpose.

As Roth came in for the kill, Gilbert twisted his blade to one side. It sliced through his palm, cutting to the bone with each edge, but that was a small thing. At the same time, Gilbert simply lifted his sword and Roth, sensing at the last moment what had happened, opened his mouth to cry out, "No!"

But he was too late. The force of his lunge brought him in range, and Gilbert felt his blade penetrate the tough membrane of the chest, grate on bone, then slide easily up to the hilt.

Roth stood there staring at Gilbert with a terrible brightness in his eyes. Then he looked down at the hilt of the sword nestled against his chest. For a long moment he seemed to be meditating what to do about it. He put his hand up, touched the hilt of Gilbert's sword tenderly—then his legs buckled and he sprawled limply on the floor, a bright crimson flood spreading out from beneath his body.

Gilbert stared at Roth's body, took one step forward on his wounded leg, and fell headlong, his legs tangled with the body of his adversary.

He looked at his left palm, noting impersonally the white gristle and bone in the red slashes, then at his thigh which was pumping a throbbing stream of his blood on the floor with each steady beat of his heart.

He heard Humility say, "We must leave! There'll be others!"

Looking up, he saw her face, but it was as if she were behind a thin red curtain. Her voice was thin and reedy, as though she were in a distant far-off room.

He knew he was dying, bleeding to death, and he desperately wanted to tell them both how he had changed out under the stars—but when he opened his lips, no sound came out.

He heard Humility say, "Leave him!" Then came a roaring in his ears, and then—nothing.

CHAPTER TWELVE

"They Knew They Were Pilgrims . . ."

★ ★ ★ ★

Consciousness came to Gilbert suddenly. One moment he was unaware of anything; then he was looking up at a crude picture of a horse with very stiff legs. Fascinated, he stared at it, thinking, *I could draw a better horse than that!* Then he felt a thrill of fear, for he realized that he didn't know where he was—nor even, for a fraction of a second, *who* he was.

"You're awake," a voice said, and he rolled his head to one side to see a face that looked familiar—an elderly man with a full beard and eyes that were kind. "About time, my boy!"

Then it all came back—the cottage in the valley and the duel with Lord Roth. "Elder Brewster . . ." he croaked, and could not say more, so parched were the tissues of his throat and lips, until Brewster held his head up and gave him a few swallows of tepid water from a pewter tankard. "Let me sit up."

"Careful with your leg!" Brewster warned as he helped pull Gilbert into a sitting position. "We've got too much invested in you to lose you now."

Gilbert's head swam as he sat up, but that passed and he stared around the room, a small, low-ceilinged affair with one small window allowing a thin shaft of sunlight through a dingy glass. "This isn't your house! Where are we—and how. . . ?"

"Now, there's time for that," Brewster said. He got up and brought a bowl from the small chest by the door. Taking a large wooden spoon he said, "You try to eat some of this broth, and I'll tell you what's happened."

The broth was cold, filmed with grease—and the most delicious thing Gilbert had ever tasted! He gobbled down the contents, and Brewster refilled it twice from a black pot as he talked.

"Well, when you went down bleeding like a slaughtered steer, we got the bleeding stopped; then we did the needlework. We had no way of knowing how soon somebody would appear looking for Lord Roth and Johnson, so we managed to get you into my little two-wheeled cart, hitch up my donkey, and somehow—by God's grace!—we got you back to Gabriel's house."

"Is this it?"

"Oh, no, Gilbert! That would have been fatal! We stayed until dark the next night; then we put you in a wagon, covered you with fresh cut hay, and Humility and I lay beside you to keep you still. Gabriel has a brother with a tiny farm about ten miles from Scrooby, and that's where we are now."

"How long have I been here, Mr. Brewster?"

"This is August 6—that makes it five days."

"Five days! Why, you can't stay here—you've got to get to Southampton at once! The *Mayflower* is due to sail—"

Brewster pushed Gilbert back into bed, and said in a gentle voice, "The ship sailed yesterday, Gilbert."

"Oh, no!" He struggled to break the grip of Brewster, but he was too weak, and finally fell back, despair etched on his face. "What will. . . ?"

He stopped abruptly when the door opened and Humility came in.

He almost failed to recognize her, so changed was she from what he remembered. She was very pale—he could not see how anyone could lose so much color in such a short time! The rosy cheeks and the pert cherry lips were washed to a pale gray, faded and lifeless, and there was none of the sparkle in her green eyes that had been so beautiful. She gazed at him as she approached, and there was no anger that he could read, but more of a stolid indifference. Her eyes seemed cloudy, obscured by a thin film that blocked out all the warmth and charm of her spirit. "I found some food," she said quietly, and there was the same deadness in her voice that was in her eyes—none of the vivacious element that had been there before.

Gilbert swallowed and said with an effort, "Humility—and Mr. Brewster—it may not mean anything to you now—I suppose it doesn't—but what I said to Roth, about deciding not to deliver you up? It was the truth!"

"I believe you," Humility said, but it seemed to have no meaning to her; there was nothing in her voice or in her face to remind him of the woman he had known.

"And so do I, Gilbert!" Brewster patted his shoulder. He gave Humility a quick glance and then said hurriedly, "You must put it all behind you, and start all over again, my boy!"

Gilbert put his hand out to Humility and said huskily, "I'm sorry for all of it!"

She took his hand, but it might have been the hand of a marble statue he held—so cold and motionless it was. And her eyes were somehow brittle and empty as she said tonelessly, "I forgive you, Gilbert." Then she turned and left, saying, "I'll be downstairs if you need me."

Brewster waited until she was gone, then said, "Don't despair, Gilbert. She'll change."

"Why should she?" Gilbert asked angrily. "I've pulled her world apart—yours as well. If I hadn't been involved, you'd both be on the *Mayflower* right now!"

"You can't *know* that, can you? A thousand things might have happened to keep us from being there. Do you remember the word from the Bible: 'All things work together for good to them that love the Lord'? So this tragedy is part of God's plan."

"Doesn't seem possible!"

"And did it seem *good* to Joseph when his brothers threw him in a pit to die? But years later when he saved his whole family, he told them not to worry about what they'd done. Remember that? He said, 'You thought evil against me, but God meant it unto good, to save much people alive.' "

"I can't see how murdering a man and wrecking your life can be *good*!"

"Well, to be honest with you, my boy, neither can I—right now. But I'm an old man, and one thing I've learned is that God has a sovereign will in every situation. So we must wait and see what He plans to do with *this* one!"

He was out of the bed in a week, dizzy and clinging to the wall for support. But it took three more weeks for him to move with anything like a normal walk. He used the days to exercise in the small room, and after dark he limped painfully around the confines of the small farm. There were other farms so close that there was always a chance of someone seeing them, so Gabriel came to bring them food and give them news.

Gilbert had given up on any response from Humility. She was locked in, barricaded behind a wall that baffled his many attempts to get through. Brewster had said, "Give her time, Gilbert. She'll come out one day and be herself again."

He marked a little calendar that he had made, checking off each day, and on the 4th of September Gabriel came bursting into the house, calling, "Mr. Brewster! Mr. Brewster!" in stentorian tones loud enough to rattle the dishes.

Gilbert fell downstairs and saw the huge Gabriel practically shaking the slender form of Brewster, his face wild with excitement.

"I tell ye, she's not gone yet!"

"Who's not gone, Gabriel?" Gilbert asked.

"The ship—the *Mayflower*—she's at Plymouth!"

Brewster was trying to read a note, apparently a letter that Gabriel had passed to him. "It's true, Gilbert! This is from Bradford . . ." He paused to scan the contents, and then looked up with excitement in his face. "The two ships left Southampton together, but the *Speedwell* proved to be unseaworthy, so they turned back to have her repaired."

"And they're at Plymouth?" Gilbert demanded.

"Yes—but Bradford says that the new plan is to leave the *Speedwell* here—to put as many as possible on the *Mayflower* and make the trip in one ship."

"When do they sail?"

Brewster looked at the letter and shook his head. "By the 6th—that's day after tomorrow!"

"You'll be on that ship!" Gilbert exclaimed.

"Impossible!" the older man exclaimed.

"With God, all things are possible," Gilbert grinned. It delighted him to have a hope; the waiting had been terribly hard on his nerves, but the worst was the total lack of any possible action. Now he took Gabriel by the arm, and said rapidly, his face glowing with excitement, "Gabriel, get your wagon piled high with hay."

"Why, it's here—I was bringing a wagon load to my brother for his stock!"

"Good! Where's Humility?"

"Gone to the stream for fresh water," Brewster said.

"I'll go get her—you throw everything we've got in the way of food and clothing together!"

He lurched out the door, breaking into a half-run. Pain ran along his leg, but ignoring it, he drove himself through the gate and halfway to the creek when he met Humility coming back in the darkness.

"Humility!" he shouted, grabbing her by both arms. "Come on! We're leaving!"

She dropped the clay pot and it smashed on the ground. "What are you talking about?" Her voice held more animation than he'd heard in a month.

"The *Mayflower* is at Plymouth, and you and Brewster will be on her when she sails in two days!"

"Oh!" That was all she said, but in the dim starlight, Gilbert could see an animation change the dead set that had fixed her features. She held a trembling hand against her cheek, and suddenly tears gathered in her eyes and trickled down her cheeks—silver tracks in the dim light.

He paused, then said, "You'll get to your New World, Humility—I promise you!"

After collecting their meager belongings, they all piled onto the farm wagon drawn by two draft horses, and Gilbert took charge of the expedition, speaking crisply, "We'll have to go through without stopping to rest the team. Gabriel, do you know any places where we can change teams on the way—maybe twice?"

"No trouble there," Gabriel nodded. "I got relatives most counties from here to Plymouth. But they'll be watching the roads pretty close."

"Do you know where the most likely checkpoints will be?"

" 'Course!"

"All right, here's the way of it, then—we'll ride in the wagon until we get close to a checkpoint. Then we get out and follow Gabriel. If he gets stopped, we go around and meet him on the far side."

"A fine plan!" Brewster said. "I have faith in it."

He had, perhaps, more faith in the plan than Gilbert, but it was the only hope. They left at once, and all night long they lurched along the narrow country road, striking the Great North Road at dawn.

Three times during the journey they had to abandon the wagon and they changed horses twice, with great difficulty the second time. It was close to dawn when they pulled up with footsore animals at the dock in Plymouth.

"She may have sailed!" Gabriel whispered.

"Let me have a look," Gilbert said. "I got a look at her at Southampton."

He began walking along the wharf, peering desperately into the dusky darkness. By the starlight and part of a moon, he could make out several ships anchored, but none of them seemed to be the *Mayflower*. He went to the end of the wharf and began the search in the other direction. He was about to give up hope when a cloud that had obscured the moon shredded and there she was—rising lightly at anchor not two hundred feet offshore—the *Mayflower*!

He hurried back to the wagon and said, "She's still here—just off shore!"

"Praise God!" Brewster breathed, then asked, "But we must get aboard without being seen—and quickly!"

"There's a dory that will serve," Gilbert said. "Let's get our things in it."

Soon they were ready, and after bidding farewell with many thanks to Gabriel, they were underway, the dory sliding easily over the small swells as Gilbert rowed.

They were almost to the ship when Brewster exclaimed, "This boat, Gilbert—it will be missed!"

"No, I'll bring it back as soon as you're aboard."

"But—how will *you* get aboard?"

Then Gilbert finally expressed what he had long since de-

cided. "I won't be coming with you, Mr. Brewster." He saw
Humility look at him with a strange expression, but he paid no
heed. "The New World's not for me. All I wanted was to make
up a little for what I'd planned to do to you. Maybe getting you
here will do that!"

Brewster was struck dumb for an instant. He had never
considered but that Gilbert would go with them. He said then,
"Why, my boy, there's no need to speak of *that*! You must go!
There's no place for you in England!"

"I'll be leaving," Gilbert said, "perhaps I'll go to France."

The prow of the dory bumped into the hull of the ship, and
there was no more time for talk. Gilbert stood up, grabbing the
small steps on the side of the *Mayflower* and held the dory still
while the other two climbed awkwardly out. "I'll go aboard with
you," he whispered. "Maybe there's no watch tonight. It would
be good if you could get aboard without their knowledge. You
won't be safe until you're underway."

That would have been well, and indeed there was no watch.
Humility made the long step that brought her to the top rail, and
cleared it despite her skirt, but when Elder Brewster attempted
it, he lost his footing and fell backward, driving into Gilbert,
who was caught off balance.

They fell into the dory, and Gilbert's bad leg took the full
force of both their weights. The gunnel of the small boat struck
his thigh a sharp blow, and Brewster's body crashed down, striking exactly on the wound.

Gilbert felt the wound gape open, and the warm rush of
blood confirmed his worst fears. He lay there struck dumb by
pain and sick to the heart with despair.

"Gilbert—I'm so sorry! Are you hurt?"

"Yes—you'll have to get some help to row me ashore!"

"Yes!"

Brewster scrambled up the ladder, and was gone so long
that Gilbert feared the morning watch would come. Finally, however, he heard sounds, and then Edward's voice said, "Gilbert!
What's the matter!"

He looked up in the growing light and gasped, "Edward,
you've got to get me ashore!"

Edward looked down at the bloody trousers, shook his

head, and said, "You'd be helpless with that wound, Gilbert. You must go with us."

"No! I *can't!*"

Edward paid no heed, but called out softly, "John? Lend me a hand—help me get him aboard!"

John Howland's face appeared, and his strong arms plucked Gilbert up as if he were weightless.

The two men carried him aboard, and there was Bradford, who looked at Gilbert with a strange expression.

"The leg's torn open," Brewster said. "Can you hide us someplace where we can work on it, John?"

"Are you certain you want this man to go with us?" Bradford stood there, his face stern, and Gilbert would have given his hope of heaven to have been able to get off the boat.

"Let me go!" he cried out, thrashing wildly, but was held in the vise of Howland's mighty arms.

"Gilbert, you have no choice," Edward said. "We have to get that leg fixed *now.*"

Gilbert was half carried down to the main cargo deck. Bradford led the way with a candle. He led them past rows of wooden barrels carrying the water supply to the forward end of the cargo hole. "This is the sail locker, William," he said, opening the door and holding the candle up to illuminate the interior.

Howland helped Gilbert inside, and put him down gently on a thick slab of folded canvas. "I'll get Fuller to take care of the wound," Bradford said, and Gilbert lay there gritting his teeth against the pain.

Brewster spoke a word of comfort once, and Edward pressed his shoulder, saying, "This will be a good place for you and William, Gilbert. The crew never comes here—except after a sail's been damaged. We'll not mention your presence to Captain Jones—not until we're several days out of Plymouth."

Fuller came quickly, his dark eyes burning. "Let me see . . ." he said brusquely. "Ah—need some restitching." He set to work, but Gilbert saw that there was a difference in his manner. He had been a warm friendly man at Leyden; now there was a hardness in his attitude.

"Get it done, Fuller!" Gilbert gasped. "I won't stay on this ship!"

Then Fuller put the needle through his flesh, and the pain was unbelievable. Halfway through the operation, Gilbert went limp.

When he woke up, Brewster was sitting beside him, reading from his Bible.

"We've left England!" Gilbert gasped.

"We'll be out of port soon, Gilbert." Brewster put the book down. "Lie still now. Fuller said the damage wasn't as bad as it might have been—but you don't want to pull the thread out again!"

"Oh, God!" Gilbert cried out, and the tears ran down his cheeks as he rolled his head helplessly. "I can't bear it! I must get off this ship!"

"Easy, son—rest easy!" Brewster said. His thin face was filled with compassion for the young man who writhed in agony of spirit before him, but he knew that for the present, there was little that anyone could do to comfort him. "There's no turning back now. You'll just have to cast in your lot with us psalm-singers."

"But everyone on this ship knows me for a traitor!"

"Not so. There's *one* who doesn't—" Brewster struck his breast lightly, then pointed upward, adding, "And there's another!"

"God? God doesn't care about me!" Gilbert moaned. He had been braced for the danger that lay before him in England—but not for the prison of the New World!

"God cares, Gilbert," Brewster said evenly. "We're not wrong, you know. All of us leaving homes and friends to risk death in a strange land, why, God knows our names! And He cares, Gilbert, oh, how He cares!"

"I can't believe that!"

"You must believe it." A prophetic light appeared in the old man's face, and he said in a soft cadence, "What's happening in the world, Gilbert? Right now? How interested is anyone in a little group of 'psalm-singers' on a tiny ship headed for an obscure corner of the globe? In London, they're talking about King James's deplorable weakness in dealing with Spain; war has broken out in Bohemia, and Spain will send a terrible army rampaging across the Continent. The English court is in an uproar, with the king hysterically denouncing Spain and vowing that the long-talked-of marriage between the Spanish infanta and Charles, the Prince of Wales, is forever cancelled. Along the borders of Holland, Spain is ready to launch an attack on the Dutch."

Brewster paused, and his beard moved lightly as he shook his head; then he looked at Gilbert and asked, "With Europe about to go up in flames, who will stop to notice a handful of tattered exiles sailing west in a weather-beaten freighter under the absurd delusion that God is interested in their endeavor and will protect them in their amateur assault on a wilderness that has swallowed thousands of tougher, better-equipped pioneers?"

Gilbert had risen on his elbow to stare at Brewster as he spoke these words. Now he thought of them, and in a voice filled with doubt, yet with a fragment of hope in his eyes, asked, "And you still say that God is in all this, William?"

Brewster's lips moved silently; then he touched Gilbert's hand and said, "God is in everything, son. He's in your life and He will bring you to harbor. You're tied to us now, and I'd like you to remember a phrase that was in Bradford's letter, when he spoke of the saints that left Leyden—risking life and all for God in this voyage."

"What did he say, Elder Brewster?"

Brewster quoted the lines softly: "They left Leyden, that goodly and pleasant city which had been their resting place for near twelve years—" and here the old man's voice broke as he completed the sentence . . . *"but they knew they were pilgrims!"*

Gilbert Winslow, fugitive from the King's justice, his life in ruins, every dream dead—gazed at the old man's face. The flickering yellow flame of the candle that guttered in a flat dish highlighted Brewster's features, forming a corona of golden light around his face. The wash of golden shadow threw his face into deep relief so that only the gleam of his black eyes was seen; and against the dusky gloom of the sailroom, his face seemed to be coated with thin gold foil, incised with tiny wrinkles etched by time.

Gilbert sat there listening to the creaking of the ship's timbers as she strained from side to side in a slow roll. He felt the plunge as she nosed down, then the rise as she rose like a phoenix and crested the waves. He thought of England, of the wreckage of his career—and he thought with a keen, almost physical pain of Cecily.

He was a Winslow, and the men of his family had been molded by the hard life of the Middle Ages. They had died amidst the ring of sword on shield; they had enriched the soil of England with their blood, their sweat. Part of that blood, at least, went back to the golden-haired Vikings who came to plunder the land; part of it to the lowly Saxons, men of the soil, and some to the proud-eyed Normans who breached the land in 1066 under William.

None of them had been cowards as far as Gilbert had heard.

Slowly he set his jaw, pulled himself up to a sitting position, then looked at William Brewster with a fierce light in his light blue eyes—perhaps like that in the eyes of his forefather when with Drake he had boarded a mighty Spanish galleon with his dirk between his teeth and his cutlass cutting down his enemies like ripe grain.

"So be it then!" he said with a mixture of exaltation and sadness in his tone. Brewster looked up in surprise at the steely note in Gilbert's voice.

"I'll be a pilgrim, too!"

Brewster smiled, his eyes filling with tears, and he said in a voice not quite steady, "That's wonderful, Gilbert! And God will be your guide!"

"No, Mr. Brewster, not God. I've tried God—and although I honor your faith, it's not for me."

Brewster raised a hand in shock, let it fall, then in a weary voice asked sadly, "No God for you, Gilbert? What will you trust, then?"

"This!"

With a cry, Gilbert reached down and unsheathed the sword made by the hand of a man long dead. The blade gleamed with reflected light, and there was a strange beauty in it, deadly as it was.

"This, Mr. Brewster," Gilbert said intently, as he lifted the blade toward heaven. "This is where I put my faith!"

"Gilbert! I thought you'd chosen the pilgrim way!"

Gilbert Winslow gave a slight salute with the blade, then said in a voice as cold as the steel itself: "So I am—*a pilgrim with a sword!*"

PART TWO

THE MAYFLOWER

★ ★ ★ ★

CHAPTER THIRTEEN

THE SWEET SHIP

★　★　★　★

The *Mayflower* was a "sweet ship," her hold full of pleasant odors, in contrast to the foul fumes that rose from some ships. She had carried cargo rather than passengers for most of her fourteen years—taffeta and satins from Hamburg, hats and hemp to Norway, wine and cognac from France.

In the gray light of morning a crowd of Plymouth people gathered on the quay to bid farewell. The tide rose full and began to drop as the male passengers gathered on the waist deck. The heads of the families, along with Bradford, Carver, and Sam Fuller, watched the thin rays of morning cut through the haze that lay over the harbor, talking quietly in low voices.

After nearly an hour Captain Christopher Jones appeared on the high aft deck. His black figure climbed out of the poop hatch and turned abruptly before the mizzenmast; with his hands on his hips, he looked down on the ship. His face was pale in the morning light, and his stiff hair was plastered down with water. He put his hands to his mouth and sent his voice bellowing down the length of the ship: "Mr. Clarke, Mr. Coffin, Mr. Duff! Break out the anchor. We get underway."

Six sailors in breeches, shirts open to the waist, and bare feet, trooped back through the hole; after working the 'tween-deck capstan to lift the forward anchor, the stairway was cleared for them to pass above.

Women and children awoke and began stumbling about as the heavy square doors of the ports, held up by chains on the outside, were dropped; they had been open day and night since anchoring; now they thudded down until darkness filled the first hold.

"Let fall your main!" Mr. Clark, the bosun, yelled.

Coffin gave William White a hard shove when the small man got in his way. White was driven forcefully against the broad chest of young John Alden who prevented him from falling, then said in a slow Yorkshire brogue, "Ye needn't be so rough, mon!"

Coffin whirled and appeared to consider giving the same rough treatment to Alden—but the immense shoulders and heavily corded arms of the young man gave him pause, as did the steady look he received from Alden's deep-set blue eyes.

"Stay clear or get stomped!" Coffin sneered, then moved to the forward mast.

Susanna White had come to stand beside her husband, and as his thin body was racked with an explosive series of coughs, she put her hand on his arm and said, "Don't mind him, William. Go lie down for a while."

"No," White said when he got his breath. "This is my last look on England, Susanna. I'll not miss that."

Susanna shot a quick look at Edward Winslow who had moved toward the scene, and something in her husband's word carried a foreboding of gloom. Winslow caught Susanna's eyes, shrugged imperceptibly, then said, "We'll be back, William, never fear."

William White looked at Winslow, gave a small shake of his head, and said quietly, "No fear, Mr. Winslow. God is with us. But it's the New World for me—I'll not look on this old one again."

The fore and main topsails were flown, as were the two big square sails and the lateen sails on the poop; the ship moved slowly down the water and the town diminished into the distance, a sharp black outline of rooftops against a cold sky.

As they came around, trimmed, into the wind so that a sudden gust filled the mainsail out with a resounding slam, William Bradford said to Dorothy, "We are free at last! Now the New World!"

"I'm afraid, William!" There was something pitiful in the small figure of Dorothy Bradford as she stood hunched over the rail, filling her eyes with the dim outlines of her homeland. "I'm so afraid!"

But an expression of exhilaration filled William Bradford's craggy face as the *Mayflower's* blunt cutwater rose and fell heavily, smashing through the dark frills of water. He was rejoicing that the thing was done at last. They were out on the open sea to live or die.

If he had taken his eyes from the horizon to look down at Dorothy's face, he would have seen exactly the reverse—for she stared wild-eyed at the rolling ocean as if it were a demon out of hell. As it was, he did not notice at all when she wheeled and ran below, her hands over her face in a helpless gesture of futility.

The day proved bright and fresh, and the sun shed warmth upon the ship as it drove into the deep swells. After the crew had set the tackle and cleared the deck, the women and children began to come up, peering fearfully at the vast expanse that met their eyes. They had their first meal at sea at noon—biscuit-bread, smoked bacon, and mugs of beer served in the first hold by candlelight.

On a ship for the first time in her life, Dorothy Bradford lay on her plank bunk in the tiny cabin shifting from hot to cold and hot again, not caring if she lived or died, while her husband wiped up the mess. Then he himself took sick and had to lie down, and Humility came into the cabin to take care of them.

Humility waited until Dorothy fell into a fitful sleep, then left the cabin. Below deck the enclosed air was soured by seasickness, although those women who were well kept the spruce planking swabbed clean with salt water. Walking was not easy, for the great width of the *Mayflower* in proportion to her length made her subject to the push-and-pull of the waves. With every change of wind, she waltzed with a thunderous flapping of canvas. The ship was built for roominess and carrying capacity. Below the deep hold and the upper deck was a gun deck about twenty-six feet wide and seventy-eight feet long. It was here that most of the passengers were settled. Humility had to step carefully, for most of the deck was covered with quilts and bedding. Beyond the gun deck the ship's sides bowed together until she was only nineteen feet wide on her upper deck.

Humility wandered aimlessly over the ship, hoping to take her mind off her queasy stomach. She peered into the forecastle, where the crew lived. A good portion of it was taken up by the galley, and the foremast came through the forward end of it. *Not much space for thirty men,* she thought. But sailors traveled light, and half the men were always on duty.

She did not go below the poop deck, the sailors being active in that area, but later she discovered it contained the poop house, a cabin about thirteen by seventeen where the master's mates dined and relaxed. There also was the Great Cabin where the captain slept and ate in lonely splendor.

Humility had heard a fragment of discussion between Captain Jones and Elder Bradford, learning that the poop house had been divided in half and that about eighteen passengers were accommodated there—a situation that did not endear the pilgrims to the crew! But some arrangement was necessary, for there were eighteen married couples, and eleven unmarried girls, many in their early teens, as well as eight or ten very young children aboard. Most of these were in the after-house cabins, where there was some degree of privacy. That left, Humility figured, as she made her way downward to the lower parts of the ship, about fifty-four people to be taken care of on the gun deck—married men without wives, bachelors, and grown boys. Some slept in the shallop, a large fishing boat taken apart and stored in sections; others had crude bunks built into the ship's sides, and a few imitated the sailors in their hammocks.

In one of the dark passageways she suddenly encountered one of the crew, a swarthy thick-bodied sailor, who deliberately pressed his rank body against her in the narrow space. He grinned broadly, exposing a wide gap in his upper teeth, and said in a thick, slurred voice, "Well, naow, looky 'ere wot we finds!" He put out a stubby finger to touch her face, and when she whirled and made her way quickly back toward the gun deck, he roared with laughter, calling after her, "You can't run far, can yer now, missy? And the gals don't get away from Jeff Daggot—no, they don't!"

In her haste to get away from the man, Humility ran headlong into the arms of a surprised Sam Fuller. He held her up as she fell backward, gave a deep laugh, and said, "Well, where could you be going in such haste, Humility?"

"Oh, it's you, Sam!" she gasped, taking a deep breath. She glanced over her shoulder and decided it would do no good to complain, so shrugged and gave him a smile. "Just exploring a little. What are you doing?"

"A mite of doctorin', lass." His large eyes crinkled in a grin, and he shrugged, adding, "Nothing to do for seasickness."

"Dorothy is very bad!"

"Yes—and I'm thinking it's a bit more than just the usual trouble at sea." He leaned back against the bulkhead, and there was a frown on his broad face. "I've said all along that some people ain't fitted for the hard life. Mrs. Bradford, why, she's a fine lady, but she is pretty delicate. I told William all along he ought to leave her home until we get a little comfort built into the new land."

Fuller looked at the tall girl with sudden interest. "You had some pretty rough handling, Humility—the business with young Winslow?"

"I'm all right, Sam."

He shifted uncomfortably, for there was something in her brief statement that did not seem good to him. He pulled at his beard, finding it hard to put into words what he wanted to say, and finally murmured, "Don't be a sour woman, Humility."

She managed to give him a smile, and patted his arm, "I—I won't get sour, Sam. I promise!"

"There's my girl!" He nodded vigorously and then said, "I don't think anyone has given any thought to our two *friends* in the sail locker. Wouldn't do, either, for the captain to be introduced to them this close to England. They must be getting a mite hungry, eh, lass?"

She saw his design, testing her to see if she could face Gilbert, and she laughed suddenly, saying, "You're not very subtle, are you, Sam? All right, I'll see to it."

"God love you, lass! That's the sweet spirit I like to see in a gal!"

Humility made her way to the galley and wheedled some biscuits and two portions of cold meat from the gnome of a cook. Thomas Hinge was very slight and crippled, but was friendly, especially with the children who crowded around his small fire hoping for tidbits as he cooked. He smiled crookedly at Humility, saying in a surprising bass voice, "You 'as quite an appetite for a young lady!"

"Oh, that's because you're such a fine cook, Mr. Hinge!" she laughed, and was rewarded by a dish of plum duff from the little man.

Finding her way below was easier now, though she had to grope her way along until she got to the cargo hold. There she found a small door at the forward end of the cargo hold.

When the door opened, William Brewster peered out, holding a candle high, and when he saw who it was, he smiled and said, "Ah, Humility! Come in, come in!"

She entered the small room, and found herself looking down at Gilbert who was sitting on a bundle of sailcloth with his back against the bulkhead.

He was, she saw, very pale, and the leg stretched out in front of him was wrapped in a thick roll of bandages. He looked startled as she stood over him, his eyes widening as she entered and set the lantern down on a small table—the only furniture in the compartment.

"Hello, Gilbert," she said steadily, willing herself to meet his eyes. She nodded and asked, "How's your leg?"

"I'm all right," he said finally. "Leg hurts some."

"You must be hungry," she said quietly and set the food down.

"You thought of us," Brewster nodded with a smile. "That's like you, Humility." He took a bite of biscuit, then nodded to Gilbert. "Try to eat, Gilbert. You lost a lot of blood."

She was not comfortable, and got up to leave.

"Can I get you anything, Mr. Brewster?" Humility asked.

"I have what I need, thank you." He held up his worn Bible.

"Can I bring you anything—" she faltered for the first time over his name, and covered up the omission by saying, "Maybe you'd like your Bible, too?"

Gilbert did not lift his head as he answered, "No Bible—but my green notebook I would like."

She did not miss the bitter note in his voice as he mentioned the Bible, but said only, "I'll bring it."

She left quickly, and the two men ate the food. Brewster noted that Gilbert was only picking at his meal, but said nothing. Finally he ate his share of the duff and handed the bowl to the younger man, saying, "Eat all the rest of this, Gilbert. It's fine duff; it'll help you get your strength back more rapidly."

"For what?" Gilbert asked, his voice full of bitterness. Impatiently he spooned the food out of the dish, then flung it onto the sailcloth. "What difference does it make? I'm not going anywhere—have nothing to do!"

William Brewster was too wise to rush the young man. He knew that Gilbert Winslow was, for all his swordplay and toughness, finely wired and as sensitive as a woman. The old man made no attempt to speak to the despair that shrouded Gilbert, but spoke of other things until Humility came back with a leather-bound book which the young man took with a curt nod.

"Mr. Bradford said to tell you he'll come and talk with you tonight. He said it would be better if you didn't leave this room for a day or perhaps two."

"Yes. I expect that would be wise."

"I'll bring your food in the morning," she said, and left without a glance at Gilbert.

Brewster sat down and opened the large black Bible with a sigh of contentment. There was a swallow of light beer left in his cup, and he drank it down, saying wryly, "I'm a very carnal man! Look, here's the Word of God—and here's my beer, and you see which of the two I mind first?"

"Man shall not live by the Bible alone—doesn't it say that somewhere?"

Brewster glanced swiftly at his companion, well aware that the caustic remark was the fruit of a bitter spirit, but he only smiled and answered gently, "Well, something like that, I think."

He read steadily, immersing himself in the Scripture, noting after a while that Gilbert had found a worn pen and a small quantity of ink. He had hitched himself up painfully with the book on his good knee and was slowly writing.

Brewster had slept little since they had scrambled on board the *Mayflower*, and now as the regular rocking of the ship rolled him in a soothing cadence, his eyes grew heavy, and the last thing he knew was the sound of Gilbert's pen making a thin scratching in the small cabin.

September 7, 1620

The keeping of a journal is the business of lovesick maidens.

Yet here am I, Gilbert Winslow, sitting in the dark sail locker of the *Mayflower*, scribbling away by the light of a stubby candle, my only companion a religious fanatic.

The cabin is no darker than my own heart. How quickly life can reverse itself! Was it only a few brief hours ago that I was secure in the certainty of place and fortune in the service of the most powerful Lord in all of England, happy in the hope of the love of a beautiful woman? And now, here I sit in this dank hole with my life wounded far worse than my leg—which, by the way, throbs as if a demon were pounding a white-hot spike into it!

Brewster has gone to sleep, and I do not need to write any longer. I began writing to keep him from talking to me, nothing more. He is so confounded *cheerful* in the face of everything! Of course, *he* is safe now, bound for his New World where he can preach to the naked savages to his heart's content. To give him his due, he is an honest man, quite convinced that this world is but a bit of practice for the world to come. They all think that, actually seeming to *enjoy* suffering! They claim hardship endured for God is like money in the bank, that it will build up compound interest until they get there to enjoy it!

But trying to talk to these fanatics about hard *fact* is like talking to a tree! They just give you a smile dripping with sweetness and ask, "Why, where's your faith, brother?"

In a few weeks, after scurvy hits and teeth start dropping out, I'd ask a few of them, "Where's *your* faith, brother!"

No, I will not. That's the bitterness of my own heart.

I pity them, for it will not be as they think—no paradise on earth!

I have only one hope. I am strong and I will endure this voyage. I will endure the beginnings—and I will be aboard the first ship that comes to the accursed place!

One thing I will *not* do—I will not join these people in any way. My lad Tink is a likely chap. But I will be leaving him as soon as I can, so no need to get emotionally involved in him. Brewster is a fine man—one of the few in this earth who would forgive another for such as I planned to do to him. But he'll starve or be killed by savages like the rest. Humility— I cannot write about her . . .

I will give these people the strength of my arm—but not one inch of ground in my heart—so help me God!

CHAPTER FOURTEEN

STOWAWAYS

★　★　★　★

Gilbert's wound began to knit almost at once, and three days after leaving Plymouth, he began to get sick of the sailroom. There was nothing to read but Brewster's Bible, and when the older man was absent, Gilbert was driven from sheer boredom to read the mystic visions of Ezekiel and the lists of clean and unclean food in Leviticus.

He spent long hours thinking of Cecily and of the lost opportunities of their life together. Now that she was lost to him, she seemed more desirable than ever, and the wealth and power which had been a mere possibility as Lord North's man, in his imagination became more solid and real than ever. A dark streak of fatalism imposed itself on his spirit, and the optimism that had been a part of his character faded as the lonely days dragged on.

William Brewster noted this, of course, and he said to Edward on the first Sunday at sea, "Edward, I'm worried about Gilbert. He does nothing but lie in that little place and mope."

They were standing at the starboard rail, watching the passengers come up for the first service since leaving England. The small deck was crowded; everyone who was not seasick came topside, most of them rather pale from the close confinement below.

"There's no help for it, I suppose," Edward answered

shortly. There was a reserve in his face that was unusual as he said, "I'm still finding it hard to believe that my own brother betrayed us!"

Brewster pulled at his grizzled beard and in his gentle voice said, "There's one thing we can take comfort in, Edward."

"What's that, William?"

"He couldn't go through with it. When the time came, there was something in him that *refused*! He has great good in him, Edward."

Edward studied the face of the older man; then a smile touched his lips. "There is that, isn't there? It gives me hope that he may come out of this business a man."

"I'm sure of it, Edward—but it's going to take all our prayers. He's bitter now, you know. I think if you'd have a word with him, it might help."

"All right, I'll do it." Edward saw that Bradford was mounting the poop deck, and said, "I think the service is beginning."

As Bradford was preparing to speak, Brewster looked down from the upper deck, seeing for the first time all the passengers together, and it gave him a sense of uneasiness to see how small the Leyden group was. Only twenty-seven in all, less than a sixth of the church—a minority that showed up clearly as he saw the bulk of the *strangers* on the crowded deck.

There were about eighty of these, volunteers whom Thomas Weston and his business friends had recruited in London and its vicinity to fill out the plantation's quota.

Some, like Christopher Martin, were dissatisfied with the Church of England and quite ready to join the kind of church the Leyden exiles had created. Others had obviously succumbed to the Weston vision of profits in the wilderness and, like millions who would follow, were headed for the New World to make their fortunes. Stephen Hopkins, Brewster thought, was certainly one of these. He had already made one voyage to Virginia, and had survived a harrowing shipwreck in Bermuda. Now he was sailing on the *Mayflower* with his pregnant wife Elizabeth and their three children. He was a man of considerable means and had brought along two servants, Edward Dotey and Edward Leister, both of London.

Another "stranger" was John Billington, a surly, contentious character, Brewster knew, with a viper-tongued wife and two unruly teenaged sons.

Scanning the crowd, Brewster nodded with more approval on William Mullins, boot and shoe dealer of Dorking. He was a devout man bringing his wife and two children, Joseph and Priscilla. Mullins had bought nine shares in Weston's company—equal to an investment of about one hundred pounds—and he had a large supply of shoes in the ship's hold—the last of his stock.

Some of the men were servants hired by more affluent members of the group, such as husky John Howland hired to do the heavy labor in the wilderness for Carver. Twenty-two-year-old William Butten was to do likewise for Samuel Fuller.

Important to the venture were two master mariners—Thomas English and John Allerton—two ordinary seamen who were to man the ten-ton shallop stored between decks on the *Mayflower*. They were under contract for one year, and were essential for helping explore the shallow waters along the coast.

One other hired man of considerable importance was Captain Miles Standish, a short, stocky, tough ex-soldier who had been assigned to handle the plantation's defenses. Now thirty-four, Standish had served with the English army sent by Queen Elizabeth to aid Holland against Spain. The last English troops had been withdrawn from Holland in 1609, about the time the first of the Scrooby exiles were making their way to Amsterdam and finally Leyden. Standish had met some of the leaders of the Green Gate congregation in Leyden, and Bradford had remembered the pugnacious warrior as the right man to superintend their military affairs. For Standish, whose only trade was soldiering, it was a welcome offer; between wars, the English government had an unpleasant habit of discharging its best men, leaving them either to steal or starve. Childless, the captain brought along only his wife Rose.

Bradford raised his voice and began a hymn, and as the others joined in, the crashing of the green waves on the plunging bow, the whistling of the wind through the rigging, and the creaking of masts and spars muffled the reedy voices.

After several hymns and a long reading from the Bible, Bradford preached a short message. He took his text from Deuteronomy 8:7: "For the Lord thy God bringeth thee into a good land, a land of brooks of water, of fountains and depths that spring out of valleys and hills."

Bradford raised his seamed face and said, "This is the promise of our God—we will rejoice and be glad in it!" Then he exhorted the people to remember that it was God and not man who had delivered them and would provide for their needs. He spoke briefly, ending by saying, "I call your attention to verse 11 of this chapter, where we are warned: 'Beware when thou hast eaten and art full that thou forget not the Lord thy God, in not keeping his commandments!' "

He closed the Bible, and the service closed with a long prayer from Bradford. Edward said, "William, there's a meeting called by Martin. You had better come."

"More complaints, I take it?"

"What else?" Edward growled as he led the way toward the stair.

The meeting was to be in the section of the poop house used by several of the passengers, and by the time Brewster and Winslow got there, Bradford was ringed by Billington, Martin, Hopkins, and several others, none of them from the Green Gate congregation.

Billington, a tall, heavy man with thick features and only one tone of voice—a half shout—was waving his thick forefinger under Bradford's nose, saying, ". . . Let no mistake be made, Mr. Bradford; we won't be put upon! Your man Cushman found out I'm a man wot's gets 'is rights! I got me rights, see?"

"No one denies that, Mr. Billington—" Bradford tried to interrupt, but was overpowered by the weight of Billington's foghorn voice.

"We ain't in Leyden, I says, so don't think we a'goin to be like them sheep wot you brought with yer!"

"Not likely," Steven Hopkins piped up. He was as small as Billington was large, and his small, pointed face was in contrast to that of the larger man. He waved his hands about as he talked, his features working nervously as he insisted, "I been a traveler, Mr. Bradford, all the way to Virginia. Was shipwrecked and made my way home safe despite it all." He nodded and looked around proudly, and then he said shrewdly, "What it comes to,

Mr. Bradford, is this: on a trip like this there's got to be some
'justments made!''

"Adjustments?" Bradford asked quietly. "What sort of adjustments?"

"Why, ain't it plain? All this talk about who's the governor
and such! When that time comes, it'll be up to *all* of us to have
a say, won't it?"

"Certainly you are entitled to have a voice in the government," Bradford nodded, but then he added with a trace of iron
in his voice as well as in his dark eyes, "but we began this voyage
under the hand of God—and God, Mr. Hopkins, is not a dem-
ocratic leader. He is a Sovereign King."

"Oh, *that's* the way it's going to be!" Christopher Martin,
tall, cadaverous, and usually angry over some imaginary slight
to his dignity, grew red and swelled up. "Why, I didn't leave
England for a New World to be lorded over by nobody! No more
lords and nobles for me!"

"That's *treason!*"

Every man in the group started at the loud voice that cut
through the argument, and the crowd parted to allow the captain
of the *Mayflower* to stand in the center.

Captain Jones was a solid, tightly built man, though neat
and short, in his early thirties. He had a pair of direct gray eyes
that ran around the crowd with no attempt to conceal the anger
in them.

"I warned you, Mr. Bradford, there'll be no treason on my
ship!"

"There is none, Captain Jones," Bradford said quickly. "Mr.
Martin was speaking in general terms."

"I heard what he said!" Jones snapped. "And I heard what
you said as well. Did I not warn you there'd be no fanatical
treason preaching on my ship? Why did you ignore my order?"

"Sir, it was Sunday. We merely had our usual worship."

"You spoke against the King!"

"Not against the King, Captain Jones."

"Did I not hear you talk of freedom for every man? What
would that be if not treason? Is not every Englishman under the
King?"

"I spoke of the soul of man, Captain, not politically."

Jones stared at him, then shook his head stubbornly. "The King is the King—no matter about *souls*!"

"I must disagree. Only God can rule over our souls."

"I am the master on this ship. Every soul 'board ship stands under the master, and likewise every Englishman stands under the King!"

"Their souls?"

"Yes!" Jones nodded emphatically, sending his curly black hair wildly bobbing. "Know, sir, that I am aware of your views. I am not unaware that some of your group offended the King and are fleeing his wrath! Deny it not to be so. You would lead people away from their duty to the King under your pretense of holiness. Beware, Mr. Bradford, for you will not do so on my ship!"

"Captain Jones!" Edward Winslow moved to stand directly in front of the captain. "There is no treason here. You are not unaware that I have been for many years in the King's service. Would such a man as I be a part of any group bent on treason?"

Jones faltered, for there was an air of distinction in Winslow's bearing, in addition to which Jones was aware of the service of this man to the King.

"I make no accusation against *you*, Mr. Winslow," Jones said in a calmer voice, "but you are not in good company. I urge you to take heed to yourself!"

The captain felt that he had made his point, so saying bluntly, "I have my eye on you—do not provoke me!" he left the hold.

"I see no point in this meeting," Winslow said, looking with distaste at the group of dissidents. "We are bound to one another, and we must have a ruler. Otherwise we are no better than beasts!"

"But who's to say who's to be the ruler?" Billington asked loudly.

"God will always raise up a man," Bradford said at once. He nodded and said, "I have nothing to say to you on this matter."

He turned and left, followed by Brewster and Winslow.

When they got up on deck again, Winslow said moodily, "That'll not satisfy them, William."

"It will have to be prayed about, I fear." Bradford looked across the rolling ocean, then down toward the hold, saying sadly, "If we cannot agree on matters before we reach our land, how will we manage there?"

"God will make our way plain!" Brewster said at once. "One step at a time, William!"

William Bradford nodded, but there was a break in his intense air of faith. He finally looked up and said, "God is all!" and then he walked away to stand beside the mizzenmast staring moodily into the west.

Humility had not felt easy over her failure to visit Elder Brewster. He was as much of a father as she had known, but to avoid contact with Gilbert, she had kept away from the sail locker for nearly a week.

Now it came to her that she was being unfair, so she made her way toward the galley to wheedle a goody or two from Hinge for the pair.

She was by now familiar with the manner of cooking aboard ship. Every third day a charcoal fire was lighted over the sand on an iron hearth, a cauldron of porridge made from soaked oats and another cauldron of stew; the porridge was eaten hot every third morning, cold every other two. Fumes from the bad charcoal made them cough, but this was thought a small inconvenience in return for a steaming bowl of food. The porridge was eaten for breakfast with a lump of biscuit-bread and a cup of beer or water, everyone sitting down around the hold with their bowls on their knees. The midday meal was usually cold stew or mush, or biscuit-bread with a slice of smoked bacon or smoked beef.

In the evening their frugal meal was again mainly biscuit-bread, with which they could have a small portion of cheese, heavily smoked, and salted sausage meat, soaked peas, raw onion, finnan haddie, kippered herring, or dried tongue, and a mug of beer.

The few delicacies—apples, prunes, raisins and pickled eggs, of which the store was small—were given only to the children, the sick, and the pregnant. All food was carefully rationed out by the orderlies. Meals took a long time; the food was small in bulk but tough in substance. Most of the meat had to be chewed at great length, and even then was hardly digestible. They were always hungry, but it lay in their own hands; they could eat well now, if they chose, while idle, and starve later on when perhaps they would have heavy labor to perform.

Humility had made a fast friend of the little gnome of a cook, Thomas Hinge. He was a lonely fellow, twisted in his legs, and most of the crew looked upon him as a menial servant.

She found him stirring a pot of stew over a small fire, and with a smile she said, "Hello, Thomas."

"Why, here you are, miss!"

"We have a sick man who would get well on a bowl of this wonderful stew."

He squinted at her, grinned and gave her a helping in a large vessel. "See you bring that bowl back, now!" Then as she rose to go, he teased her, "Sure that ain't for some young gentleman you're sweet on, miss?"

She looked at him directly, her green eyes suddenly losing their light. "No," she said evenly. "No, there's nothing like that, Thomas."

After she left, the little cook stared after her for a long time, then said, "Scratch me now—I reckon I said the wrong thing, but bless me if I know what it was!"

Making her way down the dark stairs, Humility bit her lip to keep back the tears. She had never cried a great deal, but lately she had found her eyes flooded for no reason, and now she forced herself to blink the stinging tears away.

The odors of the ship were rank, thick with the air of unwashed bodies, stale bedding, night soil, and the old grease. On land it would have been unbearable, but it had become part of the world for her and she paid no heed.

She had reached the cargo hold, and as she made her way along the dark passageway, a man moved out of the darkness ahead of her.

"Well, if it ain't my gal!" Jeff Daggot grinned broadly, moving to block her way. His massive body completely blocked the passage, and she drew back at once. He had taken every opportunity to force himself on her, brushing against her whenever they happened to meet, and more than once reaching out to touch her face with a blunt finger or give a tug to her clothing. She had heard him make a coarse remark about her to Mr. Coffin, and had tried to avoid him.

There was an unholy gleam in his small eyes, and she took a step backward, only to have him reach out and take her by the arms.

"Let me go!"

"Not likely!" he grinned through his broken teeth. "It took me a while to figure it out, but finally it come to me. I been watching you come down here, and so here I am."

He pulled her forward; in his massive arms she was powerless. His arms went around her, and she cried out, "Let me go!"

"Why, sure—in a while!" Daggot said. He put his hand behind her head and forced his huge lips on hers—fear shot through Humility in a way she'd never known. She dropped the bowl of stew, and with both hands beat against Daggot's broad chest, trying to break free from his embrace.

"That's right!" he grinned, holding her even tighter against his body. "I likes it when a gal fights a bit—makes it all the sweeter!"

He pulled her to one side of the corridor and attempted to force her to the deck. With both hands she reached in blind fear for his face, raking as hard as she could with her nails.

"Ow!" he cried out, and instinctively released her, his hands flying to his eyes. "I'll show you . . . !"

She realized the door leading up to the next deck was too far, so she ducked under his arms and plunged straight down the dark hall. She heard his heavy footsteps right at her heels, and he was cursing in a vile way as she reached the door of the sailroom, opened it, and fell inside with a gasp.

Brewster and Gilbert had heard the noise of the struggle, but had not dared open the door. Now the older man stood there and as Humility fell against him, he held her protectively as Daggot plunged into the room.

The huge sailor stopped abruptly, for he had not supposed anyone was on the cargo deck. "What's this!" he shouted. "Who are you?"

"I think you'd best be going," William Brewster said. The

frightened girl was weeping in his arms, and his face was stern as he said, "I think the captain would be most severe on you if he were to discover your treatment of this young woman!"

Daggot stared, his piggish eyes suddenly filled with apprehension. He knew what the old man had said was true. All the crew made fun of the pilgrims, but it went no further, for Captain Jones had made it clear that any of the crew actually molesting the passengers would be flogged.

But then Daggot had a thought. "Wait a minute," he growled. "I ain't never seen you—nor him either." He stared at Gilbert who had risen to a sitting position and was standing up, his face pale with the strain of standing on the wounded leg. "What you doin' here?"

"That's none of your business," Brewster said. "Just be on your way and we'll forget this."

Daggot shook his head, a frown on his face. "Stowaway, ain't you?" He caught the look that the older man and the younger man gave one another, and then he laughed hoarsely, "Well, I caught you fair, didn't I? Come on, up with you!"

Daggot grabbed Brewster by the arm, and the power of his grasp shot the frail body of the older man toward the door. Humility quickly took his arm, saying, "I'll report you to the captain, Daggot!"

"Haw! We'll see who gets reported," Daggot sneered. "Come on, now. You're all goin' to the Great Cabin!"

"Why, you can't take this man up those steep stairs!" Brewster protested. "He's got a severe wound."

"Ain't that a *shame!*" Daggot grinned. He shoved Brewster and Humility out of the compartment and grabbed Gilbert by the arm. "Now, you can walk topside, or I can drag you!"

Pain ran down Gilbert's leg, but he said steadily, "I'll walk."

It was one of the most difficult things he could remember, climbing the three flights, even with Brewster and Humility helping him. By the time they got to the Great Cabin, and Daggot rapped sharply on the door, his leg was aflame and a red mist had dropped before his eyes.

"What's this, Daggot?"

"Stowaways, Cap'n!" Daggot said. "I been seeing this gal

take food down to the cargo hold, so I sets me a trap, and these two is what I caught!"

"What's your name?" Jones demanded.

"William Brewster."

The name meant something to Jones. He nodded and said, "Wait outside, Daggot."

When the burly sailor was outside, Jones said at once, "You are a fugitive from the King's justice, Mr. Brewster."

"Yes."

The simplicity of the reply caught Jones off guard, and he said angrily, "You think I will shelter you on my ship?"

"Will you put about, Captain Jones?"

Christopher Jones reddened and snapped, "You know I can't do that—but I can take you back with me—in irons! And you, sir, what is your name?"

"Gilbert Winslow."

Captain Jones stared at the young man, shook his head and said in wonder, "It seems I have a pair of fugitives. You, too, are sought by the King."

"I have no doubt."

Jones stared at Gilbert, and there was a guarded admiration in the captain's eyes at the courage of the two men.

"Well, you are more likely to bleed to death than to hang, if I'm any judge." He looked at Humility and said, "Get that Fuller who passes for a doctor."

As they waited for Fuller, Captain Jones seated himself in the chair behind his desk and stared at the two men. There was a vague air of wonder in his face, and with a hint of humor he said, "I've hauled many a cargo in this ship, but none that gave me so much trouble as you good Christian folk. Why do you suppose that is, Mr. Brewster?"

Brewster smiled at him, and said with a touch of wry humor in his thin voice, "Why, I suppose that people are always more trouble than *things*, Captain Jones. Souls are, after all, trouble-some things!"

"True, sir," Jones nodded and added under his breath, "and in the future I will haul a cargo that does not have such pesky souls!"

Brewster heard him, however, and said, "The real trouble,

Captain Jones, is that you have a soul of your own."

Jones stared at him, and said nothing to that, but there was a nervous air in the way he ran his fingers up and down the cord that looped his neck, and he did not speak again to the old man.

CHAPTER FIFTEEN

ON DECK

★　★　★　★

Christopher Jones sat in the Great Cabin munching on an apple. He swallowed a tot of gin and ran his eyes over his log.

Log: September 12.
　　Yesterday two stowaways were discovered. One of them, Mr. William Brewster, has been a fugitive from the King's justice for some years as a result of certain writings. The other is a young man named Gilbert Winslow. Since there is no possibility of escape, I have not placed them under arrest, but on the return to England, I will do so and turn them over to the proper authorities.

A knock on his door interrupted his reading, and he closed the log, saying, "Come in."

Edward Winslow entered, nodded and said, "Good morning, Captain Jones."

"Yes, what is it?"

Ignoring Jones's gruff reception, Winslow said evenly, "I want to speak to you concerning my brother, Gilbert, and Mr. William Brewster."

"There's naught to be said!" Captain Jones snapped. He slapped his palm hard on the desk and there was an angry light in his gray eyes. "They are criminals and will be so treated!"

Winslow shook his head, saying mildly, "I realize you have been put in a difficult position, but as you get to know these two men, I'm sure you'll realize that they are not criminals in the strictest sense of that word. Mr. Brewster is a godly man of impeccable character with years of faithful service to his King and his country. His *crime* is a matter of a fine theological point." Winslow was a trained diplomat and used his full powers of persuasion as he spoke. "There was a great theological argument, I believe, among the Pharisees in the Lord's day, over how many angels could dance on the point of a needle."

"The charge against Brewster is not so frivolous as that—he is charged with sedition and plotting against the King of England!"

"Technically, that is true, but as you get to know Mr. Brewster—and my brother—you will see that they are both honorable men. Since you are an honorable man yourself, Captain Jones, I feel sure that you will find their true qualities."

"They will go back to England under arrest, Mr. Winslow." Captain Jones had been brought up in a hard school, and he was not about to gamble his ship or his reputation for the sake of two fanatics.

Winslow saw the folly of forcing the argument, so he merely smiled and said, "I hope you will see things differently before the voyage is over, Captain Jones."

He bowed, left the Great Cabin and proceeded along the deck to where Gilbert stood at the rail, staring glumly at the waves.

"Well, here you are!" Gilbert turned to face his brother, and grudgingly admitted that Edward's face was open, without a trace of the accusation he half expected to see there.

"Hello, Edward."

"Leg is doing *very* well, isn't it?"

"Yes. Much better."

"Good! Good! Expect this fresh air and exercise will work miracles for you, Gilbert. But we Winslows are a tough breed, eh?"

Gilbert smiled briefly, appreciating that Edward was doing his best to restore brotherly feelings. "By the time Captain Jones gets me back to England, I'll be in excellent health—just right for the hanging."

Edward stared at him, then laughed shortly. "Nonsense! You're not going to hang."

"No? I hadn't heard that King James had stopped executing those convicted of treason." Gilbert despised himself for unleashing on the one person who *did* have an affection for him, but the confinement had soured him, and he seemed to have no control over his tongue. He slapped the rail with his hands, then, saying sheepishly, "Your pardon, Edward. I'm not fit company for anyone."

Edward's face relaxed and he clamped his large hand on Gilbert's shoulder. As the two stood there, the family resemblance was very evident. Both were tall, and though Edward was heavier, there was a natural grace and athletic air about them both. The cornflower blue eyes were common to all the Winslow men, and the auburn hair of both glowed like burnished gold in the sun. Both had strong features, defiant cheekbones rising to broad foreheads, and both had the wedge-shaped face, and a slightly jutting jaw which suggested a deep and stubborn will.

Edward, the more intellectual of the two, was quick to reply, "No reason why you shouldn't be pretty tightly strung, I'd say. You must be out of your mind, being tied to that bunk so long."

"Well, it is getting pretty boring, Edward."

"Been catching up on your reading, I expect?"

"No. Nothing to read."

"What? Why, that's a *crime*, Gilbert! I have plenty of books. What'll you have?" He allowed a glint of humor to crease his broad lips, and suggested gently, "A good book of sermons?"

Gilbert laughed despite himself, "I'd read *tombstones*, Edward!"

"Well, some of the sermons I've heard aren't as interesting as a good stone," Edward laughed. "What would you say to a folio of Master Shakespeare's work, eh?"

"Now, that's business!" Gilbert smiled. "Thank you."

Edward turned to go and said, "I'll get it for you . . ." He paused, then said in a hesitating manner, unlike his usual forceful speech, "I say, Gilbert, don't—well, don't expect too much of us." He pulled at the lace on the front of his shirt, embarrassed, and added, "I mean to say, it may take a little *time* before people forget . . ."

Seeing Edward bog down, Gilbert gave a tight smile and finished the statement, ". . . forget that I sold Mr. Brewster for thirty pieces of silver?"

"Well . . ." Edward still could not find what to say, so he shrugged and murmured, "I know. It's hard, Gilbert. But you have to remember that all of us are flesh and blood. If you cut us, do we not bleed? But it's in your favor that when the time came, you put your life in jeopardy to save William and Humility. That will sink into people's minds after a time. Give them a chance, man!"

"Of course," Gilbert said; Edward gave him a good smile and left to get the book.

Gilbert found a place to sit down and spent the next hour reading a play about two "star-crossed lovers." The confusion that brought the youthful Romeo and Juliet to such a disastrous end caught at his mind, and from time to time he would lift his gaze to follow the drifting clouds. Once he murmured softly, "Mr. Shakespeare, you know the heart—at least the confusion of it!"

The *Mayflower* was a little world, sailing through the rolling, trackless water much as a single star cleaves through the ebony blackness of space. There was a difference, however: the star had fellows (invisible though they were to the eyes), while the ship was solitary.

Bobbing like a cork on the tossing waves, she was smaller than the leviathan that sometimes surfaced close enough for the passengers to see the waterspouts. But though dwarfed by the miles that lay beneath her keel, by the sky that unscrolled blankly over her mainmast, and by the mighty ocean stretching in every direction, she kept a life and order running through the ship—an image of the macrocosm of the planet.

Captain Christopher Jones was the archtype ruler: master, potentate, king, prince, emperor, congress, parliament, court. He ruled the little world with the power of an absolute despot, the Great Cabin no less the seat of authority than the Vatican or Buckingham Palace.

The ship was its own cathedral, chapel, monastery, nunnery; there were as many divergent views among the inhabitants of the bobbing little world as the babble of tongues in the larger one. From the dim, superstitious thought of Richard Salterne—common sailor, little better than a half-wit, who thought of God only as a sort of murky stew engulfing the earth—to the profound meditations of William Brewster, philosophies of God were as diverse on the little ship as were the staggering varieties of life that teemed beneath her keel.

Sam Fuller, sitting on the edge of the poop deck with his feet dangling, felt godlike as he watched the teeming quality of the deck. He was a man not given to idealism, and was constantly amazed to find himself on such a preposterous voyage. In truth, Fuller was an incurable romantic—and terribly ashamed of it! He covered the soft streak with a hard shell that fooled all but a few who knew him best.

Now as his eyes swept the deck, he saw half a dozen dramas unfolding, and his wise old eyes took them in—weighing, balancing, judging.

He saw Edward Winslow approach his brother Gilbert, and it was clear from his face that he was trying to cheer up the younger man. Then, after Edward left, young Tinker, who had been watching the pair from behind the mizzenmast, edged out, and Fuller saw the fear and grief in his pale face turn to joy as Winslow apparently made something right with the lad.

A smooth talker! Fuller thought grimly. *He put it over all of us—even me! But he won't do it again! Not likely!* There was a hard streak in the burly man's makeup, and he was especially sensitive since he took pride in his knowledge of men. He had taken to the young fellow as he had to few, and it had hit him hard when his faith had proved to be misplaced.

He saw William Mullins, his wife Alice, and his daughter Priscilla in a tight group over on the starboard side. And he saw husky John Alden leave his seat on the forecastle and amble along toward them, whistling, apparently quite aimless.

Fuller smiled, thinking: *Young Alden ain't so simple as he seems! Looky there how he was all surprised to see that pretty Miss Mullins sitting there—as if he didn't have the foggiest idea she was on the ship at all! Why, I've seen the young buck mooning over her since the day she come on board, and now, look at that! She's just as surprised to see him! And poor old William Mullins and Alice—why, they're so fuddled by this journey they ain't got the sight to see that pair being drawn to each other like magnets! Well, they'd better keep their eyes on that young woman! She ain't bad, but she ain't above usin' her eyes on a man, either!*

He grinned at the thought, a ribald streak running through his spirit.

Then he saw a group knotted beside the mainmast, and he frowned. The physician knew men, and the men who were engaging in a meeting were objects of scorn. Hopkins' pale blue eyes were darting constantly toward where Bradford and Carver sat in the bow, and it was obvious that Hopkins' companions—Martin and Billington—were speaking of them.

As eminent a set of ditch dogs as I've seen! Fuller thought. *They'll bring this ship to grief if they're not stomped on—and soon. I've warned Bradford, but he's so full of theology he can't see a mutiny when it's taking place under his nose. Winslow can, though!*

Sam Fuller shook his head wearily and pulled himself up to leave the poop deck.

He encountered Captain Jones who was scanning the horizon with a glass, and would have passed by, but the captain glanced at him and said, "Would you like to take a look, Mr. Fuller?"

Fuller shook his head. "Nothing to see, I know that."

"There's a school of dolphin—see?"

Fuller took the glass and watched the creatures come racing by the ship, plunging and diving in something of a marine minuet, and said grudgingly, "That's pretty, ain't it now?"

"Never get tired of watching the beasts of the sea," Jones said. He looked down at the thick knots of passengers on the waist deck and sighed. "It would be nice if people were as regular as dolphins. You always know what a dolphin's going to do, every time. Can't say as much for people, can you, Mr. Fuller?"

"No."

"On the other hand, maybe one way you can count on them."

Fuller saw that he was watching Humility Cooper washing some clothes in seawater, and the captain added, "You can count on there being trouble when a pretty woman is on ship—never fails!"

"She's a good girl!"

"Don't doubt it, but look at that," Jones pointed to where Daggot and some of his mates were lolling on the forecastle deck.

"Daggot is a fool. He's after that girl, and he'll keep it up until there's trouble."

"Keelhaul the swine!" Fuller snapped.

The captain shrugged, his gray eyes taking in the scene. "Can't keelhaul a man for what he's *going* to do—or for what wrong things he *wants* to do." He smiled suddenly at Fuller. "Guess we'd all be keelhauled if that happened, wouldn't we, Mr. Fuller?"

Sam Fuller felt weary. He looked out over the crowd below and said, "I thought we were going to the New World to work for God. Now it looks like we may never get there with a principle left intact."

"You've lost your faith?" Jones asked instantly. He was highly skeptical of the Separatists—indeed, of religion in general—and he would not have been displeased to find one of the pillars of the church beginning to crumble; it would confirm his belief that it was all humbug.

Fuller pulled himself up, looked at the people, then said, "No, Captain Jones, I've not lost faith—not in God."

He turned to leave, but said with a shrug of his heavy shoulders, "But I wish sometimes God would speak to me a little louder so I could get a better idea what He's up to!"

Jones watched the big man lumber below deck, and there was a strange smile on his lips as he looked down at his passengers, then up toward heaven. He said in a quiet voice, "Amen." Then he laughed at himself and went back to studying the dolphins.

CHAPTER SIXTEEN

CAPTAIN SHRIMP

★ ★ ★ ★

A driving wind scoured the deck as Captain Miles Standish looked with disgust at the ragged line made by the settlers along the waist deck, waiting impatiently for Mr. John Carver to finish his speech.

The snow-white hair of the man chosen as governor two days earlier blew over his face, and several times he had to pause to brush it away from his mouth. He was small and thin, but there was an erectness in his figure and a clear light in his brown eyes.

"We must be prepared to defend ourselves as soon as we land," he said in a clear, thin voice, "and we are very fortunate to have Captain Standish as our military advisor. He has served in the wars against the papists."

"Don't need no man to teach me how to fight!" John Billington rapped out sullenly. "Besides, I thought we was a Christian settlement!"

"David was a man of war, Mr. Billington," Carver said. "We will hope that we shall make a quick peace with the savages— but we must know the use of our weapons. And you must remember that we will have need of skill with weapons to bring down game for food."

Gilbert had joined the group at the urging of Edward, though he had no hope that would gain the good graces of the settlers by such an action. But his leg was improved, and he was bored with reading and staring at the empty horizon, so he agreed.

Now looking at the old, rusty matchlocks leaning against the rail, he thought with a quick grin: *I think I'd rather be in front of one of those relics than doing the firing!*

He did like the looks of Standish, though. The captain was a small, sinewy man with bright red hair and a florid complexion, wearing seasoned leather breeches and a leather-lined jacket belted and buckled. A burnished steel helmet sat on his head, decorated with a crimson band. *He looks like what he is*, Gilbert thought, *a seasoned veteran.*

Standish waited until Carver had finished, then picked up one of the matchlocks. Holding it up, he said, "You will learn to use this weapon. This is a matchlock, the most simple made. It is touched off with a wick or a match cord. There are no wheels, flints, or steel to misfire. Treat it well, and it will not fail you—unlike human beings."

"Ho, now, hear how the soldier boy talks!"

Gilbert looked up to see half a dozen of the crew gathered on the forecastle deck, grinning down at the little group. Daggot was in the center, flanked by his mates Salterne and Bart O'Neal—a stubby Dubliner with a fierce black beard and one eye milky. The pilot, Coffin, was there, standing to one side with a sardonic look in his muddy eyes.

Standish ignored the crew, and proceeded to give a stiff lecture in a crisp voice. "The first rule is to carry your length of wick in your left hand, your gun under your right arm, or on your right shoulder. You will never touch your weapon off by accident if you do this." He gave detailed instructions on how to take care of the weapon, washing out the barrel with boiling water, keeping the powder dry in rainy weather, how to form lead into shot with a ball mold, how to measure a charge. He illustrated the use of a ram, with dire warnings on the danger of putting home second and third measures of powder on previous, unexploded charges and the risk to life and limb occasioned by carrying gunpowder carelessly near the fire.

Finally, he sent John Howland below to light the slow match, and when he returned with end aglow, Standish poured a charge of powder down the muzzle of a gun, slid in the ramrod and patted it gently home and dropped in a ball. He shook a few grains of black powder over the touchhole, put some more in the flashpan by its side, and slid the flashpan cover while he screwed the glowing end of the slow match into the movable arm, which would jerk it down and dab the spark in the primed pan.

"Get below deck, mates!" Salterne shouted. "The soldier boy is likely to blow us all to kingdom come!" He was a slow-witted young man of twenty with the vilest vocabulary on board, and he loosed a few choice specimens of lower-deck language as Standish stared up at him.

Standish turned his back to the wind, holding the gun above his right hip and pointing upward, to port. Deftly he cupped his powder-blackened hand around the flashpan, protecting the powder from the wind as he slid back the cover; and all in one movement changed his position, gripped the gun with both hands and squeezed the trigger. The serpentine and wick jabbed down, a little puffing explosion of muffled fire and black smoke hissed up out of the flashpan, followed by a red belch of flame and sooty smoke from the muzzle. The heavy weapon buckled back under his arm alarmingly. A cloud of soot and sulphur fumes drifted across the deck and some of the group applauded the feat.

"Gor! 'E done me in!" Salterne shouted and fell back, clasping his heart as one with a deadly wound. His mates rocked with laughter, and Standish looked up to see Captain Jones standing on the poop deck, arms folded and wearing an amused smile on his lips.

"Captain Jones," Standish called. "Can you not find work for these men?"

"They are on their own time, Captain Standish."

"They are disturbing the drill!"

"The ship is small. Where would you have them go? Besides, you would not begrudge them a little amusement, surely."

Standish stared at Jones, his face dusky with anger. But he understood military law, and the captain of the *Mayflower* was the iron law of discipline.

Ducking his head, he bit his lip and said, "Very well. Now, who will be first to practice?"

Billington stepped forward, his eyes ugly. He towered over the small, neat form of Captain Standish, and there was a bullying light in his closely spaced eyes. "You got no right to rule over us, Captain Shrimp!" He used the term some of Standish's enemies used to deride the small man, but it brought instant retribution to Billington.

Quick as flash, Standish reached out, and grabbing the larger man by the arm, he whirled him about as if he weighed nothing. Avoiding with ease a ponderous blow that Billington made toward his head, the little captain with a smile on his face gave a hard shove with his hands and at the same time drove his boot upward in a hard kick that caught Billington in the haunches. The force of those twin blows shot the bulky form of the settler toward the longboat, and he crashed into it with his arms cartwheeling helplessly. His big belly took the force of the collision, and there was an audible *whoosh* as the air was driven from his lungs. He flopped over, sliding to the deck, and he looked like a huge sick frog as he sat there with his wide mouth open trying to draw air into his lungs.

There was a dead silence on the deck as Captain Standish ambled across the deck, with one motion grabbing Billington by the collar and jerking him to his feet. "Now, sir, *you* load that gun!"

Gagging and gasping, Billington stood there, and then Governor Carver said gently, "I believe you received a command from our captain, John."

That settled the question of the captain's authority, and one by one they took their turns, loading and firing the weapons.

Most of them had no experience at such things, but when Gilbert loaded the gun with practiced ease and got his shot off in a remarkably quick time, Standish glowed with pleasure. "Well now, Mr. Winslow, you've done that before!"

"I've had some experience," Gilbert said diffidently.

"Good! We can use some of that! And is it possible that you've handled a sword as well?"

"A bit of that, also."

"Splendid! Perhaps you might be willing to help the others with that part of the training?"

Gilbert shrugged, but said, "Well, *I* would be willing, Captain. As to whether the others would accept . . .?"

"I'll plant my foot in their backsides if I hear one word!"
The words were rough, but there was a kindly twinkle in the
little man's eye, and he clapped a friendly hand on Gilbert's
shoulder. He lowered his voice, saying, "I've heard all the gossip
about you, Winslow—but it's my way to judge a man on what I
see—not on scandalmongers!"

Gilbert warmed to the man, admiring his bluff honesty, and
for the next three days he spent much time in his company.
Standish's wife Rose was a tiny, silent woman who seemed
oddly mismatched with her firecracker of a husband. They had
no children, and Rose Standish spent much of her time caring
for the children of the settlers.

"She loves the little ones," Standish said to Gilbert while
they were sitting on deck late one afternoon. "Lost three of them,
and none has come since." He shook his head sadly. "Nothing
a man can do to help a woman in that way."

Humility Cooper, Priscilla Mullins, and Bess Tilley were sitting by the mizzenmast, laughing and talking, a pretty sight to
the captain, who had been quite a dandy in his younger days.
He caught a glimpse of Gilbert looking at the women, and asked
softly, "Now any one of those three would be a fine wife for a
young fellow, would you agree?"

"I suppose so, Miles," Gilbert said. He moved his shoulders
nervously and added, "I don't think about such things."

"And why not?" the fiery little man demanded. "I'd like to
hear your story, Gilbert—if you'd care to tell a stranger."

"You really would?"

"I would, lad. I've taken to you."

Gilbert had kept his own counsel, but Miles Standish, for
all his toughness, had a good heart, and for the next hour Gilbert
spoke steadily, reliving the history of the past few months.

He faltered at first, but Standish simply waited, and then it
began to flow. They were alone on their corner of the deck, and
as the wind luffed the square sails, slapping them with powerful
gusts that drove the little ship along swiftly, he lost himself in
the story. He made no attempt to defend his actions; indeed,
there was such bitter self-accusation in his words that more than
once Standish stared at Gilbert and gave a silent shake of his
head.

Finally he ended, almost out of breath with the effort. "And here I am, a fugitive with a guilty past—and no future to speak of."

Standish did not speak at once. He dug into his pocket, found an old pipe, then a black tobacco pouch, slick with age. Filling the bowl, he rose and walked over to where some of the matches were still glowing from the day's practice, lit the pipe, then returned to sit beside Winslow.

Finally, he said, "Boy, you can't scare me with your tales of a misspent youth. When I was your age I was studying for the gallows." He smiled at some fleeting memory, and there was a furry soft quality to his voice as he said, "I'm not a man for preaching, but one bit of scripture I think is straight . . . how does it go? Oh, yes: 'Though a just man should fall seven times, the Lord will lift him up again.' Now *that's* good sound walking around theology!"

Gilbert stared at him, seeking to understand what the soldier was saying. "Are you telling me that it doesn't count—what I did?"

"Not that!" Standish protested. "I guess what we do stays with us—in some ways. But I'm one of the roughs, lad. Maybe I've had to be. And I don't rightly know as I understand much about the God these preachers keep talking about. I read the Bible, right enough, but only about the Man."

"The Man? You mean Jesus Christ."

"That's it. Oh, I know what they say, that He's God. And so He is, but what strikes me is that when the good Lord on earth gave himself a title, it was 'The Son of Man'! Now, that's what I'm putting my hope in—the Son of Man!"

"I—I guess I'm too dense to understand, Miles."

"Not you, Gilbert," Standish smiled. "You're maybe *too* smart! Get yourself all tangled up with all kinds of high thinking about God! What I say is, Jesus Christ came here to be a *man*! And that meant He found out what it was like to be in the middle of this life! Don't you know He got dirty, got tired? People let Him down, didn't they? He bled and died, just like I've seen many a fellow do!"

Gilbert nodded slowly. "That's all true, Miles, but . . ."

"Well, that's my religion, lad! Jesus Christ was a man who

knows what this world's really like. So when I fall, which is pretty often, I just say something like, *Lord, you were a man, so you know all about this!*"

Seeing that Standish was finished, Gilbert shook his head, saying stubbornly, "That's too *easy*, Miles. There's got to be more to it than that!"

"See? I said you were too smart! But I've been there where the last drop of blood was dripping out, lad, and men who are dying get *simple*—they just come down to one thing. Have they served God or not?"

The words of Standish caught at Gilbert. He had heard of repentance many times, but as he stood there, he experienced a stab of remorse at his past sins in a way that was almost a physical pain. He yearned suddenly for a new heart—a cleanliness of spirit. And he felt with all his being that this was to be found only in Jesus Christ! But *how*? He shook the thought off regretfully.

Then Standish laughed and slapped Gilbert on the shoulder. "Bless me, lad! We got a ship packed with preachers, and here's a reprobate of a soldier preaching to you! A plague on it now!" He saw that Winslow was biting his lip with a worried scowl on his smooth brow, and added, "You'll be all right, Gilbert. I know men, and you and that brother of yours are two I'd stand for!"

They sat there talking, unconscious of the glances that touched on them from the three young women on the deck.

"I wonder how Captain Standish ever came to marry such a pale little creature?" Bess Tilley mused. "He's so full of fire and she's so drained and pale."

"Maybe she was pretty when she was young," Priscilla shrugged. "I think being the wife of a soldier would be very hard. Always traveling to strange places."

"No," Bess shook her head vigorously. "She's never been pretty, you can tell." She was a girl of strong opinions and often got into trouble for voicing them. "Lots of good-looking men marry women that are homely. Look at Edward Winslow. Why, he's so handsome it's a sin—and there he is married to poor Elizabeth!"

Priscilla pulled at a strand of her honey-colored hair and argued in a dulcet voice, "I don't think looks are very important,

Bess. It's what's in a person's heart that counts."

"Oh, you little tease!" Bess laughed. She looked at the shining hair, the startling violet eyes, and the flawless complexion of Priscilla, saying, "That's what the preachers say, but I notice you won't have anything to do with that ugly little man Richard Warren. He follows you around like a lap dog, and you don't even know he's alive! You're too busy keeping your eyes on that *beautiful* figure of Mr. John Alden!"

"Why—" Priscilla's mouth opened and her cheeks flushed scarlet. "You mustn't *say* things like that, Bess!"

"Why not? Everybody on board knows you're moonstruck with him!"

"Bess, don't tease her," Humility said quickly. She patted Priscilla's hand and smiled at her, adding, "Don't mind Bess."

"Why, you're just as bad, Humility," Bess began and then thoughtlessly prated on. "Didn't you fall head over heels in love with that Gilbert Winslow?" Instantly Bess clapped her hand over her mouth and her eyes flew open wide.

Humility did not say a word, but her face went pale, and then she got to her feet quickly and said, "I promised to take care of Resolved for Susanna."

The two girls watched her go, and as soon as she was out of hearing, Priscilla said in exasperation, "There, you see what you did, Bess! I declare you ought to have your tongue cut out!"

"How can I be so stupid?" Bess mourned. "She never liked any man before."

"No, she didn't, did she?"

"And she's the kind who sticks to things! If she were flighty like some, it wouldn't be so bad, but I'm afraid she's the kind you see sometimes who never get over a first love."

"It's too bad! He's such a handsome man, and his brother Edward is so nice." Priscilla rose and said, "You're right about the way I feel about John, Bess." She laughed and added, "I just get goose bumps looking at him!"

Bess rose with a laugh. "Isn't it *awful*? I do the same thing with my John! But I'd never let him know it!"

They left the deck, giggling and talking. After they disappeared, the sound of coarse laughter rose from the poop deck. Salterne, Daggot, and O'Neal had been lying down flat, invisible to the young women, and they had kept silent, eavesdropping.

"Now we know why you ain't never been able to get a hand on that Humility Cooper, Jeff," O'Neal crowed. "She's pinin' away for her true love—that Winslow fellow!"

Daggot's gap-toothed smile was savage, but he laughed and said, "This voyage ain't over yet, mates. I'll have her eatin' out of me hand before we drop anchor!"

"You'll get yourself a flogging, Jeff. You know how the captain is."

"Oh, I knows that, right enough," Daggot said with a wave of his meaty hand. "But all I got to do is show that little gal how much more of a man I am than that stick of a Winslow!"

"Aw, you're just sounding off, Jeff!" Salterne said. "You ain't got the guts to do nothin'!" Salterne looked thin and pale, and he loosed his customary string of blasphemy adding, "I feel like a dying buzzard. You reckon I ought to see that sawbones?"

"Drink a quart of gin, Salterne!" Coffin's voice grated behind them. Then he warned Daggot, "Do what you want to that Winslow—but be slick, Jeff!"

"Oh, I got me a plan, Coffin. You know how Winslow's teachin' them to use swords every day?"

"Yes. What then?"

"Why, I'm gonna wait until he's doing that—and until Miss Humility Cooper is watchin'—and then I'm gonna give him a lesson of my own!"

Coffin said, "You'll hang if you kill him, Jeff."

"Who said anything about killing him?" Daggot spread his hands expressively. "But if I'm letting him *teach* me, why, you know how it goes, Coffin—a man can get pinked through the shoulder—or maybe even in a bad leg, eh?"

"Now that's an evil thing!" Coffin said, but there was a cruel smile on his lips. "And besides, you don't know but what he's a better blade than you."

"No fear, Coffin! I been watchin 'im, and I can touch him anytime."

Coffin liked the idea. Winslow was not unlike the man he'd killed in a duel, and there was a perverse hatred in the pilot for all aristocrats.

"Do it then, Jeff!"

CHAPTER SEVENTEEN

THE STORM

★　★　★　★

The storm that struck on the morning of September 17 was like nothing Captain Jones had ever seen. Coming out on deck, he stopped dead still, so suddenly that Sam Fuller rammed into him. "Look at that!" he breathed in a small whisper.

"What is it?" Brewster asked.

"Storm coming—faster than I've ever seen!"

A black cloud dropped down, making a shelf across the horizon and moving so fast across the choppy waters they could trace its progress.

"All hands!" Jones shouted. "Man the sails! Batten down! Batten down!" As the crew came tumbling out of the ship, Jones said, "Get to the passengers, Brewster! This is going to be pretty bad!"

In a matter of minutes the main top sail ripped up one side and blew out in ribbons, cracking like gigantic whips.

The ship began beating back and forth before the terrible force of the headwind, like an animal running up and down. The light of day failed as the blackness of the cloud wrapped a sable blanket around the plunging ship, and the last flag of daylight, a thin streak of silver-white, was blotted out by the rolling cloud. The dull roaring rose at times to a high-pitched scream, drowning out the creaking of the timbers and the fluttering of the tattered sails.

The seamen fought their way along the tilting decks, grabbing desperately to rails, masts, lines as they tried to control the ship.

"Take in sail! In with your top sails. Lower your main sails, lower the foresail . . ." Jones shouted.

Stripped of all canvas, the *Mayflower* was thrown about like a ball. "Get a few feet of canvas up on the poop or she'll founder!" the captain shouted, and Coffin was nearly washed overboard as the crew rigged a small sail.

The masts swayed crazily against the dark sky, and the bow lifted over mountainous swells, a terrific shudder shaking her as she plowed into the head of the mountain of water. She was flooded below as wave after wave broke over her.

Below deck there was bedlam. Water ran everywhere—through the hatch covers, under the two doors opening out onto the waist deck, and through many loosened seams in the main decking, trickling and seeping down from deck to deck till it reached the bilge in the bottom of the ship.

William Brewster peered through the darkness cut only by the occasional glow of a single candle through panes of an opaque lantern, thinking with the others that each roll of the ship might be the last.

Many of the women were crying as well as the children, but suddenly William Bradford's voice rang out over the screaming wind, "Lord, do not grind our people and let them be lost! Deliver us, as you delivered Jonah and Daniel!"

Then he raised his voice in a psalm, and there, in the depths, the voices of others joined in:

Jehovah feedeth me, I shall not lack
In grassy folds he down doth make me lie
He gently leads me quiet waters by
He doth return my soul, for his name sake
In paths of justice leads me quietly.

But still the wind thundered and the ocean smashed at the ship; then as their quaking voices began the next verse, with a crash like a cannon shot, a main beam amidship cracked and buckled!

Dorothy Bradford raised a face pale as death, and cried out, "Oh, God! The ship is breaking up!"

Pandemonium broke, both from men and weather. The captain and mates rushed below to gaze up from the gun deck at the sagging beam, the splintered deck around it. Water gushed from the new openings, and the terrified passengers huddled against the ship's sides to escape it. Half a dozen of them put their shoulders to the job while the freezing water poured down on them. It was like trying to raise the roof beam of a house. The massive piece of timber only sagged a little more. A spare beam was dragged up from the hold, and the men tried using that as a ram. No success.

For two hours they fought the waves, and the carpenter exhausted his resources trying to pull the ruptured beam into place.

"We'll have to go back to England, Captain!" Mr. Clark insisted. "There's no hope of a repair where we're headed!"

"We've come too far," Jones said grimly. "She'll never make it—to the New World or the old."

A great cry went up from many of the passengers to turn back, while forward in the hold, out of the way, Bradford, Carver, Brewster, and Edward Winslow held a conference.

"We must not turn back," William Bradford said quietly. He was the type of man who performed better under pressure, and now there was a rocklike set to his craggy features.

"I agree," answered Brewster. "It will be the end of our dream. Ruin for all of us!"

Gilbert had not been invited to the meeting, of course; it was mere chance that he happened to be in the hold close to where the men met. He sat on a box, and his eyes met those of his brother. Edward said, "It's beyond the power of man, brethren. We must seek God!"

Gilbert's lips turned up sardonically, and he did not bow his head as the three men began to pray for deliverance. He got up and left, hearing William Brewster pray fervently, "Oh, God, give wisdom to deliver this ship!"

Shaking his head, Gilbert thought, *Too late for that. We'll never make it back to land.* He made his way to the spot where the carpenter, together with John Howland and John Alden, was trying to lift the beam with a long board for a lever. Putting his hands on the lever, he threw his weight on it, and the sudden strain snapped the piece.

Howland and Alden sprawled out as the deck collapsed, then got to their feet. The carpenter said, "I didn't think it would work—that beam must weigh two tons!"

"Where are the others?" Alden panted, his huge chest rising and falling with the effort.

"Up there . . ." Gilbert nodded, then added, "praying for a miracle."

"You don't believe in miracles, Winslow?"

Gilbert whirled to see the captain, his face a mask, standing behind him.

"No."

"Well—neither do I," Jones said, biting his full lower lip. "But that's about what it's going to take to get that beam in place!"

They stood there racking their brains, trying to find a way to lift the beam. In a few minutes William Bradford and Brewster came in followed by Carver and Winslow.

"We have had an answer from the Lord, Captain."

Jones started, and almost looked overhead for the Deity, but quickly covered this with a sardonic smile. "Well, it's good to have men on the ship with a direct line to God. What is the answer?"

"It came to Brother Brewster and Brother Carver almost simultaneously," Bradford smiled. "A word of prophecy based on Acts, chapter 27 and verse 24: "Fear not, God hath given thee all them that sail with thee."

"Yes, and then the 25th verse says, 'I believe God that it shall be even as it was told me,' " Brewster nodded.

Captain Christopher Jones stared at the wreck of the beam, settling slowly, knowing that it would sooner or later snap, and that when it did the *Mayflower* would break in two. He heard the cries of the women and children, and the shouts of the seamen on deck trying to keep the ship aright. The look he gave to Brewster was filled with unbelief, and he grated out in a harsh voice, "You are like all prophets that I've met—filled with pompous words that have nothing to do with living in this world!"

At that moment the ship spun her head out of the wind and lay broadside to the crested swells, instantly battered by a gargantuan wave that tore its huge weight over the deck, snapping cleats and ropes and heeling the ship so far onto her beam-ends that her spars almost entered the water and the men in her hung on a vertical wall.

Tons of water muffled the screams and cries of the women and children, and Gilbert was flung so hard against the bulkhead his head rang and pain shot through his bad leg.

Pulling himself upright, he waited for the ship to right itself. There was a long moment when he was sure that the slow roll would continue, but the *Mayflower* came upright. He shook his head and left the first hold to go to the sail locker.

He passed through the cargo hold, went to the sail cabin, pulled on a heavy coat that was drenched already, then left. As he passed through the cargo hold, there was a tremendous groaning as the timbers creaked, and only a feeble light from the swinging lantern gave any illumination.

His eyes running over the barrels and equipment, he wondered how long it would be before they slipped loose and went crashing through the planking.

Back in the first hold, he found the captain urging the carpenter to come up with a solution, and it was clear to Gilbert that Jones was a desperate man.

He joined the others as they tried to wedge a piece of heavy timber under the ruptured spar, but it was evident there was no hope.

Then something happened in Gilbert's mind. He could never explain it afterward, but it was as close to a vision as he ever came in all his days. Suddenly he saw an object—as clearly as he had ever seen anything in his life with physical eyes.

Then—the sound of the breaking sea rolled back into his head, and he looked up, startled to find himself still pushing at the futile timber.

"Wait!" he shouted, and the strident tone of his voice brought the crew to a halt.

"What is it?" Edward asked at once. "Are you all right, Gilbert?"

"I know how we can brace that timber, we can . . . !"

"Mind your business!" Coffin rasped acidly. "This is ship's matter."

"What's your idea, Winslow?" Captain Jones asked quickly.

He stared at Gilbert with a faint glow of hope in his eyes. Not much, perhaps, but he realized more than anyone there, unless that timber was braced immediately, they were doomed.

Gilbert said quickly, "Alden, you remember you were showing me the equipment in the cargo hold?"

"Yes, but . . . ?"

"I wasn't very interested, but now I remember one thing—that big iron jack!"

"That's *it*!" Alden shouted. He struck himself in the forehead with his palm and started for the ladder at a run.

"What are you talking about?" Jones demanded.

"It's some kind of device used for jacking up boats for repairing the hulls—that's what Alden told me. It's big enough to do this job, Captain."

An optimistic hubbub of talk ran through the hold, and when John Alden came back bearing the heavy black jack in his powerful arms, Jones shouted, "That's the thing! Get it under this beam!—Where's that timber, Mr. Clark? All hands bear on here!"

"Put this timber crossways, to rest it on," Alden said. "Otherwise it'll shove right through the decking."

They laid a heavy timber down, put the jack on it, then balanced another timber on its flat lip. "Get a short piece to put under this thing!" Jones urged, and when that was done, he commanded, "Raise the jack, Coffin!"

A cheer went up as the upright jack pressed against the beam and slowly pushed it up until it was even.

"That'll hold until calm weather," the carpenter said. "Then we'll spike a splint across that break and repeg it to the upper deck."

Suddenly William Brewster's voice cut through the hold like a trumpet—feeble, perhaps, but reaching every ear: "The Word of the Lord has come to pass! He has sent deliverance!"

Christopher Jones was flooded with relief. The *Mayflower* was his livelihood, his love, his security. Five minutes ago, he would not have given a farthing for the chances of saving her; now it was a matter of riding out the storm.

He raised a hand that was not entirely steady to wipe the water from his face, then he turned to face Brewster who was standing knee-deep in water with his hands raised to heaven and a light of joy on his thin face.

"I think Mr. Winslow really deserves some credit," he said softly. "It was quick thinking, man, and I'm in your debt!"

Gilbert stood there, staring at the jack, saying nothing, and then he felt a hand on his shoulder and looked up to see William Bradford standing beside him.

"Mr. Winslow, we are all in your debt."

Gilbert was caught off guard. Bradford had said not one good word to him since he had come aboard, and yet the honesty of the man was not to be doubted. He looked at the angular planes of Bradford's face, and asked impulsively, "Surely you can't think the Lord would use a sinner to do his work—with so many saints around?"

William Bradford was a strong man, but he bowed his head at that question, and there was a look of pain in his dark eyes as he looked around at the people in the hold—saints and sinners.

"I am not as certain as I once was in some things. When I was younger, I felt that it was a simple matter to identify God's children. Lately, I have wondered if I was not often hasty in my youthful judgments."

Gilbert stared at him, then said in a hard tone, "Well, there's no doubt in *my* mind about this business. I saw the jack, and when we needed it, I remembered it. Nothing of God in it!"

He sounded like a man trying to convince himself, but Edward put a hand up and said quietly, "There's some of God in everything, Gilbert—as you'll know before He's finished with you!"

Gilbert made a brief entry in his journal:

September 17
I am not sure of anything. I suppose a man has two sides and there never will be a world which will please both sides. One side of him is going to be hot and the other side cold. Maybe this earth is for right-handed folks—maybe for left. In the world of right-handed people, the left-handed ones will cry in it!
Which is my world? England seems as alien as Venus. Would I go there, get rich, marry Cecily? Why do I still look in Humility's eyes and think of New Testament verses?

I guess there is God and the devil in me—maybe in everyone.

What happened today in the hold? They prayed and I thought of a jack. Did the God who flung those millions of stars in space give a hang for this fragment of a ship on an insignificant journey to savage land? Brewster says God stepped in. He claims that I was given the answer, and that may be true—but I can't believe it! Whatever God is up there has forgotten about us long ago. But how comforting it would be to believe in Brewster's God!

CHAPTER EIGHTEEN

ANOTHER KIND OF STORM

★ ★ ★ ★

The sun breaking through the next day brought calm weather, but there was a taste of snow in the air. For the next three days Miles Standish drove the men hard at musket practice. His sharp voice harrying the settlers rang out for long hours, and more than once, one of the elders found it necessary to reprove him for his language.

"Aye, Reverend Bradford, it's not best for a man to use foul language, but do ye realize we'll be moving through enemy territory in a few days? Our lives will depend on these butter-fingered yokels! Why, sir, the whole colony could go down if these men don't do better!"

"I'll pray about it, Captain," Bradford said; his giving way marked how determined he was to plant a colony for God. He spent night and day going about the ship, encouraging the weak, nursing the sick, and for long hours he retreated to the lower deck to pray.

Standish gave Gilbert, who was standing by, a sly wink, saying, "Right! You do the praying and I'll do the drilling!"

The first day of sword drill, Gilbert had been challenged by Standish, who said, "Let me see what stuff you have, Winslow!" There had been astonishment in his eyes, however, when Gilbert toyed with him, balancing on his good leg. Time and again Standish had tried to drive through for a touch, but Gilbert had smiled and with the tip of his blade sent that of Standish wide. It was obvious that the younger man could have won at any time, and finally Standish stood there puffing with effort. It was a tense moment, for the little man fancied himself a fighter and did not like to lose.

Then he had smiled and said, "I'm not much on religion, Winslow, but if I get around to prayers any time soon, I'll give a thanksgiving for you! I've never seen a better blade—where'd you pick up the skill?"

Gilbert had not gone into details, and no one had seen the encounter, so Standish had not been shamed before the crew.

Most of the men were on deck for the drill, as were many of the women and children. There was no danger from flying lead, and quite a bit of rivalry had sprung up. The saints, Gilbert had learned at Leyden, loved simple games; and the fencing and drill, pitting man against man, took their fancy, breaking the dull monotony of the long days.

As Gilbert gave a few instructions and stood back to watch the participants, he glanced around the deck, noting that the voyage had not dissolved the factions and sects on the *Mayflower*.

The saints were crowded together in a group over on the starboard rail—the Allertons, Carvers, Tilleys, Tinkers, Whites.

The strangers, perhaps not by chance, took station on the port deck—the Billingtons (the largest family on board), Chilton, Eaton, Hopkins, and Mullins families.

Ranging around the poop deck many of the ship's crew lounged, taking in the sight with half-whispered jokes from Daggot and O'Neal. Captain Jones and First Officer Clark leaned against the mizzenmast.

Jones had requested that those members of the crew who wished might be instructed, and Standish had agreed. It was obvious that of the crew only Daggot had any skill, though there was a light in Coffin's eyes that warned Gilbert that he was no beginner.

Daggot had clowned through the basic instructions, entertaining his mates and some of the passengers with his remarks. He had attempted several times to engage Gilbert in a debate, but had been disappointed.

"He's not bad, Winslow," Standish had said, watching carefully as Daggot ran through the preliminaries with careless skill. "And he's not in love with you, I see."

"No."

"He'll try to show you up. Don't let him have a chance."

Although there was no doubt in Gilbert's mind about his ability to meet any challenge from the seaman, he knew only mischief could come of a direct conflict with the man.

As he called the men off from practice, he saw a glint in Daggot's eyes, and followed his glance. He saw Humility watching from the rail, and the sudden swagger in Daggot's walk warned Gilbert that he was going to have trouble from the man.

"All right, heed this now," he said clearly. "You've not got to face skilled fencers or trained swordsmen . . ."

"Which is a good thing, ain't it now?" Daggot said loudly, with a wink at O'Neal. " 'Cause if any of these babies ever did face a *real* man, they'd run 'ome to their nannies!"

Gilbert ignored the laugh from the crew, and continued with his lesson.

"But the principles are much the same. If you have a sword in your hand in a fight, your man will come at you with *something*—a rock, a spear, a stick. And you need to be so familiar with your blade that you don't even have to think about it . . ."

"Ain't no need to warn these babies not to think!" Daggot called out, casting a contemptuous look at the passengers.

". . . your blade must become like a member of your body . . ."

Daggot laughed and made a rude remark, and a ribald laugh went up from the crew, even from some of the strangers.

"Must we put up with this?"

Gilbert looked around to see that Peter Brown, his best pupil, was glaring at him. Brown had had some training in the use of the sword, and in the man-on-man exercises had easily won. He gave one quick glance over his shoulder to where Humility was standing, and then looked back to Gilbert. "Mr. Winslow, I think we might do without the crew for the exercise."

"Why, you ain't very polite!" Daggot spoke up, again winking at O'Neal. He took an aggressive step forward, adding, "But I guess you preachers ain't used to bein' around *real* men."

Gilbert saw the thing getting out of hand. He shot a quick

glance toward Captain Jones, who merely shrugged his shoulders. The affair amused him, and he whispered something to Clark that made the First Officer nod and smile.

Miles Standish, his face red with anger, stomped up to Daggot and stared up into the large seaman's face. "You want a little action, Daggot? Come on, then!"

Daggot shook his head as the fiery little soldier whipped out his blade. He raised his hands in a gesture of innocence, protesting, "Why, Captain, you're a professional soldier! You wouldn't take advantage of a poor ignorant sailor boy, would you now?" There was an arrogance in his tone, but the words were nothing that Standish could challenge.

"Well, *I'm* not a paid soldier!" Peter Brown cried. He whipped out his sword, and lifted it in the air. "Let me have a bout with the fellow, Winslow—if you won't do it yourself!"

He's calling me a coward, Gilbert thought. *But I'm no boy to rise to a foolish dare. I know more about my courage than he does.*

He was about to dismiss the men when Daggot suddenly whipped out his blade and said, "Why, then, sonny, let's just find out who's the real man!"

A circle was formed when the others drew back, and as the two men touched blades, Gilbert had an evil thought. *Daggot hates me and will sooner or later try to kill me. Brown is in love with Humility and will do what he can to show me up for a coward as well as a traitor. No matter which one of them wins, or even gets pinked with a blade, why, it's no problem of mine!*

He shook his head at the wicked thought and stepped forward to prevent the match, but was stopped by Standish's iron grip. "Let 'em have at it, Gilbert!" he said. "They can't hurt each other much with those blunted tips—and it wouldn't matter much if they *did*! These lads need to see a little blood to get 'em ready for what's to come!"

Gilbert shrugged and watched as the two men circled each other. The space was small and there was a vivid contrast in the antagonists. Daggot was broad as a door, bulging with muscle, while Brown was tall and lean as a sapling.

The blades rang again and again as the two met, engaged, then stepped back. Ordinarily Gilbert would have picked Brown to win easily. He had the reach and some formal training, but they did not serve him well.

Daggot's bulk did not allow him to cover ground as fast as his smaller opponent, but his reflexes were amazing, Gilbert saw at once. His blade ran in and out like the tongue of a serpent, and he had been well taught in the art of defense, probably by Coffin, Gilbert decided.

The contest soon became uneven, as Brown weakened, no doubt, from the bad food and inactivity of the voyage. He began to breathe with a rasp, and his arm began to droop with fatigue.

Gilbert moved quickly forward, seeing the young man about to be humiliated, but Daggot saw him coming and with a lightning parry drove home a stroke straight at Brown's face—a violation of the rules.

The blunted tip of the blade caught the young man in the mouth, splitting his lower lip and breaking off a tooth.

"Enough!" Gilbert cried, springing forward furiously. "You swine! I ought to run you through!"

Daggot stared at him, malice in his hot eyes. He said softly, "Why don't you, Winslow?" He waited, then when Gilbert hesitated, he raised his voice loud enough to carry to the poop deck, "Come on! Are you a man or not?"

There was a silence then, broken only by the rasping wheeze of Brown's breath, filled with pain as he held a handkerchief to his broken mouth.

Gilbert had come upon a stag once, worn down by the chase and surrounded by a pack of red-eyed wolves, their eyes cruel as death. Something of that was in the faces of the onlookers—some of them, at least. The quick look showed him that most of the crew of the *Mayflower* wore that cruel lupine expression, wanting only to see a good fight. Billington, among the strangers, looked much the same, even crying out, "Go on, Winslow, give the scoundrel a foot of steel in his belly!"

Brewster and Bradford, standing together, seemed struck dumb by the violence that had exploded in their faces, but Edward's face was red with fury, and he nodded at Gilbert, saying, "Have at him, boy!" in a voice shaking with anger.

The one face that seemed to leap out at him was Humility's. Her green eyes were enormous in her wide face, and her lips were stretched tightly against her teeth. She was not a girl to let her emotions show, Gilbert knew, but now she was holding back her feelings so strongly that the knuckles pressed against her wide mouth were white with strain.

Gilbert felt the pressure on his back, and suddenly he was tempted to cut the man down. It would not be difficult, he knew, for while Daggot was a good journeyman with the sword, he was not in Gilbert's class.

But he waited, and as he did, a mutter went across the crowd, and he heard the word *coward* several times.

It raked across his nerves, and he looked around the deck, hating the look in the eyes of most of the spectators.

I won't put on a show for you! he thought grimly, then put up his sword, saying, "Put your weapon away, Daggot. You know better than to make for a man's face. Even with a blunted tip, it's possible to blind or cripple. Stay clear of the drill in the future."

Daggot waved the sword in his hand in front of Gilbert's face, his voice filled with contempt, "And if I don't?"

Gilbert said, "Captain Jones will have something to say about it, I would think."

He looked up and saw something like disappointment in the captain's face, but Jones said, "Daggot, stay away from the passengers. I'll not warn you again!"

Angrily, Daggot threw his sword to the deck, glared at Gilbert and said, "You're a coward, Winslow! Hiding behind the captain!"

"Daggot! Did you hear me!" Jones bellowed. "One more word and we have a keelhauling!"

Fuller stepped forward, a bleak light in his face, but he said nothing to Gilbert. "Let me have a look at that mouth, Peter," he said, and he led the wounded man off to one side for a closer examination.

Standish waited until the deck had cleared, then said, "Bad business. I thought for a minute there you were going to skewer the rogue!"

"That's what everyone seemed to want!" Gilbert said wearily. "And didn't you warn me, Miles, not to let the man trap me?"

The answer came slowly. "Aye, you did the wise thing—but it must be hard to be labeled a coward."

Gilbert smiled grimly down at Standish. "I'm getting used to it, Miles. First a traitor, now a coward. Not much left, is there?"

"You're none of that!" the doughy little soldier snapped. "Why didn't you cut the man to ribbons?"

Gilbert stared out at the sea, watching the gray expanse unbroken and creased by myriad whitecaps. There was no more expression on his face than on the blank sky that stared down on the little ship bobbing on the waves.

"It didn't seem to matter much, Miles." He lifted his cornflower blue eyes, startling in his tanned face, and there was a sadness that ran deep in his husky voice that caught the attention of Standish.

"Why, you're too young to be so tired of life, Gilbert Winslow. You've got a whole lifetime ahead of you!"

Gilbert gave him a short, bitter smile before turning to leave the deck. "I know, Miles—and do I dread it!"

CHAPTER NINETEEN

LAND!

★　★　★　★

As the temperature outside fell, so did the strength of Young William Butten, Samuel Fuller's servant. He had remained in the sail cabin with Brewster and Gilbert instead of returning to his bed behind the shallop, Fuller hoping that the relatively warm, dry conditions would help him.

"He don't seem to get on," he said to Humility as they ate the meager portion of beef passed along by the cook. "I wish I'd not brought him on this trip."

Humility said quickly, "You meant well. It's the late start that's brought us into this cold weather."

"Maybe—but it's a rough life we're heading into, lass." He chewed on the tough piece of stringy beef thoughtfully, and there was a rare discouragement in his voice as he added, "We're in bad condition, Humility. Half the passengers are down with some ailment now—and what it will be like when we're put ashore in the dead of winter, I hate to think. I'm going to see to Dorothy."

"I thought she was better since she got over her seasickness."

"There are worse things than upset stomachs, lass," Fuller grunted. He pulled his hand through his tangled beard, and added, "Dorothy has problems in her mind."

"I know, Sam." Humility got up, took the man's dish and

added, "She sometimes talks—well, in a peculiar way."

"She'll lose her mind if something doesn't happen."

"Sam! No!"

"I know you work hard, lass, but I wish you'd spend all the time you can with her. Try to encourage her if you can. She needs a friend." He paused and said tightly, "Far as I can see, she opens up more to that Winslow fellow than to anybody else—which is not right!"

They parted and Humility, passing across the deck, saw that Dorothy was talking to Gilbert Winslow in the bow section. She hesitated, then made her way forward.

"Oh, there you are, Humility," Dorothy said brightly. The cold air nipped at her cheeks, grown thin during the voyage, and she smiled faintly. "Sit with us, won't you? Gilbert was just telling me about a ball he attended at St. James Place."

"I can't stop now, Dorothy, but later on maybe we can read some more out of the book you liked so well."

"All right," Dorothy said, and added as the girl disappeared down into the lower parts of the ship, "Humility's such a sweet girl! I hope she gets settled with a good man who'll take care of her."

"What book is that she spoke of?"

"Oh, a book of poetry. I don't understand much about it, but Humility reads so well, I just love to listen."

"How's your husband?"

Her face, which had been lively, tensed as if in fear. "He's very ill."

"He and I are not well acquainted, but I admire him greatly."

"Oh, he's very admirable. I—I sometimes wonder that he married me. I mean, he was older and a great scholar and I was just a silly girl—only sixteen."

Gilbert hesitated, fearing to go too far, but he had a brotherly feeling for Dorothy, and he finally asked, "Have you been happy?"

"When I was a little girl, I was very happy!" she said, and her small face lit up with pleasure at the memory.

"I mean since you married."

"I don't know," she said slowly. And then a strange thing happened, something that Gilbert didn't understand. Dorothy was staring across the rolling sea, apparently thinking of her past as a child, and suddenly she turned and said in a voice very different from her normal voice, "I want some melon, Papa!"

A chill ran over Gilbert. She had a blank look in her eyes, and her features sagged, making her look older, but the voice was that of a child.

"Can I please have some of the melon, Papa? Robert has had *two* pieces already!"

Gilbert had never encountered a disturbed mind, at least not in such a form, and he sat there petrified. There was no *danger*, of course, from this frail woman, but a streak of fear cold as ice ripped through him. He wanted nothing so much as to get up and flee from her, but could not move.

He said carefully, "Dorothy—are you all right?"

Instantly her eyes cleared, and she said in a normal voice, "Why, yes, Gilbert, I'm fine. A little cold, perhaps."

At once he said, "I'll get you a coat."

"No, I must go inside and see about William." She rose, and there was a terrible fragility in her face that Gilbert understood. She patted his arm, saying, "If I didn't have you to talk to, Gilbert, I think I'd lose my mind!"

He sat there, his mind in a whirl, and finally he rose and sought out Elder Brewster. But he found him deep in conversation with Governor Carver, and feeling that he must say something to somebody, he made his way to the small cabin that Edward and Elizabeth shared.

"Gilbert? Come in—if you can get in, that is." Edward's face was lined, for he had lost his cheerful expression. His tremendous vitality had been sapped by the illness of his wife, and he had a haunted look as he turned to say, "Gilbert's here, Elizabeth."

There was no answer from the woman who lay on her back covered to the nose with a mound of blankets. She was staring at the ceiling dully, and did not respond when her husband said, "I'll just go along with Gilbert for a time. You try to sleep."

"How is she?" Gilbert asked as they stepped out on deck.

Edward filled his large chest with fresh air, lifting his head to meet the stiff breeze. "Ah, that's good after that foul cabin!" he exclaimed. He began walking vigorously up and down the deck, swinging his arms and stamping his feet. His face grew flushed and the tension left, smoothing his features. "Elizabeth is as well as she's going to be, I suppose."

It was as close to a critical word as Gilbert had heard from his brother concerning his wife, then Edward paused and said in a softer voice, "She's not fitted for this life, Gilbert. I shouldn't have brought her."

"I think there are several who shouldn't have come. Fuller is much afraid for William Butten—and I wanted to talk to you about Mrs. Bradford."

"Dorothy?" Edward shook his heavy head, muttering sadly, "She's not doing well, is she?"

Gilbert hesitated, then told his brother of the incident that had so shaken him. He saw that it disturbed Edward greatly.

"It's not the first time, Gilbert. All of us who are close to her have had forebodings."

"Something must be done!"

"What?" Edward shook his head sadly. "Fuller can give her a purge or a blood-letting, but who can minister to a broken heart—save the Lord himself?"

"Does her husband know?"

"Why, William knows she's unhappy and not well, but he's been so busy ministering to the needs of others, he's had scarcely a word with her. I've tried to tell him, as has Elder Brewster—but he's such a single-minded man it's almost impossible to catch his attention."

Gilbert's anger flared out suddenly. "Doesn't he know the Scripture says that he who doesn't care for his own is worse than a heathen?"

Edward frowned and there was a puzzled look in his eyes. "I tell you the truth, Gilbert, I think that William Bradford is a great man—greater than we know. If this venture succeeds at all, it will be his doing. Others have been more visible, but he's been the hub on which the whole thing has turned."

"But his own wife . . . !"

"He's a great man, but great men can destroy others with their dreams!"

Edward struck the rail with his hand, and there was a fire in his blue eyes as he said angrily, "Bradford can see a New

World and all its destiny—but that vision so fills his eyes he can't see that his own wife is going insane!"

"Tell him!"

"He's a *great man*, Gilbert; you don't simply tell that breed something. It's like trying to reason with a glacier that's slowly moving along, taking everything with it—trees, rocks, hills. William must love his wife—but his vision fills his heart and his soul. He won't allow anything or anyone to come before what he sees as God's will for his life!"

"Well, I'm happy that I'm not one of the great men," Gilbert said moodily, then grinned at his brother. "Like you."

Edward spat over the rail and stared moodily at the horizon. "I'm in worse shape than Bradford in a way, Gilbert."

"I don't believe that!"

"No? You aren't blind, so you must have seen that my marriage is a farce."

"Well . . ."

"Oh, don't bother to be polite!" Edward said, almost angrily. "It would be a relief to have somebody say just once, 'Edward Winslow, you are a fool!' "

Edward's passionate speech broke off abruptly. "I'm—sorry, Gilbert," he said finally, and managed to dredge up a smile of sorts. "Don't usually let myself go like this." Then he said, "It's too late for me—but not for you. When you marry, Gilbert, be sure you get a woman who won't *bore* you to death—better to have one who'll smash your head with a chamber pot!"

Gilbert had to laugh at the idea. "Not much for me to worry about, I suppose. Can't see myself married at all."

"You're thinking about being hauled back to England? God won't let that happen. You'll marry, and I'd give anything if you'd find a woman that could keep you entertained for a lifetime in two ways."

"Two ways?"

"In body and in mind!" Edward nodded. "Now, you're not a blabbermouth, so you just keep what I've said about myself under your bonnet."

Dorothy Bradford sat below deck with the Whites, playing Fox and Hounds with Resolved, listening to Susanna and William with part of her mind. They were talking about the problems that would beset them when they arrived, and Susanna was trying to encourage her husband.

"I can't see how we can get anything planted before May," White was saying. He coughed almost constantly now, his weak lungs unable to stand the harsh air of the Atlantic. "Then we'll have to wait for the harvest—if there is one."

"God will provide for us." Susanna was close to her time, and most women would have been in need of support, but there was no fear in her eyes. She leaned forward, still graceful in spite of her girth, and held William's thin hand. "Remember the Scripture cautions us to trust in God, not in the arm of flesh."

White lifted his arm and stared at it, saying with a wry smile, "This arm hasn't got much flesh on it, has it, Susanna? Not much to trust in!"

"You'll get better, William."

"I wish I had your faith." He stared at the emaciated arm, coughed sharply, then said in a low voice that Dorothy could barely hear, "It's not myself I fear for—you know that. It's you and Resolved, and the little one. Who will care for you if I die?"

"God." Susanna smiled and put down her sewing to move to his side. "If it did come to that—God would be my help. He is the father of the fatherless."

Dorothy looked at them, and thought, *Why can't I ever talk to my husband like that?* Then she looked down at Resolved and the sight of his face brought memories of her boy John, and she began to cry. She was always crying it seemed, and she was ashamed, but there was no help. She rose and left before the Whites could see, thinking, *If only this journey were over!* But then the thought struck her, *What then?* And terror filled her, for she realized that when she got off the *Mayflower*, she would not leave the dark fears behind, but would take them with her, ghastly things that pulled at her mind and dragged her spirit downward. *Why can't it all end?* she cried out in her heart over and over, but there was no relief.

"How's the boy, Fuller?" Captain Jones asked. He was attempting to shoot the sun with his cross-staff, a graduated bar of wood about thirty-six inches long, with a sliding bar about twenty-six inches long attached at right angles.

"Bad, I'm afraid. The miserable diet of salt meat, biscuit,

and dried peas we've had for weeks hasn't been any help."

Jones did not take his eye from his staff. Absently he remarked, "Try a little extra of dried fruit and lemon juice."

"He can't keep it down." Fuller stepped closer and watched as the captain jotted down a figure in a small notebook, and asked, "Does that thing tell where we are?"

"Not exactly. Gives the latitude pretty well, but there's no way to get the longitude."

"Well, doesn't that thing the seamen fool with every day tell how far we've come? If you know how far the New World is, seems as though you could subtract and tell when we'd get there."

"All that does is judge the speed." The log line was a quadrant of wood weighted on one side with a line about 150 fathoms long attached to it. The line was knotted at regular intervals, and by counting how many knots ran out while the line ran through the log glass, the number of knots or miles per hour could be roughly figured. But in heavy weather such as they had experienced it was useless.

"We *must* be getting close!" Fuller insisted.

Jones suddenly grinned, and jibed at Fuller, "I thought you people all believed that God was in control—fall of the sparrow and all that?"

"So He is—but He gave us intelligence to look to our ways. 'A wise man looketh well to his going,' the Scripture says."

"Well, I'm keeping the Scripture then," Jones argued good-naturedly. "I'm looking well to our going—that's what a captain does." He leaned against the mast and studied Fuller, wondering for the hundredth time what went on inside the Separatists. At the beginning of the voyage he had been adamantly certain that they were only another crew of wild-eyed fanatics, but his views had changed. He had discovered that the leaders were better educated than he, and men like Edward Winslow always excited his admiration. William Bradford he did not like, but William Brewster and Governor Carver were men of such evident piety he had to believe in their sincerity.

"We'll get there, Fuller," he said gently. "I know it seems long to you—the sea seems evil at times, even to me. He waved his hand at the rolling swells, and went on in a soft voice, "What can we know about the sea? We seem to be caught in the same old circle, always the same in every direction. Sometimes it seems that no matter how we feel the ship move through the water, we haven't made any progress—just glued in place while the sky and sea moves under and over us!"

Fuller stared at him, then smiled. "Well, now you know how we feel about God, Captain Jones."

"What's that?" Jones asked in surprise.

"Why, you sail your ship toward some spot you may have never seen and you have plenty of doubts, I see. Wonder if you'll make it? Get to looking at that huge, trackless ocean and it all seems very unlikely you'll ever arrive?" Fuller's broad face broke into a smile and he said, "That's what we call 'faith,' Captain Jones!"

Jones shook his head and mused, "Sounds dangerous to me, Fuller—I mean the way you people are leaving hearth and home. I have my charts and the stars to steer by, but what do you have?"

"We chart our course by the Word of God, Captain Jones— which is more stable than all your stars. 'The Word of the Lord changeth not, it endureth forever!' "

Jones considered this, then said seriously, "You will need all your faith, Fuller. It's very late for an endeavor such as yours. You should have timed your voyage to arrive on site in May or June. Winters in this latitude are fierce as tigers, I understand. How will you live—what will you eat?"

Fuller dropped his head and for one instant he looked tired and defeated, but then he looked up at the rolling banks of clouds that raced overhead, and then back to Jones.

"God is not dead, brother."

The simplicity of the reply was exactly the sort of thing that both disturbed the captain and paradoxically drew him to the settlers. Being a practical man, he was irritated at what appeared to be improvident planning—yet he longed to possess that serenity of soul that kept them secure.

"We cannot be many days out," he said firmly. "You'll be in your new Eden in a week, I'd venture."

Fuller nodded, then a figure caught his eye. Gilbert Winslow had appeared on deck and was making for the poop deck. "What will you do about that fellow?"

"Take him back to England."

"And Mr. Brewster?"

The captain hesitated, then was spared making an answer as Gilbert approached. "Mr. Fuller, I think you'd better come."

"Is it Butten?" Fuller asked quickly.

"Yes. He's having some sort of spell."

Fuller left without a word, and Gilbert turned to follow, but paused when Captain Jones caught his arm. "Is the boy dying, Winslow?"

Gilbert gave a slight shake of his head, his eyes cloudy, and he said briefly, "He looks very bad, Captain."

"Too bad! Too bad! I wish I could do something."

Gilbert stared at the captain curiously. His impression had been that the seaman was a rather hard specimen, but now there was a concerned furrow on the face of Jones. He said, "It does you credit to be concerned, Captain."

Jones gave him a direct look. "You think I am a heartless man, I take it."

"I don't know you, Captain Jones," Gilbert shrugged.

"No, nor I you. And with a certain matter between us, we may never get to know one another."

"You mean the matter of a gallows in England to which you will take me?"

Jones bit his lip, then nodded. "I could wish it were otherwise, Winslow. But as captain I am accountable to the Crown. If it became known that I allowed a fugitive to go free, it is not inconceivable that I might take your place on the gallows."

"I believe our Royal Sovereign is quite capable of such an action," Gilbert remarked with a grim smile; then he said, "I hold no malice toward you, Captain. But surely you must have some feelings about returning Mr. Brewster to the executioner?"

The question stung Jones and he said defensively, "He is an enemy to the Crown!"

"You know how false that is, Captain, I think." Gilbert shrugged and added, "You have spent much time with him on this voyage. I know that, for he has told me. Now can you, on your honor as a gentleman, say that there is anything in William Brewster that could possibly harm King James?"

Jones struggled for an answer, then rapped the deck with

his staff, saying fiercely, "No! On my honor, he is no threat to anyone on earth!" Then he paused and there was pain in his gray eyes as he turned to leave. "I wish the two of you would sprout wings and fly off my ship!"

Gilbert watched him leave, then descended from the poop deck. He was turning to go below when a small body shot up the stairs and collided so abruptly with his legs that he nearly fell.

Gaining his balance, he saw Tink, his face white with fear, trying to scramble around him. Catching his arms he said, "Tink—what's wrong?"

At that moment the huge form of Jeff Daggot appeared on the landing below. He was evidently chasing Tink, but stopped abruptly when he saw Winslow.

"What's this about?" Gilbert said.

"That boy stole me tot!" Daggot said. He advanced up the stairs in a threatening position, pointing a dirty finger at Tink. "See? That's me own ale—and I'll have a piece of 'is skin! Teach 'im to steal from Jeff Daggot, I will!"

"Hold it right there, Daggot," Gilbert said at once. "What about this, Tink?"

Tink kept his small body behind Gilbert. He held up a pewter tankard and said in a frightened voice, "Dr. Fuller sent me to get some ale—for William. And I found this—but I didn't know it was *his*!"

"Liar!" Daggot spat out. He reached out a thick hand for the boy which Gilbert knocked away. "Keep your hands off this boy, Daggot! Tink, give me the ale!" Taking the tankard from the boy, he handed it to Daggot, saying, "There's your property."

Daggot stared at it, then suddenly threw it straight into Gilbert's face, shouting, "*You* can 'ave it yourself, Mr. High-and-Mighty!"

Gilbert gasped as the ale caught him open-eyed, and as he threw his hands reflexively to his face he felt Daggot's mighty hands close on his throat, then a smashing blow caught him full in the mouth driving him backward to sprawl helplessly against the steps. He cried out, "Run, Tink!" at the same time kicking out with his good leg.

He had guessed that Daggot would follow up and, blinded though he was, he caught the sailor a solid kick in the groin. Daggot yelled and staggered backward, and Gilbert wiped his eyes free and leaped to his feet.

Daggot's face was a red mask of pain and rage as he started up the stairs with his hands held out like claws. "I'll pop yer eyeballs out like a pair 'o grapes!" he yelled, and with a curse threw himself up the stairs.

Gilbert was struck in the stomach by Daggot's huge head, and the back of his legs struck the top stair. He fell backward, rolling his head to one side just in time to avoid the jabbing thumb which Daggot drove toward his eye. It caught him on the cheek, the dirty nail slicing a gash as neatly as a blade along his cheekbone. He felt the blood well up, but ignoring the pain he drove a knee into the man's belly. It was tough as a board, but it gave. Daggot's wind belched out and he went lax just long enough for Gilbert to roll free and get to his feet.

Daggot was up instantly, and drove a hard blow that crushed Gilbert's mouth against his teeth. He was hit in the belly and lost his wind, then fell backward as he took a low blow. Great sheets of pain flowed upwards and he pulled his knees up to protect himself from the kick he felt sure was coming. It caught him on the bad leg, and when he scrambled to his feet, he was in bad shape.

Daggot was a barroom brawler, and he was out to kill or maim. Gilbert backed away, knowing that he had no chance in such a fight. Someone cried out, but he could not make out the words. Daggot did not hear; he had lain awake nights thinking of this time, and now he would smash the man before him even if he were flogged for it. "I'll smash yer pretty face so she won't love you no more!" he grated between clenched teeth, and he drove toward Gilbert in a rush of flailing fists.

He battered Gilbert's tipped-down head and his fist scraped along the smaller man's chin and nose. He hooked into Gilbert's temple, and then the blows came like deadly rain, starting up a blaze of lights in Gilbert's brain. He felt them and he heard them, but could not stop them and was driven back against a hard object.

His hand closed on an object, and when he pulled at it, it

came loose in his hand—a belaying pin. He had only strength enough to lift it, and as Daggot came roaring in, he brought the heavy weapon down, catching Daggot on the side of the head.

It was a blow that would have knocked a lesser man unconscious, but Daggot's matted hair and thick skull protected him. He went to one knee, his head down, and blood sprinkled the deck from the gash over his left ear.

Gilbert backed away, and Clark came running up. He grabbed Daggot's arm, yelling, "You fool! You'll be . . ." He was not able to finish, for Daggot came to his feet and striking out blindly, caught the First Mate in the stomach with such a powerful blow he fell to the deck gasping for breath.

Daggot stared at the belaying pin in Gilbert's hand, then his eyes drifted to the oak cabinet to his left, just under the rim of the poop deck. It was a small closet used for gear, but Standish had persuaded the captain to let him use it as a storage place for the weapons of the settlers. It was locked, but Daggot ripped the door open with a mighty heave, and when he turned, he had a sword in his hand.

Other voices were crying out, and Gilbert thought he heard the captain, but his vision narrowed until he saw only the glittering blade in Daggot's hand. A silence fell on his ears, and he heard the ragged breathing of the man who was moving toward him with murder in his eyes.

Daggot lunged, blade lowered, and it was a good thrust. Only barely did Gilbert manage to turn the blade aside with a quick movement of the belaying pin, and Daggot recovered quickly, saying under his breath, "That's all right—that's all right—Daggot will get you—that's all right!"

To stand was to die, so Gilbert took his only chance. As Daggot fell into position for another thrust, Gilbert waited until the last possible moment, then threw the pin straight into the man's face. It caught Daggot in the chest, and Gilbert whirled and ran around the longboat making for the bow.

Daggot laughed then, and Gilbert heard the sound of bare feet close on his heels! He reached the forecastle and in one mad leap scrambled on top, hearing the hiss of Daggot's blade as he made a cut.

He rolled over, and looked wildly around, but there was

only the sea in front, and now Daggot was on the deck, his sword poised.

They stood there outlined against the sky, Daggot crouched in the classic pose of the fencer ready to drive home the final thrust; Gilbert standing on the edge of the deckhouse, his hands widespread and waiting.

Daggot laughed, ignoring the voice of Captain Jones. "I'm a'goin' to kill you now," he said, and moved forward.

Gilbert awaited the thrust, knowing that Daggot was too good a swordsman to miss, and there was no fear in him—only regret that it had to end like this. Then a voice cut across the air like a trumpet.

"Gilbert!"

Looking up, Gilbert saw John Howland's head just over the lip of the forecastle deck—and in his hand was a sword!

"Here!" Howland yelled and threw the blade toward Gilbert.

It cartwheeled in the sun, sparkling like glass as it rose. Twice it turned and Gilbert thought, *It's too high!* but he gave a leap and the hilt slapped into his palm with a solid sound.

His feet touched the deck just as Daggot made his lunge, and it must have seemed like magic to the man's eyes.

One second he was driving his blade toward the body of an unarmed man—the next moment he was facing a sliver of steel that drove his own blade to one side and rammed through his chest like an icy dart.

Daggot's lunge carried him face-to-face with Gilbert, and for one moment he stared into the blue eyes, and then the incredible pain wrenched at him. He opened his mouth and said, "You— you ain't . . ." and then his body arched over backward, ripping the sword out of Gilbert's hand.

His body twisted as he fell, and he seemed to be trying to reach the hilt of the blade that nestled against his chest. His own sword hit the deck with a clatter, then he fell.

His lower body hit the top of the forecastle deck, but the heavy torso cleared the side, and he turned a complete somersault, striking the deck a lifeless hulk.

Captain Jones was on the far side of the deck, and he rushed around to find John Alden standing there, but no Daggot.

Alden's eyes were blazing, and there was blood on the front of his jerkin. As the captain stopped short, Alden nodded toward the sea, and there was a challenge in his face as he said calmly, "Man overboard, Captain."

Log: September 20
  Sighted land at dusk. It appears to be Cape Cod, somewhere off the high bluffs at Truro. It being late, we will search the coast for a harbor on the morrow.
  Seaman Jeffery Daggot was lost at sea after falling overboard. Attempts to recover his body were in vain. May God have mercy on his soul.

CHAPTER TWENTY

MUTINY ON THE *MAYFLOWER*

★　★　★　★

They were sixty-five days out from Plymouth, ninety-seven from Southampton. Shouts of joy and tears of relief rang on the morning air as the entire company met to view their new home.

They were close enough to see high brown bluffs and the tops of tall trees, but all was in outline. Captain Jones dared not venture too close to shore, and the leadsman was hard at work feeling for the bottom. "Forty fathoms, thirty fathoms, twenty fathoms."

For half a day they continued this cautious progress down the coast, and it was late when the lookout from the maintop shouted, "Breakers ahead!"

"We'll find a harbor tomorrow," Jones said to the anxious group, and then there was an anticlimactic lull. Passengers wandered over the small deck interfering with the work of the crew, and had to be driven below by orders from the Cabin.

Far into the night the leaders talked, planned for the coming days, and they were caught off guard when a group led by Billington demanded an audience.

"We ain't satisfied with the way things is going, Mr. Bradford," Billington said bluntly. "And we have come to a decision."

William Bradford lifted his head slowly, taking in the group, and he asked quietly, "What is your decision?"

"Why, when we come ashore, we intend to use our own liberty."

"That's right!" Stephen Hopkins piped up, his rabbit-like face twitching eagerly. He nudged Billington, adding, "There's none with the power to command us—not if we land at this spot."

"And why not?" Bradford asked.

"Because this ain't Virginia like we signed for."

"In that you are correct," Bradford nodded. "The charter calls for us to settle south of latitude 41. But we are hundreds of miles north of the Hudson River, and the captain informs us that to beat our way there would be very dangerous. In addition, the captain insists on taking the ship back to England as quickly as possible."

"What this amounts to," Carver said gently, "is that we really have only two choices—settle here, or go back to England."

"We signed for Virginia!" Hopkins said stubbornly. "And if we stay here, we don't see as how we're under your authority."

"It's all Virginia," Bradford said steadily; "this part is called New England."

"I don't know anything about New England," Billington said loudly. "We won't be bound by any power if we don't settle in Virginia."

"We'll elect our own governor!" Hopkins said.

"And you are a candidate, I take it?" Bradford asked acidly.

"Why . . ."

"You were on a voyage to Virginia once before, I believe." Bradford pinned the little man with his eyes.

"Why, yes, I was, and . . ."

"And there was a rebellion against the authority of Sir William Gates, was there not?"

Hopkins' mouth dropped open, and he wiped his chin with a nervous hand. "I don't remember . . ."

Bradford's voice chopped at the little man relentlessly. "And there was a trial in which the members of the conspiracy were convicted of mutiny and rebellion."

"Yes." Hopkins' face was sallow now, and his voice could hardly be heard.

"And all were executed—with one exception, I believe. The man who organized the entire affair was let off because, as the record says, 'He made so much moan alleging the ruin of his wife and children in his trespass.' And the name of that man is—Stephen Hopkins!"

"It wasn't my fault!" Hopkins began to cry, his face contorted with shame. "They made me do it, I didn't want to!"

"And are *they* making you lead this mutiny?" Bradford asked sternly. He pointed his finger at the group, saying, "You will drop this matter at once, do you hear me!"

He did not wait, but pushed by them, saying, "Mr. Carver, Mr. Brewster, come with me."

The rest of the day they spent in the captain's Great Cabin, and the ship was abuzz with rumors. When Bradford stood on the poop deck late in the afternoon and called for a meeting, there was a rush to get a place.

The cabin was crowded, for although no women were there, most of the able-bodied men were. Discontent was in the air, and the faces of the leaders were gray with strain. The thing was settled when Brewster said to Bradford, "William, some sort of terms must be offered to all, strangers as well as saints. We must have a written document embodying the idea that everyone would have fair treatment under the new government."

That paper was in the hands of William Bradford, and he waited until the room grew quiet, then in a steady voice read the Compact:

IN THE NAME OF GOD, AMEN

We whose names are underwritten, the loyal subjects of our dread Sovereign Lord King James by the Grace of God of Great Britain, France, Ireland, King, Defender of the Faith:

Having undertaken, for the Glory of God and advancement of the Christian Faith and honour of our King and country, a voyage to plant the First Colony in the northern parts of Virginia, do by these presents solemnly and mutually in the presence of God and of one another, covenant and combine ourself together into a Civil Body Politic, for the better ordering and preservation and furtherance of the ends aforesaid, and by virtue hereof do enact, constitute and frame such just and equal law, ordinances, acts, constitutions and offices from time to time, as shall be thought most meet and convenient for the general good of the Colony, unto which we promise all due submission and obedience. In witness whereof we have hereunder subscribed our names at Cape Cod, the 11th of November, in the year of the reign of our Sovereign Lord King James of England, France and Ireland, the eighteenth, and of Scotland the fifty-fourth. Anno Domini 1620

"This will be the foundation of our government," Bradford said. He put the paper on the captain's desk, picked up a quill and signed it. Those that were entitled to the term "Master" stepped up, led by John Carver, followed by William Brewster, Edward Winslow, Isaac Allerton, Miles Standish, Samuel Fuller, William White. Then the leaders of the London group signed—Christopher Martin, William Mullins, Richard Waren, Stephen Hopkins.

Then the goodmen were invited to sign—the next social rank below master. Twenty-seven of these signed; then four servants signed on orders from their master. A total of forty-one of the sixty-five males aboard signed. The women were excluded, of course, for they were not free agents, being legal chattel and servants of their husbands.

"We will now proceed to elect a governor who will serve for one year," Bradford said. He stared straight at Stephen Hopkins and John Billington, daring them with his dark eyes to speak, then added, "I offer the name of John Carver."

"I second that name," William Brewster said, and almost before Carver knew what was happening, he was the first popularly elected official in the New World.

Brusquely Bradford dismissed the meeting, and they all trooped up to take a look at their New World.

Captain Jones had invited himself to the meeting, and since it was *his* cabin, there had been no way to exclude him. Now he sat with his back against the bulkhead watching as William Bradford remained to gather up the documents and writing materials. Rising to his feet, he walked to the table and stared down at the long sheet of paper the men had just signed.

Finally he looked up with sober eyes, saying, "This is an unusual thing, Mr. Bradford."

"Yes, Captain, it is—but then, we are leaving the *usual* behind in our venture."

"A Civil Body Politic," Jones read aloud. "That would not

be pleasing to His Majesty, I think. Nor would your manner of choosing a governor. The Crown has always appointed governors of the colonies."

Bradford gave the captain a curious smile, saying, "It is the way we choose our pastor for our congregation—by popular vote."

Jones laughed suddenly. "Well, *that* doesn't sit too well with the King either, you know." Then he added, "Carver is a good man—but it is obvious, Mr. Bradford, that you are the natural leader of the group. Why were you not elected?"

"I would be unacceptable at this time," Bradford said. "Carver is not as—" he sought for a word, then found it. "Not as *direct* as I."

"He is a meek fellow," Jones agreed. "But you will be the power behind the throne, so to speak?"

"I will serve as best I can," Bradford said slowly. "But the heart of our government will lie in this: the people will elect their own rulers."

"That is a dangerous practice!" Jones said. "What if they elect a man who is not able, or who is dishonest?"

"Then others may get together and elect a better man in his place!" Bradford smiled at the perplexity on the captain's face, and added gently, "The Greeks called it 'democracy.' "

"Sooner or later the King will realize that the end of this 'democracy' is the abolition of his own power. What then, Mr. Bradford? Will you deny the power of the Crown?"

"We will follow God's leading, Captain."

Jones stared at him, then shrugged, "Well, I wish you well, Mr. Bradford. I had little use for your ideas when we first met— but I have been most favorably impressed by the behavior of your people."

"Thank you, Captain Jones," Bradford nodded, and then with a look of rare humor in his sober eyes, he asked suddenly, "Does this charitable spirit extend to allowing Mr. Brewster to remain with us when you depart?"

"You *are* a polititian, Bradford!" Jones laughed and slapped the table with his hand. "Well, officially he does not exist on the *Mayflower*—at least under that name. I feel safe enough on that score, so he may stay."

"And Mr. Gilbert Winslow?"

Captain Jones bit his lip and shook his head. "Ah, that's different. He is a violent man—as Mr. Brewster is not."

"He is not really one of us, Captain," Bradford said slowly. "I suspect that you have found out most of his story . . ."

"I have some of it—and it does him no credit." Jones looked inquiringly at Bradford, asking, "He betrayed you—and yet you intercede for him, Mr. Bradford?"

" 'If the Lord should mark iniquities, who should stand?' " Bradford quoted. "I behaved in a very uncharitable manner to the man when he betrayed us—but there is something good in him. His brother Edward is one of the best men I have ever known, and I see some of him in Gilbert Winslow."

"The business yesterday with Daggot—!"

"Surely you of all men will not hold that against him? Your man gave Winslow no choice, did he?"

"No—the fellow was always a troublemaker! And I would have done the same," Jones admitted. "I have noted in my log that he was lost overboard—which is the truth, in a way."

"You must follow your own way in this matter, Captain," Bradford said. "But it is a serious matter to hold a man's destiny in your hands. I suggest that you pray much before you commit yourself to any action."

"Pray?" The suggestion came as a shock to Jones. "I've not been accustomed to praying about such things."

"It is not a bad way," Bradford nodded. He rolled the Mayflower Compact into a tight roll, and there was a stoop to his shoulders as he turned to go topside.

Preparations for the first exploratory voyage were underway. Miles Standish scurried around the deck, seeing to the arms of the men selected to participate, and the crew labored to swing the longboat over the side.

From the crowded decks, the passengers gazed out at the long white sandhills that reminded them of the dunes of Holland; on the other side, bristling forests marched to the water's edge. They roamed from port to starboard, from stern to stem, studying the land before them, their faces a mixture of joy at the arrival and apprehension of what was to come now.

Humility did not join those that watched. She was in the galley begging Hinge for some broth for William Butten.

"Ah, well, we can have a *real* fire now!" the little cook grinned. "Plenty of firewood instead of this cursed charcoal!"

"This is good, Thomas!" Humility said, taking a sip of the steaming broth. "It may help the boy."

"How is he now, miss? The doctor was none too hopeful yesterday."

Humility bit her lip, and there were diamonds in her wide green eyes as she said, "He is very bad, Thomas. Very sick."

"Ah, too bad! Too bad!"

She hurried down the ladder past the crew's mess, then down one more flight to the cargo hold. Balancing the bowl carefully, she pushed the door open and entered.

"Hullo, miss." Tink was sitting in the gloom of the tiny cabin, and he had a frightened look on his face. "William—William is real sick, miss!"

Humility took one look at the pale face of the boy under the blanket, and put the soup down. She knelt by the sick boy and laid her hand on his chest. It did not move, and she was suddenly paralyzed with the thought that he was dead! Then the frail chest heaved, and there was a rasping rattle in William's chest and his eyes opened. He moved his lips and she had to lean forward to catch his words.

"Are—we there? Are we—at—the New World?"

"Don't try to talk, William," she said. Then she rose and whispered, "Has Dr. Fuller been here?"

"No, miss." Tink wiped a tear from his eyes, saying, "William, he keeps askin' for Mr. Winslow. Do you know where he is?"

"I'll get help, Tink," she said quickly. She ran along the lower deck, then up to the waist deck where Fuller was busily engaged in getting ready to go ashore with the party.

"Sam! You've got to come with me! William is dying, I think!"

Fuller stopped probing at the musket in his hands, then he looked directly into Humility's eyes and said, "The boy, he don't need me, lass." Then he dropped his eyes and fumbled with a button on his frayed black coat. "I can't do anything for him now."

"Sam!"

"You ain't blind, lass," Fuller said. "He's been sinking for two days now—I expected to see him go last night."

"But you can't go with him dying!"

Fuller looked haunted, then he sighed and shook his heavy head. "I'm a coward, lass. I just don't have the heart to see the boy go. Get one of the elders to go—Carver would be good. He can pray for the boy—" He broke off abruptly and stepped away from her, joining the small group at the weapons cabinet.

Humility stared at him, angry and frightened. She turned blindly and tried to think, but her mind was spinning.

I can't go back and see him die! she thought wildly, but there was no other way. With the faint hope that Fuller might be wrong, she turned and went down the ladder.

When she got to the cargo deck, a thought came to her, and she turned to enter the water cask room. Directly behind it was a tiny room where a few things were stored, including spirits— mostly beer and ale. *Maybe some wine will help him*, she thought, and with a faint hope she opened the door and began feeling around blindly for a bottle.

She had been there before, watching Alden as he checked the water barrels and the stores, but there had been light then. Now the only light was a faint glow from a lantern that swung halfway down the cargo deck.

The wine—it was in a case by the wall, she thought, and she groped her way along the wall.

She was almost there when her extended hand touched warm flesh!

She gasped as a pair of strong hands grasped her and pulled her into a hard embrace. Blank terror filled her as the smell of alcohol on the man's breath came to her, and the pressure of his body on hers was like fire.

"Let me go!" she cried out, and with both hands she beat at her captor, but she was helpless against his strength. "Help me!" she screamed, and then he spoke.

"Go on—scream all you want, Humility!"

She stopped struggling and whispered, "Gilbert? Is it you?"

"Who else would be getting drunk and attacking innocent girls in the wine cellar?"

The reply was bitter, and his voice was slightly slurred with the wine. He pulled her even closer and suddenly kissed her before she knew what he was doing.

The touch of his lips was a shock that ran along her nerves, and suddenly she felt herself yield to his embrace! There was no reason in it, and her mind was screaming, *No! Don't let him touch you!* but her body rebelled and she felt herself relax as he pulled her closer; to her horror she felt herself raising her arms to put around his neck.

With a cry of disgust—not at him, but at herself—she pulled herself back and slapped his face with a quick blow.

"You—you *beast!*"

He laughed, and pulled her closer. "The scum of the earth!—and he's holding you in his arms, Humility." Then he added, "And you don't hate it as much as you pretend, do you?"

She felt her face burn, for he had sensed her response to his embrace. She ceased to struggle, and said quietly, "All right, Gilbert, shame me if you will—you can't say anything to me I haven't said to myself."

At once he dropped his arms, and they stood there in the darkness, memories of the past brushing against them.

Finally he said, "Don't blame yourself, Humility—you've done nothing wrong."

"The way I let myself love you—*that* was wrong!" she cried out.

"No, you just didn't have any defenses against a scoundrel," he said wearily.

She could not bear the scene, so she said, "William is dying—I came to get him some wine."

"All right." His voice was dead, and he said only, "Let's go to him."

They left the room, and she saw by the pale amber light of the lantern his face was swollen, the raw wound made by Daggot's thumbnail crusted with blood that he had not bothered to wash away.

"You'll get an infection if that cut isn't taken care of."

He had a brown gall bottle in his hand, and he looked at it, saying, "This may help him."

She stared at him. "You could die from that kind of infection. Don't you care?"

"No."

She stared at him, then wheeled and led him swiftly to the sail room. William lay still, his breath coming in a short, choppy rasp. He opened his eyes, and whispered, "Are we—home—Mr. Winslow?"

Gilbert knelt beside the boy, lifted the thin body hot with fever and poured a few drops of brandy into the trembling lips.

"You're almost home, William."

"Mr. Winslow—I—I—" He broke off, and his eyes rolled backward for a moment, then they came back to fasten on Winslow's face. "Me—and Tink—we're going to—to have—" He faltered again, and his body was suddenly rent by a racking cough.

"We'll have us a place, William!" Tink cried. He wiped the streaming tears from his thin face and patted the dying boy's hand. "We're home."

"Will you—take me—to see it—Mr. Winslow?" William gasped.

Gilbert looked over the boy's head and met Humility's tear-stained face. The anger toward him was gone, and she nodded numbly, her lips forming a *yes!*

Gilbert scooped the thin form up, and Humility tucked the worn blanket around him; they made their way along the dark corridor and up the three flights of steps.

The sky was dark, but William closed his eyes tightly. "It's so bright!"

Everyone stopped to stare at them, and a quiet fell on the busy deck. Gilbert's bloodstained, beaten face, Humility's expression of grief, and the thin form of the dying Butten threw a blanket of silence over the deck.

Gilbert carried the boy to the bow, and he felt Humility close beside him. When they got in the very apex of the deck, he turned and held the boy high, facing the shore.

"There's your New World, William," he said gently.

The boy's eyes opened slowly, and as he stared at the shore, a smile came across his parched lips.

"Ain't it—ain't it—*good*—Mr. Winslow?"

"Yes, William," Gilbert said hoarsely, his voice breaking so that he could say no more.

As the sea lifted the *Mayflower* gently, Gilbert felt Humility press closer, and Tink grabbed him by the waist sobbing uncontrollably.

The sky was gray as ashes, featureless and stark. Gusts of cold wind swept across the deck, and the shore seemed alien and hostile where it touched the sullen breakers. The harsh cry of a gull seemed an evocation of doom, and there was a brittle, fragile quality about the ship thrown into relief against the eternal whisperings of the sea.

Bradford saw that the scene was evoking sharp fears in the spectators. He raised his voice, piercing the gloom with his words, "Put away your fears, dear brothers. It is true we have no friends to welcome us. We have no shelter at hand, and winter is nigh. We hoped for a paradise, but we will be content with a desert if God so wills."

The sharp wind caught at his words, making them weak and ragged, so he cried out in a powerful manner, like an Old Testament prophet, "One day our children will say, 'Our fathers were Englishmen who came over this great ocean and were ready to perish in this wilderness. But they cried unto the Lord and He heard their voice and looked upon their adversity.' Let us therefore praise the Lord because He is good and His mercies endure forever!"

As Bradford began to pray, Gilbert felt a slight movement in the frail body he held, and then heard a single brief sigh.

"William?" Humility whispered. She gripped Gilbert's arm tightly and then looked up into his face.

He looked down into William's still, pale face, now relaxed with no trace of strain—then he looked back into the face of Humility and spoke in a gentle voice, the tears running freely down his scarred face:

"William has gone home, my dear."

PART THREE

THE
NEW WORLD

★ ★ ★ ★

CHAPTER TWENTY-ONE

FIRST LOOK AT EDEN

★ ★ ★ ★

They buried William Butten at sea, sewn into a canvas tarp with a bag of sand for ballast.

Gilbert's face was set like flint as the tiny body slid off the board, making a small splash in the sea, and as he turned to go, he met Humility's eyes, but she at once whirled and turned to avoid him.

The next day was washday, the women being put ashore early under an armed guard to do the family wash. While they were beating, scrubbing, and rinsing heaps of dirty clothes and bedding, the children ran wildly up and down the beach under the watchful eyes of sentries. The men brought in the shallop stored between decks on the *Mayflower* and beached her for repairs, for she had been badly battered and bruised by the storms at sea and her seams had been opened up.

As a gang went to work under the direction of Francis Eaton, the ship's carpenter, the rest prowled the beach and tidal flats in search of shellfish. Ravenous for fresh food, they made a great feast that night on tender soft-shell clams and succulent young quahogs, and also put away many large mussels—which proved to be a grave error, for the mussels made them deathly sick.

That night, against Governor Carver's will, they decided to send an exploring party inland. "There is a river, the captain says, and it would be safer to take the shallop in by that means."

"The craft won't be ready for days," Edward Winslow objected at once.

"And the weather is getting foul," Bradford added. "We *must* find our ground as quickly as possible."

"But what about the savages?" Carver asked.

"And the wild beasts?" William Mullins shook his head fearfully. "There may be elephants!"

"Elephants?" Standish snorted in derision. "Nonsense, Mr. Mullins—there are no fabulous beasts here."

Mullins triumphantly lifted a book, crying, "But here is proof!" He opened the book and showed them a crude picture of very fat animals being hunted by savages. "This is the book by John White, his pictures, the first ever made in Virginia!"

The men crowded around to stare, and he flipped the pages proudly. "See, there's the prince of the savages, Saturiba, walking with his queen!" He pointed to an engraving of mostly naked figures of noble-looking Indians. By the chief's side walked young men carrying great fans, while behind him walked another wearing gold and silver balls hanging from a little belt around his hips.

"I've seen those books!" Miles Standish growled. "They're made to sell—not to tell the truth."

They argued back and forth, and finally Bradford said waspishly, "Well, we can't sit here in this ship waiting for a royal welcoming committee. Tomorrow, Captain Standish, you will take fifteen men on an expedition. We must locate as soon as possible!"

The next day Edward put a hand on Gilbert's arm. "I want you with us on this exploration."

"Why? I'll not be staying here." There was a bitter light in Gilbert's eyes, but Edward ignored it.

"You need to get away from this ship. And who can say about what's to come?"

Gilbert stared at him, then smiled. "All right. I'll come."

Fifteen able men joined on deck at dawn, including Miles Standish, William Bradford, Edward and Gilbert, John Alden, Stephen Hopkins, William White, John Billington, Christopher Martin, Isaac Allerton, Sam Fuller, and the three hired sailors, English, Trevore, and Ellis.

The distance from the *Mayflower* was something under a mile, a matter of thirty minutes' pulling. The men piled out on the sandy beach, sending the boat back with the sailors.

The party turned down a gully where the growth was sparse and proceeded up through the trees. There were evergreens here and there, but otherwise the dead hand of winter had stripped the trees. Nevertheless they managed to identify a goodly number of species: boxberry, shrub oaks, oaks, aspen, beech, wild plum and cherry, holly and juniper.

As they filed across a stretch of marshy ground, a huge crane rose into the air, followed by the quicker flight of a cloud of waterfowl. Early winter dusk was already darkening the air, and they had seen no sign of human life. Confused in the wasteland, they unwittingly turned north and came upon the beach again, and decided to advance, hoping to find a better path inland. Again the men began to straggle so that Gilbert and Standish forged ahead about four hundred yards.

Suddenly Gilbert lifted his head, and squinted into the falling darkness. "Look, Miles!" he said, pointing down the beach.

Three quarters of a mile away Standish saw the black dots of human figures. Five or six men were coming along the shore toward them, and they had a dog with them. "Come up! Come up!" Standish called to the party, and as they halted, he passed his smoldering slow wick and each set a glowing tip to the end of his own cord and clipped it into his gun in readiness.

"Tightly, now," Standish commanded, and led the little troop forward. As they progressed, the figures in the distance suddenly turned and disappeared.

Standish led the group to the spot, pointing down at imprints of bare feet in the sand.

"We'll follow," he said, and stalked up the incline toward the sand hills. The men plunged over the dunes, and Standish called out, "Be ready for attack!"

"This is a little dangerous, Miles," Gilbert panted as they slid and stumbled through the undergrowth. "A perfect spot for an ambush."

"So it is, but I want to make contact—find what we're up against."

They found nothing, though, and by noon when they were

permitted to rest, they were hungry as bears. Washing down their cheese and biscuit-bread with water from a spring, they rested for almost two hours, then Standish roused them up, and they thrashed around all afternoon, coming back to the beach to make night camp. William Mullins was so afraid that he slept little, muttering deliriously and crying out in fear at every owl hoot, but most of them lay like stones. The stars came out, and Gilbert rose once to feed the fire with juniper sticks. He relieved Standish who was standing guard, and the two talked quietly for a short time sitting under the distant stars. So the night passed.

They were up at dawn, and traveled a long distance, but mostly in wavering lines; they never got more than five miles from the beach, and it was about two in the afternoon when they found the cornfield.

Standish spotted it first, and called to the others, "Here's something!" He was standing on the edge of an irregular field of stubble. It was a large-stalked, thinly spaced stubble, but obviously not wild. "A planted field!" Bradford exclaimed. They spread out and found another field adjoining, and there, half buried in the sand, were four weather-beaten timbers—ship's planks, obviously the remains of some sort of man-made hut.

"See here!" John Alden cried, stooping to scoop something up. "A kettle!" He held up a rusty iron pot, and insisted on taking it along as they continued their exploration.

At the edge of the field Billington found a small mound, and called them over, saying, "Maybe it's buried gold!"

"Looks more like a grave to me," Mullins muttered.

They fell into an argument, Billington leading those who felt they might find something valuable, and Bradford reluctant to disturb a grave. Finally, he agreed, and they began feverishly throwing the earth high in the air.

"Who knows?" Billington cried out. "Maybe an Indian king with jewels in 'is ears! Maybe gold nuggets!"

Finally they came against a hard surface, and scooping out the last of the dirt, Billington pulled out a woven basket. He instantly turned it over and a shower of yellow fell to the ground.

"Gold!" Billington shouted, and they all took it up.

"Corn, you fool!" Standish said in disgust.

Bradford picked up a handful of the grain and there was a prophetic gleam in his dark eyes as he said quietly, "To think that God led us to this very spot—out of all the vast empty spaces in this land!"

"We ought to put it back, cover it up as we found it," Edward said.

"No!" Billington shouted. "It's ours now."

"Take it," Standish said at once, and there was a sharp debate; Gilbert exchanged amused glances with Edward as the men wavered between greed and their holy duty. They finally dug farther into the mound and found a larger basket also filled with corn.

Finally Bradford said, "Very well, we'll take what we can carry—for seed corn. But we'll make every attempt to find the natives and explain our intentions—to pay for what we have taken."

Since such a thing seemed highly unlikely, Billington's faction agreed, and they left with bulging pockets filled with corn.

They got sick of the kettle, for it was heavy and awkward, and by nightfall they were glad to make their second camp. The next morning they wandered back toward the shore, discovering the river mouth that had been seen from the *Mayflower*, and later on a sandy bank, a dugout canoe, consisting simply of a tree trunk shaped by fire into a long narrow boat. Mullins suggested they might put the heavy iron pot in it and paddle back to their starting point, but Bradford insisted on leaving it in place, and Standish led them back toward the harbor. Night overtook them, and they were forced to make camp again. The next afternoon, Friday, the seventeenth of November, they reached the harbor and fired the signal shot that brought the longboat to return them to the *Mayflower*.

As they were on their way back to the ship, Edward leaned forward and said quietly, "Not the paradise most people are expecting, is it Gilbert?"

The sober look on Gilbert's face was broken as a wry grin drew his broad lips upward, and he murmured, "As Edens go, I expect it's about average."

"You're right, but dreams don't follow logic," Edward mused. He cast his eyes back toward the barren shore, then shook his head sadly. "This place is likely to break the spirit of the fainthearted."

"Are you having second thoughts, Edward?"

"*Second* thoughts!" Edward frowned. "Man, I've had a *hundred* thoughts, wondering what in God's name brought us to this place!"

"A dream, Bradford says."

"Aye, a dream, but is it a good dream—or will it turn out to be a nightmare?"

"I wonder if Bradford or Carver ever have doubts?" Gilbert asked. "They seem so certain that God is in all this."

"I doubt they ever think of it," Edward snorted. "They're visionaries, Gilbert. Prophets who've heard from God. The rest of us are risking everything on their vision."

A cold wind stung Gilbert's face, and he stared at the rolling water that tossed the longboat like a chip. All morning the sun had been muffled with fat, dark clouds, and even now there was an ominous keening as the winds gathered up and cut across the sea. He stared at his hands, red with cold, and then looked up, saying, "I've never been much for dreams, Edward. Right now the whole thing looks pretty grim to me. I won't be here if Jones has his way, but if I were staying, there'd be some fear in my heart, I think."

"Don't give up, Gilbert," Edward said instantly. He put his hand on his brother's shoulder and added, "I'm not much on theology myself, but I can't think God brought you this far for no purpose."

"You think God is in such dire need of men He has to use a traitor and a murderer to build a New World?"

"Ah, Gilbert!" Edward shook his head and said energetically, "Forbear that, I beg you! You're no murderer, nor traitor either, not in your soul. You've taken a fall—well, what young man doesn't, I ask ye?"

As the men piled onto the deck, there was an excited hum of voices, and Priscilla Mullins caught at John Alden with her eyes wide, saying, "John, what was it like?"

The big cooper smiled down at her, and pulled her off to sit beside the rail. He did not note the hard look that her father gave him, but began spinning the tale to the delighted girl.

Bradford smiled at the crowd, but shook his head. "We have good news. The land is fertile." He reached into the kettle held by Allerton and Billington, allowing the golden grain to trickle through his fingers. "See, the grain of the new land!"

As everyone crowded close to see, Brewster came close and said in a low tone, "William, you'd best go see Dorothy."

"Dorothy? Why? Is she ill?"

"I think so."

Bradford nodded, and leaving Edward to tell of their findings, he followed Brewster into the first hold. "What's wrong with her, William? She was fine when we left."

Brewster stopped so abruptly that Bradford bumped into him. "No, she was not. She hasn't been well for some time."

Bradford stared into the eyes of William Brewster, perplexity scoring his craggy face. He tried to think, then said, "I hadn't noticed she was ill."

"You must pay more heed to her, William. She's not strong."

"Why, I hadn't thought . . . !"

"No, you've been so caught up with the people, it's escaped your notice. But she needs your love and assurance more than anyone else on this ship."

They found her in the tiny cabin, sitting on the bunk with her hands folded in her lap. The light of the flickering candle threw a shattered light over her face, and the sight of her drew a sudden gasp from William Bradford.

She was staring emptily at the wall, her face etched by the rigors of the journey. She had been plump and pretty, but there was a cadaverous look about her as she sat there. Her cheeks were drawn in, and the outline of her teeth could be seen through her thin lips.

But it was not that which shocked Bradford so much as the emptiness of her eyes. She had always had bright eyes, her best feature, but now they were dull, almost as if filmed with some opaque material.

She was singing under her breath, so faintly that Bradford had to lean forward to hear. It was a nursery rhyme, one he had heard her sing often to John when he was an infant.

Bradford leaned forward and caught the faint words: *I'm a*

little lost lamb—a little lost lamb—Far, far away from home!

"Dorothy," he said gently. "Dorothy, are you all right?"

She did not respond, but kept her eyes fastened on the wall, and sang again, *I'm a little lost lamb . . ."* Then she smiled and murmured softly, "I found the doll you made me, Papa. It was under my bed."

Shock raked across Bradford's face, and he could not seem to move. He stood there, leaning over his wife, his eyes wide, his heavy lower lip drooping. Finally he straightened up and stared blindly at William Brewster. He formed the words with his lips: "She's mad!"

William Brewster's face was filled with pain as he nodded. "She is indeed a little lost lamb, William. A little lost lamb!"

CHAPTER TWENTY-TWO

DOROTHY

★ ★ ★ ★

Log: Friday December 4
   Cape Cod. Weather continues to worsen. Temperature falling, and rain threatening to turn to snow. Settlers have been in conference daily trying to make a decision on place of final settlement. Many want to settle at Corn Hill, while others cite its want of adequate water supply. They would have to depend on fresh-water ponds which would dry up in summer. Coffin has volunteered to guide an expedition to a good harbor not far across the bay. Much weakness among people. Thompson, servant of William White, dies.

The news of Edward Thompson's death came as no shock, for he had been failing for days. The men were in one of the endless debates on where to settle when Sam Fuller entered the hold, sat down heavily, his head bowed.

"What's wrong, Mr. Fuller?" Hopkins asked.

"Edward just died."

A silence settled on the group; then Billington shrugged, saying, "He'd not have lasted the winter."

The death of Thompson sobered both sides, and they finally agreed to make one more exploration. Coffin, the man who knew the coast best, vowed there was a navigable river and a good harbor less than twenty-four miles around the coast.

O'Neal asked the pilot why he was giving aid to the settlers when he'd never had anything but contempt for them.

"Because I'm interested in my own hide, that's why!" Coffin cursed and went on, "The captain, he's bewitched by these whey-faced psalm-singers! You ain't heard him say nothin' about going home, have you? No! Gone soft, 'e has! He'll stay around this cursed place all winter, and what'll we have to eat on the way home, I ask you? We'll starve, that's what! And that's why I'm gonna' show 'em a good spot; then they'll be off the ship and we can get away from this place!"

As soon as the expedition left, the weather began playing diabolical games with the *Mayflower*. Rolling swells and gusty blasts of freezing rain combined to roll the ship till she heaved and strained at her anchor. There was no possibility of going ashore, and what was happening to the small force caught in such weather, they dared not think.

Gilbert had not gone on the expedition, his place being taken by Peter Brown. The only warmth on the ship was in the small galley, and he had joined Tink there on the second afternoon after the departure.

They were hugging the small fire when Samuel Fuller came in and poured himself a cup of the hot tea that Hinge kept for a favored few. The burly physician was thinner than when they had left England, and Gilbert noticed that his hands were not steady.

He drank the tea silently, not seeming to taste it, then looked at Tink and said, "You know the forecastle, lad?"

"Yes, sir!"

"Well, there's a small leather bag in a wooden box under my bunk. Go fetch it, and I shouldn't be surprised but what there was a treat in it for you. Run now!"

Waiting until Tink dashed away in search of his prize, Fuller stared moodily at the fire, then lifted his broad face to Gilbert. "I've no liking for you, Winslow."

"That's clear enough, Mr. Fuller." Gilbert stared at him, shrugged, and said, "I can't blame you."

Fuller slapped his thigh angrily, and said loudly, "I'm too hard—too hard! That's what I am!"

Gilbert asked, "Something's wrong, isn't it?"

"Yes!" Fuller turned the cup over in his hands nervously, then looked up and said, "It's Mrs. Bradford."

"She's worse?"

"Every day she slips a little deeper into that black pit that's swallowing her up. I told Bradford not to go on that expedition!"

"Doesn't he know how sick she is?"

"He don't know anything but his New World! Blind—blind as a mole!"

"Can't you do anything?"

"You're a smart man, Gilbert Winslow. You know doctors can't do much, even for physical ailments. What can we do about a mind that's dying?"

Gilbert stared at Fuller. "It frightens me, Fuller. I suppose I have as much courage as the average man, but this is—well, it sends cold chills all over me when I look into her eyes."

"Ay, that's the way it strikes all of us."

"Is there nothing that can be done?"

Fuller squinted at Gilbert, nodded slowly, and said, "Stay with her, man. I know it's hard, but she likes you. You and Humility—she seems less likely to go into one of those spells when someone she likes is there."

"All right." Gilbert stood up and gave a long look at the physician. "I'll go see her now."

Fuller mustered a small smile. "Good man!" and there was a warmer light in his brown eyes than Gilbert had seen for some time.

Leaving the galley, Gilbert made his way along the deck slippery with rain, then down the ladder to the first hold. With an effort of will he knocked on the door, and when Dorothy said, "Come in," he entered the small cabin.

She got up and put her hand out, a smile on her face. A wave of relief swept through him as he saw that she was herself—pale and wan, but without the blank expression he had dreaded to find.

"I thought you went with the others," she said. Her hand in his was fragile, like a tiny bird's bones, and her face was hollow and sunken. Only her eyes were alert, and she pulled him toward a chair. "Sit down and put that cover over you. You must be frozen!"

They sat and talked for thirty minutes, mostly of things they had left behind in England. She seemed to have blocked the new life out of her mind, for she spoke only of her garden in Holland, of her friends she had left, of the activities of the Green Gate Church—never of anything in the future.

When the conversation lagged, Gilbert spotted a folio on a shelf and picked it up.

"Ah—Mr. Shakespeare's play, *The Tempest*, have you been reading it?"

"Oh, I don't understand such things," she answered. "Mr. Bradford says that such things are dangerous."

Gilbert scanned the pages, and she watched him. Then she said, "Read some of it, Gilbert."

He paused at the page he was on, looked up, then began to read:

> Our revels now are ended. These our actors,
> As foretold you, were all spirits, and
> Are melted into air, into thin air:
> And, like the baseless fabric of this vision,
> The cloud-capp'd towers, the gorgeous palaces,
> The solemn temples, the great globe itself—
> Yea, all which it inherit—shall dissolve
> And, like this insubstantial pageant faded,
> Leave not a rack behind. We are such stuff
> As dreams are made on, and our little life
> Is rounded with a sleep.

He lifted his eyes, about to comment on the lines, but she said in a weary tone: "That's what I've been feeling, Gilbert."

"What, Dorothy?"

"Why, like the poem says, everything is so frail! The earth is going to dissolve. That's what I've been feeling lately." She gave him a trembling smile, then brushed her hand across her eyes. "It's true, isn't it? Nothing lasts."

Gilbert was trapped, wishing desperately that Carver or Brewster were on hand to handle the question. His own mind was not clear on such things, but he knew he had to give her some encouragement.

"Why, things change, of course," he said. "But when the old things pass, new ones come along. Like your garden in Leyden," he said quickly. "It was beautiful, but you'll have one here, too."

She did not respond, but kept her eyes fixed on the candle that threw a flickering light over the dark room. It seemed to fascinate her, and as she spoke, her speech was slower, slurred as if she were very sleepy.

"But—it's not real. Like the poem says, we are made of stuff like dreams. That's what life is, Gilbert—a dream—like a dream. . . ."

Her voice trailed off, and he saw with a shock that her eyes were fixed and glassy. Taking her arm he gave her a shake, saying loudly, "Dorothy! Life's not like that at all!"

She did not hear, and her hand was limp and lifeless as he took it, cold as ice.

"It's all a dream . . ." she murmured, and then she started singing the song he had heard her sing before. "I'm a lost lamb . . ." and over and over in the darkness she sang the song and said, "It's a dream."

He sat there holding her hand, from time to time saying her name, and the horror of it rived him like a sword. This was not Dorothy sitting beside him, he knew, but something else. Where was the attractive, witty woman who had charmed him in Leyden? What held her in such a fell embrace and left him sitting with an empty shell of a woman? As time dragged on, he fought valiantly, forcing himself to remain when every nerve cried out to flee the dark cabin and the thing that sat beside him.

Finally, the door opened and Humility stood there. She was outlined against the door, her face still and yet moving as she looked into the countenance of her friend. Then she entered and asked, "She's bad, isn't she?"

"Very bad!" Gilbert breathed. He got up, and his hands were trembling.

She looked up at him, and there was some of the old affection in her eyes as she said, "You've been good to stay."

"I wish—!"

She shrugged and sat down, taking Dorothy's thin hand. "I know. It's in God's hands. I'll stay with her now."

He nodded, and the last thing he saw was Humility pulling Dorothy's head against her breast as she would a sick child.

Humility remained with Dorothy in the small cabin for twenty-four hours, and finally dropped, exhausted, into sleep.

Dorothy had slept off and on, but when she awakened and found her hand released and Humility lying on the floor asleep, she lay there for a long time staring at the candle.

The winds were whistling through the sails, and the motion of the boat was hypnotic.

"I'm a poor lost lamb—I'm a poor lost lamb . . ." she breathed softly, then put the cover aside and stood up. The cabin was cold, and she shivered as the air struck her. She leaned forward peering at Humility intently; then a small smile touched her lips and she put a finger on her lips and whispered, "You sleep, Mama—I'll go outside and play with my dolls."

Softly she tiptoed through the cargo hold, carefully avoiding the sleeping forms, and when she got to the ladder leading upward, she giggled with her hand over her mouth. She climbed the stairs and went out on the deck.

The ocean was a beast, rolling from side to side and growling deep, but she did not heed the crashing of the waves against the sides, but made her way quickly to the bow. There she leaned out and stared down at the water that seemed to be alive.

"I'm a little lost lamb . . ." she murmured, and leaned farther to see into the green depths of the great water that licked the sides of the dark hull.

The prow went down sharply, and then rose high in the air, and the sudden movement frightened her. She began to cry, calling out, "Papa! Papa! Where are you, Papa?"

Her thin cries were swallowed up by the roar of the wind, and waves licked higher up on the hull. She turned to go back along the deck, then came to a large box beside the rail.

Carefully she climbed up on top of it, then turned to look over the rail, now up to her knees. The ship seemed to drop, then lurched sideways as she started to step down, and the sudden movement threw her off balance.

Her feet slipped, and she shot over the rail crying once before she reached the freezing water, *Oh, William!* Then she struck the hard green water; darkness enveloped her as she went down, head over heels. The icy coldness seared her lungs, and she opened her mouth to scream, but it filled with salty water. Then she slid into utter darkness, dragged down by the claws of a powerful undercurrent.

The tide rolled her gently toward the deep sea, her skirts wafting slowly, a sea flower, her hands white fingers of coral, her hair fine streaming sea grass.

When the shallop approached the *Mayflower* on Wednesday, the sun shone brightly and the air was milder than it had been for days—almost like a fine fall day.

Gilbert was standing in the bow, his head down, exhausted from the search he had made in the small boat for Dorothy's body. He had driven himself long after Fuller and Humility had said, "It's no use, Gilbert—she's gone."

A shout rang out, "There's the craft!" and a moment later the rail was lined with women looking for their husbands. They waved as the shallop came in, bending on the wind, crying out to the small figures in it.

Nearer and nearer came the craft, until they could be identified: old John Carver, Alden, Edward Winslow, Hopkins, Billington, White, and the rest.

As the boat was made fast and the men started up, Brewster made his way forward, his face a mask. He must be the one to tell Bradford.

Hopkins jumped to the deck, yelling "Arrows!" and began to tell of the Indian attack; then the others piled on deck.

William Bradford was one of the last to mount the ladder, and as the others were shouting and hugging their wives, Brewster took him and drew him beneath the projecting weather-beaten deck of the poop.

Bradford looked quickly at the older man, noting the sorrow in his eye and the silence in the midst of the uproar.

Quickly he said, "Dorothy—she's worse?"

Brewster took a deep breath, then said quietly, "She's gone, Will—our Dorothy's gone to be with the Lord!"

The rawboned, harsh-featured man stood there staring at Brewster, and then without a word he turned and made his way below, going down into the dark recesses of the deck, into the cabin where her things still were, and shut the door. He stumbled about with little half-formed cries, seeking a corner in which to hide, finally falling on his face, grinding his forehead into the rough planking and calling her name again and again.

CHAPTER TWENTY-THREE

"It Will Be All Right!"

★ ★ ★ ★

"I think we must go to Plymouth Harbor, Captain."

Christopher Jones, looking up in surprise to see William Bradford standing before his desk, did not answer for a moment, so shocked he was at Bradford's appearance. It had been three days since the party came back, and Bradford had kept to his cabin all that time.

There was something pitiful to Jones about the way the minister held his back straighter than usual, but he said only, "I agree, Mr. Bradford. Are your people agreed on settlement at Plymouth Harbor?"

Bradford stared at him, then said quietly, "I will do the agreeing, Captain Jones. Please get underway as soon as is convenient."

Bradford wheeled and marched directly to the lower deck. As he came to the small area used for meetings, a silence fell on the group of men who had been loudly debating the issue of choosing a harbor.

"Well, Mr. Bradford," William Mullins said haltingly, "you've come to help us decide on which harbor we will choose for our permanent settlement." Mullins cast a look around, seeking encouragement from the others, and added, "Some would have us settle at Corn Hill, while others would like—"

"We set sail at once for Plymouth Harbor." The tone of Bradford's voice was no softer than the rocks on the harbor half a mile away; he settled back on his heels, rifled the group with a steady gaze, and said, "We have no choice. Corn Hill has no permanent water supply, and that alone is sufficient reason to eliminate it."

"But we must discuss . . ." Billington raised his voice, but was cut off at once by Bradford.

"Governor Carver has made the decision, and we sail at once."

Every eye turned to the elderly Carver, who suddenly seemed uncomfortable. He twisted this way and that, and finally nodded reluctantly, saying, "Yes, that is what we must do."

Everyone knew instantly that Mr. Carver was incapable of such a radical decision, that William Bradford was the power behind the throne; but none dared challenge the direct stare of the small man standing there like a rock.

Suddenly there was a loud rattle as the anchor chain began to draw, and Bradford said with a nod, "We will begin work on our first building as soon as Captain Jones can drop anchor."

As the group broke up, Edward said to Sam Fuller, "He's changed, Sam."

"Right enough! And for the better, I say!"

"I thought he'd die in that cabin for three days. I don't think he ate a bite."

"He's always been a driving man, but he's got a look in his eye, ain't he, Edward?"

Edward nodded slowly. He stared at the departing Bradford, and said, "He's the one man who can make a plantation in this place, Sam. Too bad it took the loss of his wife to get a fire built in him."

"There's going to be more than Bradford losing their people—and not as far away as all that, either." The heavy face of the doctor reflected the strain that he'd worked under, and he gave a helpless gesture with his hands as he turned and left Winslow alone.

The *Mayflower* weighed anchor and headed for Plymouth. With a stiff breeze blowing from the northwest, Jones slipped between the long sandspits that almost enclosed the harbor. He hauled around to the north, dropping anchor just as dark fell.

The entire company came on deck, ignoring the cold, to stare at the land, their journey's end.

A long arm of sand lay between the ship and the land. In the opposite direction a mile of uneven mud flats stretched from inner water to shore, intersected by many pools. It looked barren, huge, like the earth after the Flood receded and exposed a dying world. But far off lay the solid land, a virgin land of timber, hill, and plain.

"A miracle that we got in," Captain Jones said quietly to William Brewster who stood by him. "Another hour and the wind would have changed again."

"A miracle, Captain?" Brewster said quickly, with a sly gleam in his eye. "I thought you didn't believe in such things."

Jones ducked his head, then raised a hand to scratch his nose. "Well . . ." he finally grinned, "I suppose there are always exceptions."

Then the voice of Coffin giving instructions to the seamen up in the yards came loud and clear: "Drop the mainsail—but reef it for easy flyin'. This is their graveyard, ain't it now? We'll be off in a couple of days and they can start their dyin'!"

Jones opened his mouth to rebuke the man, but Brewster put a restraining hand on his arm. "He's partly right, you know."

"What?"

"Why, the land has only two uses for man—to live on and to bury each other in. And if we do the first according to God's will, why, the other will not be difficult."

The next day was the Sabbath, and once more the saints from Leyden refused to violate it. Many of the crew had come to respect the iron-firm convictions of the settlers, even to admire the way these people lived their faith. "They ain't no Sunday men!" was the way John Parker put it. "Always the same!"

Early on Monday, a party was sent ashore to explore. They probed the wide mouth of a brook which emptied into the bay and found good soil, supporting a thick cover of pine, walnut, beech, ash, birch, hazel, and sassafras. But the ground was too heavily wooded to be cleared quickly. They called on God for direction, and decided to settle on the high ground along the brook in the southern part of the harbor, just behind the huge rock that reached up out of the sea.

That night Mary Allerton, the tailor's wife, was brought to bed and delivered of a son, but he was stillborn.

"God grant we get off this ship before we all die," William Mullins groaned. He was ill, and a dozen others lay prostrate in their bunks. That night Richard Bitteridge of London was sewed into his shroud. He had died on shore at dawn, and braving the wind and rain, they dug a shallow grave for him on the low hill just above the shore. All that day and all the next day the storm continued to beat down on the shivering men ashore, but then the weather improved and on Monday, December 25, work began in earnest.

All able-bodied men went ashore—some to fell timber, some to saw, some to rive, and some to carry. On the north side of the brook, just above the beach, they chose a site and laid the foundations of what they called their Common House. Close by, to house the workers left ashore each night, they threw up a number of temporary shelters, conical huts of branches and turf. Late in the afternoon an Indian alarm had sent all running for their muskets, but nothing came of it.

Captain Jones watched the weary men drag themselves on board. "Not much of a Christmas for them, is it?"

Brewster smiled and tugged at his gray beard. "We don't observe the day, Captain. To us it's just a human invention—a Roman corruption—just a survival from heathen days."

"No special meal, no gifts?"

"Well . . ." Brewster admitted slowly, "We *do* like to have a good meal, a little better than usual. But I suppose we'll have to forego that. We drank the last of our beer some days ago, and the larder is pretty lean."

Jones smiled and excused himself. Later as the settlers were sitting down to a sparse meal with plain water, he appeared with seaman O'Neal behind him carrying a keg, and Davis, a hulking sailor with one arm, carrying a large box.

"Why, Captain Jones!" Carver said in surprise, looking up from his plate. "You've come to join us?"

"If I may. And since I'm unexpected company, I brought a little something to add to the supper."

A hum went up as the seamen set their burdens down, and Jones asked innocently, "I am not familiar with your customs,

Governor. Are you allowed to drink beer?"

"Beer!" Carver beamed, and looking around with pleasure, he nodded rapidly and said, "There's nothing in our doctrine that forbids that!"

"Ah—and nothing against plum cake and these few dainties?"

"Indeed not!" Carver said. He looked on the neat form of Jones and said, "Bless you, Captain Jones!"

"I was afraid you might think I was trying to corrupt you into celebrating Christmas, Mr. Carver," Jones said with a sly smile touching his gray eyes.

Carver gave him a direct look, then said seriously, "No, sir. You are a good man, Captain. We all know that. I would that you were of our faith."

Jones stared at Carver, started to say something, then apparently changed his mind. "That is a rare compliment, and I shall treasure it, Mr. Carver," he said simply.

Humility had found Peter Brown seated beside her at the meal, and for the next week, he found an excuse to talk to her every day. She wrote to her best friend in Leyden, Hope Stewart:

> My dear Hope, there is no way to mail this letter, of course, but one day a ship will come and bring it to your door.
>
> The men started building our houses on December 25, and although the weather was bad the next day, on Wednesday and Thursday, all was clear and the party was back at work.
>
> It was decided to assign unmarried men to each family to save time, so there will only be nineteen houses, the size of the plot adjusted to the size of the family.
>
> Building the houses is very difficult, not at all like at home. A foundation of stone must be laid, then an open frame erected. Trees have to be cut and trimmed to square sections with a broadax, then finished with an adze. Are you impressed with my knowledge? I have been talking a great deal to a young man named Peter Brown, one of the strangers from London. He is not really a carpenter, but has done some work in that line. He is teaching me how to sharpen tools so that I can be of some help.
>
> I can hear you say, "Oh, Humility, what does he look like? Is he handsome? Is he married?" Well, perhaps you would ask that last question *first*! He looks very well, he is not married. I might add, at the risk of being vain, he is the

most eligible bachelor on the ship, and I would be blind if I had not noted the attention he pays to me. But I am not ever going to marry.

I find this hard to write, my dear Hope, but I have no one to talk to here. It is a great sin on my part, but I must confess it, even if just in this letter that may never be seen by any eyes other than mine—I have not been able to forgive Gilbert Winslow for his behavior toward me.

I have prayed and wept and tried to *feel* that I have forgiven him, for has not God said we must forgive if we would be forgiven?

The worst of it is that I hate him not because he planned to betray Mr. Brewster, which was the real evil. No, I must set it down—I hate him because he made me love him—and he did not love me!

Now, it is down, and I look at it, read the words. But Hope, he had done me more wrong than he knows, for I gave him my love—my first love—and when the discovery came that he cared not for me, something happened deep in my soul. I do not know how to say it right, but I know that never will I be able to love a man again!

Peter Brown was satisfied. There had been a drawing for the position of lots, and he had drawn one at the foot of the street, right next to William Brewster and his large household, which included Bradford and others.

He drew Humility down to see it, and she smiled at his excitement.

"It's the best lot of all, Peter," she smiled. "It's very close to the brook, isn't it?"

She listened as he drew in the air with his hands the plan of the house, and he went on to outline how he intended to have his fields and his stock just over a rise to the east. He had been talking rapidly, his eyes bright with excitement, and suddenly he gave her a look, then laughed shortly, his face reddening. He picked up a large stick and broke it in two. Throwing half of it away, he began to trace lines in the hard earth. There was a shyness in him that drew his eyes down, but finally he looked up and said quietly, "You know why I wanted you to see this, Humility?"

She stirred and shook her head, but there was a knowing light in her green eyes. "Why?"

"Because a house without a wife in it is just a pile of sticks."

He threw the stick away and pulled her to her feet, holding on to her shoulders and there was a rough insistence in his voice. "You must know that I've thought about that!"

She said slowly, "I—I've seen your interest, Peter."

He bit his lip, then said quickly, "Is there any hope for me, Humility?"

She did not move, did not stir. Far away there came from the deep woods the cry of a hunting bird, and over the cold air she heard the sound of someone chopping a tree down.

When she did not move, he suddenly pulled her into his arms and kissed her.

She did not resist; indeed, she moved forward to meet him. He was an attractive man, full-blooded and strong. He stirred her in a strange way; whatever Gilbert Winslow had done to her, he had not destroyed or warped that side of her nature.

"Humility!" Brown smiled and nodded his head. "You care for me a little, I know."

"Peter . . . I can't say. . . !" she began, then bit her lip. With a quick shake of her head, she added, "You must not ask me to marry you, Peter."

"Why not?"

"Because I don't think I'll ever marry."

With a laugh, he seized her hand and kissed it. She had shared his kiss, and he had caught a glimpse of the passion that lay beneath her smooth, even ways. "I know—I know," he laughed. "You women have to be courted. I'll ask, and you'll say no. But finally, I'll ask often enough and you'll say yes— maybe just to hush me up."

The two of them were often together, and soon they were firmly linked in the minds of most.

Gilbert heard of it, of course. Alden asked him once, "Did you know Brown is courting Miss Humility?"

The question did queer things to Gilbert. He had noted the pair, but to hear it said made him restless. "No, I didn't know that, John."

"I suppose they'll get married. Won't do for a girl not to get married in this place."

Gilbert had met her later, at the beach. It had been almost dark, and the wind was cold as they encountered each other on a short walk—he coming from the north, she from the south.

They were both looking down at the sand, and were startled when they glanced up. Each waited awkwardly, a silence that comes when two alienated people are forced to speak.

Finally she said, "Your brother got a nice lot. I suppose you'll be staying with him?"

"No, Humility, I'll be going back with Captain Jones to be hanged." Her trivial remark irritated him, and he planted his feet firmly, and looking down on her, added, "That should make you very happy."

"That's—that's not fair!" she cried, and a wave of anger colored her high cheekbones. "I wouldn't want anyone to hang!"

He felt a stab of remorse, but there was a perverse spirit in him that made him declare, "You've not been much of a Christian, have you now?"

She stared at him, and her face grew agitated. "I—I don't know what you mean."

"It sticks out like a sore thumb!" he snapped. Taking her arm in a strong grasp, he said, "You've hated me from the second you found out what I'd done!"

She grew pale in the fading light, and the streak of honesty that ran deep in her surfaced. "Yes! And I always will!" Then tears filled her eyes and she broke his grasp and ran sobbing along the beach, nearly stumbling over the driftwood.

"Nicely done, old boy!" Gilbert nodded. He kicked viciously at a half-submerged log, and the pain gave him a savage sense of delight. He stared at the figure of the sobbing girl fading into the twilight and shook his head.

Why shouldn't she hate me? She can't despise me any more than I despise myself!

He slept on the shore that night, walking the beach, and the chilling wind was a match for his spirit.

By January 3, New Plymouth was beginning to take shape, but the progress was slow. Fieldstone had to be gathered for fireplace and hearth, two-inch planks had to be sawed for walls, and the joints and cracks had to be daubed with clay.

One of the most difficult and time-consuming tasks was thatching the roofs. They were made as they had been for generations in England, but thatch was hard to come by in Plymouth. It meant miles of tramping through the meadows and along the creek banks to gather it, with the constant possibility of being cut off by a surprise Indian attack.

"Have you seen the columns of smoke over to the west, Miles?" Gilbert asked one morning.

"I'm taking a small party out this morning to have a look. Come along, will you, Gilbert?" Standish asked.

Sick of the grinding labor, Gilbert readily agreed, and an hour later Standish took four men on a scouting expedition. They stumbled onto a few abandoned Indian huts, but saw no fresh signs. Gilbert shot a fish hawk, and they stopped long enough to cook and devour it.

"Not bad," Standish said. He licked his fingers, adding, "Once in Spain we had nothing to eat but an owl for six of us. Made a pretty fair soup."

Gilbert grinned, tearing at the tough meat with his strong white teeth. "You soldiers are a rude bunch. You'd eat anything." He got up, wiped his hands on his shirt, and asked, "You think we'll be attacked sooner or later, Miles?"

"Probably."

Gilbert grinned at the stolid pessimism of the soldier; then a sober light crossed his face. "I suppose Jones will be taking the ship back to England soon."

Standish was whittling a toothpick out of a twig, and he finished it carefully, then began probing his teeth before he gave the younger man a sharp glance, saying, "You going back with him?"

"What choice do I have?"

Standish waved his hand in a wide circle and shook his head. "There's a million square miles in this land. Our royal sovereign King James may be an idiot in many ways, but even *he* has enough sense to realize a man couldn't be caught by ten regiments if he wants to hide out."

"You mean go native?"

"There are worse things, old boy—hanging is one of them."

Gilbert stood up, stared out at the rugged woods that rose up to the west, then shrugged. "Get mighty lonesome out there."

"Take a woman with you," Standish grinned.

"Oh, yes. Why didn't I think of that?" Gilbert answered cynically. "There'd be a long waiting line, wouldn't there, Miles—women just dying to go into the wilds of America with a fugitive. Have to beat them off with a stick!"

"Don't know about a line, but all you need is one." Standish studied Gilbert intently. He had a real affection for the young man, and finally he said, "You wouldn't have to go native—not altogether. We're a long way from the King's justice out here, Gilbert—a long way." The dark eyes of Standish grew thoughtful, and he mused on an idea that had been forming in his mind for some time.

"This land—America—it's not going to be like people think. Everybody seems to think that it'll be another little colony that the King can put in his pocket. But it won't."

"Why not?"

"It's too big, too far away from England; and the wrong kind of people are coming here." He threw the toothpick away, stood up and stretched hugely. "By the *wrong* kind of people, I mean the wrong kind who won't rest easy under authority. Look at this bunch, these saints. Why, they left England to get away from having their necks stepped on by royal authority. You think they'll be more humble now that they're thousands of miles from that authority? No! There's something in the air of this place, Gilbert, something that makes a man feel—oh, I don't know! Bigger, I guess."

Gilbert had been watching Standish curiously, for something of the things the little soldier was trying to say had been in his thoughts. Finally he said, "In most of that, I'd say you were right, Miles—but I can't see running away into the woods."

"That's what I'd do if I were in your shoes," Standish shrugged. "Get that Cooper girl and go build her cabin. Raise a bunch of kids."

"Not her. She's looking at Brown."

"Is she now? Well, women are pretty much alike, boy, so just pick another. That Desire Minter, now, she's after anything in pants."

Standish got to his feet, called the other men from the woods where they were looking for signs, and as they came, he said,

"Think on it, Gilbert. This won't be the last colony. You can change your name and start a new life." In a rare gesture of affection, he threw his arm around Gilbert, having to reach high to do so, and said, "I've not got so many friends, boy, that I can spare you for the gallows!"

As they made their way back to the settlement, the words of Standish kept coming back to Gilbert's mind.

He was still turning it over when they got back to the settlement. "Something's happened," Standish said.

A crowd was milling around the beach, and when they got there, Bradford met them with a tense look on his long face. "Did you see anything of Brown and Goodman?"

"No," Standish said. "Haven't they come back?"

The two men had left on a thatch-gathering trip the day before, and had not returned before dark. "Have you looked for them?" Standish demanded.

"Only in places close by," Bradford admitted. "All the thatch close by has already been pulled. They were going over toward those hills."

"That's where we've seen smoke the last few days, Miles," Gilbert said.

"Well, we'll have to search for them." He looked up at the lead-gray sky and grimaced, "Too late to do anything today. I'll take five men out at dawn."

That night the snow that had been lurking in the biting air began to sift out of the sky. By dawn it lay in strips of white on the ground and capped the treetops. Standish led the party out, and they circled through the woods all day, returning at dusk with no sight of the pair.

"We'll try more to the north tomorrow," he said. "But it'll be fool's luck if we run on to them."

"You think the Indians may have taken them?" Humility asked. She had stayed overnight to help with the work, and she fed the scouting party, filling their plates with a stew made from herring Tink and John Alden had caught that day. When she gave Gilbert his plate, she kept her face averted and did not speak.

"I hope they're just lost," Standish said. "That's not hard to do in this place."

On Saturday at midday, Brown and Goodman came stumbling into camp, almost too weak to walk. Humility saw them first, staggering out of a clump of pines to the west of the camp, and she cried out, "Peter!" and flew to meet them.

Brown was half-carrying Goodman, and when he saw Humility running toward him, he stopped, put Goodman on the snow, and waited for her.

"Peter!" she cried and grabbed at his arms. His face was raw with the cold and exposure, and his hands were blue and stiff. "I've been half crazy!" she exclaimed.

His lips, flaked with a coat of thin ice, turned upward into a faint grin, and he whispered in a cracked voice, "Have you now? Then it's all worth it."

She touched his cheek, and then Allerton and Mullins came running up, and there was no time to say anything. Alden and John Howland came, and they picked Goodman up and carried him to one of the huts. Brown waved aside all efforts to help, leaning on Humility. "I think John's feet are frozen—but I'm all right."

As he wolfed down the fish stew, Brown told them what had happened: they'd seen a deer and gone after it, getting lost in the process. Then the snow had come, wiping out all familiar landmarks and they'd wandered around the entire time, wet and miserable. "I think I'll sleep for a week!" he declared.

Humility walked with him to the hut, and at the door he paused and looked down at her. Snow was still falling—just a few flakes, but one of them fell on her cheek and he touched it with a finger. "I thought for a while we wouldn't make it."

"What did you think about then?" she asked seriously.

"Why, I thought about you, of course," he said, surprised that she had to ask. "I thought: 'The worst thing is we'll never have a life together!' That was the worst of it all!"

She was moved by his words, and when he leaned down to kiss her, she lifted her face. It was a good kiss, not demanding, and when he lifted his head he said, "Is it all right, Humility? About us, I mean?"

She did not speak for a moment, and he was afraid she was trying to think of some gentle way to refuse him. But finally, she lifted her face; when she spoke, there was a resignation in her tone, like the turning of a key in a lock.

"It's all right with us, Peter."

His face lit up, then a thought sobered him. He said slowly, "About Winslow—that's over?"

She nodded and said evenly, "Yes, that's over." Then she added, "I was in love with him, Peter. You have a right to know that."

"But no more?"

She turned her face away, looking down gathering darkness toward the beach, then came back to him. "No more, Peter. Whatever I felt for him is gone."

He studied her face, then nodded and said, "We'll have a good life, Humility."

He did not kiss her again, but touched her cheek with his hand, then ducked inside the hut. Humility wheeled, but before going back to her cabin, she looked up into the tiny flakes crisscrossing the sky, and she said intently, as if to convince herself, "It *will* be all right!"

Then she hunched her shoulders against the cold and made her way to her cold bed.

CHAPTER TWENTY-FOUR

THE GENERAL SICKNESS

★　★　★　★

Log: January 14th

Follows the order of deaths since landing: Edward Thompson, the first to die in the New World; Jasper Moore, James Chilton, Dorothy Bradford, 11th December; Richard Britteridge, 21st December; Degory Priest, 1st January; John Langemore, Christopher Martin, 8th January, Mrs. Martin the following day. Weather continues cold, with snow and ice in abundance. Crew is restless, desiring to return to England while supplies permit. My decision is to remain at least until shelter is completed for all settlers.

"Mr. Winslow . . ."

Gilbert turned to see William Bradford looking up at him from where he sat with his back against one of the huts.

"Yes, Mr. Bradford?" Gilbert went to him at once. Snow was falling in occasional flakes, and Bradford's hair was hoary in the fading light.

"Would you have a moment for me?" Bradford looked frail, and the sickness had drained his strength. "I find myself a little weak . . ."

"Why—of course," Gilbert said. "Can I take you to your hut?"

"That would be most kind of you." Bradford put out a hand and Gilbert helped him to his feet. He led him down the hill toward the hut, and Bradford clung to his arm, almost stumbling over the rough ground. Gilbert suddenly reached around Brad- ford with his right arm, letting the older man hold to his left, and held him tightly, "Let me be your legs this once, sir," he said gently.

Bradford didn't answer as they moved along, and Gilbert thought he had offended the man's tremendous sense of self- sufficiency, but then he felt the body of Bradford surrender and lean close, accepting help with an uncharacteristic mildness.

When they reached the cabin, Gilbert helped the sick man inside and lowered him onto his bed. He lifted his feet, and Bradford lay back with a sigh. He closed his eyes, but as Gilbert turned to go, he said, "Thank you, Mr. Winslow—or perhaps I can call you by your familiar name—since you've practically car- ried me like a baby."

A small gleam of humor touched Bradford's dark eyes, and he smiled suddenly, the first Gilbert had seen since they left Holland.

"It's hard for a man like me to accept help," he said.

"You're more accustomed to giving it, Mr. Bradford."

He waved his hand and said, "That's not always a virtue, Gilbert. It can be a form of pride—the sin of Lucifer." He opened his eyes fully, musing almost to himself, "If I would change one word of Holy Scripture, it would be to make the verse read, 'It is more blessed to receive than it is to give.' "

Gilbert thought that over. "Doesn't sound right."

"That's because you're a strong man—and a proud one, like me," Bradford answered at once. There was a calculating look in his eyes not unmixed with kindness as he went on, "I never liked to have things done for me, even when I was a child. I liked to dress myself, cut my own food—all the things that par- ents do for children, I wanted to do for myself."

"Most children are like that," Gilbert argued. He pulled a chair over and sat down beside Bradford. He'd never liked the man—had despised him, in fact, for the way he'd treated his wife. But there was something in him now that had been lacking, and he wanted to discover what it was.

"When I became a man I should have put away childish things," Bradford quoted. "But the older I got, the more I prided myself on being strong enough to handle anything that came to me—without help."

He drew his knees up suddenly and placed his bony hands on them. They were roughened by the grueling labor of the past days, but they were the hands of an artist, a scholar—long, tapering, sensitive. He raised them to his face, made a pyramid of them, and touched them with his lips. A cloud passed over his eyes, and there was an unsteadiness in his voice as he met Gilbert's gaze and said, "If I had not been so independent, my wife would be alive."

Gilbert felt the force of the simple statement like a blow. He blinked and licked his lips, unable to answer. Bradford had confessed his guilt without apology, direct as a stone.

"You can't know that, Mr. Bradford," he said finally.

"No. We can never know what *would* have been had we taken a different course." Then he looked at Gilbert and forced a smile. "You are not a priest, are you, Gilbert?"

"A priest?"

"It occurs to me that I am making my confession to you like a loyal Catholic. And I could not say this to your brother—or to anyone else in this place. But you and I are much alike, so I burden you with my guilt."

Gilbert suddenly was struck with the incongruity of the thing. He grinned widely at Bradford and said, "No one would ever believe such a thing. You're a saint—I'm the sinner!"

Bradford did not smile. Instead, he put his thin hand on Gilbert's wrist. "There was a time when I cataloged men like that—saint or sinner; heaven or hell. But I was wrong." He sighed deeply. "And what about you, Gilbert?" Bradford continued at last.

"Me?"

"I have it in my mind that you are like the man mentioned in the Scripture—the one who was not far from the kingdom of God."

Gilbert shrugged, but an angry light suddenly smoldered in his blue eyes. The weight of Bradford's gaze became uncomfortable and he said, "I've tried that way—it may be all right for you, but not for me."

Bradford closed his eyes, and then opened them, saying, "You have tried religion, Gilbert. But you have been too strong to try Jesus Christ. You have to be desperate."

Gilbert laughed bitterly. "Desperate! I've killed two men, betrayed my friends—I'm on my way back to England to hang— and you say I'm not *desperate*?"

Bradford stared at him, shook his head, and murmured, "You're too strong, my boy. Tell me the truth; you are thinking that somehow you'll get out of it. That by some means you'll escape and everything will be all right for you, isn't that so?"

Gilbert opened his mouth to deny it, then suddenly realized what Bradford said was true. "Well—I suppose that's so, but . . . !"

"You see? You haven't come to the place where you can ask for help."

Suddenly Gilbert felt stifled in the small hut. He got to his feet, stopping long enough to say, "I'd better help the others, Mr. Bradford." He left, but not before he heard Bradford say, "Run away as hard as you can, Gilbert—the day will come when you'll be caught in a trap with no place to run!"

All that week Gilbert avoided Bradford. The weather cleared and he threw himself into the work with all his strength. Tink was with him every day, and he often had to say, "You're working too hard, Tink."

"Oh, I ain't tired, not a bit!" the boy would say. But he had developed a hacking cough and his cheeks were often tinged with an unnatural red.

On Saturday the 20th of January the Common House was finished, and on the next day the entire company of the *Mayflower* came ashore, as many as possible crowding into the small structure.

The largest building in Plymouth was only about twenty feet square, of wattle and daub construction with a high steep roof. Against one side was a lean-to for tools and supplies.

Gilbert did not go inside, but from the door he had a good view of the congregation—many of them too sick to stand, lying on beds. Humility, he saw, was with the Tilleys, and at her right was Peter Brown. She met his eyes once, and there was an adamant expression on her face, marring its softness. Brown caught the glance and stared at Gilbert intently for a moment, then ignored him.

Bradford looked around, opened his little Bible and began

to read. "Lord, thou hast been our dwelling place in all generations . . ." and as he read the 90th Psalm a hush fell over the congregation. He closed the Bible and began to speak, and there was none of the harsh directness which had been part of his manner in Leyden.

"This is the psalm of Moses, and it is now our psalm. Where is our dwelling place? Is it in Plymouth?" He smiled and lifted his hand toward heaven. "No, the Lord is our dwelling place—for when this Plymouth is no more, when the earth ceases to be, we will not be wanderers, for the Lord is our home."

As Bradford went on, encouraging his flock, Gilbert saw that his hearers were struck by the new humility of his manner. They were not bound to this man as people in England were bound to their ministers, but there was a power in him that held them all. *People believe him*, Gilbert thought. *That's the secret of being a leader.*

The sermon was short, and the boat returned to the *Mayflower* at once. As soon as Captain Jones' feet touched the deck, he sensed something was wrong. Wheeling around, he saw some of the crew advancing. Instantly, he recognized their purpose; he had been expecting it for some time.

"Cap'n Jones, we needs to have a word with you."

"Yes, what is it, Coffin?"

"We've been talking, sir, and what it comes to is—we think it's time to go back home."

"Why, so it is time," he nodded easily. "And I can't say I'll be sorry to leave this shore. Of course, we must wait just a little longer. You wouldn't throw sick people off the ship without a roof, would you, men?"

"And what about food, Captain?" Coffin asked at once.

"You won't starve—I'll see to that!"

Coffin shrugged, and glanced at his followers. "How can you feed us, Captain? There's only so much food to be had, and the longer we stay here the more of it goes to these psalm-singers. Can't deny that, can you?"

Jones forced himself to smile. "Why, I think you've sailed with me long enough to know that I've never let a man starve, Coffin! Just a few more days, and we're off—and here's the best of it—" A thought came to him, and he smiled broadly, winking at the men lined up behind the pilot's lean form, "You'll all be getting a bonus for the time you spend here."

He noted the smiles of the crew, and before Coffin or O'Neal could speak, he closed the matter in his usual dogmatic fashion. "Now, to work with you—and think about what that bonus will buy in England."

Coffin did not try to argue, but Jones knew he had only postponed the matter.

Sooner or later I'll have to keelhaul that man! he thought as he went to his cabin.

The last week in January wore the work force down, some of the workers taking to their beds with what was called the general sickness.

"What *is* this thing, Sam?" Edward Winslow asked in despair.

"It's not *one* thing, I'd say, but half a dozen—scurvy, pneumonia, tuberculosis, bad diet, lack of sanitation—take your pick."

"And not the least is the fact that sick people are working in the worst weather imaginable when they ought to be in bed." Winslow shook his head and added, "But how much worse can it get? Half of us are sick now."

"And some of the crew are pretty bad as well, so Captain Jones tells me," Brewster said.

"That man is a marvel to me," Edward mused. "Many men would have thrust us off on this shore and made for home."

"God's hand was in his choosing," Brewster said simply. "He will be rewarded for his faithfulness to us."

Fuller gave him a heavy glance and shook his massive head. "I been listenin' to some of the crew—Mr. Clark, mostly. He says if Captain Jones don't haul anchor soon, the crew will mutiny."

"No, I can't think they'd do that!" Winslow stated flatly. "They'd hang."

"According to Clark, they'd rather risk hanging as a maybe, than starving as a sure thing," Fuller grunted. He rose heavily to his feet and said, "I'm going to try a new medicine on Rose Standish."

"What is it?" Brewster asked.

"Some red berries that grow in the scrub oaks. Maybe they'll do her some good."

"You mean you're going to give her some medicine, and you don't know what it is!" Brewster was horrified. "Why, Sam, you might kill her."

Fuller stared at him, and said quietly, "She's going to die anyway, William. I'm just doing it to make Captain Standish feel better."

His blunt assertion caught both men off guard. They looked uneasily at each other, then back to Fuller. Winslow asked, "Is it that certain, Sam? There's no hope?"

Fuller dropped his head, then lifted it, and there was a finality in his eyes as he said, "She's lived a week longer than I'd thought, Edward. It will be a blessing."

"Does Standish know?"

"The funny thing is, he doesn't," Fuller mused. He pulled at his bottom lip, and added, "He's such a sharp fellow in so many ways, but he's like a child where she's concerned. I tried to tell him once that it might be well to consider the possibility of losing her—and he just stared at me as if I'd said something he couldn't understand."

"Poor fellow!" Brewster said. "I'll go with you, Samuel. Maybe I can comfort them with a scripture."

Brewster and Fuller made their way to the Common House, and found Miles Standish sitting beside Rose. He asked eagerly, "Did you bring the new medicine, Dr. Fuller?"

"Aye, right here, Captain." Fuller held out a small glass bottle and said, "Can you pull her up long enough to swallow this?"

"Sit up, Rose," Standish whispered, pulling her thin form up. She was semiconscious, and when Fuller ladled some of the medicine into her mouth it ran down her chin and off onto the cover.

"Now that will do you good, Rose," Standish murmured. "You'll be up and around in no time; isn't that right, Dr. Fuller?"

"We must pray much for her, Miles," Samuel Fuller said. "Mr. Brewster came to do that—for both of you."

"Why, there's nothing wrong with me!" Standish protested,

but he moved back as Brewster came to kneel beside his wife and began to pray.

When the prayer was over, Brewster turned to Standish and said gently, "She's a godly woman, Captain. I know she's made her peace with God."

"No! I won't have that kind of talk!"

Standish got up and left the room at once, his face pale and there was a madness in his eyes.

Brewster shook his head. "He's not a Christian man, Samuel. It's going to go hard with him when she dies."

"Somebody must be here at all times, William. She could go at any moment."

"I'll see to it."

Brewster got several of the women to stay with the dying woman, and she seemed to improve the next day. Standish went to get some sleep about seven o'clock, for he had not left her side.

It was long after midnight when all three men—Gilbert, Edward, and Standish—awoke instantly when a woman's voice called out, "Mr. Standish!"

Miles leaped out of bed, pulled the door open and found Humility standing there with a lantern. He stared at her, unable to say a word. Finally, she said gently, "You must come now, Mr. Standish. She's going."

"No!" Standish whirled and ran across the room. Putting his forehead on the wall, he rolled his head from side to side, saying, "No! No! No!"

Edward glanced at Gilbert and then went to the soldier. "It's hard, Miles—but you must go!"

Slowly Standish straightened, and when he turned, his face was shattered with fright. He moved like a man in his sleep, and before he reached the door, he turned and said, "Gilbert—will you go with me? I can't bear it alone!"

"Of course—but maybe you'd like one of the elders . . . ?"

"No—you come!"

Edward nodded, and Gilbert took Miles' arm and followed Humility as she went forward holding up the light.

Fuller was inside standing beside Rose, but he moved at

once to come and whisper, "She's not got long, Miles—be quick!"

Standish did not release the grip he had taken on Gilbert's arm, so the younger man was practically forced to advance and kneel with Standish. Humility came forward, her face highlighted by the lantern she held high, and Fuller stepped back into the shadows.

"Rose?" Standish put his hand on the woman's brow, and for a moment Gilbert thought she was dead. But then her eyes opened, and for the first time in days, her mind was clear.

"Miles—" she whispered, and she tried to raise her hand to touch his face.

"Sweetheart mine!" he said, the tears running down his face. He began to shake so violently that Gilbert feared he might fall, but then he caught himself and leaned forward, his lips almost touching her ear. "I love you more than life!"

Rose's face was drawn by her illness, but there was a peace in her countenance. She managed to raise her hand and put it around the neck of her husband, and he fell on her breast.

"Don't leave me, Rosie!" he sobbed.

She smiled and pulled his face up so that she could see his eyes. "I'm so tired, Miles—so very tired."

The light moved and Gilbert looked up to see Humility swaying from side to side. Her eyes were filled and her free hand was held over her mouth to stifle the sobs. She began to fall, and he leaped up, took the lamp and held her upright with his free hand. He dared not move, for the tide was going out for Rose Standish.

"Do you remember the roses you gave me—the first time— we met?" she asked, and the words came harder, "And—what you—told me?"

Standish reached down and pulled her up, holding her with both arms. "Aye! I said it was a shame that the flowers were forced to look so bad—next to your face!"

"And—you said—you loved me!"

"And so I have—so I have!"

Once more she pulled back, and looking right into his face, she whispered, "I—have loved you—always—but now, I—must go—I must go to my Lord."

She tried to touch his face, but suddenly she took one deep breath, then her hand dropped, and her head fell back.

"She's—she's gone, Miles," Fuller said. He came forward and put his heavy hand on the soldier's shoulder, and added, "She's with the Lord God."

Standish remained silent, unmoving, and Gilbert was afraid of his reaction. But carefully lowering Rose to the bed, he folded her hands, leaned over and kissed her, then stood up. His eyes were filled, but there was no panic in his voice as he said, "I never loved another woman in my life!"

Humility suddenly realized that she was being held in Gilbert's embrace, and she pulled away at once, dashing the tears from her eyes. "I'll take care of Rose, Captain Standish," she said.

Gilbert walked outside with Miles and Sam Fuller, and as they stood there looking up, a star broke through the winter sky. "See that?" Standish said quietly. "That's what she was to me— like that point of light in the dark sky." He reached up as if he could touch the star, then added, "Now my sky is dark—not a speck of light in it, Gilbert."

Gilbert Winslow wanted to say something to comfort his friend, but there was nothing in him, for his own sky was dark also.

It got darker when Fuller came to him early at dawn. "The Tinkers—they're all sick."

"Even . . . ?"

Fuller knew how much Gilbert loved Tink, and his face was grave as he nodded and put a hand on Winslow's shoulder.

"He's the worst of all, Gilbert. I fear for him—he's in God's hands!"

And since Gilbert had given up on God, who was there for him to pray to? The skies overhead were blank as he stumbled across the frozen ground to the Tinkers' hut, with not a single star to break the dull arch of the heaven.

CHAPTER TWENTY-FIVE

"LOVE IS NOT COLD!"

★ ★ ★ ★

None of the firstcomers who survived ever forgot the month of February. Whatever visions of a summery Eden remained were drowned by the rain, the sleet and snow, and the keen winds that whipped across the sea to scrape faces raw and cut the lungs with a razor's edge.

No one was ever wholly dry, and the sickness claimed new victims almost daily. There was a fever to get houses built, for the *Mayflower* could leave any day. Indians were never seen, but smoke signals were visible and more than once they came to scream at the settlers in the night.

Death became such a common visitor that the first morning thought of Fuller was, *Who will lie dead in their beds this morning?* Rose Standish's death surprised no one but her husband, and there was great grief at her funeral and afterward concern for her husband. But as soul after soul slipped off into death, it became a ritual that had lost its primeval power.

"They go different," Edward remarked to Gilbert as they were digging the graves for Edward Fuller and his wife Ann. "There was Christopher Martin, like a bull roaring and thrashing—but he had to go. And the Fullers, why they slipped away so quiet! No final words to anyone."

Gilbert paused to rest, and looking across the open field to the row of half-finished huts, he shook his head. "How many died this month?"

"Five already this month."

"That makes twenty dead in all. That means there's fewer than twenty men and boys to stand guard, build houses, trade, and hunt food."

"Standish said that we must bury the next one at night."

"Why?"

"He doesn't want the savages to know how few we are."

Gilbert smiled grimly. "They must know that already." He struck the frozen earth a blow with his mattock, "I've been surprised at how Miles has taken his loss." Standish had joined with John Bradford to become one of the most indefatigable nurses, working all day and ministering to the sick most of the night.

Edward arched his aching back, measured the depth of the grave and said, "Miles is different. He's a pretty hard fellow—never came up against something he couldn't handle with a musket until Rose died. I think he'll not be able to get away from her going."

"You mean he might become a Christian just to get to be with Rose?" Gilbert asked. "I always hated that sort of thing!"

Edward paused, looked across at Gilbert, then smiled. "I know that. But I've come to think that even a poor motive for serving God can turn out well. In Miles' case, he'll be thinking at first, *I've got to be a Christian if I'm ever to see Rose again*, but if he keeps at it, sooner or later he'll develop more than that."

"Develop what, Edward?"

"Why, a desire to see more than Rose. He'll want to see God."

Such talk made Gilbert uncomfortable, and he asked, "Isn't this deep enough?"

"Ought to do. Let's get back." Edward paused. "I'm taking Elizabeth to the ship today. It's warmer there, and there's more room in the cabin."

"Can I help?"

Edward shook his head. "No. I know you don't like to leave the boy alone too much." A thought struck him, and he added, "You might bring him on board. He might have more chance there—and his parents won't object."

Gilbert added bitterly, "No, they wouldn't care." He thought it over, and before they got to the settlement, he had made up his mind. "I think it might be good for him to be there. When are you taking Elizabeth?"

"Right away. Alden and Ellis are taking us in the shallop."

"I'll get Tink and we'll go with you."

He went straight to the Tinkers' house and knocked on the door. Thomas Tinker, a thin man with watery blue eyes and a scraggly beard, opened the door. "Wot is it, Winslow? You want to see the boy again?"

Both Tinker and his wife had recovered from the sickness, at least enough to get around. Neither of them had been strong to begin with, and the rigors of the voyage and the sickness had weakened them more.

"I'd like to take him to the ship, if you agree," Gilbert said. "It would be easier to take care of him there."

Tinker rubbed his chin with a dirty hand, and turned round to stare at the small form of Tink on the cot. He shrugged and said, "Might as well."

Gilbert at once stepped inside, and bent to pick the boy up. Tink was awake and gave him a small smile. "Well, Tink, you think you could stand a move?"

"Where to, Mr. Winslow?"

Gilbert wrapped him in an extra blanket against the cold and picked him up. "To the ship for a little while. Say goodbye to your parents."

Tink looked over at the man and the woman who were watching without much interest. "Goodbye," he said quietly.

"Mind your manners, boy, you hear me?" Mr. Tinker threatened, then lay back on his bed.

Tink had never been large, but he seemed to weigh nothing now. His eyes seemed large in his face and there was a red spot in the center of each pale cheek. As the cold wind hit his lungs, the racking cough that had plagued him began, and Gilbert pulled the blanket over his face, saying, "You just stay under there for a bit, Tink. And when we get to the ship, I'll bet we can get cook to fix you up something nice and hot!"

Edward met him, holding Elizabeth in his arms, and they

walked down to the harbor together. Alden, Ellis, and two of the other men were at the oars of the shallop, and they rowed them to the ship, helping them up the ladder with their burdens.

The first hold, which had been packed to the bulkheads, seemed empty now. "The Mullins have the cabin next to ours," Edward said. "But the small one the Hopkins had is vacant. Why don't you put the boy in there?"

Fuller came out of one of the cabins and looked up, surprised to see them. Then he nodded and said, "I'm glad you brought her here, Edward. Who's this we have?" he asked. Lifting the blanket, he peered at Tink and smiled. "Well, now, here's my fine young helper! I shouldn't wonder but what you're up and about soon, eh?"

As soon as they got the patients into bed, Gilbert pulled Fuller off to one side. "Edward and I will have to work during the day, but we'll stay with them at night."

Fuller shrugged his burly shoulders. "Some of us will be here. Mrs. White will have her baby any time now, so I'll not stray far. The Mullins are both low, so Priscilla will be here—and some of the other women. I'll see he's not forsaken."

"Has Captain Jones said when he's leaving?"

Fuller stared at him, then shook his heavy head. "No, and I thank God for that! Half his crew is down now, and the other half is on the verge of mutiny. Think what it would be if all these sick people were dumped ashore right now!"

Gilbert nodded, and left to go see Hinge. He passed through the forecastle, filled mostly with seamen, sick on their bunks and poorly cared for. One of them, a sailor named French, lifted a thin hand and whispered feebly, "Mr. Winslow—a drink of water!"

Gilbert went to him at once, and was shocked at his appearance. He had been a muscular fellow with bright black eyes, but now he was a skeleton with cloudy eyes sunk in deep cavernous sockets.

"Why, French, I'm sorry to see you like this!" He picked up a pewter pitcher, saw it was empty and said, "I'll fetch you some water right away."

He went directly to the galley and got the little gnome of a cook to warm some broth for Tink, and added, "French wants some water."

Hinge nodded at a water barrel, and said, "It's a shame the way there ain't nobody to take care o' them chaps." He stirred something into a black pot, and added, "One of 'em died last night, went out cursin' his mates, but they didn't not a one of 'em stay with the poor chap when he went out!"

Gilbert filled the pitcher with fresh water and made his way back to French. "Here we are—let me help you sit up." The man had not been cared for in any way, and the stench from his soiled clothing and filthy blanket struck Gilbert like a blow. He forced himself to smile, however, and the poor fellow gripped the glass, drinking in noisy gulps.

"Thankee! Thankee, Mr. Winslow!" he gasped as he lay down.

Gilbert looked around the room, taking in the six other seamen who were lying in the room, some in hammocks some in bunks. "You're in poor shape here, French," he said. "Who takes care of you?"

"Why, nobody. Them as can takes care of themselves. 'Course, Mr. Fuller he come by yesterday, I think it was. But he's mighty busy with his own sick folks." A sadness rose in the haunted eye of French, and he mumbled, "We already lost five men—and I reckon as how I won't be here long."

Gilbert forced himself to smile and speak heartily, "Now, that's not like you, French. Cheer up! I'll see if something can't be done for you. A little care and you'll be fine!"

"You think so, Mr. Winslow?" The little encouragement brought tears to French's eyes, and he turned his face to the bulkhead, mumbling, "Thankee!"

Gilbert went at once to the Great Cabin. Finding Captain Jones inside, he said directly, "Captain, your sick seamen are not being cared for."

Jones put down the pen he was writing with and stared at Gilbert, his eyes frosty. "Are you telling me I'm remiss in my duty, Mr. Winslow?"

"I didn't say that; you're a busy man, but the men are in bad shape."

Jones got up and went to stare out the window. He said suddenly, "I know it—but there's no way I can force the men to take care of them."

"I can do a little, with your permission."

"Certainly you have it," Jones said at once. Then he came back and sat down in his chair. He toyed with a compass, then looked up with a strange expression in his eye. "You may have an opportunity to be a nurse to them on the way back to England."

"You still intend to take me back with you?"

"I don't know!" Jones leaned back, and suddenly there was a light of humor in his gray eyes. "I don't know anything that a captain of a vessel should know. I don't know why I've stayed in this frozen land so long; don't know why I've given our food and beer to a bunch of fanatics. Don't know why I'm having trouble making up my mind about you." He grinned and summed up: "Don't know much do I?"

Gilbert met his smile, and said, "Let me know when you decide if I'm going back to hang or not. In the meanwhile, I'll see what I can do for the men."

He went back to the galley, got the broth from Hinge, and carried it to Tink. He spooned it down, and the warm food along with the clean warm blankets made the boy so sleepy he dropped off at once in a natural sleep.

Gilbert heard Fuller's voice rumbling in the Mullins' cabin and waited until he came out. "How are they?" he asked.

"Bad!" The stark answer came out sharply, and Fuller shook his head. "Don't expect them to make it. How's the boy?"

"Like for you to keep him under your eye. He's sleeping now."

"The young ones are standing it better than the older people."

Gilbert thought about that, then nodded, turned to go, then paused. "Those sailors are in poor shape, aren't they? French said you were in to see them."

"They'd be better off if the well ones would look after the sick—but they won't do it."

Gilbert gnawed his lip, considering the matter. He hated sickness, and except for Tink, had spent as little time as possible with sick people. He wanted to let it drop, but then thought of Miles Standish and the way he had done the most menial sickroom tasks since Rose's death.

"Well, I thought I'd try to do a little for them, Fuller."

The doctor stared at him; then turning his head to one side he remarked, "Never would have taken you for such a thing."

Defensively Gilbert hastened to add, "I'll be working days, but I've got the rest of today and after I get through on shore. I'll be sleeping here anyway to be near the boy. Guess it'll not kill me to give the poor chaps a hand."

"All right. I'll see to it you get some supplies and a little help."

Two hours later Gilbert was exhausted. *Why, this is worse than digging graves!* he thought as he went around the forecastle picking up the filthy clothes and blankets on the beds, emptied the chamber pots, put fresh water in the pitchers, and tried to say a word of cheer to each of them.

While he had been busy with this, Coffin and another seaman had trooped through on their way to the galley. Taking in what Gilbert was doing, Coffin said loudly, "Well, we got us one of the holy ones here today, ain't we now?"

French raised himself up on an elbow, stared with angry eyes at the pilot, and said, "You let us lie here like dogs, Coffin! Shut your foul mouth!"

Coffin cursed and moved toward French, but Gilbert moved one step, placing himself between the two. Coffin's hand dropped to the dirk in his belt, but when Gilbert merely smiled at him, he cursed and led the other sailor out of the forecastle.

As Gilbert stooped to pick up some of the soiled blankets, a sailor named Pike raised his voice. "We all thanks you, Mr. Winslow—'deed we do. You're a real Christian!"

The others were echoing Pike's sentiment when Gilbert heard the door open behind his back. Expecting Fuller, he was taken off guard when he turned to find Humility standing there.

"Mr. Fuller sent me to help," she said quietly. Their eyes met, and something stirred in him at the sight of her. The weather had roughened her skin, but the sea-green eyes were still bright and her figure erect as a soldier. He felt a loss, for a wall had sprung up between them. Suddenly he thought back to the time they had stood on the small bridge that arched the canal in Leyden, staring down at the ripples in the water, talking about love.

"Why, that's good of you," he said hastily. Then he looked down at the soiled blanket, aware that he had absorbed some of the rank smells of the sick men, and he was embarrassed. "I—I guess I'll take these blankets to be washed."

"I'll help you." She picked up the rest of the clothes and blankets, then smiled at the men. "Cook is making you something tasty, and the captain says you're all to have something special to drink for supper. I'll be back with it soon."

She turned and Gilbert followed her up on deck. "Just put those things here; I'll take them to shore tomorrow and see they're washed in fresh water."

"They're pretty filthy." He looked down at himself, and added, "So am I, for that matter."

She looked at him squarely, and there was a determined set to her jaw. Leaning back against the rail, she said, "I'm marrying Peter Brown."

"I see." He stood there waiting, for he knew she had taken this opportunity to tell him. The ship lifted and fell gently, and there was a salty tang in the wintry air. A lantern hanging on the mainmast cast flickering gleams over the deck, and her face looked like an Indian mask—planed down to simple curves and hollows.

"You love him?" he asked finally. He did not miss the quick response that swept her face—not disgust, but distrust that hardened the soft green eyes.

"I respect him; he's a good man."

"You could say that of Mr. Brewster or Mr. Bradford, I dare say. Is that enough for you—respect?"

"It's better than what I got from you!" she cried out, and despite her intention to keep her emotions under control, anger raced through her as she faced him. "I got *love* from you, didn't I? Kisses and promises that made my head swim! Oh, what a fool I was!"

He bowed his head, taking the force of her wrath as he would submit to a rightful judgment. But he could not let it all go.

"All right, I was wrong—I've admitted that. But I want to tell you two things, Miss Humility Cooper."

"What could you tell me that I would possibly want to hear?"

"When I first met you, it was all a hoax. All I wanted to do was to use you." He paused and their eyes locked, and he said intently, "But later on, after I got to know you—it wasn't all pretense."

She laughed harshly, then said mockingly, "Oh, don't tell me that you really fell in love with me! I'm not as gullible as I was then, Gilbert!"

He shrugged and said, "All right, think what you will, but I'm telling you the truth. The other thing, Humility, is that even if I am the world's greatest hypocrite and liar, that's no excuse for you to run away from love."

"You don't know what love is!"

"I know one thing—love is not cold!"

A streak of anger ran through him, and he caught her wrist as she turned to leave. "You can't bear to hear the truth, can you? But you're going to hear it this once!"

"Let me go!"

He ignored her struggles and taking her other arm, held her fast. "Rogue I am and will probably always be, Humility—liar, traitor, manslayer! But I tell you this one thing, when I kissed you on that bridge, it was not treason! It was the beginning of something I'd never known. I'd kissed other women, some as beautiful as you, but there's something in you that held me!" He forced himself to speak quietly, but there was an intensity in his blue eyes that held her fixed in his grasp.

"You are a woman of God," he continued. "But you are flesh and blood, as you found out when I kissed you. Can you deny it?"

She whispered, "You taunt me with that?"

"No! You were honest then—but you are not now."

"I am!"

He shook her like a reed and said passionately, "You are *not*! How can you be honest and marry a man you don't love? Marriage is not spirit; it's flesh and blood, Humility! And you were more honest then than now."

"It's a lie!" she whispered. "I don't want that sort of thing!"

He suddenly pulled her closer, saying, "You're afraid of love—that's why you're afraid of me right now!"

She braced herself against him, her face pale in the flickering yellow light. Desperately she cried out, "I'm not! I'm not afraid of love—nor of you either!"

He had no hopes, but he had a strong memory of her from the past, fragrant and clear as a flower. He would never have her, but he hated to see her turn into a dry-lipped, sour woman. He pulled her forward until the soft curves of her body pressed against him, and whispered, "Is this what you're afraid of, Humility?" and then he gathered her closer until they made one shadow on the deck.

She uttered one short cry before his lips silenced her, and she beat at his back with her fists, but she might as well have beaten on the huge rock in Plymouth Harbor. Furiously she struggled, kicking at his legs with all her might, but he swung her around and trapped her against the rail so that she could not move.

His lips were hard against hers, and there was no gentleness in him. His muscular arms pulled her even closer and she stopped struggling. Her hands rose involuntarily and rested on his neck, and she was aware of nothing but the pressure of his lips and the warmth of his body against hers.

Then he lifted his head, and whispered, "Never be afraid of what you're feeling right now."

She came to herself with a jerk, and her cheeks flushed as she pushed him away. With a trembling voice she said, "You're stronger than I am—that's all you've proved! You think all you have to do is touch a woman and, no matter who she is, she'll fall in love with you!" She was close to tears, but she bit her lip and made herself say coldly, "I've asked you to leave me alone, and you take advantage of me the first chance you get. Is there no honor in you, Gilbert Winslow?"

He saw that she was locked in, incapable of understanding anything he might say. He nodded once, and said, "Don't marry a man who can't make you angry—or one who can't stir your blood."

"I'm marrying Peter Brown," she said steadily. "Please don't ever make any of your foolish advances to me again!"

"I can promise you that," he said quietly. He stepped back, and she left the deck, walking unsteadily down the ladder to the first hold.

Blindly Humility went to the cabin she shared with Bess Tilley, and for a long time she sat on her bunk, fists clenched tightly together, staring at the wall.

Finally she got up, lit the lantern, and began to add to her letter to Hope Stewart.

February 28, 1621.
Dear Hope,

I cannot tell you how dark the future is for us. Over half our number lies sick, and the rest of us are half dead with fatigue.

Only one thing makes life bearable, at least for me. I have agreed to marry Peter Brown. This will be difficult for you to understand, since only a few weeks ago I expressed my intention never to marry. That was false pride on my part. I see clearly now that marriage is a duty ordained by God. I am only grateful that my earlier delusions about "romance" and "love" have been replaced by a more sensible and mature attitude.

Peter Brown is a good man, and I will make him a good wife. Neither of us expect the "romance" some people put such stock in. Thank God that it's all settled!

A knock at the door interrupted her, and she started up, thrusting the small notebook into a chest and shoving it under the bunk. Opening the door, she saw Sam Fuller, who said at once, "Can you help me, Humility? Susanna's baby is coming."

"Of course." She followed him to Whites' cabin, and for the next four hours they were both very busy.

Edward Winslow was getting ready to go to shore at dawn when Fuller approached, his face lined with fatigue. "Well, the first baby in the New World is here."

"Susanna?" Winslow asked quickly.

"Very well. She had a hard time."

"Sam, would it be all right if I saw her?"

He went quickly to the cabin and entered; Susanna looked up at him with eyes like diamonds. Out of a bundle of white, a tiny black crown stuck out, and he thought he had never seen anything more beautiful than the two of them.

"His name is Peregrin," she smiled.

"An odd name," he murmured softly. Pulling the blanket back, he asked, "What does it mean, Susanna?"

"It means 'pilgrim,' " she said.

"A little pilgrim," he mused, and the tiny fist waved in the air and grasped the tip of his finger. "Peregrin White. That's a fine name—and he's a fine boy. Now Resolved will have a little brother to play with."

"Yes—but no father."

Winslow started and cried out, "Susanna, no!"

"You didn't know?" she said. In a gesture old as the world, she held the baby to her breast and kissed his head. "He and Mr. Mullins went together yesterday."

Death had become so common that the chilling shock should have passed, but Winslow's mind was numb. "Both of them gone! I—I can't grasp it!"

Susanna rocked the child slightly, and he began to cry feebly. "He hated to go before the baby came—but he knew it was time, and he endured his going better than anyone I've ever known."

"He was a good man, Susanna—no, he was a noble man! Great courage!"

She nodded. "I think he knew he'd never stand this trip— but he wanted the little ones—and me, to have a better chance."

He rose and stood over her for one moment. "I must catch the longboat." He leaned down and touched the tiny crop of hair in a gentle caress. "Peregrin, may you be as good a man as your father and a blessing to your good mother!"

Then he nodded and left her. She stared at the door, listening to his footfalls, then looked at the child. As he began to cry, she smiled a secret smile, and fell asleep.

CHAPTER TWENTY-SIX

MIRACLES ARE TROUBLESOME

★ ★ ★ ★

February was Plymouth's worst month. Seventeen of their number perished, and work came to a complete standstill. The weather continued to be miserably cold and rainy. Gilbert had worn himself to a fine edge, working in all kinds of weather during the day and caring for the sick of the *Mayflower's* crew and for Tink through the nights.

He had finished his chores one night and gone to the galley to see if there was anything to eat. To his surprise he found Captain Jones and Samuel Fuller sitting before the small fire talking.

"Come in, Winslow," Jones said. He took a heavy pot and scooped some of its contents into a bowl. "Have a little of this warm soup."

"That would go down well," Gilbert said wearily.

Jones turned to Gilbert, considered him with a direct glance, then, said, "You've been a great help, Winslow, with the sick men."

Gilbert answered, "I think French will make it now."

"How's the boy?"

Gloomily Gilbert said, "No better. Would you have a look at him before you go to bed, Fuller? I couldn't get him to eat much."

"The boy's parents died last week, didn't they?" Fuller

asked, getting to his feet. "Maybe he's grieving for them."

"Perhaps. But he's had that fever for so long!"

"I know. I'd bleed him, but he's so weak already," Fuller said. He left the galley, saying, "I'll look in on him."

The two sat there, not speaking for some time. Winslow was an enigma to the captain. He had failed completely to find an answer to his problem: what to do with him when the ship left.

Jones got up, stretched and then gave Gilbert a long look. "Been expecting you to make a run for it, Winslow. Hide out in the woods until after the ship left."

"Thought about it."

"But you haven't gone." The fact brought perplexed lines across Jones's forehead, and then he slapped his leg and said, "This is a rough crew; it wouldn't be hard for the mutineers to take over and sail the ship back to England themselves."

"What about you?"

"Maybe washed overboard in a storm. Maybe just put ashore. They'd be long vanished by the time I could file a report against 'em."

Gilbert asked suddenly, "Why haven't you left, Jones? You're not getting rich sitting here in this harbor."

"Scratch me if I can say!" Christopher Jones exploded, and there was a strange mixture of wonder and anger in his gray eyes. "I think I must be getting old!"

Gilbert smiled wryly, humor lurking in his face. "I think you're getting religion, Captain."

"No, it's worse than that, Winslow," Jones said shaking his head. "I've had religion for a long time. What I may be coming down with is a bad case of whatever fanaticism these people have."

"It can be dangerous to your health." Gilbert got to his feet, started for the door, then paused to look back. "Best be on your guard, Captain Jones. I'd hate to see you lose this ship to Coffin and the rest."

Leaving the captain to stare at the fire, Gilbert trudged wearily down to the cabin. The single candle guttered low in its own pool of wax, stretching his shadow, grotesque and malformed, from deck to ceiling. Fatigue dragged him down; he moved like an old man and his thinking was sluggish. He took a long drink from the waterjug, replaced it, and went to look down at the boy.

Tink was so thin he could see the pulse in his throat, beating irregularly. He put his hand on the boy's forehead. *Burning up! He'll die if that fever doesn't go down!*

Despair ran through him, and he sank down on his bunk, throwing his arms over his face.

Sleep eluded him, and when he dozed he had fitful dreams that flitted across his mind like stones skipping across water. Once he dreamed of a dog he'd had when he was ten—then of his mother, whom he could barely remember. Finally he drifted off into a fitful half sleep, tossing and turning on the narrow bunk.

Gilbert awoke to Tink's coughing spasm. He held the helpless boy in his arms, trying to get a swallow of water down the dry throat, but the racking coughing did not stop until it seemed even a strong heart would burst.

The words of William Bradford came floating into his mind: *"You're not desperate enough to trust God."*

Sitting there in the murky darkness with the dying boy, the hopelessness of his life settled on him like a leaden blanket. He put his head back on the bulkhead and closed his eyes, trying not to think of the future, to block everything out completely, hearing Tink's labored breathing and rasping cough.

He had almost dropped off to sleep when he was awakened by a sound from Tink. He sprang up and was beside him in a heartbeat. The boy's eyes were rolled back in his head, his chest was heaving wildly, and the cabin was filled with a rattle that came from his throat.

Then there was a *clicking* sound and the boy's body went completely limp, the arms and head flopping down nervelessly.

"Tink! Don't die, Tink!" Gilbert cried wildly. He leaped to his feet and holding the motionless boy up high in his arms, he called on God as he never had before.

"O God! Don't let Tink die!—Please!"

The tears streamed down his upturned face, and even as the echoes of his plea died out, he called again, "I love him, Lord God—don't you love him, too?"

He stood there in the murky darkness listening to the echoes of his own voice fade away until there was no sound at all save his own sobbing.

Then something happened.

Gilbert had never been a mystic, never believed in such things. When people had said, "God told me to do this," he had scoffed.

He realized suddenly that his wild fear was gone; his trembling had ceased and the racking sobs had stopped. His breathing slowed and then there was a faint ringing in his ears, like little silver bells far, far away. The cold of the cabin seemed to fade, and he felt warm. His eyes were closed, but he had the sensation of light surrounding him.

Somehow he was aware of words coming together in his mind. At first they were blurred and distorted. Then they began to come together forming a complete thought—but still not his own thought. Of that he was very sure, both then, and for the rest of his life.

Standing there holding Tink, with his mind cut off from fear and the terror of death, the words came before him:

Yes, I love him, and I will give him life. One day you will love me even more than you love this boy. You will love me more than your own life.

The cold and the darkness came back with a rush, when Tink's body twitched suddenly. The boy caught a great gulp of air, then expelled it like a swimmer surfacing after being too long under water.

"Tink!" Gilbert said huskily, and the boy's eyes opened slowly, and then he smiled.

"Hello—Gilbert . . ." he said; then he closed his eyes, and for one dreadful instant the man thought he was gone. Then he saw the boy's even breathing, and put him gently on the bed.

Two hours later, Sam Fuller came in yawning and scratching. "You better eat a good breakfast this morning, Gilbert. It's going to be cold out there. Well, let me have a look at—"

He had stepped beside Tink and bent over to look at the boy's face, placing his hand on the forehead at the same time.

"Bless my soul!" he exclaimed, then turned wildly to Gilbert, he cried, "Look at this, man! It's a miracle!"

Gilbert came to look down at Tink. "He's better, isn't he, Sam?"

"Why, his fever is completely gone—and his breathing is— why, I can't hear a thing in his chest, Gilbert!"

Tink opened his eyes then and saw the two men bending over him. "Hello," he said cheerfully though in a weak voice. Then he licked his lips and said, "I'm awful hungry! Could I have something to eat? And a lot of it, please?"

Fuller gave a burst of roaring laughter and rubbed his hands together with pleasure, "I should say so, my boy! Well, I must be a better doctor than I've been thinking lately, eh, Winslow?"

Gilbert was staring at Tink's face, and he murmured quietly, "I'll get you something right away, Tink." He touched the boy's cheek with his hand, and there was wonder in his blue eyes.

As he walked toward the galley with Fuller, the doctor could not contain himself. He clapped Gilbert on the back and cried, "I told Edward last night the boy couldn't last two days—and now look at him! Good color, clear eyes, and a ravenous appetite! Thank God! We've lost so many I was about to lose my faith, but this boy is a miracle, Winslow!"

Gilbert stopped so suddenly that Fuller stumbled. He put one hand on the rail, then with the most sober look the doctor had ever seen on his face, he said, "I never believed in miracles. But now I've seen one."

Fuller stared at him, then said, "Well, what will it do for you, son?"

Gilbert rubbed his jaw, stared out over the rail at the rolling tide, and then finally said softly, "A miracle, now, can be a pretty troublesome thing, Fuller. Once you've seen one, you can't ever go back to the old ways of thinking."

"Would you want to?" Fuller inquired gently.

Gilbert thought it over for a long moment, then said, "No, if there's something like that in this universe, I wouldn't want to miss it." Then he moved along the deck toward the galley, leaving Fuller to stare at him with open eyes.

"Well, now," the physician said in wonder, "What'll be the end of *that*, I wonder?"

March brought the end of the general sickness—and the Indians.

On March 16, Standish had called a meeting to reorganize the men into a more efficient body when they were interrupted in a most astonishing manner. Armed with bow and arrows, a tall powerful warrior emerged from the wood, crossed the clearing, and came striding down toward the Common House where the meeting was in session. He walked right up to the astonished group, raised his hand in friendly salute, and said in English, "Welcome."

There was a sudden burst of activity, and the men surrounded the Indian, everyone trying to talk at once. Finally Standish shouted, "Silence!" Then while the others listened, he questioned the Indian.

His name, he said, was Samoset. He talked for a long time, answering freely all questions put to him. He was an Algonquin and had spent much time with an English sailor named Captain Dermer, a name they all knew well. He had been sent out by the Council for New England to explore the coast but had not returned when they had sailed from England.

When they asked him about Plymouth, he explained that the place was called Patuxet in his tongue, but that a terrible plague had wiped out the tribe that had planted the corn they had found. He told them the Wampanoags ruled by Massasoit were the most powerful tribe in the area.

Finally he ate a meal of biscuit, butter, cheese and pudding washed down with beer.

There was some disagreement about what to do with him. Billington and others thought he should be held lest he be a spy come to discover their strength, but Bradford demurred, and the next morning, he left, promising to return soon with some of the leaders of the surrounding tribes.

A week passed and Gilbert met Edward as he came in from working on Standish's emplacements. There was such a pallor on his brother's face that Gilbert was alarmed. "Edward, what's wrong?"

"Elizabeth is dying."

Gilbert stood there helpless to say a word; then he put his arm around his brother's shoulder, and walked with him to their little house. Inside they found Fuller, Priscilla, and Humility watching over the dying woman.

Gilbert took a seat on a stool, his back against the wall, while Edward slumped in a chair holding his wife's hand.

Fuller came over and sat down by Gilbert, whispering, "She'll not see another day, I'm afraid."

She died an hour later without awakening. One minute she was laboring for breath, then she coughed once and the breathing stopped.

Edward stood up as Fuller went quickly. He searched for life, and then turned and said softly, "She's gone, Edward."

Edward Winslow stood there, tears in his eyes. For a long time he looked down at the dead face; then he whispered huskily, "I was not a good husband to you, Elizabeth. God forgive me!"

At once Humility, who had been standing with her back to the wall, went to him. She took his arm, turned him to face her, then said, "You were a wonderful husband, Mr. Winslow! You cared for her these last months as no other man in the world would have done! I—I never knew a man could be so loving and kind to a woman!"

She turned her head and looked directly at Gilbert as she ended, then whirled and left the room.

Later that week, Samoset returned with another Indian named Squanto. His story made that of Samoset seem pale and insignificant.

He had been to England with Captain George Weymouth, and returned to Plymouth with Captain John Smith. He spoke better English than Samoset, and informed the men that Massasoit with about sixty of his braves were on their way to Plymouth. None that were there that day ever forgot the sight of the great chief striding out of the woods, wearing about his neck his badge of office, a great chain of white bone beads. His face was dyed a deep mulberry, and he was oiled from head to foot so that his body gleamed in the sun. Behind him came sixty tall, grim-looking warriors, all painted on the face and body, some black, some red, some yellow, some white, decorated with crosses, and some with grotesque loops and squares. A few wore skins. Many were naked. All were tall, muscular men.

Captain Standish and William Brewster met him at the Town Brook with a half dozen musketeers as a guard of honor. They exchanged salutes and marched together down the little main street to an unfinished house. There they had spread a green rug and three or four cushions. The chief and his most important warriors sat on these, and then Governor Carver appeared, preceded by a drum and trumpet. Miles Standish was the stage manager for this performance. He was determined to impress the Indians with all the military pomp and bravado that his handful of soldiers could muster.

All afternoon the business went on, and Tink finally got his fill of watching. "Do we have to stay for all this?" he asked.

"Why, you're seeing history made, Tink!" Gilbert said in amusement. "What would you rather do?"

"Catch a fish!"

Gilbert nodded and said, "Me too, son. Let's let these folks make history while we try our luck at that deep pool by the big elm."

Late that afternoon when they came back with a stringer of fish, the Indians were gone.

"What happened, Miles?" Gilbert asked as he pulled off his shoes and went to bed.

Standish rolled over and gave him a roguish look. "Same thing that always happens at these meetings. We agreed to be nice to them, and they did the same."

Gilbert closed his eyes and asked, "Think it'll work?"

"Certainly—until one side gets a better offer! Not much different here than in the courts of Europe."

Gilbert lifted his head at that, then shook his head. "Think you might be wrong, Miles. These people are different. They'll do what they say."

Standish thought about that, then let his head fall back, as he muttered, "Well—*that* will be a change, won't it now?"

CHAPTER TWENTY-SEVEN

A NEW SERVICE

★ ★ ★ ★

Tink grew better every day, but now that others were getting out of their beds and making rapid recoveries, Gilbert developed a nagging cold accompanied by a dry cough and a ringing in his ears. He said nothing about it, but Edward noted it.

Since the night in Tink's cabin, he'd been quieter, spending his time alone, walking in the woods. He read a great deal from William Brewster's small library—mostly books of sermons and from the Bible. He hadn't told anyone about the experience, but it was impossible for him to forget it; rather, as time went on, the memory of it burned more deeply into his consciousness.

The closest he came to speaking of it was once when he'd been sitting late one night reading, and Edward had sat across from him writing a history of New Plymouth.

His eyes began to burn, and he coughed and put the book down. Edward looked up and said, "You ought to get some rest. You look terrible!"

"I'm all right." Then he leaned forward and stared at his brother, and asked suddenly, "Edward, do you love God?"

"Do I love God? Of course I do!"

"Tell me how it is."

Edward looked confused. He started to speak once, then cleared his throat and thought hard. Finally he said, "Why, man was made to love God. I'd be a heathen if I didn't!"

Gilbert rubbed his eyes, then shook his head. "I don't love Him." He looked across at Edward with a strange expression in his eyes, and said almost to himself, "I love people that I can see and touch and hear. But God is far away and I've got no picture of Him in my mind. It's like trying to love a dim fog."

Edward put his pen down, folded his hands and put them on the table as he considered what Gilbert had said. "You're not the first to have a problem with that. The Scripture says, 'No man hath seen God at any time.' And that's what the gospel is all about, Gilbert. Did you ever hear the word *Emmanuel*? Well, that means literally 'God with us.' And that's what Jesus is—the God who cannot be seen became flesh and dwelt among us."

"And do you love Jesus Christ?" Gilbert asked at once. "You haven't seen Him either."

"In one way I have—or rather, in two." Edward touched the Bible in Gilbert's hand, saying, "In the Gospels we have the picture of the Lord Jesus. As I read about His life—how He went about giving sight to the blind, healing the lame, it soaks into me and I get an impression of Him that way."

"I can understand that," Gilbert nodded. "He isn't like any other man, is He? I mean can you imagine any other human being saying to another, 'I forgive your sins'? And not sins done against Him, either—just sins." He paused then asked, "What's the other thing that makes you love Him?"

Edward shifted uncomfortably, and there was a trace of embarrassment in his eyes. "Well—I don't know exactly how to put it without sounding like some sort of wild-eyed prophet. It's something that some people go into error on quite often." He searched for a way of putting it, then shrugged. "I can only say that in some way I can't explain, since I gave my heart to God, there's been a—a *presence* inside me."

"A presence!" Gilbert's head came up and there was a sharp light in his eyes.

"That sounds fantastic to you, I suppose, but I can't think of any way to explain it."

Gilbert stared across the table, then asked tensely, "Do— have you ever *heard* anything?"

Edward laughed and slapped the table. "Do I hear voices, you're asking! Well, not really, but several times I've had what you might call *impressions*. Thoughts that came from somewhere outside my own mind—and that keep coming back."

He glanced at his brother, "Having quite a struggle with God, aren't you, lad?"

Gilbert retreated behind the Bible and nodded, "Just thinking about things, Edward."

He never missed the services held in the Common House, and it came to him once as he sat there listening to Bradford preach, how much more real God was in his life than ever before. Always before, God had been something academic, a vague force that had to be acknowledged. But as he listened to the sermons and the day-by-day conversation of the people around him and as he immersed himself in the Scripture, the figure of Jesus Christ loomed ever larger in his thoughts.

One day you will love me with all your heart.

A hundred times a day that flickered through his mind, but he still had not sense of what it all meant.

Two days later he was eating a quick breakfast with Miles and Edward when they heard footsteps approach; then a knock sounded on the door, loud and urgent.

"Come in!" Edward called, and they looked up to see the door open and Captain Christopher Jones enter.

He had been there often, seeming to enjoy the company of the three men, but now his eyes were burning with anger, his lips white and compressed.

"What's wrong?" Standish demanded, as all three of them got to their feet.

"The crew's taken the ship," he said tightly.

"Mutiny?" Edward breathed, then shook his head. "I didn't think they'd dare!"

"They dared, right enough," Jones said. "And they'll get away with it, too!"

"We'll put a stop to this nonsense!" Standish said angrily. "Get the men up, Edward—we'll send a boarding party and take that ship!"

Jones shook his head, saying bitterly. "Not a chance of that, Standish. Coffin is in charge, and he was a gunner in the navy. He's got your cannon in place, and he says he'll blow any craft out of the water that comes near enough."

Standish stood there, breathless with rage. He blustered and swore, but Edward said, "We must have a meeting at once! When will they leave, Captain? A week or so?"

A bitter light gleamed in Jones's gray eyes. "They weigh anchor at dusk tonight—when the tide rises enough to get them over the shoals."

"Tonight! Why, we'll have to do something right away!" Edward said.

"Nothing to do, Winslow," Captain Jones shrugged. "There's only about fifteen of them, and only about six who are mutinous. But Coffin knows his business. He can navigate and he can do what he says with the gun. They'll be on their way at dusk."

In less than half an hour every man who could walk was crowded into the Common House. Edward asked Captain Jones to repeat his story, which he did, adding only, "It's bad luck, for me—and for you, too. I wish we'd gotten all your tools and supplies off the ship before this happened."

"Why, most of our seed corn is on the ship!" Governor Carver said in a shocked tone.

"And my cannon! How can we defend ourselves without arms?" Miles Standish cried, his face red with anger. "And most of our powder hasn't been moved to the powder house."

Everyone began talking at once, and finally Bradford held up his hand for silence. "We are helpless—but God is not. Let us pray that God will help us as He has done so often in the past. And let us be specific in our prayers. The Savior said, did He not, 'Whatsoever things ye ask believing, ye shall receive'? We are His people and the sheep of His pasture, so let us call upon the Great Shepherd to meet our dire need."

Gilbert was familiar with this method. He had seen it often used in Leyden, and it took one specific form. A need would be voiced, the people would pray, and then after a time of waiting, quite often someone would stand and give a simple message of some sort. Sometimes no one did, but often one of the congregation would give a "word of exhortation" in which the congregation would be encouraged to have faith until God answered.

Expecting something like this from one of the leaders, shock ran along Gilbert's nerves when out of the long silence he heard the voice of William Brewster say clearly, "The Lord will deliver us from this calamity—and He will do so by the hand of Gilbert Winslow!"

A wave of silence filled the room and Gilbert's face flushed as every eye turned toward him. He leaped to his feet.

"I'm not one of your number, Mr. Bradford." He took a deep breath and added so softly that those in the back had to lean forward to catch his words. "I—I am not a man of God like the rest of you."

The silence ran so deep that the sound of a woodpecker far off rang clearly through the room, and Gilbert coughed twice, then lifted his head and stared straight at William Brewster, saying, "You must be mistaken in this instance, sir. I am not a man that God would care to use."

"God longs to use all men, Gilbert!" Brewster nodded, and then he added with a fine smile, "Especially those men who are willing to confess their inadequacy. I ask you plainly, do you have anything to say concerning this trouble we are in?"

Then William Bradford said, "Perhaps this time you are desperate enough, Mr. Winslow."

Suddenly Gilbert raised his head and he said clearly. "I make no claim to being God's agent—but a way of taking the ship has been taking shape in my mind."

A hubbub of voices began, but the voice of Christopher Jones rose above it. "For God's sake, man, out with it!"

A burden lifted from Gilbert's shoulders, and from where she stood, Humility saw his wide lips break into a reckless grin, lightening the gloom that had rested on his face for so long.

"The thing is impossible," he began, "but you of all people should not be put off by that. One thing is clear, they'll watch the shallop like a hawk!"

"That they will!" Jones nodded. He had his attention fixed on Gilbert, and added, "There'll be no using that craft to get on board."

"No, but there's a way to board the ship," Gilbert said.

"How do you propose to get on board?" Bradford asked, his face perplexed.

"The only way there is—swim."

"What!" Jones yelped. "Why that's insane, Winslow! The

ship is half a mile out—and you'd have to circle behind—!"

"It'll be about a mile and a half, Captain," Gilbert said quietly. "I've done that distance and more many a time."

"That he has," Edward said. "But not when you were sick. That water is icy still with the winter's chill."

"Besides, what could you do if you *did* get there?" Standish asked. "You couldn't carry a pistol of any kind in the water."

"I could take my sword."

Something about the way he said the thing—so simply and so quietly—caught at them all. He made a flat high shape outlined against the shadows of the lanterns; there was a tough and resilient vigor all about him, a hard physical power to his body. Discipline lay along the pressed lines of his broad mouth, but a rash and reckless will was in his eyes, struggling against it.

"One sword against a crew of armed men? It makes no sense!" Samuel Fuller lowered his head, staring at Gilbert steadily, doubt in his face.

"Not the whole crew," Gilbert said. "Get to Coffin, and the rest will be easier."

Standish said, "Man, I'd go with you in a second—but I can't swim no more than a nail!"

Gilbert shrugged. "Not too many can, Miles." He looked around the room and asked, "Any of you men think you can make it to the ship?"

"I can."

Peter Brown stepped forward to stand in front of Gilbert. "I grew up on the sea, Winslow. Once I swam three miles to a reef, then back five hours later."

There was a challenge in Brown's face, and Gilbert met it directly. "There'll be a little more to it than a long swim."

"Don't worry about that, Winslow. I'll do my share of the fighting."

William Bradford stepped in to say, "I am not at all certain of this. Captain Standish, you must decide, since this is a military affair."

Miles Standish stared at Gilbert, his eyes stern, and he nodded. "It's the only way, Mr. Bradford. If Mr. Winslow has luck, it could work."

"I dislike the word *luck*," Bradford insisted, "I would much rather he had the favor of the Lord."

"Amen—Amen!" A wave of agreement swept the crowd; then Standish said, "All right, we'll do it, but with one change in your plan. We'll make a run at the ship with loaded muskets and grappling hooks in plain sight. We'll carry all the loaded muskets we can handle and keep up what fire we can. Probably won't hit anything but it'll keep those scoundrels' attention, I'll warrant!"

"What about the cannon?" Jones asked.

"If we keep the bow of the shallop straight, she'll be a mighty small target. They won't be able to get off more than two or three shots."

"But they'll be firing at us with muskets as well," Edward said.

Standish gave him a tight grin. "Yes, Mr. Winslow, that's what happens when men fight in a war. You get shot at—and sometimes you get killed."

Bradford said, "I feel that the thing must be attempted. Mr. Brewster, Governor Carver, do you agree?" Receiving their nods, he turned and went to Gilbert. Putting both his hands on the young man's head in a gesture going far back in history, he blessed him, then turned to Peter Brown and did the same.

"God will be with you," he said softly.

Gilbert looked into the older man's eyes, and there was a peace in his face as he murmured with a tone of wonder, "He already is, Mr. Bradford!"

All day the preparations for the attack kept the men busy. The skies were beginning to turn dark when Gilbert came to look at the shallop. Howland had made, in effect, a shooting platform in the prow of the craft.

Gilbert stepped in to stand on the platform with Standish, and the little captain's face beamed as he picked up one of the muskets from the rack built midway in the shallop. "Look! Just the right height to rest a musket on—and only my head's exposed to their fire!"

"Can't hurt *you* with a shot to your head," Gilbert grinned. "Just so they don't shoot you in the foot, where your brains are."

Standish gave him a wide grin, then, leaning the musket

against the rail, he grew serious.

"It's a wild thing, Gilbert—and your chances are not good. According to Jones those rascals are a pretty tough bunch, and if there's one slip they have you."

Gilbert stared out at the *Mayflower* sitting quietly in the harbor half a mile off. "Miles, one thing I'd like to be sure of—in case I don't make it."

"Name it, boy!"

"Watch out for Tink, will you?"

"Like he was my own son!" Standish said instantly. "Have no fears on that score." He hesitated and then with some difficulty asked, "Have you any fears about what happens if you die?"

Gilbert rested his hand on the upper plank of the barricade, then put his chin on it. A squadron of gulls wheeled by, dipping down to touch the long, low swells of gray water, then with cacophonous screams, rose high in the sky. "I've thought of that, Miles. Most men do before a thing like this, I suppose."

"Always before a battle," Standish agreed.

"I've never had much use for deathbed confessions—seems like a cheap way for a man to act. Live like the devil, then when death comes, go whining to God making promises to be good." He lifted his head, turned to face Standish and there was no strain in his wedge-shaped face. His eyes were steady and his broad lips were half smiling. When he spoke his husky voice was even, as if he were talking about fishing instead of his own death.

"I've not given God much thought, Miles—but these people have forced me to it. You know, I'd always thought that getting into heaven was a matter of accounting. I'd stand before some angel, and he'd put all my good deeds in one arm of the balance and all my sins in the other—then if the good weighed a pound or so more than the bad, why, I was all right."

Standish nodded. "Aye, I've thought about the same most of my life."

"It's not like that, Miles," Gilbert said soberly. "I'm not sure about many things, but I have learned this from Brewster and Bradford: getting to heaven is tied up with where you stand with Jesus Christ—and right now all I can say, I guess, is that I'm looking for Him."

"From what I get from the preaching of these men," Standish said, "I think Christ is looking for you—even more than you're looking for Him."

Gilbert nodded, then said, "God be with you when you make the attack, Miles."

"And with you, boy!" Awkwardly Standish threw his arm around the taller man, gave him a fierce hug, then wheeled and leaped out of the boat, embarrassed by his own action.

Gilbert grinned, then saw Brown standing by watching. "Ready?" he asked.

"Yes." The young man's face was pale, and he was holding a sword and a sheathed knife in his hands, looking at them strangely.

"I've been thinking about a way to carry our weapons, Peter," Gilbert said. He took the sword and measured it carefully with his eyes. "Can't carry the swords as we normally would—too much in the way for swimming. I think we can make some sort of harness out of thin strips of leather. Tie them around the neck so that the blade is out of the way on our backs."

"Yes, I think that might work," Brown said.

"I've got some leather in the hut. I'll run up and get it. We'll need to start in ten minutes."

He turned and ran up the hill, and after a short search he found several strips of leather. Picking up his sword and a dagger and a couple of sheaths, he left the hut and turned toward the sea.

"Gilbert!"

Humility had appeared from higher up the hill, and she came to stand stiffly before him. Her hands were long and slender and supple as she held a piece of cloth. A feeble slanting beam of sunlight reached through the clouds to accent the yellow luster in her hair; and that rich color deepened the ivory tints of her skin.

"I—I wanted to speak to you," she said, and color touched her cheeks as she stood before him. "There's been a wrong feeling in my spirit about you, Gilbert." The words came hard, but she kept her back straight, and her eyes fixed on his. "I've hated you for what you did—but I ask you to forgive me for that. Will you?"

"Of course!"

"Thank you." She put out her hand and he took it in his own. "I can't lie to you. I never could, could I? You know I loved you."

He nodded and started to speak, but she took her hand back and said quickly, "No, don't say anything. I don't know why you're doing this thing—risking your life, but I do know that you're not what I thought. You're honest. But we can never be more than friends."

"Humility—!"

"Peter is a reliable man. You're like the wind, Gilbert—wild and exciting, but I'd never know what to expect. That's important to me, you know."

He looked at her, then said soberly, "I know you think that." He searched her face carefully, then shook his head, saying, "You're wrong, Humility! You're more of a woman than you know—but I guess you'll never find that out."

"Why do you *say* things like that!" she cried, clenching her fists.

"Sorry." He glanced up toward the sky, then back to her. "I must go. Goodbye, then."

He turned and ran down toward the beach. If he had turned he would have seen her drop the cloth and throw her arms up in a strange manner—then put her hands over her face and retreat back up the street with her shoulders shaking as she went blindly along.

"You'd best be on the way," Standish said as he returned. "By the time you get out there, it'll be almost dark."

"All right. Here's the leather, Peter." He fashioned a simple harness for Brown's sword that allowed freedom of action and kept the blade resting on his back. "That ought to do." He made another for himself and Brown helped him settle the sword into position. "This will do for the knives." They belted the knives about their waists and then were ready.

"God be with you!" Standish cried as the two men left, running quickly up the beach.

"This will do," Gilbert said. He kicked off his shoes and Brown did the same, then they stripped out of their breeches. Wearing only undergarments and their weapons, they ran together and plunged into the sea.

The cold water hit Gilbert like a knife, taking his breath for a moment, but he forged ahead with long, slow strokes. The sea was calm inside the reef, but he could see that the water was choppy farther out. *Make it harder for them to see us,* he thought.

They passed the reef and the water became rougher, slapping at their faces and lifting them high, then dropping them down in the troughs.

After fifteen minutes he turned to float on his back, calling out, "Are you all right?"

Brown gave him a wide-eyed look and yelled back, "Yes—how about you?"

"Cold—but not too tired. Can you see the ship?"

Brown looked over his shoulder, peered into the falling gloom. "No, I can't."

Gilbert had excellent eyesight; he looked south and said, "She's right over there. We can bear south now."

They made the swim without another pause, Gilbert fearing that they'd cut it too fine. *Got to be in position when Miles attacks— if I know him, he won't stop until he rams the ship and tries to board her. Got to be on deck by then—they'd cut our men to pieces as they try to board!*

Brown got confused and finally dropped behind, but he was swimming strongly. Gilbert stayed less than two hundred yards north of the ship, then swung south and finally pulled up. Lying on his back and gasping for breath, he said, "I'm about done! How about you?"

"I—I'm pretty tired."

They lay there getting their breath back, and watching the dim shadow of the *Mayflower* outlined in the falling darkness.

"When we go up, we'll use the ladder. I'll go first, but I'll wait until you're on the ladder."

"What then?"

"The problem will be with Coffin, O'Neal, Davis, and a couple more. Some of the men aren't really in this. Don't hurt French or Pike." He suddenly threw his head back. "There's a shot—let's go!"

He threw himself forward, making for the ship as fast as he could propel himself through the sea, and by the time he pulled himself up the wooden ladder and helped Brown up beside him, the firing from the deck had started.

Gilbert pulled his knife, sliced the harness and, holding his sword in readiness, moved up the ladder, Brown right behind him. The cannon went off just as they reached the rail, and Gilbert raised his head carefully.

Four men, including French, Pike and another seaman named Morton served the gun, with Coffin standing behind it to aim the weapon.

Stationed along the rail seven seamen were ranged firing their muskets at the approaching shallop.

"Give it to 'em!" Coffin screamed, and he touched a match to the venthole. The cannon boomed, and recoiled to the end of the rope that made it fast to the rail.

"Hi! Good shot!" O'Neal yelled. "Not more'n a foot wide. You'll get a hit next time, Coffin!"

Gilbert risked standing up and saw the shallop coming full at the ship, Standish ignoring the barricade and standing up to get a better shot with his musket. He fired and splinters flew from the rail between two of the seamen.

"They're coming in," Gilbert said leaning over to speak to Brown. "I'll take Coffin and you try to put O'Neal down."

"You mean—kill him?" Brown said. There was a wild look in his eyes, and every time a gun went off he flinched.

"Put him down any way you can—or those men in that boat will be butchered! Come on!"

He had not much hope Brown would be of help, but there was no time to think. As he leaped over the rail he saw that two of the men were busy loading their muskets, and two others fired off a shot. *Three with charged muskets*, he thought, but he concentrated on Coffin who was cursing the gun crew for their slowness.

Gilbert knew that the action would last only a few seconds, and that he and Brown would not live if they failed. Coffin's narrow back was toward him, and every instinct in him urged him to drive his blade home, but he did not. Switching his sword to his left hand he lifted his right arm high and brought his forearm down on Coffin's neck with a tremendous blow that snapped his head backward and drove him to the deck, his arms and legs flapping loosely.

"What . . . !" A muscular seaman named Prine had just dropped the ball down the mouth of the cannon. He looked up to see Coffin sprawl on the deck, and his eyes caught sight of Gilbert who had put his sword in his right hand. Prine howled, "O'Neal! Over here!" He pulled a sword from his belt and glanced over his shoulder. "French—get 'em!"

French and Pike looked up at the same time, with startled eyes, and taking one look at Gilbert, they both stepped back. The other man, a seaman that Gilbert didn't know, drew his sword and joined Prine in a sudden attack on Gilbert.

Neither of them were expert, and in a single duel, Gilbert would have played with them—but they came at him in tandem, and he took a step back, parrying the blade of Prine, then with a slashing backstroke struck the other's sword with a force that drove it out of the man's hands to the deck.

Prine backed off, looked where the others were attacking by the rail, and over his head Gilbert saw that everything had gone wrong.

Brown must have been slow or had been too scrupulous, for O'Neal had avoided him. Even as Gilbert watched, the thick sailor took a step back, snatched a loaded musket from one of the men along the rail, and cried out, "Shoot them!"

Gilbert saw Prine and the other man, who had recovered his sword, closing in on him, but there across the deck he saw that Peter Brown would soon be a dead man!

Both O'Neal and one of the other men were swinging their muskets around toward the helpless Brown, and there was no doubt about their intention. They could not miss at that range. Brown turned his head suddenly, his fear-stricken eyes meeting those of Gilbert.

In that split second, with the sound of firing around him and with the blades of the two men reaching for him, Gilbert made a decision. With a catlike leap he sprang past his own adversaries. There was a low railing around the mainmast, and without breaking stride, he used it for a springboard. The muzzles of the weapons were lowering as he crouched, then drove himself in a headlong drive at O'Neal and the other man. As he flew through the air, he twisted his body, so that he went crashing with his torso on O'Neal's squat body, driving him into the rail and touching off his musket with a roar of explosion right in his face. His legs hit the other man waist high, but though he was staggered, he didn't go down.

"Peter! Cut them down!" Gilbert yelled, and a red mist seemed to fall over his eyes, the rage of battle driving him beyond logic or reason.

Gilbert saw Brown being backed to the mast by two men beating his sword down with their blades, and others were rushing to help them and Prine.

He did his best, twisting as Prine's naked blade shot forward, and by twisting his body to one side, he managed to take only a minor wound, a raking shallow cut across his back, high up.

Then he was through, for he was practically on his face after his last lunge. *Now it's over*, he thought; he was sad at what he would never have, but not afraid.

Then he heard a chorus of yelling and, rolling over quickly, saw Pike, French, and two other men come up to attack Prine.

He heaved himself to his feet, grabbed his sword and with a yell threw himself at the two men about to finish off Brown.

One of them turned with a startled look of rage and made a pass at Gilbert. He parried it with ease and drove his own blade through the man's heart, withdrew it and turned to meet an attack from the rear.

It was well he did, for he found himself face-to-face with Coffin!

The tall, thin form of the man was twisted sideways, one foot out with knee bent, left foot back and at right angles—the classic position, and the moment their blades touched, Gilbert knew he had never crossed blades with a better swordsman.

He saw in a flash that men, led by Standish, were swarming over the rail, and that the loyal portion of the crew had united with them to herd the renegades into a huddle next to the rail.

"It's over, Coffin!" he cried. "Throw down your sword."

"No, it's not over, not till you're dead meat!" Coffin snarled and moved ahead with a rapid attack such as Gilbert had never seen!

Coffin's blade darted faster than a snake's tongue, and only by falling back in a half-stumble did Gilbert survive. He was exhausted after the swim, and the wound in his back was draining his strength. Back, back he went, staving off death by the last fraction of a second as he pushed aside Coffin's darting blade time and time again.

His back struck the wall of the quarterdeck, and he twisted to one side, missing death by inches as Coffin's blade struck the wood where he had been an instant earlier.

Gilbert turned, driven back by the brilliance of the man's swordsmanship; never once was he able to mount an attack of his own. Dimly he was aware that the fight below was almost over; soon, Standish and others would come to his aid—but it would be too late.

For he could back up no more. His legs struck the rail, and for a few seconds the blades made a ringing clash so rapid it was impossible to separate them. He was fighting on instinct now, his mind not able to keep up with Coffin's tactics. Parry, parry, parry—twist and turn. But now he was getting slower and he saw the fiery light of victory in Coffin's eyes as he crouched for the final lunge.

Do what he nevair expect! The words came to his mind like a flash of light from his past—the words of his old master, Dupree. And in a desperation born of despair, he did exactly that. He threw the book away in one instant. With a wild yell he leaped at Coffin, lifting his sword high over his head like a club! If Coffin had kept his head he could have run Gilbert through the body at that moment, but he did not.

The wild yell and the totally unexpected abandonment of the classic style for the rough, vicious swing of the sword rattled him. He took one step back and when the downward stroke of his raging opponent struck, it nearly tore his own blade from his hand!

He had only time to lift his blade to catch the next wild sweep which Gilbert threw at him crossways like a scythe.

Screaming like a banshee, Gilbert drove Coffin across the deck by brute force. None of the smooth exact science he had spent years learning! He swung his blade like a wild Irishman swings a shillelah in a brawl, and it shattered Coffin's cool confidence.

He caught himself for one last try, but as he went into the

classic stance, Gilbert kicked him in the knee and Coffin went down with a cry of agony.

Instantly Gilbert was over him, his eyes mad with battle fury, his sword poised over the fallen man's body.

Coffin looked up, and there was no fear in his eyes. He spat out, "Do it, then! I ain't afraid to die!"

Still Gilbert stood there, the sword drawn back, quivering and ready to drop.

"Well, you going to kill him or not?"

Gilbert twisted his head to see that Standish had come up the ladder and was watching the scene with clinical interest.

The roar of blood in Gilbert's ears quieted, and he looked down at Coffin, glaring at him with pale-eyed hatred.

Then he slowly pulled his sword back and there was a look of wonder in his cornflower blue eyes.

"No, I'm not—and there's your miracle right there!"

Even as he spoke, a violent tremor shook his body, and Standish at once whipped off his cloak and draped it over his shoulders. "We'd best get you to Fuller at once. That's a bad cut you took—and that freezing swim didn't do you any good!"

By the time they'd returned and Fuller had finished taking a few stitches in his back, Gilbert's head was swimming, and he seemed to be burning up.

"W-what's wrong with m-me?" he asked feebly.

Fuller threw the needle down and cried, "Curse it all, you've got a case of the sickness coming on, or I'm no doctor! Just when the thing has left, it comes back and tries to take another one of us!" Then he caught himself and said quickly, "But we'll pull you through, my boy—don't doubt it!"

But Gilbert heard only the first part of his statement. His head was swimming and he slipped into a black hole that seemed to be waiting to swallow him up like a huge beast.

CHAPTER TWENTY-EIGHT

THE *MAYFLOWER* SAILS

★ ★ ★ ★

Sometimes he was falling down into a dark hole, and he would tense his muscles for the terrible moment when he would strike the bottom. A roaring would fill his ears, like a mighty rushing wind, but when he opened his mouth to cry out, the wind rushed in, stifling him like a massive blanket.

At other times he seemed to be floating lightly in air, in a strange quietness so hollow that tiny sounds seemed to echo deep down in his brain. At those times there would be a bright light, not harsh but soft and gentle, bathing him in warmth, shielding him from the bone-cracking chill that racked him.

"It's all right, Gilbert! You're not falling!"

His eyes opened and closed abruptly as the light hit them, but he blinked and his vision cleared.

He was sitting up in bed, in a room that was dark except for a low-burning lamp on the table. The shadows flickered over the woman who was kneeling to hold him by the shoulders as he swayed and tried to throw the covers off.

"Humility!" He recognized her, and his lips were so dry her name came out in a croaking sound.

Keeping a hand on his shoulder, she picked up a mug from a table, held it to his lips, saying, "Drink this."

He found he had a raging thirst, and swallowed frantically at the water until she pulled it back, saying, "You can have more later." Putting the mug down, she asked, "How do you feel?"

He licked his lips and answered slowly, "All right. How long have I been here?"

"About ten days." She took her hand off his shoulder and said, "Can you eat something?"

"Anything!" He had a hunger to match his thirst. He ate the bowl of soup she brought him and asked for more.

"You'd better wait until Mr. Fuller gets here. Too much at first might be bad for you." She turned to leave, but came back and put her hand on his chest. Shoving him back flat on the bed, she said, "You'd better rest—you haven't had much normal sleep."

Her face was thinner, he thought, and lined with fatigue. "Have you been here all this time?"

She hesitated, then nodded. "Some of the time. Edward stayed with you as well."

He was so sleepy he couldn't keep his eyes open, but he said as he dropped off, "I don't think Peter will like it."

He woke up some time later to find clear light streaming in through the open window. A bird was singing, and the room seemed stuffy. He sat up in bed, swung his feet to the floor, then stood up. The room swung round in an alarming fashion, but he held to the wall until it stopped.

He was wearing only a pair of short underpants, and could not find his clothes, so he wrapped the blanket around him and staggered outside. He sat down at once on a rude bench against the side of the hut and looked around.

Spring had made an assault on Plymouth during his sickness, driving out the cold winds and clammy air. He took a deep breath of the warm April breeze, smelling of the sea and of green trees and warming earth, and for a long time he sat there, enjoying the warmth.

A slight figure was wending up the steep hill, and he recognized Captain Christopher Jones. There was an odd look on the seaman's face, Gilbert saw, as he came closer, but he smiled when he came up to the cabin, saying with energy, "Why, you're not dead, are you, Winslow?"

"I guess not, Captain."

"You came pretty close, I can tell you! I sat with you a few times with Edward, and it looked like you weren't going to make it." His face crinkled in a smile and he added, "If it hadn't been for that young woman caring for you like a sick baby, why, I reckon you'd not be sitting here enjoying this sunshine."

Gilbert stared at him. "She did that?" he asked.

Jones cocked his head, suddenly sober as he remarked. "I tell you, it's hard to figure these folks out, Winslow. I got the idea she had nothing but hate for you after what you did; then she goes and pulls a stunt like this!"

Gilbert bit his lip, then shook his head. "These folks believe in turning the other cheek. Humility believes in doing her Christian duty."

"That so?" Jones asked, and there was a light of humor in his gray eyes. "Well, I guess there's more to it than that—but in any case, you're looking better."

Something in Christopher Jones's face made Gilbert consider him more closely. He finally asked, "I think you've got something to tell me."

"Well, I didn't know how I'd find you . . ."

"What is it, Captain?" He glanced toward the sea, and it came to him. "You're taking the *Mayflower* back home?"

"Well, yes. Today's the fourth—we'll set sail tomorrow."

Gilbert dropped his head and considered it. He was still weak and his thinking was confused. Finally he said, "I'll be ready."

"Well, the thing is . . ." Jones cleared his throat, and seemed to be having trouble with his words. Then he slapped his thigh and cried out, "Oh, a plague on it! Why didn't you stay sick!"

"What?"

"Why, I couldn't take a dying man on board, could I? I had my plan all made to get away while you were still unconscious—then you have to wake up and spoil it all!"

Gilbert smiled at his red face, and said, "Sorry to be such a bother, Captain."

Jones stared at him, gnawing at his lip. "You saved my ship, Winslow. Chances are those roughs would have piled her up or sold her for scrap when they got home. It was you that gave her back to me. What do I do about *that*?"

"You might make me a partner," Gilbert said.

Jones grinned. "Well, that would be going a little *too* far. But you won't be going back with me to England." He grew serious then and said, "I'd never be able to look myself in the face if I took you back to face a rope—and it's not only that you saved the ship. You're not the same man that stowed aboard, are you?"

Gilbert shook his head. "No, I'm not—but I'm still a fugitive and you can get in trouble for concealing me."

"I'll be careful to keep myself clear," the captain said. "But you have to realize that the next ship that comes will probably have someone aboard with a warrant from the King." He shook his head then added, "I'll do this for you; let me take you. When we're in the Channel and I touch at Calais, you can hide yourself in France."

Gilbert shook his head at once. "I'm grateful to you, Captain—but I'll take my chances here."

Jones rose with a puzzled look on his face. "Scratch me! I knew you'd say that! I've offered to take anybody who wants to go back home, and you know how many have accepted my offer?"

"Not many, I'd venture."

"None! Not a bloody one!"

"I'm not too surprised. Even Billington and Hopkins have found something here they'll never give up."

"Found what?" Jones demanded.

"I guess it's freedom, Captain." Gilbert knew that was not altogether right, but he shrugged, and then a thought struck him. "Could you take a letter for me to England?"

"I'm taking one for everybody else, so why not?"

The next morning, despite dire warnings from Sam Fuller and Edward, Gilbert insisted on walking down to the harbor to see the departure.

In the morning light fifty-six people stood watching as Captain Jones stood on the poop deck of the *Mayflower* waving his hand. Gilbert studied them as the sails were being run up. "Why are they all staying, Edward?" he asked quietly. "Only fifty-six people, and twenty-five of those are children. Just thirty-one adults perched on the edge of a continent so big we can't even imagine how far it stretches!"

Edward nodded, and his eyes sought out Susanna White where she stood holding the baby in one arm and Resolved with the other. His cheeks were hollowed, making his large nose seem even larger, but there was a satisfaction in his clear blue eyes. "I know, Gilbert. It looks foolish to the world, but I tell you, there's a victory here! The sickness got half of us—but not a one accepted Jones's offer to go back to an easy life in Holland or England. Listen—" He broke off as Bradford raised his voice in a hymn of thanksgiving. They sang, their thin faces tear-marked, but radiating a joy that could not be denied. "The God of this universe has not let us go unnoticed!"

The women's headcloths flapped in the breeze and men's hair and beards ruffled as they sang. Old John Carver, Brewster, Bradford, and Allerton sang at the top of their lungs as the wind puffed the sails of the ship; soon only the declining speck of the *Mayflower* could be seen, then nothing broke the flat plane of the wide horizon of the sea.

The firstcomers were alone in their New World.

Gilbert regained his strength quickly, and only Edward commented on his remaining in Plymouth instead of returning with the *Mayflower*. "Jones couldn't take you back. He talked about it quite a bit while you were ill."

"I'll have to go back sometime, Edward. They won't forget about Lord Roth back in England."

But he put that in the back of his mind, working hard with the others at planting their corn under Squanto's direction. He often hunted and fished with Tink, the two becoming proficient at finding both game and a variety of ocean and freshwater fish. The boy was happy, but from time to time he got a worried look, and Gilbert knew he was worried about the next ship which might separate them. Gilbert forced the thoughts of that from his mind.

He saw Brown often. The first time they'd met, Brown had been awkward. "You saved my life on the ship. I'm—grateful to you, Winslow."

"You did a good job, Peter. I couldn't have done it without your help."

The tall young man ducked his head, his neck red with

embarrassment; then he looked up and said quietly, "I'm sorry about—about the way it turned out for you. About Humility, I mean."

"You're getting a fine woman, Peter. Any man would be proud to have a wife like her."

"Yes—but what . . . ?"

Gilbert cut off his question. "I wish you both the best, Peter."

Humility had met his gaze with her steady eyes the first time they'd met, but she avoided his company whenever possible.

On Sundays the entire town assembled in the main street, and with every man carrying his musket, they followed Governor Carver to the Common House, where they worshiped. They wore their best clothes for the occasion, Carver having on a fine red cloak. The blues, red, and greens of their coats and smocks made a splash against the plain walls, and William Brewster had a violet suit that almost hurt the eyes. The bands, flat white collars worn by the men, were white and glistening, and some of them wore high-crowned hats.

Elder Brewster served as pastor. He did not give communion since he was not ordained, but he was an excellent preacher. Bradford recorded of him in the history he was writing: "In teaching he was very stirring, and moving the affections; also very plain and distinct in what he taught; by which means he became the more profitable to the hearers. He had a singular good gift in prayer, in ripping up the heart and conscience before God."

They suffered a loss that month, in Governor Carver. The old man had insisted on working alongside the younger men in the fields, and on a very hot day he suddenly dropped his hoe and complained of a terrific pain in the head. Everyone assumed he had too much sun, but after lying down for a few hours, he lapsed into a coma and died two days later.

After the old man was buried with a guard of honor, the next order of business was the election of a new governor. William Brewster was the most obvious choice, but he was eliminated by his position as ruling elder of the church.

"We must always keep the church and the state separate,"

Brewster said, when asked to serve. "We have seen the disastrous effects of its union in England!"

Unanimously, the choice fell on William Bradford, and from his first days in office, a new vigor entered Plymouth's public affairs. Up to this time affairs had rested largely in the hands of Elder Brewster, Pastor Robinson, Deacon Cushman, and Deacon Carver—all older men. Now this group was scattered—one was dead, another in London, a third in Leyden, so the thirty-two-year-old Bradford picked up the reins firmly.

Edward Winslow worked as hard as any man, but something drove him to walk in the woods in the twilight hours. He became absent-minded with Gilbert, his attention hard to hold.

He was walking back to the town late one night, tired and dissatisfied with he knew not what. The spring peepers in the brook made a shrill chorus as he walked slowly, not looking up at the moon that was beginning to peer with a silver face through the velvet sky.

"Edward."

He lifted his head instantly, knowing the voice at once. "Susanna . . ."

He hesitated, then stepped to her side. She stood before him, watching his face in the close and personal way she had; and the warm light of her eyes grew and her face was changed in a way he could not describe. Suddenly she was a shape and a substance before him, and a fragrance and a melody all around him, so that the loneliness that had lived in him so long grew insupportable. The wall he had built against tradition and ritual went down. She was before him, and there was nothing between them. But still he hesitated.

"Edward, would you think of marrying me?" she asked quietly.

He was caught by her direct honesty, and he moved ahead and put his arms around her. Watching her lips lift, he saw that she was smiling—and so he kissed her.

When they broke into the cabin to find Gilbert sitting at the table reading, their faces shone. He rose at once, a wide smile on his face, and put his arms around Susanna, saying, "Well, I have a new sister!" and they all laughed.

Edward Winslow and Susanna White were married in May

when the wild plums put on their white blossoms. The soft, sweet warmth of New England's spring was all about them, and everyone was delighted to have something to celebrate after the long winter of sickness, disaster, and gloom.

They were low on some food, but Gilbert and Tink saw that there was enough fish to cover a wide table in the Common House, and Peter Brown brought down two fat deer.

As Gilbert watched the festivities, he remarked to Bradford, who had joined him, "I remember how I once thought all you people sat around dressed in black and hated mirth and singing . . ."

Bradford gave Gilbert a smile and said, "You have changed many of your ideas recently, haven't you?"

Gilbert said soberly, "I can't believe what a fool I was, Elder! I can't think of a thing I was *right* about!"

Bradford studied him, then asked, "What will you do with your life?"

"I don't know."

"Will you go back to England?"

"To the gallows?" Gilbert stared at the people moving along and piling their plates high with food. There was a strong streak of fatalism underneath his light manner, and he said thoughtfully, "Only a little while ago I was headed for a promising career under Lord North. Money, pleasure—and maybe even a marriage with his daughter. Now I'll probably spend the rest of my life waiting for a door to open and some officer to come through it with the warrant to drag me back to a rope."

Bradford's dark eyes fixed on the face of the younger man, and he let the silence run on before he said, "You think that would have brought you happiness, Gilbert?"

The question raked against the young man's nerves. "Why, I don't know. Why wouldn't it, Elder? Aren't those the things every man wants?"

"And were the people you met in the higher realms of society happy? Did they have peace and contentment?"

Gilbert was suddenly silent, for he knew that such was not the case. "No, they weren't. Most of them wore themselves out chasing after money or pleasure."

"If you were free to do so, would you go back and take up that life?"

Gilbert did not answer; he was glad that John Alden had stood up suddenly and called for quiet.

"Friends, we celebrate the wedding of our good friends, and we all wish them long life and happiness." A chorus of "amen's" met this, and when they subsided, John continued, "I want to invite you to another wedding—mine and Miss Priscilla Mullins!"

This came as no great shock to anyone, but there was a wave of applause and there was much hugging of Priscilla by the women and much beating on John's broad back by the men.

Then Peter Brown moved out from the side of the room where he had been standing with Humility, and with a slight pallor under his tan, he said, "Friends, since weddings and marriage is the purpose of our gathering, I congratulate Mr. and Mrs. Winslow, and I wish Mr. Alden and Miss Mullins joy." He cleared his throat before he added, "And Miss Humility Cooper and I invite you to share in our joy as well."

He moved back to take Humility's hand, and the two were surrounded at once by a wave of people crowding around to congratulate them.

Gilbert was startled to hear a voice in his ear, "It would be nice if you would join in with the well-wishers, Gilbert."

He turned to see Edward standing beside him, and Gilbert at once said, "Thank you, Edward." He moved forward slowly, and finally stood before the two. A silence fell on the room, and all eyes were fastened on the three.

"You are to be congratulated—both of you," he said quickly. Humility took Peter's arm in a quick gesture. She was not smiling as she had been, but her voice was steady and clear as she said, "Thank you, Mr. Winslow."

Brown put his hand out, and when Gilbert gripped it, he said, "I appreciate your good wishes, Gilbert."

Then it was over, and someone started a song. "That was well done," Edward said quietly as Gilbert returned to stand beside him.

"All my loose ends tied up, eh, Edward—" Then his wide mouth turned up in a sudden wry smile as he added, ". . . except the one the hangman's probably getting ready for me at the tower!"

Gilbert discovered that it was impossible to maintain his spirit of apprehension. As the weeks went by he was less and less likely to gaze at the sea and wonder if a sail would appear with the law on board.

The work kept him busy. He helped all the other families finish their houses, and since he had no house or fields of his own, he got to know all of them. The three families still intact were allotted houses, and they each took in several single men and women. Young Priscilla Mullins lived with Elder Brewster and his family, while Humility and Bess stayed with the Allertons.

Gilbert had seen Humility practically every day for months, but had said nothing more intimate than, "Would you pass the water jug?"

He had gone down to the creek to fill two water buckets and met her, awkwardly trying to fill one of the large, wooden kegs from the stream. The brook was deep only in the middle, and she was trying to shove the keg out to deeper water without getting her shoes muddy.

"Let me help you."

She whirled at his words and dropped the keg, which would have floated downstream if Gilbert had not abandoned his buckets and plunged in to retrieve it. "This is too heavy for you," he remarked as the cool water spilled into the container.

She stood there watching him, and finally she said, "I have something to say to you." She spread her hands over the front of her dress, looked out across the woods, then brought her gaze back to meet his. "You said something to me once that I feel is unfair."

"I know." He filled the keg, carried it back to the bank, then turned to face her. She took a step back as if he meant to attack her, and he smiled. "I said you were afraid of life." A loon gave his eerie cry, and then in the silence that followed, he said directly, "I still say it."

She was a tall girl, and the strong lines of her body were outlined beneath the plain dress she wore by the pressure of the

October wind. Her high cheekbones and wide-spaced eyes gave her face an Oriental cast, but the firm chin and green eyes were English. She had been hurt by this man, more than she had dreamed a woman could be hurt, and often she had found herself feeding on her bruised pride, greedily hoping that someday she would find a way to pay him back in kind.

Now she cried out, "You're wrong! So very wrong!"

"I've been wrong about almost everything—but not about this." He asked her suddenly, "When are you marrying?"

The question flustered her, and she raised one hand to tuck a blonde tress under her cap. She was restless under his gaze, and finally burst out, "Oh, I don't know! Why do you ask?"

When he didn't answer, she suddenly struck his chest with her fist, crying out, "You think you're better than Peter, don't you?"

Catching her hand, he held it, shook his head. There was a sadness in his lean face as he said slowly, "No, I don't. I don't think that at all."

She stared at him. "Then what *is* it, Gilbert? Why do you look at me like you do?" A bitterness ran through her tone, and she flushed as she said, "You didn't want me—but you don't want another man to have me, is that it?"

He was unhappy with the scene, and could not answer her question. She was not the woman he'd imagined in his own life, but he could not dislodge the pictures of her that kept coming back to his mind.

"I've made a ruin of my own life, Humility," he said finally. "I hate to see you do the same."

She stared at him, her cheeks suddenly still. He was not the same man she'd known in Holland; not even the same as when they'd landed in Plymouth. The soft lines of his face, the easy laugh, and the confident manner had faded. Now he looked older, and there was a maturity in his face that had been lacking. He smiled often, but it was not the same, for now beneath the smile there was a knowledge of the razor-sharp edge of life that can cut a man down in one instant.

She shook her head, then asked without warning, "You're still in love with that woman, Cecily."

He stared at her, then shook his head. "That's over. She's

in England. Probably married to some Count by now."

"You called her name when you were sick. You wouldn't have done that if you'd forgotten her."

He shrugged, saying quietly, "We don't forget anybody. But . . ."

Whatever he was going to say was cut off by the boom of the cannon, followed by another.

"Both guns," he said looking toward the town. "Something's happened!"

They began to run, and she was as fast as he was. When they got to the edge of the woods, they saw a crowd gathered around the rampart that Standish had built for the weapons. The captain was standing beside one of the cannons, pointing with his sword out toward the sea.

Gilbert looked that way, and saw a tiny flash of white, a sail catching the sun.

"It's a ship." He stared at it steadily, then felt her touch on his arm.

"Run away!"

"What?"

"You can go stay with Squanto and the Indians," she said, and there was an urgency in her manner. "Don't go back to England!"

He stood there, caught by her intense manner, but then he shook his head. "I can't run like a frightened rabbit every time a ship appears." He left her and started to walk down toward the beach, then turned and said with a warmth in his blue eyes, "Humility, whatever happens, I'll always have one thing."

"One thing? What will you have?" she asked.

He grinned and lifted his hand as if he held his sword in a salute.

"I'll always remember that once at least, I loved a real woman!"

As he walked away, her lips trembled, and she whispered, *You fool! You fool! You're throwing yourself away!*

She could not bear to see the straight set of his back as he went to meet whatever fate had for him. Blindly she turned and walked slowly away from the beach and the ship that came closer with every gust of wind.

CHAPTER TWENTY-NINE

OUT OF THE PAST

★ ★ ★ ★

Every man, woman, and child in Plymouth gathered at the beach to welcome the longboat from the ship. Standing slightly apart from the main body, Gilbert ran his eyes over familiar faces, and was swept with a wave of regret; there was little doubt in his mind that he was seeing the last of them.

The prow of the boat grated on the beach, then two seamen jumped out and made her fast, while the passengers disembarked.

"Elder Brewster!" a smallish man cried out, and he was greeted warmly by Brewster and many others. Gilbert heard the name *Cushman*, and looked with interest at the man whom he had met at Southampton.

There was a swirl of people talking and moving, but Gilbert's attention was riveted on William Brewster. He stood there in the midst of the crowd like a statue, his eyes fixed on a man who got off the longboat last. Gilbert had never seen him, but he thought at once, *This is Brewster's son.* He was in his late twenties, and was in size and appearance what William Brewster must have been like as a young man. The older man's face was moved with emotion, and then he held out his arms and his son stepped into them.

There was much confusion as Cushman began introducing

the newcomers to the settlers, but one by one all were made known.

All but one. A tall, thick-bodied man with inquiring brown eyes had stood slightly apart from the group. He was well dressed in a gray suit, over which he wore a black greatcoat with a beaver collar turned up. There was an air of authority about him, and at first Gilbert thought he might be the captain of the ship, yet he did not seem to fit in that role.

Bradford raised his voice above the babble of talk. "Friends, let us go to the Common House. You must be hungry for fresh food after your long voyage." He led them up the hill, but Gilbert noted that the tall man in the brown suit stopped John Alden to ask a question. Alden paused, looked surprised, then looked around. Finding Gilbert with his eyes, he nodded his head, said something briefly, then with a long look at the man, turned and followed the others up the hill.

The man came at once to stand before Gilbert. For all his size he was light on his feet, and paused slightly before saying, "Mr. Gilbert Winslow?" His voice was deep and resonant, giving the impression that if he cared to raise it, the volume would overcome all other sounds.

"That is my name."

A light of interest stirred in the man's quick glance, eyes running over Gilbert as though taking inventory. Then he said, "My name is Wellington. Caleb Wellington of London."

Gilbert nodded but made no reply. Everything about the man signaled power and authority. His hands were strong but well cared for, and the diamond on the ring finger of his right hand would have fed the colonists for six months. His lips were broad with deep creases running along the corners, and the cleft chin was like the prow of a ship, invincible, daring anyone to get in its way. The eyes were set in deep sockets and shadowed by heavy brows, and his forehead was broad, with a mane of thick brown hair that sometimes fell over it in the brisk breeze.

"We have some business to discuss, Mr. Winslow," Wellington said finally. "Would you come aboard to my cabin?"

His manner puzzled Gilbert. There was no question of his mission, since he had asked by name for Gilbert Winslow. *He's not one of the new colonists,* Gilbert thought swiftly. *He's come for me—but why this smooth approach? Why not a brace of armed guards and a pair of manacles for me?*

"Why not here, Mr. Wellington?" Gilbert was curious to see what effect resistance would have on him. This was obviously a man accustomed to being obeyed, but he was surprised at the reaction.

"Why, if you please, but this air is chilly and our business may take a little time."

"Very well." Gilbert followed him to the longboat and they seated themselves. The six sailors manning the oars put about quickly.

"What ship is this?" Gilbert asked.

"The *Fortune*—fifty-five-ton, Robert Logan, captain. Four months out of Southampton." Wellington rattled the facts off in a practiced manner, then asked, "Has your plantation here been successful, Mr. Winslow?"

Gilbert gave him a direct stare, then shrugged. "Half our number are dead. I'm sure most would say that's a high price to pay for a dozen huts and a few acres of Indian corn."

The blunt speech jarred the big man out of his smooth manner. "Half dead! Did the savages attack?"

"Sickness."

Wellington shook his head. "I spent quite a few hours playing chess with Mr. Cushman. He talked quite a bit about his people here. Must say he's not what I expected, Mr. Winslow." His direct brown eyes searched Gilbert's face, and he asked curiously, "I've been wondering how you fit in with these people— different in so many ways from yourself."

"How am I different, Mr. Wellington?"

Gilbert's instant question broke through the man's calm. He blinked, and there was a trace of irritation in his manner as he realized he'd said more than he meant to. He was not a man to endure much pressure, so he turned to face Gilbert squarely, and a hard-edged streak surfaced, breaking the smoothness of his face. "You're not of the Brownist persuasion, Mr. Winslow— or you were not a year ago."

"Who are you, Mr. Wellington?" Gilbert asked. "Are you an agent of the Crown?"

"We're almost to the ship," Wellington said. He looked up

at the red and white cross of St. George flying from the mast. "Our business can wait until we are alone."

The firm set of Wellington's jaw told Gilbert that it would do no good to protest. He had the feeling that he was caught up in some force that was pulling him closer to a dangerous end, but there was no fear as the longboat made fast, and he followed Wellington up the ladder to stand on deck.

"This way." Gilbert followed Wellington as he walked toward the stern, and entered the oak door under the poop deck. Ordinarily there would be a single door inside leading to the captain's Great Cabin, but there were two, one of them old and one obviously new. Removing a key from his vest pocket, Wellington unlocked the one on the left, stepped back to wave Gilbert inside, then followed him.

The room was not large, not more than ten feet wide and twelve feet long. A new partition had been built, Gilbert saw, taking space from the Great Cabin. Most of the space was taken up by a bed, a large oak cabinet that almost touched the low ceiling, two upholstered chairs, a small desk and a small table by the bed. The only decoration was a colorful blanket or shawl on the newly built wall. It looked Oriental and was made of some fine material.

"You must have a very hospitable captain."

"Ah?"

"To allow you to take part of his space." Gilbert nodded at the wall to his left. "You had that put in just before you sailed, I take it."

Wellington was surprised; then he smiled. "You have sharp eyes, Mr. Winslow."

Gilbert didn't respond to that, but said, "About our business?"

"Ah, yes. Well, sit down, Mr. Winslow. Perhaps a glass of wine?"

Gilbert stared at him, then sat down with a smile and took the glass of wine that Wellington poured from a small glass decanter on the table, and tasted it.

"Very fine, sir." He took another swallow and said with a smile, "Probably the best wine I've ever shared with a man who's taking me to the gallows."

He had expected to catch Wellington off guard with the statement, but the big man merely looked at him, then sipped his own wine.

Gilbert grew angry then, and put the glass down before saying, "You like to torment the mouse a little before the kill—is that it?"

"Is it?"

Gilbert leaned forward, his cornflower blue eyes snapping, and he raised his voice. "You're a policeman—but you must be a lawyer too, judging from the way you hate plain speech!"

"Are you married, Mr. Winslow?"

It was the last question Gilbert expected. He blinked and stared blankly at Wellington, who returned the stare with bland attention. "No, I'm not married. Why do you ask—don't you arrest married men?"

"You expect to be arrested?"

"Another question!" Gilbert said. He stood up and his voice was hard as he said, "I won't play your game, Wellington. Put me in irons, but I'll not be questioned!"

Wellington leaned back in his chair, laced his strong fingers, and said coolly, "A year of hard labor hasn't done much for your temper, has it now? Hasn't it gotten you into enough trouble?"

"The death of Lord Roth was not a matter of temper!"

"Was it not? As I understand the thing, you were employed to run William Brewster to earth and then turn him over to the authorities. Why did you turn on Roth and Johnson?"

"It's—very personal," Gilbert said.

"Murder is usually a personal business, Mr. Winslow!" Wellington's voice was sharp, but he moderated it at once. "Look now, I know you have no reason to trust me . . ."

"*That* is true!"

" . . . but we are alone here, and I may be more of a friend to you than you now believe."

"A friend? How can that be? I don't know you."

"But I know you—or to put it more literally, I know *about* you," Wellington smiled. "Now, I have a proposition to make you, sir. In short, I may be able to help you to some degree. . . ." He put up his hand to ward off Gilbert's question. "Now I said *may* be able to help you, and I said to *some* degree."

"Why should you?" Gilbert knew he was no match for the wits of the man across from him, but he could not for the life of him think of any reason why Wellington or anyone else should help him.

"That question I will answer—after you have done one thing for me."

"Which is?"

"I want a complete and thorough report of your activities from the time you entered the service of Lord North until this day."

Gilbert stared at him. "You must think me quite a fool, sir, to think that I would give such a thing to a stranger."

"You would be exactly that, Mr. Winslow, if you spoke so freely to anyone else—but you would be foolish *not* to speak to me. For believe me, I am one of the very few who have the means of getting you out of this snare you have gotten yourself into. But I will not beg. This is my final offer, if you will do as I ask, and give me a complete and thorough account of the period I mentioned, I shall—if I am convinced that you are honest—let you know my reasons for being here. Now, I will not add to that. What is your decision?"

Wellington settled back, laced his fingers, and there was an adamant set to his face that told Gilbert he meant exactly what he said. The thought flashed through Gilbert's mind, *It's a trap— say nothing!* But the more he considered the man, the more inclined he was to comply with his strange request. Finally he shrugged, "You realize that what I say here, I will not repeat in a court of law?"

"Of course." Wellington got up and pulled his chair around to the small desk. He picked up a pen, trimmed it with a silver knife from his vest pocket, dipped it into the ink well. Then he pulled a sheet of paper close and with his pen poised, said, "Proceed, Mr. Winslow. I may interrupt you from time to time for fine details. It would save time if you give them on your own. I must ask you to give me—insofar as possible—not only what you *did*, but *why* you did it. In other words, lay your soul bare." He looked up with a slight smile on his heavy mouth and added, "I have seen a bit of the world, Winslow, so do not fear you'll shock me with your confession."

Gilbert turned his head to stare out of the mullioned windows cut into the high stern of the *Fortune*. The ship was anchored with the bow facing away from the shore, thus he could see the harbor and the main street of Plymouth plainly. For months he had worked on the small houses that mounted up the slope, but only now as he sat across from the man who might take him away from the small group of people he had been tied to, only then did it strike him forcibly that he might be taking his last look at Plymouth.

He thought of how he'd come to revere Brewster and Carver—and even Bradford, though he'd disliked the man at first. He thought of the young men he'd worked beside—John Alden, John Howland, Thomas Fletcher. Of the children who had stood the trip better than most of the adults. He thought of those now buried in shallow graves or in the sea. He thought of Humility.

Then he said, "I've done many foolish things in my life, Mr. Wellington. Putting my confidence in you will probably wind up at the top of that list . . ." He watched Wellington's face closely, but there was not a break in the smooth countenance of the man. Gilbert smiled grimly, then went over to stand beside the window.

"I hated my brother Edward because I thought he had robbed me of my inheritance . . ." he began, and for the next hour he went over the whole thing, beginning with his first meeting with Lord North down to the time the sails of *Fortune* had appeared over the horizon.

He began awkwardly, embarrassed to lay his memories before a stranger. But Wellington never looked up from his writing desk. He sat there motionless, making a note from time to time, but he spoke only to ask a few questions.

The questions were not the ones Gilbert had expected. He was prepared for snares concerning the death of Lord Roth, but Wellington seemed to have more appetite for other things.

"This young woman—Humility Cooper," he asked quietly. "Did you find her attractive?"

"Very much."

"So that made your task easier?"

"No, sir, it did *not!*" Gilbert shot back at once.

"You did have relations with her, of course." There was no rebuke in the smooth voice; Wellington might have been stating that it was a pleasant day.

Gilbert turned from the window, his face flushed; he took one step toward Wellington, then stopped.

The big man did not even look up from his notes. "Did you hear me, Mr. Winslow? I asked if you had intimate relations with the woman."

Gilbert forced himself to be as calm as Wellington, at least outwardly. "No, I did not."

That brought Wellington's head up, and his dark piercing eyes met Gilbert's. "Why not?" he asked.

"It's not a question I care to answer, sir. If you insist on one, the interrogation is over."

Wellington stared at the young man as if he were an interesting specimen he had discovered, then smiled slightly, turned back to his notes, and said calmly, "Proceed with the account."

Gilbert went on with his story, and Wellington stopped him at one point with a question about his relationship with Lord North.

"I admire him very much."

"And his daughter?"

"Why, she's one of the loveliest women I've ever seen."

"Is that all?"

"I—I don't understand you."

"I think you do."

Stung by the man's calm assurance, Gilbert bit his lip, then said, "Well—I will admit, sir—it *was* more than admiration."

"I see. How much more?"

Gilbert shrugged. "I was very much attracted to her—but you know how little that means, Mr. Wellington. I was a poor man, with no name and no fortune."

"There have been matches of that sort, I believe."

Gilbert struck the windowsill with his fist, and cried out, "Yes! and what is your opinion of poor young men who marry wealthy women?"

"I would have no general opinion," Wellington said, giving Gilbert a straight glance. "I know there are some scoundrels who have married women for their fortune; I know some men of impeccable honor who have married women of wealth for love. I am asking you, Mr. Winslow, what was your feeling for Cecily North?"

Gilbert sat down in the chair, poured himself a glass of wine, drank it down. Then he asked quietly, "Did you ever go through a bad time in your life, Mr. Wellington?"

"Yes."

Gilbert smiled and said, "You're no lawyer, as I thought at first. No lawyer ever spoke so certainly and so shortly. But— during that difficult time, did you ever dream of earlier days when things were better?"

"Yes, many times."

"Well, how accurate were those dreams, in all honesty? Weren't they shaped by the agony of the present trial?"

"I believe that's very accurate," Wellington nodded. "And that is, I take it, your answer as to how you felt about the young woman at that time."

"I was intoxicated by her—who wouldn't be?" Gilbert murmured. "Those brief times we shared—I've dreamed about them over and over during this past year. When death was at my right hand every day, those memories kept me sane, I think."

Wellington let the silence run on, then he said, "I have one more question. It has to do with the tragedy of Lord Roth."

Gilbert said evenly, "I thought we'd get to that!"

"Yes, now, Mr. Winslow, think carefully before you answer my question." Wellington put his paper down and leaned forward holding Gilbert's eyes with his own.

"You left Leyden with the intention of being faithful to the task you'd committed yourself to?"

"Yes."

"Then when the moment came for you to do that, you did just the opposite."

"Yes."

"My question is this: *why* did you change your mind? I have heard Johnson's story—I warn you of that—and he indicates that Lord Roth threatened to have you charged with being derelict in your duty. He was not correct, was he?" Wellington's eyes narrowed and Gilbert knew that the answer to this question was the one that could lead him to the gallows.

He looked straight at Wellington, saying, "Lord Roth was quite correct in believing that I intended to help William Brewster escape."

"But—you did not feel that way when you left Leyden, by your own statement. Why did you change your mind?"

Gilbert paused, searching for the right words, but nothing he thought of sounded like the sort of thing that would satisfy this man. Finally he looked Wellington in the eye and said simply, "I found out I couldn't be a traitor. It was a matter of honor."

"I see." Clearly that answer was a problem for the big man, but Gilbert could not find another way to put it.

"I suggest, Mr. Winslow, that it is possible that you did this for the young woman? That you had fallen in love with her and could not bear to betray her. Am I correct?"

"No, sir, you are *not*!" Gilbert spoke crisply, and got to his feet. "I would have done the same if she had been ninety years old, or if William Brewster had been the only one involved."

Wellington's large eyes narrowed. Letting the silence run on until it grew uncomfortable, finally he nodded and said, "Very well, I think that will do."

"Now perhaps you can tell me who you are."

"You have been most cooperative, Mr. Winslow." Wellington rose to his feet, walked to the door, and turned to face Gilbert with the suggestion of a smile on his lips. "If you will remain in this room for just a short while, you will receive your reward."

"But—!" Gilbert started to protest, but the big man stepped through the door and shut it firmly. The key turned, and Gilbert said under his breath angrily, "Remain in this room—where in the name of heaven could I go?"

He paced about the room, pausing at the desk to open a drawer and look through the contents thoroughly. There was nothing to indicate the profession of Wellington—only a few small books on the New World, well-thumbed, with his name on the inside cover.

He moved toward the windows to look outside, and as he passed the colorful hanging on the inner wall, his eye caught a faint movement of the fabric. He was within arm's reach, and when he stopped to face it, he heard a small sound—very much like an intake of breath.

It was a trap! he thought at once, assuming that whoever was behind the drapery had been put there so he might serve as a witness at a murder trial. Anger swept him, and he plucked up one of the heavy chairs, intending to drive it through the colorful fabric; then a thought came, and he put it down softly.

He crouched slightly in front of the hanging, his knees bent, his arms outstretched, and uncoiled his body in an explosive drive that sent him through the thin material like a cannon shot. His outstretched arms wrapped around a figure, as he had expected, but he was surprised at the small size of Wellington's man—more like a boy than an adult, and the strength of his powerful arms wrapping around his prey cut off all resistance.

The hanging ripped from its fastenings made a shroud of sorts, and when he fell on the helpless body, there was a cry of pain as the breath was driven out.

Gilbert rolled off, and cast a quick look around, noting that the room was furnished in a much more elaborate fashion than the adjoining room. But it was empty save for whoever was squirming wildly beneath the folds of the covering at his feet.

He reached down and plucking up the figure, ripped the thin fabric away from the head, saying, "All right, if you're so interested in me, take a good . . . !"

Gilbert stopped abruptly as the emblazoned cloth fell away, and he found himself face-to-face with Cecily North!

He stood there in total disbelief, his mind reeling, but it was no other. He licked his lips, and said finally, "Cecily! I can't believe it!"

Cecily had a slight redness on her right cheek—accentuated, no doubt, by the pallor brought on by the shock of Gilbert's charge. But the sleek black hair still framed a face that had haunted Gilbert for months. The bold black eyes opened wide, only inches away from his own, and she said breathlessly, "Are you going to hold me like this forever, Gilbert?"

He realized that he was holding her tightly, and there was a light of laughter in her eyes as her smooth lips turned upward in a smile. "Well, since you evidently refuse to let me go—what are your intentions?"

The pressure of her body against his suddenly awakened all the old hungers, and the past and the future faded like mist—

there was only this time and this place and her full red lips.

Finally she leaned back, then whispered huskily, "It's been a long time!"

She pulled away, her hands going up to her hair—they were not steady, Gilbert noted. His thoughts were confused, and the kiss had brought back many memories.

"I remember that dress," he said, more to gain time than for any other reason. "You wore it the night we went to the Duke's ball in Bath."

She was wearing a gown with vertical stripes of silver set off by sky blue trim. Suddenly she laughed and her black eyes danced. "I love that! Here we meet for the first time in months— you're running from a hangman—and you pay compliments on my dress!"

Her laughter forced him to smile, and he shrugged, "I still think I'm having a dream."

She sobered, and pulled him to a small sofa covered with green embroidery. "Sit down—we have a lot to talk about."

Gilbert shook his head, and asked, "First, what are you doing here?"

She lay back against the thick cushion, her lips curving upward. "You can't guess?" she asked.

"Well, surely not for a holiday!" he answered with a frown and a wave toward the land. "This isn't exactly the land of Eden the travel books make it out to be."

"But it has *one* feature that interests me—Gilbert Winslow!"

He kissed her hand, and that simple gesture stirred him so that he shifted uncomfortably and shook his head. "Does any mental problem run in the North family, Cecily?"

"Why, no!"

"Then you are the first to lose your mind," he said, and a grim line etched itself between his eyes. He got up suddenly, walked to the window, and stared out blindly at the coast. "It's all very romantic, Cecily, but so hopeless!"

"Why do you say that?" Cecily asked. She got up and went to him, turning him with a hand on his arm. "It's not very complimentary to me, Gilbert, is it? Here I sail thousands of miles to see you, and all you can say is that it's hopeless."

He looked down at her and smiled. "You are the same," he said.

"Yes. Are you the same, too?"

He bit his lip, and then said quietly, "No, I'm not. A year ago I didn't have name or fortune, and I still don't. But no man can kill another as I have—and spend a year in this place—without being changed."

She nodded, her face still, then said, "You've struggled with thoughts of the future—about Roth, I mean."

"Why, of course," he said in surprise.

She looked down at the floor, and her hand toyed with a small silver chain around her neck. Then she looked up with a strange light in her dark eyes. "Suppose all that were settled, what would you do then, Gilbert?"

He smiled grimly, his jaw tense and his lips thin. "Why even think about it? It's not going to disappear."

She stood there, and then said slowly, "I've thought about you a great deal this year. For a long time I didn't do anything. I stayed at home, went to France—anything to fill the time. All the time I was trying to forget you."

"I see."

"Do you? I doubt it!" Her eyes flashed then, and she was sober. "I was sure that you'd fallen in love with that woman you were mixed up with in Leyden. I think I would have killed both of you if I'd had the chance!"

"Cecily—!"

"Wait, I want this to be very clear," she said, putting her fingers over his lips to cut off his protest. "I hated you both, and when it didn't pass away—as some said it would—I knew I had to find out the truth about us. That's why I came to this new Eden."

He stared at her blankly. "But—don't you realize it doesn't *matter* how I feel about you! No matter how much I loved you, I could never speak, for what could I offer you except an invitation to watch me hang!"

She kept her eyes fixed on his for a long moment, then walked to the door. Before she opened it, she said, "We'll have the truth about us in a few moments."

She opened the door, and said, "Come in, sir."

Caleb Wellington must have been less than a foot from the door, for he came in at once, planted his feet and said, "Now, Mr. Winslow, it is your turn to interrogate *me!*"

"Who are you?" Gilbert threw the question at him sharply, and got an instant answer.

"A lawyer in the service of Lord North." He laughed quietly, adding, "*Not* an agent for the King looking for wayward theological students, as you have supposed."

"And what is your purpose, sir?"

"To bring you back to England with me."

Shock ran along Gilbert's nerves, but he only asked mildly, "And the charges against me?"

"There are no charges, Mr. Winslow."

"It is no longer against English law to slay a peer of the realm?"

Wellington did not rise to meet Gilbert's ironic manner. He said evenly, "Certainly it is—or any other man in the English kingdom."

Gilbert stared at him, then asked directly, "What about Lord Roth?"

"Lord Simon Roth was slain approximately one year ago. His assailant remains at large, but the authorities have little hope that he will be found after all this time, and with no witnesses."

"But there *was* a witness," Gilbert said at once. "What about the man named Johnson? Surely he must have had something to say to the law."

"There *was* a certain Johnson who was alleged to be in the company of Lord Roth during the time of his death—but he cannot testify."

"Why not?"

"Because he is dead." Wellington did not blink as he said this, but he went on to explain. "I will tell you two facts about Johnson, and no more. First of all, you may know that Johnson did talk not long after Lord Roth's death to Mr. Lucas Tiddle, a gentleman in Lord North's service."

"What did he tell Tiddle?"

"Ah, that is between the two of them!" Wellington said with a frown. "And I have not found Mr. Tiddle a man who takes his calling lightly. It is highly unlikely that you will ever know what passed between the two. All I can say is that Johnson talked to Mr. Tiddle, then immediately left England on a ship—the *Defiant*, bound for Australia."

Tiddle bought him off! Gilbert knew instantly. "And he died—how?"

"The *Defiant* went down in a storm in May—broke up on the Great Barrier Reef, with all hands lost."

"I see." Gilbert stared at Wellington, trying to see past the smooth face and the hooded eyes. Finally he asked slowly, "Then—I can go back to England a free man?"

A trace of humor broke the expression of Wellington. "I doubt that any of us are completely free, Mr. Winslow—but the answer to your question is—'yes'!"

The suddenness of it caught Gilbert unprepared. He covered his confusion by saying, "I—I'm grateful to you, Mr. Wellington—"

"I am very well paid, Mr. Winslow, for carrying out Lord North's wishes. In this case, his wishes were that I accompany his daughter on a voyage and give you an item of information." He reached into his inside pocket and took out a thin envelope which he handed to Gilbert. "This is from Lord North."

Gilbert stared at the envelope, then opened it.

> Winslow, if you have finished making a fool of yourself, you may come home and pick up your duties where you left off with Tiddle. If you have *not*, I will attempt to carry on without you.

Gilbert looked at Cecily. She did not speak, but her eyes met his with reckless invitation.

Folding the paper carefully and tucking it away into his pocket, he said softly, "Not many men get a second chance, do they? Thank God I've been given one!"

Wellington gave him a careful stare. "I was afraid that you might have changed your views, Winslow. I mean, these people are rather unworldly, aren't they? Denying the flesh and all that sort of thing? The way Deacon Cushman put it, it would be difficult to be a pilgrim and at the same time keep both feet planted in this world—as any man of Lord North's will surely have to do."

This was no idle remark, Gilbert sensed instantly. *North told him to check me out*, he thought. *And Tiddle will have had something to say about my sense of "honor."*

He looked at Cecily, then back to Wellington. Finally he laughed and said, "You know, I once told Brewster that I'd never be able to trust God completely—that if I were ever to be a pilgrim, why, I'd be a pilgrim with a sword." His eyes narrowed and he took a deep breath and looked straight toward Cecily.

"There are only two swords for a man to carry in this world—his own blade to cut his way to the top against all odds—or the Sword of the Lord." He paused and there was regret in his face as he dropped his head and said, "I have had some hope of being the kind of man who would love God with all his heart—but I am not that man." Gilbert smiled grimly, then went over to stand beside the window. From deep within rose the words, *You will love me with all your heart*, and he began very rapidly to drown them out.

CHAPTER THIRTY

"WITH ALL YOUR HEART!"

★ ★ ★ ★

The arrival of the *Fortune* stirred every member of the small settlement, and for two days there was joy and sorrow over the letters and reports that Deacon Cushman brought from Leyden. Death had come for some that had remained behind as well as for the firstcomers. Cushman was so shocked over the decimation among the ranks through the sickness that he was past comfort for a time, but when he saw that the faith of the others remained unshaken, he plunged into action with zeal.

On Wednesday, November 13, two days after the arrival of the ship, Bradford assembled the men for a meeting in the Common House, saying, "Our brother, Mr. Cushman, has news for us," and then sat down with the others.

Cushman smiled and held a parchment high for them to see; it was tan with a bright red ribbon around it. Unrolling it, and spreading it so that all present could see, he said, "This is the most important document our colony could have, brethren. As you all know, New Plymouth does not lie within the territory of our original charter. This could be very serious—we could be ordered to leave by the Crown."

"They'll not push me off my land!" Stephen Hopkins cried out, red-faced and angry.

As several others began to take up the cry, Cushman raised his hand for silence and said, "We have been in the hands of

God; this document that I hold in my hand is a patent signed by Sir Ferdinando Gorges and the other members of the Council for New England."

"What is that?" Samuel Fuller demanded.

"It is a reorganized form of the Plymouth Company."

"I hope it's better than the old one!" Billington snapped.

"You will think so, Mr. Billington, when you hear that under this patent every one of you will receive 100 acres of land at the end of seven years!"

A shout of joy went up, and every face was beaming.

"It is the hand of the Lord!" William Brewster said after Deacon Cushman went over the details, which were indeed more generous than any of them had expected.

Then John Alden asked, "May I ask if—if Mr. Brewster will be . . . ?" He seemed unable to get his question out, and his face grew red with embarrassment. All of them knew his question dealt with the legal status of Brewster; most of them had heard that Captain Jones had ignored the matter, but the *Fortune* was another thing.

"I've heard that there's a man aboard the ship sent to bring back Mr. Brewster," Isaac Allerton said. "That's not so, I hope, Mr. Brewster?"

"No, it is not. I will be staying on," Brewster said with a smile. "I think the King has more important things to do than send for a poor preacher clean across the ocean."

"What about Gilbert? Is he going to stay, too?"

All looked to Edward, who shifted uncomfortably, then shook his head, saying, "I believe my brother will return to England."

"What about the—the charges we heard were lodged against him?" Peter Brown asked.

"There have been no charges." Edward Winslow's tone shut the door on further discussion, and the meeting moved on to other matters.

After the meeting, Peter Brown left and went directly to the Common House. As he expected, he found Humility helping the other women as they cooked and prepared, decorating the place as well as they could with such little trimming as they could manage.

"How was the meeting?" she asked when he came to stand beside her. She was cutting a large cod into steaks for baking, her hair bound underneath a white cloth.

"Very good." He told her the details, ending by saying, "We'll have 100 acres, Humility, after only seven years. Of course, that's just a beginning. We can get more later on."

"Why should you want more?" she asked. Her eyes rested on him, and there was a puzzled look in them. "You can't farm even *that* much, can you?"

"I'll hire men to work it, then buy more. Before we're through, why, I'll have as much land as any man in Plymouth."

"If that's what you want, Peter." The subject seemed to hold no interest for her, and she picked up the knife and began slicing fish.

He was disappointed in her reaction, for he was an ambitious man and wanted her to share in his dreams. "Don't you want to get ahead?"

A wry smile crept across her lips, and she said, "Is a man with 200 acres ahead more than a man with only 100?"

"Why, of course!" The question troubled Brown, and he bit his lip, staring at her. She was not one for small talk, but he had run on this streak in her before, and it bothered him. "Shouldn't a man do his best, Humility?"

"Yes—but there's more to a person's best than getting and spending."

He stared at her, then a thought struck him, and he said diffidently, "Winslow—he's going back to England."

He watched her very closely, and did not miss the fact that she paused in her work, the knife suspended for an instant after he spoke.

Carefully she resumed cutting and did not look up as she asked quietly, "Is he?"

"Humility, don't do that to me!"

She was startled at the quick anger in his voice. He never showed bad temper to her, but now as she looked up there were harsh lines on his face and his lips were drawn thin.

"Why, what did I do?" she asked in confusion.

"You're an honest girl, but you aren't being honest now,"

he said. "You cared for the man once. I can't believe you've no interest in him now."

She started to shake her head, but instead lifted her eyes to his, and there was a faint color in her face. "I *was* dishonest, Peter," she said suddenly. "Maybe I'm still ashamed of—of being interested in him. . . ."

"Why don't you say it—being in love with him!"

She stiffened her back and said quietly, "All right, then, if you think it's important, Peter. I was in love with him. I suppose you can't be indifferent to someone you've been in love with, can you?"

"I hope so!" Brown answered like a shot. "I'd hate for my wife to have thoughts of another man."

She stared at him, as if seeing something in him she'd never noted. "But you have your thoughts and your memories, Peter, that I can never really share."

He was confused and angry, but could not tell why. If he had been calmer he would not have said what he did then.

"You're still in love with him!"

She put down the knife carefully and wiped her hands on the cloth tied around her waist. "If you think that, Peter, you'd be a fool to marry me. Do you want me to release you from that?"

"Oh, no! No, Humility!" Brown caught up her hand and said earnestly, "I'm sorry—I didn't mean to say that! Why, I can't lose you, Humility!"

"You could do better." She stated this as a fact, and there was a steady look in her eyes as she added, "I'm not ambitious, Peter."

He smiled in relief, kissed her hand, then said, "I'll be ambitious for the two of us."

"Very well." She picked up the knife and began to slice the pink steaks. "I knew he would go—and I've been worried about what awaits him when he gets to England."

Brown laughed then, which surprised her. He said, "So *that's* it! I'm glad to hear it—but you can worry about someone else. Winslow's going back to what most men would love to have!"

"But—he's going back to be tried for murder!"

"I've been talking to Deacon Cushman," Brown said. "He's a natural gossip, I fear, and it didn't take long to get out of him that the charges have all been dropped."

"Dropped!" Humility stared in unbelief at him. "That's impossible! How could—?"

"My dear girl," Brown smiled sourly, "with money all things are possible. Evidently Winslow was in favor with Lord North, and when that gentleman wants something, he usually gets it!"

"I can't believe it!"

"Can you believe this—" Brown watched her closely, and continued evenly, "Lord North's daughter is on board the *Fortune*—and it's Cushman's feeling that she's come for Winslow."

"Cecily!" The word slipped out before Humility thought, and she reddened. "He—called for her when he had the sickness."

"Well, he called well," Brown said with a wry smile. "She heard him, apparently, and will wed him as soon as she gets him back to England."

Humility said slowly, "She'll be coming to the reception this afternoon along with the rest." She looked around the rough-hewn logs making up the Common House. "This won't impress her much after a mansion, will it?"

"I suppose she'll do the impressing," Brown shrugged, then kissed the cheek that Humility offered and left.

Peter Brown was neither a prophet nor the son of a prophet—yet his words came to pass.

The area around the Common House served as a dining room for many, and the weather was good. Tables were set up outside for those who could not get inside the single community building, and the air was filled with laughter and singing as the new settlers—thirty-five in all, joined with the firstcomers in the festive affair.

They had just seated themselves when there was a scraping of chairs, and the men rose as a small group entered. A middle-aged man, balding but with quick, intelligent eyes entered first, and Cushman said at once, "Friends, may I introduce Captain Robert Logan—and this is Mr. Evans, his mate—and Mr. Caleb Wellington of London."

There was a slight pause, then a silence as Cushman said,

"Mr. Gilbert Winslow, you know, of course, and this is Lady Cecily North."

He was partly mistaken, for the company did not "know" the Gilbert Winslow who stepped through the door. They were not looking at the plainly dressed brother of Edward who had labored in the mud and cold. Gilbert wore a smooth dark blue velvet coat trimmed in light blue ribbon. It was long, reaching halfway to his knee, but loose with a short line of silver buttons down the right side. His neckband carried a shortfall of lace, down over a long red satin waistcoat slashed with white. The dark blue velvet breeches and the snowy white hose completed his dress, except for the Clemens Hornn sword buckled under the coat at his left hip.

Startled as they were at Gilbert's transformation, he was forgotten as they took in Lady Cecily North.

She wore a short pellise of black ermine which reached to her elbows, which she removed at once and handed to Mr. Wellington. Her gown had vertical stripes of black and scarlet, with a very low bodice edged in small white and black ruffles. A small purse, gold-dusted and set with a circle of rubies swung at her right hip, and her skirt flared in vivid scarlet; under it she wore so many petticoats that when she moved she sounded like a small rain shower.

A cluster of fiery stones hung from her neck, suspended by a golden chain; two diamonds flashed from her earlobes. She had full red lips and flawless olive skin; a small mole on her left cheek, far from being a flaw, served as a natural beauty mark.

Bradford indicated their places, and soon the meal was under way. Peter was sitting at Humility's left, and he talked easily to the man across from him—a new settler named Duncan—about the year's events in England.

After the meal there were many speeches, and Humility was relieved when finally Captain Logan thanked them for their hospitality, but said he wished to get back to his ship before dark.

"You must see my guns, Captain," Standish said, and the captain, being an ex-soldier himself, gave in. The two men left and most of the crowd followed them up the steep hill to the miniature fortress overlooking the town.

As the room cleared, Humility moved around stacking the

trenchers and mugs. Hearing a sound, she turned and found herself face-to-face with Cecily North and Gilbert.

"It's a little cool for such a long walk," Cecily said with a smile. "Do you mind if we wait inside?"

"No. Of course not."

Cecily waited for a moment, then looked at Gilbert. "I have not met this lady," she said.

Gilbert cleared his throat, then made the introduction. "This is Miss Humility Cooper—Lady Cecily North."

Instantly Cecily's eyes riveted on the girl in front of her, taking in the plain gray smock, the lack of adornment. She did not, however, miss the fine green eyes set off by blonde hair and fair skin.

A challenge filled Cecily's dark eyes suddenly, and she drew herself up, saying, "Ah, yes, Miss Cooper—I've heard of you."

Knowing what she had heard brought the color to Humility's cheeks, but she said, "We're happy to have you here, Lady North."

"Even if I'm taking part of your small company away from you?" It was a playful remark on the surface, but Cecily took Gilbert's arm with a possessive gesture, and a predatory curl marred the line of her full lips as she watched the effect of her words on the other woman.

Humility deliberately looked from the dark girl into Gilbert's face. He was watching her intently, and the vertical lines between his heavy brows indicated he was displeased. He met her gaze, and there was a short, charged silence.

"Mr. Winslow will be a great loss to the colony," Humility said, and a shock ran along her nerves as she discovered it was true. "He has served the company well, and will be greatly missed."

Gilbert blinked his eyes in surprise, then bit his lip. "That's kind of you; but then, you're always one to find something good in the worst of us."

Cecily did not care for the sudden flash of intimacy that seemed to exclude her. "Perhaps," she said with a small smile, her voice drawing Gilbert's attention, "you'll come to visit us after we're married."

Humility did not miss the startled glance that Gilbert shot

at Cecily, but ignored it. "That's very kind of you, Lady North—but very unlikely."

"Well, you *are* cut off out here, aren't you, Miss Cooper?"

"From what?"

"Why—!" Cecily was taken off guard and looked confused, "Why, from the world, I suppose I meant."

Humility stood there, and the smile on her face softened her features. The quietness that Gilbert had learned to appreciate was never so clearly in evidence as at that moment.

"We're far from England," she said, "but we're not far from God." Then she nodded and said, "I hope you enjoy your visit, Lady North."

After she left, Cecily stared at the door, and then looked directly into Gilbert's eyes. "You didn't tell me she was so attractive."

Gilbert said at once, "She is very beautiful, Cecily—and very strong."

"Yes, that's true. I wonder she's not married."

Gilbert's gaze swept Cecily's face, and he said tonelessly, "She's engaged to marry a man named Brown."

"How nice!" Cecily's dark eyes sparkled and she leaned against him, saying, "We must send them something very nice for a wedding gift."

"When did you say we sail from this dreadful place, Mr. Wellington?"

Cecily threw her book down and went to stare at the bleak coastline out of the windows of her cabin.

Caleb Wellington lifted his big head from where he sat beside an oil lamp. "We've been here three weeks. Logan says we'll leave soon—next week, I'd venture."

"How can they stand it?" Cecily threw herself down, and raked her nails across the fabric of her chair. "I'd go *insane* if I had to spend a winter here!"

"Well, you won't have to, my dear," Wellington said calmly. Then he asked curiously, "Where's Mr. Winslow been the last three days?"

"How should *I* know?" Cecily said shortly. "He said something about making some sort of trip inland for Mr. Bradford—

business with the Indians of some sort."

"Well, he'll be back soon, and we'll sail—then it'll be over."

Cecily stared at him, and there was a puzzled look on her face. She asked, "Have you found Gilbert—different lately?"

"Different? How different?"

"I don't know how to put it," she said. "He's attentive—but when I try to talk about our life when we get home, why, he just doesn't seem *interested*."

"He's been through a lot. He'll be all right when we get him away from these preachers."

She stared at him, then nodded, saying, "I think you've hit on it—he's more caught up with all this holy living than he knows. I noticed it almost from the first day we got here. And lately it's worse! He's always reading the Bible or some sermon. He reads parts of them to me and I try to be interested, but they're so *dreary*."

The big lawyer shrugged, "You'll take that out of him soon enough, I should think. Get him back home, give him a taste of good living and what service with your father can bring—he'll forget all this!"

Cecily leaned back and there was a calculating light in her eyes as she said softly, "He'll have to, Mr. Wellington—there's no room for pilgrims in my world!"

At the very moment they were speaking, Miles Standish was giving Edward Winslow a report on his brother.

"You talked to him before he left, Miles?" Edward asked. There was a worried frown on his face, and he shook his head doubtfully. "We're in for bad weather. He could get lost and freeze." They were standing on the hill looking down on the scattered houses lightly coated with fine-grained snow. "I don't understand why he went. He was all tied up with that North woman on the ship."

Miles looked at the larger man, and there was a flicker of humor in his sharp eyes. "Well, if you want my opinion, he's coming down with a bad case of God-fearing conviction."

"What?"

Standish smiled and said, "You're on your honeymoon, Edward, and you don't notice things. Gilbert hasn't been happy.

Truth to tell, he's been bone-achin' miserable!''

"But he's got what he wants, Miles!" Edward protested. "He's always wanted to rise in the world, be rich—now he'll have it."

"Well, all I know is, he came to me three days ago, and he was at the end of his tether! I thought he was sick, he looked so bad, but then after a while, I saw it was something else." Standish was a man of action, and he had trouble finding his words, but finally he shrugged and said, "He came to me because he didn't want any sermons, Edward. He knew I'd been through the fire after Rose died, and he knew I wouldn't have a sermon for him." Then the fiery little captain laughed and said, "He was wrong about that!"

"What did you tell him?"

"Well, I listened to him at first. He went over the whole thing, all his life wanting to be somebody, to be rich. And when he was finished, he looked at me with pure misery in his eyes, and he said, 'Now I've got it, Miles—so why am I so unhappy?' "

Edward stared at Standish, then shook his head. "I should have seen it! Should have helped!"

"I think the boy covered it up pretty well," Standish observed.

"Why'd he leave town?" Edward asked.

"Well, I told him how I'd forgot about God until it was a shame—and then I said, 'You'll never be happy, Gilbert, until you get Christ!' Well, it touched a nerve, I tell you! He turned pale as a ghost and seemed to melt. So I told him he ought to do what I had to do—back when I lost Rose and just about went crazy."

Edward stared at him, then said quietly, "I failed you, too, Miles. What did you do?"

"Why, I went out into the forest and stayed until I found God," Standish said simply. "Like I told your brother, I went out there, and if God hadn't done something to help me, why, I'd never have come back, Edward."

Edward stared out into the gathering darkness, and there was a sadness in his voice as he said, "Poor boy! I wish I could be there to help him!"

Miles Standish said quietly, "No, he's got to that place we

all have to come to, Edward. Nobody can help us there—not father, mother, brother, or friend. A man can get help with most things, but when he goes to find God, he goes alone!"

Miles away, the object of their concern was trudging along, head down and tired to the bone. He had taken a message to Massasoit for Bradford. It had given him an excuse to leave town, and he had carried out his mission with no problem. Massasoit had attempted to convince him that he should delay his return to Plymouth, but Gilbert ignored his warning and had reached the halfway mark when the snow began to thicken, falling in chunks from an iron-gray sky.

He had thought about Cecily and England and a new life until it made his head ache. The worst thing was that he took no joy in the prospect, and he could not understand *why*.

"It's all there, Miles, all I've ever dreamed about," he had told Standish. "All I have to do is reach out and take it—but when I think about it, I just feel—I feel *empty!*"

Night was closing in, and a streak of fear ran through him as the power of the sudden winter storm rocked him with a blast of freezing wind that seared his lungs. *Got to get some shelter!* he thought, and as the last shreds of light flickered from the west, he cut a few saplings and managed to tie them together at the top, then cut evergreen boughs to make a top.

It was a pitiful sort of thing, but there was nothing else. He managed to make a fire in the small space between a tree trunk and the door to his shelter, and all night long as the rain changed to snow, he kept feeding it with small twigs.

With a shock, he realized he had only a handful of hard-baked bread and a little dried bacon. "Should have been more careful," he murmured.

When morning came, the snow turned to freezing rain, and he had to make several attempts to get to his feet. His muscles were slow to respond to the commands from his brain, and he knew then that he was in trouble.

He was halfway between Massasoit's camp and Plymouth—at least twenty miles to either, probably more. He considered heading back to the Indian camp. *Might run across some Indians*, he thought, but then realized that no one would be out in this storm.

All afternoon he floundered through the falling snow, stopping just before dark to make another shelter. He was moving so slowly that it took him a long time, and by the time he got a small fire going, he was half unconscious with cold and fatigue.

He ate the rest of the small portion of bread as slowly as possible, saving the handful of bacon for morning.

The temperature fell quickly, and he forced himself to get up and jump in the snow until the slugging blood pumped through his body, but each time it took longer. He was using up the energy he would need to fight his way through the drifts when morning came.

Some time before dawn, he drifted off to sleep, and as the cold seeped into his body, he began to lose body heat. The small fire died to a single glowing stick, and he did not move.

He never knew why he awakened, if an animal made a cry or a snow-laden branch crashed to the ground nearby.

It was like coming out of a warm bed into an icy room—there was the intense desire to slip back into the warmth, to flee from the biting cold.

You're freezing! part of his mind said, but when he tried to move, his limbs were powerless. Desperately he tried to roll over, even to lift one arm, but it was as if he were frozen in ice.

Over and over he tried, then he stopped. He knew he was dying. Part of his mind was awake enough to tell him that. He could not feel anything—neither cold nor pain.

A great regret came to him. He thought of all the things that he would never do—simple things, like watching Tink's face when a thumping fish jerked the boy's quill under, or the first bite of food after a long hunger.

Then in the midst of these last thoughts, he was conscious of something different—something that was *not* within. He was suddenly thinking some words that came from outside, somehow. For a long time they seemed to come and go, floating around his head, and he could not understand them.

Then he heard inside his head the words he'd thought of a thousand times: *Someday you'll love me.* He saw no figure; there was no strange light, but his mind suddenly became sharp and clear as a steel blade.

He began to think of all the sermons he'd heard from the

pilgrim ministers, and the words of the Scripture beat against his consciousness. "Except you repent, ye shall all likewise perish . . . Come unto me and I will give you life . . . except a man be born again, he cannot see the kingdom of God . . . confess with thy mouth the Lord Jesus . . . he that hath the Son hath life . . ."

Then he was conscious that he was in the presence of God, and he remembered how Standish had told him the same thing had happened to him when he had gone deep into the woods after Rose's death.

He lay there thinking of his misspent youth, spotted with sins of the flesh, and he knew that even if he survived, he could not go on living as he had. He opened his eyes, blinking against the light. Gathering his strength, he pulled himself to his knees, and then he lifted his hands toward the lead-gray heavens. His voice was feeble, but the cry that came through his cracked, frozen lips sounded loud in the silence of the forest: "Oh, my God . . . I—I am lost! Lost!"

Tears scored his cheeks, and in an agony of spirit, he lifted his head and with utter despair, cried, "I can't help myself, Lord God! I am only a sinner . . . but I believe you care—that you love me. I want to love you, God!"

Raw grief shut his throat, but he ignored it, and dropped face downward in the snow, crying out, "In the name of Jesus Christ, O God, save me!"

A wolf howled far off, and then there was silence. As Gilbert Winslow lay with his face pressed into the snow, something strange was happening. The agonizing bitterness in his spirit seemed to move away, and he was filled with a sense of such complete peace and joy that he was unable to move. He lay there for a long time, and finally he was aware that his tears were flowing, but they were tears of joy! He climbed to his feet, lifted his face toward heaven, and with wonder in his voice, cried out, "O God! I love you!"

Then not in words, but with a gust of knowledge, came the thought, *You love me now as a babe—but you will grow in the faith and will be my servant.*

Gilbert finally stood upright, his face stiff, his eyes slits, weaving like a tall tree cut almost in two at the base and about to topple.

He stared out into the first light, a sickly gray feebly staining the ink-black sky, and knew he could never make it back to Plymouth.

But something inside said, "Walk!" and he left the shelter, staggering through the drifts, wallowing and falling often, but always floundering to his numb feet and beginning again. He could not make a mile, he knew, and Plymouth was almost twenty miles—but there was always the feeling that he could take one more step. *Don't quit—just one more now—that's the way—good!*

Thirty minutes later he ran blindly into what he thought was a tree. His eyes had been shut, and when he opened them, he saw that he had run into one of the pine supports for the small cabin that Miles Standish had insisted on building as an outpost the previous spring.

As Gilbert fell inside the door, he remembered with a grim streak of humor he had told Standish, "It's a waste of time, Miles! The Indians will tear them down and steal the supplies."

But they hadn't. Not this one.

He stumbled around, getting a fire going in the small stone-and-clay fireplace, melting snow to make water, and cooking the best meal of his life—boiled corn that tasted like ambrosia to him.

As he sat there eating and soaking up the heat from the fire, he reached into his pocket and pulled out a small black book—the Bible.

He stared at it until he finished his meal, then put a few branches on the fire.

Settling with his back to the fire, he opened the Bible and said softly, "God, I'll not leave this place until I find your will!"

He stayed there for two days, going outside only three times for wood. The rest of the time he was either reading from the Bible or praying.

The snow fell intermittently, but he paid no heed. Sometimes he would eat a little food, but he didn't sleep at all, or not for long.

He could never tell anyone much about what went on in that cabin, any more than he could tell them how, out of all the directions he might have gone, he'd taken the only one that had led to the outpost.

What he did say to a few people later on was simple and to the point: "When I went inside that hut, I didn't love God much. When I came out, I loved Him with all my heart!"

When he came walking into camp, he was met with a great shout by the first man he saw, John Howland, who ran and caught him with a wild embrace.

"Gilbert! You're alive!"

He gave a shout, and soon Gilbert was inside the Common House telling his story to all that could get inside. His shoulders were sore with the thumping they had taken, and looking around at his friends, he got a lump in his throat and his eyes burned.

"Here, let the lad be," William Bradford said, seeing the trouble Gilbert was having. "It's a miracle, but we don't want to kill him with kindness, do we now?" He patted Gilbert's shoulder fondly, which was unusual for him, and added in a gentle voice, "You're home now, Gilbert. We've been praying for you constantly."

Gilbert raised his head, and there were tears in his eyes and on his cheeks. He looked around the room and noted each face, dearer to him now than anything in England.

"Mr. Bradford, He heard your prayer—and He saved more than my body—Jesus Christ is now my Savior!"

A cry went up from Bradford's throat, and that stern man threw his arms about Gilbert, and someone began to sing a song of praise as they all tried to get closer—to touch the newest pilgrim.

The hull of the *Fortune* dipped below the horizon two days later; the sails followed, and finally she was gone, leaving nothing but a smooth, clean line for Gilbert to watch.

He had climbed the hill to watch her clear the harbor, and now stood beside one of Miles' guns. He had left early, and for a long time he'd stood there after the ship left, his mind going over the last few days.

"Gilbert!"

He wheeled, startled, and there she was, her face flushed with the exertion of the climb, her sea-green eyes wide and her lips parted as she stood before him.

Gilbert looked past her, but saw no one. "You came alone?"

Humility didn't answer, but came to stand so close that he could smell her hair. She faced him squarely, tall and slim in the bright November sunshine. Her face was filled with wonder. "You didn't go back!"

"No. There's nothing there for me to go back to."

She shook her head and asked with a catch of her breath. "But—I thought you and Lady North . . . ?"

He laughed and his eyes crinkled as he said, "Well, I thought so, too, but she told me that she'd never be satisfied with half a man!"

"She said that?"

"Yes—and she was right," Gilbert said. "I told her that something had come into my life, something wonderful, but that it would make a difference in our plans. Then when I told her that the New World was for me, she couldn't believe it." He laughed and said, "I guess living in a cabin with a minister didn't appeal to her much."

Humility stared at him. "With a minister!"

He seemed embarrassed, and the smile he gave her wasn't very strong. He dropped it, and his face was honest and open in some new way. "I'm so ignorant, Humility! Here I've wasted my life, and now I stand here saying I'm going to be a minister! Isn't that the most insane thing you ever heard of!"

"No."

He stared at her. "You—you don't think so?"

"Gilbert Winslow!" Humility said with a gust of emotion, "I expect you can do just about anything you set your mind to!"

His mouth dropped open, and he stared at her. "Why, I've never done anything *right* in my whole life, Humility! Look at what I did to you, and—!"

She put her hand on his lips, and he felt her tremble. "Hush! I want to ask you a question. Do you love God with all your heart?"

He took her hand from his lips with his own, but did not release it. "Yes!" he said firmly.

She nodded, and made no attempt to reclaim her hand. "Then you'll be His man, Gilbert Winslow!"

He stared at her, stirred as always by the clean beauty of

her face. "Humility, I wish that you and I—" he broke off suddenly, then dropped her hand.

"I have another question for you," she said, and her voice was so unsteady that he looked up quickly.

"Another question? What is it, Humility?"

She swallowed and her voice trembled as she whispered, "Would—would you marry me?"

He stared at her, thinking he had misunderstood, but she returned his look, her eyes shining like diamonds.

"But—what about you and Peter Brown?"

She shook her head, saying, "He told me he needed more than half a woman! He said . . ." She turned away from him, then, and her voice was so soft he had to lean forward to hear it— ". . . he said that any fool could see I was still in love with you—just like I've always been!"

A great joy filled his heart, and he turned her around. He looked down at her, and she tried to smile, saying with a sob, "And he was—he was *right*! I'll always love you!"

She tried to turn and run, but his strong arms made her captive, and he waited until she grew calm.

"I love you, Humility Cooper!" he whispered in her ear. Then he kissed her, and there was a union as they held each other, their lips sealing what they felt in their hearts.

Finally he pulled his head back, and there was light of pure joy in his brilliant blue eyes, and a wide smile on his lips. "What a life we're going to have!"

Humility leaned back to gaze into his face, and her lips curved into a beautiful smile, then she asked quietly, "Will you ever miss it all, dear?"

He shook his head, "Never! I'll have *you* and I'll have my sword! What man could ask for more?"

"Your sword?" she asked. "But . . . !"

He pulled the worn black Bible from his pocket and held it high, as if it were his Clemens Hornn blade.

"The Sword of the Lord, Humility!" he cried out gaily.

"The sword that gives life," she murmured, "and a man who wields it well. Who could ask for greater adventure?"